1987 Poet's Market

1987

Poet's Market

Where & How to Publish Your Poetry

Edited by
Judson Jerome
Assisted by
Katherine Jobst

Writer's Digest Books

Cincinnati, Ohio

If you are a poetry publisher and would like
to be considered for a listing in the next
edition of *Poet's Market*, please request a
questionnaire from *Poet's Market*,
9933 Alliance Road, Cincinnati, Ohio 45242.

Distributed in Canada by Prentice-Hall of
Canada Ltd., 1870 Birchmount Road,
Scarborough, Ontario M1P 2J7.

Managing Editor, Market Books Department:
Constance J. Achabal

International Standard Serial Number
0883-5470
International Standard Book Number
0-89879-244-4

ALSO BY JUDSON JEROME

Light in the West (poems)

The Fell of Dark (novel)

Plays for an Imaginary Theater (verse plays
and autobiographical essays)

*Culture out of Anarchy: The Reconstruction of
American Higher Learning*

I Never Saw . . . (poems for children)

*Families of Eden: Communes and the New
Anarchism*

Poetry: Premeditated Art

The Poet and the Poem

Thirty Years of Poetry: Poems 1949-1979

Myrtle Whimple's Sampler

Publishing Poetry

Public Domain

The Village . . .

Partita in Nothing Flat

The Poet's Handbook

On Being a Poet

1   **From the Editor**
3   **Using Your Poet's Market**
6   **Launching Your Poems into the Public Sea**

The Markets

13   **Publishers of Poetry**

Close-ups

38   **Peter Davison, Editor and Poet**
*Advice from the man who has been called
"a major force in contemporary American poetry"*

49   **Robert Wallace, Bits Press**
*This publisher has an idea which could bring
back an audience for poetry*

75   **Nikki Giovanni, Poet**
*The poet laureate of young black women offers
encouragement – and a challenge – to new writers*

101   **Barbara Holley, Earthwise Publications/Productions**
*Earthwise is a "beginner's market," but its editor demands
structure, form, contents and craft in poetry submissions*

137   **Andrew Hudgins, Poet**
*Keep your reader in mind, advises this
Pulitzer-nominated poet*

143   **Esther M. Leiper, Inkling**
*This poet/editor offers her definition
of "a good poet"*

181   **Judith Viorst, Poet**
*How does this writer succeed in reaching such
a large audience with her poetry?*

221   **Gail White, Piedmont Literary Review**
*Here's one answer to the often-asked question,
"Why do poets write?"*

223   **Ed Ochester, Pitt Poetry Series**
*Read the reason why this prestigious publisher
believes in publishing poets' "second" books*

Contents

237 Vi Gale, Prescott Street Press
Everybody gets paid at this regional market,
but it's still primarily a labor of love

261 Merritt Clifton, Samisdat
An exceptional definition of poetry
from an exceptional publisher

311 John Stone M.D., Poet
Dr. Stone tells how he juggles the demands of his
profession with his need to write poetry

342 Contests and Awards
357 State and Provincial Grants
359 Alternative Writing Opportunities

Resources

362 Conferences and Workshops
367 Writing Colonies
369 Organizations Useful to Poets
375 Publications Useful to Poets
379 Close-up: Noel Peattie, Sipapu
This editor offers an inside look at many of
the presses and publications listed in Poet's Market

380 Glossary

Indexes

381 Subject Index
386 State Index
392 General Index

From the Editor

Putting together this second annual **Poet's Market** has taught me more about the world of publishing than I ever learned in 40 years of professional writing. Every day I discovered in the ads or exchange columns of little magazines, the names and addresses of other little magazines or publishers of chapbooks (literally "cheap books," usually meaning saddle-stapled pamphlets of under 40 pages); books; anthologies; cassettes; broadsides; postcards or posters of poetry.

Wonderland of Poetry

Some publish over the air waves of TV (see Word-Fires) or radio. Some publish with a mimeograph machine on the kitchen table. Others (see, for example, Mosaic Press) publish original poetry in beautifully crafted miniature books less than an inch in height. Richard Mathews of Konglomerati Press is a devoted scholar and teacher of book arts while Ric Soos of Realities Library simply tries to get poetry out to as many readers as possible in very inexpensive formats. Some magazines such as *Assembling* publish exactly what you send in the form in which you send it. *Assembling* asks you to submit a thousand copies of each page, printed both sides, to include in the thousand magazines they assemble without editorial intervention, but submissions are by invitation only. *Poetalk/Poemphlet*, tries to print at least one poem, under 20 lines, from each poet who submits.

Finding one's way around this wonderland is nearly impossible without some such guidebook as this volume hopes to be.

Poetry Editors

Publishing for many of those listed in this directory is a labor of love. Many subsidize it with contributed labor, space and funds. Their personalities, feelings and tastes create a colorful landscape as one surveys the publishing scene. Poets should remember, when they submit or correspond with editors, that real people open those envelopes and react to what is written. Usually they are busy people who have no secretaries or staff but whose "office" can be a bedroom desk surrounded by diapers or the dining room table just cleared (or uncleared) of dinner dishes. The word "press" does not imply they own any printing equipment; they may well publish their magazines or chapbooks by taking the copy to the jiffy printer on the corner. An editor's mood may be modified in the middle of reading a poem by junior obnoxiously asking to use the family car—or the cat sleeping on his or her feet may inspire a relaxed personal response to what you have written. Many are quite young—poets themselves, perhaps as much neophytes as those they publish. Some are erudite and some apparently (judging by their comments) relatively unlearned. Some are passionately ideological and some are loftily dedicated only to what they regard as the highest aesthetic standards, regardless of content.

"**Poet's Market** is an oxymoron," commented one editor. That is, the adjective contradicts the noun, as in "sweet poison," or "sad optimist." Most of these publishers pay nothing at all, other than contributor's copies. (But a surprising number of the specialized markets, such as religious magazines, magazines for children, and trade publications actually pay—and reach a far wider audience than literary magazines.) Not even the best poets make a living from sales of poetry alone. Most have jobs or other income; pick up honoraria for readings (where they also sell books and chapbooks); receive grants or awards; or they may gain reputations through poetry which make it easier for them to find publishers for more lucrative prose. But the side benefits could not accrue unless their work appeared in print. And printing poetry is the reason hundreds of these magazine and book publishers exist, many of them publishing nothing *but* poetry.

1987 Poet's Market

The 1986 edition of **Poet's Market** was an immense success, even going into a second printing. But the book must be done again each year because new publishers are constantly emerging—there are more than 400 new listings in this 1987 edition—or moving, or changing their plans or formats. I also asked editors who were listed last year not only to check the accuracy of the information in their old entries but to freshen them with new sample lines, new comments, and more explanation of their operations. In arriving at final copy, I quote them liberally. While I make few evaluative comments, and each entry is approved by the publisher, you can often read between the lines as you consider these comments and samples of poetry and make a realistic assessment or find the personalities and tastes which seem to match your own.

But I also kept in mind that, unlike most directories, this is a book to be *read*, not merely referred to. One of its most popular features is the quoting of sample lines, which constitute a kind of mini-anthology of the whole range of poetry being published today. I know you will enjoy and be edified as I have been by simply reading this array, even of publishers to whom you may never submit your work.

Actually, it is as important to know where *not* to send your poetry as it is to know where to send it. For this reason, this year I use a new market category symbol (V) to mark those listings who do not accept unsolicited manuscripts. See the section Using Your Poet's Market for a full explanation of all the market categories, I-V.

Unfortunately some publishers refuse to be listed because they have no (or inadequate) staff to deal with a flood of submissions. The names and addresses of the most important of these are given at the end of the Publishers of Poetry section.

On the other hand, I exclude publishers who seem to me to be exploitative of poets. But some quite respectable publishers are open to subsidy arrangements, and are probably a much better choice for poets than the big subsidy publishers who advertise in writer's magazines. Some editors charge reading fees. Many who are especially open to work by beginners do not pay even contributor's copies, so you have to buy a copy to see your work in print. I have included many of these because some poets find them of great value, and they make it possible for virtually any poet to be published. Moreover, the editors often comment on submissions and try to be genuinely helpful to those just getting started.

Editors also are "helpful" in the Close-up interviews you will find throughout the book. Other close-ups are with representative poets who give you some insight into their work and their experiences with the publishing world. At the back of the book are a series of other features. In the Alternative Opportunities section I discuss some ways poets can use their talents to support themselves, other than writing poetry for publication in magazines and books. There are dozens of "Major" and hundreds of "Minor" contests and awards, and a discussion of how such contests are to be regarded—and the kinds you should avoid. Conferences and workshops, organizations useful to poets, publications useful to poets, and writing colonies are listed.

Indeed, I have tried to include in this second edition of **Poet's Market** everything I know of which can lend support to working poets.

Judson Jerome

Using Your Poet's Market

Before studying the listings and making your marketing plans, read these suggestions for the most productive use of all the features in **Poet's Market**. Especially note the explanations of the information given in the sample listing.

• This directory has been simplified by listing all activities of one publisher in one listing. For instance, if you would look up Kenyon Hills Publications in another directory you would not know that *New England Review* and *Bread Loaf Quarterly* are also published at the same address, and you would have to look in three different places to find each one's marketing information. In **Poet's Market** you will find all of them under Kenyon Hills Publications. **Therefore, look first in the General Index to find the page number of a specific publication or publisher.**

• A double dagger symbol (‡) appears before the names of publishers new to this edition.

• All magazines are distinguished by asterisks before their names in the listing head.

• Listing names are followed by one or more Roman numerals to enable you to identify quickly five market categories. Observe the categories carefully and submit only to the listings which publish your level or type of poetry. (Some publishers fit more than one category, in which case more than one numeral is assigned to them.)

  I. Publishers very open to beginners' submissions. For acceptance, some require fees, purchase of the publication or membership in an organization, but they are not, so far as I can determine, exploitative of writers, and they often encourage and advise new writers. They publish much of the material they receive and often respond with criticism and suggestions.

 II. The general market to which most poets familiar with literary journals and magazines should submit. Typically they accept 10% or less of poems received and usually reject others without comment. A poet developing a list of publication credits will find many of these to be respected names in the literary world.

III. Prestige markets, typically overstocked. They do not encourage widespread submissions from poets who have not published elsewhere—although many do on occasion publish relatively new and/or little-known poets. So little chance is there of acceptance, I personally would be unlikely to submit to prestige markets, considering it probably to be a waste of my time and that of the editors.

IV. Specialized publications which are limited to contributors from a geographical area, a specific age-group, specific sex or sexual orientation, specific ethnic background, or who accept poems in specific forms (such as haiku) or on specific themes. In most IV listings we also state the specialty (IV, Religious).

 V. Listings which do not accept unsolicited MSS. You cannot submit without specific permission to do so. If the press or magazine for some reason seems especially appropriate for you, you might query (write, with SASE). But, in general, they prefer to locate and solicit the poets whom they publish. I have included them because it is just as important to know where NOT to submit. Also, many are interesting publishers to know about and because this book is widely used as a reference by librarians, researchers, publishers, suppliers and others who need to have as complete a listing of publishers of poetry as possible.

● Note these features illustrated by this sample listing:

(1)PAYCOCK PRESS, (2)*GARGOYLE MAGAZINE (3)(II), Box 3567, Washington, (4)D.C. 20007, phone 202-333-1544, (5)founded 1976, (6)poetry editor Gretchen Johnson. *Gargoyle* comes out twice a year—a (7)hefty, flat-spined, beautifully printed literary journal containing quality fiction, poetry, interviews and reviews. (8)Sample $4 postpaid, subscription $10. The emphasis is on (9)**"innovative and unusual work by new, little-known and/ or neglected writers and artists** . . . We hope to function as a catalyst/crossroads for widely divergent groups, their styles, attitudes, and objectives." Recently published poets include Roy Fisher, Lee Upton, Carlo Parcelli, Nigel Hinshelwood and Doug Messerli. (10)Here are some lines from a poem by Amy Gerstler:

> *Not a soul heard me call out, felled by*
> *his soft karate. The phrase "Flight from*
> *Egypt" popped into my head while I focused*
> *my eyes on the whitewashed ceiling . . .*

(9)**"We don't exclude work in traditional forms, but have rarely published it.** We do not publish political poetry when it is primarily a vehicle for political messages." They (9)**prefer short poems (page or less) but will consider longer work. The poetry should show "an awareness of design and its relation to the subject of the poem."** (11)They estimate that they receive 30,000 submissions a year, of which they use about 30, but they have only a month's backlog and (12)report within a month. (13)The magazine has a circulation of 1,500, 100 subscriptions (25 libraries). (9)**"We prefer to see a group of poems—5 or so.** (14)Any legible format. (15)Submit anytime, no query necessary. (16)Payment: 1 complimentary copy, additional copies half price." In addition, as Paycock Press, they publish one perfect-bound chapbook (about 50 pp.) by an individual poet each year, and they project an anthology for 1987. (9)**Advisable for poet to have seen an issue of the magazine before submitting to the chapbook series. Send sample of 5-10 poems, brief bio and note on publications.** If your manuscript is published as a chapbook you get (16)10% (average 100 copies) of the press run, and half the net profit, if any. Sample $5.95 postpaid. They are likely to comment on submissions, "especially if the work is close to what we're looking for." Gretchen Johnsen advises, (17)**"**Read as widely as possible the contemporary journals of poetry to find out what's new and relevant to your experience and style and to avoid duplications. Submit to those publications which are most interesting to you as a reader."

(1) In most cases the editor decides on the main name for the listing, in this case under the name of the publishing company rather than the magazine.

(2) Asterisk in the main heading indicates the title of a magazine.

(3) Roman numeral indicates the market category.

(4) Two-letter codes are used for all US states and areas (in this case District of Columbia) and Canadian provinces. For a complete list of these codes, see the Glossary in the back of this book.

(5) Date of founding helps you judge the stability of the publication or publisher. Recently founded publications may be more in need of material and thus more open to submissions—but they have not yet established continuity.

(6) Names of contact persons are provided by the publisher. If no name is given I would address a submission to "Poetry Editor." Sometimes there are special instructions, even a separate address, for the poetry editor. Note and follow such instructions carefully.

(7) Description of the physical appearance and quality of the publication. See the Glossary for definition of special terms. I have given as much information about the appearance of the publication as possible because poets, especially, like to imagine in what form their

work will appear and the quality of the printing and binding.

(8) Almost all editors advise you to read sample publications before submitting—and to obtain guidelines if they are available.

(9) Boldface text indicates information important to keep in mind when submitting—the preferred themes and the specifics of actual submission policies. Quotation marks indicate the description is in the words of the editor. I often quote when the language seems ambiguous or unclear to me—not true in this case—or to enable you to sense the personality and attitudes of the editors.

(10) I ask the editors to select sample lines, but in some cases they prefer that I do it or simply do not select samples. In those cases I make the selection (if I have a sample of the publication), trying to find a brief excerpt that seems representative of the quality of the poetry published and, if possible, an excerpt that is somewhat self-contained in form and meaning. Samples are indented and italicized to make them easy to spot.

(11) Information about how many poems are received and accepted is based on approximations by the editors. It gives you some indication of the likelihood of acceptance of any given submission and helps you analyze the market.

(12) Reporting time—the length of time a publisher needs to respond to your submission—is approximate and can fluctuate greatly. If you have had no response within the reporting time plus a week or so, it is appropriate to query politely (with SASE) whether the manuscript is still under consideration. If a second or third query, spaced a few weeks apart, gets no response, it is appropriate to notify the editor that you are submitting the manuscript elsewhere. (Always, of course, keep copies of manuscripts submitted! Sometimes you will be unable to get them returned.)

(13) Circulation figures are the total of subscriptions (individual and library) plus off-the-shelf sales.

(14) This editor is open to any *legible* submission; others are much more selective, especially with computer printouts, and will tell you in the listing exactly what they will accept. In the early days of word processing there were many dot-matrix printers of poor quality on the market and many editors object to manuscripts printed on them. Now the quality of dot-matrix printing has improved, and many dot-matrix manuscripts, especially when photocopied on a good machine, cannot be distinguished from those printed on "Letter-quality" machines.

(15) This editor does not mention "simultaneous submissions" (submitting the same material to more than one publisher at the same time) so she does NOT accept them. Most editors of magazines refuse to accept such submissions. Some publishers of books and chapbooks do not object to simultaneous submissions; if that is the case, the listing will say: simultaneous submissions OK. If your manuscript is a simultaneous submission, always mention it in a cover letter.

(16) Payment is a contributor's copy. Most publishers pay copies only. A few (all in category I, for beginners) do not pay even a copy, so the poet has to buy the magazine (or book) to see the work in print.

(17) This editor's advice.

• Always include SASE (self-addressed, stamped envelope) or, for foreign publishers, SASE with IRCs (self-addressed envelope with International Reply Coupons purchased at the post office) when submitting; querying; asking for a catalog, sample or other response. Be sure you have enough return postage to cover the amount of material you want returned and that the return envelope is large enough to hold such material. This information is so important that we repeat it at the bottom of many pages throughout this book rather than include it in individual listings.

• Consult the Glossary in the back of this book for explanations of any unfamiliar terms you might encounter while reading the listings.

Launching Your Poems into the Public Sea

by Judson Jerome

Those of you who read my poetry column in *Writer's Digest* have met there Myrtle Whimple, a figment of my imagination who pours out her heart in Guthrie, Oklahoma. In one of her poems she describes in her inimitable and folksy style a classical cure for writer's block:

A Rhyme in Time

(For my granddaughter, Patti Lorelei, who, assigned to write a poem for her fifth-grade composition class, said she couldn't think of one.)

If you've got to write a poem,
    And you haven't got a thought,
And your tummy's got the jitters,
    And your tongue in throat is caught,
And your brow is sort of sweaty,
    And your hand can't make a start,
There is just one place to find a poem:
    Child, look into your heart.

Sometimes a piece of paper can
    Seem blank and hard as stone,
And the pencil you pick up to use
    Seems blunt as any bone,
And the words that came so easy when
    You were talkin' on the phone
All scattered like the blackbirds that
    Left the king alone.
And you're sittin' there all bound and gagged,
    Your senses blown apart.
There's only one thing left to do:
    Child, look into your heart.

I know you are too big to cry
    And much too nice to curse:
Just listen to your quiet heart
    A-pumpin' out a verse.
No need to bite your pencil or
    To pout and make a frown.
Inside you is a ticker that
    Will never let you down,
That will straighten out your tangles,
    Put your horse before its cart,
And flood your emptiness with song:
    Child, look into your heart.

Well, you've done that, haven't you—children of all ages? And having done so, you're now wondering what to do with the product.

Consider the case of Deckard Ritter. In the little Ohio village where I live there are dozens of poets like myself whose poetry regularly appears in literary journals. But the unquestioned village bard, until his recent death at 92, was a man named Deckard Ritter, whose poems during his lifetime were published almost nowhere other than in the letters section of our local weekly, *The Yellow Springs News*. It is a publication unlisted in this directory (as are most other newspapers, but many use poetry). Deckard had something even poets of greater literary reputation might well envy: an eager audience of friends, family and neighbors who actually *wanted* to read his poetry. And his poetry had qualities that modern poetry in general seems to lack: clarity, broad public relevance, optimism tempered by realism, steady joy, and graceful form. Here's a little sample:

If There's One

Why should I labor on in verse
And strive to mingle sense with sound?
Almost none will hear my song—
But if there's one, I'm bound.

In the Beginning

Before you send out poems hither and yon, you might well consider his example. If you are a beginner, stop and think of your writing goals. Whom do you wish to reach? What do those people read? Or what do they listen to on the radio or watch on television? Many local stations offer opportunities for listeners to participate. There are thousands of church and organizational newsletters, special interest magazines, bulletin boards and other means of publication which might suit your needs for communicating with those near and dear (or far, but sharing common interests).

This volume tells you of hundreds of publications in which your poetry might be welcome. Study the listings which have a (I) market code. Many of the specialized magazines categorized as (IV) in this volume are also quite open to the work of beginners, provided they also meet the magazines' special requirements. The word *beginners* should not be interpreted too narrowly. Deckard Ritter had been writing poems for most of a century. His poems were insightful, sophisticated and highly crafted, mostly in traditional metrical forms. But had he sought a market beyond Yellow Springs he would have been most likely to find the right magazines for what he wrote in categories (I) and (IV) including some in (IV) that want writing only from elderly people.

The Next Step

But, once you have some experience in submitting poetry and having it accepted and then have aspirations of being recognized as a poet by the literary world, it is probably to publications in categories (II) and (III) you should look. Yours is quite a specialized search. You are not primarily concerned with reaching neighbors or your family or friends or masses of common readers. And though you may have dreams of reaching an audience you can never know, posterity, you realize that matter will have to take care of itself. Now you have to concern yourself with contemporary literary taste, that of the editors of respected journals and publishing houses, the critics and reviewers, the academic teachers of literature, the folks at the National Endowment of the Arts, or those in the foundations, or of those handing out the literary prizes and the opinions of the hundred or so poets who are "recognized" at any given time in the United States, or Canada, or England, or some other nation of the world.

There are some advantages in aiming for this elite audience. That's about the only way, for instance, of reaching posterity, of gaining a seat on Olympus alongside Homer, Keats, Yeats,

Frost and Emily Dickinson. That last name reminds us that posterity may eventually seek out the manuscripts stored in our attic trunks, as it found Emily's little beribboned packets after her death. Yet she had sent out some half-dozen harbingers before she died, poems which appeared in enough magazines and anthologies to suggest that a mother lode might be buried somewhere. She had gained enough attention from a few of the literati to whet their interest. Had she not let out such peeps the American literary heritage might lack one of its greatest women poets to date.

Another advantage of working toward reaching the audience of those seriously concerned about literature, is that you can actually learn how to do it, provided you have some background, taste and intelligence. Most of the instruction, as in my own columns and books about how to write poetry, and in workshops, writers' conferences, and creative writing courses, is geared toward this kind of audience. You can read the literary journals, study the contemporary critics, or learn from poetry readings. In spite of the diversity of modern poetry—represented in this volume by the many quoted sample lines—there are still many shared premises and tastes. Each poet is different, yet in their assumptions about what is admirable and to be emulated, literary poets are more alike than the poetry they write would lead you to expect. Hang around the poets at a writers' workshop, or in the accompanying cocktail parties, and you'll know you are entering a rather coherent and predictable world.

The Marketing Game

To some extent you must play the game, and I would like here to help you play it successfully. A "game" it sometimes seems—akin to analyzing trends and doing market research. Careful, now. Not too much. One editor who wrote me scorned the evidence he sees in many submissions of "career-mongering": poets whose cover letters were too obsequious, or too self-congratulatory, or too phonily professional (talking about such things as "first American serial rights only"). I rarely use cover letters myself, unless there is something quite specific I want to explain about the enclosed manuscript, so unwilling am I to venture among those particular hazards. Some editors like cover letters—and say so in their entries. Some are insulted unless there is one. But unless the listing specifically asks for a cover letter, you are safe to submit without one. At most it should be, for those not requesting more, a brief note regarding your most important prior publications. If you have none of those, silence is your best friend. Let your poems speak for themselves.

But for your own mental health it is important that you maintain perspective about "success" in the current literary world. In *On Being a Poet* I say:

> Obviously, the judgment of the professionals of any given time may or may not coincide with the judgment of the ages (and even the "judgment of the ages" is relative). In the mid-seventeenth century, when Donne and Milton were writing, the professionals were betting all their chips on Abraham Cowley, the T.S. Eliot of his day. Cowley is now regarded primarily as a historical curiosity. Since Eliot's death his reputation, which so dominated the literary world for nearly half a century, has similarly diminished. He is currently most widely known as the author of *Cats*.

At least in seventeenth century England there was some consensus, however mistaken in the long run, about the best poets. Today there is no such consensus. After the deaths of Eliot and Frost, many in the United States regarded Robert Lowell as our greatest living poet (though I thought they were overlooking the much greater Archibald MacLeish). Since the deaths of Lowell and MacLeish there has been no one recognized in that position, though I have nominated Richard Wilbur, a choice with which few can be found to agree. There is no dominant school, nor even a dozen major poets nationally or internationally recognized as such. In this era we seem to have a plethora of poets whom many regard as very good—but none as great, none of the stature of the giants of the early part of this century.

Increasingly reputations are regional, often sub-regional. One cannot talk about West Coast poets, but one may of Bay Area Poets, of Los Angeles Poets, of Northwest Poets. I have the impression that in some localities, especially in cities, the "known" poets are known primarily in their neighborhoods. I have asked editors and publishers listed here to name a few of the better-known poets they have recently published. I recognize very few of the poets on those lists. Some recur often, but I still have not often seen their poetry.

The lesson you can learn (if you're playing the game) is to know what is going on in your immediate area. Look at the listings by state, province and nation in the back of this book. Where, if anywhere, is the "scene" you might be most likely to participate in? Where are readings being given? Sponsored by what groups? The newsletters of such organizations as the Poets League of Greater Cleveland or the Long Island Poetry Collective reflect seething activity, readings, publications parties. In less populous regions, the state poetry societies (members of the National Federation of State Poetry Societies) often have local chapters in which poets may get together and create their own scene.

If you are beginning to break into magazines, those near you geographically are often your best bets. If you have a collection of poems (most of which have already appeared in magazines) and are seeking a chapbook or book publisher, one nearby offers you the advantage of collaboration with the publisher both in designing and producing the book and in distributing it. Sell it at local readings. Send it to nearby magazines for review. Find out whether your state arts council has grants or other opportunities for poets. Like Deckard Ritter, start where you are and with the folks you can personally know.

Submission Mechanics

But, no matter where you are sending your work, learn first how to go about it properly. Remember that in many cases you are dealing with the editors of small presses who own not a single item of publishing equipment. These aren't giant companies. They don't have offices, secretaries, often not even stationery. If a registered letter or one with postage due arrives, a guy or gal like you or me has to get on a bicycle or into a car and make a trip to the post office to get it, which doesn't cultivate a cheery mood. If your return envelope flap gets glued shut—which many seem to do (I used to imagine the poets who sent them lived in the tropics)—there just might not be a reusable envelope suitable for replacing it. Most of the editors you deal with are also poets, many of them young, trying to make it just as you are. Remember that a submission is communication between human beings, both living and hurting and hoping and hollering at their respective ends of the line.

Okay, your envelope arrives and waits its week or so (at most magazines) in the inbasket. When an editor opens it, what does he or she assume? First, that the work is submitted for publication—so you don't have to say that on an extra piece of paper. (Tell them if it *isn't*.) Most likely it will be a packet of 3-6 poems, folded twice, in a #10 ("business-size") envelope, with another such envelope, your SASE (self-addressed stamped envelope), folded twice and tucked in with the poems.

Suppose you want to be different. Perhaps you decide to use a 9x12" envelope with cardboard backing for the MS, an odd-size return envelope, or a MS in beautiful calligraphy instead of typewriting. Or you use a typewriter with cute italics or Olde English type, or YOU PUT YOUR POEM IN ALL CAPS TO MAKE IT STAND OUT, or you put " " around your titles, or you leave your name and address off the MS because it's on the outside of the envelope (the editor just threw away). Instead of standard 8½x11" white typing paper you use small violet stationery or a poster-size piece of brown wrapping paper rolled like a scroll. Your typewriter being broken (or nonexistent), you borrow a spiral notebook from your daughter, write out your poems on its ruled pages, rip them out and send them with ragged edges. Or you have some other individualistic variation on standard submission practices. Many editors will assume right off (I would) that you are an amateur. Now it's no sin to be an amateur, but you're not likely to get into a category (II) magazine if you behave in a category (I) fashion.

It's not you or your manuscript which should be different, but the poetry itself, and then, different only in being of unusual force and beauty, of distinctive imagination, of searching insight and freshness of language—not *decorated* differently. Ordinarily put no more than one poem to a page (except some publishers will accept several haiku or very short poems to a page). If the poem is longer than one page, put your name and the poem's shortened title at the top of each page after the first. A few publishers in category (I) and in category (IV) (for the elderly, primarily) will accept handwritten MSS, but most won't. Type or use a word processor. Use good quality white paper—not the slippery erasable stuff. Some poets put the line-count of each poem at the top of the page, which is all right but not essential.

Okay, you make it past the first barrier. The editor has opened your envelope without forming prejudices about your amateurishness. Your name and address are on each poem (either right or left upper corner). Poems are single-spaced, double-spaced between stanzas (unless the guidelines for the publication indicate otherwise). Your submission is not a single poem, or a massive collection, but a reasonably tasteful, small packet. Most editors will accept high-quality photocopies (indeed, cannot tell them from typed or word-processed originals), and that's what I usually send, saving the clean original for reproduction as needed (when MSS become tattered or stained from too many trips to editors' desks). Unless you say otherwise the editor will assume that the poems are unpublished, and are not simultaneously submitted elsewhere.

And then you wait. To the litany of editors complaining about such matters as unsuitable submissions, nuisance calls and queries, discourteous letters, and amateurish-looking manuscripts I could add the litany of poets complaining about the delays, the occasional rudeness of editors, the practices of a few who write on MSS or staple them and make retyping necessary, their unresponsiveness in shipping out sample copies or answering inquiries, and the assumption that they are God's gift to the poets because they occasionally deign to use for free the material submitted. None of us is perfect. But we can improve the situation by behaving toward one another with common decency and intelligence.

Copyrighting Your Work

You *can* write the Copyright Office, Library of Congress, Washington, D.C. 20559, and get the forms to copyright your poems for a small fee, if you wish. Then you can mark each poem with © _____ (filling in the year and your name). But it's unnecessary, and I don't advise it. No one is going to steal your poem. (You should be so lucky!) Besides, in my opinion, a copyright notice on your MS also looks amateurish. Most little magazines are copyrighted when printed, which covers your poem. You can use the poem elsewhere, as in a book, unless you gave the editor, in writing, more than first rights for his copyrighted magazine. If that's the case, you should write the editor for permission to use the poem, or to have the copyright assigned to you, a request that will be granted automatically (and without cost) by almost all publishers. Book publishers ordinarily take out a copyright in the name of the author (if it is a collection of work by an individual; if it's an anthology, the same procedures apply as are used in magazines). But you have signed a contract for the book which authorizes only the publisher to reprint your work. If you want to use the poetry elsewhere you must request permission from the publisher, which is almost always granted as a courtesy.

Sharks in the Water

You have probably seen (I hope you haven't fallen for them) ads in writers' magazines and elsewhere saying "Poems Wanted" or "Song Lyrics Wanted" or inviting you to enter contests with a "chance" to be included in some forthcoming anthology. Send them any piece of nonsense on a scrap of paper, and you'll get that "chance"—provided you buy a copy of the book at some excessive cost. When it arrives, usually quite a fat book, you'll probably find your poem in small type on a page with many poems by others who have agreed to buy the anthology. Hundreds of poets will be included. Multiply what you paid for the book by the number of poets and estimate how much profit was made.

Use your head a moment. Who could afford such advertisements other than people who were making money off the poets who respond? I get sad letters from poets who say they have been published in three famous anthologies and wonder why no magazine will take their work. Such publication is not an honor. Quite the opposite. These anthologies are never reviewed or read by anyone with any literary knowledge because it is clearly understood how they work and why. If you have been published in one, keep quiet about it. For some reason these businesses particularly ply upon poets. Maybe poets have more vanity than their counterparts in the other arts, vanity which enables one after another of these arrangements to work. They are perfectly legal, by the way. If you fall for them, you have only yourself to blame.

These are variations on what is known as the "vanity press," or the "subsidy publisher." If you contact these publishers you will be sent publicity pointing out, quite accurately, that there are many instances in literary history of self-publication, and that many controversial and important points-of-view would be suppressed if our "free press" did not provide opportunities for any author to pay for publication. If you send a MS, you will probably be flattered into thinking you are one of the chosen few, too unconventional, original, innovative and eloquent for the crass commercial world, but the publisher would be honored to add you to his list—if you pay the freight. Such publishers may even imply that your book will sell—a claim no reputable publisher would ever make concerning poetry.

And the cost is high. Sometimes the author, who has already paid to have a whole press run printed and bound, will be granted only a few "author's copies" and must buy any additional ones from the publisher (at a special author's discount), over and above the cost of printing. Sometimes copies are not even bound, but stored in the warehouse until sufficient time has passed to send them to the recycling plant. Review copies are sent out, but, fair or not, reviewers ignore them because they recognize the names of the publishers and know how the books got into print.

There are many honorable ways to self-publish, but these large vanity houses are, though not dishonorable, possibly one of the worst ways. You will do much better to go to a printer, or to one of the various subsidy publishers listed in this directory (see, for example, Northwoods Press) which offer reasonable alternatives to poets wishing to self-publish. Robert Olmstead, the editor at Northwoods, explains a great deal in his listing about the economics of publishing poetry. His realistic description of what it takes to make poetry pay will help you understand why a support operation is necessary for many poets. As in regard to the sharks in the water, suppress your vanity for your own protection.

Off and Running

With the savvy you can gain by what I have said here and in the other introductory sections of this book and, above all, what you can learn from the diverse and colorful range of editors represented in this book—their comments about what they want, how they work, and the advice they have to give—you will soon (if you're not already) be piling stacks of contributor's copies in your closet (though not money in your bank account). Read them. Get acquainted with your fellow poets. Write them letters with comments on their poems. Try to develop penpals for critical exchange. Though the editors themselves are not likely to have much time for correspondence, I have found that most writers, including poets, are usually grateful for personal comments about their work—provided you don't come across as seeking primarily to draw attention to your own work.

It is in the give and take of informal exchange, networking (primarily through the mails), that you can learn most and link yourself most comfortably to the literary world you are becoming part of. If you show genuine interest and appreciation, your correspondents or new literary acquaintances may well show genuine interest in and appreciation of you. But for that to happen, you have to *be* interesting, to write well enough to *be* appreciated. In my other books and in my monthly column in *Writer's Digest* I have been trying for the past 25 years to help you in those respects.

Meanwhile, I will, through the year, be preparing for next year's edition of **Poet's Market**. I always appreciate news, tips and comments, and I answer my mail. I usually will not comment on poetry you send me: I get far too much to make that possible. But I will be interested in learning of your experiences, good and bad, with the publishers listed here, or of new publications emerging, changes in address or editorial policy, and other matters which will help me help you and your peers stay informed.

Market listing information

- Listings are based on questionnaires and verified copy. They are not advertisements *nor are markets reported here necessarily endorsed by the editor.*
- Information in the listings comes directly from the publishers and is as accurate as possible, but publications and editors come and go, and poetry needs fluctuate between the publication of this directory and the time you use it.
- **Poet's Market** *reserves the right to exclude any listing that does not meet its requirements.*

The Markets

Publishers of Poetry

Last year in the first edition of **Poet's Market** I said several times: "Any poet who fails to get published (without paying for the privilege) has simply run out of stamps or persistence." I want to repeat that phrase again this year, and as you read the wealth of listings in this section you'll understand why.

Many thousands of magazines and journals around the world publish poetry. Hundreds publish nothing but poetry. In addition, hundreds of presses are churning out a mountain of chapbooks, pamphlets, broadsides, paperbacks and hardcovers of poetry each year.

No poet should be stifled by a lack of publishing opportunity.

For advice on the proper methods of submitting your poetry to these publishers, see the Manuscript Mechanics section in "Launching Your Poetry into the Public Sea." Also make sure you study "Using Your **Poet's Market**" in order to understand well all the information given in the listings. One piece of information in that section is so important it is worth stating here also:

All publishers require that submissions and queries, requests for guidelines, catalogs or other information be accompanied by SASEs (self-addressed, stamped envelopes), or, for those in countries other than your own, SAEs (self-addressed envelopes) and sufficient IRCs (International Reply Coupons, purchased at your post office) for reply or return of your manuscript.

The editors and publishers of the publications in this section would *like* to assume that you have studied the magazine to which you are submitting. It's always a good idea to buy a sample copy if you haven't seen the magazine—not with, but *before* your first submission. Most presses are shoestring operations and sales of samples are a big help to them, as studying them is a big help to you. But few of us can afford to buy samples of *all* the publications to which we submit. If you are familiar with the *Antioch Review*, you perhaps need not also read the *Indiana Review* or the *Virginia Quarterly Review*. But if you are submitting to *Kaldron* and have no idea what "visual poetry" is, or to the *Magazine of Speculative Poetry* and wonder (as I did—and still can't well explain) what speculative poetry might be, a sample copy is in order.

If you live near a big library, especially a university library, you might find there a collection of publications of little magazines and small presses. Some bookstores, especially in bohemian or university neighborhoods, carry selections of such magazines. Or send for a few. But don't abuse editors by sending manuscripts indiscriminately the way poets did to the one who wrote me:

First, a very heartfelt Thank You! for the lovely write-up in your **Poet's Market**! I found myself reading and rereading it. . . . ("Gosh, that's OUR magazine he's talking about!") Second, I would like to complain politely about the submissions we've been getting since it came out. We've been receiving an average of 10-12 letters per week, containing 2-12 poems each for a couple of months now! Incredible! I know you've often written about inappropriate submissions . . . now I know why. It has been a real "education" to see how many people seemingly mail out their work without any consideration of suitability for the market. And out of over 100 submissions now we've had exactly TWO requests for sample copies! (I wish we could afford to offer free copies, maybe it would encourage people to be a little more discerning.) Enough grumbling. Thanks again for the exposure, Jud. We have received some very lovely poetry; it's great to be able to share thought- and feeling-provoking verse with our readers.

That very little, very specialized magazine edited by the woman who wrote me and her husband in their home, uses very little poetry on very specific themes—all explained clearly in their entry. If readers use this directory like a phone book it will be a disservice to all of us.

Speaking of phone books, though many publishers give their phone numbers, there is almost never a good reason to phone them about poetry. Nor to send queries before submitting, except to those in category (V). Just send along your poems and SASE. They'll know what to do with them.

ABATTOIR EDITIONS (II), University of Nebraska at Omaha, Omaha, NE 68182-0190, phone 402-554-2787, founded 1972, poetry editor Bonnie O'Connell, publishes **first, limited editions of new poetry** or short prose printed by hand, chapbooks, pamphlets, hardbacks. They will consider "**work that's fresh, original.**" They have published poetry and prose by Charles Gullans, Dana Gioia, Art Homer, James Merrill, Philip Gallo, Weldon Kees, Norman Dubie, Charles Martin, W.S.D. Piero and Richard Wilbur. Forthcoming writers include Sam Pereira and Brenda Hillman. As a sample, they offer these lines by Timothy Steele:

> . . . *I see*
> *That evil is the formless and unspoken,*
> *And that peace rests in form and nomenclature,*
> *Which render our two natures—formerly*
> *Discomfited, self-conscious-second nature*

They publish 2 chapbooks and 2 hardbacks a year. **Query. MS should be legibly handwritten, typed or photocopied. Include return postage. Considers simultaneous submissions. Payment is 10% royalties and 2 author's copies. They sometimes comment on MSS.**

‡****ABBEY (II)**, 5360 Fallriver Row Court, Columbia, MD 21044, phone 301-730-4272, founded 1971, editor David Greisman, a "small press litmag, so cheaply produced that it's embarrassing but with a persistence that quality writers seem to like." **The editor will not describe the kind of poetry he wants or quote lines, but he did say that he doesn't want "political and/or pornographic." The purpose of** *Abbey* is to "give the same 'buzz' to the reader that your first Molson Ale gives on a hot July afternoon." The magazine has published poetry by Gretchen Johnson, Harry Calhoun, Ron Androla, Vera Bergsheim, John Elsberg, and Steven Ford Brown. *Abbey* appears 2-4 times a year; it is magazine-sized, 14-26 pp., photo-reproduced, with pen and ink artwork. Circulation is 200 (controlled); subscription price is $2 for 4 issues. **Sample available for 50¢ postpaid. Pay is 1-2 copies. Writers should submit no more than 10 short poems. Reporting time is "2 days-2 years" and time to publication is 6 months. For chapbook publication, poets should query first, sending 14-20 poems plus credits and bio. Queries will be answered in 1 month and MSS reported on in 2 months. Pay for chapbook is 30-50 author's copies.** Mr. Greisman publishes 1-2 chapbooks/year, "cheap Xerox" format, with an average page count of 14.

ABRAXAS PRESS, INC. (II.), 2518 Gregory St., Madison, WI 53711, founded 1968, poetry editor Ingrid Swanberg. *Abraxas*, a literary quarterly which uses "**contemporary poetry of outstanding quality**" and reviews of poetry has published poets such as Ivan Arguelles, Charles Bukowski, Janet Gray, Andrei Codrescu and Roberta Hill Whiteman. It has a circulation of 600; 300 subscriptions of which a third are libraries. They receive about 2,500 submissions per year, use 100, have a 3-5 month backlog. The editors chose these sample lines:

the sleepers in the leaf each in a separate world
hear the wind's cadaver soughing through hair
heaven is as far from the hand's reach
as ever on this beautiful bleak day

Sample: $4 postpaid. Submit up to 5 poems, no simultaneous submissions, no unsolicited reviews. Reports in 1-5 months, pays in copies.

‡ACHERON PRESS (II), Bear Creek at the Kettle, Friendsville, MD 21531, founded 1981, editor-in-chief Robert E. Pletta, a press that publishes poetry anthologies as well as supplemental college texts, historical sketches. Poetry **"can be any length, subject matter, style, or purpose, but should not be experimental or naive. "We have a traditional bent."** The press has published **Knife Gift** by Kevin Sheehan and **Masked Avenger** by Doug De Mans. They publish about 6 poetry titles per year, digest-sized, 75-100 pp., flat-spined paperbacks. **When submitting, poets should send sample poems with bio and aesthetic aims. Simultaneous submissions, photocopied, dot-matrix, or discs compatible with IBM are acceptable. Royalties are 7½-10%, plus advance, honorarium, and author's copies (amount and number unspecified). Catalog free for 4x10" SASE.** "We do run limited editions in cooperation with [partially subsidized by] the author." Because of the general relevance of Robert Pletta's advice, I quote him at length: "Many more new poets would and could be published if more of them were also readers of materials that are published by the smaller presses. Acheron received more than 4,000 submissions last year, but our mailing records show no more than a handful of those potential authors ordering and, we hope, reading our publications. New authors should realize that the 'small press scene' is exactly that—small. . . . For it to exist at all, it must often survive harsh, financial realities. The small presses can only maintain their integrity by support from their *readers* as well as authors. . . . Most would be poets really do need more *reading* experience. Far too many are only vaguely aware of the poetic heritage. . . . It should be obvious . . . that a passing familiarity with the publications of the press with whom one is considering publication is well advised."

ACTION, LIGHT AND LIFE PRESS (IV, Nature), 901 College Ave., Winona Lake, IN 46590, phone 219-267-7656, press founded 1886, *Action* started in 1981, poetry editor Vera Bethel, is an 8-page leaflet used for **Sunday school take-home material. They use nature poems for children 9-11, 8-16 lines, for which they pay $5. Reports in 1 month. Sample for SASE. Guidelines available**. As a sample I selected "Spring Surprise" by Mildred Grenier:

When I awoke this bright spring morn,
A warm wind whispered through the pines,
Our lawn was wearing a new green dress,
All buttoned up with dandelions!

They receive about 200 submissions per year, use 15. Their circulation is 35,000.

ADASTRA PRESS (II), 101 Strong St., Easthampton, MA 01027, 413-527-3324, founded 1980 by Gary Metras, who says, "I publish poetry because I love poetry. I produce the books on antique equipment using antique methods because I own the equipment and because it's cheaper—I don't pay myself a salary—it's a hobby—it's **a love affair with poetry and printing of fine editions**. I literally sweat making these books and I want the manuscript to show me the author also sweated." All his books and chapbooks are **limited editions, handset, letterpress**, printed with handsewn signatures. The chapbooks are in square-spine paper wrappers, cloth editions also handcrafted. If sales warrant, he'll reprint offset, perfect-bound editions. He wants **no rhyme, no religious. Poetry is communication** first, although it is art. **Long poems and thematic groups** are nice for chapbooks. No subjects are tabu, but topics should be drawn from **real life experiences**. I include accurate **dreams** as real life. He has published books by W. D Ehrhart, Peter Oresick, Constance Pierce, Harry Humes, Zoe Anglesey, and others, including himself. Here are some lines from "Pastoral" by Richard Jones:

Distant guns; the evening sky is red.
When will it end, those explosions
inside you, the doves who live
inside the heart, being shot, one by one?

ALWAYS submit MSS or queries with a stamped, self-addressed envelope (SASE) within your country or International Reply Coupons (IRCs) purchased from the post office for other countries.

That's from the chapbook, *Innocent Things*, published in an edition of 220, which sells for $4. He brings out 1-3 such chapbooks and 1 or 2 each of perfect-bound paperbacks (48-56 pp.) and clothbound books (18-56 pp.) per year. **Author gets 10% of the press run in copies. Query first. Considers simultaneous submissions. He has a catalog he'll send you for a SASE, and you might buy some of the books to decide whether it's for you.**

‡*ADRIFT (II, IV, Irish, Irish-American), 4D, 239 East 5th St., New York, NY 10003, founded 1980, editor Thomas McGonigle, who says, "The **orientation of magazine is Irish, Irish-American**. I expect reader-writer knows and goes beyond Yeats, Kavanagh, Joyce, O'Brien." The literary magazine is open to all kinds of submissions, but does not want to see "junk." Simultaneous submissions OK. Poets recently published include James Liddy, Thomas McCarthy, Francis Stuart, and Gilbert Sorrentino. As a sample, the editor selected this poem, "Mussel" by Beatrice Smedley:

> eating with
> friend his other
> pleasure now
> more limpid

Adrift appears twice a year and has a circulation of 1,000 with 200 subscriptions, 50 of which go to libraries. Price per issue is $3, subscription $7. **Sample: $4 postpaid. Magazine pays, rate varies; contributors receive 1 copy.** Magazine-sized, 32 pp., offset on heavy stock, cover matte card, saddle-stapled.

AEGINA PRESS (I, II), 4937 Humphrey Rd., Huntington, WV 25704, founded 1983, poetry editor Ira Herman, **is a subsidy press** strongly committed to publishing new or established poets. "We try to provide a way for talented poets to have their collections published, which otherwise might go unpublished because of commercial, bottom-line considerations. Aegina Press was established to publish quality poetry that the large publishers will not handle because it is not commercially viable. We believe it is unfair that a poet has to have a 'name' or a following in order to have a book of poems accepted by a publisher. Poetry is the purest form of literary art, and it should be made available to those who appreciate it." The editor selected these sample lines are from Kirk Judd's "Field of Vision":

> Time
> is not enemy or friend
> but element, as rain or wind
> eroding immortality

"**The poetry books we accept are subsidized by the author (or an institution).** In return, the author receives all sales proceeds from the book, and any unsold copies left from the print run belong to the author. Our marketing program includes submission to distributors, agents, other publishers, and bookstores and libraries." **Manuscripts should be typed and no shorter than 45 pages. There is no upper length limit. Simultaneous and photocopied submissions OK.** They publish perfect-bound (flat-spined) paperbacks with glossy covers. **Sample books are available for $5 each plus $1 for postage.**

‡*AERIAL, SLIPPERY PEOPLE PRESS (II), Box 1901, Manassas, VA 22110, phone 703-368-5614, founded 1984, poetry editors Rod Smith and Wayne Kline, a twice-yearly publication that wants "**intelligent, energetic writing by poets moving forward from Black Mountain, New York, the Beats, objectivists, L-A-N-G-U-A-G-E, etc.**" They have recently published work by Hannah Weiner, Gretchen Johnsen, Deirdra Baldwin, and Douglas Messerli. The magazine is 6x8½", offset, 50-60 pp. Circulation is 500, of which 75 are subscriptions and 300 are newsstand sales. Single copy price is $3.50. **Sample available for $3.50 postpaid. Pay is "only for solicited material. Contributor's copy to unsolicited material." Poets should submit 5-10 pages. Reporting time is 1 week-1 month and time to publication is 6-18 months.** The editors say, "One hears so much about the 'sad state of contemporary poetry'—fact is, there are a great number of truly exciting artists working today. You just have to look for them."

*AGADA (IV, Jewish themes), 2020 Essex St., Berkeley, CA 94703, phone 415-848-0965, founded 1981, poetry editor Reuven Goldfarb, "**is a Jewish literary magazine replete with illustrative graphic art, which is published semiannually.**" They want "**quality work with Jewish subject matter or sensibility. Send SASE for guidelines. We welcome original lyric or narrative work, translations of Scriptural or other Hebrew, Yiddish, or Ladino poetry**—or from any language which has success-

✚ *The double dagger before a listing indicates that the listing is new in this edition. New markets are often the most receptive to freelance contributions.*

fully incorporated at least some aspects of the Jewish experience. Form doesn't matter as long as the forms are used well—with some awareness of what masters of that technique have achieved. Don't like: inappropriate line breaks; poems that degenerate into prose—that break rhythm—that never really take off; loading excessive meaning on key words which are often placed on a line of their own; verse that is preponderantly intellectual; clichés. Admire: fresh ways of looking at familiar material; original use of language and metaphor; fusing various levels of meaning into an allusion; real humor; tenderness." They have published poetry by Isaac Mozeson, Julia Vinograd and Karl Dardick. The editor selected these sample lines by Suzanne Bernhardt from "Like Some Image of the Sea":

> in the pool house
> mothers take their time,
> dark wood baking
> their bones

The issue I examined (Winter, 1984) contained a long poem in Spanish by García Lorca, "Cementario Judio," translated into English by Hylah Jacques. The 7x10" professionally-printed, saddle-stapled magazine has a circulation of 1,000, 250 subscriptions of which about 35-40 are libraries. Each issue uses about 14 pp. of poetry. They receive over 200 submissions per year, use "a couple of dozen," have as much as a 6 month backlog. **Sample: $6 for current issue, $5.75 for back issue. Subscription: $12/ year. Submissions acknowledged. Submit up to 6 poems, typed, double-spaced. (Photocopy OK "but don't really like 'word processor' poetry".) Include SASE and return postcard. Advise if submitted elsewhere or if it has been published elsewhere. "No objection to republishing if there is no serious overlap in audience.** Likewise, a commitment to request credit being given to *Agada* if it should be published again is appreciated. **Reports within 3-4 months. Payment in copies.** The editor advises, **"Learn from the greats, pay attention to small details in daily life, play with words, listen deeply."**

AGENDA EDITIONS, *AGENDA (II), 5 Cranbourne Ct., Albert Bridge Rd., London, England SW11 4PE, founded 1959, poetry editors William Cookson and Peter Dale. *Agenda* is a 7x5", 80 pp. (of which half are devoted to poetry) quarterly (1 double, 2 single issues per year), circulation 1,500-3,000, 1,500 subscriptions of which 450 are libraries. They receive some 2,000 submissions per year, use 40, have a 5 month backlog. **Sample: £2.50 postpaid. "We seek poetry of 'more than usual emotion, more than usual order' (Coleridge). We publish special issues on particular authors such as T. S. Eliot, Ezra Pound, David Jones, Stanley Burnshaw, Thomas Hardy, etc."** Some of the poets who have appeared in *Agenda* are Peter Dale, Geoffrey Hill, C. H. Sisson, Patricia McCarthy and W. S. Milne. The editors selected these sample lines (poet unidentified):

> How will you want the snowy impermanence of ash,
> your dust, like grass-seed, flighted over heathland,
> drifting in spinneys where the boughs clash,
> with matted needles laying waste beneath them.

Reports in 1 month. Pays. To submit book MS, no query necessary, "as little as possible" in cover letter. Reports within a month. They offer 7% royalty, £100 advance, 12 copies. The editors say poets "should write only if there is an intense desire to express something. They should not worry about fashion."

THE AGNI REVIEW (III), Box 660, Amherst, MA 01004, phone 413-367-9506, founded 1972, bi-annual, publishes some of the best-known poets such as Jorie Graham, Craig Raine, Ai, Derek Walcott, Seamus Heaney, Wiliam Logan, and Melissa Green. **Submit 3-5 poems, photocopy, multiple submissions OK, reports in 5 weeks, payment: 3 copies.** They have a circulation of about 1,200. A fat (136 pp.) digest-sized, flat-spined, finely printed format, **sample: $4 postpaid.**

AG-PILOT INTERNATIONAL MAGAZINE (IV, Agricultural aviation, crop dusting), Drawer R, Walla Walla, WA, 99362, phone 509-522-4311, "is intended to be a fun-to-read, technical, as well as humorous and serious publication for the ag pilot and operator." It appears monthly, 48-60 pp., circulation 10,200. Interested in all **agri-aviation (crop dusting)-related poetry. Buys 1 per issue, pays $5-25.**

AHNENE PUBLICATIONS, POETRY 'N PROSE (I), Box 456, Maxville, Ontario, K0C 1T0 Canada, founded 1982, poetry editor M. K. Williams, primarily publishes the typescript newsletter, *Poetry 'n Prose*, though they are collecting material for an anthology, **Future Classics**. Says editor Williams, "We are information, entertainment, literary publishers of paperbacks and periodicals. **We are committed to introducing new or unknown writers.**" They offer an annual poetry contest, the "top poem of year award—voted by readers of **Poetry 'n Prose.**" **Open to all forms, but "no smut."** The magazine is an inexpensively produced offset, saddle-stapled, with a typescript cover on the same paper as the inner pages, amateurish art, chatty style, with news and advice about marketing, a crossword puzzle, interspersed with poems, including some by children (**sample $1.50 postpaid**, subscription $10—Canadian). I selected these lines from "Growing Old," by Barbara Clark, as an example:

> And I pray
> I shall never be like you,
> Old wrinkled, claw-like, man.
> But I'm afraid. . . . some day . . .

They have 470 subscriptions, 8% libraries, **use 15-25% of material submitted. Submit any time, any form, payment 1 copy, guidelines available. Be sure always to enclose Canadian postage or IRC. If you want to submit to Future Classics, enclose $3 reading fee for up to five poems. $10 reading fee for chapbook submissions.** Williams advises, "Keep writing; keep sending poems out; try not to get discouraged . . . Write what *satisfies you*."

AHSAHTA PRESS (IV, Regional/Western American), 1910 University Dr., Boise, ID 83725, 208-385-1246, founded 1975. This is a project of Boise State University to publish **contemporary poetry of the American West**. But, say editors Tom Trusky, Ory Burmaster and Dale Boya, "**Spare us paens to the pommel, Jesus in the sagebrush, haiku about the Eiffel Tower, 'nice' or 'sweet' poems**." The work should "**draw on the cultures, history, ecologies of the American West**." They publish collections (60 pp.) of individual poets in handsome flat-spined paperbacks with plain matte covers, with an appreciative introduction, about 3 per year. Occasionally they bring out an anthology on cassette of their authors. **And they have published an anthology (94 pp.) Women Poets of the West**, with an introduction by Ann Stanford. Some of their poets are Susan Deal, Leo Romero, David Baker, Richard Speakes, Philip St. Clair, Judson Crews. Here are some lines from Marnie Walsh's "Dakota Winter," in the collection **A Taste of the Knife**:

> it is where the long-fingered
> hand of winter
> clangs down a crystal lid
> to the sound of snow

You may submit only during their January-March reading period each year—a sample of 15 of your poems with SASE. They will report in about 2 months. Multiple and simultaneous submissions, photocopy, dot-matrix OK. If they like the sample, they'll ask for a book MS. If it is accepted, **you get 25 copies of the 1st and 2nd printings and a 25% royalty commencing with the 3rd**. They seldom comment on the samplers, frequently on the MSS. Send SASE for their catalog and order a few books, if you don't find them in your library. "Olde advice but true: read what we publish before submitting. **75% of the submissions we receive should never have been sent to us. Save stamps, spirit, and sweat.**"

AILERON PRESS, *AILERON: A LITERARY JOURNAL (II), Box 891, Austin, TX 78767-0891, founded 1980, poetry editor Mike Gilmore, is a periodical (at least once a year, sometimes twice) consisting **entirely of poetry**, with some photos and art. The editor says they offer a journal "wherein **new authors may see their work side by side with that of more seasoned poets.**" He wants "**no sentimental garbage**" and selected these lines, by Elkion Tumbalé, as an example of what he likes:

> Athwart gills of the blow-fish
> bulbous fricaine amina
> Myco-porcelain lying scratch
> I sing of the billows O! final swells

Recent poets published there include Albert Huffstickler, Gene Fowler, Charles Behlen, Marc Widershien, Janet Cannon, Pat Ellis Taylor, Janet McCann, Christopher Middleton and Naomi Shihab Nye. It's a digest-sized format, saddle-stapled, typeset (in small type), stiff cover with art. Circulation is 300-500, with 15 subscriptions. **Sample $3 postpaid**, subscription $8 for 3 issues. Each issue contains 40-60 pages of poetry garnered from 400-500 submissions each year of which 60-100 are used, 6-8 month backlog. **All formats acceptable; multiple submissions OK; must have name & address on each page; payment is 2 copies; no limitations on form or subject matter; guidelines available for SASE.**

*AIM MAGAZINE (I, IV, Social), 7308 S. Eberhart Ave., Chicago, IL 60619, phone 312-874-6184, founded 1974, poetry editor Henry Blakely, is a magazine-sized quarterly, circulation 10,000, glossy cover, "**dedicated to racial harmony and peace.**" They use 3-4 poems ("poetry with social significance mainly") in each issue, **paying $3/poem. They ask for 32 lines average length, but most poems in the sample issues I have seen were much shorter, and some were by children.** They have recently published poems by Elsen Lubetsky, Henrietta Hopper, Leonard Cirino, Daniel Brady and Barbara Foster. The editor selected these sample lines from "The Clock is Ticking" by Juliana Lewis:

> *The clock is ticking . . .*
> *have you shared today?*
> *Tick-tick-ticking . . .*
> *cared today?*
> *The clock is ticking . . .*
> *did you serve today?*
> *Tick-tick-ticking . . .*
> *Observe today?*

They have 3,000 subscriptions of which 15 are libraries. Subscription: $8; per issue: $2. **Sample: $3 postpaid. They receive only about 30 submissions per year of which they use half. Photocopy, simultaneous submissions OK, no dot-matrix. Reports in 3-6 weeks.** The editor's advice: "Read the work of published poets."

‡*AKWEKON LITERARY JOURNAL, *AKWESASNE NOTES (IV, Native Americans), Box 223, Hogansburg, NY 13655, phone 518-358-0531, founded 1985, co-editors Alex Jacobs and Peter blue Cloud. *Akwesasne Notes*, a tabloid publication, comes out 6 times/year; it is a political, cultural, and information network for native American and indigenous peoples. *Akwekon* is a national native North American quarterly that publishes native writers and authors; its contents deal with native issues. The sample of *Akwesasne Notes* I have contains one double-page spread of poetry by one author; *Akwekon* contains several pages of poetry, each by a single author. **The editors do not want to see "crying, self-indulgent, immature" poetry.** They have published work by Wendy Rose, Joe Bruchac, John Trudell, Ray Young Bear, Charlotte DeClue, and Barney Bush. As a sample, they chose the following lines by Linda Hogan:

> *What soft edges the earth has. Nothing is lost.*
> *The deer have gone over into birds*
> *and the birds fly through me*
> *a breath apart*

Akwekon Literary Journal is magazine-sized, nicely printed on slick paper with handsome b/w graphics, photos, and cartoons, 72 pp. flat-spined with glossy card cover and four-color illustration. The journal has a circulation of 830, of which 300 are subscriptions, 50 go to libraries, and 300 are sold on newsstands. Price per copy is $7, subscription $20/year. **Sample available for $7 postpaid, guidelines for SASE. Pay is 2-3 copies. Poets should submit 3-6 short poems or 1 longer, typed double-spaced or clearly legible photocopy; simultaneous submissions OK; selected reprints are sometimes published.** *Akwesasne Notes*, official publication of the Mohawk Nation at Akwesasne, near Rooseveltown, NY, is published in February, April, June, August, October, and December each year. It is tabloid-sized, printed on newsprint, with b/w photos and graphics. Newsstand price price is $1.75, subscription $10/year in the US and Canada. **I have no submission information other than that for** *Akwekon.* The editors' advice to native poets is: "Submit to all native presses, start within your region, then nationally. Do not dwell on past problems, do not cry or complain or be romantic about the past; the contemporary moment, pop-culture, the future is what's important. Talk to elders. Non-native poets writing 'Indian' poems: very difficult situation; most native presses will reject unless the story you are telling rings true and reaches both grassroots and progressive Indians. The story, not the symbols."

‡UNIVERSITY OF ALABAMA PRESS (II), Box 2877, University, AL 35486, director Malcolm MacDonald. They publish the University of Alabama Poetry Series, general editors Dara Wier and Thomas Rabbitt. The sample I have seen is a glossy covered paperback, flat-spined, $5\frac{1}{2}$x$8\frac{1}{2}$", 68 pp., nicely printed on buff stock. The book is called **A Belfry of Knees**, by Alberta Turner, and I have selected the following whole poem, "Cloth" as a sample:

> *I envy nuts their dense flesh*
> *I love my ears   soft   and no sound too swift*
> *I can braid rain*
>
> *Weaving sky takes most of the day*

Pays maximum 10% royalty on wholesale price after the first 1,000 copies are sold; no advance. Computer printout submissions acceptable. Free book catalog.

THE ALCHEMIST (II), Box 123, Lasalle, Quebec, Canada H8R 3T7, founded 1974, poetry editor Marco Fraticelli, is a 100 pp. small digest-sized, flat-spined literary magazine, handsomely printed and illustrated with b/w drawings, irregularly-issued literary journal, using mostly poetry. **No restrictions on form, style or content, (though in the issue I examined, #8, there is a section of haiku and a useful catalog of haiku markets.** They have a print-run of 500, 200 subscriptions, of which 30 are libraries, and they send out some 200 complimentary copies. Subscription $10 for 4 issues, $3 per issue. They have a 6 month backlog **Sample: $1 postpaid. Reports in 1 month. Payment: 2 copies.** I selected these sample lines, the opening of "Dreams" by A. D. Winans:

> *the dreams will not leave me alone*
> *they come and go through my skull*
> *opening the memory bank*
> *like an overfilled suitcase*

ALCHEMY BOOKS (II), Suite 514, 711 Market St., San Francisco, CA 94103, chief editor Phillip Grahem, is a general publisher, primarily of nonfiction, which publishes some fiction and poetry. Send SASE for catalog to buy samples.

*ALCOHOLISM & ADDICTION MAGAZINE, RECOVERY! (IV, Social), Alcom, Inc., Box 31329, Seattle, WA 98103, phone 206-527-8999, is a six-times-a-year magazine covering alcoholism, treatment and recovery, circulation 30,000. **They use 3-4 poems/issue, free verse, light verse, and traditional (lucid). Wants recovery-oriented material only relating to chemical dependency and co-dependency. Poems can illustrate recovery principles or feeling states. Humor is especially valued.** Sample lines from "Flight" by Devon Cave:

> *I sit upon the branch*
> *Looking down*
> *The world spreads beneath me*
> *It is my decision*
> *To soar*
> *Child of the wing*
> *Returning no more.*

‡ALDEBARAN (I), Student Senate, Roger Williams College, Bristol, RI 02809, founded 1971, president Steve Mastovich, a semi-annual (December and May) college literary magazine that publishes poetry and short fiction. **"We look for well-done work in any style. Emphasis on craftsmanship."** Two poets they have published recently are Fritz Hamilton and Karla Hammond. The magazine (which I have not seen) is digest-sized, 60-70 pp., saddle-stapled; art work or photography is used on the covers. Circulation is 200, price per issue $2, subscription $3.50/year. **Sample available for $2.50 postpaid. Pay is 2 copies. Submissions should be limited to 5 poems at a time; no simultaneous submissions; computer printouts are OK if legible. Reporting time is 1 month during semester.** The editor says, "We are a college magazine; we respect good work and are open to new styles. But we have deadlines. **No submissions are read from April 15 until September 1. No submissions are read from November 15 until February 1. Send nothing during these times, your letter will wait.** We appreciate a poet's patience."

ALICE JAMES BOOKS (IV, Regional/New England, women), 138 Mt. Auburn St., Cambridge, MA 02138, phone 617-354-1408, founded 1973. "An author's collective, which publishes exclusively **poetry, with an emphasis on poetry by women; authors are exclusively from the New England Area.**" Offers Beatrice Hawley Award for poets outside New England. They publish flat-spined paperbacks and hardbacks of high quality, both in production and contents, no children's poetry, and their books have won numerous awards and been very respectably reviewed. "Each poet becomes a working member of the co-op with a two-year work commitment." That is, you have to live close enough to **attend meetings and participate in the editorial and publishing process.** In 1983 they published Helena Minton's collection, **The Canal Bed**, Joan Joffe Hall's **Romance and Capitalism at the Movies**; **Night Watches**; **Inventions on the Life of Maria Mitchell**; and Fanny Howe's **Robeson Street**. These lines by Celia Gilbert are an example of the poetry they publish:

> *Close as the finger*
> *running over the blade*
> *daring it to be itself,*
> *we are that close, mother.*

They publish about 4 books, 72 pp., each year in editions of 900 paperback, 300 hardback. **Query first, but no need for samples: simply ask for dates of reading periods. Reports in 2-3 months. Send two copies of the MS.**

ALIVE! FOR YOUNG TEENS (IV, Teen), Christian Board of Publication (founded 1910), Box 179, St. Louis, MO 63166, phone 314-371-6900, founded 1969, is a monthly magazine which uses poetry **"of interest to young adolescents in a church audience, usually under 20 lines."** They have recently published poems by Emily Councilman and Helen Shepherd. The editors selected these lines by a 13 year-old-boy as a sample:

> *The sound of a rainbow is like the*
> *"swoosh" when you slide down a slide;*
> *The "Ahhh" with your first breath of morning air;*
> *The "crackle" when you crunch over fallen leaves.*

There are about 5 pp. of poetry in each issue, 7½x10½," 32 pp., glossy paper cover with photo and graphics, circulation 10,000. Subscription: $13.50. They receive over 500 submissions per year, use 60. Minimum of 11 months between acceptance and publication. **Sample: $1 postpaid. Simultaneous submissions, photocopies, dot-matrix OK. Poetry from young adolescents given first priority. Pays 25¢/line. Send SASE for guidelines.**

ALL IN WALL STICKERS (IV, Illustratable poetry), 27 Harpes Rd., Oxford OX2 7QJ England. Founded 1968 by Nina Steane who publishes **only posters. She wants short illustrated or illustratable poetry, previously unpublished, exciting, original, and adventurous**. She doesn't repeat authors, and has published posters by George MacBeth, Brian Patten, and Ted Hughes. Here are some lines from "Summer's Day" by Rakiyah Beswick:

> Come let me tell you sparrow
> This is no day for dying in,
> For crying in
> Look how the Father's eyes
> Silvered in the sun
> Spangle their jewels on you

She publishes an average of one a year, for which she **pays 10£ on acceptance and 6 copies on publication**. No query—just good poetry and drawings. Send **one£ for a sample**. Her advice to poets: "Be alive!"

‡ALLARDYCE, BARNETT PUBLISHERS (V), 14 Mount St., Lewes BN7 1HL, England, founded 1982, editorial director Anthony Barnett. Allardyce, Barnett publishes important substantial collections by current English language poets; "our financial situation does not currently allow for an extension of this programme into other areas. **We cannot at this time encourage unsolicited manuscripts.**" Some of the better-known poets they have published are J. H. Prynne, Andrew Crozier, and Douglas Oliver. The press publishes simultaneous cloth and paper editions, currently less than 1 per year, with an average page count of 320, digest-sized. In the U.S., their books can be obtained through Small Press Distributors in Berkeley, CA.

ALLEGHENY PRESS (IV, Nature), Box 220, Elgin, PA 16413, founded 1967, poetry editor Bonnie Henderson, publishes **poetry books concerned with outdoor and nature topics.** The editor selected these sample lines:

> You ride to me upon a different horse
> Special riding tricks, lofty circus stunts
> Come mount the steed, together we shall fly
> Dark silhouettes of love against the sky.

They have published 3 books of poetry, 1 anthology, and 4 chapbooks since 1967. **Query with 2 samples. Cover letter should tell how many pages are estimated for the proposed book. Replies to queries in 2 weeks, to submissions (if invited) in 2 weeks. Simultaneous submissions, photocopy ok, no dot-matrix. Publishes on 10% royalty contract plus 2 copies.** Editor sometimes comments on rejections, but "We don't like people to send MS to us expecting AP to improve their skills." She comments, "Poetry has never paid its way in our publishing program. We still plan to publish meritous (as suits the fancy of our editors) poetry even though it represents a financial loss, not to mention time and effort of our make-up and editorial staff. We do not like poets who write poetry but do not read other's poetry or buy books of poetry."

*THE ALLEGHENY REVIEW (I, IV, Specialized), Box 32, Allegheny College, Meadville, PA 16335, founded 1983, poetry editors Thomas J. Stout and Terrie S. Williams. "Each year *Allegheny Review* compiles and publishes a review of the nation's best **undergraduate literature.** It is entirely composed of and by college undergraduates and is nationally distributed both as a review and as a classroom text, particularly suited to creative writing courses. We will print **poetry of appreciable literary merit on any topic, submitted by college undergraduates. No limitations except excessive length (2-3 pp.)** as we wish to represent as many authors as possible, although exceptions are made in areas of great quality and interest." They have published poetry by Nathan Copple, Christine Hines, Dorothy Harbeck and Ron Tisdale and selected these lines by Joel Hanan (Brown University) as a sample:

> This spring I'll take a gardener for a lover
> Not . . . like the girls that flirt and husband hunt down
> around Simpson Square.
> But to push down a patch of MacIntosh's woods
> and become the ends of the green-eyed grass, my body, like
> earth, blooming.

The *Review* appears in a 6x9", flat-spined, professionally-printed format, b/w photos and b/w art on glossy card cover. **Submissions should be accompanied by a letter telling the college poet is attending, class standing, personal basis for the poem, any background, goals and philosophies that the author feels are pertinent to the work submitted. Short capsules about each author will be published along with the accepted piece(s). Reports 1-2 months following deadline. Submit up to 3 poems, typed, double-spaced, photocopy, dot-matrix OK. Sample: $3 and 11x18" SASE. Poem judged best in the collection earns $50 honorarium and invitation on alternating years with fiction winner, to read on campus with nationally recognized poets.**

‡**ALLY PRESS CENTER (V)**, 524 Orleans St., St. Paul, MN 55107, founded 1973, owner Paul Feroe, **publishes and distributes work by Robert Bly, Chapbooks, cassette tapes, and newsletter. The press is not accepting any unsolicited MSS at this time.** They publish two chapbooks per year, 54 pp., paperback, flat-spined. Book catalog is free on request.

ALTA NAPA PRESS (IV, Specialized), 1969 Mora Ave., Calistoga, CA 94515, founded 1976, publishes a variety of kinds of books, but the imprint **Gondwana Books is for epic poetry only**. A number of the books in their catalog (available for 9x12" SASE and $1) are by the editor, Carl T. Endemann. He **publishes other authors on a "co-operative basis,"** which means partial or full subsidy but gives no details of how that works. Write directly for information, and when you do **send three poems, and your covering letter might include biographical background, personal or aesthetic philosophy, poetic goals and principles, and the hour, date and place of your birth.** He says "No, I am not a fortune teller!" but he is apparently interested in **astrology and reincarnation**. He says he wants poetry which is **"clear, clean, concise/ rhythm, reason and 'rammar/ rare rational rhymes"** on any subject of **universal appeal; spiritual OK, but effusions of personal frustrations no. No trite drivel. Sex yes, Porno NO, no spectator sports.** Here are some lines from his own **Voyage Into the Past**:

> *Whence do we come and whither do we go*
> *We better had make plans while there is time*
> *To draw the plans for our next life, and then*
> *Submit designs to the Great Architect Divine*

He publishes 3-4 chapbooks (30-148 pp.) and 3-4 flat-spined paperbacks (50-240 pp.) per year. Advice: "Join a GOOD Creative Writing Class now for three years and read *Writer's Digest* in depth. That's what I did. Poetry is not a commercial endeavor, but it can eventually pay for itself—mainly give you the feeling of having done something *worthwhile* which *no* money can buy. He offers **criticism for $1.30 per page of MS**.

*****THE ALTADENA REVIEW (II)**, Box 212, Altadena, CA 91001, founded 1978, poetry editors Robin Shectman, Carl Selkin, comes out **twice a year with about 32 pages of poetry per issue**; also reviews and interviews making a 48 pp. saddle-stapled magazine, typeset on typewriter, offset. "We want **good strong poems with concrete imagery—no vague mush, no rambling self-indulgence**. They have recently published poetry by Margot Treitel, Kay Ryan, Carol Dunne, Vincent Spina, Antony Oldknow, Ivan Argüelles and B. Goodenough. By Kim Bridgford:

> *The old woman stroking the hard, yellowed fingernails*
> *of her dying husband like maps;*
> *The man and woman who follow the variegated trails*
> *Of color behind each other's names.*

This is a modest but attractive little magazine, 250 print run, 35 subscriptions (of which 10 are libraries), sending out about 30 complimentary copies. Subscription $5, **sample: $2.50 postpaid**. They receive about 1,200 manuscripts a year and take about 50 (pointing out that these are often two or three at a time from a single submission). From three months to a year between acceptance and publication. **No query necessary (except for reviews or interviews), send "any reasonable number" of pages, name and address on every page, with SASE. Photocopies OK, but nix on dot-matrix. Warn them if it's a simultaneous submission. Reports in 4-6 weeks, pays in copies**. They do *not* publish books. If a MS "comes very close we will say so and sometimes say why." Advice: "We would like to see every poet go into his or her neighborhood bookstore at least once a month, **buy a book or magazine of poems, and complain to the manager that not enough poetry is being stocked there.**"

*****ALURA (II)**, 29371 Jacquelyn, Livonia, MI 48154, phone 313-427-2911, founded 1975, poetry editors Ruth Lamb and Dorothy Aust, is a poetry quarterly whose "aim is to reach the general public with understandable poetry. We also have a cable TV program 4 times monthly featuring various poets." Its format is 51 pp., saddle-stapled, with colored matte cover illustrated (as are many inside pages) with b/w amateur drawings. The magazine is typeset with small, dark type. They use **"well-written poetry in all styles but not 'typewriter gymnastics' nor uninterpretable symbolism. Poems must communicate. Prefer poems of not more than 48 lines and spaces. All subject-matter in good taste. Do not waste reader's time with obscure meanings."** They have recently published poetry by Alex Blain, John

Wilkie, Joe Cardillo, Lou Cantoni, Alma Reith, Irene Warsaw and Kathleen Leo. The editors selected these lines by Héctor Martinez M. as a sample:

> *Now, years later, you write,*
> *"When I hear that song,*
> *it fills my ears with the sound of the sea*
> *and my eyes with your image"*

They have a circulation of 325, 93 subscriptions of which 5 are libraries, receive 1,500-2,000 submissions per year and use about 350. **"Submissions should be folded and sent in a regular business envelope. We accept simultaneous submissions and previously published poems IF poets have retained all rights. Poets published in** *Alura* **do retain all rights. Prefer no more than 5-6 poems at a time. Photocopy, simultaneous submissions OK." They report in 6 weeks, pay 2 copies. "We appreciate loose stamps (4) to help with postage."** The editors comment, "Poets should search the market for periodicals that publish their style of poetry . . . religious, pornographic, etc. The trend to traditional poetry is due to return. Very little poetry being written today would lend itself to memorization or recital. We think many of the students are being deprived of learning the beauty of poetry. Many poems we receive are nothing more than prose broken down into lines. Surely poetry should be more than that."

‡**AM HERE BOOKS (II)**, 242 Ortega Rigde Road, Santa Barbara, CA 93108, proprietor Richard Emmet Aaron, who says, "Am Here Books solicits hard hitting essays and **poems which may serve the purpose of reminding the reader of a time when men and women walked on two legs and talked a common language.**" The sample book of poetry I have seen is magazine-size, offset on white paper, cover of slightly heavier stock, "laboriously hand-stapled [on the side] in an edition of 250 copies." The book, *Born Again*, by Ray Bremser, is "an 11-page long poem combining all that is comical and tragic in the nature of man and, indeed, all life forms" (it had been previously published in *New Blood*). As a sample, I selected the following lines (the beginning of the poem):

> *in a past life*
> *i was a field of wheat*
> *which was mowed & ground*
> *into a bag of grain*
> *which a cow ate,*
> *who, which later, i ate..*

Am Here books are available from the publisher for $2.50 each postpaid. **"Work is solicited for future publications."**

*AMAZING STORIES (IV, Science fiction), Box 110, Lake Geneva, WI 53147, founded 1926, editor Patrick L. Price, "is the world's first and oldest science fiction magazine, a bimonthly primarily devoted to fiction," but **uses a small amount of poetry. Must have science fictional or fantastic content, clearly expressed. Any form or style is OK as long as it's not obscure. In poetry, as in any other type of writing, say what you mean.** They have recently published poetry by Thomas Disch, Gene Wolfe and Esther M. Friesner. The issue I examined had 5 poems. The following sample is from "All Hallows Eve" by Robert E. Howard:

> *Now anthropoid and leprous shadows lope*
> *Down black colossal corridors of night*
> *And through the cypress roots blind fingers grope*
> *In stagnant pools where burns a witches' light.*

The digest-sized, flat-spined magazine, newsprint with glossy cover with art, has a circulation of 13,000 including 2,500 subscribers, receives "several hundred" submissions per year, of which they use 30. **Sample: $2.50 postpaid. Submit double-spaced, typed (photocopy OK, no dot-matrix). No queries. Reports in 3 weeks, pays $1 per line.**

*AMELIA (II), 329 "E" St., Bakersfield, CA 93304, founded 1983, Frederick A. Raborg, Jr. poetry editor, is a quarterly magazine that publishes chapbooks as well. Central to its operations are a **series of contests, most with entry fees, spaced evenly throughout the year, with cash and other awards, but they publish many poets who have not entered the contests as well**. Among poets published in their first two years are David Ray, Larry Rubin, Knute Skinner, Gary Fincke, Fredrick Zydek and Lawrence P. Spingarn. These sample lines are by Pattiann Rogers:

> *If I could bestow immortality,*
> *I'd do it liberally—on the aim of the hummingbird,*
> *The sea nettle and the dispersing skeletons of cottonweed*
> *In the wind, on the night heron hatchling and the heron*

They are "**receptive to all forms to 100 lines, as well as the occasional longpoem of unlimited length. We do not want to see the patently-religious or overtly-political. Erotica is fine; pornography, no.**" The digest-sized perfect-bound magazine is offset on high quality paper, with a circulation of about 1,000, 326 subscriptions, of which 24 are libraries. **Sample: $4.75 postpaid. Submit 3-5 poems, photocopies OK, dot-matrix acceptable but discouraged, no simultaneous submissions. Reports in 2-8 weeks. Pays $2-25 per poem plus 2 copies.** "Almost always I try to comment." This new magazine represents one of the most ambitious and promising ventures in publishing poetry I know of. The editor comments, "*Amelia* is not afraid of strong themes, but we do look for professional, polished work even in handwritten submissions. Poets should have something to say about matters other than the moon. We like to see strong **traditional pieces as well as the experimental. And neatness** *does* **count.**" *Cicada,* **consisting entirely of haiku and senryu, and** *SPSM&H,* **consisting entirely of sonnets,** are quarterly supplements to *Amelia.* **Three awards of $10 each will go to the three best poems in** *Cicada* **each issue; two awards of $14, to the best sonnets in** *SPSM&H.* Subscribers to *Amelia* will receive *Cicada* and *SPSM&H* automatically and without charge; others who wish *Cicada* or *SPSM&H* alone may subscribe to either or both for $2 per issue or $8 per year. Subscriptions to *Amelia* are $15 per year, $28 for 2 years. *Amelia* offers the widest range of prize contests of any magazine I know of. All winning poems are published in *Amelia* and each winner also receives two contributor copies. The following annual contests have various entry fees: The Amelia Awards (six prizes of $200, $100, $50 plus three honorable mentions of $10 each, annual deadline December 1); The Anna B. Janzen Prize for Romantic Poetry ($100 or silver coffee service, poet's choice, annual deadline January 2); The Bernice Jennings Traditional Poetry Award ($100, annual deadline January 2); The Georgie Starbuck Galbraith Light/Humorous Verse Prizes (six awards of $50, $30, $20 plus three honorable mentions of $5 each, annual deadline March 1); The Charles William Duke Longpoem Award ($100, annual deadline April 1); The Lucille Sandberg Haiku Awards (six awards of $50, $30, $20 plus three honorable mentions of $5 each, annual deadline April 1); The Grace Hines Narrative Poetry Award ($100, annual deadline May 1); The Amelia Chapbook Award ($250, book publication, 50 copies and 7½ percent royalty, annual deadline July 1); The Johanna B. Bourgoyne Poetry Prize ($150, annual deadline July 1); The Douglas Manning Smith Epic/Heroic Poetry Prize ($100, annual deadline August 1); The Hildegarde Janzen Prize for Oriental Forms of Poetry (six awards of $50, $30, $20 and three honorable mentions of $5 each, annual deadline September 1); The Eugene Smith Prize For Sonnets (six awards of $100, $50, $25 and three honorable mentions of $10 each, annual deadline October 1); The A&C Limerick prizes (six awards of $50, $30, $20 and three honorable mentions of $5 each, annual deadline October 1); The Montegue Wade Lyric Poetry Prize ($100, annual deadline November 1). Submit to Box 2385, Bakersfield, CA 93303 or 329 "E" Street, Bakersfield, CA 93304. (805)323-4064.

AMERICA (II), 106 W. 56th St., New York, NY 10019, phone 212-581-4640, founded 1909, is a Jesuit weekly which is a good general "think" magazine. They primarily publish opinions on religious, social, political and cultural themes, with usually **one and occasionally two poems of 10-30 lines per issue, and sometimes a whole page of poetry but infrequently longer poems. Payment $1.40 per line plus 2 author's copies.** The poetry editor, John Moffitt, has written **guidelines (send SASE)** which provide good guidance for poets submitting to most magazines of high quality: "Our preference is for poems written in *contemporary prose idiom,* **only very occasionally a more traditional idiom if not too predictable rhyme and meter. No needless obscurity, vagueness parading as profundity, or too blatant statement;** but a surface clarity that will speak to the average intelligent reader. Requiring that our poems should flow without break from beginning to end, I am constantly on the alert for moments when the way a thing is said distracts a reader's mind from what is being said. Poems should be evocative enough to allow readers to share the poet's experience as if it was their own. Those that seize the reader's attention from the first line and hold it throughout are most likely to be accepted. For the most part I am interested in work of a **spiritual nature**, by which I mean work with relevance for the understanding and enrichment of the human spirit. It **need not be 'religious,'** though such poems are welcome so long as they do not repeat well-worn ideas and images." Some recently published poets: Fred Chappell, Anne Kilmer, Dorothy Donnelly, Larry Rubin, William Stafford. Moffitt chose these lines by Stephen Applin as a sample:

> The rain beats the color from these cold hills,
> Filling the crimson buds with their gold breaking.
> the freshet becomes a turbulence; stream swell
> With this first waking. Beneath the banks frogs thaw,
> Snakes loosen, and roots curl upwards away from the crystalline cold.

Circulation: 33,000 subscriptions of which 10,000 are libraries; receives 800-1,000 submissions per year, uses 40-50. **Submit any time (one month ahead for seasonal poetry). Sample (and price per issue): $1.** Moffitt offers comments "only if a poem is almost deserving of publication." He advises, "Do not send large amounts of verse, or explain what the poems are intended to accomplish or what they are about, do not supply details of biography, or imitate other poets."

AMERICAN ATHEIST PRESS, GUSTAV BROUKAL PRESS, *AMERICAN ATHEIST (IV, Atheism), 2210 Hancock Dr., Austin, TX 78756, phone 512-458-1244, founded 1958, editor R. Murray-O'Hair, publishes the monthly magazine **with 30,000 circulation,** *American Atheist* and, under various imprints some dozen books a year reflecting "concerns of Atheists, such as separation of state and church, civil liberties, and atheist news." **Poetry is used primarily in the poetry section of the magazine. It must have "a particular slant to atheism, dealing with subjects such as the atheist lifestyle. Anticlerical poems and puns are more than liable to be rejected. Any form or style is acceptable. Preferred length is under 40 lines**." Poets they have published recently include E. Krall, Gerald Tholen and Chris Brockman. The editor chose these lines as a sample:

> Bless us for we have sinned;
> We have no enemies except old Charlie;
> Dear Lord, striketh Charlie with a lightning bolt.
> Amen.

Of their 17,000 subscriptions, 1,000 are libraries. The magazine-sized format is professionally printed, with art and photos, glossy, color cover; subscription, $25, single copy price $2.95, **sample: free**. They receive over 800 submissions per year, use about 36. **Submit typed, double-spaced (photocopy, dot-matrix, simultaneous submissions OK). Time-dependent poems (such as winter) should be submitted 4 months in advance. Reports within 6 weeks. Pay "first-timers" 10 copies and 6 month subscription; thereafter, $10/poem. Guidelines available for SASE, but a label is preferred to an envelope**. They do not publish poetry in book form, but are open to subsidy arrangements on variable terms. **Sometimes comments on rejected MSS.**

‡*AMERICAN LAND FORUM (IV, Landscape)**, 5410 Grosvenor Lane, Bethesda, MD 20814, phone 301-493-9140, founded 1980, executive editor Sara Ebenreck. Magazine is an **"interdisciplinary quarterly for land resource professionals and concerned citizens; focus is on American land. Each issue has a featured poet section with 5-7 short (50 lines or less) poems (by the same author) centered on a particular landscape or land-area theme. Interested in poems that evoke the land and people's relation with the land—but not romantic poetry or 'cause' poetry**." As a sample I selected the complete poem called "Sage Plane" by Mary McGinnis:

> i long to grow dry and brittle as the sage
> a seed attaching myself for being reborn
> flying into Sleeping Ute Mountain
> without regret

American Land Forum is magazine-sized, typeset and printed on quality paper with b/w graphics and photography feature, no ads. Frequency is quarterly, circulation 3,000, subscriptions $20. **Sample: $7.50 postpaid. Guidelines available for SASE. Payment is $75, on acceptance, per feature section, plus two free copies. Submissions reported on within 6 weeks.** 1987 will be first available issues.

*AMERICAN POETRY REVIEW, WORLD POETRY, INC. (III)**, Temple University Center City, Rm. 405, 1616 Walnut St., Philadelphia, PA 19103, founded 1972, is probably the **most widely circulated (24,000 copies bimonthly) and best-known periodical devoted to poetry in the world**. Poetry editors are Stephen Berg, David Bonanno and Arthur Vogelsang, and they have **published most of the leading poets writing in English and many translations**. The poets include Gerald Stern, Brenda Hillman, John Ashbery, Norman Dubie, Marvin Bell, Galway Kinnell and Tess Gallagher. As a sample, I selected some lines of my own published there, from "Encounters Of Kind," a poem based on a journal entry by Anton van Leeuwenhoek of Delft:

> The ladder down into the well appears
> to have infinite and ever-smaller rungs.
> Look up into the dark sky where it reaches
> and hear the wind stirred by those alien tongues.

15,000 subscriptions, of which 1,000 are libraries, tabloid format. **Sample and price per issue: $1.95**. They receive about 4,000 submissions per year, use 200, **pay $1 per line, 8 weeks to report, 1-1½ year backlog, no simultaneous submissions**. The magazine is also a major resource for opinion, reviews, theory, news and ads pertaining to poetry.

‡*AMERICAN ROWING (IV, Rowing-related)**, (formerly *Rowing USA*), U.S. Rowing Association, Suite 980, 251 N. Illinois St., Indianapolis IN 46204, phone 317-924-2444, editor M. Merhoff, is a bimonthly magazine, circulation 12,000 for competitive and recreational rowers (mostly sliding-seat boats) which uses some free verse, haiku, light verse and traditional poetry which is rowing-related only. Pays $50 maximum.

*THE AMERICAN SCHOLAR (III)**, 1811 Q St. NW, Washington, DC 20009, phone 202-263-3808, founded 1932, associate editor Sandra Costich, is an academic quarterly which **uses about 5 poems per issue, pays $50 each**. Offers Mary Elinor Smith Memorial Award. They have published poets such as

Robert Pack, Alan Shapiro and Gregory Djanikan. "**We would like to see poetry that develops an image, a thought or event, without the use of a single cliché or contrived archaism. The most hackneyed subject matter is self-conscious love; the most tired verse is iambic pentameter with rhyming endings. The usual length of our poems is 30 lines. From 1-4 poems may be submitted at one time;** *no more* **for a careful reading.**" Study before submitting (**sample: $4.75, guidelines available for SASE**).

AMERICAN STUDIES PRESS, INC., MARILU BOOKS (II, IV, Americana), 13511 Palmwood Lane, Tampa, FL 33624, founded 1977 publishes under a variety of imprints: **ASP Books, Rattlesnake Books**, and **Harvest Books**, but poetry primarily as **Marilu Books**, which includes **HERLAND (poems by women about women and WOMAN)**. These are generally low-budget, offset, typeset, saddle-stapled or flat-spined chapbooks of 30-50 pp. with simple art, but some good poetry. Editor-in-chief Don Harkness says he wants "**poetry with a central (and American) theme**—possibilities are wide." He has recently published work by Normajean MacLeod, Lynn Cheney-Rose, Rochelle Lynn Holt, Chick Wallace, Hans Juergensen and offers these lines by Evelyn Thorne as a sample (the opening of her "School Marms Late 19th Century" from **Of Bones and Stars**):

> *Ubiquitous stench of wet wool rubber chalk dust*
> *At night the icy sheets of a rented room*
> *but through the smog of monotony sometimes*
> *a keen young face a flowering moment*

Send SASE for a free catalog and buy a **sample ($2-5)**. Submit 4 or 5 poems with a cover letter giving **publications, biographical background, personal or aesthetic philosophy, poetic goals and principles—but keep it short! Simultaneous submissions OK. Reports in 1-2 months, pays 10% royalties after printing expenses are met plus 10 copies. Poets have earned from $6 to $250 on their books.** Don Harkness advises, "(1) Poetry began in rhythm, meter and rhyme; the current pathological avoidance of same has begun to pall. (2) I generally find, in poems which I reject out of hand, an excessive solipsism."

*THE AMICUS JOURNAL (IV, Nature based), 122 E. 42nd, New York, NY 10168, phone 212-949-0049, poetry editor Brian Swann, is the **journal of the Natural Resources Defense Council, a quarterly with a circulation of about 55,000, which pays $25/poem**. Brian Swann says the poetry should be "nature based, but not 'nature poetry.'" They have used poems by some of the best known poets in the country, including David Wagoner, Gary Snyder, David Ignatow, Marvin Bell and William Stafford. As a sample, I selected the opening stanza of Mary Oliver's "Starfish":

> *In the sea rocks,*
> *in the stone pockets*
> *under the tide's lip*
> *in water dense as blindness*

The Amicus Journal is finely-printed, saddle-stapled, on high quality paper with glossy cover, using much art, photography and cartoons. They use about 5% of the 200 submissions they receive each year. **No simultaneous submissions, nothing over 1 page; reports within 3 weeks.**

& (AMPERSAND) PRESS (IV), 141 Barrack St., Colchester, Essex, U.K., publishes a series of chapbooks of poetry in keeping with their aesthetic aims. Send SASE for guidelines and catalog to order sample, or query with 2-3 pp. (at most) discussion of your aesthetic principles and samples of your poetry.

ANDROGYNE BOOKS (II), 930 Shields, San Francisco, CA 94132, founded 1971, publishes the "infrequent" magazine, *Androgyne* (**an issue about every 18 months**), books and chapbooks of poetry. Poetry editor Ken Weichel says he wants "**experimental and new surrealism**" and has published Steve Abbott, Allen Cohen, Mel Clay, Ira Cohen, Ed Myche, Rebekka Whetsyne, Jeff Zabel and James Broughton. I selected these lines as a sample from "Blue Paint" by Francine Lake, published in 1984 in the magazine:

> *The tapestry unravelled leaving a pool of blue blood on the floor.*
> *The blue raven tore at its sodden feathers.*
> *The windows of the palace were covered with rose*
> *flavoured drapery emblazoned with violets.*

Weichel describes the magazine as "a rebus of poetry, fiction and college" with about 60 pages per issue (flat-spined paperback, 500 copies, 23 subscriptions), **sample: $3. Simultaneous submissions OK, reports in 1 month, payment 2 copies**. He publishes two 30 pp. collections per year, and an 80 pp. anthology. **Query first with samples; payment 10% of press run (for collections).**

‡ANEMONE PRESS, *ANEMONE (I), Box 425, RD 2, Chester, VT 05143, founded 1982, editor Nanette Morin, a small-press publisher of "**poetry that is well-written and relates to the reality of the**

world we live in—emotion, idea, point of view, feeling, happening." The press publishes a quarterly tabloid-style magazine, *Anemone*, as well as chapbooks, special editions, postcards and broadsides. The editor says, "**We encourage new writers but are also open to established writers. We look for the different, that which is not likely to be accepted in your average publication. We do encourage political poetry. We exist to raise our consciousness as artists of the world.**" She does not want to see "**Poetry on the horrors of living. Much of the work is rejected because it is so negative. Is everyone out there depressed—or is it a sign of the times?**" She has recently published poetry by Diane Glancy, Kathleen Spivack, Janice Powell, William Vernon, Truman Nelson, and Roque Dalton (translated by Jack Hirschman). Though in response to my request for sample lines the editor said, "All our poetry is so different I cannot possibly do that," I selected the following stanza from "Before the Lisbon Earthquake," by Lee Slonimsky to suggest the quality of poetry used:

> In an asylum a madman dreamed
> The entire event in vivid detail.
> Because he claimed God gave him the news,
> He was threatened with death, or a crueler jail.

The 12-page unstapled tabloid, offset on newspaper stock, contains mostly poetry with b/w photographs and art work and book reviews, interviews, one-color cover. Circulation is 3,000 price per issue $1.50, subscription $6. **No samples or guidelines available; pay is a subscription. The editor says, "Would rather receive work than queries." Submission will be reported between 3 weeks to 3 months.**" They publish chapbooks "only when contests are in progress." Writers should send 5 sample poems. "**$1 reading fee is appreciated.** All submissions are read with care and comments are made, which is why returns are not always that quick. For new poets: Remember Ezra Pound." I am reminded that in his last days Pound said to an interviewer, "Save the young from the influence of Ezra Pound."

ANGELTREAD, THE LYRIAN RUSE (I,II), c/o T.W. Phillips, Apt. 114, 102 S. 2nd St., Grayville, IL 62844, founded 1984, poetry editor T. W. Phillips, is a photocopied newsletter, circulation 20, of photos, art, miscellaneous thoughts, fiction excerpts and poetry. Appears 3-4 times a year. They want "**unself-conscious discoveries leading to truth, beautiful and careful language. Do not want pedantic or obscene matter, or greeting card language. Any form or style.**" They have recently published poetry by Frederick A. Raborg, Jr., Paul Weinman, Michael Ketchek and Mary Peck. There are 4-8 pp. of poetry in each issue, which are usually typed, one side of page only, stapled at the upper left corner. Some issues are hand colored. "Angel theme yearly. **Sample: $2 postpaid. Subscription: $8/year. Submit maximum of 5 pp., donations with submissions appreciated. No similtaneous submissions. Photocopy OK. Reports in 1 month. Pays in copies. Query with SASE regarding contests. Editor sometimes comments on rejections. Negotiable terms for criticism.** The editor advises, "We use poetry that will still be good in ten years. Any serious writers out there? I mean writers who also read other poets, study writing, eat, live, and breathe it? Then please send to *Angeltread.*"

ANHINGA PRESS (II), Box 10423, Tallahassee, FL 30302, phone 904-562-1209, founded 1972, poetry editors Donald Caswell and Van Brock, publishes "**books, chapbooks and anthologies of poetry. We also offer the Anhinga Prize for poetry-$500 and publication—for a book-length manuscript each year. We want to see contemporary poetry which respects language. We're inclined toward poetry that is not obscure, that can be understood by any literate audience.**" They have recently published poetry by Sherry Rind, Yvonne Sapia, Leon Stokesbury, Judith Kitchen, Ricardo PauLlosa, Michael Mott, Cynthia Cahn and Rick Lott. These sample lines are by Sherry Rind.

> Do not believe birds sing for the sun.
> Walking is the surprise
> to which they cry
> I'm here, I'm here

Send SASE for rules (January 31 deadline) of the Anhinga Prize for poetry, which requires a $10 entry fee, for which all contestants receive a copy of the winning book. The contest has been judged by such distinguished poets as William Stafford, Louis Simpson and Hayden Carruth. "We encourage poets who don't already know us to enter the Anhinga Prize for Poetry competition. Query only if suggesting a book not eligible for this prize." A sample chapter is $3; sample full-sized book is $6.

ANIMA; AN EXPERIENTIAL JOURNAL (II, IV, Women, feminist), 1053 Wilson Ave., Chambersburg, PA 17201, founded 1973, "celebrates the wholistic vision that emerges from thoughtful and imaginative encounters with the differences between woman and man, East and West, yin and yang—*anima* and *animus*. **Written largely by and about women** who are pondering new experiences of themselves and our world, this equinoctial journal welcomes contributions, verbal and visual, from the known and unknown." Poetry editors John Lindberg, Rebecca Nisley, and Harry Buck say, "**We publish very few poems, but they are carefully selected. We are not interested in simply private experiences. Poetry must communicate. Advise all would-be poets to study the kinds of things we do**

publish. No restrictions on length, form, or such matters." As a sample I chose the first stanza of Kay Ryan's "Why Animals Dance":

> *Because of their clickety hoofs*
> *Because of their scritchety claws*
> *Because of their crackety beaks*
> *Because they don't have any boots*

There are 5-10 pages of poetry in each semi-annual issue of the elegantly-printed and illustrated 8½" square, glossy-covered magazine, circulation 750, 700 subscriptions of which 150 are libraries. Price per issue: $5, but **sample: $2. No dot-matrix, slow reporting—sometimes 4-6 months, payment: offprints with covers**.

ANOTHER CHICAGO PRESS, *ACM (ANOTHER CHICAGO MAGAZINE) (II), Box 11223, Chicago, IL 60611, founded 1976, poetry editors Barry Silesky and Lee Webster, wants "**no religious verse**." They have recently published poetry by Barny Bush, June Jordan, Wanda Coleman, William Matthews and Joy Harjo. As a sample the editors selected this line by Tom McGrath: "This mission of armed revolutionary memory I'm here to sing." *ACM* comes out twice a year, digest-sized, 144 pp., flat-spined, professionally printed with glossy color card cover with art, circulation 1,000, 350 subscriptions of which 60 are libraries, using about 80 pp. of poetry in each issue. Subscription: $9. They receive about 1,500 freelance submissions of poetry per year, use 160. **Sample: $5 postpaid. Name and address should be on each work. They do not read during August and December. Simultaneous submissions OK, but they want to be notified immediately if you are withdrawing from submission. Send SASE for guidelines. Reports in 2-6 weeks, pays $5/poem. For book publication, query with 5 samples, bio. Replies to queries in 2 weeks. Simultaneous submissions, photocopies, dot-matrix OK. Publishes books on 10% royalty contract, advance (about $100) and 50 copies. Send SASE for catalog to order samples.**

ANSUDA PUBLICATIONS, *PUB (II), Box 158JA, Harris, IA 51345, founded 1978, "is a small press operation, publishing independently of outside influences, such as grants, donations, awards, etc. Our operating capital comes from magazine and book sales only." Their magazine *The Pub* "uses some poetry, and we also publish separate chapbooks of individual poets. We **prefer poems with a social slant and originality—we do *not* want love poems, personal poems that can only be understood by the poet, or anything from the haiku family of poem styles. No limits on length, though very short poems lack the depth we seek—no limits on form or style, but rhyme and meter must make sense. Too many poets write senseless rhymes using the first words to pop into their heads. As a result, we prefer blank and free verse.**" They have recently published Real Faucher, Mark Kramer, Joe Brandt, Christine D. Beyer and Dianna Garcia, but offer no sample because "most of our poems are at least 25-30 lines long and every line complements all other lines, so it is hard to pick out only four lines to illustrate." *The Pub*, which appears irregularly (1-3 times a year) is a low-budget publication, digest-sized, mimeographed on inexpensive paper, making it possible to print 80 or more pages and sell copies for **$2 (the price of a sample)**. Its minimum print-run is 350 for 130 subscriptions, of which 7 are libraries. Each issue has 8-12 pages of poetry, but "**we would publish more if we had it; our readers would like more poetry.**" Everything accepted goes into the next issue, so there is no backlog; **reports immediately to 2 weeks, payment 2 copies, guidelines available for SASE**. They also publish 1-2 chapbooks (24-28 pp.) per year. For these, **query with 3-6 sample poems**. "We need cover letters so we know it's for a book MS query, but you should only include information *relevant* to the book (education, experience, etc.). We are *not* interested in past credits, who you studied under, etc. Names mean nothing to us and we have found that small press is so large that big names in one circle are unknown in another circle. In fact, **we get better material from the unknowns who have nothing to brag about (usually)." Replies to queries immediately, reports in 1-2 months on submissions, no dot-matrix, simultaneous submissions only if clearly indicated. Payment: royalties plus 5 copies**. They will also subsidy publish if poet pays 100% of costs, picks own press name (**Ansuda** does not appear on subsidy publications), and handles distribution. Prices on request. Daniel Betz adds, "About all I have left to say is to tell the beginner to keep sending his work out. **It won't get published in a desk drawer**. There are so many little mags out there that eventually you'll find homes for your poems. Yes, some poets get published on their first few tries, but I've made first acceptances to some who have been submitting for 5 to 10 years with no luck, until their poem and my mag just seemed to click. It just takes time and lots of patience."

ANTI-APARTHEID NEWS (IV), 13 Mandela St., London NW1 0DW, England, phone 01-387-7966, founded 1965, is a newspaper (10 times per year) "for **freedom in Southern Africa" which uses 1-2 poems per issue**, payment in copies. As a sample, I selected these lines from "Walking Out of Step" by Ducus Fambai:

> *Playing only the white keys*
> *leaving the blacks to rot and rust*
> *how harmonious the tune?*
> *"Right! Left! Right! Left!"*

They receive 50-60 submissions per year, use 10-20, have a 1-2 month backlog.

*ANTIETAM REVIEW (II), Washington County Arts Council, 33 W. Washington St., Hagerstown, MD 21740, an annual founded 1981, poetry editor Ann B. Knox, **uses about 10 poems per issue, up to 30 lines each, pays $20/poem, depending on funding**. Poets they have published include Joan Aleshire, David Huddle, Ann Darr and Warren Miller. They have a press run of 1,000, 8½x11" saddle-stapled, **sample: $3 postpaid.**

*THE ANTIGONISH REVIEW(II), St. Francis Xavier University, Antigonish, Nova Scotia, Canada B2G 1C0, phone 902-867-3269, founded 1970, poetry editor Peter Sanger, "is a literary quarterly. We like all kinds of good poetry, but no erotica." No specifications as to form, length, style, subject-matter or purpose. They have recently published poetry by R.J. MacSween, Francis Stuart, John Cage, Michael Hulse and Alistair MacLeod. They have 50 pp. of poetry in each issue, circulation 900, 600 subscriptions of which 200 are libraries. Subscription: $14; per copy: $4. They receive about 600 submissions per year, take 75, have a 6-9 month backlog. **Sample: $2 postpaid. Submit any time up to maximum of 6-8 poems. Photocopy, dot-matrix OK; no simultaneous submissions, no queries. Reports in 2-3 months. Pays copies.**

*THE ANTIOCH REVIEW (III), Box 148, Yellow Springs, OH 45387, founded 1941, "is an independent quarterly of critical and creative thought . . . **For 45 years, now, creative authors, poets and thinkers have found a friendly reception . . . regardless of formal reputation**." Poetry editor: David St. John. "We get far more poetry than we can possibly accept, and the competition is keen. Here, where form and content are so inseparable and reaction is so personal, it is difficult to state requirements or limitations. Studying recent issues of *The Review* should be helpful. **No 'light' or inspirational verse**." Recently published poets: Molly Peacock, Joyce Carol Oates, Debra Nystrom, Karen Fish, Michael Collier, Andrew Hudgins. I selected these sample lines from Craig Raine's "Inca":

> *And the swans display*
> *their dripping beaks for us,*
> *but your lips are parted:*
> *to kiss, or to speak.*

Circulation is primarily to their 4,000 subscriptions, of which half are libraries. They receive about 3,000 submissions per year, publish 12-16 pages in each issue, have about a 6 month backlog. **Pays $10/ published page plus 2 copies, general guidelines for contributors available for SASE, reports in 4-6 weeks.**

APALACHEE QUARTERLY, D.D.B. PRESS (II), Box 20106, Tallahassee, FL 32316, founded 1971, editors Barbara Hamby, Allen Woodmont and Monica Faeth, want **"no formal verse."** They have published poetry by David Kirby, Peter Meinke and Jim Hall. There are 55-95 pp. of poetry in each issue, circulation 500, 200 subscriptions of which 15 are libraries, a 1-12 month backlog. **Sample: $3.50 postpaid. Submit clear copies of up to 5 poems, name and address on each, no dot-matrix, photocopied, simultaneous submissions OK. Payment 2 copies. Guidelines available for SASE. Sometimes comments on rejections.**

‡APAEROS: READER-WRITTEN FORUM ABOUT SEX AND EROTICA (IV, Erotica), Sylvia % Correspan, Box 759, Veneta, OR 97487, is just what its subtitle implies. Sylvia Carlson, who calls herself "clerk" because the magazine has no editor, says, **"Each subscriber may but needn't contribute up to two pages per issue, which will be published (unedited) at no extra charge. A nonsubscriber may send submissions which will be included IF I especially like any and IF I have space left.** This is actually more of a service and newsletter than a magazine." The three poems (including one by e.e. cummings) in the first issue all seem to be by poets other than the persons who sent them in. **Send SASE for guidelines. Sample $2 postpaid. Your submissions are photo reduced to about half-size and printed as they appear, so they must be very legible.** Each of the first two issues consisted of three sheets of paper, stapled at the corner, with 24 pp. of submissions in reduced type on both sides of the pages.

‡*APPALACHIAN HERITAGE (IV, Regional/Southern Appalachian), Hutchins Library, Berea College, Berea KY 40404, phone 606-986-9341, ext. 289 or 290, founded 1972, editor Sidney Saylor Farr, a literary quarterly with Southern Appalachian emphasis. The journal publishes several poems in each issue, and the editor wants to see **"poems about people, places, the human condition, etc., with**

Southern Appalachian settings. No style restrictions but poems should have a maximum of 25 lines, prefer 10-15 lines." She does not want "blood and gore, hell-fire and damnation, or biased poetry about race or religion." She has recently published poetry by Jim Wayne Miller, Louise McNeill and Bettie Sellers. As a sample, she selected the following lines by James Still:

> They have come down astride their bony nags
> In the gaunt hours when the lean young day
> Walks the grey ridge, and coal light flags
> Smooth-bodied poplars piercing a hollow sky.

The flat-spined magazine is 7x9½", professionally printed on white stock with b/w line drawings and photos, glossy white card cover with four-color illustration. A sample copy may be obtained by writing. **Contributors should type poems one to a page, simultaneous submissions are OK, and MS are reported on in 2-4 weeks. Pay is 5 copies. The editor criticizes rejected MS.** She says, "Study potential market. Study and learn different forms of poetry. Learn the discipline of writing to forms—only in discipline can there be true freedom."

APPLEZABA PRESS (II), Box 4134, Long Beach, CA 90804, founded 1977, poetry editor D. H. Lloyd, is "dedicated to printing and distributing poetry to as wide an audience as we can." They publish both chapbooks and flat-spined collections of individual poets and occasional anthologies, about 3 titles per year. **"As a rule we like 'accessible' poetry, some experimental. We do not want to see traditional."** They have recently published poetry by Leo Mailman, Gerald Locklin, John Yamrus, Toby Lurie and Nichola Manning. These sample lines are from Lyn Lifshin's "Parachute Madonna":

> either quite manic or depressive
> either up and flying or down
> with a huge crash.

No query. Submit book MS with brief cover letter mentioning other publications and bio. Report in 3 months. Simultaneous submissions, photocopy OK, dot-matrix accepted but not preferred. Pays 8-12% royalties and 10 author's copies. Send SASE for catalog to order samples. The samples I have seen are digest-sized, flat-spined paperbacks with glossy covers, sometimes with cartoon art, attractively printed.

‡*AQUA/ART NODE (I)**, Box 4218, Langely Park MD 20787, phone 301-465-1118, founded 1984, poetry editor Valerie Russell, who says that for poetry they want "fish stories"—actually **anything with a halfway political bent, yet with some degree of artistic inspiration." They do not want "growing pains or living abortion poems (we have enough of them)."** They have recently published poetry by Charles Plymell and Herbert Huncke. As a sample, the editor chose the following lines from "Nuclear Christ," poet unidentified (about Norman David Mayer):

> A van full of air and will
> he was there
> at the biggest phallic symbol
> of them all
> It looks like a missle how sleek
> And defined, pointed at God,
> Now what do they have in mind

Aqua, which appears three times a year, is described as "alternative in true sense of word—homeless stories, jailhouse odes, drug allures, etc." It is digest-sized, 40 pp., cardstock cover, lots of art. Circulation is 500, of which 28 are subscriptions; most circulation seems to be complimentary. Price per issue is $2, subscription $6/year. **Sample available for $3 postpaid, pay is 1-2 copies "if requested." MSS should be typed. Reporting time is 5 weeks and time to publication is 6-8 weeks.** The editor's advice is, "Laziness doesn't pay—we expect stuff to be worked over at least as much as a basket. Having been rejected by much of the academe, we don't put much faith in established venues. Make your own."

AQUARIUS (II), Linden, Flat 3, 114 Sutherland Ave., London, England W9, is a literary biannual publishing quality poetry. Sample: £2.50.

AQUILA PUBLISHING CO., *PROSPICE, *PRINTERS PIE, IOLAIRE ARTS FOUNDATION, PHAETON PRESS, CLUB LEABHAR, THE MOORLANDS PRESS (II), Box 1, Portree, Isle of Skye, Scotland 1V5 0BT, founded 1968. **Aquila: Ireland, *Tracks*,** founded 1983, Box 1, Drogheda, Co Louth, Ireland. All Divisions of **Johnston Green & Co. (Publishers) Ltd.** This company was founded in Glasgow and later moved to Birmingham in England where it was operated by husband and wife Jim and Anne Green as a spare time activity connected with their printing business and Jim's work as a producer for the British Broadcasting Corporation's Radio output of literature and arts programmes. In 1974 the owners returned to Scotland to live and work in the scenic Isle of Skye. The press merged with another Scottish company, Club Leabhar Ltd., and since 1977 has been more or less a full time occupation publishing poetry and many other types of books. It is now a division of Johnston Green International Ltd., based in Skye. They have recently published **Selected Poems** by Knute Skinner from whose "A Cat's Purr" I selected the first stanza as a sample. *The nice thing about a cat's purr is knowing your cat is happy and taking credit for it. Wives and children don't work that way.* "As 'book people' we care about books, about writing, writers, etc. We aim to publish and produce a diversity of material, good work of whatever type. **We want GOOD poetry of any style. We do not publish racist or sexist material. We are not prudes, but uncalled-for pornography or violence are not read. Eroticism yes. We publish a lot of translation titles. We receive many thousands of submissions a year, and we use a large proportion in some way—pamphlets/magazines/books/cards/anthologies, etc. We aim for a 1 month turn-around on queries, and 3 months on a final decision. We suggest that poets submit non-returnable photocopies if from outside UK, and 3 IRC's. We will then acknowledge receipt, and if no decision is received by air-mail 3 months later, query again. UK submissions will be acknowledged if a SAE is provided. Again, query if no reply within 3 months. Good copies essential—new carbons, good copier, or fresh ribbon. Dot-matrix OK, simultaneous submissions OK so long as the editor is informed at time of submission. To submit book MSS, no need to query, include brief biography, details of other publications, particularly important magazine credits, awards, etc., but, please, not masses of mentions for every little mag or local paper ever to carry something by the poet. Mention non-poetry books if relevant. For pamphlets we may well ask the poet to purchase some copies for his/her own sales; we give 50% discount. We do like authors who are willing to promote their books and have confidence in their work—otherwise why should we? Usually no payment for poetry, though 10% royalties on other books. 12-20 authors copies. Catalogue available for 3 IRCs. Criticism can be arranged for a negotiable fee, which goes to a qualified reviewer, not the press**." Jim Green had these general comments, helpful for poets at any level: "Publishing poetry is not a particularly easy way to make a living, but this company was founded to do just that, on a part-time basis. Poets must realize that they are most unlikely to be able to live from their writing alone, but some poets manage a kind of living editing, reviewing, and above all reading or lecturing about their work or some aspect of poetry, or another poet. They are few, though, and most poets depend on other, possibly related activities to earn their bread. Please bear in mind that almost always the editor who reads your work does so on a part-time basis, and if paid at all is rather poorly paid. Poetry is a diverse field, and virtually all types of poetry can find a home, but only if the writing poet is prepared to read and research the market. This is more important for poets than most other types of writer. Small magazines and small presses work on a shoestring, and the best way to ensure publication of poetry is via these outlets. However if no one buys their output, they won't survive, and if they don't survive poets will be left with the choice of vanity/subsidy publishing, or the liklihood or otherwise of finding a place on the list of a *big* publisher. **Aquila is still a small press, even though we publish more poetry titles than any other British publisher**. I would estimate that if all the small presses, went out of business, a great deal of good poetry would not be published commercially, and that in numbers in Britain the remaining big publishers would publish only about the quantity of titles that we ourselves publish now. **Buy poetry magazines and publications, not just to support them, but to learn what they publish, and learn from reading that work. NEVER pretend in a letter that you have read a magazine, or a press's output if you have not so done. We are not fools, you always give yourselves away** . . . *Prospice*, appearing May and November, "Scotland's International Literary Magazine" has a proportion of Scottish writers but is open to all others, 60 pp. of poetry in each issue, a flat-spined, book-like magazine with fine printing and art, **hopes to pay in addition to providing free copies**. Print run 2,000, 800 subscriptions of which 80% are libraries (many in North America). **Sample $4 postpaid by surface mail.** *Tracks*, poetry editor John F. Deane, published January and July, "Ireland's International Literary Magazine," is also open to writers from any other country. About the size and shape of *Prospice*, print run 1,000, with 200 subscribers, of which 10% are libraries, maximum of 20 pages of poetry. About 500 submissions received of which 20% are used, **translation featured quite heavily. Payment plus copies. Sample $4 postpaid by surface mail.** *Printers Pie*, a quarterly, uses no poetry but is a valuable resource for poets, containing reviews, news, information and advice. Print run 2,500, of which 90% goes in subscription sales, **sample $3 postpaid by surface mail. Iolaire Arts Foundation Competitions**—a continuing search for 2 manuscripts per quarter for poetry chapbooks (22 pp.) published by **Phaeton Press** at the Foundation's expense in print runs of 250, 10% royalties. $10 entry fee. Send query and IRC for rules.

ARACHNE (IV, Rural), 162 Sturges St., Jamestown, NY 14701, founded 1979, is a digest-sized quarterly, 50+ pp., circulation 500, publishes **conservative poetry of rural America. Sample: $4.**

‡***ARETE: THE JOURNAL OF SPORT LITERATURE (IV, Sports)**, San Diego State University, San Diego CA 92182, phone 619-265-6220, founded 1983, poetry editor Robert W. Hamblin, Professor of English, Southeast Missouri State University, Cape Girardeau, MO 63701. *Arete* publishes a variety of sport-related literature, including scholarly articles, fiction, poetry, personal essays, and reviews; 6-

10 poems per issue; two issues annually; fall and spring. **Subject matter must be sports-related; no restrictions regarding form, length, style or purpose. They do not want to see "doggerel, cliche-ridden, or oversentimental" poems.** Some poets recently published are Robert Fink, Charles Ghigna, William Heyen, Robert Gibb, Barbara Smith, and Don Welch. As a sample, the editor selected the following lines by J. F. Connolly:

> *Like those first newsreels, we all move too fast,*
> *solid foot soldiers who block out the sound*
> *and face in the dark and grainy fame film.*
> *And then number ten, the quick one, breaks loose:*

The magazine is digest-sized, an offset, flat-spined paperback with illustrations and some ads, 200 pp. per issue. Circulation is 1,000 of which 750 are subscriptions, 400 to libraries. Price per issue is $12.50; subscription is included with membership ($30) in the Sport Literature Association. **Sample $12.50 postpaid. Contributors receive 6 offprints. Submissions are reported on in 4-6 weeks and the backlog time is 6-12 months; "only typed MSS with SASE considered."**

*ARGO (INCORPORATING DELTA) (II), The Old Fire Station, 40 George St., Oxford, England, founded 1979, appears three times a year; poetry editors Hilary Davies and David Constantine. *Delta* began in 1953 and combined with *Argo* in 1979, and since has "pursued a policy of openness to a wide variety of poetic thought and styles; it has drawn on British, American, Australian, Canadian, Israeli and Indian writing in the belief that familiarity with both regional and international idioms of English can only be beneficial in avoiding the sometimes narrow interpretation put on English poetry and fiction. . . . Each issue contains unpublished work by both lesser-known and established poets . . ." They are **"ready to consider all types"** and have published Dannie Abse, Milton Acorn, John Matthias, Brad Leithauser, Michael Hamburger, Jenny Joseph and Carol Rumens. As a sample the editors chose the opening stanza of George Szirtes "The Swimmers":

> *Inside the church the floor is like black ice:*
> *The past moves underneath it as it glimmers*
> *In the light of the long windows, and you read*
> *In brass the images of the dead swimmers.*

Print run 800, **sample: $3.50**. They receive about a thousand submissions a year of which they use about 20 in 14-20 pages of poetry in each issue. It's a handsomely printed digest-sized perfect-bound magazine with photos and drawings. 6 months-1 year backlog. **Submit no more than 5 poems at a time, reports in 1-2 months. No limit on length of poems. Pays $5/contributor plus 2 copies and a gift subscription.** "We look for the objective, not the confessional unless it has some wider application. Excessive personalization is not in general a recipe for good poetry."

ARIES PRODUCTIONS, *DOORWAYS TO THE MIND: JOURNEY INTO PSYCHIC AWARENESS (IV, Inspirational), Box 29396, Sappington, MO 63126, founded 1973, poetry editor Michael Christopher, is the **Journal of the Mind Development Association**, appearing quarterly. They want **poetry that is "inspirational but not religious, metaphysical, or spiritually oriented. Do NOT want love, contemporary experience, narrative, the 'what a joy it is to do dishes' type. Prefer short, succinct 8-12 lines."** They have recently published poetry by Orin H. Jones, Sr. and John C. Aultly, and offer this passage (of prose-poetry?) by Joyce A. Chandler as a sample: "The Dichotomy of Earth and Heaven: Man walks the earth, trembling and unsure; his eyes long blinded by the strident lights, his head lowered, he absorbs the poisons of the earth. Once upright like the stable horse, he knows not where his feet will go; but waits to be led, racing to his sudden end." The magazine is inexpensively produced, photocopied from typescript, in a digest-sized, saddle-stapled format with paper cover and simple art. They have 2,500 subscriptions (including 10 libraries), circulation of 5,000. Subscription is $7.50 ($13 foreign), individual copy $1.50, **sample: $1 + 2 stamps and large return envelope.** Michael Christopher says they receive "zillions" of submissions, use 20-25 per year, have a backlog which is "enormous. We have instituted a department of rotten rhymes/ putrid poetry, another for those who don't include return postage. **No query. Should buy a copy of the magazine before submitting. Prefer typed, double-spaced, 1 page. No dot-matrix. Simultaneous submissions OK. Pays 5 contributors copies and $2 "if exceptional." Guidelines available for SASE. They comment "if good or very very bad."** For $2 per poem the editor will supply criticism upon request. "We like good poetry, rhymed poetry coming back. Our subjects are specialized, not much available. We've seen so much bad poetry handwritten in pencil, misspelled terribly: He done, we was, she has did. We would like to tell them to take a course in creative writing/grammar. Beginners will never get published with submissions of this type."

*ARIZONA QUARTERLY (II), Main Library B-541, University of Arizona, Tucson, AZ 85721, phone 602-621-6396, founded 1945, A. F. Gegenheimer, editor, is a handsomely printed, conservative-looking academic journal, 6x9", flat-spined, **sample: $1.50 postpaid**. They receive a lot of poetry, use little. The sample I have has four in its 90 pp. I chose the opening lines of Robyn Wiegman's "La Mujer" as an example:

> *In Argentina, despair rises.*
> *There are no wings, only the crush*
> *of fingers held too long in one place*
> *and a night coming on with nothing but sorrow.*

Submit 1-5 poems, no longer than 30 lines each. No simultaneous submissions, previously published poems. Photocopy OK. Reports in 3 weeks (slower in summer). Pays in copies and a one-year subscription beginning with issue in which published.

ARJUNA LIBRARY PRESS, *JOURNAL OF REGIONAL CRITICISM (IV, Specialized), 1025 Garner St., Box 18, Colorado Springs, CO 80905, founded 1979, seems to be very much a one-man operation, that of Joseph A. Uphoff, Jr., who has developed a personal aesthetics and is much involved with publishing (or circulating in manuscript) his own work in the arts. He describes his operation as "limited productions by means of xerography, fine arts, poetry, calculus and mathematical theories of literature, fiction, art, surrealism, mathematical criticism" and says he publishes "monthly manuscript copy and **limited (10 or less each) editions in chapbooks**." He wants "**free verse, surrealist, dadaist, general audience or censorable (by quotation)**" which I quote without understanding. "**Prefer length and cohesive irrationality (dreamstyle)**." In addition to himself he has published Thomas Hibbard:

> *. . . in their yards, children played their blind games.*
> *Many times a distant train signaled its passing.*
> *Your mother picked up all your scattered toys*
> *and stored them in the bedroom closet . . .*

He publishes two or more issues of the *Journal* a month with five or more pages of poetry in **a usual print-run of two**. The sample he sent me, *The Plastic Metaphor*, by himself, consisted entirely of poems written in mathematical symbols (with footnotes). For **sample, send 10¢/page plus postage**. (I guess you'll have to ask him how many pages of what.) To the question, "How many freelance poetry submissions do you receive per year?" he answered "0 to one." He says manuscripts should be "**clearly readable, will not be returned, notification upon acceptance, reports in one month and pays in "commentary**." Considers simultaneous submissions. "Letter style manuscript copy mailed to museums and libraries. Examples have been exhibited in juried fine art shows. "**Biography requested but not required; we prefer theoretical dissertations in illustration of work submitted**." How can poet obtain or see samples of books you have published? "Exchange, page for page, book for book. Will comment if work is salvageable by us, will criticize by contract upon acceptance of manuscript for this purpose, will subsidy publish for cost plus labor." None of this makes much sense to me, but it may to others, and the man is eager to get in touch: "We are interested in forging relations between poets, artists, critics, and the market; collaboration is the key to success. Communication is the only viable means of exposing work to the reading, viewing public. Letters are all-important!" So write him a letter!

THE ARK (II), 20 Tufts St., Cambridge, MA 02139, phone 617-876-0064, founded 1970 (as BLEB), poetry editor Geoffrey Gardner, publishes books of poetry. "**We will consider work of *any* form or style. Depth, power and excellence are what we want. We are especially interested in new translations of poetry from all languages and periods. We look for seriousness of purpose and brilliance of execution.**" They have published poetry by David Budbill, Kenneth Rexroth, John Haines, Joseph Bruchac, Elsa Gidlow, W. S. Merwin, Eliot Weinberger, Kathy Acker, George Woodcock, Kathleen Raine, Marge Piercy and Linda Hogan. The editor selected these lines by Kenneth Rexroth (translated from the Sanskrit) as a sample:

> *You think this is a time of Shiva's waking*
> *You are wrong*
> *You are Shiva*
> *But you dream*

Query with at least 10 pp. of poetry and a cover letter giving such things as publication credits, bio, personal or aesthetic philosophy, poetic goals and principles. Replies to queries at once, to submissions in 3-12 weeks. Typescript only. Pays 10% royalties and 5% of press run. The editor sometimes comments on rejected MSS. He says, "The number of poetry MSS read by editors every year far exceeds the number of books of poetry sold each year. We do not want to contribute to this situation and suggest that poets seek publication (especially with us) only if they are convinced they have something urgent and stunning to say to the world." To see samples of their publications, order from the Ark, or find them in bookstores or libraries.

THE UNIVERSITY OF ARKANSAS PRESS (II), McIlroy House, Fayetteville, AR 72701, founded 1980, poetry editor Miller Williams (Director of the Press), publishes flat-spined paperbacks and hardback collections of individual poets. Miller Williams says, "**We are not interested in poetry that says, 'Guess what I mean' or 'Look what I know.'** They have published poetry by Ronald Koertge, Debra Bruce and George Garrett. I selected these sample lines from the late John Ciardi's **Selected Poems:**

> *Men marry what they need. I marry you,*
> *morning by morning, day by day, night by night,*
> *and every marriage makes this marriage new.*

Query with 5-10 sample poems. Replies to query in 2 weeks, to submissions in 2-4 weeks. No replies without SASE. MS should be double-spaced with 1½" margins. Clean photocopy OK. No dot-matrix. Discs compatible with CPT OK. Pay: 10% royalty contract plus 10 author's copies. Send SASE for catalog to buy samples.

‡**ART TIMES: Cultural and Creative News (II)**, Box 730, Mount Marion, NY 12456, phone 914-246-5170, editor Raymond J. Steiner, a monthly tabloid newspaper devoted to the arts that publishes some poetry and fiction. The editor wants to see "**traditional and contemporary poetry with high literary quality."** He does not want to see "**poorly written, pointless prose in stanza format."** The most well-known poet he has published recently is Helen Wolfert. As a sample, he selected the following lines by Anne Mins:

> *Your finical ear, my friend*
> *Neat file of images, pile of esoteric words*
> *Compendium of rhymes, blend of assonance,*
> *Your pyrotechnic metric, Spare me, spare me.*

Art Times focuses on cultural and creative news of the Catskill and Mid-Hudson region; contributors do not, however, have to be from that region. The paper is 16-20 pp., on newsprint, with reproductions of art work, some photos, advertisement-supported. Frequency is monthly and circulation is 15,000, of which 450 are subscriptions; most distribution is free through galleries, theatres, etc. Subscription is $15/year. **Sample: $1 postage cost. Guidelines available for SASE. Pay is 6 free copies. Submissions are reported on in 2 months; publication is in 6-8 months. There is a 20-line limit for poetry. Simultaneous submissions OK. Typed MSS should be submitted to the editor. Criticism of MSS is provided "at times but rarely."**

ARTEMIS (IV, Regional/Virginia), Box 945, Roanoke, VA 24005, founded 1977, is a literary annual publishing work by poets from the Blue Ridge Mountains of Virginia. "*Artemis* considers submissions in the fall through November 15th. We use very little formal poetry, simply because we receive little that is good. If you write in form, and consider poetry to be more than a hobby, send something along. While general submissions are restricted to our region, our contest is open to all." Sample: $4.75. Pays 1 copy.

‡*****ARTFUL CODGER AND CODGERETTE, *SNOWY EGRET (IV, Elderly)**, 205 S. 9th St., Williamsburg, KY, 40769, phone 606-549-0850, founded 1984, editor and publisher Humprhey A. Olsen. *Artful Codger* is a "mini-monthly" (10 times/year) dealing with nostalgia plus a realistic approach to problems facing older persons. *Snowy Egret* **(a semi-annual) accepts poetry related to natural history,** *Artful Codger* **wants poems (limit 45 lines) about nature, older persons, of general interest, and nostalgia. They do not want "abstruse, long poems."** As a sample, the editor selected the following lines by an unidentified poet:

> *Four honking geese*
> *ostentatiously wing*
> *down Third River*
> *as if on their way*
> *to a military display.*

The Artful Codger is 7x8½", 8 pp., mimeographed and folded, with b/w decorations. Circulation is 450, mostly free local distribution, but subscriptions are available for $4/year. **Sample available for SASE. Pay is 10 copies plus a 1 year subscription. Reporting time is 1 month, and there is no backlog.** The editor advises, "Be sure to send material that meets our requirements."

THE ARTHUR PRESS (II, IV, Theme, style), 7301 S. 70 E Ave., Tulsa, OK 74133, phone 918-494-5653, founded 1984, poetry editors Andrew Bixler and Berniece Estey, has so far published only 2 books, both by B. E. Bixler, but they are now open to submissions from others and are considering publication of a magazine. They want to "**publish poetry—avant-garde, not rhyming, any subject, feminist slant, have contests in poetry with prizes, a non-profit regional organization which is just getting underway to fulfillment. No 'cute' folksy poetry, no haiku, no long, narrative poems, no vulgar eroticism. Short poems preferred—any subjects, if not too light-weight. Serious thought, rhythm, form."** As a sample the editors chose these lines by B. E. Bixler:

> *"Where are the great women artists?" men ask.*
> *Imagine a woman trying to become an artist!*

> *Imagine a woman aboard Klee's magic boat*
> *Afloat in Algerian color, shades of blues & yellows*

They charge a reading fee of $2 per poem. Simultaneous submissions, photocopies, dot-matrix OK. MS should be double-spaced, clear print. They will pay on royalty contracts with 50 copies. Buy samples for $4. If asked, editor will give free criticism (i.e., to those who have paid the reading fee). Andrew Bixler says, "Rilke's advice to a young poet will do very well: 'Between my good and my *best* writing there is a chasm.' I agree. Beginning poets must read the *best* poets to improve their own— like Dylan Thomas, Sylvia Plath, Rilke, Neruda, Paz, Wallace Stevens, Ann Sexton."

ARTS END BOOKS, *NOSTOC MAGAZINE (II),, Box 162, Newton, MA 02168, founded 1978, poetry editor Marshall Brooks. **"We publish good contemporary writing. Our interests are broad and so are our tastes. People considering sending work to us should examine a copy of our magazine and/or our catalog; check your library for the former, send us a SASE for the latter**.*"* Their publications are distinguished by excellent presswork and art in a variety of formats: postcard series, posters, chapbooks, pamphlets, flat-spined paperbacks and hardbacks. As a sample Brooks chose Rogue Dalton's "The Captain" (translated by Sesshu Foster):

> *The captain in his hammock the captain*
> *asleep under the chirping of the night*
> *the guitar hanging against the wall*
> *his pistol set aside his bottle*
> *awaiting like a rendezvous with love*
> *the captain the captain*
> *—he should know—*
> *under the same darkness as his prey.*

The magazine appears irregularly in print-runs of 300-500, about 30 pp. of poetry in each, 100 subscriptions of which half are libraries. **Sample: $2.50 postpaid**. They receive a few hundred submissions per year, use 25-30; "modest payment plus contributor's copies." To see samples of their other publications, "Order books from the catalog or have local bookstore or library order them. A cover letter is a very good idea for any kind of submission; we receive *very* **few good, intelligent cover letters; what to include? That's up to the writer, whatever he/she feels important in terms of the work, in terms of arousing our curiosity, interest. Tries to report within a few weeks," discourages simultaneous submissions, frequently comments on rejected MSS**. Marshall says, "We respond warmly to writers interested in making genuine contact with us and our audience; we respect people with a commitment to good writing and who want to share that commitment with us; we admire people dedicated to communicating or perhaps I should say **COMMUNICATING** . . . they're rare."

‡*ARTS INSIGHT (IV, Regional/Indiana), Suite 403, 47 S. Pennsylvania, Indianapolis, IN 46204, phone 317-632-7894, founded 1979, poetry editor Cynthia Blasingham, a tabloid-sized review on visual, performing, and literary arts in Indiana. "The mission of *Arts Insight* is to expand, throughout Indiana, informed participation in the arts. **There must be an Indiana connection." They use "all varieties" of poetry except that "not related to Indiana." They buy 12 poems/year, and a maximum of 3 can be submitted at any one time.** The issue I have (January, 1986) contains a selection of poems from "Poetry on the Buses," and annual contest co-sponsored by *Arts Insight*; all of the "Poetry on the Buses" winners are published in a small chapbook. As a sample, I chose the beginning lines from "Keepsake" by Barbara Koons:

> *My grandmother lives*
> *in my top bureau drawer*
> *beneath scented handkerchiefs*
> *behind old jewelry*

Arts Insight is 32 pp., professionally printed on heavy stock (not newsprint), a folded, non-stapled tabloid. It is attractively designed with many b/w illustrations. The magazine comes out 10 times a year (September through June); it is supported by a grant from the Indiana Arts Commission and the National Endowment for the Arts. Circulation is 8,000. Single copy price is $1.50 and a subscription is $14/year. **Pay for poems is $2.50 plus 1 copy and a free subscription to the magazine.**

AS IS/SO & SO PRESS, *SO & SO, *BAD BREATH MAGAZINE, AND STILL IT MOVES (V, IV, Specialized), 1003 Keith Ave., Berkeley, CA 94708, phone 415-526-3207, founded 1973, poetry editor John Marron, who describes his operation this way: "irregular, issue specific, visual poetry, national-international-CA/SF Bay Area/NYC concentrated, some multicultural oral tradition/political work, some language-centered serialistic and minimist/Buddhist writing, some reviews, letters to editor, and books and magazines received section. Idiosyncratic!" He says he wants **"multilingual, visual, sound specific, photo-narrative prose-poetry, visually precise, *not* reproducing T. S. Eliot, Berryman, Olson, James Dickey or Robert Hass! Short, detailing with the writing moment, 4-6**

pp., **narrative or not,** *not* purely imagistic, descriptive." They have recently published poems by Kathleen Fraser, Diane Ward, Kathy Acker, Lyn Hejinian, Juan Felipe Herrera, Loris Essary, Ron Silliman, Doug Skinner, Doris Cross, Chris Knowles and Cindy Lubar. The editor selected these sample lines:

> 1) *"Everything I seek to hide structures a face.—Barry Watten*
> 2) *"out of mai lai, watts, wounded knee, mission st. barrios*
> *we sing hurimentado blues."—Al Robles*
> 3) *"Asphalt reminds me of you. Shush completely."—Diane Ward*
> 4) *"Lemons shaped like the eye of a tiger*
> *bitter as the world around me"—Yolanda Ann Brown*

So 'n' So appears irregularly (1-4 a year) in various formats: idiosyncratic, dependent on poets and materials at hand—visually elegant, word to word relations intact, musical, language centered, place and culture specific." Two of the sample issues I examined were digest-sized, about 20 pp. saddle-stapled, offset on colored mimeo paper from typescript, matte card covers. Another (Summer, 1980) was professionally printed, flat-spined, 7x9", about 100 unnumbered pp. There are "28-128" pp. of poetry per issue, print run 300-500, 52 subscriptions of which 10 are libraries. Doesn't publish unsolicited mss. **Sample: $3 postpaid. "Poets should query maybe with 1 poem as example of work and/or check magazine out** *first.* **Reports in 1 month, pays contributor's copies. Query regarding book publication.** No information on *Bad Breath Magazine.* And Still It Moves is a beautifully printed "SF Neighborhood Multicultural Poetry Calendar," $8, published in 1984, 1985 and 1986. The editor will provide criticism for $5 per page only upon request. John Marron advises, "Do it, write it, think it, absorb it, read closely, diversity, do something else (learn it early) for a living, never stop, don't underestimate the gentle support and savage wisdom other poet-egos can provide, sing, hide, share it with your lovers, children, friends and perfectly estranged readership. Let everyday poems, ordinary miracles, and task-art remain in *con*-text. Love and best love to you all."

‡**ASHLEY BOOKS, INC. (II)**, Box 768, Port Washington, NY 11050, phone 516-883-2221, founded 1971, associate editor Gwen Costa, a small-press publisher of fiction, non-fiction, biography, medical books, black and gay literature, cookbooks, and poetry. Some of their books are hardcover, some are flat-spined paperbacks. The editors says, **"Will consider all types [of poetry]. Very flexible in terms of form, subject, etc., but most interested in collections, not submissions of individual poems."** She has recently published work by Anne Frost. As a sample, she selected the following lines by an unidentified poet:

> *The sound of pounding waves,*
> *the constant wind,*
> *the flow of tears down pallored cheeks;*
> *for naught.*

Ashley Books publishes 4 poetry chapbooks per year with an average page count of 100. **Writers should query before submitting "typewritten, completed manuscripts (may be photocopy)." Queries will be answered in 2 weeks, MSS reported on in 4 weeks; simultaneous submissions will be considered. The press pays royalties of 10-15%, an advance (negotiable), and 10 author's copies. Criticism of rejected MSS is provided.**

ASHOD PRESS (IV, Armenian), Box 1147, Madison Square Station, New York, NY 10159, founded 1980, publishes poetry translated from Armenian or expressive of Armenian culture. Send SASE for catalog to buy samples.

‡**ASSEMBLING PRESS, *ASSEMBLING ANNUAL (IV, Print art)**, Box 1967, Brooklyn, NY 11202, founded 1970, editor/publisher Charles Doria. "Our activity is the publication and distribution of poetry, fiction (experimental and otherwise), criticism, artists' books and anthologies. We sponsor readings, performances, and exhibits. **The anthology is a spontaneous event where no editor and contributor dominates.** We produce every type of book including artists' books. We are not restricted to any specific format." **Poetry can be "any type that interests us" but not "any type that bores us."** Poets recently published include Rose Drachler, Richard Kostelanetz, Charles Doria, John Cage, Dick Higgins, Michael McClure, Tim Reynolds, Ellen Zweig, Tom Savage, Lawrence Ferlenghetti, Fred Truck, and Jackson MacLow. As an "atypical" sample I selected the poem "poolwater" by Howard Robertson:

> *rp tpero wpaotoelr owalt lw*
> *P O O L*
> *W A T E rp O O L*
> *W A tpeoro L*
> *wpaotoelr*
> *P owoalt E R*

POOlwATER
WATER

Assembling Annual is "a collaborative anthology wherein each invited contributor sends 1,000 copies of 1 page, which can contain art, text, etc. Each artist wishing to participate must first send a sample. No unsolicited material will be used." Freelance submissions are accepted for chapbooks, but "occasionally we must first discuss the matter with the writer." The annuals are titled by their order of publication, for example: *Eighth Assembling* (1978). They are magazine-sized, composed by binding together one of each of the 1,000 copies submitted by each author or artist. Some of the pages are on colored, heavy stock but most are b/w; some MSS are hand-written; there are a few photographs. It is impossible to describe the contents because it seems that anything from a postage cancellation to an advertisement, menu, postcard or personal letter is acceptable. The editors say, "As no invited submission was refused, nothing expressed in the following pages can be considered the responsibility of Assembling Press or its compilers." Circulation is 1,000, of which 100 are library subscriptions and 300 are newsstand sales. Price per issue is $10. **Sample $10 plus $2 postage and handling; guidelines are available for SASE. Invited contributors receive 1 to 3 free copies. Submissions are reported on immediately and publication is within a year. Invited contributors should submit 1,000 copies of 1 to 3 pages with a 1½" left margin on 8½x11" paper; copies should be offset litho, silkscreen, typeset or photocopied. Black and white copies are not encouraged.** The press occasionally publishes chapbooks of poetry, 3x5", 40 pp. paperbacks or hardcovers. **Writers should query before submitting. Simultaneous submissions are not acceptable. Photocopies, dot-matrix MSS, or discs compatible with Kaypro, IBM, or Radio Shack are OK. Payment for chapbooks is royalties of 5-10%. Book catalog is free on request for SASE.** The editors commment "endlessly" on rejected MSS, and the reading fee is a "free dinner." Their advice is: "Keep the work short and sweet. Think of us before you think of Random House. We seek impact and innovative concepts."

‡*ATHENA INCOGNITO MAGAZINE (I)**, 1442 Judah St., San Francisco, CA 94122, phone 415-665-0219, founded 1980, editor Ronald Rosen, a photocopied quarterly **"with open-minded acceptance of poetry; especially responsive to avant-garde/surrealist, dada. The editor does not want** "trite, hackneyed, slangy poetry." The sample issue I have contains poems by Ken Delponte, Greg A. Wallace, John Curl, and others. As a sample, I chose the first stanza from "Night Winds" by B.D. Anthony:

> *The trees from a window at night*
> *Ashamed to let Aurora ignite*
> *forms of grey*
> *block the whisper of winds*

Athena Incognito is photocopied from various styles of typed copy on ordinary photocopy paper, 9 pp. printed on both sides, stapled in top right-hand corner, b/w line drawings and decorations. It comes out 3 times/year and has a circulation of "100 or so." Single copies are $2/each, subscriptions $6.50/year. **Sample available for $2 postpaid. Pay is 1 copy.**

ATHENEUM PUBLISHERS, (III), 115 5th Ave., New York, NY 10003, phone 212-486-2700 publishes about 6 books of poetry per year by poets they have published in the past. Their **"list has been closed for ten years, and will not be opened. All materials submitted will be returned un-read, and only if a stamped, self-addressed envelope is included; if it is not, the material will automatically be discarded."**

*****THE ATLANTIC (III)**, 8 Arlington St., Boston, MA 02116, phone 617-536-9500, founded 1857, poetry editor Peter Davison, publishes 1-5 poems monthly in the magazine. **Some of the most distinguished poetry in American literature** has been published by this magazine, including recently work by William Matthews, Mary Oliver, Stanley Kunitz, George Starbuck, Rodney Jones, May Swenson and L. E. Sissman. The magazine has a **circulation of 440,000**, of which 5,800 are libraries (**sample: $3 postpaid**). They receive some 70,000 poems per year, of which they use 35-40 and have a backlog of 6-12 months. **Submit 3-5 poems, no dot-matrix, no simultaneous submissions, payment about $3/line.** Peter Davison says he wants "to see poetry of the highest order; we do *not* want to see workshop rejects. **Watch out for workshop uniformity. Beware of the present indicative. Be yourself.**"

*****ATLANTIS, A WOMEN'S STUDIES JOURNAL, REVUE D'ETUDES SUR LA FEMME (II, IV, Women's/feminist)**, Mount St. Vincent University, 166 Bedford Highway, Halifax, Nova Scotia B3M 2J6 Canada, founded 1975-6, poetry editor Hilary Thompson, "is an interdisciplinary journal devoted to critical and creative writing in English or French on the topic of women. Published 2 times a year, *Atlantis* contains scholarly articles, essays, book reviews, art work and poetry intended to encourage women's studies. We publish a few poems in each issue of the magazine on **women's concerns,**

Close-up

Peter Davison
Editor and Poet

Peter Davison has been, as he says, "on three out of four sides of the editorial desk." Poet, editor, and publisher, Davison has been labeled by the *New York Times*, "A major force in contemporary American poetry."

Davison is poetry editor of *The Atlantic* magazine, and until recently, Senior Editor at Atlantic Monthly Press, where he began as an editor in 1957. Poets he has edited include Stanley Kunitz, Mary Oliver, and Robert Penn Warren. Four books he has edited have won Pulitzer Prizes.

And, of course, Peter Davison is a poet, with his recent work, *Praying Wrong: New and Selected Poems 1957-1984* (Atheneum, 1984) receiving both critical and popular praise.

Now, Davison is beginning a new publishing venture, as head of a Houghton Mifflin trade imprint bearing his name.

When considering such a distinguished career, the obvious question is, which came first—the poet or the editor? Odd though it may seem, Peter Davison did not begin writing until he was 30. "I had a terrible handicap," he explains. "My father was a poet. It was a great benefit in that the air was always buzzing with poetry, but it was difficult to believe that poetry could be written by someone my age. I didn't feel entitled to write until I was 30, though I was an editor at 22.

"I actually started writing because of Stanley Kunitz—I was reading a manuscript by him in 1957. Something about it upset me. So I put it down, walked over to my desk, and started writing my first poem. It was a terribly important moment in my life."

Peter Davison reads a lot of poetry, as both editor and poet. He finds the range of emotion in contemporary American poetry broader in the work of women poets. He cites Mary Oliver, Marge Piercy, Louise Gluck, Marilyn Hack, Carolyn Kizer, and May Swenson as examples of quality in American poetry. "They seem, for whatever reason, to be able to command a wider, more compassionate range of emotion, and a more coherent, continuous kind of narration in poetry. It seems to me that an awful lot of male poets are kind of writing themselves into a corner, whether it's the present-tense corner of the neo-surrealist, or the private reference of the New York school, or the reference of the writing programs. I don't see many young male poets with a wide range of emotions.

"The male poets whom I see with a full range of emotion," he adds, "tend to be older. Robert Penn Warren and Galway Kinnell, for example."

Davison's primary advice to new authors is "Don't stop!" He also advises writers to "use the language as completely as possible. One of the things I find most depressing about the poetry I see is self-limitation. So much of the writing is in the present indicative, which is a very, very narrow kind of poetry, with the author trying to be immediate and personal. Poets should try everything the language can offer."

Davison recommends several poets to writers. In particular, he cites Stanley Kunitz as a model. "Emulate his patience as a writer." Other authors Davison feels are worthy of study include Robert Coles, Farley Mowat and William Least Heat Moon.

Davison stresses the role of the poet as more than that of recorder or observer. "Robert Penn Warren talks about poetry as a way of seeing, a way of living, rather than a mode of writing, and I think that's close to the truth. A poet is someone who sees to the center of the human condition, or tries to."

And Peter Davison seems to live close to Warren's ideal. "I write poetry," he says, "because only when finishing a poem do I possess a sense of having got things right. The word is the way to understanding."

—*Michael A. Banks*

---

poetry reflecting feminist attitudes. We cannot accept long poems. We want clear, original images sustained in a relatively short poem. A journal with long articles like ours needs to be punctuated by poetry." They use 2-3 pp. of poetry in each issue, circulation 800,400 subscriptions of which 400 are libraries. Individual subscription: $15. They use 10 of 100 freelance poems submitted per year. **Sample: $7.50. Reports in 1-3 months. Pays by copy if submission is accepted. Editor sometimes comments on rejections.**

AUDIO/VISUAL POETRY FOUNDATION (I), 400 Fish Hatchery Rd., Marianna, FL 32446, phone 904-482-3890, founded in 1971, poetry editor Wilbur I. Throssell, is not really a publisher but a taped poetry exchange. Wilbur Throssell, who does this for a hobby and calls himself "The Pied Piper of Poetry," **immediately accepts any poem received, if it's not offensive—one poem on a C-60 cassette of no more than 3 minutes reading time. Preface with title and your name. Simultaneous submissions OK. No fees or dues except for return postage. The editor combines all submissions and returns your cassette with poems by others and a newsletter. You listen to them all and send $1 to the poet whose poem you liked best. It is a continually quarterly contest. Send SASE for guidelines and sample of the** *Bulletin* in which listener reactions are reported. Wilbur Throssell sent these lines of his own poetry as a sample:

> *George A. Custer's troops come thundering*
> *to the ambush slaughter blundering . . .*
> *through the low hills boldly riding*
> *where the Sioux braves lurk in hiding*

‡*THE AUGUSTA SPECTATOR (IV, Regional/southeastern United States), 200 Walton Way, Augusta, GA 30910, founded 1980, poetry editor Dr. John May, is a regional magazine appearing 3 times a year using 2 pp. of poetry **of interest to southeastern U.S.** in each issue. I selected these sample lines, the opening of "Advance Notice" by Joan Ritty:

> *It is only November, but already*
> *I see teeth in the moon's mouth,*
> *and wind lances the prairie heartland*
> *purging summer's soft aches, pretending*
> *to heal what has not been sick.*

The 48 pp. magazine-sized publication is professionally printed on glossy stock using 4-color printing, ads, circulation 4,000, 2,000 subscriptions of which 15 are libraries. $2 per issue, $5 per year. **Sample guidelines: $1. Pays 5 copies. Reports in 1 month. Editor seldom comments on rejections.**

‡*AURA LITERARY/ARTS MAGAZINE (I), Box 76, University of Alabama at Birmingham, Birmingham, AL 35294, phone 205-934-3216, founded 1974, editor Andrea Mathews, a semiannual magazine that publishes "fiction and art though majority of acceptances are poetry—90-100 per year. **Length—open, style open, subject matter open except to pornography. We are looking for quality poetry. Both first-time and often published poets are published here. We look for literary quality of tone, style, theme, etc.**" *Aura* has recently published work by Gilbert Horigfeld, J. B. Goodenaugh, and Carl Morton, poet laureate of Alabama, whose four lines below the editor selected as a sample:

> *But there within the curling concept of desire*
> *between the living and that peaceful nether world*
> *(between the now of time and now of space and mood)*
> *One sat alone, wearing such fragile loveliness*

The 8x8" magazine has 90-120 pp., flat-spined, nicely printed on white stock with b/w photos, lithography, and some one-color art. The matte card cover has a b/w drawing on colored stock. Circulation is 500, of which 40-50 are subscriptions; other sales are to students and Birmingham residents. Price per issue is $3, subscription $6. **Sample available for $2.50 postpaid, guidelines for SASE. Pay is 1 copy. Writers should submit "6-10 poems, with SASE, no simultaneous submissions, will take** photocopies or even neatly hand written." Submissions are reported on in 2 months and time to publication will be another 2 months. The editor says, "Quality is our quantity. If it's good we will find a place for it, if not this issue, the next."

*AURORA: SPECULATIVE FEMINISM, SOCIETY FOR THE FURTHERANCE & STUDY OF SCIENCE FICTION (IV, Feminist, science fiction, fantasy), Box 1624, Madison, WI 53701-1624, founded 1975, poetry editor Terry A. Garey, who says, "We want poetry that deals with science fiction and/or fantasy in a feminist, or at least nonsexist, way. Usually no longer than 1 typed page (double-spaced). We do theme issues, so it's a good idea to query about upcoming themes first." Of their various publications, *Aurora* is the one which primarily uses poetry, 34 poems in each of the biannual issues. They have published poetry by Sheila Fitch-Raynor, Robert Frazier, Terry A. Garey, Wendy Rose, Elissa (Hamilton) Macohn and Jessica Amanda Salmonson. These sample lines are by Suzette Haden Elgin:

> How do you assemble a rose window
> in a universe
> which has no curving surfaces?

Their circulation is 500-700 with 100 subscriptions, of which 10 are libraries, price per issue $3, subscription $8 for 3 issues ($10 foreign), **sample: $3.50 postpaid**. They use about 10 of the 100 submissions they receive a year, have an average backlog of 6 months. **"Simultaneous submissions OK. Please query with SASE; we will send guidelines." Reports in 2 weeks with acknowledgment. Pays 1 copy.**

*THE AWAKENER MAGAZINE (IV, Religious), 938 18th St., Hermosa Beach, CA 90254, founded 1953, is an annual **philosophical, religious journal "devoted to the teachings of Avatar Meher Baba, his life and work**." They have a circulation of 1,000, 700 subscriptions, of which 6 are libraries, **sample: $3 postpaid**. Their backlog is "tremendous," and **"since we have such a specialized audience of 'Babalovers,' outside poets seldom intrigue us."** Reports "immediately." No pay.

‡AWEDE PRESS (II), Box 376, Windsor, VT 05089, phone 802-484-5169, founded 1975, editor, Brita Bergland. *Awede* is a small press that publishes letterpress books, sewn with drawn-on covers, graphically produced. The editor wants **"contemporary, 'language' poetry with a strong visual interest."** They have recently published poetry by Charles Bernstein, James Sherry, Rosemarie Waldrop and Hannah Weiner. the editor selected these sample lines (poet unidentified):

> No priority other than the vanished
> Imagination of some other
> Time—inlets of dilapidated
> Incredulity harbored
> On the deleterious Bus to Air Landing

Awede publishes two poetry chapbooks per year, 32 pp. 6x9", flat-spined. **Freelance submissions are accepted, but author should query first. Queries are answered in 2 weeks, MSS reported on in 4-5 months, simultaneous submissions are acceptable, as are photocopied MSS. Pay is in author's copies, 10% of run. Criticism of rejected MSS is provided.** No subsidy publishing, book catalog free on request, sample books available at list price of $4-8.

*AXE FACTORY REVIEW (II), Box 11186, Philadelphia, PA 19136, phone 215-331-7389, founded 1984, poetry editors Louis McKee and Joseph Farley. **First issue, March 1986**. They are starting with the annual magazine and hope to publish chapbooks and full-sized collections in the future as **Axe Factory Publications**. Their first issue includes poetry by Charles Bukowski, Etheridge Knight, Arthur Knight, William Stafford, George Myers Jr., and Stephen Dunn. Sample lines by Daniel Reinhold:

> Felica slept with a stuffed marlin.
> It was seven feet long and shiny blue.
> She had been sleeping with it
> since nineteen sixty-eight. . .

"We publish what we like—open to any school/style. As editors, we want to 'enjoy' our magazine. We want our readers to feel the same way." They use 50% poetry, approximately 32 pp. per issue, a printrun of 500. **Reports in 2-5 weeks, pays in copies. Regarding possible chapbook publication, query with 5-10 samples and cover letter conveying "personality as well as background info (publications, bio, personal aesthetics/philosophies, etc.)" They comment "when so moved and have time to do so."**

*AXIOS (V), 800 S. Euclid St., Fullerton, CA 92632, phone 714-526-2131, founded 1980, poetry editor Daniel Gorham, is a monthly magazine **"to present the view and lifestyle of the Eastern Orthodox Christian and their worldview**. We're not accepting unsolicited submissions."

AYA PRESS POETRY SERIES(IV), Box 1153, Station F, Toronto, Ontario M4Y 2T8 Canada, founded 1978, poetry editor Bev Daurio, is "a small Canadian literary house producing 5 books per year in limited fine editions. We attempt to produce **aesthetically and emotionally stimulating books of poetry** and fiction. No subject criteria, but for funding reasons we are **generally restricted to Canadian writers**." They have published poetry by Steven Smith, Rikki, Robert Sward and A. F. Moritz. As a sample, the editor selected lines from "blind zone," by Steven Smith:

> *We walk among familiar secrets*
> *while things we've known*
> *slip between the cracks*
> *and we mistake*
> *the things we see*
> *for what they are*

The book is a flat-spined paperback, 6x9", with an abstract cream and burgundy cover, 64 pp. $8 (Canadian). **Query with sample of 45 poems and list of other publications. Reports in 2 months, payment 10% list royalties or 10% of run. Send SASE for catalog to order samples**. The editor advises, "Make sure your ms is clean and double-spaced; send your best—fewer but better poems make a better impression; include a SASE; have patience."

‡***AZTEC PEAK (I, II)**, 542 S. 35th Circle, Mesa, AZ 85204, phone 602-830-8363, founded 1985, editor Marsha Ward, associate editor Elsie Lindahl, a "quarterly showcase newsletter with writing emphasis and upbeat philosophy: Ascend to the PEAK through the joy of writing." For poetry, the editor wants: **"Celebrations of life in rhyme or exceptional blank verse; up to 20 lines, will rarely publish longer poems; on writing themes or nature or life, mostly of a positive slant; lyric preferred over narrative or dramatic, but there will be exceptions."** She has recently published poems by Clay Harrison, Sigmund Weiss, and Martin Musick. As a sample, she chose the following lines from "Mountain Mystery" by Jean Conder Soule:

> *From the peak of the mountain a misty cascade*
> *Of burgeoning waterfall, rainbow-arrayed,*
> *Tumbles and gambols in silvery haze*
> *To a verdant meadow where shy deer graze.*

Aztec Peak is a 10 pp. quarterly newsletter, magazine-sized, offset from typed copy on ordinary paper, side-stapled, masthead and text on cover. Its circulation is 100, of which 35 are subscriptions and 20 go to writer's clubs. Price per issue is $2, subscription $7.50/year. **Sample $2 postpaid, guidelines available for SASE. Pay averages $1/poem. Poems should be submitted in batches of 5, 1/page, name and address on each page; photocopy, dot-matrix OK if legible, also legible handwritten poems; simultaneous OK "if we know; give line count." Reporting time is 3-4 weeks and backlog is 3-6 months.** The newsletter sponsors various contests; "as we grow we will give cash prizes to more than just the top winner." The editor says, "Our function is to publish and showcase writers and poets who haven't hit the big-time. . . . We do encourage, because we are writers too, and understand the delicate balance between professional attitude and personal feelings. We love beautiful language. Poets: read what you like, study what makes it tick, practice, and *persist* in submitting."

‡**BALANCE BEAM PRESS, INC. (IV, Children, feminist, peace)**, 12711 Stoneridge Rd., Dayton, MN 55327, phone 612-427-3168, founded 1979, editor Mary Ellis Peterson, a small press publisher of poetry and short fiction in chapbooks and anthologies. they want **"Work by children; work related to war/peace, feminist, working toward relationships, which are not stereotyped but are fully human; spirituality, environment, sensitively political, surprising, insightful."** No pornography. They have recently published work by Grace Sandness. As a sample, the editor selected these lines from "Heartbreak" by Sheila Hertel:

> *In the corner a broken toy*
> *an apple on a tree too high to touch*
> *the pen he signed her yearbook with*
> *running dry*

Freelance submissions for chapbooks are accepted; they report in 1 month and time from acceptance to publication is 6 months. Simultaneous submissions should be so identified. Writers should send sample poems, bio and SASE. Queries will be answered in 4 weeks. Photocopied or dot-matrix MSS are OK, as are discs compatible with Apple II-C, but hard copy is preferred. Pay depends on grant/award money. Book catalog is free on request with #10 SASE. The editor comments on rejected MSS if she feels she can be helpful. The press publishes 2 paperback, flat-spined chapbooks each year, 24 pp; they are priced at $2.50 to $4.95 (for an anthology). **Writers can receive samples at 30% discount.** The editor advises: "Find a writing support group. This helps in dealing with the isolation inherent in writing, also gives contacts for potential publishing and feedback on writing. A writer's work usually sounds very different read out loud to a critical audience than read in his/her own home just after writing."

*BAMBOO RIDGE (IV, Regional), Box 61781, Honolulu, HI 96822-8781, founded 1979, poetry editor Eric Chock, is a quarterly using **poetry by and about Hawaii's people.** Poets they have recently published include Juliet Kono, Wing Tek Lum, Dana Naone, Debra Thomas and Diane Kahanu. I selected these sample lines from "Meditation on Bones," which happens to be by the editor:

> Tonight, my fingers down your spine
> massage the trail of vertebrae
> like the goat bones I carried
> out of the river with us today,

The digest-sized saddle-stapled magazine is professionally printed, matte cover with art, ads, circulation 600-1,000, 200 subscribers of which 20 are libraries. They use about 20 pp. of poetry in each issue. There are two special issues per year for which material is solicited. They receive about 400 poetry and prose submissions annually, use 60, have a 1 month backlog. **Sample: $3 plus $1 for postage and handling.** Reports in 3 months. Pays $10/poem plus 2 copies. The editor comments "when writing merits criticism."

BAPTIST SUNDAY SCHOOL BOARD, BROADMAN PRESS, *LIVING WITH PRESCHOOLERS, LIVING WITH CHILDREN, LIVING WITH TEENAGERS, *HOME LIFE (IV, Religious), 127 Ninth Ave. N., Nashville, TN 37234, the publishing agency for Southern Baptists. "We publish magazines, monthlies, quarterlies, books, filmstrips, films, church supplies, etc., for Southern Baptist churches." Books of poetry are published under the Broadman Press imprint. **Query with samples.** For most of their publications they want **"inspirational and/or religious poetry, no longer than 24 lines," typed, double-spaced, no simultaneous submissions. Reports within 60 days, rate of pay figured on number of lines submitted.** The biggest of the monthlies is *Home Life*, which began in 1947. Circulation 750,000, 20,000 subscriptions—a magazine-sized 60 + pp., saddle-stapled slick magazine, illustrated (no ads). Its poetry editors, Reuben Herring and Mary Darby, say they want **"religious poetry treating from a Christian perspective marriage, family life, and to some extent the Christian life generally. We rarely publish anything of more than 25 lines."** As a sample, the editors chose these last four lines from "Reality" by Candice Cook-Darby:

> I didn't destroy you with my displeasure
> You didn't bleed with my acceptance of your faults
> Forgive me, but I thought we both needed you to be perfect
> What a strain you have endured

Sample: free to authors with SASE! Submit no more than 6 poems at a time. "Prefer original, but photocopy and dot-matrix acceptable. Query unnecessary." Send SASE for guidelines. Reports in 4-6 weeks, pays $15-24.

BARE NIBS (II), 24 The Ridgeway, Ware, Herts., SG12 0RT England. Founded 1983, editor Steve Woollard, is a low-budget quarterly, "providing a forum for new and established writers in all areas and to assist in the development of the Ware Arts Centre." The pamphlet-like book, digest-sized, photocopied from typescript, 36 pp. saddle-stapled, with cartoon-like art, **uses about 6 pp. of poetry per issue—"descriptive, social, political, satirical and generally outward-looking. We don't like introverted or 'angst' poetry."** They have published poems by Godfrey Marriot, Tom Bingham, Jon Daunt, Edmund Harwood, Julian Le Saux and Zbigniew Sas. The editor selected these lines by Brian Bes as a sample:

> The editor, couched in a casting role,
> Reels off the copy in reams.
> Another month over, a little more soul
> Is sold in each issue, it seems.

It has a circulation of 200, 30 subscriptions of which 8 are libraries. **Sample: please inquire. Submit up to 10 poems in any shape or form; reports within 2 months, pays one copy**. The editor advises, "My own feeling is that (in this country) there is a **trend away from free form, 'instant expression' poetry, toward the much more structured and carefully considered poem, however, no style or subject matter should be dismissed out of hand. Intellectual poetry with serious meaning can be fine, even uplifting, but there is also a place in** *Bare Nibs* **for humor and joviality.** Personally I like a good laugh."

BARNWOOD PRESS COOPERATIVE, BARNWOOD (II), Box 11C, RR 2, Daleville, IN 47334, founded 1978, poetry editor Tom Koontz. "The Barnwood Press Cooperative is a nonprofit organization of writers and readers who **share the costs (energy, time, money) and the pleasures of publishing poetry**, and, occasionally, fiction." Their chapbooks, books, broadsides, cards and experimental formats are distinguished by fine printing and artistic design. *Barnwood* is a quarterly leaflet, 7x10½", 12 pp., circulation 500, which includes in each issue 5-6 poems by such poets as Marge Piercy, William Stafford, Robert Bly, Grace Butcher, Jared Carter and Lewis Turco. The editors offer these sample lines by Sonya Dorman:

in the festive bowl oranges
huddle above tangerine cousins
a white hand arranges black grapes
the mother makes one clean cut
through an apple's heart
and her child's astonished.
by the star's dark population

Subscription: $2.50. **Sample: $1 postpaid. Pays $10 per poem.**

‡*BARQUE (II)**, 779 14th St., San Francisco, CA 94114, phone 415-621-3606, founded 1986, editor Joseph Lerner, a literary quarterly whose first issue was published in June, 1986. It includes **"humor/satire, surrealist, Third World, oral tradition and esoterica, dream, fantasy, open and concrete poetry. No horror/sf, no limericks. Otherwise open to most genres."** At the time of this writing, there were no samples to be quoted. The magazine was planned to be 8½x7", 60 pp. typeset and stapled with graphics and cover art. It was going to appear 3-4 times a year and have a print run of 1,000. **Pay is 1 copy. Reporting time is 4-6 weeks and time to publication 8-12 weeks. "Photocopy and simultaneous submissions, near letter-quality printing OK."** The editor says, "Covering letters are welcome, but we're generally not impressed by long lists of credits, comments by teachers or other poets, or your own opinion of your work."

BARRINGTON PRESS (II, IV, Specialized), 4102 East 27th St., Tucson, AZ 85711, founded 1983 (purchased Cole & Sherwood, Inc., 1983), poetry editors Yvonne Taylor and Nancy Thomas, publishes nonfiction, monographs and **poetry. "We operate in two extremes: social commentary, and light or dramatic metric verse. We** co-op with other publishers, some of them major houses. **We find much appeal in clear, light, rhymed poetry à la the old Ogden Nash genre. We do not consider rambling, sorrowful free verse. We want poetry, not self-directed philosophy. Skill, compression, image, identity—light and observant at one end; biting social commentary at the other."** They have recently published poetry by Derek Simpson, Gretchen Wyler, Wren Badger and Bill Safford. As a sample the editors selected these lines by William Hester:

Consider how lucky we are
To know there is always a bar,
A tavern or club,
A bistro or pub,
That's thankfully, not very far.

Query with 4 samples, cover letter "no longer than one page; a few credits, exactly who you are." Replies to queries in 2 weeks, to submissions (if invited) in 6 weeks. Simultaneous submissions OK if editors advised. MS should be "traditional, clean, single-spaced." Photocopy, dot-matrix OK. Pays $500 advance, 12 copies, no royalties for book-length prose; copies for poetry. Send SASE for booklist to order samples. The editors comment, "Regrettably, a good 80% of what we have received is rather bad. We might say (here we go again), LEARN YOUR CRAFT. We get a lot of dirges, fugues, philosophical tragedies. They tell us nothing, but evidently fulfill some sort of ego fortification for the writer." Carol Showell adds, "we are putting some emphasis on a new subject during 1986 . . . **UFO material. Coincident with a renewed public consciousness of this area, we would like to see verse that might fit—scientific or esoteric.** We expect to form an association/book club in this field during 1986, and have the support of the country's top three experts in this fascinating field of research and commentary."

‡*BASEBALL: OUR WAY, *FOOTBALL: OUR WAY, OUR WAY PUBLICATIONS (IV, Baseball, football)**, 3211 Milwaukee St., #1, Madison WI 53714, phone 608-241-0549, founded 1984, editor and publisher Dale Jellings, two newsletters covering all aspects of baseball, or football, from humor to poetry to trivia. The editor says he **likes to see poetry about baseball (or football) only, but "the connection can be as distant as watching one's son play the game to poems about baseball parks or players or people acquainted with either. We generally publish shorter poems, but are open to any length."** He has recently published poems by Diane Glancy, Paul Weinman, and himself. As a sample, he chose "A Day at the Ball Park" by Micah Jenkins:

A hanging curve ball
like a badly finessed opera note
held too long—
Crack!
It's gone,
a memory forever . . .
and a souvenir
for a little boy
grown old.

Baseball: Our Way is an 8-page photocopied newsletter, stapled at the top left corner, with one page of poems. It appears ten times per year and has a circulation of 100, of which 60 are subscriptions. Price per copy is $1 ("but a hay-penny will do"), subscription $9/year. **Pay is 2 copies. Poems should be submitted in any readable typewritten form, no more than 1/page. Reporting time and time to publication are 2-6 weeks.** The editor says, "Poetry about sports need not be any different than poetry about other subjects. Do your homework! Learn about what poetry is. Read poetry. Avoid the trite and the literal. Use the language. Don't simply describe or report. Always attempt to move the reader intellectually or emotionally."

THE BASILISK PRESS (II), Box 71, Fredonia, NY 14063, phone 716-934-4199, founded 1970, poetry editors David Lunde and Marilyn Masiker, is a **"very small, non-profit press founded to publish books by deserving new writers and those whose work we think has been undeservedly neglected."** They publish perfect-bound paperbacks and chapbooks and have published postcards from time to time. **"No restrictions on style, form, or content, but work sent here should show evidence that its author has read English and American poetry and learned from it. We look for professionalism, craftsmanship, honesty, imagination, passion. Religious or mystical poetry would have to be pretty remarkable to stand a chance of overcoming our bias against it. We don't like polemics of any sort."** They have recently published Tom McKeown, Harley Elliott, Toni Zimmerman, Tom Disch, Eileen Owen, and though they feel that any quotation would be misleading, as their taste is too varied, I selected these lines from Lyn Lifshin's **Blue Dust, New Mexico**:

> *mother holding her*
> *sick child close*
> *feels the bad heat*
> *slip from his body*

They publish one flat-spined paperback, 50-100 pp., per year. **Submit either whole MS or query with sample of at least 5 poems and cover letter telling "whatever they would like us to know." Usually reports within 2 weeks. Payment consists of copies—5% of press run.** "The proceeds from book sales are used to publish more books." They comment "if work interests us or author requests it." For advice they say, "Read what other poets have written and practice a lot."

BAY AREA POETS COALITION (BAPC), POETALK (I), 1527 Virginia St., Berkeley, CA 94703, phone 415-845-8409, founded 1974, poetry editor Maggi H. Meyer. The Coalition sends its monthly poetry letter, *Poetalk* to over 400 people. They also publish an annual anthology giving one page to each member of BAPC who has had work published in the monthly letter (which uses 40-55 poets in each issue). Though *Poetalk* has announcements of events, contests and activities of BAPC's over 150 members, it circulates to many more and *anyone can submit.* **At least one poem from each new submitter will usually be printed if it's under 20 lines, typed single-spaced.** The editor cuts and pastes to fit as many poems as she can on the 2-3 legal-sized pages. Quality, obviously, is uneven. Here is a sample by Winona Kernan Champagne:

> *On a dreary day,*
> *I dusted my antique doll*
> *and found a young smile.*

Send 4-5 poems, preferably camera-ready so they don't have to be retyped. One will generally be used upon receipt, you'll get 1 copy of the letter in which it appears. Write (with SASE) and get put on the mailing list for 2 month's free copies. Anyone can join BACP for $12, which brings you 12 monthly letters, a copy of the anthology, and, if you live in the area, other privileges. The group holds open readings, contests and other activities, has a mailing list available to local members, and a PA system members may use for a small fee (which BAPC bought by getting 200 people to contribute a word each, and $1, to a nonsense poem "which turned out amazingly well"). This organization might be a **useful model for poets in other areas.** Their membership includes people from 25 states other than California and 5 countries, and their 6 contests have drawn entries from all over.

BAY WINDOWS (IV, Gay/lesbian), 1515 Washington St., Boston, MA 02118, founded 1983, poetry editors Rudy Kikel and E.J. Graff. *Bay Windows* **is a weekly gay and lesbian newspaper** published for the New England community, regularly using "**short poems of interest to lesbians and gay men. Poetry that is 'experiential' seems to have a good chance with us, but we don't want poetry that just 'tells it like it is.' Our readership doesn't read poetry all the time. A primary consideration is** giving *pleasure*. **We'll overlook the poem's (and the poet's) tendency not to be informed by the latest poetic theory, if it** *does* **this: pleases. Pleases, in particular, by articulating common gay or lesbian experience, and by doing that with some attention to form. I've found that a lot of our choices were made because of a strong image strand. Humor is** *always* **welcome—and hard to provide with craft. Obliquity, obscurity? Probably not for us. We can't presume on our audience**." They have recently published poetry by Edward Field, Joan Larkin, Felice Picano, Jewel Gomez, Gregg Shapiro,

Rid Sawyer and Jane Barnes. As a sample Rudy Kikel selected these lines by Arthur Lipkin:

> No jungle hues for now
> for now no orgiastic rites—
> just phone calls in the morning,
> Bach, and breakfast glances.

"We try to run two poems (one by a man, one by a woman) each month, print-run 13,000, 700 subscriptions of which 15 are libraries. Subscription: $35; per issue: 50¢. They receive about 200 submissions per year, use 1 in 10, have a 3 month backlog. **Sample: $1 postpaid. Poems by gay males should be sent to Rudy Kikel, by lesbians to E.J. Graff. "3-5 poems, 10-30 lines are ideal."** Reports in 4 weeks, pays $10/poem. Editors "often" comment on rejections.

BB BKS, *GLOBAL TAPESTRY JOURNAL (II), Spring Bank, Longsight Road, Salesbury, Blackburn, Lancaster, BB1 9EU England, founded 1963, poetry editor Dave Cunliffe. "**Experimental, avant-garde—specializing in exciting high-energy new writing. Mainly for a bohemian and counter-culture audience.**" In addition to the magazine, *Global Tapestry Journal*, BB Bks publishes anthologies, greeting cards, posters and pamphlets. "We want honest, uncontrived writing, strong in form and content. We don't want 'weekend hobby verse' and poetry without energy. They have published Chris Challis, A.D. Winans, Chris Torrance, Geoffrey Holloway, Richard Mason and George Montgomery. These sample lines are by Lyn Van Eimeren:

> I will be vaporized
> at any moment by the
> sad wild end of
> america's paranoia

Global Tapestry Journal "tries to be quarterly." Dave Cunliffe describes it as "**a mind-blowing mosaic of exciting writings, poetry and graphics. Only present United Kingdom magazine of its kind.**" There are about 40 pages of poetry in each issue, circulation 1,000, 500 subscriptions of which 20 are libraries, **sample: $1.20 postpaid.** They receive about 2,000 submissions per year, use 250, and have a **two-year backlog. Submit 2-10 poems, photocopy OK,** reports "as soon as possible," **payment: one copy.** The digest-sized magazine is crammed with writing in a variety of type-styles, some in red ink, graphics (often poorly-reproduced photos, careless paste-up), on inexpensive paper with a card cover. They also publish four 30 pp. anthologies per year, sometimes larger ones, and are open to submissions of book manuscripts: **send complete MS with cover letter about yourself, reports soon, pays 20 author's copies, $1 for a sample.** The editors comment, "UK poetry reading audience is declining and so are consequently its publishers and platforms. Beginners are best advised to concentrate on submissions to the literary press and avoid commercial and vanity press operations."

BEACH & CO., PUBLISHERS, CHERRY VALLEY EDITIONS, SYLVIA BEACH AND JACK KEROUAC AWARDS (II), Box 303, Cherry Valley, NY 13320, founded 1974, poetry editor Charles Plymell, is basically a **subsidy publisher**, with an unusual "buy-back" arrangement. **You buy half the press run at wholesale** (e.g., 500 copies of an edition of 1,000 of a 64-100 pp. book, flat-spined, paperback, for $2.50 per copy). "**The remaining 500 copies would be promoted and distributed by the publisher. The author would earn 10% royalty 'off the top'** of the $4.50 price of the books sold (minus promotional/review copies)." There is a **reading fee of $10** for consideration of the MS, and you are expected to **participate in a seminar, for which there is tuition. Query with a sample of 10 poems and cover letter describing your other publications, biographical background, personal or aesthetic philosophy, poetic goals and principles. Considers simultaneous submissions.** Write for details regarding the Jack Kerouac and Sylvia Beach Awards (which have $7 entry fees)—offering cash prizes and royalty contracts for book publication. As a sample of the poetry they publish, I chose these lines from Victor Vacarno Dove's **Blood in the Hourglass**, a 64 pp. digest-sized, flat-spined, glossy-covered paperback:

> I've been burned 'n drowned, kicked around
> Hung all up in trees
> Shot 'n stabbed, thrown 'n nabbed
> But yet I still show glee

BEAR TRIBE, *WILDFIRE NETWORKING MAGAZINE (IV, Nature, ecology), Box 9167, Spokane, WA 99209, phone 509-326-6561, founded 1965 (with the magazine's former name, *Many Smokes Earth Awareness Magazine)*, poetry editors Eleanor Limmer. The magazine uses **short poetry on topics appropriate to the magazine, such as earth awareness, self-sufficiency, barter, sacred places, native people, etc. Send SASE for guidelines and brochure.** They have published poetry by Gary Snyder, W. D. Ehrhart, P. J. Brown and Evelyn Eaton. The quarterly devotes 1-2 pp. to poetry each issue. They want a **"positive and constructive viewpoint, no hip or offensive language." No pay. The Press publishes books that incorporate Native American poems and songs, but no collections by individuals. They comment on rejections, "especially on good poetry."**

‡*BEATNIKS FROM SPACE, NEITHER/NOR PRESS (I)**, Box 8043, Ann Arbor, MI 48107, founded 1980, editor Denis McBee. *Beatnicks from Space*, which is "irregular" in its times of appearance, is "the magazine that makes trendy people grit their teeth." The editor wants **"Poetry that sings, swings, and moves with the pulse of modern life. Length, style, and form are not as important as the simple gut-feeling your verse imparts to readers."** He does not want **"self-centered whimpering verse bemoaning the poet's inability to find anyone who truly understands them. Not interested in profanity, glorification of self-destruction, sexual excess, or knee-jerk criticism of the establishment."** He has recently published poems by David Cope, Jeffrey Zable, De Villo Sloan, Joy Walsh, and Joel Dailey. As a sample, he chose the following lines by Duke O'Realo:

> *I don't wanna see you crawl*
> *in search of easy answers*
> *or hear how life has smacked you down*
> *and pounded you with problems.*

The magazine is 7x8½", "offset and Xerox" (I have not seen a copy), 48 pp. saddle-stitched, "contains various ads, graphics, and comics. Circulation is 600, of which 100 are subscriptions and 12 go to libraries; newsstand sales are 100. Price per copy is $3, subscription $10/4 issues. **Sample available for $3 postpaid. Pay is 1 copy. "We'll look at anything legible."** Reporting time is 3 months and time to publication 6-12 months.

BEFORE THE RAPTURE PRESS (IV, Religious, social), Box A3604, Chicago, IL 60690, founded 1980, poetry editors Cynthia Gallaher and Carlos Cumpian. This press began as a magazine, *Before the Rapture: Poetry of Spiritual Liberation*, which has ceased publication, and they now publish poetry chapbooks in an effort **"to show the literary and contemporary side of Christian poetry with emphasis on social issues, social justice and world problems**." They have recently published John Tagliabue, Richard Kostelanetz, Carmen Conde (Spain) and Fina Garcia Marruz (Cuba). These sample lines are by Harry Brody:

> *They went out and asked him*
> *to come live in their city.*
> *They couldn't see that soon*
> *He would live everywhere.*

For more examples, **buy one of the four back issues of the magazine for $2.50**. In 1985, they published their first chapbook **Amphora Full of Light** by Denver poet, Ida Fusel. More chapbooks will be published as funds are available. They comment, "Poetry need not be out of the reach of anyone. A good poet is one who loves poetry and has a deep respect for words. The best poet seeks and upholds the truth. And every poet must have the discipline and openness to read many, many other poets and write in a variety of styles to seek his best voice."

THE BELLEVUE PRESS (II), 60 Schubert St., Binghamton, NY 13905, phone 607-729-0819, founded 1973 by Gil and Deborah H. Williams. **"publishing art, photography and poetry postcards; signed letter-press poetry broadsides, and small and large letter-press books of poetry and art**." Their presswork is elegant. They are looking for "original work which reflects current or future trends in style, not work which simply rehashes styles of the past!" They have recently published poetry by John Yau, Leonard Nathan, Stephen Sandy, Mark Porteus, L. Fixel, Carole Stone and Edouard Roditi. These sample lines are from a postcard, Lewis Turco's "Lineage":

> *White and yellow, its flight*
> *outlined in black, the butterfly*
> *cuts a trace among lilies*
> *of the valley and a hedge*
> *of lilac.*

Their average production of books is two 30 pp. chapbooks per year. **Query with about 5 samples and "a one-page mini-bio listing some publications (preferably book or anthology appearances) and recent accomplishments." MS should be "as the poet intends the book to appear." Photocopy OK. Replies to query in 2-3 weeks, to MS in 6 weeks. Payment: 10% of press run.** Gil Williams comments "when I'm asked to, or sometimes when I have extra (?) time. But everyone in America has a poetry manuscript these days! Yet for every order we actually get at the Press, we must receive 10 letters from hopeful poets seeking publication! Poets had better start BUYING books and using our postcards or there will be NO Bellevue Press! As I write, I sit surrounded with some 3,000 poetry books I have BOUGHT!"

‡*BELLOWING ARK (II)**, Box 45637, Seattle, WA 98145, phone 206-545-8302, founded 1984, poetry editors Robert R. Ward and Crysta Casey, a bi-monthly literary tabloid that **"publishes only poetry which acknowledges in some way the proposition that existence has meaning, or, to put it another way, that life is worth living. We have no strictures as to length, form or style; only that**

the work we publish is to our judgment life-affirming." They do not want "academic poetry, in any of its manifold forms." Poets recently published include Camille Hayward, Lisa Davidson and Mary Wenner. As a sample I have selected the final stanza from "Writing between the four lines given to me by my writing group" by Sheila Bender:

> When writing something, how important is the relative clause?
> *Love has no clauses;*
> *it is always present or past*
> *I have loved. I am loving. I love.*

The paper is tabloid-sized, 16 pp. printed on electrobright stock with b/w photos and line drawings. Circulation is 1,000, of which 100 + are subscriptions and 600 + are sold on newsstands. Price is $2/issue, subscription is $12/year. **Sample: $1 postpaid. Pay is 2 copies. The editors say, "absolutely *no* si**multaneous submissions, prefer not to see dot-matrix or photocopy." They reply to submissions in 2-6 weeks and publish within the next 1 or 2 issues. Occasionally they will criticize a MS if it seems to "display potential to become the kind of work we want."

*THE BELOIT POETRY JOURNAL (II)**, Box 154, RFD 2, Ellsworth, ME 04605, phone, 207-667-5598, founded 1950, editor Marion K. Stocking, a well-known, long-standing quarterly of quality poetry and reviews. **"We publish the best poems we receive, without bias as to length, school, subject, or form**. It is our hope to discover the growing tip of poetry and to introduce new poets alongside the better-established writers. We publish occasional chapbooks to diversify our offerings." They want **"fresh, imaginative poetry, with a distinctive voice. We tend to prefer poems that make the reader share an experience rather than just reading about it, and these we keep for up to 3 months**, circulating them among our readers, and continuing to winnow out the best. At the quarterly meetings of the Editorial Board we read aloud all the surviving poems and put together an issue of the best we have." They have recently published Brooks Haxton, Marianne Boruch, Lola Haskins, Albert Goldbarth, and Karen Snow. The guidelines have a section, **"How to submit poems—to us or to any magazine**," which is valuable advice. **Submit any time, without query, any legible form, "NO SIMULTANEOUS SUBMISSIONS." (If you send photocopies or carbons, include a note saying the poems are not being submitted elsewhere.) "Any length of MS, but most poets send what will go in a business envelope for one stamp. Don't send your life work." Payment: 3 copies**. It's an attractively printed digest-sized, 40 pp. format, with tasteful art on the card covers. Sample copy: $1, includes guidelines, or SASE for guidelines alone. They have a circulation of 1,100, 575 subscriptions, of which 325 are libraries. No backlog: "We clear the desk at each issue."

*BERKELEY POETS COOPERATIVE (WORKSHOP & PRESS) (II)**, Box 459, Berkeley, CA 94701, phone 415-524-9797, founded 1969, poetry editor Charles Entrekin (plus rotating staff), is "a nonprofit organization which offers writers the opportunity to explore, develop and publish their works. Our primary goals are threefold—to bring to the Berkeley community a literary magazine of high quality, to maintain a free workshop open to writers, and to publish outstanding collections of poetry and fiction by individual writers." The *New York Times* has called it **"the oldest and most successful poetry co-operative in the country**." They publish a biannual magazine, *Berkeley Poets Cooperative* and flat-spined chapbook collections of poets who have been published in the magazine (open to poets everywhere). Chapbooks recently published by Carla Kandinsky, Gerald Jorge Lee and J.D. Woolery. Charles Entrekin says he prefers **"modern imagist—open to all kinds, but we publish very little rhyme**." Recently published are Alicia Ostriker, Lyn Lifshin, Ivan Arguelles, Bruce Hawkins and Lucile Day. These sample lines are by Gail Rudd:

> *We must lean our bodies together*
> *fill the rooms with the noise of children.*
> *There is nothing out there. Nothing.*

The 72-92 pp. magazine is beautifully printed, glossy cover, with fiction and graphics as well as 40-50 pp. of poetry. **Sample: $3. Its circulation is 1,600, with 150 subscriptions (about half of which are libraries). They receive over 500 submissions per year, of which they use 80, and the backlog is sometimes up to 9 months. Submit 1-5 poems, none of which is over 3 pp., October-January or April-July. Payment: 2 copies plus 50% discount on additional copies. Guidelines available for SASE.** They publish one 48 pp. chapbook by an individual who has appeared in the magazine each year, for which the poet receives 50% of the profit and 20 copies. You can order a sample book for $3. **Criticism sometimes provided on rejected MSS. Poets elsewhere might consider BPWP as a model for forming similar organizations.**

‡BEST CELLAR PRESS, *PEBBLE (II)**, Department of English, University of Nebraska, Lincoln, NE 68588, editor Greg Kuzma. Each issue of *Pebble* seems to be a book—a small collection of poetry, an anthology, or a collection of essays and letters; the periodical appears irregularly, although a subscrip-

tion is available at $10 for three issues. I have seen issues #22 and 23 of *Pebble*, one of which is *Poems for the Dead*, a collection edited by Greg Kuzma which contains work by such poets as Kenneth Rexroth, James Wright, and Conrad Hillberry. The other chapbook is *The Big Parade*, by Alfred Starr Hamilton. As a sample, I have selected from it the following complete poem, "Sky":

> *Why didn't you say an inkstand*
> *Why didn't you say all of this was for the blue sky*
> *Why didn't you say a sheet of writing paper was for a cloud*

The books are 4¼x7", nicely printed on white stock, with one-color glossy card covers, flat-spined; the anthology has 95 pp.

‡*BEYOND (IV, Science fiction/fantasy), Box 136, New York, NY 10024, phone 212-874-5914, founded 1985, editor Shirley Winston, a 3-times-a-year magazine of science fiction and fantasy. For poetry, the editor wants **"anything short of a major epic"** on those themes. **She does not want anything longer than 120 lines.** She has recently published poetry by David Vosk and Scott Green, from whose "Spacewalker" she chose the following lines as a sample:

> *When a child*
> *I read Verne and Heinlein*
> *Dreamt among the stars.*
> *Drifting out from the shuttle*
> *I enter the sky*
> *Becoming a star.*

The magazine-sized *Beyond* is 40 pp., saddle-stapled, offset from typed copy with b/w drawings to illustrate the pieces and a b/w decoration on the matte card cover. Circulation is 400. Price per issue is $3, subscription $4/year. **Sample available for $4 postpaid. Pay is 2¢/line plus 1 copy. Submissions "must be legible (dot-matrix is OK)." Reporting time is 1 month and there is no backlog at present. The editor "always" provides criticism on rejected MSS.**

*BIFROST (IV, Science fiction, fantasy), 4020 Woolslayer Way, Pittsburgh, PA 15224, started originally (as *Antithesis*) in 1978, folded, and restarted June, 1985, as a publication of **Southern Circle Press**. Poetry editor: Cathie Whitehead, describes it as "a **quarterly SF/Fantasy magazine**, with a blend of stories, art and poems." She says, "**I want any style, free verse, blank verse or rhymed and metered. I do *not* want sexually explicit poems. Poems *must* conform to strict science fiction or fantasy format. Any length or form accepted**." She gives these lines as an example, by Susan Matthews:

> *tonight*
> *will I walk*
> *with legends, through the halls*
> *of nightmare, to the sound*
> *of weirding waltz*

3-5 poems per issue, mimeographed format, sample $5 after June, 1985. Submit no more than 3 at a time, no handwritten submissions. Photocopy, dot-matrix OK, simultaneous submissions if the editor is notified. Payment in copies. Cathie Whitehead says, "I would like to warn neophytes about the importance of keeping to strict forms if they insist on writing 'form' poetry. I hate to see wandering rhyme schemes, improper scansions, and atrocities committed to the language just to force the rhyming word to fall at the end of the line."

‡*BIG TWO-HEARTED (I, IV, Regional/Michigan, nature), 424 Stephenson Ave., Iron Mountain, MI 49801, phone 906-744-3005, founded 1985, editor Gary Silver, a tri-quarterly literary publication of Mid-Peninsula Library Cooperative through its Ralph W. Secord Press. *"Big Two-Hearted* **will consider all forms of poetry but does show preference for subject matter about nature, Michigan's Upper Peninsula, and the out-of-doors. Local or Michigan authors are shown preference. Authors should remember that *Big Two-Hearted* is published by a group of public libraries, and "we will not publish erotica, morbidity, or profanity."** They have published Tom Blessing and Gary L. Williams, among others. As a sample, the editors chose the following lines from T. Kilgore Splake's poem "Upper Peninsula Reminiscence":

> *Matured in tall, deep, cold Keweenaw snows,*
> *sustained by bleeding red Vulcan tailings,*
> *born by clam Manistique waters, and reared*
> *with large, straight Baraga firs,*

ALWAYS submit MSS or queries with a stamped, self-addressed envelope (SASE) within your country or International Reply Coupons (IRCs) purchased from the post office for other countries.

Close-up

Robert Wallace
Bits Press

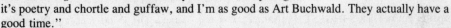
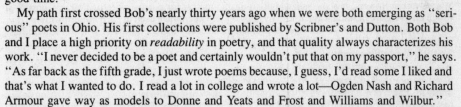

Poets have tried to save the world in many ways. Bob Wallace would have them do it through laughter. Of the annual anthology of light and humorous verse, *Light Year*, he edits for his Bits Press, he says "If it's the bridge that brings readers back to poetry, it just may be that it is the most important thing going on in poetry right now. When I read from *Light Year* to a nonliterary audience, they forget it's poetry and chortle and guffaw, and I'm as good as Art Buchwald. They actually have a good time."

My path first crossed Bob's nearly thirty years ago when we were both emerging as "serious" poets in Ohio. His first collections were published by Scribner's and Dutton. Both Bob and I place a high priority on *readability* in poetry, and that quality always characterizes his work. "I never decided to be a poet and certainly wouldn't put that on my passport," he says. "As far back as the fifth grade, I just wrote poems because, I guess, I'd read some I liked and that's what I wanted to do. I read a lot in college and wrote a lot—Ogden Nash and Richard Armour gave way as models to Donne and Yeats and Frost and Williams and Wilbur."

And, for the talented who learn their craft, publishing follows writing as the day the night: "The natural thing to do with poems, when you have them, is to send them to editors. You hope they're good, that editors buy them. But that probably doesn't matter. Good or not, poems are a way of getting something inside, outside. If the transaction is roughly honest, it's valuable enough—like whittling or growing string beans. They don't have to be World Famous Golden String Beans. Pulitzer Beans. Nobel Beans.

"I didn't decide to get into publishing and editing any more than I'd decided to be a poet. In 1974 I bought a tabletop letterpress, like the one Leonard and Virginia Woolf took home, and set up on the kitchen table. I was struck by A. J. Liebling's remark: 'The freedom of the press belongs to the man who owns one.' "

Bits Press has brought out works in fine editions by such poets as X. J. Kennedy, John Updike, Linda Pastan, Richard Wilbur, and, most recently, David R. Slavitt's *The Elegies to Delia of Albius Tibullus*.

"That's one fork of the road," Bob says. "The other fork is *Light Year*." Each year sales of the anthology have increased, and it is getting more and more critical attention. "What do we want for *Light Year*? The best damn funny poems anybody can write. Not just clever quatrains, but the whole possible range of forms and subjects—and *new* kinds of funny poems. Just as no one could have imagined Ogden Nash or Don Marquis before they did it, I'm looking for the new funny poems nobody's dreamed of yet."

"The problem for poetry in our time is that nobody much reads it. There are probably as many fine poets as ever—perhaps more. But nobody is listening. Certainly not the general reader. A part of the solution can be funny poems. Poems that can be read just for pleasure. No critical or intellectual or aesthetic intimidation, such as you get in high-toned reviews and in the teaching of poetry in schools and colleges." His aim is now to find the poetry that can compete with movies and TV. Whether *Light Year* does *that* or not, it will bring readers—and its editor—a lot of fun in the process.

—Judson Jerome

The magazine is digest-sized, offset on fairly lightweight paper, 34 pp. saddle-stapled with one-color matte card cover illustrated by a line drawing. Single copy price is $4.50 and a subscription (3 issues) is $9.00. **Payment for stories and poems is in copies, responding time will be 1-90 days. "While *Big Two-Hearted* will publish 'name' and 'previously published' writers, our commitment is to writers who have never before published."**

‡*BILL MUNSTER'S FOOTSTEPS, *FOOTSTEPS (IV, Horror)**, Box 75, Round Top, NY 12473, founded 1982, editor Bill Munster, is a horror magazine that appears twice a year, using poetry of "**any length. No rhymes. Must be rich in imagery. I want to stuff a poem into a projector and watch it on the screen. Do not want philosophical poetry, gore.**" As a sample the editor selected these lines by Janet Fox:

> A red sea of wildflowers and goldenrods parted
> leaves mushroomed
> until he darted momentarily out of sight
> behind a cluster of tall grass and rustling milkweeds

The magazine is digest-sized, photo reduced from typescript, glossy b/w cover with art, using b/w horror cartoons, illustrations, and advertising. It comes out twice a year, circulation 600-1,000. **Sample: $4 postpaid. Guidelines available. Submit no more than 3 poems. Prefers photocopies. Simultaneous submissions OK. Reports in 2-4 weeks. Pays 2 copies. Editor sometimes comments on submissions.** Bill Munster says, "The most important tip I can offer to any poet considering to submit to *Footsteps* is to study an issue first. In other words, know your market."

*BIRD WATCHER'S DIGEST (IV, Nature)**, Box 110, Marietta, OH 45750, founded 1978, editor Mary Beacom Bowers, is a specialized but promising market for **poems of "true literary merit" in which birds figure in some way**, at least by allusion. **2-3 poems are used in each bimonthly issue and earn $10/poem**. Some poets who have appeared there recently include Maxwell Wheat, Eleanor Bush, Irene Zimmerman, Julia Older and Herb Kenny. I liked these lines from David Hopes' "The Kingdom of the Birds," describing cranes:

> pointed upward, flight a repose
> between two agonies, striving and beating
> as though together all might lift
> the swamp up rung by rung into the sky.

"Preferred: no more than 20 lines, 40 spaces, no more than 3 poems at a time, no queries." Sample copy postpaid: $2.50. They have up to a year's backlog and use 12-20 of the approximately 500 poems received each year.

BITS PRESS, LIGHT YEAR (II,IV, Humor, light verse), English Department, Case Western Reserve University, Cleveland, OH 44106, phone 216-795-2810 (press founded 1974, **Light Year** in 1984), poetry editors Robert Wallace, C. M. Seidler, Bonnie Jacobson and Nicholas Ranson. Robert Wallace says, "**Bits Press is devoted to poetry. We publish chapbooks (and sometimes limited editions) by young as well as well-known poets. Our main attention at present is given to the annual Light Year, an anthology of the best light verse and funny poems being written**." The chapbooks are distinguished by elegant but inexpensive format. **Light Year** is a cloth-bound trade book of wide distribution (250 pp., 3,500 print-run). They have recently published chapbooks by John Updike, X.J. Kennedy and George Starbuck. These sample lines are from Richard Wilbur's "A Finished Man":

> Seated, he feels the warm sun sculpt his cheek
> As the young president gets up to speak
> If the dead die, if he can but forget,
> If money talks, he may be perfect yet.

Sample copy of *Light Year*: $9 postpaid for poets (lists $13.95). Of the 5,000 + submissions each year they use 300-350, **pay $5/poem plus 15¢/line and a copy. Contributors may buy additional copies at 50% discount. Annual deadline, February—for September publication. Poems recently in periodicals are okay.** The few chapbooks they publish are mostly solicited. **Send $2 for a sample or two of the chapbooks; payment to poet in copies (10% + of run).** Wallace adds this advice: "A word to beginners: Writing good poems isn't easy. Count on working at it, not on luck." He **sometimes offers criticism with rejections.**I recommend his textbook, **Writing Poems**, published by Little, Brown, distributed by Writer's Digest Books.

❝Watch out for workshop uniformity. Beware of the present indicative. Be yourself.

Peter Davison, The Atlantic ❞

*BITTERROOT (II), Box 489, Spring Glen, NY 12483, founded 1962, poetry editor Menke Katz, tries "to inspire and discover talented, promising poets. We **discourage stereotyped forms that imitate fixed patterns** and encourage all poets who seek their own identity through original poetry. **We do not send printed rejection slips." They are looking for "rich imagery which leaves an individual mark. Up to 50 lines, unless we consider it an unusual, inspiring poem. We are more interested in** *how* **the poet writes than what he says, though; this is important. Translations.**." Among poets they have recently published are Sister Mary Ann Henn, Harland Ristau, B.Z. Niditch, Gary Fincke. "We don't necessarily look for famous names but for new talent, which we hope will take a place in American poetry one day." As a sample he chose these lines:

> Only spurned lovers
> Know why weeping rocks can not
> stop oozing tears, why
> suicides are in love with
> the ill light of late sunsets

The 72 pp., digest-sized, flat-spined magazine appears 3 times a year, has a circulation of 850, 50 of which are libraries and colleges, **sample: $3.75 postpaid. Submit 3-4 poems, typed legibly, double-spaced, with name, address and zip code on each page. Clear photocopies OK, no simultaneous submissions. Payment: 1 copy. Reports within 6 weeks. Send SASE for guidelines, rules for William Kushner and Heershe David Badonneh Award contests: poems up to 40 lines (no more than 3 poems to each contest), any subject, any form, any level, no fee. December 31 deadline.** They are hoping for a grant to begin paying contributors. Menke Katz advises, "Poets must place poetry in the center of their lives—to beware of clichés, to find their own path, close to earth or fantastic. Just as every face is different, so must every poet be himself in reality as well as in dreams."

‡BIZARRE PRESS, *THE BLUE GLOW/EGAD! (II), Suite 134-PM, 21738 South Avalon Blvd., Carson, CA 90745, phone 213-835-5474, founded 1985, editor/publisher Tom James, a small-press publisher of a semi-annual poetry anthology. The editor wants to see **poetry of "any form. Length: up to 100 lines. Prefer experimental, avant-garde, free and blank verse; traditional poetry is OK only if it has some sort of twist. There are two categories: 'The Blue Glow' (serious, emotional), and 'Egad!' (experimental, avant-garde and/or humorous). Also satires, and parodies."** He does not want "Iambic pentameter with rhymed endings, unless it has an unusual twist. **Poems about nature or religion would need to be pretty good to be accepted here."** Bizarre Press's magazine has yet to be published as of this writing; however, the editor says that it will be digest-sized, offset, with some graphics, 25 pp. Price per issue was planned to be $2.50. **Guidelines are available for SASE. Pay is 1-4 copies, or $10/poem for contest winners. Poets should submit "any number" of poems, typed, handwritten, photocopy, computer printout—so long as legible. Prefer previously unpublished; if accepted elsewhere, poet must have permission to resubmit." Reporting time is 1 week-4 months; "allow 6 months between acceptance and publication."** The editor's advice is, "Avoid archaic or cliche-ridden language. Don't be afraid of bold language or ideas. . . . Experimental and/or humorous poetry is always in demand at Bizarre Press. Poems that have a strong emotional impact fare better than intellectual poems."

*BLACK AMERICAN LITERATURE FORUM (IV, Ethnic), Parsons Hall 237, Indiana State University, Terre Haute, IN 47809, founded 1967 (as *Negro American Literature Forum*), poetry editors Sterling Plumpp and Thadious M. Davis, is a "magazine devoted to the analysis of Afro-American literature. Poetry is more supplemental than central to our enterprise." **One issue per year focuses on poetry by black American poets only. No specifications as to form, length, style, subject matter or purpose.** They have recently published poems by Amiri Baraka, Gwendolyn Brooks, Leon Forrest, Jan Carew, Clarence Major, Dudley Randall and Owen Dodson. As a sample I selected the opening lines of "on the line" (with 11 million unemployed 9/3/82) by Mel Donalson:

> and still they wait
> no less in need than the generation before
> their names altered to percentage rates
> their faces mere decimal points along economic indicators

The *Forum's* format changed in Spring 1986 to 6x9", 128 pp. with photo on the cover. Individual subscriptions: $12 USA, $15 foreign. They receive about 500 submissions per year, use 50. **Sample: $3 postpaid. Submit maximum of 6 poems to editor Joe Weixlmann. Pays in copies. Reports in 2-3 months. Send SASE for guidelines.** The editors sometimes comment on rejections.

‡BLACK BEAR PUBLICATIONS, *BLACK BEAR REVIEW, POETS ELEVEN . . . AUDIBLE (II, IV, Specific themes), 1916 Lincoln St., Croydon, PA 19020, phone 215-788-3543, Privecode #373, founded 1984, poetry editors Ave' Jeanne and Ron Zettlemoyer. *Black Bear Review* is a semi-annual international literary and fine arts magazine that also publishes chapbooks and holds an annual poetry contest and a chapbook contest. A new poetry project is *Poets Eleven . . . Audible*, which released its first cassette in the summer of 1985. Poets recently published in *BBR* are William Vernon, Lyn Lifshin, Alan Catlin, James Humphrey, Elliot Richman, and Gail White. *Poets Eleven . . . Audible* has released poetry on tape by A. D. Winans, Belinda Subraman, Tony Moffeit, Ric Soos, Van Matre, and Tom House. As a sample from *BBR*, the editors selected lines from "The Ocean Brings its Tidings to a Desert," by Jon Daunt:

> *dried leeches the color of salt/ they cling*
> *to motionless bones: the buffalo, a horse's*
> *agony in rodeos,/ we hold skulls up to our*
> *ears and listen*

Circulation of *BBR* is 300, of which 150 are subscriptions; 15 libraries. Price: $3/issue; subscription $5. Subsidy publishing will be considered. Book catalog is free for SASE. The magazine is digest-sized, 50 pp., offset from typed copy on buff stock, with line drawings and woodcuts, one-color matte card cover, saddle-stapled. The editors explain that *Poets Eleven . . . Audible* was started for accommodation of longer poems; **the author may submit up to 7 minutes of poetry. "We like well crafted poetry that relates to our times.** *Black Bear Review* **wishes to see energetic poetry, avant-garde, free verse and haiku which relate to the world today. We seldom publish the beginner, but will assist when time allows. No traditional poetry is used.** We suggest that the poet read a lot of the good poets writing today as well as listening to them read. The underlying theme of *BBR* is ecological and environmental, but the review is interested also in political, war/peace, and minorities themes." Receive over 2,000 submissions. **Pay: 1 copy. Black & white artwork (5½x8) or smaller is also welcomed. Photocopies of the original only. Also publishing 45 minutes on cassette of individual poets. Write for guidelines before submitting. Recently published THE REAGAN PSALMS by A.D. Winans on cassette.** Pay: 1 copy. Receives over 2,000 submissions per year. Submissions are reported on in 2 weeks, publication is in 6-12 months, any number of poems may be submitted, one to a page, photocopies are OK but they prefer not to read dot-matrix. The editors do accept freelance submissions for chapbook publication; they publish one chapbook per year. Writers should query first, sending credits and 10 sample poems. For book publication, they would prefer that "*BBR* has published the poet and is familiar with his/her work, but we will read anyone who thinks they have something to say." Queries are answered in 2 weeks, MSS in 4; simultaneous submissions are not considered. Sample of *BBR*: $3 postpaid; back copies when available are $2 when postpaid. Guidelines available for SASE. "Cover letters are appreciated, but please tell us about *you* the poet and omit the degrees and the fact that you're a brain surgeon. We take pride in the fact that all submissions are handled personally and that quite often rejected manuscripts are given encouragement and directed to other interested markets."

BLACK BUZZARD PRESS, *VISIONS: THE INTERNATIONAL MAGAZINE OF ILLUS-TRATED POETRY, THE BLACK BUZZARD ILLUSTRATED POETRY CHAPBOOK SE-RIES, (II), 4705 S. 8th Road, Arlington, VA 22204, founded 1979, poetry editor Bradley R. Strahan, associate editor Shirley G. Sullivan, art editor, Ursula Gill. "We are an independent nonsubsidized press dedicated to publishing fine accessible poetry accompanied by original illustrations of high quality in an attractive format. **We want to see work that is carefully-crafted and exciting work that transfigures everday experience or gives us a taste of something totally new; in all styles except concrete and typographical 'poems.' Nothing purely sentimental. No self-indulgent breast beating. No children's poems. No 'workshop' poems. No sadism, sexism or bigotry. No two finger exercises. No unemotional pap. No copies of Robert Service or the like. Usually under 100 lines but will consider longer.**" They have recently published Walter McDonald, Philip Dacey, Elisabeth Murawski and Aaron Kramer; and though he protests that "no 4 lines can possibly do even minimal justice to our taste or interest!" Bradley Strahan offers these lines from "Open-Air Concert" by Veno Taufer as a sample:

> *he climbs the stairs and winds his heart up*
> *nude bodies drown in sand from the hourglass*
> *fish flick through their veins*
> *with dark designs concealed in their bloody gills.*

Visions, a digest-sized, saddle-stapled magazine finely printed on high-quality paper, appears 3 times a year, uses 42 pages of poetry in each issue. Circulation 650, 235 subscriptions of which 40 are libraries, **sample: $2.50 postpaid**. They receive over a thousand submissions each year and use 100, have a 3-18 month backlog. **"Poems must be readable (not faded, light photocopy or smudged) and *not* handwritten. We resent having to pay postage due, so use adequate postage! No more than a dozen pages, please." Reports in 3 days-3 weeks, pays in copies or $5-10 "if we get a grant**. We are international in both scope and content, publishing poets from all over the world and having readers in 43 + US states, Canada and 16 other foreign countries." **To submit for the chapbook series, send samples (5-10 poems) and a *brief* cover letter "pertinent to artistic accomplishments." Reports in 3 days-3 weeks, pays in copies, usually provides criticism. Send $3.50 for sample chapbook**. Bradley Strahan adds that in *Visions* "We often publish helpful advice about 'getting published' and the art and craft of poetry."

*THE BLACK MOUNTAIN REVIEW (V, I, IV, Theme), Box 1112, Black Mountain, NC 28711, phone 704-669-6211, founded 1969, poetry editor David A. Wilson. *The Black Mountain Review*, 2 issues/year, is specialized: **"the basic theme being the intelligence of man. It is important to send for the guidelines (SASE) to know what to submit. Samples: $5 postpaid. Payment is $2.50 per published page plus 2 copies. Photocopy OK, no simultaneous submissions.** Subscription: $8/year. Lorien House takes its name from Lothlorien, the land of the elves. He publishes books by others on a subsidy basis—**50% of cost, 50% of income received. "The goal has been to create quality books which are informative and inspirational. We like poetry which is thought-provoking, metaphysical, descriptive (no sex, violence or offensive language). Themes which have been presented: the Dream; the Soul; the Seeker. Book must have a definite theme—beginning, middle-ground, positive ending. 30-60 poems/pages."** They have published poetry by David Wilson, Aly Goodwin, Phillip Harrell and Charles Baar. As a sample the editor chose these lines of his own:

> *The sky stood forth today,*
> *blue immensity*
> *filling ever the distant corners*
> *of my mind.*

The sample chapbook I have examined, **the Song of the Sea, poetry by David Wilson**, is 34 pp., digest-sized, neatly composed in typescript, matte cover with art. It sells for $1.50. **Query with 4 samples, "publishing record, bio, goals: the theme and specifics of the book, number of pages, illustrations, what is involved." Reports on queries in 1 week, on submissions (if invited) in 1 month. MS should be standard, typed, arranged in book sequence. Photocopy OK, no dot-matrix or simultaneous submissions. Poet gets 20 copies. Send 50¢ for catalog to buy samples. Editor comments on rejected MSS and is willing to provide detailed criticism for a fee.** David Wilson advises, "Poetry is the most difficult form of writing to sell and the results are many times disappointing. The sales of a book is a long term effort, and must be a cooperative effort by the publisher and the author. I am therefore *extremely* selective.

‡*BLACK RIVER REVIEW, STONE ROLLER PRESS (II), 855 Mildred Ave., Lorain, OH 44052, phone 216-244-9654, founded 1985, poetry editor Michael Waldecki, editorial contact Kaye Coller, is a literary annual using "**contemporary poetry, any style, form and subject matter, 50 line maximum (usually), poetry with innovation, craftsmanship and a sense of excitement and/or depth of emotion. Do *not* want Helen Steiner Rice, greeting card verse, poetry that mistakes stilted, false or formulaic diction for intense expression of feeling.**" They have recently published poetry by James Proctor, Gary Nemes, Marci Janas, John M. Bennett, Gus Shanower and Raymond McNiece. The editor selected these sample lines from "Learning Repentance" by Phyllis M. Lee:

> *The nuns at St. Anthony's*
> *pried the lid off hell every Saturday—*
> *let us feel the heat:*
> *see the worms that never die.*

The magazine-sized annual is photocopied from typescript on quality stock, side-stapled with matte card cover with art, about 50 pp., using ads, circulation 300 (sold in college bookstore). **Sample: $2.50 postpaid. Pays 1 copy. Submit between Jan. and May 1, limit of 10, photocopy OK, no simultaneous submissions. Will consider previously published if acknowledged. Address to Jack Smith, editor. They conduct contests with cash prizes, $1 entry fee. Approximately half the magazine is devoted to contest winners. Send SASE for rules. Editor may comment on submissions, not on contest entries.** Kaye Coller comments, "Many poems written in traditional forms are poor imitations of earlier poets. Find your own voice. Make your form fit the content, not vice versa. Also, many poems we've been reading are technically well-written, but are missing something—heart, emotion, soul, whatever. We're more likely to publish a poem that makes us feel something than a well-created poem that is empty. What we really want is a technically perfect poem that hits us hard. Very rare! We are not a charitable organization devoted to giving poor poets a chance to see their words in print. We do not want poets who believe poetry come in a flash of inspiration and should not be changed once it's on paper. Our major purpose is to attract quality writers, whether or not they've been published before, and to publish poetry in which talent and skill are obvious enough to demand publication."

BLACK SPARROW PRESS (III), Box 3993, Santa Barbara, CA 93130, founded in 1966 by John Martin, who is still editor and publisher, has a prestige list of **avant-garde poetry**, fiction and criticism, including poets such as Charles Bukowski, Diane Wakoski, Tom Clark, Paul Bowles, John Fante, Wyndham Lewis, John Sanford and Wanda Coleman. John Martin says, "**We only want to see submissions by poets who are familiar with our list and understand the goals of Black Sparrow Press**." According to Richard Kostelanetz in *The New York Times Book Review*, Martin specializes in poets associated with the **Black Mountain school** of American Poetry—Robert Creeley, Charles Olson, Robert Duncan, Fielding Dawson and Paul Blackburn. Martin publishes editions of at least 2,500 copies, and Bukowski's *War All the Time*, published in 1984, has already sold about 15,000 copies—all this, according to Noel Young of Capra Press, in spite of the fact that he disregards the procedures of publishing, doesn't advertise, apply for grants, get loans, go to book fairs or booksellers conventions, and doesn't do commercial books to support his literary titles.

THE BLACK WARRIOR REVIEW (II), The University of Alabama, Box 2936, University, AL 35486, phone 205-348-7839, founded 1974, poetry editor Janet McAdams, wants **"serious, literary work only**." They have published poetry by Annie Dillard, James Tate, George Garrett, Dave Smith and Michael Pettit. **Submit any number of poems, simultaneous and photocopy submissions OK, awards two $500 awards annually, and they plan to pay all contributors beginning in 1985. Reports in 3-8 weeks**. It is a semiannual of 128 pp., 6x9'', circulation 1,500, **sample: $3.50 postpaid**. Send SASE for information.

BLACKBERRY BOOKS,(IV, Ethnic), Box 687, South Harpswell, ME 04079, phone 207-729-5083, founded 1974, poetry editor Gary Lawless, wants **"Native American poetry, women, poetry dealing with place, the natural world, mythology and anthropology."** He has published poetry by Ted Enslin, Kate Barnes, Miriam Dyak, Elizabeth Coatesworth, Peter Blue Could and Tim Koller. For book publication query with 5-10 poems and "a friendly letter actually written by one living person to another—not an application for a position as professor." Pays 10% royalties and 10% of print run. Comments on rejections "only if I feel the writer has some idea of where they were sending the manuscript."

BLIND BEGGAR PRESS, LAMPLIGHT EDITIONS, NEW RAIN (IV, Ethnic), Box 437, Williamsbridge Station, Bronx, NY 10467, founded 1976, poetry editor Gary W. Johnston, publishes **work "relevant to Black and Third World people, especially women."** New Rain is an annual anthology of such work. **Lamplight Editions** is a subsidiary which publishes "educational materials such as children's books, manuals, greeting cards with educational material in them, etc." They want to see **"quality work that shows a concern for the human condition and the condition of the world**." They have recently published work by Judy D. Simmons, Catherine Sanders and Bernard V. Finney. As a sample I chose the first four lines of Jayne Cortez' "Big Fine Woman From Ruleville":

> *How to weave your web of medicinal flesh into words*
> *cut the sutures to your circumcised name*
> *make your deformed leg into a symbol of resistance*
> *Big fine woman from Ruleville*

New Rain is a digest-sized saddle-stapled, 60 pp. chapbook, finely printed, with simple art, card covers. **Sample: $4 postpaid**. They also publish about 3 collections of poetry by individuals per year, 60 pp., flat-spined paperback, glossy, color cover, good printing on good paper. **Sample: $5.95. For either the anthology or book publication, first send sample of 5-10 poems with cover letter including your biographical background, philosophy and poetic principles. Considers simultaneous submissions.** They reply to queries in 1-2 weeks, submissions in 1-2 months, **pay in copies (the number depending on the print run)**. Willing to work out individual terms for subsidy publication. Catalog available for SASE.

BLIND SERPENT (II), Tighbeg, 15 Wood Rd., Birkhill, Dundee, Angus, Scotland, phone 580328, founded 1984, poetry editors Hamish Turnbull, Andrew Fox and Dr. Brenda Shaw, is a **4-page broadsheet of poetry**, elegantly printed, with art, on heavy paper. They get about a dozen poems into that striking format several times a year. "We started the Broadsheet to encourage **new up-and-coming poets and at the same time expect a high standard of poetry. We also try to encourage poets by answering their correspondence**". As a sample, I selected a short poem, "Moon," by Andrew Fox:

> *Big white moon*
> *white as the bones*
> *of the fresh fish*
> *I've just eaten.*

They print 500 copies, which sell for 35 p. each. **No pay at present, but they hope to pay in the future. Submissions should be "typewritten if possible. Must be clear, easy to read." Photocopy OK. Reports within 2 weeks**. Hamish Turnbull advises, "Read as much poetry as possible. Join a writers' group. Study style and work on your poetry."

BLOODROOT, INC., BLOODROOT (II,IV, Women), Box 891, Grand Forks, ND 58201, phone 701-775-6079, founded 1976, poetry editors Joan and Dan Eades, publishes **"quality poetry and fiction with special interest in publication by women authors and a preference for long poetry as opposed to short verse."** They have recently published such poets as Joan Joffe Hall and Crystal MacLean Field and offer these lines by Georgia Tiffany as a sample:

> *Edges of Antarctic currents*

> *cut colder than immersion.*
> *If deep is but a motion*
> *descend to where it moves*
> *and rise.*

Bloodroot appears irregularly (9 issues since 1976) though it nominally appears "three times a year", 6x9" saddle-stapled, quality paper, printing and art, 72 pp. of which about 15 are poetry, printrun of 800, 250 subscriptions of which 90 are libraries, **sample $3.50 postpaid**. They receive hundreds of submissions per year, use about 40, have a 6 month backlog. **Reports within 6 months, pays (if funds allow) $5/page, guidelines available for SASE**. They also print chapbooks in the same format. **Query first about chapbook submissions, with sample of poetry and biographical background; immediate response to queries. Payment for chapbooks $5/page (depends on grant or award money). Sample chapbook for $3.50 postpaid**.

*THE BLOOMSBURY REVIEW (II), Box 8928, Denver, CO 80201, phone 303-455-0593, founded 1980, poetry editor Ray Gonzalez, is a bimonthly tabloid-sized, saddle-stapled "book magazine," handsomely printed, with photos and art, with a quality newsprint color cover, which **uses about 24 poems per year, for which it pays $5-15 for each. Sample: $2 postpaid**. In the issue I examined there were several substantial reviews of small press publications of poetry, an interview with poet Wendell Berry, and poems by Ramona Weeks, Roger Finch, and Zona Teti, from whose "Exercise of Roosters" I chose these opening lines as a sample:

> *In memory of ancestral buzzards*
> *fighting it out on cliffs,*
> *the roosters come at each other*
> *putting up their ruffs*
> *like umbrellas. . . .*

Submit 5-8 poems, none longer than 65 lines, not previously published, not simultaneously submitted elsewhere. Photocopy OK. Report in 3 months.

‡*BLUE BUILDINGS (II), Apt. F, 1215 25th St., Des Moines, IA 50311, phone 515-274-9103 or 277-4298, founded 1978, poetry editors Tom Urban, Ruth Doty, Lyn Wegrich, and Judy Keyser, an international magazine of poetry, prose poetry, translations, and graphic art; they have occasionally published chapbooks. The editors want **"free verse of intense imagery, character and unique voice. Long poems and prose poems accepted. Experimental poetry accepted."** They do not want **"bad rhymes, haiku, tankas."** They have recently published work by Peter Wild, Roger Weingarten, Albert Goldbarth, Alberto Rias, and Gary Fincke. As a sample they chose the following lines from Pablo Neruda, translated by Hardie St. Martin:

> *Poetry is not static matter but a flowing current that*
> *quite often escapes from the hands of the creator*
> *himself. His raw material consists of elements that*
> *are and at the same time are not, of things that*
> *exist and do not exist . . .*

Blue Buildings is magazine-sized, 30-60 pp., with b/w photography and graphic art. It appears once or twice a year. Circulation is 250, of which about 20 are library subscriptions. Price per issue is $2, subscription $4/2 issues. **Sample available for $1.50 postpaid, guidelines for SASE. Pay is 2 copies. Submissions should be sent to Lyn Wegrich c/o** *Blue Buildings***, no more than 5 long or short poems at a time, no simultaneous submissions; photocopied MSS are OK. Reporting time is 2-3 months** ("sometimes longer; please be patient") and time to publication is 6 months or more. They are not currently publishing any chapbooks but may in the future. **Writers who are interested in chapbook publication should query, sending 5 sample poems.** The editors ask that poets "please read a copy of *Blue Buildings* before submitting, in order to get an idea of the type of poetry we are looking for. Please be patient after submitting."

BLUE CLOUD QUARTERLY PRESS, *BLUE CLOUD QUARTERLY (IV, Native American), Blue Cloud Abbey, Box 98, Marvin, SD 57251, phone 605-432-5528 (press founded 1954, became a poetry magazine in 1971), poetry editor Brother Benet Tvedten, OSB, is devoted to publishing **poetry by contemporary Native American and occasional translations of ancient songs, poetry and legends**. The press has published an anthology of Native American poets, **Wounds Beneath the Flesh**, but most **issues of the quarterly are, in effect, chapbooks by individual poets**. They have published poets such as Lance Henson, Diane Glancy, Anita Endrezze-Danielson, Joseph Bruchac and Maurice Kenny. These sample lines are from Elizabeth Cook-Lynn's "Grandfather at the Indian Health Clinic":

> *This morning the lodge is closed to the dance*
> *and he reminds me these are not the men who*
> *raise the bag above the painted marks; for the young*
> *intern from New Jersey he bares his chest*

Each issue of the *Blue Cloud Quarterly* contains 24 pp. of poetry, digest-sized, saddle-stapled, handsomely typeset. The *Quarterly* has 1,000 subscribers, of which 200 are libraries, sells for $1 a copy (**sample free!, guidelines available for SASE**). Considers simultaneous submissions. Brother Benet Tvedten receives about 50-60 manuscripts per year, uses 4, **reports in 2-3 weeks**, has accepted a couple of manuscripts ahead for each year's work. **Pays in copies**.

BLUE LIGHT BOOKS, *BLUE LIGHT REVIEW (II), Box 1621, Pueblo, CO 81002, founded 1979 (chapbook series), 1983 (magazine), poetry editor Paul Dilsaver. The *Review* is a semiannual literary magazine, circulation 200, which uses about 30 pp. of poetry in each issue: inexpensively printed (offset from various varieties of typescript) in a digest-sized saddle-stapled format. **Sample: $3. Reports in 3 months. Pays 1 copy.** I selected these sample lines, the opening stanza of "November Morning" by Victoria McCabe:

> *Someone is walking behind,*
> *walking very deliberately behind,*
> *as if he had a mission*
> *he walks, whoever he is, behind.*

About twice a year Paul Dilsaver publishes a chapbook, 12-24 pp. **To submit for the chapbook series, query with 5 samples and cover letter "describing project and potential audience. Author might be asked to buy a number of copies. No dot-matrix. Pays 10% royalty and 2 copies. Send SASE for list of titles in print to buy sample.** The editor's advice: "Write till it hurts."

BLUE MOUNTAIN ARTS, INC. (II), Box 1007, Boulder, CO 80306, is a publisher of **"distinctive notecards and related products such as calendars, gift and greeting books which feature unrhymed poetry and watercolor, airbrush and pastel illustrations. We are interested in unrhymed poetry on friendship, love, philosophies, family, etc. We are not interested in rhymed greeting card poetry. We prefer more honest person-to-person style . . . on the deep significance and meaning of life and relationships."** Leonard Nimoy and Peter McWilliams have been published by Blue Mountain Arts. They offer as an example these lines by Susan Polis Schutz:

> *It is so essential*
> *to have you in my life*
> *Thank you for being*
> *my friend*

They use very little freelance material, pay $150/poem. "New material is always welcome and each manuscript is given serious consideration. Please always include SASE with sufficient postage. Since we buy world-wide exclusive rights to what we publish we discourage simultaneous submissions, but we will still consider them."

*BLUE UNICORN, A TRIQUARTERLY OF POETRY (II), 22 Avon Rd., Kensington, CA 94707, phone 415-526-8439, founded 1977, poetry editors Ruth G. Iodice, B. Jo Kinnick and Harold Witt, wants **"well-crafted poetry of all kinds, in form or free verse, as well as expert translations on any subject matter. We shun the trite or inane, the soft-centered, the contrived poem. Shorter poems have more chance with us because of limited space."** Some poets they have published recently are Charles Edward Eaton, Beth Bently, Joseph Bruchac III, R.T. Smith, Josephine Miles, Walter McDonald, Karl Patten and Elisavietta Ritchie. These sample lines are from "Skunk in the Pipe" by Tom McDaniel:

> *You slant the load again, Into the high end*
> *you pour in drinking water, about a glass,*
> *and one crumpled skunk slides out into the wind*
> *and humbly humps away through pasture grass.*

The magazine is **"distinguished by its fastidious editing, both with regard to contents and format."** It is 48-56 pp., narrow digest-sized, saddle-stapled, finely printed, with some art, **sample: $3 postpaid**. They receive over 35,000 submissions a year, use about 200, have a year's backlog. Submit 3-5 poems on normal typing pages, original or clear photocopy or clear, readable dot-matrix, no simultaneous submissions or previously published poems. Reports in 1-3 months, payment one copy, guidelines available for SASE. They sponsor an annual contest with small entry fee to help support the magazine, with prizes of $100, $75 and $50, distinguished poets as juges, publication of 3 top poems and 6 honorable mentions in the magazine. **Criticism occasionally offered**. "We would advise beginning poets to read and study poetry—both poets of the past and of the present; concentrate on technique; and **discipline yourself by learning forms before trying to do without them**. When your poem is crafted and ready for publication, study your markets and then send whatever of your work seems to be compatible with the magazine you are submitting to."

BLUE WIND PRESS (III, V), Box 7175, Berkeley, CA 94707, founded 1970, poetry editors George and Lucy Mattingly, is one of the most highly respected publishers of **avant-garde literature**. In striking, unusual, high-quality editions they have published poetry by Ted Berrigan, Anselm Hollo, Merrill Gilfillan, David Gitin, Jack Marshall and Lorenzo Thomas. Reviewers have said, "**liveliest anti-mainstream books**, *Choice*; "most interesting book designer in the country," *San Francisco Review of Books*; "happy, mad books," *Library Journal*; "excellent fiction and poetry,"*Los Angeles Times*. **Send SASE for catalog to buy samples. "No plans to publish any new titles. No manuscripts accepted."**

BLUELINE (IV, Regional/Adirondack Mountain area), Blue Mountain Lake, NY 12812, founded 1979, poetry editors Alice Gilborn, Jane S. Carroll and guest editors, "is a semi-annual literary magazine dedicated to prose and **poetry about the Adirondacks and other regions similar in geography and spirit." They want "clear, concrete poetry pertinent to the countryside. It must go beyond mere description**, however. **We prefer a realistic to a romantic view. We do not want to see sentimental or extremely experimental poetry."** Usually 44 lines or less, though "occasionally we publish longer poems" on "nature in general, Adirondack Mountains in particular. **Form may vary, can be traditional or contemporary**" They have recently published poetry by Phillip Booth, George Drew, Norbert Krapf, L. M. Rosenberg, John Unterecker, Lloyd Van Brunt, Laurence Josephs, Maurice Kenny and Nancy L. Nielsen. As a sample they offer these lines from "Eagle Lake" by Noelle Oxenhandler:

> Sometimes the lines fall this way,
> the canoe's narrowness
> filling my mind, and my arms
> sending their weight through the water.

It's a handsomely printed, 56 pp., 6x9" magazine with 20-25 pp. of poetry in each issue, circulation 700. **Sample: $2.75 postpaid**. They have a 3-11 month backlog. **Submit August 1- February 1, no more than 5 poems with short bio. Occasionally accepts simultaneous submissions. Photocopy, dot-matrix OK if neat and legible. Reports in 2-10 weeks. Pays copies and subscription. Contributors are encouraged to buy copies, but it's not mandatory. Guidelines available for SASE. Occasionally comments on rejections**. "We are interested in both beginning and established poets whose poems evoke universal themes in nature and show human interaction with the natural world. We look for **thoughtful craftsmanship rather than stylistic trickery. We'd like to see less narcissism in the poems we receive and more perspective and humor**. We don't care much about what a poet *feels* about a mountain or a lake or a tree unless he or she can vividly convey the objective world that calls forth emotion.

BOA EDITIONS, LTD. (III), 92 Park Ave., Brockport, NY 14420, phone 716-637-3844, founded 1976, poetry editor A. Poulin, Jr., **generally does not accept unsolicited MSS**. They have published some of the major American poets, such as W. D. Snodgrass, John Logan, Isabella Gardner and Richard Wilbur, and they publish introductions by major poets of those less well-known. For example, Richard Wilbur wrote the foreword for Thomas Whitbread's **Whomp and Moonshiver, from whose title-sonnet I selected these sample lines:**

> Whomp and moonshiver of salt surf on sand,
> Beer cans, rocks, seawall: Galveston night vision
> Anyseawhere hear-and seeable, incision
> Cut into land, incessasnt dentist's hand
> At drill, letless force, without countermand
> Order thump order order thump intermission
> Thump order thump thump thump order No Permission
> For surfers Danger Deep Holes yet all how grand.

Query with samples. Pays outright grants or royalties.

‡***THE BODY ECLECTIC, GIMLET PRESS/GIMLET PUBLISHING (I)**, Box 6287, Longview, TX 75608, founded 1985, managing editor Julie Allen, a quarterly whose goals are to be **"a respected market for good poetry; a communicative tool for aspiring poets throughout the United States; a learning experience for you and us; and a publication in which you'll be proud to display your work."** The 10-page issue I have seen contains poems by Gene Liminac, Gregg Lozaw, Jon Rod Stearns, and others. As a sample, I selected the beginning lines from "If Spring Could Ever Be Estatic," by Ted Vund, M.D.:

> Washington Dee
> Scene of a blossoming
> cherry in the bald happy bosom
> of gorilla. April
> is bad weather for apes to escape
> from the zoo.

The magazine-sized newsletter is photocopied from a variety of photo-reduced typescripts on offset paper, with b/w illustrations, unstapled and folded for mailing. Subscription price is $8/year. **Submissions are invited; they will purchase a minimum of eight poems for each issue at $2/poem plus complimentary copies. "You may have your poetry considered for publication without payment; please indicate on your submissions if you would like this consideration." Submissions must be typed, 1 poem/page, on 8½x11" sheet with name and complete address in upper right hand corner. All poems must be titled. Unlimited entries, but 20 lines maximum length. "An author may be showcased at the discretion of the editorial staff; additional payment is made for a showcase page."**

*THE BODY POLITIC (IV, Lesbian/gay), Box 7289, Station A, Toronto, Ontario, Canada M5W 1X9, phone 416-364-6320, founded 1971, poetry editor Richard Summerbell, is a monthly tabloid magazine **for gay liberation, serving the lesbian and gay community. The poetry they use "must appeal to our audience by including gay/lesbian theme."** They have published poetry by David MacLean and Scott Tucker. These sample lines from "Between the Folds" by Terri Jewell:

> *They remark*
> *how stunning we are together*
> *my arm eclipsing the flash*
> *of your shoulder, your hair*
> *embroidering the velour of my own.*
> *We twist like taffy in argument,*
> *show all shades of exotic peppers*
> *then purr apologies like calicoes.*

They have a circulation of about 8,000, 2,500 subscriptions of which 40 are libraries. They receive "several" freelance submissions of poetry and use one each month. **Sample: $2 plus postage. "We accept any legible submission." Address to: "Reviews and Features." Reports within 4 weeks. No pay but copies. Will comment on rejections if asked.**

BOGG PUBLICATIONS, *BOGG (II), 422 N. Cleveland St., Arlington, VA 22201, founded 1968, poetry editors John Elsberg (USA) and George Cairncross (UK: 31 Belle Vue St., Filey, N. Yorkshire YO 14 9HU, England). "We publish *Bogg* magazine and occasional free-for-postage pamphlets. The magazine uses a great deal of poetry in each issue (one poem usually per author per issue): **poetry in all styles, with a healthy leavening of shorts (under 8 lines). Our emphasis is good work per se, and Anglo-American cross-fertilization and encouragement.**" This is one of the liveliest small press magazines published today. It started in England, and in 1975 began including a supplement of American work; it now has roughly equal US and UK sections with reviews of small press publications in both. It's thick (60 + pp.) and large (magazine-sized), typeset, side-stapled, with occasional crude English cartoons. They have recently published work by Ann Menebroker, David Hilton, Lyn Lifshin, Gerald Dorset, Robert Peters, Harold Witt, Ron Androla, David Spicer, Steve Sneyd, Tina Fulker, Andy Darlington, and offer these lines by Bernard Lionel Einbond as a sample:

> *I am a bit of an Englishman,*
> *I write nonsense like Dodgson and Lear,*
> *I write nothing at all of the slightest importance;*
> *Do I make myself perfectly clear?*

All styles, all subject matter. "We look closely for good shorts; a long poem, over 1 page, has got to be very good to justify the space. Overt religious and political poems have to have strong poetical merits—statement alone is not sufficient. Prefer typewritten manuscripts, double-spaced, with author's name and address on each sheet. Photocopy OK. We will reprint previously published material, but with a credit line to a previous publisher." No simultaneous submissions. Prefers to see 6 poems. About 40 pp. of poetry per issue, print run of 600, 350 subscriptions of which 20 are libraries, **sample $3 postpaid.** Subscription: $8, for 3 issues. They receive over 5,000 poems per year and use 100-150. "We try to accept only for next 2 issues (so publication could be up to nearly a year away). SASE required or material discarded (no exceptions)." **Reports in 1 week, pays 2 copies, guidelines available for SASE.** Their occasional pamphlets and chapbooks are by invitation only, the author receiving 25% of the print run, and you can get **samples free for SASE.** Better make it at least 2 ounces worth of postage. John Elsberg advises, "Always read a magazine before submitting to it. Always enclose SASE. Long lists of previous credits irritate me, as if I should be influenced in my own judgment of the material submitted to *Bogg*. Short notes about how the writer has heard about, and what he finds interesting in, *Bogg* I read with some interest."

BOREALIS PRESS, TECUMSEH PRESS LTD., *JOURNAL OF CANADIAN POETRY (V, IV, Canadian writers), 9 Ashburn Dr., Ottawa, Canada K2E 6N4, founded 1972. Borealis and Tecumseh are imprints for books, including collections of poetry, by Canadian writers only, and they are presently not considering unsolicited submissions. Send SASE (or IRC's) for catalog to buy samples. Poets published recently include John Ferns, Giorgio Di Cicco, and Russell Thornton. These sample lines are by Russell Thornton:

> *My longing brought me a far distance*
> *to your kisses, flying slowly for my mouth like melting birds,*
> *to your braided river hair and faun-brown skin*
> *and your eyes, lighting like hazel flames of candles.*

The annual *Journal* publishes reviews and criticism, not poetry. Sample: $6.95 postpaid.

*BOSTON REVIEW (II), 33 Harrison Ave., Boston, MA 02111, founded 1975, a bimonthly tabloid (newsprint), uses about a **half-page of poetry per issue, or 10 poems a year**, for which they receive about 700 submissions. Circulation 10,000, of which 3,000 are subscriptions (200 libraries), 2,000 are sold on newsstands and the rest sent out as complimentary copies. (**Sample: $3 postpaid.**) They have a 4-8 month backlog. **Submit any time, no more than 6 poems, photocopy OK, simultaneous submissions discouraged; reports in 2 months, pay varies**. The editor selected these lines, the opening of Alice Fulton's "Obsessions"as a sample:

> *steady as the heat*
> *bugs' drone, a rip of white*
> *water too violent*
> *to support much*
> *life. Only, only, only*
> *that's the song, self-*
> *absorbed and hardly knowing*

The editors advise, "To save the time of all those involved, poets should be sure to send only *appropriate* poems to particular magazines. This means that a poet should not submit to a magazine that he/she has not read. Poets should also avoid lengthy cover letters and allow the poems to speak for themselves."

‡BOTTOM DOG PRESS (IV, Regional/Ohio), % Firelands College of Bowling Green State University, Huron, OH 44839, phone 419-433-3573, founded 1984, publisher Larry Smith, a small-press publisher of a chapbook series by Ohio writers. **"We are looking for long poems, journal poems, cycle poems that have a sense of unity, not a selection of your work. Our slant is toward writing with a direct human voice and clean, clear images. Sense of place writing is preferred, as is poetry of social or greater consciousness. We prefer the personal but not self-indulgent, simple but not simplistic, writing of value to us all."** The press has recently published chapbooks by Terry Hermsen, Milton, Jordan, Marci Janas, Philip O'Connor and Larry Smith. As a sample, the editor selected these lines by Larry Smith:

> *The logs in the back bay*
> *have acred themselves*
> *into a kind of wooden rainbow. . .*

The press publishes 3 chapbooks/year with an average page count of 36; they are digest-sized, saddle-sewn, numbered and signed paperbacks. **Freelance submissions are accepted; poets should send no more than 30 poems and bio. Simultaneous submissions are OK if noted, photocoied MSS OK. Royalties are 10-15% plus 15-30 author's copies. "We want to work with the poet on the publication, sales, distribution. We do our part and expect cooperation from the writer." Book catalog free for SASE; sample books available for $4.50 postpaid.** The editor says "We plan to continue our Ohio Writers Series of chapbooks and to do at least one book a year of translations. My advice to poets seeking initial publication is to be realistic and to work with a publisher you can trust. . . . Write what is meaningful for you, find the book it makes of itself, and send it off with a short cover letter. If you care about it, continue; your writing will improve, as will your chances. Don't confuse sentiment with sentimentality, but also don't forget sentiment that is authentic."

‡*BOTTOMFISH (II), De Anza College, Creative Writing Program, 21250 Stevens Creek Blvd, Cupertino CA 95014, editor Frank Berry. This college-produced magazine appears annually. The Spring, 1985 issue *(Bottomfish 8)* contains poems by R. E. Brock, Janice Dabney, Gage McKinney, Chet Leach, and several others. From a special section of poetry and prose by Edward Kleinschmidt, I selected the first stanza of "Orbit of the Eye" as a sample:

> *Without trying, see.*
> *See if you can watch*
> *waves flash at the water.*
> *You've walked down there,*

Bottomfish is 7x8¼", well-printed on heavy stock with tasteful b/w drawings (many of fish), 55 pp. flat-spined, white matte card cover illustrated by a fish print. Circulation is 500, free to libraries, schools, etc., but **$3,50/copy to individual requests from writers who will submit. Reporting time is 6-8 weeks, except during the summer. Pay is 2 copies.**

‡*BOWBENDER (IV, Archery), Box 192, Carstairs, Alberta TOM ONO, Canada, phone 403-337-3023, founded 1984, editor Kathleen Windsor, a quarterly magazine that publishes material on **archery, hunting with a bow, hunting, the outdoors sportsmanship, and family recreation. Poems can be of any form or length, but short poems are preferred. Poems should not defame or malign sport hunters. The editor says that she "has little appreciation for much free verse, and Canadian poets are too 'survivalist' for [her] liking."** One of the poets she publishes is Dan Walker. As a sample, she chose the following lines by an unidentified poet:

> *'Tis the time of year when I hasten to fear*
> *the coming of the men.*
> *In their blaze orange coats with bows they tote,*
> *And they smell like a grizzley's den.*

Bowbender is magazine-sized, printed by offset web, with 4-color cover, artwork and graphics done by staff. Circulation is 10,000, of which about 8,000 are newsstand sales. Price per issue is $2.50, subscriptions $9/year. **Sample available for $2.50 postpaid, guidelines for SASE. Pay is 10¢/word plus 1 copy. Submissions can be in any form and will be reported on in a maximum of 2 weeks. Time to publication is approximately 6 months. Criticism of rejected MSS is always provided.** The editor's advice to poet's (and, I suppose, to archers) is: "Get a second job."

**BOX TURTLE PRESS, *MUDFISH (II), 184 Franklin St., New York, NY 10013, phone 212-219-9278, founded 1983, poetry editors Jill Hoffman and Jill Gallen. *Mudfish* is an annual art and poetry journal. Recent contributors include John Ashbery, James Applewhite, Marge Piercy, Stephen Sandy, John Godfrey, Carolyn Maisel, Michael Malinolitz, Stuart Kaufman, Marc Cohen, Kathy Andrews, Evelyn Horowitz, Frank Kuenstler, Elaine Edelman, Theodore Weiss, Michael Andre, Amy Bartlett, Ann Lauterbach, Billy Collins, Cheri Fein, Joseph Bruchac, Glenda Frank, Susan Baran, David Lehman, Charles North, Jane Flanders, Roland Flint, Ruth Danon, David Ray, Gerrit Henry, Jill Gallen and Jill Hoffman. Sample is from Jill Hoffman's "I am a kind of burr; I shall stick."

> *I say this to myself and fall asleep*
> *wandering through fields of various endearments*
> *of yours that astonish with their insensate*
> *candour, painted on both sides.*

In addition, Box Turtle Press publishes flat-spined paperback collections. **Query. Immediate reply. Editors provide comment on rejected MS.**

BRANDEN PUBLISHING CO., INC., INTERNATIONAL POCKET LIBRARY, DANTE UNIVERSITY OF AMERICA PRESS (II), Box 843, 17 Station St., Brookline Village, MA 02147, poetry editor Adolph Caso, publishes "very little poetry and on a standard contract-royalty basis—no subsidy accepted. We give authors a 10% royalty and *very very* **small advance. Branden is small but puts out quality books.** Our most recent book of poetry is **The Ruin Revived** by Mark Rudman, with illustrations by Susan Laufer—a mixture of poetry, prose and art dealing with Italy's ancient monuments and ruins." I selected this sample from **Words Ready For Music: Poems of a Young Teenager** by Rachel A. Hazen:

> *Again I'm all alone with myself*
> *In a room that's filled with fools.*
> *Again I write my poetry,*
> *With paper and pen as my tools.*

Queries only with SASE.

‡*BREAKTHROUGH! (I),** % Aardvark Enterprises, 192 Balsam Place, Penticton, BC, V2A 7V3 Canada, founded 1986, editor J. Alvin Speers, is a new quarterly "dedicated to life improvement, starting with the primary resource—the individual." **Sample: $4 postpaid. No profanity or porn. Prefers rhyming poetry.** They are conducting a poetry contest with a December 31 deadline, fees and prizes "to be announced."

‡*BREATHLESS MAGAZINE (I),** 910 Broad St., Endicott, NY 13760, phone 607-785-7790, founded 1984, poetry editor Jeff Rinde. *Breathless* is a "literary annual that prefers to publish work that is realistic in nature, but will also publish other genres if the writing is exceptional. As implied in our title, we will publish just about anything that **exhibits a strong sense of vitality, energy and originality. Of course, it must also be well written. As far as poetry is concerned, we are not prejudicial as to what subject matter or style our MSS exhibit, but please, don't submit anything that is ridiculously long . . . no single poem that is longer than 10 pages. We also tend to automatically disregard any poem that uses the rhyme technique; they're usually not very well done."** He does not want to see **"rhyme, religious or radically experimental poetry."** Some poets recently published are A. D. Winans, Andy Tang, Jeff Oaks, and Vonie Crist. As a sample, the editor chose these lines by C. W. Spinks:

> *Is now the moment of uncertainty*
> *Or the time of tolerence at night's end?*
> *And will words of the world's winking wisdom*
> *Break, fall, and shatter like old statuary?*

Breathless is handsome, magazine-sized, about 50-60 pp., saddle-stapled, offset from typescript on white stock, glossy white card cover with b/w photograph, no art inside but, they say they use photos and graphics, plan ads in future. The magazine appears annually with a circulation of 500, price $2.50/issue, subscription $5/2 issues. **Sample: $2.50 postpaid, guidelines available for SASE. Pay is 1 or 2 free copies. Submissions are reported on within 1-2 months, time to publication is up to 1 year. MSS must be typed, photocopied or dot-matrix OK, no simultaneous submissions. Criticism of rejected MSS is sometimes provided.** Some kind of award or competition is planned for the near future.

*BRIDE'S (I, IV, Marriage, love, romance), 350 Madison Ave., New York, NY 10017, a Condé Nast Publication, founded 1934, poetry editor Susan Kuziak ("Love" column), is a thick, slick magazine for "the couple planning a wedding, a marriage, a home, a honeymoon—and for their friends and families." It comes out bimonthly, with a **circulation of 400,000, pays $25/poem plus one copy. The poetry is by "readers. Doesn't use poetry every issue. Most are previously unpublished—the bride-to-be or groom-to-be, their parents, relatives, friends, relating to relationships, marriage, love, life together, feelings about marriage**." They receive about 260 submissions per year, have a 6-month backlog. **Submit short (no more than one page) poems, no simultaneous submissions, home address, day and evening phone numbers; include SASE. Reports in 6-8 weeks**. I selected this sample stanza, from "Those Words" by Robin Martin:

> *You carefully caressed my body*
> *And sent me higher than the trees.*
> *You held my heart in your hands*
> *I was truly under siege.*

The editor advises, "Please read the publication thoroughly, to understand its readers," and supplied these specifications: "average 23.2 years old (brides), 25 years old (grooms), engaged for 10.5 months. They are optimistic about the future, yet keenly aware of the lifestyle decisions facing them: finances, two careers, family planning, housing."

*BRILLIANT STAR (IV, Children), Bley, Suburban Office Park, 5010 Austin Rd., Hixson, TN 37343, is a Bahai bimonthly for children, appearing in a magazine-sized format, using some poetry fostering Bahai's very general spiritual values. The editor selected these sample lines from "In Celebration of Black History" by Mary Lou McLaughlin:

> *Then, a springtime arrived*
> *with colors, colors alive!*
> *Black is Beautiful, red and*
> *yellow blossomed above the*
> *richness of the brown earth.*
> *Hues by which to measure*
> *the standard,*
> > *and so it is*
> > *a challenging delight.*

No pay. Considers simultaneous submissions. Sample: $2 postpaid, in which the objectives are printed in the masthead.

*BROADSIDE MAGAZINE (IV, Political), Box 1464, New York, NY 10023, editor Jeff Ritter. *Broadside*, a monthly magazine of 20 pp., offset, with a circulation of 1,000 (750 subscriptions), publishes **"political songs and poems."** It has 25 library subscriptions and newsstand sales of 200. **Sample: $2 postpaid; no guidelines available. Pay is 2 copies. Submissions are reported on in 1 month. There are no specifications as to how poems should be submitted. The editor says poets should submit works that are** "personal/political, topical—humorous."

*BROKEN STREETS (I, IV, Religious), 57 Morningside Dr. E., Bristol, CT 06010, founded 1981, poetry editor Ron Grossman, is a **"Christian-centered outreach ministry to poets. Chapbooks are sent free to encourage poets."** The digest-sized magazine, photocopied typescript, 40-50 pp., card covers, appears 4-5 times a year—100 copies, and though he gives them away, he charges the publishing cost, **$3.50, for a sample. The editor wants "Christian-centered, city poetry, feelings, etc., usually 5-15 lines, haiku, no more than 5 poems at a time, not necessary to query, but helpful." Reports in 1 week. Uses about 150 of the 200 poems submitted per year, almost everything he gets—by children, old people, etc. No pay, but copies**. He has published recently B. Z. Niditch, Bettye K. Wray, Ruth Wilder Schuller. I selected this poem by Crystall Carman, age 10, as a sample:

> *The sea runs against the shore*
> *while thunder roars beyond the distant sunset*
> *and God smiles at his creations*
> *while the thunder drifts away*

BROKEN WHISKER STUDIO (II), Box 1303, Chicago, IL 60690, founded 1976, "is a small independent press and art studio that publishes primarily short fiction, poetry and juveniles in limited edition paperback books, chapbooks and broadsides. **"Strong writing, not slick, interests us, and we welcome new authors. We enjoy experimental writing (but not self-conscious syntactical gymnastics). We have no restrictions on theme or subject. Because the work is able to stand on its own we do not need to know about the author's biography, degrees, prior publications, or any other matters unrelated to the manuscript. We prefer to see the first 10 pages or so of the manuscript, and we will ask for more if we are interested in publishing the work. Presentation should be clean and neat: typed, double-spaced with 1" margins, on 8½x11" white paper. We dislike receiving dog-eared pages. We write comments on the title sheet and will mark on the manuscript itself if the author indicates that comments are welcome.** Since we publish infrequently we must be highly selective, and sometimes we have to reject a manuscript that we like." Send SASE for guidelines—most of which I have quoted here.

*BROOKLYN REVIEW (II), Dept. of English, Brooklyn College, Brooklyn, NY 11210, founded 1974, is a flat-spined, 80 pp., digest-sized annual, professionally printed, with glossy, color cover and art. They have published poets such as John Koethe, Ann Lauterbach, James Liddy, Paul Hoover, John Yau, Bink Noll, John Ashbery and Marc Cohen. They offer these sample lines by Benjamin Sloan:

> *You wake up early*
> *And play a glass of gin*
> *On your ukelele*
> *While out on a suburban lawn . . .*

They have a circulation of 500, **sample: $3 postpaid, pays in copies. Sometimes comments on MSS.**

BRUNSWICK PUBLISHING COMPANY (II), Box 555, Lawrenceville, VA 23868, founded 1978, poetry editor Walter J. Raymond, is a **partial subsidy publisher. Query with 3-5 samples. Response in 2 weeks if postage enclosed with SASE. If invited, submit double-spaced, typed MS (photocopy, dot-matrix OK). Reports in 3-4 weeks, reading fee only if you request written evaluation. Poet pays 80% of cost, gets same percentage of profits for market-tester edition of 500, advertised by leaflets mailed to reviewers, libraries, book buyers and book stores.** The samples I saw were flat-spined, matte-covered, 54 pp. paperbacks, inexpensively printed. **Send SASE for "Statement of Philosophy and Purpose,"** which explains terms, and catalog to order samples. I quote from that Statement: "We publish books because that is what we like to do. Every new book published is like a new baby, an object of joy! We do not attempt to unduly influence the reading public as to the value of our publications, but we simply let the readers decide that themselves. We refrain from the artificial beefing up of values that are not there. . . . We are not competitors in the publishing world, but offer what we believe is a needed service. We strongly believe that in an open society every person who has something of value to say and wants to say it should have the chance and opportunity to do so."

BRUSH HILL PRESS, INC., *EIDOS MAGAZINE; EROTIC ENTERTAINMENT FOR WOMEN, (IV, Erotica/women), Box 96, Boston, MA 02137, founded 1982, poetry editor Brenda Loew Tatelbaum. **"Our press publishes erotic literature, photography and artwork. Our purpose is to provide an alternative to women's images and male images and sexuality depicted in mainstream publications like *Playboy, Penthouse, Playgirl*, etc.** We provide a forum for the discussion and examination of two highly personalized dimensions of female sexuality: desire and satisfaction. We do not want to see angry poetry or poetry that is demeaning to either men or women. We like **experimental, avant-garde material**." *Eidos* is professionally printed, slick, magazine-sized, with fine photography and art, **including 1-6 pages of poetry in each issue**, print run 5,000, over 500 subscriptions of which 1% is libraries. **Sample: $5 postpaid.**. They receive hundreds of poems per year, use about 100. Backlog 6 months to a year. **1 page limit on length, format flexible, photocopy, dot-matrix, simultaneous submissions OK, reports in 4-8 weeks, payment: 1 copy, guidelines available for SASE. Sometimes accepts sexually explicit material.** Some poets they have recently published include Judith Arcana. *Comment or criticism provided as often as possible*. Brenda Loew Tatelbaum advises, "There is so much poetry submitted for consideration that a rejection can sometimes mean a poet's timing was poor. We let poets know if the submission was appropriate for our publication and suggest they resubmit at a later date. Keep writing, keep submitting, keep a positive attitude."

*BUFFALO SPREE MAGAZINE (II), 4511 Harlem Rd., Buffalo, NY 14226, founded 1967, poetry editor Janet Goldenberg, is the quarterly regional magazine of western New York. It has a controlled circulation (21,000) in the Buffalo area, mostly distributed free (only 3,000 subscriptions, of which 25 are libraries). Nestled between luxury ads on its glossy pages are general-interest features about local culture, plus book reviews, fiction and poetry contributed nationally. They receive about 300 poetry submissions per year and use about 25, which have ranged from work by Robert Hass and Carl Dennis to first publications by younger poets. They use 5-7 poems per issue, **paying $20 for each; these are selected 3-6 months prior to publications; (sample copy, $3.75 postpaid).** As an example, the editor chose 5 lines of Martha Bosworth's "Alien in Spring":

> *I am a tall pale animal in boots*
> *trampling forget-me-nots and scaring birds*
> *from the lemon tree: with my long-handled claw*
> *I pull down lemons—tear-shaped, dimpled, round,*
> *bouncing they vanish into vines and weeds.*

‡*BUMBERSHOOT (II)**, Box 21134, Seattle, WA 98111, phone 206-448-5233, founded 1973, producing director Louise DiLenge, an annual publication issued in conjunction with a literary arts festival at the Seattle Center on Labor Day weekend. "Thousands of glossy, 4-color cover magazines will be published for mailing prior to and distributed at the Festival. Included will be selected works by the Writers-in-Performance and winners of the Written Works Competition as well as the official Literary Arts Program Schedule for the Festival." **Six $125 honoraria will be awarded for written works. Poets must submit a book, chapbook or typewritten manuscript. Previous publication required although submitted works may be new. Deadline for application was April 17 in 1986. Application forms and further details can be had from** *Bumbershoot* at the address above. *Bumbershoot* was planned to be magazine-sized, 32 pp. with 4-color cover, interior illustrations and photos. Circulation was planned to be 4,000, prices per issue $1. **Sample available for $1.50 postpaid, guidelines for SASE. Pay is 1 copy. Reporting time is 1 month and time to publication 3 months.**

BURNT LAKE PRESS (IV, Haiku), 535 rue Duvernay, Sherbrooke, P.Q., Canada J1L 1Y8, phone 819-566-6296, founded 1983, poetry editor Rod Willmot, is "devoted to publishing **haiku by North American haiku poets.** All books are printed letterpress on tone paper. Chief market is the readership already interested in haiku, but by printing attractive books I hope to assist poets in reaching a wider audience." Their books are hand-sewn paperbacks sidestitched under a glued cover with flat spine, up to 90 pp. The editor expects to print chapbooks also in the future. He prefers **contemporary haiku over "traditional."** He has published a book by Penny Harter and selected this haiku by Nicholas. A. Virgilio as a sample:

> *the far graveyard*
> *quivering in the heat wave:*
> *river at my feet*

Query with a dozen sample haiku. "No conditions except high quality. Poets who have not already done extensive work in haiku are unlikely candidates. I'm most interested in poets who have proven themselves in the haiku magazines, who have made themselves known for at least a couple of years." **Replies to queries and submissions in about a month. Photocopy, dot-matrix OK. Pays 10% royalties. Rod Willmot "definitely" comments on rejections.** He says, "Since I'm well-known as a reviewer in the magazines, most poets specifically ask for comments. Over the last 20 years the haiku movement in North America has matured and grown to the point where it encompasses a wealth of competent writers and knowledgeable readers and a surprising number of truly excellent poets. Haiku is now on the point of entering the mainstream of literary awareness, not as an exotic hobby (as it may have been 20-30 years ago) but as an authentic literary form. I believe it has the potential to arouse the interest of a vast readership."

*BYLINE MAGAZINE (IV, Writers, writing)**, Box 30647, Midwest City, OK 73140, founded 1981, is a **magazine for the encouragement of beginning writers and poets, using 10-15 poems per issue about writers or writing, paying up to 55¢ per word**. They prefer short, humorous poems but often purchase longer, serious poems. They have over 2,200 subscriptions (a figure rapidly growing), of which 64 are libraries, receive 6,000 submissions per year, of which they use 600-700. I chose this sample by Charlotte Hatfield, "Be-Mused":

> *You played me a dirty trick, O, Muse;*
> *You sent me ideas by the flock.*
> *Now I don't even know where to begin.*
> *I might as well have writer's block.*

Byline is professionally printed, magazine-sized, with illustrations, art, cartoons, ads, **sample: $2.75 postpaid. They have a 6 month backlog. No more than 4 poems per submission, photocopy OK, no simultaneous submissions, reports within a week, rates $2-50, guidelines available for SASE**. They are also publish books for writers generated in-house under the Byline Books imprint. Mike McCarville advises, "STUDY MARKETS before submitting."

‡*CABARET 246, RED SHARKS PRESS (V, IV, Friends), 122 Clive St., Grangetown, Cardiff, UK CF1 7JE, phone 31696, founded 1983, publisher Christopher Mills. *Cabaret 246* is a magazine-sized, flat-spined periodical that appears 3 times a year; Red Sharks Press publishes flat-spined paperback chapbooks—**"anything possible given the right sort of financial incentive." In other words, Mr. Mills does do subsidy publishing: "He/she pays part of print costs. Money back as soon as made (we always cover print costs in sales), then 50% of profits."** As for what kind of poetry he wants to see, he says **"I don't want to see any,"** although he does accept freelance submissions for chapbooks. He has recently published poetry by Peter Finch, Chris Torrance, Robert Minhinnick, Ian Mc-Millan, Matthew Sweeney, R. S. Thomas, and John Harrison. As a sample, he selected the following lines by himself:

> *It's like riding a bike*
> *Once you've forgotten*
> *You never remember*
> *How to fall off.*

Cabaret 246 has a circulation of 250 and subscriptions are $20/year. "Sales are greatest at Cabaret 246 performances." **Sample: $5 postpaid. Since no contributors are wanted, contributors are not paid. Writers who wish to submit poems for book publication should query first, sending 6 sample poems and bio. Queries will be answered in 2 months or sooner. Simultaneous submissions will be considered, and photocopied or dot-matrix MSS are OK, but discs are not.** "$2 for a copy of a chapbook; $8 for a paperback, perfect-bound." Mr. Mills's advice to would-be poets is: "Become dentists!"

*CACHE REVIEW (II), Box 3505, Tucson, AZ 85722, founded 1981, poetry editor Steven Brady, "is a small press magazine in search of writers, who have something to say and know how to say it. We listen for **honest, original voices. Poems of any length, any style**. We shoot for variety in every issue." Poets they have published recently include Edward Mycue, Roger Dunsmore, Joseph Semenovich, Tony Moffeit, Wilma McDaniel and Ellen Celano. These sample lines are by Clyde Kessler:

> *I buy the ground for them, I free*
> *scutch and fescue I see their graves*
> *Starting mud rock and black vines*

The magazine appears twice a year, 25 pp. of poetry in each, with a circulation of 250, 50 subscriptions of which 10 are libraries. It's a magazine-sized format, mimeographed, side-stapled (taped) spine, neat, non-nonsense appearance. **Sample: $2** They use about 100 of the 1,500 submissions they receive each year. **Send 5 or more poems, any length, originals or good copies; simultaneous submissions OK. Payment: 2 copies. Guidelines available for SASE. Comments on MSS that show promise**. Steven Brady advises, "Know your markets, be persistent, especially with editors or markets that show interest. Publish wherever you can. **Small markets are as important as large ones when it comes to establishing your credentials.**"

*CAESURA (II), English Dept., Auburn University, Auburn, AL 36849, founded 1984, editor R. T. Smith, a twice-yearly literary journal with poetry emphasis. The poetry editor wants poems **"under 100 lines, no form or format restrictions beyond intelligent good taste (not cute, kitch)."** He does not want "religious, surreal experimentation, haiku, light verse—we do not print poems that sound like prose or that fail to go beyond literal reports." He has recently published poetry by Fred Chappell, Jared Carter, David Citino, Jordan Smith, Ted Morison and James Applewhite. He says that the purpose of the journal is "to provide a forum for serious writers and to provide stimulation for Auburn University and the Auburn community." The editor offers these sample lines (poet unidentified):

> *. . . an old negro at roadside*
> *Waved, his creased palm still*
> *convivial, though calloused,*
> *still strangely blue*
> *with the cash crop stain*

The magazine is digest-sized, offset, 64-80 pp., with a little art and graphics. Its circulation is 400, of which 100 are subscriptions and 20 go to libraries. **Samples $2 postpaid. Contributors receive two copies per work published. Writers should submit no more than 5 poems, no photocopied or dot-matrix MSS, no simultaneous submissions. The editor reports on submissions in 3 months and there is no backlog. He holds one annual contest, to which anything published is automatically eligible.** His advice is: "Don't settle for the almost right word. Rewrite. Invest emotion, instinct, intellect and viscera in your work. And rewrite."

CALLALOO POETRY SERIES, *CALLALOO (IV, Regional), Dept. of English, University of Kentucky, Lexington, KY 40506-0027, phone 606-257-6984, founded 1976, editor Charles H. Rowell. Devoted to **poetry dealing with the Black South, Africa, Latin and Central America, South Ameri-**

ca and the Caribbean. Their magazine and chapbooks are elegantly printed, flat-spined glossy-covered paperbacks. They have recently published poetry by Gayl Jones, Jay Wright, Brenda Osbey, Alice Walker, John A. Williams. These sample lines are by Clarence Major:

> They've forced me to pose
> in the picture with them.
> I'm the unhappy one
> standing next to the man
> with sixty smiles
> of summer in his smile

The magazine is a thick triannual with a varying amount of poetry in its nearly 200 pp., circulation 1,000, 600 subscriptions of which half are libraries, $7/issue—**sample free! "We have no specifications for submitting poetry except authors should include SASE." Reports in 8-12 weeks, payment in copies.** In the chapbook series they publish 4 flat-spined paperbacks a year, 65-80 pp. **"Please inquire before submitting to chapbook series."**

‡*CALLIOPE, BENSALEM ASSOCIATION OF WOMEN WRITERS (I)**, Box 236, Croydon, PA 19020-0940, founded 1985, editor Joann Marie Everett, a newsletter of the BAWW that publishes poetry, contest information, and "information on the basics of writing," and runs a critique service. "We will be merciless in our evaluation of your written creation, but oh, so tender with your writer's ego." Cost of critique service is $10 for 3 short poems or 1 "epic" (50 line limit). **You must subscribe to submit. The BAWW is "open to all kinds of writing. Each issue runs different contests with different themes. [A recent contest paid a $30 first prize, $2 entry fee.] We like to see poetry with meaning and a clear, fluid style; no pornography."** *Calliope* has recently published poems by Marion Ford Park, Rochelle Lynn Holt, and Alice MacKenzie Swain. The editors selected as a sample the following lines by an unidentified poet:

> I am Halloween fire
> born to light the blackest pot
> glowing in the darkest night
> of medieval mystical mayhem.

Calliope is magazine-sized, offset from typed copy on colored stock, 20 pp., stapled in top left corner, no cover. Circulation is 150 + and "still growing"; members of BAWW receive the newsletter as part of their membership, which is $15/year. Single copies are $4. **Sample $2.50 postpaid; guidelines available for SASE. Pays contributor's copies. Writers should "ask for info" before submitting; simultaneous submissions OK. Reporting time is 2-3 weeks.** The BAWW is "dedicated to aid women in the development and growth of their writing as it pertains to the world they live in and their personal lives. It is a circle of women writers who adopt as their keywords: knowledge, sensitivity, and creativity."

CALLI'S TALES (I, IV, Wildlife, pets, nature)**, Box 1224, Palmetto, FL 33561, founded 1981, poetry editor Annice E. Hunt, is a **typescript quarterly newsletter "for animal-lovers of all ages,"** stapled at the corner, with a colored paper title-page, illustrated with simple art. They want **"any type of poetry that is in good taste, poems of 16 lines or less, about wildlife, pets or nature in general**." As a sample I chose this complete poem, "Spring Snow," by Patricia Crandall:

> A blizzard in the greening stage!
> Bird talk once cheery
> sounds eerie
> in a spring snow!

The editor says she uses about a fourth of the poetry submitted, has a 6-month backlog, wants poems typed one to a page, reports in a month, pays 1 copy. Will accept multiple submissions; considers simultaneous submissions. Guidelines available for SASE. Sometimes comments.

CALYX, A JOURNAL OF ART & LITERATURE BY WOMEN (IV)**, Box B, Corvallis, OR 97339, phone 503-753-9384, founded 1976, poetry editors M. Donnelly, C. McLean, E. Wilner, L. Domitrovitch, R. Gordon, J. Alexander and R. Malone, **publishes poetry, prose, art, reviews and interviews by and about women.** They want **"excellently crafted poetry that also has excellent content."** Some poets they have published recently are Paula Gunn Allen, Cherrie Moraga, Wendy Rose, Coleen McElroy. I selected these sample lines from "To Praise" by Ellen Bass as a sample:

> I want to praise muscle
> and the heart, that flamboyant champion
> with its insistent pelting like
> tropical rain, fierce and fast

Each issue is 7x8", handsomely printed on heavy paper, flat-spined, glossy color cover, 125-200 pp., of which 50-60 are poetry. **Sample for the single copy price, $6.50 plus 75¢ postage. "Send up to 6 poems with SASE and short biographical statement. We do not encourage simultaneous submis-**

sions—queries not necessary. We accept copies in good condition and clearly readable. Reject immediately; if interested, we report in 2-6 months. Guidelines available for SASE. Sometimes comments on returned MSS.

CAMAS PRESS, *THE ARCHER (II), Box 41, Camas Valley, OR 97416, press founded 1941, magazine 1951, is the one-man operation of Wilfred Brown, who both edits and handsets the Goudy 12 pt. (⅛ inch) type for *The Archer* and prints it on a hundred-year-old letter press. (**Camas Press** no longer actively publishes books.) A review describes *The Archer*: "Each 32-page issue is an appealing assemblage of personal poetry from far-flung, unpaid contributors. Some is fairly standard amateur verse. Some flashes with sharply expressed feeling. And **all of it, contributions and presentation together, is clearly a labor of love.**" It appears 3 or 4 times annually. Wilfred Brown says he wants "**lyrical verse, sonnets, tankas, haikus, limericks. We do not publish explicit sex. Neither do we often publish what might be called religious poems. Tributes to spring are rarely accepted because they tend to be trite. We welcome humor but, sadly, do not think most of that received is very funny. Both rhymed and unrhymed verse, but rhymes should fill a purpose and not be there soley to match the vowel sound of another word.**" In recent issues have appeared Frederick Raborg, Jay Giammarino, Anona McConaghy—"however names, per se, mean little to us." These sample lines are by Janet Elcano:

> *I wonder what my life is worth;*
> *I don't know but I care—*
> *For if I get the chance to sell*
> *My soul—what price is fair?*

Sample: $1 postpaid. He gets "close to 10,000" submissions per year, of which he uses about 300. "Our aim is to publish within a year, to report within a month but sometimes don't succeed. **We prefer not to receive more than about 4 poems at a time. A poem taking more than 1 page (32 lines) must be very appealing.**" I quote his advice at length, because many poets are not sufficiently aware of these details: "Read your MS closely before sending it out to see if improvements might be made. Please put both name and address on *each* poem. It is surprising how many poets do not, thereby adding a lot to troubles of the editor and resulting in accidental loss of many MSS. From our viewpoint the best envelopes are #10, long, with SASE folded in thirds inside. Sending a small SASE requires troublesome refolding and MS will almost certainly have to be retyped before being sent out again. Elinor Henry Brown [the editor's deceased wife] claimed she could tell a MS was 'no good' if it came in a large (9x12") envelope. Her judgment was probably too harsh, but I tend to put such MSS at the bottom of the pile. We still get frequent MSS with *no SASE*. They get put aside and usually not returned (for at least a considerable while). Most "little" mags already are in the red, as *The Archer* has been for over 35 years. Re: *punctuation*. Many poets avoid it like the plague. Our view is that it should be used if it aids in the quick understanding of what the poet is trying to say!"

*CANADIAN LITERATURE (IV, Regional, Canadian poets), 2029 West Mall, University of British Columbia, Vancouver, B.C., Canada V6T 1W5, phone 604-228-2780, founded 1959, poetry editor W. H. New, is a quarterly review which publishes **poetry by Canadian poets. "No limits on form. Less room for long poems."** They have recently published poems by Atwood, Ondaatje, Layton and Purdy. The following sample lines are from "Riddle" by Robert Bringhurst:

> *A man with no hands is still singing.*
> *A bird with no hands is asking the world,*
> *and the world is answering every day:*
> *earth is the only flesh of the song.*

Each issue is professionally printed, large digest-sized, flat-spined, with 190 + pp., of which about 10 are poetry. It has 2,000 circulation, two-thirds of which are libraries. **Sample for the cover price: $7.50 Canadian.** They receive 100-300 submissions per year, of which they use 10-12. **No photocopy, round-dot-matrix, simultaneous submissions or reprints. Reports within the month, pays $10/ poem plus 1 copy.**

‡***CANDLE: A WORKING PERSON'S RAGAZINE, TIPTOE PUBLISHING (I, IV, Humor)**, Box 206-V, Naselle, WA 98638-0206, founded 1985, editor A. Grimm-Richardson, who says, "Tiptoe to publish staff-generated works. *Candle*—small press magazine, general international, family interest, for working people, unemployed, retired (& US) military, Western Hemisphere topics, political; use a *little* verse in magazine." The editor wants "**short (4- to maximum-12 lines) humorous, political or for children. Want material from (and about) anywhere in The Americas—especially open to material from Latin America (in English) and Caribbean countries.**" She does not want poetry that is "vague, R or X-rated, four-letter words, exploitive." She has recently published poems by Doreen Bulzomi, Everett Whealdon, L. E. Cornelison, and Cicely Johnston. As a sample, she selected the following lines by an unidentified poet:

> *This day is mine on loan*
> *I give it back to sleep*
> *The time which stitched my memories*
> *is never mine to keep*

The slick-paper, magazine-sized journal (24 pp.) is computer printed (dot-matrix) and hand lettered, with graphics and cover design. It appears 10 times/year (at 36.5 day intervals), and circulation is "growing internationally." Single copy price is $2, subscription $15. **Sample $2.25 postpaid, guidelines available for SASE. Contributors of poems receive 1 copy. The editor wants 3-5 1-page poems at a time; photocopied or dot-matrix OK, as are simultaneous submissions "if we know."** She reports in 45 days and time to publication is 1 to 3 months. She "plans to run various contests, with minimal 'recognition' but no charge for entry." Her notes to authors are, "We do not look for 'fine poetry' but verse. Want humor or political comment. Shorter has best chance with us. We use verse to make point or counterpoint to fiction, columns, cartoons and other graphics."

‡**CANNON PRESS, SHOTGUN POETRY SERIES (II)**, Box 912, Station A, Hamilton, Ontario L8N 3P6, Canada, phone 413-521-9196, founded 1985, editor Jeff Seffinga, a small press that publishes quality poetry chapbooks. The editor wants **short MSS (20-36 short poems, perhaps 1 long), thematic. He does not want any "confessional, 'I' centered, overly religious meditations."** As a sample, he chose the following lines from "Wasyl Szewczyk" by James Strecker:

> *. . . He was attuned, like*
> *spring, to the delicacy*
> *of creation.*

Mr. Seffinga publishes 2-3 poetry chapbooks each year with an average page count of 32, 7x4½" paperbacks, stapled. **Poets wishing to submit should send credits, 8-10 sample poems, bio, and philosophy. Queries will be answered in 2-3 weeks and MSS reported on in 4-10 months. Simultaneous submissions and photocopied MSS are OK. Pay is 10 author's copies.** A book catalog is in preparation; it will be available for a #10 SASE.

‡***CAPE COD LIFE (II)**, Box 222, Osterville, MA 02655, phone 617-428-5706, founded 1979, managing editor Mary Shortsleeve, who says, **"Short poems on nature and coastal life are especially welcome, but we are open to all kinds of poetry."** She has selected the following sample lines by an unidentified poet:

> *How I saw you in everything.*
> *A thousand years of reaching out,*
> *calling, knowing the strange quiet*
> *long before*

Cape Cod Life is an elegant, upscale bi-monthly magazine that has not published poetry consistently in the past but plans to include it on a regular basis from now on. Magazine-sized, glossy stock, full-color illustrations, ads, and cover, flat-spined. **Pay is $20/poem plus 2 free copies. Simultaneous submissions OK. Submissions reported on within 1 month, publication in 4-8 months.**

***THE CAPE ROCK (II)**, Department of English, Southeast Missouri State University, Cape Girardeau, MO 63701, founded 1964, appears twice yearly and consists of **64 pp. of poetry and photography, with a $200 prize for the best poem in each issue and $100 for featured photography**. It's a handsomely printed, perfect bound (square back) digest-sized magazine, **sample: $2, guidelines available for SASE. "No restrictions on subjects or forms. Our criterion for selection is the quality of the work. We prefer poems under 70 lines; no longpoems or books, no sentimental, didactic, or cute poems."** They have published such poets as Stephen Dunning, Joyce Odam, Judith Phillips Neeld, Lyn Lifshin, Virginia Brady Young, Gary Pacernik and Laurel Speer. I selected these sample lines from Kevin Woster's "November Night":

> *The rough paved streets*
> *have crystalized with sudden beauty*
> *Even trash cans find*
> *an edgeless sort of grace*

Their circulation is about 500, with 200 subscribers, of whom half are libraries. They have a 2-8 month backlog and **report in 1-3 months. Pays in 2 copies**

CAPPER'S WEEKLY (I), 616 Jefferson St., Topeka, KS 66607, founded 1879, poetry editor Dorothy Harvey, is a biweekly tabloid (newsprint) going to **425,000 mail subscribers, mostly small-town and farm people**. Uses 6-8 poems in each issue—**payment $3-6 per poem. They want short poems (8-10 lines, lines of one-column width) "relating to everyday situations, nature, inspirational, humorous."** They have recently published Helen Harrington, Elizabeth Searle Lamb, R. H. Grenville and Anne Kilmer. The editor selected a complete poem called "Pigeons" by Parker Kimball:

> *Pigeons strutting*
> *Sidewalk parade grounds . . . each one*
> *Playing drum major . . .*

They receive about 5,000 submissions per year, use about 140. Their backlog "depends on space, season, etc. We've held some for years before publishing; others have been used immediately after acceptance." **Submit 4-6 poems at a time with return postage, no photocopies or simultaneous submissions. Reports within a month. Send 55¢ for sample. Not available on newsstand.**

CARAVAN PRESS (II), 343 S. Broadway, Los Angeles, CA 90013, founded 1980, poetry editor Olivia Sinclair-Lewis, is "a small press presently publishing approximately four to five works per year including poetry, photojournals, calendars, novellas, etc. We look for quality, freshness and that touch of genius." In poetry, "**we want to see verve, natural rhythms, discipline, impact**, etc. We are flexible but **verbosity, triteness and saccharine make us cringe**." The example I have of one of their poetry collections, **Razor Candy**, by Scott Sonders (90 pp.,$5.95), has a glossy cover with black-and-white photos front and back, and the type is a mixture of typescript (rather light) and set type, with illustrations. As a sample of poetry they publish the editor chose these lines from Sonders' "Legacy":

> *now you lie somewhere strange and new*
> *cancer stole your hair*
> *and you stare with vacant eyes*
> *at the long blue arms of God.*

Query first, with 2-3 poems and resume. If invited to submit, send double-spaced, typed MS (photocopy, dot-matrix OK). They reply "ASAP." They offer 20% royalty contract, 10-50 copies, advance or honorarium depending on grants or award money. Send SASE for catalog and order sample. Criticism offered on rejected MSS. (Note: Fee charged if criticism requested.) As advice for poets, the editor adapted Emily Dickinson: "[you] never know how high [you] are/ till [you] are called to rise/ and then if [you] are true to plan/ [your] stature will touch the skies."

*CARDINAL PRESS (V), 76 N. Yorktown, Tulsa, OK 74110, phone 918-583-3651, founded 1978 poetry editor Mary McAnally, publishes 1-3 chapbooks a year, **poetry on a subsidy basis, co-operative contact for labor and costs on varied terms, payment a percentage of the print run. No unsolicited MSS. Query with 3-6 samples and cover letter giving background, publications, personal or aesthetic philosopyy, poetic goals and principles. Simultaneous submissions, dot-matrix, photocopies OK. Reports on submissions in 1-3 weeks with comments.**

*CARIBBEAN REVIEW (IV), Florida International University, Tamiami Trail, Miami, FL 33199, phone 305-554-2246, founded 1969, poetry editor Elizabeth Lowe, is a slick magazine-sized quarterly "dedicated to the **Caribbean, Latin America and their emigrants." Poetry must relate to these subjects, but there are no other specifications**. In one sample issue I found 2 rather long poems (2 pp. each, with art and illustrations): Geoffry Philp, "Florida Bound: A Jamaican Complaint," and Julia Alvarez, "Homecoming: A Dominican Reverie." As a sample, I quote the opening lines of the latter:

> *When my cousin Carmen married, the guards*
> *at her father's finca took the guests' bracelets*
> *and wedding rings and put them in an armored truck*

Circulation is 5,000. **Sample: $3 postpaid. They receive 12-24 submissions per year, of which they use about 6. Up to 6 months backlog on hand. No simultaneous submissions. Pays copies**.

*CARNEGIE-MELLON MAGAZINE (II), Carnegie-Mellon University, Pittsburgh, PA 15213, phone 412-268-2467, editor Ann Curran, is the **Alumni magazine** for the university and favors writers connected with the university but considers submissions from others: **avant-garde or traditional, no previously published poetry, no payment. Direct submissions with SASE to Gerald Costanzo, poetry editor.** The issue I examined had one poem, "A Daughter," by Lee Upton (who had read her work at the Carnegie-Mellon Visiting Writers Series), from which I selected the opening stanza as a sample:

> *Water on the white blossoms,*
> *warm, almost like the touch of oil.*
> *To be ridiculous and beautiful was*
> *one task for a daughter.*

‡CARNEGIE-MELLON UNIVERSITY PRESS, *THREE RIVERS POETRY JOURNAL (III), Box 21, Schenley Park, Pittsburgh, PA 15213, phone 412-268-2861, poetry journal founded in 1972, press in 1975, director Gerald Costanzo, poetry editor Laurie Schorr. The journal publishes poetry, some short fiction; the press publishes 6 poetry titles a year in both cloth and paper editions. **The editor**

says they are "completely open (we think)" to all types of poetry submissions. They have recently published work by Stephen Dunn, Rita Dove, and Brendan Galvin. *Three Rivers Poetry Journal* appears twice yearly and has 80-100 pp. flat-spined. Circulation is 1,000, of which 450 are subscriptions; 90% of those go to libraries. **Sample available for $2 postpaid. Pay is 2 copies.** In regard to books published by the press, the editor says, "Of the 6 books published in our poetry series each year, at least 2 by poets who have not been published by us previously. **Such MSS must be postmarked only during October each year. They must be accompanied by stamped, self-addressed packaging suitable for return and by a reading fee of $7.50** (checks made payable to "Carnegie-Mellon University Press").

*CAROLINA QUARTERLY (III), Greenlaw Hall 066A, University of North Carolina, Chapel Hill, NC 27514, founded 1948, poetry editor Margaret Bockting, is a small literary magazine that appears three times a year using poetry of "**all kinds, though we seek excellence always.**" They have recently published poets such as Albert Goldbarth, Richard Kenney, Charles Simic and Mary Kinzie. As a sample I selected the first stanza of "The Business of Bees" by Michael Finley:

> *When prices are normal*
> *and weather cold, bees clump*
> *in a knot, suck sugar*
> *and hum to stay warm.*

It's a professionally printed, 6x9" flat-spined magazine, glossy cover, with 90 pp. of which about 30 are poetry, circulation 800, 400 subscriptions, of which about half are libraries. They receive thousands of submissions per year, use 40-60. **Sample: $4 postpaid. Submit no more than 2-6 poems. Use of poems over 300 lines is impractical. No simultaneous submissions. Reports within 3 months. Pays $5/poem plus 2 copies. Guidelines available for SASE. Comments sometimes on rejections**.

CAROLINA WREN PRESS (IV, Regional), 300 Barclay Rd., Chapel Hill, NC 27514. founded 1976, poetry editor Judy Hogan, publishes "**primarily NC authors; primarily people whose work I have come to know through teaching, readings, consultation; focus on women and minorities, though men and majorities also welcome.** *I won't read unsolicited MSS*, before 1987, but I do send them information about my consultation services." Judy Hogan is one of the most broadly experienced editors in the small presses and **offers "consultation" at $25 for 12 pages or "NC authors can sometimes consult me free if they can come to Durham.**" The consultation consists of "feedback, advice about acquiring writing skills, where to publish, support groups, classes and other community resources, and help with book-length projects." Some published poets are Jaki Shelton-Green, Li Ch'ing-Chao (in translation), Gene Fowler, T.J. Ready and Tom Huey. The editor chose this sample from Mirand Cambanis' "The Traffic of the Heart":

> *When poetry sleeps, she is fatally wounded. Her breasts lie still under*
> *her red dress and her voice surrenders to inarticulate shrieks that freeze*
> *the tears and put a gun on the temple of those who reject their own*
> *heartbeat and believe they can cross reality when they can only lift it.*

Pays 10% of print run in copies. Send catalog to purchase samples. Some free advice: "Become good and for feedback use friends and community resources."

*THE CATHARTIC (II), Box 1391, Ft. Lauderdale, FL 33302, phone 305-474-7120, founded 1974, edited by Patrick M. Ellingham, "is a **small poetry magazine devoted to the unknown poet** with the understanding that most poets are unknown in America. It tries to provide a place for poets to meet and be met." He says, "While there is no specific type of poem I look for, **rhyme for the sake of rhyme is discouraged. I seek poems that speak to readers in language and with emotions they can identify with. Any subject matter except where material is racist or sexist in nature. Overly-long poems are not right for a small magazine normally**." Recently published poets include H. E. Knickerbocker, Joy Walsh, Lyn Lifshin, Aisha Eshe, Patrick Mckinnon, Arthur Knight, P. T. Lally, and Sheila E. Murphy. These sample lines are from a poem by Eileen Eliot:

> *you're not used to descriptions like this*
> *all your rituals that keep life like a fossilized fern*
> *tight under glass are unraveling you pick the edge*
> *of your blanket, wanting more*

It's a modest, 28 pp. pamphlet offset printed from typescript, consisting mostly of poems, which appears twice a year. **Sample: $2 postpaid**. He receives over a thousand submissions per year, of which he uses about 60. No backlog. **Photocopy, dot-matrix, simultaneous submissions OK, submit 5-10 poems. Reports in 1 month.** Uses reviews of small press books as well as some artwork and photography. **Guidelines available for SASE. Contributors receive 1 copy, but $15 cash award is given for "the best poem of each issue as decided by reader input."** The editor comments "when time and work load permit". He advises, "The only way for poets to know whether their work will get published or not is to submit. It is also essential to read as much poetry as possible—both old and new. Spend time with the classics as well as the new poets. Support the presses that support you—the survival of both is essential to the life of poetry."

*CATHEDRAL VOICE, ST. WILLIBRORD PRESS (IV, Peace), Box 98, Highlandville, MO 65669, phone 417-587-3951, founded 1965, poetry editor Karl Pruter, is a quarterly magazine serving as a "voice for the World Peace Academy and the Cathedral Church of the Prince of Peace," of the independent Catholic and Orthodox Movement. They use **preferably short poems "ONLY about peace and issues concerning peace." Pays $10 and up. Sample: $1 postpaid. Please do not query**. They have a 3 month backlog, circulation of 1,800, 1,500 subscriptions of which 50 are libraries.

*CEILIDH: AN INFORMAL GATHERING FOR STORY & SONG (II), 986 Marquette Lane, Foster City, CA 94404, phone 415-572-9338, founded 1981, poetry editors Patrick S. Sullivan and Perry Oei, is interested in "**experimental, translations, long poems, and language poetry. Not interested in satire, word play or other less than literary poetry**." In recent issues they have published Patrick Smith, John Moffitt, Sarah Bliumis and Kate Adams. These sample lines are from "Vega: Lies of Ascent" by Traise Yamamoto:

> I want to write a poem that forgets about loneliness.
> And saying that makes me think of the afternoon
> we stood on the hill looking at the cows. We laughed some
> said those were a poet's cows, wondered whose they
> really were.

There are 32-64 pp. per issue. Winter and summer issues are devoted to fiction, spring and fall issues each use about 30 pages of poetry. Circulation of 400 subscribers, of which 100 are libraries. **Sample: $3.50 postpaid**. They have a 2-3 month backlog. **The best time to submit is January-March and July-September 1. Photocopy, dot-matrix OK, but no simultaneous submissions. Reports in 6-8 weeks. Pays 2 copies. Guidelines available for SASE. Usually a contest with each issue with prizes from cash to gift certificates to poetry books**. Some of their contest judges: Gerald Frassetti, James K. Bell, Michael Thornton. **Occasional criticism of rejected MSS**.

‡*CELEBRATION (I), 2707 Lawina Road, Baltimore, MD 21216, phone 301-542-8785, founded 1975, editor William J. Sullivan, a poetry magazine, "published occasionally—in the past about once every two years." **Poems can be "any form; length; what will fit on about two printed pages or shorter; any subject; contemporary style; we do use much rhyming poetry." They do not want "greeting-card-type verse; nothing which is hand-written."** *Celebration* has recently published work by Ivan Arguelles, Sheila E. Murphy, Robert K. Rosenburg, and Michael L. Johnson. As a sample, the editor selected the following lines from "Hair Poem" by Lisa Yount:

> Has anyone sung of the wonders of hair?
> Has anyone said how it blows in your eyes and makes rainbows?
> How it nuzzles its way into a kiss

The magazine is digest-sized, 22 pp., offset on white paper, saddle-stapled, with b/w illustration on one-color matte card cover. Circulation is 300. Price per copy is $1.45, subscription $5 for 4 issues. **Sample available for $1.45 postpaid. Pay is 2 copies. No dot-matrix. Reporting time is 3-6 months and time to publication 6 months-1 year**. The editor says, "We do accept work from beginning poets. We recommend that all poets submit about five poems at a time and include a note about oneself and/or a list of some previous publications."

*THE CELIBATE WOMAN: A JOURNAL FOR WOMEN WHO ARE CELIBATE OR CONSIDERING THIS LIBERATING WAY OF RELATING TO OTHERS (IV, Celibacy/women), 3306 Ross Place, NW, Washington, D.C., 20008, phone 202-966-7783, founded 1982, poetry editor Martha Allen, is a communications network among women **on the issue of celibacy and uses approximately 5 poems on that subject in each issue**. It appears irregularly, approximately annually, a digest-sized, saddle-stapled, 32 pp. format, finely printed in small type with tasteful drawings. **Sample: $4 postpaid. Reports in "a few weeks."**

*THE CELTIC LEAGUE, CARN (IV, Specialized), 9 Br Cnoc Sion, Áth Cliath 9, Ireland, founded 1973, poetry editor Alan Heusaff, is a magazine-sized quarterly, circulation 2,000. "The aim of our quarterly is to contribute to a **fostering of cooperation between the Celtic peoples**, developing the consciousness of the special relationship which exists between them and making their achievements and their struggle for cultural and political freedom better known abroad. Contributions to *Carn* come **through invitation to people whom we know as qualified to write more or less in accordance with that aim. We would welcome poems *in the Celtic languages* if they are relating to that aim, and, exceptionally, poems in English, the contents of which would be in agreement with it**. If I had to put it briefly, we have a political commitment, or, in other words, *Carn* **is not a literary magazine**."

CENCRASTUS (IV, Scottish), 34, Queen St., Edinburgh, Lothians, Scotland EH2 1JX, phone 031-226-5605, founded 1979, poetry editor Geoff Parker, is a quarterly magazine "**to create the intellectual and imaginative conditions for a new Scottish nation" which uses "no light verse; long poem a specialty; all poetry to be relevant to Scotland or peripheral living.**" They have published poetry by Edwin Morgan, Kenneth White, Sorley Maclean, Gael Turnbull, Douglas Dunn and international poets. There are 3-8 pages of poetry in each issue. Circulation to 1,000 subscriptions of which a fourth are libraries. **Sample: £1.75 postpaid from USA.** They receive over 400 submissions per year and use 30. 1-2 issue backlog. **Submit 4-8 poems, typed, no query, reports in 1-2 months. Pays £7.50 per poem or £30 per page.**

*THE CENTENNIAL REVIEW (II), 110 Morrill Hall, Michigan State University, East Lansing, MI 48824, phone 517-355-1905, founded 1955, poetry editor Linda W. Wagner, is a well-established quality quarterly, which **uses free, "organic" poetry, especially by women.** They have published poetry by Joyce Carol Oates, David Ignatow and Susan Fromberg Schaeffer. It is an elegant 6x9" format, flat-spined (80 + pp.), **sample $1.50 postpaid, subscription $5 for 4 issues. Submit 3-5 poems, no longer than a page each, no photocopy or simultaneous submissions. Pays 2 copies and year's subscription.** Circulation: 1,200.

*CENTRAL PARK: A JOURNAL OF THE ARTS AND SOCIAL THEORY (IV, Experimental, political focus), Box 1446, New York, NY 10023, founded 1979, poetry editor Eve Ensler, fiction editors Richard Royal, Stephen-Paul Martin, is a beautifully printed, flat-spined (90 + pp.), 7x8½' biannual with quality photography and art, uses **poetry which "is either overtly political in its tone, radically experimental in its form, or—ideally—the combination of both**. It should "reveal an advanced political consciousness, but be conveyed in sensitive and not ideological terms." They have recently published poetry by Charles Culhane, Robert Bly, Marie Cartier, García Lorca, Catherine-Marie Sanders and Marc Kaminsky. As a sample, I selected these lines from Christine Zawadiwsky's "Missing Kisses":

> *you hear the rain sliding down the windows*
> *'til the world is rain, the world is bone,*
> *the bones of the world that are miser.*

They have a circulation of 750, with 100 subscriptions of which 10 are libraries. Of hundreds of submissions received each year they use about 20 and have a 3-4 month backlog. **Sample: $5 postpaid. Considers simultaneous submissions. Reports in 6 weeks, pays 1 copy**. The editors say, "*Central Park* is a place. It is where art and socio-political sensibilities merge. It is not a clearinghouse of literary paraphenalia, but rather a place readers can come to in the hopes of finding the best questions to ask in an increasingly complex and inscrutable society. We expect to alert the reader to new ways of examining the world around him/her, to sensitize him/her to the surrounding environment. Apathy has reached critical stages, and the policies of reactionary leaders have made this kind of heightened awareness necessary to the survival of the race. New and even disturbing literature can help people to crawl out of their numbing fear, to pursue what cause they feel is more lastingly effective than materialism. As a group, we stage readings, benefits and dances so that we can celebrate life together in a supportive way." **They try to provide comment or criticism on each rejected MS.**

*CHANDRABHAGA (IV, Third World), Tinkonia Bagicha, Cuttack, Orissa, India 753001, phone 20-566, founded 1979, poetry editor Mr. Jayanta Mahapatra, is a biannual magazine which **uses poetry "with an Indian/Third World bias suitable for English teaching departments at universities." No sex/gay themes.** They have recently published poetry by A. D. Hope, C. B. Cox, Satchidanandan, and Banshidhar Sarangi. These sample lines, chosen by the editor, are by Bal Sitaram Mardhekar:

> *A little white on black*
> *This sinner is able to scratch*
> *then. O the rest of my days*
> *Only this—some black on white.*

Chandrabhaga is an attractively printed 5½x9½" flat-spined format, using 80-88 pp. per issue, circulation 500, 250 subscriptions of which 50 are libraries. They have a 2 year backlog, receive about 100 freelance submissions of poetry per year, use 30. **Sample: $5 + $3 postage for airmail. "Foreign postage rates have gone up considerably, hence we are trying NOT to take in contributions from abroad, but we will consider poetry which deals with India or Indian problems." Send 4-7 poems, original typescripts. Reports in 8-12 weeks. Pays copies.**

*CHANGING MEN: ISSUES IN GENDER, SEX AND POLITICS (IV, Feminist), (formerly *M. Gentle, Gender, Sex & Politics*), 306 N. Brooks, Madison, WI 53715, founded 1979, poetry editor Franklin Abbott (also poetry editor of *RFD*) is described as "**a pro-feminist journal for men—politics, poetry, graphics, news.**" Franklin Abbott wants "**personal, creative use of language and im-**

age, relevant to journal themes, political themes. "We try to publish as many poets as we can and tend to publish shorter poems and avoid epics." They have published poetry by James Broughton, Sidney Miller, Steven Finch, Louie Crew, Ed Mycue and Denis O'Donovan. Though the poetry is "so varied" the editor felt he could not select 4 representative lines, I chose the opening lines of James Broughton's "Afternoon in Ceylon" illustrated the quality, if not variety, of poetry in the magazine:

> Luncheon had made us hungry for one another
> After the curry and fried bananas
> we added our own heat to the hot afternoon
> simmering in sweat and coconut oil

Uses about 44 pp. of poetry in each magazine-sized issue, circulation 2,000, 1,000 subscriptions of which few are libraries. They have a backlog for 2-4 issues. **Sample: $4 and 9x12" SASE. Submit up to 5 poems, photocopy, simultaneous submissions ok.** Reports in 2-6 months. Pays copies. Send SASE for guidelines. Editor sometimes comments on rejections.

‡*CHANNELS (IV, Christian)**, 1615 Parkinson, Vincennes, IN 47591, phone 812-882-4289, founded 1975, editor Kevin Hrebik, a tri-annual magazine of the Christian Writer's Leage of America. They **"prefer non-controversial Christian material, especially good poetry and fiction, also special forms with Christian content, such as haiku."** They use 150-200 poems/year, 3-25 lines. Pays in contributor's copies. Photocopied, simultaneous, previously published and dot-matrix submissions are acceptable. Reporting time is 2-4 weeks. Sample available for $2.95 postpaid, guidelines free. Uses original art and photography; will consider submissions (nature scenes with water) for cover. The editor says, "Just send 4-6 good poems. Don't write Christian 'baby' material, assume reader is intelligent, literate and mature. Write clearly, make specific points, yet try to be artistic. Make poems flow smoothly, show off your skill."**

CHANTRY PRESS (III), Box 144, Midland Park, NJ 07432, phone 201-423-5882, founded 1981, poetry editor D. Patrick, publishes **perfect-bound paperbacks of "high quality" poetry. No other specifications**. They have published work by Laura Boss, Maria Gillan, Anne Bailie, Ruth Lisa Sckecter, Joanne Riley. These sample lines are from **Winter Light** by Maria Gillen:

> Remember me, Ladies,
> the silent one?
> I have found my voice
> and my rage will blow
> your house down.

That's from an 80 pp. book (usually books from this press are 72 pp.), flat-spined, glossy cover, good printing on heavy paper, author's photo on back, $5.95. **Send SASE for catalog to order sample. Don't send complete MS. Query first, with 5 sample poems, no cover letter necessary. Considers simultaneous submissions. Replies to query in 3 months, to submission in 3 months. Simultaneous submissions OK, photocopy OK. 15% royalties after costs met and 10 author's copies. Very short comment sometimes on rejected MSS**. The editor advises: "Do not be rude in inquiring about the status of your manuscript."

*CHAPMAN, LOTHLORIEN (IV, Scottish)**, 35 E. Claremont St., Edinburgh, Scotland EH7 4HT, phone 031-556-5863, founded 1970, poetry editor Joy Hendry, **"provides an outlet for new work by established Scottish writers,** for the discussion and criticism of this work and for reflection on current trends in Scottish life and literature. But *Chapman* is not content to follow old, well-worn paths; it throws open its pages to new writers, new ideas and new approaches. In the international tradition revived by MacDiarmid, *Chapman* also features the work of foreign writers and broadens the range of Scottish cultural life." As a sample I selected this poem by Fred Cogswell, "Of All the Forms . . .":

> Of all the forms of lesbian venture
> The most innocent and free from censure
> Is the love affair, piquant yet abstruse,
> Between the female poet and her muse.

Chapman appears 3 times a year in a 6x9" saddle-stapled format, 2 issues of 72 pp., 1 issue of 144 pp., professionally printed in small type on matte stock with glossy card cover, art in 2 colors, circulation 2,000, 700 subscriptions of which 200 are libraries. They receive "thousands" of freelance submissions of poetry per year, use about 200, have an 8-12 month backlog. **Sample: £1.50 (overseas). Pays £6 per page. Reports "as soon as possible."** The press, Lothorien, is not interested in unsolicited MSS.

*CHARIOT (I)**, Box 312, Crawfordsville, IN 47933, phone 317-362-4500, founded 1895, editor Loren w. Harrington, is a quarterly "fraternal insurer publication informing **members of the Ben Hur Life Association** of activities and other items of general interest" which uses poems as filler pieces. The sample I have has a full-page poem in large type on the cover, "Hurry Spring," by Mary Kay Hummel, which begins:

> *Some people say they like the snow;*
> *The early winter sunset glow;*
> *Ice crystals hanging on the trees*
> *That sound like wee bells in the breeze.*

They want **"light upbeat humor or poignant items applicable to season or holiday. Nothing of an obscene or sexually-oriented nature."** They have a circulation of 11,000, mailed to members' households (5 libraries). Minimum of 2 months backlog, **reports in 2-4 week, pays $1 and up plus 1 copy, guidelines available for SASE. Multiple and simultaneous submissions OK if advised of circumstances. For sample send 80¢ and a magazine-sized SASE.**

THE CHARITON REVIEW PRESS, *THE CHARITON REVIEW (II), Northeast Missouri State University, Kirksville, MO 63501, phone 816-785-4499, founded 1975, poetry editor Jim Barnes. *The Chariton Review* began in 1975 as a twice yearly literary magazine, and in 1978 added the activities of the Press, producing "limited editions (not chapbooks!) of **full-length collections . . . for the purpose of introducing solid, contemporary poetry to readers**. The books go free to the regular subscribers of *The Chariton Review*; others are sold to help meet printing costs." The poetry published in both books and the magazines is, according to the editor, **"open and closed forms—traditional, experimental, mainstream. We do not consider verse, only poetry in its highest sense, whatever that may be. The sentimental and the inspirational are not poetry for us."** They have recently published poets such as David Ray, T. R. Hummer, Ruth Good, Marcia Southwick, Robert Lietz, J. V. Brummels, Albert Goldbarth and Dagmar Nick. These lines offered as a sample are from "Earthquake Weather" by Richard Robbins:

> *If we walk, it's the same story: quiet and moving*
> *tangles of wave and kelp, a blurred island*
> *seeming to pitch with its mute floating.*
> *Weather inside us stills. Discreetly . . .*

There are 40-50 pages of poetry in each issue of the *Review*, a 6x9" flat-spined magazine of over a hundred pages, professionally printed, glossy cover with photographs, circulation about 560 with 400 subscribers of which 50 are libraries. **Sample: $2 postpaid.** They receive 7,000-8,000 submissions per year, of which they use 35-50, with never more than a 6-month backlog. **Submit 5-7 poems, typescript single-spaced, no carbons, dot-matrix or simultaneous submissions. Payment: $5/printed page. Contributors are expected to subscribe or buy copies. To be considered for book publication, query first—no samples. Payment for book publication: $500 with 20 or more copies**. Usually no criticism is supplied. The sample book I have seen, **The Tramp's Cup**, by David Ray, has an appearance much like the magazine and sells for $3. The prices of both the magazine and books seem remarkably low in view of the high quality of production. Jim Barnes advises poets "Bury your naivety. Ask; don't assume."

‡*THE CHATTAHOOCHEE REVIEW (I, II), 2101 Womack Road, Dunwoody, GA 30338, phone 404-393-3300, ext. 170, founded 1980, editor-in-chief Lamar York, a quarterly of poetry, short fiction, essays, and plays, published by Dekalb Community College, North Campus. **"We like to publish beginners alongside professional writers. We are open to poetry from traditional forms to avant-garde and any subject matter or length or style."** They have recently published poems by Fred Chappell, Rosemary Daniell, Robert Lietz, Lyn Lifshin, and William Paulk. The Review is 6x9", professionally printed on white stock with b/w reproductions of art work, 90 pp., flat-spined, with one-color glossy card cover. Circulation is 1,000, of which 500 are complimentary copies sent to editors and "miscellaneous VIP's." Price per issue is $3.50, subscription $15/year. **Sample available for $3.50 postpaid, guidelines for SASE. Pay is 1 copy. Writers should send 2 copies of each poem and a cover letter with bio material. Reporting time is 3 months and time to publication is 3-4 months. Queries will be answered in 1-2 weeks. No simultaneous submissions. Photocopied or dot-matrix MSS are OK but discs are not. There is a $100 prize for best poem and short story; all authors published in current volume are automatically eligible.**

‡CHAWED RAWZIN PRESS (V), 101 E. Magnolia, San Antonio, TX 78212, founded 1974, editor/publisher Charles Behlen, a small press publisher of poetry chapbooks and poster/broadside series. He has recently published poetry by Albert Huffstickler. The editor chose as a sample these lines from "topping the" by Todd Moore:

> *. . . we didn't say*
> *anything just stood*
> *watching wind pour*
> *fire off the horses*

Sample chapbooks I have seen vary from digest to magazine-sized. Some contain poems by several authors, some by a single author. They are sometimes typeset, sometimes offset from typescript. Stock is white with buff or colored covers, some with illustrations, some saddle-stapled. He also publishes poster/broadsides containing a single poem. The editor says, **"I don't consider unsolicited manuscripts but I never return anything cold."** He publishes **"poems with guts and grace"** after he has **"seen that work in magazines and/or anthologies and contacted the author."** Payment is half the press run. His advice is, "Support the best periodicals and presses in your region with money and your best work. Make occasional forays into the sometimes bigger and/or better-known mags . . . but resist the temptation to start at the top. Stay cold and alone."

*CHICAGO SHEET (II), Box 3667, Oak Park, IL 60303, founded 1984, poetry editor Jeremy A. Pollack, is a tabloid (newsprint) 8-page monthly which the editors call "a conversation through fiction, essay, poetry, and interview, blending current authors/artists with those of the past." They use **a few poems in each issue. They want poetry "such that its meaning and impact are immediate. We try not to be concerned with length**. However, while poetry is necessary to our periodical, we do not focus on it." They have published Chicago-based poets such as Julie Parson, Anthony Fitzpatrick and Grace Chaplin, poets from elsewhere such as Harley Joens and Timothy Pratt, and those of the past, such as Edward Lear, Matthew Arnold and John Milton. These sample lines are the opening of "Uncommon Man" by Scott A. Momenthy:

> I have a yearning.
> It casts this town as a ball and chain.
> But I can take the strain.
> I'm the son of a working man.

They have a circulation of about 250 and have accepted about 10 of the 20 poems submitted their first year. **Free sample for SASE. Prefer typed, double-spaced MSS, report within 4-6 weeks, pays 3 contributor's copies.**

‡**CHICORY BLUE PRESS (II)**, East Street North, Goshen, CT 06756, phone 203-491-2271, founded 1985, publisher Sondra Zeidenstein, a small press publisher of fiction and poetry; the first publication, an anthology of work by writers "who have made their major commitment to writing *after the age of 45*, will be issued in late 1986 in both hardcover and paperback. For future books she wants **the work of poets who take their craft seriously and are continuing to develop and deepen."** MSS can be in **any typed form; simultaneous and freelance submissions are accepted; writers should send 10 sample poems. Queries will be answered in 4 weeks and MSS reported on in 3 months. Pay is in author's copies.** She says, "The paperback edition of the anthology will be *reasonably* priced."

CHILDREN'S BETTER HEALTH INSTITUTE, BENJAMIN FRANKLIN LITERARY AND MEDICAL SOCIETY, INC., *HUMPTY DUMPTY'S MAGAZINE, *TURTLE MAGAZINE FOR PRESCHOOL KIDS, *CHILDREN'S DIGEST, *CHILDREN'S PLAYMATE, *JACK AND JILL, *CHILD LIFE, (IV, Children's health), 1100 Waterway Blvd, Box 567, Indianapolis, IN 46206. This publisher of magazines stressing health for children has a **variety of needs for mostly short, simple poems, for which they pay $7 minimum. Send SASE for guidelines**. For example, *Humpty Dumpty* is for ages 4-6; *Turtle* is for preschoolers, similar emphasis, uses many stories in rhyme—talking animals, etc.; *Children's Digest* is for ages 8-10; *Jack and Jill* is for ages 6-8. *Child Life* is for ages 7-9. All appear 8 times a year in a 6½x9" 48 pp. format, slick paper with cartoon art, very colorful. The editors advise that writers who appear regularly in their publications **study current issues carefully. Samples: 75¢ each, postpaid.**

‡***CHIMERA (I)**, 4215 N. Marshall Way, Scottsdale, AZ 85251, phone 602-946-7056, founded 1981, poetry editors Agnese Voinotti, Marilyn Szabo, and Neal Berg, a literary and visual arts quarterly journal that wants **poetry of** "any subject and every style; quality is the criterion." They have recently published poetry by David Chorlton, Ken Stone, and Paul Weinman. As a sample, the editors chose the following lines by Agnese Voinotti:

> A bullet; horrible noise of disaster
> and the color red covers the earth.
> I never knew blood, so beautiful
> when spilled on virgin snow

Chimera is 8¼x8¼", 54-60 pp. with a hand-printed cover, "printed on a limited edition basis." Its circulation is 500-1,000; "we sell out." Price per issue is $3.50, subscription $17.50/year. **Sample available for $3.50 postpaid, guidelines for SASE. Pay is 1 copy. Writers should send 5 poems at a time. Reporting time is 4-6 weeks and the backlog is 2 issues.**

‡***CHIMERA CONNECTIONS (I, II)**, 3712 NW 16th Blvd., Gainesville, FL 32605, phone 904-378-0251, founded 1985, poetry editors Jeff VanderMeer and Duane Bray, appearing three times a year, is "**open to all submissions, any style, any length. Please send letter of inquiry first. We appreciate**

Close-up

Nikki Giovanni
Poet

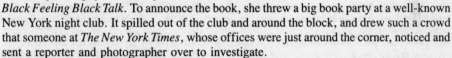

Nikki Giovanni's philosophy in writing is direct and to the point. "You look for your own market," she says, "and if you can't find it, you create it. You have an obligation to present your work, to make sure as many people know about it as possible, to maximize your visibility."

Giovanni's introduction to the world as a writer exemplifies this philosophy. She self-published her first book, *Black Feeling Black Talk*. To announce the book, she threw a big book party at a well-known New York night club. It spilled out of the club and around the block, and drew such a crowd that someone at *The New York Times*, whose offices were just around the corner, noticed and sent a reporter and photographer over to investigate.

"We got a lovely story out of the *Times*, and a picture on the second front page," Giovanni relates. "But it was not a 'break'—I worked a lot for that one."

The author of twelve books of poetry for children and adults, as well as books such as *A Dialog: James Baldwin and Nikki Giovanni* and *Gemini* (a book of essays), Giovanni has been called "the poet laureate of young black women and sensitive souls everywhere"—a title well deserved. Her poetry succeeds in bringing a substance to feelings often undiscussed, but felt by many, as she writes of mothers and children, love, the reality of life in many venues—a near-infinity of concerns, images, and emotions. And she brings a special voice to writing about being black—a voice neither self-conscious nor intimidating, but a voice that demands attention.

That voice springs from her character. Nikki Giovanni is impressive and memorable both as a writer and as a person. It is easy to feel that Giovanni and her work are thus because of the honesty of her motives in writing—motives that she passes on to other writers in her advice to "believe in what you are doing. Write what you believe in. Don't be afraid to break new ground."

Like her writing, Giovanni's observations on contemporary American writing are right on target. She sees poetry as a fairly constant field, with not all that many newcomers, but she does believe that the field is wide open. "I don't believe that most writers will be able to take advantage of this," she adds, "because they can't make the sacrifices involved."

And what are those sacrifices? According to Giovanni, there is some measure of sacrifice in believing in oneself, in breaking new ground—something that she feels that few poets are doing—and in having the courage to communicate with honesty.

"Of necessity, publication is a prerequisite to success. As a writer, you should want to be published. But before you would want to be published, you must be sure of who you are. Actors can be fixed up, but writers are who they are, and it shows. That's where young writers lose it . . . they want to get something out there very quickly. They are trying to adjust to the market. One of the problems with American arts and letters now is that too many people are trying to satisfy a market that doesn't exist."

She also cites persistence as an element of success in writing poetry. "If there are 200 million people in this country, there are 199 million who think they can write poetry. So it's a real stick-to-it business." She welcomes competition, however, in the form of talented poets whose work will attract an audience to poetry in general. "You always want a real strong poet out there, because the more people who come in and say they want poetry, the better it is for all."

Giovanni offers her strongest encouragement to new writers in urging them to do as she has. "You have to make up your mind what your writing means to you. Don't take anyone's word for it as to whether or not you are a poet."

—*Michael A. Banks*

---

cover letters. No religious or inspirational poetry, no matter how good the poem may be." They have published poems by Erskine Carter, Kenneth Geisert, Agnes Homan, Jan Kovach, and Donna Thomas. As a sample the editors selected the following lines from Kenneth Geisert's "Candlelight Contemplation":

> Off in the distance, I discerned the hollow calling,
> as if in supplication, one of nature's
> feathered creatures, frightened of the dark
> as am I.

Chimera Connections is digest-sized, 50 pp., photocopied with saddle-stapled textured cover. Circulation is about 200. Each issue has a contest with a $2 entry fee and $25, $15 and $10 prizes. Winning entries, including honorable mentions, are published in the magazine, along with accepted general admissions. A subscription, $7.50 for 3 issues, brings contest and magazine information and newsletters; or one may become a *Chimera Connections* colleague, $16, to receive the above plus 3 in-depth critiques per issue and a reduced contest entry fee of $1/poem. **Sample: $2.50 postpaid. Pays 1 copy. MSS should have name and address on each page of single-spaced typescript or printout. Submissions are reported on after each contest deadline, and there is no backlog. Simultaneous submissions OK. "All rejected poetry is sent back with a mini-critique and suggestions for improvement."**

*CHINESE LITERATURE (IV, Translations), 24 Baiwanzhuang Road, Beijing, China, founded 1951, is a quarterly of **"translations of Chinese fiction, poetry, art, etc., for readers abroad." They do not accept foreign submissions, but choose poetry reflecting Chinese life by such poets as Ai Qing and Lu Yuan. They pay their contributors, have a circulation of 50,000. For samples, write for catalog** from China International Book Trading Corporation, Box 399, Beijing, China.

*CHOICE MAGAZINE (IV, Religious), (formerly *Solo: The Christian Magazine for Single Adults*), Box 1231, Sisters, OR 97759, phone 503-549-0443, poetry editor Ann Staatz, is "to provide the Christian single adult, ages 25-45, practical information and Biblical inspiration that will enable them to grow and live victoriously; to remind the single adult that they were created for a purpose, and are loved mercifully by the Heavenly Father, to challenge the reader to be all they can be for God's glory. **We prefer free verse, poetry that's feeling-oriented and relational. We don't want greeting card-type verse. Don't use much rhyming poetry. Poems should be 20 lines or less, should deal with life from a Christian world view."** They have recently published poetry by Mari Hanes and Barbara Penwarden. The magazine-sized quarterly, 54 pp., glossy paper, circulation 28,000, 22,000 subscriptions, uses less than 1 page of poetry per issue. (The issue I examined had none.) They receive 150 + submissions of freelance poetry per year, use 3-4. **Sample: $2 plus 9x12" SASE. Submissions should be double-spaced, no more than 2 at a time. "Query preferred but not required." Dot-matrix OK. Reports in 60-90 days. Pays $15-$75 per poem. Send SASE for general writers' guidelines.** The editor comments, "I see a lot of poetry, but very little that is creative in ideas or artfully crafted."

‡*CHRISTIAN EDUCATORS JOURNAL (IV, Christian education), 639 Ridge, Ripon, CA 95366, phone 209-599-2265, founded 1960, managing editor Lorna Van Gilst. A quarterly journal geared toward Christian day school educators, the magazine wants poetry to fit on one page, magazine-sized; **focus must be Christian day school education.** Poets recently published include Luci Shaw, Richard French, and Joan Mills. The editor selected the following lines from Luci Shaw:

> That the glory may be of God
> Each day he seems to shine
> from the more primitive pots
> the battered bowls . . .

The magazine is published quarterly during the school year, 36 pp., enamel cover. Circulation is 3,550 with 3,500 subscriptions. **Sample: $1 postpaid. Payment is $10/published poem plus 1 free copy. Submissions are reported on in 4-6 weeks, but the magazine has a 1-2 year backlog.**

THE CHRISTIAN SCIENCE MONITOR (II), 1 Norway St., Boston, MA 02115, phone 617-262-2300, founded 1908, a national daily newspaper with a weekly international edition. Poetry used regularly in The Home Forum. Pays $25 and up.

‡*CHRISTIANS WRITING (I, IV, Christian), 2/724 East St., Albury 2640, New South Wales, Australia, founded 1980, publisher Paul Grover, a small-press literary quarterly "with **contents focusing upon the Christian striving for excellence in poetry**, prose and occasional articles relating Christian views of literary ideas." In poetry, the editors want **"shorter pieces with no specification as to form or length (necessarily less than 3-4 pages), subject matter, style or purpose. People who send material should be comfortable being published under this banner—'Christians Writing'."** They have recently published poetry by John Foulcher and other Australian poets. As a sample, the editors selected the following lines by Andrew Lansdown:

> *. . . His gaze is distant.*
> *He is dreaming. To be a blower,*
> *he says, to be a didgeridoo-man*
> *is good. You know? Get respect. Get proudness.*

Christians Writing is digest-sized, printed in brown on heavy beige-colored stock, 25 pp. saddle-stapled, matte card cover of the same color with brown decorations, graphics and line drawings. Circulation is 270, all subscriptions. Price per issue is $5 (Aus), subscription $15 (Aus). **Sample available (air mail from U.S.) for $7 (Aus). Pay is 1 copy. Submissions may be "typed copy or dot-matrix or handwritten or simultaneous—or even calligraphy!" Reporting time is 2 months and time to publication is 6 months.** The magazine conducts a bi-annual poetry and short story contest. The editor says, "Trend in Australia is for imagist poetry and poetry exploring the land and the self. Reading a magazine gives the best indication of their style and standard, so send a few dollars for a sample copy before sending your copy. Keep trying, and we look forward to hearing from you."

*CIMMARON REVIEW (II), 208 Life Science East, Oklahoma State University, Stillwater, OK 74078, founded 1967, poetry editor Michael J. Bugeja, is a quarterly 64-pp literary journal "reflecting humanity in contemporary society. We seek literary examples of **Man Triumphant in a technological world. We emphasize quality and style. We like clear, evocative poetry (lyric or narrative) that uses images to enhance the human situation. No obscure poetry. No sing-song verse. No quaint prairie verse. No restrictions as to subject matter, although we tend to publish more structured poetry (attention to line and stanza)**. Also, we are conscious of our academic readership (mostly other writers) and attempt to accept poems that everyone will admire." Among poets they have published are Robert Cooperman, James McKean, David Citino and Lynn Domina. Michael Bugeja selected these representative lines by Patrick Lawler:

> *Maybe the taptaptap of distant hammers*
> *Will stop. Maybe the pine turning to stone*
> *Will be still for a moment. Ask the worker*
> *Whose daughter was alive for two hours.*

There are 8-10 pages of poetry in each issue, circulation of 500, 350 subscriptions of which about 300 are libraries. They get about 1,500 submissions per year, of which they use 20-30, and have a 6 month backlog. **Free sample. Submit to Jeanne Adams Wray, managing editor, any time, 3-5 poems, name and address on each poem, typed, single or double-spaced. Clear photocopies acceptable, but no dot-matrix and no simultaneous submissions. Replies within 2 weeks-2 months. They pay when they have a grant to do so. "Nearly all rejections have some sort of personal comment, from suggested revisions to encouragement or advice."** The editor advises, "Many beginning writers confuse creativity with freedom of expression. We define it as the ability to rise above the limitations of poetic form (free verse included) and to inform, entertain or evoke emotions from your readers. By the same token, **we believe in editing our poems (with permission from writers, of course) to make them more readable, clear, powerful, etc**. All changes are worked out carefully with writers before poems are accepted."

CITY LIGHT BOOKS (III), 261 Columbus Ave., San Francisco, CA 94133, phone 415-362-8193, founded 1955, poetry editors Lawrence Ferlinghetti, Nancy Peters and Robert Sharrard, achieved prominence with the publication of Allen Ginsberg's **Howl** and other **poetry of the "beat" school**. They publish flat-spined paperbacks and hardbacks. **Simultaneous submissions OK, payment varies, reporting time 4 weeks.**

CITY MINER BOOKS (IV, Regional/northern California), Box 176, Berkeley, CA 94703, founded 1975, editor Michael Helm, is a **regional press which primarily publishes northern California writers and expects to publish no more collections of poetry through 1987. Query with five samples. Catalog available for SASE.**

‡THE CITY PAPER (II), Washington Free Weekly, Inc., 919 6th St., N.W. Washington, DC 20001, phone 202-289-0520. Founded 1981. Associate editor: Kara Swisher. *The City Paper* is a typical big-city "what's-going-on-in-our-town" weekly tabloid newspaper. This one is distributed free and is very heavy on advertising. The 63 pp. contain mostly reviews and listings of activities, plus one page of poetry in the copy I have. Poets published on that page were John Glassie, Janice Lynch, John B. McCarthy, Kathryn Rhett, and Reuben M. Jackson, from whose "late october blues (for bessie smith)":

> *if houdini returns*
> *give him my address*
>
> *loan him cab fare*
>
> *tell him not to be afraid*
> *of coming*
> *into a black neighborhood*
>
> *cause I need him to*
> *make all this heartache disappear*

The paper will publish **"any kind of poetry except bad poetry." It pays $10/poem and will give contributors as many free copies as they want. Considers simultaneous submissions. Submissions are reported on in 2 weeks, and the editors sometimes provide critiques of rejected MSS.**

*THE CLASSICAL OUTLOOK (IV, Translations, classical, original Latin), Classics Dept., Park Hall, University of Georgia, Athens, GA 30602, founded 1924, poetry editor Dr. Jeffrey Duban, "is an internationally circulated quarterly journal (3,000 subscriptions, of which 250 are libraries) for high school and college Latin and Classics teachers, published by the American Classical League." They invite **"submissions of verse translations from Greek and Roman authors of all periods, of original poems on classical themes, and of original Latin verse. 'Free verse' is discouraged. Translations should exhibit consistency of rhythm, syllabification and diction, and the adroit handling of rhyme whenever rhyme is used. Limit of 50 verses [lines]."** They have recently published work by David Middleton, Robert Lindsay and Herbert Huxley. As a sample I selected the first stanza of John S. Anson's "Iphigenia":

> *The wind has disappeared for days,*
> *becalmed because the king has sinned.*
> *His daughter's death alone can raise the wind.*

There are 2-3 magazine-sized pages in each issue, and they use 58% of the approximately 100 submissions they receive each year. They have a 6-12 month backlog, 4 month lead time. **Submit 2 copies, double-spaced. Receipt is acknowledged by letter. Poetry is refereed by poetry editor, and, in the case of Latin, by two additional outside readers. Reports in 3-6 months. Pays in 5 complimentary copies. Guidelines available for SASE.**

‡*CLOCK RADIO, TEN MILLION FLIES CAN'T BE WRONG (I, II), 116 Northwood Apts., Storrs, CT 06268, phone 203-429-7516, founded 1984, editor Jay Dougherty. *Clock Radio* is a small press magazine of "a-formal" poetry, published 2-3 times per year. *Ten Million Flies Can't Be Wrong* is a newsletter-style supplement which publishes mainly poetry but also letters, listings of other little magazines, and sometimes reviews; it appears 3 times a year. **Both accept concrete poetry or "typewriter" poetry; they do not want to see pedantic or religious pieces.** Some of the poets they have published recently are Alta, Tom Clark, Lyn Lifshin, Charles Plymell, Robert Peters, Gerald Locklin, and Ivan Arguelles. As a sample, the editor selected the following lines from Charles Bukowski's "working out" about Van Gogh's cutting off an ear to give to a prostitute:

> *Van, whores don't want*
> *ears*
> *they want*
> *money.*

Clock Radio is 6x9", 20 pp., typeset then photocopied, saddle-stapled, yellow matte card cover with black lettering and design by Markus Grossner. *TMFCBW* is magazine-sized, typeset then photocopied, with art by Markus Grossner. Circulation of *CR* is 500, price $1.50/issue, 3 issues for $4. Circulation of *TMFCBW* is 400. **Sample: $1.50 plus a business-sized envelope, postpaid. Pay is in copies. Submissions are reported on in 1 week, MSS published in 1-4 months. MSS should be typed, single-spaced, with name and address on each page. Freelance submissions for chapbooks are accepted. Photocopied or dot-matrix MSS are acceptable.** The editor advises, "Read other poets and, if budget allows, *Clock Radio*."

*CLOCKWATCH REVIEW, A LAKE COUNTRY CHRISTMAS, CHRISTMAS IN WATERTOWN (I, II), Driftwood Publications, 737 Penbrook Way, Hartland, WI 53029, phone 414-367-8315, founded 1982, "publishes primarily *Clockwatch Review* **and two annual Christmas booklet**

fundraisers, A Lake Country Christmas and Christmas in Watertown, both with circulations of 2,400. James Plath is editor, and Elizabeth Balestrieri, John Blum, and Mary Ann Emery are associate editors. "It is our belief that the **audience for contemporary poetry/fiction could and should be broader**, and it is our goal to try to accomplish that by producing **a quality journal in a visually appealing style/format**. We publish a variety of styles, leaning toward poetry which goes beyond the experience of self in an attempt to SAY something to other people, without sounding pedantic or strained. We like a **strong, natural voice**, and lively, unusual combinations in language. **Something FRESH, and that includes subject matter as well as word combinations. It has been our experience that extremely short/long poems are hard to pull off**. Though we'll publish exceptions, we prefer to see poems that can fit on one published page (digest-sized) which runs **about 32 lines or less**.They have recently published James Dickey, Dave Etter, Margaret Gibson, John Judson, David Ignatow, Lisel Mueller, Howard Nemerov, Ronald Wallace and Pat Hutchings. Asked for a sample, the editors say "trying to pick only four lines seems like telling people what detail we'd like to see in a brick, when what we're more interested in is the design of the HOUSE." Nonetheless, they selected these sample lines from Jared Carter's "Damaged Money":

> *Now in each handful given to you*
> *See how hammers have blurred old monuments,*
> *Industrial wastes dribbled across*
> *The profiles of the great, the illustrious.*

The 56 pp. biannual *CR* is printed on glossy paper with colored, glossy cover (with striking art—so that it "might serve as a coffee table book, allowing people the chance to read it bit by bit"). They use 7-10 unsolicited poems in each issue, and 9-12 pp. of featured poets. Circulation is 1,300, 82 subscribers, of which 12 are libraries. They send out 200-300 complimentary copies and "The balance is GIVEN out as promotion for the magazine and made available to the general public . . . which is our goal in the first place. For example, we've placed sample copies in the waiting rooms of doctors and dentists, given copies out at art fairs and symphony concerts, polo matches, and conventions in order to reach people who would not normally spend money to buy a poetry/arts magazine." **Sample: $3 postpaid.** They receive 350-400 submissions per year, use 15-20. No backlog. **Prefer batches of 5-6 poems. "We are not bowled over by large lists of previous publications, but brief letters of introduction or sparse minivitas are read out of curiosity. One poem per page, typed, single-spacing OK, photocopy OK if indicated that it is not a simultaneous submission (which we do NOT accept). We do not guarantee that we will wade through submissions sent on dot-matrix." Reports in 2-8 weeks. Payment (other than 2 copies) only to featured poets**; but we're working on a 'years best' incentive program. We hope to get into the chapbook/awards 'game' in the future, but only when we feel we can do a first-rate job of it, to make it special in some way, and different from the run-of-the-mill press competitions where the $6-7 reading fee pays the freight." **They will comment if asked**, but "cringe as we do so because we anticipate the reaction on the other end. It has been our experience that when a writer asks for criticism, what he or she really wants is praise." James Plath comments, "Give your poems time to cool down before you send them off . . . The act of the 'high' to wear off. I suspect that too many writers are taking poems right from the typewriter rollers and stuffing them in envelopes with SASE enclosed . . . only to get them back a month later and be able to see flaws in the work." **Amateurs and children might submit to the Christmas booklets in August and September; address envelopes to Christmas Booklets**. I chose this sample poem from **Christmas in Watertown** for 1983. It's by Shannon O'Donnell, Grade 6:

> *White snow drifts slowly,*
> *The freezing snow strikes faces.*
> *Tears of loneliness.*

"**No droll retellings of Christ's birth, and no epic narratives. We look for upbeat poems that are well-crafted, on the general subjects of Christmas and/or winter." Reports in 2-8 weeks, payment: 2 copies**.

CLOUD RIDGE PRESS (V), Box 926, Boulder, CO 80306, founded 1985, editor Elaine Kohler, a "literary small press for unique works in poetry & prose." They publish letterpress and offset books in both paperback and hardcover editions. In poetry, they want **"strong images of the numinous qualities in authentic experience grounded in a landscape and its people."** The first book, published in 1985, was **Ondina: A Narrative Poem**, by John Roberts. As a sample, the editor selected the following lines:

> *Then sinuous as shedding snakes,*
> *They part the robes,*
> *reveal the opening*
> *of naked fullness in the night.*

The book is 6x9¼", handsomely printed on buff stock, cloth bound in black with silver decoration and spine lettering, 131 pp. Eight hundred copies were bound in Curtis Flannel and 200 copies (of which mine is one) bound in cloth over boards, numbered and signed by the poet and artist. This letterpress edition, priced at $18/cloth and $12/paper, is not available in bookstores but only by mail from the press. The trade edition, due in the fall of 1986, will be photo-offset from the original, in both cloth and paper bindings, and will be sold in bookstores. The press plans to publish 1-2 books/year. **Since they are not accepting unsolicited MSS., writers should query first. Queries will be answered in 2 weeks and MSS reported on in 1 month. Simultaneous submissions are acceptable, as are photocopied or dot-matrix MSS. Royalties are 10% plus a negotiable number of author's copies. A brochure is free on request; send #10 SASE.**

*CLUBHOUSE, YOUR STORY HOUR (II), Box 15, Berrien Springs, MI 49103, founded 1949, poetry editor Elaine Meseraull, **pays about $10 for poems under 24 lines. The publication is printed in conjunction with the Your Story Hour** radio program which is designed to teach the Bible and moral life to children. The magazine, *Clubhouse*, started with that title in 1982, but as *Good Deeder*, its original name, it has been published since 1950. Elaine Meseraull says, "**We do like humor or mood pieces. Don't like mushy-sweet 'Christian' poetry. We don't have space for long poems. Best—16 lines or under.**":

> *From out of my bedroom window*
> *I can look on a beach of sand,*
> *And some nights I hear feet pounding*
> *Across the silvery strand.*

The magazine has a circulation of 15,000-17,000, 15,000 subscriptions of which maybe 5 are libraries. It is free (10 times a year) for the first year to kids 9-13 years old; otherwise $3. **Sample: 3 oz. postage. Writer's guidelines are available for SASE, simultaneous submissions OK. The "evaluation sheet" for returned MSS gives reasons for acceptance or rejection.**

THE CLYDE PRESS (IV, Folk), 373 Lincoln Parkway, Buffalo, NY 14216, phone 716-875-4713, 834-1254 and 268-5789, founded 1976, poetry editor Catherine Harris Ainsworth, specializes in folklore, oral literature, ethnic tales and legends, games, calendar customs, jump rope verses, superstitions and family tales—all edited and left in the words of the informants, and all taken from collections that cover about 30 years, 1952-82. They will consider submissions of **folk poetry and songs from bona fide folk collections, "i.e. recorded from the folk or written by the folk, really sung or recited." Query with samples. Provides 2 author's copies and payment after expenses of publication are met. Send SASE for booklist to order samples.**

COACH HOUSE PRESS (II), 401 (Rear) Huron St., Toronto, Ontario Canada M5S 2G5, phone 416-979-2217, founded 1965, poetry editors Michael Ondaatje, B. P. Nichol and Frank Davey, publishes "mostly living Canadian writers of 'post-modern' poetry and fiction. Some U.S. and U.K. They have printed finely-printed flat-spined paperback collections by such poets as Phyllis Webb, Michael Ondaatje, Diana Hartog, Sharon Thesen and Bill Griffiths. They want "**no religious, confessional stuff." Query with about 15 samples. Cover letter should cover bio and other publications but "please—no aesthetic philosophy." Double-spaced, photocopy or dot-matrix OK. Reports in 4-16 weeks. Contract is for 10% royalties, 10 copies**. To see samples, send SASE for catalog and buy direct, or "Beyond Baroque Foundation and Northwestern University receive everything we do." Clifford James says, "We encourage poets to publish a number of individual poems in magazines before expecting to interest a publisher in a book-length MS. A poet must have developed an audience in order to sell even 500 books, and work appearing in magazines is the best way to develop a following."

COBBLESTONE PUBLISHING CO., *COBBLESTONE, *FACES (IV, Children), 20 Grove St., Peterborough, NH 03458, phone 603-924-7209, founded 1979, *Cobblestone* is a monthly history magazine for young people ages 8-14; *Faces* is a magazine about people (cultural anthropology) for the same age group; they also publish *Classical Calliope*, on the classics, but it is done inhouse. **Each issue is planned around a theme, so contributors should send SASE for guidelines to learn themes for future issues. They want clear, objective imagery in serious or light verse up to 100 lines, for which they pay on an individual basis.** The issue of *Cobblestone* I have seen was finely printed, saddle-stapled, 48 pp. of heavy 7x9" pages with glossy cover (with photo), richly illustrated—on the theme of the Wright Brothers and the Story of Aviation.

‡COFFEE HOUSE PRESS, MORNING COFFEE CHAPBOOKS (V), Box 10870, Minneapolis, MN 55440, phone 612-338-0125, publisher Allan Kornblum, a small press publisher of fiction, poetry, and children's books. The editor says, "**We strongly discourage poetry submissions. Our poetry titles are primarily solicited.**" Some poets the press has published are Anne Waldman, Faye Kicknosway, Alice Notley, and Ed Sanders. They publish 10 poetry chapbooks each year, flat-spined paperbacks, some hardcovers. **Writers should query, sending credits, sample poems (½ of the MS), and bio. Accepted poets are usually previously published or award-winning. Simultaneous submissions and photocopied or dot-matrix MSS are OK. Royalties are 7.5-10%, "sometimes." Criticism of rejected MSS is provided. Catalog is free on request.** Though I have not seen samples, accor-

ding to the catalogs the chapbooks are priced from $5 to $7.50 and average 24 pp. Offset trade books are $8.95-12.95 and average 94 pp. The catalog says, "The Coffee House Press has made the chapbook form its own, blending the energy of the varied voices of American poetry with the patient craft of fine printing. . . . We hope that each book, featuring original art, signed by author and artist, and designed according to the needs of the work at hand, reflects the joy our work gives us."

‡*CO-LABORER, WOMAN'S NATIONAL AUXILARY CONVENTION (IV, Religious), Box 1088, Nashville, TN 37202, phone 615-361-1010, founded 1935, editor Lorene Miley, is "a quarterly publication to give women a missionary vision and challenge. **We'll consider any length or style as long as the subject is missions.**" **They do not want to see poetry which is not religious or not related to missions**. As a sample I selected this quatrain from Lorene Miley's pamphlet. **A Guide to Better Poetry:**

> Only God can make a snowflake
> As it flutters to the ground;
> Make it shine like lustery silver
> Let it fall without a sound

The digest-sized 32 pp. magazine uses one poem on the back page of each issue, circulation 18,000. **Sample: free for SASE. The WNAC (Free Will Baptist) also publishes an annual collection of poetry. Guidelines are available in a "Creative Arts Contest." For Free Will Baptist women only. Reports immediately. Pays 3 copies.**

COLD-DRILL BOOKS, *COLD-DRILL (IV, Regional/Idaho), Dept. of English, Boise State University, Boise, ID 83725, phone 208-385-1246, founded 1970, publishes **primarily Boise State University students, faculty and staff, but will consider writings by Idahoans—or writing about Idaho by 'furriners.'**" They do some of the most creative publishing in this country today, and it is worth buying a **sample of** *cold-drill* **for $5** just to see what they're up to. This annual "has been selected as top undergraduate literary magazine in the US by such important acronyms as CSPA, CCLM and UCDA." It comes in a box stuffed with various pamphlets, postcards, posters, a newspaper, even 3-D comics with glasses to read them by (which I couldn't make work). **No restrictions on types of poetry**. As yet they have published no poets of national note, but Tom Trusky offers these lines as a sample, from Patrick Flanagan, "Postcard From a Freshman":

> The girls here are gorgeous, studying hard,
> many new friends, roommate
> never showers, tried to
> kill myself, doctor says
> i'm getting better

Circulation is 400, including to 100 subscribers, of which 20 are libraries. **"We read material throughout the year, notifying only those whose work we've accepted Dec. 15-Jan. 1st. Manuscripts should be photocopies with author's name and address on separate sheet, simultaneous submissions OK. Payment: 1 copy.**" They also publish two 24 pp. chapbooks and one 75 pp. flat-spined paperback per year. **Query about book publication**. "We want to publish a literary magazine that is exciting to read. We want more readers than just our contributors and their mothers. Our format and our content have allowed us to achieve those goals, so far." I would advise discretion in regard to mothers.

*COLLEGE ENGLISH, Dept. of English, University of Alabama, Drawer AL, University, AL 35486, founded in 1937, poetry editor, James Tate, appears 8 times a year, uses 5-7 pp. of poetry each issue. Circulation: 15,000, in addition to 2,000 library subscriptions. Sample: $4 postpaid.

‡*COLONNADES (IV, College students), Box 5246, Elon College, Elon College, NC 27244-2010, editor Lauri S. Crowder, a publication **open to all college students** that holds contests in poetry, short stories, graphics, and arts. **"We want to promote the up and coming poets found in the general student body." They do not want works by "professional" poets or those that want to only establish public credits.**" The journal appears once a year in the spring. It is magazine-sized, 32 pp. Circulation is 3,000, evidently free to the student body. **Submissions are accepted through the end of January for each spring publication. Student competitions have awards of $50 and $25.**

*COLORADO REVIEW (II), (formerly *Colorado State Review*), English Dept., 359 W. O. Eddy Bldg., Colorado State University, Ft. Collins, CO 80523, phone 303-491-6428, founded 1977, poetry editor Bill Tremblay, is a literary journal which appears twice annually—one fiction issue, one poetry issue. **"We're interested in poetry that explores experience in deeply-felt new ways; merely descriptive or observational language doesn't move us to want to print it. Poetry that enters into and focuses on experience, weaving sharp imagery, original metaphor, and surprising though apt insight together in compressed precise language is what triggers an acceptance here**." They have recently published poetry by Paul Nelson, William Hathaway and Lyn Lyfshin. They have a circulation of 350, 150 subscriptions of which 75 are libraries. They use about 10% of the 500-1,000 submissions they receive per year. **Sample: $2 postpaid. Submit about 5 poems, typewritten or clear photocopy. "We do not look kindly on having poems we accept being withdrawn because the poet has accepted publication with another magazine (so much for simultaneous submissions)." Reports no later than 6 months, usually 3. Pays $5/page and copies. "When work is a near-miss, we will provide comment**." Bill Tremblay says, "Our attitude is that we will publish the best work that comes across our editorial desks, regardless of subject, theme, or obsession, though we want work of substance, ambition, clarity of language and focus, as well as originality. We see poetry as a vehicle for exploring states of feeling, but we aren't interested in sentimentality (especially metaphysical)."

*COLORADO-NORTH REVIEW (II, IV, Avant-garde), University Center, University of North Colorado, Greeley, CO 80639, founded 1968, "is a student-staffed and student-funded magazine which prints 3 issues per year, none summer months." They want "**avant-garde poetry. Please no Longfellow-esque tomes, no overdone constructs. Only rhyme if not trapped by a metronome. Short poetry (no more than 40 lines) preferred; a light heart and heavy editing pen should rule a poet who submits here. We are receptive to any theme as long as it is approached in a fresh way**." They have recently published poetry by Lyn Lifshin, Ken Poyner, Veronica Patterson, Rita Kiefer. B. Z. Niditch, Mitch Clute, Alber Huffstickler, Brother Eddie, John E. Ames, Richard Dean, Dieter Weslowski and Paul Witherington. These sample lines are by James Sutherland Smith from "On Parliament Hill":

> *I should compose a sentence for us*
> *Slender and bare of complication*
> *As a poplar becomes in Winter.*
> *It should be singular as a bench on a hill.*

They have a circulation of 3,000 with 105 subscriptions of which 53 are libraries. It's a digest-sized flat-spined 68 pp. format with 30-40 pp. of poetry in each issue. They receive about 600 submissions per year, use around 110. **Sample: $2.50 postpaid. Submit no more than 15 pieces. Simultaneous submissions, photocopy, dot-matrix OK. Reports in maximum of 2 months. Pays 2 copies. "We critique if requested to do so**."

COLUMBIA: A MAGAZINE OF POETRY & PROSE (II), 404 Dodge, Columbia University, New York, NY 10027, founded 1977, appears 1-2 times yearly, 200 + pages, 5x8", circulation 200, offers an annual Editors' Awards contest, $200 prize for poetry, entry fee $5.

COMET HALLEY PRESS, *COMET HALLEY MAGAZINE, *COMET WITH NO NAME, COMET COMPANION, (II), 1363 Oliver Ave., San Diego, CA 92109, phone 619-270-0327, founded 1984, poetry editor Brian C. Clark, assistant editor Sheila Seiler-Clark. *Comet Halley Magazine* is quarterly; each magazine has a companion chapbook. *Comet With No Name* is published irregularly along with a broadside series called *Kamikazee Comet*. They want "**no porn for porn's sake. Want well-written poetry full of image that gives the reader a memorable experience**." They have recently published poetry by Fred Raborg, Ken Sutherland, Michael Hemmingson. The editor offers these sample lines by Darin Peabody (from "Naked Is the Night"):

> *There we were modern-day stranded*
> *in the middle of the vast wasteland*
> *Southern California, known as the Mojave Desert.*

All their publications are inexpensively produced, photocopied from typescript (with card covers on the chapbooks). Some are single-sheet folded leaflets. *Comet Halley* is a "magazine-sized 22 pp. side-stapled format, photocopied magazine with a circulation of 200 + , 75 subscriptions. **Sample: $2 postpaid. "We will not hold work more than 3 months. Will read any legible submission and write specific, personal reply within 1 week. Photocopy and simultaneous submission OK, as long as so stated**." Guidelines and book catalog available for SASE. For chapbooks, submit complete MS with cover letter telling bio, publications, personal or aesthetic philosophy, poetic goals and principles. Payment for chapbooks 10% of print run, for magazine copies. Brian C. Clark says, "I always write a note explaining why MS has been rejected/accepted, often suggesting specific rewrites. Be persistent. Write letters to your editors. Proofread! Always put name and address on every page. Many submitters to *Comet Halley* receive free information, poetry publications, etc. I try to stay on top of the small press publications and often inform my submitters of new publications, old ones closing shop, special issues, and on and on."

*COMMON LIVES/LESBIAN LIVES; A LESBIAN QUARTERLY (I, IV, Lesbian), Box 1553, Iowa City, IA 52240, founded 1981, edited and published by "a collective of lesbians committed to reflecting the diversity among us by actively soliciting and printing in each issue the work and ideas of lesbians of color, Jewish lesbians, fat lesbians, lesbians over 50 and under 20 years old, physically challenged lesbians, poor and working-class lesbians, and lesbians of varying cultural backgrounds. *CL/LL* feels a strong responsibility to insure access to women whose lives have traditionally been denied visibility and **to encourage lesbians who have never thought of publishing to do so.**" It's a flat-spined, glossy-covered, professionally printed paperback, digest-sized, 100 + pp., with a circulation of around 2,000, 700 subscriptions of which 30 are libraries. 3 month backlog. **Sample: $4 postpaid. "We prefer non-'abstract,' experiential/narrative/poetry. Submit 10 pp., typed. Photocopy OK, dot-matrix discouraged, no simultaneous submissions. "Bio must accompany all submissions—non-academic preferred." Reports in maximum of 6 months. Payment: 2 copies**.

*COMPASS: POETRY & PROSE, AUSTRALASIAN WRITING (IV, Regional/Australia, New Zealand), Box 51, Burwood, N.S.W. Australia 2134, founded 1978, poetry editors Chris Mansell, Joanne Burns, Dorothy Featherstone Porter, is a quarterly which **publishes Australian and New Zealand poets almost exclusively. They want "adventurous" poetry, do not want to see poetry from "hobbyists."** They have a circulation of 600-700, use about 5% of the submissions received. **Sample: $5 foreign, $3 Australian, postpaid. Pay varies. Will comment if requested**. The editor advises, "Read as much contemporary poetry from all over the world, especially Australia, as possible."

‡CONDITIONED RESPONSE PRESS, *CONDITIONED RESPONSE (II), 361 Hayes Ave., Ventura, CA 93003, founded 1982, poetry editor John McKinley, a small-press publisher of poetry only—magazine and occasional chapbooks. The editor says, **"We accept all forms. Poems can be of any subject matter and the acceptable length depends upon the poem. We want to see an ingenious use of language and a conscious awareness of the effects of run-on lines and endstops and their function within the poem. We do not want to see archaic verse, light verse, or poems about kittens or puppies."** He has recently published poetry by Randall Kennedy, Nancy Lopez, and Ronald Edward Kittell. As a sample, he selected the following lines by an unidentified poet:

> *a mute menagerie of corpses*
> *assembled for our introspection*
> *a gathering of the dead*
> *responding to death's reveille call*

Conditioned Response appears "annually or more" and has a circulation of 100 +; there are no subscriptions. The digest-sized publication contains poetry only, no illustrations except a cover photograph. It is professionally printed on lightweight stock, 24 pp., matte card cover, saddle-stapled. **Sample: $2.50 postpaid; pay is 2 copies. The editor says, "Prefer 5-10 poems in one batch, typewritten, simultaneous submissions not encouraged, but who's going to know anyway right?" Submissions are reported on in less than 1 month and publication time is up to 1 year.** The press publishes no more than 1 chapbook per year, 24 pp., same format as the magazine. **For chapbook consideration, writers should send 15 sample poems, credits, bio, philosophy, and "why does the poet wish to publish with us?" Photocopied MSS are OK, but not dot-matrix or discs; personal replies with all submissions. Pay for chapbooks is 15 author's copies. Sample books: $3.** The editor advises, "Wanda Coleman explained her struggle to stay afloat in this way—'cuz poetry doesn't pay.' Poetry markets is an oxymoron. Unlike many other arts, poetry begets little financial reward. Write it and live it because you love it . . . but being a lawyer helps too."

CONFLUENCE PRESS, BLUE MOON PRESS, INC. (IV, Native American or western poets), Spalding Hall, LC Campus, Lewiston, ID 83501, phone 208-746-2341, editor changes each semester, founded 1975, publishes paperback collections of poetry by **Native Americans and poets from western states. Pays copies. Query with samples. Decision in 2 months.**

*CONFRONTATION MAGAZINE (II), English Dept., C. W. Post of Long Island University, Greenvale, NY 11548, founded 1968, poetry editor Winthrop Palmer, is "a semi-annual literary journal with **interest in all forms.** Our only criterion is high literary merit. We think of our audience as an educated, lay group of intelligent readers. **We prefer lyric poems. Length generally should be kept to 2 pages. No religious or overly sentimental verse.**" They have recently published poetry by Siv Cedering, T. Alan Broughton, David Ignatow, Colette Inez, Donald Junkins, Joseph Brodsky. As a sample I selected the first stanza of David Galler's "Rotten Dreams":

> *It's no disgrace*
> *To dream you look in a mirror*
> *And see your mother's face,*
> *Or the kitchen floor.*

Basically a magazine, they do on occasion publish "book" issues or "anthologies." It's a digest-sized professionally-printed, flat-spined, 190 + pp. journal with a circulation of about 2,000. **Sample: $2 postpaid.** They receive about 1,200 submissions per year, publish 150, have a 6-12 month backlog. **Submit no more than 10 pp., clear copy (photocopy OK). "Prefer single submissions." Reports in 6-8 weeks. Pay: $5 to $40.**

THE CONNECTICUT POETRY REVIEW (II), Box 3783, New Haven, CT 06525, founded 1981, poetry editors J. Claire White and James William Chichetto, is a "small press that puts out an annual magazine. We hope to be a bi-annual magazine by '86. **We look for poetry of quality which is both genuine and original in content. No specifications except length: 10-40 lines**." The magazine has won high praise from the literary world; they have recently published such poets as William Virgil Davis, Robert Peters, Sue Standing and Ruth Feldman. Each issue seems to feature a poet. These sample lines are by John Updike:

> They were old friends. She held up a paw, and he
> injected a violet fluid. She swooned on the lawn,
> and we watched her breathing slowly ebb to naught.
> In the wheelbarrow up to the hole, her fur took the sun.

The flat-spined, 60 pp. large digest-sized journal is "printed letterpress by hand on a Hacker Hand Press from Monotype Bembo." Most of the 60 pp. are poetry, but they also have reviews. Circulation is 400, with 80 subscriptions of which 25 are libraries. **Sample: $3.50 postpaid.** They receive over 700 submissions a year, use about 20, have a 3 month backlog, **report in 3 months, pay $5/poem plus 1 copy.** The editors advise, "Study traditional and modern styles. Study poets of the past. Attend poetry readings. And write. Practice on your own."

*CONNECTICUT RIVER REVIEW (II), 30 Burr Farms Rd., Westport, CT 06880, founded 1977-8, poetry editor Peggy Heinrich, a semiannual, wants "**poetry of depth—emotional—but well-controlled. Strong, down-to-earth themes. No haiku.**" They have recently published poetry by Dick Allen, Ruth Krauss, Kathleen Spivack, Lyn Lifshin and Philip Miller. I selected these sample lines, the first stanza of Ralph Nazareth's "The Water Path":

> Now that you are here
> to pay your last respects
> I must be brief. My breaths are scarce
> as stones in a ravaged quarry.

Each of the plain but attractively printed, digest-sized issues contains about 35 pp. of poetry, has a circulation of about 300, with 175 subscriptions of which 5% are libraries. They receive about 1,500 submissions per year, use about 70. **Sample: $4 postpaid. Submit no more than 6 poems. Rejections within 2 months, acceptances could take 3-6 months. Pays 2 copies. They offer an annual Brodine Award. Rarely comments.**

‡*THE CONNECTICUT WRITER (II), Box 10536, West Hartford, CT 06110, an annual publication of the Connecticut Writers League, founded in 1980 (previously called "Harvest"), poetry editor Fay Manus. **The magazine sponsors annual awards in both poetry and short fiction, with first and second prizes of $50 and $25, plus publication and complimentary copies. They are "open to all kinds of poetry—short has a better chance"** (65 lines maximum for contest). **They do not want "very long, dense."** Poets recently published include Ann Zoller, Christine Swanberg, and Charles Darling. As a sample, I selected the beginning lines from the 1985 first-prize winning poem, "Ole Mike's Harp" by Robert E. Nelson:

> When Ole Mike blow his harp
> all them black days come out.
> He close his eyes,
> and he open his insides,
> and summertime come out like steam.

The magazine is digest-sized, professionally printed on white stock, flat-spined with glossy card cover illustrated with b/w photo of a Connecticut writer. Circulation is 500. Price per issue is $5 (or $5 postpaid). **Sample: $5 postpaid, and guidelines are available (after April of each year) for SASE. Pay is 2 copies plus reduced rates for contributors.** As to submissions the editor says, "I struggle with poor quality typing or printouts. We do not keep a backlog from year to year. All submissions are considered for that one issue only." Criticism is rarely provided, and there are no reading fees except that there is a $2 reading fee to enter the annual contest.

‡*CONNECTIONS MAGAZINE (II), Bell Hollow Road, Putnam Valley, NY 10579, phone 914-526-3420, founded 1973, editor Toni Ortrer-Zimmerman, a small press publisher of fine quality poetry in its annual magazine, *Connections*. **The editor wants "free verse, modern" but no "cliche, sentimental, sexist, violent, end rhyme."** Her emphasis is on women poets, both well known and unknown; she has recently published Natalie Robins and Lyn Lifshin. She says the magazine, which I have not seen, is 7½x9", "offset on fine quality paper with cover art and excellent line drawings." Circulation is 700. **Sample available for $3.50 plus 85¢ postage. Pay is 1 copy. Writers should submit 5 poems at a time, typed, no photocopies or simultaneous submissions. Reporting time is "immediate" and time to publication varies. SASE required.** The editor comments, "My plans for *Connections Magazine* are open right now—I am still selling off backlog on issues six and seven."

COOP. ANTIGRUPPO SICILIANO, CROSS-CULTURAL COMMUNICATIONS, TRAPANI NUOVA (II), Via Argenteria, Km 4, Trapani, Sicily, Italy, 91100, phone 0923-38681, founded 1968, poetry editor Nat Scammacca, is a group of over 100 poets involved in international activities pertaining to poetry including readings, sponsored visits, and publication in the weekly cultural newspaper, *Trapani Nuova*, or in collections or anthologies. **Free samples**. Scammacca says, " **We translate and publish short poems every week in *Trapani Nuova* and, on occasion, in our anthologies**. This year we have published several thousand American poems and have included 20 American poets including Simpson, Stafford, Bly, Ferlinghetti, Corso, Ignatow, etc. We like **ironical poetry, committed poetry (anti-atomic), intelligent poetry; we do not want poetry that makes no sense, rhetorical stuff, sentimental, or poets who think each word or line is God-sent. The poem must *communicate*. We prefer short poems, but if the poem is exceptional, we want it. Short poems we can translate into Sicilian and Italian and use in our weekly in a week's time**." The editor selected a sample from Scammacca's "A Love Poem at 60" from *Schammachanat* Nov. 1985, 4x8", 96 pp. blue & white cover with art by Nicole D. Alessandro and Gnazino Russo:

> "*I feel great today, my love,*"
> *I say to my wife, nibbling at her ear from behind.*
> "*Good," she says,*
> "*when you go out, take the garbage with you.*"

Send poems of 4-15 lines to Nat Scammacca. "The poet must send his best poetry. If it is difficult but makes sense he can explain why he wants us to publish the poem, why he wants us to suffer. We want, otherwise, enjoyable, witty, intelligent and if possible great poetry." Apparently one gets acquainted by submitting to the weekly. If you want **to send a book MS, query first, with cover letter giving biographical background, personal or aesthetic philosophy. Payment in copies of the published book**. "They are lucky when we publish them," says the editor. The nonprofit cooperative is supported by government funds; it organizes poetry tours, radio and TV appearances and readings for some of the authors they have published. "We want other poets to be sufficiently confident in themselves so as not to ask for our opinion concerning their poetry. We prefer having the poet himself explain why he writes, for whom and why he writes as he does. We do not want to substitute our methods for his methods."

COPPER BEECH PRESS (II), Box 1852, English Dept., Brown University, Providence, RI 02912, phone 401-863-2393, founded 1973, poetry editor Edwin Honig, publishes **books of all kinds of poetry**, about three 48 pp. flat-spined paperbacks a year. They have recently published poets such as Blasing, Schevill and Jane Miller. I selected these lines by Keith Waldrop as a sample:

> *Even in dreams I hear*
> *nothing but songs of passion*
> *sung by a cardinal*
> *from a sycamore behind the house.*

Query with 5 poems, biographical information and publications. Replies to queries in 1 month, to submissions in 3 months, payment: 10% of press run.

‡**CORDILLERA PRESS (II, IV, Spanish)**, 4 Marshall Road, Natick, MA 01760, 617-653-3354, founded 1976-78, re-established 1983, managing director Raffael DeGruttola. Cordillera is a small-press publisher of **poetry chapbooks including some bilingual editions. The editor wants to see serious political poetry, as well as new forms, experimentation in feeling and form, moderate length, 100 or less pages, preferably around 60 pp., including haiku. He does not want traditional academic poetry**. He has published books by Ted Thomas, Jr., Martin Espada, and Sura Ting. As a sample, he selected the following lines by an unidentified poet:

> *and there was clapping*
> *that grew louder and louder*
> *clap clap clap clap clap clap clap clap*
> *and the compas*
> *commemorating the dead*
> *ahahahahahah ayyyyyyyyyy*

Cordillera publishes one or two chapbooks per year; the page count and the format vary (haiku books are smaller with fewer pages). Of the samples I have seen, some are typeset and some are offset from typed copy, but all are beautifully done and some have illustrations. Paper varies from heavy buff stock to glossy, as do the covers. Some books are saddle-stapled and some are flat-spined. Prices are $3 and $4. **Cordillero pays royalties; 15% minimum, 20% maximum. Writers should query before submitting, sending 6-10 sample poems, bio, philosophy, and aesthetic or poetic aims. Queries will be answered in 1 month, MSS accepted or rejected in 1 month. Both photocopied and dot-matrix MSS are acceptable**. There is no subsidy publishing; book catalog is available on request; sample books can be purchased at 40% discount. They offer no grants or awards, but do provide criticism of rejected MSS.

The editor comments: "New writing in this century has followed many divergent trends—from symbolism, imagism, surrealism, dada, the different fusing of the arts, experiments with language, sound-text poetry, concrete poetry, the influence of the wars, the vision of self (confessional poetry) and today's exploits into changing syntax or meaning in how language works. Cordillera Press hopes to keep an open mind with respect to experimentation and the evaluation of feeling, sense, and form."

*CORNERSTONE; THE VOICE OF THIS GENERATION (IV, Religious), Jesus People USA, 4707 N. Malden, Chicago, IL 60640, phone 312-561-2450, editor Dawn Herrin, is a mass-circulation (100,000), low-cost ($1.75 per copy, bimonthly **directed at youth, covering "contemporary issues in the light of Evangelical Christianity." They use avant garde, free verse, haiku, light verse, traditional—"no limits except for epic poetry. (We've not got the room.)" Buys 10-50 poems per year, uses 1-2 pp. per issue, has a 2-3 month backlog. Submit maximum of 10 poems. Pays 10¢ per word. Send SASE for guidelines.**

CORNERSTONE PRESS, *IMAGE MAGAZINE (II), Box 28048, St. Louis, MO 63119, editors A. Summers, J. Finnegan, F. Brungardt and T. Adams, phone 314-296-9662, founded 1972, publishes chapbooks, flat-spined paperbacks and anthologies of poetry in addition to *Image*, "a magazine of the arts," appearing three times a year, which the editors describe as a "typical small press and literary magazine, except we tend to be **a bit off the wall. We'll look at any kind of poetry if it's well-written. 5-10 pages with each submission; longer works require our consent.**" They have published poetry by Guenther, Neruda, Schwartz, Fericano, Clifton and Montesi. Generally 60-75% of each issue (40-180 pp., usually flat-spined) is devoted to poetry. They have over 500 subscriptions of which 10-20 are libraries, receive 4,000-5,000 submissions per year and use about 10% of those. **Sample: $3.50 postpaid. MSS may be in "any legible format, no simultaneous submissions." Reports in 1-4 weeks and pays "sometimes—$1-100." Guidelines available for SASE.** In addition, the Press is open to submissions of collections. **Query with 5-10 pages of sample poems.** Reply to queries is "ASAP," to submissions in 4-6 weeks. They publish on **royalty contract (percentage varies) and minimum of 10 copies. They comment on MSS "usually—and if it is requested, certainly**." The editor advises poets to "read literary magazines and standard classical fare."

*CORONA (II), Dept. of History and Philosophy, Montana State University, Bozeman, MT 59717, phone 406-994-5200, founded 1979, poetry editors Lynda and Michael Sexson, "is an interdisciplinary annual bringing together reflections from those who stand on the edges of their disciplines; those who sense that insight is located not in things but in relationships; those who have deep sense of playfulness; and those who believe that the imagination is involved in what we know." In regard to poetry they want **"no sentimental greeting cards; no slap-dash."** They have recently published poems by Richard Hugo, X. J. Kennedy, Donald Hall, Philip Dacey, Wendy Battin, William Irwin Thompson, Frederick Turner and James Dickey. Asked for a sample, they said, "See journal for examples. We are not interested in cloned poems or homogenized poets." Journal is flat-spined, 125-140 pp., professionally printed, using about 20-25 pp. of poetry per issue, circulation 2,000. **Sample: $7 postpaid. Submit any number of pages, photocopy and dot-matrix ok, no simultaneous submissions. Reports in 1 week to 3 months. Payment is "nominal" plus 2 contributor's copies.** The editors advise, "Today's poet survives only by the generous spirits of small press publishers. Read and support the publishers of contemporary artists by subscribing to the journals and magazines you admire."

*COSMOPOLITAN (III), 224 W. 57th St., New York, NY 10019, founded 1886, is a monthly magazine "aimed at a female audience 18-34," part of the Hearst Conglomerate, though it functions independently editorially. They want **freshly-written free verse, not more than 75 lines, either light or serious, which addresses the concerns of young women. Prefer shorter poems, use 1-4 pages each issue,** they say, though the sample they sent me happened to have none. They have recently published poems by Erica Jong, Rod McKuen and Tricia McCallum. They have a **circulation of 2,987,970. Buy sample at newsstand. Reports in 3-5 weeks, pays $25 and up.** "Please do not phone; query by letter if at all, though queries are unnecessary before submitting."

‡COTEAU BOOKS, THUNDER CREEK PUBLISHING CO-OP (II, IV, Western Canada), Box 239, Sub #1, Moose Jaw, Saskatchewan S6H 5V0, Canada, phone 306-693-5212, founded 1975, managing editor Heather Wood, a "small literary press that publishes poetry, fiction, drama, anthologies, children's, resource books, primarily those written by western Canadian writers." **Poetry should be "of general interest to Canadian or American audience."** They have recently published poetry by Lorna Crozier, Gary Geddes, and Mick Burrs. **Writers should submit 20-50 poems "and indication of whole MS," typed; simultaneous submissions accepted; letter should include publishing credits" and bio. Queries will be answered in 2-3 weeks and MSS reported on in 2-4 months. Pay is 10 author's copies.** They publish 1-3 paperback flat-spined books of poetry per year and 1-3 hardcover volumes. Their attractive catalog is free for 6x9" SASE. It says: "The Thunder Creek Co-op presently has two divisions—Coteau Books and Caragana Records. Membership has changed through the years in the co-op, but now stands at 10. Each member has a strong interest in Saskatchewan writing and culture."

‡*COTTON BOLL/THE ATLANTA REVIEW (IV, Regional), Box 76757, Sandy Springs, Atlanta, GA 30358-0703, founded 1985, "reflections of the contemporary South." Poetry should be "high in good imagery, any style or length although in long poems preference is for narrative. No rhyming couplets in iambic pentameter; no pornography, religion, lovelorn or racism." Poets recently pulbished include R. T. Smith, Bettie Sellers, Suzanne Paola, Kenneth Anderson, and Marianne Andrea. As a sample, the editor selected the following lines from "Tipsy Lawson" by William Sullivan:

> Over a hundred for twenty-nine days
> no rain and none in sight. Bean vines are little
> puffs of pale yellow spiderweb wafted
> between bleached sky and parched earth, turning to . . .

Cotton Boll is digest-sized, nicely printed on buff stock (prose is double-spaced), 115 pp. flat-spined with one-color matte card cover illustrated by a drawing of a cotton boll. Circulation is 1,000, of which half are newsstand sales. Price per issue is $5.50, subscription $20/year. **Sample is available for $5.50 postpaid, SASE absolutely required for guidelines. Pay is 1 copy plus 25% off any additional copies of issue in which author appears. Poems, 3-6 in a batch, should be typed single-spaced within stanzas, double-spaced between stanzas, one poem/page, author's name on each page. Reporting time is 1-6 weeks and backlog from 3-6 months. "No dot-matrix, no multiple submissions, must not have been printed elsewhere."** A contest was planned for August, 1986. The editor's advice is: "Study the magazine."

COTTONWOOD PRESS, *COTTONWOOD (II,IV, Regional/Midwest), Box J, Kansas Union, Lawrence, KS 66045, founded 1965, poetry editor Philip Wedge. The Press "is auxiliary to *Cottonwood Magazine* and publishes material by authors in the region. Material is usually solicited. We will not be reading new material for book submissions in 1986." For the magazine they are looking for "strong narrative or sensory impact, non-derivative, not 'literary,' not 'academic.' Emphasis on midwest. Don't prefer rhyme. Poems should be 1 page or less, on daily experience, *perception*. We also have an upcoming special issue on black Midwest writers, for which we need submissions." They have recently published poetry by William Stafford, Jed Carter, Stephen Hind, Victor Contoski, W.S. Merwin, Jack Anderson and Kathleen Spivack. The editors selected these sample lines by Robert Harlow:

> my gas cap locked
> against the sudden
> need
> of deer.

The 6x9", flat-spined (80 + pp.) magazine is published 2-3 times per year, attractively printed though from typescript, with photos, using 20-30 pages of poetry in each issue. They have a circulation of 300, 150 subscriptions of which 75 are libraries. They receive about 750 submissions per year, use about 70, have a maximum of 1 year backlog. Price per issue, $4, **sample: $3 postpaid. Submit up to 5 pp., dot-matrix, photocopy OK. They sometimes provide criticism on rejected MSS.** The editors advise, "Read the little magazines and send to ones you like." Payment: one copy.

‡*THE COUNTRYMAN (IV, Rural), Sheep St., Oxford OX8 4LH, England, phone Rurford 2258, founded 1927, editor Christopher Hall, a quarterly magazine "on rural matters." The editor wants **poetry on rural themes, "available to general readership but not jingles."** I have not seen the magazine so cannot give a description or quote samples, but it does **pay: a maximum of £12/poem. Submissions should be short. Reporting time is "within a week usually," and time to publication is "3 months-3 years."**

*CRAB CREEK REVIEW (II), 806 N. 42nd, Seattle, WA 98103, phone 206-634-3199, founded 1983, poetry editor Linda J. Clifton, appears 3 times per year, 32 pp., attractively-printed on newsprint. Their **guidelines (available for SASE) indicate that they want poetry which is "free or formal, with clear imagery, wit, voice that is interesting and energetic, accessible to the general reader rather than full of very private imagery and obscure literary allusion. Translations accepted—please accompany with copy of the work in the original language. Prefer poetry under 40 lines; occasionally use longer work, and prefer 80-120 lines there to fit our page size and layout. Payment: 2 copies. (We're working on establishing enough funding to pay in actual cash.)"** They have published poetry by Mark Halperin and Ernesto Cardenal and offer as a sample these lines from "Charlotte McAllister at She-Nah-Nam" by Shannon Nelson:

> *This land's more than you can imagine—like*
> *A husband's hands, a child moving from your blood*
> *Into the air.*
> *Pinpoints of light poke through the door of hides.*
> *In the air, the smell of the fir needles giving up.*

They have about 20 pp. of poetry in each issue, circulation 500, 150 subscriptions of which 10 are libraries, receive 400-500 submissions per year from which they choose 50-60 poems, have a 1 year backlog. **Sample: $3 postpaid, subscription $8 per year. Listed in** *Index of American Periodical Verse.* **Submit up to 6 pp., photocopy, dot-matrix OK, no simultaneous submissions; reports in 6-8 weeks. Sometimes comments on rejections.** Linda Clifton advises poets to "read a sample of the magazine, but don't try to clone what you've seen there for your submission."

THE F. MARION CRAWFORD MEMORIAL SOCIETY, *THE ROMANTIST, *THE WORTHIES LIBRARY (IV, Form/style), Saracinesca House, 3610 Meadowbrook Ave., Nashville, TN 37205, founded 1975, is dedicated to "**Romanticism as a valid literary credo**—renamed the more accurate 'Romantism' . . . ignoring those few over-studied early Romantics such as Byron, Shelley and Keats who mostly stressed the personal and subjective . . . . Instead, we are providing a forum for studying the more subtle, wide-ranging Romantists who emphasized the Ideal and the Imaginative. We especially incline toward fantasy poems." They publish *The Romantist* magazine, single poems in various formats ("Occasional Verse" series) and are open to publishing book-length collections of poems by individuals and anthologies. They want to see, "**Romantic verse but NO mush love poems; Poe, Clark Ashton Smith, George Sterling and Robert Frost are good examples of our taste. Preferably 16 lines or less, lyrical strength a must. Free verse seldom accepted, prefer rhymed and metrical, no ugly modern verse; no homespun, trite rhymed verse; no clichés.**" They offer these lines by Marianne Andrea as a sample:

> *Amidst the flowering Judas,*
> *Leaves turned a brown and angry hue;*
> *October firethorn was starkly red,*
> *Sun hardened as its blood withdrew.*

(One of the few publishers I know of who would take a poem using the word *amidst*.) *The Romantist* is an annual, magazine-sized, flat-spined collection published in an edition of 300 for 200 + subscribers (of which about 30 + are libraries). Samples not available because of limitation to 300 copies. They **use 10-15 freelance submissions per year. Send no more than 3, no simultaneous submissions. Stocked through 1986. Reports in 30 days.** No pay, but author may purchase a copy at half the $8 price. To **submit book MS, query with samples. Replies in 30 days. 10% contract with 5 copies. Subsidy publication can be arranged with 10% royalties after production costs are recovered. Criticism of rejected MSS.** The editors advise, "Read good poetry from the library. Shun forced rhymes, clichés, poeticisms; strive for images and language; avoid modern ugliness and obscurity."

*CRAWLSPACE (I), 908 W. 5th St., Belvidere, IL 61008 (address all correspondence to editor Dennis Gulling), founded 1980, "a **scrappy, no-frills, hardtop mag that publishes scrappy, no-frills, hardtop poems.**" It looks more like a newsletter, photocopied on typing paper, folded, making about 16 pp., with cartoon-like art on the front. It comes out twice a year, with a circulation of 100-150. **Sample free for 39¢ postage on 6x9" envelope.** Each issue is on a theme. I have seen "The Housewife Issue" and one called "TV Edition," from which the editor selected these sample lines, from "6:30 NEWS" by Kirk Robertson:

> *the toll had risen to 11*
> *and they'd found 11 glasses*
> *that once held blood*
> *all with lip prints*

"Want: poems that are hard-edged, wiry, snappy, passionate, honest and cinematic. Don't want: poems that are wimpy, academic, sentimental, trendy, clumsy, anemic, cut, self-important or 'poetic.' **Prefer poems less than 50 lines. I avoid rhyme (unless it sounds like a drinking song), haikus and limericks. Writers should query first to see what the upcoming theme will be.**" He receives 100-150 poems per year, uses 40-45, has a 1-6 month backlog. "**Poems should be typed, single-spaced (photocopies OK). One poem per page.**" No simultaneous submissions. Reports in 1-4 weeks. No pay."

‡*CRAZY QUILT QUARTERLY (II), Writer's Bookstore and Haven, 3341 Adams Ave., San Diego, CA 92116, founded 1986, poetry editors Jackie Cichetti and Bill Jarosin, is a quarterly literary magazine "**seeking good poetry, any style or length, other than long.**" **Simultaneous submissions, previously published poems, photocopies OK. Sample: $3.95 postpaid.** They have a press run of 500, use about 100 poems/year.

‡*CREAM CITY REVIEW (II), Box 143, University of Wisconsin, Milwaukee, WI 53201, founded 1975, poetry editor Marcia Hesselman, is "a small university-based, student-run literary magazine. We publish local and national talent in the magazine, broadsides and posters." They want to see "**all kinds of high quality poetry. Form is open. The only prohibition is hackneyed verse or pornography. We're especially interested in poems dealing humanely with human relationships but we are open to any topic and form. We judge quality as freshness or uniqueness of form, style, and content with a genuine sincerity of tone.**" They have recently published poetry by Maxine Chernoff, Amy Clampitt, Lawrence Ferlinghetti, May Sarton, Marilyn Hacker and Lewis Turco. The magazine appears twice a year with 20-30 pp. of poetry in each issue, circulation 1,000. $3.50 per issue, $6 per year. **Sample: $4 postpaid. Type one per page, name and address on each page. Photocopies, dot-matrix OK. Simultaneous submissions OK if so noted. Reports in 8-10 weeks. Pays 1 copy. Editor usually comments on returned MSS.** Marcia Hesselman says, "Beginners shouldn't be discouraged if they aren't accepted on the first try. I'm happy to work with poets of merit and have often published poets who have sent poems several times before acceptance."

CREATIVE LOAFING (II), 750 Willoughby Way, NE, Atlanta, GA 30312, editor Deborah Eason, is a weekly 50+ pp. tabloid newspaper, circulation 100,000, which uses some **poetry, pays $2.25/14 picas and $3/19 picas. Sample: free for SASE.**

‡*THE CREATIVE URGE, *DARK STAR (I, IV, Science fiction), Drawer 417, Oceanside, CA 92054, phone 619-722-8829, founded 1984, editor and publisher Marjorie Talarico. *The Creative Urge* is a monthly magazine that publishes poetry, articles on and about writing, stories and essays, with monthly theme contests: *Dark Star* is a new (1986) quarterly with fantasy/horror, science fiction emphasis. For the former, the editor wants "**poems/prose of any subject/length unless specified by monthly contest theme**"; for the latter, "**poems/prose with horror/occult/sci-fi/mystery themes; any length unless specified in contest.**" For both magazines, she does not want to see anything "**pornographic/highly erotic, political. We use religious/inspirational poetry in one issue a year.**" She has recently published poetry by Clay Harrison and Kay Gibson. As a sample of poetry from *The Creative Urge*, she selected the following lines by Jan Maxwell Stephens:

> You cannot mask your candid eyes
> For, this has long been proven wise.
> With empty words and vacant deed
> You cannot heal a heart in need.

The Creative Urge is magazine-sized, 20-30 pp., illustrated with pen and ink drawings; it uses 25-30 poems/month. Circulation is about 300, price per issue $2, subscription $15/year. **Sample available for $2 postpaid, guidelines for both magazines available for SASE. Pay is up to 4 copies. "We accept photocopy, dot-matrix printed, handwritten (legible, please), simultaneous submissions." Reporting time is 4-6 weeks and time to publication is 2-4 months. "We offer publishing grants, reports, cash prizes for contests. Fees are charged only if writer wishes help in revising material and terms are negotiable then."** The editor says, "Subscription rates [for *Dark Star*] will be $4 single issue, $12/year. *The Creative Urge* will be using four 'guest columnists' each issue . . . They'll be 'paid' in copies and their column will appear with their byline for 12 issues. We'd like to hear from people with something to say about the craft of writing."

CREATIVE WITH WORDS PUBLICATIONS (C.W.W.), SPOOFING (I, IV), Box 223226, Carmel, CA 93922, phone 408-625-3542, founded 1975, poetry editor Brigitta Geltrich-Ludgate, **offers criticism for a fee**. It focuses "on furthering a. **folkloristic tall tales** and such; b. creative writing abilities in **children** (poetry, prose, language-art); c. creative writing in **senior citizens** (poetry and prose). The editors organize and sponsor an **annual poetry contest, offer feedback on MSS submitted to this contest**, and publish on a wide range of themes relating to human studies and the environment that influence human behaviors. **$2 reading fee per poem, includes a critical analysis.** The publications are anthologies of children's poetry, prose and language art; anthologies of senior citizen poetry and prose; and *Spoofing: an Anthology of Folkloristic Yarns and Such*, which has an announced theme for each issue. "**Want to see: folkloristic themes, poetry for and by children; poetry by senior citizens; topic (inquire). Do not want to see: too mushy; too religious; too didactic; expressing dislike for fellowmen; political; pornographic poetry.**" Guidelines available for SASE, catalog for 25¢. The samples I have seen of *Spoofing!* and an anthology of poems by children are low-budget publications, photocopied from typescript, saddle-stapled, card covers with cartoon-like art. **Submit 20-line, 40 spaces wide maximum, poems geared to specific audience and subject matter.** They have published poetry by Richard M. Watson, Douglas Dwyer, Nona Brown Thompson, Margaret Goings and Mary V.L. Traeger, offering as a sample these lines by Anne Webb Armentrout:

> Is this all I shall have of eternity?
> Sitting here, bare feet dangling

> *Over muddy, moving water,*
> *Leaning my head against your arm.*

"Query with sample poems, short personal biography, other publications, poetic goals, where you read about us, for what publication and/or event you are submitting." Their contests have prizes of $15, $10, $5, $1, but they hope to increase them. "No conditions for publication, but **CWW** is dependent on author/poet support by way of subscription and/or purchase of a copy or copies of other publications." The editor advises, "Trend is proficiency. Poets should research topic; know audience for whom they write; check topic for appeal to specific audience; should not write for the sake of rhyme, rather for the sake of imagery. Feeling should be expressed (but no mushiness). Topic and words should be chosen carefully; brevity should be employed."

CREDENCES: A JOURNAL OF 20TH CENTURY POETRY & POETICS (II), 420 Capen Hall, SUNY, % Poetry Collection, Buffalo, NY 14260, focuses on "special collection librarianship" and articles on 20th century poetry, but **wants original poetry and essays. Sample: $5 postpaid.**

‡***CREEPING BENT (II)**, 433 W. Market St., Bethlehem, PA 18018, phone 215-691-3548, founded 1984, editor Joseph Lucia, a literary magazine that focuses on serious poetry, fiction, book reviews and essays, with very occasional chapbooks published under the same imprint." **"We publish only work that evidences a clear awareness of the current situation of poetry. We take a special interest in poems that articulate a vision of the continuities and discontinuities in the human relationship to the natural world." The editor does not want "Any attempt at verse that clearly indicates the writer hasn't taken a serious look at a recent collection of poetry during his or her adult life."** He has recently published work by Joan Colby, Charles Edward Eaton, Robert Gibb, Harry Humes, Walter McDonald, and Patricia Wilcox. As a sample, he chose these lines by an unidentified poet:

> *To see this flower,*
> *you must lie down*
> *in old leaves, moss, the peaty rubble*
> *of years, tilt the brown bell upward,*
> *and with your eyes descend : .*

Creeping Bent is digest-sized, nicely printed on heavy stock with some b/w artwork, 48-64 pp. saddle-stapled with glossy white card cover printed in black and one other color. It appears twice a year, spring and fall; issue No. 2 was a special one featuring poetry and fiction by women. Circulation is 250, of which 175 are subscriptions, 25 go to libraries, and 25 are sold on newsstands. Price per copy is $3, subscription $6/year. **Sample available for $3 postpaid, guidelines for SASE. Pay is 2 copies plus a 1-year subscription. "Absolutely no simultaneous submissions!" Photocopied and dot-matrix MSS are OK. Reporting time is usually 2-3 weeks and time to publication is 6 months at most.** The editor says, "Before submitting to any magazine published by anyone with a serious interest in contemporary writing, make certain you understand something about the kind of work the magazine publishes. Be familiar with current styles and approaches to poetry, even if you eschew them."

***CRITERION REVIEW, CRITERION WRITING COMPETITION (I)**, Box 16315, Greenville, SC 29606, founded 1982, poetry editor Terri McCord, is "to publish and inform writers of competence who are not writing for a living." They also publish occasional chapbooks. They have recently published poetry by Philip Bird and Thomas Allen. The editor selected these sample lines by Jonathan F. Lowe, from "Riddle":

> *Quarrelling, the first gull flies.*
> *The surging foam has swallowed down the beach.*
> *Without its claw a sandcrab dies*
> *Grappling out of reach.*

Criterion Review is a quarterly using about 5 pp. of poetry in each issue, circulation 750, 600 subscriptions. Subscription: $8. They receive 200-300 submissions per year, use 20-30, have a 4-month backlog. **Sample: $2.50 postpaid. Submit up to 4 poems. Reports in 2 weeks. Pays copies and up to $5/ poem. The Criterion Writing Competition, December 31 deadline each year, has $1 entry fee per item, poems up to 16 lines, with cash awards of $75, $50 and $25 in both fiction and poetry. The editor offers criticism for $5 per poem or per 1,000 words, if requested.** He advises, "Writing is rewriting."

CRONE'S OWN PRESS (IV, Feminist), 310 Driver St., Durham, NC 27703, phone 919-596-7708, founded 1981, poetry editor Elizabeth Freeman, **"publishes the work of older women who are feminists and women-identified."** Elizabeth Freeman says, **"I am an older woman with limited resources both physical and monetary. I expect the women I publish to do some of the work of producing and distributing the book."** The digest-sized chapbooks are attractively printed, 40 pp., saddle-stapled with colored matte cover. She has published work by Bonnie Davidson and offers these opening lines from "Shape Of a Load," by Margaret Budicki (from **Splinters**) as a sample:

> *In the string bag against my leg*
> *potatoes are heavy but benevolent,*
> *books have corners that hurt.*
> *I hollow my muscles against the load.*

Query with 4-5 samples and cover letter indicating "strong feminist consciousness. Replies very soon. Poets help with layout, art work, proofreading and distribution. Pays in copies. Write for sample.

*CROSS TIMBERS REVIEW (II), Cisco Junior College, Cisco, TX 76437, founded 1983, is a literary biannual, circulation 350, which uses poetry of quality, pays 3 copies. Sample: $3.50.

‡***CROSS-CANADA WRITERS' QUARTERLY (IV, Regional/Canadian)**, Box 277, Station F, Toronto, Ontario, Canada M4Y 2L7, founded 1979, editor Ted Plantos. The editor describes the quarterly as "the Canadian literary writer's magazine," and says that he wants poetry that is **"under 100 lines, accessible (not obscure), highest quality Canadian literature." He does not want to see "private 'diaries,' obscurity, doggerel, experiment for its own sake without adequate attention to content."** He has recently published Al Purdy, Susan Musgrave, Glen Sorestad, Robert Kroetsch. As a sample, he selected the following lines from "Neighbourhoods" by Barry Dempster:

> *Some men pray with shovels, trowels,*
> *others speak in waterfalls.*
> *A scent of marigolds,*
> *a wisp of rainbow on the breath.*

Writers' Quarterly is professionally printed, magazine-sized, 32 pp., saddle-stapled, with photographs, ads, glossy card cover in one color with b/w photo. Circulation is 2,000 with 900 subscriptions, 150 of which go to libraries, and 800 newsstand or bookstore sales. Price $3.95 per issue, subscription $14 in Canada, $16 US. **Guidelines are available for SASE and sample copy for $3.95 postpaid. Pay is $5/ poem plus one free copy. MSS rejections are made in 3 weeks, acceptances may take up to 3 months. Writers should allow up to one year until publication. MSS should be typed with name and address on each page. Send 6-8 poems. Dot-matrix is acceptable if clear.** The magazine offers an annual "WQ Editors' Prize" for poetry and short fiction with a total of $1,500 in prizes; the competition is now open to all writers. In 1986 they will offer a special international prize for writers outside Canada. The editor advises, "Read widely; learn *craft*."

*CROSSCURRENTS, A QUARTERLY (III), 2200 Glastonbury Rd., Westlake Village, CA 91361, founded 1980, poetry editor Elizabeth Bartlett, **has two issues per year open to submissions** (the other two being by invitation only). It has an elegant 6x9" format, 4-color card cover, 176 + pp., flat-spined, finely printed on heavy paper with much white space, photos and drawings. They want **highest quality literary poetry. Very long poems are always harder to place; no political poems; no more than 5 poems per submission, please. Unsolicited submissions accepted between June 1 and November 30 each year. Photocopy OK, dot-matrix "marginal". Reports in 4-8 weeks. Pays $15. Sample: $5 postpaid.** They have published work by Jaroslav Seifert, William Stafford, Linda Pastan, Joseph Bruchac, Leonard Nathan and Yannis Ritsos. As a sample I selected these line from "Don't Let it End Here" by Marvin Bell.

> *Trees that say things unheard of . . .*
> *Mountains in the clouds . . .*
> *Also, clouds inside the mountains!*
> *And you, who mean everything to me,*
> *hardly speak at all. Look!*

Elizabeth Bartlett comments "when time permits (but please don't ask—we're swamped)." She advises, "Study a sample copy to determine if your work seems appropriate for our publication. BEGINNERS: First, study the marketplace widely, and wait to submit until your work is as good as what's in print."

*CROTON REVIEW (II), Box 277, Croton-on-Hudson, NY 10520, founded 1978, executive editor and founder Ruth Lisa Schechter, is published annually. It is part of the literary program of the Croton Council on the Arts, Inc., a tabloid-size format: issues #1-7, issue #8 and #9 changed to 7x10 book format, 64 pp., **original, unpublished poetry welcome. "We prefer contemporary poetry which indicates evidence of language, craft, substance, music and we appreciate imagery, imagination from known and unknown writers throughout the USA. Work is read by entire staff of editor and poets. Sentimentalized, wornout, cliché writing is rejected. We enjoy poems with a sense of history and wit, poems on love, life, death, birth, loneliness—up to 75 lines. We are impressed by respect for the craft of poetry, vitality and honesty."** They have published poems by Marge Piercy, John Menfi, Susan Fromberg Schaeffer, Maria Gillan, Clarence Major, Yvonne Wanda Coleman, T. Allan Broughton, Veronica Patterson and interviews with Carolyn Forché and John Gardner. There are 40 to 50 contributors in poetry and prose in each annual issue, plus a Section on Special Themes. Issue #8 features a "Tribute to Jazz" by poets and artists. Circulation 2,000, 600 subscriptions of which 200 are libraries, single copy: $3, Issue #8: $4, **sample back issue: $2, add 75¢ postage on each copy ordered. Subscription: $10, 2 annual issues (post paid).** They receive about 3,000 submissions per year, use work of 30-40 poets. No backlog. *CR* **reads only September to January deadline for spring annual issues. Reports in 4-16 weeks. Submit 3-5 poems, single-spaced, clear and legible. Pays honorarium "according to grant provisions" plus 1 copy. Guidelines available for SASE.** They offer Annual *Croton Review* **Awards in Poetry and publication to winners. Prizes of $200 first prize, $100 second prize. Ruth Lisa Schechter advises, "Beginners might consider studying poetry seriously to learn important basics: the tools, nuts and bolts, same as a pianist or visual artist does. They might also read more poetry and often should think of improving writing skills and heightening talent rather than seeking to rush poems into print. Literary newsletters and magazines are valuable aids to sensing trends."** *CR* **is published with support of NEA, CCLM, DAW, NYSCA; member of CCLM and COSMEP.**

*CROWDANCING (II), Box 1562, Crescent City, CA 95531, founded 1983, poetry editors John R. Campbell and Holly V. Pink, is a "literary quarterly interested in high quality poetry and fiction; encourages new authors." They want **"nature poetry, imagery work and narrative—straightforward and unpretentious, 1-80 lines in any form."** Some of the poets they have recently published are D. Nurkse and Karen Reich. *Crowdancing* is a 7x8½" magazine, 60 pp., saddle-stapled, offset from typescript, $3.50. The magazine appears in 2 combined issues twice a year with 30-40 pp. of poetry in each, circulation 300, 10 subscriptions of which 4 are libraries. They use about 90 of 250 freelance submissions they receive each year, have a 4-12 week backlog. **Sample: $3.50 postpaid. Submit any time, any number; photocopies, simultaneous submissions OK. Reports as soon as possible, 4-12 weeks. Pays 1 copy. The editor "would be happy"** to comment on rejections if requested. The editor says, "Don't feel that it's a losing battle. Readers are out there. We're trying to put readers and poets together and are starting out small but have had terrific feedback from around the country."

‡CROWN CREATIONS ASSOCIATES, *MYTHOS, *COSMOS PRIME (I, IV, "mythopoeic"), Box 11626, St. Paul, MN 55111-0626, phone 612-698-0051, founded 1982, editor Steven Mark Deyo. *Mythos*, which has been a bi-monthly, photocopied, 8-page, corner-stapled magazine, is "going annual for 1986" and "taking on a twin"—*Cosmos Prime*—according to the editor. He reports that the combined 1986 annual will contain "108 pages of art, articles and humor on mythopoeic science fiction, fantasy and myth and will go quarterly, 20 pp. in 1987." He wants to see **poetry of "any meter, rhyme or style; subjects must touch on classical mythic themes or created/alternative worlds. Theology permissible only from Judeo-Christian viewpoint, mythopoeic preferred. Parody welcome, "nothing nihilistic, anti-heroic (unless whimsical), experimental or contemporary in the bad sense of the words."** As a sample, he selected the following lines by Bernard Hewitt:

> *Natural events still amaze,*
> *Eliciting a wide-eyed gaze:*
> *A shower of shooting stars.*
> *Some believe in dreams . . .*

Mythos is "handsomely bound in pastel soft cover." Price of the annual volume is $10, mailing around July. **Guidelines are available for $1. Pay is up to 4 copies. Submission instructions are: "five maximum a shot, 2-page single-spaced maximum per poem, original preferred, simultaneous not OK, dot-matrix OK." Reporting time is 1-6 weeks and time to publication is 2 issues, or 2-8 months.** The editor advises, "The fresh view should be your view. Rethink your assumptions, your prejudices: Are you coming at the subject all left-brain-sided, or are you letting your intuitive right side feed the images, the 'spiritual senses,' to your verbal left side? Try to go through a Lonerganian dialectic of consciousness, try to practically speak from your heart the thoughts and visions you receive. Finally, a solid Christian prayer life aids in attuning the practice of mythopoeia, 'worship through creativity.' Read J.R.R. Tolkien, C.S. Lewis and Charles Williams for hints."

*CUMBERLAND POETRY REVIEW (II), Box 120128, Acklen Station, Nashville, TN 37212, phone 615-373-8948, founded 1981, is a biannual with a 100 + pp., 6x9" flat-spined format which has published such poets as Donald Davie, William Stafford, Elder Olson, Richard Eberhart, Seamus Heaney, and Donald Hall. **Sample: $5 postpaid. Submit poetry or poetry criticism with SASE or IRC. Reports in 3 months.** Their circulation is 500.

CURLEW PRESS, *POETRY QUARTERLY (II), Hare Cottage, Kettlesing, Harrogate, UK, founded 1972, poetry editor P. J. Precious, publishes *Poetry Quarterly* and booklets of poetry. *PQ* appears "infrequently (name is a joke)." **Each issue has a theme. Pays 1 copy.** The booklet I have seen,

Selected Short Poems Vol. 1, by the editor, P.J. Precious, is 6x8", 22 pp., offset from typescript with hand-lettered contents and copyright page. As a sample I selected the entire poem, "Never":

> *I'll never make a pop star*
> *can't even move the hoover*
> *without tripping over the wire*

Simultaneous submissions, photocopy, dot-matrix all OK. Editor responds "by return post where possible." Sample free for postage. Editor sometimes comments on rejected MSS.

‡**CURVD H & Z, *INDUSTRIAL SABOTAGE (II)**, 729A Queen Street East, Toronto, Canada M4M 1H1, phone 416-463-5867, founded 1978, editor J. W. Curry, who says "Both the press & magazine focus on a 'the book as object' ideal. **Great attention is paid to creating formats that expand on their contents rather than just contain them.**" He produces "leaflets, chapbooks, boxes, envelopes, postcards, broadsides printed by rubberstamps, silkscreen, handtyping, Xeroxing—whatever." The samples he sent me are all **extremely small, on stiff paper which may be folded once or twice. Inside there might be something resembling a poem or there might be only one word.** In any case, he lists as recently published poets: loris essary, Hans Arp (translated by Yves Troendle), bp Nichol, John M. Bennett, and Stuart Ross. As a sample, he quoted "sinillogical translations" by Mark Laba:

> *and body*
> *frame of sound*
> *in a sound*

Industrial Sabotage appears at "very random" intervals and its format varies (I have not seen it). Circulation also varies, from 50 to 400, and price and number of copies to contributors vary too. **Reporting is "quick" but time to publication seems to follow the varying pattern; it's certainly best to be a very patient individual."**

CUTBANK (II), English Dept., University of Montana, Missoula, MT 59812, phone 406-243-5231, founded 1973, editor Pamela Uschuk, a biannual publishing "the best poetry, fiction, reviews, interviews and artwork available to us." Offers 2 annual prizes for best poem and piece of fiction in two issues, The Richard Hugo Memorial Prize and The A. B. Guthrie Fiction Prize (1985 judges: Sandra Alcosser and Rick MeMarinis)—$100 first prize/$50 honorable mention in each category. Winners announced in spring issue. Past contributors include James Crumley, William Pitt Root, Patricia Goedicke, Jim Hall, Richard Hugo, William Stafford, Harry Humes and Rita Dove. Sample lines by Hillel Schwartz:

> *the miniatures are the essential us, . . .*
> *the last condensed edition.*
> *We have always wanted good*
> *uncluttered copy. Here we are,*
> *less than breviary, pruned*
> *to the absolute.*

There are about 35-50 pp. of poetry in each issue, which has a circulation of about 350, 140 subscriptions of which 10-20 are libraries. **Price per issue: $4, sample: $2 postpaid. Submission guidelines: 50¢. Submit 3-5 poems, single-spaced. Photocopies OK, dot-matrix discouraged, no simultaneous submissions. "Please don't query." Reports in 8-10 weeks. "We don't read during the summer." Deadlines: March 1 and October 1. Pays in copies.**

‡***CV2 (IV, Regional/Canadian)**, Box 32 University Centre, University of Manitoba, Winnipeg, MB R3T 1EO, poetry editors are an editorial collective, is a quarterly of Canadian poetry and criticism. The CV in the title means "contemporary verse." I selected these sample lines from "Primum Mobile" by James Hutchison:

> *In performance precise*
> *as firebird's dance on eggshell legs*
>
> *a kid slouches through the park*
> *cartwheels twice and saunters on.*

They have about 45 pp. of poetry in each magazine-sized issue, circulation 500, 350 subscriptions of which 200 are libraries. The magazine is professionally printed on buff stock with a card matte cover with black-ink drawing, b/w drawings used inside. **Sample: $4.50 postpaid. Submit groups of 3-6, typed. Editor comments "if it's close." Reports in 6-8 weeks. Pays 1 copy.**

DAN RIVER PRESS (I, II), Box 123, South Thomaston, ME 04858, phone 207-354-6550, founded 1976, poetry editor Richard S. Danbury III. They publish an annual *Dan River Anthology* . They want **"no bad versy stuff that rhymes, no triteness, but good, serious work. No specifications as to length, style, subject, purpose, etc. No query needed."** Dan River Press books are marketed with **Northwoods Press Books (send SASE for catalog to order samples). Photocopies, dot-matrix—or**

discs compatible with Sanyo 1160 CPM or Compugraphic 7300 or TI 99/4A computer typesetter OK. Response "each year in April."

‡*DAUGHTERS OF SARAH (IV, Feminist, religious)**, 2716 W. Cortland, Chicago, IL 60647, phone 312-252-3344, founded 1974, editor Reta Finger, a bimonthly magazine "integrating feminist philosophy with biblical-Christian theology, and making connections with social issues." The magazine includes only "occasional" poetry. The editor says, **"Do not prefer rhyming poetry; must be short enough for one 8½x5½ page, but prefer less than 20 lines. Topics must relate to Christian feminist issues, but prefer specifics to abstract terminology."** She does not want **"greeting-card type verse or modern poetry so obscure one can't figure out what it means."** As a sample she chose the following lines by Deborah May:
> *I believe*
> *When the Messiah comes*
> *he will not be*
> *a white man with blue eyes*
The magazine is digest-sized, 36 pp., with photos and graphics, web offset. Its circulation is 3,700, of which 3,600 are subscriptions, including about 250 library subscriptions; bookstore sales are 50. Price per issue, $2; subscription $12/year. **Sample: $2 postpaid; guidelines are available for SASE.** *Daughters of Sarah* **pays $10-15/poem plus 2-3 copies. Poets should submit two copies of each poem to the editor, who reports in 1-2 months; time to publication is 3-18 months.**

*DAY TONIGHT/NIGHT TODAY (II)**, Box 353, Hull, MA 02045, founded 1980, poetry editor S. R. Jade, appears 7 times a year, and wants poetry that is **"personal, gutsy, tough, *not* racist, sexist, sticky sweet, rhyming**." They have recently published poetry of Doris Davenport, Wilma E. McDaniel, Dee Anne Davis, Cynthia Golderman, Lyn Lifshin, Terri Jewell, Jill Divine and Janine B. Canan (i.e., **women**). Though the editors say the poetry is too diverse to be represented by a sample, I selected these lines from "Hard Gloss" by Wanda Coleman:
> *fingers caress it fingers all hot dream orange*
> *creamy smooth reach for the nob turn it on*
> *first the buzz and then glimmer to light/throbs*
> *focus: a blonde with broad grinning teeth*
Every 7th issue is devoted entirely to one writer's work. They have a print-run of 750, 287 subscriptions, of which 15 are libraries. It's a digest-sized format, saddle-stapled, printed from photo-reduced typescript with narrow margins, about 48 pp. of poetry per issue. **Sample: $3.04 postpaid**. Backlog 3-12 months. **Submit no more than 10 pages. Photocopy, dot-matrix, simultaneous submissions OK. "Will consider requests for criticism if there's time that day**." They receive no government or state funding. "We subsist on subscriptions and donations." Payment is contributor's copy. Rights revert to author upon publication.

‡*DAYBREAK (I)**, 178 Bond Street North, Hamilton, Ontario, Canada L8S 3W6, editor Margaret Sanders. *Daybreak* **publishes haiku and longer than haiku poems, "will consider work from beginners and established poets. But it must be good poetry."** Poets recently published include Don Polson, Marianne Bluger, and Herb Barrett. I have selected a sample of a haiku by Lorraine Ellis Harr:
> *Out in the harbour—*
> *snowflakes and her ashes*
> *scatter on the wind*
Magazine is digest-sized, offset printed on bond, with woodcut illustration and cover design. **Payment is 1 copy of magazine; copyright remains with author.**

‡*DEAR CONTRIBUTOR (IV, Publishing)**, 227 East 11th St., New York, NY 10003, phone 212-473-2739, founded 1981, editor-publisher Jeri Blake, a newsletter for professional writers, editors, and allied persons, published by Inter-Verba, a literary agency. **They publish "short poems only on writing/publishing themes; humor a definite plus."** They don't want any **"envelopes full of stuff that has obviously been around the world a few dozen times."** I have not seen samples of the publication so cannot describe it or quote lines. The editor says there is "**token**" pay plus 1 copy. "**Limit quantity to what will fit in a No. 10 envelope."** Reporting time "**varies**," and time to publication is "**immediate.**"

*DECISION (IV, Christian, inspirational)**, 1300 Harmon Place, Minneapolis, MN 55403, phone 612-338-0500, founded 1960, poetry editor Viola Blake, is the monthly magazine of the **Billy Graham Evangelistic Association. It uses occasional poems of 4-20 lines, "free verse and some rhymed poetry, no 'cutsie' forms, fresh, perceptive with take-away value for the reader" in keeping with** the magazine's objective: "To set forth the Good News of Salvation in Jesus Christ . . . with such vividness and clarity that he will feel drawn to make a commitment of his life." The editor says, "We would like more poems by men." **Pays on publication. "We are usually inundated with poetry"** and so they have a year's backlog. **Send SASE for guidelines.**

*THE DEKALB LITERARY ARTS JOURNAL (II), 555 North Indian Creek Dr., Clarkston, GA 30021, is a magazine of literature and the arts published 3 times a year by DeKalb College and open to "*any* interested writer." It has a professionally-printed, flat-spined, digest-sized format, about 100 pp. **Photocopies discouraged. Sample: $4 postpaid. Annual subscription: $10-12 outside USA.** I selected these sample lines by scholarship winner Perry Thompson, the opening stanza of "From a Room Downtown":

> the city's got soul.
> music curls like snakes along the avenue.
> through traffic noise the beat takes hold.
> black shoes click on main.

‡**DELONG & ASSOCIATES, *SHORELINES, (II)**, Box 1732, Annapolis, MD 21404, phone 301-263-5592, poetry editor Rosemarie Peria. DeLong & Associates Quarterly Poetry Review is a **quarterly contest with an entry fee of $5 for 3 poems, prizes of $250, $150, $50, and $10 each for 12 honorable mentions. Winners are published in** *Shorelines* **and given complimentary copies in addition to their cash prizes.** The editor selected these lines as a sample (author not indicated):

> No other souls were even near,
> You loved it
> When I kissed your ear;
> Then I softly touched your breast

The editor comments, "As the DeLong & Associates Quarterly Review expands, we will begin to select poets who have participated in our program and invite them to submit book-length poetry MSS for publication," for which they intend to **pay royalties, and advance, and author's copies.** The editor advises beginners, "participate in legitimate contests to sharpen skills and get maximum exposure to award-winning poetry of all types and styles."

*DELTA SCENE (IV, Regional), Box B-3, Delta State University, Cleveland, MS 38733, is a quarterly magazine, 32 pp., circulation 2,000, using material, including **poetry, relating to the Mississippi Delta region—traditional forms, free verse and haiku. Simultaneous, photocopies, previously published material OK. Buys 1 per issue. Pays $5-10. Sample: $1.75.**

‡***DENVER QUARTERLY (II)**, University of Denver, Denver, CO 80210, phone 303-871-2892, founded 1966, poetry editor Bin Ramke, a quarterly literary journal that publishes fiction, poems, book reviews, and essays. **There are no restrictions on the type of poetry wanted.** They have recently published poetry by James Merrill, Linda Pastan, and William Matthews. As a sample, the editors selected the following lines from "The Inns and Outs of Irony" by William Logan:

> All Britain this hospital between the guts
> and what scavanges after, vulture blood fledged
> with lies, light: lab where the dusty wish
> of culture cultures the dawn in its dish

Denver Quarterly is 6x9", handsomely printed on buff stock, average 160 pp., flat-spined with two-color matte card cover. Circulation is 1,000, of which 600 are subscriptions (300 to libraries) and approximately 300 are sold on newsstands. Price per issue $5, subscription $15/year to individuals and $18 to institutions. **Samples of all issues before Spring 1985 are available for $4 postpaid, guidelines for SASE. Pay is 2 copies. No submissions read between May 15 and September 15 each year. Reporting time is 2-3 months.** The editors say they are planning a competition soon.

*DESCANT (II), Box 314, Station P, Toronto, Ontario, Canada M5S 2S8, founded 1970, poetry editor Karen Mulhallen, calls itself " **The magazine that sings** . . . a quarterly journal of the arts committed to being the finest in Canada. **While our focus is primarily on Canadian writing we have published writers from around the world.**" Some of the poets they have recently published are John Hollander, Peter Redgrave, Gwen MacEwen, Earle Birney and Irving Layton. As a sample, I selected the opening stanza of Lyn King's "Joyce and the Broken Window":

> The day your hand fell to pieces
> and spilled itself like squeezed fruit
> into my fingers, I ran
> for towels, help, from you.

It is an elegantly printed and illustrated flat-spined publication with colored, glossy cover, over-sized digest format, 140 + pages, heavy paper, with a circulation of 750 (400 subscriptions, of which 20% are libraries). **Sample: $7.50 postpaid**. They receive 500-800 freelance submissions per year, of which they use 60-80, with a 9-12 month backlog. **Guidelines available for SASE. Submit typed MS, unpublished work not in submission elsewhere, photocopy OK, name and address on first page and last name on each subsequent page. Reports within 4 months**. They pay "approximately $50" Karen Mulhallen says, "Best advice is to know the magazine you are submitting to. Choose your markets carefully."

*DESCANT (II), English Dept., Texas Christian University, Fort Worth, TX 76129, founded 1956, is a literary biannual, 6x9", 90 pp., circulation 450, using **quality poetry up to 40 lines. Submit 4-5 at a time. Considers simultaneous submissions. Pays in copies.**

‡*DEVIANCE (I, IV, Feminism), Box 1774, Pawtucket, RI 02862, phone 401-722-8187 (weekends best time), founded 1985, editor Linda R. Collette. *Deviance* published its first issue in Spring 1986; it is a literary quarterly that wants **"work exploring the 'female experience' in free verse, traditional, light, etc. Length—usual maximum should be 120 lines—exceptions could be made for right material; try not to ape Marge Piercy or May Sarton, but be as original as possible. The editor does not want to see poetry that is homophobic, sexist (of either sex), racist, anti-ethnic or anti-religious, or rewrites of things Piercy, Lifshin, Sarton have done."** As a sample she offers the following lines by an unidentified author:

> *October, she said, is when the trees burn*
> *with raging beauty in a dying glory.*
> *October is when you die and I die*
> *And when the world will come to an end.*

Deviance is magazine-sized, 20-28 pp., offset, uses b/w art when available, expects to take ads in future. Circulation is approximately 500. Price is $2.50/issue; subscription $12. The bimonthly magazine **"provides an arena for very original material on the female experience, whether lesbian or not, feminist or not—what it means to be a woman today."** They offer an annual prize for best work; **pay, 1 or 2 free copies. Sample: $2.50 postpaid. Guidelines available for SASE. Submissions are reported on within 3 weeks and should be in standard format, a maximum of 6 at a time, simultaneous submisions are OK, photocopies and dot-matrix MSS OK if legible. Criticism of rejected MSS is provided. Reading fee (negotiable) will be charged only if asked to critique a major work.**

*DIALOGUE: A JOURNAL OF MORMON THOUGHT (IV, Latter-Day Saints Market), 202 W. 300 North, Salt Lake City, UT 84103, founded 1966, poetry editor Michael R. Collings, "is an independent quarterly established to express Mormon culture and to examine the relevance of religion to secular life. It is edited by Latter-Day Saints who wish to bring their faith into dialogue with the larger stream of Judeo-Christian thought and with human experience as a whole and to foster artistic and scholarly achievement based on their cultural heritage. The views expressed are those of the individual authors and are not necessarily those of the Mormon Church or of the editors." **They publish 1-4 poems of each issue, "humorous and serious treatments of Mormon topics or universal themes from a Mormon perspective. Under 40 lines preferred. Must communicate with a well-educated audience but not necessarily sophisticated in poetic criticism. Free verse OK but only if carefully crafted."** They have published poetry by Emma Lou Thayne, Robert A. Rees, Michael Collings and Mary L. Bradford. The editor selected these sample lines from "Repapering the Kitchen" by Randall L. Hall:

> *We probe and scrape and peel away the faded*
> *Multicolored layers of a lifetime,*
> *Like Schliemann*
> *(Who?) Grandmother asks . . .*

They have a circulation of 3,500-4,000 subscriptions of which 150 are libraries. The journal has an elegant 6¾x10" format, 170 + pp., with color, artistically decorated cover and tasteful b/w drawings within. They receive about 50 submissions/year, use 8-14. **Sample: $7 postpaid. Submit typed MS in triplicate, 1-2 poems per page. Acknowledges in 10 days, reports in 2 months. Payment is 10 offprints plus two contributors' copies.**

*DIALOGUE, THE MAGAZINE FOR THE VISUALLY IMPAIRED (IV, Traditional, for visually impaired), 3100 Oak Park Ave., Berwyn, IL 60402, phone 312-749-1510, founded 1962, poetry editor Bonnie M. Miller, "is a general interest quarterly produced on ½ speed cassette in recorded disc, braille and large-print editions." **They use 6-8 poems in each issue, want poems up to 20 lines, not avant-garde. No light verse. "Our readers prefer traditional forms of poetry, blank verse, free verse and haiku. We do not want erotic poetry that is too graphic or religious poetry."** The poets they publish are "all blind and visually impaired readers of *Dialogue.*" The editor selected these sample lines from "Broken Time" by Valerie Moreno:

> Brittle Feelings,
> sharp as bones,
> Crack against the pressure
> of silence.

In all editions they have a circulation of 50,000, many reading through the Library of Congress. They have 6,375 subscriptions of which 4,000 are libraries. They receive about 125 poems per year, use 32-38, try to keep the backlog under 1 year. **Samples are free to the visually impaired. Enclose a note indicating nature of serious visual impairment, request guidelines and read several issues. No returns or acknowledgements without a SASE. Submissions can be in any medium (including braille and tape) except handwriting, 3 poems. They pay in copies, report within 6 weeks, usually with comment.**

‡DICKENSON PRESS (V, IV, Appalachian), 1012 Chesapeake Court, Huntington, WV 25701, founded 1982, editor/publisher Llewellyn McKernan. *Dickenson* is a small press that publishes small poetry chapbooks and flat-spined paperbacks. I have selected the following selection from **Short and Simple Annals** by Llewellyn McKernan:

> It is May Day
> and Momma is doing the washing.
> The scrub board bubbles with blue,
> her fists make knots of our clothing

The sample book I have seen is 40 pp., flat-spined, professionally printed in small type on heavy buff stock with b/w illustration on the matte card cover, selling for $2.50. The editor says, **"I will not be publishing any poetry chapbooks in the next two years (1986-87) due to lack of funds."** Considers simultaneous submissions. Freelance submissions are not accepted, no subsidy publishing, no grants or awards, no reading fees.

*DICKINSON STUDIES, *HIGGINSON JOURNAL, DICKINSON-HIGGINSON SOCIETY PRESS (II, IV, Emily Dickinson, lyric), 4508 38 St., Brentwood, MD 20722, phone (after 1 PM) 301-864-8527, founded 1968, poetry editor F. L. Morey, are publications of the Emily Dickinson Society (membership $30 individuals, $60 for libraries for 3 years). Both magazines are semiannuals, sometimes with bonus issues (e.g. in 1984 there were 9 issues instead of the minimum 4 promised to members), all distributed free to about 250 subscribers of which 125 are libraries. *Dickinson Studies* is principally for scholarship on Emily Dickinson, but **uses poems about her.** *Higginson Journal* **has a special poetry issue about every two years and uses a few poems in each issue—"lyric, no didactic, narrative or long dramatic; all styles welcome. No sentimental, moral; up to 50 lines in any form.** They have published poems by Lyn Lifshin, Roger White and Cherry Kelly. As a sample, I chose the opening stanza of a villanelle by Miriam Rose Paisley, "Song of Life":

> My song is greater than the blare of Rock.
> It holds within me lilting joy and cheer.
> The blatant beat of Rock will only mock.

The address of each poet is printed with the poem. The journals are both digest-sized, about 30 pp., saddle-stapled, typeset with card covers and b/w art. **Sample: $3 postpaid. Submit 3-6 poems no longer than a page each. Reports in 1-2 weeks. Payment: 1 copy.** F. L. Morey, a retired professor, says he receives about 20 submissions for *DS*, of which he uses 10, 50 for *HJ*, of which he uses 20. "I am really not wishing for a deluge of poems." The Dickinson-Higginson Society Press also has subsidy-published one collection of poems, the poet putting up $500 and the publisher $600 for printing a flat-spined paperback on quality paper.

‡*DINOSAUR REVIEW (II, IV, Western Canada), Box 294, Drumheller, Alberta, Canada T0J 0Y0, founded 1981, poetry editor Monty Reid. A literary quarterly with western Canadian emphasis, *Dinosaur Review* wants to see **"contemporary poetry, no specs as to length, form, etc.—in fact we often publish lengthy selections of poetry. We do want to see poetry that is aware of current intellectual and literary trends, although it certainly does not have to approve of them."** They do not want to see devotional verse. Poets published recently include Pat Lane, Erin Moure, Michael Ondaatje, bp Nichol, and Andrew Suknaski. As a sample I selected the following stanza from "The Politics of Fall," by Barbara Curry Mulcahy:

> The wind, a demagogue drunk
> on his own words, breaks the lock
> of a liquor store
> and the looting begins.

Dinosaur Review (formerly the *Camrose Review*) is published three times yearly and has a circulation of 600, of which 350 are subscriptions and 50 go to libraries. Price per issue is $3, subscription $8. **Sam-**

ple: $3 postpaid. The review is magazine-sized, 72 pp., professionally printed on heavy stock with occasional graphics. **Pay rate is $5/page plus 2 free copies. Submissions are reported on in 3 months, publication is in the next issue.** The editor advises: "get familiar with the magazines before you submit; don't give up easily; if you don't like it, start your own publication."

DISTRICT LINES (IV, DC school children), Box 32325, Washington, DC 20007, 202-333-1026. founded 1985, co-editors Laurie Stroblas and Nan Fry. *District Lines*, whose first issue appeared in September, 1985, publishes creative writing, especially **poetry, by students (grades 4 through 9) who attend school in the District of Columbia**. The magazine takes "all types of poetry: rhymes, free verse, haiku, concrete, experimental, no restrictions on subject matter or style." As a sample, the editors selected the following poem by San San Truong, grade 5:

> *A lake:*
> *Frozen and can't move*
> *People ice-skating fast*

The magazine is digest-sized, 64-80 pp., typeset, saddle-stitched. It appears twice a year, in fall and spring. Circulation of issue #1 was 1,000. Price per issue is $4, subscription $6/year. **Sample available for $4 postpaid, guidelines for SASE. Pay is 1 copy. Writer should "print legibly or type. Student's name, address, phone, school grade, name of teacher must be on each entry. We cannot return material submitted from outside District of Columbia." Reporting time "could be 2 weeks-4 months;" time to publication "could be 3-8 months." Simultaneous submissons, photocopied or dot-matrix MSS are OK.** The editors' advice to students is: "*Read* your peers' work & well-known poets too!"

DRAGON GATE, INC. (II), 6532 Phinney Ave. N., Seattle, WA 98103, phone 206-783-8387, founded 1979, editor and publisher Gwen Head, editor-in-chief Marlene Blessing, publishes "work of high literary quality, work we expect to endure. We publish 4-5 books each year, some poetry and some fiction. We pride ourselves not only on the quality of the works, but on the quality of the book design, cover art, and bindings. Each book is simultaneously published in cloth binding and in sewn paper binding. **We are not actively seeking new poets, as we have a continuing commitment to the 10 we presently publish. We will give serious consideration to the works of people who seem likely to fit our needs and meet our literary standards, whatever the form, style, or subject of the poems."** Among poets whose books they have published are Laura Jensen, Liam Rector, Linda Gregerson, Richard Ronan, Richard Blessing, Jeanne Murray Walker, Joan Swift, Caroline Finkelstein, Henry Cartile and Eve Triem. The editors (reluctantly—as they recognize as we all do the impossibility of choosing a short sample that is fairly representative of a publisher's taste), provide these lines from John Woods' "Striking the Earth":

> *Every few years we need the quick downpour,*
> *like rivers on end, seeing the oak stump*
> *hammering the pilings, the car light shining*
> *at the bottom of deep wells. These are our wars.*

Their edition of Eve Triem's **New As a Wave** was selected by Robert Penn Warren for one of the Western States Book Awards in 1984. **Send 7x10" SASE for catalog to order samples. Considers simultaneous submissions. To submit, query first with 6-8 samples and publication record.**

*DRAGONFLY: A QUARTERLY OF HAIKU, WESTERN WORLD HAIKU SOCIETY (IV, Haiku), 7372 Zana Lane, Magna, UT 84044, founded 1967, poetry editors Richard Tice and Jack Lyon, is intended "to further the knowledge and the writing of Classical/Traditional Haiku, to adapt it from the Japanese language into a specific and understandable genre of English language literature." They want: **"NO 3-line POEMS! We believe that haiku is a unique genre. That it is unlike our poetry. We believe that it can be made a part of English literature keeping its unique identity. With time, it can be recognized as English language HAIKU . . . not POEMS. We avoid free verse as haiku, prose as haiku, poems as haiku. We follow the Classical/Traditional concepts of what haiku is by studying the haiku poets of Japan. We consider haiku a Way-Of-Life."** Some of the poets they have recently published are "Tombo (Lorraine Ellis Harr's pen name), H. C. Acton, M. G. Robinson, A. R. Mendenhall, G. Barton, R. Hansen, J. Baranski, S. L. Lehmer, D. G. Neher and H. J. Sherry." As a sample, the editor offers this haiku of her own:

> *Clouds that cross the moon*
> *cross the moon's reflection-*
> *in the autumn pool.*

She says it won first place in the *Mainichi Daily News* (Tokyo, Japan) annual contest, 1982. *Dragonfly* is in a digest-sized 68 pp. saddle-stapled format, has a circulation of 350 + of which 20 are libraries. They receive 3,000-4,000 submissions (usually with numerous haiku) per year, accept 1,400-2,000, have a 3 month backlog (a few holdovers from quarterly issue to issue). **Sample: $3 postpaid. Submit 1** haiku per page, 5 haiku per submission, full name and address on upper left corner. "Legal size envelopes for both submissions and returns." Reports by return mail or within 2 weeks. No pay, but there are awards in each issue. Send SASE for guidelines, and, advises the editor, "STUDY THEM. Study haiku as published in *Dragonfly*."

DRAGON'S TEETH PRESS, LIVING POETS SERIES, NEW POETIC DRAMA (II), El Dorado National Forest, Georgetown, CA 95634, founded 1970, poetry editor Cornel Lengyel. *New Poetic Drama* is "a quarterly devoted to the encouragement of dramatic poetry through the publication of living playwrights, with essays on various aspects of poetic drama in world literature." It is a flat-spined, professionally printed paperback, 70 + pp. As a sample, I selected the speech of a harlot in George Hitchcock's **The Devil Comes to Wittenberg**:

> *Listen to him brag! I don't claim to have invented*
> *what I have to sell, but it's a wonderful product*
> *all the same. They bring me their dreams and I*
> *fill them with flesh and garnish them with kisses.*

Collections of poetry in the Living Poets Series have a format similar to that of the quarterly. Dragon's Teeth Press "**subsidy publishes 25% of books** if book has high literary merit, but very limited market"—which no doubt applies to books of poetry. They publish other books on 10% royalty contract. Simultaneous and photocopied submissions OK, computer printout acceptable. Reports in 2 weeks on queries, 1 month on MSS.

THE DRAGONSBREATH PRESS, *DOOR COUNTY ALMANAK (II, IV, Regional, issue's theme), 10905 Bay Shore Dr., Sister Bay, WI 54234, phone 414-854-2742, founded 1973, poetry editor Fred Johnson. Dragonsbreath is a "small press producing a very small number of handmade, **limited edition books aimed at art and book collectors. Prefer to work cooperatively with authors to produce handmade books, sharing expenses and any profits,**" but other arrangements are possible. *Door County Almanak* is a regional annual, each issue having a major theme of local interest. The magazine has 5-10 pp. of poetry in each issue. The editor says he receives "very much" poetry and accepts "very little." **Sample: $5.95 postpaid. Query regarding current theme. Submit September-April, 3-5 poems, photocopies, simultaneous submissions OK.** If interested in book publication, query with 3-5 samples and cover letter with bio, publication record, and personal or aesthetic philosophy. Fred Johnson says, "Writers should be more selective of what they send out as samples. I am not at this time looking for any book manuscripts."

*DREAM INTERNATIONAL QUARTERLY (IV, Dreams), 1-17-7 Ushita Waseda, Higashi-Ku, Hiroshima, Japan 732, or 333-B Autumn Dr., San Marcos, CA 92069, founded 1980, Les Jones and Charles, World Editors, is devoted "to stimulate **interest in and research related to dreams and sleep.**" The poetry they use can be "**any form and style but must be related definitely to dreams. No restrictions except that of good taste (may be erotic if not offensive).**" They have published poems by Diana Henning, Linda Ravenwulf and Zbigniew Konofalski. These sample lines are from "You Are" by Joan M. Sherer, Lebanon, Oregon:

> *Somewhere in this world you are,*
> *and, because you are, I am.*
> *We meet in the twilight of dreams*
> *and awake, I can't know you.*
> *But, because you are, I am.*

They have a circulation of 250, 31 subscriptions, receive about 420 submissions per year and use 60, have a 4 month backlog. **Sample: $3 postpaid. Submit no more than 7 double-spaced pages, photocopy, dot-matrix OK, queries unnecessary. Pays in copies. Reports in 6 weeks. Guidelines available for SASE. Awards (subscriptions or cash) for annual best contributions. Sometimes comments on MSS.** Les Jones advises, "the essence of poetry is similar to the essence of dreaming. Contemplate *dreaming* and you should be able to write good poetry."

DUCK DOWN PRESS, WINDRIVER SERIES, (II), Box 1047, Fallon, NV 89406, phone 702-423-6643, founded 1973, poetry editor Kirk Robertson, publishes quality contemporary poetry, fiction, art and photography. They want "**no rhyming verse; quality contemporary post-modern only.**" They have published poetry by Shelton, Bukowski, Masarik, Tom Clark, Norbert Kraft, Jo Harvey Allen and Albert Drake. These sample lines are from "The Muse" by Michael Hannon:

> *I don't go to her, she comes to me still red*
> *with the blood of unspeakable crimes, and her hair*
> *is a black wind annihilating worlds to get at the door in my*
> *bed.*
> *It takes me forever to get her clothes off and I don't have*
> *forever.*

Duck Down Press, Windriver Series, has many distinguished poets on its list such as Joanne de Long-champs, Ronald Koertge, Greg Kuzma, Leo Mailman and William Stafford. **Query with 5-8 samples, record of publications and biographical background.**

DUENDE PRESS (IV, New Mexico), Box 571, Placitas, NM 87403, founded 1964, poetry editor Larry Goodell, publishes **"books of poetry and broadside incidentals from the time warp of New Mexico."** They have published poetry by Judson Crews, who wrote these sample lines:

> *So you would walk*
> *where Bulltoven walked sniffing*
> *a bush here and there, shouting*
> *he peed here, right here!*

In what form should the MS be? "Personal." Pays 20 copies. For sample, send $5. The editor will consider publishing a book by any poet/publisher who will in turn consider publishing a book by him.

*EAR MAGAZINE (IV, Music and performance), Rm. 208, 325 Spring St., New York, NY 10013, founded 1973, editorial board, **uses some poetry related to music and performance. Sample: $3. Pays copies. Reports in 3 months.** There are 1-2 pages of poetry in each issue (5 times per year), and poets such as Jackson Maclow, John Cage, Edmund Chibeau and Charles Bernstein have appeared there. The magazine has an international circulation of 6,000. The editor advises poets to "start your own press. It's a free country, i.e., no pay for artists (myself included)."

EARTHWISE PUBLICATIONS/PRODUCTIONS, *EARTHWISE: A JOURNAL OF POET-RY, EARTHWISE NEWSLETTER, EARTHWISE LITERARY CALENDAR, *TEMPEST RE-VIEW, MIAMI-EARTH CHAPTER, FLORIDA STATE POETRY ASS'N. INC. (N.F.S.P.S.), T. S. ELIOT CHAPBOOK CONTEST (I), Box 680-536, Miami, FL 33168, founded 1978, poetry editors Barbara Holley and Frank S. Fitzgerald-Bush, "began with a small folio of poems, expanded with the *Newsletter* for informing writers, took on *Tempest* to feed *EW* both financially and aesthetically, found that the *Calendar* brought new members into the National Federation of State Poetry Societies and showcased poets/artists as well. We focus on simply fine work and often emphasize environment, the issues, when we can. We want **no porn, little confessional or religious. We tend to like well-crafted contemporary rhymed or free verse. We are currently involved with themes (list on request) and prefer poems less than a page long (unless very well-crafted and skilled). We like poetry that 'says something,' that folks can often relate to, poetry that lives, so to speak**." They have published poems by Richard Wilbur, Jorge Valls, Lola Haskins and Knute Skinner; and interviews on John Davies, Ester Wagner and Richard Wilbur. These sample lines are by Wang Wei (translated by Joseph Lisowski) from T'ang Dynasty called "Clear Bamboo Ranges":

> *Sandalwood is reflected in the empty turn*
> *Blue-green waves flash, flowing to a pool*

> *But gloom penetrates the Shang Mountain Road*
> *So deep even the woodman cannot know*

Earthwise is biannual and they hope to make it a quarterly, a digest-sized flat-spined format, using a variety of type-styles, photos of poets and cover art, printed on heavy paper with matte cover. *Tempest*, irregularly published, "is now a vessel for material which is fine, sometimes more 'avant' than seems right for *Earthwise*, has 'themes.' " It is also digest-sized, saddle-stapled, otherwise much like *Earthwise* in format. The *Calendar*, also annual, incorporates original poetry, quotes from poets, and b/w art work and photography. All submitting are invited to join the NFSPS and the Miami Earth Chapter of FSPS, for which you receive a free subscription to the criticism service and newsletter. *Earthwise* has a circulation of 350+ to subscribers, of which about 100 are libraries. They receive about 7,500 submissions per year, use about 1,200-1,500 in various publications, have an approximate 2 year backlog (less if the poems fit current themes). **Sample of *Earthwise*: $5 postpaid. Send SASE for guidelines. Submit to any of these publications with name and address on SASE and each MS page. "Send some bio re: past publications, awards, etc. with MSS. We send release form if accepted, stating issue planned, publication in which MS to be used and asking for more bio. We try to get back within 1-3 months." Both magazines pay $3 per poem, calendar ($6.95 to non-members, $5.95 to members) guarantees publication for member; non-member as space permits. Newsletter pays in copies. To submit for chapbook publication query with 3 samples, cover letter about publications, awards or "beliefs, credo, etc. $10 reading fee for annual T. S. Eliot Chapbook Contest. Deadline Nov. 30.** ("A reading fee of $100 is paid to a judge and the balance of fees collected go to producing the 200+ copies of which the author receives 100 and to promotional material.") Barbara Holley adds, she has also produced 2 cable TV programs, **Impromptu,** interviewing poets and other artists and personalities, and **Poet Tree.**

Close-up

Barbara Holley
Earthwise Publications/Productions

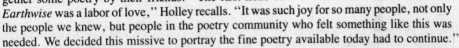

Artist: Lawrence Goodridge

Earthwise is a lot like its editor—busy, varied, and intriguing. The biannual, digest-size magazine is among the better publications of its type, in both content and production.

The first issue of *Earthwise* was put together in late 1978 and published in early 1979 by Barbara Holley and her friend, Pauline Harden. Their purpose was to get together some poetry by their friends. "The first issue of *Earthwise* was a labor of love," Holley recalls. "It was such joy for so many people, not only the people we knew, but people in the poetry community who felt something like this was needed. We decided this missive to portray the fine poetry available today had to continue."

Later, when Harden moved to California, Holley faced the question of whether or not to continue publication. She went ahead, and with the support of her husband and numerous editorial helpers, she has expanded *Earthwise* into two other publications—*Tempest* and *Earthwise Newsletter*, both of which materially support the original *Earthwise*. They also have quarterly contests, and "our yearly T.S. Eliot chapbook contest." Holley also does two cable television interview programs—*IMPROMPTU* and *The Poet Tree*—dealing with artists and writers.

"The idea was to get poetry to pay something. In the beginning, I had to worry about how to get the money together for each issue, and that's when I decided that maybe *Tempest* would help. The other projects evolved naturally."

Earthwise itself features an eclectic mix of poetry of all types and on all topics, supported by a handsome format that includes tasteful line drawings and photos of contributors.

A Pulitzer Prize nominee (for her chapbook collection, *Pieces of a Woman*, Red Key Press, 1982), Holley says that her own work has suffered some for that decision to continue, but "my soul has flourished."

Holley's advice for poets wanting to be published centers on persistence. "Keep learning and do not give up," she says. "Often an editor will accept a poet after many, many years of rejection. Never be satisfied with yourself; that is disastrous." Holley defines a "good" poem as "one that kind of grabs you, makes you 'feel' what the poet is saying." She further advises, "The new poet needs to find ways of making the reader sit up and take notice."

The same advice applies to getting published in *Earthwise*, for which Holley seeks poetry with structure, form, content, and craft. "We usually adhere to the standard of good moral ethics in *Earthwise*, and our criteria is basically good literature. Everybody sees something fine and different in a piece of good writing. Basically, though, a poem for *Earthwise* should be going somewhere, and have something important to say in an interesting way."

She also suggests that the writer "Improve his or her vocabulary to the point where he or she knows how to spell important words and use them competently. Use of the language is important in giving the reader a complete feel for the piece . . . what I call 'being there', although simple language is often best." Holley urges writers to be, above all, themselves. "The same rules don't work for every writer. Everyone has his own set of rules. You have to find your own voice, your own faith and work with it."

—Michael A. Banks

ECCO PRESS, *ANTAEUS (III), 18 W. 30th St., New York, NY 10001, phone 212-685-8240. founded 1970, editor Daniel Halpern; managing editor Katherine Bourne. *Antaeus*, a prestige semi-annual publishing such poets as Robert Hass, Robert Pinsky and Carolyn Kizer, James Merrill, Carolyn Forché, and Octavio Paz, **buys 30-35 poems per year, "avant-garde, free verse and traditional," for which it pays $5/page. Submit maximum of 8 poems, no simultaneous submissions, no submissions June-October. Reports in 6 weeks; send SASE for guidelines.** They use about 1% of the many submissions they receive each year. The magazine has an elegantly printed, flat-spined, 6½x9" format, circulation 5,000. The Press has published books by such poets as Sandra McPherson, Jon Anderson and Stanley Plumly. **Send SASE for catalog to order samples. Submit 4-6 samples with query. Replies in 1 week. If you are invited, they will read a MS of 65-80 pp., report in 2 months.** They publish 1-2 new selections per year.

‡**EDITIONS NEPE: *DOC(K)S, ZERROSCOPIZ, ANTHOLOGIES DE L 'AN 2.000 (II)**, Le Moulin de Ventabren, 13122 Ventabren, France 13122, phone 42288561, founded 1971, poetry editor Julien Blaine, who uses **"concrete, visual, sound poetry; performance; mail-art; metaphysical poetry."** He does not want **"poesie à la queue-leu-leu"** . . . whatever that means. He has recently published work by J.F. Bory, Nani Balestrini, F. Beltrametti, A. Arias, E. Miccini, E. Limonov, A. Spatola, and M.A. Desheng as well as himself. The magazine *Doc(k)s* is published 4 times a year and has a circulation of 1,100, of which 150 are subscriptions. **Pay for poetry is 5 copies. There are no specifications for submissions.**

*ELECTRUM, MEDINA PRESS (II), 2222 Silk Tree Dr., Tustin, CA 92680-7129, phone 714-730-4046, quarterly, founded 1977, poetry editor Roger Suva. "Each issue of *Electrum* is packed with the best in contemporary poetry. Special emphasis is given to a **multi-cultural selection of work from around the country." They use all kinds of poetry on any subject.** Some poets they have recently published are Deena Metzger, Robert Peters, and Eloise Klein Healy. The editors selected these sample lines from "She Wants The Ring Like He Wants The Suit . . ." by Juan Felipe Herrera:
> I want liquid diamonds of music from a window when it fractures
> doors fresh emeralds eyes from a blaze against ice/all
> that screams torsos petals of an inmortal stone of rain
> legs of a metallic sea in serach of fruit ground.

Electrum is an 8x10⅞" quarterly, 60 pp. of which 35 are poetry, circulation 2,500, 300 subscriptions of which 10 are libraries, subscription: $10. A photo of each contributor is included in each issue. They use tasteful b/w art and ads, glossy three-color cover, professional printing and graphics. They accept about 15% of the thousand or more submissions they receive each year, have a 1-3 month backlog. **Sample: $3.50 postpaid. Put name and address on every poem. Limit submission to 5 poems. Recommended maximum length is 80 lines. Reports in 1-3 months, pays copies. Send SASE for guidelines.** Subscription: $7 per year. Each year they award an Alice Jackson Poetry Prize—with $200, $100 and $50 awards. Entry fee is $2 per poem. Deadline is August 30.

‡**EMBER PRESS, *ACUMEN (II)**, 6 The Mount, Furzeham, Brixham, South Devon TQ5 8QY, England, press founded 1971, magazine 1985, editors Patricia and William Oxley. *Acumen* is a twice-yearly literary magazine with poetry emphasis; Ember Press publishes books and pamphlets. The magazine wants **"well crafted poems that are more than verbal experiments or merely descriptive pieces."** They do not want **"mere verbal exercises, pointless experiment, wholly descriptive or academic exercises."** They have recently published Dannie Abso, Roy Fuller, John Heath-Stubbs, Philip Gross, R.S. Thomas, C.H. Sisson, and Ken Smith. As a sample I selected the first stanza of "Prose and Verse" by Freda Bromhead:
> Until that time in Warsaw
> Prose was enough for all my needs,
> Verse I did not dare—poetry
> Was a high calling, not for me.

Acumen is 6x8", 100 pp. flat-spined, offset in small print on high-quality stock with glossy card cover, using b/w line drawings. Circulation is 500, single copy price £1.75 or $5, subscription £3 or $9 for 2 issues. **Sample available for £1.75 or $9 postpaid. Pay is "by negotiation" plus 1 copy. Poets should submit a maximum of 5 poems with IRC(s), name and address on each page. Reporting time is 1-2 months, and there is no backlog.** Ember Press's list includes 9 pamphlets or chapbooks plus 16 publications of the University of Salzburg, several by Mr. Oxley. Mrs. and Mr. Oxley say, "The learning of the craft of poetry is a matter of long experience, hard work and wide reading. Poets should continue to send their work around to a variety of magazines and not give up in the face of numerous rejections. They should read and subscribe to as many magazines as possible."

‡*EMBERS (II), Box 404, Guilford, CT 06437, phone 203-453-0303, founded 1979, poetry editors Katrina Van Tassel, Charlotte Garrett, Mark Johnson, a "poetry journal of talented new and well-known poets." The editors say, "**no specifications as to length, form or content. Interested in new poets with talent; not interested in way-out verse, porn, or poetry that is non-comprehensible.**" They have recently published poetry by Derek Walcott, Amy Clampitt, Donald Hall, Maxine Kumin, and Marge Piercy. As a sample, the editors chose the following lines by Margaret Gibson:

> From the crest of the first dune
> the shoreline hooks like a moon fresh from darkness,
> a margin of tangible light I can feel in my feet

Embers is digest-sized, nicely printed on white stock with an occasinal b/w photograph or drawing, 52 pp. flat-spined with one-color matte card cover handsomely printed in black; it appears twice a year—spring/summer and fall/winter. There are approximately 150 subscriptions. Price per issue is $4.50, subscription $9/year. **Sample available for $2 postpaid, guidelines for SASE. Pay is 2 copies. Submissions must be typed, previously unpublished, with name, address and brief bio of poet.** Poetry contests with a prize of $75 are held for each issue; material will be sent with cover sheet. Submissions are reported on in March and November, and publication depends on time of receipt. The editors say they "encourage changes to make poems possibly acceptable for publication." Their advice is, "Send for sample copies of any publication you are interested in; follow the directions issued by that publication as to kind of work, how to submit, etc. Be patient. Most editors read as quickly as they can and report likewise. If a poet sends in work at the beginning of a reading time, or long before a deadline, he/she will have to wait longer for answers."

EMBERS PRESS, MOONJUICE COLLECTIVE (IV, Santa Cruz women poets), 540 Meder St., Santa Cruz, CA 95060, founded 1975, publishes an anthology of **poetry by women in the Santa Cruz area** every 2 years. Send SASE for catalog to buy samples.

‡*EMPIRE FOR THE SCIENCE FICTION WRITER, UNIQUE GRAPHICS, *OWLFLIGHT (IV, Science fiction), 1025 55th St., Oakland, CA 94608, 415-655-3024. Editor Ms. Millea Kenin founded Unique Graphics 1980, took over *Empire* in 1983. *Empire* accepts poems of **"any form or style, serious or humorous, preferred length 4 to 30 lines, *must* be on SF/fantasy theme or about being a writer of SF/fantasy. Poems about rejection slips will always garner one more."** Poets recently published include Robert Frazier, Julia Vinograd, and Janet Fox. As a sample, the editor selected these lines from Bruce Boston:

> Poets have velvet wings.
> Novelists have no wings at all,
> but oh how they can hop.

Empire, which will resume a quarterly schedule in 1986, is magazine-sized, offset, with b/w cover art and interior spots, saddle-stitched. Circulation is 2,000, of which 1,500 are subscriptions. Price per issue is $2.50/subscription $9 for 4 issues. **Sample $2.50 postpaid. Guidelines are available for #10 SASE (39¢); one packet includes complete guidelines for all Unique Graphics publications.** Pay: 1 copy. Submissions must be typed, double-spaced, near-letter quality, photocopies OK, simultaneous submissions and previously published material must be identified. Submissions are reported on within 6 weeks. The editor says that she "always rejects with at least a brief comment." She does not require a contributor to subscribe, nor does she charge reading fees, saying emphatically "That's unethical!" *Owlflight* is also a magazine-sized publication, 64 pp., offset from typed copy with many b/w graphics, two-color matte card cover, saddle-stapled. Price per copy is $3, subscription $10 for 4 issues. **"Before submitting art and/or writing to *Owlflight*, please send a SASE and request information as to whether *Owlflight* is open for submissions."**

*ENCOUNTER (III), 59 St. Martin's Lane, London, England WC2N 4JS, editors Melvin J. Lasky and Richard Mayne, a prestige monthly (except August and September) which has published many of the major British and American poets. **Sample: $4.50 postpaid (surface mail). Submit maximum of 6 poems, 12-100 lines. Simultaneous submissions not welcome. Pays variable fee.**

‡*ENVOI, ENVOI POETS PUBLICATIONS (II), Pen Ffordd, Newport Dyfed SA42 0QT, Wales, phone 0239-820285, editor Anne Lewis-Smith plus an "editorial panel of 30." *Envoi*, which publishes

❝Amelia is not afraid of strong themes, but we do look for professional, polished work. Poets should have something to say about matters other than the moon.

Frederick A. Raborg, Amelia ❞

new poetry and short reviews, was founded in 1957, Envoi Poets Publications, founded in 1985, publishes flat-spined paperbacks. The editors want **"high standard new poetry, more than 40 lines not welcome unless exceptional; well crafted."** They do not want **"political, slang, badly crafted work."** *Envoi* has recently published Pam Croome, Ann Born, Howard Sergeant, David Holiday, and Isobel Thrilling. As a sample, they selected the following lines by an unidentified poet:

> *Procedure complete, with a flurry of leggings and breeches*
> *And sooty-black cassocks, they flap like angels in air,*
> *Thrice circling the sunlit meadow, up to the crest of a*
> *spinney*
> *To broadcast from pulpits of elm their resonant speeches.*

The magazine is digest-sized, "litho printed to a high standard," 40 pp., glossy card cover; it has a competition in each issue. Its circulation (international) is 500 + , of which 50 are library subscriptions. Price per issue is £1.75, subscription £5 for 3 issues. **Sample available for £1, guidelines for SASE. Pay is 2 copies.** Writers should submit 1 poem/page with name and address on each page, preferably not hand written, not previously published. **Reporting time is 3-6 weeks, publication is in next issue.** Freelance submissions of poetry for chapbooks are accepted, but all chapbooks are subsidy published; arrangements are "personal with each poet." Poets should query first, sending credits, 10 sample poems, and bio. "We like them to be subscribers and to have had poetry printed in *Envoi*." **Photocopied, dot-matrix are OK. Queries will be answered in 1 week, MSS reported on in 3-6 weeks.** The press publishes 12 chapbooks each year with an average page count of 28, flat-spined with card cover. **Sample chapbooks are available for £2 or $4 plus postage. "We prefer dollar bills to checks."** The editors say, "Apart from publishing good new poetry, our great strength is that each poem has a free criticism slip attached when returned. All 30 of the editorial panel work at this, all of them known poets. Advice to beginners—put your new poems away for 6 months, then look at them anew with a fresh eye. Also read established poets."

*EPOCH (III), 251 Goldwin Smith, Cornell, Ithaca, NY 14853, founded 1947, has a distinguished and long record of publishing **exceptionally fine poetry** and fiction. They have published work by such poets as Ashbery, Ammons, Eshleman, Wanda Coleman, Molly Peacock, Robert Vander Molen and Alvin Aubert. The editor selected these sample lines from "that they were at the beach—aeolotropic series," by Leslie Scalapino:

> *So it's sexual coming—anyone—but corresponds to the*
> *floating world, seeing men on the street*

The magazine appears 3 times a year in a professionally printed, 6x9" flat-spined format with glossy b/w cover, 100 + pp., which goes to 900 subscribers. They use less than 1% of the many submissions they receive each year, have a 2-12 month backlog. **Sample: $3.50 postpaid. Reports in 2 months. Pays $1 per line. Occasionally provides criticism on MSS**. The editor advises, "I think it's extremely important for poets to read other poets. I think it's also very important for poets to read the magazines that they want to publish them. Directories are OK, but reading them and not acquainting oneself with the magazines (or some of the magazines) they list is like reading the Cliff's Notes version of **Moby Dick** and not Melville's novel. If you don't want to buy a sample of *Epoch* send us a self-addressed, stamped postcard and we'll direct you to the closest library which carries it."

EPOS (II), English Dept., Troy State University, Troy, AL 36081, phone 205-566-3000, poetry editors Theron Montgomery and Ed Hicks, an annual, **wants poetry that is "imagistic—*but* in motion. Will look at anything."** They have published poetry by Larry McLeod, Coleman Barks, Leo Luke Marcello and George Ellenbogen. I selected these sample lines, the beginning of "Washington Starting Out: 1791" by P. B. Newman:

> *The white carriage with its gilded springs*
> *backs with the trembling horses, confused*
> *grooms cajoling, seamen making wisecracks*
> *and whoops, hoping that something will go wrong.*

The beautifully printed 40 + pp., 7x10" magazine, matte cover with art, b/w art and some colored pages inside, receives 150 submissions per year, uses 20, has a 6 month backlog. **Sample: $1.50 postpaid. Query not necessary. Reports in 2 weeks. Pays copies. Sometimes comments on rejections.**

ERIE STREET PRESS, *LUCKY STAR (II), 221 S. Clinton, Oak Park, IL 60302, phone 312-848-5716, founded 1976, poetry editor Henry Kranz, is "a not-for-profit corporation that publicizes poetry through books, magazines, readings and other literary events, focusing our activities on the west side of Chicagoland." They want **"no religious or blatantly political poems, no greeting card verse."** Some poets they have recently published are Dan Campion, Rob Patton, Lyn Lifshin, Marvin Bell, Rick Duffey and Carl Watson. These sample lines are by Frederick Rimms:

> *The shakers hate me, although the movers laugh*

> when they see my furniture. Every planet shaped fruit
> leaks in the arena I'm allowed.

Lucky Star appears twice a year, a 7x8½" saddle-stapled format, 50 + pp. photocopied from various typescripts with cartoon-like art on the matte cover. It has a circulation of 400, 225 subscriptions of which 40 are libraries. They receive 200-300 submissions per year of which they use 50-60, have a 3-12 month backlog. **Sample: $4 postpaid. Photocopy, simultaneous submissions OK, no dot-matrix. Send brief bio note with poems. Pays 1 contributor's copy. For chapbook publication, query with 5-10 samples.** Send SASE for catalog. Henry Kranz advises, "Read published poetry; study famous poets from antiquity and the last 3-4 generations. Attend public readings and absorb as much as possible. Do not attempt to publish until the poems have lived with you 2-5 years."

EUROEDITOR, *NEW EUROPA(II), case postale 212, Luxemburg-Grand Duchy, P. M. Oostveen, Manager, publishes **"all kinds of good poetry"** and has recently published work by De Andrade Guillevic, Guillen, Sjostrand, and Alberti. As a sample I selected the opening stanza of "Green Shutters" by Rose Mary Rowley:

> Green shutters on terra cotta,
> recall franchised lives in the sun,
> Clean linen,
> The shroud of the land
> And the humid valley.

The 6x9" quarterly, *New Europa*, is 80 pp. flat-spined, printed on coated stock with a 2-color card cover. **I have no information about submission or payment.** Euroeditor specializes in bilingual editions in 10 European languages.

‡*EUROPEAN JUDAISM (IV, Jewish)**, Kent House, Rutland Gardens, London, England SW7 1BX, 01-584-2754, founded 1966, poetry editor Albert H. Friedlander, is a **"twice-yearly magazine with emphasis on European Jewish theology/philosophy/literature/ history, with some poetry in every issue. It should preferably be short, as it is often used as filler, and should have Jewish content or reference. We do not want hackneyed, overblown rubbish."** They have recently published poetry by Alan Sillito, Erich Fried, Ruth Fainlight and Carol Adler. I selected these sample lines from "Victims" by Bernard Kops:

> their songs of praise will rise
> with the smoke of our bones
> and journalists will weep
> and history will shrug

It is a glossy, elegant 7x10" flat-spined magazine with no ads, rarely art or graphics, 48 pp. They have a print-run of 950, about 50% of which goes to subscribers (few libraries). $4 per issue; subscription $7.95. **Sample: $4 postpaid. Pays 2 copies.**

EVANGEL (IV, Nature, religious), 901 College Ave., Winona Lake, IN 46590, weekly since 1897, poetry editor Vera Bethel, publishes Sunday-school literature, curriculum and **take-home papers—an 8-page paper for children and another for adults. They use nature and devotional poetry, 8-16 lines, "free verse or with rhyme scheme**." The circulation of these papers is 35,000; they are sold in bulk to Sunday schools. **Free sample. Pays: $5. Photocopy, simultaneous submissions OK. Reports in 1 month.** These sample lines are from "Spring Rain" by Darlene Workman Stull:

> A punctured sky is leaking gentle rain
> Upon the rosery, the lawn, the hay.
> An iris wears a beading on its mane.
> And moisture films the mushroom's fawn beret.

The editor advises, "Do not write abstractions. Use concrete words to picture concept for reader."

***THE EVANGELICAL BEACON (IV, Religious)**, 1515 E. 66th St., Minneapolis, MN 55423, phone 612-866-3343, is the denominational magazine of the Evangelical Free Church of America, published every third Monday. Sample copy and guidelines: 75¢. It **uses very little poetry—which must be in keeping with the aims of the magazine—"helpful to the average Christian" or "presenting reality of the Christian faith to non-Christians." Pays variable rate—$3.50 minimum.** "Some tie-in with the Evangelical Free Church of America is helpful but is not required."

***EVENT (II)**, Douglas College, Box 2503, New Westminster, B.C., Canada V3L 5B2, founded 1978, poetry editor Dale Zieroth, is "a literary magazine publishing **high-quality contemporary poetry**, short stories, reviews and graphics. "**Any good-quality work is considered**." They have recently published Earle Birney, Dorothy Livesay, Alden Nowlan, Roo Borson and Lyn Lifshin. These sample lines are by Bronwen Wallace:

> it takes me a day to remove
> their fingerprints from the walls
> and hours of scrubbing before
> the tub gives up its dead cell scum

It appears twice a year as a 6x9" flat-spined, 140 + pp., glossy-covered, finely printed paperback with a circulation of 900, 450 subscriptions, of which 50 are libraries. **Sample: $4 postpaid**. They have a 6 month backlog, **report in 1 month, pay $20/poem** plus one free copy of issue. Sometimes they have special thematic issues, such as on "work," "feminism," "coming of age." **They comment on rejections.**

‡*EXIT, ROCHESTER ROUTES/CREATIVE ARTS PROJECTS (II)**, 193 Inglewood Dr., Rochester, NY 14619, founded 1977, editor and publisher Frank Judge, a small-press publisher of a literary review and occasional chapbooks. *Exit* publishes poetry, fiction, translations, interviews, and art work. **"We are interested primarily in quality and prefer shorter pieces."** The editor says, "There is no 'typical' poem we can quote. Styles of acceptable material range from Bly to Wilbur, Dickey to Creeley to Merwin to concrete and 'pop'." The magazine (which I have not seen) is digest-sized, offset, 32-69 pp., with art, graphics, and ads. Circulation is 1,000, of which 50 are library subscriptions. Price per copy is $5, subscription $15/3 issues. **Sample (if available) costs $6 postpaid. Pay is 3 copies. "We like to see a good sample of a poet's work (5-10 poems); short (1-2 pp.) preferred; photocopies, dot-matrix, disc (Apple II +)** acceptable; writers should send 10 sample poems with credits and bio. Pay for books is 25 author's copies. They publish 1 poetry book per year, digest-sized, saddle-stitched, with an average page count of 32.

*EXPECTING (IV, Expectant mothers)**, 685 3rd Ave., New York, NY 10017, is a mass-circulation quarterly (1,200,000) for expectant mothers which **occasionally buys subject-related poetry; all forms. Length: 12-64 lines. Pays $10-30. Send SASE for guidelines.**

EXPEDITION PRESS (II), 311 W. Vine, Kalamazoo, MI 49001, phone 616-345-9345, founded 1978, poetry editor Bruce W. White, who says, "We publish poetry chapbooks composed of long-poems, experimental poems, tone poems, existential poems, whole books, or parts of longer works." He likes to see **"fresh new approaches, interesting spatial relationships, as well as quality art work. We dislike political diatribes."** Some poets he has published are J. Kline Hobbs; Jim DeWitt, Martin Cohen and C. VanAllsburg. As a sample he chose this "Haiku" by himself:

> The sun low in the West.
> The warm clay courts. A
> moment of peace.

The sample chapbooks I have seen are by Bruce White, digest-sized 20 pp., offset from typescript, saddle-stapled, matte-colored card cover with drawings, $2 each. Submit MS of 20-30 pp. and brief bio. Photocopy, dot-matrix, simultaneous submissions OK. MS on cassette OK. Reports in 1 month. Pays 100 copies.

‡*EXPLORATIONS 87, (II)**, 1120 Glacier Highway, Juneau, AL 99801, phone 907-789-4423, founded 1980, student editor Danielle Davee, advisor Ron Silva. The annual literary magazine of the University of Alaska, Juneau, *Explorations 87* (or appropriate year) publishes **"The best quality poetry, any form, style, purpose; form fits meaning, meaning fits form; classical forms, new forms." They do not want to see loose free verse, "poetry," sentimental or religious poetry.** Some of the poets published recently include Susan Bazett, Wendy Taylor, and Sheila Nickerson. The editors selected the following haiku as a sample (poet unidentified):

> Undulating to
> deep throbbing drumbeats,
> She echoes ancient rhythms.

The publication is mainly for writing by students of UAJ, but it also publishes work by other authors. Digest-sized, nicely printed, with front and inside back cover illustration in one color, saddle-stapled. **Pay is 2 free copies. Submissions are reported on promptly, publication is annual. MSS should be typed, with name and address, photocopies OK, simultaneous submissions OK.** The editor says "Be proud of your work and submit accordingly."

‡*EXPLORER MAGAZINE, EXPLORER PUBLISHING CO. (I,IV, Inspirational)**, Box 210, Notre Dame, IN 46556, phone 219-277-3465, founded 1960, editor and publisher Raymond Flory, a semi-annual magazine that contains short inspirational, nature, and love poetry as well as prose. The editor wants **"Poetry of all styles and types; should have an inspirational slant but not necessary. Short poems preferred—up to 16 lines. Good 'family' type poetry always needed. No real long poetry or long lines; no sexually explicit poetry or porno."** He has recently published poems by Ma-

rion Schoeber-Lein, Edna James Kayster, Carrie Quick, and others. As a sample, he chose the entire poem, "The Poet," by Jim Wyzard:

> *He puts his pen to paper,*
> *In hope that he might find,*
> *A spark of new conjecture,*
> *And a stairway to the mind.*

Explorer is digest-sized, photocopied from typed copy (some of it not too clear) on thin paper, 31 pp., cover of the same paper with title superimposed on a water-color painting, folded and saddle-stapled. Circulation is 200, subscription price $3/year. **Sample available for $1.50 postpaid, guidelines for SASE. Pay is 1 copy. Subscribers vote for the poems or stories they like best and prizes of $5-10 are awarded. Writers should submit 3-4 poems, typed or photocopied; dot-matrix OK. Material must be previously unpublished; no simultaneous submissions. Reporting time is 1 week and time to publication 1-2 years.** Explorer Publishing Company does not presently publish books except for an anthology about every 4 years; it is a paperback, digest-sized book with an average page count of 20. The editor says, "Over 90% of the poets submitting poetry to *Explorer* have not seen a copy of magazine. Order a copy first—then submit. This will save poets stamps, frustration, etc. This should hold true for whatever market a writer is aiming for!"

‡*EXPRESSIONS: FIRST STATE JOURNAL (I, IV, Regional)**, Box 4064, Greenville, DE 19807, poetry editor Joanne Petrizzi. **Beginners submissions are accepted but magazine publishes only one page per issue called "New Voices." They are "open to all types of poetry. We do want quality—be it prose, traditional, historical, nature . . . We like to see all styles, and each issue falls together as the submissions roll in. Our purpose is to be able to introduce Delaware to the world . . ." They do not want to see "Moon, June, Spoon" poems, although they do enjoy rhyming poetry.** As a sample the editor selected these lines from an unidentified poet:

> *In all the temples ever wrought to gods,*
> *in all recorded works for all mankind;*
> *there comes no finer total peace in life*
> *than that absorbed in miles left behind.*

The semi-annual magazine **does not pay but will send 2 free copies to contributors. Submissions are reported on in 3-6 weeks, time to publication will be about 4-6 months. Poems, which may be more than 1 page long, should be submitted 1 per page; photocopied or dot-matrix MSS are OK. Sample: $4 postpaid.** The editor comments, "Our format is open to expression. We like to see quality poetry from Delaware as well as international, translations, and from anywhere in the good ole U.S.A. . . . We prefer to have bio sent with all submissions and enjoy the cover letters we receive. We are open to suggestion, and want to encourage people to submit. We have accepted several re-written poems, which we helped to edit. We read from April through July and October through January for issues." Advice? Re-read, and then submit! . . .

*EXQUISITE CORPSE (II)**, Dept. of English, Louisiana State University, Baton Rouge, LA 70803, founded 1983, is a monthly cultural magazine, 6x16", 20 pp., circulation 2,000, which publishes avant-garde poetry. Sample: $2.

*FANTASY AND TERROR (IV)**, Box 20610, Seattle, WA 98102 (published c/o Richard H. Fawcett, 61 Teecomwas Dr., Uncasville, CT 06382), founded 1973, poetry editor Jessica A. Salmonson, publishes **new works of lyric verse in the dark-romanticism vein, macabre-surrealist symbolist, allegorical vignettes (prose poems), and "other odd, cynical kinds of writing about death, the supernatural—anything gloomy and *brief*.** Not even one submission from our 1986 listing came close to our very carefully defined needs. I think you got the needs across excellently, but 'tis a hopeless task. Though it says very clearly 'prose-poems' ('poems-in-prose' might've been more descriptive; the term prose-poem does sometimes get misused and some might not know what it is) I've seen not one poem in prose. Though it says even more clearly that I'll also consider 'lyric' verse (again, perhaps 'metrical' would've been an even clearer term, but I doubt it) I haven't even seen dreadful kitchen-verse. It's just *all* blank verse, experimental, and perhaps the term 'surrealism' caught the eyes of some of these poets, but dark-romanticism and macabre did not. Reams and reams of junk! I pity the trees that died in vain! I've a sneaking suspicion that the artistic temperament, especially the old-fashioned romantic, scribbling insane visions of damnation, is not the sort of nurd to go look in *Poet's Market* in the dire hope of someone publishing their cynical ravings. Rather, they're readers themselves, antequarian collectors, haunters of the streets and wood of night—and I find my kindred spirits in the dark corners of the planet by means incomprehensible but reliable." They have published work by Jane Yolen, Bruce Boston, Tom Ligotti, Thomas Wiloch, Mary Elizabeth Counselman, Michael Bishop, Robert Frazier and Frank Belknap Long. As a sample of the sort of thing they're looking for, the editor offers these lines by Thomas Bailey Aldrich (1836-1907), titled "Romeo and Juliet":

> *From mask to mask, amid the masquerade,*
> *Young Passion went with challenging, soft breath:*
> *"Art Love?" he whispered; "art thou Love, sweet maid?"*
> *Then Love, with glittering eyelids, "I am Death."*

It appears "occasionally" (4 issues in 1984), circulation 500. The sample I have is 37 pp. with cover, digest-sized, offset printed from reduced typescript, saddle-stapled. **Sample: $2.50, from publisher, address above**. The editor says, "I don't want submissions from anyone who hasn't a deep-rooted knowledge of supernatural fiction and poetry. This is **not a "horror magazine" per se, since it leans more to Baudelaire than to Lovecraft; Leonora Carrington or Renee Vivian rather than Stephen King. Payment: copies. Reporting time: usually within a week**. They also publish chapbooks. Send the editor a large SASE for the **Weird Poetry Chapbook Catalog** to order samples.

*FANTASY BOOK (IV, Fantasy), Box 60126, Pasadena, CA 91106, founded 1981, poetry editor Nick Smith, is a quarterly devoted to illustrated fantasy fiction but which uses **2-3 fantasy-oriented poems in each issue, whenever possible**. "We prefer short works to longer ones, though we will consider anything oriented toward the fantastic. We prefer story-poems." They have recently published poems by Robert Frazier, Esther M. Friesner, Jim Neal and Nancy Springer. The magazine has a circulation of 4,500, 650 subscriptions of which 20 are libraries. Sample: $4 postpaid. Reports in 4-6 weeks. Pays 50¢ a line. Send SASE for general guidelines.

*FANTASY REVIEW (IV, Horror, fantasy, science fiction), (formerly *Fantasy Newsletter*), College of Humanities, Florida Atlantic University, Boca Raton, FL 33431, founded 1978 poetry editor Robert A. Collins, is a monthly review of *all* the titles in the fields of fantasy, horror and science fiction, which uses **1-2 poems in each issue, pays: $10 per poem plus contributor's copy**. "Highly imaginative, even bizarre images, relating to fantasy, horror and science (or science fiction). No long narrative works, no clichés. (No talking rabbits, little green men, etc.) Length a factor: we need 'em short." They have recently published poetry by Ardath Mayhar, Steve Rasnic Tem, Bruce Boston, Janet Fox, Larry Cuthbert and Margaret Flanagan. These sample lines are by Tom Rentz:

> *This one looks so real, old woman,*
> *With every feature so detailed.*
> *and each hair neatly placed,*
> *I can't help but wonder—*
> *Whose soul is trapped within?*

They have a circulation of 2,800, with 1,500 subscriptions, of which 300 are libraries. They receive over 150 submissions per year, use about 20, have a 5-6 month backlog. **Sample: $2.50 postpaid. Guidelines available for SASE. Submit packet of 3-4 poems. Those over 1 page unlikely to be considered**. The editor comments, "For our kind of poetry they should consult *Star*Line, Velocities* and Owlswick Press's *Burning With a Vision*."

*FARMER'S MARKET, MIDWEST FARMER'S MARKET, INC. (IV, Regional), Box 1272, Galesburg, IL 61402, founded 1981, editors Jean C. Lee, John Hughes and Gail Nichols, is a biannual seeking "to provide a forum for the best of regional poetry and fiction." They want poems that are **"tightly structured, with concrete imagery, specific to Midwestern themes and values, reflective of the clarity, depth and strength of Midwestern life. Not interested in highly abstract or experimental work, or light verse**." They have recently published poetry by Kathryn Burt, Jim McCurry, Joan Rohr Myers, Richard Behm, Victoria McCabe, and Michael McMahon. As a sample, they offer these lines by Bradley Steffens:

> *The fierce grey whistle disturbs*
> *commonplaces of an Iowa morning: linens*
> *rolled in soaking wads, drip*
> *through a varnished wicker basket;*

The format is digest-sized, saddle-stitched with card cover, handsomely printed with graphics and photos. Circulation 500, 50 subscriptions, of which 10 are libraries. **Sample: $3 postpaid**. They receive about 500 submissions per year, of which they use 20-30, have a 6 month backlog. **Submit up to 10 pages, typed or letter-quality print out, photocopies OK, would rather not have simultaneous submissions. Reports in 2-6 weeks (summer replies take longer). Pay: 1 copy. They comment on rejections, "only if we think the work is good**."

*FAT TUESDAY (II), Suite 104, 419 N. Larchmont, Los Angeles, CA 90004, founded 1981, poetry editors F. M. Cotolo, B. Lyle Tabor, Lionel Stevroid, is an annual which calls itself "**a Mardi Gras of literary and visual treats featuring many voices, singing, shouting, sighing and shining, expressing the relevant to irreverent**. On Fat Tuesday (the Tuesday before Ash Wednesday, when Lent begins) the editors hold The Fat Tuesday Symposium. In five years no one has shown up." They want "**prose**

poems, poems of irreverence, gems from the gut. Usually shorter, hit-the-mark, personal stuff inseparable from the voice of the artist. Form doesn't matter." Poets they have recently published include Mark Cramer, Mary Lee Gowland, Chuck Taylor, Patrick Kelly and Randy Klutts. As a sample they offer these lines by John Quinnett:

> It is enough to be alive,
> To be here drinking this cheap red wine
> While the chili simmers on the stove
> & the refrigerator hums deep into the night.

The digest-sized magazine is typeset (large type, heavy paper), 36 pp., saddle-stapled, card covers, with cartoons, art, ads. Circulation 200, 20-25 pp. of poetry in each issue. **Sample: $5.00 postpaid**. They receive hundreds of submissions each year, use 3-5%, have a 3-5 month backlog. **No previously published material. "photocopy, dot-matrix, handwritten OK; we'll read anything." Reports in 1-2 weeks. Pay: 1 copy.** The editors say, "Our tip for authors is simply to be themselves. Poets should use their own voice to be heard. Publishing poetry is as lonely as writing it. We have no idea about current trends, and care less. Poetry is nothing more than pure expression. Timed correctly, a belch or a fart can be as poetic as the most eloquent line of verse. Nor is poetry limited to the tired forms verse has to offer. It can be as delicious in a sentence, a thought fragment, a black line drawing as it is in perfect meter. Self-expression is the trend. Beginners need only write what they mean to reflect how they feel, and worry not about reason or rhyme. And if it takes a trillion words to find that truth, only the naturals will write the trillion-and-first one."

FEMINIST STUDIES (IV, Women), %Women's Studies Program, College Park, MD 20742, founded 1969, poetry editor Rachel DuPlessis, **"welcomes a variety of work that focuses on women's experience, on gender as a category of analysis, and that furthers feminist theory and consciousness**." They have recently published poetry by Marilyn Hacker, Kathleen Fraser, Cheryl Clark and Naomi Replanski. As a sample, they offer this prose poetry by Eleanor Wilner: ". . . She had the reticence of passion, the terror of the early wounded, and the courage of those who try to write their way past repetition . . ." The elegantly-printed, flat-spined, 360 + pp., paperback appears 3 times a year in an edition of 7,000, goes to 3,500 subscribers, of which 1,500 are libraries. There are **4-10 pp. of poetry in each issue. Sample: $8 postpaid**. No pay.

*THE FIDDLEHEAD (II, IV, Canada), The Observatory, University of New Brunswick, Box 4400, Fredericton, NB E3B 5A3, Canada, founded 1945, poetry editors Robert Gibbs, Robert Hawkes, Yvonne Trainer. The quarterly magazine seeks "to publish excellent *literary art that is a distinctive expression of Atlantic-Canadian culture and also to publish solidly worthwhile works from the rest of Canada and abroad*." As the oldest continuing Canadian literary journal, it has a distinguished tradition and maintains very high standards of excellence. Among the poets whose work they have published are Eric Trethewey, Alden Nowlan, Milton Acorn, Hillel Chwartz, Lesley Choyce, and Richardo Pau-Llosa. As a sample, I chose the first stanza from "Man in the Moon" by Don Domanski:

> at night when I fill my shoes with ether
> when my heart makes the sound
> of eggs boiling away in the dark
> I often lie there thinking of you

The Fiddlehead is a handsomely printed, 6x9" flat-spined paperback (140 + pp.) with b/w graphics, glossy colored cover, which, on the copy I have seen (January, 1983, #135), is illustrated with a detail from a painting. Circulation is 1,200. Subscription price is $12/year. **Sample available for $4.25 plus postage. Pay is $12/printed page. They use less than 10% of submissions. Reporting time 6-8 weeks, backlog 6-12 months.**

‡FIDDLEHEAD POETRY BOOKS, GOOSE LANE EDITIONS (II), 132 Saunders ST., Fredericton, NB, E3B 1N3 Canada (no connection with *The Fiddlehead*), phone 506-454-8319, publisher and general editor Peter Thomas, founded 1958, a small press that publishes perfect-bound paperback collections of poetry. The book I have is **From the Bedside Book of Nightmares** by Suniti Namjoshi. As a sample, I selected the first poem in a sequence called "From Baby F with Much Love":

> In those early photographs you (and my father)
> look so very young that I'd be inclined
> to weep—as people do at weddings—
> if I weren't implicated.

The book is 6x9", handsomely printed on heavy buff stock, 70 pp., flat-spined with a glossy two-color card cover; its price is $6.95. The spring, 1985, catalog of Fiddlehead Poetry Books/Goose Lane Editions lists 12 new publications of which most are poetry; prices range from $6.95 to $12.95. **"Unsolicited MSS considered, SASE essential (IRC's or Canadian postage stamps only)."**

*FIGHTING WOMAN NEWS (IV, Women's martial arts), Box 1459 Grand Central Station, New York, NY 10163, founded 1975, poetry editor Muskat Buckby, provides "a communications medium for **women in martial arts, self-defense, combative sports**." They want **poetry "relevant to our subject matter and nothing else**." Poets they have recently published include Pam Parker, Kate MacLaren, Kristen Noakes-Fry, Miriam Frank, Pat James, Sandy Feather, Oreithyia, J. W. (Joyce Wadler), Quintus Smyrnaeus, Torquato Tasso, and "Anonymous (I like her best)," says the editor. As a sample she offers these lines by a poet whose name is actually D. Duck, "For Them As Likes to Vegitate":

> *Sitting cross-legged peacefully,*
> *Looking very mature,*
> *Is nothing to drinking a lot of sake*
> *And making a riotous noise.*

Fighting Woman News appears quarterly in a magazine-sized, saddle-stapled format, 32 pp. or more, finely printed, with graphics and b/w photos, circulation 6,500. **Sample copy $3.50 including postage,"and if you say you're a poet, we'll be sure to send a sample with poetry in it."** Only about a quarter of a page of poetry in each issue, and they are overstocked—6-24 month backlog. **"If it** *really* **requires an audience of martial artists to be appreciated, then send it." Simultaneous submissions, photocopy OK, no dot-matrix. Replies "ASAP." Pays: copies**. "Because our field is so specialized, most interested women subscribe. It is not a requirement for publication, but **we seldom publish a non-subscriber**." The editor advises, "Read the magazine FIRST. To guarantee publication of your poem(s), submit a hard core martial arts non-fiction article. Those are what we really need! Fighters who are also writers can have **priority access to our very limited poetry space by doing articles**. Something I would *really* like: A good translation of the Anglo-Saxon *Judith*."

‡*FINE MADNESS, *HAD WE BUT, INC, (II), Box 15176, Seattle, WA 98115, phone 206-526-2494, founded 1980, editorial contact person James Snydal. *Had We But* is an international poetry biennial, *Fine Madness* is a twice-yearly magazine. The editors say, **"We want writers with their own distinctive voices, and writing which shows that a mind is working, not just a tongue; that the form works for the piece and not against it. We do find ourselves reluctant to spend much time on Victorian-sounding verse."** Poets recently published include Leslie Norris, Glyn Jones, William Matthews, Colleen McElroy, Marc Hudson, Greg Kuzma, Sam Hamill, and Lyn Lifshin. As a sample, I selected this complete poem, "West Coast Nature Poetry II" by Hart Schulz:

> *In California*
> *—when the frogs*
> *won't quit*
> *we put alligators*
> *in the pond*
> *and call*
> *the new silence*
> *poetry*

Fine Madness is digest-sized, 64 pp., saddle-stapled, letterpress printed with cover art, matte card cover. Circulation is 1,000 most of which is newsstand or bookstore sales. $4/copy, subscription $8. **Sample: $2.50 postpaid, guidelines available for SASE. Payment is 2 free copies. Reports on submissions in 2-3 months, publishes in 6 months-1 year**. "We would appreciate original typed MSS. No blurred photocopies, smudged carbons, or dot-matrix productions, please. Two $50 prizes are given each year for the editor's favorite submissions."

FIREWEED PRESS, VANESSAPRESS (IV, Regional), Box 83970, Fairbanks, AK 99708, founded 1976, publishes **"only anthologies of contemporary Alaskan writing** (including works by writers with "a significant relationship" to the state) and books resulting from special contests. The subsidiary, Vanessapress publishes poetry, fiction and non-fiction by **contemporary Alaskan women writers**. Fireweed has recently published poetry by Pat Monaghan, Katherine McNamara, Joe Enzweiler, John Haines, and Jane Hixon. Vanessapress has published a visionary long poem by Sheila Nickerson. These sample lines are from "Words for a Granddaughter" by Linda Schandelmeier:

> *The same crows in the morning, fogbound on the*
> *pilings, the ocean shuffled into the slough*
> *like always, but the children*
> *were sinking like dead stars.*

"For Fireweed, write for current MSS sought; do not send unsolicited work unless it meets current contest or anthology categories." Only Alaskan women should submit—query with 5-6 samples to Vanessapress, noting these quarterly reading deadlines: **January 14, April 15, July 15 and September 15. Include $5 reading fee**. Both Fireweed and Vanessapress work closely with the author on distribution and marketing, reply to queries in 1 month, to submissions in 3 months. Simultaneous submissions, photocopies and dot-matrix OK, contracts on 7% royalty basis with 10 author's copies.

THE FIRST EAST COAST THEATER AND PUBLISHING CO., INC. (II), Box A244, Village Station, New York, NY 10014, phone 718-296-1979, founded 1979, poetry editors Paul Buccio and Karen Corinne Boccio, publishes flat-spined paperbacks of **"serious contemporary and fresh poetry"**—no "greeting card" type verses, jingles, seasonal, etc. "Otherwise our publications are varied in style. We publish MSS from 30-70 pp., consistent style, thought-provoking material." They have recently published poets such as Stuart Kaufman and Roger Steigmeier. I selected these sample lines from Anna Adams, "The Candle Hops in the Bog Broadside: for Bobby Sands," in **The Ratio of One to a Stone**:

> Empires change shapes like amoeba
> Our tycoons are tomorrow's dodos,
> Castles well we'll rent to the yanks
> But what'll we do with the London Tower

The book is a digest-sized matte-covered paperback, neatly printed with large type, very readable. **Submit 3-5 sample poems first with cover letter concerning biographical background, personal or aesthetic philosophy, poetic goals and principles. Replies to queries in 1 month, to submissions (if invited) in l month. Simultaneous submissions, photocopy, dot-matrix OK. Pays 10% royalties, 10 author's copies. They comment "almost always,"** and advise, "Having individual poems published helps with credits but isn't essential. Poetry is an on an upswing. Small press is where it's at for many serious poets."

*FIRST HAND (IV, Gay, lesbian), Box 1314, Teaneck, NJ 07666, phone 201-836-9177, founded 1980, poetry editor Jack Veasey, is a **"homosexual erotic publication written mostly by its readers**." The digest-sized monthly has a circulation of 70,000, 3,000 subscribers of which 3 are libraries, and uses 1-2 pp. of poetry in each issue, for which they **pay $25 a poem**. Poems by Chuck Ortleb, Felice Picano and Dennis Cooper have appeared there recently. I selected these sample lines from "Blue Boys" by Mark Benoit:

> Blue boys leave without dinner they
> leave without a cordial or
> tea they leave only the water
> that drips from their raincoats they
> Leave without me

Submit poems no longer than 1 typed page. No queries. Reports in 6 weeks. Jack Veasey or Assistant/editor Bob Harris sometimes comment on rejected MSS. They have a 4-6 month backlog. The editor advises, "Make sure what you're writing about is obvious to future readers. Poems need not be explicitly sexual, but must deal overtly with gay situations and subject matter."

‡*FIRST TIME (I, II), The Gables, 80 St. Helen's Rd., Hastings, E. Sussex, England, phone 0424-428855, founded 1981, editor Josephine Austin, who says the magazine is **open to "All kinds of poetry—our magazine goes right across the board—which is why it is one of the most popular in Great Britain."** The magazine appears twice a year; from the recent issues I have seen, I selected the following lines from "Flowers" by Daphne Schiller, "our featured poet:"

> I could start a religion with snowdrops,
> Spring's votive candles born of black loam,
> I could invent a philosophy from crocuses,
> Important globes pulsing with light

The digest-sized magazine, 24 pp. saddle-stapled, contains several poems on each page, in a variety of small type styles, on lightweight stock, b/w photographs of editor and 1 author, glossy one-color card cover. Price per issue is £1.25, subscription £2.50/year. **Sample: 50p plus postage. Pay is 1 copy. Poems submitted must not exceed 30 lines, must not have been published elsewhere, and must have name and address of poet on each. Maximum time to publication is 2 months. Poets should send 10 sample poems. There is an annual competition with money prizes, and a poetry festival.** The editor advises, "Keep on 'pushing your poetry.' If one editor rejects you then study the market and decide which is the correct one for you. Try to type your own manuscripts as long hand work is difficult to read and doesn't give a professional impression. Always date your poetry — C1985 and sign it. Follow your way of writing, don't be a pale imitation of someone else—sooner or later styles change and you will either catch up or be ahead."

‡*FIVE FINGERS REVIEW, FIVE FINGERS POETRY (V, IV, Social Issues), Suite 303, 100 Valencia St., San Francisco, CA 94103, founded 1984, poetry editors Lisa Bernstein and others, a literary bi-annual publishing "diverse, innovative writing by writers of various aesthetics who are **concerned with social issues**." Some of the better-known poets they have published are Denise Levertov, Robert Bly, C.D. Wright, Kathleen Fraser, and Ron Silliman. An occasional poem is published in both English and Spanish, such as "Lejos Esta Mi Patria," by Roque Dalton, translated by Barbara Paschke and

David Volpendesta; as a sample I selected its first stanza, in English:

> *Far from the world, far*
> *from the natural order of words;*
> *far away,*
> *twelve thousand kilometers*
> *from where iron is a house for man*
> *and grows like a rare flower enamored of the clouds;*

Five Fingers Review is 6x9", nicely printed on buff stock, 78 pp., flat-spined with one-color glossy card cover. Circulation is 750 copies, 25% of which go to libraries. Price per issue is $5, subscription $8/year. **Sample available for $5 postpaid. Pay is 2 copies. Reporting time is 3-6 months and time to publication is 4 months.** Five Fingers Poetry has published one chapbook, **Anorexia**, by Lisa Bernstein (a case-study of anorexia in poems). It is 6x9", 27 pp. saddle-stapled with glossy card cover. **No freelance submissions are accepted for chapbooks.** The advice of the editors is: "Form a company. As in an ensemble. Publish yourselves."

‡*FLAME POETRY MAGAZINE (I)**, 20 Brooklyn Dr., Lymm, Cheshire WA13 9DN, England, phone 092-575-4726, founded 1985, editor N.A. Stone. **"No special type [of poetry] demanded, nor certain forms, subjects, styles. I prefer poetry of little more length than would fill 1 or 1½ sides of A5 [digest] sized paper." The editor wants nothing "racist, sexist, war mongering, or haiku."** He has recently published poems by Hugh McMillan, Dave Cunliffe, Alan Dunnelt, and Steve Sneyd. As a sample, I chose the following stanza from "Suicide" by Alan Dunnett:

> *Ah, Smith! the fire brigade*
> *Will soon be here and an ambulance. With an axe*
> *And jacket will you be tended*
> *And a little injection to make you relax*
> *And a stomach pump if you've been silly,*
> *Smith.*

Flame, which appears "several times a year, depending on submissions," is digest-sized, photocopied from typed copy on ordinary paper, 22 pp. folded and saddle-stapled, with b/w decorations. Circulation is "less than 300" and a subscription is "free for return postage." **Sample available for "things of interest and postage." Pay is as many copies as requested.** Submissions should be typed; "prefer original unpublished; no simultaneous submissions. **Each separate sheet** *really* **must bear name and address of poet."** Reporting time is 1-8 weeks and time to publication is 6 months.

FLUME PRESS ANNUAL POETRY CHAPBOOK CONTEST (II), 644 Citrus Ave., Chico, CA 95926, founded 1984, poetry editors Elizabeth Renfro and Casey Huff, is "a small not-for-profit press that will publish **one chapbook a year**, the winner of an annual poetry chapbook contest—the $5 entry fees going toward prizes, judge's fee, and production. We will **concentrate primarily on newer poets. We have few biases about form, although we appreciate control and crafting, and we tend to favor a concise, understated style, with emphasis on metaphor rather than editorial commentary. Sample copy: $14.** The sample I have seen, Tina Barr's At Dusk On Naskeag Point, is handsomely printed, matte cover with color, 32 pp. hand sewn, 6x9", using high quality paper. As a sample I selected the first stanza of her "Eclipse":

> *Spiked silhouettes emerge*
> *as the pinks and purples of the lupine fade.*
> *Further off, pines repeat the image.*
> *Behind them—the moon, full grown, white.*

"MSS submitted to our contests should be 30 pp. maximum with name, address, phone and appropriate acknowledgments on a separate cover sheet." Simultaneous submissions OK. Winner receives $50 honorarium and 50 copies.

FOLDER EDITIONS (II), 103-26 68th Rd., New York, NY 11375, phone 718-275-3839, founded 1953, poetry editor Daisy Aldan, is "a small press with a fine **reputation for printing excellent poetry**, translations and occasional fiction of a high quality." They have published poetry by Angeln Ray, Ruth Lisa Schecter, Alexander Grillikhes, Albert Steffen (Swiss) and Harriet Zinnes. I selected these sample lines from "Even If I Founder" by Daisy Aldan (in **Between High Tides**):

> *Water salamanders are writing joyful tidings*
> *in black water under ice, wrecking the framework of winter.*
> *The beehive lake is melting.*

The book is a 74 pp. flat-spined paperback with slipcover over card cover, digest-sized, using small type, purple ink. To be considered for publication by this press, **query with 6 samples, photocopy OK. Replies to query in 2 weeks. If accepted, publication is on a 15% royalty contract with 10 author's copies**. Daisy Aldan advises, "Remain true to highest standards of the word, Do not compromise for material gains."

*FOLIO: A LITERARY JOURNAL (II), Dept. of Literature, Gray Hall, American University, Washington, DC 20016, phone 202-885-2973, founded 1984, editors Gregg Shapiro and Tammy Lillis, a biannual, wants **no light verse, pornography; nothing over two pages**. They have published poetry by Walter McDonald and D.C. Berry. The editor selected these sample lines from "The Felsenmere" by Elaine Magarrell:

> *Ceremony begins*
> *in a zone of partial*
> *melting, magma*
> *Wells up in the mantle,*
> *Spews onto the oceanfloor.*

There are 25-30 pp. of poetry in each 64 pp. issue, narrow digest-sized, thin flat spine, matte cover, neatly printed from typeset. **Sample: $3.50 postpaid. Submit from August to mid-October or January to mid-March, up to 6 pp., include a brief bio/contributor's note, photocopy, dot-matrix OK. Pays in one contributor's copy. Comments on rejection "if it came close to acceptance." They also sponsor a contest open to all contributors with a $50 prize for the best poem of the issue.**

*THE FOLIO: AN INTERNATIONAL LITERARY MAGAZINE (I, IV, Subscribers), 82 Dresden Close, Corby, Northants, England NN18 9EN, poetry editor Tom Bingham, who describes it as, **"an independent OPEN magazine that publishes some 50 poets per issue (3 times a year). We accept work from USA but only from subscribers to the magazine.** USA is too expensive for us. Few actually send the correct return postage, and even fewer subscribe. We do not reply to ANYONE who does not send 3 IRC's or dollar bills. We publish at least 6 USA poets each issue." **No religious work;** anything else will be considered. 25-30 lines preferred. Work acceptable: feminist/political/satirical/etc. "We specialize in publishing poets and writers without telling them on the basis if they don't buy a copy they don't care if their work appears or not. We also publish individual poets' short-run booklets." The magazine's stationery bears the slogan, "There's Room for Everyone," and judging by the samples sent me, that may be the case. As a sample I selected the opening lines of a poem entitled "Stan's Legacy (Paula)"—poet unidentified in the magazine:

> *As clear as yesterday enslaves me,*
> *I remember well the look you gave me*
> *When bitten by a dog, and in pain*
> *To your Apothecary I came.*

‡*FORUM (BALL STATE UNIVERSITY) (II), Department of English, RB238, Ball State University, Muncie, IN 47306, phone 317-285-8584, poetry editor Darlene Mathis-Eddy, an "eclectic literary quarterly with emphasis on poetry, short stories, and essays. One issue per year devoted to poetry; eight to ten poems used in each of the other three issues." They want **"Quality poetry—traditional and innovative—no restrictions on form. Basically we seek lyric poetry of the highest quality from both established and new poets. Interested in diversity of themes and approaches, landscape and nature poetry, translations, satires." They don't want** "tasteless or imitative verse, lengthy narrative poetry, or prose poems." They have recently published poetry by Nancy Westerfield, Louis Brodsky, Thom Tammaro, Mattheu McKay, and Hillel Schwartz. As a sample, the editors chose the following lines from "Below" by Susan Fromberg Schaeffer:

> *Seaweed of the mortal life.*
> *In the quiet chambers*
> *On a dry beach,*
> *Such fossils we become.*

Forum is a 6½x9½", professionally printed on white stock, 80 pp. saddle-stapled, buff matte card cover with illustration of a painting by Millet. Single copy price is $3, subscription $10/year. **Contributors should follow the** *MLA Style Manual* **and send no more than 3-5 poems at a time. Pay is 3 copies. Reporting time is 3-6 months and time to publication is usually 10-15 months.** The magazine expects to hold contests in 1987-88 and thereafter. The editors advise, "Patience, Perseverance, A Sense of Humor."

*FOUR BY FOUR: A SELECTION OF POETS, VILLENEUVE PUBLICATIONS (I,II), 4646, rue Hutchinson, Montreal, Quebec, Canada H2V 3Z9, founded 1982, is a serial anthology which features **four poems by each of four poets in each issue. "We welcome beginners' submissions, and as a matter of policy reserve one slot per issue for some comparatively 'unknown' poet."** On the other hand, they cannot accept many manuscripts without creating a very large backlog; so that **"if we cannot publish a poet within one or two foreseeable issues we will return the ms with an invitation to re-submit at a later date." Submit a sufficient sample to enable the editors to make a selection. Simultaneous submissions OK, but notify editor if submission is to any other** *Canadian* magazine. Translations welcome (but enclose copy in original language with proof that rights have been acquired). Pays 5 copies + year's subscription. Sample: $1.50 postpaid. The magazine is a narrow digest-sized 33 pp. saddle-stapled format.

‡*FRANK: AN INTERNATIONAL JOURNAL OF CONTEMPORARY WRITING AND ART (II)**, 6 rue Monge, Paris 75005, US address, %editor David Applefield, Mixed General Delivery, APO New York, NY 09777, founded 1983. *Frank* is a literary semi-annual that **"encourages work of seriousness and high quality which falls often between existing genres. Looks favorably at true internationalism and stands firm against ethnocentric values. Likes translations. Very eclectic." There are no subject specifications, but the magazine "discourages sentimentalism and easy, false surrealism. Although we're in Paris, most Paris-poems are too thin for us. Length is open, but we prefer poems that don't exceed 3 pages."** Some poets published recently include Derek Walcott, Ginsberg, Alain Bosquet, Edouard Roditi, Pierre Seghers, James Laughlin, Breytenbach, Michaux and many lesser known poets. The journal is digest-sized, flat-spined 96 pp., offset in b/w with graphic art, photos, drawings, and manuscript pages, 10 pages of ads. Circulation is 2,500, of which 1,000 are bookstore sales and other copies are distributed through galleries and cultural centers. Price per issue is $4.50, subscription $15 for 4 issues. **Sample: $4.50 postpaid airmail from Paris. Pay is two copies. Guidelines available for SASE. Poems must be previously unpublished. Submissions are reported on in 8-10 weeks, publication is in 1-4 months. "Send 2 or 3 of your *best* poems and a short cover letter."** The editor provides criticism on rejected MSS **"almost always, but if poet agrees to subscribe I feel more generous with my comments."** Editor organizes readings in US and Europe for *Frank* contributors.

*THE FRIEND (IV, Religious)**, 50 E. North Temple, Salt Lake City, UT 84150, a publication of The Church of Jesus Christ of Latter-Day Saints, **for children 4-12, circulation 200,000.** Issues feature different countries of the world, their cultures and children. They have special issues for Christmas and Easter. Submit seasonal material 6 months in advance. **Send SASE for guidelines and sample copy. Poetry can be serious, humorous, or for the holidays—any form with child appeal. Pays $15.**

‡FROM HERE PRESS *XTRAS, OLD PLATE PRESS (V, II)**, Box 219, Fanwood, NJ 07023, phone 201-889-7886, founded 1975, editors William J. Higginson and Penny Harter, a small-press publisher of a chapbook series called *Extras* and flat-spined paperback anthologies and solo collections. The editors want **"contemporary work; we have a particular interest in haiku, but also have done everything from haibun and renga to long poems." They do not want "5-7-5 nature poems, poorly crafted traditional verse."** The *Xtras* series of books are published on a co-op basis; the author pays half the cost of production and receives half the press run. Other book contracts are individually negotiated. They have recently published poetry by Alan Ginsberg, Elizabeth Searle Lamb, and themselves. I have seen two sample volumes a chapbook of haiku, **Casting Into a Cloud**, by Elizabeth Searle Lamb, and a flat-spined paperback, **Lovepoems**, by Penny Harter; as a sample, I chose the beginning lines from Harter's "Our Hair Is Happy":

> *Our hair is happy.*
>
> *You pull the brush through my hair.*
> *It crackles, lifts, curls on your wrist.*
> *My head streams into your hands.*

Lovepoems is handsomely printed on heavy beige stock with b/w drawings by Gilbert Riou, 70 pp. **Casting Into a Cloud**, which is *Xtras #11*, is also attractively produced. **The editors are accepting no freelance submissions in 1986-87; for 1988, "please query with 10 pp. first." MSS should be "clear, typed double-spaced, no simultaneous submissions." Queries will be answered in 2 weeks. Pay is usually ½ of the press run in author's copies.** The press publishes 2-4 books each year, mostly digest-sized, with an average page count of 40. A catalog is free for #10 SASE; average price of books is $2.50. The editors say, "If you do not read 10-12 books of poetry by living authors each year, please do not consider submitting work to us."

*FRONTIERS: A JOURNAL OF WOMEN STUDIES (IV, Feminist)**, Women Studies, Box 325, University of Colorado, Boulder, CO 80309, founded 1975, is published 3 times a year, circulation 1,500, magazine-sized format, flat spined, 80-92 pp., sample: $8. **Uses poetry on feminist themes. Recently published Marilyn Krysl, J.B. Goodenough, and Debra Bruce. Pays 2 copies.**

‡*FRUGAL CHARIOT (II)**, 102 Wayland Ave., Providence, RI 02906, phone 401-272-7683, founded 1986, editor Elizabeth Gordon, a "little, low-budget poetry quarterly." The editor says, **"Prefer shorter poetry (40 lines or less); any style is welcome, from traditional to experimental, although the work must show that the poet is *in control* of his/her form and not vice versa. We want work that shows conviction. Also, it would be pleasing to hear distinct, individual voices coming**

through. We reject anonymity; don't be afraid to stand out." She does not want anything "racist, sexist, etc. No clichés or otherwise dull language. Don't preach or teach (people can and do learn from poetry, but this doesn't mean that a poem should be a 'lesson'." As a sample, she chose the following lines from "a night of silk" by taro tsuzuki:

> . . . *the moon is up*
> *behind budda's [sic] head. he,*
> *whose shade hides me from the*
> *silver wolves, has no face . . .*

At press time *Frugal Chariot* had not yet appeared; it was planned to be digest-sized, 28-36 pp., photocopied from typescript, with matte card cover. circulation for the first issue was expected to be 100. Price per issue is $1.50, subscription $4.50/year. **Sample available for $1 postpaid. Pay is 1 copy. Poets should submit 6-8 poems; photocopies and simultaneous submissions are OK. Reporting time is 2 weeks and time to publication a maximum of 3 months.**

*FRUITION (IV, Nature), Box 872, Santa Cruz, CA 95061, founded 1979, is a magazine-sized biannual, 8-12 pp., circulation 300, which uses some **poetry pertaining to public access nut and fruit trees, re-establishing Eden, horticulture, natural diet and natural hygiene. Pay: subscription and/or back issues. Sample: $2. Simultaneous submissions OK.**

FULL COURT PRESS, INC. (V, II), 138-40 Watts St., New York, NY 10013, founded 1976, editors Anne Waldman, Joan Simon and Ron Padgett, publishes collections of avant-garde and experimental poetry. Pays. Send SASE for catalog to buy samples. Currently not considering unsolicited mss.

GALAXY BOOKS (II), 71 Recreation St., Tweed Heads, NSW 2485 Australia, phone 075-361997, founded 1980, by Lance Banbury who says, "to date, publications have been limited to works (poetry, a drama, criticism) by myself; however, this has brought 'enlightenment' and the decision to cease self publishing and to begin on **anthologies of other poets exclusively, in a paperback series. Any kind of poetry (rhyme, blank verse, experimental) dealing with personal emotion, socialization, abstraction. Explicit sex not OK. No more than 100 lines per poem.**" As an example of what he likes he offers these lines by Rozanna Sanzo:

> *Babble on tape:*
> *Subway blues*

He says, "**Send some info on submissions of individual poems desirable. Philosophy and theory, mainly.**" He is not presently considering book MSS, only poems for the anthology. **Simultaneous submissions OK. Reports in 4 weeks, pays $5 per poem, one copy of the anthology. He comments on MSS, "especially if some work has been selected for inclusion**." And he advises, "Study the historical poets for a direction to the avant-garde now."

*A GALAXY OF VERSE, AN INTERNATIONAL POETRY MAGAZINE (I), 200 S. Chandler Dr., Ft. Worth, TX 76111, founded 1974, poetry editors Esther Lee Thompson and Don E. Peavy, is a semiannual publication of a membership organization, **A Galaxy of Verse Literary Foundation**, which poets accepted for publication may join for $10 per year. Poems by members published in *Galaxy* are considered in **nine annual contests open to members only (with no entry fees), as well as in other contests open to all poets (for which entry fees are required). Offsprings of members (who are students) may compete without charge in contests open to members only.** The magazine is in an inexpensive format, digest-sized, typescript (of various type faces), some of it photo-reduced, with simple drawings and photographs, photocopied on offset paper, permitting the publication of many poems on its 50 + pp. They use "**traditional, free verse, narratives, any form or school, from fixed forms to avant-garde. We want poems alive with emotion, but controlled by good taste.** *Galaxy* wants serious poems that echo the aspirations of the heart; the frustrations and triumphs of life. They must be expressed in vivid imagery, utilizing metaphors, similes, etc. **Short poems preferred, but will accept a few poems of 50-60 lines in narrative form if very good.**" Some of the poets they have recently published are Edna Meudt, Carl Bode, Jack E. Murphy, Pat Stodghill and Anne Marx. These sample lines are from "The Wall Builders" by the late John Williams Andrews, Editor-in-Chief of *Poet Lore*:

> *Proudly we crampon to the highest hills, corking the canyons—*
> *the moon stripped of its wonder, death reparcelled in bitter packages*
> *because we move with egos in our eyes. I have built my own walls . . .*
> *I worship them, raising my hands in panic as they teeter.*

Circulation is 500, with 456 subscriptions, of which 4 are libraries. **Sample: $1.50 postpaid**. They receive 50 or more submissions per year and use 40-45. **Submit batches of 4-6. Reports in 2 weeks. No pay other than contest awards. Guidelines available for SASE. Comments on all rejections. In-depth critiques available for $3 for short, $5-7 for longer poems**. The editor says, "I would advise poets to study a publication before submitting. Write for guidelines and follow them religiously. Poetry should be timely, in that it should reflect the age in which we live; also current events can trigger the creative process. Use your imagination. **Learn to think in word-pictures. Do not preach, nor obviously teach, but let the poem tell its own truth in situations.**"

THE GALILEO PRESS, GALILEO BOOK SERIES (II), 15201 Wheeler Lane, Sparks, MD 21152, founded 1981, poetry editors Julia Wendell and Jack Stephens. The imprint **Galileo Books** is used for collections of poems by individuals, 60 pp., flat-spined, hard- and paperback editions. **"Have published (to date) 3 poetry titles:** *Keeping Still, Mountain* by John Engman (1984), *The Maze* by Mick Fedullo (1985) and *New World Architecture* by Matthew Graham (1985), expect to publish two poetry collectories in 1987." Query regarding book publication with publishing and biographical information. Replies to queries immediately, to submissions in 1-2 months. Considers simultaneous submissions. Payment: $800 honorarium and 10% of print run in copies. Send SASE for catalog. The editors often comment on rejections.**

‡***THE GALLEY SAIL REVIEW (II)**, Suite 42, 1630 University Ave., Berkeley, CA 94703, phone 415-486-0187, editor Stanley McNail. *The Galley Sail Review* was originally founded in 1958 and published until 1971 in San Francisco; now it has been revived (Spring, 1986) and is based in Berkeley. Publication is planned three times a year: spring, summer, and fall-winter. The editor says, "GSR is like many other "littles" in that it **compensates its contributors in copies.** Since its inception it has survived without recourse to governmental or foundation grants, but is supported out of the editor's pocket and produced as a "one-man" magazine entirely. We (editorial "We") do not conduct contests or offer prizes, but **we endeavor to find and publish the best, most insightful and imaginative contemporary poetry extant. We do not promote any literary "school" or ideological clique."** The sample copy I have contains only poetry, although it says "submissions of poetry and reviews are invited." Forty-four different poets are represented. As a sample, I chose the first stanza from "The Hunter" by Jory Sherman:

> *The heart is squeezed sometimes*
> *too hard to pulse, the breath hugged*
> *like cotton in the lungs so long*
> *it explodes, catches fire.*

The Galley Sail Review is digest-sized, offset on fairly thin paper, 44 pp. saddle-stapled, with cover of the same paper, printed in black on yellow and illustrated by a landscape photograph. Single copy price is $3, subscription $8/3 issues.

***GAMBIT (II, IV, Regional)**, OVLG, Box 1122, Marietta, OH 45760, phone 614-373-7391, founded 1969, poetry editor Jane Somerville "is a joint publication of the Ohio Valley Literary Group and Parkersburg Community College. They want "**serious contemporary poetry. No trite-end rhyme or religious verse. We want to present a cross section of writing from our region (West Virginia, Virginia, Ohio, Kentucky, Pennsylvania) by professionals and talented beginners. We try to keep a balance between the work of well-known regional writers and promising work of the ordinary people of our region. One of our goals is to keep awareness of literature, as something people do, alive in our area.**" They have recently published poetry by James Bertolino, David Citino, Wayne Dodd, Stuart Friebert, Elton Glaser, Gordon Grigsby, Elizabeth Ann James, Valery Nash and Wyatt Prunty. As a sample, they offer these lines by Jeff Nichols:

> *we whisper the bread away,*
> *you pass the wine, sure*
> *the sky makes concessions.*

The handsomely printed 6x9" flat-spined annual magazine, with glossy cover featuring b/w photo, has a circulation of about 500. **Sample: $3 postpaid.** They receive about 1,000 freelance submissions of poetry per year, of which they take 50. **Submit 5-6 poems. Photocopy OK. Include brief bio. Reports in 1 month. Pays 1 copy. Sometimes comments on rejections.**

***GAMUT (II)**, 171-238 Davenport Rd., Toronto, Ontario, Canada M54 1J6, phone 416-963-9730, founded 1980, poetry editors Haygo Demir and Alfredo Romano, is "a magazine of culture and ideas." **We read all types of poetry, but publish only serious poets. We are not particularly interested in inspirational or 'romance' poems. All forms, lengths and styles are acceptable. We do not censor subject matter as long as the poems are of high quality and innovative..**" They have recently published poetry by Giorgio Di Cicco, Simon St. Sabbas, Bill Bisset, Bruce Cockburn and Richard Stevenson. The editors selected these sample lines by Susan Musgrave:

> *at the core there was only terror,*
> *a compass of blood in the heart's*
> *wreckage and blood and more blood*
> *in every direction.*

The quarterly is 8½x11," saddle-stapled, handsomely printed on heavy paper with color, glossy cover, 70+ pp., circulation 2,000, 400 subscriptions of which 100 are libraries. They use 5-10 pp. of poetry in each issue and usually have a 2 issue backlog. They receive about 1,500 submissions per year, use 20. **Sample: $5 postpaid. Submit no more than 7 poems, photocopy, dot-matrix, simultaneous submissions OK. SASE Canada only, IRC U.S. No queries! They report in 8-10 weeks.**

*THE GAMUT, A JOURNAL OF IDEAS AND INFORMATION (II, IV, Serious, experimental), Cleveland State University, Cleveland, OH 44115, phone 216-687-4679, founded 1980, poetry editors Leonard Trawick and Louis T. Milic, is "a general interest journal for educated readers" which **includes some poetry for which they pay an average of $25 per poem** + 2 copies. Leonard Trawick says, "Most of what we publish is related to this region," but that probably doesn't pertain to (or limit) poetry submissions. They have recently published poetry by Robert Creeley, David Citino, Karl Kempton and Cyril Dostal. As a sample I selected this prose poem by Michael Cole inspired by a photograph by Jerry N. Uelsmann, "Myth of the Tree":

> It is said that should the beholder of this great oak see in its branches or bark the face of a sleeping dryad, his or her life's sleep will be restful and death will come in sleep. Last April during a thunderstorm, I thought I saw her ebony face far up the bole. This insomnia is killing me.

Gamut appears 3 times a year in a 7x10" flat-spined, 96 pp. format, professionally printed in small type on heavy stock, glossy two-color card cover with art, includes b/w photos and graphics. **"We do not want doggerel or anything resembling greeting card verse. Interested in any serious poetry (including humorous poems) and concrete experimental works." Sample: $3 postpaid. Photocopy OK, simultaneous submissions "OK if acknowledged." They report in less than 3 months.** The magazine has a circulation of 1,200, 1,050 subscriptions of which 100 are libraries. Price per issue: $5, subscription: $12 (3 issues).

‡*GANDHABBA, NALANDA UNIVERSITY PRESS (IV, Post beat, themes), 622 East 11th St., New York, NY 10009, phone 212-533-3893, founded 1983, editor Tom Savage, a yearly poetry magazine with **"emphasis on post-Beat, New York school and language works. Each issue is thematically oriented." The editor does not want "Academic, rhymed verse. also, self-indulgent, egotistical 'punk' poetry that extols violence, toughness and brutality. Also, no religious poetry, please."** He has published poems by Allen Ginsberg, Joel Oppenheimer, Anne Waldman, and Jackson Mac Low. As a sample, I chose the beginning lines from "Talking to your Answering Machine" by Nina Zivancevic:

> I am sorry   I am not able at the moment
> to answer your needs and
> meet your demands
> because it is exactly 6 o'clock Friday afternoon and
> I think
> they are going to spill Acid Rain over China

Gandhabba is thick (98 pp.), mimeographed on fairly rough paper, magazine-sized, with white glossy card front cover illustrated in b/w, stapled on left side. Circulation is 400, of which 50 are subscriptions, 10 go to libraries, and 100 are newsstand sales. Price per copy is $3, subscription $10/3 issues. **Sample available for $4 postpaid. Pay is 2 copies. Submissions are reported on in 6-12 months and time to publication is the same.** The editor says, "My tastes are broad but my intentions for each issue are quite specific. In my second issue, I asked each poet for a poem longer than a page. In my third issue, I asked each poet for two completely dissimilar works to be published together. **In order to avoid time wasting and disappointment, it seems better that anyone wishing to submit to *Gandhabba* at least write to me requesting a copy and inquiring as to the theme of the next issue."**

‡GAZ PRESS (V), 277 23rd Ave., San Francisco, CA 94123, phone 415-751-6852, founded 1983, editor Larry Price, a small press publisher of poetry (flat-spined paperbacks). The editor says, **"I read and comment upon all received unsolicited MSS, but I publish none of it."** He has recently published books by Carla Harryman, Jean Day, Ted Pearson, Barret Watten, and himself. **Queries will be answered in 1 week and MSS reported on at the same time. Pay is in author's copies, 10% of press run.** All books are priced at $5 and can be ordered directly from the press at list price.

*THE GENEVA REVIEW (V), 19 rue Centrale, 1580 Avenches, Switzerland, editor Jed Curtis, is a literary magazine "serving much the same function that *The Paris Review* did before it relocated to the U.S." Serves intelligent English-speakers in Europe. A paying, prestige market, but they are overstocked with poetry and prefer to have no submissions. **Query with IRC before submitting.**

*GEORGIA JOURNAL, AGEE PUBLISHERS, INC. (IV, Regional/Georgia, the south), Box 526, Athens, GA 30603, phone 404-548-5269, poetry editor Janice Moore. The *Georgia Journal* is a bimonthly magazine, circulation 5,000, covering the state of Georgia. **Send SASE for guidelines. Sample: $3.** They use poetry about the South, especially Georgia—or at least no poetry dealing specifically with another region. It must be suitable for young adults. "Most of our school-age readers are high school." Buys 20 poems per year. Submit maximum of 4 poems, maximum length 25 lines. Pays in copies.

‡**UNIVERSITY OF GEORGIA PRESS (II)**, Terrell Hall, University of Georgia, Athens, GA 30602, phone 404-542-2830, founded 1938, poetry editor Bin Ramke. The press publishes four books of poetry each year in the Contemporary Poetry Series, two of which are by previously unpublished poets, in simultaneous hard cover and paperback editions. **Freelance submissions are accepted, but writers should query first for guidelines. There are no restrictions on the type of poetry submitted, but "familiarity with our previously published books in the series may be helpful."** They have published books by Dannie Abse, Lynn Emanuel, Terese Svoboda, and X.J. Kennedy, from whose work the editors selected the following lines as a sample:

> *Under the parked car in the driveway, shadows seep.*
> *From somewhere the cry of a child protesting bed*
> *Comes blundering in again and again, a stick of driftwood.*

Poets who have never had a full-length book of poems published can submit MSS during September each year. "Chapbook publication does not disqualify a writer . . . nor does publication of a book in some other genre." **Poets with at least 1 full-length book of poems published should submit MSS during January. Poets should query first, asking for guidelines. There is a submission fee of $10 per book-length collection. Photocopied MSS and simultaneous submissions are OK. Reporting time is 3 months. Royalties are a maximum of 10% plus author's copies (usually 12).** The press says, "90.95% of our contemporary poetry books are subsidized by grants (e.g. from the NEA). We do not solicit or accept subvention from authors."

*****GESAR: BUDDHISM IN THE WEST, DHARMA PUBLISHING (IV, Buddhism)**, 2425 Hillside Ave., Berkeley, CA 94704, founded 1973, is a quarterly (circulation 3,500, 7x10", 64 pp.) which uses **poetry related to Buddhism. No pay.**

‡**GHOST PONY PRESS (V)**, 2518 Gregory St., Madison, WI 53711, phone 608-266-3259 (see also *Abraxas*), founded 1980, editor and publisher Ingrid Swanberg, a small-press publisher of poetry chapbooks and books, "with some emphasis on first books as well as books of outstanding quality by established American poets." **Poets should inquire before submitting.** They have published books by Ivan Arguelles, Connie Fox, and Peter Wild. As a sample, the editor chose the following lines by W.R. Rodriquez:

> silver   nickel   copper   *pure from the outstretched*
>   *arms*
> *of the barely poor   too heavy with work*
> *too thin with youth   to pump music from the grind*
>   *and drone*
> *the clatter and chatter of the trolley shaken*
>   *cobblestones*

Ghost Pony Press publishes 1-3 books of poetry each year with an average page count of 44, 6x9", flat-spined paperbacks. The sample I have, **Getting Ready for a Date**, by Peter Wilde, is very handsomely printed on heavy buff stock with a two-color matte card; it is priced at $15. **When querying, writers should send 2-5 sample poems and list of credits. Royalties are 30-50% plus 20-30 author's copies. Book catalog is free for 4x9" SASE.**

‡*****GIANT STEPS, GIANT STEPS PRESS (II, IV, Yorkshire)**, The Beeches, Riverside, Clapham via Lancaster LA2 8DT, England, founded 1982, editors Maggie and Graham Mort, a semi-annual magazine and a press that publishes collections of poetry. "*Giant Steps* concentrates on a few poets only in each issue; in this way it is possible to offer new and established writers much more space than other magazines. As a natural consequence of this policy *Giant Steps* **has come to specialize in the long poem and poem-sequence, but by no means exclusively.**" They have recently published work by U.A. Fanthorpe, Anna Adams, Margaret Toms, and Geoffrey Holloway. As a sample, the editors chose the following lines from "The Fire-Taint" by David Craig:

> *Our words bear the fire-taint:*
> *Launch, formation, flight-path, take off-*
> *Is there a word that does not say kill?-*
> *Jet, aim, button, touch-down,*
> *Marine, magazine, muzzle, sight . . .*

The magazine is digest-sized, offset (reviews are in smaller type than poems), 47 pp. flat-spined, matte card cover with one-color decoration. Circulation is 400, of which 100 are subscriptions and 6 go to libraries. Price per issue is £1, subscription £2.50 (in the US, add 50% to cover postage; the editor prefers payment in sterling). **Sample available for £1. Pay is 5 copies. Writers should submit 6-10 poems, typed on 1 side of paper only. Reporting time is 6 weeks and time to publication 6 months.** The press publishes 3 poetry collections/year, digest-sized, 40 pp., flat-spined paperbacks. **Freelance submissions for books are accepted from the UK only. Writers should query first, sending credits, 10 sample poems, and bio. Queries will be answered in 6 weeks and MSS reported on in 6 months. Photocopied MSS are OK but not dot-matrix or discs.** Poetry collections are priced at £2.50 postpaid in the UK. The editors say, "Currently subsidised by Yorkshire Arts Association to produce 3 books by Yorkshire poets in 1986—hoping to expand to publish books by poets from elsewhere. (Poetry for magazine accepted from anywhere.)

‡*GILA REVIEW (II)**, Box 969, Thatcher, AZ 85552, phone 602-428-1133, founded 1984, editors David Tammer and Norman Lanquist, publishes poetry and fiction with Southwestern emphasis in *Gila Review*, plus two chapbooks a year. The editors will consider any kind of poetry, **with emphasis on Southwestern experience, but no haiku.** *Gila Review* has recently published William Stafford, Keith Wilson, Howard McCord, and G. S. Sharat-Chandra. As a sample the editors selected these lines from an unidentified poet:

> So the land of the Apache has become
> the land of the Circle K

Gila Review is 7x8¼", published quarterly, with handsome layout, typesetting and printing by Graphic Arts Class, Fort Grant Arizona (two-color), including illustrations by Ned Sutton. Cover is glossy with attractive design in color, saddle-stapled, price $2. **Submissions are reported on in 6 weeks, publication is in 1-2 months. Writers should submit 3 or 4 poems, 1-2 pp. each, on any typewritten or computer-produced form. Freelance submissions for chapbooks are accepted only in response to contests, which are announced in January.** Format of the two chapbooks per year is the same as that of *Gila Review*; the average page count is 17.

‡GLOBE PUBLISHING, *SEATTLE PULP (I)**, 3625 Greenwood N., Seattle, WA 98103, founded 1985, editor Dale J. Sprague, a publisher of "prosepoetry" for general audiences. The first **Seattle Pulp** will be published probably in December, 1986. The editor says that he needs **"metaphor/imagery set in exposition, dramatic, or mythic prose that communicates to general audience. Any length, any style, any theme."** He does not want **"modern, post-modern trends or verse."** As a sample, he chose the following lines, an excerpt from a large MS in process:

> Apparitions of unending darkness prevail.
> Faces appear and forever vanish; faceless,
> Sadness drips from darkness. A familiar feeling
> Becomes a fleeting figment of a dream.

Dale Sprague plans to publish 1 flat-spined paperback, digest-sized, in 1986 and 2 in 1987, with an average page count of 80-120. **Contributors to the Seattle Pulp are selected from a semi-annual competition. Writer's should query for submission guidelines. The editor plans to pay 15% royalties to contributor group. He will provide a critique of a rejected MS for a potential contributor.** The editor's advice to beginning poets is, "If you want a reading audience to experience you, the reading audience must be able to find some part of themselves in some part of your work."

‡GMP PUBLISHERS (IV, Gay)**, Box 247, London N15 6RW, England, phone 01-800-5861, founded 1980, editors Martin Humphries for gay men and Gillian Hanscombe and Suniti Namjoshi for lesbian women. The press wants **"poetry by lesbians and gay men; particular interest in work that is informed by feminist and gay liberation politics." They don't want anything "racist, sexist, etc. Not keen on poetry which is so subjective as to exclude everyone except those with personal knowledge of the poet."** They have published poetry by Thom Gunn, Lee Harwood, Felice Picano, James Liddy, and others. As a sample the editors chose (although they said "this is a mad request!") the following lines by Isaac Jackson:

> The homelife of black homosexuals
> is powerful when scribed for paper
> or painted on paper
> or wrapped up in gift paper

They publish 4 poetry books each year, digest-sized, with an average page count of 64, flat-spined paperbacks. **They rarely publish unsolicited material, but writers may send 10 sample poems plus bio, "each poem on a new page cleanly typed/printed." Queries will be answered in 1 month and MSS reported on in 3 months. Simultaneous submissions, photocopied or dot-matrix MSS are OK. They pay royalties of 7½-10% plus an advance of £50 and 6 author's copies.** Average price of their books is £2.95; they can be ordered from the catalog (free for #10 SASE) at list price plus 50p for postage. The editors says, "We are interested in seeing the work of beginning poets who feel sure they have something of interest to say. Our list is new. We are establishing the market in Britain and want our list to reflect current concerns of lesbians and gay men as well as contributing to the growing richness of lesbian and gay writing."

‡**GOLD ATHENA PRESS (III)**, Box 2521W, Melbourne, Vic., Australia 3001, founded 1985, contact the managing secretary. Gold Athena **does not accept freelance submissions of poetry without a preliminary inquiry**. Simultaneous submissions OK. It is a small press book publisher specializing in arts and humanities, and aiming to support works "disadvantaged in the commercial market by intellectuality and in the academic market by unfashionability." The press publishes **"Poetry of enduring significance (aesthetically and intellectually) by international, trans-historical standards; anthologies or sizable collections; originals or translations; bias towards 'classical humanistic' ideals, as exemplified in Classical Greek, Renaissance, and Chinese cultures; also towards modern contributions to important traditional forms, e.g., sonnet, ode, etc." They do not want to see "Experimental, regional, humorous, narrowly religious, narrowly satirical, or narrowly socio-political" poetry**. A recent publication is an anthology titled **English Philosophical Sonnets** (over 110 poets from the 16th to the 20th centuries), which can be ordered directly for $11.95 (Australia) plus $2.00 (Australia) for airmail delivery outside Australia. Payment is "not by any fixed policy but arrangements are made to suit the project concerned. Subsidy publishing has not been done but is a possibility." The editor says, "We do not believe that much worthwhile poetry is being written today, and thus it will be only in exceptional cases that we will publish poetry titles." Standard format of *Gold Athena* books is a flat-spined paperback with laminated 4-color cover.

‡***GOLDEN ISIS, *AQUARIUS ANTHOLOGY (I)**, Box 9116, Downers Grove, IL 60515, founded 1980, editor, Gerina Dunwich, a literary journal "devoted to New Age awareness, fantasy, and mystical art. **Our main interest is mystical poetry that is creative and well-written. Themes range from love & emotion to cosmic fantasies & abstract mind trips. Poems that are metaphysical, surrealistic, Egyptian and occult-oriented are also needed. We are always open to new ideas and we welcome the work of poets who are rejected by other poetry journals because they dare to be different. Avant-garde, blank verse, free verse & haiku, 40 lines maximum. We are not interested in poetry that is cute, religious, Satanic, unimaginative, or obscene. Please do not send anything in obvious bad taste."** The copy I have contains work by many different poets; as a sample I chose the beginning lines from "Midnight Seance" by Gypsy Electra:

> *A midnight seance on a night*
> *Of ice and rain.*
> *Upstairs, a circle of silhouettes joined in concentration*
> *call out to the reflections of life from another dimension*

The magazine is digest-sized, 48 pp., offset from copy typed in a script type face, saddle-stapled, one-color matte card cover. Circulation is 400. Single copy $2.95, subscription $10/year. **Sample available for $1.95 postpaid; no payment for poetry. Submit 1 poem/page, typed double-spaced, name & address on upper left corner & number of lines on upper right corner; photocopied submissions OK.** The magazine sponsors a "Poem of the Year" contest that offers a prize of $200 plus subscription to Golden Isis and quarterly newsletter; winning poem is published in the winter issue of *Golden Isis*. Entry fee for 1-2 poems is $1, 3-5 poems $2, deadline December 1. Poems should be up to 30 lines, any form. *Aquarius* is a yearly anthology of 1960's nostalgia, poetry, psychedelic and pop art!

GOLDEN QUILL PRESS (II), RFD #1, Avery Rd., Francestown, NH 03043, publishes a great deal of poetry, 90% on a subsidy basis, "depending on past sales record." **Pays maximum 10% royalties. Submit complete MS. Photocopy, dot-matrix OK. Reports in 2 weeks on queries, 1 month on submissions.**

***GOOD HOUSEKEEPING (II)**, Hearst Corp. 959 8th Ave., New York NY 10019, **circulation 5,000,000, women's magazine, uses up to 3 poems per issue for which they pay $5 per line. Light verse and traditional. Usually overstocked.**

***GRAHAM HOUSE REVIEW (II)**, Box 5000, Colgate University, Hamilton, NY 13346, phone 315-824-1000, ext. 262, founded 1976, poetry editors Peter Balakian and Bruce Smith, appears 1-2 times per year. "We publish contemporary poetry, poetry in translation, essays, and interviews. **No preferences for styles or schools, just good poetry.**" They have recently published poems by Seamus Heaney, James Dickey, Richard Hugo, Madeline DeFrees, Michael Harper and Dave Smith. As a sample I selected the first stanza of "Light Opera" by Michael McFee:

> *Before the sun, light*
> *tips day's scale, lifting*

> *birds from sleep into song*
> *amplified by silence into unison,*

GHR is digest-sized, flat-spined, 86 pp., professionally printed on heavy stock, glossy color card cover with photo, using 65-70 pp. of poetry in each issue, circulation 500, 300 subscriptions of which 50 are libraries. They receive about 1,500 freelance submissions of poetry per year, use 0-40. **Sample: $5 postpaid. No photocopy. Reports in 2 months or less, pays 2 copies.**

*GRAIN (II)**, Saskatchewan Writers' Guild, Box 1154, Regina, Saskatchewan, Canada S4P 3B4, phone 306-757-6310, poetry editors Brenda Riches and Garry Radison, is a literary quarterly "that seeks to explore the boundaries of convention and challenge readers and writers." They have recently published poems by Maggie Helwig, Richard Stevenson and Jerry Rush. It is a digest-sized format, professionally printed using rather small, light type, with chrome-coated cover, 64 pp., circulation 900, 512 subscriptions of which 76 are libraries. Subscription: $9. They receive about 600 freelance submissions of poetry per year, use 6-10. They use 40-60 poems per year. I selected as a sample the opening of "Love Words" by Janice Kulyk Keefer:

> *Your tongue in my mouth as*
> *suddenly you kiss me*
> *burns hot honey.*
> *I lie. Not honey.*
> *No such stuffed sweetness—it is*
> *no taste but the*
> *grained feel of flesh. . .*

Sample: $3 + IRC (or 64¢ Canadian). They want "no poetry that has no substance." Submit maximum of 8 poems, 3-200 lines. Photocopies OK. Prefers letter-quality to dot-matrix. Pays $20 per poem. Send SASE for guidelines. The editor comments, "Only work of the highest literary quality is accepted. Read several back issues. Get advice from a practicing writer to make sure the work is ready to send. Then send it."

GRAYWOLF PRESS (II, V), Box 75006, Saint Paul, MN 55175, phone 612-222-8342, founded 1975, poetry editor Scott Walker, **does not read unsolicited MSS.** They have published poetry by Tess Gallagher, Linda Gregg, Jack Gilbert, Chris Gilbert and William Stafford. They **pay 7½% royalties, 10 author's copies, advance negotiated.**

‡**GREAT ELM PRESS (IV, Rural),** Box 37, RD. 2, Rexville, NY 14877, phone 607-225-4592, founded 1984, Walt Franklin, editor/publisher. Great Elm is a small press dedicated to the writing of rural affairs, to bio-regionalism, to the universal qualities found in local life. The press produces chapbooks and anthologies in limited editions. The editor says, **"We hold no specifications as to form, length or style. Subject matter is often traditional, Native American, mythical or geographically informed." They do not want to see "abstract, self-involved, confessional rantings."** Some poets the press has published recently are Ken Stone, Walt Franklin, and Peter Franklin. The editor chose these sample lines from an unidentified poet:

> *Come story us again*
> *with the seldom*
> *heard. Come sing*
> *the magic songs.*

The press publishes 2-3 chapbooks/year, 35-40 pp., digest-sized, flat-spined paperbacks. **The editor suggests querying for theme and guidelines before making freelance submissions. Queries are answered in 1 week, as are MS submissions. Simultaneous submissions will be considered, photocopied MSS are OK. Number of author's copies and honorarium are negotiable. "We are not subsidy publishers—to date. Authors are published at our expense, with payment in copies and hopefully with 25% royalty on each copy above and beyond the printing cost."** T. Parkins says, "We appreciate writers with a sense of Williams' 'no ideas but in things.' Our primary interest lies in the 'bioregional,' that buzzword indicating that a given locale is more than a simple reading of humanity, is, in fact, an intricate and interrelated realm of man, animal and plant—their histories reflected in a geographic place. We are currently working on an anthology of poems and fiction inspired by the upper Susquehanna River watershed." Sample publications I have seen are photo-offset from typewritten copy on buff or white stock, matte card cover with illustration, price $2.50 each.

*GREAT RIVER REVIEW (II, IV, Regional/midwest)**, 211 W. 7th, Winona, MN 55987, phone 507-454-6564, founded 1977, poetry editor Orval Lund, a biannual, is especially interested in **quality, literary poetry from or about the Midwest.** Some of the poets they have recently published are Thomas McGrath, Phil Dacey, Jill Breckenridge, Marisha Chamberlain and Alvin Greenberg. The magazine has 150+ pp., flat-spined, 6x8". **Sample: $3.50 postpaid. Submit 4-6 poems. Photocopy acceptable. Pays 2 copies.**

‡*THE GREEN BOOK (II)**, 72-74 Walcot St., Bath, Avon BA1 5BD, England, phone Bath 62546, founded 1979, poetry editor Linda Saunders, a "visual and literary review of the arts," published quarterly. **The editors want "well crafted contemporary poetry" but no "therapeutic rubbish."** They have recently published poetry by Anne Stevenson, Tom Rawling, and Phillip Gross. As a sample, they chose the following lines from "The Coming Land, in tribute to Max Beckmann" by Duncan Tweedale:

> *For every journey, the legends say,*
> *a starting-point: perhaps this city*
> *of heads wagging together, of narrow*
> *trees and thought:*

The Green Book is a very handsome volume (although the poems are crowded on the page), 5³⁄₄x8¹⁄₄", about 60 pp., professionally printed with lots of b/w illustrations (photographs of works of art, etc.). It is flat-spined and the glossy white card cover is decorated with a colored reproduction of a painting. Its circulation is 2,000, of which 200 are subscriptions. Price per copy is £1.75, subscription £9/year. **Pay is 2 copies. "All poetry must be typed/photocopy sent to poetry editor." Reporting time is about 6 weeks, time to publication approximately 2 issues.** The only book they publish is an anthology of work from their annual contest, The Green Book National Poetry Competition, which awards prizes of £500, £250, £150, and £50, March 31 deadline (send SAE with IRC for rules). The editors say, "We intend to publish selected poets from time to time."

*****GREEN FEATHER MAGAZINE, QUALITY PUBLICATIONS, S-W ENTERPRISES (II)**, Box 2633, Lakewood, OH 44107, founded 1978, editors Gary S. Skeens and Robin S. Tibbitts. *Green Feather Magazine* is a magazine-sized literary quarterly (5-8 pp.) with a circulation of 150 that **pays in copies. Send SASE for guidelines.**

GREEN TIGER PRESS, STAR & ELEPHANT BOOKS, ENVELOPE BOOK LIBRARY (IV, Children), 1061 India St., San Diego, CA 92101, phone 619-238-1001, founded 1971, poetry editor Harold Darling, publishes elegantly written and illustrated books, mostly for children, "**containing a romantic, visionary or imaginative quality**, often with a mythic feeling where fantasy and reality coexist. We try to invoke a sense of wonder through creative means." The editors say their "**use of poetry is very limited; we seek children's poetry for** *Dream Pedlar* annual and some poetry for the Envelope Book Series. We are not interested, for the most part, in adult poetry, and seek children's poetry or other kinds of poetry with an imaginative or visionary quality." They have published poetry by John Theobald and Jacques Yvart and recommend that poets study anthologies of children's poetry with special attention to such poets as Walter de la Mare and Robert Stevenson. **Query with 5 samples. Cover letter should mention previous publications. Replies to queries in 4-6 weeks, to submissions in 8-10 weeks. Photocopy OK. Dot-matrix discouraged. Payment on royalty contract. Send SASE for guidelines and catalog.**

THE GREENFIELD REVIEW PRESS, *THE GREENFIELD REVIEW (II), Box 80, RD 1, Greenfield Center, NY 12833, phone 518-584-1728, founded 1971, poetry editor Joseph Bruchac III, all from a nest of literary activity, The Greenfield Review Literary Center, which publishes a regular newsletter, has a poetry library and offers workshops and lectures in a former gas station. **Send large SASE with 2 oz. postage for guidelines, a handout on "marketing tips" and sample copy of the newsletter. The biannual** *Greenfield Review* **wants "multi-cultural, contemporary poetry, no doggerel."** They have published poetry by Leo Connellan, Judith McDaniel, Derek Walcott, Hayden Carruth, Linda Hogan, Edward Brathwaite, Kofi Awoonor, Meene Alexander and Elizabeth Cook-Lynn. It has a circulation of 1-1,500, 500 subscriptions of which 150 are libraries—a handsome digest-sized flat-spined format, 160+ pp., glossy color cover. They use 200-300 of the 5,000 submissions received each year, have a 6 month backlog. **Sample: $3 postpaid. Typed originals only—no photocopies, no simultaneous submissions. No submissions considered June 1-August 31. Guidelines inform you of times to submit. Reports in 2-7 days. Payment varies. No submissions for books until 1987, then query with samples.** Joe Bruchac advises, "Buy books of poetry and literary magazines. The community you support is your own. Don't be in too much of a hurry to be published."

*****GREEN'S MAGAZINE, CLOVER PRESS (I)**, Box 3236, Regina, Sask., Canada S4P 3H1, founded 1972, editor David Green. *Green's Magazine* is a literary quarterly with a balanced diet of short fiction and poetry; Clover Press publishes chapbooks. They publish **"free/blank verse examining emotions or situations." They do not want greeting card jingles or pale imitations of the masters.** Some poets published recently are Sheila Murphy, Mary Galazs, Robert L. Tener, David Charlton, Alison Reed, Ruth Schuler. As a sample I selected the complete poem called "psalm" from **Notebook of an Immigrant**, by Marion Beck:

> *having a garden helps*
> *kneeling in the sun eyes see only earth*

fingers in warm soil
press seed in firmly
delighting in how quickly all things grow
i never lift my eyes

The magazine is digest-sized, 100 pp., with line drawings. A sample chapbook is also digest-sized, 60 pp., typeset on buff stock with line drawings, matte card cover, saddle-stapled. Circulation is 400, subscriptions $10. **Sample: $3 postpaid. Guidelines available for SASE. Payment is 2 free copies. Submissions are reported on in 8 weeks, publication is usually in 3 months. The editor prefers typescript, complete originals. Freelance submissions are accepted for the magazine but not for books; query first. Comments are provided on rejected MSS.**

*THE GREENSBORO REVIEW (II), English Dept., University of North Carolina, Greensboro, NC 27412, phone 919-379-5459, founded 1966, poetry editor Linda L. Fox, appears twice yearly and has published poetry by R.T. Smith, Thomas Heffernan and Timothy Steele. As a sample I selected the first stanza of "The Past" by Victoria McCabe:

You must take it whole,
Swallow each ingredient
As in a casserole—It's good
For you, will make you strong.

The digest-sized 100 + pp. flat-spined magazine, colored matte cover, professional printing, uses about 25 pp. of poetry in each issue. Circulation 500, 300 subscriptions of which 100 are libraries. Uses about 10% of the 800 submissions received each year, has a 3-month backlog. **Sample: $2.50 postpaid. No simultaneous submissions, reports in 2-6 weeks, pays 6 copies.** They offer an Amon Liner Poetry Award and a $250 Greensboro Review Literary Award in poetry and in fiction each year.

‡*THE GRENDHAL POETRY REVIEW (II), 116 Tamarack St., Vandenberg AFB, CA 93437, founded 1986, editor Ann Salazar, a bimonthly magazine "directed towards a scholarly audience." **They use poetry that is "post-modern, beat, New York School, anything we find interesting." There are no length restrictions.** In the first issue (January/February 1986), there were selections of poems by Barbara Holland, Rhett Moran, and Richard Davidson. As a sample, I chose the following "Poem" by Ray Dipalma:

desert
horse penetrating the frontier
small hard footed short back
lumbar fusion shapes the continent

The magazine is digest-sized, offset from typed copy on ordinary paper (smaller type is used for long poems), 32 pp. saddle-stapled with glossy white card cover. Circulation is 500, subscription rate $10/year. **Sample available for $2 postpaid. Pay for poems is in copies. Writers should submit 5 or more poems. Reporting time is 1 week if the work is not needed and 2-4 weeks on acceptance. "We will look at photocopies if clear."** The editor says, "We are also looking to publish 2 or 3 chapbooks of poetry per year, 24-28 pp. **For chapbook consideration, submit complete manuscripts only. To be considered for this series you'd have to be a published poet that we'd read before in journals and magazines that we respect (such as** *Unmuzzled Ox, Parix Review, Wormwood Review, Vagabond*."

GREY WHALE PRESS, *BLOW (II), 4820 SE Boise, Portland, OR 97206, founded 1980, poetry editors Mike Bonner and Karol Kleinheksel. *Blow* appears irregularly (about twice a year), a literary magazine using about 20 pp. of poetry in each issue, circulation 100, 30 subscriptions. They receive about 500 submissions per year, use 50, have a 6 week-6 month backlog. They have published poetry by Bob Warden, Diane Wakowski and Charles Bukowski. Sample: $3 postpaid. Prefer short poems. Payment in copies (usually 2). They also publish chapbooks and broadsides, but with submissions by invitation only.

*GRINNING IDIOT: A MAGAZINE OF THE ARTS (II), Box 1577, Brooklyn, NY 11202, phone 718-447-2312, founded 1982, poetry editor B. A. Levy, is a semiannual, "impecuniously chaotic, anarchic, always attempting to steer away from the pretentious, we seek **quality in the obscure and unknown scribblers, primarily.**" In addition to the magazine, they publish chapbooks and pamphlets. B. A. Levy says he wants to see "**anything driven to the page by unknown forces from earnest hearts and minds**." They have recently published poems by Charles Bukowski, William S. Burroughs, Tom Whalen, and Ivan Arguelles (none exactly "unknown scribblers"!). The editor selected these sample lines by John Clellon Holmes:

Rodin's Balzac: the mystery lodged in stone,
The great animal head staring, impervious,
the body swathed in the obscuring robes,
that swaddle babes and wind a corpse.

The editor describes the magazine as "art-wind." It is 48 pp., magazine-sized, saddle-stapled, containing prose, verse, satire, drawings and cartoons, with 2-10 pp. of poetry in each issue, circulation 500, 100 subscriptions of which 35 are libraries. $2.50 per issue, $5 for subscription. They receive about 300 submissions per year, use 2-3. **Sample free for postage. Reports in 2-6 months, pays 3 copies, guidelines available for SASE. Editor "always" comments on returned MS. To submit for chapbook publication, send 3 samples. Simultaneous submissions, photocopy OK, no dot-matrix. Submission on Atari disks permissible but hard copy preferred.** Their books can be found "in book stores throughout NYC, Toronto and LA."

GRIT (I), 208 W. 3rd. St., Williamsport, PA 17701, phone 717-326-1771, founded 1882, poetry editor Joanne Decker, is a weekly tabloid newspaper for a general audience of all ages in rural and small-town America. They **use traditional forms of poetry and light verse, 16 lines maximum, for which they pay $6 for 4 lines and under, 50¢ each for each additional line. Send SASE for guidelines.** These sample lines are the first stanza of James Dykes, "Across the Miles":

> Thoughts of you go homeward winging,
> when I'm far away . . . alone!
> But my sad heart starts a singing
> just to hear you on the phone.

‡**GROVE PRESS (III)**, 196 West Houston St., New York, NY 10014, phone 212-242-4900, founded 1952, publisher Barney Rosset, poetry editor William Matthews. Grove is a highly respected press that publishes about 6 books of poetry each year, both hardcover and paperbacks. **Freelance submissions are accepted. "Form can be anything, length—same; subject matter—not "sentimental"; style— very original, very developed; purpose—of a literary nature and hard-hitting." They do not want anything "oversentimental, religious (straight religion)."** They have recently published books by Julia Alvarex, Richard Jackson, Donald Axinn, and Paul Mariani, from whose **Prime Mover** they chose the following lines as a sample:

> the mind's eye straining draws at last
> upon the single candle of the self
> left to gasp and sputter in the dark

Grove Press's books of poetry are usually 100 pp., either flat-spined paperbacks or hardcovers. **Writers should send 10 sample poems, with credits and bio ("a brief introduction of self and work"). Simultaneous submissions are OK, as are photocopied or dot-matrix MSS. Queries will be answered in 6 weeks, MSS reported on in 2 months. A negotiable advance is paid, plus royalties and author's copies (amount and number not specified). Book catalog is free on request.**

‡*GRUE MAGAZINE (IV, Horror)**, Box 370, New York, NY 10108, founded 1985, editor Peggy Nadramia, a horror fiction magazine "with emphasis on the experimental, offbeat, rude." The editor wants **"Poems of any length including prose-poems, with macabre imagery & themes. Not interested in Poe rip-offs, (although we'll look at rhyming poems if subject is weird enough), 'straight' vampire, ghost or werewolf poems."** She has recently published poems by Ardath Mayhar, Denise Dumars, Jessica Salmonson, Wayne Sallee, Joey Froehlich, and Billy Wolfenbarger. As a sample she selected the following lines by T. Winter-Damon:

> Baptize me with the wanton venom of your serpent kisses!
> Thrust your thorns of pleasure deep into my skull!
> Hammer your rusted spikes into my outstretched palms,
> My courtesans of darkness!

The magazine is digest-sized, 80 pp., offset, with a glossy b/w cover, "sharp" graphics, and "a center-fold that is unique." It appears 3 times a year and has a circulation of 1,000, of which 300 are subscriptions and 100 are newsstand sales. Price per issue is $3.50, subscription $9/year. **Sample: $2.50 postpaid; guidelines are available for SASE. Poets receive 2 copies. They should submit up to 5 poems at a time, photocopied or dot-matrix MSS are OK. Submissions are reported on in 3 weeks and time to publication is 9 months. The editor "always" provides criticism of rejected MSS.** Her advice is: "Strong controlling images are important. Don't twist the language to suit your ideas. Be honest with yourself & the reader, and we can't fail to respond!"

The double dagger before a listing indicates that the listing is new in this edition. New markets are often the most receptive to freelance contributions.

*GRYPHON (I, II), Dept. of Humanities, the University of South Florida, Tampa, FL 33620, phone 813-974-2260, founded 1974, editor Hans Juergensen, associate editor Ilse Juergensen, is published 3 times a year to **"give new poets a chance and publish known ones as well." Occasionally a poet is featured with about 5 pp. of work. They** describe their needs as: **"contemporary subject and diction, good rhymed work, very eclectic, translations, humor. We avoid crudities of subject and language, no sentimentalism, no explicit sex."** Poets they have published recently include Richard Eberhart, William Stafford, Anne Marx, Lyn Lifshin, Van K. Brock, Peter Meinke, Laurel Speer, A. McA. Miller, Edna Meudt, Colette Inez, B. Z. Niditch and "students and poems from Italy". I selected these sample lines, the first stanza of Dudley Randall's "Woman of Ghana":

> *There are forests in your eyes,*
> *Shaded with silk cotton trees*
> *Trailing snowy filaments.*

There are usually about 50 pp. of poetry in each issue. The magazine is neatly printed from typescript, magazine-sized, flat-spined. They use about 300 of the 1,200 submissions they receive each year, have about a 4 month backlog. **Sample: $2.69 postpaid, overseas $2.96. Submit up to 4 pp., usually single-spaced, name and address on each sheet. Reports in 8 weeks or less, pays 1 copy.** Hans Juergensen comments that *Gryphon* is not supported by the university, "though it alleges to be proud of it," but by subscriptions and patrons. He advises, "Read much, write much; find an expert critic, submit and subscribe to mags. There are too many trends in poetry and art; it is difficult to project final judgment. I go poem by poem."

GUERNICA EDITIONS, ESSENTIAL POET SERIES, OPEN WINDOWS, COMPUTER DISC SERIES, BROKEN IMAGES EDITIONS, (IV, Specialized), Box 633 Station NDG, Montreal, Quebec, Canada H4A 3R1, founded 1978, poetry editor Antonio D'Alfonso. "We wish to bring together the **different and often divergent voices that exist in Quebec and Canada. We are interested in translations. We are mostly interested right now in prose poetry and essays."** They have recently published poetry by Gaston Miron, Antonio Porta, Nichole Brassard, and Italian writers of Canada. **Open Windows** is a series of books of haiku. **Computer Disc Series** is a poetry series on Apple II discs. **Broken Images Editions** is, like the **Essential Poetry Series**, a general series of Canadian poetry. **Query with 1-2 pp. of samples. Send SASE or IRC (Canadian stamps only) for catalog to buy samples. The editor comments, "We enjoy reading what other people are doing, to go beyond our country and study and learn to love what we originally thought little of."**

GULL BOOKS (II, V, Invitation), Box 273A, Prattsville, NY 12468, phone 518-299-3171, founded 1980. Poetry editor Carolyn Bennett says, "We are interested in the diversity of cultural experience in contemporary American writing and hope that our publishing program reflects this. **At present, we are accepting MSS by invitation only;** however, we hope this will change in the future, when we don't now know." They publish handsomely printed, flat-spined paperbacks with glossy covers, and have published poetry by such poets as Daniel Gabriel, Tom Smario and Bill Miller. As a sample, I chose these lines from "Doc's Oyster House" by Rochelle Ratner:

> *The closed eyes of fish*
> *underwater*
> *stare at the diners*
> *in the same way that we,*
> *eating, stare at the sunset.*

Carolyn Bennett says, "I'm **not interested in rhymed poetry, or poetry with a specific religious message**. As to what I do want, a solid manuscript which can only be encountered, in my opinion, on a one-to-one basis." Their books are published on a **10% royalty contract with 10 author's copies.** Send SASE for catalog. This editor's advice to poets is, "Poetry workshops can be important sources of friendship, criticism and support. Poetry collectives are also important alternatives to finding a publisher and can help build an audience for the poet's work. Poets should know something about the magazines and presses they wish to submit their work to. But, most important, beginning poets should *read* poetry, contemporary or otherwise."

*GYPSY, *SANCTUARY, VERGIN' PRESS, (II), 105 Elledge Mill Rd., North Wilkesboro, NC 28659, phone 919-670-2355, founded 1984 (in Germany), poetry editors Belinda Subraman and S. Ramnath, is "a vehicle for sharing and promoting the literary arts; we have the time/talent and care to answer submissions personally: PERSONAL TOUCH—HANDSOME FORMAT. Material will be considered for poetry/art posters. At present, chapbook by invitation only. We want to see **something with impact, something you'll want to read again. Don't want self-conscious or shallow work. 3-18 lines are best, but the only real requirement is quality. Will read any length."** They have recently published poetry by William Burroughs, Edward Mycue, A.D. Winans, Todd Moore, and Al Masarik. As a sample, the concluding lines of "Thursday Seeing You" by Lyn Lifshin:

> *a room full of stamps*
> *the roof leaks wildly*
> *in gluing what should*
> *not be together together*

Gypsy appears twice a year, magazine-sized, 72 pp. offset from typescript, flat-spined, glossy color card cover, with full-page and decorative b/w graphics, circulation 400 ("and growing"), 180 subscriptions of which 15 are libraries. Subscription: $7 (includes 2 issues of *Gypsy* and chapbooks and posters from Vergin' Press). They receive over 3,500 submissions of freelance poetry per year, use 40 per issue. **Sample: $3 postpaid. Photocopied submission OK (if not previously published). Reports in 2 weeks-3 months. Pays 1 copy. Editor comments on rejections: "oh yes, and encouragement; we don't kick anyone in the teeth."** *Sanctuary* is a magazine on cassette of poetry and original music. Belinda Subraman advises, "Keep writing, growing, refining. Don't give up. It takes a while to become polished. It may take a while to get into print."

*THE HAGUE REVIEW, THE HAGUE PRESS, (II), Box 385, Norfolk, VA 23501, phone 804-853-4661, press founded 1980 and *The Hague Review*, 1986. Poetry editors Roger Hunt Carroll and Allan Mason Smith. The Press is a subsidy arrangement which I'll let Roger Carroll describe, as it is fairly typical of the direction many small presses are going today, and he gives poets a realistic understanding of what's involved: "It was begun for the main purpose of providing an imprint for collections, etc., of poetry or other literary work by individuals who want to bring out their own things. Because the few of us who are involved in the little venture have some background and experience in self-publishing and are also persons who have worked in publishing and printing of one sort or another, we are able to be a kind of guide to the author, helping same to go through the editing, designing, typesetting, printing, binding process. What we do, you see, is help the author get the thing into his hands as a physical item. From then on it is the author's undertaking to do the real publishing by way of distribution, sales, etc. We do very little marketing for an author. For a fee which varies enormously according to what the author wants his or her chapbook to be, we will see to the entire production of the work. It is not possible to quote a fee schedule because fees would have to be figured after the author had made decisions about what the book would be like—i.e., cheap paper, exquisite paper, etc., etc. Generally the fee would be considered on the amount of time we had to spend in preparing and walking the thing through production. We are then what you might call a 'literary contractor.' We will *not* work with those who write junk verse. And we will reserve the right to decide what's junk and what ain't. Our object is to help put serious artistic stuff out in artistic presentations." *The Hague Review*, an annual collection of poetry, has been created by the Press. "The object," say the editors, "is to provide exposure of poetry that is formed essentially from two elements: the one being the poet's conviction that she or he has something to relate which can *only be related in the medium of verse*; and the other, the poet's ability to create verse that bears witness to an understanding of the craft of poetry and to the fact that poetry is the fraternal twin of music. So what kind of poetry do we want? **Pieces that will fall into the concept of** *verbal music*. **We want incantatory, lyrical, oracular, rhetorical and—yes—perhaps even hermetic verse that appeals to the** *metasensibilities* **of a reader/hearer. It is not traditional form only, nor is it sugary fluff (music is created from both harmony AND discord).** If Hart Crane were around today, we'd beg, borrow and steal to use his work. The *Review* will also look at essays of 3,000 words max on a topic germane to the art of prosody. **Translations will be considered too.** Payment is one copy and encouragement from an outfit that has found your work to be *artistic*. **All candidates for inclusion must write for our more detailed guidelines. Send only a first class stamp and we'll give you the envelope. No deadline.**

HAIKU SOCIETY OF AMERICA, HAROLD G. HENDERSON AWARD, *FROGPOND: QUARTERLY HAIKU JOURNAL (IV, Theme, style), % Japan House, 333 E. 47th St., New York, NY 10017, has been publishing *Frogpond* since 1978, now edited by Elizabeth Searle Lamb, and **submissions should go directly to her** at 970 Acequia Madre, Santa Fe, NM 87501. *Frogpond* is a stapled spine quarterly of about 45 pp., 5½x8½", of haiku, senryu, haiku sequences, renga, more rarely tanka, and other poems related to haiku and translations of haiku. It also contains book reviews, some news of the Society, contests, awards, publications, and other editorial matter—a dignified, handsome little magazine. Poets should be familiar with modern developments in English-language haiku as well as the tradition. **Modern haiku, according to Ms Lamb, "has developed far beyond the 5-7-5 (syllable) 'pseudo-Japanese nature poem' which has in the past passed for haiku."** Recent contributors include Ann Atwood, James Minor, Hiroa Ki Sato and Cor van den Heuvel. Considerable variety is possible, as these two examples from the magazine illustrate:

> *The family gathered—*
> *a tear of embalming fluid runs*
> *from my brother's eye*
> George Swede © 1985

> *One paw off the ground, cat listens to winter.*
> Virginia Brady Young © 1985

Each issue has between 25 and 35 pages of poetry. The magazine goes to some 280 subscribers, of which 10 are libraries. **Sample, postpaid—$5,** They receive about 5,000 submissions per year and use about 400-450. **Accepted poems usually published within 6-12 months, reporting within 6 weeks. They are flexible on submission format: haiku on 3x5" cards or several to a page or one to a page or half-page. Ms Lamb prefers 5-20 at one submission, no photocopy or dot-matrix. They hope contributors will become HSA members, but it is not necessary, and all contributors receive a copy of the magazine in payment. Send SASE for Information Sheet on the HSA.** The Society also sponsors the Harold G. Henderson Award Contest and gives Merit Book Awards for books in the haiku field. A "best-of-issue" prize is given "through a gift from the Museum of Haiku Literature, Tokyo."

*HAIKU ZASSHI ZO (IV, Style), Box 17056, Seattle, WA 98107-0756, founded 1984, poetry editor George Klacsanzky, a biannual (June and December) provides **"a liberal forum for Haiku poets writing their poems originally in English**. We promote a better understanding of the Japanese culture and its integration into American life. (Closeness to Nature, etc.) We provide Haiku writing parties and other activities such as the annual 3-day retreat." George Klacsanzky says, **"I like to see clear well-realized Haiku. Poems in which all unnecessary words have been eliminated. Will consider Haiku between 8 and 22 syllables long. I also will consider entire collections of Haiku for publication in book form. This coming year we plan to publish three books of poetry."** They have recently published Francine Porad, Mark Allan Johnson, Miriam Sagan and Yuki. This haiku is by Yuki:

> *Dead seagull*
> *on the beach—eyes still*
> *looking for fish.*

The magazine appears in a format of about 50 saddle-stapled pages on tan paper with tasteful oriental b/ w art, circulation about 400-500, 150 subscriptions. **Sample: $3 postpaid. Submit up to 15 poems, all can be on same page, photocopies, dot-matrix "and any other form" acceptable. Simultaneous submissions OK. SASE required. Reports in 1-2 months, pays in copies. Sometimes comments on rejections.** They hold one annual contest with deadline of December 1 each year. The editor comments, "Outside of truth there is no poetry. Every word must be an experience."

‡*HANDICAP NEWS (IV, Handicapped), 272 N 11th Ct., Brighton, CO 80601, phone 303-659-4463, founded 1984, editor-publisher Phyllis A. Burns. A 3-page (printed on both sides) newsletter, *Handicap News* **accepts poetry submissions from handicapped persons and their families. The editor says that she will print any type, form, or style of poem except horror.** She has recently published work by George C. Koch and Kimberly Harrison. The editor selected these sample lines from a poem entitled "Two of a Kind" by Nedine Davis:

> *The wink I give the boy*
> *in the sporty wheelchair*
> *at the amusement park*
> *unleashes a smile*

The purpose of the newsletter is to disseminate news to handicapped people and others interested; it goes to associations, non-profit organizations, and handicapped people. Frequency is monthly, circulation 500, subscriptions 100. Ads are available for 20¢/word, no graphics. **No sample back issues available. Guidelines cost $1 (US currency) plus SASE. Pay in 2 free copies. The editor reports on submissions in 1 month, publishes in 3 months, and requests no more than 3 submissions per envelope; she will accept photocopies or simultaneous submissions.** "Content means more to me than particular style—although I would appreciate seeing something besides religious poems. Handicapped people, be creative and tell the world of your place in the world and how you see it."

HANDSHAKE EDITIONS, *CASSETTE GAZETTE, *PARIS EXILES (II), for all but the last the address is: Atelier A2, 83 Rue de la Tombe-Issoire, Paris, France 75014, phone 327-1767, founded 1979, editors John Strand and Randy Koral. For *Paris Exiles*, write Randy Koral, Ed., 118 Rue Vieille du Temple, Paris, France 75003. *Cassette Gazette* is an audio cassette issued "from time to time," and *Paris Exiles* appears 4 times a year in a print-run of 5,000, "a mag of new fiction and faction, poetry, images and ideas from Paris and the world flowing through it." Some of the poets published in these various forms are Ted Joans, Yianna Katsoulos, Judith Malina, Elaine Cohen, Carol Pratl, Joseph Simas, Amanda Hoover and Jayne Cortez. **Payment in copies. Handshake Editions does not accept unsolicited MSS** for book publication. Jim Haynes, publisher, says, "I prefer to deal face to face."

*THE HARBOR REVIEW (II), % English Dept., University of Massachusetts at Boston, Boston, MA 02125, founded 1982, editors Stephen Strempek, Charles Grace Anastas and Linda McPhee, publishes "primarily poetry with an occasional piece or two of fiction. **We tend to publish poetry**

which is clear, direct and *not* written in traditional (i.e., ABAB, iambic pentameter, etc.) form. No restrictions on length. Style and subject matter & purpose: best to read a sample copy of the *Review.* While we look for and publish younger and lesser known writers, we have published Marge Piercy, Amy Clampitt, Jared Carter and Tom Wayman." Instead of sample lines the editors provided a couple of titles to suggest the taste and quality of the magazine: "Practical Dreams," by Pam Annas, and "The Poetry of Tire-Urns," by Amy Clampitt. Puzzled by the latter, I discovered it referred to planters one finds in yards in Maine. As the poem says:

> There is something about the original structure
> of an automobile tire that gives it, turned inside out,
> the curve of an urn: much flattened, but urnlike nevertheless.

The twice yearly digest-sized 48 pp. review, saddle-stapled, matte cover with 2 colors and art, uses 30-40 pp. of poetry in each issue, circulation 300, 100 subscriptions of which 25 are libraries. Subscription (3 issues): $7; per copy: $2.50. They receive 1,500-2,000 submissions per year, use about 40. **Sample: $2.50 postpaid. No simultaneous submissions. Reports in 3-4 months, pays 2 copies. Send SASE for guidelines. Comments on rejections "only when we have something to ask or say."** Stephen Strempek says, "We really do look for unpublished writers and give careful consideration to such submissions; we will write an 'unknown' writer if we feel s/he has written something worthwhile."

HARCOURT BRACE JOVANOVICH, PUBLISHERS, CHILDREN'S BOOKS (IV, Childrens), 1250 Sixth Ave., San Diego, CA 92101, phone 619-699-6781, publishes hardback and trade paperback books for children. **Submit complete MS. No dot-matrix. Pays favorable advance, royalty contract and copies.** Send SASE for guidelines and book catalog.

HARD PRESS (II), 340 E. 11th St., New York, NY 10003, phone 212-673-1152, founded 1976, poetry editor Jeffrey C. Wright, publishes postcard series and occasional chapbooks. The "**Hard Press Poetry Card series publishes poetry with graphics, pairing the celebrated with exceptional younger writers.** Our idea is to reach a larger audience than poetry usually does by publishing striking postcards." They want poetry which is "accessible, mysterious, relevant, sexy, with rock & roll shock value and intelligent display of vast poetry input (reading). 1-20 lines are most suitable, integrated graphic preferred." They have recently published poetry by Alice Notley, Tom Disch, Amiri Baraka, Pedro Pietri, Maureen Owen, and they offer these lines by Robert Creeley as a sample:

> If it's not fun
> don't do it.

They publish three series of 4 postcards per year in print-runs of 500. They have 50 subscribers, of which 5 are libraries. A subscription costs $2.50 for all three sets. They receive about 100 submissions per year, use 2, have a 12-18 month backlog. **Sample: $2.50 postpaid. Query with brief cover letter. Reports in 1 month. Pays 10% of press run.** They also publish books under the imprint of Chronic Editions but do not consider freelance submissions. Jeffrey Wright says he comments "always if poet shows promise. Beginners should read as much as possible, correspond a lot and submit material widely. A beginner should also start a project of use and interest to the poetry community, such as a reading series or press of some kind."

‡**HARPER ROW, COLOPHON BOOKS (V)**, 10 East 53rd St., New York, NY 10021, founded 1817, editor F. Lindley. Harper and Row, as you can tell from the date of founding, is an old-line, highly respected publishing house; Colophon Books is their paperback imprint. Among the 300 titles Harper's publishes each year only 3 are books of poetry. **They accept no unsolicited MSS, but the questionnaire they returned does say that poets can submit 6 sample poems.** The poets they publish are, obviously, likely to be fairly well-known before Harper's publishes them; on my shelves I have, for example, volumes published by Harper and Row by William Stafford, Hayden Carruth (in the Colophon imprint), Yehuda Amichai, and Gwendolyn Brooks. All are handsomely produced. As a sample I chose the beginning lines from Gwendolyn Brooks's "Jessie Mitchell's Mother":

> Into her mother's bedroom to wash the ballooning body.
> "My mother is jelly-hearted and she has a brain of
>   jelly:
> Sweet, quiver-soft, irrelevant. Not essential.
> Only a habit would cry if she should die."

If your poetry is good enough to be published by Harper and Row, you probably don't need this directory.

HARTMUS PRESS (II, V), 23 Lomita Dr., Mill Valley, CA 94941, founded 1957, poetry editor Catherine Moreno, publishes an average of **one paperback of poetry "every three years or so. At that time notices go out that Hartmus Press is looking for such and such, submissions welcome just for that project."** Payment is 10% of press run. "Hartmus Press continues its existence today as it began, a protest against the stifling of a commercial publishing world which, for financial reasons, selects only a narrow band of the most broadly popular taste in writing." The sample of their publishing I have seen, **Captive of the Vision of Paradise,** $4.95, by Ivan Arguelles is a 6x9" flat-spined paperback, side-stapled with matte end papers and cover glued over (a format which makes it difficult to open flat but the margins are wide to compensate). It is beautifully printed and decorated with drawings in colored ink. I selected these sample lines, the opening of "The Seducer":

> *in his eye a single bright lawn*
> *but in the other one a black pebble*
> *the moon's indecipherable rune*
> *his tongue is a fuse contaminated by logic*

Send SASE for catalog to buy samples.

‡*HAT, IDAD PRESS (I),** 1A Church Lane, Croft, Linconshire, England PE24 4RR, founded 1975, editor Ian Hogg, publishes "all kinds of poetry" in their magazine and booklets. They have recently published poetry by Jim Burns, Andy Darlington, Phil Carradice, Max Noiprox, and Steve Sneyd. As a sample the editor chose these lines by himself:

> *The Japanese have been*
> *importing and exporting*
> *mushrooms for years*
> *but never like the one the Americans sent.*

The sample of *Hat* I have seen consists of 4 sheets of tabloid-sized paper side-stapled, printed in various colors of ink, a crowded jumble of drawings and photocopied typescript and print, pasted up casually, ads mingled with art and editorial matter. The editor seems to have a special interest in the occult. **Sample: 1£ postpaid. Pays 1 copy.** Idad Press publishes a variety of 32-48 pp. booklets. For book publication, **query with 12 pp. sample poems and "as much as possible" about your bio and philosophy. Simultaneous submissions, photocopy OK.** *Hat* conducts the annual contest for F.A.I.M. deadline October 31, for poems of no more than 32 lines, prizes 10£-40£, entry fee 50p/poem or 1£/3 poems.

‡*THE HAVEN; NEW POETRY (I),** 5969 Avenida la Barranca NW, Albuquerque, NM 87114, phone 505-898-7954, founded 1985, editor Michael McDaniel, assistant editor Miquel Montaño, a literary quarterly "with emphasis on quality writing." The editors say, **"All types of poetry considered, with no restrictions, as long as the writing has merit." They do not want "greeting card verse, doggerel, unless used to make a valid artistic statement."** In their first issue they published work by 21 new poets. As a sample, they selected the following lines from "you sleep through the storm" by Katherine Flanagan:

> *i awake with lightning*
> *ripping black velvet night*
> *exposing mountains outlined*
> *like gloved seductive fingertips*

The magazine is digest-sized, printed on fairly thin paper, 34 pp. saddle-stapled with one-color matte card cover. Some of the issues will have themes; for instance, Fall 1986 will feature poems about the writers' home states, and Winter 1987 will be devoted to haiku (there is a haiku contest with cash prizes). **Sample available for $2.50 postpaid, contest guidelines for SASE. "Work should be legible, preferably typewritten, one poem to a page, centered, with name and address at top left." Pay is $5-10 upon acceptance plus one copy. "We try to respond within 4 weeks."** Michael says, "My advice can only echo Jerome's. Check his books." Miguel says, "We hope that each poem we accept will have the power to change readers' lives. The poems are destined for *readers*, not for one's self. The reader should be conscious of gain to him/herself after reading your poem."

UNIVERSITY OF HAWAII PRESS, PACIFIC POETRY SERIES (II), 2840 Kolowalu St., Honolulu, HI 96822, phone 808-948-8694, founded 1947, poetry editor Stuart Kiang, currently limits publication in poetry to the annual **Pacific Poetry Series competition. Book MS (64-96 pp.) by poets who have not previously published a book of poetry—no age, residency or nationality requirements—are received during the month of March only, $5 entry fee. Send SASE for contest rules.** Recent judges of the competition have been William Stafford, W. S. Merwin and David Wagoner. The aim of the series is to publish work that adds significantly to the literature of the Pacific Region. The author of the winning MS receives the usual royalties. They have recently published books of poetry by Gary Kissick, Marina Makarova, and Cynthia Huntington.

‡*HAWAII REVIEW (II),** %English Dept., University of Hawaii, 1733 Donaghho Rd., Honolulu, HI 96822, phone 808-948-8548, founded 1972, editor Rodney Morales, a small-press semi-annual magazine that publishes poetry, fiction, and reviews. I have not seen a copy, and the editors do not specify any particular type of poetry they want or do not want. As a sample, they selected the following lines by Frank Stewart:

> *Circling slow and dipping like a fat June bug in the rain,*
> *turbos throbbing in the labored*
> *dark over Chicago, the Electra turned, one wing*
> *pivoted up, like an old dog tilted on three legs*

Hawaii Review is 6x9", 100-150 pp., with cover art, graphics, and a few ads. Its circulation is 3,000; most copies are distributed to students at the University. Price per issue is $3, subscription $6/year. **Sample available for $3 postpaid, guidelines for SASE. Pay is $10 plus 2 copies. Writers should submit a clean, typed original or good quality photocopy, 3-4 poems at a time, no simultaneous submissions. Reporting time is 2-12 weeks and time to publication is usually 6-8months.**

‡*HEARTLAND JOURNAL (IV, Elderly)**, 3100 Lake Mendota Dr., Madison, WI 53705, phone 608-238-3408, founded 1983, editors Lenore Coberly and Jeri McCormick. The editors describe *Heartland Journal* as **"excellent writing by older writers for readers of all ages." They use all types of poetry, but do not want to see "general non-specific commentaries."** I have not seen the magazine, so I cannot quote samples. **"We accept hand-written easy to read MSS. We want fresh material by older writers." Writers should submit 1-5 poems at a time; they publish 20-40 poems/year. Pay is copies and an annual prize. Photocopied and previously published submissions are acceptable. Time to publication averages 6 months.**

‡**HEIRLOOM BOOKS, A SMALL PRESS (I)**, Box 15472, Detroit, MI 48215, founded 1983, editor C.M. Burke. The press publishes **"an annual poetry anthology of works from new writers across the country,"** poetry chapbooks, and special collector's editions of "handmade clothcover books lettered in calligraphy and bound in the ancient Chinese concertina (fold-out) form." The editor wants **"poetry from all races, ages (over 21), backgrounds . . . beginning poets, minority poets, handicapped, blind, deaf poets, ill or physically injured poets, etc. Poems should be no more than 30 lines; short poems of up to 16 lines are most often published. No excessive use of vulgar language."** They have recently published poems by Christine Beyer, Laurie Ochsner, Adam Szyper, Chris Christian, and Jani Johe Webster. As a sample the editor chose the following lines by an unidentified poet:

> *My niece has the name of bedspreads I slept under when I was little and*
> *thought that people had center-holes where souls swirled about serenely or*
> *in discontent. Chenille says angels are butterly ladies*
> *and I again see beautiful life through a child's eyes.*

The annual volume, call **Heirloom Poetry Sampler**, is digest-sized, 20 pp., saddle-stapled with green card cover printed in black. Thirteen poets are included in the volume I have seen. Titles are done in calligraphy. The press publishes 3 chapbooks of poetry each year. **Writers should query before submitting, sending bio and poetic aims. Queries will be answered in 3 weeks and MSS reported on in 9 weeks. No previously published material or simultaneous submissions. Photocopied or dot-matrix MSS are OK. Pays is 1 author's copy. Sample available for SASE and $3.** The editor says, "Beginning this year, the annual Heirloom poetry anthology will be compiled, dramatically read and produced with music on cassette tapes as "talking books." Heirloom will continue to publish printed chapbooks and artful concertina books and scrolls."

*****HELICON NINE: THE JOURNAL OF WOMEN'S ARTS AND LETTERS (II, IV, Women)**, Box 22412, Kansas City, MO 64113, phone 913-381-6383, founded 1977, poetry editor Pat Breed, "provides a forum for the **creative accomplishments of women in the fields of literature**, music, the visual and the performing arts. It juxtaposes works from one generation with another, thereby covering the broad range of past and present talent." The magazine, appearing 3 times a year, is distinguished by its elegant format: 7x10", flat-spined, 90 + pp., glossy card cover, richly illustrated inside and out with full color reproductions and photographs and b/w art, each tri-annual issue containing a recording (floppy LP) of a musical or oral performance. **They want "intelligent and perceptive poetry by women," no specifications as to form, length, style, subject-matter or purpose. Recently they have published poetry by Joyce Carol Oates, Ruth Whitman, Edna St. Vincent Millay, David Ray, Doris Radin, Martha McFerren, Colette Inez and Grace Paley. The editor selected these sample lines (poet unidentified):**

> *As I cross the brook*
> *and walk up the hill towards your grave*
> *a humming fills the air,*
> *a giant motor is working among the trees.*

There are 15-20 pp. of poetry in each issue, circulation 2,000, 1,000 subscriptions of which a quarter are libraries. They receive about 1,500 submissions per year, use 60-75. **Sample: $7.50 postpaid. Subscription: $15. Submit typed, double-spaced MS. Reports in 3-6 months. Payment: 2 copies and 1 year subscription. Editor occasionally comments on rejections.**

HELIKON PRESS (II), 120 W. 71st St., New York, NY 10023, founded 1972, poetry editors Robin Prising and William Leo Coakley, "**tries to publish the best contemporary poetry in the tradition of English verse. We read (and listen to) poetry and ask poets to build a collection around particular poems. We print fine editions illustrated by good artists. Unfortunately we cannot encourage submissions.**" They have published books by John Heath-Stubbs, George Barker, Michael Miller, Carolyn Harris, Thom Gunn and Helen Adam, from whose "Limbo Gate" in Selected Poems & Ballads the editors selected these sample lines:

> *Towers of atoms fall and rise*
> *Where gigantic Adam lies.*
> *Adam lies in Limbo Gate*
> *Dwarfing night and day.*

The poets they select are paid on royalty contracts and 12 author's copies. **Send SASE for list of their publications.** William Leo Coakley comments, "The only advice to a poet is to write and rewrite from the heart of one's experiences of the joy and the sorrow of life or the stories and epiphanies which embody those emotions, until one has refined, expressed, communicated them to other human beings in song. We hope to continue to publish such poems in the future, as many as our limited resources make possible."

HERESIES: A FEMINIST PUBLICATION ON ART AND POLITICS (IV, Specialized), Box 766, Canal St. Station, New York, NY 10013, founded 1976, is a 90 + pp. magazine-sized quarterly, circulation 8,000, which uses poetry, but only on specific themes announced in advance. Send SASE for guidelines, $3 for sample.

HERMES HOUSE PRESS, *KAIROS (II), Apt. 10D, 900 West End Ave., New York, NY 10025, founded 1980, poetry editors Alan Mandell, William Rasch and Richard Mandell. The press is "dedicated to the publication of **works neglected, forgotten, or ignored, of known, little known, or unknown authors**, generally in limited editions." *Kairos*, a magazine appearing twice a year since 1981, is a "journal of contemporary thought and criticism" which uses 1-5 pp. of poetry in each issue. They want poetry which is "**sensitive, with an ear for language, an eye for images; evocative**." They have recently published poems by William Rasch, Christine Farris and Michael Stephens. I selected these sample lines (poet unidentified):

> *Things longed for unattained . . .*
> *one sees plaster flake*
> *and feels strength of brain*
> *slow blur and die away:*

They have a circulation of about 500, receiving 50 submissions per year, using 5, having a 6 month backlog. **Sample: $5, plus $1 postage and handling. Send any number of poems. Photocopy OK, dot-matrix "not encouraged but accepted." Reports in 4-6 weeks, pays in copies. To submit a collection, no need to query. Send MS with brief bio. Reports in 4-6 weeks. Payment: percentage of profits, 10 copies, discounts on additional copies.** The editors "almost always" comment on rejected MSS.

THE HEYECK PRESS (II), 25 Patrol Ct., Woodside, CA 94062, phone 415-851-7491, founded 1976, poetry editor Robin Heyeck, is "essentially a private press, publishing very fine poetry in letterpress editions. We are able to produce only 2-3 books per year and not all of these are going to be poetry in the future. We sometimes do dual editions of paperback and fine volumes on handmade paper with special leather and marbled paper bindings." They want to see "**well crafted, well organized poetry which makes sense—poetry which shows particular sensitivity to the precise meanings of words and to their sounds.**" They have published poetry by Adrienne Rich, Frances Mayes, Sandra Gilbert, William Dickey, Susan MacDonald, Charlotte Muse and Frank Cady. Robin Heyeck selected these sample lines from Rich's book *Sources*:

> *I refuse to become a seeker for cures.*
> *Everything that has ever*
> *helped me has come through what already*
> *lay stored in me. Old things, diffuse, unnamed, lie strong*

The sample books I have seen are, indeed, elegantly printed on heavy stock, lavish with b/w drawings. **The Summer Kitchen,** poems by Sandra Gilbert, drawings by Barbara Hazard, is a series of poems on vegetables, titles on the cover and on individual poems in red ink; and **Herbal,** poems by Honor Johnson, drawings by Wayne and Honor Johnson, is a series on herbs. **Query with 5-6 samples and cover letter stating other publications, awards and a "brief" biography. Replies to query in 3 weeks. Photocopy, dot-matrix OK. Contract is for royalties 10% of net sales.**

HIBISCUS PRESS, *HIBISCUS MAGAZINE (II), Box 22248, Sacramento, CA 95822, founded 1972, editor-in-chief Margaret Wensrich, poetry editor Joyce Odam. This press formerly published *In a*

Nutshell, 1975-9, and revived it under a new name (January, 1985) as a tri-annual, *Hibiscus*, **which uses "traditional—but fresh—stories and poetry of today: sonnets, villanelles, haiku, cinquains, ballads—vigorous and adventurous—and free verse."** They have published poetry by James Breeden, Martha Bosworth, Jack Tootell, and Harold Witt. These sample lines are by Nancy G. Westerfield:

> *Now that we go nowhere, mostly the cats*
> *Keep track of the luggage in dark*
> *Closeted corners, climbing those alpinical*
> *cases on their chase of one another*
> *Through a nether world.*

There are about 4 pp. of poetry in each issue, print-run of 3,000. They receive about 1,000 submissions per year, use 16-20, have a 1 year backlog. **Sample: $3 postpaid. Submit 1 poem per page, photocopy OK. Reports in 4-8 weeks (poems held longer if under serious consideration). Pays $5-25 per poem plus copies. Send SASE for guidelines.** They commission the books of poetry they publish (on a co-operative basis). Send SASE for catalog. The editors advise: "Keep writing and keep submitting. Believe in yourself. Poets enrich the world in ways that cannot be measured in board feet."

‡**HIEROGLYPHICS PRESS (I)**, Box 906, Hwy. 19, Maggie Valley, NC 28751, phone 704-926-3245, founded 1983, editor/publisher Carolyn E. Cardwell. The press publishes **poetry anthologies of work submitted by beginning poets; the poet must buy a copy ($5) in order to see his work in print. Poems may be 3-20 lines, on any subject (but no porn), typed or printed, any style. The editor does not want "illegible handwriting, poor spelling!"** I have seen 3 anthologies, entitled *My Heart Speaks to Thee, From the Heart of a Poet*, and *Odes to a Cockroach*. As a sample, I selected the title poem from the last named book, by Debra McClure; the first stanza is:

> *Here's to my enemy the cockroach*
> *You make my nights so fun*
> *When I turn the kitchen light on*
> *I watch you scurry and run.*

The anthologies are digest-sized, thick—140-196 pp.—flat-spined, offset from typed copy on light-weight paper with many b/w decorations, white glossy card cover with b/w drawing. **Writers may submit up to 3 poems for any anthology but only 2 will be accepted for each book. Simultaneous submissions are OK, name and address should be on each poem.** The editor says, "Care enough about your work to use a dictionary! Books are published as they fill. New titles are announced in *Writer's Digest*. We encourage poets of all ages, from all over the world. Ethnic differences in expression and vocabulary are not removed during editing."

HIGH COUNTRY NEWS (IV, Environmental), Box 1090, Paonia, CO 81428, founded 1970, is a bi-weekly tabloid, 4,400, devoted primarily to **environmental issues of the mountain region, it also does four poetry center spreads each year. Sample: free for SASE.**

HIGH/COO PRESS, *MAYFLY*, *HAIKU REVIEW* (IV, Haiku), Rt. #1, Battle Ground, IN 47920, phone 317-567-2596, founded 1976, poetry editors Randy & Shirley Brooks. *Mayfly* **is an irregular "very selective, lean, letterpress magazine of haiku. Haiku is best savored in small servings. Each haiku will have its own page so the reader may give full attention to it. Submissions are open to subscribers only with a limit of five submissions per issue."** The editors selected this sample by Peggy Willis Lyles from their first issue:

> *a mayfly*
> *taps the screen—*
> *warm beets slip their skins*

I have not seen *Mayfly*, so cannot describe its format. **Sample: $3.50 postpaid. Subscription (necessary for submission) is $10/3 issues. Pays $5/poem.** The editors say, "We also publish postcards, booklets, paperbacks, chapbooks, and handbound cloth books of the poems which result from the sustained attempts to master the challenge of significant expression within maximum conciseness. The poem's effect on the reader is our primary interest, not whether it fits any rules, definitions, or concepts of literature. We prefer poetry written with such care and precision that all chatter, rambling thoughts, philosophy, word games, poetic conceits, and clever metaphors are eliminated. Any imperfection is magnified, thus drawing the reader's attention away from the desired response. We want poems to eat like a green apple freshly picked from the branch. We seek poetry which presents the aliveness of this eternally changing present existence. All of our experiences occur in moments, a continual flux of now, now, now. Concise poems are very effective at expressing these instants of being alive and the resulting emotions. We also publish *Haiku Review*, a reference book appearing every 2-3 year (since 1980). It includes reviews, directory of books in print, lists of publishers and magazines, bibliogrpahy of essays, and new critical scholarships—all on haiku." Send business-sized SASE for catalog.

AARON W. HILLMAN PH.D., PUBLISHER, *THE CONFLUENT EDUCATION JOURNAL, THE CONFLUENT EDUCATION TEACHERS HANDBOOK, (formerly *Bibliotherapy, Inc.*), 833 Via Granada, Santa Barbara, CA 93103, phone 805-569-1754, founded 1972. Publishes two magazines; *The Confluent Education Journal* and *The Confluent Education Teachers Handbook* (a book in process with quarterly supplements). "**Experimental poetry is appreciated**." Poets recently published are Judy Cantera, Judy Belfield, WS-Allen-Bolt and David Ogden. These sample lines are from "Resolution" by Judy Belfield:

> What is the question,
> old man
> The question you were about to ask
> before time froze you in this pose?

Submit no more than 3 poems, no query, any format (but no handwritten submissions). Payment is a year's subscription. The editor advises, "Read, study, contemplate and sing. Take poetry back to where its meaning was clear."

HIPPOPOTAMUS PRESS (II), 26 Cedar Rd., Sutton, Surrey, U.K., phone 01-643-1970, founded 1976, poetry editors Roland John and Anna Martin, specializes in **collections of individual poets** printed in flat, printed spine paperback and cloth editions, 50-150 pp., with wrap-around covers, original or translations, "**in a recognizable English, works that comply with the usual standards of diction, syntax and technique. We want to see work that has grown out from the Modernist movement of Pound/Eliot—but it has to be technically competent. In the past we have published work in strict meters as well as the longer looser lines of contemporary free verse. Our criterion is the quality in the chosen technique. We are not interested in glimpses into the workshop**." They have published books by Peter Dale, William Bedford, G. S. Shart Chandra and David Summers. I selected these sample lines from "What's all this about fish?" by Shaun McCarthy (in **The Banned Man**):

> Cod on the slab ooze brine like blood
> my dreams give them life, but grilled
> they leave a skeleton the cartoon cat
> pursues through his comic adventures.

The book is handsomely printed, digest-sized, 60 pp. **Submit complete MS, simultaneous submissions OK. No cover letter: "Nearly every publication has been unsolicited. We don't care what the hell the author believes. We do care for *good* poetry." Reports in 2-3 weeks. Royalty contract with 20 author's copies.**

*HIRAM POETRY REVIEW (II), Box 162, Hiram, OH 44234, founded 1967, poetry editors Hale Chatfield and Carol Donley, is a semi-annual with occasional special supplements. "**We favor new talent—and except for one issue in two years, read *only* unsolicited MSS." They are interested in "all kinds of high quality poetry"** and have published poetry by Grace Butcher, Hale Chatfield, David Citino, Michael Finley, Jim Daniels, Peter Klappert and Harold Witt. They offer these sample lines from "Buttons" (1943) by Nina Dorfman:

> I hold a small cluster of small moments now in a dream
> Childhood I'd forgotten, in which I'd dreamed out the war
> and my real childhood, stuck to my real skin.

There are 30 + pp. of poetry in the professionally printed digest-sized saddle-stapled magazine (glossy cover with b/w photo). It has a circulation of 400, 250 subscriptions of which 150 are libraries. $2 per subscription, $1 per copy. They receive about 7,500 submissions per year, use 50, have up to a 6 month backlog. **Sample: free! No carbons or photocopies. "Send 4-5 fresh, neat copies of your best poems." Reports in 2-3 months. Pays 2 copies plus year's subscription.**

*HIS MAGAZINE (IV, College life), Box 1450, Downers Grove, IL 60515, phone 312-964-5700, editor Verne Becker, is a magazine issued monthly, October-April, for Christian college students. "It is an interdenominational, Biblical presentation of insights on campus life." They are interested in **sophisticated humor as well as serious poetry. Publication typically 1-2 years after acceptance. Pays $25-45 per poem.**

*HOB-NOB (I), 715 Dorsea Rd., Lancaster, PA 17601, phone 717-898-7807, founded 1969, poetry editor Mildred K. Henderson, began in 1969 "as a general publication with emphasis on crafts & hobbies. In the early 70's it acquired male readers and shifted emphasis to the literary, with short prose and poetry both being featured. It is currently a semi-annual, may revert to quarterly. **Short poetry to 16 lines preferred (or up to 35 letters/spaces per line to fit 3 column pages). *All styles OK*, but NO EROTICA or objectionable language. Occasional longer poems or "prosetry" of a narrative nature will be included. "I do NOT like poems with lots of capitalized words, or *all* caps! This detracts from the inherent merit of a poem."** Some of the poets they have published (59 in current issue) are Kenneth Siegelman, Viola Berg, Sigmund Weiss and Curtis Nelson. The editor selected these sample lines from "Shells" by Charles A. Waugaman:

> *Moments come when I would gladly*
> *Gather treasures from the low tides*
> *Of my life, such as I salvage now*
> *From the crest of this sand bar—*
> *Frail castoffs of what once was worthy.*

Each issue is magazine-sized, 52 or more pp., colored matte covers, photocopied from typescript, some art (including poets' illustrations of their own work). The circulation is 200-300. **Sample: $2.25 postpaid. "Any CLEAR copy acceptable, even neatly hand-printed work. No more than 4 poems please (or 8 haikus or other *short* poems). We do not accept submissions from new poets and writers between March 1 and September 1 of every year. Material received during this period will be returned unread. Rejections within 2 weeks. Acceptances take longer. Pays 1 copy for first appearance. After that poets are expected to subscribe for further appearances. Guidelines printed in the magazine. Comments—especially for new or young poets who appear to *need* help. "I do review a few poetry books per issue (if submitted)."**

*THE HOBOKEN TERMINAL, LITTLE FATHER TIME SOCIETY (PRESS) (II), Box 841, Hoboken, NJ 07030, phone 201-798-1696, founded 1981, poetry editors Jack Nestor, C. H. Trowbridge, Eliot Schain, is a tri-annual literary-art journal publishing poetry, fiction, art, photographs and reviews of small-press books. They are interested in **"all kinds, all forms"** of poetry. Poets they have recently published include Barbara A. Holland, D. Nurkse, Paul Barry and Christopher Buckley. There are about 30 pp. of poetry in each digest-sized 80 pp. issue, circulation about 500. They receive 1,000 submissions per year, use 60-80, have a 6 week-6 month backlog. **Sample: $2 postpaid. Submit 3-5 poems. Reports in 4-6 weeks. Payment in copies. They suggest that poets examine a copy before submitting.** Their advice: "Younger poets—or more specifically, less experienced poets professionally speaking—should not become discouraged by rejection. We find that sometimes poets we rejected yet encouraged to resubmit do not. When editors ask to see more of your work, show them."

*THE HOLLINS CRITIC (II), Box 9538, Hollins College, VA 24020, phone 703-362-6316, founded 1964, editor John Rees Moore, publishes critical essays, poetry and book reviews, appears 5 times yearly in a 20 pp. magazine-sized format, circulation 550, **uses a few short poems in each issue, interesting in form, content or both.** They recently published poetry by Lyn Coffin, David Citino, and Joan Colby. The issue I have (October 1985) contains two poems, one by William Slaughter and one by David Galler. As a sample, I selected the first stanza of Galler's "Keep Away!":

> *If someone very dear*
> *Fell down before me, dead,*
> *I think I wouldn't shed*
> *A tear.*
> *What may be worse,*
> *I wouldn't even curse.*

Sample: $1.50. Submit up to 5 poems, none over 35 lines. No photocopies. Reports in 6 weeks (slower in the summer). Pays $25/poem plus 5 copies.

HOLMGANGERS PRESS, KESTREL CHAPBOOK SERIES (II, IV, Regional, history), 95 Carson Ct., Shelter Cove, Whitethorn, CA 95489, phone 707-986-7700, founded 1974, poetry editor Gary Elder, was "founded primarily to bring out **young and unjustly ignored 'older' poets.** We have since published as well collections of fiction, novels, history, graphic art and experimental works. We want **poetry with a sense of place, time, wonder. No confessionals, self-analysis, polemic, field-notes, grocery lists, academic playtoys.**" They have recently published books by Gene Detro and Rian Cooney. Gary Elder selected these sample lines by Rodney Nelson:

> *The finger aims a shadow, blue and green,*
> *At ranks of birches on the other shore.*
> *They touch the dark lake like a ribbon:*
> *The whiteness of a north of North to be.*

They publish four Kestrel Chapbooks (24 pp., saddle-stapled) and two 80-pp. flat-spine paperbacks per year in elegantly printed editions, but future publishing schedule is now uncertain. Poets should **query with a sample of 5 poems. Responds to queries in 2 days, to submissions (if invited) in a month. Simultaneous submissions, photocopy OK. Authors receive 10% royalties; number of copies negotiable. Editor sometimes provides criticism on rejections.** Send SASE for catalog to buy samples. "Advice—Len Fulton said it long ago, editorializing in an early *Dust* magazine: 'young poets would do well to learn humility.' "

*HOME EDUCATION MAGAZINE (V, IV, Home schooling), Box 218, Tonasket, WA 98855, founded 1984, poetry editors and publishers Mark and Helen Hegener, is a national monthly for parents who teach their own children at home. They will consider "**anything that relates to the family, the parent-child relationship, no restrictions on form, length, style. We'd love to see some poetry relating directly to homeschooling.**" They have recently published poetry by R.J. Larbes and Robin C.P. Vernuccio. The editors chose these sample lines by Casey Parr:

> Sometimes, sometimes I can't even look at her
> The pain is too sweet, the joy too painful
> She is leaving me and I'm helping her go
> I want her to go and become her own
> But oh I want her to stay.

"We no longer use a quarter page of poetry in each issue, but we would if we could find some good poetry. Magazine-sized, saddle-stapled, 24 pp. printed from typescript on heavy beige paper. Circulation is "blasting off—right now it's about 2,700." **They receive few poems, and those they use—most!—are published in the next issue. Sample: $2 postpaid. Simultaneous submissions OK. Reports in one month. Payment $5-10 and up plus one copy.**

*HOME PLANET NEWS (II), Box 415, Stuyvesant Station, New York, NY 10009, phone 718-769-2854, founded 1979, editors Enid Dame and Donald Lev, is a 3-4 times a year tabloid (newsprint) journal presenting a "lively, eclectic and comprehensive view of contemporary literature." They want "**honest, well-crafted poems, open or closed form, on any subject, but we will not publish any work which seems to us to be racist, sexist, agist, anti-semitic, or has undue emphasis on violence. Poems under 30 lines stand a better chance. We lean somewhat toward poetry with urban sensibility but are not rigid about this.**" They have published poetry by William Packard, Virginia Scott, Kirk Robertson, nila northSun, Daniel Berrigan, Will Inman, Toi Derricotte, Fritz Hamilton, Paul Genega, Leo Connellan and Eleni Fourtouni. The editors selected these sample lines by Sparrow from "My New Neighbors Play the Rolling Stones":

> Lying in bed
> reading G.K. Chesterton
> I have the sudden
> urge to dance.

They use approximately 13 full 11x16" pp. of poetry in each 24 pp. issue, circulation 1,000, 300 subscriptions of which 6 are libraries. Of 1,200 submissions per year, they use about 30-40. Publication could take one year from acceptance. **Sample: $1.50 postpaid. Submit 3-6 poems typed double-spaced. Reports within 3 months. Payment: 4 copies and year's subscription.**

‡*HOOFSTRIKES NEWSLETTER (IV, Equine themes),, Box 106, Mt. Pleasant, MI 48858, phone 517-772-0139, founded 1982, editor Cathy Ford, a 20-page, magazine-sized newsletter "intended to meet the esoteric needs of creative writers, poets and artists whose work involves equine themes. All equines are included: horse, zebras, pegasus, centaurs, etc. Work can be of any genre." **For poetry, all forms are acceptable as long as they have equine themes; should not be over 40-50 lines.** As a sample, the editor chose the following lines from "Farewell, Eohippus" by Ralph E. Vaughan:

> White breaths lace the air
> When the little ones come to drink
> At the flowing valley streams;
> Tiny footprints in mud, of stallion and mare

Hoofstrikes Newsletter pays up to $25/poem plus 1 copy. Submissions should be "good clear copy of any type of 8½x11" white paper." Reporting time is 2-4 weeks and time to publication 2-6 months. Sample copy available for $2 postpaid. The editor says, "I look at poetry as art with words. Poetry which is creatively constructed appeals to my tastes. I also like unusual themes."

‡*HORIZONS S F (HORIZONS SCIENCE FICTION MAGAZINE) (IV, Science fiction), Box 75, Student Union Bldg., University of British Columbia, Vancouver, BC, Canada V6T 2B5, founded 1979, poetry editor Kyle R. Kirkwood, a twice-yearly (fall and spring) literary journal specializing in science fiction and fantasy. **"Poetry should be short, humorous, and definitely with a SF or fantasy slant. They do not want to see "anything sophilistic,"** (which I take to mean solipsistic). As a sample, the editor selected his own poem "To a Gobe-Mouche" (form—a pastiche to Robbie Burns):

> Wee, sombulent, cow'rin, tum'rous Ronnie,
> O, what a panic buttons in thy brestie!
> Thou need na start a war sae hasty,
>   wi' bickering battle

Horizons S F is "digest-sized, laser copy, cover ticket paper, with b/w art" (I have not seen a copy). Circulation is 125 of which 51 are subscriptions, 5 go to libraries, and 20 are newsstand sales. Price per issue is $1. **Sample: $1.75 postpaid; no guidelines available. Pay is one copy. MSS should be double-spaced between lines, triple spaced between stanzas. Photocopied and dot-matrix MSS are OK. Reporting time is 6 months, and there is "never a backlog for a well written poem." There is a writers' competition, held usually in February, sponsored by the University of British Columbia Science Fiction Society.** The editor says, "Recommend reading poetry by Robert Zend, Randall Garret, and any of the more outrageous poets of SF. Be humorous and light hearted, unusual poems such as an 'Ode to Sum Function S called Entropy'—science related poems always are well received. **Simple rhymes, limericks, other forms encouraged also involving palindromes or pastiches."**

*HOT SPRINGS GAZETTE, THE DRIFT GROUP (IV, Specialized, thermal springs), Box 61, Burbank, CA 91503, phone 818-845-8627, founded 1977, poetry editor Christopher Reiner. The publications of this press are "to extol the virtues and liabilities of recreational hot spring use." The magazine (digest-sized, 50 + pages, issued about every 9 months) uses poems which are "**mainly thermal spring related but definitely nature related." No restrictions on form, length, style.** He has published poetry by Susan Haumpfleish, Suzanne Hackett and Jake Swartz. Print run is 1,000, 500 subscriptions of which 20 are libraries. He receives about 6 submissions per year, uses 3-4. Considers simultaneous submissions. **Reports in 1 month. Pays with free subscription.**

‡HOUGHTON MIFFLIN CO. (V), 2 Park St., Boston MA 02108, founded 1850, poetry editor Peter Davison. Houghton Mifflin is a high-prestige trade publisher that puts out both hardcover and paperback books, but **poetry is by invitation only.** They have recently issued poetry books by Galway Kinnell, Ai, Thomas Lux, and David St. John. **Authors are paid 10-15% royalties; advance is $750.**

‡*HOWLING DOG (I), 10917 W. Outer Drive, Detroit, MI 48223, founded 1985, editor Mark Donovan, a quarterly literary journal of "letters, words, and lines." The editor likes "**found poetry, graphically interesting pieces (4½x7½ if possible, avant-garde, experimental, fun and crazy. All forms. All subjects, but we tend to have a light satirical attitude towards sex and politics."** He has recently published poems by Airhead, Kinky Reggae, Richard Weaver, and Robert C. Lyons. As a sample, he chose the following lines by Susan Osterman:

> today i decided to write a poem
> nothing was forthcoming
> i wasn't even coming
> you came too soon

Howling Dog is digest-sized, offset from typed copy on buff stock, 32 pp. saddle-stapled, one-color matte card cover with illustration in black. Circulation is 250, price per issue $3, subscription $10/year. **Sample available for $1 postpaid, guidelines for SASE. Pay is 5 copies. Submit 3-15 poems with name on each page. Reporting time "varies," time to publication is 2-3 months.** Mr. Donovan publishes 3 spiral-bound, magazine-sized chapbooks of poetry each year with an average page count of 50. **Writers should query before submitting; queries will be answered in 6 months. Simultaneous submissions, photocopied or dot-matrix MSS are OK.** The editor says, "There is probably something in everyone's piles of papers from the past or present for the *Howling Dog*. We provide a forum for friends and folks who have found different ways of expressing ideas creatively that can be reproduced on the 8x5" page. Beginners are invited to send in their best and veterans are encouraged to send in whatever they wouldn't send anywhere else. We are unbiased towards race, sex, religion, politics, or poetical clique."

‡*HURRICANE ALICE (IV, Feminist), 207 Lind Hall, 207 Church St. SE, Minneapolis, MN 55455, phone 612-376-7134, founded 1983, acquisitions editor Toni McNaron, a quarterly feminist review that publishes a maximum of 1-2 poems per issue; "we are not willing to read much poetry." Poems should **be infused by a feminist sensibility (whether the poet is female or male) and should have what we think of as a certain analytic snap to them."** They have recently published poems by Alice Walker, Ellen Bass, Meridel LeSueur, Patricia Hampl, and Nellie Wong. The magazine is a "12-page folio, T of C on cover, plenty of graphics." Circulation is 500-1,000, of which 350 are subscriptions and about 50 go to libraries. Price per issue is $3.50, subscription is $9 (or $7 low-income). **Sample available for $2 postpaid. Pay is 5-10 copies. Reporting time on submissions is 3-4 months and time to publication 3-6 months.** The editor says, "Poets—read what one another are doing. If someone has already written your poem(s), listen to the message. Read what good poets have already written. Spare the trees—."

*HYSTERIA (IV, Women/feminist), Box 2481, Station B., Kitchener, Ontario, Canada N2H 6M3, phone 519-576-8094, founded 1980, poetry editor Catherine Edwards, is a quarterly for feminists—social, cultural and political articles and essays, fiction, graphics and **poetry by women. "We select poems on the basis of their appeal to feminists".** Some of the poets they have published are Dale Loucareas, Julie McNeill, Marilyn S. Boyle and Cynthia Ingle. The editors selected these sample lines

Close-up

Andrew Hudgins
Poet

Saints and Strangers, nominated for a Pulitzer Prize, is Andrew Hudgins' first book of poems. Hudgins has little to say about the publisher's (Houghton Mifflin, New Poetry Series) nominating *Saints and Strangers*, except he won't be chosen as a winner. "There are some very strong books out this year [1986] and it almost invariably goes to an established writer."

Who are the saints, and who are the strangers? ". . . there are few saints in a world of strangers," says John Frederick Nims in his introduction to Hudgins' book. Hudgins says there are saints *and* strangers in "all of the characters and they overlap on some of those themes." They also portray "what it means to be part of the elect and not [part of it]." Like most writers' work, parts of Hudgins' life show up in his poems, ". . . especially as I get older and further away from my childhood." But most, he says, is imagined. Of his writing style, he says his poetry is becoming more narrative. He is more and more of a "storyteller."

Hudgins began writing in high school. He grew up in Montgomery, Alabama, where writers like Dickey, Faulkner, Welty and O'Connor influenced him because they were also from the South. He also admired Robert Lowell for his sense of history and intensity; Shakespeare for his line and creation of characters. Finally, the Bible influenced him with its persisting rhythm.

Hudgins didn't always admit to being a poet. In college he studied to be a teacher and if asked, claimed education as his profession. He later received a Master of Fine Arts from the University of Iowa. One of the most important things he learned at Iowa "was that it's okay to be a writer." That is the area where he feels creative writing classes and poetry workshops are the most beneficial. They teach technique too, but "they provide an atmosphere for writers. Mostly they free you to think about writing among people who take it very seriously."

There are fewer people who take writing seriously. Fewer who read, or at least, fewer people who read poetry. "But too many writers today don't even think of a general audience, so some of the decline in poetry reading is on our own heads." Hudgins says writers should put themselves in the place of the reader and then write what they as readers would enjoy. "If you're not writing for somebody else, why do you expect them to read it?"

What is going to be out there for people to read? Hudgins thinks poetry is becoming more formal. Not necessarily a movement away from free verse and back to traditional but "more of a concern for the formal qualities of a poem, the measure of a line, the rhyme."

There will be another book by Hudgins out soon. It will be a collection of poems written in the voices of historical poets. A poem in *Saints and Strangers*, "Sidney Lanier in Montgomery: August 1866" is similar to Hudgins' works in progress.

—Katherine Jobst

from "This is What Happened" by (K.) Jane Butler:

> *He kissed her on the forehead, and she wet her pants*
> *No, No, that didn't happen. This did:* `
> *He kissed her on the forehead, and she thanked him.*
> *okay, okay. Honestly?*
> *He kissed her on the forehead and she thought, well at*
>   *least he kissed me.*

The magazine-sized, professionally printed quarterly, 40 + pp., saddle-stapled, with glossy color cover, uses 2-4 pp. of poetry in each issue. Their circulation is 1,200, 650 subscriptions of which 75 are libraries. They receive about 200 submissions per year, use 40. **Sample: $2 postpaid. Submit any length, "although we prefer shorter poems," typed in the style the author wants for typesetting. Photocopies, dot-matrix, simultaneous submissions OK. Include SASE, or IRCs for non-Canadian submissions. No query. Reports within 4 months. They will pay about $5 a poem as well as 2 contributor's copies beginning in 1985. "If requested to do so, we pass along our readers' comments."**

‡**IDEALS PUBLISHING, *IDEALS MAGAZINE (I, IV, Nostalgia),** Nelson Place at Elm Hill Pike, Box 141000, Nashville, TN 37214-1000, phone 615-889-9000, founded 1944, poetry editor Ramona Richards. *Ideals* is a slick, lavishly illustrated four-color magazine that is published 8 times a year; the issue I have is *Ideals—Christmas.* They publish **"mostly short (20-30 lines) poems which are seasonal or nostalgic about life in North America during the first half of the 20th century. They should inspire or invoke pleasant memories in our readers (mostly women over 50). Prefer iambic pentameter, but work with other forms as well." They do not want "pessimistic, free verse, social concerns, complex structures."** They sometimes publish poems by such poets as Frost, Whittier, and Ogden Nash, but the copy I have has seasonal poems by lesser-known writers. As a sample I selected the following first stanza from "Interlude," by Hilda Butler Farr:

> *The week that follows Christmas*
> *Is to me the best of all;*
> *The rushing days are over*
> *And friends have time to call.*

The next issue is to be called *Ideals—Sweetheart*—perhaps to coincide with Valentine's Day. The magazine-sized periodical has 80 pp. flat-spined, four-color photographs and one-color art, with no advertising. A single issue is $3.50, subscription (8 issues) is $15.95. **Pay is $10/poem plus 1 copy, and guidelines are available for SASE. MSS should be typed with name and address on each poem, simultaneous submissions are OK, dot-matrix is OK if run with new ribbon. They report on submissions within 2-3 months and publication is in 8-12 months.**

UNIVERSITY OF ILLINOIS PRESS (II), 54 E. Gregory Dr., Champaign, IL 61820, phone 217-333-0950, founded 1918, poetry editor Laurence Lieberman, publishes **collections of individual poets, not anthologies, no translations, 65-105 pp.** Some poets they have published are Josephine Miles, Michael S. Harper, Dave Smith, T. R. Hummer and Emily Grosholz. **Query with "brief resumé of publications, awards, etc." Samples optional. If invited to submit MS, there is a $5 reading fee. Simultaneous submissions OK. Reports in 2 months. Typescript preferred. Royalty contract and 10 copies. Editor comments on many submissions.** Laurence Lieberman (one of our best-known poets) comments: **"Poets would do well to acquaint themselves with at least a few books from our list before deciding whether to submit their work to Illinois." Send SASE for catalog.**

ILLUMINATI, *ORPHEUS: THE MAGAZINE OF POEMS, PICTOGRAMS, TADBOOKS, TALLTALES (II), Box 67e07, Los Angeles, CA 90067, founded 1978, editor P. Schneidre. "Illuminati brings out 25 publications per year, including 10 trade books, approximately half of which are poetry collections or single long poems; a couple are usually somewhere between poetry and prose; usually 1 art book. Beyond those 10 full-size titles, we publish the following: **tadbooks,** a series of limited-edition (225 copies, of which 50 are signed and numbered) volumes by a single author, often of prose fragments, usually of poetry. Contents of the tadbooks are often drawn from *Orpheus,* our poetry journal issued 3 times yearly, and often reappear yet again in the larger trade books by the same authors. Recent tadbooks are by Herbert Morris, Tom Clark and James Krusoe. We publish 3 tadbooks per year. **PictoGrams,** published 4 times a year, are a series of small illustrated books, often poetry (again, in some cases drawn from the more serious collections of Illuminati-published authors) and sometimes cartoons, designed to sell from card racks rather than poetry sections of book stores. **Talltales,** also four per year, are novellas or single short-stories published in a tall format. Our purpose could be said to be the making-public of the art and literature that seems valuable to us in formats that are intriguing enough to be noticed by a public at best only marginally interested in the forms of writing we most admire, *viz.* poetry. **Hard to generalize about what works for us, but we tend not to like surrealism, politics; heavily**

rhymed trochaic tetrameter, poems about poetry editors, mean-spirited portraits in general, or excessively light verse. Not terribly thrilled by Western haiku synthetics. **Every poem must contain poetry, and every piece of poetry must take the shape of a poem.**" They have recently published poetry by Lyn Lifshin, Greg Kuzma, Herbert Morris, David St. John, William Pillin, Nichola Manning, Tom Clark, Robert Peters, F. A. Nettelbeck, and Amy Gerstler. As a sample, the editor selected these lines from **To Pull Out The Peachboy,** a tadbook by Janet Gray:

> *If you pluck a rose apart—*
> *carefully!—*
> *and arrange the parts in rows*
> *by size and color—*
> *what you have is:*
> *the parts of a dead rose;*
>
> *and there are those*
> *who will be grateful*
> *that, at last,*
> *the heart is exposed.*

All of their publications are elegantly printed, bound and illustrated. *Orpheus* is a large-format (6¾x11") spacious magazine of poetry only, each issue in 2 parts, the first a long-poem or sequence by a single author, the second a collection of single poems by 12 or so authors. Circulation varies, most of 400 subscriptions is to libraries. **Sample copy: $4. They receive 7,000-8,000 submissions per year and about 50 are used, 1 year backlog. No query but submit "5-6 pages preferred in legal-sized envelope—not in manila mailer nor on onionskin nor word-processed. Of course we'd prefer new submitters to order a sample copy, but this has nothing to do with how the work will be received editorially." Reports within a week. Pays $5-25.**

‡**ILLUMINATIONS PRESS (II)**, 2110-9th St., #B, Berkeley, CA 94710, phone 415-849-2102, founded 1965, poetry editor Norman Moser, an independent publisher of limited circulation books of poetry, plays, and fiction, average press run 400-800. Norman Moser says, **"I prefer visionary, mystical and/or lyrical or nature poetry. However, I've also aired quite a lot of experimental or political poetry (or prose-poetry) in my mag *Illuminations* in the past & I imagine the book-series will eventually have that (eclectic) character too."** He does not want to see "rhyming verse, light verse, religious (especially Christian) verse. Blatantly propagandistic or political tracts sans literary quality." He has recently published poetry by Hadassah Haskel, Morton Felix, and himself. As a sample, he selected the following lines from *The Forester Whacks,* a book by Tim Holt:

> *Dusty children chant against that sky:*
> *A shingling of motives define me.*
> *And pulling out all my weight,*
> *The chanced and accidental abjure cry.*

The press publishes 1-2 chapbooks/year with an average page count of 64, paperback, flat-spined. The editor says, **"Usually prefer query first since so far all contributors have been taken from current subscription list or past contributors' lists." Requirements for publication? "Yes, first they must subscribe at current $30 rate. Then they'll be expected to offset some agreed-upon percent of overall costs (usually not more than 50%, sometimes less) and to help sell the book in their area, especially help with mailings and the like." Royalties are 15%.** Book catalog free for #10 SASE; book prices are $4 and $5. The editor comments, "I am extremely eclectic in my own work and in my publishing too. Yet at the same time I feel the **language should be kept to simplicity and even to lyricism wherever possible. Somewhat Beat and/or Black Mountain influenced, I'm quite fond of visionary and/or nature poetry a la Ginsberg, Snyder, Bly *et al.*,** but I strive mightily to keep myself open to new styles and am quite ashamed of the tame poetry in academic mags."

IMAGES (II), English Dept., Wright State University, Dayton, OH 45435, founded 1974, poetry editor Gary and Dorothea Pacernick, is a triannual tabloid printed on high-quality newsprint, **12 pp. of poetry of high literary quality spaciously laid out and attractively presented with b/w photo illustrations. Submit any number of poems, none over 150 lines. Photocopy OK. Reports in 4 weeks. Pays 3 copies.** They have published work by such distinguished poets as William Stafford, Marge Piercy, Harvey Shapiro, James Schevill, Edwin Honig, David Ignatow and Elizabeth Bartlett, though unknowns and newcomers are also used in each issue. I selected these sample lines by Grace Butcher:

> *Sleep is all we know of innocence anymore;*
> *we darken with daylight.*
> *Every night we are lifted by love*
> *and yearn towards the silences of stars.*

They have a circulation of 1,000. **Sample: $1 postpaid.**

IMPLOSION PRESS, *IMPETUS (I,II), 4975 Comanche Trail, Stow, OH 44224, phone 216-686-9800, founded 1984, poetry editor Cheryl Townsend, publishes the quarterly literary magazine, chapbooks, special issues. The editor would like to see **"anything but rhyme for the sake of rhyme, oriental, or 'Kissy, kissy I love you' poems. Any length as long as it works. All subjects okay, providing it isn't too rank."** They have published poetry by Ron Androla, John Bennet, Ella Blanche, Merritt Clifton, Bruce Combs, Todd Moore, Tom House and Lyn Lifshin. The editor selected these sample lines by Steven Doering:

> *The red shirt*
> *I love to peel*
> *from her flesh*
> *is now wrinkled with*
> *dark designs of*
> *desire*

The 7½x9" magazine is photocopied from typescript, saddle-stapled, with matte paper with photos, cartoons, ads (some sexually explicit). Circulation about 1,000, 150 subscriptions. Generally a 3 month backlog. **Sample: $2.50 postpaid. The editor says, "All I ask is that they send me what best represents them, but I prefer shorter, to-the-point work. Previously published work OK if it is noted when and where. Prefer cover letter and bio note, saying what they want known about themselves."** Usually reports the same day. Pays 1 copy. Send SASE for guidelines. For chapbook publication, query with up to 5 samples. In her comments on rejection, the editor usually refers poets to other magazines she feels would appreciate the work more. She says, "Bear with the small press. We're working as best as we can and usually harder. We can only do so much at a time. Support the Small Presses!"

*IMPULSE MAGAZINE (II), 471 Richmond St. W., Toronto, Ontario, Canada M5V 1X9, founded 1971, is a large-format, beautifully printed, slick, colorful quarterly which publishes **contemporary, experimental art in all fields from all over the world. They have used little poetry in recent years but are open to it.** As a sample I selected these lines from the Spanish of Nicaraguan poet Yolanda Blanco:

> *Here they are*
> *These are the ones*
> *One by one*
> *The Flowers of horror*

They have a circulation of 6,000, 1,500 subscriptions of which 500 are libraries. **Sample: $5 postpaid. Sometimes pays and provides copies.**

*INDIANA REVIEW (II), 316 N. Jordan Ave., Bloomington, IN 47405, founded 1982, associate editor Pamela Wampler, is a triquarterly of new fiction and poetry. "In general the *Review* looks for poems **with an emphasis on striking or elegant language. Any subject matter is acceptable if it is written well. We do not want to see poetry that is clichéd, amateurish or faked.** Although we have published such writers as David Wagoner and Lisel Mueller, we also publish new or little-known poets. Content is more important than 'name recognition.' The magazine uses about 20 pp. of poetry in each issue (6x9", flat-spined, 100 + pages, color matte cover, professional printing). The magazine has 1,200 subscriptions of which 60 are libraries. They receive about 6,500 submissions per year of which they use about 60, have a 3-4 month backlog. **Sample: $4 postpaid. Submit no more than 7-8 pp. of poetry. Photocopy, dot-matrix OK if readable. Please indicate stanza breaks on poems over 1 page. "Cover letter useful but not required."** Pays $5 per page plus 2 copies and remainder of year's subscription. They are also looking for short, detailed analyses of *individual* poems and on "detailed, appreciative criticism of the works writers and readers generally admire . . . the means by which contemporary poets . . . achieve their effects. What makes a contemporary poem 'work'?" The editor advises, "read before sending out MSS. Read the publication, not just ours, but any you wish to submit to. And don't just recycle poems—editors can tell when a batch of poems has been shuffled across more than one desk. Keep your work neat."

*INDRA'S NET (II), 78 Center St., Geneseo, NY 14454, founded 1984, poetry editor Wendy Innis, is a "small quarterly that tries to show the inter-connectedness of people, environment, and culture. Upbeat. Some topics covered: third world, nutrition, some lighter subjects and Zen poetry. Non profit." They want poetry which is **"up-beat, lyrical, excellent, free verse (usually), punchy, to lift the heart, to make one** *see*. **Write with precision, whether it's about planting potatoes or studying a camellia. This does not exclude humor. No more than 50 lines."** They have published poetry by Alan Brooks and Nancy L. Nielsen. The editor selected these sample lines by Miranda Beth Arnold:

> *Abstract ideas flow,*
> *half chocolate half ocean,*

through his mind
and return to him in his music.
They usually have 1 page of poetry in their 20 pp. issues (digest-sized, saddle-stapled, small type, narrow margins, no cover—a no-nonsense, packed format). **Sample: $1 postpaid. Submit any number of poems, "neat format, prefer original typed (or computer typed), no query." Pays in copies. Reports in about 2 weeks. Covering letter appreciated, SASE mandatory.**

‡*INFINITUM (IV, Science fiction, fantasy), 5737 Louetta Rd., Spring TX 77379, phone 713-376-9693, founded 1985, editor William H. Doyle. This semi-annual magazine publishes **Blank verse and traditional poetry, no avant-garde, on science-fiction and fantasy themes.** They publish only 5 poems/year. Since I have not seen a copy I cannot quote samples. Circulation of *Infinitum* is 400. **Sample available for $3, guidelines for SASE. Photocopied and previously published submissions are OK. Writers should submit no more than 4 poems at a time, maximum length 40 lines. Reporting time is 6 weeks.**

INKBLOT PUBLICATIONS, *INKBLOT (IV, Style), 1506 Bonita, Berkeley, CA 94709, founded 1981, poetry editor Theo Green, "publishes a selection of international writers focusing on alternative fiction and poetry, plus some visuals, in chapbooks, books and the biannual *Inkblot* magazine. **We only will consider experimental, concrete, avant-garde, cut-up poetry**." They have recently published poetry by Dick Higgins, F. A. Nettelbeck, Gellu Naum and Dale Jensen. As a sample, Theo Green selected these lines by Sebastien Reichmann:

> *Day in front come from everywhere,*
> *waiting for it,*
> *the voices have lowered little by little,*
> *nothing will ever be the same.*

Inkblot is magazine-sized 60 pp., offset from typescript, with b/w graphics and ads, using 15-20 pp. of poetry in each issue, circulation 1,000, 100 subscriptions of which 20 are libraries. They use 5 of some 30-40 submissions received each year. **Sample: $3 postpaid. Reports in 2-3 months. Pays in copies. Send SASE for guidelines. For book or chapbook publication, query with 3 samples. "Cover letter not essential, but could be useful." Replies to queries in 3 months, to submissions (if invited) in 3 months. Simultaneous submissions, photocopy OK. Pays 10% royalties, advance ($100-200) plus 10 copies on book contracts. Send SASE for catalog to buy samples.** The editor comments, "We will be publishing 5 books of poetry per year. Advice: something different. Style is much more important than content."

INKLING PUBLICATIONS, INC., *INKLING LITERARY JOURNAL *FREELANCE WRITER, *WRITING UPDATE(II), Box 128, Alexandria, MN 56308, phone 612-762-2020, founded 1980, poetry editor Esther M. Leiper. *Inkling* **is a monthly journal "for writers and poets which offers advice and guidance, motivation, inspiration, to both beginning and publishing writers" and market information as well as poems. Esther Leiper has a regular column in which she analyzes and discusses poems sent in by readers. They want all forms of poetry—no erotica, vulgar, religious or badly written. Prefers shorter to longer.** Some of the poets they have published are Arthur A. Greve, Richard Solly, Bruce Souders, Esther M. Leiper and Ann Zoller. As a sample I selected the opening quatrain of a sonnet that won first prize ($125) in one of their two annual poetry contests (entry fee $2), "Old Pemberton" by Leonard Helie:

> *Old Pemberton, they said, had cut so much*
> *Firewood and piled it up so far ahead*
> *That there were pieces he would never touch*
> *Unless he aimed to empty out his shed.*

It is magazine-sized, professionally printed, 28-32 pp. (including paper cover), using 2-4 pp. of poetry in each issue. Circulation 2,400, with 2,000 subscribers of which 12 are libraries. They receive about 300 submissions per year of which they use 40-50, have a 3 month backlog. **Sample: $2 postpaid. Photocopy, dot-matrix OK, no query. Reports in 3-4 weeks, pays 25¢ a line, $4 minimum. Inkling Publications is newly undertaking publication of two 40 pp. collections by individuals per year. Query with 5-6 samples, bio and publication credits. They pay 10% royalties and 10 copies.** For sample send $5 for a copy of their anthology, **The Inkling Selection**, poems that appeared in the magazine. They have also published the **International Directory of Writers' Groups & Associations**.

*INKSTONE: A QUARTERLY OF HAIKU (IV, Haiku), Box 67 Station H, Toronto, Ontario, Canada M4C 5H7, founded 1982, poetry editors Keith Southward, Marshall Hryciuk and J. Louise Fletcher, "**publishes haiku and related forms plus reviews, articles, etc., related to haiku. Poems must be haiku or related, but we use a broad definition of haiku.**" They have published haiku by Le Roy Gorman, Michael Dudley, Alexis Rotella, George Swede and this sample by Roger Ishii:

> *the path divides*
> *dawn peeling off*
> *the birch bark*

There are roughly 20 pp. of poetry and reviews/articles in the digest-sized format, 40 pp., offset from typescript, matte card cover, circulation 100, accepting "perhaps 10%" of the poems submitted each year, poems appear as space permits, usually in the next issue after acceptance. **Sample: $5.50 postpaid. Submit any number of poems, preferably 1 per 5½x8½" sheet, typewritten. Reports within 6 weeks. Pays 1 copy.**

INKY TRAILS PUBLICATIONS, *INKY TRAILS, *TIME TO PAUSE, *PATHWAYS, *BIRTH OF AMERICA (I), Box 345, Middleton, ID 83644, founded 1967, poetry editor Pearl L. Kirk, are inexpensively produced publications (typescript, side-stapled in magazine-sized format) which you have to buy one copy of the issue in which your work appears if your poem is to be included. "Non-subscribers don't have to subscribe to be published," order in advance. *Inky Trails* and *Time to Pause*: $8. *Pathways*: adults $5.50; children $4.50. They run various contests with small cash prizes. Beginners and children have a good chance of acceptance. Send SASE for guidelines and information. The editor quotes a sample stanza from "A Peaceful Night" by Virginia West, which appeared in *Inky Trails*:

> *Soon the world is hushed in slumber*
> *Broken only as an owl hunts nearby*
> *Stillness reigns in the forest*
> *When night winds croon a lullaby*

"We accept material from 2-3 years in advance, so be patient. No horror, porno or sexually explicit material and any sent won't be returned either." 1 poem per page; 1 side only; name and address at bottom of MS. Always include SASE; for copy of magazine send 9x12 SAE with cost of magazine plus 70¢ postage. Query for information on contests.

*INLET (II), Virginia Wesleyan College, Norfolk, VA 23502, phone 804-461-3232, ext. 283, founded 1971, associate editors H. Rick Hite, L. Anderson Orr and Gordon Magnuson, is an annual "**publishing the best poems and stories we can get, by established or unknown writers. Well-written, serious poetry—even if humorous; no sentimental stuff, no doggerel, and nothing that is indistinguishable from prose. Short (8-16 lines) in great demand; poems of 36-46 lines had better be** *very* **good; anything longer had better be immortal.**" They have published poetry by David Madden, Sister Mary Ann Henn, Carol Reposa, Caryl Porter, Ruth Moon Kempher, Bruce Guernsey, Brenda Nasio and Mary Balazs. As a sample I selected this complete poem by Heather Downey, "Man":

> *Oneness of Design*
> *a million mirrored minds*
> *images the same*
> *intelligence in kind, find*
> *each in his time, rhyme*

18-24 pp. of poetry are used in each 32 pp. issue, 7x8", pebbled matte cover with art, circulation 500, distributed free. Sample: 75¢. **MSS accepted from September 1st through March 1st; publishes in August. Address submissions to H. Rick Hite, photocopy OK, with name of the poet and number of lines on the first page of each poem; 7 poems or fewer, prefer 8-30 lines but will consider longer ones. Reports within 3 months,** "*usually.*" **Payment in copies.** The editor advises, "Write as well as you can and present neatly typed, readable manuscripts worthy of a professional. Don't wait for one batch to come back before trying *other* magazines with new poems."

*THE INQUIRER (IV, Religious, social issues), 59 Barton Rd., Cambridge, England CBJ 9LL, founded 1842, is a biweekly magazine dealing with **religion and social issues and using some poetry relevant to those concerns. Sample: free for postage.**

*INSIGHT (IV, Teens), The Young Calvinist Federation, Box 7259, Grand Rapids, MI 49510, is a Christian monthly (except June and August), 28 pp., circulation 18,500, for **teens 15-19. Uses 10 free verse poems per year, 4-25 lines. Pays $10-20. Simultaneous, photocopied and previously published submissions OK. Send 9x12" SASE for guidelines and free sample copy.**

‡INSIGHT PRESS, *ROAD RUNNER (V, Invitation), Box 25, Drawer 249, Ocotillo, CA 92259, founded 1983, publishers John and Merry Harris. The Harrises publish short poetry chapbook anthologies (one per year) containing the work of "**pre-selected writers (no submissions without invitation, please.)" The work published must be "short, non-academic poetry for the layman—clarity and lucidity a must. Prefer humorous, inspirational poetry.**" They have recently published poems by Gloria Procsai and Merry Harris, who selected as a sample the following "4-liner" from "Laughter: A Revelry" by Geraldine Plomb:

Close-up

Esther M. Leiper
Inkling

Artist: Lawrence Goodridge

Although her literary accomplishments are considerable, Esther Leiper admits that she has no "typical" schedule. "Not that I don't aspire to more sacrosanct hours," she says, "but with job, kids (Hannah Margaret, two and a half years old, and Thomas, eleven months), house and garden, interruptions are frequent."

Despite the interruptions, Leiper is poetry editor of *Inkling* literary journal; a columnist for the *North Country Weekly*, a New England newspaper; a poet whose work has appeared in over 200 magazines and won more than 600 national poetry contests; a lecturer at conferences and workshops; and author of *How To Enter Poetry Contests to WIN* (Inkling Books) and a soon-to-be-published book on poetry patterns, as well as numerous articles and stories in both literary and commercial publications.

Such accomplishments obviously demand persistence and determination, two of the qualities Leiper considers fundamental to success. She displayed these attributes early in life. "I started a journal when I was eight that lasted till college, when I discovered poetry and fiction could preserve what I wanted preserved in an infinitely more interesting manner." She says that, as a teenager, she felt some of her friends wrote with more verve and skill than she did, but they didn't care to become writers, "the drive wasn't there." By the time she was in college, she began seeing her work in print and other doors opened. She was a poet in the schools in Cookeville, Tennessee, and started lecturing and teaching classes and workshops.

Leiper, whose work has appeared in *Touchstone*, *Shenandoah*, *Mississippi Review*, *Cape Rock Journal*, *Amelia*, and many other publications, has won success with a remarkable diversity in her poetry, using many patterns and styles from free verse, to sonnets and French patterns, to stylistic prose. In today's published poetry, she sees a trend toward "understandability," rather than the obscure, vague and abstract.

As poetry editor for *Inkling*, she likes to see variety and diverse styles. "I try to be open to all kinds of verse," she adds. She wants to see poems that are clear, concise and filled with imagery. "Take me there (the world of the poem) and make me want to stay."

Inkling has published a number of "name" poets, but Leiper doesn't actively seek names. "Nothing pleases me more than a fine effort by someone I have never heard of," she says.

A wide variety and diversity of backgrounds are represented in poets published in *Inkling*: a pediatrician, a missionary MD, a professional dancer, teachers, a factory worker, a science-fiction writer, a policeman, a movie director, a computer processor—to name a few.

Her advice to beginning poets: "Read—write—revise." But she believes there is no "right way" to write. "You write anyway that works; write what demands to be written."

As an editor, she cautions poets to be especially concerned with presentation and professionalism. "Show me you respect your work," she stresses. This means submissions that are neatly typed with the poet's name and address on each poem, and a SASE. Unlike some editors, Leiper enjoys a cover letter with submissions.

What makes a good poet? Leiper says, "An openness of life and the willingness to take infinite pains. Poetry may end as a fine art, but starts as a trade."

—Pat Beusterien

> *Male and female*
> *Created he them.*
> *From this fact*
> *All troubles stem.*

The chapbooks are paperback, flat-spined, 40-50 pp. "We sell our chapbooks at cost and send out at least 50 of first run for promotion of our poets, who are then widely reprinted." **Sample: $2 for "Laughter: a Revelry."** Merry Harris advises, "1) one tip for beginners: Join United Amateur Press Assn., as I did 40 years ago, to learn basics while being published. Amateur does NOT mean 'Amateurish.' AMAT = LOVE! 2) Join a local writers' co-op. 3)*Avoid those who exploit writers.*"

‡*INTERIM (II)**, Department of English, University of Nevada, Las Vegas, NV 89154, phone 702-739-3172, originally published in Seattle 1944-55, now being revived (spring 1986), editor A. Wilber Stevens, a twice yearly (spring and autumn) literary magazine that publishes **"the best poetry we can get from anywhere."** Some poets scheduled to be published in forthcoming issues are John Heath-Stubbs, X.J. Kennedy, James Laughlin, Stephen Stepanchev, William Stafford, James Ragan, and Peter Cooley. The magazine is 6x9", circulation 600-1,000, single copy $3, subscription $5/year. "Subscriptions are eagerly solicited." **Pay is "under discussion." Reporting time is 1 month.**

‡*INTERNATIONAL POETRY REVIEW (II, IV, Translations)**, Box 2047, Greensboro, NC 27402, phone 919-273-1711, founded 1975, editor Evalyn P. Gill, a semi-annual (spring and fall) magazine that publishes **translations of contemporary (including original) poetry and poetry originally written in English; any form, but no haiku.** Poets recently published include Fred Chappell, Willis Barnstone, William Stafford, and Charles Edward Eaton. There are 100-148 pp. of poetry in each issue, and the usual print-run is 400. Price per issue is $3, subscription $6/year, $11/2 years, $16/3 years. **Sample: $3.50 postpaid. Writers should submit 3-5 poems, up to 100 lines; no query is necessary. Time to publication is 3-6 months. No guidelines: payment is in copies. Past contests have awarded a prize of $150 each for the best translation and the best poem in English.** The magazine appears in a flat-spined, 6x9" format.

INTERNATIONAL PUBLISHERS CO., INC. (IV, Anthologies), Rm. 1301, 381 Park Ave. South, New York, NY 10016, founded 1924, does not publish collections by individuals, only special anthologies (for example, by black Americans, Native Americans) by independent editors. Watch for announcements in such publications as *Coda* for forthcoming anthology themes and the address of the editor to whom to submit. **Terms for poems selected vary, usually $5-10 per poem plus 50% of all reprint fees (which are usually $50 per short poem). Do not send submissions to the address above, but send SASE for flyers and announcements.**

INTERNATIONAL UNIVERSITY PRESS, *INTERNATIONAL UNIVERSITY POETRY QUARTERLY (II), 1301 Noland Rd., Independence MO 64055, phone 816-461-3633, founded 1974, editor Dr. John Wayne Johnston. The magazine-sized quarterly, circulation 1,095, uses **quality poetry, pays in copies.** The press subsidy publishes 30% of their 100 titles per year. "Such decisions are made by a committee based on internal criteria. **We will consider poetry MSS of 50 pp. or more either in form of long, epic poems or a collection of shorter works."** Submit complete MS.

‡*INTERSTATE (II)**, Box 7086, University Station, Austin, TX 78712, editors Loris Essary and Mark Loeffler, a numbered magazine (the copy I have is *Interstate 16*) that appears once or twice a year. The editors say, **"*Interstate* continues to pursue an eclectic editorial policy. Submissions are welcome.** *Interstate* traditionally opens each issue with an essay, often non-traditional itself, which creates a milieu . . . for the usually non-traditional work that follows." *Interstate* opens with poetry that relates to a Degas painting, which is faintly reproduced in b/w. Some of the poems are by Jack L. Anderson, Carmen Musolino, and Bagi Ali Diaab. As a sample, I selected these lines from "Women" by John Paul Minarik:

> *In the foreground,*
> *with orange hair gathered from the neck,*
> *in the purple wings, leaning on a green dressing stool*
> *is the dancer of the adjusting slipper:*
> *the mother dressing children in snowsuits,*
> *the fixer of the home.*

Interstate is digest-sized, offset from typed copy on ordinary paper with occasional b/w photographs or decorations, 90 pp. flat-spined with one-color glossy card cover. Circulation is 500, price $5 per copy, subscription $10 for 2 issues. **Sample available "by arrangement." Pay is in copies, and reporting time is "as soon as possible."**

INTERTEXT (II), 2633 E. 17th Ave., Anchorage, AK 99508, founded 1982, poetry editor Sharon Ann Jaeger, is "devoted to producing lasting works in every sense. We specialize in poetry, translations and short works in the fine arts and literary criticism. **We are looking for work that is truly excellent—no restrictions on form, length, or style. Cannot use religious verse.** Like both surrealist and realist poetry, poetry with intensity, striking insight, vivid imagery, fresh metaphor, musical use of language in both word sounds and rhythm. Must make the world—in all its dimensions—come alive." She has published poetry by James Hanlen, Louis Hammer, Tim Hunt, Barbara Ann Blatner and Elaine Handley. To give a sense of her taste she says, "I admire the work of Louise Glück, Louis Hammer, William Stafford, Jim Wayne Miller, Antonio Ramos Rosa, Rainer Maria Rilke, Eleanor Wilner, Wallace Stevens, Frank O'Hara." The sample of their publishing I have seen, 17 Toutle River Haiku by James Hanlen, is beautifully printed and illustrated with "oil and mixed media" and calligraphy: sells for $12. **Query first with 3-5 samples only.** "Cover letter optional—the sample poems are always read first—but no form letters, please. If sample poems are promising, then the complete chapbook MS will be requested." Photocopy OK. Simultaneous queries OK. Payment: 10% royalty after costs of production, promotion, and distribution have been recovered. Send 6x9" SASE for catalog to purchase sample. Comments briefly on rejected sample poems or, "if we ASKED for entire MS, on MS."

‡**INVERTED-A, INC., *INVERTED-A HORN (I)**, 401 Forrest Hill, Grand Prairie, TX 75051, phone 214-264-0066, founded 1977, editors Amnon Katz and Aya Katz, a very small press that evolved from publishing technical manuals for other products. "Publishing is a small part of our business. Our interests center on justice, freedom, individual rights, and free enterprise." The catalog of Inverted-A, Inc., lists Flight simulation, computers and peripherals, electronics, telephone equipment, and [last] books and publications." *Inverted-A Horn* is a periodical which I have not seen but the editors describe as magazine-sized, offset, usually 6 pages, which appears irregularly; circulation is 300. **Freelance submissions of poetry for chapbooks are accepted. The editors do not want to see anything "modern, formless, existentialist."** As a sample, they quote the following lines by an unidentified poet:

> Cursed be he who in peace tends his hand,
> Cursed be he who partakes of the pot,
> Cursed be they who can understand,
> Cursed be they who advise: avenge not!

The sample chapbook I have seen, **A Fistfull of Filk**, contains satirical lyrics by several different authors to be sung to various popular tunes. It is magazine-sized, 20 pp., offset from typed copy (some of it faint), with illustrations inside and on the one-color matte card cover, saddle-stapled. **Pay is one reduced-price copy. Queries are reported on in 2 weeks, MSS in 2 months, simultaneous submissions are OK, as are photocopied or dot-matrix MSS.**

*IOWA REVIEW (II), 308 EPB, University of Iowa, Iowa City, IA 52242, phone 319-353-6048, founded 1970, editor David Hamilton (first readers for poetry and occasional guest editors vary), appears 3 times a year in flat-spined, 170-200 pp., professionally printed format. The editor says, "We simply look for poems that at the time we read and choose, we admire. **No specifications as to form, length, style, subject-matter, or purpose**. There are around 30 pp. of poetry in each issue and currently we are giving those pages to about 5-6 writers only." Circulation 1,200-1,300, 1,000 subscriptions of which about half are libraries. They receive about 5,000 submissions per year, use about 100. **Sample: $5 postpaid. Their backlog is "around a year. Sometimes people hit at the right time and come out in a few months." They report in 1-4 months, pay $1 a line, 2-3 copies and a year's subscription.** Occasional comments on rejections or suggestions on accepted poems. The editor advises, "That old advice of putting poems in a drawer for 9 years was rather nice; I'd at least like to believe the poems had endured with their author for 9 months."

*IRON MOUNTAIN: A JOURNAL OF MAGICAL RELIGION (IV), Box 2282, Boulder, CO 80306, founded 1983, is a biannual, 50 pp., 7x8½", focusing on **magical religion and using some poetry relevant to their theme. Send SASE for guidelines before submitting. Sample: $2.**

IRON PRESS, *IRON (II), 5 Marden Terrace, Cullercoats, North Shields, Tyne & Wear, NE30 4PD England, phone 091-2531901, founded 1973, poetry editors Peter Mortimer and Ian McMillan, "publishes contemporary writing both in magazine form (*Iron*) and in individual books. Magazine concentrates on poetry, the books on prose and drama." They are "**open to many influences, but no 19th century derivatives please or work from people who seem unaware anything has happened poetically since Wordsworth.**" Peter Mortimer says, "Writing is accepted and published because when I read it I feel the world should see it—if I don't feel that, it's no good. What's the point of poetry nobody understands except the poet?" The poets they have recently published include Ken Smith, Ann Born, and Ray Tallis. For a sample try the opening stanzas from "Canteen Assistant" by Maurice Rutherford:

> *She arrives for work by taxi*
> *she and three others*
> *have filled with smoke*
>
> *Two years from school her wedding*
> *pregnant, a stillbirth, the marriage*
> *guttered, and went out.*

Iron is 8¼" wide x 7¾" tall, flat-spined, professionally printed in small type, 1-3 columns, using b/w photos and graphics, three-color glossy card cover, about 50 pp. of poetry in each issue, circulation 750, 300 subscriptions of which 30 are libraries. **Sample: $5 postpaid, or £1.50. Submit a maximum of** *five* **poems. "Just the poems—no need for long-winded backgrounds. The poems must stand by themselves." He reports in "2 weeks maximum," pays £10 per page. He always comments on rejections "provided poets keep to our maximum of 5 poems per submission."** They do not invite poetry submissions for books, which they commission themselves. The editor advises, "don't start submitting work too soon. It will only waste your own and editors' time. Many writers turn out a few dozen poems, then rush them off before they've learnt much of the craft, never mind the art." And about his occupation as editor, this journalist, poet, playwright and humorist says, "Small presses are crazy, often stupid, muddle-headed, anarchic, disorganized, totally illogical. I love them."

*IRONWOOD, IRONWOOD PRESS (II), Box 40907, Tucson, AZ 85717, founded 1972, editor Michael Cuddihy, is one of the most highly respected and influential of our literary journals, "an independent poetry magazine with no institutional ties, published twice yearly. Now in our fifteenth year, we continue to grow in size, readership, prestige. We keep an eye out for the new, the experimental, yet remain loyal to those values found in the best contemporary poetry. **Imagination. Intelligence. Moral seriousness. A concern for language.** *Ironwood* is known for its clean, clear format, the quality of its design and materials." It is 200 pp., flat-spined, 6x9", professionally printed with full-color glossy card spine, circulation 1,200-2,000. "Our special issues on individual poets and aspects of poetry have become indispensible to poets and literary scholars in all parts of the country as well as dozens of foreign countries. These issues contain a wealth of original poems, memoirs, photographs, letters, and exhibit a wide spectrum of critical opinion. Special issues have featured George Oppen, James Wright, Linda Gregg, Hilda Morley, Czeslaw Milosz, Robert Duncan, Thomas Transtromer and César Vallejo. Others have dealt with Chinese Poetry and the American Imagination or 'Language' Writing." As a sample I selected the opening lines of "Clarity: A Knife" by Patrick Lawler:

> *They settle on invisibility the way some men*
> *Settle on a price. Farmers: men who are certain*
> *Of their equipment, obstinate like crowbars. Sceptical*
> *Men who sharpen their collars; men ready with a dent.*

Subscription: $8. Sample: $4 postpaid. Pays $10 per printed page when possible (less for long poems).

ISHTAR PRESS, *PAINTBRUSH: A JOURNAL OF POETRY, TRANSLATIONS AND LETTERS (II), Dept. of English & Foreign Languages, Georgia Southwestern College, Americus, GA 31709, founded 1974, editor Ben Bennani. *Paintbrush* is a 6x9", 64+ pp. literary biannual, circulation 500, which uses **quality poetry. Sample: $5.** Ishtar Press publishes collections of poetry. Send SASE for catalog to buy samples.

*ISLANDS: A NEW ZEALAND QUARTERLY OF ARTS & LETTERS (II), 4 Sealy Rd., Torbay, Aukland 10, New Zealand, is a literary quarterly which suspended publication for several years but resumed in July, 1984. They publish **quality poetry. "Little, if any room at the moment for material from outside the South Pacific basin." Send IRCs for guidelines. An annual overseas subscription is $36. Sample copy $10 in NZ; $15 (NZ) from overseas—payment with order, please. Four lines from Allen Curnow's "The Loop in Lone Kauri Road"** (Islands 35):

> *So difficult to concentrate/a powerful*
> *breath to blow the sea back*
> *and a powerful hand to haul it*
> *in, without overbalancing.*

‡***ISSUE MAGAZINE (II)**, 1651 Larkin St., San Francisco, CA 94109, founded 1983, editor/publisher T. Baron, a literary magazine with emphasis on post-modern poetics. **The editor wants to see postmodernist work including translations, but no "self exploring i.e. confessional or Bukowski type—no haiku, no poems of 'feeling,' no 'pop art' poems."** He has recently published poetry by Rosemarie Waldrop, Paul Vangelisti, Gerald Burns, and Guilia Niccolia. As a sample, he selected the following lines by an unidentified poet:

> *Divinity, what it*
> *means to one who would not sleep or rather dream, is*
> *the shelf of endurance where the license to talk is*
> *reversed, through "Villages of Ether" the words*
> *are not mine . . .*

Issue appears approximately once every 9 months. It is 4½x7", 65 pages, "I-Tech printing, cover done by artist." Circulation is 400, of which 200-300 are newsstand sales; subscriptions go only to libraries. Price per issue is $4. **Sample available for $4.60 postpaid. Contributors receive free copies (number varies). Submissions are reported on ("if I even get to look at unsolicited") in "perhaps 1 month"; time to publication is approximately 8 months.** The editor advises, "Don't simply send work 'out' to get published—with *Issue,* as I hope with others. Read the publication first. Support what needs support. Don't only think of publication of your work!"

ISSUE ONE, EON PUBLICATIONS (II), 2 Tewkesbury Dr., Grimsby, South Humberside, England DN34 4TL, founded 1983, poetry editor Ian Brocklebank, is an attractive quarterly **pamphlet,** professionally printed on colored card stock folded accordian-style into 5-8 letter-sized panels. A typical issue contains 8-10 short poems. The editor says he "aims to publish not only a broad mix of styles of poetry by new and established poets the world over but also strives to a consistently high standard with regard to the actual presentation of this work. **I prefer short pieces with modern themes, concise but comprehensive images. Metre etc. unimportant. Poems with a point to make. My own criterion for selection is based firmly on whether images within the poem stir something, anything else in my imagination than what seems to be the subject. No epics required. Usually nothing above 14 lines overall. Bad taste, racism, sexism are not encouraged. Humour is welcome but no limericks please!** *Issue One* will intermittently use guest editors." He has recently used poetry by George Cairncross, Dale Loucaraeas, Andrew Darlington, Shaunt Basmajian, Mark Roberts and Carol Hamilton. As a sample, I selected this complete poem by Peter Mortimer (of *Iron*), "Tomorrow":

> *When the passion has run*
> *and we two are done*
> *"I will love you forever"*
> *will sound, like the never*
> *quite still vibration*
> *of some great tolling bell*

Issue One has a circulation of about 75, 50 + subscriptions of which 5 are libraries. He receives 300-500 submissions per edition of which he uses a maximum of 15. No backlog: "I do not hold over work but will allow re-submission." **Sample free for envelope and postage. Submit no more than 5 typed or photocopied pages "with a covering note and SASE/IRC if they require a response. Simultaneous submissions OK. General queries will be welcome with a SASE/IRC." Reports in a maximum of 2 months. Pays in single contributor's copies. Send SASE for guidelines. Prefers not to comment but "will provide observations if specifically requested."** Book publication by Eon Press is by invitation only. Ian Brocklebank says, "For someone starting out writing poetry I would advise trying out as much of your poetry on as many different magazines as you can afford. Do not become discouraged by rejection of your work. Try to keep variety in your subject matter."

ISSUES (IV), Box 11250, San Francisco, CA 94101, founded 1973, is an 8 pp. newsletter of **Messianic Judaism** distributed free, circulation 50,000, which uses some **poetry relevant to that cause. Send SASE for free sample. Pays.**

‡*THE ITALIAN TIMES OF MARYLAND (IV, Italian), Italian-American Publications, Inc., Box 20241, Baltimore, MD, phone 301-337-0596, founded 1985, editor Stephen J. Ferrandi, a monthly magazine with a circulation of 32,574 that publishes **"anything of interest to Italian-Americans." They take most types of poetry (no avant-garde), except "mafia or organized crime poetry or anything that is anti-Italian." Sample available for $1 postpaid. They buy 6 poems/year with a maximum length of 50 lines. Pay is $2-125. Simultaneous or previously published submissions are acceptable. Reporting time is 4 weeks and time to publication is 3 months.** The editors say, "We encourage good writers who haven't been published to send MSS for consideration. We welcome phone calls to answer any questions (9-5)."

ITHACA HOUSE, *CHIAROSCURO (II), Box 6484, Ithaca, NY 14851, founded 1970, poetry editors John Latta and Chris Henkel, is one of the longest-going and highly respected small press publishers of poetry in the country. The press produces "letterpress editions of 600-1,000; 3-4 books per year; we generally see more good MSS than we can afford to publish. The Ithaca House Poetry Series numbers over one hundred volumes now. The books are generally 50-80 pp. in length. No chapbooks. Lately we have begun publishing *Chiaroscuro,* an annual poetry magazine. **We look for lively language, strong**

imagery, a kind of authenticity of vision. We generally return the work of easy versifiers." They have recently published poetry by Carol Frost, Maxine Chernoff, Christopher Buckley, E.G. Burrows, Jack Driscoll, Deborah Tall, Roy Marz and Eileen Silver-Lillywhite. I selected as a sample the first of eight stanzas of "Uncle Groundhog" by Patricia Goedicke (from *Chiaroscuro #4*):

> He peers out at us, enraged
> cork stuck in the bottle
> of his own doorway. Pulling the brown ruff
> up over his head

The magazine is a beautifully printed digest-sized flat-spined paperback (90 + pp., colored matte cover), illustrated with colored woodcuts, circulation about 300, 30 subscribers of which 25 are libraries. They receive 150-200 submissions per year, use 3-5. Poetry accepted appears in the subsequent issue. Sample: $5 postpaid. Submit 5-8 pp. of poetry. Photocopy OK. Reports in 2-3 weeks. Pays variable rates "when grants allow payment." Contributors should be familiar with the publication before submitting. For a book MS, query with 8-10 samples, publication record and bio. They pay no royalties (but "would if a book took hold and demanded a large second edition"), pay honorarium "if grants allow it," 20-50 author's copies and 40% discount on additional copies. Send SASE for catalog to buy samples. They sometimes comment on rejections. "We manage to continue because we do all of the production work on our books ourselves—printing, binding, etc. This with a lot of volunteer labor, and occasional blessings of grant monies."

‡*IWI REVIEW, ILLINOIS WRITERS, INC., IWI POETRY CONTEST (IV, Members)**, Box 1087, Champaign, IL 61801, phone 217-398-8526, founded 1976, poetry editor Deborah Bosley. **The *IWI Review* publishes reviews of current literature and excerpts; the *Monthly* has notices, announcements, MS wanted, etc. In 1986 they had a poetry contest for members. The winner will have a chapbook published by IWI. No poetry submissions are accepted from non-members.** The *IWI Review* is magazine-sized, 12-36 pp. with glossy cover, photo or graphic art, appearing semi-annually. Its circulation is about 300, of which 250 go to members. A subscription is included with a $10/year membership fee. Price per issue is $4. **Sample: $2 postpaid "if available; most aren't." Pay varies, but was $25 in 1985 plus 1 copy. Submissions are reported on within a few weeks and there is usually no backlog.** The group has published no chapbooks yet but plans to issue 1 each year of about 30 pages. **Queries will be answered in 1 week, and photocopied or dot-matrix MS are OK. An honorarium will be paid "if we can."** The editors say, "We would like to become an annual poetry and fiction competition, for members publishing 1 fiction and 1 poetry chapbook/year in addition to the *Review* and *Monthly*."

‡JACKSON'S ARM (V)**, 179 Wingrove Rd., Newcastle upon Tyne NE4 9DA, England, phone (091)273-3280, founded 1985, editor Michael Blackburn, a small-press publisher of poetry chapbooks and translations. **"No specifications as to subject or style. The poetry I want to publish should be vigorous and imaginative, with a firm grasp of everyday realities. Nothing bland, safe, or pretentious."** The press publishes 3 chapbooks per year with an average page count of 18, saddle-stitched paperbacks. However, the editor says **he does not usually accept freelance submissions. Writers should query, sending 6 sample poems, credits, and bio. Queries will be answered immediately. Pay is in author's copies equivalent to royalties at 10% of total.** A book catalog is free for IRC. Mr. Blackburn advises, "Read everything you can, in particular *contemporary* poets and writers. Get hold of all the 'small' poetry magazines you can, as well as the more commercial and prestigious."

*JAM TO-DAY (II)**, Box 249, Northfield, VT 05663, founded 1973, poetry editors Don and Judith Stanford "publishes poetry and, beginning with the 1980 issue, fiction. The editors are concerned more with quality than quantity, and so only 12 issues have appeared since the magazine began in 1973. *Jam To-Day* is not affiliated with any institution. **Contributors are paid—not much, but something.** Money is, perhaps unavoidably, the dominant standard of value in our society, and poetry and fiction are worth at least something. At least to some people. The editors make a positive effort to be **open to new voices. Don't send light verse. Send experimental work only if you know clearly why your work is experimental (rather than just impenetrable) and what you are trying to accomplish (other than reader bewilderment). We are biased against poems about poets and poetry, poems telling the world how awful it is (the world knows that already), and poems preaching God's love in rhyme** (that doesn't mean we shun religious topics; few aspects of life are as important). **We are biased in favor of work that is emotionally honest, sensitive to the English language, genuinely concerned with life's strange twistings and turnings. The best way to get a sense of what we look for is to purchase a sample copy."** To my request for names of poets recently published they responded, "Since we emphasize work by unknowns, it doesn't tell anyone much to list their names. However, occasionally we cannot control ourselves, and we solicit well-known authors for material. Recent are X. J. Kennedy and Marge Piercy. Those instances are abberations. *Jam To-Day* is built almost entirely from unsolicited

MSS." As a sample they offer this haiku by William J. Harris:

> On the phone, my grandfather's voice
> So frail
> No, my father's

The magazine is a handsomely printed digest-sized flat-spined, 90 + pp., format with b/w art using 40-50 pp. of poetry in each issue, circulation 300. They receive about 720 submissions, averaging 4 poems, each per year, use 40-50. There is up to a year between acceptance and publication. **Sample: $3.50 postpaid. Submit no more than 4 poems. Photocopies, dot-matrix OK. Reports in 6 weeks. Pays $5 per poem or more if it is more than 3 pages plus 2 copies.**

‡*JAMES DICKEY NEWSLETTER (II)**, Dekalb College, 2101 Womack Rd., Dunwoody, GA 30338, founded 1984, editor Joyce M. Pair, a bi-annual newsletter devoted to study of James Dickey's works. They **"publish a few poems of *high* quality."** The copy I have, which is 30 pp. of *ordinary* paper, neatly offset (back and front), with a card back-cover in blue, stapled top left corner, contains 1 poem, "Mourner," by Marion Hodge. Its first stanza is:

> A sky god—sword and shield against the Horns,
> three stars stiff beween his legs
>   for love—

The newsletter is published in the fall and spring. Single copy price is $3.50, subscription $5/year. **Sample available for $3.50 postage. Contributors should follow MLA style and standard MS form, sending 1 copy, double-spaced.** The editor's advice is: "Acquire more knowledge of literary history and grammar."

‡*JAMES JOYCE BROADSHEET (IV, Joyce)**, School of English, University of Leeds, Leeds LS2 9JT, England, founded 1980, editor Richard Brown, a "small-press specialist literary review, mainly book reviews connected with James Joyce; we include relevant poems in the magazine." **Poems must be short, of good quality, and connected with James Joyce. They do not want anyting "long, self-indulgent."** The issue I have contains two poems, "The Ballad of Erse O. Really?" by Gavin Ewart and "Keeping Awake Over Finnegan" by Alamgir Hashmi; they have also published poems by Seamus Heaney and Jim Morgan. As a sample, the editor chose the following lines (poet unidentified):

> Then I knew him in a flash
> out there on the termac among the cars
> wintered hard and sharp as a blackthorn bush.

The magazine is "literally a broadsheet folded into digest sized." It is professionally printed on good paper and includes b/w line drawings and other art work. When unfolded, it is 4 pages, 11½x16¼". It appears in February, June, and October and has a circulation of 700, of which 70 go to libraries; complimentary copies go to "eminent Joyceans." Subscription price is £4 (UK or Europe) or $10 (US), sent by air. Sample available for £2 or $4. Pay is 3 copies. Writers should send 2 copies of their work. Reporting time is 1 month and time to publication 4 months. Simultaneous submissions photocopied or dot-matrix MSS are okay.

*JAPANOPHILE (IV, Japan)**, Box 223, Okemos, MI 48864, phone 517-349-1795, founded 1974, poetry editor Earl R. Snodgrass, is "a literary quarterly about Japanese culture (not just in Japan). Issues include articles, art, a short story and **poetry (haiku or other Japanese forms or any form if it deals with Japanese culture). Note: karate and ikebana in the U. S. are examples of Japanese culture.** They have published poetry by Mary Jane Sanadi, F. A. Raborg, Jr., Geraldine Daesch, Anne Marx, Egean Roggio, Catherine K. Limperis and reprints of Basho. As an example the editors selected this haiku by Michael Elsey:

> The glass sings crystal
> a moist finger gently
> dancing on the rim.

There are 10-15 pp. of poetry in each issue (digest-sized, about 50 pp., saddle-stapled). They have a circulation of 700, 100 subscriptions of which 30 are libraries. They receive about 500 submissions a year, use 70, have a 6 month backlog. **Sample: $3 postpaid. Summer is the best time to submit. Photocopy OK. Reports in 6 months. Pays $1 for haiku to $15 for longer poems. Send SASE for guidelines.** They also publish books under the Japanophile imprint, but so far none have been of poetry. Query with samples and cover letter (about 2 pp.) giving publishing credits, bio, personal or aesthetic philosophy, poetic goals and principles.

‡*JEAN'S JOURNAL (I)**, Box 791693, Dallas, TX 75379, phone 214-241-9574, founded 1963, editor Jean Calkins, a literary quarterly publishing poetry **"rhymed, free verse, haiku in good taste." Ms. Calkins does not want to see "extreme avant-garde, smut."** She has recently published poems by Minnie Klemmie, William Walter DeBott, Jaye Giammarino, and Viola Berg. As a sample, she se-

lected the following lines by Alice Mackenzie Swaim:

> *Today is not for pruned austerity, or insisting*
> *that pen and paper be obedient slaves.*
> *Sun chases shadow between unfolding leaves*
> *and down the flagstone path*

The purpose of **Jean's Journal** is to provide "an outlet for new and established poets, critique and help for novices." The quarterly is digest-sized, offset with card cover, completely illustrated. Circulation is 300, of which 200 are subscriptions. Price per issue is $2.50, **sample available for $1 postpaid, guidelines for SASE. If contributors want a copy of their poem, the editor will send a photocopy for SASE. Poems should be submitted 1/page, name and address on each page; the editor prefers typewritten MSS or computer printouts. She reports on submissions in 2-3 weeks and publication is in 3-12 months.** She publishes 2 anthologies per year, soft cover, page count 30-60. **Writers should send sample poems. There is a purchase requirement of $3/page; 1 copy is given for each page.** The editor's advice is: "Be willing to consider suggestions; if you don't agree, do try other markets."

*JEWISH CURRENTS (IV, Jewish themes), Suite 601, 22 E. 17th St., New York, NY 10003, phone 212-924-5740, founded 1946, editor Morris U. Schappes, is a magazine appearing 11 times a year that uses **poetry on secular Jewish themes or Jewish point-of-view. It is in a digest-sized format, usually 48 pp., saddle-stapled. Sample: free for 2 oz. postage. Submit 3-4 poems. Photocopies OK. Pays 6 copies plus year's subscription. There is an annual Avrom Jenofsky Award of $200 for services to Yiddish in translation.**

ANNE JOHNSTON/THE MOORLANDS PRESS (II), 11 Novi Lane, Leek, Staffs. England ST13 6NS, phone 047852-257, founded 1982, poetry editor J. C. R. Green. See **Aquila.** This press is related (same editor) but is an independent operation at an English rather than Scottish address. Initially they published chiefly pamphlets and **The Moorland Review**, which has now merged with **Prospice** (described under Aquila). J. C. R. Green says Anne Johnston/The Moorlands Press is "an archetypical LITTLE PRESS. WE PUBLISH FOR FUN. Good general poetry required." They expect to bring out about 8 titles in poetry per year. **No query needed. Submit MS with cover letter with brief bio and main previous publications, not over 1 page maximum. Reports in 3 months. Simultaneous submissions OK if advised in advance. Photocopies, dot-matrix OK. Publishes on 10% royalty contract plus 12 copies. Send SASE for catalog to buy samples.** I have examined a 24 pp. pamphlet, **The Survivor**, by Sally Lucas, 5x7", neatly but inexpensively produced with green mat cover, selling for £75 (about $1.50). As a sample I selected the first of three stanzas of the title poem:

> *The undefined, warm edges of September*
> *Nudging the frost and sun of either side*
> *Collect new moments as the eyes remember*
> *Others that drowse beneath the harvestide.*

‡*JOURNAL OF NEW JERSEY POETS (IV, Regional/New Jersey), English Dept., Fairleigh Dickinson University, Madison, NJ 07940, phone 201-377-4700, ext. 243, founded 1976, managing editor Marjorie Koyishian. This annual volume uses poetry from **current or former residents of New Jersey. They want "serious work (including humor) by poets familiar with current potential and practice of the art. They do not want sentimental, greeting card verse."** Poets recently published include Simon Penchik, Judah L. Jacbowitz, John V. Chard, and Andonis DeCavalle. As a sample, the editor selected the following lines by W. Lanf:

> *At dusk there is*
> *silence in the little, three-sided barn*
> *light in the cracks between the boards*
> *is pink and gray*

The annual is digest-sized, offset, with an average of 40 pp. Circulation is 300, price per issue $1.50. **Pay is 2 copies. There are "no limitations" on submissions; reporting time is 2-3 months and time to publication within 1 year.**

*JOYFUL NOISE (IV, Handicapped writers), 5500 Monroe Ave., Evansville, IN 47715, editor **Brad Chaffin, is a quarterly literary magazine** "originated, published and written by impaired persons, serving as an outlet for handicapped writers, artists and puzzle makers." It is a 14 pp. magazine-sized format, saddle-stapled, with much art and varied typography. Most of the many poems in the issue I examined had a religious/inspirational emphasis. Subscription: $10. I selected these sample lines, the first of four stanzas, from "The Awful Truth," one of a pageful of "Poems by Bush," James Bush:

> *Spring comes later every year,*
> *The winters are so long and cold.*

> *Autumn comes so soon these days;*
> *Can it be I'm growing old?*

Send SASE for instructions for submitting and terms. Pays in copies.

JUNIPER PRESS, *NORTHEAST, JUNIPER BOOKS, THE WILLIAM N. JUDSON SERIES OF CONTEMPORARY AMERICAN POETRY, HAIKU-SHORT POEM SERIES, INLAND SERIES, GIFTS OF THE PRESS (II), 1310 Shorewood Dr., La Crosse, WI 54601, founded 1962, poetry editors John and Joanne Judson, is one of the oldest and most respected programs of publishing poetry in the country. *Northeast* is a semi-annual little magazine, digest-sized, saddle-stapled. **Most poets published in book form have first appeared in *Northeast*.** A subscription to *Northeast/Juniper Press* is $30 per year, which brings you 2 issues of the magazine and the Juniper books, haiku-short poem booklets, WNJ Books, and some gifts of the press, a total of about 5-8 items. (Or send SASE for catalog to order individual items. Sample: $2.50 postpaid.) The Juniper Books are perfect bound books of poetry; the WNJ Books are letterpress books on quality paper; the haiku booklets are 12-40 pp. each, handsewn in wrappers; Inland Sea Series is for larger works; Gifts of the Press are usually letterpress books and cards given only to subscribers or friends of the Press. **Payment to authors is 10% of the press run of 300-500.**

*JUST ABOUT ME (JAM), A MAGAZINE FOR KIDS 10-15 (IV, Childrens, teens), Suite 202, 56 The Esplanade, Toronto, Canada M5E 1A7, editor Ulla Colgrass, is a bimonthly magazine, circulation 40,000, with **Canadian readership and contents, which uses avant-garde, free verse, haiku, light verse and traditional poems appropriate for its readership. Pays $10 maximum per poem. Sample: $2.60. Send SASE (2 Canadian stamps or IRC) for guidelines.**

‡*KALDRON: AN INTERNATIONAL JOURNAL OF VISUAL POETRY AND LANGUAGE ART (IV, Visual), Box 7036, Halcyon, CA 93420-7036, phone 805-489-2770, editor and publisher, Karl Kempton *Kaldron* is a "journal of visual poetry and language art interested only in works which are a true wedding of language/poetry/literature and the other arts. This is a journal which publishes works from around the world." Mr. Kempton says, **"A visual poem is a poem which takes the patterns and densities of language and molds them with other art forms, mainly the visual arts in such a way that without either element the work falls apart, that is to say the entire image is what is on the page."** The tabloid-sized, 24 pp. newspaper has no recognizable English text except the masthead, a list of contributors, short reviews, and a list of magazines with visual literature. It is impossible to quote works from the magazine without photographing them; recent contributors include Doris Cross, Scott Helmes, Loris Essary, Alan Satie, Hassan Moussady, Paula Hocks, Shoji Yoshizawa, and Giovanni Fontana. *Kaldron* appears "once or twice a year" and has a circulation of 800; single copy price $5. **Sample $5 postpaid. Contributors receive 2 to 10 copies. The only instruction for contributors is: "no image should be larger than 10¼x16." Submissions will be reported on in "one day to a month," and time to publication "varies, but contributor kept informed of any delays." Criticism will be given "if submissions are accompanied with a cover letter."** Mr. Kempton says, "Visual poetry and language art published in *Kaldron* may be considered examples of an ongoing development of an international meta-language/poetic/artistic gesturing which attempts to express what language is unable to express. Such concerns have created a strong international dialog. The roots of this expression are ancient; the modern roots are found in movements like futurism and dadaism in the early part of this century and the more contemporary roots are found in the concrete poetry movement of the 50's and 60's, a poetry held by many to be the first true international poetic expression. Around 100 serious visual poets and language artists are at work in this country and hundreds more at work around the globe."

KALEIDOSCOPE PRESS, *KALEIDOSCOPE: INTERNATIONAL MAGAZINE OF LITERATURE, FINE ARTS, AND DISABILITY (IV, Disability), 326 Locust St., Akron, OH 44302, phone 216-762-9755, founded 1979, editor Dr. Darshan C. Perusek consulting poetry editors Vassar Miller, Christopher Hewitt and Dr. Joseph Baird. *Kaleidoscope* is based at United Cerebral Palsy and

❝ Poems should be evocative enough to allow readers to share the poet's experience as if it were their own. Those that seize the reader's attention from the first line and hold it throughout are most likely to be accepted.

John Moffitt, America ❞

Services for the Handicapped, a nonprofit agency, and has the mission "to provide a viable national and international vehicle for literary and artisitic works dealing with the experience of disability, stimulate ongoing literary and art programming among organizations which serve persons with disabilities, provide an international Poetry, Fiction and Art Award Contest, and reflect the issues inherent to the experience of disability that popular culture and most serious art forms neglect." "Poems of any kind including experimental. Can deal with being disabled but not limited to that. Photocopies with SASE. Reports in 3 months, pays up to $50 for a body of work. Any well-written short story, play or poem will be considered, including children's literature. All submissions must be accompanied by an autobiographical sketch. "Sketch should include general background information, any writing experiences, artistic achievements, a listing of previous publications (if applicable), and nature of disability (physical, mental, or emotional). If applicable, a photo is optional but welcome." The editor says, "People need to understand the craft of poetry and the magic it can produce. Poetry can be based on personal experience, though it must reach beyond the particular and must communicate vividly." They have recently published poetry by Christopher Hewitt, James Weigle, Deborah Kendrick, Felix Pollack and Vassar Miller. As a sample, they offer these lines by Zana:

> What is
> the typical day
> of an easter islander?
> maybe you should
> send in an anthropologist,
> to observe my ways

Circulation 1,500, including libraries social service agencies, health professionals, disabled student services, literature departments, and individual subscribers. A subscription is $8, single copy $4, but samples free upon request (for SASE). *Kaleidoscope* **International Poetry, Fiction and Art Awards** of cash are given to professional and non-professional entries. Alex Gildzen, poet, has been a judge for these contests. The editor advises, "**We are looking for tough-minded poetry, free of maudlin expressions.**"

‡*KALLIOPE (IV, Women)**, 3939 Roosevelt Blvd., Jacksonville, FL 32205, phone 904-387-8211, founded 1978, managing editor Sharon Weightman, a literary/visual arts journal published by Florida Junior College at Jacksonville; the emphasis is feminist. The editors say, "**We like the idea of poetry as a sort of artesian well—there's one meaning that's clear on the surface and another deeper meaning that comes welling up from underneath. Odds are we'll reject anything too sentimental or 'rhymed up' but there are always those irresistible exceptions. We'd like to see more poetry from Black, Hispanic, Native American women, and more translations. Nothing sexist, racist, conventionally religious.**" Poets recently published include Susan Fromberg Schaeffer, Marge Piercy, Kathleen Spivak, and Denise Levertov. As a sample, the editors selected the following lines by Laurie Duesing:

> Now I am rapt and looking for the still point
> between earth and air. I am willing
> to wait while the world turns red,
> to watch while everything comes at me.

Kalliope calls itself "a journal of women's art", and it publishes fiction, interviews, essays, drama, and visual art in addition to poetry. The magazine, which appears 3 times a year, is 7¼x8¼", handsomely printed on white stock with b/w photographs of works of art and, in the sample copy I have, a photographic (no words) essay. Average number of pages is 72. On my copy, the glossy card cover features a b/w illustration of a piece of sculputre; the magazine is flat-spined. The circulation is 1,000, of which 400-500 are subscriptions, including 50 library subscriptions, and 200 copies are sold on newsstands. Price per issue is $3.50, subscription $9/year or $17/2 years. **No free sample copies are available, but guidelines can be obtained for SASE. Contributors receive 3-10 copies. Poems should be submitted in batches of 3-10 with bio note and phone number and address. Submissions will be reported on in 3 months and publication will be within 6 months. Criticism is provided "when time permits and the author has requested it.**" The editors say, "Just as your first-grade teacher told you, 'Neatness counts.' Send out clean, professional MSS to 'medium-range' journals and don't get discouraged until (at least) your hundredth form rejection."

*KANSAS QUARTERLY (II)**, Denison Hall 122, Kansas State University, Manhattan, KS 66506, phone 913-532-6716, founded 1968 as an outgrowth of *Kansas Magazine,* poetry editors W. R. Moses and H. Schneider, is "a magazine devoted to the culture, history, art and writing of mid-Americans, but not restricted to this area." It publishes poetry in all issues. They say, "**We are interested in all kinds of modern poetry except humorous verse, limericks, extremely light verse, or book-length MSS.**" They have recently published poetry by Lewis Turco, Richard Gillum, David Baker, Daniel Lusk, David Citino, Lyn Lifshin, Anita Skeen, Roger Finch, Dave Etter, A.D. Winans and R.T. Smith. As a sample the editor offers these lines from "School in the Bird's Eye," by Mary Tisera:

> *His hands squeeze the reuben so hard*
> *sauerkraut slips from the bread,*
> *off his plate. I am too dumb-*
> *founded to reply. Instead,*
> *I practice him gone: how I live*
> *the celibate life, write him every day,*
> *how he longs for me so much*
> *he returns to face*
> *whatever made him desperate. Then*
> *I exercise the darker skill:*
> *how I write him every day while he . . .*

There are an average of 80 pp. of poetry in each creative issue, circulation 1,150-1,350, 719 subscriptions of which 50% are libraries. They receive 10,000 submissions per year, use 300-400. There is at least a 14-18 month backlog unless a poem fits into a special number—then it may go in rapidly. **Sample: $4 postpaid ($6 for double number). Submit "enough poems to show variety (or a single poem if author wishes), but no books. Typed, double-spaced, photocopy OK, but no dot-matrix. No queries." Reports in 1-3 months. Pays 2 copies and yearly awards of up to $200 per poet for 6-10 poets.** The *Kansas Quarterly*/Kansas Art Commission Awards are $200 (1st prize), $150 (2nd), $100 (3rd), $50 (4th), and up to 5 honorable mentions. There are also similar prizes in the Seaton Awards (to native-born or resident Kansas poets). The editors **often comment on rejections, even at times suggesting revision and return.** Editors say, "Our only advice is for the poet to *know* the magazine he is sending to: consult in library or send for sample copy. Magazines need the support and their published copies should provide the best example of what the editors are looking for. We believe that we annually publish as much good poetry as nearly any other U.S. literary magazine—between 250 and 400 poems a year. Others will have to say how good it is."

*KARAMU (II), Dept. of English, Eastern Illinois University, Charleston, IL 61920, phone 217-581-5614, founded 1966, editor John Guzlowski, poetry editor Beth Kalikoff, is an annual whose "goal is to provide a forum for the best contemporary poetry and fiction that comes our way. We especially like to print the works of new writers. **We like to see poetry that shows a good sense of what's being done with poetry currently. We like poetry that builds around real experiences, real images, and real characters and that avoids abstraction, overt philosophizing, and fuzzy pontifications. In terms of form, we prefer well-structured free verse, poetry with an inner, sub-surface structure as opposed to, let's say, the surface structure of rhymed quatrains. We have definite preferences in terms of style and form, but no such preferences in terms of length or subject matter. Purpose, however, is another thing. We don't have much interest in the openly didactic poem. If the poet wants to preach against or for abortion, the preaching shouldn't be so strident that it overwhelms the poem. The poem should first be a poem."** They have recently published poetry by Ruth Moon Kempher, Jared Carter, Don Baker, Lyn Lifshin and John Ditsky. The editor chose these sample lines from "The Boomerang" by Bruce Guernsey:

> *To hold these abstract wings*
> *is to feel the glide of the falcon—*
> *the curve of this beakless bone,*
> *flight itself in your hand.*

The format is a 60 pp. 5x8", matte cover, handsomely printed (narrow margins), attractive b/w art. Each issue has about 20 pp. of poetry. They have a circulation of 350, 300 subscriptions of which 15 are libraries. They receive about 200 submissions per year, use 15-20. Never more than a year—usually 6-7 months—between acceptance and publication. Payment is one contributor's copy. **Sample: $1.75. "Poems—in batches of 5-6—may be submitted to John Guzlowski at any time of the year. Photocopied work as well as dot-matrix is OK, although we don't much care for simultaneous submissions. Poets should not bother to query. We critique many of the better poems—about 1 out of 5. We want the poet to consider our comments and then resubmit the poems.** My only advice is the standard advice: know your market. Read contemporary poetry and the magazines you want to be published in."

‡*KATUAH: BIOREGIONAL JOURNAL OF THE SOUTHERN APPALACHIANS (IV, Regional), Box 873, Cullowhee, NC 28723, phone 704-252-9167, founded 1983, edited by a collective group. *Katuah* is a quarterly tabloid journal "concerned with developing a sustainable human culture in the Southern Appalachian Mountains." **The editors want to see poetry "oriented" to that region.** They have recently published poems by Jim Wayne Miller, Kay Byers, and Bennie Lee Sinclair. The issue I have contains two poems by Stephen Knauth; as a sample, I selected the beginning lines of his "1836. In the Cherokee Overhills":

> *In a pasture of the Milky Way*
> *where the Little Pigeon glides down over the dark*
> *rocks*
> *of Tennessee,*
> *a man has landed on his belly,*
> *drinking water from a cup made of hands,*

The tabloid has 32 pp., offset on newsprint, nicely laid out with attractive b/w drawings and other illustrations, folded for mailing, not stapled. Price per copy is $1, subscription $10/year. Circulation is 2,000, of which 200 are subscriptions; 80% of circulation is newsstand sales. **Sample available for $2 postpaid, guidelines for SASE. Pay is 10 copies. Reporting time and time to publication are both 6 months.**

KATYDID BOOKS (V), English Dept., Oakland University, Rochester, MI 48063, founded 1973, poetry editors Thomas and Karen Fitzsimmons, is currently fully committed to a series of books of **Japanese poetry in translation and cannot consider unsolicited MSS.** As a sample I selected the opening lines of "Every Thirteen Seconds" by Tamura Ryuichi as translated by Christopher Drake in **Dead Languages: Selected Poems 1946-1984, a 300 + pp., flat-spined paperback, glossy cover with author's photo, bilingual:**

> *I don't like new houses*
> *the one I was born in was already old*
> *they have no tables to share with the dead*
> *no space where sentient beings can be born*

*KAVITHA (II), 4408 Wickford Rd., Baltimore, MD 21210, phone 301-467-4316, founded 1982, poetry editors Thomas Dorsett and Kammaha Nirmala, a poetry journal published once a year, has **"no fixed policy regarding length, but we rarely publish poems longer than 40 lines or so. The first criterion is language that lives. Second: evidence that behind the language that lives there is an author who knows what living means."** They have recently published poetry by Gary Fincke, Joan Colby, Christine Zawadiwsky and Shaya Kline. The editors selected these sample lines by Robert L. Tyler:

> *How can this loneliest of jobs,*
> *of ghost, dasein, or merely things,*
> *straighten my crooked love of them,*
> *give this odd business some wings?*

Their magazine is characterized by "good printing, good poems," about 45 pp. of poetry in each issue, circulation 500, 175 subscriptions of which 25 are libraries. They receive 300-500 submissions per year, use 40, have a 6-8 month backlog. Sample: $3.50. Submit in batches of 5. Contributors are encouraged to buy copies. No pay. Send SASE for guidelines.

THE KEEPSAKE PRESS (II), 26 Sydney Rd., Richmond, Surrey, TW9 1UB England, phone 940-9364, founded 1958, poetry editor Shirley Toulson, is a "private press, printing in letter press inhouse." In addition to chapbooks and books they publish poemcards and other items. "**Policy recently changed. Established poets only. Can't sell newcomers unless absolutely of genius quality." For this reason he considers only English poets who are known. Query with samples and publication credits.** Send 8x9" SASE (or IRC) for catalog to buy samples. Those I have seen are good poetry, quality printing, but in rather small type. Editor-publisher Roy Lewis says he has published poetry by Florence Elon, Charles Maude, Edward Lowbury, Kathleen Nott and Stan Cook. Though he says it is "ridiculous" to quote 4 lines which "represent the taste and quality you want in your publications," I was impressed and amused by these lines about T. S. Eliot from "No Land is Waste, Dr. Eliot" by James Simmons, which I quote not as representative but for enjoyment:

> *What roots? What stony rubbish? What rats? Where?*
> *Visions of horror conjured out of air,*
> *the spiritual D.T.s. The pompous swine . . .*
> *that man's not hollow, he's a mate of mine.*

Roy Lewis advises poets to "*buy* and *read poetry. They so often never do. Some of them cannot write— or read, I often think.*"

‡KEITH PUBLICATIONS, *WRITER'S RESCUE, *WRITE TO FAME, *CONTESTS & CONTACTS (I), Box 1028, Litchfield Park, AR 85340, founded 1985, editor Mary L. Keith, who says the three publications are "newsletters created out of my desires and needs as a writer. *Write to Fame* specializes in materials directed at beginners, young writers, interested parents and teachers. *Writer's Rescue* covers all areas of writing. *Contests & Contacts* specializes in contests and poetry directed at Poets/Writers. All three of these newsletters are open markets . . . Each has its own contests and offset from typed copy with b/w graphics, cover on the same stock, saddle-stapled, 7-13 pp. **Payment for poems is**

"up to $1." I have selected the following sample stanza by Sharon Lynn Drake:

> *Thunder in the distance,*
> *The landscape is hazy,*
> *Ninety degress and humid—*
> *Enough to make one lazy*

Anyone submitting material must be a subscriber to one of the newsletters. "Material will be accepted from non-subscribers but pay will go toward a subscription of one KP Newsletter of this choice. Same holds true for young writers. Anyone can work toward a subscription be it for themselves or another writer." Subscription rates are $12/year for *Writer's Rescue* and *Write to Fame* and $18/year for *Contests and Contacts*, which publishes information about many poetry contests.

KENNEBEC: A PORTFOLIO OF MAINE WRITING (IV, Regional), University of Maine, Augusta, ME 04330, founded 1975, editors Carol Kontos and Terry Plunkett, is an annual tabloid of creative writing by Maine writers (whether or not currently residents) supported by the University of Maine at Augusta. 5,000 copies are distributed free as a service to the community in an effort to bring Maine writers to the attention of a wide public. **Qualified writers may submit (with a statement of their relationship to Maine) between September 15 and December 1 each year. Sample free for SASE. Pays copies.** I selected these sample lines from "North Into Love" by David Adams:

> *A little on we inspect the ponds for frogs,*
> *guess at the names of shrubs,*
> *transversing a green geometry, like*
> *a dream through a dream.*

*KENTUCKY POETRY REVIEW (II), 1568 Cherokee Rd., Louisville, KY 40205, founded 1964, poetry editor Wade Hall, appears twice yearly publishing "**good poems of all types. No restrictions on style, structure or subject.**" They have recently published poems by James Dickey, X. J. Kennedy, Wendell Berry, Ruth Whitman, Robert Penn Warren, Philip Appleman and James Still. As a sample, the editor selected these lines by Janet Lewis:

> *That one small garden*
> *Should yield such treasure,*
> *Thanks be to God, at noon, at dawn.*

There are approximately 52 pp. of poetry in each issue, circulation 350, 250 subscriptions of which 45 are libraries. Price per issue: $5; subscription: $8. They use about 70 of 200 submissions received each year, have a 1 year backlog. **Sample: $5 postpaid. Submit up to 3 poems, photocopy OK, no line limit but prefer under 40 lines; reports within a month, pays in one contributor's copy.**

KENYON HILLS PUBLICATIONS, *NEW ENGLAND REVIEW AND BREAD LOAF QUARTERLY (NER/BLQ) (III), Box 170, Hanover, NH 03755, founded 1978. *NER/BLQ* is a prestige literary quarterly, 6x9", 160 + pp., flat-spined, elegant make-up and printing on heavy stock, glossy cover with art. **Pays.** As a sample the editors selected the last lines of "Souls" by C.K. Williams, describing teddy bears on a dump truck:

> *Their stuffing hasn't been so crushed in them as to affect their jaunty,*
> > *open-armed availability,*
> *but when their truck stops at a light, their faces instantly assume the*
> > *fanatical expressionlessness*
> *of Soldiers, who, wounded, captured, waiting to be sent away, now are being*
> > *photographed.*

That poem introduces an essay by Mandel, "The Poetry of our Climate: Slouch, Bric-a-brac, and Decayed Statement," a protest against the prevailing slovenliness in contemporary American poetry. The New England Review also sponsors an annual narrative poetry competition. Query with SASE. Send $4 for sample copy.

THE KINDRED SPIRIT, GROOVY GRAY CAT PUBLICATIONS (I, II), Rt. 2 Box 111, St. John, KS 67576, phone 316-549-3933, founded 1982, poetry editor Michael Hathaway, is a semiannual newsprint tabloid "**which publishes *mostly* short unrhymed experimental/avant-garde poetry under 30 lines, or poetry with any of the following: powerful feelings, vivd images, guts, substance, originality, creative style, punch, twist or humor. No self-indulgent therapeutic poetry or Helen Steiner Rice/Rod McKuen type of work.**" They have published poetry by Patrick McKinnon, ave jeanne, Padi Harman, Rhonda Poynter, Ruth Moon Kempher and D. Roger Martin. These sample lines are by C.K. DeRugeris:

> *Salina Sloan speaks of war and peace*
> *on other planets she sings of the bomb*
> *& solar dynamics while waiting in darkness*
> *for a chance at nuclear love*

Each 12 pp. issue contains dozens of poems. Its circulation is about 1,000, 800 distributed as complimentary copies, 200 subscriptions of which 2 are college libraries. Samples: $1, or $3 overseas, U.S. funds, postpaid. **Send SASE for guidelines. Send "interesting introductory letter" and 5-10 poems "typed or printed legibly." Photocopies, simultaneous submissions, previously published poems OK. Must include SASE or IRC coupons. Reports in 2-4 weeks. Pays 1 copy.** Michael Hathaway comments, "The sample I selected should not be considered the only style I use. I like to receive all kinds of poetry so my magazine can be eclectic and have a good variety. I'll read and consider almost any style, length or subject and welcome all submissions and correspondence."

KING AND COWEN PRESS, *BRAVO, *THE POET'S MAGAZINE (II), 1801 Trafalgar St., Teaneck, NJ 07666, phone 201-836-5922, founded 1979, poetry editor José Garcia Villa, managing editors John Cowen and Robert L. King. *Bravo*, a 6x9" literary journal, appears irregularly, circulation 500, 350 subscriptions of which 50 are libraries, using about 50 pp. of poetry in each issue. *"Bravo* **believes that poetry must have formal excellence; poetry must be lyrical; poetry is not prose. We want lyrical poems, not prose poems. We do not want formless poetry. Models: Cummings, Moore, Donne, Wylie, Schwartz, Thomas, Hopkins. Experimental lyrics are possibilities; crafted poems that are clean, economical."** They have recently published poetry by Robert L. King, John O. Stevenson, Mort Malkin, Gloria Potter and Nick Joaquin. The editor selected these sample lines by John Cowen:

> *(a grief)(and a grief)*
> *and a grind after all*
> *and to those with too much,*
> *rose, the presages of*
> *death impose*

They receive about 100 freelance submissions per year of which they use "few." **Sample: $3.50 less 20%. Read a sample before submitting. Reports immediately. Pays 2 copies.** The press also publishes collections by individuals. **Query with 5 samples. "If interested we will ask to see more." Prefers MS typed, double-spaced. Photocopies OK, dot-matrix "not preferred." Pays in copies. Inquire about buying samples.**

KITCHEN TABLE: WOMEN OF COLOR PRESS (IV, Third World), Box 2753, New York, NY 10185, phone 212-308-5389, founded 1981, is "the first publisher in North America committed to producing and distributing the **work of Third World women of all racial/cultural heritages, sexualities, and classes.**" They publish flat-spined paperback collections and anthologies. **"We want high quality poetry by women of color which encompasses a degree of consciousness of the particular issues of identity and struggle which women of color face."** The editors selected these sample lines from "A Comrade Is As Precious As a Rice Seedling" by Mila D. Aguilar:

> *There is something about*
> *The heaviness of summer*
> *The kept humidity*
> *That will not break out into rain*

That book is a digest-sized, flat-spined paperback, glossy card cover, 55 pp., $4.95, with critical praise on the cover by Adrienne Rich, June Jordan and Audre Lorde. They publish an average of one book of poetry every other year and have published three anthologies, two of which contain poetry. All books are published simultaneously in hardback for library sales. **Submit a sample of 10 pages of poems with background information about your writing and publishing career and a general description of the poetry collection as a whole. They reply to queries in 4 weeks, to full MS submissions (if invited) in 4 months. Simultaneous submissions OK if they are informed. MS should be typed, double-spaced. Clear photocopies OK. No dot-matrix. Payment is 8% royalties for first 5,000 copies, 10% thereafter, and 5 copies. Write for catalog to purchase samples. General comments usually given upon rejection.** The editors say, "We are particularly interested in publishing work by women of color which would generally be overlooked by other publishers, especially work by American Indian, Latina, Asian-American and Afro-American women who may be working class, Lesbian, disabled or older writers."

‡KONGLOMERATI PRESS, *KONGLOMERATI (V), Box 5001, Gulfport, FL 33737, phone 813-323-0386, founded 1971, editor-publisher Richard Mathews. Konglomerati Press publishes very high quality, limited edition letterpress books, pamphlets, broadsides—mostly poetry. *Konglomerati* magazine publishes fiction, nonfiction and poetry. **At present they are not accepting unsolicited manuscripts. But when they do, they want "original, professional, inspired work, concrete and visual poetry, any length." They do not want "derivative and imitative work."** As an indication of the quality of their work, the press had published *Florida Poems. 1981* by Richard Eberhart ($15.95 paper; $30 cloth) and *Lines from Neuchatel* by Peter Meinke (1974, OP). As a sample of work from

Konglomerati magazine, I chose the beginning lines from "My Death" by Erica Jong:

> My death
> looks exactly like me.
> She lives to my left,
> at exactly an arm's length.
> She has my face, hair, hands;
> she ages
> as I grow older.

The press and the magazine are part of the functions of the Konglomerati Foundation (Florida Foundation for Literature and the Book Arts), which is partially supported by the National Endowment for the Arts, Florida Arts Council, and B. Dalton Bookseller/Dayton Hudson Foundation. The foundation has a turn-of-the-century letterpress studio in Gulfport where it produces its beautifully printed limited editions. The foundation also offers classes, workshops, literary readings, public lectures, and exhibits. *Konglomerati* magazine appears irregularly and has a circulation of 150-300. It is 6¼x9½", 45 pp. flat-spined, extremely handsome in every way, printed on buff stock with a one-color matte card cover, **Contributors receive 3 copies and a 10% discount on other publications.**

KONOCTI BOOKS, CANNONADE PRESS, *SIPAPU* (V), Rt. 1, Box 216, Winters, CA 95694, phone 916-662-3364, founded 1973, poetry editor Noel Peattie, has "published poetry books by Ramona Weeks, Gloria Bosque, Doc Dachtler, and Karl Kempton." Cannonade Press publishes short poems on a Kelsey handpress. *Sipapu* consists of reviews and interviews and conference news, **no poetry.** The editor says he is **"overcommitted. I do not want to see any more at this time." Query first with 5 samples. "Never mind the letter—I can tell with 5 poems. Usually I send them back by return mail. MS should be typewritten. Photocopies OK. No dot-matrix."** Asked if he provided criticism on rejected MSS, Noel Peattie said, "No—I reject them and then they send them back. Please tell your readers that No means NO."

‡*KOYO (I), #5, 809 King St. West, Hamilton, Ontario L8S 1K2, Canada, phone 416-529-3125, founded 1985, editor/publisher G.J. McFarlane, a "literary quarterly open forum, open to all writing. Responsive to the excellence of writers rather than us to them. **Particularly interested in innovative work concerning the human condition." There are no particular specifications for poetry.** *Koyo* has recently published work by Michael Dennis, James Strecker, P.E. Stenord, and Bayla Winters. As a sample, the editor chose the following lines by an unidentified poet:

> No, please leave the light on
> i want to see your skin
> i want to take what i see
> the darkness could only be a contradiction.

Koyo is 8x7", 51 pp. photocopied on fairly thin paper, saddle-stapled, grey matte card cover with black decoration. It appears "quarterly or as often as money and material allow." Circulation is "50 and growing"; subscriptions are "20 and growing." Single copy price is $2, subscription $5 for 3 issues. **Sample available for $2 postpaid. Pay is 1 copy. Submissions are reported on ASAP, and time to publication is 2-3 months.**

*KRAX (II, IV, Rump Booklets/Specialized), 63 Dixon Lane, Leeds, Yorkshire, LS12 4RR England, founded 1971, poetry editors Andy Robson et al. The press "publishes short stories, poetry, graphics, personality interviews, related photography and novelty material—i.e. calendars, card games, postcards." *Krax* appears twice yearly, and for this they want poetry which is **"light-hearted and humorous; original ideas. Undesired: anything containing the words 'nuclear' or 'Jesus.' 2,000 words maximum. All forms and styles considered.** Sample from title piece "Better than Valium" by Samantha Dee:

> Love should be
> Available on prescription
> A neatly packaged potent potion
> Amongst the kelp and ginsing

Krax is a 6x8", 48 pp. of which 30 are poetry, saddle-stapled, offset with b/w cartoons and graphics. Price per issue: £1 ($1.50), per subscription: £3 ($6). They receive up to 1,000 submissions per year of which they use 6%, have a 2-3 year backlog. **Sample: $1.50 (75p). "Submit maximum of 6 pieces unless less than 6 lines in length. Writer's name on same sheet as poem. SASE or IRC encouraged but not vital. Simultaneous submissions discouraged unless overseas." Reports within 4 weeks. Pays 1 copy. Rump Booklets are 16 pp. collections. Query with "detailed notes of projected work." Send SASE for catalog.** He says, "Don't send money to publishers, etc., without written proof of their existence. Keep copies of your work—all things may be lost in transit, so query if no reply. Name poets tend to shun us in favor of glossy paperbacks and hard cash, but diamonds don't come in garish packages and no-one can start at the top."

KROPOTKIN'S LIGHTHOUSE PUBLICATIONS (V, IV, Foreign, political), (home) 186, Dunstans Rd., London, England SE22 0ES, (business) Box KLP Housmans Bookstore, 5, Caledonian Rd., London, England N1, founded 1969, poetry editor Jim Huggon. "**We publish anarchist-pacifist material and poetry, postcards, posters, calendars, one anthology so far, one volume of short stories.**" Send SASE for catalog to buy samples. Editor prefers no unsolicited MSS, but has "very occasionally" published collections by individuals. Query with samples. Bio info later if requested. Reports by return mail. Prefers typed MSS, photocopies OK. "We would give a percentage of the print run free to an author in lieu of royalties." Jim Huggon's advice is, "Do what I did in the beginning and publish, promote, sell *yourself*—rather than collect rejection slips. If you have enough belief/confidence in your work it is the obvious way!"

LA JOLLA POETS' PRESS (IV, Established poets), Box 8638, La Jolla, CA 92038, poetry editor Kathleen Iddings, publishes "established, excellent poets." The sample I have seen, **Survival, Evasion, & Escape**, by Hank Malone, is a 92 pp. flat-spined paperback with glossy cover, professionally printed in small type on heavy, textured stock. The titles and page numbers are hand-scrawled with a felt marker—unusual and attractive. I selected as a sample the final stanza (after 8 quatrains in which various animals describe themselves) of "The Menagerie":

> THE POET: I am a poet, inside me fighting
> with all the other animals, taming each quality, rending
> subduing each skill, each chill, haunting the deeps, a creature
> searching for a creature never seen before in the menagerie.

Considers simultaneous submissions.

*LABEL MAGAZINE (II), 57 Effingham Rd., Lee Green, London, SE12 8NT, England, founded 1981, editors Paul Beasley and Ruth Harrison, a twice-yearly publication that "represents the work of writers and artists from all over the UK, Europe and North America. Especially those who question physical, social and philosophical prejudices and challenge limited and limiting conceptions of poetry. **Publishes post-modern, experimental, concrete, performance, jazz, dub poetry. There is an emphasis on social and/or innovative poetry.**" The most recent issue I have, *Label 6*, contains poetry by Nick Rogers, earle birney, Emile Sercombe, and several others; some of it is visual. As a sample, I selected the beginning of "Parable of the Sidewalk Tellers" by Tom House:

> Earbob and the painted carnivores
> are dancing on the corner
> in 5-inch, gleaming platforms,
>
> twirling their pleats,
> rearranging their chains,

Label 6 is 8½x6", "printed on recycled paper" in various colors, 42 pp., folded and glued, green matte card cover with brown decorations. Copy is offset in various sizes of type; there is an occasional piece of two-color artwork. Circulation is 600-700, of which 70 are subscriptions. Price per issue is £1 or $3, subscription £2 or $6. **Sample available for £1 or $3 postpaid, guidelines for SASE. Pay is 1-4 copies; contributors are "encouraged" to subscribe. Poets should submit 1-6 poems at a time, any length. Reporting time is 1-3 weeks and time to publication 1 week-12 months.**

*LADIES' HOME JOURNAL (IV, Humorous), 3 Park Ave., New York, NY 10016, phone 212-340-9343, founded 1883, a slick monthly, circulation 5½ million, no longer accepts serious poetry unless submitted by an agent or from famous poets. But they do consider **light verse for the "Last Laughs" page. Put "Last Laughs" on the outside of the envelope. No SASE necessary because they neither return nor acknowledge submissions. If your poem is accepted you'll know when you get the check for $25.** For a sample (and to lighten the pages of this directory) I chose, "The Power of Christmas" by Eric Brand:

> Never mind the ribbons,
> And never mind the bows;
> Never mind the stockings,
> Or when and if it snows;
> Never mind the wrappings
> That you picked with extra care;
> And never mind the presents
> That you searched for everywhere.
> Initial squeals of happiness
> Will all dissolve to naught
> When you find out that the batteries
> Are what you haven't bought.

‡**LAKE SHORE PUBLISHING, *SOUNDINGS, GEMINI PRESS (I)**, 373 Ramsay Rd., Deerfield, IL 60015, phone 312-945-4324, founded 1983, poetry editor Carol Spelius, is an effort "to put out decent, economical volumes of poetry." **Reading fee: $1 per page. They want poetry which is** "understandable and *moving*, **imaginative with a unique view, in any form. Make me laugh or cry or think. I'm not so keen on gutter language or political dogma—but I try to keep an open mind. No limitations in length, but would like each poem to fit each page—4x6½" space. Single space."** In their first annual volume, 1985, they published poetry by Alice MacKenzie Swaim, Vesle Fenstermaker, Helen Degan Cohen, Pat Rahman and many others. The editor selected these sample lines (poet unidentified):

> *The suitors spoke hoarsely of apartments*
> *And TV, beds, money, children, and*
> *Two promised a car of her own.*
> *She ran alone to wrap night around her.*

The 253 pp. anthology included 100 poets in 1985, was published in an edition of 2,000. One appears every 2 years. It is flat-spined, photocopied from typescript, with glossy, colored card cover with art, and sells for $7.95. **Pays 1 copy and half-price for additional copies. Submit any number of sample copies, with $1 per page reading fee, and a covering letter telling about your other publications, biographical background, personal or aesthetic philosophy, poetic goals and principles. Simultaneous submissions, photocopy, dot-matrix, all OK. Reports within 4 months. Contest with 31 prizes ranging from $5-15, judged by Ted Schaefer. Carol Spelius comments on returned MSS. She subsidy publishes under the imprint Gemini Press: "I split the cost if I like the book."** She advises, "Keep reading classics and writing modern. Try all forms. Pray a lot."

LAKE STREET PRESS, *LAKE STREET REVIEW (II), Box 7188, Powderhorn Station, Minneapolis, MN 55407, founded 1975, poetry editor Kevin FitzPatrick. *Lake Street Review* **is a Minneapolis-St. Paul literary magazine that focuses on the work of both developing and experienced poets and prose writers.** The Press has published a chapbook of poems and an anthology of 6 poets, but chapbook and anthology publication are not open to unsolicited MSS. For the magazine, **both traditional and free verse are considered. "We rarely publish a 'long' poem—more than 50 lines."** Poets they have recently published include Robert Bly, Ethna McKiernan, Eugene McCarthy, Dorian Brooks Kottler, Jonathan Sisson and Monica Ochtrup. The editor selected as a sample the complete poem, "Repeat After Me" by Dick Donaldson:

> *The Doberman pinscher*
> *properly trained*
> *has a sane mind.*

The magazine is published once a year in a 7x8½" 40+ pp. format, neatly photocopied from typescript with attractive b/w art, matte cover with art, circulation 600, 150 subscriptions of which 50 are libraries, 15 pp. of poetry in each issue. They receive some 800 freelance submissions per year, use 30-40, have a very small backlog as poems are usually selected for the coming issue. **Sample: $2 postpaid. Submit readable copies, typed or photocopied. Reports in 2 months maximum, deadline is October 1 of each year, pays 2 copies. Send SASE for guidelines. Usually short comments on rejections.** The editor says, "Read a sample copy. I am looking for **accessible poems that convey meaning with impact but in an engaging or aesthetically pleasing way. Vivid detail, figurative language, conciseness, use of sound, alliteration, assonance, etc. are looked for."**

‡**LANCASTER INDEPENDENT PRESS *(LIP) (I)**, Box 275, Lancaster, PA 17603, founded 1969, poetry editor. The small, liberal community newspaper, called *L.I.P.*, is a tabloid with a poetry section; they say they are the oldest continuously published alternative newspaper in the country, "staffed by volunteers and idealists." An anthology, "The Best of *L.I.P.*," is being planned. Most of the writers published are from the local area. Poets recently published include Jala Magik, Paul F. deUriarte, and Carol Sahady. As a sample, the editor selected the following lines from an unidentified poet:

> *Like the animal who strays from the pack*
> *or is rejected*
> *or unwanted in the first place*
> *some lambs walk alone*

The tabloid, which appears monthly, has 12-16 pp., web offset, with b/w graphics and halftones. Its circulation is 3,500-4,000, of which 1,500 are subscriptions and newsstand sales are about 1,500. Price per issue is 50¢, subscription $10/year. **2 Samples: $1 postpaid. Contributors receive as many free copies "as required." The editors do not report on submissions; time to publication is 1-2 months.** The press publishes occasional poetry chapbooks, digest-sized, saddle-stapled or side-stapled, 32 pp. **Poets should query before sending poems. Queries will be answered in 6-8 weeks and MSS reported on in the same period of time. Photocopied or dot-matrix MSS are OK but not discs. There is no pay for chapbook authors.**

*LAPIS, LAPIS EDUCATIONAL ASSOCIATION, INC. (IV, Jungian psychology, spirituality), % Karen Degenhart, 1438 Ridge Rd., Homewood, IL 60430, founded 1977, is a digest-sized 64 pp. annual journal with a **psychological (especially Jungian) and spiritual (especially Christian) focus which uses some poetry relevant to its concerns. Sample: $1.50. Simultaneous submissions OK. No payment.**

‡LATIN AMERICAN LITERARY REVIEW PRESS, *LATIN AMERICAN LITERARY REVIEW (IV, Romance language), Box 8385, Pittsburgh, PA 15218, phone 412-351-3987 (Calls taken by Three Rivers Decorating Company), poetry editor Yvette E. Miller. *Latin American Literary Review*, founded in 1972, publishes semiannually. Number of pages of poetry is variable; total circulation 1,500, subscriptions 1,000, of which 800 are libraries. $14/issue; institutional subscription $27. **Sample copy $8.25 postpaid; they use 25% of submitted material. Send up to 10 pages, photocopies OK, reports within 3 months, no pay, contributors are expected to subscribe or buy copies. The** magazine is 200 pp., flat-spined, 6x9". Latin American Literary Review Press, founded 1977, publishes books in any Romance language and in English or English translation. Bilingual format is used for poetry. The Press publishes anthologies, flat-spined, paperbacks, and hardbacks. **Poetry is "not restricted on subject but we object to political themes. No explicit sex."** Poets recently published include Jose Emilio Pacheco, Isabel Fraire, Alejandra Pizarnik, and Violeta Parra. As a sample I selected the first stanza of "La Danza" by Marjorie Agosin, as translated by Cola Franzen:

> As I dance submerged
> on the blue perch
> that was floating between my mother's legs
> and in her belly danced
> dark signals to announce myself.

The press publishes 3-4 poetry chapbooks/year of about 100-160 pp., 1,000 paperbacks (100-160 pp.), 100 hardbacks in special editions, and 2 anthologies. **Freelance submissions are considered but poets should include bio and list of other publications. Replies to queries in 1 month, reports on submissions in 3 months. Occasional reading fee of $100/book is charged. Photocopied MS OK. Royalties 10% of print run and 10 copies.** No subsidy publishing. Book catalog free on request with 9½x12½" envelope. Poets can request books at 10% discount. Book samples we have seen are handsome, professionally printed, with glossy card covers, flat-spined.

‡LAUGHING WATERS PRESS (IV, Peace), 1416 Euclid Ave., Boulder, CO 80302, founded 1980, Gary E. Erb, publisher. The press is **"primarily a publisher of literary work dealing with peace and non-violence,"** with no restrictions as to length or style. The editor does not want to see **"solipsistic 'poor little old me' bitching."** He has recently published poetry by J. Janda as well as by himself. The editor selected these sample lines (poet unidentified):

> The Blood of Guatemalans
> Watered the berries for my coffee.
> Ragged, bony Chileans
> Mined the copper for my telephone.

The sample chapbook I have seen has 85 pages, is flat-spined, offset from typed copy, with colored matte card cover. **The editor does not accept freelance submissions for chapbooks, but he does publish anthologies and will evidently accept freelance poetry submissions for them. He reports on queries within 1 week, MSS in 3 weeks, and will consider simultaneous submissions, photocopied and dot-matrix MSS. Payment is ten author's copies.**

*THE LAUREL REVIEW (II, IV, Appalachia), Department of English, West Virginia Wesleyan College, Buckhannon, WV 26201, phone 304-473-8000, Ext. 8240, founded 1960, poetry editors Mark DeFoe, David McAleavey, Constance Pierce, Marc Harshman, Joan McIntosh and Bill Trowbridge, is a literary biannual "publishing **quality poetry, fiction and general interest essays from Appalachia and from across America, Canada and abroad. We publish excellent writing— from the traditional to the untraditional."** There are 40 pp. of poetry in each issue, circulation 500, 150 subscriptions of which half are libraries. They receive about 2,000 submissions per year, use 80, have a 1-4 month backlog. **Sample: $4 postpaid. Subscription $8/year; pays 2 free copies and 1 year subscription. Submit 3-6 poems, photocopies, dot-matrix, simultaneous submissions OK.** "Of course we often comment, make suggestions, criticize. Among poets they have recently published are Sonia Gernes, Michael Bugeja, Marlene Youmans, Margot Treitel, Jeff Daniel Marion, Cheri Fein, Robert Powlowski. Lines from Sonia Gernes' villanelles "Playing the Bells:"

> Notes ending, I will the resonance to stay—
> to be stronger than twilight, stronger than rain,
> five stories up in the Steeple where we play
> lest we return to darkness as surely as to day!

‡*LEGERETE (IV, Human rights), Post Office Drawer 1410, Daphne, AL 36526, editor Kimberly Coale," an international journal concerned with literature and with human rights: the source for the very best in translations and in emigre literature, and for current news of **human rights abuses, and essays and letters from prisoners of conscience.**" Formerly quarterly, it is now published monthly. The 1985 issues contained poetry by Krzysztof Ostaszewski, Asher Torren, Jerzy Jarucki, Elemer Horvath, Bernard Hewitt, and Albert Russo. **Each issue has a special theme**; in 1986, the August issue was devoted to poetry. The 6½x8" journal is published by Legerete International Writers' Union, an organization of writers and others who are "committed to achieving the worldwide liberalization of literature from government controls." Dues are $45/year, including subscription to *Legerete*. Regular subscription price is $24/year plus $12 for airmail. **I have no submission or payment information.**

‡L'EPERVIER PRESS (III), 4522 Sunnyside N., Seattle, WA 98103, founded 1977, editor Robert McNamara, a "small press publisher of contemporary American poetry by little known and known poets in perfect bound and casebound books." **The editor does not want to see "confessional" poetry.** He has recently published books by Bill Tremblay, Christopher Howell, Linda Bierds, Frederic Will, Paul Hoover, and David Rigsby. As a sample, he chose the following lines by an unidentified poet:

> She watched the woman steal down bayside rocks
> under a hooded moon through shadows black as judges
> to the inlet where pebbles gleamed in the sucking tide.
> Surfing toward her from the sea's sleep the sealman . .

The press publishes 4 poetry books each year, 5x8" with an average page count of 64, some flat-spined paperbacks and some hardcovers. The book they sent me, **Second Sun** by Bill Tremblay, is handsomely printed on heavy buff stock, 81 pp., with glossy card cover in grey, yellow, and white; there is a b/w landscape photo on the front cover and a photo of the author on the back; the book is priced at $6.95. **Freelance submissions are accepted, but writers should query first, sending 6 sample poems, bio, and poetic aims. Queries will be answered in 3 months and MSS reported on in 6 months. Simultaneous submissions will be considered, and photocopied MSS are OK. Pay is in author's copies, 10% of press run. Catalog is available for #10 SASE.**

A LETTER AMONG FRIENDS (II), Box 1198, Groton, CT 06340, founded 1977, poetry editors Lee Howard, Patricia Jordan, Norma Walrath, Raymond Ellis and Gilbert Purdy, is a tri-annual of **poetry and art**, circulation 400, 200 subscriptions of which 12 are libraries, $9 per year or $3 per copy. They have a backlog of about 2 months, receive about 350 submissions a year of which they use 120. As a sample I selected a complete poem, "Of Julie" by Larry Sowell:

> She accepts passions idea
> gently, dreaming
> a pure star—
> her heart's brilliance

The digest-sized 56-64 pp. perfect-bound magazine is professionally printed on good paper with b/w art, matte cover with cartoon art. **Sample: $2.50 postpaid. Submit 1-6 poems with biographical information. Reports in 1-6 months. Pays 1 copy. Send SASE for guidelines and rules for an annual poetry contest. Sometimes comments on rejections.** They also sponsor writing workshops and open readings.

LIBRA PUBLISHERS, INC. (I), Suite 207, 4901 Morena Blvd., San Diego, CA 92117, phone 619-273-1500, poetry editor William Kroll, publishes two professional journals, *Adolescence* and *Family Therapy* plus books, primarily in the behaviorial sciences but also some general nonfiction, fiction and poetry. "At first we published books of poetry on a standard royalty basis, paying 10% of the retail price to the authors. Although at times we were successful in selling enough copies to at least break even, we found that we could no longer afford to publish poetry on this basis. Now, unless we fall madly in love with a particular collection, **we require a subsidy. The amount is based on the production costs and the author receives 40% of the retail price of all copies sold.** If we ever hit it big with a particular book and find that we can afford to channel those funds into publishing more poetry that we like, we'll certainly do so without requiring a subsidy. But unless the market for poetry suddenly changes for the better, we could not be optimistic about the chances of offering many royalty contracts." They have published books of poetry by Martin Rosner, William Blackwell, John Travers Moore and C. Margaret Hall, the author of these sample lines selected by the editor:

> Writing poetry means
> That I can take up the brush at any minute,
> That I can put down the thought
> That was flying high.

Query with 6 sample poems, publishing credits and bio. Replies to query in 2 days, to submissions (if invited) in 2-3 weeks. MS should be double-spaced. Photocopy, dot-matrix OK. Send 9x12 SASE for catalog. Sample books may be purchased on a returnable basis.

THE LIGHTNING TREE (II), Box 1837, Santa Fe, NM 87504-1837, phone 505-983-7434, founded 1972, Jene Lyon publisher and editor is "a privately owned and financed trade press. We publish books in history, alternate technology and development, cook books, poetry and regional nonfiction—an average of 3-5 new titles per year. Our books of poetry are primarily paperbacks, but we always bind some copies in cloth editions for libraries and collectors. **At the present we are only considering MSS that will adapt to the 64 pp. format for the Lightning Tree Contemporary Poets series. We do not ask poets (or any authors) to invest in publication costs. We pay 10% royalty based on list price . . . after the sale of the first 300 copies of a book of poetry. Authors receive 10 free copies of their books**, and the right to purchase any TLT books at trade discount. Publication is by contract, and we copyright in the author's name. While we do not really expect many profits from the publishing of poetry, those books that have succeeded have always had **full cooperation in promotion and marketing from the writers. We want poetry which shows a knowledge of the English language, has universality, something significant to say.**" They have published poetry by Ann Fox Chandonnet, Roger Hecht and James C. McCullagh. I selected this complete poem, "Still Life" by David Nolf in **Surviving the Raw and the Crooked** as a sample:

> The bird flies into the pudding;
> the tree grows into the sky.
> The worm suicides on a flower's thorn—
> such a rosy way to die.

The book is 5½x7", flat-spined, 64 pp., with matte cover and cartoon art by Marc Krebs. **Query with 5-6 samples, publication credits, bio. Replies to query in 2-4 weeks, MS (if invited) 2-4 months. MS should be typed, double spaced. Send SASE for catalog to buy samples. Editor "very frequently" comments on rejections, "especially when we see talent."** She advises, "Read and write and don't expect economic rewards."

LIMBERLOST PRESS, *THE LIMBERLOST REVIEW (II), Box 1563, Boise, ID 83701, founded 1976, is a digest-sized 45 pp. poetry biannual, circulation 500-1,000. **One issue each year to a single poet. Limberlost Press publishes individual collections.** "Limberlost + 14 (1985) is devoted to *Gone In October: Last Reflections on Jack Kerouac*, by John Clellon Holmes. Limberlost + 16 is devoted to '*What Thou Lovest Well Remains': 100 Years of Ezra Pound*, featuring essays by Jim Harrision, Charles Bukowski, James Laughlin, Allen Ginsberg, John Clellon Holmes, Hayden Carruth and others." Pays copies. Sample: $5.

LINDEN PRESS (II), 3601 Greenway, Baltimore, MD 21218, founded 1960, poetry editor Robert K. Rosenburg, publishes small collections of poetry. They have published a book by the editor and one by Hans Juergenson, from which the editor selected these sample lines:

> How shall I locate
> My Body
> Cellular muscle-mechanic
> When that "I" has unlearned
> Its existence

Query with 3 samples, publication credits, bio. Replies to query in 2 weeks, to MS (if invited) in 4-6 weeks. Typewritten, photocopies OK. Pays minimum royalties. Send SASE for guidelines.

LINTEL (II), Box 8609, Roanoke, VA 24014, phone 703-982-2265 or 345-2886, founded 1977, poetry editor Walter James Miller, who says, "**We publish poetry and innovative fiction of types ignored by commercial presses. We consider any poetry except conventional, traditional, cliché, greeting card types, i.e., any artistic poetry.**" They have recently published poetry by Sue Saniel Elkind, Helen Morrissey Rizzuto and Adrienne Wolfert, and the editor selected these lines from Edmund Pennant as a sample:

> Not until the landing gear locks down
> with a thump and the turbines howl
> will she take me into her dream.
> Descending, we become one tapestry.

The book from which this was taken, **Mis/apprehensions and other poems**, is 80 pp. flat-spined, digest-sized, professionally printed in small bold type, glossy, color cover with art, the author's photo on the back. I notice that the author's first collection was published by Scribners, and it is typical that poets "discovered" and then neglected by major publishers turn to noncommercial presses for subsequent publication. Walter James Miller asks that you **query with five sample poems. He replies to the query within a month, to the MS (if invited) in 2 months.** "We consider simultaneous submissions if so marked and if the writer agrees to notify us of acceptance elsewhere." MS should be typed, photocopy OK. Pays royalties after all costs are met and 100 copies. To see samples, send SASE for catalog and ask for "trial rate" (50%).

LINWOOD PUBLISHERS (II), Box 70152, North Charleston, SC 29415, phone 803-873-2719, founded 1982, poetry editor Bernard Chase, was "organized as an independent small press and publisher, primarily to publish the poetry of known, unknown, and little known poets." They publish anthologies, postcard series, posters, calendars, art prints and collections in both paper and hardback editions. The editor says he is interested in **"quality poetry of any form."** They have recently published poetry by Simon Perchik, Karla Hammond, George Gott, Carl Lindner, Conis Burke and J. B. Moore. The editor selected these sample lines by Emily Bampha's **Coming Up . . .**

> *For charge of despair and fear unmeasured*
> *To the glory and light of all his treasures*
> *I can see pain of hope and love to come*
> *We can wait for, and dream of songs unsung.*

They will consider freelance submissions of book MSS. **It is your option whether to query first and send samples. Your cover letter should give your publication history and bio. They reply to queries within 30 days, to MSS within 30-60 days. Preferably typed MS: photocopies, dot-matrix, simultaneous submissions OK, and discs compatible with TRS-80 or Adam. Contracts are for 5-10% royalties plus honorarium and author's copies (negotiated). Send SASE with 7x10" envelope, 3 oz. postage, for catalog, or send SASE for "local listing of availabilities" in local or school libraries or bookstores to see samples.** Bernard Chase advises, "Feel no intimidation by the breadth, the depth of this craft of which you have chosen to become a part."

LIONHEAD PUBLISHING/ ROAR RECORDING (II), 2521 E. Stratford Ct., Shorewood, WI 53211, phone 414-332-7474, founded 1969 as Albatross Press, name changed in 1976 to Lionhead; Roar added in 1980, editor/publisher Dr. Martin J. Rosenblum. The press publishes experimental poetry utilizing print media as well as vinyl and cassette recordings. **The editor is "particularly interested in post-Projectivist and post-Objectivist poems and in long poems . . . We are not interested in highly literary poetry that is mainstream abstraction and, of course, we don't want any 'calendar' poems from beginning writers."** He has published Carl Rakosi, Toby Olson, Karl Young, and himself; as a sample he selected the following lines by Cicero DeWestbrook:

> *lite over tree bark*
> *& into flooring*
> *but first! upon window*
> > *sill the quality sticks.*

The press publishes 1 or 2 chapbooks each year, with 25-75 pp. The format varies; some books are paperback, flat-spined, some are hardback, some are tapebooks. **Freelance submissions are accepted "sometimes," but the writer should query first with SASE. Payment is 10 copies. Criticism of rejected MSS will be provided if there is a cover letter.** The editor advises, "Stop writing unless you are causing structural changes in the art form: content is a type of structure, too."

‡***LIONSONG MAGAZINE, LIONSONG PRESS (II)**, #3E, 6901 Shore Road, Brooklyn, NY 11209, phone 718-745-8151, founded 1985, editor Mark Ari. *Lionsong Magazine* publishes poetry, fiction, drama, essays, journalism and art. **"We are open to all mediums of expression as long as the submissions are of high quality. We have a special interest in Dada, Zen, and Anarchism. We prefer poetry that is not overly academic or banal."** *Lionsong* has recently published poetry by Irving Stettner, Beth Jankola, and Mark Ari. As a sample, the editor chose this one line by Tommy Trantino:

> *The crack in the wall is not sunlight*

Lionsong, which appears 3 times a year, is 8½x14", 50-75 pp., "printing variable," card covers sometimes hand painted. It has a circulation of 2,000, of which 500 are subscriptions, 20 go to libraries, and the rest are sold in bookstores. Price per copy is $3, subscription, $9/year, no back issues available. **Guidelines available for SASE. Pay is 3 copies. Submissions are reported on within 6 weeks and time to publication is 6-12 months. Reading fees are not charged, but the editor will provide "a critical report with suggestions at rate of $30 per 5 pages of poetry."** He says, "Keep writing no matter what!"

***LIPS (III)**, Box 1345, Montclair, NJ, 07042, founded 1981, poetry editor Laura Boss, "is a quality poetry magazine published 3 times a year, average 60 pp, digest-sized, flat-spined, circulation 550, 200 subscriptions of which approximately 100 are libraries, which takes pleasure in publishing previously unpublished poets as well as publishing the most established voices in contemporary poetry. We look for quality work: the strongest work of a poet; work that moves the reader; poems take risks that work. We prefer clarity in the work rather than the abstract. Poems longer than 6 pages present a space problem." They have recently published poems by Gregory Corso, Allen Ginsberg, Richard Kostelanetz, Lyn Lifshin, Robert Phillips, Marge Piercy and Ishmael Reed. The editors selected these sample lines by Michael Benedikt (from "Americans Are Certainly Lousy Lovers—a European Couple, in Possible Nonsensical Conversation, for L. Z. or, el Contradictor"):

> *Generations of American women, at their mixing bowls*
> *with pestles, mortars, wooden objects*
> *Of various sizes . . . oh I see those cleverly-shaped*
> *kitchen objects & the husbands, curiously jealous . . .*

They receive about 8,000 submissions per year, use less than 1% for 1985/1986, have a 6 month backlog. **Sample: $4 postpaid. Poems should be submitted between September and March to Laura Boss, editor, 6 pp., typed or clear photocopy OK, no query necessary. She tries to respond in 1 month but has gotten backlogged at times. Pays 2 contributor's copies. Send SASE for guidelines.** Her advice to poets is, "Remember the 2 T's: Talent AND Tenacity."

‡*LITERARIA (I)**, 1302 East "F" St., Russellville, AR 72801, founded 1985, editor Chuck Rector, a "magazine of general items" that wants poetry of **"general types, not Marxist-Leninist."** In the first issue (December, 1985), *Literaria* published poetry by Loy Banks, Ronald Edward Kittell, Dean Ewing, Craig Peter Standish, Michael L. Johnson, and Janet McCann, from whose work the editor chose the following lines as a sample:

> *Spaces are clouding over*
> *as if for snow*
> *but it will not snow*

Literaria is magazine-sized, offset on ordinary paper from typed copy, no cover, stapled in top left corner, 10 pp. The magazine appears "2-3 times a year," has a circulation of 20, price per issue $1. **Pay is 1 copy. All formats are OK for submissions, which will be reported on in 1 month; time to publication is 1-3 months.** The editor advises, "Don't plagiarize, be creative; want historical and epic (Homeric) poetry."

*THE LITERARY REVIEW (II)**, 285 Madison Ave., Madison, NJ 07940, phone 201-377-4050, founded 1957, poetry editors Walter Cummins, Martin Green and Harry Keyishian, a quarterly, seeks **"work of high literary merit with sophistication of presentation by poets familiar with the form."** No specifications as to form, length, style, subject matter or purpose.** They have recently published poetry by David Citino, Geraldine C. Little, Gary Fincke and Susan Fromberg Schaeffer. The editors selected these sample lines by William Doreski:

> *I want to harvest this undulant*
> *sea-glow the way Turner could,*
> *but haven't his way with cream*
> *and vermillion, his capacity*
> *to liquefy with a glance.*

The magazine is 6x9", flat-spined, 170 + pp, professionally printed with glossy color cover, using 20-50 pp. of poetry in each issue, circulation 1,100, 800 subscriptions of which most are libraries. They receive about 1,200 submissions per year, use 100, have a 3-12 months backlog. **Sample: $4.50 postpaid. Submit no more than 5-6 poems at a time, clear typing or dot-matrix, simultaneous submissions OK, no queries. Reports in 2-3 months. Pays copies.** There are 3-5 annual Charles Angoff Awards of about $100 each for poems published in the magazine. At times the editor comments on rejections. The editors advise, "Read magazine carefully before submitting."

LITTLE BALKANS PRESS, *LITTLE BALKANS REVIEW: A SOUTHEAST KANSAS LITERARY AND GRAPHICS QUARTERLY (II, IV, Regional/Kansas authors), 601 Grandview Heights Terrace, Pittsburgh, KS 66762, founded 1970, poetry editor Gene DeGruson. The Press publishes books by Kansas authors only, no unsolicited MSS. The quarterly "regional magazine of national interest, exploring the works of Kansans and former Kansans who have made an impact on national and international culture," wants **any poetry of quality (not only by Kansans).** They have recently published poetry by William Stafford, Barbara Shirk Parish, Elizabeth Sargent and Al Ortolani. The editor selected these sample lines by Fred Chappell:

> *I have a sorrow that no tear can cool.*
> *I know a ghostly bird sings out of tune.*
> *I find the parts that never make a whole,*
> *The broken halves that never join as one.*

The digest-sized 100 + pp., flat-spined magazine, matte cover with b/w art, circulation 1,200, 1,000 subscriptions of which 250 are libraries, is professionally printed, uses drawings or photos of each poet. Each issue has about 96 pp. **They receive about 2,000 submissions per year, use 45, have a year's backlog. Sample: $2.50 postpaid. Send no more than 5 poems at a time; reports in 6 weeks, pays 3 copies.** Send SASE for guidelines. The editor sometimes comments on rejections.

THE LOCKHART PRESS (IV, Dreams), Box 1207, Port Townsend, WA 98368, phone 202-385-6413, founded 1982, poetry editor Russell A. Lockhart, Ph.D, began as a publisher of fine handmade hardbound books, now expanding to chapbooks and paperbacks, is interested in, **but not limited to, poetry having its origin in or strongly influenced by dreams." No specifications as to form, length or style.** They have recently published Janet Dallett's **Midnight's Daughter**, which won the Letterpress Prize in the Small Press Book Show Festival of the Arts, Seattle, 1983; Marc Hudson's **Journal for An Injured Son**; and Peter Levitt's **Homage: Leda as Virgin**, all handmade editions including special readings by the poets on tape issued in limited deluxe editions costing $75 or more. Sample lines from Hudson's **Journal**:

> *My boy also is a swimmer, for whom desire*
> *annihilates distance. He is my dolphin, my little Odysseus.*
> *Death could not steal from his eyes*
> *the dawn of his homecoming.*

Query with 5 samples, usual bio, credits information. Replies to query in 2 weeks, reports on submission (if invited) 90 days. MS should be clear in any form—simultaneous submissions, photocopies, dot-matrix, or discs compatible with Apple II or Macintosh OK. Contract is for 15% royalties plus 10 copies. To see a sample, you may ask for one on approval. Sometimes comments on rejections.

THE LOFT PRESS, *GLENS FALLS REVIEW (II), 42 Sherman Ave., Glens Falls, NY 12801, phone 518-798-8110, founded 1982, editors Walter Lape and Jean Rikoff: "We print an annual literary review—prose, poetry, articles of general interest—and we publish one or two chapbooks a year, both in prose and poetry. We are interested in **all kinds of good poetry." No specifications as to form, length, style, subject matter or purpose.** They have recently published Norman Dube, William Kennedy, William Bronk, Gus Pelletier and Jeannine Savard. The editors declined to quote a sample because "this would assume we have a special *kind* of poetry we like, which isn't true. We're very democratic in our taste." *GFR* is a beautifully printed magazine-sized 56 pp. journal which is about a third poetry, using photos of many of the authors, circulation 1,000. They receive some 500 submissions per year, use "as many as are suitable," and have no backlog. Sample: $5 postpaid. MS should be "typed—neat—address on each page." Submit between January 1 and May 1. "We pay in copies."

*LONDON REVIEW OF BOOKS (III), Tavistock House, Tavistock Square, London, England WC1, founded 1979, editor Karl Miller, is published 22 times a year, mostly reviews and essays but some stories and poems. They have published some of the most distinguished contemporary poets, such as Ted Hughes, Frederick Seidel and Thom Gunn. As a sample I selected the opening stanza of "My Fuchsia" by Ruth Fainlight:

> *My fuchsia is a middle-aged woman*
> *who's had fourteen children, and though*
> *she could do it again, she's rather tired.*

The paper has a circulation of 15,000, 10,000 subscriptions. Considers simultaneous submissions. **Sample: £1.25 plus postage (available at some bookstores). They pay £30/ poem.**

LONESTAR PUBLICATIONS OF HUMOR, *LONESTAR: HUMOR DIGEST (FORMERLY LONE STAR—A MAGAZINE OF HUMOR) THE LONE STAR COMEDY MONTHLY, LONE STAR: A COMEDY SERVICE AND NEWSLETTER (IV, Humor), Suite 103, Box 29000, San Antonio, TX 78229, founded 1981, poetry editors Lauren Barnett and Ashleigh Lynby. "**Our only interest is humor, but we're interested in every aspect of it. We use poetry in** *The LoneStar: Humor Digest.* **Any kind of poetry as long as it's funny (and not too long). Limericks, Clerihews, free verse, cheap verse, designer verse—all of this is OK. Don't want to see anything that runs more than two typed pages.**" They have recently published poems by Robert N. Feinstein, Julie Eilber, Virginia Long, Lauren Barnett and Christine Sutowsky. As a sample the editors selected these lines from "Old Blue" by Neal Wilgus:

> *I've sure got to hand it to Blue:*
> *Quest's disguise Blue had quickly seen through.*
> *For Quest was six guys—all Neptunian spies,*
> *held together with some kind of glue.*

The book appears 2 to 3 times a year, digest-sized, 60 pp. with glossy card cover with cartoons, offset from various styles of typescript on colored paper, circulation "over 1,200." It uses 1-2 poems per issue. They receive about 400 submissions of poetry per year, use about 5% of them. "For the next several months, we will be generating much of our material 'in-house'. Poets should inquire before submitting material. **Sample: inquire. Submit to poetry editor any time, no more than 5 poems per submission. Photocopy OK, dot-matrix no. Reports within 8 weeks. Pay: inquire. Send SASE for guidelines.**" The editors comment, "Good 'serious' writers are abundant; good writers of humor are rare. Poets who feel that humorous poetry is less important or easier than 'serious' poetry should not send their material to *Lone Star*. It's not likely that their endeavors will be good enough to interest us."

*THE LOOKOUT (IV), Seamen's Church Institute of New York and New Jersey, 50 Broadway, New York, NY 10004, phone 212-269-2710, founded 1834, poetry editor Carlyle Windley, is the "external house publication of the Institute and has been published continuously since 1909, 3 times a year, circulation 5,700. Basic purpose of the publication is to engender and sustain interest in the work of the Institute and to encourage monetary gifts in support of its philanthropic work among merchant seamen. Emphasis is on the *merchant marine*; NOT Navy, power boats, commercial or pleasure fishing, passenger vessels." It is magazine-sized, normally 20-24 pp., printed offset in two color inks. Subscription is via a minimum contribution of $5 a year to the Institute. It "**buys small amount of short verse (sea-faring related but *not* about the sea per se and the clichés about spume, spray, sparkle, etc.), paying $10.**" They have published poetry by Kay Wissinger, June Owens, Irene Abel and L. A. Davidson. The editors selected these sample lines by Wendy Thorne:

> *Tides rise and ebb with small heed of season;*
> *Yet, subtle change a new coast carves,*
> *The salt air tang, the call of the gull*
> *Where fathoms are great*

Sample: free for 9x12" SASE. Submit any number of poems. No photocopies. Typed originals. Reports within 2 weeks. Send SASE for guidelines.

‡LOOM PRESS *LOOM (II), Box 1394, Lowell, MA 01853, founded 1978, editor Paul Marion, a small-press publisher of poetry chapbooks and broadsides. The broadside series, which appears irregularly, is called *Loom* and publishes *"good contemporary poems in any form, style."* Poets recently published include Helena Minton, Maurya Simon, and Eric Linder. As a sample, the editor selected the following lines by an unidentified poet:

> *Morning after rain*
> *and the scant leaves of injured*
> *trees dangle like Purple*
> *Hearts.*

The broadsides range from magazine-sized to 11x17". They have a circulation of 100-500. Price per issue varies, but a **sample is available for $2. Pay is 10 copies. "Clear copies" are OK for submissions which will be reported on in 1 month; time to publication is 3-6 months. Writers should query first for chapbook publication, sending credits, 5 sample poems, and bio. Queries will be answered in 2 weeks, MSS reported on in 4 weeks. Simultaneous submissions will be considered, and photocopied or dot-matrix MSS are OK. Royalties of 10% are paid on chapbooks, plus 10% of print run. Sample chapbooks are available at $3 each. The editor comments on MSS "when time allows."** The chapbooks are saddle-stitched, 6x9", with an average page count of 20. The editor advises, "1) Read what your contemporaries are writing; 2) buy new books of poetry."

LOTUS PRESS, PENWAY BOOKS (II), Box 21607 (18080 Santa Barbara Dr.), Detroit, MI 48221, phone 313-861-1280, founded 1972, poetry editor Naomi Long Madgett. "With one exception of a textbook, we publish **poetry only—usually books by individual authors,** although we have one anthology and three sets of broadsides, one with a teachers' guide for use in secondary schools. We occasionally sponsor readings. **Most, but not all, of our authors are black. We want to see poetry by serious poets who have learned their craft. Subject matter is not important, although we tend toward books acceptable in most schools. We are not interested in unbridled emotion, nor do we have a preference for black subjects. No preference regarding form and length except that anything highly experimental may not be accepted.**" They have published collections by Sybil Kein, Dolores Kendrick, Toi Derricotte, Gary Smith, Paulette Childress White, Dudley Randall and Gayl Jones. The editor selected these sample lines from "Baton Rouge Poems" in *I Never Scream* by Pinkie Gordon Lane::

> *Cleansed, purged,*
> *exorcised to silence*
> *I slip into the valleys*
> *of my mind, fused*
> *to a green landscape*

Query with about 5 sample poems. Cover letter "not required, but no objection. Information concerning other publications is sometimes helpful but not necessary." Reports on "some almost immediately; we aim at response within 6 weeks." MS should be typed, double-spaced. Photocopy, dot-matrix OK. Pays 25 copies. Catalog available for 6x9" SASE. To the question, "Do you ever comment or provide criticism on rejected MSS?" Naomi Madgett says, "As much as we would like to do so, we simply do not have the time."

LOUISIANA STATE UNIVERSITY PRESS (II), Baton Rouge, LA 70893, phone 504-388-6618 or 388-6294, founded 1935, poetry editor Beverly Jarrett, is a highly respected publisher of collections of poets such as Richmond Lattimore, William Hathaway, Fred Chappell, Susan Ludvigson and Lisel Mueller. As a sample I selected the conclusion of "On Being Instructed by a Nude," from **The Meaning of Coyotes** by William Mills:

> *. . . as you stand nude in the sun*
> *Casting for our supper's trout,*
> *Your brown body gathering the world to it.*
> *As you gather fish*
> *The world to be fished falls silent.*

Query with 6-8 sample poems, publication credits and regional bayou. Replies to query in 2-3 weeks, to submission (if invited) in 3-4 months. Simultaneous submissions, photocopies OK; no dot-matrix. Royalty contract plus 10 author's copies. The editor sometimes comments on rejected MSS.

‡***LUCKY JIM'S JOURNAL OF STRANGELY NEGLECTED TOPICS (II)**, 3806 St. Denis, Apt. A, Montreal, PQ, Canada, H2W 2M2, phone 514-286-0418, founded 1984, co-editors William Hall and Gary Clairman. **There are no specifications about the kind of poetry the editors want to see, but they do not want anything by "bad poets in love."** The magazine, which appears three times a year, is photocopied with hand-made covers, 51 pp., with three-color linoleum block print soft cover, stapled. Edition is limited to 300 numbered copies. **Guidelines available for SASE. Pay is unspecified number of copies. Time to publication "can be months, but will hopefully improve. Content is decided by whatever is good that comes in the mail. A special science fiction issue is planned for 1986."**

***LUDD'S MILL, EIGHT MILES HIGH HOME ENTERTAINMENT (IV, Music)**, 44 Spa Croft Rd., Teall St., Ossett, West Yorkshire, England WF5 0HE, founded 1971, is a 36 pp. biannual exploring the **rock/industrial/jazz/pop music and alternative beat/dada/avant-garde using poetry in keeping with that focus. Sample: $2.**

  LUNA BISONTE PRODS, *LOST AND FOUND TIMES (IV, Style), 137 Leland Ave., Columbus, OH 43214, founded 1967, poetry editor John M. Bennett, may be the zaniest phenomenon in central Ohio. John Bennett is a publisher (and practicioner) of **experimental and avant-garde writing** and art in a bewildering array of formats including the magazine, *Lost and Found Times,* post card series, posters, chapbooks, pamphlets and labels. You can get a **sampling of Luna Bisonte Prods for $2 + $1 postage and handling. Numerous reviewers have commented on the bizarre** *Lost and Found Times,* "reminiscent of several West Coast dada magazines"; "This exciting magazine is recommended only for the most daring souls"; "truly demented"; etc. He wants to see "**unusual poetry, naive poetry, surrealism, experimental, visual poetry—***no* **poetry workshop or academic pablum.**" He has published poetry by I. Arguelles, G. Beining, B. Heman, R. Olson, J. Lipman, B. Porter, C. H. Ford, P. Weinman, E. N. Brookings, F. A. Nettelbeck, D. Raphael, R. Crozier and himself. As a sample he selected this short poem from *Footnotes For The Future*, a chapbook by Bob Heman:

> *it is lacking and loud. its mole is the perfect library. it*
> *joins the image of masked hands and frowns at the extinct*
> *fish. it invites a new form of measurement.*

The digest-sized 28 pp. magazine, photoreduced typescript and wild graphics, matte card cover with graphics, has a circulation of 200, 35 subscriptions of which 18 are libraries. **Sample: $3 postpaid. Submit any time—preferably camera-ready (but this is not required). Reports in 1-2 days, pays copies. Luna Bisonte also will consider book (and chapbook) submissions: query with samples and cover letter (but "keep it brief"). Photocopy, dot-matrix OK.** He will also consider subsidy arrangements on negotiable terms.

‡***LUNA TACK(II)**, Box 372, West Branch, IA 52358, 319-643-7324, founded 1981, editor David Duer, a journal of art and literature that, in addition to the magazine, publishes occasional letterpress postcards. The editor wants to see "**poetry that engages the world in a direct fashion; poetry that challenges and experiments with form and style.**" He does not want "**poetry that is not careful and disciplined in its use of language.**" He has recently published Cid Corman, Sam Hamill, Paul Hoover, Greg Kuzma, Susan Howe and Anselm Hollo. *Luna Tack* is a semi-annual, digest-sized, 56 pp., offset, with art, no advertisements, circulation 400 with 65 subscriptions, $3 per copy, subscription $10 for two years. **Sample: $3.50 postpaid. Pay is 2 copies. Submissions, which should be at least 5 to 6 pp. of poetry, are reported on in 1 month, publication is in 1 year maximum. The editor occasionally comments on rejected MSS. His advice is, "Read everyone, then follow your own heart, mind and tongue."**

*THE LUTHERAN JOURNAL (IV, Religious), 7317 Cahill Rd., Edina, MN 55435, editor The Rev. Armin U. Deye, is a family quarterly, 32 pp., circulation 136,000, for Lutheran Church members, middle age and older. They use **poetry "related to subject matter," traditional, free verse, blank verse. Pays. Sample free for SASE. Simultaneous and photocopied submissions OK.**

*LUTHERAN WOMEN (IV, Religious), 2900 Queen Lane, Philadelphia, PA 10129, phone 215-438-2200, founded 1962, appears 10 times a year, circulation 32,000-35,000, is a "magazine of informed opinion for Christian audiences about some of the social and critical concerns of the times, **especially concerns of or involving women in this country and worldwide."** They use "**mostly serious verse on general Christian themes, often specifically for female audience. Some humorous verse accepted. No doggerel. No 'housebound' themes. Length is generally 25 lines or less. Occasional exceptions are made.**" They have published poetry by Emily S. Councilman, Marilyn E. Scott, Paula Denham, Clara Baldwin, Ramona C. Carroll and Gladys McKee. The 7x10, 32 pp. magazine uses "0-1" page of poetry per issue, (the two I examined had none), and they have a 1-2 year backlog. **No form specifications. No queries. Simultaneous submissions OK if indicated as such. Reports in 3 months. Pays $35 or less plus 2 copies. Sample: 75¢ postpaid. Send SASE for guidelines.**

*THE LYRIC, (II), 307 Dunton Dr., SW, Blacksburg, VA 24060, founded 1921 ("the oldest magazine in North America devoted to the publication of **traditional poetry**"), poetry editor Leslie Mellichamp, uses about 45 poems each quarterly issue. "**We use rhymed verse in traditional forms, for the most part, with an occasional piece of blank or free verse. 35 lines or so is usually our limit. Our themes are varied, ranging from religious ecstasy to humor to raw grief, but we feel no compulsion to shock, embitter, or confound our readers. We also avoid poems about contemporary political or social problems—grief but not grievances, as Frost put it. Frost is helpful in other ways: if yours is more than a lover's quarrel with life, we're not your best market. And most of our poems are accessible on first or second reading. Frost again: don't hide too far away. Poems must be original, unpublished, and not under consideration elsewhere.**" **Pays 1 copy, and all contributors are eligible for quarterly and annual prizes totaling over $600.** They have published poetry by Anne Barlow, John J. Brugaletta, Maureen Cannon, Rhina P. Espaillat, W. Gregory Stewart, Alfred Dorn, Gail White and Tom Riley. The editor selected these sample lines by Bernhard Hillila:

> There is no fire but needs some tending
> True lovers learn.
> Good neighbors know there is no fence
> but needs some mending.

The digest-sized, 24 pp. format, professionally printed with varied typography, matte card cover, has a circulation of 850, 800 subscriptions of which 290 are libraries. They receive about 2,000 submissions per year, use 200, have an average 5 month backlog. **Sample: $2 postpaid, subscription $6. Submit up to 5 poems. Photocopy, dot-matrix OK. Reports in 3 weeks. Send SASE for guidelines and, if you are a college student, for rules of the College Student Annual Contest (prizes totaling $500).** Leslie Mellichamp comments, "Our *raison dêtre* has been the encouragement of form, music, rhyme and accessibility in poetry. We detect a growing dissatisfaction with the modernist movement that ignores these things and a growing interest in the traditional wellsprings of the craft. Naturally, we are proud to have provided an alternative for over 60 years that helped keep the true roots of poetry alive."

M.A.F. PRESS, *THIRTEEN POETRY MAGAZINE (I, IV, Form), Box 392, Portlandville, NY 13834, phone 607-286-7500, founded 1982, poetry editor Ken Stone. *Thirteen Poetry Magazine* "**publishes only 13 line poetry; any theme or subject as long as in 'good' taste. We seek to publish work that touches the beauty of this life.**" The M.A.F. Press publishes a chapbook and an anthology series with open submission—**no reading fee. Chapbooks must be a total of 24 pp.** They have published poetry recently by Shirley Murphy, Lynne Cheney-Rose, T.K. Splake, Lyn Lifshin, Bernhard Frank, Margot Treitel, and Alan Catlin. As a sample—"The Voice Inside" by David Chorlton:

> God sprouts hair along his spine
> His claws open the clouds
> and drops a litter on the world
> to grow in his image

Thirteen appears quarterly in a magazine-sized 40 pp., saddle-stapled format, photocopied from typescript, matte card cover with b/w cartoon, circulation 200, 104 subscriptions of which 20 are libraries. Ken Stone accepts about 100 of the 300 submissions he receives each year. **Sample: $2.50 postpaid. Submit 4-6 poems. Photocopies are acceptable, no reprint material. "We have even taken handwritten poems. As to queries, only if 13 lines gives the poet problems." Reports "immediately to 2 weeks." Pays 1 copy. Send SASE for guidelines. For chapbook submission, send complete MS, no query, with short bio. Reports in 2-3 weeks. Photocopy OK; no dot-matrix. Pays 50 copies. Com-**

ments on rejections "**especially if requested.**" The editor advises, "Send more poetry, less letters and self-promotion. Read the 'want lists' and description listings of magazines for guidelines. When in doubt request information. Read other poets in the magazines and journals to see what trends are. Also, this is a good way to find out what various publications like in the way of submissions."

‡**M.O.P. PRESS, *PUNCLIPS (I, IV, Humor)**, Rt. 24, Box 53C, Fort Meyers, FL 33908, phone 813-466-4690, M.O.P. Press founded in 1979, poetry editor Shirley Aycock. *Punclips*, founded spring 1985, an inexpensively produced, 16 pp. publication the editor describes as "**a quarterly magazine of humorous poems, under 30 lines, free verse preferred, good taste please; should be subtle, not slapstick or clownish.**" She has published poetry by Carrie Quick and Ken Stone. As a sample, the editor selected this poem, "Weather or Not," by Leo Wiener:

> *Outside's meows and*
> *Barks inside's*
> *Only a bird*
> *In a guilty cage.*

Punclips is digest-sized, photocopied from typescript, saddle-stapled on white bond with b/w cartoons, wrap-around paper cover, $1.50/issue, subscription $5. **Sample: $1.50 postpaid. Reports in 2 weeks, publication in maximum of 3 months. No pay; you must buy a copy to see your work in print. Send SASE for guidelines. M.O.P. Press publishes occasional collections of poetry by individuals and occasional anthologies. No pay.** Samples available for postage (37¢ up). Occasional competitions or awards, occasional comments on rejected MSS, criticism available for $3.

‡***MAAT (II)**, 1223 South Selva, Dallas, TX 75218, phone 214-324-3093, founded 1985, editor Katherine Flanagan, a trice-yearly literary magazine which publishes primarily poetry, sponsors an annual chapbook contest, and occasionally publishes extra issues on announced themes. "**No restrictions on theme or style though we publish haiku infrequently and almost never publish rhymed work because we rarely see any of high quality. Tend to prefer personal/emotional themes over descriptive; want nothing contrived. We'll take a look at any type of poetry, and we always comment.**" *Maat* has recently published work by Lyn Lifshin, Tony Moffeit, Harry Calhoun, Tom House, Ave Jeanne, Sue Marra, and Patrick McKinnon. As a sample, the editor chose the following lines by Elliot Richman:

> *The revelers are long silent.*
> *The earth hurls one year closer*
> *to the night*
> *of the sun's death.*

Maat is digest-sized, offset from typed copy, 40-60 pp., with gold matte card cover, saddle-stapled. Circulation is 200+ with about 60 subscriptions ("we're new"). Price per copy is $3. **Guidelines are available for SASE. At present *Maat* pays only in copies, but the editor hopes to be able to pay a token amount to her contributors. She prefers submissions of 5-10 pp., photocopies OK. "We return all simultaneous submissions, though we do not accept previously published material." Submissions will be reported on in 1-6 weeks and time to publication will be no longer than 3-4 months. She accepts freelance submissions for chapbooks between Jan. 1 and Feb. each year;** 1-3 chapbooks are published during a year, digest-sized, matte card covers, side-stapled, 30 pp. **Writers should query before submitting, sending "whatever information the poet feels applicable." Queries will be answered in 1 week and MSS reported on in 2-6 weeks. Photocopied or dot-matrix MSS are OK but discs are not. Pay for chapbooks is in author's copies; the number varies. Sample of chapbook: $3. There is an annual chapbook contest and "some other infrequent contests which we announce 6 months or so before deadline."** Katherine Flanagan advises: "read and write as much as possible and then *more*. Don't let rejection discourage you. There is far less space in journals today than there are talented poets and writers. Keep trying. There is a market for almost everyone, but it takes time and persistance to locate those markets."

‡ **MACFADDEN WOMEN'S GROUP, *TRUE EXPERIENCE, *TRUE LOVE, *TRUE STORY, *MODERN ROMANCES (I)**, 215 Lexington Ave., New York, NY 10016, 212-340-7500. **Address each magazine individually; do not submit to MacFadden Women's Group.** Each of these romance magazines uses poetry—usually no more than one poem per issue. Their requirements vary, and I suggest that readers study them individually and write for guidelines. Paula Misiewicz, editor of *True Experience*, says these are their requirements: "**1. Short (3-8 verses); 2. All subjects, especially love, marriage, family, life, seasonal (no religious or historical); 3. Keep tone light, optimistic, pleasant, emotional; 4. Uses 1 poem per issue, as *space permits*; 5. SASE, rates vary; pays on publication; 6. Beginners always welcome; 7. No simultaneous submissions.**" As a sample from that magazine 1 selected the last stanza of "The Sooner it's Spring the Better!" by Florence Boutwell:

> *I want to find, for just us two,*
> *A green, romantic glade*
> *Sweet with grass and tumbling stream*
> *And lazy, leafy shade.*

Requirements for the other magazines are similar. These mass-circulation magazines (available on newsstands) are obviously a very limited market, yet a possible one for beginners—especially those who like the prose contents and are tuned in to their editorial tastes. One poet who had published in *True Story* wrote me of her experience: "I have never seen a listing for *True Story* for poetry, but I just took my chances and submitted poetry to them over and over. They are extremely slow in replying. It took them 8 months to reply to the last submission I made, and that is the time they purchased one of my poems. I've sent them some of my best and been rejected while one of my worst was purchased."

‡*THE MACGUFFIN (II)**, Schoolcraft College, 18600 Haggerty Rd., Livonia, MI 48152, phone 313-591-6400, ext. 400, founded 1983, editor Arthur Lindenberg, who says, "*The MacGuffin* is a literary magazine which appears twice each year, in April and November. We publish the best poetry, fiction, non-fiction and artwork we find. We have no thematic or stylistic biases. **We look for well crafted poetry. Long poems should not exceed 300 lines. Avoid pornography, trite and sloppy poetry."** The MacGuffin has recently published poetry by Helen Hoffman, Michael Hogan, Chet Leach, and A. Wilber Stevens. As a sample, the editor selected the following lines from "The Blue Handkerchief" by Danny Rendleman:

> *The death in you seemed to rise*
> *like music up through a bewildered juke-box.*
> *Toward the end, in the hottest summer*
> *Laurel, Mississippi could recall*

The MacGuffin is digest-sized, professionally printed on heavy buff stock, 84 pp. with matte card cover, flat-spined, with b/w illustrations and photos. Circulation is 500, of which 25 are subscriptions and the rest are local newsstand sales, contributor copies, and distribution to college offices. Price per issue is $2.50, subscription $4.50. **Sample: $2 postpaid. Pay: two copies.** "The editorial staff is grateful **to consider unsolicited manuscripts and graphics." MSS are reported on in 2-4 weeks and the publication backlog is 1-6 months. Writers should submit no more than 6 poems of no more than 300 lines; they should be typewritten, and photocopied or dot-matrix MS are OK.** "We will always comment on 'near misses.' " The magazine recently sponsored a contest with a $25 first prize for Michigan poets only; they hope to be able to sponsor a national competition soon.

THE MADISON REVIEW (II), Dept. of English, Helen C. White Hall, 600 N. Park St., Madison, WI 53706, founded 1978, poetry editor Garrison Pettit, wants "**original, serious, shorter poems— generally not over 100 lines. Probably would not want: translations, longer poems, or obviously light verse."** They have recently published poetry by Donald Finkel, Laurel Speer, George Bradley, Ted Kooser, Ron Wallace, Naomi Shihab Nye, Stuart Dybek, Simon Perchik, Carl Lindner and Jim Daniels. As a sample the editor selected these lines from "Song for a Hotspell" by David Keller:

> *That cat is dead years ago,*
> *and the curve in the roofline of that house*
> *taken up in your shoulders, the pain*
> *in your knee like a birthday present.*
> *But that will come later, Mother, we know.*
> *Just that it is so hot.*

There are usually 2 issues per year, 350 plus, 30-40 pp. of poetry, 80 pp. with fiction in each issue, for which they receive about 500-550 submissions, use 25-45. **Sample: $2 postpaid. Submit maximum of 5 poems. Photocopy OK. Often not reading over summer months. Usually reports in 8-12 weeks. Pays 1 copy.** "We do appreciate brief cover letters with submissions. They help us get to know our contributors. We sometimes comment on rejections; we try to be helpful and encourage more work, more submissions. Beginners: *read* before, during and after writing. Please be neat and treat your poems *better* than job applications! We *do* appreciate thoughtful, clever, careful work. Thank you."

> 66 **Most would-be poets really do need more reading experience. Far too many are only vaguely aware of the poetic heritage.**
>
> *Robert E. Pletta, Acheron Press* 99

*THE MAGAZINE OF SPECULATIVE POETRY (II), Box 564, Beloit, WI 53511, founded 1984, editors Roger Dutcher and Mark Rich, a quarterly magazine that publishes **"the best new speculative poetry. We are especially interested in narrative form, but interested in variety of styles, open to any form, length (within reason), purpose. We're looking for the best of the new poetry utilizing the ideas, imagery and approaches developed by speculative fiction and will welcome experimental techniques as well as the fresh employment of traditional forms."** The issue I have (Vol. I, No. 3) has poems by Bruce Boston, Robert Frazier, S. R. Compton, Peggy Sue Alberhasky, Stan Proper, Bonnie Morris, John Oliver Simon, Mark Rich, Harry Bose, Michael Finley, Robert Randolf Medcalf, Jr., and a translation from Krzysztof Ostaszewski. As a sample, I have selected the first stanza from "A Clone in the House of Mirrors" by Elissa Malcohn:

> *It is the perfect copy that bothers her,*
> *that spies on her reflection,*
> *takes notes, judges her speed*
> *of recognition. Who is real?*
> *Who is not real?*

The digest-sized magazine, 20 pp., is offset from typed copy with a colored matte card cover featuring an illustration by Mark Rich; it is saddle-stapled. Price is $2 per issue; subscription price (4 issues) is $7.50. Print run is 400. **Sample $1.50 postpaid. Submit in any format. Photocopied MSS are OK. Submissions are reported on in 1 month. Pay begins at $1 per poem plus copies.**

‡*THE MAGE (IV, Science fiction), Colgate University Student Activities, Hamilton, NY 13346, founded 1984, poetry editor David Gregg, a student-run journal of science and fantasy fiction and essays, poetry, and art. It publishes 5-8 poems in each issue. The editors say, **"We will consider poems of science fiction and/or fantasy themes or subjects. We do not have any categorical specifications as to form or length. We do not print erotic poetry or limericks."** They have recently published poems by Mark Rich and Darryle Stephen Douglas. The editors preferred not to quote lines, but I have selected, in order to suggest quality, the beginning lines from "Bramblebeard" by t. Winter-Damon:

> *his words trail him like a cloak of velvet*
> *they flow moss-soft dream-warmed as cats' purr*
> *he breathes a charm that tastes of rich brown loam*
> *beneath his feet the beard of the earth grows*
> * wilder greener*

The Mage is magazine-sized, professionally printed with occasional pen-and-ink illustrations, 52 pp. saddle-stapled with white textured card cover illustrated by a b/w drawing. The magazine appears each semester (twice a year) and has a press run of 250, including 11 subscriptions and about 80 newsstand sales plus individual sales by the staff. Price per issue is $1 and "we try to discourage subscriptions." **Sample available for $2.50 postpaid. Pay is 1 copy. Submissions "only have to be readable. Desired punctuation and spacing should be clear so that we don't have to write for clarification during typesetting." Reporting time is 1-6 weeks, and accepted work is published in the next issue. "We usually endeavor to make some constructive criticism on all MSS."** The editor offers two pieces of advice: "1) Avoid the cliches which are all too common in these genres. Be original, it is the surest way to publication, and 2) An unusual interest grabbing first line is *much* better than an unusual format (with apologies to e. e. cummings)."

*MAGIC CHANGES (II), Suite 14, 8 Huntington Circle, W, Naperville, IL 60540, phone 312-355-3275, founded 1978, poetry editor John Sennett, is a literary annual in an unusual format. Photocopied from typescript on many different weights and colors of paper, magazine-sized, stapled along the long side (you read it sideways), taped flat spine, full of fantasy drawings, pages packed with poems of all variety, fiction, photos, drawings, odds and ends—including reviews of little magazines and other small-press publications, it is **intended to make poetry (and literature) fun—and unpredictable. Each issue is on an announced theme.** There are about 100 pp. of poetry per issue, circulation 500, 28 subscriptions of which 10 are libraries. They have published poetry by Sri Chinnoy, Roberta Gould, A. D. Winans, Lyn Lifshin and Dan Campion. For example, I open to a yellow page dominated by photos of mountains, inset one on another. In the air is the drawing of an otter (abalone on his belly)—reminding me that they originally called themselves The Celestial Otter Press. Inset on the upper left heaven are pieces of paper cut like mountains with these lines:

> *going home from the mountains*
> *for a shower and soft bed*
> *I find the smoke smell like*
> *pine needles caught in my clothes*

Below that, typed on another inset strip, is the name of the poet, John Rothfork. Below it somewhat randomly, on another piece cut with a mountain-like outline, is typed "The Subtlety of Mountains," presumably the name of the poem. **Sample: $5 postpaid. Submit 3-5 poems anytime. Photocopy OK.**

He says "no query," but I would think poets would need to know about upcoming themes. The editor sometimes comments on rejections and offers criticism for $5 per page of poetry, $2 per page of fiction. Pays 1 or 2 copies.

*MAGICAL BLEND (IV, Spiritual), Box 113003, San Francisco, CA 94101, founded 1980, is a magazine-sized quarterly, 96 pp., using material, including **poetry, of an uplifting, metaphysical, occult and spiritual nature. Send only 2 poems per submission. Sample: $4. Pays copies.**

MAINE WRITERS' WORKSHOP, MAINESPRING PRESS, *LETTERS MAGAZINE, Box 905 RFD, Stonington, ME 04681, phone 207-367-2484 (winter: Sapphire Bay West, St. Thomas, VI 00802), phone 809-775-7956, founded 1969, poetry editor G. F. Bush, **"accepts only high quality material in all ethical fields of literature." Readership: general public.** Poets they have published include Eberhart, Boyle, Buckminster, George Garrett, Carlos Baker, Fuller and S. F. Morse. *Letters* is a **quarterly which uses poetry. Cash payment varies. The press considers book MSS after query with SASE. Submit complete MS. MS should be "legible," no photocopies, no dot-matrix. Cash payment "depends." Sample free with SASE. Sometimes comments on MSS. Fee "depends."**

MAIZE PRESS (IV, Chicano/Latin American), Box 10, The Colorado College, Colorado Springs, CO 80903, phone 619-473-2233, ext. 624, founded 1977, poetry editors Alurista and Xelina R. Urista, is **"dedicated to the publishing and the public performance of Chicano and Third World—particularly Latin American—works of poetry,** short story and novels. They publish poetry chapbooks. **"Third World, socially conscious, feminist, and concrete imagery poetic production is our focus."** They have published poetry by Cordelia Candelaria and Ricardo Cobian, and they selected these sample lines by Leo Griep Ruiz, a Salvadorean residing in Colorado Springs:

> *is there room for me*
> *in your fallout shelter we could laugh*
> *in harmony*
> *in time to the rhythm of our hair*
> *it falls*
> *in clumps to the floor . . .*

Individuals wishing to submit a freelance book should **query first with at least 15 poems, some bio, where published, what literary awards. Replies to queries in 3 weeks, to MS (if invited) in 6 weeks maximum. Clean, typewritten MS. Photocopy OK, dot-matrix no.**

*THE MALAHAT REVIEW (II), Box 1700, University of Victoria, Victoria, British Columbia, Canada, V8W 2Y2, phone 604-721-8524, founded 1967, editor Constance Rooke, is "a high quality, visually appealing literary quarterly which has earned the praise of notable literary figures throughout North America. Its purpose is to publish and promote poetry and fiction of a very high standard, both Canadian and international. **We are interested in various styles, lengths and themes. The criterion is excellence."** They have recently published poems by Gary Gildner, Paulette Jiles, Erin Mouré and John Newlove. The editors selected these sample lines from "Invisible Presences Fill the Air" by P. K. Page:

> *I hear the clap of their folding wings*
> *like doors banging or wooden shutters.*
> *They land and settle—giant birds*
> *on the epaulettes of snowed-on statues.*

They use 30-50 pp. of poetry in each issue, have 900 subscriptions of which 250 are university libraries and 50 are public libraries. Subscription: $15. They use about 100 of 1,500 submissions received per year, have a 3 month backlog. **Sample: $7 postpaid. Submit 5-10 poems, double-spaced, addressed to Editor Constance Rooke. Reports within 3 months, pays $12.50 per poem plus 2 copies and reduced rates on others. Send SASE for guidelines.** The editors comment if they "feel the MS warrants some attention even though it is not accepted."

THE MANDEVILLE PRESS (V), 2 Taylor's Hill, Hitchin, Hertfordshire, SG4 9AD England, founded 1974, poetry editors Peter Scupham and John Mole, publishes hand-set pamphlets of the work of individual poets, but will not be considering new submissions through 1986. Send SASE for catalog to buy samples.

*MANHATTAN POETRY REVIEW (III), 36 Sutton Place South, 11D, New York, NY 10022, founded 1982, is a biannual poetry journal, digest-sized, 80 pp., circulation 1,000, which uses **quality poetry, pays 1 copy. Submit 3-5 poems, publication credits. Send SASE for reply. Sample including postage: $5.73.**

MANIC D PRESS (I, II), 1853 Stockton, San Francisco, CA 94133, founded 1984. **manic d** is interested in books/broadsides/etc. of **poetry by young unknowns who are looking for an alternative to** establishment presses. Considers simultaneous submissions. Pays copies. Send SASE for catalog to buy samples (or $3.50 for one of their books of their choice).

‡*MANKATO POETRY REVIEW (II)**, Box 53, English Dept., Mankato State, Mankato, MN 56001, phone 507-389-5511, founded 1984, editor Roger Sheffer, a semi-annual magazine that is **"open to all forms of poetry. We will look at poems up to 60 lines, any subject matter."** They have recently published poets by Laurel Speer, John Solensten, William Elliot, and Candace Black. As a sample, the editor chose the following lines from a poem by Ron Robinson:

> The rain paints late Monets at Hennepin and Lake;
> Water and glass show both through and back to,
> Headlights, taillights, neon: Rainbow Cafe,

The magazine is 5x8", typeset on fairly thin paper, 30 pp. saddle-stapled with buff matte card cover printed in one color. It appears usually in May and December and has a circulation of 200. Price per issue is $2, subscription $4/year. **Sample available for $2 postpaid, guidelines for SASE. Pay is 2 copies.** "Readable dot-matrix OK. Please indicate if simultaneous submission, and notify." Reporting time is about 2 months, "we accept only what we can publish in next issue." The editor says, **"We're interested in looking at longer poems—up to 60 lines, with great depth of detail relating to place (landscape, townscape)."**

*MANNA (I)**, 4318 Minter School Rd., Sanford, NC 27330, founded 1980, poetry editor Nina A. Wicker, is "a small poetry, prose magazine for the **middle-of-the-road poet. We like humor, short poems, farm poems, inspirational poetry; we use rhyme and free verse, also form poems such as limericks. We do not want long poems. Short ones to the point, poems with feelings, not sentimental! Good images and use of the language."** They have recently published poetry by Curtis Nelson, Jean Pasternik, Ellen T. Johnston-Hale and Leon Hinton. The editor selected these sample lines by Martha McKay:

> My purse is diminished, patience finished,
> sanity is in doubt, I've suffered a clout.
> Now I sign on the line
> and swear I'm no liar.
> A check I enclose and relief flows
> from head to toes and comes to repose
> in mind. Taxes behind
> I look ahead . . . to bed!

The digest-sized, 45 pp. magazine, photocopied from typescript, matte card cover with simple art, comes out twice a year, using nothing but poetry, circulation 200 +, 100 subscriptions. They receive 1,000 submissions per year, use about 200, and have less than a year's backlog. **Sample: $2.50 postpaid. Submit 3-5 poems any time, reports in less than 2 weeks. No pay, but they give 3 small prizes ($5, $3 and $2) for the best in each issue. Contributors are expected to buy a copy. Editor sometimes comments on rejections.** She advises, "Rewrite, rewrite and rewrite again! REMEMBER your reader—hardly anyone is interested in a long drawn out spill on what you feel about a rejected lover. Show in vivid language and images. Don't tell it all unless it's funny!"

‡*MAROVERLAG (II)**, Riedingerstr. 24, 8900 Augsburg, West Germany, phone 0821/416003, founded 1970, editor Lothar Reiserer. **Maroverlag publishes paperbacks and some hardcover books of poetry, one a year, averaging 80 pp.** The books are in German, but they have published a number of English and American poets (for example, Charles Bukoski). Submit sample of 8-10 poems and bio. Pays 5-10% royalties.

*MARRIAGE AND FAMILY LIVING (IV, Religious)**, St. Meinrad, IN 47577, phone 812-357-8011, a monthly magazine, circulation 40,000, for Christian couples and parents; supports, deepens, awakens the conviction of God's presence in the communion of family life. Pays $15 on publication. Sample $1.

THE UNIVERSITY OF MASSACHUSETTS PRESS, THE JUNIPER PRIZE (II), Box 429, Amherst, MA 01004, phone 413-545-2217, founded 1964. The press offers an annual competition for the **Juniper Prize, which consists of an award of $1,000 and book publication. $7 entry fee, deadline October 1. Send SASE for rules.**

*THE MASSACHUSETTS REVIEW (II)**, Memorial Hall, University of Massachusetts, Amherst, MA 01003, founded 1959, editors John Hicks and Mary Heath, is a distinguished literary quarterly which uses **quality poetry. Pays 35¢ per line or $10 minimum. Sample: $4 + 50¢ postage. SASE a must.**

MATILDA PUBLICATIONS, BRUNSWICK POETRY WORKSHOP, *MATILDA LITERARY & ARTS MAGAZINE (I), 7 Mountfield St. Brunswick, Victoria, Australia, phone 03-386-5604, founded 1974, poetry editors Mr. Fonda Zenofon and Kathleen Moore. "In Australia we are specialists in poetry. Yet we cater for the beginner thru to pro. It is not just a press but we have many resources. Poetry should fill the spirit/heart and drive out hate/alienation/depression which inspire suicide and jealousies; thus conflict; blood spill! We publish chapbooks verse/non-fiction. Our magazine: *Matilda* publishes a good proportion, we produce audio albums; discourses/poetry, etc. One music album; words & music. **Poster cards/seek more card/poster/light and humor for these formats.** Poetry is not like inventing/science; in a sense, you see you can't go outside the laws of nature; poets should not be hung up with tearing boundaries—it's the content that must be arranged. Then again it is like science with regard to its metre/form & measure." **He wants: poems with illustrations or those suitable for such. Humor to break the concentration of reader. Traditional forms must have modern theme; not outmoded styles. No abuse of syntax or grammatical flow; if you mean the running water, don't say THE RUN WATER."** He has published poetry by Arthur Hall, Jean Opperman and Pam Cooney. As a sample Fonda Zenophon selected these lines written by him:
> *Poetry is not meant to be sold;*
> *like truth it is meant to be told.*

The Brunswick Poetry; The First Official Poetry Body in Australia. Workshop offers a variety of publications, including subscription to *Matilda*, "free critical reports," and attendance at workshops. Membership: $18 per year. *Matilda* is a quarterly, circulation 1,000 + , 380 subscriptions of which 28 are libraries, which uses 6-23 pp. of poetry in each issue. They receive about 200 freelance contributions per year, use 60, have a 3 month backlog. **Sample: $1 postpaid "or send us yours; we'll barter. All contributions will be considered for print and audio and workshop discussion. We would like a quota of international flavour, U.S.A. especially, but we get too many hip man types; we are serious about our work."** Reports in one month if not sooner. Pays 1 copy. **Contributors are not expected to subscribe or buy copies "but those who help are remembered." Send SASE for guidelines. For chapbook consideration, query with 10 samples, "Comprehensive bio and brief auto- and reasons for taking up poetry, the most uncommercial area. No photocopy, no dot-matrix. Disks compatible with Tandy acceptable but hard copy preferred. Pays author's copies. Send 4x9" SASE (or IRC) for book catalog. Criticism free to members, by fees to others who ask.** Fonda Zenophon comments: "We find that the poets of today, the new generation, are arrogant and display a spoiled attitude. They lack the discipline and magic of better times. We find poets write for the wrong reasons. Eventually pay the price, they suffer, but worse, people won't read their poems."

*MATRIX (IV, Canadian), Box 510, Lennoxville, Quebec, Canada J1M 1Z6, founded 1975, is a literary biannual which publishes **quality poetry by Canadians without restriction as to form, length, style, subject matter or purpose. They have recently published poems by Irving Layton, Michael Harris, David Solway, Elizabeth Woods, Dorothy Livesay and Ken J. Harvey. The editor selected these sample lines by Don Kerr:**
> *the world gets smaller*
> *but I don't she said*
> *and expanded at 3% a year*
> *and became her own conglomerate*

There are 10-15 pp. of poetry in each issue. The magazine is 6x9", 72 pp., flat-spined, professionally printed, glossy cover with b/w art and graphics, circulation 400, 200 subscriptions of which 70 are libraries. Subscription: $6. They receive about 300 submissions per year, use 20-30, have a 6 month backlog. **Sample: $3 postpaid. Submit 6-10 poems. Reports in 8 weeks. Pays $15 per poem. Editor sometimes comments on rejections.** They run contests "when we have the money."

‡*McCALL'S (I, II), 230 Park Ave., New York, NY 10169, phone 212-551-9500, founded 1876. This well-known monthly women's service magazine publishes poetry which **"must be immediately accessible to our readers. However, the need for clarity should not result in oversimplified thoughts and emotions. There is still room for original ideas, lyrical turns of phrase, subtlety, humor and deep feeling. Any subject that interests women is acceptable. A partial list would include love, family, children, relationships with friends and relatives, familiar aspects of domestic and suburban life, Americana and seasonal poetry. In addition, we are always interested in seeing limericks and light, comical verse for our humor page. The poetry should not be lengthy, as we do not have space to print anything longer than 30 lines."** They do not want to see "sexy, violent, obscure, sick" poetry. Since *McCall's* is familiar to most everyone, I won't describe it here; samples are easily obtained on any newsstand. Circulation of the magazine is 6.2 million. **Guidelines are available for SASE. Pay is $10/line, payment upon acceptance. Contributors receive 1 copy. Time to publication is 2 months. They are currently severely overstocked.**

MCCLELLAND AND STEWART LIMITED (IV, Canada), 25 Hollinger Rd., Toronto, Ontario, Canada M4B 3G2, publishes "around six new collections of poetry each year, and while the primary criterion is high literary quality, virtually all our books at the press are by **authors who are citizens of Canada or permanent residents of this country.**" Send SASE for catalog to buy samples.

*ME MAGAZINE, POST ME STAMP SERIES (IV, Visual art, Maine), Box 1132, Peter Stuyvesant Station, New York, NY 10009, founded 1978, editor Carlo Pittore. *ME* stands for Main(e), among other things. The magazine "published at odd intervals" is devoted to **mail art—the exchange of visual poetry.** It is a magazine-sized 8 pp. newsletter for the mail art movement in which Carlo Pittor publishes **himself and his "friends and long time correspondents."** Considers simultaneous submissions. $5 for the magazine and a sheet of **Post Me** stamps. "We only consider poetry on the theme of *ME*, and/or on themes of visual art."

*MEMPHIS STATE REVIEW (II), English Dept., Memphis State University, Memphis, TN 38152, phone 901-363-2668, founded 1980, editor William Page, wants "to see serious, well-crafted poetry with vital imagery and emotional honesty. We do not want to see: verbosity, stilted or contrived diction, needless obscurity, works with no sense of form or direction.**"** They have recently published poetry by James Dickey, Philip Levine, Maxine Kumin, John Ashbery, Robert Penn Warren, W. D. Snodgrass and Mary Oliver. I selected as a sample the first stanza of "The Boxer and the Queen of Hearts" by Jeanne Lebow:

> The taste of blackberries from sixty summers
> sweetens her memories. Now, she feels
> her fingers thin as berry canes in winter
> and thinks God leaves her too long in a cold sun.

The biannual is 7½x10", saddle-stapled, 60 pp., 20-30 pp. of poetry in each issue, professionally printed, two-color matte cover, circulation 2,000, subscription: $3. They receive about 3,000 submissions per year, use 47, have a 12-18 month backlog. **Sample: $2 postpaid. Submit no more than 5 poems, none June-August. Photocopy OK. Reports in 2-12 weeks. Pays 2 copies (and have paid as much as $500 per poems when grant funds were available). $100 Hohenberg Award is given annually to best fiction or poetry selected by the staff.**

MENDOCINO GRAPHICS, *THE MENDOCINO REVIEW (II), Box 1580 or Box 888, Mendocino, CA 95460, phone 707-964-3831, founded 1974, poetry editors Peter Lit and Camille Ranker. The *MR* is an annual literary journal, "collection of previously unpublished works (short stories, poetry, illustrations and photography) of new and established writers, poets, artists and photographers from around the world. **We look at all forms of poetry. No politics or religion, please.**" They have recently published poetry by Tony Zurlo, Bill Bradd, Don Shanley Kiva, Sharon Dubiago and Lydia Rand. The editors selected these sample lines from "T/Our" by Richard Miller:

> Take for instance
> me please
> this fine piece of
> the American Dream I am

The *MR* is large (7¼x10½", 190+ pp.), professionally printed, glossy card cover with art, liberally illustrated with b/w drawings and photos and ads ("our country businesses support us well), circulation 5,000-8,000, 500+ subscriptions of which 50 are libraries. They receive 300-400 multiple submissions per year, use about 60 poems. **Sample: $8.95 postpaid. Send SASE for guidelines. "Submit up to 6 poems, one poem per page, centered, with name and address on each. Simultaneous submissions OK. Send enough poetry to truly sample your work. Key word is TYPED. No originals—only copies. We acknowledge receipt immediately, report in 60-90 days." Pays copies.** The editors advise, "Don't oversubmit . . . allow time to consider one batch of poems before you send another. Mostly, though, treat your work with respect. Don't send throw-aways or copies that have obviously made the 'rounds.' If you respect your work, we will."

MENNONITE PUBLISHING HOUSE, *PURPOSE, *CHRISTIAN LIVING, *STORY FRIENDS, *ON THE LINE, *GOSPEL HERALD, *WITH (IV, Religious), 616 Walnut Ave., Scottdale, PA 15683, phone 412-887-8500. The official publisher for the Mennonite Church in North America seeks also to serve a broad Christian audience. Each of the magazines listed has different specifications and the editor of each should be queried for more exact information. *Purpose* is a weekly, circulation 18,800, devoted to "discipleship for young and old. Seeks to explore **life issues in relation to faithfulness to Jesus Christ.**" They have recently published poetry by Thomas John Carlisle, Marlowe C. Dickson, Wayne B. Dayton, Janice Wise, Emily Sargent Councilman, Joyce Chandler, Mary M. Pronovost, Chris Ahlemann, May Richstone, Clare Miseles, Hilda Ingles and Marilyn Black Phemister. The editors selected these sample lines (poet unidentified):

> *The orphan*
> *send off*
> *the sacrifice of giving*
> *what will I offer?*
> *Losing nothing.*

Purpose uses 3-4 poems per week, receives about 2,000 per year of which they use 150, has a 10-12 week backlog. **Submit to editor, one poem per page, up to 12 lines, typewritten, double-spaced, one side of sheet only. Considers simultaneous submissions. No query. Reports in 6-8 weeks, pays up to $1 per line. Send SASE for guidelines.** *On the Line* **is for children 10-14,** weekly, circulation 12,000, uses light verse and religious, pays $5-15. *Story Friends* **is for children 4-9, weekly, circulation 11,500, uses traditional and free verse 3-12 lines, pays $5. Free sample (for SASE).**

‡*MENSUEL 25, ATELIER DE L'AGNEAU (I)**, 39 Rue Louis de Meuse, Herstal, Belgium, phone 41-36-37-22, founded 1972, editor Robert Varlez. *Mensuel 25* is a bi-monthly magazine of new poetry and graphics that is **open to all styles of poetry except classic.** They have recently published work by Jacques Izoard, Eugene Savitzkaya, and James Sacre. As a sample, the editor chose the following lines by an unidentified poet:

> *Let light*
> *loosen the mind's*
> *clenched fist*
> *the five senses*
> *fit like fingers*
> *into the warm glove*
> *of the world*

The magazine is 21x27 cm, 72-112 pp., offset with graphics and art. It has 200 subscriptions. Price per issue is 200 FB, subscription 1200 FB. **Sample available for 250 FB postpaid. Pay is 1 copy. Writers should send "10 pages translated in French." Time to publication is 1-4 months.** Atelier de L'Agneau publishes books only in French.

‡**MERGING MEDIA (V, Invitation)**, 516 Gallows Hill Rd., Cranford, NJ 07016, phone 201-276-9479, founded 1978, publisher D. C. Erdmann. Merging Media publishes 2-3 chapbooks of poetry each year, but **submissions are only by invitation. Poets should query first with 5 sample poems.** The press has recently published Geraldine Little, Alexis Rotella, Adele Kenny, Dorothy Rudy, Virginia Love Long, and Susan Sheppard. As a sample, the publisher selected the following lines from "Mendsongs & Soulspace" by Rochelle Lynn Holt and Linda Zeiser:

> *Often dying awake*
> *or in our sleep*
> *we speak as ghosts*
> *haunting shores already known . . .*

The sample chapbook I have seen is digest-sized, 33 pp. offset from typescript, with glossy card cover, flat-spined, b/w cover illustration; it sells for $3.50. **The editor subsidizes books by having the author agree to buy all but 50 copies. Other pay depends on grant/award money. Queries will be answered in 1 week, MSS reported on in 1 month. Simultaneous submissions are OK, as are photocopied or dot-matrix MSS. Criticism will be provided for a reading fee of $10/hour or $50/manuscript.**

MERIDIAN (I), Bottom Line Design, Inc., Box 40511, Indianapolis, IN 46240, is a monthly mini-tabloid (newsprint, saddle-stapled), distributed free (circulation 25,000) in the Indianapolis area, supported by advertising, focusing on **social activities, entertainment and political affairs of Indianapolis, using 1 page of poetry per month. Extremely flexible in range of topics, but long ballads are discouraged.** These sample lines are from "Here's to Life," by Chris Laux:

> *Everyday's a holiday*
> *and every meal a feast*
> *I have no enemies*
> *man or beast*

*METROSPHERE LITERARY MAGAZINE (II)**, English Dept., Box 32, Metropolitan State College, Denver, CO 80204, phone 303-629-2495, founded 1983, poetry editor Robert J. Pugel, is a magazine-sized literary biannual **"to provide a literary showcase for the creative and artistic talents of fresh, new, exciting writers and artists." They use "any kind, any style" of poetry, maximum 50 lines.** They have published poetry by Allen Ginsberg "and a host of new poets (some previously published)." As samples, the editors chose lines from 'Gordway Goal" by Bobbie Ware:

> *. . . A fat gray moth with dusty wings*

> *lay like a crashed airplane in the leaves*
> *and the sky grew dark.*
> *The rain pelted the windows, like black marbles*
> *and left round fingerprints in the mud.*
> *Plans dropped heavy on torn moth wings . . .*

Over 40 pp. of each 80 + pp. per issue are devoted to poetry. The magazine has a circulation of 3,000 (so far local distribution), 1,000 subscriptions of which 100 are libraries, 2,000 copies are given away. It is elegantly printed on various shades of heavy matte stock, liberally illustrated with b/w photos and graphics. They receive about 2,000 submissions of poetry per year, use about 10%, have a 3 month backlog. Subscription: $2.50, per copy: $2. **Sample: $1 postpaid. Submit batches of 6 poems. Previously published, simultaneous submissions, dot-matrix, photocopies all OK. Send SASE for guidelines. Reports in 3 months. Pays copies. Criticism supplied on rejections "if requested."**

*MICHIGAN QUARTERLY REVIEW (II), 3032 Rackham Bldg., University of Michigan, Ann Arbor, MI 48109, phone 313-764-9265, founded 1962, poetry editor Laurence Goldstein, is "an interdisciplinary, general interest academic journal that publishes mainly essays and reviews on subjects of cultural and literary interest." They use **all kinds of poetry except light verse. No specifications as to form, length, style, subject matter or purpose.** Poets they have recently published include Edward Hirsch, Alice Fulton, Diane Ackerman, John Updike, Philip Levine and James Merrill. As a sample, the editors chose these lines by William Stafford:

> *New people need what time passing gives:*
> *they lean over the calendar and slowly trace*
> *voluptuous numbers, 2's and 3's,*
> *and—three times a month—an elegant 8.*

The *Review* is 6x9", 160 + pp., flat-spined, professionally printed with glossy card cover, b/w photos and art, has a circulation of 2,000, 1,500 subscriptions of which half are libraries. Subscription: $13; per copy: $3.50. They receive 1,500 submissions per year, use 30, have a 1 year backlog. **Sample: $2 postpaid. They prefer typed MSS, photocopies OK. Reports in 4-6 weeks. Pays $8-12 per page.** Laurence Goldstein advises, **"There is no substitute for omnivorous reading and careful study of poets past and present, as well as reading in new and old areas of knowledge. Attention to technique, especially to rhythm and patterns of imagery, is vital."**

*MID-AMERICAN REVIEW (II), English Dept., Bowling Green State University, Bowling Green, OH 43403, phone 419-372-2725, founded 1980, editor Robert Early, is a 200 pp., digest-sized biannual, **sample: $4.50, which uses poetry with strong imagery and strong sense of vision. They buy 60 poems per year, pay $5 per page, and offer an annual prize for the best poem.**

‡*MIDLAND REVIEW (II), English Dept., Morrill Hall, Oklahoma State University, Stillwater, OK 74078, phone 405-624-6138, founded 1985, poetry editors Alice Bolstridge and Marinelle Ringer, a literary annual that publishes "poetry, fiction, essays, ethnic, experimental, women's work, contemporary feminist, linguistic criticism, drama, comparative lit., interviews." Each issue seems to have a theme; for April 1987 it will be contemporary Irish women writers, for December 1987 contemporary Native American writers. The editors say, **"style and form are open." They do not want long or religious poetry."** Poets recently published include Amy Clampitt, William Stafford, Brenden Galvin, and Richard Kostelanetz. As a sample, the editors chose the following lines by Robert Siegal:

> *The snow throws itself down in pity*
> *From the order of heaven where things are clear*
> *as the horizon retreating from a space shuttle*
> *or the edge of Africa, a calm and simple line.*

Midland Review is digest-sized, 80-100 pp., with photography and ads. Circulation is 530, of which 500 are subscriptions. Price per issue is $5. **Sample available for $5 postpaid. Pay is 1 copy. Writers should submit 3-5 poems, typed MS in any form; simultaneous submissions are OK if indicated. Reporting time is 6-8 weeks and time to publication 3-6 months.**

*MIDSTREAM: A MONTHLY JEWISH REVIEW (IV, Jewish themes), 515 Park Ave., New York, NY 10022, phone 212-752-0600, poetry editor Joel Carmichael, is a magazine-sized, 64 pp., flat-spined national journal, circulation 10,000, appearing monthly except June/July and August/September, when it is bimonthly. It uses **short poems with Jewish themes or atmosphere.** They have published poetry by Yehuda Amichai, Albert Memmi and Else Lasker-Schüler. The editors selected these lines by L. M. Rosenberg as a sample:

> *The angel of death flies slower*
> *in his eternal circle. Blown weakly in,*
> *he closes the door, locks it, sits, and begins*
> *to drain the dark wine brimming at the empty place.*

Subscription: $15; per issue: $2. They receive about 300 submissions per year, use 5%. **Sample: free. No query. Reports in 1 month. Pays $25 per poem.**

MIDWEST ARTS & LITERATURE, SHEBA REVIEW, INC. (II, IV, Regional), Box 1623, Jefferson City, MO 65102, founded 1978 (as *Sheba Review*, name changed 1981), poetry editor Sharon Kinney-Hanson, is a tabloid (and sometime chapbook) appearing irregularly as an effort "to promote writers and artists in the Midwest." They want "no erotica/porno, generally do not publish long/lengthy epic poems." Prefer poems of one page up to 3 pp. double-spaced. "We try to utilize the work of people living and working in the Midwest." They have published many known and unknown poets such as Alice G. Brand, Mona Van Duyn, Pamela Hadas, Joan Yeagley, Pete Simpson and Charles Guenther. The editor selected these sample lines from "Photo from the Times" by Jane Schapiro:

> For a moment forget your past
> and become a still-life poised for the camera.
> Forget you are among the ragged
> who line this city like sidewalk cracks . . .

The tabloid format on slick stock, 12 pp., circulation 500, consists of poetry, fiction and nonfiction pertaining to all the arts plus book reviews. **Sample: $3 postpaid. Submit maximum of 5 poems, double-spaced. SASE a must. Simultaneous submissions, photocopy (if dark, clear) OK. Pays 1 copy. The editor makes a personal reply with commentary as time permits.** "We are a not-for-profit service/educational/cultural corporation. We offer consultation/assistance in securing grants; function as corporate sponsor to individual writers, poets, translators, etc." Sheba Review, Inc. Occasionally publishes books—such as a guide to museums in Missouri—and will "rarely" consider submissions of book MSS. Query. Sharon Kinney-Hanson comments, "Poets should READ poetry, join writers groups, take writing classes and attend writers' conferences when possible periodically; and writers should experiment with language in order to develop voice, skill, talent."

*MIDWEST POETRY REVIEW, RIVER CITY PUBLICATIONS (V), Box 776, Rock Island, IL 61202, founded 1980, poetry editors Tom Tilford, Grace Keller and Jilian Roth, is a "subscriber-only" quarterly, with no other support than subscriptions—that is, **only subscribers ($15 per year) may submit poetry and/or enter their contests. Subscribers may also get help and criticism on one poem per month.** "We are attempting to encourage the cause of poetry and raise the level thereof by giving aid to new poets, to poets who have lapsed in their writing, and to poets who desire a wider market, by purchasing the best of modern poetry and giving it exposure through our quarterly magazine. We want **poetry from poets who feel they have a contribution to make to the reader relating to the human condition, nature, and the environment. Serious writers only are sought. No jingly verses or limericks. No restrictions as to form, length or style. Any subject is considered, if handled with skill and taste.**" They have recently published poetry by Elizabeth Hartman, Kay Harvey, Patricia Hladik, Barbara Petosky, Nancy Alden, Esther Leiper, Timothy Ward, Fritz Wolf, Peter Wessel and C. R. Mannering. The editors selected these sample lines from "Deliverance" by Pamela Pitkin (Texas—the editors identify every poet in the magazine by state):

> Choking in the wind of endless dust,
> burned earth flung skyward, never to return,
> And Papa said, pack the truck.
> We're heading west to Kansas, the land is done for, here.

The digest-sized 48 pp., saddle-stapled magazine is professionally printed in various type styles, matte card cover, some b/w art. They have quarterly and annual contests plus varied contests in each issue, with prizes ranging from $25-500 (the latter for the annual contest), with "unbiased, non-staff judges for all competitions. There are Junior Awards in the annual and quarterly contests. Paid up subscribers enter the contests without fees—but have to purchase additional subscriptions to enter more than one poem in each. **Sample: $2.50 postpaid. Subscription fee of $15 must accompany first submission. No photocopies. Reports in 2 weeks. Pays $5-500 per poem. Send SASE and $1 for guidelines.** River City Publications is not currently publishing books. The editor advises, "We are interested in serious poets, whether new or published. We will help those who wish to consider serious criticism and attempt to improve themselves. We want to see the poet improve, expand and achieve fulfillment."

*THE MIDWEST QUARTERLY (II), Pittsburg State University, Pittsburg, KS 66762, phone 316-231-7000, ext. 4317, founded 1959, poetry editor Stephen Meats, "publishes articles on any subject of contemporary interest, particularly literary criticism, political science, philosophy, education, biography, sociology, and each issue contains a **section of poetry from 0-30 pages in length.** In the past we have published poetry only in regular issues of the *Quarterly*; in spring '85, however, we published our first chapbook and may publish others (by invitation only) in the future. I am interested in **well-crafted, though not necessarily traditional poems that see nature and the self in bold combinations, from writers striving to find an expression for the ineffable, the inexplicable, the irrational, the un-**

known either in themselves or in the world around them. 60 lines or less (occasionally longer if exceptional)." They have recently published poetry by Michael Heffernan, Linda Girard, Laurie Sheck, Lolette Kuby, Ben Howard and Michael Burns. I selected these sample lines from "False Spring" by the editor, Stephen Meats:

> Each dawn, like blood
> returning again and again to the heart,
> cardinal and mate
> return to the feeder nailed to the sycamore.

The digest-sized , 130 pp., flat-spined, matte cover, magazine is professionally printed, has a circulation of 650, 600 subscriptions of which 500 are libraries. Subscription: $6; per issue: $2. "My plan is to publish all acceptances within 1 year." **Sample: $2. MSS should be typed with poet's name on each page, 10 pp. or fewer. Unsolicited poetry also published; photocopies OK; simultaneous submissions accepted, but first publication in** *MQ* **must be guaranteed. Reports in 6 weeks, usually sooner. Pays 5 copies. Send SASE for guidelines. Editor comments on rejections "if the poem or poems seem particularly promising." He says, "Keep writing; read as much contemporary poetry as you can lay your hands on; don't be discouraged by rejection."**

*MILKWEED CHRONICLE, MILKWEED EDITIONS, MOUNTAINS IN MINNESOTA SERIES, LAKES AND PRARIES SERIES (II), Box 24303, Minneapolis, MN 55424, phone 612-332-3192, founded 1979, poetry editor Emilie Buchwald. *Milkweed Chronicle* "is a journal (3 times a year) of essays and graphics designed to bring words and images together, to publish excellent work in poetry, essays and visual arts, and to act as a focal point for collaboration. Milkweed Editions are books of poetry, fiction, essays, and, in the future, artist's books. Mountains in Minnesota and Lakes and Praries are contests for chapbook publication. We want to see **poetry with an individual's voice; not derivative or imitative of a school or movement. We don't want overtly religious, political work, or poems for children or (usually) rhymed verse.**" They have recently published poetry by Michael Dennis Browne, Denise Levertov, Howard Nemerov, Philip Dacey and David Wagoner. As a sample, I selected some lines from the winning book in the Mountains in Minnesota competition, 1984, a contest to encourage collaboration between artists. Two poets, Jim Moore and Deborah Keenan, collaborated on **How We Missed Belgium**, each writing alternate poems that told a fictional story—until the last poem when each wrote alternate lines. These are the first four of that final poem, "A Different Ending":

> To come to the end is to begin
> nothing, at least for awhile, I've learned that much
> as a child learns to ask for one more story before sleep
> we have had to learn about the nightlight going out,
> footsteps down the stairs

The Milkweed Chronicle: A Journal of Poetry and Graphics, is a beautifully printed, 11x13" format, glossy cover, saddle-stapled, rich with photos and graphics, using about 30 pp. of poetry in each issue, circulation 2,000, 700 subscriptions of which 40 are libraries. Subscription: $9; per issue: $4. They receive about 4,000 submissions per year, use 180, have a 1-2 month backlog. **Sample: $4. Submit 5 poems maximum, any legible format. Reports in 2-3 months. Pays $10. For chapbook publication, query about current competitions and send no more than 5 samples, bio, publication credits. Replies to queries in 1 month, to MS (only if invited) in 2 months. Pays $300 advance, 10 copies. Send SASE for catalog and price list (and contests for the Mountains in Minnesota competition for collaborations and Lakes and Praries Series for individual chapbooks.** Emilie Buchwald advises, "Be professional; excellent quality of MS presentation. Recognize that there's lots of competition."

MINA PRESS (II), Box 854, Sebastopol, CA 95472, phone 707-829-0854, founded 1981, poetry editors Adam David Miller and Mei T. Nakano, selects MS "more for their literary merit than for their marketing value. This makes the going tough. We give particular attention to previously unpublished writers and non-mainstream writers, though we consider other works too. We reject, out of hand, MSS containing material that tends to glorify war, portray gratuitous violence, or demean a group of human beings like Third-World persons, the elderly, or women. We like children's books which convey some meaningful, learning experience, which is not all fluff and prettiness." They have recently published *Quadrille for Tigers* by the Jamaican poet Christine Craig. I selected the first stanza of "Crow Poem" from that book as a sample:

> I want so much to put
> my arms around you but
> extended they are feathered
> vanes, snapped, tatty things
> no longer curving.

Query with 5 samples and cover letter with "whatever information the writer deems pertinent." Replies to query in 1 month, to submission (if invited) in 3 months. Each poem should be on a sepa-

rate sheet. Simultaneous submissions and photocopies OK, dot-matrix no. Pays 10% royalties, 10 copies. To see a sample, order the book I mentioned: $5.95 plus 75¢ postage.

*MINAS TIRITH EVENING-STAR: THE JOURNAL OF THE AMERICAN TOLKIEN SOCI-ETY (IV, J.R.R. Tolkien), Box 277, Union Lake, MI 48085, editor Philip W. Helms, "serves as the meeting ground for the exchange of ideas and joy generated by J. R. R. Tolkien's monumental works. Each issue features a variety of art, fiction, **poetry**, scholarly research, games, reviews and columns each **directly linked to the life and/or works of the good professor. These are special poetry issues. Membership in the ATS is open to all, regardless of country of residence, and entitles one to receive the journal. Dues are $5 per annum to addresses in the U.S. and $10 elsewhere.** *Minas Tirith Evening-Star* is magazine-sized, offset from typescript with cartoon-like b/w graphics. Pays copies. The issue I examined was largely taken up with photocopies of proclamations and congratulatory letters and contained no poetry, with the possible exception of "delving" by Nancy Martsch:

> there once was a gardener named Tuck
> Who was quite a lusty young buck.
> "Rose Rowan, and Tansy,
> May, Myrtle, and Pansy,
> Each Flow'r I see I want to pluck,

MINOTAUR PRESS, *MINOTAUR, BONUS BOOKS (II), Box 4094, Burlingame, CA 94011, founded 1973, poetry editor Jim Gove. *Minotaur* is "scheduled quarterly, sometimes less frequently." It features **"contemporary poetry, some experimental (little or no 'language' poetry)—some poetry reviews (poetry scene, poet interview or book review), oriented, but far from exclusively, to San Francisco Bay Area poets and poetry. Uses contemporary free and blank verse, literate but non-literary. Classic rhymed poetry or doggerel is not wanted. We are open to all lengths, forms and styles (except classic rhymed), are not interested in separatist or bigoted material. All other subjects welcomed."** They have recently published poetry by Gerold Locklin, Paul Mariah, James Broughton, Judson Crews, Will Inman, Peter Brett and George Montgomery. As a sample I selected a complete poem by Miriam A. Cohen, "remembering Mommy alive: poem #1":

> i was told—
> to fear black men,
> & Jews are better than other people,
> & that I am a monstrosity.

The magazine is inexpensively produced, offset from typescript with card cover with b/w art, saddle-stapled, using 35-60 pp. of poetry in each issue, circulation 450, 300 subscriptions of which 20 are libraries. Subscription: $4; per copy: $1. They receive at least 500 submissions per year, use 140. **Sample: $1.50 postpaid. All forms except handwritten OK. Simultaneous submissions OK. Reports in 2 weeks minimum. No pay. Send SASE for guidelines. For chapbook publication, query with 5 samples and bio information. Chapbooks are $1 plus 50¢ postage, so buy samples.** Bonus Books is a newly reinstituted practice of distributing all chapbooks published during the year free to subscribers. Jim Gove advises, "Write about what you know, whether that knowledge be experientially gained or intellectually, emotionally. Be real."

*MIORITA (IV, Romanian), Department of Foreign Languages, Literatures and Linguistics, University of Rochester, Rochester, NY 14627, is a scholarly annual, digest-sized, 100 pp., circulation 200, focusing on **Romanian culture and using some poetry by Romanians or on Romanian themes. Sample: $5. Pays copies.**

MIRIAM PRESS, *DEROS; UP AGAINST THE WALL, *MOTHER (I, IV, Specialized, women), 6009 Edgewood Lane, Alexandria, VA 22310, phone 703-971-2219, founded 1980, poetry editor Lee-lee Schlegel. The two quarterlies are "both concerned with poetry as therapy first, literary excellence second. Our philosophy is that there are many good literary markets but few who 'help' those in trouble. *Deros:* **anything on Viet Nam and its aftermath.** *Mother:* **anything on women in crisis (we deal with the darker side here—death, rape, abuse, the frustrations of mothering/ wives, etc.).** *Deros* has recently published poetry by James Humphrey, Gerard Bufalini and Ralph Carlson. *Mother* has recently published poetry by Nita Penfold, Patrick McKinnon, Jean Youell Johnson and Ruth Wildes Schuler. Lee-lee Schlegel selected these sample poems—from *Deros*, "Ambush," by Bufalini:

> it is over in a priest's blessing
> the massacre is ended
> go in peace
> the benediction of the body count begins.

And from *Mother*, "I Am a Phoenix" by Shubb:

> I am wounded
> weary carion meat
> for my family who
> preys together.

Close-up

Judith Viorst
Poet

Artist: Lawrence Goodridge

"I am a short, plump, blonde, Methodist woman who lives on a farm in Iowa. I think you are a tall, thin, dark-haired, Jewish woman who lives on the East coast. But we live the same life." That is an excerpt from one of Judith Viorst's favorite letters and probably the most revealing clue to her success in reaching large amounts of people with her poetry.

Judith Viorst's seven slim volumes of adult verse and prose, and seven volumes of children's books have sold more than a million copies. Her light verse finds and emphasizes the humor in being a contemporary woman. As a writer, Viorst is difficult to categorize. "I am very comfortable with all the different modes of writing." In addition to poetry and children's books, Viorst writes a column for *Redbook* and recently finished a book on loss. "What I love is having a writing career that allows me to play out all the different parts of myself. I am somebody who's interested in eyeliner *and* the meaning of the universe."

Viorst's first published poems appeared in *New York Magazine* in the 60's. The magazine normally didn't publish poetry, but Viorst became their "house poet." Those poems later appeared as her first book, *The Village Square*.

For poets wanting to be published Viorst says, "Send out. Send out. Send out. You need a very strong stomach because you're going to get a lot of rejection slips." She has been submitting poetry since the age of eight. "I really didn't want to write just for myself, I wanted to make contact with those people out there."

Viorst grew up a voracious reader, something she learned from her mother. "The idea that thoughts and feelings could be put into words on a page influenced me." Eliot, Yeats and Hopkins are among some of Viorst's favorite poets, though not any one writer influenced her. I think I have set very specific goals for myself, which are on a considerably smaller scale than 'The Love Song of J. Alfred Prufrock'. Within the limits and expectations that I set for myself, I am satisfied that I have come reasonably close to fulfilling them."

Viorst works at home, as does her husband Milton, who is also a writer. Besides writing, Viorst lectures, which she keeps to a maximum of 10 times a year. She also belongs to a poetry group that reads and discusses poetry. "It puts you on your mettle and reminds you about the economy of language." Viorst thinks reading poetry is the best continuing training for poets. "You really have to be exposed to what gifted people do with words."

Inspiration for Viorst's poetry comes from life. Hers. Other people's. "I don't go to parties taking notes . . . but conversations I hear. The life stories I'm told." Viorst says she's never really had writer's block. "I was published for the first time simultaneous with being married and having my first child. So I didn't really have time for writer's block. I had to write when I had the time."

Viorst's next book of poetry will probably be in keeping with her general style and deal with the topic of "being 50." It will have more of the poetry that Viorst terms "aggravation recollected in tranquility."

—Katherine Jobst

Each issue of each digest-sized magazine has 29-52 pp. of poetry. Each has a circulation of about 500, 400 subscriptions of which 25 are libraries. They are inexpensively produced, offset from typescript, card covers with simple art. They receive about 6,000 submissions per year, use 800. **Sample: $3 for** *Mother,* $2.50 for *Deros.* **Submit 4-6 poems. Simultaneous submissions, photocopies, dot-matrix OK. Usually reports the same or next day. No pay. Send SASE for guidelines. Criticism on rejections "if requested.** I do it because I feel it's important to encourage new poets, guide them in the right direction, foster their care and feeding. We are a friendly press open to all. We are also very poor and appreciate support. Our immediate goals include being able to pay poets in copies, eventually money. Advice: 1) study your market, 2) always send SASE, 3) please don't tell me how good your poetry is!"

*****MISSISSIPPI REVIEW (II),** Box 5144, Southern Station, Hattiesburg, MS 39046, founded 1971, is a semiannual, 125-200 pp., digest-sized literary journal, circulation 1,500, which uses **quality poetry, pays copies. Sample: $4.50.**

*****MISSISSIPPI VALLEY REVIEW (II),** English Dept., Western Illinois University, Macomb, IL 61455, phone 309-298-1514, founded 1973, poetry editor John Mann, is a literary magazine published twice a year which uses **poems of high quality, no specifications as to form, length, style, subject matter or purpose.** They have recently published poetry by Susan Fromberg Schaeffer, Ralph J. Mills, Jr., Daniel J. Langton and Tony Curtis. The editor selected these sample lines by Walter McDonald:

> We'd ease down into cockpits
> wired to explode, hook up
> and pressure-test pure oxygen
> of our other planet.

MVR uses a handsomely printed, digest-sized, flat-spined, 60 + pp. format, glossy, color cover, circulation 400. Subscription: $6; per copy $3. They have about 25 pp. of poetry in each issue, receive 500-1,000 submissions per year, use about 30, and have a 6-12 month backlog. **Sample: $3 postpaid. Submit 5 pp. or less. Report in 3 months. Pays 2 copies. Editor comments on rejections "occasionally, particularly if we are interested in the MS."**

UNIVERSITY OF MISSOURI PRESS (II), 200 Lewis Hall, Columbia, MO 65211, phone 314-882-7641, founded 1958, holds a Breakthrough competition in odd-numbered years, choosing 6 MSS of poetry and short fiction by authors who have published in other media but have not had a book published. Books of poetry are eligible for the Devins Award of $500 advance against royalties. Some of the poets they have published are Harry Humes, Mary Kinzie and Jane Wayne. The winner of the Devins Award for 1983, judged by David Wagoner, was Wesley McNair, *The Faces of Americans in 1853,* from which I selected these sample lines, the opening of "Holding the Goat":

> holding the goat is when the man who appears
> to be my father is pulling a hammer
> out of the sky again
> and again and the goat is on its knees

It is a professionally printed digest-sized paperback, glossy card cover, flat-spined, 64 pp. The judge for the Breakthrough Series and Devins Award in 1985 was George Garrett. **To submit a MS in the Breakthrough competition, send SASE for rules after October 1986. Submissions accepted February and March, odd-numbered years** *only.* **Photocopy and dot-matrix OK. Reports in 3-4 months. 10% royalty contract. Send 9x12" SASE for catalog to buy samples.**

MISSOURI REVIEW (II), University of Missouri, 231 Arts & Science, Columbia, MO 65211, phone 314-882-6066, founded 1978, poetry editors Sherod Santos and Garrett Hongo, is a quality literary journal, 6x9", 250 pp., which appears 3 times a year, **buys 100 poems per year at $10 minimum per poem. Submit maximum of 6. Photocopies, dot-matrix OK. Reports in 8 weeks. Sample: $4.50.**

MR. COGITO PRESS, *MR. COGITO (II), U.C. Box 627, Pacific University, Forest Grove, OR 97116, or 3314 S.E. Brooklyn, Portland, OR 97202, founded 1973, poetry editors John M. Gogol and Robert A. Davies. *Mr. Cogito,* published 1-2 times per year, is a tall, skinny (4½x11") magazine, 24 pp. of poetry. The copy I examined was printed in a variety of type styles on blue paper. The editors want **"no prose put in lines. Yes: wit, heightened language, craft. Open to all schools and subjects and groups of poets."** They have published poetry by Peter Wild, Patrick Worth Gray, Norman H. Russell and Ryszard Krynicki. As a sample the editors selected these lines from "The Three Kings" by Stanislaw Baranczak

> . . . as bewildered as a new-born babe,
> you'll open the door. There will flash
> the star of authority.
> Three men. In one of them you'll recognize . . .

They use both poems in English and translation, "preferably representing each poet with several poems." The magazine has a circulation of 400, sells for $1.50 a copy. **Sample: $1. Submit 4-5 poems. Simultaneous submissions and photocopies OK. Pays copies.** Mr. Cogito Press publishes collections by poets they invite from among those who have appeared in the magazine. Send SASE for catalog to buy samples. They also make the Pacific Northwest Translation Award and conduct special theme contests. The editors advise, "Subscribe to a magazine that seems good. Read ours before you submit. Write, write, write."

‡*MOCKERSATZ ZROX (II), 104 Woodgate Ct., Sterling, VA 22170-1630, phone 703-430-7021, founded 1984, editor Zen Sutherland, a "very irregular" magazine that publishes language oriented poetry and reviews of small press material. The editor wants **"a wide variety of content and form of expression. Length varies, but prefer less than 40 lines. Subject matter is diverse, from clean teeth to pedophilia, as long as valid. Prefer even surreal material."** He does not want **"self-conscious nature poems, 'the world is neat & snappy' poems, pornography for its own sake."** He has recently published Todd Moore, Don Wentworth, Tony Moffeit, Kyle Laws, and Ron Androla. As a sample I chose the following entire poem by Edward Mycue (with / for line breaks):

> Just looking into the wind/ Twilight/ Endeavor/ Cheers/
> Momentum/ Military Music/ Heroes/ Flesh offered-up/
> Resources spent/ Starvation/ Wounds/ Wonderful Music/
> Heroes/ Cheers/ Endeavor/ Twilight/
> Just looking into the wind

The publication is magazine-sized, photocopied from typed copy on paper with b/w illustrations, 40 pp. side-stapled, matte card cover. Author's name is not printed with the poems but a few lines about each writer are usually given in "Contrib Notes" at the back of the book. The magazine appears "1-2 times a year"; circulation is 150-250, single copy price $1, subscriptions are being phased out." **Sample is "free for postage" ($1), guidelines available for SASE. Pay is an unspecified number of copies. "Photocopy, dot-matrix, handwritten, simultaneous submissions (if mentioned up front), all acceptable." Reporting time is 2 weeks-2 months,** and time to publication varies. The press also publishes 3-4 small poetry chapbooks/year, digest-sized, 6-12 pp., saddle-stapled, matte card covers with b/w illustrations. **Writers should query first, sending 5 sample poems and bio. Queries will be answered in 2 weeks-1 month. Pays is 10-12 author's copies. Book catalog is free on request for #10 SASE; sample book available for "2 regular [Canadian] postage stamps.** The editor says, "As a poet you *have* your vision. This is a large, wonderful world; find an editor who shares your vision, talk and listen closely to him/her."

*MODERN BRIDE (IV, Marriage, love), 1 Park Ave., New York, NY 10016, a slick bimonthly, occasionally buys **poetry pertaining to love and marriage. Pays $20-30 for average short poem.**

*MODERN HAIKU (IV, Style), Box 1752, Madison, WI 53701, founded 1969, poetry editor Robert Spiess, "is the foremost international journal of English language haiku and criticism. It has received 3 consecutive award-grants for excellence from the National Endowment for the Arts and is considered by several Japanese persons knowledgeable in haiku [e.g., Kazuo Sato of the International Division of the Museum of Haiku Literature in Tokyo—ed.] to be the best English language haiku magazine. It is the only currently published English language haiku magazine to be cited in the 'Haiku' entry in the new 9 volume English language **Kodansha Encyclopedia of Japan.** We are devoted to publishing only the very best haiku being written and also publish articles on haiku and have the most complete review section of haiku books. The magazine is illustrated with many ink brush paintings." They use **haiku only. No tanka or other forms. "We publish all 'schools' of haiku, but want the haiku to elicit intuition, insight, felt-depth."** They have published haiku by Alexis Rotella, LeRoy Gorman, Geraldine Little and Johnny Baranski. The editor selected this sample (poet unidentified):

> Becoming dusk—
> the catfish on the stringer
> swims up and down

The digest-sized magazine appears 3 times a year, printed on heavy quality stock with interior and cover illustrations especially painted for each issue by the staff artist. There are 44-50 pp. of poems in each issue, circulation 565. Subscription: $9.65; per copy: $3.45. They receive 15,000-16,000 freelance submissions per year, use 700. **Sample: $3.45 postpaid. Submit on "any size sheets, any number of haiku on a sheet; but name and address on each sheet." Reports in 2 weeks. Pays $1 per haiku (but no contributor's copy). Send SASE for guidelines.** The editor "frequently" comments on rejected MSS. Robert Spiess says, "In regard to haiku, Daisetz T. Szuki said it succinctly well: 'A haiku does not express ideas but puts forward images reflecting intuitions.' "

*MODERN MATURITY (IV, Senior citizen), American Association of Retired Persons, 3200 E. Carson St., Lakewood, CA 90712. Editor-in-Chief Ian Ledgerwood, is a slick bimonthly magazine, circulation 13,700,000, going to the membership of the AARP ($5 per year, which includes subscription). They use **poetry up to 40 lines appropriate for their readership of persons over 50. Pays $50 + . Send 9x12 SASE for free sample and guidelines.** I selected this sample, the opening lines of "Commitment" by Polly Thornton (a poem which happens to be 45 lines, in spite of limit indicated):

> You lie beside
> My restless form, asleep.
> I am no bride. You wed me long
> Ago and now you snore
> And lay your arm
> As you have done
> So many times before
> Around my waist. You really are
> An ordinary man . . .

‡*MOMENT MAGAZINE, JEWISH EDUCATIONAL VENTURES, INC., (III)**, Suite 301, 462 Boylston St., Boston, MA 02116, phone 617-536-6252, founded 1975, assistant editor Josh Gamson, **is a monthly of Jewish politics, art, culture, and education which uses fiction and occasional poetry. The poetry should have "Jewish subject matter—though we occasionally accept poems without** *explicit* Jewish content. Open to differing styles and lengths and forms. Must be a *new* presentation, perhaps a surprising one. No cliches." They have recently published poems of Yehuda Amichai and S. Y. Agnon. The editor selected these sample lines:

> What are we doing in this dark land that casts
> yellow shadows slashing our eyes . . .
> shed blood is not tree roots,
> but it's the closest to them that man can come

The magazine—sized monthly is professionally printed, 64 pp., glossy color paper cover, b/w art inside, circulation 30,000, with 26,000 subscriptions of which 300 are libraries. $2.95 per copy, subscription $27. **Sample: $3.83 postpaid. Pays varied rates and 2 copies—or more on request. Reports in 6-8 weeks publishes in 1-6 months. Editor sometimes comments on rejected MSS.**

MONITOR BOOK COMPANY, INC., ANTHOLOGY OF MAGAZINE VERSE & YEARBOOK OF AMERICAN POETRY (II), Box 3668, Beverly Hills, CA, phone 213-271-5558, founded 1950, poetry editor Alan F. Pater. The annual **Anthology** is a selection of the **best poems published in American magazines during the year and is also a basic reference work for poets.** Alan F. Pater says, "We want poetry that is 'readable' and in any poetic form; we also want translations. All material must first have appeared in magazines. Any subject matter will be considered; we also would like to see some rhyme and meter, preferably sonnets." They have recently published poetry by Margaret Atwood, Richard Eberhart, Stanley Kunitz, Stephen Spender, William Stafford, Robert Penn Warren and Richard Wilbur. Indeed, the anthology is a good annual guide to the best poets actively publishing in any given year. For the most part selections are made by the editor from magazines, but some poets are solicited for their work which has been in magazines in a given year. The 1985 edition, 736 large pp, is listed at $35.95.

‡**MOONSQUILT PRESS (V)**, 16401 NE 4th Ave., N. Miami Beach, FL 33162, phone 305-947-9534, founded 1977, editor Michael Hettich, a small-press publisher of poetry chapbooks. The press publishes **"poetry concerned with tradition, though not necessarily 'traditional'." However, they do not accept freelance submissions.** The press, which issues one chapbook per year, has published books by Stephen Sandy and Burton Raffel. Their chapbooks are saddle-stapled paperbacks with an average page count of 30. **Pay is 50 author's copies.** All books are priced at $3.

‡**MOSAIC PRESS (IV)**, 358 Oliver Rd., Cincinnati, OH 45215, phone 513-761-5977, poetry editor Miriam Irwin. The press publishes fine hardbound small books (under 3" tall); **they want "interesting topics beautifully written in very few words—a small collection of short poems on one subject." The editor does not want to see haiku.** She has recently published collections by Robert Hoeft and Marilyn Francis; the following lines, selected by her, are from "The Tin Snips" by Robert Hoeft:

> A metal woodpecker
> jaws like sharpened sin
> harmless to lumber
> nemesis to tin.

The sample miniature book the editor sent is **Water and Windfalls**, by Marilyn Francis, illustrated by Mada Leach. It is ⅝x⅞", flat-spined (⅛" thick), an elegantly printed and bound hardback, with colored endpapers and gold lettering on spine and front cover. The press publishes 1 book per year, average page count 64. **She does accept freelance submissions but the writer should query first, sending 3** or more sample poems and "whatever you want to tell me." She says, "We don't use pseudonyms." Simultaneous submissions are OK, as are photocopied and dot-matrix MSS, although she doesn't like the latter. Payment is in author's copies (5 for a whole collection or book) plus a $50 honorarium. She pays $2.50 plus 1 copy for single poems. Criticism will be provided only if requested and "then only if we have constructive comments. If work is accepted, be prepared to wait patiently; some of our books take 4 years to complete." The press publishes private editions but does not call it subsidy publishing. A catalog is free for SASE, and a writer can get on the mailing list for $3. The editor advises, "Type neatly, answer letters, return phone calls, include SASE."

MOSAIC PRESS, VALLEY EDITIONS (IV, Canadian authors), Box 1032, Oakville, Ontario, Canada L6J 5E9, phone 416-825-2130, founded 1974, poetry editor Mike Walsh, publishes some of the finest and most established authors in Canada—**but primarily Canadian authors because they receive assistance from Canada Council and Ontario Arts Council to encourage writing in Canada.** Mike Walsh wants **"no concrete or experimental, illogical, self-indulgent crap. Poetry with craft and a serious purpose."** He has published poetry by **Irving Layton, R. A. D. Ford, Anne Marriott, Patrick Lane** and **Seymour Mayne. I selected these sample lines from "The Desert," one of the T. E. Lawrence Poems** (in which Lawrence is imagined to be speaking) by Gwendolyn MacEwen:

> Only God lives there in the seductive Nothing
> That implodes into pure light. English makes Him
> an ugly monosyllable, but Allah breathes
> A fiery music from His tongue, ignites the sands, invents a terrible love that is
> The very name of pain.

Query with no samples but a letter giving bio, publication credits, personal or aesthetic philosophy, poetic goals and principles. Replies to queries in 1 month, to submissions (if invited) in 3. MS should be typed, double-spaced. Photocopies OK. Publishes on royalty contract (6-10%) plus 5-10 copies. Send SASE for catalog to buy samples.

MOTHER DUCK PRESS, BISBEE PRESS COLLECTIVE (IV, Invitation/Southwest authors, environment), Box 25A, Rt. 1, McNeal, AZ 85617, founded 1975, editor Michael Gregory, **"publishing poetry, art and prose by environmentally-oriented Southwest authors, at present by invitation only.** We have published works by Lawrence Ferlinhetti; Bisbee poets Michael Gregory, Jon Horn, Elizabeth Thornton and Chris Dietz; Richard Nonas; and two anthologies of Bisbee poets. Write for more information."

‡MOTHER OF ASHES PRESS, *THE VILLAGE IDIOT (I), Box 135, Harrison, ID 83833, phone 208-689-3738, press founded 1980, magazine 1970, "poet-in-residence" Joe M. Singer. *The Village Idiot*, an irregular periodical," prints "poems, pictures, stories, technical articles on graphic arts for the small press, miscellaneous nonsense." **The only specification for poetry is that it should "breathe." The poet-in-residence does not want to see "dead poetry."** He has recently published poems by Annalee Wade, Bagla Winters, and Don Chotro. As a sample, he chose the following lines by Darlene McGregor:

> The way to begin is to begin
> the way to write is to write
> tell a story
> tell a Darlene story tonight

Mr. Singer refused to categorize his magazine, saying "I am not familiar enough with the contemporary poetry 'scene' to know who is being published and who is not. And I have absolutely no regard whether a poet is developing a list of publication credits. In fact, I have very little regard whatsoever for poets—only for poems. I try to treat the poem's authors with some basic human consideration, but what the magazine publishes is poetry, not poets"; I have therefore put it in category I. The sample of *The Village Idiot* I have seen is digest-sized, rather fuzzily offset on photocopy paper (folded and saddle-stapled) from copy typed with a fabric ribbon, with b/w drawings, photos of Ronald Reagan, and a botanical illustration of male and female marijuana plants. Mr. Singer expresses appreciation to several people for help in preparing the edition, which took from October 1982 through October 1984; it is called the "Poetic Justice" edition. Circulation is 80, price per issue $3.50, subscription (for 5-7 editions) $16.50. **Sample available for $3.50 postpaid; pay is "nominal" plus 1 or 2 copies. Submission information is: "Keep it simple, legible, and manageable." Reporting time is "within 3 months,"** and time to publication is, obviously, variable.

‡*MOUNTAIN CAT REVIEW, MOUNTAIN CAT PRESS, (II), #1, 14 Washington, Denver, CO 80203, founded 1976 as Society for the Advancement of Poetics, editor Jess Graf. Mountain Cat Press is the sponsor of readings in Denver and publishes chapbooks, occasional broadsheets, and an irregularly published ("when material dictates") review. The editor wants **"variety of style but usually short,**

compact, 'fresh lines' " He does not want "lame, stale self-pity, religious, party line, women's, men's, anyone's movement except human." He has recently published Frankie Rios, Tony Scibella, James Ryan Morris, John Loquides, and himself. As a sample, he selected the following lines by Stuart Z. Perkhoff:

> turned loose in the streets
> we eat the earth itself in
> search of visions
> earth tastes like 50 million years

The *Mountain Cat Review* publishes poetry and reviews of books of poetry; size varies from a few pages to 30 or so; circulation is under 100. **Sample: $4 postpaid. Pay is 1-5 free copies. MSS are reported on "sometimes quick, sometimes never." The editor says, "I have never requested submissions but I get stuff anyway. I am not commercial, obviously. I gotta know them [poets] and their work real well. The sounds of falseness only serve to discourage me. I will try not to pass those things on to anyone who reads my stuff, as editor or as poet."** He publishes no more than one chapbook a year, about 40 pp., paperback, saddle-stapled, offset from typed copy. The sample I have seen is printed on buff stock with plain black matte card cover and blue dust jacket with art work. The editor advises, "Read your work in public a couple of times a year and never turn down a request to publish your work."

THE MOUNTAIN LAUREL (I, IV, Traditional, nostalgic), Rt. 1, Meadows of Dan, VA 24120, founded 1983, poetry editor Susan Thigpen. "We are a monthly journal in newspaper format of mountain life preserving the day-to-day history of the Blue Ridge. **We want traditional style poetry, nothing crude—short poems to fit the mountain, nostalgic format**." The editor selected these sample lines from "Drinkin' Tea with Mabel," by Diana J. Felts:

> He ain't much for lookin' back
> (things don't change by wishin')
> Still, sometimes, when he's alone
> In the fields or fishin'
> What he wouldn't give to be
> Settin' at the table,
> Tellin' jokes and swappin' lies,
> Drinking tea with Mabel.

"We are geared to articles but occasionally include a poem, but it really has to fit and really has to be good by our standards. We publish less and less poetry because most doesn't fit our needs. We like **old fashioned sentimental verse, but 'corn-ball' doesn't stand a chance. We like truth, honesty, well-expressed human feelings—nothing vague or abstract.**" The tabloid has a circulation of 25,000 wholesale distributed in 6 states—subscribers in every state, Canada and several foreign countries, sells for 75¢ a copy. Send for sample. They get about a thousand poems submitted each year, take 1 out of 200, have a year's backlog. They want traditional/rhyming poems with good cadence. Reports within month. Pays copies. The editor "practically always" comments on rejections.

*MS. MAGAZINE (IV, Feminist), 119 W. 40th St., New York, NY 10018, phone 212-719-9800, editor Yvonne, is "for women and men; varying ages, backgrounds, but committed to exploring new lifestyles and changes in their roles and society." Monthly, circulation 450,000. **"We do read unsolicited MSS: poetry, fiction, and nonfiction articles or profiles . . . Send MSS to Manuscript Reader and indicate on envelope what type of piece is being submitted. Accepts only 1 in 1,000 unsolicited MSS. Pays on acceptance, competitive magazine rates. Publishes an average of 4 months after acceptance."**

MULTIPLES PRESS, *MULTIPLES (II), 1821 S. 4th West, Missoula, MT 59801, phone 406-543-6502, founded 1982, poetry editors Paul S. Piper and Bill Borneman: "We are dedicated to **experimental and investigative poetics of all styles, poetry that explores its origin and definition. We are not interested in poetry which is content to languish in past definitions or clichés. 3 pages of any one artist is about all we will print.**" They have recently published poetry by Clayton Eshleman, Tom Clark, Charles Bernstein, Jed Rasula, Anne Waldman and Clark Coolidge. As a sample the editors selected these lines by Michael Palmer:

> All those Words we once used
> For things but have now discarded
> in order to come to know things.

Multiples started as *Zetesis* in 1981. It appears 1-2 times per year, magazine-sized, 30-40 pp., innovative designs and covers, 30-40 pp. of poetry in each issue, circulation 200, 50 subscriptions of which 2 are libraries. Subscription: $12 for 3 issues; per issue: $3. They receive a hundred submissions per year, use about 5 have a 6-8 month backlog. **Sample: $3 postpaid. Submit with "brief explanation of why you are writing the stuff." Reports in 2-6 weeks, no pay.**

‡**MUNDUS ARTIUM PRESS (IV, Translations)**, Box 688, University of Texas/Dallas, Richardson TX 75080, phone 214-690-2092, founded 1968, director Rainer Schulte, a small-press publisher of **international poetry in translation of younger poets; all are first English publications.** The number of books published each year varies; they are 6x9'' flat-spined paperbacks. **Freelance submissions are accepted, but writers should query before submitting. Queries will be answered in "weeks" and MSS reported on in "months." No simultaneous submissions. Photocopied or dot-matrix MSS are acceptable. Pay is 10-20 author's copies plus an honorarium that depends on project and grant funding.**

*MUSCADINE (I, IV, Mature)**, 1111 Lincoln Place, Boulder, CO 80302, phone 303-443-9748, founded 1977, poetry editor Lucille Cyphers, is a magazine with the aim "**to awaken or reawaken creativity in old people, so we limit our publication of works of professional writers. They have to compete much harder for spaces. We turn 'prose poems' into prose and put it in the general section—100-150 words. Poetry must be understandable by old people. Brief. Not trite.**" They have recently published poetry by Grace Scott, Jean Kalmanoff and Harold Chambers. The editor selected these sample lines by Irene Palmer:

> She threads a colored ribbon
> Through the liquid drops of heaven
> And paints a glorious pattern in the sky;
> Soon she tires of this diversion

Muscadine appears 6 times a year, magazine-sized, 24 pp., inexpensively produced—offset from typescript on paper of various colors, colored paper cover, simple art throughout, circulation 400. They receive 800 submissions per year, use 90, usually with a backlog of 4 months. **Sample: $1.25 postpaid. "Poets must be 60 years old. We want an honest view of the whole of life—no subjects are banned (if in good taste). Multiple submissions OK. Very little use for narrative poems. MSS need not be typed. We report in 2 weeks. Pays in copies. Priority is given to unpublished writers. We 'tutor' a lot through the mail."** The editor advises, "Use short, concise forms, use images, including other senses besides sight. Don't explain (show, don't tell). Find a direct treatment of the subject in common language. The cadence should fit the mood of the line. In *Muscadine* space limits the way we respace the poem.

*MUSE'S BREW POETRY REVIEW (II)**, Box 9484, Forestville, CT 06010, founded 1983, poetry editor Kathy Raymond, is a semiannual, digest-sized, 28 pp., poetry magazine, circulation 200, which wants "**poetry that can be read and understood by the general public, as well as college professors. High-quality free verse and original adaptations of traditional forms are preferred.** Radical departures from free verse result in too many unsuccessful, obscure arrangements of words. Most experimental poetry demonstrates that writers do not know the difference between poetry and amateur graphic design. **No restriction on length but a poem over 75 lines better nearly measure up to 'The Love Song of J. Alfred Prufrock.' All types of personal poems, political poems welcome. The editor reserves the right to publish material promoting liberalism and human rights. I believe good political poems are very effective picket signs. Readers mustn't only seek entertainment or escape—they should get fired up enough to want to change the things they don't like."** Pays 1 copy per printed page.

‡*MUSIC WORKS (IV, Musical themes)**, 1087 Queen St. W., Toronto, Ontario, Canada M6J 1H3, phone 416-533-0192, founded 1978, managing editor Tina Pearson, a tabloid quarterly journal of contemporary music. The editor says, "**The poetry we publish usually directly relates to the musical themes we are dealing with—almost always it is poetry written by the (music) composer we are featuring.**" None of their recently published poets are known as poets; the composers were Murray Schafer, Pauline Oliveros, and John Cage. The tabloid paper is published on newsprint, 22 pp., with b/w visuals, b/w photography, some illustrative graphics and scores. Circulation is 550, of which 350 are subscriptions. Price is $2.50/issue or $6.50 for the paper plus cassette. **Sample: $2.50 postpaid. The paper pays Canadian contributors $20-50 per contribution plus 2-3 free copies. They report on submissions within 1 month, and there is no backlog before publication.**

THE MYTHOPOEIC SOCIETY, *MYTHLORE, MYTHPRINT, MYTHELLANY, MYTHOPOEIC FANTASY AWARD, MYTHOPOEIC SCHOLARSHIP AWARD (IV), 740 S. Hobart Blvd., Los Angeles, CA 90005, phone 213-384-9420, founded 1967, poetry editor Ruth Berman. The Society is "a literary and educational organization devoted to the study, discussion, and enjoyment of all the **works of J. R. R. Tolkien, C. S. Lewis, and Charles Williams.** It believes these writers can more completely be understood and appreciated by studying the realm of myth; the genre of fantasy; and the literary, philosophical, and spiritual traditions which underlie their work, and which they have drawn from and enriched." Send SASE for brochure, price list and more detailed description of the various publications. Several use poetry **relevant to the purposes of the society. "No limit on form or length."** They have recently published poetry by Marilyn Jurich, Alice P. Kinney, Joe R. Christopher, Darryl Schweitzer and Martha Benedict. The editor selected these sample lines (poet unidentified):

> They live within their storied rhyme,
> Untarnished and untouched by time
> But we are born, we live, we die—
> The faintest breath, a wistful sigh

Mythlore, a quarterly, uses 3-4 pp. of poetry per issue, 800 subscriptions of which 20% are libraries. They receive 15-30 freelance subscriptions per year, use 6-10, have a 6 month backlog. **Sample: $3.50 postpaid. Reports in 1 month. No pay. Editor sometimes comments on rejected MSS.**

NADA PRESS, *BIG SCREAM (II), 2782 Sixie SW, Grandville, MI 49418, phone 616-531-1442, founded 1974, poetry editor David Cope, *Big Scream* is **"a brief anthology of mostly 'unknown' poets**, 2 times per year. Nada press publishes also 1-2 yearly chapbooks. We are promoting a continuation of objectivist tradition begun by Williams & Reznikoff. We want objectivist-based short works; some surrealism; basically short tight work that shows clarity of perception and care in its making. Also poems in Spanish—*not* **translations."** They have published poetry by Antler, James Ruggia, Richard Kostelanetz, Andy Clausen and Janet Cannon. As a sample David Cope selected some lines of his own:

> an old blind black vet blows
> "Camptown Races" *on his harp,*
> stomping his one foot in time;
> another, legless, claps his hands

Big Scream is 35 pp., magazine-sized, mimeo on 60 lb. paper, side-stapled, "sent gratis to a select group of poets and editors; **sample copies $2**; subscriptions to institutions $5 per year." He has a print run of 100. He receives "several hundred (not sure)" freelance submissions per year, uses "very few." **Submit 10 pp. Simultaneous submissions OK. Reports in 1-14 days. Pays copies. To submit chapbook MS, query first with 10-15 samples. No cover letter. "If poetry interests me, I will ask the proper questions of the poet." No dot-matrix. Pays as many copies as requested. Order sample chapbooks $2 each. Comments on rejections "if requested and MS warrants it."** David Cope advises: "Read Pound's essay, "A Retrospect," then Reznikoff and Williams; follow through the Beats and NY School, especially Denby & Berrigan, and you have our approach to writing well in hand. I expect to be publishing *BS* regularly 10 years from now, same basic format."

*NAKED MAN (II), % Mike Smetzer, English Dept., Kansas University, Lawrence, KS 66045, founded 1981, poetry editor Mike Smetzer, "is a one-editor operation and reflects my interests rather than those of any group or school. I prefer to present **several poems by each poet when possible.** Contributors receive proofs. I have eclectic tastes but **most often respond to suggestive images, distinctive insights, or humor. I dislike poetic posing, stock sentiments, and simplistic rhyming. Give me something fresh."** He has recently published poetry by Victor Contoski, Jared Carter, Michael Lassell, Philip St. Clair, J. B. Goodenough and David Rice. As a sample he selected some lines from "First Sunday in Advent," by Vanessa Furse:

> Our trail moved between two waters.
> Kingfishers ran the sky upon their backs
> along the mirrorlight.
> A huddle of geese rested stiffly on the stones.

The digest-sized 48 pp., saddle-stapled, matte card cover with simple art, offset from typescript, appears irregularly, uses 20 pp. of poetry in each issue, circulation 250-400. Subscription: $8.50 for 4 issue; per copy: $2.50. He receives about 1500 freelance poems per year, uses 10-20, has a 2-12 month backlog. **Sample: $2. No query. Photocopies ok. Simultaneous submissions must be identified as such. Reports in 2-3 weeks, pays 2 copies.**

‡*NANCY'S MAGAZINE (I), 336 E. Torrence Rd., Columbus, OH 43214, founded 1983, editor Nancy Kangas, who describes her product as a "variety magazine." **She wants to see "short, experimental, everyday life, rhythmic" poetry, but not "Christian, pornographic, lengthy."** She has recently published poems by Pat Reed and Jessica Grim, and she chose the following lines from "Dog Tired" (poet unidentified) as a sample:

> The trick is to find a corner
> that hasn't been marked
> A naked one with rubbery white
> paint strokes frozen fresh

Nancy says that her magazine is "often thematic" (the sample I have is called "The Mood Issue") and "leaning towards literary (without ever getting there)." It is 7x8½", 36 pp., offset from various sizes of photoreduced copy (some of it upside down), with b/w drawings on light blue paper (except for a "polyester pull-out," which is on yellow). Cover is the same weight paper—color, mauve with orange illustration—saddle-stapled. Frequency is twice a year, circulation 350, of which 50-75 are newsstand sales. Price is $1/issue. **Sample available for $1 postpaid, guidelines for SASE. Pay is 1 copy. "No dotmatrix." Submissions will be reported on in 1 month and time to publication is 6 months maximum.** The editor's advice is: "Just keep writing. Don't be discouraged about magazines not publishing your stuff—it's all a matter of finding the right one."

‡*THE NATION (III), 72 Fifth Ave., New York NY 10011, founded 1865, poetry editor Grace Schulman. *The Nation* is an old-line, highly respected, national weekly magazine that is politically oriented with a liberal slant. **Their only requirement for poetry is "excellence,"** which can be inferred from the list of poets they have recently published: W.S. Merwin, Maxine Kumin, Donald Justice, James Merrill, Richard Howard, May Swenson, and Amy Clampitt (and, not so recently, Judson Jerome). **Pay for poetry is 1 copy.** The magazine co-sponsors the Leonore Marshall/Nation Prize for Poetry which is an annual award of $7,500 for the outstanding book of poems published in the U.S. in each year; and the "Discovery"/ The Nation Prizes ($200 each plus a reading at The Poetry Center, 1395 Lexington Ave., New York, NY 10128 (submit up to 500 lines by mid-February. (See under Contests and send SASE for rules and application).

‡NBJ, *LA NOUVELLE BARRE DU JOUR (IV, French), C.P. 131, Outremont, Quebec, Canada H2V 4M8, phone 514-653-8372, founded 1965, director Michel Gay, a small-press publisher of poetry chapbooks (15 titles yearly) and a periodical (24 issues yearly). The editor wants to see **"5-10 pages modern or post-modern poetry (in French)."** He has recently published Nicole Brossard, Normand de Bellefeuille, and Maurice Roche. The magazine, *La Nouvelle Barre du Jour*, is digest-sized, with 32, 48, 64, or 96 pp., offset flat-spined, with graphics. It is published 3 times monthly in each of 8 months. Circulation is 600-800, of which 300 are subscriptions and 65% of those go to libraries. There are 200 newsstands sales. Price per issue is $4.50 (Candian), subscription $45 (Canadian). **No samples or guidelines available. Pay averages $5/page plus 3-4 copies. Submissions are reported on in 4 weeks and time to publication is 6 months.** Poetry chapbooks have an average page-count of 24, handsomely printed, with graphics, glossy card covers, flat-spined. **Writers should send 4-5 sample poems with bio and publication credits. Queries will be answered in 3 weeks and MSS reported on in 4 weeks; photocopied MSS are OK. Honorarium for chapbooks averages $50 Canadian.**

*NEBO: A LITERARY JOURNAL (II), English Dept., Arkansas Tech University, Russellville, AR 72801, founded 1982, poetry editor Paul Lake, is a digest-sized 60pp. biannual, circulation 500, which uses **quality poetry. Sample: $1.**

*THE NEBRASKA REVIEW (II), ASH 212, University of Nebraska, Omaha, NE 68182-0324, phone 402-554-2771, founded 1973, co-editor Art Homer, a semi-annual literary magazine publishing fiction and poetry with occasional essays. The editor wants **"Lyric poetry from 10-200 lines, preference being for under 100 lines. Subject matter is unimportant, as long as it has some. Poets should have mastered form, meaning poems should have form, not simply 'demonstrate' it."** He doesn't want to see **"concrete, inspirational, poesa vivsa, didactic, merely political."** He has recently published poetry by Dave Etter, Peter Wild, William Kloefkorn, Carol Ann Russell, Richard Robbins, and Candace Black. As a sample, he selected the following lines from "Moonlight Caves In" by David Henson:

> . . . *she folds snapping*
> *sweaters that bristle*
> *the soft, clear hairs on her arms,*
> *breaks his ankles*
> *in a dozen pairs of socks*

The magazine is 6x9", nicely printed, 60 pp. flat-spined (but the glue doesn't hold), glossy card cover with b/w illustration on green. It is a publication of the Writer's Workshop at the University of Nebraska and it was formerly called *Smackwarm*; it retains the volume and issue number of that publication. Circulation is 400, of which 80 are subscriptions and 20 go to libraries. Price per issue is $3.50, subscription $6/year. **Sample available for $2 postpaid. Pay is 2 copies and 1-year subscription. "Clean typed copy strongly preferred. Dot-matrix strongly discouraged." Reporting time is 3-4 months and time to publication is 3-6 months.** The editor says, "Your first allegiance is to the poem. Publishing will come in time, but it will always be less than you feel you deserve. Therefore, don't look to publication as a reward for writing well; it has no relationship."

*NEGATIVE CAPABILITY, NEGATIVE CAPABILITY PRESS (II), 6116 Timberly Rd. N, Mobile, AL 36609, founded 1981, poetry editor Sue Walker. *Negative Capability* is a quarterly of verse, fiction, commentary, music and art. The press publishes broadsides, chapbooks, perfect-bound paper-backs and hardbacks. They want **both contemporary and traditional poetry. "Quality has its own specifications—length and form."** They have recently published Betty Adcock, W.D. Snodgrass, Andrew Glaze, Helen Norris, Leon Driskell and Eugene Walter. Sue Walker selected these lines from "Deserters", by William Stafford:

> At first the old people hesitate—
> time scares them; they fear to go back.
> But necessary jobs have been faced before,
> that's how they have survived.

The editor says, "Reaching irritably after a few facts will not describe *Negative Capability.* Read it to know what quality goes to form creative achievement. Shakespeare had negative capability; do you?" In its short history this journal has indeed achieved a major prominence on our literary scene. It is a flat-spined, elegantly printed, digest-sized, 150+ pp. format, glossy card color cover with art, circulation 1,000. About 60 pp. of each issue are devoted to poetry. Subscription: $12; per copy: $3.50. They receive about 6,000 freelance submissions per year, use 250. **Sample: $3.50 postpaid. Reports in 4-6 weeks. Pays 2 copies. Send SASE for guidelines. For book publication, query with 10-12 samples and "brief letter with major publications, significant contributions, awards. We like to know a person as well as their poem." Replies to queries in 3-4 weeks, to submissions (if invited) in 6-8 weeks. Photocopy, dot-matrix OK. Payment arranged with authors. Editor sometimes comments on rejections.** They offer an Annual Eve of St. Agnes Competition with major poets and judges.

‡*NEOPHYTES (I),** Box 22, RR #7, Anderson, IN 46011, founded 1985, poetry editor Nancy Pope, aims **"to publish poets (new and publishing) and provide communication between them." It is a newsletter (photocopied from reduced typescript on colored paper, stapled at the corner) which appears 6 times a year.** Only subscribers may submit, and anyone who subscribes may have 3 poems published—each 1 page maximum, typed. Anything not in bad taste. Names and addresses are published with the poems to encourage comments and communication. **Sample: $1; subscription $6. As the intention is "to help poets make new friends" the newsletter prints letters, comments and articles on poetry as well as the poems.** Nancy Pope says, "Poets have a *need* to have their poetry published. **Neophytes** helps fulfill this need. I receive comments from subscribers saying, 'I got a card from _____ today, they said how much they liked my poem _____. It really made my day. Printing our address with our poems is a great idea—thanks.' "

*NEW AGE JOURNAL (II),** 342 Western Ave., Brighten, MA 02135, phone 617-787-2005, is a monthly magazine, covering "contemporary thought and lifestyle. Readership currently exceeds 400,000. Publishes poetry occasionally." Send SASE with submission.

‡*NEW CICADA (IV, Haiku),** % Tadao Okazaki, 40-11 Kubo, Hobara, Fukushima, Japan 960-06, phone 0245-75-4226, founded 1984, editor Tadao Okazaki. *New Cicada* is "the only Japanese publisher of English language haiku poetry magazine." **Haiku poems must be no longer than 3 lines with subject matter of nature or man and nature. The editor does not want "plain humor, pornography, hatred, concrete poems, or moods or feelings explained or expressed in direct words."** He has recently published haikus by Cor van den Heuvel, Teijo Nakumura, Lorraine Ellis Harr, Atsuchi Azumi, Catherine M. Buckaway, and Seishi Yamaguchi. As a sample, he chose the following by an unidentified poet:

> I will take a nap
> in this heavy shower of white
> mountain cherry petals.

The purpose of the magazine, which appears twice yearly in March and September, is "to raise the quality of haiku in English, and to let the public understand what a true classical haiku is." Volumes 1 through 5 were published in Toronto, Canada, by Eric W. Amann, founding editor. The digest-sized publication is offset from dot-matrix copy with a b/w frontispiece; one-color matte card cover, saddle-stapled. Price is $3/issue, $5 for a 1-year subscription. **Sample: $3 postpaid by US personal check or 7 international reply coupons; no guidelines available. Pay is 1 copy. The editor says, "No MSS returned; no SASE if no report requested, needed."** If reports are requested, it will take 6 months to get one. The editor says, "*Good* short (3 lines or less) poems can easily be a haiku; you don't have to be Japanese, you have to be a being in nature."

NEW COLLAGE MAGAZINE (II), 5200 N. Tamiami Trail, Sarasota, FL 33580, phone 813-355-7671, ext. 269, founded 1970, poetry editor A. McA. Miller. *New Collage* provides "a forum for contemporary poets, both known and undiscovered. We are **partial to fresh slants on traditional prosodies, and issues are often thematic, so query before sending. We want poetry with clear focus and clear imagery. No greeting-card verse. We prefer poems shorter than five single-spaced pages. We**

like a maximum of 3-5 poems per submission." They have recently published poetry by X. J. Kennedy, Peter Meinke, Yvonne Sapra, Lola Haskings, Van Brock, Judith Ortiz Cofer and Ruth Moon Kempher. The editor selected these sample lines, "The New South" by Harry Brody:

> *Lounging in lawn chairs*
> *on white skillet porches,*
> *we chew soft drawls of tobacco*
> *and wait for the tourists.*

The magazine appears 3 times a year, 20-28 pp. of poetry in each issue, circulation 1,000, 150 subscriptions of which 30 are libraries. They receive about 5,000 poems from freelance submissions per year, use 90. Subscription: $6; per copy: $2; **sample: $4. Photocopy OK. Simultaneous submissions not read. Reports in 3-4 weeks. Pays 3 copies and "sometimes token cash." Send SASE for guidelines. Editor sometimes comments on rejections.** Editor "Mac" Miller advises, "Sending a MS already marked copyright is absurd and unprofessional, unless your name is Robert Lowell. MSS may be marked "first North American Serials only," though this is unnecessary."

*NEW DEPARTURES (V), Piedmont, Bisley, Stroud, Glos, GL6 7BU England, founded 1959, poetry editor Michael Horovitz, is an irregularly published (approximately annual) magazine-sized, 64 pp., avant garde literary journal, circulation 4,000-5,000, which **wants no submissions at this time. Sample: £5 or $2 ($3 extra for conversion with check) postpaid.** They sponsor an annual "Poetry Olympics" in the Young Vic Theater in London, with readings by major and unknown poets, especially many young ones. Here are some sample lines from "Hate" by Adam Horowitz who was 12 at the time the poem was published in *New Departures #15:*

> *I have seen films of pastures of hate,*
> *Bombed buildings, burnt-out cars,*
> *Wallpaper floating on the wind*
> *Like the souls of the ones*
> *Who once lived in these battered buildings.*

‡*NEW HOPE INTERNATIONAL (II), 23 Gambrel Bank Rd., Ashton-Under-Lyne, U.K. OL6 8TW, (they expect to change their address by 1987), founded 1969, editor Gerald England, is a "**bi-yearly magazine of poetry, fiction, literary essays, news and reviews.**" They also publish chapbooks. "**Most types of poetry are acceptable, no limit on length. Content without form and form without content are equally unacceptable. Poems must be well-written within the form chosen but also have something to communicate in the widest sense. Don't want to see doggerel, anti-Christian work, depressive self-examinations.**" They have recently published poetry by B. Z. Niditch, Thomas Kretz, Tony Austin, Novin Afrouz, Teresinka Pereira and Brian Merrikin Hill. The editor selected these sample lines from "Futures" by Christine England:

> *I can, also*
> *laugh, enjoy, hear, walk*
> *so I know*
> *what might have been*

The digest-sized magazine, 48 pp., is lightly photocopied from a variety of type faces, mostly typescript, some of it italics, mimeograph paper, saddle-stapled, color paper cover, using b/w line drawings and decorations. Circulation 350, 250 subscriptions of which 20 are libraries. $3 per issue, $10 for 4 issues. **Sample: $2 postpaid. "Those who subscribe can expect much more in the way of feedback. Manuscripts read at anytime but those received in January or June can expect speedier replies." Reports in "maximum 6 months." Pays 1 copy. Put name and address on each sheet; not more than 6 at a time; simultaneous submissions** *not* encouraged. Photocopy OK, dot-matrix OK. For book publication, query first with 50 samples and bio. "Poets must fully participate in book marketing—buy copies at 50% discount for resale." The editor advises, "New poets should read widely and keep their minds open to work of different styles. 'Progress is a going forward from—not towards.' "

*THE NEW LAUREL REVIEW (II), 828 Lesseps St., New Orleans, LA 70117, founded 1971, editor Lee Meitzen Grue and assistant editor Calvin Andre Claudel, "is an independent nonprofit literary magazine dedicated to fine art. Each issue contains poetry, translation, literary essays, short fiction reviews of small press books, and visual art." They want "**poetry with strong, accurate imagery. We have no particular preference in style. We try to be eclectic. No more than 3 poems in a submission.**" As a sample I selected these lines, the opening of "Children" by Evelyn Thorne:

> *Their heads are so round*
> *we want to fit our big hands upon them*
> *as the soothsayer over the crystal*
> *and look in there.*
> *What are the portents, demons and angels*
> *Swaying together in the ferny tides*
> *of those secret skulls*

The *Review* is handsomely printed, generous with photos and graphics, flat-spined, 80 + pp., pebbled mat cover with fine drawing. Pays in contributor's copies. It has a circulation of 500, subscription: $8; per copy: $4. **Sample: $4 postpaid.**

*NEW LETTERS (II), University of Missouri-Kansas City, Kansas City, MO 64110, phone 816-276-1168, founded 1934 as *University Review*; became *New Letters* in 1971, poetry editor James McKinley, "is dedicated to publishing the best short fiction, best contemporary poetry, literary articles, photography and art work by both established writers and new talents." They want "**contemporary writing of all types—free verse poetry preferred, short works are more likely to be accepted than very long ones.**" They have recently published poetry by Lyn Lifshin, Hayden Carruth, Geoff Hewitt, James B. Hall, Louis Simpson, Vassar Miller and John Tagliabue. As a sample I selected the first 2 of 9 stanzas of "Unrequited Love" by Marilyn Chin:

> Because you stared into the black lakes of her eyes
> you shall drown in them.
> Because you tasted the persimmon on her lips
> you shall dig your moist grave.

The flat-spined, professionally printed quarterly, glossy 2-color cover with art, 6x9", uses about 65 (of 120 +) pp. of poetry in each issue, circulation 1,845, 1,520 subscriptions of which about 40% are libraries. Subscription: $15; per copy: $4. They receive about 7,000 submissions per year, use less than 1%, have a 6 month backlog. **Sample: $4 postpaid. Send no more than 6 poems at once, no simultaneous submissions. "We strongly prefer original typescripts rather than photocopy or dot-matrix. We don't read between May 15 and September 15. No query needed." They report in 2-6 weeks, pay a small fee plus 2 copies. Occasionally James McKinley comments on rejections.** They also publish occasional anthologies, selected and edited by Mckinley.

‡*NEW METHODS: THE JOURNAL OF ANIMAL HEALTH TECHNOLOGY (IV, Animals), Box 22605, San Francisco, CA 94122, phone 415-664-3469, founded as **Methods** in 1976, poetry editor Ronald S. Lippert, AHT, is a "monthly networking service in the animal field, open forum, active in seeking new avenues of knowledge for our readers, combining animal professionals under one roof." They want poetry which is "**animal related but not cutesy**" They get few submissions, but if they received more of quality, they would publish more poetry. They publish a maximum of one poem in each monthly issue, circulation 5,600 to subscribers, of which over 73 are libraries. Price per issue, $1.50; subscription $18. **Sample: $3.60 postpaid, $2 if *Poet's Market* is mentioned as source.** Reports in 1-2 months. Double space with one-inch margins, include dated cover letter. Everything typed. Guidelines are available for SASE. Rarely pays, but "open to discuss." Comment on rejected MSS? "Always!" Ronald Lippert advises, "Keep up with current events."

*NEW MEXICO HUMANITIES REVIEW (II, IV, Regional), Humanities Dept., New Mexico Tech, Socorro, NM 87801, phone 505-835-5200, founded 1978, editor Jerry Bradley, a tri-quarterly which invites MSS "**designed for a general academic readership and those that pursue Southwestern themes or those using interdisciplinary methods.**" There are no restrictions as to type of poetry; "*NMHR* publishes first class, literary poetry," but does not want "sentimental verse, shallow, pointlessly rhymed ideas." Poets recently published include George Garrett, Ralph Mills, Jr., Fred Chappell, Peter Wild, and Walter McDonald. As a sample the editor selected the following lines by M. L. Hester:

> Stainless steel is the percentage sink.
> It will not chip, rust scratch or peel.
> And it shines. The beauty of light
> bouncing in the AM kills all germs democratically;

The review is digest-sized, 100 pp., printed by offset on white stock, with an embossed, one-color matte card cover, flat-spined; there are graphics and ads. Circulation is 650, of which 350 are subscriptions; other copies are sold at poetry readings, writers' workshops, etc. Price per issue is $3, subscription $8/year. **The NMHR pays $10/poem plus 2 copies and a free one-year subscription. Sample copy is $3 postpaid. They report on submissions in 60-90 days, publication is in 10-14 months. Submit no more than 6 poems or 10 pages. MSS must be typed.**

‡NEW ORLEANS POETRY JOURNAL PRESS (III), 2131 General Pershing St., New Orleans, LA 70115, phone 504-891-3458, founded 1956, publisher/editor Maxine Cassin, poetry editor 1985-86 Richard Katrovas. Maxine Cassin says "**We prefer to publish relatively new and/or little-known poets of unusual promise or those inexplicably neglected—'the real thing.'** " She does not want to see "cliche' or doggerel, anything incomprehensible or too derivative, or workshop exercises." Query first, with six samples; she does not accept freelance submissions for her chapbooks, which are flat-spined paperbacks. She has recently published books by Vassar Miller, Everett Maddox, and Charles Bluck. As a sample, the editor selected these lines from "Going Public" by Martha McFerren:

> *I have poems I've never shown a living soul,*
> *he says to me,*
> *smiling at his cuticle.*
> *It's, you know, a personal thing.*

The chapbook I have seen, **Struggling to Swim on Concrete**, by Vassar Miller, is nicely printed on buff stock, 77 pp., flat-spined with matte card cover printed in black on grey, price $5. **The editor reports on queries in 2-3 months, MSS in the same time period, if solicited. Simultaneous submissions will possibly be accepted, and she has no objection to photocopied MSS. Pay is in author's copies, usually 50 to 100.** Ms. Cassin does not subsidy publish at present and does not offer grants or awards. For aspiring poets, she quotes the advice Borges received from his father: "1) Read as much as possible! 2) Write only when you *must* (i.e. have the urge), and 3) Don't rush into print!"

THE NEW POETS SERIES, INC., CHESTNUT HILLS PRESS (II), 541 Piccadilly, Baltimore, MD 21204, phone 301-321-2863 or 878-0724, founded 1970, poetry editor Clarinda Harriss Lott. The New Poets Series, Inc. brings out first books by promising new poets, providing 20 copies to the author, the sales proceeds going back into the corporation to finance the next volume (usual press run: 750). "It has been successful in its effort to provide these new writers with a national distribution; in fact, The New Poets Series was recently named an Outstanding Small Press by the prestigious Pushcart Awards Committee, which judges some 5,000 small press publications annually." Chestnut Hills Press publishes author-subsidized books—"High quality work only, however." The New Poets Series also publishes a biannual anthology drawn from public reading series. They have recently published books by Jan Sherrill, Josephine Jacobsen (in an anthology), Donald Richardson and Elizabeth Stevens. Though Clarinda Harriss Lott says "out-of-context poetry troubles me," I selected "Poetry as a Religion of Skin," a whole poem from **Religion of Skin** by Dyane Fancey as a sample:

> *The Flesh become words again.*
> *The wine*
> *rain water*
> *on grapevines,*
> *the simplest*
> *equation*
> *brought to its roots*
> *language of lips on lips.*

Query with 10 samples, cover letter giving publication credits and bio. "Please—no 'philosophy.' " Replies to queries in 1 week, to submission (if invited) in 6 months. Simultaneous submissions, photocopies OK. No dot-matrix. Editor sometimes comments briefly on rejections. Send 6x9" SASE for samples.

*the new renaissance (II), 9 Heath Rd., Arlington, MA 02174, founded fall, 1968, poetry editor Stanwood Bolton. *the new renaissance* is "intended for the 'renaissance' person, the generalist rather than the specialist. Seeks to publish the best new writing, to offer a forum for articles on topics of public concern, and to highlight interest and/or neglected writers and artists in its essay/review section. *tnr* **has always welcomed all styles of poetry except the overly sentimental or vulgarity for its own sake. We encourage the poetry of ideas but discourage narrowly 'academic' poems.** *tnr* **features 'literary', 'street', free verse, rhymed and, occasionally, light poetry. Experimental poetry is less common but we read and occasionally publish it. In keeping with** *tnr's* **international focus, we strongly encourage translations, accompanied by the original poems as we publish translations vis-a-vis in almost all issues. Our only criterion is excellence; our only limitation, excessive length."** Recently published poetry by Joan Colby, Yannis Goumas, Janet Grillo, Janet McCann, Tambuzi, Margot Treitel, David Hopes, and translations of poems by Luis Cernuda, Talat Sait Halman, Fazil Husnu Daglarca, Nana Issaia, and Abdel Kader Arnaut. The poetry editor selected these lines from "Blues for Robert Jonson (d.1938)" by Louis Mazzari:

> *They are faint blinking pinpricks*
> *Over an autumn evening halo*
> *Over its levee-bank juke joint;*
> *But later, they ride moonglow,*
> *Vex Cleopatra's curtains;*
> *Pointed yellowed teeth in the electricity of a fingertip.*

tnr is flat-spined, professionally printed on heavy stock, glossy, color cover, 124-136 pp., using 16-34 pp. of poetry in each issue; usual print run 1,600, 600 + subscriptions of which approximately 132 are libraries. Subscriptions: $10.50/3 issues; per copy: $5.90. **They receive about 500-525 poetry submissions per year, use about 32-45, have about an 18-month backlog. New submitting dates: January 2 thru July 2nd each year; no submissions the rest of the year. Submit up to 6 poems of 1-3pp, each doubled-spaced, typed. If long poems, submit 1-3 poems only.** Editor sometimes comments on rejections, "especially if we want to see the poet's work again or feel that we can offer some help. We like to receive submissions from poets whom we have personally encouraged in this manner." Contributors are expected to buy copies—$5.15 for 2 back issues or $5.60 for a current issue or $4.30 for special poetry back issue #4 (now a collector's item). "We feel justified in asking writers for support through purchase because:) *tnr* is an unsponsored independent literary with no permanent funding sources; 2) the general public has little interest in modern literature, particularly in poetry, and we're trying to change that to some small degree; 3) since 1968, we have published 92% of our 'creative sections' (i.e., fiction and poetry) from unsolicited submissions. No other highly acclaimed literary magazine can make that statement; and 4) we make acceptances on merit, not on celebrity status, prior publications, friendships, social or literary contacts, political justifications, etc." Like any other respected literary magazine *tnr* likes to be thought of as a first or early choice, so clean, freshly typed mss are a plus but faint photocopies or dot-matrix or dogged-eared mss do the writer no favors. "Beginners should read and re-read poetry from all eras. Of course, they should be familiar with the magazine they're sending to."

‡*THE NEW REPUBLIC(II)**, 1220 19th St. NW, Washington, DC 20036, phone 202-331-7494, founded 1914, poetry editor Richard Howard. *The New Republic* is an old-line politically liberal weekly magazine that publishes occasional poetry. The issue of February 4, 1986, contained one poem, "Our Days," by Gary Soto. As a sample, I chose the following lines:

> *We get up to our feet, stretch, and throw practice kicks*
> *At the air, and bowing to one another,*
>
> *Begin to make bruises where the heart won't go,*
> *A hurt won't stay. I like that, the trust of bone,*
>
> *And how if I'm hit I'll step in, almost crazed,*
> *And sweep, back fist, and maybe bring him down.*

The New Republic is magazine-sized, printed on slick paper, 42 pp. saddle-stapled with 4-color cover. Subscription rate $48/year, back issues available for $2.50 postpaid. **I have no submission or payment information.**

NEW RIVERS PRESS, INC. (II, IV, Specialized), 1602 Selby Ave., St. Paul, MN 55104, founded 1968, publishes collections of poetry, translations of contemporary literature, collections of short fiction, and is also involved in publishing Minnesota regional literary material. Send SASE for catalog to buy samples.

***NEW SOUTHERN LITERARY MESSENGER, THE AIRPLANE PRESS (IV, Local)**, 400 S. Laurel St., Richmond, VA 23220, phone 804-780-1244, editor Charles Lohmann, is a digest-sized, 35 pp. quarterly featuring short stories, political satire, and **local poetry. Sample and guidelines: $1 plus 6x9" SASE double-stamped. Pays $1-5.**

NEW TRADITIONS PRESS (II), Allen Coit Rd., Huntington, MA 01050, founded 1979, poetry editor Stephen Sossaman, produces "a very few poetry items each year on letterpress as the owner's time permits. **We do not seek unsolicitied MSS but will read whatever comes our way. To save time, however, we will not return any submissions. For this reason, writers are encouraged to send photocopies or word-processed submissions. If we are interested, we will respond very quickly. Our primary interest for the immediate future is in poetry postcards, thus in short poems. We want no clumsy, obese, trite or didactic poems. We prefer short, well-crafted and tight, rhymed or free verse. We like poems inspired by Japanese and Chinese poetry and poetry with wit."** They also publish occasional chapbooks and broadsides. I selected this sample from a postcard, the complete poem "February Night," poet unidentified:

> *Falling under the watchful eye of its father the sun*
> *last summer, this wood sang out loud to the woodcutter's axe.*
> *Now it sings again, more softly, in the woodcutter's fire,*
> *rising in silent smoke to its mother, the moon.*

When submitting, "**The cover letter should include the poet's current assessment of the intent and achievement of the work submitted, and (for chapbooks) a statement of what unifies the individual poems." No reply to queries. Reports on submissions in 1 week if interested. Simultaneous submissions, photocopy, dot-matrix OK. Poet receives 20-50% of the printrun in copies. For sample, send $1 for poetry postcards.**

***NEW WORLDS UNLIMITED (I)**, Box 556-PM, Saddle Brook, NJ 07662, phone 201-796-5429, founded 1974, poetry editors Sal St. John Buttaci and Susan Linda Gerstle, publishes "an annual anthology of poetry containing the poems of writers here and abroad. The anthology contains high-quality poems in a hardcover edition only of about 140 pp. Winners of two contests (fall and spring) held annually [fees $1-2, cash prizes $5-20], along with their winning poems are given special recognition in the anthology along with prizes of free books, award certificates and money. Contest judges are local poets and teachers of poetry. **We cannot afford to distribute even one copy free to each contributing poet or library. However, at no time have we ever (nor would we ever) require that a poet purchase a copy or more in order for his poetry to be included. In fact, we have some poets who've been published in each of the 11 annual anthologies, not one of which they've purchased! It is absolutely not a prerequisite to being published. I would say that about 20% of the included poets do not buy a copy."** The copy of an anthology I examined had a fine, heavy hardback cover. The contents were photocopied from typescript—138 pp. containing hundreds of poems. **Sample: $5 postpaid.** The modest price of the anthology and the policy stated by the editor make this quite a different matter from the vanity anthologies which will "accept" practically any poem submitted on the condition that the poet buy at least one copy of an expensive (usually $25 or more) book. Sal St. John Buttaci says, **"We prefer poems rich in imagery without being overly sentimental. Contrived rhymes are a turnoff, as is the use of archaic language and illogical premises. Only poems 2-14 lines long are considered. Any style is fine, and the subject matter is open except for pornographic, scatological themes."** Among the poets they have published are Mary Frances Langford, George Kessler, Mike Maggio, Clo Weirich, Jo Starrett Lindsey, Virginia West, Sara Lewis Kline and Ann Caroline Kabel. The editor selected these sample lines by Frank McCoy:

> Here is the death
> The land made black and wet . . .
> Of love and dead November
> The drunk falling of the sun . . .
> I miss the praying to idols
> I miss the clubs at nights

Send SASE for guidelines and contest rules. Replies to queries immediately, to submissions "from immediately to up to 9 months. Include a self-addressed stamped postcard for immediate notification, if desired. We won't publish a poem already published elsewhere." MS should be "preferably typed or at least neatly and legibly written," dot-matrix, photocopy OK. The editor advises, "Beginners ought best to do a lot of poetry reading, to see what is being written today, and to try at first to imitate what they read. In so doing their own style will emerge. Moreover, they should study the techniques of poetry writing, attend poetry readings, and join local poetry associations that hold meetings that are instructive."

*NEW YARN, TOKYO WOMEN'S ARTS FESTIVAL (IV, Asian, Japanese women), Fujicho 6-5-20, Hoyasi, Tokyo 202, Japan, phone 0424-67-3809, founded 1982, poetry editors Barbara Yates and Cheiron McMahill. The Tokyo Women's Arts Fesival is conducted by the Arts Council of International Feminists of Japan, which edits *New Yarn,* most of which is presented at the Festival, but some is collected during the year from women who are not able to be present. The digest-sized 64 pp., flat-spined magazine, printed on heavy, slick stock, includes poetry in Japanese and English and b/w art reproductions. "We wish to encourage writers in Asian countries and to make their work available to the English-reading public and publish western women writers and make their work available in Japan and the East." They **"will consider any subject matter, prefer Japanese, Asian women's material."** They have recently published poetry by Mieko Watanabe, Satchiko Yoshihara, Cheiron McMahill and Marilee Morinaga. The editors selected these sample lines by Barbara Yates:

> . . . welding and grinning beneath the skein masks,
> Inventing seams we never dreamed would hold
> Indeed
> We are all the women quietly knitting a New Yarn

The magazine appears twice a year. **Submissions should be accompanied by short bio, be in readable handwriting or, preferably, typed, double-spaced. Photocopies, dot-matrix OK. Reports in 1-2 weeks, pays 2 copies. Send SASE for sample. Editors sometimes comment on rejections.**

*THE NEW YORK QUARTERLY (II), Box 693, Old Chelsea Station, New York, NY 10113, founded 1969, poetry editor William Packard, after an interval of several years of suspension, resumed publication 3 times a year February, 1985. They seek to publish "a cross-section of the best of contemporary American poetry" and, indeed, **have a record of publishing many of the best and most diverse of poets**, including W. D. Snodgrass, Gregory Corso, James Dickey, Charles Bukowski, Leo Connellan, Helen Adam and even a crusty old conservative like Judson Jerome. It appears in a 6x9" flat-spined format, thick, elegantly printed, color glossy cover. Subscription: $10 to 305 Neville Hall, University of Maine, Orono ME 04469. **Submit 3-5 poems. Reports within 2 weeks. Pays copies.**

*THE NEW YORKER (III), 25 W. 43rd St., New York, NY 10036, founded 1925, poetry editor Howard Moss, circulation 500,000, uses **poetry of the highest quality—light verse or serious—and pays top rates. MSS not read during the summer.** Sample: $1.50 (available on newsstands).

‡*NEXT EXIT (IV, Regional), RR #3, Harrowsmith, Ontario K0H 1V0, Canada, founded 1980, editor Eric Folsom, a twice-yearly magazine that features poetry and reviews and focuses on **Kingston and Eastern Ontario writers. The editor wants to see poetry that is "lyric, narrative, meditative, concrete, explorative; any form done well," but nothing "misogynist."** He has recently published work by Bronwen Wallace and Tom Marshall. As a sample, he chose the following lines from "Stoning the Moon" by Carolyn Smart:

> *You are thinking about women*
> *you thought you'd comforted*
> *tell me everything you said*
> *and some do*

The magazine is 7x10", offset from typed copy on slightly rough paper, 36 pp. saddle-stapled and folded with black lettering and illustration on cover. Circulation is 200, of which 50 are subscriptions and 10 go to libraries. Price per issue is $3, subscription $6/year. **Sample available for $2 postpaid. Pay is 1 copy, more if requested. Submissions will be reported on in 90 days and time to publication is 6 months.**

*NEXUS (II), 006 University Center, Wright State University, Dayton, OH 45435, phone 513-873-2031, founded 1967, Nexus is a "student-operated creative magazine, featuring short stories, poetry, art work and photos (b/w). Open to poets anywhere. We usually prefer concrete visual imagery that transmits feeling and ideas. We will consider anything." They have recently published poetry by David Garrison and Marcia Gale Kester. These sample lines have been selected from "For All the Marbles," by Vance Wissinger Jr.:

> *sky so deep as to blue clear air & marble*
> *clouds, like I was in god's own*
> *aggie where one summer day lasts*
> *forever and victory is a 2 bit jawbreaker*
> *that lasts all afternoon.*

Nexus appears 3 times a year, using about 15 pp. of poetry (of 48-56) in each issue, circulation 4,000. They receive 100-150 submissions per year, use 30-50. **Send SASE for free sample. Submit up to 6 pp. of poetry, Sept. to May. Photocopy and simultaneous submissions OK. Send bio with submissions. Reports in 6-10 weeks. Pays 3 copies. Send SASE for guidelines. Editor sometimes comments on rejections.**

‡*NIGHT CRY: THE MAGAZINE OF TERROR (IV, Horror), 800 Second Ave., New York, NY 10017, founded 1984, editor Alan Rodgers, a quarterly mass-market horror magazine "from the editors of Rod Serling's *The Twilight Zone* magazine." The editor says, **"We look for literate, well-written, and most especially frightening and unsettling poetry. We don't want to see poems that are fundamentally horrific nursery rhymes; we aren't interested in light verse with horrific props."** Poets recently published include Robert Frazier, Susan Sheppard, and Rochelle Lynn Holt. As a sample, I selected the following lines from "The Shaman's Meal," by Ronald Terry:

> *What food attracts the dead?*
> *Does wine intoxicate them?*
> *Or do they demand blood*
> *to sharpen their forms?*
> *I wait to offer.*
> *I am hungry.*

The magazine is digest-sized, 191 pp., printed on pulp paper with the usual lurid pulp-magazine cover, flat-spined. Circulation is 30,000, all of it at newsstands or bookstores. Price per issue is $2.95; **sample available postpaid for the same price. The magazine pays $30-150 to its contributors, plus two free copies. It reports on submissions in 2-3 months and publishes in 6 months to 1 year. "Submissions should be readable; the more readable they are, the more likely they are to get a sympathetic reading. It's hard to be sympathetic to a writer who obviously has no concern for our ability to read his work."** The editor says that they respond personally to submitted MSS pretty often, but generally critique only things that they would like to see revised.

*NIGHTSUN (IV, Specialized), Philosophy Dept., Frostburg State College, Frostburg, MD 21532, founded 1981, is a 128 pp. digest-sized literary annual **of poetry on specific topics. You have to subscribe ($6 plus postage) to submit, and the theme for each year is announced in advance. Query regarding theme. Sample: $6.95. Pays in contributor's copies.**

*NIMROD MAGAZINE, PABLO NERUDA PRIZE FOR POETRY (II), 2210 S. Main St., Tulsa, OK 74114, phone 918-584-3333, founded 1956, poetry editors Mark Johnson and Fran Ringold, "is an active 'little magazine,' part of the movement in American letters which has been essential to the development of modern literature. *Nimrod* publishes 2 issues per year: an Awards Issue featuring the prize winners of our national competition, and a thematic issue, so that in addition to bringing new, vigorous writing to the reading public, we also focus each year on the literature of an emerging nation." They want "**vigorous writing that is neither wholly of the academy nor the streets, typed MSS.**" They have published poetry by Pattiann Rogers, Denise Levertov, Willis Barnstone, Francois Camoin, Tess Gallagher, McKeel McBride, Bronislava Volek and Ishmael Reed. As a sample I selected the opening lines of "Trail Blazing" by Carol Barrett:

> *My brother is stacking rocks by a mountain pool.*
> *I sit on a flat stone near Indian paintbrush*
> *and fireweed, tracing the tips of the mountains*
> *with my eyes. The clouds, white gauze.*

The 6x9" flat-spined, 80 + pp., journal, full-color glossy cover, professionally printed on coated stock with b/w photos and art, uses 40-50 pp. of poetry in each issue, circulation 2,000, 400 subscriptions of which 50 are libraries. Subscription: $10; per copy: $5.50. They use about 1% of the 2,000 submissions they receive each year, have a 3 month backlog. **Sample: $5.50 postpaid. Reports in 3 weeks-4 months, pays copies. Send SASE for guidelines and rules for the Pablo Neruda Prize for Poetry ($1,000 and $500 prizes), which has an April 1 deadline each year, $10 entry fee for which you get a one year subscription to** *Nimrod.*

*****NINTH DECADE**, 52 Cascade Ave., London N10, England, editor Robert Vas Dias, founded 1983, It is published in conjunction with Oasis Books and Shearsman Books and comes out three times a year, about 60 pages, finely printed, saddle-stapled. Co-editor Robert Vas Dias says the magazine "**exists to publish postmodern, innovative writing, translations of contemporary French and other European writing, and critical articles on important but neglected poets**. Each issue contains the work of about 10 writers—of prose as well as of poetry. One of these is 'featured'—usually a British or American poet who has published significant work over a sustained period but who has received inadequate critical attention; 10-15 pages of his or her work appears, together with a specially commissioned review/essay. *Ninth Decade* tries to give a meaningful representation of the work, so that **at least 5 or 6 pages is devoted to each poet**. *Ninth Decade* is not a hobbyist's magazine so no competitions are run and no "theme" issues are dreamed up as a substitute for indifferent submissions. Potential contributors should definitely be familiar with the magazine before submitting." They have published Gilbert Sorrentino, Christopher Middleton, John Yau, Jon Silkin, Karin Lessing, Tess Randolph, Tom Pickard. Here are some lines from George Evans, "Evacuation":

> *They drive their pigs*
> *at the ends of long sticks*
> *down the road as if the road's a book*
> *they're writing with their feet*

About 40 pages of poetry in each issue, print run 500, 300 subscriptions, of which 50 are libraries. **Sample: $3 postpaid.** Annual subscription: $10. They receive about 1,000 submissions each year, use 3%. **Submissions should contain at least 6 pages of poetry, typed double-spaced. Photocopy OK, no dot-matrix, no simultaneous submissions. Do not send from June to August. Be sure to include sufficient postage or IRC's. If it's OK to dispose of the poetry, 2 IRC's are sufficient for airmail reply. Reports in 1-2 months. Payment is 2 copies.** (see also Permanent Press).

*****NIT & WIT: CHICAGO'S LITERARY/ARTS MAGAZINE (II)**, Box 627, Geneva IL 60134, phone 312-232-9496, founded 1977, poetry editor Larry Hunt, is "a bi-monthly magazine that regularly features the cultural arts, music, film, theatre, dance, photography, design, architecture, fiction, and, of course, poetry. **The poetry can be serious or humorous. We prefer poems of 30 lines or less, but overall quality will decide acceptance.**" Recently published poets include Richard Holinger, Joyce Schenk, and Joseph Somoza. As a sample, the editors chose the following lines from J.R. Ransom's "Dreaming, then—":

> *The man took his trombone*
> *from its casket and launched bubbles*
> *that spun gold and green and rose*
> *to the parent globe. The woman danced,*
> *her nightgown glowed and rippled.*

They use about 6 poems per issue. *Nit&Wit* is magazine-sized, printed on heavy coated stock, with ads, b/w photos, and art. **Sample available for $2.50 postpaid. Pay is in copies. Reporting time is 2-3 weeks, backlog no more than 6 months or 3 issues.** The magazine also sponsors an annual poetry contest with prizes totalling a minimum of $500.

‡*****NO MAGAZINE (I)**, 826 West Belmont, #3F, Chicago, IL 60657, founded 1985, editors Brad Johnson and Ann Meyer. Vol. 1, No. 1 of this quarterly publication of poetry, prose, and artwork appeared in summer, 1985. The editors say, "**The pay is one copy and there are no limits on style**

though rhyming poetry is discouraged." The digest-sized publication, unpaged, offset from typed copy, contains poems by Jim O'Malley, C. Shore, Layla Brick, Y. B. Fletcher, Bob Kimbell, Brigitte Pavich, M. Bernstein and B. Wilson, Michael L. Miner, Nancy Hamm, James Loverde, Nancy Jo Zaffaro, Eileen Forslund Woolman, and Brad Johnson, as well as prose and b/w illustrations. As a sample, I have selected this complete poem by Nancy Szymanski:

> *The strings inside of us have broken,*
> *we no longer play silver tunes.*
> *All this sadness makes no noise.*

The magazine has a one-color matte card cover and is saddle-bound with string. Price is $3 per copy.

‡*NORTH AMERICAN POLITICAL SPECTRUM, FLEUR DE LEAF WORLDWIDE, INC. (IV, Political)**, Box 10352, St. Petersburg, FL 33733, phone 813-323-4827, founded 1985, publisher Andre Begin. *North American Political Spectrum* is "a thematic magazine published on a yearly basis" and Fleur de Leaf is a subsidy publisher of chapbooks. For the magazine, the editor wants to see **"any form or length or style of poetry with a political theme. 'Political' meaning nearly anything subject to debate in the modern arena of intelligent thought. We are not opposed to work that is very free or very tight in form. We care only about content."** As a sample, the editor chose the following lines by an unidentified poet":

> *Traditions march on in vengeance, culture coughs up*
> *another souvenir,*
> *and all the world is a riot, and how many martyrs*
> *shall rise from the dead?*

The magazine, which had not yet appeared at the time of this writing, was planned to be digest-sized, 160 pp., with "85-line screened photos, b/w illustrations, etc." **Camera ready copy and art should be provided by the contributor.** The magazine was planned for free distribution to several college campuses. Single copy price was $1.50 for the first edition, no subscriptions. **Sample available for $2.75 postpaid, guidelines for SASE. Pay is 2 copies. Poets should submit no more than 5 poems at a time, no simultaneous submissions, photocopied or dot-matrix MSS are OK. Reporting time is within 2 weeks and "we only accept enough material for the year in question." Fleur de Leaf press accepts freelance submissions of political material only; chapbooks must be 75% financed by the author.** They also sponsor an annual contest. The editor says, "We are non-aligned politically and would enjoy opinions from left, right, or center. *The poet should say what he/she feels without worry as to what we may feel.*"

‡THE NORTH CAROLINA HAIKU SOCIETY PRESS (IV, Haiku)**, Box 14247, Raleigh, NC 27620, phone 919-828-5551, founded 1984, editor/publisher Rebecca Rust. The press was established **"solely as a vehicle for publishing books by those authors who have received a grant from the North Carolina Haiku Society. Applicants must apply for the grant to be published. This is open to anyone."** They publish flat-spined paperbacks of, or about, haiku only. Poets recently published include Lenard D. Moore and Rebecca Rust. As a sample, the editor selected:

> *Sring noonday river—*
> *an old canoe just twists*
> *in the thunderstorm*

and as a one-line she selected:

> *a blade of summer grass moving moonlight*

The sample book I have seen is attractively printed on white stock with line drawings, shiny card cover with b/w art work, priced at $6.50 plus 75¢ postage and handling. **Freelance submissions are accepted in the form of application for the North Carolina Haiku Society grant. Currently the editor would rather not have any unsolicited MSS because she has a backlog. When applying for a grant, the writer should submit 30-50 haiku in any legible form copy, it is best to query first. Queries are answered in 2 weeks, MSS are reported on in 1 month.** There is no subsidy publishing. The editor says, "Please, please read *all* of the classical books of, and about, haiku and *study* before attempting to submit."

‡*NORTH DAKOTA QUARTERLY (II)**, Box 8237, University of North Dakota, Grand Forks, ND 58202, phone 701-777-3323, founded 1910, poetry editor Jay Meek, a literary quarterly published by the University of North Dakota Press that includes material in the arts and humanities—essays, fiction, interviews, poems, and visual art. **"We want to see poetry that reflects an understanding not only of the difficulties of the craft, but of the vitality and tact that each poem calls into play."** They do not want to see **"poems by writers who do not read poems."** Poets recently published include Thomas McGrath, Peter Wild and David Citino. The issue I have (Fall 1985) contains an "anthology of rural poetry" with work by 23 different poets. As a sample, I selected the first stanza from "Drought" by John N. Miller:

> *Our neighbor squints, glowering at the sun*
> *Glowing at him through a thick sky.*
> *Furrows harden in his forehead,*
> *In his fields the corn shrouds its stalks*
> *With dry tatters. His sheep forage*

This issue of *North Dakota Quarterly* is 6x9", 261 pp. flat-spined, professionally designed and printed with b/w artwork on the white matte card cover and b/w photographs inside. Circulation of the journal is 700, of which 500 are subscriptions and 200 go to libraries, 100 are newsstands sales. Price per issue is $4, subscription $10/year. **Sample available for $4 postpaid. Pay is 2 copies. Poems should be typed or otherwise mechanically reproduced. Reporting time is 4-6 weeks and time to publication varies.** The press does not usually publish chapbooks, but "we will consider."

NORTHEASTERN UNIVERSITY PRESS (IV, Translations), Northeastern University, 360 Huntington Ave., Boston, MA 02115, will consider **poetry in translation particularly from French. They also offer the Samuel French Morse Poetry Prize. Send SASE for guidelines and rules to English Dept., Northeastern University, 360 Huntington Ave., Boston, MA 02115.**

***NORTHERN LIGHT (IV, Neo-surrealistic)**, 605 Fletcher Argue Bldg., University of Manitoba, Winnipeg, Canada R3T 2N2, founded 1967, poetry editor Douglas Smith, is a biannual of **neo-surrealistic poetry from Canada, the U.S. and abroad (also work in translation). They would like to see others as well as neo-surrealistic poetry.** They have recently published poetry by Lyn Lifshin, Rolf Jacobsen, Hans Artmann and Susan Fromberg Schaeffer. The editor selected these sample lines by Bill Tremblay:

> *The self is the vehicle of*
> *expression, not a defense, flying with ice and song,*
> *dark wings of longing for what is hidden within us.*

The sample issue I have seen (#6, Summer 1981) is flat-spined, 52 pp., professionally printed on good stock with much white space, glossy card cover with b/w black and gold graphics. They use 60 pp. of poetry in each issue, circulation 500, 350 subscriptions of which 200 are libraries. They receive "thousands" of submissions each year, use 75-100. **Sample: $2.50 postpaid. Reports in 4-6 weeks. Pays $5 page plus copies.**

‡*NORTHERN LIT QUARTERLY (II)**, 10 Murphy Hall, University of Minnesota, Minneapolis, MN 55455, phone 612-373-3381, founded 1984, poetry editor Scott Gilchrist, a tabloid-type literary quarterly, published in two sections, that publishes poetry and fiction "by up and coming writers as well as established/well known writers." **The focus is on "free verse, non-regional, thought provoking, poetry that is eclectic,"** but no "self-indulgent, first draft type." Poets recently published include Dave Etter, Paul Zarzyski, Phil Dacey, and Chet Corey. As a sample, the editors selected the following lines by an unidentified poet:

> *Tornadoes unscrew farm sheds*
> *from the flat boards of Kansas.*
> *For the first time, chickens fly!*
> *A farmhouse roof gapes—its throat a red score.*

The free tabloid, printed on newsprint, contains 60 pp. including many campus-related ads in its two sections. Circulation is 40,000 + , of which 1,000 copies are distributed on newsstands and the rest are given out on campus, at request, shows, or for promotion. Subscriptions (3 issues) are $3, to cover postage. **A sample issue is free, and guidelines are available. The magazine pays $20/poem, and $1.25/ column inch for fiction plus 2 copies or more on request. Submissions must be previously unpublished material; they are reported on in 3-4 weeks and publication is December, March and June.** Criticism of rejected MSS is not given due to volume.

‡*NORTHERN PLEASURE, NORTHERN PLEASURE PRESS, NORTHERN PANIC MAIL, HYDRAULICS POETRY PUBLICATIONS CO., PRESS-PRESS PRESS, MARIJUANA MOMENTS (V, Invitation)**, 1547 W. 24th St., Erie, PA 16502, founded 1980, publisher Ron Androla, who describes his operation as a "small-press, independent publisher of true, intense, personal, avantgarde, prelapsarian, sexual, violent poetry against all otherwise moronic yawning." **The publications listed above include a magazine, chapbooks, chapettes, broadsides, and an anthology,** "invitation only in resubmissions of manuscripts." **Mr. Androla has recently published work by Charles Bukowski, Rick Peabody, Todd Moore, Jack Kerouac, and Allen Ginsberg. The magazine,** *Northern Pleasure*, **appears irregularly, has 40 photocopied pp., circulation 200, price per issue $10, subscription $100 (patron).** No samples or guidelines available; contributors receive 1 copy. No freelance submissions for chapbooks are accepted; however, queries will be answered in "weeks." Simultaneous submissions, photocopied or dot-matrix MSS are OK but no discs. Pay is in 15 author's copies. Sample chapbooks can be obtained for $5 cash. **In case you didn't already know, Mr. Androla informs you, "Art is madness!! Poetry is terror."**

*NORTHWEST MAGAZINE (IV, Poets of the Pacific Northwest), 1320 SW Broadway, Portland, OR 97201, phone 503-221-8228, poetry editor Paul Pintarich, is the Sunday magazine of the *Oregonian* newspaper. They use poems only by **poets living in the Pacific Northwest. Pays $5/poem. No restrictions or specifications as to type, length, etc.** As a sample I selected the first quatrain of "Sonnet: On Sonnets" by Dana E. Scott:

> *The manufactured cadence of desire,*
> *Each measured foot true to an inner song,*
> *Recalls to mind the days when we were strong,*
> *Our life imbued with power to inspire.*

*NORTHWEST REVIEW (II), 369 PLC, University of Oregon, Eugene, OR 97403, phone 503-686-3957, founded 1957, poetry editor John Witte, is "seeking excellence in whatever form we can find it" and uses "**all types**" **of poetry**. They have recently published poetry by Alan Dugan, Olga Broumas, William Stafford and Richard Eberhart. The 6x9" flat-spined magazine appears 3 times a year, uses 25-40 pp. of poetry in each issue, circulation 1,300, 1,200 subscriptions of which half are libraries. They receive 2,500 submissions per year, use 4%, have a 0-4 month backlog. **Sample: $3 postpaid. Submit 6-8 poems clearly reproduced. "NEVER simultaneous submissions." Reports in 8-10 weeks, pays 3 copies. Send SASE for guidelines.** The editor comments "whenever possible" on rejections and advises, "Persist."

NORTHWOODS PRESS, CONSERVATORY OF AMERICAN LETTERS (CAL)(II), Box 88, Thomaston, ME 04861, phone 207-354-6550, founded 1972, poetry editor Robert Olmsted, is an attempt to face reality and provide a sensible royalty-contract means of publishing many books of poetry. **If you are at the stage of considering book publications, have a large number of poems in print in respected magazines, perhaps previous book publication, and are confident that you have a sufficient following to insure sales, send 8½x11" SASE (3 oz. postage) for "descriptions of the Northwoods Poetry Program and CAL."** Robert Olmstead says, "The publishing of poetry has long been an economic disaster. Poets pay printers, bribe publishers, pay publishers, become publishers. Publishers gamble and gradually disappear. Poets and publishers pray for and wait for grants that seldom come. Professors talk their schools into financing their work and college presses grow weaker. Over the past 12 years I have helped about 150 poets get their books published. Neither the poets nor I have made a dime. I have experienced economic ruin as I struggled to do the impossible. I have learned much and hope I may have learned a way to do the impossible. That is, get excellent books of poetry into print without economic hardship to the poet, or to me. . . . Northwoods Press is designed for the excellent working poet who has a following which is likely to create sales of $1,500 or more. Without at least that much of a following and at least that level of sales, no book can be published. Request 15-point poetry program." Poetry must be non-trite, non-didactic. It must never bounce. Rhyme, if used at all, should be subtle. One phrase should tune the ear in preparation for the next. They should flow and create an emotional response." Query with cover letter dealing with publication credits and marketing ideas. The program pays 10% royalties plus 10 copies (and 50% discount on additional copies). Emphasis is less on whether your poetry suits the editor's taste than on your economic viability as a poet, which he will help you determine by means of a questionnaire.** If your work is good but not considered commercially viable, perhaps you should look into a subsidy program such as that offered by CAL. Robert Olmsted says, "Publishing is NOT a reward for good writing. Publishing is a commercial activity engaged in for profit. Poets—especially good ones—should spend more time developing markets and *being* a poet—doing readings, autograph parties, being proud of his/her art, not apologetic. The poet should be creating an audience. Poets should, in about 99.9% of all cases, consider their poetry a hobby and not a commercial endeavor. Like any other worthwhile hobby, they should expect it to cost, not pay. That may not be a popular statement, but for all of us, it is the truth. Do not consider a hobby to be a frivolous or inconsequential activity. They almost *never* are."

‡W. W. NORTON & COMPANY, INC. (III), 500 Fifth Ave., New York, NY 10110, phone 212-354-5500, founded 1925, poetry editor Kathleen Anderson. W. W. Norton is a well known commercial trade publishing house that publishes only original work in both hardcover and paperback. They want "**quality literary poetry**" **but no "light or inspirational verse."** They have recently published books by Ellen Bryant Voigt, Rosanna Warren, Norman Dubie and Eugenio Montale. W. W. Norton publishes two books of poetry each year with an average page count of 100. The samples I have are flat-spined paperbacks, attractively printed (one has b/w illustrations), with two-color glossy card covers; they are priced at $5.95 and $6.95. **Freelance submissions are accepted, but authors should query first, sending credits and 15 sample poems plus bio. Norton will consider only poets whose work has been published in quality literary magazines. They report on queries in 2-3 weeks and MSS in 16 weeks.** Simultaneous submissions will be considered if the editor is notified, and photocopied MSS are OK. Royalties are 10%, but there are no advances. Catalog is free on request. Criticism of rejected MSS is sometimes given.

‡*NOTEBOOK: A LITTLE MAGAZINE, ESOTERICA PRESS (II, IV, Chicano, historical), Box 26B43, Los Angeles, CA 90026, press established 1983, magazine 1985, editor MS. Yoly Zentella. Esoterica is a small-press literary publisher. *Notebook,* a semi-annual magazine. "Every year its winter issue is devoted to writing by and about Chicanos and other Latin Americans. Will accept Spanish." The editor wants to see "serious poetry with a message. Especially interested in historical, cultural, literary, travel, art themes. For Chicano/Latin American issue interested in all aspects involved. No frivolities, explicit sex, obscenities or experimentation." As a sample, she chose these lines from "Ash Wednesday" by Gabriela Cerda:

> The church is full, noisy, praying, kneeling
> and I am writing, one of your children of the
> race of eagles and serpents and the inquisition,
> out of place. That I could belong.

Notebook is digest-sized, 26 pp. saddle-stapled, offset from typed copy, with b/w illustrations inside and one-color matte card cover. **Sample: $4 postpaid, guidelines available for SASE, pay 1 copy,** subscribing "not expected but would be appreciated." The editor wants MSS "typewritten and proofread with name and current address on top of the page. No limit in number of poems or length. Solicits unpublished work. Will not consider multiple submissions but will consider previously published. Address all submissions with bio to editor." She reports on submissions in 8-12 weeks. Esoterica Press has published 1 chapbook, 6 pp.—a mini-book attached to the magazine. She will accept freelance submissions for chapbooks. Queries will be answered in 4 weeks and MSS accepted or rejected in 8-12 weeks; no simultaneous submissions. Original copy submissions only. Pay for chapbooks is 1 copy plus 40% off all other copies. The editor's advice is: "Write and submit, but don't forget to re-read, edit and re-write. For beginners: There are editors like myself that do not regard beginners as 'beginners' but writers with little exposure."

‡*NOW AND THEN (IV, Appalachian), Box 24292, ETSU, Johnson City, TN 37614, phone 615-929-5348, founded 1984, editor Fred Wagge, a regional magazine that deals with northern and southern Appalachian history and culture. **The editor does not want any poetry not related to the region. Some of his issues have themes—for instance Fall, 1986, will be Cherokees; Winter 1986-87, Appalachian childhoods; Spring, 1987, the world of the Appalachian writer. Poetry should be "not too long."** He has recently published poetry by Anne Shelby, Jo Cavson, and George Ella Lyon, from whose "The Foot Washing" he chose the following lines as a sample:

> They kneel on the slanting floor
> before feet white as roots,
> humble as the stumps . . .

I have not seen *Now and Then*, which appears three times a year. It is magazine-sized, offset, with photos and line drawings and cover art. Circulation is about 500. A subscription is $5/year or $11/2 years. **Sample available for postage plus 8½x11" SASE. Pay is 2 copies. Submissions are reported on as soon as possible, and time to publication varies.**

‡*NYCTICORAX (II), Box 8444, Asheville, NC 28814, phone 704-254-1359, founded 1985, poetry editor John A. Youril, a literary magazine published 3 times/year that wants **poetry of "highest quality only. No restrictions on theme or length. No light verse, sentimental poetry."** They have recently published poems by David Hopes, Ivan Arguelles, Christina Zawadiwsky, and Jerry Ratch; I have not seen a copy so cannot quote samples. The magazine is digest-sized, offset, 64 pp. Circulation is 650, price per issue $4, subscription $10/year. **Sample available for $3 postpaid, guidelines for SASE. Pay is 1 copy. Writers should submit 4-6 poems, previously unpublished. Reporting time is 6 weeks and time to publication averages 6 months.**

O.ARS (II), Box 179, Cambridge, MA 02238, founded 1981, poetry editors Don Wellman, Irene Turner and Cola Franzen, publishes anthologies of **"innovative poetry and prose, poetics,"** each on a specific theme: **Coherence, Perception, Translations. They are interested in "anything except lyrical drivel about cats. Read before submitting."** They have recently published poetry by Bernstein, Andrews, Simic, Creeley and Waldrop. As a sample I selected the opening lines of "A Merz Sonata" by Jerome Rothenberg:

> world of the crying man
> is death's world
> money acids him, he sucks
> hard on his tongue
> but can't unjunct the word

The anthologies are 6x9", flat-spined, 200 + pp., professionally printed, glossy card cover. **Sample: $3.50 postpaid. Query with brief, factual cover letter and 3 poems. Replies to queries in 2 weeks, to submissions in 2 months. MS should be typed, no dot-matrix, photocopy OK. Pays 3 copies.**

OASIS BOOKS, O BOOKS SERIES, *OASIS (II)*, 12 Stevenage Rd., London, England SW6 6ES, founded 1969, poetry editor Ian Robinson. They seek "**to promote poetry and prose writing of a kind that probably won't be contemplated by commercial houses—writing often of an, for want of a better word, experimental nature—and this includes translations, which form a large part of our publishing programs.**" They have published poetry by Tomas Tranströmer, Gunnar Harding, John Ash, Marcel Béalu, D. E. Steward, David Ignatow, Christopher Middleton, Gael Turnbull and David Wevill. Though Ian Robinson says that selecting 4 lines "which represent the taste and quality" they want is "an impossible request—the work we have published is so varied," I selected as a sample the opening lines of "Calafawnya" by Gilbert Sorrentino:

> *Involved in peripheral necessities*
> *In which lakes certainly had a part*
> *And why not? the man was seen by witnesses*
> *To be buying furniture. Purportedly.*

Oasis Books is associated with Permanent Press in publishing the magazine *Ninth Decade*. They also publish irregularly a magazine, *Oasis*, which consists of excerpts of poetry to be published by Oasis Press and other original material, "but it cannot be subscribed to, nor will it receive submissions." Sample: £80 plus postage. To have a book considered for Oasis, query first, no samples. They pay for the books they publish in copies (20-25). Write for the catalog to buy samples.

‡***ODESSA POETRY REVIEW (I)**, Box 39, RR 1, Odessa, MO 64076, founded 1984, editor and publisher Jim Wyzard; "Missouri's largest poetry magazine." The editor says, "**We would like to see more poetry of traditional forms dealing with the special, human, and political issues which face today's world. However, we are open to poems of various forms and subject matter, as long as they are 24 lines or less, and are socially acceptable. Nothing dealing with sexual variations, pro-drugs, anti-American, female/male superiority, white/minority superiority, etc.**" They have recently published poetry by Esther Leiper, Rod Kessler, Sal Burraci, Moraeg Wood, and Linda Hutton. As a sample, the editor selected the following lines from "In America" by Adrienne Wolfert:

> *I light my Sabbath candles*
> *From the fires of Auschwitz.*
> *Invisible, my sisters*
> *surround me as I pray:*

Odessa Poetry Review is digest-sized, typeset in fairly small type on thin paper. One issue I have contains 44 pp. and another has 108, saddle-stapled. B/w photos (mostly of the west) are used as illustrations and on the glossy card cover. The magazine appears quarterly and a circulation of 3,000 was expected for 1986. Price per copy is $4, subscription $16/year. **Sample available for $4 postpaid, guidelines for SASE. Evidently all poems must be submitted as contest entries with a $1/poem entry fee, limit of 10 poems per submission. Photocopied and simultaneous submissions are OK. Submissions are reported on "1 week after deadline," and time to publication is 1 month.**

*THE OHIO JOURNAL (II), English Dept., Ohio State University, 164 W. 17th Ave., Columbus, OH 43210, founded 1973, editor David Citino, appears twice yearly with reviews, essays and quality poetry. "**We're open to all forms; we tend to favor work that gives evidence of a mature and sophisticated sense of the language.**" They have recently published poetry by Albert Goldbarth, David Ray, Miller Williams, Martha Collins, Jane Shore, Beth Spires, and Howard Nemerov. The following sample is from the opening stanza of "Beyond" by William Stafford:

> *The world needs to be more than itself—*
> *at night its caves to become even darker*
> *and stiller, and any river we follow*
> *to murmur and begin to put silver*
> *on evening. Sky sounds of birds or spirits*
> *descend. Trees come nearer and wait.*

The *OJ* is magazine-sized, professionally printed on heavy slick stock with b/w graphics, glossy cover with art, 44 pp., of which about 20 in each issue are devoted to poetry, circulation 1,000. Subscription: $5; per copy: $3. They receive about 3,000 submissions per year, use 200, and have a 3-6 month backlog. **Sample: $3. Photocopy, dot-matrix OK. No restrictions on number of poems per submission. "Cover letter helpful." Reports in 2 weeks-3 months. Pays copies.** There is an annual President's Award of $100 for the best poem appearing that year in the magazine. On occasion editor comments on rejections. David Citino advises, "However else poets train or educate themselves, they must do what they can to learn our language. Too much of the writing that we see indicates that poets do not in many cases develop a feel for the possibilities of language, and do not pay attention to craft. Poets should not be in a rush to publish—until they are ready.''

OHIO RENAISSANCE REVIEW, INFINITY PUBLICATIONS (II), Box 804, Ironton, OH 45638, phone 614-532-0846, press founded 1969, *ORR* began fall, 1984, publisher/editor James R. Pack, poetry editor Ron Houchin, "a totally independent labor-of-love operation dedicated to publishing the works of new poets with creative imagination and personal integrity and to challenging established poets to greater creative heights. We want **concrete poetry, germinal with ideas and expressing a clear, natural voice. We don't want traditional, rhyming, abstract or artificial forms. Free verse; no length limit; style conversational or experimental; no subject matter restraints but tasteless obscenity not appreciated.**" They have recently published poetry by Lyn Lifshin, J.F. DaVanzo, Edward Romano and Tammy Chapman. The editor selected these sample lines from "A Show of Hands" by Ron Ikan:

> Note the deaf man's
> Handiwork; his words are handmade,
> Individually signed (like an artist)
> And his meaning speaks purely for himself

ORR is a quarterly, 7x10'', 64 pp., saddle-stapled, elegantly printed on coated offset paper, cover 8 pt. color cast stamped and embossed in gold (the metal, not the color). In addition to 20 pp. of poetry it uses science fiction, fantasy, mystery, creative art and photography, circulation 1,000, 500 subscriptions of which are "lifetime merit awards to famous people all over the world, including poets, novelists, performing artists, scientists and world leaders." Subscription: $20; per copy: $10. **Sample: $4 postpaid. Submit any time, any number of poems, typed 1 to a page. Readable photocopy, dot-matrix OK. Reports in 4-6 weeks, pays 25¢ per line ($5 minimum) plus 1 copy.** Editor comments on rejections "occasionally, if requested and time permits." They plan to publish books and chapbooks within the year and to offer best-of-year awards for publications in the magazine. Ron Houchin says, "We hope to combine in *Ohio Renaissance Review* the most talented and innovative of new and established poets and to make the magazine a pre-eminent voice in literature today."

*THE OHIO REVIEW, OHIO REVIEW BOOKS (II), Ellis Hall, Ohio University, Athens, OH 45701-2979, phone 614-594-5889, founded 1959, editor Wayne Dodd, attempts "to publish the best in contemporary poetry, fiction and reviews" in the *Review* and in chapbooks, flat-spined paperbacks and hardback books. They use "**all types**" of poetry and have recently published poems by Reg Saner, William Matthews, Patrica Dobler, Hayden Carruth and Sandra Agricola, from whose work the editor selected these sample lines:

> In my mother's house china kewpie dolls touch.
> If I pull them apart they bob and sway
> on a worn-out spring. No way out but back
> together so I leave them as I left them
> twenty years ago, eyes closed kissing.

The *Review* appears 3 times a year in a professionally printed, flat-spined, 140 + pp. format, matte cover with color and art, circulation 2,000, featuring about 18 poets per issue. Subscription: $12; per copy: $4.25. They receive about 3,000 freelance submissions per year, use 1% of them, and have a 6-12 month backlog. **Sample: $4.25 postpaid. Reports in 1 month. Pays $5 per poem plus copies.** Editor sometimes comments on rejections. **Send SASE for guidelines.** They are not at present accepting freelance submissions of book MSS. Query with publication credits, bio.

*OINK! MAGAZINE (IV, Specialized), 1446 Jarvis, Chicago, IL 60626, phone 312-764-1048, founded 1971, poetry editors Maxine Chernoff and Paul Hoover, is an annual which **poetry "in the progressive tradition associated with the New York School and post-modernism in general**." They have recently published poetry by Anne Waldman, Charles Simic, Charles Bernstein, Ron Padgett, James Laughlin, Ron Koertge and Kenward Elmslie. The digest-sized 120 + pp. flat-spined journal is professionally printed, glossy, color card cover with art, circulation 600, 40 subscriptions, all libraries. There are approximately 80 pp. of poetry in each issue, 10% of the "hundreds" of submissions they receive each year. **Sample: $5 postpaid. Submit no more than 5 poems. Photocopy OK. Reports in 1-4 weeks. Pays $5 per poem "when funds are available" plus 1 copy.** Editor sometimes comments on rejections.

*THE OLD RED KIMONO (I, II), Box 1864, Rome, GA 30163, phone 404-295-6312, founded 1972, poetry editors Jo Anne Starnes and Jon Hershey, a publication of the Humanities Division of Floyd Junior College, has the "sole purpose of putting out a magazine of original, high quality poetry and fiction. **We are open to all quality poetry and are willing to consider any type of good work.**"

They have recently published poetry by William Evans, Dev Hathaway, Martha Wicklehaus, Lynne Davis Spies, John C. Morrison and Mark R. McCulloh. The magazine is an annual, circulation 800, 7½x10½", 50+ pp., professionally printed on heavy stock with b/w graphics, colored matte cover with art, using approximately 40 pp. of poetry (usually several poems to the page). Sample copy $2. They receive 400-500 submissions per year, use 60-70. **Sample free with 9x12" SASE. Photocopy OK. Reports in 4-6 weeks. Pays copies. Editors sometimes comment on rejections.**

THE OLEANDER PRESS, OLEANDER MODERN POETS (V), 210 5th Ave., New York, NY 10010 and 17 Stansgate Ave., Cambridge, England CB2 2QZ, founded 1960, poetry editor Will Marston, **accepts *no* submissions.** They publish major writers from any language but "approach authors or translators from seeing their work in print in magazines, etc." They have recently published poetry by Osten Sjöstrand, Hans-Juergen Heise and César Moro. The editors selected these sample lines from Sue Lenier's first book, **Rain Following**, 1984 ($8.95 in paperback, $15 in hardback):

> *And what a night, A night full of spades*
> *A silver night blinking at its own damnation*
> *A night when you and I loved*
> *And the world lay hushed and blindfolded . . .*

Poets they publish must have been widely published first in magazines. They offer 10% royalty contracts plus 6 copies. Send SASE for catalog to buy samples. The editors comment, "As Oleander has to survive on sales, we have to be very careful that our poets are of major stature before we publish them. Sjöstrand, for example, has won the Bellman Prize, the major poetry prize in his native Sweden. Poetry can only survive if enough poets *read* the great poets of past and present and *buy* books. Most poets do not read at all, but write and expect to be published without making any effort to support the very poetry publishers to whom they submit. We had to give up accepting submissions in order to devote all our precious time to the thankless task of selling what we have already published."

OMMATION PRESS, *SALOME: A LITERARY DANCE MAGAZINE, *MATI MAGAZINE, OFFSET OFFSHOOTS (I, IV, Dance), 5548 N. Sawyer, Chicago, IL 60625, founded 1975, poetry editor Effie Mihopoulos. They publish "**all kinds**" of poetry and have recently published poetry by Lyn Lifshin, Susan Fromberg Schaeffer, Douglas MacDonald and Ted Berrigan. The editor selected these sample lines from "Finger Point" by Emilie Glen from *Salome*:

> *Dancing is for fingers*
> *fingers on piano keys*
> *dance faster than feet*
> *Pierrot dancing on the black and whites*

Mati, an annual, is all poetry and graphics, 40-60 pp. of various colors and weights, offset from typescript with elaborate decorative drawings on every page, saddle-stitched, printrun 500. *Mati* uses about 30% of the 500 submissions received each year. **Sample: $1.50 plus 69¢ postage.** *Salome: A Literary Dance Magazine*, a magazine-sized quarterly, printrun 500, 50 subscriptions of which 15 are libraries, saddle-stapled, offset from typescript with b/w photos and graphics, matte card cover with colored art, 100+ pp., uses 25 pp. of poetry per issue. **Sample: $4 postpaid for double issue of *Salome*. They take about 85% of the 1,000 submissions received each year, have a 1-2 year backlog. Submit up to 10 poems, clean copy. Simultaneous submissions OK if editor notified. Reports "as soon as possible," pays copies. Send SASE for guidelines. Ask for list of chapbooks (Offset Offshoots series) and other publications to buy samples. Pays 50 copies (and $100 if grant money available) for chapbook MSS. Prefers submission of whole MS to query. Provides criticism for $1 per poem (no longer than 2 pp.) Annual chapbook contest (Omation Press): query for deadline; $8 entry fee per book ms, no longer then 60 pp. Prize: $50 plus 50 copies.**

*ON BEING (IV, Religious), 2 Denham St., Hawthorn Vic., 3122 Australia, founded 1974, editor Owen Salter, an Evangelical Christian monthly magazine whose readership "is from all denomiations, all age groups and theological commitment within the Christian church." **Poetry submitted can be from 4-30 lines.** In a recent issue they published poems by L. Stewart and A. Lansdown, from whose "Behind the Veil" I chose the following lines as a sample:

> *How often my grandparents allude to death, now.*
> *The simplest plans and preparations for the new year*
> *They preface and conclude: If we're still here.*

The magazine is magazine-sized, and averages 56 pages. It is printed by web offset with some color; "graphics/art have a high profile." **A sample copy and writer's guidelines are available free. They buy only 3-5 poems/year; there is no pay. Previously published, photocopied, and dot-matrix submissions are acceptable.**

*ON THE EDGE (II), 32 Churchill Ave., Arlington, MA 02174, founded 1983, editor Cathryn McIntyre, "is a literary magazine which includes poetry, short-short fiction, essays and interviews. Wants material dealing with contemporary attitudes, behavior and beliefs. Will consider **any style of poetry, prefer a contemporary outlook and non-traditional forms and themes. Length can vary, though poems longer than 30 or so lines are unlikely to be accepted."** They have published poetry by Kathleen Spivak, Bill Costley, Connie Fox, Richard Weekley and Sigmund Weiss. The magazine is scheduled to appear 3 times a year, 7x8½" offset from typescript with 6-10 pp. of poetry per issue. They receive about 450 submissions per year, use less than 50, have a 4-6 week backlog. **Sample: $2 postpaid. Submit no more than 10 poems. Prefer typed, easily readable originals, but photocopies are OK if clear and readable. Reports in 1-8 weeks, pays 2 copies.** "In some cases" editor comments on rejections.

*ONE EARTH, THE FINDHORN PRESS (IV, Spiritual), The Park, Forres, Morayshire, Scotland IV36 0TZ, founded 1979, is a bimonthly 32 pp. magazine, circulation 2,500, expressing the **spiritual goals of the Findhorn community and uses some poetry, mostly written by members of the community, relevant to that theme. Sample: $2.**

‡*ONE SHOT (IV, Rock and roll), 3379 Morrison Ave., #, Cincinnati, OH 45220, phone 513-861-1532, founded 1986 (first issue March, 1986), editor Steven Rosen, a quarterly described by the editor as "an irreverent magazine, with both creative writing and journalism, dedicated to the great one-hit wonders of rock 'n roll and related music." **All types of poetry about rock 'n roll are acceptable; the magazine expects to buy 100 poems/year.** As a sample, I selected these lines from the second stanza of Betsy Greiner's "What the Blueswomen Knew:"

> *Before there was rock 'n' roll there was Bessie Smith singing*
> "Down Hearted Woman" *for all*
> *down-hearted women of the world.*
> *Ethel Waters finding Jesus after*
> *forty years swinging on the road.*

Since the magazine was not yet published as we went to press, I have not seen it; however, it was planned to be digest-sized, typed on word processor with line justification, letter-quality printer, then photocopied, 40 pp. saddle-stapled, matte card cover with illustration. **Sample available for $2 postpaid, guidelines for SASE. Pay is an unspecified number of copies. Poets can submit any number of poems at a time, no minimum, or maximum length. Simultaneous, photocopied, or previously published submissions are OK. Reporting time is 1 month.** The editor says that "Obviously, publication is for people who love writing and music and have some sympathy with the philosophy that 'anyone who once made us happy deserves to be remembered forever'."

*THE ONTARIO REVIEW (II, V), 9 Honey Brook Drive, Princeton, NJ 08540, editor Raymond J. Smith, Associate Editor Joyce Carol Oates, invites "contributions of all kinds, especially fiction and poetry." They "wish to encourage dialogues between the humanities, creative arts, and human sciences. They welcome essays, especially of an intercultural nature, that deal with 20th-century American and Canadian writers and artists, particularly those who have not received much critical attention in the past. **Contributors are asked to include a brief biographical note." Overstocked and cannot consider any unsolicited poetry submissions for the time being.** It is a biannual, subscription: $8; per copy: $3.95, 6x9", flat-spined, 100 + pp., professionally printed on book stock, glossy card cover with photo, using b/w graphics and photos. The issue I examined had poetry by Robert DeMott, Tom Wayman, Robert Phillips, Barry Callaghan, Richard Moore, Gary Young, Lewis Horne, Paul Shuttleworth and Frederick Feirstein, from whose "Divorced" I selected the first of eight stanzas as a sample:

> *His walls are soiled with his children's handprints.*
> *His bed is chronically unmade.*
> *He can't cook, eats junkfood standing up,*
> *Has no will to go out and get laid*

There are at least two poems, often several pages, by each poet. **Pays $5 per page.**

‡*OOVRAH (II), 249 Morris St., Albany, NY 12208, phone 518-462-3583, founded 1985, co-editors Michael Blitz and Stephen Gilson, a magazine of poetry and poetics published 3 times/year. The editors say, **"No particular forms are out-of-hand unacceptable, though we tend to seek poetry which defies convenient tags or typing. 'Risk-taking' purport to 'express' emotions or that tend toward sentimentality. If the poetry does not attend to sound, language, knowledge—it it is merely a poetic reflection 'on life'—we don't want it."** The first issue of *Oovrah* included poetry by Rosemarie Waldrop, Connie Deanovich, John Mason, Gerrit Lansing, and Judith Johnson. The magazine is digest-sized, 60-70 pp., card-stock cover, with graphics. Circulation expected to be "200-300." Price per copy is $2.50. **Sample available for $2.50 postpaid, guidelines for SASE. Pay is 1 copy. Writers should submit 10 pp. or less, photocopied or clean dot-matrix OK. Reporting time is 3-5 weeks and time to publication is approximately 8 weeks.** The editors advise, "Poetry is most interesting when it pushes the frontier of knowledge to locate itself as an instance, and an instant, of knowledge."

*OPEN PLACES (II), Box 2085, Stephens College, Columbia, MO 65215, phone 314-442-2211, Ext. 653, founded 1966, poetry editor Eleanor M. Bender. This distinguished semiannual poetry journal has recently published poetry by Sharon Olds, X. J. Kennedy, Marilyn Hacker and Margaret Atwood. *Open Places* will celebrate its 20th anniversary in 1986 with a special double issue devoted to American writers abroad. The editor selected these sample lines from "The Spider Speaks on the Need for Solidarity" by Angela Jackson:

> *We have to weave*
> *one web, a thousand-ark.*
> *We have to stick*
> *together.*

There are about 76 pp. of poetry in each issue, circulation 1,500, 1,000-1,200 subscriptions of which 70-75 are libraries. Subscription: $8; per copy: $4. They receive hundreds of submissions per issue, in each of which 7-8 poets are recognized with several poems and photograph from each. **Sample: $2. MSS are considered between September 1 and April 2 only. Poets should read a recent issue before submitting. Send 5-6 poems. Reports in 4-6 weeks. Pays in copies. Send SASE for guidelines. Editor sometimes comments on rejections.**

‡*OPPOSSUM HOLLER TAROT (I), Rt. 2, Campbellsburg, IN 47108, phone 812-755-8218, founded 1982, editor Larry Blazeh, a "true underground magazine" that publishes "short-short stories & poems about politics, sci-fi, horror, Zen Buddism and lots of other things." They want "**almost anything but over-sentimental love laments.**" They have recently published poems by Steve Srend, Susan Packie, Ed Orr and Janet Fox. As a sample, the editor chose the following lines by an unidentified poet:

> *a sourjourn flower*
> *spreads its unlovely vagina*
> *a lifetime passing*
> *a printing too complete.*

The magazine, which appears "occasionally," has a circulation of "few." Price per issue is $1.02, **sample available for same price. Pay is 1 copy. The editor says, "Please single-space, as the copies are taken direct from the manuscript, single-spacing leaves room for more material." Submissions are reported on "soon," and the backlog is from 1 week-6 months.**

*ORBIS (II), 199 The Long Shoot, Nuneaton, Warwickshire, CV11 6JQ, England, founded 1968, editor Mike Shields, considers "**all poetry so long as it's genuine in feeling and well executed of its type.**" They have published poetry by John Betjeman, Ray Bradbury, Dannie Abse, Christopher Fry, John Elsberg, Elsa Corbluth, Lain Crichton Smith, Naomi Mitchison, and James Kirkup, "but are just us likely to publish absolute unknowns." As a sample the editor selected the last stanzas of "Stop at the Bridge" by Georgia Tiffany (Spokane, USA):

> *Light wears its shadows hungry*
> *for a swallow, a long*
> *silver-tailed flight into the flesh*
> *and brooding sky*
> *I feel your throat wild and tender*
> *holding onto the fire,*
> *holding something cold.*
> *Frost crawls along the hoods of cars.*
> *The clock tower climbs out of the fog.*
> *Threaded across the once intimate blaze*
> *a web of ice,*
> *the enviable rage of spiders.*

The quarterly is 6x8½", flat-spined, 64 pp. professionally printed with glossy card cover, circulation 500, 450 subscriptions of which 50 are libraries. Subscription: £10 (or $20); per copy: £2.50 ($5). They receive "thousands" of submissions per year, use "about 5%." **Sample: $2 (or £1) postpaid. Submit typed or photocopied, 1 side only, one poem per sheet. No bio, no query. Reports in 1-2 months. Pays £2 per acceptance plus 1 free copy automatically, up to 3 on request. Each issue carries £50 in prizes paid on basis of reader votes. Editor comments on rejections "occasionally—if we think we can help."** "ORBIS is completely independent and receiving no grant-aid from anywhere," but it does associate with other organizations wishing to hold competitions—e.g. Rhyme Revival, Poems for Peace, (Barcelona, Spain), and Stanza Poets (London, UK) and also sponsors poetry weekends in England.

*ORE (IV, American folklore), 7 The Towers, Stevenage, Hertfordshire, England SG1 1HE, poetry editors Eric Ratcliffe and Brian Louis Pearce, a magazine that appears 2-3 times per year, and "**relates**

to poems which reflect the ancient atmosphere of Britain, and country atmosphere of other lands, also in Arthurian themes." Each issue is about 60 pp. It "reviews poetry booklets and refuses little in this respect, but substandard poetry is frankly referred to as such. Cuttings of reviews can only be sent if postage costs are enclosed with the booklet, or preferably cost to cover the issue in which it appears. **Sample: £1.30 surface mail, £2 airmail, by I.M.O. payable to Eric Ratcliffe. "Dollar checks should not be sent owing to excessive bank charges here to convert into sterling which would mean paying five times as much as the sterling value.** *Ore* is sent to the Lockwood Memorial, University of California and the New York libraries and is presumably available there for perusal." The editor advises U.S. poets, "Owing to the content and 'British' atmosphere of *Ore*, it will be realised that the tribal and ancient symbol predominates and that we will not be looking for poetry reflecting American city life, but on American folklore. Regarding prose about poetry, short articles relative to the poetry scene in a State are welcome if well written. Currently, subscribers are more welcome than submissions (overstocked). *Ore* can be sent in advance of payment if desired, on a continuous basis, provided the customer vouches to pay on receipt until he/she cancels. A note to this effect should be sent when requesting post-payment facilities."

*ORPHIC LUTE (II), 1675A, 16th St., Los Alamos, NM 87544, founded 1950, editor Patricia Doherty Hinnebusch, is a digest-sized 48 pp. quarterly (photocopied from typescript, saddle-stapled, matte card cover) which uses **"lyric poetry that speaks through metaphors and images, produces a strong musical effect, is subtle and natural, traditional or contemporary in theme and tone. No poems that preach. No pornography. 3-80 lines; forms and free verse equally welcome."** They have recently published poetry by Marc Jampole, B. Z. Niditch, Serena Fusek, David Craig and Charles T. Stewart. The editors selected these sample lines by Marc Jampole:

> *What a language is this color brown! An eternity of sparks*
> *streaks, motes, from which you emerge and throw off*
> *sparks through the getto smoke, lighting*
> *the surface of things*

The magazine has a circulation of 250, 200 subscriptions of which 6 are libraries. Subscription: $10; per copy: $2.50. They receive about 3,600 submissions per year, use 250, have a 2-3 month backlog. **Sample: $2.50 postpaid. Submit 3-4 poems; no simultaneous submissions, no query; clear type or photocopy. Reports in 4-8 weeks.** No pay. Send SASE for guidelines. "Whenever asked, we critique submissions. We frequently make minor revisions a condition of acceptance." The editor advises, "Every poem is a working poem. The poet can make improvements in successive revisions over many years. If it is worth saying, it is worth saying well."

*OSIRIS, AN INTERNATIONAL JOURNAL/UNE REVUE INTERNATIONALE (II, IV, Translations), Box 297, Deerfield, MA 01342, founded 1972, poetry editor Andrea Moorhead, a 6x9", saddle-stapled, 40 pp. biannual **publishes contemporary poetry and fiction in English, French and Spanish without translations and in other languages with translation, including Polish, Greek and Italian.** They also publish graphics, interviews and photographs. They want poetry which is **"lyrical, non-narrative, multi-temporal, well crafted."** They have recently published poetry by Simon Perchik, Duane Locke, Charlotte Melancon (Quebec), Jerzy Ficowski (Poland) and Jacques Bussy (France). The editors selected these sample lines (poet unidentified):

> *erase the lines etched in snow*
> *as you walk and the trees are bare now*
> *host of feathers and fallen fruit*
> *the ground under pine dark and cool*

There are 8-12 pp. of poetry in English in each issue. They have a printrun of 500, send 40 subscription copies to college and university libraries, including foreign libraries. Subscription: $7; per copy: $3.50. They receive 50-75 freelance submissions per year, use 12. **Sample: $3 postpaid. Include short bio with submission. Reports in 4 weeks. Pays 5 copies.** The editor advises, "It is always best to look at a sample copy of a journal before submitting work, and when you do submit work, do it often and do not get discouraged. Try to read poetry and support other writers."

‡*OTHER POETRY (II), 2 Stoneygate Ave., Leicester LE2 3HE, England, phone (0533) 703159, founded 1979, managing editor Evangeline Paterson, consulting editors Michael Hoyland and Gerry Wells. *Other Poetry* appears three times a year and wants **well-crafted poems on any subject, in any style, not too long,"** but doesn't want anything "too way out." They have recently published Anne Stevenson, Tom Rawling, and John Latham. As a sample, the editors selected the following lines by Dan Wylie:

> *Japheth at his desk and erudite pen . . .*
> *And Ham on a hot bright hilltop, drumming,*
> *Drumming, heartbeating, his earthy hands*
> *Cry to the tattered, bald, exuberant kraals.*

Other Poetry is digest-sized, nicely printed on white stock, 54 pp. saddle-stapled with a one-color glossy card cover; each issue is numbered (*Other Poetry: 17*). Circulation is 300-400, of which 120-150 are subscriptions. Price per issue is £1.50 and subscription price is £4.50 or £6 if mailed to USA. The magazine recently ran a poetry competition with a first prize of £25. **Sample available for £1.50 (surface mail). Pay is £2/poem and one free copy. MSS submitted should be clearly typed with name and address on each page. Photocopies are accepted. Reporting time is within 3 months, and time to publication is usually within a year.** The editors say, "*Other Poetry* is an open magazine, attached to no particular poetic school or theory. Nor do you have to be a friend of the editor. We publish what we like, and by having at least two consulting editors we try to ensure a variety of response to submissions."

*THE OTHER SIDE MAGAZINE (IV, Spiritual issues), Box 3948, Fredericksburg, VA 22402, founded 1965, poetry editor Rosemary Camilleri, is "a monthly magazine 10 times a year for Christians with an active concern for peace and justice. **We use mostly poems that relate to peace and justice issues, Christian spirituality, or appreciation and care of the created world. Any form or style. All of the poems we publish are less than 40 lines.**" They have recently published poetry by Eugene Warren, Gail White and Barbara Shisler. I selected as a sample the first of 3 stanzas of "Crab Cactus" by Rod Jellema:

> *Deformed and staunched like the stump*
> *of a claw, it hunches toward light.*
> *The stalk that it is accumulates*
> *its fleshy lack of decency*
> *time out of mind in the sands.*

The format is magazine-sized, 72 pp., saddle-stapled, with glossy color paper cover, using many graphics, photos, ads, circulation 15,000, 14,000 subscriptions of which 100 or so are libraries. Subscription: $19.75; per copy: $2.50. They receive a thousand submissions per year, use 20, have a 6 month backlog. **Sample: $2.50 postpaid. No more than 3 poems per submission. Reports in 2 months. Pays $15-20 per poem and 5 copies and subscription.**

*OUR FAMILY (IV, Religious), Box 249, Battleford, Saskatchewan, Canada S0M 0F0, phone 306-937-2663, founded 1949, editor Rev. Albert Lalonde, o.m.i., is a monthly religious magazine **for Roman Catholic families. "Any form is acceptable. In content we look for simplicity and vividness of imagery. The subject matter should center on the human struggle to live out one's relationship with the God of the Bible in the context of our modern world. We do not want to see science fiction poetry, metaphysical speculation poetry, or anything that demeans or belittles the spirit of human beings or degrades the image of God in him/her as it is described in the Bible.**" They have recently published poetry by Nadene Murphy and Arthur Stilwell. The editor selected these sample lines from "Believers" by Neil C. Fitzgerald:

> *In everyone of us*
> *there is a Thomas*
> *that sees the miracles yet does not believe*

Our Family is magazine-sized, 48 pp., glossy color paper cover, using drawings, cartoons, two-color ink, circulation 14,562 with 12,016 subscriptions of which 48 are libraries. $1.85 per issue, subscription $13.98 Canada/$17.48 US. Sample: $2.50 postpaid. Send SASE for writer's guide. 4-30 lines. Pays $.75-1 per line. Simultaneous submissions OK, prefers letter-quality to dot-matrix. Comments "if the poem did not make the grade but still shows some poetential for our readership." The editor advises, "The essence of poetry is imagery. The form is less important. Really good poets use both effectively."

OUROBOROS (II, IV, Visual, experimental), 40 Grove Ave., Ottawa, Ontario, Canada K1S 3A6, phone 613-233-4176, founded 1982, poetry editor Colin Morton. "Excellent graphic arts design and unusual formats characterize the Ouroboros Poetry Editions. We are an exceptionally small press, and see our role as being to bring to light fresh voices and fresh approaches to the **relation between poetry and other art forms—visual, musical, etc. We especially want to see poetry that breaks new ground in exploring the interplay of literary, musical and visual art, poetry that is a notation of a live performance; concrete poetry; sound poetry; etc. Any form, length, style or subject matter compatible with the above orientation will be considered. Politically engaged work, erotica, personal expression are OK.**" They have recently published poetry by LeRoy Gorman, Penny Kemp and Chris Wiod. As a sample, Colin Morton selected some lines from Robert Eady's book of prose poems, *The Blame Business*:

> *The auditors of night wait at the airport. An eye has been*
> *found under a floorboard. It cannot speak. An ear comes*
> *forward. Suddenly the facts lock up the house and run.*

The samples I have seen are, indeed, in unusual formats—paperbacks, chapbooks, folding broadsheets, posters, audio-cassettes, postcards—all elegantly printed and using sophisticated graphics. For chapbook consideration, **query with 20 samples and a letter which includes "shot bio plus any ideas on format, design, etc."** Responds to queries in 2 weeks, to submissions (if invited) in 4-6 weeks. Simultaneous submissions OK if identified. Photocopy, dot-matrix OK, or discs compatible with Apple II or Macintosh (but hard copy strongly preferred). Pays 10% royalties on books, 10 copies (and more at 40% discount). Postcards, etc: payment in copies. Send 5x8" SASE for catalog to order samples.

*OUT THERE, OUT THERE PRODUCTIONS, INC., MANHATTAN POETRY VIDEO DIVISION,(I), 156 W. 27, New York, NY 10001, phone 212-675-0194, founded 1975, poetry editors Rose Lesniak and Barbara Barg, seeks to "publish newcoming songwriter book 1986 plus produce poetry video of contributing authors. Special issues; videos, poetry-prose-songs/posters/pamphlets/flat-spined books and magazines, some mimeo." *Out There* magazine appears irregularly, 100 pp. of poetry in each issue, printrun 5,000. They use about half of the 1,000 submissions they receive per year. No samples available. Collectors issues for sale, $10. Query to find out what current book deals with. Pays $0-250 per poem. "We want *all* poetry to be read as well as seen." They have recently published poetry and have poetry videos by Eileen Myles, Tone Blevins, Anne Waldman, Bob Holman, John Giorno and Allen Ginsberg. They are currently producing a poetry video project in an effort to bring poetry into the commercial markets. **Out There Productions sponsors poetry events in the community and helps poets and writers by providing educational projects in public schools/films and video with poetry, MSS and project consultation and a networking service. Fee by donation, varies. Query; call first. They have various reading and evaluation fees—from free for the poor to donations.** The editors advise, "Find out about grants. Read all magazines. Watch and buy our videos. Perform in public. Perform community services. Go out there. Inspire/buy/rent our poetry videos."

*OUTERBRIDGE (II), English A323, The College of Staten Island, 715 Ocean Terrace, Staten Island, NY 10301, phone 212-390-7654, founded 1975, poetry editors Charlotte Alexander and Margery Robinson, publishes "the most crafted, professional poetry and short fiction we can find (unsolicited except special features—to date rural, urban and Southern, promoted in standard newsletters such as *Coda, AWP, Small Press Review*), interested in newer voices. **Anti loose, amateurish, uncrafted poems showing little awareness of the long-established fundamentals of verse; also anti blatant PRO-movement writing when it sacrifices craft for protest and message. Poems usually 1-4 pp. in length."** They have recently published poetry by P. B. Newman, Cathryn Hankla, Kenneth Frost, Marilyn Throne, Naomi Rachel, Susan Astor, Joseph Bruchac, Philip K. Jason and M. R. Doty. The editors selected these sample lines from "Discovering Musicians" by Sharyn November:

> *They understand operations better than surgeons,*
> *how the sharpness of hair against cat-gut*
> *cuts more cleanly than a scalpel.*
> *Pasteboard and velvet cases cushion their unstrung*
> *cellos, basses, instruments whose scroll-work*
> *coils into a bass clef.*

The digest-sized flat-spined, 100 + pp. annual is about half poetry, circulation 500-600, 150 subscriptions of which 28 are libraries. They receive 500-700 submissions per year, use about 60. **Sample: $4 postpaid. Submit 3-5 poems anytime except June-July. "We DISLIKE" simultaneous submissions "and if a poem accepted by us proves to have already been accepted elsewhere, a poet will be blacklisted as there are MANY good poets waiting in line." Reports in 2 months, pays 2 copies (and offers additional copies at half price).** The editor says, "As a poet/editor I feel magazines like *Outerbridge* provide an invaluable publication outlet for individual poets (particularly since publishing a BOOK of poetry, respectably, is extremely difficult these days). As in all of the arts, poetry—its traditions, conventions and variatons, experiments—should be studied. One current 'trend' I detect is a lot of mutual backscratching which can result in very loose, amateurish writing. Discipline!"

OUTPOSTS PUBLICATIONS, *OUTPOSTS POETRY QUARTERLY (I, II), 72 Burwood Rd., Walton-on-Thames, Surrey KT12 4AL England, phone 2240712, managing director Howard Sergeant, a small-press publisher of a poetry magazine and individual collections of poetry. They are **"open to all kinds and forms of good poetry."** Poets recently published include Ted Hughes, Seamus Heaney, Peter Redgrove, Elizabeth Bartlett, and V.A. Fanthorpe. The quarterly magazine is letterpress printed, 40 pp., with no art and graphics. Circulation is 2,000, of which approximately 100 are library subscriptions and about the same number are sold on newsstands. Price per issue is $4, subscription $16. **Sample available for $4 postpaid. Pay "varies with length," plus 1 copy. The editor "objects to simultaneous submissions." Reporting time is approximately 2 weeks and time to publication varies from 3-6 months.** The press publishes both hardcover books and flat-spined paperbacks; number per year varies. **For book consideration, "it is preferable that poets should first appear in the magazine."** The editor does not want photocopied, dot-matrix, or disc MSS. About the individual collections, he says, "Publication is based on advance subscriptions from buyers; amounts over costs go to author." The magazine holds an annual competition; no details are available.

OUTRIGGER PUBLISHERS LTD., RIMU PUBLISHING CO. LTD., OUTRIGGER, *RIMU, OCEAN MONOGRAPHS, *PACIFIC QUARTERLY MOANA (IV, Third World and Pacific Cultures), Box 13-049, Hamilton, New Zealand, phone 071-55-536-55-910, poetry editors Norman Simms, Theola Wyllie, et al., history, the Pacific Rim, Third World, translations and multi-cultural publications. They publish magazines and pamphlets and want **"intelligent, well-crafted poetry concerned with traditional values. No self-serving, immature, sloppy writing. Translations welcome."** They have recently published poems by Vaughan Morgan, Rob Dyer and Talosaga Tolovae. As a sample I selected the complete poem, "From a Wicker Chair in the Impala Hotel, Bangkok" by Marina Makarova:

> The Frenchmen come for the tennis weekends
> The Dutch to lord it over the native servants
> The Japanese bring suitcases full of samples
> The sad fat Australian lady buys herself jewels
> And I keep firmly to the scrambled eggs and cannot help wondering
> why the courtyards are full of Thai cats with no tails.

Rimu is a bimonthly, magazine-sized, 16 pp. on glossy paper, glossy card cover with b/w photos, graphics and ads, circulation 900-2,000, 2-3 pp. of poetry in each issue, on "art, culture and history which focuses with all of New Zealand in its multi-cultural diversity and its many languages and Maori, and other languages used in this area." *Pacific Quarterly Moana* is a "general intellectual quarterly concerned with Third World, Pacific, theory of translation, etc.," circulation 500-1,000, $12 a copy. **Neither of these magazines accepts unsolicited MSS from non-subscribers, neither pays except in copies. For chapbook or book publication, query with samples.**

THE OVERLOOK PRESS, TUSK BOOKS (III), 12 West 21st St., New York, NY 10010, phone 212-675-0585, founded 1972, are trade publishers with about 8 poetry titles. **"We prefer poets with some following. MSS should be typed, and we would rather see selections than full MSS. We *do* read everything we receive and have no specifications as to subject."** Query with sample poems. **Send SASE for catalog to order sample books.** They have published poems by David Shapiro and Freya Manfred. The editors selected these sample lines from "Mannequins" by Daniel Mark Epstein:

> This indecent procession of the undead invades
> the Avenue windows, dressed to kill, sporting
> tomorrow's clothes and yesterday's faces.

Tusk/Overlook Books are distributed by Viking Press. **They publish on standard royalty contracts with author's copies.**

OXFORD UNIVERSITY PRESS (III), 200 Madison Ave., New York, NY 10016, phone 212-679-7300, founded 1478, poetry editors Curtis Church (U.S.) and Will Sulkin (U.K.), is a large university press publishing academic, trade and college books in a wide variety of fields. "Our list includes (or has in the past included) Richard Eberhart, Conrad Aiken, e. e. cummings, and Anne Stevenson. These, with the addition of Geoffrey Hill, a major poet new to our list, indicate our direction and what we'd like to see." They have also published poetry by Peter Porter and Charles Tomlinson. **Send a "representative sample" of poetry and publication credits. Simultaneous submissions, photocopies, dot-matrix OK. Reports in 6 weeks. Pays on 10% royalty contract and 10 copies.**

*OYEZ REVIEW (I), 430 S. Michigan Ave., Chicago, IL 60605, phone 312-341-2017, founded 1965, editor Helen G. Forsythe, is an annual literary magazine published by Roosevelt Universtiy. **"We are always looking for up-beat poetry with fresh, creative and original images and statements. We encourage writers at all stages to submit their work. Visual poetry is usually not accepted due to the size of our magazine. We are not interested in poems that sound too much like letters."** They have recently published poetry by Lyn Lifshin, Mac Wellman, John Jacob and Michael Finley. The editor selected these sample lines by Molly McQuade:

> It is after the rain.
> The trees are straining upward
> as the warehouses crumble
> under boxes of cloud.

The digest-sized review is flat-spined, about 100 pp., using b/w photography and line drawings, glossy, color card cover. Circulation 400, with 20 subscriptions. It is sold at Roosevelt University events. **Sample: $3.50 postpaid. Guidelines "sometimes" available for SASE. Pays 2-3 copies. Reports in 6-8 weeks. Deadline usually in October or November; published in spring.** Helen Forsythe advises, "We encourage beginning writers to submit to us if they think their work is publishable. Remember that punctuation or lack of it, can make a difference, be sure poems are tightly woven."

PACIFIC ARTS & LETTERS, PEACE & PIECES BOOKS, *ALPS MONTHLY (V), Box 99394, San Francisco, CA 94109, phone 415-771-3431, founded 1971, poetry editor Dr. Diane Comen. Pacific Arts & Letters is a "small non-profit arts organization, publishers of *Alps Monthly* for small presses, poets and writers, sponsors of an Annual PAL Bookfair, and of Lawson & Arts, a TV program in San Francisco which does small press reviews." *Alps Monthly* **uses occasional poetry, but nothing unsolicited. The poems are short—less than 32 lines—"ecology, satire, haiku."** They have used poems by A. D. Winans, Lawrence Ferlinghetti, Jack Micheline, Janet Cannon and Beverly Brown. The editor selected a sample by Todd Lawson:

> *Jollification emits*
> *pregnant sounds.*
>
> *Frogs frolic,*
> *imagining (themselves) to be*
> *sea monsters,*
>
> *and,*
>
> *once in a while*
> *I read the Bible,*
> *but just once in a while.*

Alps Monthly, magazine-sized, 8-12 pages except for large bookfair issues, uses a half page of poetry in each issue, circulation 3,000 to subscribers of which 750 are libraries and institutions. Subscription: $28; per issue: $3. They receive 30-50 freelance submissions of poetry per year, use 5-10, have a 6-8 week backlog. **Sample: $3.50 postpaid. Contributors are "mostly subscribers." Reports in 6 weeks, pays "only subscribers."** Peace & Pieces Books is an imprint used mostly for anthologies, accepts no unsolicited material. The editor advises, "Poetry is an art and craft of love. Few make any sort of living at it—including many outstanding poets. *Alps Monthly* subscribers are informed of grants, publishing tips and resources as well as information on the poetry, prose scenes."

*PACIFIC BRIDGE (IV, Gay), Box 883903, San Francisco, CA 94188-3903, phone 415-641-4788, founded 1982, is a gay Asian (and non-Asian) personal ad magazine with some stories, poems and articles. **Contributors should be gay Asians or the poetry should "somehow be thematically relevant (no hardcore), under 2 pages in length."** As a sample, I selected the first stanza of "Nightwalk" by T. J. Ho:

> *Dear friend*
> *Walk me through the night*
> *Chase the shadows back into their hidden sanctuaries*
> *Before I am abducted and led away*

The digest-sized bimonthly, 34 pp., circulation 1,500, matte card cover, photocopied from typescript with b/w photos, uses a maximum of 2 pp. of poetry in each issue, receives a dozen submissions per year, uses 30%, have up to 4 months backlog. **Sample: $3.50 postpaid. With submission "state clearly rules for use and desired compensation (i.e., we will honor one-time use agreement, copyright retention and MS return requests)." They pay up to "$30/issue maximum; can negotiate free ad or subscription if preferred."**

*PAINTED BRIDE QUARTERLY (II), 230 Vine St., Philadelphia, PA 19106, editors Louis Camp, Joanna DiPaolo, and Louis McKee, founded 1975, after a period of suspension, revived by the Painted Bride Art Center two years ago. It is "a magazine publishing **regional writers with their peers from around the country.** *PBQ* aims to be a leader among little magazines published by and for independent poets and writers nationally." The 80 pp. perfect-bound, digest-sized magazine uses 60 + pages of poetry per issue, receiving over a thousand submissions per year and using under 150. Neatly printed, small type. It has a circulation of 750, 200 subscriptions, of which 30 are libraries. $4 per copy, $12 for subscription, **sample: $4 postpaid.** Here are some lines from a poem by Naomi Shihab Nye:

> *Once you start wanting to get out of Texas*
> *it's all over.*
> *The Land can't love you anymore.*

Quarterly deadlines: on going. Submit no more than 6 poems, any length, typed, photocopies OK, only original, unpublished work. Payment 2 copies. The editors say they comment "if we think the poet has potential or the poems we received might improve. But **if we say send more, we mean it.**"

ALWAYS submit MSS or queries with a stamped, self-addressed envelope (SASE) within your country or International Reply Coupons (IRCs) purchased from the post office for other countries.

‡ **PANCAKE PRESS (II)**, 163 Galewood Circle, San Francisco, CA 94131, phone 415-665-9215, founded 1974, publisher Patrick Smith, a small-press publisher of hand-bound paperbacks with sewn signatures. The editor wants **"poetry aware of its own language conventions, tuned to both the ear and eye, attentive to syntax, honest about its desires, clear about something, spoken or written as a member of the species."** He has recently published books by John Logan, David Ray, and Stephen Dunning. As a sample, he selected the following lines by an unidentified poet:

> *if I could sit still forever like this*
> *id be as simple as the universe*
> *my subtlety impossible to unsnarl*
> *but a vacation is just a vacation*

The two thin chapbooks I have seen are handsomely printed on fine paper; one has b/w illustrations. Covers are either matte or glossy cards, and one is illustrated with a drawing of the author. Pancake Press publishes 2-3 chapbooks each year, with an average page count of 36, flat-spined. **Freelance submissions are accepted; the author should send 5-6 sample poems, and if he/she wants to send bio, philosophy, or poetic aims, those are OK too. Queries will be answered in 2-3 weeks and MSS reported on in 4-6 weeks. Simultaneous submissions are OK if marked as such. Photocopied or dot-matrix MSS are acceptable but discs are not. Pancake Press gives advances; the amount is negotiable but is usually $100. Payment is 10% of net sales equivalent. Criticism of rejected MSS is always provided.**

*PANDORA, EMPIRE BOOKS (IV, Science fiction, fantasy), Box 625, Murray, KY 42071-0625, founded 1980, poetry editor Ruth Berman (send MSS here: 2809 Drew Ave. S. Minneapolis, MN 55416). *Pandora* is a small press **science fiction and fantasy** magazine appearing twice a year, using 2-3 poems per issue. **"Prefer 5-20 line poems; will occasionally purchase up to 50-line poems. *No longer*. Themes: science fiction, fantasy, weird, offbeat."** They have recently published poetry by Robert Frazier, Lee Ballentine, Millard Alexander, Scott E. Green, Chris Gilbert, William M. White and A. McA. Miller. The magazine has a circulation of 700, 300 subscriptions of which "maybe 10" are libraries. Subscription: $10 for 4 issues; per copy: $3.50. They receive 30-50 submissions per year, use 6-8. **Sample: $3.50 postpaid. Submit no more than 3 poems at a time. Readable dot-matrix, photocopy OK. Reports in 4-5 weeks. Pays $2 per poem. Send SASE for guidelines. Editor sometimes comments on rejections.**

*PANGLOSS PAPERS (II), Box 18917, Los Angeles, CA 90018, founded 1982, edited by Bard Dahl, is a **satirical literary magazine: "We question authority."** Offset printed from typescript, saddle-stapled, 48 pp. digest-sized, decorated with crude cartoons—**obviously not for the artsy-snobbish. 600 copies are printed quarterly and sent out free. Sample: $1 postpaid**. He uses about 4 pages of poetry per issue, gets about 50 submissions per year, has no backlog. Simultaneous submissions OK. Pays 2 copies. Here's the "Editor's Note" from the July, 1984, issue: "We are pleased to announce we have received no grants, prizes, honorable mentions, bonuses, rebates, discounts, refunds, offers to purchase or merge. We *have* received tirades, insults, threats, cries of outrage, condescending pity, and exclamations of amazement that we continue. Praise has been sparing, carefully-measured, and iridescent as old wine. This proof elates and endorses our conviction that we are fulfilling our mission. *Pangloss* marches on."

PANJANDRUM BOOKS (II), 11321 Iowa Ave., Ste. 1, Los Angeles, CA 90025, founded 1971, editor Dennis Koran, associate editor David Guss. **The press publishes a distinguished list of avant-garde books. They are interested in translations (especially European) of modern poetry, surrealism, dada and experimental poetry and accept book-length MSS only with SASE; query first.**

‡***PANORAMA OF CZECH LITERATURE (IV, Czech)**, Halkova ulice 1, 120 72 Prague 2, Czechoslovakia, published by the Union of Czech Writers, the Czech Literary Fund, and the DILIA Theatrical and Literary Agency, chief editor Ivo Kral. This annual publication, which is very handsomely printed and illustrated (though poorly glued; pages fall out when it is opened), is an overview of Czech literature and art, including poetry; it is published in both Czech and English editions. As a sample, I selected the first stanza from "Not For Me," by Ivan Skala, translated by Jarmila and Ian Milner:

> *Not for me verse about nothing,*
> *however shapely, with brilliant rhyme,*
> *while underfoot the earth is burning*
> *as we move through our searing time.*

The edition I have *Panorama 6* (1984), contains 204 pp. It is 6½x9", printed on slick paper with both b/w and four-color illustrations, glossy card cover with colored drawing, flat-spined. 5,000 copies were printed. **Reporting time: 6 months; payment according to fixed rates.**

‡***PAPER AIR MAGAZINE, SINGING HORSE PRESS (III)**, Box 40034, Philadelphia, PA 19106, founded 1976, editor and publisher Gil Ott, who says "*Paper Air* features poetry, interviews, essays, and letters in an attractive and well-designed format. Circulation is small and the magazine appears irregularly. Singing Horse Press publishes small books. Poets should read the magazine before submitting." He did not name poets he has published nor quote sample lines, and I have not seen the magazine. *Paper Air* is magazine-sized, offset, 120 pp. flat-spined; one artist is usually featured per issue, contributing a serial or thematic work. It appears "approximately annually." Circulation is 800, of which 75 are subscriptions, 25 go to libraries, and 300 are sold on newsstands. Price per issue is $5. **Sample available for $5 postpaid. Pay is 2 copies. No simultaneous submissions. Reporting time is 1-8 weeks.** Singing Horse Press publishes 1-2 poetry chapbooks/year with an average page count of 24-48; format varies. Prices, according to their catalog, range from $2.50-4. **Writers should query before submitting.**

***PARABOLA, PARABOLA BOOKS (II)**, 150 5th Ave., New York, NY 10011, phone 212-924-0004, founded 1975, poetry editor Jeff Zaleski. *Parabola* is a quarterly "to explore man's quest for meaning as expressed in myth, folklore, the great religious traditions and contemporary writing." Each issue is based on a particular theme, so **before submitting, query regarding current themes. Any form or style, but 250 words maximum length.** They have published anonymous Sufi poetry and poetry by John Updike, from whom the editor selected these sample lines:

> Coming from a chore as the day
> was packing it in, I saw my long shadow
> walking before me, carrying in the tilt of its thin head
> autumnal news

Each 128 pp. issue uses 1-4 pp. of poetry. *Parabola* has a circulation of 18,000, 14,000 subscriptions of which 300 are libraries. Subscription: $18; per copy: $5.50. They receive 150 submissions per year, use 1-5. **Sample: $5.50 postpaid. Photocopy, dot-matrix, simultaneous submissions OK. Reports in 1 month, pays $50 per poem. Send SASE for guidelines. Parabola Books is currently considering freelance submissions of poetry.**

‡**PARALLEL PROJECTS, *PARALLEL (II, IV, Thematic)**, Boterstraat 43, 2930 Hombeek, Belgium, founded 1982, editors Luc and Tania V. Fierens, uses poetry in "**all forms, all lengths, experimental, avant-garde (visual poetry, concrete poetry, mail art, correspondence art, style with symbols, images, dramatic, sadistic, satirical, absurd poetry. We try a lot, but do *not* want to see middle-of-the road poetry, lyric poetry, didactic poetry—oh no!**" They have recently published poetry by Terry Cuthbert, Max Noiprox, and A. Darlington. The editor selected these sample lines by David Banks:

> Flemish day trip
> sprinkled
> with military cemeteries
> and still
> still poppies

Parallel is a magazine-sized, 30 pp., photocopied from typescript, with b/w graphics, side-stapled with colored card cover. The **Yearbook**, which I have not seen, consists of **work on pre-announced themes**. Circulation: 300, 100 subscriptions of which 15 are libraries. **Sample $3, guidelines available for SASE, pays 2 copies. Submit no more than 3 "not *too* long," photocopies OK. Editor comments if poet asks.** "The creative yearbook is a limited edition (300 maybe 500) with poetry and creative work (graphics b/w). I organize a Mail-Art exhibition on a theme and the yearbook is the document (action) of the project." Luc Fierens comments, "I make a mag for a forum of artists and for a forum of readers from around the world. Tania and I select on a basis of 'we like it or not.' We are little, with little money. I dare not tell you about the postage money we pay here in a year to keep *Parallel* and the arts alive. It's a passion. I adore art and poetry. I mail everything around the world, I am a mail-artist: visual poet, poet certainly, no business poet or marketing poet. Write the way you are, make the world with your passion and energy. Passion creates Art."

***THE PARIS REVIEW (III)**, 45-39 171st Pl., Flushing, NY 11358, founded 1952, poetry editor Jonathan Galassi (**submissions should go to him at 541 E. 72nd St., New York, NY 10021**). This distinguished quarterly (circulation 10,000, digest-sized, 200 pp.) has published many of the major poets writing in English. **Sample: $6. Study publication before submitting. Pays $35 to 24 lines, $50 to 59 lines; $75 to 99 lines; $150 thereafter. Also sponsors Bernard F. Conners Prize.**

***PARIS/ATLANTIC INTERNATIONAL MAGAZINE OF POETRY, NEW POETS SERIES, INTERNATIONAL YOUNG WRITERS AWARD FOR POETRY (II)**, 31 Avenue Bosquet, Paris, 75007, France, founded 1982. The magazine appears 3 times a year, 70 pp., 6x8½", circulation 1,000.

According to Michael Lynch, editor, the journal "is published by the American College in Paris—all poetry, no reviews, no prose. The poets are from many different countries, and we have published in English with French translations as well as German into English and Dutch into English—many well-known poets in France and England as well as such poets as William Pitt Root and Brian Swann from the States, Seamus Heaney and Derek Mahon from Ireland, Jeremy Reed from England and a good number of previously unpublished poets from such countries as Pakistan and India. We encourage unpublished poets, but have also published some very well-known poets. We will be starting a chapbook series for unpublished poets in the next year and would like to begin to publish and establish contacts with poets from as wide a variety of backgrounds as possible." **Sample: $3 plus postage. Pays in copies.**

*PARNASSUS LITERARY JOURNAL (I), Box 1384, Forest Park, GA 30051, founded 1975, edited by Denver Stull: "Our sole purpose is to promote poetry and to offer an outlet where poets may be heard." **One copy in payment.** This is an amiable, open magazine **emphasizing uplift**. It is photo-copied from typescript, uses an occasional photo or drawing, a chunky (84 pp.) saddle-stapled, **low-budget production**. Poets they have published include Ruth Wildes Schuler, Diana Kwiatkowski, William Evans, J.B. Goodenough, B.Z. Niditch and Mary Ann Henn. As a sample, I selected the beginning lines from "Lobster" by Faye Simpkins:

> I'm an ugly red lobster
> Awful looking as a big monster
> A lady is forking me on a soda cracker
> If I weren't dead I'd try to smack 'er!

Denver Stull says, "**We are open to all poets and all forms of poetry, including oriental. Prefer 24 lines and under but will take longer poetry if it is good. Do not see enough humor**." The magazine comes out three times a year with a print run of 250 copies, 125 + subscribers (5 libraries). They receive about **1,200 submissions per year, of which they use 400**, 6 month backlog, **report within one week. Considers simultaneous submissions. Sample: $3.** (regularly $3.50 per copy, $10 per subscription). Periodic contests with small cash prizes. "**Definitely**" comments on rejected MSS. The editor advises: "Read. Read and study other poets. Study the markets. Ask for sample copy of magazine before submitting—not necessarily our magazine, but know what the editor is looking for and save postage. Be patient with little magazine editors. We are one-man operations and we are swamped. Only so many poems will go into an issue, so it may take a while for your poem to appear. The magazine says, "Contributions from non-subscribers are welcome, but in the case of two submissions of equal quality and suitability, the subscribers will be given preference."

*PARNASSUS: POETRY IN REVIEW, POETRY IN REVIEW FOUNDATION (V), 205 W. 89th St., New York, NY 10024, phone 212-787-3569, founded 1972, poetry editor Herbert Leibowitz, provides "comprehensive and in-depth coverage of new books of poetry, including translations from foreign poetry." They have had special issues on Words & Music, Charles Ives, Virgil Thompson, Charles Olson and Women and Poetry. "**We publish poems on occasion, but we solicit all material. Writer is given all the space he or she wishes. The only stipulation is that the style be non-academic.**" They have recently published poetry by Derek Walcott, Vladimir Mayakovsky and Velimir Khlebnikov. The editor selected these sample lines by Irina Ratushinskaya, translated by Pamela White Hadas and Ilya Nyksh:

> Over Russia's wheatfields once, a pre-war wind unfurled,
> And a funny high school kid, in love with all the world,
> Hunched over Magellanic maps, burning candles down
> And meanwhile growing up. All according to plan . . .

The semiannual is 350-400 pp, flat-spined, glossy card cover with art, elegantly designed and printed, with 1,000 subscriptions of which 550 are libraries. Subscription: $13; per copy: $7-10. They receive about 60 submissions of poetry per year, use 2, have a 3 month-2 year backlog. **Sample: $7.86 post-paid. "Don't like multiple submissions or dot-matrix. Photocopies if legible are OK. Reports usually within 6 weeks; during certain periods like the summer 3-4 months. Pays $25-250. Contributors are given 2 gift subscriptions and can take one for themselves. Editor comments on rejections—from one paragraph to 2 pages.** The editor comments, "Contributors should be urged to subscribe to at least one literary magazine. There is a pervasive ignorance of the cost of putting out a magazine and no sense of responsibility for supporting a mag. Our own plan is to publish more essays on and poems from foreign poetries."

*PARTISAN REVIEW (III), 141 Bay State Rd., Boston, MA 02215, phone 617-353-4260, founded 1934, editor William Phillips, is a distinguished quarterly literary journal (6x9", 160 pp., flat-spined, circulation 8,200), using **poetry of high quality. Submit maximum of 6. Buys 20 per year, pays $50 each.**

*PASSAGES NORTH (LITERARY MAGAZINE) (II), William Bonifas Fine Arts Center, Escanaba, MI 49829, founded 1979, poetry editor Elinor Benedict, is a **semiannual tabloid** (i.e., white uncoated paper, folded, unstapled), though the quality of paper and printing are higher than that term implies. "The magazine not only publishes established writers, but also encourages students in writing programs. It fosters interchange between the Upper Midwest and other parts of the nation." They have published Michael Delp, Susan Rea, Judith Minty, Danny Rendleman, Jim Daniels, Sheila E. Murphy, and Jack Driscoll, whose lines from "The Arrow" the editor offers as a sample:

> *When my father bought me this arrow*
> *he said its cutting head*
> *still held the light*
> *he'd pushed through a deer's heart.*

"**Do not want greeting card, sentimental, popular song or poster-type verse**." About 16 pages of each 24 page issue are devoted to poetry, 2,500 received and 100 used per year. The print run is 2,000, 800 subscriptions of which 10 are libraries, $1 per issue, $2 per year (**sample: $1.50 postpaid, guidelines available for SASE**). "**Prefer groups of 4, typed single-spaced, or clear copy. Multiple submissions only if informed *at once* if accepted elsewhere. Query unnecessary, reports 3 weeks to 3 months, payment 3 copies and $10 when grants are available**." They have occasional competitions and pay honoraria when grants are available. **Comments on rejected MSS "whenever possible."**

*PASSAIC REVIEW (II), % Forstmann Library, 195 Gregory Ave., Passaic, NJ 07055, founded 1979, Richard P. and Lorraine A. Quatrone, poetry editors, has published **a number of our most notable poets, such as Allen Ginsberg and David Ignatow**. Here are some lines from "June 17, 1983" by Richard Quatrone:

> *These could be the lines of a dying man.*
> *Dying here in Passaic, in the fumes and poisons*
> *of modern greed and hatred, dying in the flesh*
> *of cynicism, caught within its grip with nowhere*
> *to go, with no one to listen, with only one hope*

It comes out twice a year in an offset, typescript, saddle-stapled 48 pp. digest-sized format, with occasional artwork. The editors say they want "**direct, intelligent, courageous, imaginative, free writing**." They print a thousand copies, have 75 subscriptions (20 libraries). Each issue is $3.75, subscription $6, **sample back-issue $2.75**, have a 4-6 month backlog and **report in 4-6 months. Payment: one copy**. Rarely comment.

*PASSION FOR INDUSTRY (II), Box 1252, Athens, OH 45701, founded 1984, general editor, Joseph Allgren, is a biannual literary quarterly. "Quality is our only bias, but we do have some basic beliefs. One is that the business of literature is to turn off the robot, the automatic way we live our lives, and therefore to 'remind us of what it means to be human.' Another is that there is no dichotomy between image and idea; they are both essential and inseparable. And we believe in drive: the drive that makes a work passionately involved in the world and the drive it takes to write and rewrite until the work breathes on its own. We belive in passion and we believe in industry." **No limitations on kinds of poetry. "Poems under 200 lines please."** They have recently published poetry by Hollis Summers, Roy Bentley, Stephen Smith and Sibyl James. The digest-sized magazine, saddle-stapled, appears in June and December. They have a circulation of 100-200, 24 subscriptions of which 2 are libraries. Subscription: $5 for 4 issues. **Sample: $1.50 postpaid. No more than 20 poems, please. Photocopy, dot-matrix OK. Reports in 2-4 weeks. No pay.**

‡*PATH PRESS, INC. (IV, Black American and Third World), 53 West Jackson Blvd., Suite 1040, Chicago, IL 60604, phone 312-663-0167, founded 1969, executive vice president and poetry editor Herman C. Gilbert, a small publisher of books and poetry "**by, for, and about Black American Third World people.**" **The press is open to all types of poetic forms except "poor quality." Submissions should be typewritten in manuscript format. Writers should send sample poems, credits, and bio.** I have not seen sample books, but the editor describes them as "hardback and quality paperback."

PAYCOCK PRESS, *GARGOYLE MAGAZINE (II), Box 3567, Washington, D.C. 20007, phone 202-333-1544, founded 1976, poetry editor Gretchen Johnsen. *Gargoyle* comes out twice a year—a hefty, flat-spined, beautifully printed literary journal containing quality fiction, poetry, interviews and reviews. **Sample $4 postpaid**, subscription $10. The emphasis is on "**innovative and unusual work by new, little-known and/or neglected writers and artists. . . . We hope to function as a catalyst/crossroads for widely divergent groups, their styles, attitudes and objectives**." Recently published poets include Roy Fisher, Lee Upton, Carlo Parcell, Nigel Hinshelwood and Doug Messerli. Here are some lines from a poem by Amy Gerstler:

> *Not a soul heard me call out, felled by*
> *his soft karate. The phrase "Flight from*
> *Egypt" popped into my head while I focused*
> *my eyes on the whitewashed ceiling . . .*

"We don't exclude work in traditional forms, but have rarely published it. We do not publish political poetry when it is primarily a vehicle for political messages." They prefer short poems (page
or less) but will consider longer work. The poetry should show "an awareness of design and its relation to the subject of the poem." They estimate that they receive 30,000 submissions a year, of which
they use about 30, but they have only a month's backlog and report within a month. The magazine has
a circulation of 1,500, 100 subscriptions (25 libraries). "We prefer to see a group of poems—5 or so.
Any legible format. Submit anytime, no query necessary. Payment: 1 complimentary copy, additional copies half price." In addition, as Paycock Press, they publish one perfect-bound chapbook
(about 50 pp.) by an individual poet each year, and they project an anthology for 1987. Advisable for
poet to have seen an issue of the magazine before submitting to the chapbook series. Send sample
of 5-10 poems, brief bio and note on publications. If your manuscript is published as a chapbook you
get 10% (average 100 copies) of the press run, and half the net profit, if any. Sample $5.95 post-
paid. They are likely to comment on submissions, "especially if the work is close to what we're looking for." Gretchen Johnsen advises, "Read as widely as possible the contemporary journals of poetry to
find out what's new and relevant to your experience and style and to avoid duplications. Submit to those
publications which are most interesting to you as a reader."

*THE PEGASUS REVIEW (II), Box 134, Flanders, NJ 07836, founded 1980, is a 14 page (counting
cover) pamphlet entirely in calligraphy with drawings, on high-quality paper, some color overlays.
Poetry editor Art Bounds says, "This magazine is a bimonthly, and each issue is based on a specific
theme. These themes may be approached by means of poetry (24 lines), fiction (short short) or essays.
Any style of poetry, but the emphasis is on quality. Experimental is fine, but the work must indicate thought." They have published Susan Beard, Jack R. Justice, Mary Searle, Earl E. Squires. The
editor selected these lines as a sample (from "Winter Prayer" by T. K. Splate):

> *Oh, Lord, may bright warm sun beams continue to green*
> *the spring forest, blossom the*
> *beautifully colored woodland*
> *wild-flowers, and bleach my gray beard red*
> *Please, one more time.*

Sample: $1, subscription $5. Query to find out themes for the year; a prompt reply will be made.
150 copies are printed for 105 subscriptions, of which 3 are libraries. Reports within a month, usually
with personal reply, payment: 2 copies. There are occasional awards as funds are available, usually inscribed books useful to writers. The editor advises, "Become aware with good writing through
your local library and quality publications. *Writer's Digest* as well as other similar publications are a
must in order to be aware of the current market situation. Writers should write daily and market their
work."

‡PELLA PUBLISHING COMPANY, *THE CHARIOTEER (IV, Greek), 337 West 36th St., New
York, NY 10018, phone 212-279-9586, poetry editor Carmen Capri-Karka. Pella is a small-press publisher of academic books and journals; *The Charioteer* is an annual publication of essays and poems on
and English translations from works of modern Greek writers. "We publish translations from the
original Greek texts and original material relevant to Greece and Greek culture, and preferably *in
Greek*." Two well-known poets published recently are Regina Pagoulatou and Nikos Spanias. *The
Charioteer* is digest-sized, approximately 150-200 pp. Circulation is 1,000, of which about 700 are subscriptions and half of those go to libraries. Price per issue is $15. Sample: $15 postpaid; no guidelines
are available. Pay is 2 copies plus 4 reprints. Submissions must be hard copy if original work; if a
translation it must be accompanied by a copy of the original Greek text. Submissions are reported
on in 6 months and the backlog is 1 year.

*PEMBROKE MAGAZINE (II), Box 60, Pembroke State University, Pembroke, NC 28372, found-
ed 1969 by Norman Macleod, edited by Shelby Stephenson, a heavy (252 + pp., 6x9"), flat-spined,
quality literary annual, has published Fred Chappell, Stephen Sandy, Charles Edward Eaton, M.H.
Abrams and David Rigsbee. Here is one of A.R. Ammons' poems "Cold Rheum":

> *You can't*
> *tell what's*
>
> *snot from*
> *what's not*

Print run: 500, subscriptions: 125, of which 100 are libraries. **Sample: $3 postpaid**, the single copy price, **reports within 3 months, payment in copies, sometimes comments on rejections**. Stephenson advises, "Publication will come if you write. Writing is all."

*PENNINE PLATFORM (II), Ingmanthorpe Hall Farm Cottage, Wetherby, W. Yorkshire, England LS22 5EQ, phone 0937-64674, founded 1973, poetry editor Brian Merrikin Hill, appears 3 times a year. The editor wants **any kind of poetry but concrete ("lack of facilities for reproduction"). No specifications of length, but poems of less than 40 lines have a better chance. "All styles—effort is to find things good of their kind. Preference for religious or socio-political awareness of an acute, not conventional kind."** They have recently published poetry by Elizabeth Bartlett, Anna Adams, Pierre Emmanuel, Stanley Cook, Judith Kazantzis and Joan Downar. The editor selected these sample lines by Cal Clothier:

> The fiction of your life has made the news
> tea-time pornography; we need to know,
> we need to know what's now impossible.
> Your head's too small: how can we make
> you bear the guilt, and not diminish our
> responsibility for innocence?

The 6x8" 36 pp. journal is photocopied from typescript, saddle-stapled, with matte card cover with graphics, circulation 400, 300 subscriptions of which 16 are libraries. Subscription £3 for 3 issues (£5 abroad; £15 if not in sterling); per copy: £80. They receive about 300 submissions per year, use about 30, have about a 6 month backlog. **Sample: £80 postpaid. Submit 1-6 poems, typed or photocopied. Reports in about a month. No pay. Editor occasionally comments on rejections.** Brian Hill comments, "It is time to avoid the paradigm-magazine-poem and reject establishments—ancient, modern or allegedly contemporary. Small magazines and presses often publish superior material to the commercial hyped publishers."

‡*THE PENNSYLVANIA REVIEW (II), English Dept., 526 CL, University of Pittsburgh, Pittsburgh, PA 15260, phone 412-624-0026, founded 1985, managing editor Ellen Darion. This ambitious new quarterly was described by *Choice* as "a fine small literary magazine." **There are no restrictions on subject matter, style, or length, although they do not want to see "light verse or greeting card verse."** Some poets recently published are Sonia Sanchez, Gary Fricke, Greg Kuzma, Gary Margolis, Joseph Bruchac, Walter McDonald, and Peter Meinke. As a sample I have selected the opening stanza of "Why I Got Pregnant in 1984," by Elizabeth Kerlikowske:

> A garden is out of the question.
> There is no land here and the rules
> prohibit even sunning oneself in front
> of one's cubicle.

The Pennsylvania Review announces that it publishes "the best contemporary prose and poetry twice yearly." It is a handsome magazine, 7x10", 80 pp. flat-spined, professionally printed on heavy stock with graphics, art, and ads, glossy card cover with b/w illustration on grey. Circulation is approximately 1,000 with 300 subscriptions, price per issue $5, subscription $9. **Sample: $5 postpaid. Pay is $3/page plus one free copy. Submission deadlines are November 30 for Spring issue, April 1 for Fall issue. Submissions are reported on in 8-10 weeks, and the magazine has no backlog at present. Writers should submit 3-6 poems, typewritten only, clear photocopies OK but no dot-matrix.**

PENNYWHISTLE PRESS (IV, Children), Box 500-P, Washington, DC 20044, is a weekly tabloid newspaper supplement with stories and features for children 6-12 years old, circulation 2,600,000 which uses **"traditional poetry for children." Buys 5-10 poems per year. Submit maximum of 1 poem. Pays variable rate. Send SASE for guidelines, 75¢ and SASE with 2 stamps for sample.**

PENTAGRAM (II), Box 379, Markesan, WI 53946, founded 1974, poetry editor Michael Tarachow, who is also printer and publisher. Pentagram "is a one-man outfit publishing books of contemporary poetry on an 1893 Chandler & Price letterpress. Handset type, mouldmade or handmade papers, handbound. **Query with SASE before sending MSS."** Pentagram publishes broadsides, postcards and pamphlets in addition to books. Has recently published poetry by Bob Arnold, Barbara Moraff, Theodore Enslin, Karin Lessing and Christopher Buckley. "*Time* is the invisible factor, the hours invested/spent in producing the handmade book. One *can* judge a book by its cover, if one knows how to look—and vision's a rare commodity these days, it seems. 'If the approach isn't true, nothing is." **Replies to queries next day. Payment—variable. Catalog available.**

‡*PENTECOSTAL EVANGEL (IV, Christian), 1445 Boonville, Springfield, MO 65802, phone 417-862-2781, founded 1914, editor Richard G. Champion, is the official organ of the Assemblies of

God, a Pentecostal denomination. They want **"inspirational and devotional" poetry, usually not longer than 25 lines.** As a sample, the editor selected these lines from an unidentified poet:

> *Creation's voice speaks louder than my own!*
> *(My heart's devotion stands in awe)*
> *Still nearer to him her worship calls*
> *And stirs my mind with sweet amens.*

The weekly publication is magazine-sized, 32 pp., offset, with photos and graphics, "split color." Circulation is 290,000, price per issue 30¢, subscription $10 for the first year. **Guidelines are available for SASE. Pay is a minimum of 40¢/line plus 2 copies. Queries are discouraged. Submissions are reported on in 6 weeks and the backlog is usually 1 year.**

THE PENUMBRA PRESS, THE MANILA SERIES (II), 920 S. 38th St., Omaha, NE 68105, phone 402-346-7344, founded 1972, poetry editors Bonnie and George O'Connell, publishes "contemporary literature and graphics in the tradition of fine arts printing." Their books are "designed, illustrated (unless otherwise indicated), hand printed from hand-set type, and bound by the proprietor," Bonnie O'Connell. All are limited editions, including hard and soft cover books, chapbooks, postcards and theme anthologies. They have recently published poetry by David St. John, Brenda Hillman, Debora Greger, Peter Everwine, Laura Jensen, Norman Dubie and Rita Dove. As a sample the editor selected these lines from "Cool Dark Ode" by Donald Justice:

> *When the long planed table that served as a desk*
> *was recalling the quiet of the woods,*
> *when the books, older, were thinking farther back,*
> *to the same essential stillness . . .*

Query with 5-6 samples, some personal background and publication credits. Simultaneous submissions, photocopy OK. Editor sometimes comments on rejections. Send SASE for catalog to order samples or inquire at university libraries (special collections)—or through their distributor, Granary Books, 212 N. 2nd St., Minneapolis MN 55401.

PERIVALE PRESS (II), 13830 Erwin St., Van Nuys, CA 91401, founded 1968, editor Lawrence P. Spingarn, publishes **Perivale Poetry Chapbooks, Perivale Translation Series**, anthologies. The collections by individuals are usually translations, but here are some lines from R. L. Barth from "Da Nang Nights: Liberty Song," in **Forced-Marching to the Styx**:

> *In sudden light we choose*
> *Lust by lust our bar:*
> *And whatever else we lose,*
> *We also lose the war.*

They publish an average of one 20 pp. saddle-stapled chapbook, one perfect-bound (20-70 pp.) collection, one anthology per year, all quality print jobs. Send SASE for catalog. Perivale publishes both on **straight royalty basis (10%, 10 author's copies) usually grant supported, and by subsidy, the author paying 100%, being repaid from profits, if any. "Payment for chapbooks accepted is 50 free copies of press run. Contributors are encouraged to buy samples of chapbooks, etc., for clues to editor's tastes." To submit, query first, with sample of 6-10 poems, bio, previous books**. Spingarn, a well-known, widely published poet, offers **criticism for a fee, the amount dependent on length of book**.

*PERMAFROST (II), English Dept., University of Alaska, Fairbanks, AK 99701, phone 907-474-5239, founded 1977, poetry editors Alys Culhane and R.H. Ober. *Permafrost* is a biannual magazine of poems, short stories, essays, reviews, drawings and photographs, using "**any style of poetry provided it is well-written. Favor strong images. Avoid vague, wordy, sentimental poems. Interested in seeing poetry that demonstrates an unusual content. Poetry is more than prose with large margins.**" They have recently published poetry by David Ignatow, Miriam Sagan, Diane Reynolds, Mary Baron, Malcolm Glass, John Haines, Gunter Grass and William Stafford. The editors selected these sample lines from "Dust" by John Morgan:

> *Given a life to spend, a bank of bones,*
> *two bodies tough as any blossoms, we*
> *took each other in hand. So this*
> *is what it means to live on earth—*

The digest-sized 70+ pp. magazine is flat-spined, professionally printed, glossy card cover with b/w graphics and photos, has a circulation of 500, 160 subscriptions of which 20 are libraries. Subscription: $5; per copy: $3. They have a 4 month backlog. **Sample: $3 postpaid. Submit no more than 5 poems, neatly typed or photocopied. Pays 2 copies. Editors occasionally comment on rejections.**

PERMANENT PRESS, (II), 52 Cascade Ave., London N10, England, editor Robert Vas Dias. The press started in 1972. "The aim of **Permanent Press** is to bring to the attention of readers of poetry on both sides of the Atlantic the **work of significant new poets as well as that of more established writers from Britain and America**. Even the work of certain better-known postmodernist writers often fails to make the trans-Atlantic crossing successfully. **Permanent Press books are designed to remedy this lack by making available inexpensive and well-produced editions of poetry—both collections (about 40-45 pp. is optimum, though we have also published smaller chapbooks) and poem-sequences, long poems, or sections from longer work-in-progress.** Recently published authors include Toby Olson, Paul Blackbarn, Kelvin Corcoron and Clarence Major. Submit about 6 poems, cover letter optional, with 2 IRCs for an airmail reply (more if you wish return of MS). Reports in one month. Pays 10% royalty in author's copies. (See also *Ninth Decade*).

‡*THE PET GAZETTE (IV, Pets)**, 1309 N. Halifax, Daytona Beach, FL 32018, phone 904-255-6935, founded 1984, editor Saith A. Senior, a quarterly journal that wants **"poems about animals, nature and/or ecology. Simple and easily understood, in behalf of animals overall, short ones preferred."** She does not want "haiku, and ultra-contrived and/or highly intellectual." As a sample, she selected the following lines by Sister Mary Ann Henn:

> *Taffy was a wanderer . . .*
> *Taffy was a thief . . .*
> *Taffy was a golden cat . . .*
> *Who stole a piece of beef!*

Pet Gazette is magazine-sized, offset on ordinary paper, in many type styles with b/w photos and drawings, folded and saddle-stapled with b/w photos on cover, inserts from various organizations. Circulation is 300. Single copy price is $1.50, subscription $5/year. **Sample available for $1.50 postpaid. Pay is 3 copies. Reporting time is "upon receipt," and time to publication is "sometimes a year, usually much sooner."**

‡*PETRONIUM PRESS (V, IV, Hawaii)**, 1255 Nuuanu Ave., 1813, Honolulu, HI 96817, founded 1975, editor Frank Stewart. Petronium is a small-press publisher of poetry, fiction, essays, and art—**"primarily interested in writers in and from Hawaii, but will publish others under special circumstances.** Interested in fine printing, fine typography and design in limited editions." They publish chapbooks, trade books, limited editions, broadsides and "other ephemera," but they **are not accepting unsolicited material at this time."** They publish 3-6 poetry chapbooks per year, with an average page count of 32, flat-spined paperbacks. The editor says, **"Query letters are welcome, with SASE."** He **replies to queries within 3 weeks and reports on MSS in the same amount of time. He has "no speical requirements,"** but will not accept photocopied or dot-matrix MSS or discs. "Payment of authors is negotiated differently for each book." **The editor does not comment on rejections "unless the material is exceptionally good."** He says, "We are not really for beginners nor, in general, for people outside the Pacific region. We are not strict regionalists; but believe in nurturing first the writers around us. Beginning writers might do well to look for publishers with this same philosophy in their own cities and states rather than flinging their work to the wind, to unknown editors, or to large publishing houses. All writers should consider supporting quality publishing in their own region first." Some of Petronium's books are distributed by the University of Hawaii Press and may be obtained from them; "send for their literature catalog or ask for our titles specifically."

PHILADELPHIA POETS (II), Apt. 1701, 1919 Chestnut, Philadelphia, PA 19103, founded 1980, is a monthly 12 pp. booklet consisting of 8 pages poetry, 4 pages of news, reviews, and readers "respond" column. Special Feature: Philadelphia High School Poets Page, circulation 500, using **quality poetry. Sample: $1. Pays copies.**

*PHILOSOPHY AND THE ARTS (IV, Philosophy, Bertrand Russell)**, Box 431, Jerome Ave. Station, Bronx, NY 10468, founded 1975, is a 25 pp., magazine-sized annual using some **poetry relevant to philosophy in general and in particular Bertrand Russell. Simultaneous submissions OK. Sample: $2.98. Pays copies.**

*PHOEBE, THE GEORGE MASON REVIEW (II)**, 4400 University Drive, Fairfax, VA 22032, phone 703-323-3730, founded 1970, poetry editor Anne Wiegard, is a literary semiannual which uses **"any contemporary poetry of superior quality."** They have recently published poetry by C. K. Williams, Peter Klappert and Mark Craver. *Phoebe* is 6x9", 100+ pp., flat-spined, professionally printed with 3 to 4-color glossy cover, photos and graphics, circulation 3,500, 250 subscriptions of which 10 are libraries, using 30-35 pp. of poetry in each issue. Subscription: $13; per copy: $3.25-6.50. They receive 2,500 submissions per year, use 20, 1-3 months between acceptance and publication. **Sample: $3 postpaid. Submit no more than 4 poems, no simultaneous submissions, no dot-matrix. Submission should be accompanied by a short bio. Reports in 6-8 weeks. Pays copies.** Occasionally comments on rejections.

*PHOEBUS (IV, Illustrated poetry), Box 3085, Phoebus Station, Hampton, VA 23663, founded 1983, poetry editor Jean Nealon, uses "**illustrated/visual poetry only. Poetry and art must be by same person. No collaborations. No photography. Please don't send sentimental or pornographic material. Poetry must be accompanied by b/w art work that relates to the poem, or else be visual in itself, i.e., concrete or shaped verse.**" They have recently published poetry by Elizabeth Bartlett, Dick Higgins, Walt Phillips and Carrie Hines. The editor selected these lines by Vivian Milloy as a sample:

> Smells released in last night's rain
> rise like cool incense under my running feet
> the path to the new moon springs ahead—
> clear branch, wet-ink silhouette

Phoebus, a semiannual, circulation 150, 75 subscriptions of which 4 are libraries, is digest-sized, saddle-stapled, glossy, color card cover, using an average of 28 pp. of poetry in each issue. They receive about 550, use 10%. Never more than a 6 month's wait between acceptance and publication. **Sample: $2 postpaid.** "**Submit 3-6 typed poems to editor with b/w** *copies* **of art work—not responsible for original art. No dot-matrix. No query.**" **Usually reports in 2-4 weeks. Pays in copies and subscriptions. Send SASE for guidelines. Editor sometimes comments on rejections.** Jean Nealon says, "My advice to poets, beginners or otherwise: Don't linger on the surface. Write from the inner well-spring. Follow Rilke's advice: Pay attention to that which rises up in you."

PHOENIX BROADSHEETS, NEW BROOM PRIVATE PRESS (IV, Descriptive), 78, Cambridge St., Leicester, England LE 3 0JP, phone 547419, founded 1968, poetry editor Toni Savage, publishes chapbooks, pamphlets and broadsheets on a small Adana Horizontal Hand Press. He wants poetry which is "**descriptive—not too modern, not erotica or concrete, up to 12 lines (for the sheets)**. Also some personal background to the poet." He has recently published poems by Spike Milligan, Edward Murch, Elizabeth Bewick and John Adlard. Toni Savage selected these sample lines from "Regrets" by Diana Calvert:

> What happens to Love and Desire?
>   What puts out the white hot flame
> how do you rekindle the fire
>   and bring back joy again.

The broadsheets are letterpress printed on tinted paper (about 5x8") with graphics. **Submit no more than 3 poems with cover letter giving "personal backgrounds and feelings." No pay. Poet receives 20-30 copies.** "My *Broadsheets* are *given* away in the streets. Edition is usually 200-300. They are given away to Folk Club, Jazz Club and theater audiences. The broadsheets started as a joke. Now much sought after and collected. This is my hobby and is strictly part-time. Each small booklet takes 1-3 months, so it is impossible to ascertain quantities of publications."

PHOENIX POETS, THE UNIVERSITY OF CHICAGO PRESS (V), 5801 S. Ellis Ave., Chicago, IL 60637, poetry editor Robert von Hallberg. "Up until the late 1960s the University of Chicago Press published a small number of poets, building a selective and distinguished list under the Phoenix imprint. This tradition gave impetus to the renewal of the **Phoenix Poets. The series publishes poetry of all styles and persuasions, with the criteria for selection being superior quality and craftsmanship. Each volume will be published simultaneously in cloth and paper; cloth editions will have a distinctive three-piece binding**. Submissions by invitation only. The first two volumes in the renewed series were (1984) Alan Shapiro's **The Courtesy**, and David Ferry's **Strangers**. I selected this complete poem, "In Eden," from the latter as a sample:

> You lie in our bed as if an orchard were over us.
> You are what's fallen from those fatal boughs.
> Where will we go when they send us away from here?

The book is professionally printed, digest-sized, 64 pp., with a glossy cover on the paperback edition, which sells for $5.95.

*PIDDIDDLE (I), 1000 Timm Dr., College Station, TX 77840, founded 1985, poetry editor Janet McCann, "is just starting up. If you're wondering if it to be (a) a perfect-bound, high-class appearing journal or (b) another one of those poetry journals that looks like it was published in someone's garage, the answer is (b). **I plan to try to offer criticism to most who submit and** *at least* **to respond with a note. I'll be interested in new poets and especially student poets.**" It appears 3 times yearly, is approx. 30 pp., 4¼x5½, with 28 pp. of poetry in each issue. She wants "**no greeting card-type verse—rhymed**" **light verse"—otherwise anything goes. Right now I want short (1 page) poems only.**" Photocopy OK. Pays 1 copy. Sample: $2.50 postpaid.

*PIEDMONT LITERARY REVIEW, PIEDMONT LITERARY SOCIETY (I, II), Box 3656, Danville, VA 24541, founded 1974, poetry editor Gail White, 724 Bartholomew, New Orleans, LA

Close-up

Gail White
Piedmont Literary Review

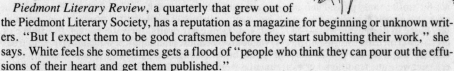

Artist: Lawrence Goodridge

"Poetry you'll enjoy reading" is a slogan for the *Piedmont Literary Review* says its poetry editor, Gail White. "Poetry can be entertaining for the reader without sacrificing intellectual quality." She cites John Donne as an example of a poet who writes eye-grabbing poetry. "Bring the reader into the poem in line one and make him want to stay."

Piedmont Literary Review, a quarterly that grew out of the Piedmont Literary Society, has a reputation as a magazine for beginning or unknown writers. "But I expect them to be good craftsmen before they start submitting their work," she says. White feels she sometimes gets a flood of "people who think they can pour out the effusions of their heart and get them published."

Many poets that submit to her need to improve. "Improvement comes mostly from reading and from growth in one's own ideas. I don't think that ever stops." White says she writes better poetry than she did ten years ago, even though she hasn't been taking formal classes. "If you continue reading and thinking, the improvement is going to come." She considers reading the King James Bible good training for a poet. "Notice that it uses very few words over two syllables long." Simple language is strong language. "To learn about fresh and vivid images study the Psalms and the Prophets."

White also tells beginning writers to read their work out loud, which she feels is as good as comment from a group. "Everything seems wonderful from the first five minutes to 24 hours after you've written it. Then come the reaction and revisions—reading aloud can speed the process along."

If a contributor's work is promising and nearly publishable, White will say so and give concrete suggestions. If they follow her advice, they almost always find their work in the *Piedmont Literary Review*.

One of the qualities that make her want to stay with a submission is clarity. "I think poetry should be written in complete sentences and obey the usual rules of spelling and grammar. Originality of thought and felicity of expression" are also important to her. She personally prefers traditional poetry. White realizes that "free verse is here to stay," though she has never really fancied it. She hopes for, believes in and looks for a revival of the traditional types of poetry, "an honest effort to work creatively with rhyme and meter." That isn't to say White won't choose poetry that isn't traditional. She will.

White is always pessimistic about poets' prospects for fame and fortune. "It's chiefly because I think new writers who are serious about poetry should know what they are getting into, and that any nonsense about being the unacknowledged legislators of the world should be knocked out of their heads." Poets get little reward in the usual ways success is measured. They receive little income and only "esteem equal to that of a schoolteacher." But "the only excuse for writing poetry is Jeremiah's excuse for prophecy—when he tried to stop prophesying 'the word became a fire in his bones'."

—*Katherine Jobst*

70117 (and **poetry submissions should go to her address**). **If you join the Piedmont Literary Society, $10 a year, you get the quarterly** *Review* and a quarterly newsletter containing much market and contest information. Gail White says, **"I prefer the conventions of spelling and punctuation. Also like to see good rhymed poems (but fewer sonnets and sestinas). Also have a haiku editor. 1 page poems have the best chance."** They have recently published poetry by Eric Thetheway, Mordecai Marcus, Miriam Sagan, Joan Colby and Lee M. Gure. As a sample I selected the opening lines of "Love & Bloom" by Sue Walker:

> *Yoga-like on the kitchen counter, you sit*
> *reading Molly Bloom's soliloquy*
> *while I set two places at your table*
> *and stir the Court Bouillon.*

The digest-sized saddle-stapled magazine is offset from typescript, matte card cover with b/w photo and graphics, circulation 500, using 40-50 pp of poetry in each issue. They receive "many!" submissions per year, use "about 8%." **Sample: $2.50 postpaid. Submit maximum of 5-6 poems. Simultaneous submissions OK. Reports ASAP. No pay. Send SASE for guidelines. They have annual contests in several categories. Write to Danville address for rules.** Editor sometimes comments on rejections.

*THE PIKESTAFF FORUM, PIKESTAFF PUBLICATIONS, INC., THE PIKESTAFF PRESS, PIKESTAFF POETRY CHAPBOOKS (II), Box 127, Normal, IL 61761, phone 309-452-4831, founded 1977, poetry editors Robert D. Sutherland, James R. Scrimgeour and James McGowan, is "a not-for-profit literary press. Publishes a magazine of national distribution, *The Pikestaff Forum*; has inaugurated a poetry chapbooks series." They want **"substantial, well-crafted poems; vivid, memorable, based in lived experience—NOT: self-indulgent early drafts, 'private' poems, five finger exercises, warmed over workshop pieces, vague abstractions, philosophical woolgathering, 'journal entries,' inspirational uplift. The shorter the better, though long-poems are no problem; we are eclectic; welcome traditional or experimental work. We won't publish pornography or racist/sexist material."** They have recently published poetry by Jared Carter, Joan Colby, Gary Metras, J. W. Rivers, Frannie Lindsay, Harold Witt, Roberta Metz Swann, David Chorlton, Nancy Nowak, David Henson, Judith Tannenbaum, Frederick A. Raborg and Bill Tremblay. I selected these sample lines from the "For John Donne and Many Others" by Gail White:

> *From the first shy, reluctant kiss*
> *to sundering of the maidenhead,*
> *poets have wasted worlds of bliss*
> *persuading ladies into bed.*

The Pikestaff Forum is an annual newsprint tabloid, 40 pp., "handsome, open layout. Trying to set a standard in tabloid design. Special features: POETRY, FICTION, COMMENTARY, REVIEWS, YOUNG WRITERS (7-17 in a special section), EDITORS' PROFILES (other magazines), The FORUM (space for anyone to speak out on matters of literary/ publishing concern)." Circulation 1,200, 200 subscriptions of which 5 are libraries. Price per copy: $2. Subscription: $10/6 issues. They receive 2,000-3,000 submissions per year, use 3%, have a year's backlog. Copyright remains with authors. **Sample: $2 postpaid. "Each poem should be on a separate sheet, with author's name and address. We prefer no simultaneous submissions—but if it is, we expect to be informed of it. No more than 6 poems per submission. Reports within 3 months. Pays 3 copies. Send SASE for guidelines. Query with samples and brief bio for chapbook submission. Replies to queries in 2 weeks, to submission (if invited) in 3 months. "Reluctantly" accepts simultaneous submissions if informed. Photocopy OK, but "reluctantly" accepts dot-matrix. Pays 20% of press run for chapbooks. The editors "always" comment on rejections.** They advise, "For beginners: don't be in a hurry to publish; work toward becoming your own best editor and critic; when submitting, send only what you think is your very best work; avoid indulging yourself at the expense of your readers; have something to say that's worth your readers' life-time to read; before submitting, ask yourself, 'Why should *any* reader be asked to read this?'; regard publishing as conferring a responsibility."

‡*THE PIPE SMOKER'S EPHEMERIS (IV, Pipe smokers), 20-37 120th St., College Point, NY 11356, editor/publisher Tom Dunn, who says, "The *Ephemeris* is a limited edition, irregular quarterly **for pipe smokers and anyone else who is interested in its varied contents. Publication costs are absorbed by the Editor/Publisher, assisted by any contributions—financial or otherwise—that readers might wish to make."** There are 66 pages, offset from photoreduced typed copy, colored paper covers, with illustrations, stapled at the top left corner. *Ephemeris* seems to publish very little poetry, but I found the following lines form "Coterie Fellowship" by R.W. on page 47 of my sample copy:

> *There is no comparable moment*
> *When I light up my briar,*
> *To tamp that bowl of contentment,*
> *And to mix that gold with fire.*

Close-up

Ed Ochester
Pitt Poetry Series

A recent issue of *Scholarly Publishing* printed the results of a poll of 140 American poets which asked respondents to indicate which house published "the best, or most significant, poetry." The Pitt Poetry Series was chosen the best of all university press poetry series, and second among all publishers.

The Pitt Poetry Series, under the umbrella organization of the University of Pittsburgh Press, published its first volume of poetry in 1968. Initially the series published the winners of the United States Award of the International Poetry Forum. Between 1967 and 1976, ten annual awards were presented to Americans who had never before published a volume of poetry. Jon Anderson, Richard Shelton and Carol Muske were some poets published during this period.

Ed Ochester, associate professor of English and director of the writing program at the University of Pittsburgh, was appointed editor of the Pitt Poetry Series in 1978. Ochester has total autonomy for choosing the books in the series. Upon his appointment as editor of the series, Ochester changed emphasis from first books to the works of established writers. Poets must have previously published full-length collections of poetry, full-length being a book of 48 or more pages.

The decision to shift emphasis of the series was based on what Ochester felt was a changing situation for poets. "In the 60s when the series was established it was extremely difficult for a younger poet to place his first book." Ochester felt that in the 70s, because of prize competitions and the aim of many university presses, the opportunities for younger poets were more abundant. "At that time it was much more difficult for poets who had broken into print for the first time to get a second book printed." The commercial publishing houses, who were for a time publishing eight to twelve books of poetry, were cutting down to one or two or none, leaving university and small presses the responsibility of taking up the slack.

When Ochester chooses books for the series, beyond the basic rules of good poetry, his cardinal principle is not to repeat style or subject matter. He reads a lot and is familiar with the work of "most poets who have published previously with a trade, university or established small press." Ochester says, "what I'm looking for consciously, is what I haven't seen before, a freshness, uniqueness in style with subject matter handled in a way I've never seen before." The series prides itself on the eclectic nature of its list. It is not tied to any particular school of writing or style—it only demands exceptional merit.

Pitt publishes at least two titles, annually; the books are selected from submissions. With over 900 submissions each year, Ochester rarely solicits manuscripts. "Our poets come from all over the United States, several live abroad." Manuscripts are accepted only during September and October. Final decisions are made by the beginning of March.

Unpublished poets, or those with chapbooks, or limited editions of less than 750 copies, can enter the Agnes Lynch Starrett Poetry Prize Competition. The Starrett Prize is the only way first books of poetry are considered. In addition to a $1,000 cash award the winner is published in the Pitt Poetry Series.

—*Katherine Jobst*

Ephemeris seems to be supported by "members" rather than subscribers, but it gives no indication as to the cost of membership.

PITT POETRY SERIES, UNIVERSITY OF PITTSBURGH PRESS, AGNES LYNCH STARRETT POETRY PRIZE (II), 127 N. Bellefield Ave., Pittsburgh, PA 15260, phone 412-624-4110, founded 1936, poetry editor Ed Ochester, publishes "**poetry of the highest quality; otherwise, no restrictions—book MSS minimum of 48 pp.**" Simultaneous submissions OK. They have recently published poetry by Larry Levis, Ted Kooser, Siv Cedering, Greg Pape, Gary Soto and Gary Gildner. "**Poets who have not previously published a book should send SASE for rules of the Starrett competition ($7.50 handling fee), the** *only* **vehicle through which we publish first books of poetry.**" **Poets who have previously published books should query.**

***PLACE STAMP HERE, PRESS ME CLOSE (IV, Visual)**, Box 250, Farmingdale, NJ 07727, founded 1983. *Place Stamp Here* is a biannual magazine, circulation 300, made entirely of **4x6" postcards, using visual poetry and graphic art. Sample: $2.**

***PLAINSONG (II)**, Box U245, Western Kentucky University, Bowling Green, KY 42101, phone 502-745-5708, founded 1979, poetry editors Frank Steele, Elizabeth Oakes and Peggy Steele, is a biannual poetry journal. "**Our purpose is to print the best work we can get, from known and unknown writers. This means, of course, that we print what we like: poems about places, objects, people, moods, politics, experiences. We like straightforward, conversational language, short poems in which the marriage of thinking and feeling doesn't break up because of spouse-abuse (the poem in which ideas wrestle feeling into the ground or in which feeling sings alone—and boringly—at the edge of a desert). Prefer poems under 20 lines in free verse. No limits on subject matter, though we like to think of ourselves as humane, interested in the environment, in peace (we're anti-nuclear), in the possibility that the human race may have a future.**" They have recently published poetry by William Matthews, Ted Kooser, William Stafford, Del Marie Rogers, Betty Adcock, Julia Ardery and Abby Niebauer. The editors selected these sample lines from "Dream of an Afternoon with a Woman I Did Not Know" by Robert Bly:

> *Frost has made clouds out of the night weeds.*
> *In my dream we stopped for coffee, we sat alone*
> *Near a fireplace, near delicate cups.*
> *I loved that afternoon, and the rest of my life.*

The 48-56 pp. 6x9", professional printed, flat-spined magazine, matte color card cover with photos and graphics, print run 600, 250 subscriptions of which 65 are libraries, uses about 100 of the 2,000 submissions received each year. Subscription: $7; per copy: $3.50. **Sample: $3.50 postpaid. "We prefer poems typed, double-spaced. Simultaneous submissions can, of course, get people into trouble, at times." Reports "within a month, usually." Payment in copies. Send SASE for guidelines.**

‡***PLAINSONGS (II)**, Department of English, Hastings College, Hastings, NE 68901, founded 1980, editor Dwight C. Marsh, a poetry magazine that "**accepts manuscripts from anyone. We consider poems on any subject in any style, although non-English poems should be accompanied by an English translation acceptable to its author. Although our past contributors have largely been Nebraskans, we have printed poems from such diverse places as Pennsylvania, Texas, New Mexico, Utah and California.**" The January, 1986 issue contains poems by 33 authors. As a sample, I selected the beginning lines from "Another Poem About Money" by Sam Umland:

> *that winter, dad turned sixty-one and They fired him*
> *after weeks unemployed, mom told him*
> *she intended to give her body to Science*
> *dad railed for hours how They cut-up a person*
> *she asked why should i care, then?*

Plainsongs is digest-sized, 30 pp. saddle-stapled, offset from typed copy on thin paper, one-color matte card cover with black logo. The editor describes the magazine as "self-subsidized by subscriptions," which cost $6/year for three issues. **Pay is 2 copies.** The editor wants the magazine to be "accessible to a wider geographical range of poets."

‡**PLANTAGENET PRODUCTIONS (V)**, Westridge, Highclere, Nr. Newbury, Royal Berkshire 2G15 9P1, England, phone Highclere 253322, founded 1964, director of productions Miss Dorothy-Rose Gribble. Plantagenet issues cassette recordings of poetry, philosophy, and narrative (although they have issued nothing new since 1980). Miss Gribble says, "Our public likes classical work . . . We have published a few living poets, but except for Edinburgh poets, whose work sells in Scotland, this is not very popular with our listeners, and we shall issue no more." They have issued cassettes by Oscar Wilde, Chaucer, Pope, as well as Charles Graves, Elizabeth Jennings, Leonard Clark, and Alice V.

Stuart. The recordings are issued privately and are obtainable only direct from Plantagenet Productions; write for list. Miss Gribble's advice to poets is: "If intended for a listening public, let the meaning be clear. If possible, let the music of the works sing."

‡**PLAYERS PRESS (II)**, Box 1132, Studio City, CA 91604, phone 818-789-4980, founded 1974, associate editor Marjorie E. Clapper, a "theatrical publisher, poetry publisher, magazine publisher, and music publisher." They issue chapbooks, flat-spined paperbacks, and hardcover books, 2-10 per year. **Freelance submissions are accepted; they are open to all submissions except "vulgar." Writers should send 20-50 "medium length" sample poems, original or quality photocopy, with bio; MSS will be reported on in 3-6 months; "we publish upon acceptance." Amount of royalties "varies with contract,"** plus 2-10 author's copies. The press does very occasional subsidy publishing. Book catalog is free on request.

***PLOUGHSHARES (III)**, Box 529, Cambridge, MA 02139, phone 617-926-9875, founded 1971, poetry editors Seamus Heaney, Tom Lux, Gail Mazur, Donald Hall, Jane Shore . . . "a journal of new writing edited on a revolving basis by professional poets and writers to reflect different and contrasting points of view." They have recently published poetry by Philip Levine, Donald Hall, Linda Gregg, Charles Simic, Robert Creeley and Ellen Bryant Voight. The quarterly is digest-sized, 220 pp., circulation 4,000, 1,500 subscriptions of which 320 are libraries. Subscription: $14 (domestic; $16 foreign). They receive approximately 15,000 submissions per year, have a 2-4 month backlog. Sample: $5 postpaid. "Due to revolving editorship, issue emphasis and submission dates will vary. We suggest attention to schedule announcements in current issue, or inquiry prior to submission. Envelopes should indicate current poetry editor." Reports in 1-4 months, pays $10 per poem. Contributors are encouraged to subscribe.

***POEM, HUNTSVILLE LITERARY ASSOCIATION (II)**, English Dept. University of Alabama at Huntsville, Hunstsville, AL 35899, founded 1967, poetry editor Nancy Frey Dillard, appears twice a year, a flat-spined 4½x7¾", 70 pp. journal, circulation 500 (500 subscriptions of which 125 are libraries), matte card cover, tinted paper, consisting entirely of poetry. "**We are open to traditional as well as non-traditional forms and we have no bias as to length so long as the work has the expected compression and intensity of good lyric poetry. We have no bias as to subject matter or theme; however we do favor poems that have inspired sentiments earned from within the poem itself and that have a high degree of verbal and dramatic tension. We welcome equally submissions from established poets as well as from less known and beginning poets. We do not accept translations or previously published works. We prefer to see a sample of 3-5 poems at a submission, with SASE. We generally respond within a month. We are a non-profit making organization and can pay only in copy to contributors. Sample copies are available at $3.**" They have recently published poetry by Charles Edward Eaton, Norman Nathan, John Ower, Emanuel di Pascale and William Virgil Davis. I selected as a sample the first stanza of "Black Purse/ White Gloves" by Kay Ryan:

> It's a small essential gesture—
> the abrupt way she takes up
> her purse, clutches it
> beneath her breasts,
> a black heart.

They receive about 2,000 submissions per year, use 210.

***POET AND CRITIC (II)**, 203 Ross Hall, Iowa State University, Ames, IA 50011, phone 515-294-2180, founded 1963, poetry editor Michael Martone, appears 3 times a year, 6x9", 64 pp. perfect bound, professionally printed with sometimes bizzare photos and graphics, matte card cover with color, graphics, photography, circulation 400, 300 subscriptions of which 250 are libraries. Subscription: $9; per copy: $3. **Sample: $3 postpaid. Submit 3-5 poems, no photocopy or dot-matrix. Reports in 8 weeks (slower in summer). Pays 2 copies (more at half price). Send SASE for guidelines.** The sample copy I examined focused on humorous poetry—10 poets, some represented by more than 1 poem, each providing a commentary on his own work (and I do mean "his," as it happened they were all men). I selected as a sample the opening of "Kong Settles Down" by William Trowbridge:

> They've locked me in with this goddam lady gorilla,
> Russian bred, bulged up on steroids
> till she's damn near big as me. Shot-putter,
> they say. Couldn't pass the hormone test.

Michael Martone advises beginning poets, "Read *Poet and Critic.*" I found I couldn't put this sample copy down! Magazine focus changes with each issue.

THE POET, FINE ARTS SOCIETY (I), 2314 W. Sixth St., Mishawaka, IN 46544-1594, phone 219-255-8606, founded 1964, editor Doris I. Nemeth, associate editor Nellie Ann Buck. *The Poet* is a huge, 330 pp. flat-spined, magazine-sized annual, offset from typescript, glossy card cover, with decorative art which uses "**all types of poetry in good taste; students, professional people, children, et al. We prefer approximately 4-16 lines. No religious, as we are usually overstocked or they simply are not well written.** Schools and universities and creative writing classes use *The Poet* and teachers send grade school art and poetry." They mention Mogg Williams "noted Welsh poet with many hardcover books to his credit" as a poet recently published and selected these lines by Mokuo Nagayama, of Japan, as a sample:

> With its wild rage
> a gale blew away
> the snows of sentiments;
> there appeared the steel-like
> blue ice of silence.

If you join the Fine Arts Society you get a chatty *Bulletin*—a legal-sized mimeographed sheet with many "mini-bios" of fellow members and other news. You are not required to join or buy a copy of the anthology to be accepted, but they don't give contributors' copies. Simultaneous submissions OK. "We send free copies to schools where students' work appears in magazine. Some free copies are sent to some of our elderly and unemployed contributors, and others that are in need."

*POET LORE, HELDREF PUBLICATIONS, POET LORE NARRATIVE POETRY PRIZE (II), 4000 Albemarle St. NW, Washington, DC 20016, founded 1889, Ed Taylor, Managing Editor, is dedicated "to the best in American and world poetry and objective and timely reviews and commentary. We look for **fresh uses of traditional form and devices, but any kind of excellence is welcome. The editors encourage narrative poetry and original translations of works by contemporary world poets.**" They have recently published poetry by Walter McDonald, Ann Darr and Ronnie McQuilken. As a sample the editor chose the first stanza of "Hieroglyphics" by Amy Rothholz:

> September is lying on its side
> So blackberry brandy and professions of love
> Can swim down my throat.
> Put another quarter in the jukebox.
> Let the pretty lies fly.

The 6x9", 64 pp. saddle-stapled, professionally printed quarterly, matte card cover, has a circulation to 400 subscriptions of which 200 are libraries. Subscription: $12; per copy: $4.50. They receive about 3,000 poems in freelance submissions per year, use about 100. **Sample: $2.50 postpaid. Submit to Ed Taylor, managing editor, typed double-spaced, author's name and address on each page. Photocopies OK. Reports in 3 months. Pays 2 copies. Send SASE for guidelines and rules of various contests.**

THE POET TREE, INC., THE SACRAMENTO POETRY CENTER, POET NEWS, *QUERCUS (IV, Regional/Sacramento area), 2791 24th St. #8, Sacramento, CA 95818, founded 1979. The monthly newsletter, *Poet News*, 12 pp., circulation 1,000 and literary biannual, *Quercus*, publish articles and **poetry by authors in the Sacramento area. Pays 10 contributor copies. Sample: $3 + $1.25 postage for *Quercus; Poet News* free for SASE.** The Poet Tree hopes in time to publish books by local authors.

*POETIC JUSTICE (II), 8220 Rayford Dr., Los Angeles, CA 90045, phone 213-649-1491, founded 1982, poetry editor Alan C. Engebretsen, publishes "contemporary American poetry. **Quality poetry is what I want—no-nos are raw language and blue material.**" They have recently published Joan Ritty, Gerry Rosenzweig, Pearl Bloch Segall, Gary Metras, Austin Straus, Philip D. Crosby and Elsen Lubetsky. The editor selected these sample lines by Suzanne Overall:

> When someday you cross an unfamiliar bridge
> into a foreign day, conjure up the essence
> kept burning through the years; a dream almost forgotten.
> revealing, unfolding and finally recognized as home.

The quarterly is digest-sized, 44 pp., professionally printed, tinted matte card cover, circulation 250, 100 subscriptions of which 2 are libraries, using 39 pp. of poetry per issue. Subscription: $10; per copy: $3. They receive about 1,500 poems per year, use 160. No current backlog. **Sample: $3 postpaid. Prefer submissions of 4 poems at a time, typewritten. No query. Reports in 2-3 days. Pays contributor's copy. Send SASE for guidelines. Editor comments on rejections "when I have something to say."**

*POETRY, THE MODERN POETRY ASSOCIATION (II), 601 S. Morgan St., Box 4348, Chicago, IL 60680, founded 1912, editor Joseph Parisi, "is the oldest and most distinguished magazine devoted entirely to verse," according to their literature, though *Poet Lore* is considerably older. Nonetheless the historical role of *Poetry* in modern literature is incontrovertible: "Founded in Chicago in 1912, it immediately became the international showcase that it has remained ever since, publishing in its earliest years—and often for the first time—such giants as Ezra Pound, Robert Frost, T. S. Eliot, Marianne Moore and Wallace Stevens. *Poetry* has continued to print the major voices of our time and to discover new talent, establishing an unprecedented record. There is virtually no important contemporary poet in our language who has not at a crucial stage in his career depended on *Poetry* to find a public for him: Edgar Lee Masters, Dylan Thomas, Edna St. Vincent Millay, Carl Sandburg, Anne Sexton, Sylvia Plath, James Dickey, Thom Gunn, David Wagoner—only a partial list to suggest how *Poetry* has represented, without affiliation with any movements or schools, what Stephen Spender has described as 'the best, and simply the best' poetry being written. Although its offices have always been in Chicago, *Poetry*'s influence and scope extend far beyond, throughout the U.S. and in over 45 countries around the world. Over the decades, the magazine has featured many special issues devoted to the poetry of France, Italy, Greece, Japan, India, Israel, and translations from the work of dissident poets in the U.S.S.R—most of whom are unpublished in their own land. In addition to these reports on the state of poetry around the world, *Poetry* has been the gauge, as it has often set the standards, of verse from e. e. cummings to A. R. Ammons." John Ciardi has said "*Poetry* is the seedbed of poetry. It is the place one turns to first to see what is coming onto the scene. For over 70 years now it has searched out and presented new talent. I doubt that there is a 20th-century poet of any consequence who did not publish his first poems in *Poetry*." I would like to add the personal testimony that this was certainly true for me. Though I had published poetry in a couple of other magazines, it was my first appearance in *Poetry* in 1955, the sonnet "Deer Hunt," that made me feel I was a genuine *poet*. Editors of other magazines began writing me asking for contributions as a result of that appearance. When, a few years later, the then-editor Henry Rago showed me my folder in the file drawer, right there between Randall Jarrell and Donald Justice, I knew I had somehow arrived. Asked to select 4 lines of poetry "which represent the taste and quality you want in your publication" Joseph Parisi selected the opening lines of "The Love Song of J. Alfred Prufrock" by T. S. Eliot, which first appeared in *Poetry* in 1915:

> Let us go then, you and I,
> When the evening is spread out against the sky
> Like a patient etherized upon a table;
> Let us go, through certain half-deserted streets . . .

The elegantly printed flat-spined 5½x9" magazine appears monthly, circulation 7,000, 6,000 subscriptions of which 80% are libraries. Subscription: $22; per copy: $2.50. They receive about 70,000 submissions per year, use 150, have a 9 month backlog. **Sample: $3.25 postpaid. Submit no more than 6 poems. "Photocopy OK; no dot-matrix; letter-quality OK." Reports in 6-8 weeks. Pays $1 a line. Send SASE for guidelines. Several prizes, awarded annually, are announced every November for the best verse printed in *Poetry* during the preceding year. Only verse already published is eligible for consideration and no formal application is necessary.** The Modern Poetry Association is the nonprofit corporation which publishes *Poetry*. All contributions to the Association are deductible for income-tax purposes.

*POETRY CANADA REVIEW, ECW PRESS (II), 307 Coxwell Ave., Toronto, Ontario, Canada M4L 3B5, founded 1979, poetry editors Robert Billings, Barry Dempster (New Voices), Rosalind Eve Conway (International). Each issue features a major Canadian poet on the cover and center spread (recent ones include Susan Musgrave, Roo Borson, Marilyn Bowering). This is a quarterly magazine; uses about 70 poems per issue; circulation 1,800, 500 subscribers. Subscription: $14 one year individual; $26 one year institutions. **Sample: $3.50 postpaid. Submit 6-12 poems with SASE. Reports in 2-8 weeks. Pays $5 per poem.** Each issue contains several columns from Canada and abroad, and some special interest columns. Also, each issue contains feature articles *by* major Canadian poets. As of issue 6:4 (June 1985) we review every book of poetry published in Canada."

‡THE POETRY CONNEXION (IV, Radio), Wanda Coleman and Austin Straus, co-hosts, Box 29154, Los Angeles, CA 90029-0154, founded 1981, contact person Austin Straus. **"The Poetry Connexion" is a radio program, usually live; poets coming to the LA area make contact in advance and send work with SASE just as though the program were a press.** The program is heard on the first, third, and fifth Saturdays of each month from 6:30 to 7:30 p.m. Its purpose is "to broaden the audience, reading and listening, for poetry in the Southern California area which is now experiencing a cultural 'boom' of sorts. **We are volunteer Pacifica Radio broadcasters and do not pay." The co-hosts say "We have a preference for the 'serious' poet who has published in recognized magazines. The poet may not necessarily have a book but must be on the verge of publishing, participating in workshops, readings, residencies, etc." Submissions are open, but they "prefer the accessible.**

We are also always most interested in poets whose lives are as committed and intense as their work."

POETRY DURHAM (II), English Dept., University of Durham, New Elvet, Durham, England DH1 3JT, edited by Michael O'Neill and Gareth Reeves, founded 1982, appears 3 times a year, 36 pp., digest-sized, circulation 400, using **quality poetry. Pays £10 or dollar equivalent per poem. Sample: $2 or £10.**

*POETRY EAST (II), Star Route 1, Box 50, Earlysville, VA 22936, phone 804-924-3509, founded 1980, poetry editors Richard Jones and Kate Daniels, "is a triannual international magazine publishing poetry, fiction, translations, and reviews. We suggest that authors look through back issues of the magazine before making submissions. **No constraints or specifications, although we prefer free verse.**" They have recently published poetry by Tom Crawford, Louis Jenkins, Rolf Jacobsen, Sharon Olds, Patricia Goedicke and Tom Paulin. As a sample I chose the opening lines of "The Voyages" by Gregory Orr:

> It's late when I try to sleep, resting
> one hand on your hip, the other on my chest
> where the rise and fall of breath
> is a faint light that brightens and fades.

The digest-sized flat-spined, 100+ pp., journal is professionally printed, glossy color card cover, circulation 1,000, 200 subscriptions of which 40 are libraries. They use 45-65 pp. of poetry in each issue. Subscription: $10; per copy: $3.50. They receive approximately 2,000 freelance submissions per yer, use 1-5%, have a 4-6 week backlog. **Sample: $4.50 postpaid. Reports in 4-6 weeks. Pays copies. Editors sometimes comment on rejections.**

*POETRY FLASH, THE BAY AREA'S POETRY CALENDAR & REVIEW (II, IV, Specialized), Box 4172, Berkeley, CA 94704, phone 415-548-6871, founded 1972, editor and publisher Joyce Jenkins, associate editor Richard Silberg, "is a monthly tabloid calendar of literary or literary-related events in Northern California, with selected national events listed. We publish mostly reviews, interviews and photos, also practical info (contests, submissions) for poets. We publish at least one poem a month. Poetry is our focus. **Long poems, especially of a romantic or metaphysical nature, are inappropriate for the *Flash*. We seek the highest craft possible. Poems which are somehow topical or current, or are about poetry and writing, or reading, are appropriate. 30 lines or under. We like translations, pithy, well-crafted poems.**" They have recently published poetry by Dick Bakken, Howard Hart, Theresa Bacon, Gellu Naum (Romanian), George Oppen and Julian Beck (of the Living Theater). As a sample I selected these lines from "My Black Sea" by Deborah Bruner:

> I sniff the cork.
> To my right, each Russian cruise ship
> leaving the dock is Plath's two-tiered wedding cake
> carrying its candles slowly off.

The newspaper has a circulation of 12,000, 750 subscriptions of which 50 are libraries. Subscription: $8; per copy: free. They receive "hundreds" of freelance submissions per year, use 1%, have a 3 month backlog. **Sample: free for 9x12" manila envelope with postage to cover 2 oz. mailing. Reports within 2 months, pays free subscription. Editors sometimes comment on rejections.** They say, "We are delighted to have published the poems which we have and are looking forward to publishing more in each issue. We frequently publish well-known or established poets, but we certainly have published unknowns and we plan to continue that policy. Our advice to beginning poets is simple: just don't jump into print too fast. So many poems we receive aren't really even finished or thought-out by the poet. Sometimes a body of work has to mature before it's ready for posterity!"

*POETRY IRELAND REVIEW (II, IV, Irish), 106 Tritonville Rd., Dublin 4, Ireland, founded 1981, "provides an outlet for **Irish poets; submissions from abroad also considered and accepted.**" They want "**lyrics and sections from long poems. No specific style or subject matter is prescribed.**" They have recently published poetry by Seasmus Heaney, Richard Murphy, John Montague and Brendan Kennelly. The 6x8" quarterly uses 70 pp. of poetry in each issue, circulation 800, 250 subscriptions of which 30 are libraries. Subscription: $12; per copy: $3 (U.S.). They receive about 2,500 submissions per year, use 250, have a 3 month backlog. **Sample: $3 postpaid. Submit photocopies, no simultaneous submissions, no query. Reports in 3 months. No pay.** The editors advise, "Keep submitting: good work will get through."

‡*POETRY KANTO (II), Kanto Gakuin University, Mutsuura, Kanazawa-Ku, Yokohama, Japan 236, founded 1967, editor William I. Elliott. *Poetry Kanto* is a literary annual published by the Kanto Poetry Center, which sponsors an annual poetry conference. It publishes original poems in English and in Japanese (the Summer 1986 issue was devoted to translations). The magazine is **"open to anything except pornography and tends to publish poems under 30 lines."** They have recently published work by William Stafford, Shuntaro Tanikawa, and Makoto Ooka. As a sample, I selected the final stanza from "The Well" by Denise Levertov:

> It was on dark nights of deep sleep
> that I dreamed the most, sunk in the well,
> and woke rested, and if not beautiful,
> filled with some other power.

The magazine is digest-sized, nicely printed (the English poems occupy the first half of the issue, the Japenese poems the second), 60 pp. saddle-stapled, matte card cover. Circulation is 500, of which 400 are complimentary copies sent to schools, poets, and presses; it is also distributed at poetry seminars. The magazine is unpriced. **Guidelines are on the editorial page. Pay is 3-5 copies. Submissions should be typed, double-spaced. Reporting time is usually 2 weeks and there is no backlog except in special cases.** The editor advises, "Read a lot. Get feedback from poets and/or workshops. Be neat, clean, legible, and polite in submissions."

*POETRY/LA (IV, Regional/Los Angeles), Box 84271, Los Angeles, CA 90073, phone 213-472-6171, founded 1980, editor Helen Friedland, assistant editor Barbara Strauss, "is a semi-annual anthology of **high quality poems by established and new poets living, working or attending school in the Los Angeles area. Otherwise, high literary quality is our only constraint.**" They have published poetry recently by Ann Stanford, Peter Levitt, Charles Bukowski, Carol Lem, Jack Grapes, Gerald Locklin, Joan LaBombard and Lee Chul Bum. As to selecting a sample, the editor says, "Since our orientation is eclectic, quoting one poem would draw too many submissions with that poem's traits." With that warning, I selected the opening lines of "Errant" by Ron Koertge, hoping his style is inimitable but does represent the quality of the magazine:

> You wanted me to take care
> of that dragon who was bothering
> you, and I was glad to. He wasn't
> much bigger than a pig and had breath
> like a kitchen match.

The flat-spined, digest-sized biannual, professionally printed, color matte card cover, circulation 500, 200 subscriptions of which 20 are libraries, uses about 120 pp. of poetry in each issue. Subscription: $8; per copy: $4.25. They receive 2,750 submissions per year, use 200. Almost all poems are published within 2-6 months from date of acceptance. **Sample: $3.50 postpaid. "We prefer about 4-6 pp., but will review all poems received. Clean photocopy is fine, simultaneous submissions are not. And, please, name and address on each poem (anonymous entries drive us crazy)."** They report in 2 weeks-3 months, pay copies only (one per printed page of the poet's work). Send SASE for guidelines. Editor comments **"in general, only if we believe the poem merits publication if certain difficulties can be resolved."**

‡*THE POETRY LETTER (II), Box 4181, San Rafael, CA 94913, phone 415-485-0267, founded 1983, poetry editor Jeanne McGahey, a bimonthly newsletter about poetry that publishes one poetry spread in each issue. **"We look for technical excellence of a kind we find very rare in current production—but no rarer among beginners than among established names. Criteria are difficult to pin down briefly. A principle is that poetry is sharply different from prose, not prose with line-breaks added."** They do not want **"pages-from-a-journal type; poetry that is (purely) propaganda; poetry that is easy to write and unrewarding to read."** Poets recently published include Jeanne McGahey, Rosalie Moore, Robert Horan, Jack Gilbert, Robert Barlow, and Josephine Miles. As a sample, the editors chose the following lines by Fred Ostrander:

> The mountain Indian died. Fell like a horse. There is a
>> prayer,
> today it softly expired. Across your
> mountains, sir, the sparse small birds, like leaflets,
>> are falling.

The Poetry Letter is magazine-sized, 12 typeset pages with "loose, open layout, emphasis on readability, no graphics." Circulation (currently free) is 1,800, of which 800 go to subscribers and 1,000 are distributed at bookstores. **Sample available for $2 postpaid. Pay is 10 copies. Multiple submissions or previously published poems are OK. Reporting time is 1 month and time to publication is 2-3 issues.**

*POETRY NEWSLETTER (II), English Dept., Temple University, Philadelphia, PA 19122, editor Richard O'Connell, founded 1971, is a 20-30 pp. magazine-sized quarterly, circulation 500-1,000, which uses **quality poetry. Sample: $1. Subscriptions $3 year. Pays 3 copies. "The poetry is the news."**

POETRY NIPPON PRESS, THE POETRY SOCIETY OF JAPAN, *POETRY NIPPON, POETRY NIPPON NEWSLETTER (II, IV, Japanese or Western poets, translations), 5-11, Nagaike-cho, Showa-ku, Nagoya, Japan 466, phone 052-833-5724, founded 1967, poetry editors Yorifumi Zaguchi and Atsuo Nakagawa (and guest editors). *Poetry Nippon*, a quarterly, uses **translations of Japanese poems into English, poems by Western and Japanese poets, tanka, haiku, one-line poems, essays on poetry, poetry book reviews, poetry news, home and abroad. They want tanka, haiku, one-line poems and poems on contemporary themes.** They have recently published poetry by Gary Snyder, James Kirkup and Tautomu Fukuda. The editor selected these sample lines by James Kirkup:

> There is no other place
> like the room we were born in,
> The moment no one remembers
> is enshrined in it for ever.

Poetry Nippon has a circulation of 500, 200 subscriptions of which 30 are libraries. Subscription: $15; per copy: $5. They use 25% of the 400 submissions they receive each year, have a 6-12 month backlog. **Sample free for 4 IRCs. Submit 2 poems, 5 tanka or 6 haiku, unpublished and not submitted elsewhere. "Deadline March 31 for nonmembers." Reports in 6 months for members. Send SASE for guidelines.** Apparently you can join the Poetry Society of Japan, receive the *Newsletter* and *Poetry Nippon* and have other benefits. For example, **the editors provide criticism "on members' MSS only."** They sponsor contests for tanka and haiku and publish collections by individuals and anthologies.

*POETRY NORTHWEST (II), 4045 Brooklyn NE, Seattle, WA 98105, phone 206-543-2992, founded 1959, poetry editor David Wagoner, is a quarterly which uses 48 pp. of poetry in each issue, circulation 2,000. Subscription: $8; per copy: $2. They receive 40,000 poems in freelance submissions per year, use 160, have a 6 month backlog. **Sample: $2 postpaid. Reports in 1 month maximum, pays 6 copies. They award prizes of $100, $50 and $50 yearly, judged by the editors. Occasionally editor comments on rejections.**

*POETRY NOTTINGHAM, NOTTINGHAM POETRY SOCIETY, LAKE ASKE MEMORIAL OPEN POETRY COMPETITION, QUEENIE LEE COMPETITION (II), 21 Duncombe Close, Nottingham NC3 3PH, England, phone 0602 584207, founded 1941, poetry editor Howard Atkinson. Nottingham Poetry Society meets monthly for readings, talks, etc., and publishes quarterly its magazine, *Poetry Nottingham*, which is open to submissions from all-comers. **"We wish to see poetry that is intelligible to and enjoyable by the average reader. We do not want any party politics. Poems not more than 40 lines in length."** They have recently published poetry by C. M. El Kadi, Louise Horton, Denise Painchaud and Margo Requard from the USA and by Tony Cosier from Canada. The editor selected these sample lines by Tony Lucas:

> I pick a cobble off the beach:
> it has the temperature of flesh,
> touch of a generous warmth
> stored from the day's bright sun.

There are 28 pp. of poetry in each issue of the 6x8", saddle-stapled magazine, professional printing with b/w graphics, color matte card cover, circulation 325, 200 subscriptions of which 20 are libraries. Subscriptions: £4.80 ($10 USA); per copy: £1.20 ($5 USA). They receive about 1,500 submissions per year, use 120, usually have a 2-6 month backlog. **Sample: $5 or £1.20 postpaid. Submit at any time 3-5 poems, not more than 40 lines each, not handwritten, previously unpublished and not currently submitted elsewhere. No need to query. Reports "within a fortnight plus mailing time." Pays one copy.** They publish collections by individual poets who were born, live or work in the East Midlands of England. The Lake Aske Memorial Open Poetry Competition offers cash prizes and publication in *Poetry Nottingham*. Open to all. The Queenie Lee Competition is for members and subscribers only, offers a cash prize and publication. **Editor comments "when I feel the poet is able to write something that I will accept."** His advice, especially for beginners, is "read the magazine before submitting anything; write the kind of poetry you believe in, which, if it is any good, will find a magazine to publish it." As a footnote, to help US poets understand some of the problems of editors in other countries, I'd like to quote Stanley Cook at length: "The price of the magazine, thanks to financial assistance from the East Midlands Arts Association, is low (£3.20 annual subscription in the U.K.). If, however, I wish to exchange a draft for $10 from the USA, the Bank charges me £3 commission (their commission being the same whether I am exchanging $10 or $10,000). An extreme example of the situation is that I have two $1 notes that someone sent me, which I cannot exchange since it would cost me more to exchange them than they are worth. I therefore much appreciate being paid with a draft for sterling and, though I do not know how much these cost the people who send them, I guess they are probably saving money. May I suggest that a general note about how to pay for small magazines from England that sell only a few copies in the USA, with a recommendation to send a draft for sterling, would be helpful to your readers."

POETRY NOW (UK) (II), Scotswood, South Park, Sevenoaks, Kent, England Tn13 1EL, formerly **The Cambridge Poetry Magazine**, founded 1983, poetry editor Ravi Mirchandani, "produces a quarterly magazine of poetry in English, mainly from the US and UK, but with a general brief to encourage appreciation of non-British poets and unpublished poets in the UK." The editor comments, "With poets touring in trains and helicopters, Tony Harrison and Norman MacCaig reading on TV, and Faber's poetry sales up by 21% over the last year, there are undeniable signs that British poetry is alive and just about kicking. . . . Our policy is to be as catholic as possible, but we would **not want to see poetry that is racist or sexist, and tend to favor longer poems and political poetry.**" They have recently published poems by Charles Bukowski, Czeslaw Milosz, Adrienne Rich, Denise Levertov, Fleur Adcock, Ruth Fainlight, R.S. Thomas, Thom Gunn and Richard Braun. As a sample I selected this stanza (of eleven) from "In Memory of My Friend the Bassoonist John Lenox" by Donald Justice:

> John, where you are now can you see?
> Do the pigeons there bicker like ours?
> Does the deep bassoon not moan
> Or the flute sigh ever?

The format is magazine-sized, handsomely printed on heavy paper with wide margins, glossy card cover, with 48 pp. of poetry in each issue, circulation 1,300, 300 subscriptions of which 40 are libraries. They receive about 350 submissions of freelance poetry per year, use 40. **Sample: 2 pounds or $6 postpaid. Submissions should be "preferably typed. Poets are advised to study a copy of the magazine before submitting, but this is not essential." Pays 5 pounds or $6 per poem, minimum. Comments on rejections "if requested."**

‡**POETRY PRESS (I)**, Box 736, Pittsburg, TX 75686, phone 214-572-6673, founded 1974, poetry editor Judith Lyn, **offers contests for publication and cash prizes (typically $100, $50 and $25), publishing the winners in anthologies, which the poets have to purchase ($5-12) if they want copies. Entry fees (for example, $3/poem, but semiannual "Amateur Poetry Contest" has no entry fee), themes, rules, line lengths vary. Send SASE for guidelines.** They have recently published poems by Ted Yund, August Moon, Donna Swope and Alice Mackenzie Swaim. The editor selected this sample line from "Satin Cats Play Leapfrog" by Jacqueline Row Gonzales:

> Young Laura weeps
> silently, as cool mist
> cries softly on the pane.

The editor advises, "Meet the needs and requirements of the publication to which you are submitting. Check your work carefully for spelling and typing errors. Deal with small presses in a professional manner. If you do not understand procedures, ASK—rather than assume you have been mistreated."

*****POETRY REVIEW (II)**, 21 Earls Court Sq., London, SW5 9DE England, founded 1909, editor Mick Imlah. This quarterly publication is the journal of the Poetry Society. The only instructions as to type of poetry wanted are **"Intending contributors should study the magazine first."** They publish "all the leading UK poets, many American and European poets." The issue I have contains poetry by many different poets, including the winners of the 1985 Gregory Awards, Graham Mort and Adam Thorpe (£4,000 each), Pippa Little (£3,000), James Harpur and Simon North (£2,000 each), and Julian May, (£1,000). As a sample, I selected the first four lines of "Think of the countless books" by Adam Thorpe:

> Think of the countless books that no-one has read,
> the eternity of lives that no-one has led.

> Think of the millions of flowers still to be seeded,
> the million constellations not yet freed

Poetry Review is 6¾x9¾", 76 pp., offset on rough paper, with b/w graphics and photos of the six winners of the Gregory Awards. Stiff card cover, printed in fuschia, black, and yellow on white, flat-spined. Circulation is 3,000, price per issue £2.50, subscription L11. **Sample available for £2.90 postpaid, guidelines for SASE. Pay is £10-15 poem, plus 2 copies. Reporting time is 10 weeks and time to publication varies.**

*****THE POETRY REVIEW, POETRY SOCIETY OF AMERICA (II)**, 15 Gramercy Park, New York, NY 10003, founded 1983, poetry editor Jerome Mazzaro. **The Poetry Society of America**, founded 1910, offers a wide range of workshops, lectures and readings, the Van Voorhis Library of poetry, and many annual contests and awards, many open only to members. Membership is $30 per year. *The Poetry Review*, a semiannual literary magazine, (digest-sized, flat-spined, 100 + pp., professionally printed with color matte card cover, circulation 3,000, 2,000 subscriptions of which 200 are libraries) "publishes poetry, essays and translations by PSA members AND non-members. Unsolicited MSS are welcome & encouraged." They use **poetry of "all kinds, any and all styles."** They have recently published poetry by Fredrick Morgan, Dana Gioia, Linda Wagner, Peter Viereck. As a sample the editors and I selected these lines from "Midsummer, Night" by Joyce Carol Oates:

> *I stepped through the house's sleeping walls.*
> *In stealth I entered the moon's wide light.*
> *Always summer, always the din of crickets,*
> *moist air and grasses, solitary cars on the highway.*
> *The romance of those travelers!—adult and unknown,*
> *headlights blinding,*
> *whipping past.*

Subscription: $5; per copy: $3. They receive about a thousand submissions per year, use about 50, have a 2-3 month backlog. **Sample: $3 postpaid. Name and address should be on each poem, typed, photo-copied or dot-matrix. "Suggest sending 4-5 poems." Reports in 2-3 months, pays $10 per page plus 1 copy. Editor sometimes comments on rejections.**

‡**POETRY: SAN FRANCISCO PUBLICATIONS, *POETRY: SAN FRANCISCO QUARTER-LY, POETS FOR PEACE (II, IV, Peace)**, Ft. Mason Cultural Center, San Francisco, CA 94123, phone 415-621-3073, founded 1983 (quarterly founded March, 1985), editor Herman Berlandt, who describes *Poetry: San Francisco* as "a quarterly for **bold and compassionate poetry, 'poems for planetary survival' for the Poets for Peace section. Poems of contemporary vision, style and content in the tradition of Whitman, Patchen, Everson and Bly, fresh, creative energy in the humanist mode." He does not want "trite, self-indulgent or contrived stuff."** They have recently published poetry by Robert Bly, Gene Ruggles, Ellen Leroe, Janice Blue and Julia Vingrad. As a sample the editor selected these lines from "City in the Fog" by Lucha Cordi Hernandez:

> *Skyscrapers, insatiable harpies feeding on stars,*
> *drinking all the moonlight*

Poetry: San Francisco is a typeset unstapled tabloid, 16 pp, with photos, graphics and ads, circulation 6,000, distributed free "to reach 40,000 literati in the Bay Area" and available to others by subscription at $5/year. **Sample: $1.25 postpaid. "Big backlog, active file for a year. Suggest poems under 32 lines. No SASEs. Just send xerox copies—if published, contributor will get copies."** No other pay "as yet. Suggest that contributors subscribe to maintain good contact." In addition to the quarterly they publish a "yearly poetry marathon collection" of 36 pp., saddle stapled. They also conduct a National Poetry Contest for National Poetry Week in April with 20 prizes $25-200, entry fee $2, winning poems published in *Poetry Week Program*, $1. Send SASE for details of this and other Poetry Week events. The editor advises, "Get yourself some strong mentors and read their work thoroughly—be it e.e. cummings, Allen Ginsberg, Nikki Giovanni, or Bob Dylan. See if you agree with them aesthetically and philosophically. Rich traditions help."

***POETRY TORONTO (II)**, 217 Northwood Dr., Willowdale, Ontario, Canada M2M 2K5, founded 1976, publisher Maria Jacobs, editors Maria Jacobs and Robert Billings, poetry editor Richard Lush, is a monthly digest-sized 36 pp. magazine, circulation 750. This directory is marketed internationally, so I include *Poetry Toronto* especially for poets outside the US, but Maria Jacob's comment is instructive—and should be heeded by all poets, especially those in the USA: "I am afraid there is little point in being listed in your directory. As it is, we receive a fair number of poetry submissions from the USA, and although we certainly would look at quality writing, most of the US submissions are more trouble than they are worth. This is not to be wondered at, since few US writers have ever seen our publication and send out blindly. I do not see how being listed in your directory would alter that fact: sending for sample copies is costly and time-consuming, and most people prefer to take a chance. But this results in a lot of unnecessary work for already overworked editors, and I do not wish to add to their burden at this point." **Sample: $2. Subscription: $11 (US subscribers pay in US currency), outside North America $14.**

❝ *Our function is to publish and showcase writers who haven't hit the big-time. We do encourage because we are writers too, and understand the delicate balance between professional attitude and personal feelings. We love beautiful language. Poets: read what you like, study what makes it tick, practice, and persist in submitting.*

Marsha Ward, Aztec Peak **❞**

Institutions: add $3. Submit maximum of 8 poems, avant-garde, free verse, haiku. **Poetry submissions should be single-spaced within stanzas, double-spaced between stanzas. Include SASE or SAE plus IRC(s). Payment: copies plus subscription.**

POETRY WALES PRESS, *POETRY WALES (II, IV, Welsh, Anglo-Welsh), 56, Parcau Ave., Bridgend, Mid-Glamorgan, Wales, founded 1965. *Poetry Wales*, a digest-sized 130 pp. quarterly, circulation 1,000, has a primary interest in **Welsh and Anglo-Welsh poets but also considers submissions internationally. Sample: £1.25. Pays.** The press publishes books of **primarily Welsh and Anglo Welsh poetry**, distributed by Dufolu Editions, Inc., Box 449, Chester Springs, PA 19425. If interested in this literature a good introduction might be their anthology, **Anglo-Welsh Poetry 1480-1980**, available from Dufolu for $19 hardbound (377 pp.) I selected the first of 6 stanzas of "The Dark" by Richard Poole from that anthology as a sample:

> And now, it seems, you are fearful
> of the dark. You people black vacancies
> with monsters of your own imagining.

POETRY WORLD (IV, Translations), (formerly *Modern Poetry in Translations*), English Dept., University of Iowa, Iowa City, IA 52242, founded 1965, poetry editor Daniel Weissbort, appears twice annually, publishes "**translations into English of foreign poetry, articles on literary translation, reviews of translations. We want translations of contemporary or earlier poetry, preferably not the universally known figures, also oral poetry. We do** *not* **consider work written in English.**" They have published poetry by Béalu, Reverdy, Rolf Jacobsen, Eskimo, Yugoslav folk poetry, etc. A durable little book. It has a circulation of 1,750, 500 subscriptions of which 200 are libraries. The new magazine is 160 pp., flat spine, back issues of *Modern Poetry in Translation* are available from the publisher, Anvil Press. Poetry, 69 King George St., London SE 10 8PX, England. "**Query advisable. 5-10 poems per individual poet. Format doesn't matter. Simultaneous submissions OK provided we are informed.**" **Reports in 3-6 months. Payment amount depends on funds available. Complimentary copies to contributors.**

‡*POETS AT WORK (I)**, RD 1, Portersville, PA 16051, founded 1985, Jessu Poet editor/publisher, a bi-monthly which runs many contests; **contributors are expected to subscribe. Jessu Poet wants to see "any form, subject matter that is within normal dictates of good taste. Limit of 21 lines. Like to have some under 6 lines. I publish every subscriber I have.**" He does not want to see "**that which is loaded with obscenity; long poetry.**" He has recently published poetry by Eddie Lou Cole, Marijane Ricketts, Ralph Hammond, June Owens, James Proctor, Vesle Fenstermaker. As a sample he selected the following lines from an unidentified poet:

> Drowsiness comes late
> Eyelids close . . . my thoughts roam now
> And sleep is denied.
> Reliving past events causes
> Insomnia to remain.

The editor describes the magazine as "exposure and entertainment for poets." It is generally 36 closely printed pages (offset from photoreduced typescript), magazine-sized, one-color paper cover with illustraton, saddle-stapled. Poetry is printed in categories such as love, death, humor, etc. Frequency is bi-monthly, subscription $12/year. **Sample: $3 postpaid. Guidelines available for SASE. Submissions are reported on in 2-3 days, poems published in 2-3 months. Previously published or simultaneous submissions are OK; the editor likes to have at least 5 poems, photocopies are OK. Free contests are run each issue.** The editor's advice is: "Make a poem *look* like a poem. It should not go clear across the page; don't rhyme for the rhyme alone—meaning must always be first; study poetry terminology; don't try free verse for your very first poem; always revise and delete; use a Thesaurus constantly; use common language; read work of good poets; use titles; prepare poetry carefully; follow guidelines of editor."

*POETS ON: (II)**, Box 255, Chaplin, CT 06235, phone 203-455-9671, founded 1976, poetry editor Ruth Daigon, is a 48 pp. poetry semiannual, each issue on an announced theme. "**We want well-crafted, humanistic, accessible poetry. We don't want to see sentimental rhymed verse. Length preferably 40 lines or less, or at the very most 80 lines (2 page poems).**" They have recently published poetry by Marge Piercy, Richard Kostelanetz, Charles Edward Eaton, Ruth Stone and Carolyn Stoloff. As a sample the editor chose these lines by Larry Rubin:

> Absorbing time, we fatten with the years,
> Storing experiences like calories,
> Each of us as rich as clocks permit
> I live on my own fat, and do not feel
> The sly contractions of the calendar.

The digest-sized, professionally printed magazine, matte card cover with b/w graphics, has a circulation of 450, 350 subscriptions of which 125 are libraries. Subscription: $6; per copy: $3.50. They use about 5% of the 800 submissions they receive each year, have a 2-3 month backlog. **Sample: $3.50 postpaid. Query with SASE to find out the current theme. Submit 5-6 poems (no more than 8-9) September 1-December 1 or February 1-May 1. Photocopy, dot-matrix OK. No handwritten MSS. Include short bio. Reports in 2-3 months. Pays 1 copy. Editor sometimes comments on rejections.** Ruth Daigon advises, "It's generally a good idea for the poet to read the magazine he/she is planning to send his/her poems to. That will save the poet a lot of postage and heartburn. The poet should make him/herself open to whatever is being done in the world of poetry, whether they like it or not, whether they agree with it or not, whether they understand it or not."

‡*POETS. PAINTERS. COMPOSERS. (II), 10254 35th Ave. SW, Seattle, WA 98146, phone 206-937-8155, founded 1984, editor Joseph Keppler, who says *"Poets. Painters. Composers.* is an avant-garde arts journal which publishes poetry, drawings, scores, criticism, essays, reviews, photographs and original art. **If poetry, music, or art is submitted, the work should be exciting, knowledgeable, and ingenious."** The journal, which appears 2 to 4 times a year, has published such poets as Richard Kostelanetz, Clifford Burke, Marion Kimes, and Arrigo Lora-Totino. As a sample from the issue I have (No. 3, Jan. 1985) I selected the beginning lines from "Setting Fire to the Road" by Scott Davidson:

> When the tailpipe busts loose
> halfway home, spraying my rearview mirror
> with sparks, I drag it thirty miles
> on this asphalt joke, through acres
> of nothing and don't slow down.

It should be noted that the above poem is one of the more conventional in the magazine; many verge on visual poetry. The very handsome, expensively printed journal is magazine-sized, 60 pp., most of it printed in black on white paper but with occasional inserts of colored paper, tissue, cutouts—one poem is even printed in its own little card folder. Mr. Keppler says, "each odd-numbered issue appears in an 8½x11" format; No. 2, for example, is published as posters; No. 4 appears on cassettes." Circulation is 300, no subscriptions. The magazine carries no price tag, but "Individuals donating $100 receive every issue." **Sample available for $5 postpaid. Contributors receive 1 copy. "Contributors' poetry receives great care. All material is returned right away unless (a) it's being painstakingly examined for acceptance into the journal or (b) it's being considered as right for some other way of publishing it or (c) we died."** He expects to publish 3 chapbooks of poetry a year and will accept freelance submissions. **For chapbook publication poets should query first "if poet prefers," sending credits, 7 sample poems, bio, philosophy, and poetic aims. Pay for chapbooks will be in author's copies, number negotiable ("We're generous"); honorariums may be given in the future.** Format of the chapbooks is expected to be "small, avant-garde, distinguished, exciting, experimental." Joseph Keppler says, "Poets' work is important work, and poetry is a most difficult art today. We maintain absolutely high standards, yet offer a hopeful critique . . . We want to develop the avant-garde here and everywhere. We expect to last well into the 21st Century and to change the way this culture understands literature. We intend to transform the role of poets in society. Advice for beginning poets? We're all beginning poets today."

POINT RIDERS PRESS, THE COTTONWOOD ARTS FOUNDATION, *RENEGADE (IV, Specialized), Box 2731, Norman, OK 73070, founded 1974, publishes **two books of poetry by midwestern poets.** *Renegade* "is an occasional publication, usually in 32 pp. chapbook format (but with special double issues and sometimes other formats). $10 for 4 issues; 4-6 per year; edited by Frank Parman." Poets published include Jennifer Kidney, George Economov, Michael Pons and Robin Schultz. No unsolicited MSS without query. The Point Riders Great Plains Poetry Anthology, 1982, edited by Arn Henderson and Frank Parman, 176 pp., 6x9" flat-spined paperback with glossy color card cover, $7.95 + $1 postage is a good regional collection from which I selected these sample lines, the opening of "Our People" by Teresa Anderson:

> For more years than I can remember,
> the crops have failed
> in this land where rain is a fugitive;
> and the people in my blood have
> lived in houses cut from the earth.

Send SASE for booklist to order samples. Pays in copies, usually 10% of print run. Considers simultaneous submissions.

PORCUPINE'S QUILL, INC. (II), 68 Main St., Erin, Ontario, Canada N0B 1T0, phone 519-833-9776 and 416-454-2001, founded 1974, poetry editor Joe Rosenblatt, is a small literary publisher who has brought out books by Robin Skelton, Jane Urquhart, Allan Salarik and Derk Wynand. I selected these sample lines by Robert Finch (from "The Legends" in **The Grand Duke of Moscow's Favorite Solo**):

> *There are three legends that concern the flute.*
> *You know them. There is Pan. He has the rating*
> *Of the first shepherd. He was too astute*
> *To limit entertainment to mere bleating,*

The book is handsomely printed, flat-spined, digest-sized, 90 + pp., three color matte card cover, photo of the poet inside: $7.95 plus postage. **Do not send unsolicited MS. Query with personal background, publishing history. Reply to query in 1 week, to MS (if invited) in 1 week. They publish on 5% royalty contract plus 10 copies. Send 6x9" SAE with 2 oz. postage for catalog to order samples.**

*UNIVERSITY OF PORTLAND REVIEW (II)**, 5000 N. Willamette, Portland, OR 97203, phone 503-283-7144, appears twice a year—"a commentary on the contemporary scene intended for the college educated layman." As a sample of their poetry I selected the first stanza of "Un-Just Spring" by Mary Comstock:

> *Nothing is right this year.*
> *Rain is beating Spring back to the ground.*
> *Grass drowns about us.*
> *Buds never blossom,*

The 6x9" saddle-stapled, 44 pp. magazine uses about 10 pp. of poetry in each issue, has 200 subscribers of which 200 are libraries, sends out 600 complimentary copies. Subscription: $1; per copy: 50¢. They receive about a hundred submissions of poetry per year, use half, have a 1 year backlog. **Sample: 50¢ postpaid. Submit any number of poems any time. Reports within 6-12 months, pays 5 copies. The editors sometimes comment on rejections.**

‡**POTES & POETS PRESS, INC., *ABACUS (II)**, 181 Edgemont Ave., Elmwood, CT 06110, phone 203-233-2023, press founded in 1981, magazine in 1984, editor Peter Ganick. "P + Pinc publishes avant-garde poetry in magazine form under the *Abacus* imprint, one writer per 16-page issue. The P + Pinc books are flat-spined and range from 80-120 pages in trade editions (first book June 1986)." **In addition to avant-garde, they want experimental or language-oriented poetry, not too much concrete poetry.**" No "*New Yorker* magazine, *Ploughshares* magazine, mainstream poery." They have recently published poems by Ron Silliman, Jackson Mac Low, Charles Bernstein, Cid Corman, and Theodore Enslin. The editors did not quote lines, and I have not seen samples. *Abacus* is magazine-sized, photocopied, no graphics, 12-18 pp.; it appears every 6 weeks. Circulation is 150, of which 40 are subscriptions and 10 go to libraries. Price per issue is $2.50, subscription $14/year. **Sample available for $2.50 postpaid. Pay is 12 copies. Simultaneous submissions are OK, as are photocopied or dot-matrix MSS. Reporting time is within 6 weeks and time to publication is 1 year. Freelance submissions are accepted for book publication. Writers should "just send the manuscript."** The press plans to publish 3 books of poetry per year with an average page count of 100, flat-spined paperbacks.

POTPOURRI INTERNATIONAL (DIVISION OF THE LITTLEFIELD GROUP) (I), Box 876-PD, Pottstown, PA 19464-0876, phone 215-327-4674, founded 1973, poetry editors Elizabeth M. Downing and Lenny Fields, publishes **3 anthologies per year, primarily of previously unpublished poets. You pay an entry fee of $3.50 for 1 poem, sliding scale for more—none over 36 lines. Simultaneous submissions OK. Each anthology is also a competition with five prizes from $10-$50 and honorable mentions. You are not required to buy the anthology ($11.45 postpaid or less if purchased in quantity) to be included. "We send copies to publishers and editors."** The digest-sized saddle-stapled, 90 pp. book is offset from typescript with simple art work. As a sample, the editors selected these lines from "Never Known" by R. L. Leonard:

> *Reaching into the air he felt God on a cloud*
> *While below him there were many who*
> *Had never known the peace he now knows.*

It appears that unpublished or lesser known poets are afforded an opportunity with this publisher.

*PRAIRIE FIRE, A DIVISION OF THE MANITOBA WRITER'S GUILD, INC. (II, IV, Canada from Manitoba)**, 3rd Floor, 374 Donald St., Winnipeg, Manitoba, Canada R3J 2J2, phone 204-943-9066, founded 1978. The Manitoba Writer's Guild, Inc. "is an arts-service organization which publishes a literary quarterly called *Prairie Fire*. It also publishes a newsletter. *Prairie Fire* **is concerned primarily with the contemporary writing of Canada's prairie provinces and appears in every library and half the schools in Manitoba.**" They have recently published poetry by Lyn Lifshin, Monty Reid and Glen Sorestad. As a sample the editor selected these lines by Thelma Poirier:

> *They want to touch the wind*

> *touch the things the wind touches . . .*
> *They want to tell what comes after*

The 6x9" flat-spined 90 + pp. quarterly is professionally printed, glossy card cover with graphics, circulation 1,000, 740 subscriptions of which 465 are libraries. Subscription: $15 (foreign subscription including US, add $5 year); per copy: $4. They receive over 200 freelance submissions of poetry per year, use less than 5%. **Sample: $4 postpaid. Submit up to 6 pp., 1 poem per page, name on page. No photocopy or dot-matrix. Reports in 2 months. Pays $10-20 per poem, also 1 contributor's copy. Editor comments "only if implored."**

‡*THE PRAIRIE JOURNAL, PRAIRIE JOURNAL PRESS (IV, Canadian literature)**, Box 997, Calgary, Alberta, Canada T3A 3G2, founded 1983, literary editor A. Burke, a literary quarterly and a small-press publisher of chapbooks; **the purpose is to promote Canadian literature. The editor wants to see "free verse, imagist, post-modern, emotional, cerebral, and original" poetry, not** "rhymed stanzas if unimaginative or imitative." They have recently published Fred Cogswell, Steve Noyes, and Ronald Kurt. As a sample, the editor selected the following lines by Richard Stevenson:

> *There is trouble on the playing fields:*
> *you would have words spread out*
> *like a line of fearful citizens*
> *looking for their corpse*
> *some kind of clue.*

The Prairie Journal is digest-sized, saddle-stapled, offset, with some graphics; exchange ads are considered. Circulation 200 + , of which about 40% are library subscriptions. Price per issue is $6, subscription $12. **Sample: $5 postpaid. Pay: 1-3 free copies. Writers should submit 8-10 pages, neatly typed or photocopied, with a covering letter. The editor reports on submissions in 2 weeks, and publication is in a year or more. Freelance submissions are accepted for chapbooks. Queries will be answered in 2-4 weeks and MSS reported in the same time. Authors of chapbooks are paid an honorarium of $100 if grant money is available.** The editor says, "We are interested in anthologies and do not pay royalties since our runs are small and not commercial." Book catalog is free on request. Samples of books: $6. He criticizes for a fee of $10 per page if detailed criticism is requested in advance. The sample chapbook I have seen is offset from typescript, with b/w illustrations, 36 pp., one-color matte card cover with drawing, saddle-stapled.

*PRAIRIE SCHOONER (II)**, 201 Andrews, University of Nebraska, Lincoln, NE 68588, phone 402-472-1800, founded 1927, poetry editor Hilda Raz; "one of the oldest literary quarterlies in continuous publication; publishes poetry fiction, essays, interviews and reviews." They want "**good poetry; that is, poems that fulfill the expectations they set up." No specifications as to form, length, style, subject-matter or purpose.** They have recently published poetry by Amy Clampitt, Marilyn Hacker, David Wagoner, Ben Howard, Kelly Cherry, Judith Ortiz Cofer, Gary Margolis, Lee Jenkins, Peter Makuck Carole Oles, Charles O. Hartman and Diane Ackerman. The editors selected these sample lines by Ted Kooser:

> *As the President spoke, he raised a finger*
> *to emphasize something he said. I've forgotten*
> *just what he was saying, but as he spoke*
> *he glanced at that finger as if it were . . .*

The magazine is 6x9", flat-spined, 120 pp., circulation 2,000, and uses 40-50 pp. of poetry in each issue. Subscription: $11; per copy: $3.25. They receive about 2,800 MSS (of all types) per year from which they choose 160-200 pp. of poetry, have a 12 month backlog (which they're trying to reduce). **Sample: $1 postpaid. "Clear copy appreciated." Reports in 2-3 months; "sooner if possible." Pays copies. The $500 Strousse-Prairie Schooner Prize is awarded to the best poetry published in the magazine each year, and the Slote Prize for beginning writers ($500) will also be awarded. Editors serve as judges.** Hilda Raz comments, "*Prairie Schooner* receives a large number of poetry submissions; I expect we're not unusual. Our staff time doesn't allow criticial comments on MSS, but the magazine's reputation is evidence of our careful reading. We've been dedicated to the publication of good poems for a very long time and have a reputation for publishing work early in the career of many poets." I was pleased that she remembered my own poems appearing there in the mid-60's.

*THE PRESBYTERIAN RECORD (IV, Inspirational)**, 50 Wynford Dr., Don, Mills, Ontario, Canada M3C 1J7, phone 416-441-1111, founded 1876, poetry editor James Ross Dickey, is "the national magazine that serves the membership of The Presbyterian Church in Canada (and over 1,000 who are not Canadian Presbyterians). We seek to: stimulate, inform, inspire, to provide an 'apologetic' and a critique of our church and the world (not necessarily in that order!)." They want **poetry which is "inspirational, Christian, thoughtful, even satiric but NOT maudlin. No 'sympathy card' type verse a la Edgar Guest or Francis Gay. It would take a *very* exceptional poem of epic length for us to use it.**

Close-up

Vi Gale
Prescott Street Press

Artist: Lawrence Goodridge

Reading the poetry she publishes one has the impression of wide open spaces, mountains and forests. But Vi Gale, who lives and works in Portland, thinks of herself as an "Ouppie" (old urban professional). Her studio office has been in the heart of the city for 18 years. "I like the routine of getting up and going to work in the morning," she says. "But more than that, I like the feeling of being involved with other people going about their lives. In the evening I go home to my husband, who is a contracting engineer, and a small house in the suburbs. Middle-America to the hilt."

She has published short stories, articles, photography, and, to date, six collections of poetry. "My press has presented the work of more than 50 poets and artists on our postcards and in our Prescott First Books." Two collections of Japanese translations from the work of Shuntaro Tanikawa grace her list—and a third is due out this fall.

"I love the look of fine print on good paper in the context of tasteful design," she comments. "It is an art form in itself and adds to the impact of the writing. That publishing poetry calls for hard, caring work on the part of everyone and very little in the way of financial return hasn't seemed to bother anyone so far. We are all immodestly pleased with the work we do. We hope we can stay with it for years to come."

I first came to know Vi's poetry in the 50s, when she was a college student and I accepted some of her work for *New Campus Writing*. I was attracted then as now by its clean taste and lucidity. "My interest in words," she says, "goes back to the time when I was a child in Sweden. I was about three or four when I began learning to recognize some of the shorter words in print. I could hardly wait to go to school, where I could learn to read and write. Before that happened, however, our family emigrated to the United States, and I went to school here and began learning American English."

Her first two collections of poetry (in 1959 and 1965) were published by Allan Swallow of Denver, who was legendary for discovering and helping new poets during his lifetime. "He had gotten in touch with me after seeing a poem in a little magazine. He gave me an ongoing interest in small press publication that helped me when I founded Prescott Street Press in 1974."

Poets who live in the Northwest or whose work has what she calls a "Northwest focus" may want to sample her publications. You can do that inexpensively by purchasing one of the postcard series, and at the same time have postcards you'll be proud to mail—an admirable way to pass good poetry around. The work at Prescott Street Press is collaborative, with poets, artists, designers and typesetters pitching in—and eventually getting paid. But, as is true throughout much of the world of poetry, publishing is a labor of love.

—Judson Jerome

Shorter poems 10-30 lines preferred. Free verse OK (if it's not just rearranged prose). 'Found' poems. Subject matter should have some Christian import (however subtle).'' They have recently published poetry by Jean Larsen, Jeanne Davis, Joan Stortz, Marlow C. Dickson, Len Selle and J.R. Dickey. The magazine comes out 11 times a year, circulation 77,777, 77,500 subscriptions. Subscription: $7.50; per copy: 65¢. They receive 50-60 submissions per year, use 10-12, have a 4-5 month backlog. **Sample: $1 postpaid. Submit seasonal work 6 weeks before month of publication. Double-spaced, photocopy OK. "Dot-matrix semi-OK." Simultaneous submissions OK. Reports usually within a month. Pays $20-50 per poem. Editor sometimes comments on rejections.**

PRESCOTT STREET PRESS (IV, Regional), Box 40312, Portland, OR 97240-0312, founded 1974, poetry editor Vi Gale: "**Poetry and fine print from the Northwest.**" Vi Gale says, "Our books and cards are the product of many hands from poet, artist, printer, designer, typesetter to bookstore and distributor. Somewhere along the line the editor/publisher [herself] arranges to pay one and all in some way. Sometimes we have had grant help from the NEA and also from State and Metropolitan arts organizations. But most of our help has come from readers, friends and the poets and artists themselves. Everyone has worked very hard. And we are immodestly pleased with our labors! **We pay all of our poets. A modest sum, perhaps, but we pay everyone something. We are not a strictly regional press, although the poets I take on are connected with the Northwest in some way when we bring out the books.**" Vi Gale brings out series of postcards and paperback and hardback books of poetry in various artistic formats with illustrations by nationally known artists. Send SASE for catalog to order copies. I selected these sample lines, the opening of "Crow Feather" by Kim Robert Stafford, from a Salal Series of poetcards:

> *At the edge of silence*
> *crack your knuckles for luck.*
> *Crow will hear and answer, declare*
> *all shadows created equal,*
> *brothers in black.*

Considers simultaneous submissions.

THE PRESS OF MACDONALD & REINECKE (II), Box 1275, San Luis Obispo, CA 93406, phone 805-543-5404, founded 1974, poetry editor Lachlan P. MacDonald. "The press is a division of Padre Productions bringing together under one imprint drama, fiction, literary, nonfiction and poetry. We publish poetry in broadsides, flat-spined paperbacks, chapbooks and hardcover. We are looking for **poetry of literary merit and also poetry suitable for travel and nature photo books. We are averse to tightly rhymed conventional poetry unless designed to appeal to the general humor market.**" They recently published Terre Ouenhand's "Voices from the Well". **Query with 5-6 samples, publication credits, bio. The editor also wants to know "do they give readings or have marketing opportunities? Some authors distribute flyers to build up pre-publication orders sufficient to justify the print order." Replies to queries in 2-4 weeks, to submissions (if invited) in 2-6 months. Simultaneous submissions, photocopy, dot-matrix OK. MS should be double-spaced. Pays minimum of 4% royalties, 6 copies. The editor "frequently makes brief comments" on rejections. Send 6x9" SASE for catalog to order sample publications.** The editor advises, "Poets should get published in dozens of magazines before they consider book publication. Most collections offered us do not have unity of theme, style or subject matter; the poet needs to develop craft that will give the book identity and some potential market."

PRESS PORCEPIC LTD.(IV, Canadian poets), 235-560 Johnson St., Victoria, British Columbia, Canada V8W 3C6, phone 604-381-5502, founded 1971, poetry editors Gerry Truscott and Shelley McGuinness. "We look for **new Canadian writers** of both poetry and fiction. Our aim is to give these promising new writers a chance to present their work in attractive, quality paperbacks at an accessible price. **Poetry must be non-sexist and deal with contemporary themes. We often publish poetry that explores mythical themes in a contemporary setting. We prefer free verse, collections with varying rhythms on all types of subjects.**" They have recently published books of poetry by Kristjana Gunnars, Marilyn Bowering, Jane Urquhart and David Halliday. **Canadian poets (or landed immigrants) fitting their description may submit complete MSS or query with 5-10 samples and cover letter which especially gives publication credits and bio, and whatever personal or aesthetic philosophy, poetic goals and principles seem relevant. Simultaneous submissions OK if so indicated in cover letter. Replies to queries in 1-3 weeks, to submissions in 8-10 weeks. Photocopy OK, dot-matrix not preferable. Pays 10% royalties, negotiable advance, plus 10 copies. Send 8½x11" SASE for catalog to order samples from distributors: Beaverbooks in Canada, Inland Books in USA. Editors sometimes comment on rejections.**

PRESSED CURTAINS, *CURTAINS (II, IV, Translation), 4 Bower St., Maidstone, Kent, England ME16 8SD, founded 1971. *Curtains* is a literary annual, 200 pp., circulation 450, which uses **quality**

poetry, especially of French poetry translated into English. **Sample: $7.** Pressed Curtains publishes books of poetry by poets who have appeared in the magazine. Send SASE for catalog to buy samples.

*PRIMAVERA (II, IV, Women), 1212 E. 59th St., Chicago, IL 60637, phone 312-684-2742, founded 1975, is "an irregularly published but approximately annual magazine of poetry, fiction and articles reflecting **the experiences of women. We look for strong, original voice and imagery, generally prefer free verse, fairly short length, related, even tangentially, to women's experience.**" They have recently published poetry by Leslie Adrienne Miller, Alice Fulton, Claire Nicolas White and Kathleen Spivack. The editors selected these sample lines by Julie Fay:

> *This swimmer who defies dimension*
> *invites me to cut through air, ease*
> *out of my body to plunge and pitch-*
> *Each time we move we rearrange infinity-*

The elegantly printed magazine-sized publication, flat-spined, generously illustrated with photos and graphics, uses 30-35 pp. of poetry in each issue, circulation 800. Price per issue: $5. They receive over 1,000 submissions of poetry per year, use 32. **Sample: $4 postpaid. Submit no more than 5 pp. anytime, legible photocopy OK, no dot-matrix or queries. Reports in less than 6 weeks. Pays 2 copies. Send SASE for guidelines. Editors comment on rejections "when requested or inspired."**

*PRIME TIME SPORTS & FITNESS, PRIME TIME PUBLICATIONS, GREENWOOD ST. PRESS, DENNIS A DORNER COMMUNICATIONS, CHICAGO TOWER PRESS (IV, Sports, humor),** Box 6091, Evanston, IL 60204, phone 312-864-8113, founded 1980, executive editor Nicholas Schmitz. Prime Time Publications are "publishers of general circulation magazines and tabloids as well as specialty sports and humor magazines and calendars." *Prime Time Sports & Fitness* is a monthly magazine "humorous and sports related." **No specifications as to form, length, and style— though the poems should be appropriate to the themes of the magazine: "sports, recreational, health-club emphasis, exercise, diet, nutrition, self-improvement."** The magazine has a circulation of 38,000, 18,000 subscriptions of which 200 are libraries. Subscription: $15; per copy: $1.50. Last year they received 200 submissions of freelance poetry, used 35. If poetry is seasonal it could be 1-10 months before publication. **Sample: $2.50 postpaid. Shorter poems wanted unless editorializing on tennis, racquetball, etc." Reports in 4-6 weeks, pays $15-100.** Greenwood St. Press, Dennis A. Dorner Communications and Chicago Tower Press are imprints under which they publish books, "**but open to chapbooks submissions. Looking for whole books of poetry. Especially *right now*." No query: submit whole book only. Reports in 4-6 weeks. Prefer no simultaneous submissions. Photocopies OK. Payment depends on grant or award money.** They also subsidy publish, the author paying 70% of costs. Nicholas Schmitz is willing to provide critiques for $50 for 60 pages or on an hourly basis. He says, "We are very open to poetry; however most that is submitted is not suitable. If you can do sports or exercise prose or poetry you can sell to us."

*PRIME TIMES, NATIONAL ASSOCIATION OF RETIRED CREDIT UNION PEOPLE (NARCUP) (IV, Mature adult),** 2802 International Lane, Suite 120, Madison, WI 53704, phone 608-241-1557, founded 1979, poetry editor Joan Donovan, is a quarterly "**targeted to pre-retirees. Its purpose is to help its readers 'redefine' mid-life in creative ways. Needs in poetry: light-toned is fine, but heavier reflective themes are agreeable. Subject matter should be suitable for mature adults. Sexual/erotic themes *fine*. We prefer poetry that is gifted and genuinely poetic, but *accessible*.**" They have not recently published poetry, but would like to consider excellent poetry. The quarterly is magazine-sized, 40 pp., glossy paper and cover with many color illustrations, circulation 61,000, 42,000-50,000 subscriptions of which a few are libraries. It is free to members of NARCUP, $10 per year to non-members. Per copy: $2. The editor reports receiving 25 submissions of freelance poetry per year and has taken "to date, none." **Sample: $1 postpaid. Submit up to 5 pp. any time. Photocopy, dot-matrix, simultaneous submissions all OK. No queries, please. Reports in 6-8 weeks. Pays $50-250 per poem. Editor "often" comments on rejections.**

‡PRINCETON UNIVERSITY PRESS, PRINCETON SERIES OF CONTEMPORARY POETS, LOCKERT LIBRARY OF POETRY IN TRANSLATION (III),** 41 William St., Princeton, NJ 08540, phone 609-452-4900, literature editor Robert E. Brown. "In both series, we publish simultaneous cloth and paperback (flat-spine) editions for each poet. Clothbound editions are on acid-free paper, and binding materials are chosen for strength and durability. Each book is given individual design treatment rather than stamped into a series mold. We have published **everything from collections of short free-verse poems to more formally structured long narrative poems. Successful works tend to reflect the poet's intellectual engagement with his/her surroundings, as well as attention to form. Do not want to see inspirational, light, humorous, or political-diatribe verse.**" They have recently published poetry by Vicki Hearne, Fred Turner and Debora Greger in the Contemporary Poets series and

Holderlin in the Lockert Library. The editor selected these sample lines by John Koethe:

> *What I want in poetry is a kind of abstract photography*
> *Of the nerves, but what I like in photography*
> *Is the poetry of literal pictures of the neighborhood.*

The editor says, "All our books in both series are heavily subsidized to break even. We have internal funds to cover deficits of publishing costs. We do not, however, publish books chosen and subsidized by other agencies, such as AWP. **Our series are both open competitions, for which the 'award' is publication. We comment on semifinalists only."** Send SASE for guidelines to submit. Send MSS only during respective reading periods stated in guidelines. Reports in 2-3 months. Simultaneous submissions OK if you tell them; photocopy, dot-matrix OK. Pays royalties (5% or more) and 12 author's copies.** Robert E. Brown advises, "Before submitting to any publisher, it is best to be familiar with what they have published recently."

PRINTABLE ARTS SOCIETY, INC., *BOX 749, *RE:PRINT (AN OCCASIONAL MAGA-ZINE) (II), Box 749, Old Chelsea Station, New York, NY 10011, founded 1972. *Box 749* is an annual of "the printable arts," including **poetry. Sample: $3.** *Re:Print (an Occasional Magazine)* reprints selected items from *Box 749* for separate sale, and the press also publishes collections of poetry. Start with *Box 749.*

*PRISM INTERNATIONAL (II), Dept. of Creative Writing, University of British Columbia, Vancouver, British Columbia, Canada V6T 1W5, phone 604-228-2514, founded 1959, editor-in-chief: Wayne Hughes. "*Prism* is an international quarterly that publishes poetry, drama, short fiction, and translation into English in all of these genres. We have no thematic or stylistic allegiances: excellence is our main criterion for acceptance of MSS. **We want poetry with something fresh to say and a distinctive way of saying it. Prosody, wit, image as opposed to symbol. We do not want avant-garde experimentation for its own sake. We read everything.**" They have recently published poetry by Robert Bringhurst, Al Purdy, Alison Reed, Charles Bukowski, Anghel Dumbraveanu. As a sample the editor selected these lines by Erin Mouré:

> *Sometimes I am only a small wound,*
> *a small hole in the skull*
> *thru which brilliant light leaks,*
> *a flaw betraying paradise.*

Prism is elegantly printed in a flat-spined 6x9" format, 80 pp., original color artwork on the glossy card cover, circulation to 900 subscribers of which 200 are libraries. Subscription: $10; per copy: $4. They receive 1,000 submissions per year, use 125, have a 1-3 month backlog. **Sample: $4 postpaid. Submit 5-8 poems at a time, any print so long as it's typed. No query. Reports in 3 weeks ("or we write to poet to tell him/her we're holding onto the work for a while"). Pays $25 per printed page plus subscription. "We ask contributors to please buy copies." Send SASE for guidelines. Editors often comment on rejections.** Wayne Hughes advises, **"Take chances—try things you've never seen poetry do before, but remember to maintain consistency of image, content and structure within each poem."**

*PROCESSED WORLD (IV, Work/information handling), 55 Sutter St. #829, San Francisco, CA 94117, phone 415-495-6823, founded 1981, edited by a collective. "*PW* is a magazine about work, especially work in 'information handling' industries. It serves as a creative outlet for those with stultifying jobs and offers critical and creative reflections on life in the processed world." They use poetry which is **"witty, short, work-related, anti-alienation."** They have published poetry by Tom Clark, John Oliver Simon, Adam Cornford, Barbara Schaffer, Carl Watson, Jeffry Zabk, Linda Thomas, Valerie Warden, Ligi, Kurt Lipschwitz and Fritz Hamilton. As a sample I chose these lines from "I Don't Want To Be a Technopeasant" by Beth Jones:

> *I wonder*
> *Will someone, using an Apple II,*
> *discover the plan to make*
> *us nothing but numbers,*

The 8½x11" 50 pp. magazine is printed in 9 point type, various tints of ink, has a glossy card cover with cartoon graphics, circulation 3,500, 850 subscriptions of which 12 are libraries. Each issue (3 times a year) uses 2-3 pp. of poetry. Subscription: $10; per copy: $2.50 (by mail). They receive 100-200 submissions per year, use 10% (8-10 poems in each issue). **Pays free copies on request. Sometimes editor comments on rejections.**

‡***PROOF (IV, Regional)**, Glenhirst, Station Rd., Swineshead, Nr. Boston, Lincolnshire, PE20 3NX, England, telephone 820314, founded 1976, editor Shirley Bell, a literary magazine of new **writing from the Lincolnshire and Humberside region. They want "good serious contemporary work.**

Part of the magazine's function is to be open to all submissions—rejected manuscripts are always returned with advice/criticism. Nationally known guest writers are featured (e.g. U.A. Fanthorpe), but mostly include a range of local writers—from beginners to poets who are developing national reputations." The copy I have contains poems by more than a dozen local poets. As a sample, I selected the beginning lines from "A Cuckoo at the Picnic" by N.S. Jackson:

> *The 'Cuck-oo!' chimes out across my satisfaction:*
> *"I've waited all winter to hear that!"*
> *"You are a fool" she says. "An absolute fool!"*
> *I have not the heart to argue with her.*

At this time of this writing, *Proof* was magazine-sized, 12 pp. including covers, printed in black on pink paper, folded and saddle-stapled, but, according to the editor, "the magazine will become 20 pp. excluding covers, printed in black on white." It has a circulation of 1,600, of which 1,500 are subscriptions, which go with membership in the local arts organization (£5/year). Price per issue is 50p but "is about to rise." **Sample available for 50p plus IRC or stamp, guidelines are printed in the magazine. Pay is £5/poem plus 1 copy. Writers should submit no more than 5 poems, clearly written, preferably typed, must be previously unpublished. Reporting time "varies," and time to publication is 2-3 months. Criticism of rejected MSS is always provided.** The editor says, "*Read* lots of good contemporary work in books/ magazines. *Write* as a late 20th century poet."

PROOF ROCK PRESS, *PROOF ROCK (I, II), Box 607, Halifax, VA 24558, founded 1982, poetry editor Don R. Conner. "We try to wake up a passive readership. We challenge our writers to search for something new under the sun; and improve on the old." The poetry they want is: "**adventure, contemporary, humor/satire, fantasy, experimental. Avoid overt sentimentality. Poems up to 32 lines. All subjects considered if well done**." They have recently published poetry by Lifshin, Locklin, Craig, Arguelles and Faucher. As a sample I chose the opening lines of "The Hidden Reader" by Kurt J. Fickert:

> *They have forbidden me to read.*
> *Go bowling, they say; watch TV.*
> *Share a pizza with a friend.*
> *But I cheat: I plummet into a book,*

The digest-sized magazine appears 2-3 times per year, is offset from typescript copy, colored matte card cover, with 30-40 pp. in each issue, circulation 300, 100 subscriptions of which 8-10 are libraries. They receive 800-1,000 submissions per year, use 120-150, have a 3-6 month backlog. Subscription: $4; per copy: $2.50. **Sample: $2.50 postpaid. Submit no more than 6 pieces, year round. No query needed, though some issues are on announced themes. Photocopy, dot-matrix, simultaneous submissions OK. Reports "usually within 30 days." Pays 1 copy. Send SASE for guidelines.** Proof Rock Press publishes an occasional anthology and collections by individuals. **Query with 8-10 samples, bio and publishing credits. Reply to queries in 30 days, to submissions (if invited) in 1-3 months. Simultaneous submissions, photocopies, dot-matrix OK. Pays copies. Send $2.50 for a sample chapbook. Editor sometimes comments on rejections.** His advice is, "Be introspective. Accept the challenge of looking within and write from experience."

PROPER TALES PRESS, *MONDO HUNKAMOOGA, WEEPING MONK EDITIONS, COPS GOING FOR DOUGHNUTS EDITIONS, PROPER TALES POSTCARDS (II), Box 789, Sta. F, Toronto, Ontario, Canada M4Y 2N7, founded 1979, poetry editor Stuart Ross, who says, "I sell my own titles out on the street. I find an empty corner or doorway, fling a sign around my neck, and sell my books. Sometimes I sell one or sometimes 20. Usually I sell about 10. And it's amazing who buys the books. People who have only read horoscopes and Harold Robbins are getting into my stuff, showing interest—not just other writers. I am interested in putting out books that wouldn't be published elsewhere. Proper Tales Press wants to inject excitement and quality into a publishing world inundated with the mundane and the repetitive. I want **surrealist poetry, bizarre, demento-primitivo. I** *don't* **want 'obscure to the point of inaccessiblity,' religious, boring or confessional 'verse.'**" He has recently published poetry by Opal L. Nations, John M. Bennett, Lillian Necakov, Randall Brock and Wain Ewing. As a sample he selected these lines from "Yapping Eyes Blues in D7th" by Mark Laba:

> *I am the tiny skulls that fill*
> *your coffee cup*
> *each morning*
> *doing the funky chicken.*

Mondo Hunkamooga, a journal of small press reviews does use poetry. The other imprints are explained by Stuart Ross: "Weeping Monk Editions is a mimeo series that so far hasn't gotten past #1. Cops Going For Doughnuts Editions are one-pagers, and you know, if you need a quick read during your morning coffee, it's just the thing. They are all single prose pieces, because poetry and doughnuts just seem too much of a cliché." Proper Tales Press books are attractively printed, mostly inexpensive chapbooks in innovative formats. **Query with 10-30 samples, "short bio, a hello, some flattery, *no* philosophies, principles, etc. Who cares? Let's see *poems*." Reports in 1-90 days on submissions. No reading fee, "but we accept donations from Texan oilmen and wealthy widows." No simultaneous submissions. MS should be "legible; no ketchup stains." Photocopy, dot-matrix OK. Poets are paid: "negotiable, but usually" and get 10% of the press run. Send 6x9" SASE for catalog to order samples—or send $2 or more: "the more $ the more books!" The editor "quite often" comments on rejections.** His advice, "Don't bother if you're just going to waste nice trees."

*PROPHETIC VOICES, HERITAGE TRAILS PRESS (II), 94 Santa Maria Dr., Novato, CA 94947, founded 1982, poetry editors Ruth Wildes Schuler, Goldie L. Morales and Jeanne Leigh Schuler. "Our goal is to share thoughts on an international level. We see the poet's role as that of prophet, who points the way to a higher realm of existence." They publish *Prophetic Voices* twice a year and chapbooks. They want **"poetry of social commentary that deals with the important issues of our time. Poetry with beauty that has an international appeal. Do not want religious poetry or that with a limited scope. Open to any kind of excellent poetry, but publish mostly free verse. Limited number of long poems accepted due to lack of space."** They have recently published A. D. Winans, D. Roger Martin, Mary Rudge, Mogg Williams, Joseph Bruchac, Naomi Long Madgett and Shiang-hua Chang. As a sample the editors selected these lines from "Marina Tsvetayeva" by B. Z. Niditch:

> *The dead cannot hear*
> *the rain of Russian cries*
> *this voice ever new*
> *her weeping over an age*
> *through cloaked*
> *amidst shower of longing*

Prophetic Voices is digest-sized, 130 pp., saddle-stapled, offset from typescript with mat card cover, colored stock with graphics. They have 100 pp. of poetry in each issue, circulation to 400 subscribers of which 10 are libraries. Subscription: $10; per copy: $5. They receive 2,000 submissions per year, use 400, have a 3 year backlog. **Sample: $5 postpaid. Photocopy OK. Submit 4 poems or less. Reports in 1-8 weeks. Pays 1 copy.** Heritage Trails does not consider unsolicited MSS. The editors advise, "Be aware of what is going on in the world around you. Even the personal poem should have universal appeal if it is to survive the test of time."

*PTOLEMY/THE BROWNS MILLS REVIEW (II), Box 908, Browns Mills, NJ 08015, founded 1979, fiction editor David C. Vajda, is a 16 pp. digest-sized literary review appearing 1-2 times a year. It has published poetry by Edward Lynskey, Dan Raphael, B. Z. Niditch, Michael McMahon, Richard Soos and Jesse Glass, Jr. **Sample: $1 postpaid. Photocopy, dot-matrix OK. Reports "as soon as possible." No pay.** David Vajda also publishes collections by individuals and anthologies. **Query. Pays copies. Sometimes comments on rejections. Query about seeing samples.**

‡*PURPLE HEATHER PUBLICATIONS, *THE TOLL GATE JOURNAL, *FIVE LEAVES LEFT (II), 12 Colne Rd., Cowling, Nr. Keighley, West Yorkshire BD22 0BZ, England, founded 1982, editor and proprietor Richard Mason, a small press publisher of literary bi-annuals. **The editor wants "Poetry of a quality that other writers will enjoy reading. Poems of social comment, peace, politics, philosophy, poems of bohemian visions, *poems that disturb*." He does not want traditional poetry.** He has recently published poetry by George MacBeth, Jim Burns, Dave Cunliffe, and Andy Darlington. As a sample, he chose the following lines from "Gauguin Nude" by David Tipton:

> *washing your black hair as you lay*
> *gold-skinned in the tub the yellow*
> *and blues of Iris's and Gauguins*
> *Et L'Or de heur Cortes on the wall.*

Five Leaves Left, which appears three times a year, is for "alternative sub-culture and high energy ideas and inspirations" (I have not seen it so cannot tell what this means). It has 64 pp., offset, with graphics and cover art. Circulation is 500, of which 20 are library subscriptions; other sales are on newsstands. Price per issue is $1.50, subscription $6 (in the US). **Guidelines are available for 6 IRCs or $3 cash. Pay is "at least" 1 copy. "Camera-ready copy is appreciated. Only unpublished poetry. Reporting time is within 1 month and time to publication is "perhaps 1 year." Detailed criticism of MSS is available for $6.** The press runs an annual competition for a poetry collection of not more than 24 pp. Mr. Mason's advice to poets is, "Imitate your peers, but be original!"

‡*PURPLE PATCH (I), 8 Beaconview House, Charlemont Farm, West Bromwich, England, founded 1975, editor Geoff Stevens, an "approximately quarterly" poetry and short prose magazine with reviews, comment, and illustrations. The editor says, **"prefer maximum of one page length (40 lines), but all good examples of poetry considered." He does not want "poor scanning verse, concrete poetry, non-contributing swear words and/or obscenities, hackneyed themes."** The copy I have contains work by many poets in many styles; as a sample, I chose the beginning lines from "Island" by Paul Seabrook:

> *I remember the river, and the sweat*
> *On the boatman's brow in bringing us, the boat*
> *A thing of wood only,*
> *And the day an animal slumped in the trees.*

Purple Patch is magazine-sized, 14-20 pp. offset on plain paper, cover on the same stock with b/w drawing, side-stapled. Circulation "varies." Price is 3 issues for £1.50 in Great Britain. **Contributors have to buy a copy to see their work in print. "All legible formats" are accepted. Reporting time is 1 month to Great Britain, longer to USA; time to publication is a maximum of 4 months.** The editor says, **Purple Patch** is a founder-member of F.A.I.M. (Federation for Advancement of Independent Magazines) with 10 member magazines at present. All present member magazines publish poetry and beginners are welcome to submit to any of them."

‡*PUBLIC WORKS (I)**, room 173, University College, The University of Western Ontario, London, Ontario, Canada N6A 3K7, an annual student magazine that **accepts submissions of poetry, prose, articles and reviews of a literary nature from non-students.** The copy I have contains poetry by Brenda Carr, John Tremblay, Cris Guiltinan, Don McKay, Beryl Baigent, Mhairi James, John Nold, Renee Ruth Read, and Heather Barclay. As a sample, I selected the first stanza from "College Street Line" by Ian MacKenzie:

> *The dog had eyes of luminescent cadmium.*
> *It moved down the aisle with the unnerving*
> *confidence of an animal. Its muscular*
> *haunches brushed past my face, leaving no*
> *detectable odour.*

The journal is magazine-sized, 60 pp., offset from typed copy on lightweight white stock with b/w decorations, tan matte-card cover with block-printed titles in red, side-stapled. Price is $2.50 per issue. **Contributors receive 1 copy.**

‡*PUBLISHED!, PLATEN PUBLISHING COMPANY (I)**, 14240 Bledsoe St., Sylmar, CA 91342, phone 818-367-9613, founded 1985. Editor and publisher Patricia Begalla, a monthly for, by and about writers with emphasis on the talented beginner. "It was conceived as a place where **serious fledglings could really get a start in the writing profession." Articles are supposed to pertain to the business of writing, but there are no specifications for poems.** The September, 1985 issue contained poetry by Ester Leiper, Gene Boone, Nola Waddington, and Joyce A. Chandler, from whose "To Be a Poet" I selected the beginning stanza as a sample:

> *to be a poet   that's my ilk*
> *to line the common ear with silk*
> *soothing redundant cares away*
> *like the court jester of yesterday*

Published! is 8½x11", offset from typeset copy on quality 60 lb paper with occasional small b/w drawings and a page of classified ads, 20 pp. saddle-stapled, grey matte card cover printed in burgundy. Subscriptions $12/year. **Don't send more than 3 poems at once (20 lines maximum); MSS should be typed double-spaced. Only one submission per author will be published at a time. "We answer everyone in chronological order, reporting in 30-45 days." Pay for poems is $10/each. Send 3 first class stamps or IRC's for sample issue and guidelines.**

THE PUCKERBRUSH PRESS, *THE PUCKERBRUSH REVIEW (IV, Regional), 76 Main St., Orono, ME 04473, is a **Maine-oriented** biannual, magazine-sized, 30-50 pp., circulation 250 + , which uses **quality poetry by poets in Maine or poets writing about Maine. Sample: $1.**

PUDDING PUBLICATIONS, *PUDDING MAGAZINE, (II, IV, Social), 2384 Hardesty Dr. S., Columbus, OH 43204, phone 614-279-4188, founded 1979, poetry editor Jennifer Welch, attempts to provide "a sociological looking glass through poems that provide 'felt experience' and share intense human experience. To collect good poems that speak for the difficulties and the solutions. To provide a forum for poems and articles by people who take poetry arts into the schools and the human services." They publish **Pudding** every five months, also chapbooks, anthologies, broadsides, VHS video tapes and audio cassette tapes. They **"want experimental and contemporary poetry, what hasn't been said before. Speak the unspeakable. Don't want preachments or sentimentality. Don't want obvious traditional forms without fresh approach. Long poems are happily considered too, as long as they aren't windy."** They have recently published poetry by Janet McCann, Fred Waage, Alan Catlin, Alfred Bruey. (And Jennifer Welch says, "Who we've turned down is more impressive!") The editor selected these sample lines from "Artifacts" by Lowell Jaeger:

Back side of the busted globe, bricks
and boards on the streets of the armistice
and my father stuffed his canvas duffle
with the wounded artifacts of fresh-dead war.
He was alive without an explanation . . .

Pudding is a literary journal with an emphasis on poetry arts in human service. They use about 80 pp. of poetry in each issue—digest-sized, 80 pp., offset from typescript, circulation 2,000, 1,800 subscriptions of which 50 are libraries. Subscription (3 issues): $10. Per copy: usually $3.75. The editor estimates that they receive 150,000 single poems per year. **Sample: $3.75 postpaid. Submit 5-25 poems. Photocopies and previously published submissions OK. Send SASE for guidelines. Reports on same day (unless traveling). Pays 1 copy—to featured poet $10 and 4 copies. For chapbook publication, no query. Send complete MS with cover letter with publication credits, bio, personal or aesthetic philosophy, poetic goals and principles. Send #10 envelope plus 2 oz. postage for catalog to order samples. Editor often comments on rejections for free, will critique on request for $3 per page of poetry or $25 an hour in person.** Jennifer Welch advises, "For beginners—don't try to share your entire philosophy in a poem. As a matter of fact, forget about your philosophy for a few years and learn to simplify. 'Take a picture of a moment.' "

QUADRANT EDITIONS (II), Concordia University, 1455 de Meisonneauveld, Montreal, Quebec, Canada H3G 1M8, founded 1981, poetry editor J. LaDuke, "publishes 9-12 titles per year of which 2-3 are poetry, either individual works or anthologies." They have recently published books by Roo Borson, Al Purdy and a translation of Baudelarie. **Query with 2-6 samples, bio and publication credits. Replies to query in 1 month, to submission (if invited) in 2-6 months. Simultaneous submissions, photocopy OK, no dot-matrix. Publishes on 10% royalty contract with 6 copies. Send SASE for catalog to buy samples.**

*QUARRY MAGAZINE, QUARRY PRESS (II), Box 1061, Kingston, Ontario, Canada K7L 4Y5, founded 1952, editor Bob Hilderley. "The Quarry Press is designed to extend the range of material, poetry and prose, generally handled by *Quarry Magazine*—that is, to represent, as accurately as may be, the range of contemporary writing. We publish chapbooks, soft-bound books of stories and poetry—collections ranging from 60-150 pp. in addition to the quarterly *Quarry Magazine*. **We are interested in seeing any and all forms of contemporary verse.** *Quarry Magazine* **maintains a practical limit on length of submissions—that we cannot consider any single piece or series by one author that would print at more than 10 pp. Quarry Press considers MSS on an individual basis."** They have recently published poetry by Roo Borson, Kim Maltman, Roger Nash, Jane Munro, Fred Cogswell and Don Bailey. The editor selected these sample lines from "i Met a Poem" by Dennis Cooley:

they say earth
shifts & glides
like a figure
skater double-axeling her way
across the screen
fine for compulsory
figures i suppose
but what about
the free
skating
the free
wheeling

Quarry is a digest-sized, 130+ pp., flat-spined publication with an unusually attractive cover—textured matte ivory card with striking b/w drawing trimmed so the front is a half-inch short—professionally printed on egg-shell stock. There are 40-50 pp. of poetry in each issue, circulation 1,000, 600 subscriptions of which 140 are libraries. Subscription: $16 ($2 surcharge outside Canada); per copy: $4. They use about 70 of over a thousand submissions of freelance poetry received each year. "We are prompt. Very small backlog if any. 3-6 month lead time." **Sample: $5 postpaid. No limit on number or time of submissions; prefer typed (or WP) double-spaced; clear photocopies acceptable; query not necessary, though it will be answered. Reports in 6-8 weeks. Pays $10 per poem plus 1 year subscription. Send SASE for guidelines. For book consideration, query with 6-10 samples, publication credits, brief bio and current projects.** "We give priority to Canadians because of our Arts Council funding and our own interest in promoting Canadian writing." **Replies to queries in 30 days, to submissions (if invited) in 6-8 weeks. Photocopy, dot-matrix OK. Contract is for 10% royalties 25-40 author's copies. Send 5x7" SASE for catalog to order samples. Editor "frequently" comments on rejections.** They conduct a High School Writers' Contest every second year; the issue I examined (Winter, 1984) contained outstanding prose and poetry by high school students, winners of this competition. The editor advises, "Read widely; avoid trends which place style above all else and which employ technique for its own sake. The excellent merging of form and content means a great deal to us here at *Quarry.*"

*QUARTERLY REVIEW OF LITERATURE (III), 26 Haslet Ave., Princeton, NJ 08540, founded 1943, poetry editors T. and R. Weiss. After more than 35 years as one of the most distinguished literary journals in the country, *QRL* has adopted a new format, the *QRL Poetry Series*, in which 4-5 book length collections are combined in one volume, each of the 4-5 poets receiving a $1,000 Colladay Poetry Award as an honorarium. The resulting 300-400 pp. volumes are printed in editions of 3,000-5,000, selling in paperback for $10, in hardback for $20. Subscription—2 paperback volumes containing 10 books: $15. For example, Poetry Series II contained: poetry of So Chongju, translated from Korean by D. R. McCann; *What the Land Gave*, by Phyllis Thompson; *Surviving the Cold*, by David Barton; *Herring, Oatmeal, Milk and Salt*, by Mairi Macinnes; and poetry of Carlos Nejar translated from Portuguese by M. Picciotto. **"Manuscripts may be sent for reading during the months of October and May. The collection need not be a first book. It should be between 50-80 pp. if it is a group of connected poems, a selection of miscellaneous poems, a poetic play, a work of poetry translation, or it can be a single long poem of 30 pp. or more. Some of the poems may have had previous magazine publication. Also considers simultaneous submissions. Manuscripts in English or translated into English are also invited from outside the U.S. Only one MS may be submitted per reading period and must include an SASE."** Since poetry as a thriving art must depend partly upon the enthusiasm and willingness of those directly involved to join in its support, the editors request that each MS be accompanied by a subscription to the series.

*QUARTERLY WEST (II), 317 Olpin Union, University of Utah, Salt Lake City, UT 84112, founded 1976, is a 6x9", 140 pp. biannual literary review which uses **quality poetry. Pays copies plus $5 per page and subscription. Sample: $3.50.**

*QUEEN OF ALL HEARTS (IV, Religious), 26 S. Saxon Ave., Bay Shore, NY 11706, phone 516-665-0726, founded 1950, poetry editor Joseph Tusiani, a magazine-sized bimonthly, uses **poetry "dealing with Mary, the Mother of Jesus—inspirational poetry. Not too long**." They have published poetry by Feznando Sembiante and Alberta Schumacher. The editor selected these sample lines (poet unidentified):

> *Mary, it was your blood that flowed that day*
> *On Golgotha when Jew and Roman led*
> *Your Son in purple raiment through the dead*
> *And buried streets lit only by His ray.*

The 48 pp. professionally printed magazine, heavy stock, various colors of ink and paper, liberal use of graphics and photos, has 8,000 subscriptions at $10 per year. Per copy: $1.50. They receive 40-50 submissions of poetry per year, use 2 per issue. **Sample: $2 postpaid. Submit double-spaced MSS. Reports within 3-4 weeks. Pays 6 copies (sometimes more) and complimentary subscription. Sometimes editor comments on rejections.** His advice: "Try and try again! Inspiration is not automatic!"

*QUEEN'S QUARTERLY: A CANADIAN REVIEW (II,IV, Canadian writers), John Watson Hall, Queen's University, Kingston, Ontario, Canada K7L 3N6, phone 613-547-6968, founded 1893, editors M. Stayer and G. Amyot, is "a general interest intellectual review featuring articles on science, politics, humanitics, arts and letters, extensive book reviews, some poetry and fiction. **We are especially interested in poetry by Canadian writers. Shorter poems preferred.**" They have recently published poetry by Robert Bowie, Peggy Flanders, Robyn Supraner, Dave Margoshes, Ruth Messenger, Marianne Andrea, Tom Wayman, Al Purdy, Naomi Rachel, Susan Musgrave, Ramona Weeks and Ralph Gustafson. There are about 12 pp. of poetry in each issue, 6x9", 224 pp., circulation 1,500. Subscription: $16 Canadian, $18 US; per copy: $4.50 Canadian. They receive about 400 submissions of poetry per year, use 40. Sample: $4.50 Canadian postpaid. Submit no more than 6 poems at once. Photocopies OK but no simultaneous submissions. Reports in 6-8 weeks. Pays usually $10 (Canadian) per poem, plus 2 copies.

‡UNIVERSITY OF QUEENSLAND PRESS (IV, Australian), Box 42, St. Lucia, Queensland 4067, Australia, poetry editor Martin Duwell, is a press which publishes scholarly works plus fiction and **poetry by Australian writers. Australians or poets living in Australia may submit. Query before sending MS.**

QUINTESSENCE PUBLICATIONS (II), 356 Bunker Hill Mine Rd., Amador City, CA 95601, phone 209-267-5470, founded 1976, poetry editor Marlan Beilke "is the largest linotype and Ludlow facility in the West; huge typography section—strictly letter-press." They publish broadsides, books and reference work. "We are interested in those who understand/ appreciate the hot metal printing process." They have published a critical work on Robinson Jeffers and poems of Jack London and **"rarely" consider poetry submissions by individuals. Query with samples and bio, publication credits, personal or aesthetic philosophy, poetic goals and principles. Reply to query in 3-4 weeks. Photocopy, simultaneous submissions OK. No dot-matrix. They publish on royalty contracts copies but are also open (but rarely) to subsidy arrangements. Send SASE for book catalog. Editor comments on rejections "only if requested."**

QUIXOTE PRESS, QUIXOTL, *QUIXOTE (II, IV, Political), 1810 Marshall, Houston, TX 77098, founded 1866, restored 1966, poetry editors Ed Ochester and Victor Contoski, aims to **"promote anti-capitalist and anti-bourgeois, pro-democratic thought; left viewpoints welcome."** They publish postcards, posters, chapbooks, pamphlets and flat-spined paperbacks. They **"want work poems, feminism, internationalist and urban; no lyrics and introspection or self-pity decadence, no glorification of violence or worship of money and success."** They have recently published poetry by Margaret Benbow, Pablo Neruda, Esther Buffler, Joel Lipman, Margot Treitl, Marge Piercy and Charles Bukowski. *Quixote* is a monthly, 4x5", offset, using 20 pp. of poetry in each issue, print run 200, 100 subscriptions of which 68 are libraries. Subscription: $15; per copy: $2. They use 40 of 100 submissions received per year, have a 6 month backlog. **Sample: $2 postpaid. Photocopies OK. Reports in 3 months maximum. Pays 2 copies. Send SASE for guidelines.** Under the imprints of Quixote Press and Quixotl they publish collections of poetry by individuals and anthologies—five 24 pp. chapbooks, 2 flat-spined paperbacks, 2 anthologies per year. **Query unnecessary. Submit complete MS. Simultaneous submissions OK. They are open to 50-50% subsidy arrangements. Send $2 for sample. Editor sometimes comments on rejections.** The editors advise, "Stay away from the suburbs, read a little Marx and learn to live on bread and water—kvass, bread soup, tea, etc. You must transcend a major in English."

‡QUIXSILVER PRESS, *MICROCOSM, POET'S SHOWCASE (I), Box 7635, Baltimore, MD 21207, phone 301-944-0661, founded 1981, editor/publisher Robert Medcalf, Jr., a small-press publisher of poetry and a literary annual (*Microcosm*) of imaginative poetry. By "imaginative poetry," Mr. Medcalf means **"science fiction poetry, horror poetry, fantasy poetry, and speculative poetry; under 40 lines; prefer poetry with rhythm and 'music,' but will consider other forms, poems with sensuous imagery."** He charges a reading fee of $1 for 5 poems and $5 for 15-20 poems submitted for chapbook publication. He has recently published poetry by Steve Eng, John Gregory Betancourt, and Janet Fox. As a sample, he selected the following lines by Jonathan Post:

> *Lady, you are walking in your sleep,*
> *Walking weightlessly*
> *Over alien-beautiful moons and planets*
> *In a spacesuit made of silk*

Mircocosm is a digest-sized, 24 pp., offset, with some art. It has a circulation of 100, of which 20 are subscriptions. Price per issue is $3. **Sample $3 postpaid, guidelines available for SASE. Contributors receive 2 copies. Submissions are reported on in 2 months and time to publication is 1-2 years. For chapbook publication, writers should query first with sample poems and reading fee, giving publication credits, bio, philosophy, and poetic aims. MSS will be reported on in 3 months. Simultaneous submissions are OK, as are photocopied MSS and dot-matrix; no discs. Royalties will be 10-15% and 10 free copies.** Robert Medcalf publishes 1 chapbook per year, digest-sized, 24 pp., price $3. He advises, "Be prepared to revise or rework new poems as a result of comments and criticism. Give financial support to publications that you submit to."

‡R.S.V.P. PRESS (I), Box 394, Society Hill, SC 29593, founded 1982, publisher-editor Gene Boone, publishes "brief inexpensive guides for poets/writers and an annual paperback anthology of poetry (saddle-stapled, color card cover). **"We prefer 'good' poetry, but this does not necessarily mean we want literary-type poetry; we will consider literary poetry, of course, but we will also accept poetry that expresses ideas in modern poetry forms—free verse, traditional, fixed-forms, etc. will all be considered. Subjects are 'open'; we encourage self-expression strongly and recommend that poets choose subjects about which they feel deeply. Nothing too obviously 'sexual' or poetry that exploits violence, in short, these matters are taboo unless justified by the contributions they bring to the poetry."** They have recently published poetry by Dale Loucareas, Dorothy Friedman and editor Gene Boone, who selected these sample lines (poet unidentified):

> *When only echoes*
> *Come to mind*
> *The World is quiet*
> *The peace is kind*

"We prefer submissions of 4-8 poems; we do not encourage simultaneous submissions. Submis-

sions should be addressed to R.S.V.P. Press Anthology." They plan to offer cash prizes or other awards for the best poems in future annual anthologies. Gene Boone, who also writes a column for *Published!*, comments, "Today we constantly hear 'poetry just doesn't sell enough copies anymore,' and I think we, as poets and lovers of poetry, should feel inclined to offer our support to this worthy cause, by supporting poetry organizations, publishers who strive to improve the dismal state of poetry sales and we should also strive to help poetry sales by purchasing copies of works by others poets."

RACCOON BOOKS, *RACCOON (II), % St. Luke's Press, Suite 401, Union Ave., Memphis, TN 38104, founded 1978, poetry editor, David Spicer, *Raccoon* journal, editor David Spicer. Though St. Luke's Press itself (founded 1975) publishes about one book of poetry a year (and doesn't read unsolicited poetry MSS), its subsidiary, **Raccoon Books publishes anthologies, a postcard series, chapbooks, and collections by individual poets** in both paperbacks (flat-spined) and hardcover, plus 16-page monographs (folded in a self-cover). They are looking for "**tightly-crafted contemporary work dealing with the dark image for *Raccoon***," and have recently published such poets as Charles Wright, Charles Bukowski, Marge Piercy, Liesel Mueller, Mary Oliver, Colette Inez, Pamela Stewart. These are lines by Gordan Osing from "The Indo-China Cafe":

> *I, too, have been treacherous for God.*
> *The moon narrowed her eye. I confess I crave*
> *to squander words carefully down this white entrance*
> *the page*

Raccoon journal comes out three times a year in one of three formats, a 48 pp. anthology, an annual chapbook of one poet's work, and a monograph of criticsm or creative work by one author. **To submit, send no more than 6 previously unpublished poems, one poem to a page, typed**. They receive about 500-1,000 poems a year and have about a year's backlog, **report within 3 months**, have an average circulation of 200-300, 75 subscriptions, of which 60 are libraries. You can subscribe for $10 a year, **$5 for a sample, postpaid. Payment: $10/poem for the anthology issue**. St. Luke's Press also publishes scholarly books for the American Blake Foundation.

*RACKHAM JOURNAL OF THE ARTS AND HUMANITIES (RAJAH), University of Michigan, MLB 4024, Ann Arbor, MI 48109, phone 313-764-2537, founded 1970, poetry editors Darcy Engholm and Nash Myfield. *RAJAH* is a graduate student sponsored annual publishing fiction, translation, poetry and critical essays in the humanities. They use 5-20 pp. of poetry in each issue, circulation 500, 300 subscriptions of which 241 are libraries. They receive about 30 freelance submissions of poetry per year, use 1. **Sample: $1 postpaid. Please send SASE with submission. "Our only stipulation is *clean* copy." Reports within a month, pays copies.**

*THE RADDLE MOON (II), 9060 Ardmore Dr., Sidney, British Columbia, Canada V8L 3S1, founded 1982, poetry editor Susan Clark, is a 6x9" flat-spined 100 + pp. varnished cover, literary biannual using "**epic, lyric and language poetry (including translations)**." They have published poetry by Mary de Michele, Marlene Cookshaw, Sharon Thesen, D. Norkse, Roo Borson, Antonio Porta, Pierre Reverdy, Crispin Elsted, Nerina Tsverayeva, Pier Paolo Pasolini, Cecelia Vicina, Ginter Eich, Marilyn Bowering, James Reaney, William Stafford and Derk Wynand. The editor selected this sample poem, "The Curse," by James Wood:

> *I swear she held the fascinated*
> *phone down to the deathbed. At this end,*
> *"doves," that instrument in my*
> *palm said, like a last heartbeat between*
> *disappearing wings.*

Their usual print run is 600 for 175 subscriptions of which 50 are libraries. Subscription: $6 (in the US). They use about 30 of 400 freelance submissions of poetry per year, have a 4-6 month backlog. **Sample: $4 postpaid. No simultaneous submissions "unless time is given for a reply; if a MSS says 'this MSS will be submitted elsewhere 1 month from today.' ". Photocopy OK. Reports in 2-3 months. Pay: 1 year subscription. Editor comments on rejections "when the work is promising."**

*RAG MAG (II), Box 12, Goodhue, MN 55027, phone 612-923-4590, founded 1982 as *Underground Rag Mag* by Andy Gunderson, poetry editor now Beverly Voldseth, appears twice a year—in April and October. They are also beginning to publish chapbooks. The editor says, "**I like to think good writing is my only requirement. I tend not to use poetry with a lot of F- words or that are pornographic or violent. I also shy away from Helen Steiner Rice types of poems. I like good images, good stories. If the poems are long they really have to be good to hold my interest.**" She has recently published poetry by Syd Weedon, Mark Arvilla, Cathy Czapla, Warren Lang, Riki Kolbl Nelson and Lynne Burgess. Beverly selected this poem, "Rune," as a sample (poet unidentified):

> *And in time may the earth call us back*
> *salt of her oceans*
> *and blood of her moon*
> *May we live again simple as animals then*
> *white roots and berries*
> *and blankets of fur*
> *enough life for our children*
> *and compost at last*
> *when earth calls us back from air.*

Each issue of *Rag Mag* has about 50 pp. of poetry, circulation 150, 50 subscriptions of which 2 are libraries. Subscription: $5; per copy: $3. She receives about 200 submissions per year, uses about 50. **Sample: $3 postpaid. Submit 6-10 pp., name and address on each. Simultaneous submissions OK. "Hate dot-matrix. A letter to editor OK but am turned off by listings of accomplishments." Reports "getting slower." Pays copies. Editor sometimes comments on rejections.**

RAINBOW BOOKS, EDWARD A. FALLOT POETRY COMPETITION (I), Box 1069, Moore Haven, FL 33471, founded 1979, poetry editors Betty Wright, Janny Vaughan, Ailsa Dewing, mostly publishes nonfiction (self-help, how-to: one of their titles is **A Guide to Writing Prize Winning Poetry**, by Patricia Lewis), but occasionally a chapbook of poetry selected through the **Edward A. Fallot Poetry Competition. To enter the contest, you pay an entry fee of $5 for the first poem, $1 for each additional one, poems of no more than 16 lines, by October 15 annually.** Prizes are $50 for the Grand Winner, $25 each for 1st, 2nd, and 3rd." Recently published poets include Pamela Pitkin, Sarah Nichols, Patricia Lewis, Mirian McNeill, Juanita Stroud Phillips. These lines by Robert Hoeft are offered as a sample:

> *She took such delight*
> *with a limber willow switch*
> *in beheading the dandelions*
> *that chanced upon our lawn.*

Send SASE for rules and guidelines. Sample chapbook, $6 postpaid.

RAMBUNCTIOUS PRESS, *RAMBUNCTIOUS REVIEW (II), 1221 W. Pratt, Chicago, IL, 60626, phone 312-338-2439, founded 1982, poetry editors Mary Dellutri, Richard Goldman, Nancy Lennon, **The *Review* appears twice a year** in a handsomely printed, saddle-stapled, 7x10" format, 48 pp. They want "**spirited, quality poetry**, fiction, short drama, photos, and graphics. **Some focus on local work, but all work is considered.**" Recently they have published John Jacob, Effle Mihopoulos, Elizabeth Eddy, and offer these lines by Phyllis Janik as a sample:

> *Light. wanton. exuding itself. less heavy than others*
> *of its kind. Be with me when it's time—time*
> *the natural bent, fall the liquid complement seeping*
> *through*
> *quietly urgent as sleep seeking its own level.*

They have a circulation of about 500, 200 subscriptions, single copy $2.50 (**sample: $3 postpaid**). They recieve 500-600 submissions a year and use 50-60, **reporting in 4 months. No special requirements for submission, will consider simultaneous submissions. No queries, payment 2 copies.** Occasional comments on MSS. They run annual contests in poetry, fiction, and short drama.

RANDOM HOUSE, VINTAGE BOOKS (III), 201 E. 50th St., New York, NY 10022, phone 212-751-2600, founded 1925, poetry editor Jonathan Galassi, is, of course **one of the major trade publishers and offers contracts on the usual basis, 10% royalty on hardbacks, 7 1/2% on paperbacks, 10 author's copies.** They have recently published such poets as Charles Wright, Molly Peacock, Gerald Stern, James Fenton, C. K. Williams, Raymond Carver, Donald Hall, Yves Boonefoy, Timothy Steele and Frank Bidart. **Query first, with sample of 5 poems and cover letter listing other publications and giving biographical information. Reports within 3 months. MS must be typewritten.**

RAW DOG PRESS, POST POEMS (IV, Humor) 2-34 Aspen Way, Doylestown, PA 18901, phone 215-345-6838, founded 1977, poetry editor R. Gerry Fabian, "publishes Post Poems annual—a postcard series. We do chapbooks from time to time and there is always a special project that crops up. **We want short poetry (3-7 lines) on any subject. The positive poem and the poem of understated humor always have an inside track. No taboos, however. All styles considered. Anything with rhyme had better be immortal.**" They have recently published poetry by Arthur Winfield Knight, Merritt Clifton, Ramona Weeks, K. S. Ernst, Marion Cohen and the editor, R. Gerry Fabian, who selected this sample poem, "The Nothing on Television" (poet unidentified):

> *It was terrible—*
> *Raw, damp and gray*
> *with weeks and weeks*
> *of Lawrence Welk rain.*

Query with 7-10 samples for chapbook publication. "We are small and any poet is expected to share half the responsibility and often that includes cost—not always, however. No photocopies or dot-matrix. Pays copies. Send SASE for catalog to buy samples. The editor "always" comments on rejections. He says he will offer criticism for a fee, "if someone is desperate to publish and is willing to pay we will use our vast knowledge to help steer the MS in the right direction. We will advise against it, but as P. T. Barnum said . . . Raw Dog Press welcomes new poets and detests second rate poems from 'name' poets. We exist because we are dumb like a fox but even a fox takes care of its own. We are grudgingly patient with new poets because we love the innocent."

RE:AL (RE: ARTES LIBERALES) (II), Box 13007, Stephen F. Austin State University, Nacogdoches, TX 75962, founded 1968, is basically a scholarly, academic journal, but it also uses short fiction, drama, and poetry **(limit about 50 lines)**. It's a handsomely printed, digest-sized saddle-stapled journal which appears twice a year, using about **10 pages of poetry in each issue. Sample $2 postpaid**. Their circulation is to some 400 subscribers, more than half of which are libraries. They have a 4 month backlog, receive about 80 submissions of poetry per year and use about 20. Here are some sample lines from "Within The Womb of This Mountain," by Jenna Fedock:

> *We will not see him again,*
> *"Lord have mercy,"*
> *but only in the black box wedged in an aisle,*
> *heavy lid crushing our heads. We chant*
> *"Vichnaya pamyat, Vichnaya pamyat, Vichnaya pamyat,"*
> *trying to cast it off—but cannot.*

Submit original and copy, reports in 3 weeks, pays in copies.

REALITIES LIBRARY (II), 2745 Monterey Hwy., #76, San Jose, CA 95111, founded 1975 by Ric Soos, is a multifaceted, one-man operation, bringing out at various intervals, **chapbooks, magazines, postcards and posters, all very low-cost publications**. Ric Soos says his aim is "to provide an outlet for experimental and/or non-mainstream writers . . . While I am bent toward the surreal, I have accepted and published sonnets, first-person experience, even rhymed couplets. I publish anything intelligent." Among the poets he has recently published are Burton Raffel, A. D. Winans, Alberto Rios, Kay Clossom, Robert Bly, Joel Daily, B. Z. Niditch, and Don MacQueen. He gives these lines, from Haywood's "Freckled Tickle," as a sample:

> *There should be a word like fuckle*
> *We need a word to represent the tender quiet kind of screwing*
> *that is done without frantic, blind, self aware intensity,*
> *without demands of frenzy, with more love than passion.*

He publishes 12-18 **chapbooks** per year, 4 **flat-spined paperbacks. For book publication, query first with sample of 4-5 poems. "A cover letter is helpful for the editor to discover the poet's interests and personality, but not necessary." Pays 15% royalties minimum and author's copies. For sample, order from catalog or "send $3 and I'll choose."**

*RECONSTRUCTIONIST (IV, Jewish), 270 West 89th St., New York, NY 10024, phone 212-496-2960, founded 1935, poetry editor Jeremy Garber, is "a Jewish cultural and intellectual review published 8 times per year, 32 pp., magazine-sized, circulation 8,500, 8,100 subscriptions. **"We publish about 12 poems per year—either on Jewish themes or in some other way related to Jewish spiritual quests—short poems up to about 30-35 lines."** They have recently published poetry by Myra Sklarew, Carol Adler, Aloma Halter, Vicki Wieselthier, Mark Bloome, Robert Hirschfield and Gabriel Preil. As a sample the editor selected these lines by Jason Sommer:

> *I have wrestled Jacob's angle,*
> *all night, nor did prevail.*
> *It was not principle we wrangled,*
> *but each minute detail.*

They receive about 100 submissions of poetry per year, use 10-12. Considers simultaneous submissions "if so states." **Sample: $3 postpaid. Reports in 1-2 months. Pays $36/poem and 5 copies.**

RED ALDER BOOKS, *PAN-EROTIC REVIEW (IV, Sexuality, eroticism), Box 2992, Santa Cruz, CA 95063, phone 408-426-7082, founded 1971, poetry editor David Steinberg. "We specialize in publication of books on re-examination of traditional male roles, and **creative, provocative erotica that is imaginative, top-quality, non-exploitative, especially if unconventional or explicitly sexual.**

It is our desire to demonstrate that erotica material can be evocative, sexy, powerful and emerging, without being cliche, exploitive of men's and women's frustrations, or male-dominant. Our work demands respect for the best of our erotic natures, for life, for love, and for our wonderful bodies." They have recently published poetry by Adele Aldridge, Michael Hill, Peter Larson, Blake Samson and Bill Berg. **Query with 5-10 sample poems, and cover letter giving "goals/perspectives." Replies to queries and/ or submissions in 2-4 weeks. Simultaneous submissions, photocopies OK. Dot-matrix: "reluctantly." Pays copies, occasional royalties. Sample book available for $6, ppd from above address.** The editor advises, "Tell the truth; avoid playing the poet; pursue humility; be useful to someone beyond yourself; in general, stop trying—rather let what you are saying decide how it wants to emerge (or stay hidden)."

*RED BASS (IV)**, Box 10258, Tallahassee, FL 32302, founded 1981, publishes the tabloid quarterly magazine (newsprint, oversize), *Red Bass*. Poetry editors: Eugenie Nable, Jay Murphy. "**We want good poetry. We want it to be original, inventive, committed to social change and good craftsmanship. We don't want academic or light verse**." Recently published poets include Amiri Baraka, Allen Ginsberg, Daniel Berrigan, Roque Dalton and Anne Waldman. I selected this sample of lines from Jayne Cortez' "Blood Suckers":

> *exploding way down in the dumps of Love Canal*
> *expanding themselves and vigorously sucking on*
> *a medley of birth defects . . .*

They have a circulation of about 2,000, over 200 subscriptions (of which 5 are libraries ("but growing"). It sells for $2 a copy (**sample: $1.25 postpaid**), get about 300-400 submissions per year and use 40-50 of these (about 3-5 pages of poetry per issue), backlog for 1-2 issues. "**Any legible copy will do. If simultaneous submission please inform us. Submit only poems that have not been previously published. No query necessary, report in 1-3 months, payment in copies**." The editors comment on MS if "**we feel the poem is close to what we want**." We favor Surrealism and politically charged works, but publish more traditional forms as well. Some forthcoming poets include Simon Oritz, new translations of Robert Desnos, new poetry from Salvador."

THE RED CANDLE PRESS, *CANDELABRUM (II, IV, Traditional), 9 Milner Rd., Wisbech, PE23 2LR, England, founded 1970, editors Basil Wincote, B.A. and M. L. McCarthy, M.A., administrative editor Helen Gordon, B.A. was "founded to encourage poets working in **traditional-type verse, metrical unrhymed or metrical rhymed**. So far we've simply been publishers, but we may extend our work to holding readings, or forming a correspondence club or critical service. We're more interested in poems than poets: that is, we're interested in what sort of poems an author produces, not in his or her personality." They publish the yearly magazine, *Candelabrum*, anthologies, occasional postcards, paperbound paperbacks (both flat-spined and staple-spined). For all of these they want "**good-quality metrical verse, with rhymed verse specially wanted. Elegantly cadenced free verse is acceptable. No weak stuff (moons and Junes, loves and doves, etc.) No chopped-up prose pretending to be free verse. Any length (up to 50 lines for *Candelabrum*), any subject, including eroticism (but not porn)—satire, love poems, nature lyrics, mildly philosophical—any subject, but nothing racist or sexist**." They have published Vernon Porter Loggins, Roy Harrison, Thomas Land, Anne Bulley, David Horowitz, Bradley Strahan, Martin Lyon, Meg Seaton, Ellen Collins, and offer these lines by Mark Wild as a sample:

> *The walls of this bedroom lean over top far;*
> *whispers from the past where unhappiness generally wins.*
> *Total demolition is called for, total war—*
> *A hand-grenade to bury the dead hurts and sins.*

The digest-sized magazine, staple-spined, small type, exemplifies their intent to "pack in as much as possible, wasting no space, and try to keep a neat appearance with the minimum expense." They get in about 36 pp. (some 50 poems) in each issue. Circulation: 900, 700 subscriptions, of which 22 are libraries. **Sample: $4 prepaid. They receive about 2,000 submissions per year, use approximately 5% of those, sometimes holding over poems for the next year or longer. "Submit any time, IRC essential if return wished, each poem on a separate sheet please, neat typescripts or neat LEGIBLE manuscripts. PLEASE no dark, oily photostats, no colored ink (only black or blue). Clear photocopies acceptable. Author's name and address on each sheet, please." Reports in about 2 months. Pay one contributor's copy**. The books published by Red Candle Press "have been at our invitation to

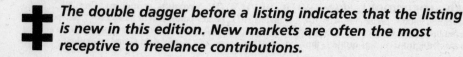

The double dagger before a listing indicates that the listing is new in this edition. New markets are often the most receptive to freelance contributions.

the poet, and at our expense." They have run a 1985-86 competition, with small entry fee and small prizes, and plan a 1987-88 competition. Send SASE for details. The editors comment, "We think traditional-type poetry is much more popular here in Britain now than it was in 1970, when we founded *Candelabrum*. We always welcome new poets, especially "traditionalists," and we like to hear from the U.S.A. as well as from here at home. General tip: We think poets should form themselves into a few large groups, not into thousands of tiny groups: more distribution, and more money, and more readers."

RED HERRING PRESS, RED HERRING CHAPBOOK SERIES, MATRIX ANTHOLOGY (IV), 1209 W. Oregon, Channing-Murray Foundation, Urbana, IL 61801, phone 344-1176, founded 1976, publishes "works of **members of Red Herring Poetry Workshop** as selected by members of the workshop." The chapbooks are generally thematic. *Matrix* is an annual anthology of members' work. They have recently published poems by Debra Thomas, Miriam Marx, Dick Ferry and John W. Edwards. The director selected these sample lines by Netta Gillespie:

> Out of sun's sway I move
> Who never could be still,
> Almost beyond the reach of love,
> Almost out of control.

Considers simultaneous submissions.

RED KEY PRESS (II), Box 551, Port St. Joe, FL 32456, founded 1982 by Margaret Key Biggs, first to publish her own work. She has gone on to publish chapbooks of the works of others and anthologies. She says, "*Red Key Press* wishes to publish poetry chapbooks of highest quality, not sterile obscurity. We sponsor contests about poets and poetry, and will publish prize-winners. We want contemporary, living poetry. We do not care to see traditional poetry from the greeting card crowd. No specifications as to form, length, style, subject matter and purpose. We do not *bridle* poets." As a sample she sent these lines by Barbara Holley:

> Meager as bones, fleshing themselves
> into ribbons of orange fire horses
> by Bonheur, a dozen dogs tear the yard
> to shards, mark our arrival.

Query first, include bio, no sample poems. Responds to query in 2 weeks, reports on submissions in 6 weeks. MSS should be typed, one poem to a page, no dot-matrix, but good photocopies OK. You may submit on disc for Kay-Pro IV. Sample chapbook: $2.50 postpaid. Those I have seen are 12 page booklets, offset, typeset, with simple art, jacket photo of the poet.

*THE RED PAGODA, A JOURNAL OF HAIKU (IV, Haiku), 125 Taylor St., Jackson, TN 38301, phone (after 6 pm) 901-427-7714, founded 1982, Lewis Sanders, editor, a quarterly journal that will consider "**haiku, modern and traditional. Renga, tanka, heibun, senryu, linked poems, articles and book reviews on books and subjects dealing with haiku." You must buy a copy to see your work in print (price is $3/copy), but poets do not have to subscribe or purchase a copy to be published.**

‡*THE REDNECK REVIEW OF LITERATURE (IV, Regional), Rt. 1, Box 1085, Fairfield, ID 83327, phone 208-764-2536, editor Penelope Reedy, an annual magazine publishing poetry, fiction, and essays **dealing with the contemporary West. The editor wants to see "any form, length, or style—not heavy on sex or politics. Want a sense of place—voices heard in the fields, at crossroads, hunting, etc." She does not want "porn; ethereal ditties about nothing; obscure."** She has recently published poetry by Bill Studebaker, Walt Franklin and Nolene Zajanc. The magazine, which appears in the spring each year, is magazine-sized, offset, spiral bound, no advertising. Circulation is 300-500, of which 100 are subscriptions and 100-150 are newsstand sales. Price per issue is $5.75 postpaid. **Sample: $3.75 postpaid. Pay is 2 copies. Rejected MSS are reported on immediately, and no accepted MSS are held beyond the next issue. Writers should submit "2-3 poems at a time, letter quality—don't like simultaneous submissions. Please send SASE with** *enough* **postage to return MSS."** Criticism is sometimes given. The editor says, "Take time—have something to say. Practice forms like sonnets, to learn how to pull images out of your head, to cover an idea completely. Read nursery rhymes to your kids, listen and observe."

*REFLECT (I, IV, Spiral, movement literature), 3306 Argonne Ave., Norfolk, VA 23509, founded 1979 by W.S. Kennedy, editor and publisher, is a typescript, zerox quarterly, 40 pp., digest-sized, staple-spine, with thin paper cover and simple art, ads. Kennedy has very specific goals: "We have become a vehicle for the presentation of poetry and prose representing the **1980's Spiral back-to-beauty movement, the euphony-in-writing school showing 'an inner-directed concern with sound,' Spiral writ-**

ing, in the terminology of the movement's adherents. Beauty is the criterion here; all forms judged and accepted with that in mind. (Pornography, hatred, sneers at one thing or another, for some reason do not seem to be written with beauty in mind; such themes are not likely to be accepted.) **Poems no longer than can be printed on one page**. They have recently published Ruth Wildes Schuler, Goldie L. Morales, Jan Brevet, and offer these sample lines from "Verlaine" by B.Z. Niditch:

> *That spiral of the lost angel*
> *by the airy stations*
> *a bottle of white wine*
> *and the counsel of trees.*

Each issue contains about 20 pp. of poetry. Their circulation is about 200, with 2 library subscriptions. **Sample: $1 postpaid, subscription $3.50. Not more than 3 months between acceptance and publication. No photocopies, dot-matrix, no need to query, reports in 1 month, no pay except a contributor's copy**. The editor says, "There is a strong back-to-beauty trend, a grassroots movement (unencouraged by the literary hierarchy to date). If the older poetry was mainly lyric (emotional) and Shucks Yes (meaning anything goes *except* beauty of style), now the trend is euphonic, mystical."

*REFLECTIONS (IV), Box 368, Duncan Falls, OH 43734, phone 614-674-4121, founded 1980, is "**a poetry magazine by students from nursery school to high school**"—a project of the 7th and 8th grade journalism students from Franklin Local Schools, Duncan Falls Junior High School, Box 368, Duncan Falls, OH 43734-0368. Editor Dean Harper says it "**is aimed at helping students become published and to focus on famous, published poets for insights into publishing**." They consider **all forms and lengths of poetry**. These are sample lines selected by the editor:

> *Closing my eyes*
> *lifting my head*
> *Dropping and becoming*
> *one of the dead.*

Reflections comes out twice a year in an elegant magazine-sized format with a glossy, color photograph by a student on the front. Its 32 large pages are filled with poems (in rather small type), often with a b/w photograph of the student, and a few ads. It has a circulation of 1,000, with 700 subscriptions, of which 15 are libraries. **Sample $2, subscription $3. Reports within 10 days, one year backlog. Send SASE for guidelines. No pay**, but this is one of the few good places publishing poetry by children. They receive about 3,000 submissions a year, use about 200. Considers simultaneous submissions.

‡*REFORM JUDAISM (IV, Jewish), 838 Fifth Ave., New York, NY 10021, phone 212-249-0100, ext. 400, founded 1972, poetry editor Steven Schnur, a quarterly Reform Jewish publication that **publishes very little poetry (there is none in the sample issues I have) but has no specification as to form or style except that poems "shouldn't be more than 1 page long and should focus on a Jewish theme."** The 32 pp. journal is magazine-sized, printed on newsprint with a two-color paper cover, saddle-stapled. It has a circulation of 280,000 of which only 100 are subscriptions. **Pay is $25-75 and 2 free copies. Writers should submit a good photocopy with cover letter to Joy Weinberg, managing editor. Submissions will be reported on in 2-3 weeks and publication is in 3 months.**

‡*REGRESSION THERAPY (IV, Spirituality), 4 Woodland Lane, Kirksville, MO 63501, phone 816-665-1836, founded 1986, editor Irene Hickman, a quarterly journal on the Association for Past Life Research and Therapy. The editor wants "**short poems dealing with immortality, spirituality, and reincarnation, no more than 24 lines; no erotic, nature, political.**" The journal is digest-sized, 64 pp., with no ads and no graphics. **No guidelines are available, but the editor says "if we like the poem we can use 1-3 per issue." Pays 1 copy. Submissions are reported on within 1 month.**

REIMAN PUBLICATIONS, *FARM WOMAN (IV, Women, rural living), Box 643, Milwaukee, WI 53201, founded 1970, managing editor Ruth Benedict. *Farm Woman* "is a monthly magazine dedicated to the lives and interests of rural women, most of whom are the working partners of farmers and ranchers. However, as our masthead states, *FW* is published for those actively engaged in farming, and those who have moved from the farm in body, but not in heart. In some ways, it is very similar to many women's general interest magazines, and yet its subject matter is closely tied in with rural living and the very unique lives of farm and ranch women. *FW* is the main buyer of poetry; however, Reiman Publications periodically publishes anthologies. **We like short (4-5 stanzas, 16-20 lines) poems that reflect on a season or comment humorously or seriously on a particular rural experience. We don't want rural put downs, poems that stereotype rural women, etc. Our poems are fairly simple, yet elegant. They often accompany a high-quality photograph, and are often published as a reflective close to the magazine, positioned on the back cover, which is a prime spot for us.**" *FW* recently published poems by Ann Blakeslee, Mary Keck, and Eileen Yoder. As a sample I selected these lines from a poem by Katherine Hanley:

> *My trowel touches in brief caress*
> *To promise my winter-weary heart*
> *That the life is there about to dance,—*
> *That the golden cycle's about to start—*
> *The Creator's taking another chance.*

FW, appearing 11 times a year, is magazine-sized, 48 pp., glossy paper with much color photography and ads, circulation to 300,000 subscriptions, $11.98 per year, $2.50 per copy. They receive about 1,200 submissions of poetry per year, use 40-50 (unless they publish an anthology). Their backlog is 1 month to 3 years. "We have a fair supply on hand, regretfully." **Sample: $2.50 postpaid. Submit maximum of 6 poems. Photocopy OK if stated not a simultaneous submission. Reports in 6 weeks maximum. Pays $40 per poem plus copy.** They hold various contests for subscribers only. I examined one of their anthologies, *Cattails and Meadowlarks: Poems from the Country,* 90+ pp., saddle-stapled with high-quality color photography on the glossy card cover, poems in large, professional type with many b/w photo illustrations.

‡*RELIGIOUS HUMANISM (IV, Humanism)**, Box 278, Yellow Springs, OH 45387, phone 513-324-8030, founded 1964, editors Paul and Lucinda Beattie, a quarterly journal of **humanistic religion and ethics.**" The issue I have seen contains two poems by the same author, Michael Wurster. As a sample, I selected the beginning lines from his "Consolidating the Revolution":

> *the flowers*
> *have been delivered*
> *their outrageous colors*
> *fill every room*
>
> *we have forgotten winter.*

The magazine is 6¾x9½", professionally printed on buffstock, 50 pp. saddle-stapled with one-color glossy card cover. Circulation is about 1,000, of which 948 are subscriptions. Single copy is $2.50, subscription $10/year (or included as part of membership in the Fellowship of Religious Humanists, $15/year). **Sample available for $2.50 postpaid. MSS should be submitted double-space, in duplicate.** "To encourage freedom of expression, the editorial staff of this journal gives to all its contributors full responsibility for opinions held or positions taken."

RFD: A COUNTRY JOURNAL FOR GAY MEN EVERYWHERE (I, IV, Gay), Box 127E, Route 1, Bakersville, NC 28705, founded 1974, poetry editor Franklin Abbott (who is also poetry editor for *Changing Man*). *RFD* "is a quarterly for gay men with emphasis on lifestyles outside of the gay mainstream—poetry, politics, profiles, letters." They want **poetry with "personal, creative use of language and image, relevant to journal themes, political themes. We try to publish as many poets as we can so tend to publish shorter poems and avoid epics."** They have recently published poetry by James Broughton, Steven Finch, Louie Crew and Ed Mycue. The issue I examined had 4 magazine-sized pp. of poetry, some dozen poems photoreduced from typescript arranged at various angles on the page, with b/w photos and drawings interspersed. As a sample I selected the opening lines of "Pussywillows" by Gary Czerwinski:

> *Winter's nervous fingers unzip*
> *The sky and you churn the air thick*
> *With gossip like sap fattening*
> *Veins from roots newly fondled.*

RFD has a circulation of 2,000, 1,000 subscriptions—per year: $18 first class, $12 second class; per copy: $4.25. **Sample: $4.25 postpaid. Submit up to 5 poems at a time. Photocopies, simultaneous submissions OK. Reports in 2-6 months. Pays copies. Send SASE for guidelines. Editor sometimes comments on rejections.** He says he is looking for "interesting thoughts, creative and succinct use of language, matching thoughts and images."

RHIANNON PRESS (IV, Regional, women poets), 1105 Bradley Ave., Eau Claire, WI 54701, founded 1977, poetry editor Peg Lauber, "**specializes in Midwestern women poets**" and publishes an annual chapbook of a Wisconsin woman poet. The poetry should be **not rhymed nor metered**. They have published Laurel Speer, Betsy Adams, Margaret Kaminski, and Peg Lauber, who offers these lines as a sample:

> *remember that your hands*
> *are yours alone. woman*
> *there are services*
> *you need never perform*

Send SASE for contest rules, catalog. They don't consider unsolicited manuscripts without a query. Responds to query within a week, to submissions within a month, sometimes charges $3 reading fee. Photocopy, dot-matrix OK. Payment is 40 copies of a run of 250. Criticism provided for

$15, making notations and suggestions for change, addition or deletion on individual poems. Their chapbooks (staple-spined) and flat-spined anthologies are quality print-jobs, carefully edited.

*RHINO (II), 3915 Foster St., Evanston, IL 60203, phone 675-6814, founded 1976, poetry editor Laurie O. Buehler, "is an annually published literary journal using poems and short prose. We seek well-crafted work with fresh insights and authentic emotion by known or new writers. **We want poems that show careful attention to form and that contain surprise. We do *not* want archaic forms, posturing or sentimentality. Poems no longer than 3 pp. double-spaced.**" They have recently published poetry by Ivan Arguelles, Lyn Lifshin, Gary Fincke, Emily Warn and Harold Witt. The editor chose as a sample the opening lines of "Riske" by Sara Esgate:

> A begonia sun
> melts the space between us.
> My eyes hide in the Mulberry leaves
> and watch our words.
> A sentence pauses on a shadowed crossbar,
> then moves across the floor,
> risking brightness.

The digest-sized 83 pp. journal, perfect bound, matte card cover with art, is offset from typescript on high-quality paper, circulation 500, 100 subscriptions of which 10 are libraries. They use 50-60 of 1,000 + submissions received. **Sample: $3 postpaid. Submit 3-5 double-spaced poems; photocopies, dot-matrix OK. Reports in 6 weeks, pays one copy. Editor often comments on rejections.** Annual *Rhino* Poetry Contest with $100 prize and publication in *Rhino*. Laurie Buehler comments, "What keeps poetry alive are the 'little magazines,' forming an underground 'network of light' which satisfies in part our contemporary hunger for truth in resonant language."

*RHODE ISLAND REVIEW (V, II), Providence, RI 02906, founded 1979. *Rhode Island Review*, now a quarterly (planning more frequent issues) is "A showcase for artists' work. Broad appeal to intelligent, non-academic readership. Not accepting unsolicited MSS."

RHYME TIME POETRY NEWSLETTER, HUTTON PUBLICATIONS CONTEST, MYSTERY TIME, WRITERS' INFO (I, IV, Humor/mystery), Box 2377, Coeur d'Alene, ID 83814, poetry editor Linda Hutton. *Rhyme Time*, founded 1981 and published bimonthly beginning in 1987, consists of 3-5 sheets of typing paper, stapled at the corner, photocopied both sides from typescript, "featuring **rhymed poetry with some free verse and blank verse. We sponsor several contests each year, both with and without entry fees. 16 lines maximum, no avant-garde, haiku or religious work.**" She has published William F. Dougherty, Dorothy Plewman Dean and M. Rosser Lunsford. This sample, "Prescience," is by Margaret Hillert:

> How could I know that you would leave
> With the last leaf blowing,
> And I be so alone to grieve,
> Left with my knowing?

Sample and guidelines free for SASE (two stamps), price regularly $1.25, subscription $7.50, circulation 200, 75 subscriptions (2 libraries). She **uses about half of the 300 submissions received annually, pays one free copy.** *Mystery Time*, founded 1983, is an annual 44-52 pp. digest-sized chapbook, stapled-spine, containing 1-2 pages in each issue of **humorous poems about mysteries and mystery writers** such as this, by Irene Warsaw:

> This brand-new whodunit is clever for sure:
> The villain's elusive and clues are obscure.
> I'm having such trouble unmasking the blighter,
> I'd like to catch up with and clobber THE WRITER.
> WHODUNIT? HE dunit!

Circulation: 100, **sample $3.50**, uses 4-6 of the 12-15 submissions received. Guidelines available. Pays one copy. *Writer's Info*, founded 1984, is a monthly consisting of 3 sheets of typing paper, stapled at the corner, offset both sides from typescript. Tipsheet for the beginning freelancer. The editor has published Betty M. Bennoit, William Borden and Tom L. Ervin. This sample, "A La Doggerel," is by Pat Campbell:

> The doggerel poet's sneered at
> By educated bards,
> But someone's got to write the verse
> That goes in birthday cards.

Sample and guidelines free for SASE (two stamps), price regularly $1, subscription $12, circulation 100, 50 subscriptions. She uses about three-fourths of the 400 submissions received annually, pays $1-10 for first rights, one copy for reprint rights. **Submit 4-5 pages, typed, double-spaced, any time,** photocopy, dot-matrix, simultaneous submissions OK, no query, reports in one month, previously published submissions welcome. Hutton Publications Contests are monthly, on a variety of themes, in various lengths and forms, sometimes subscribers only, sometimes over 55 only, $1-2 entry fees, prizes $10-50. Send SASE for current rules.

‡*RHYTHM-AND-RHYME (I)**, The Barhil Collective, 23 Liverpool St., Epsom, Auckland 3, New Zealand, founded 1985, poetry editor Hilda Phillips. The Barhil Collective was founded by Barbara Whyte, a collective's semi-annual publication. Aim of the periodical is to "help New Zealand poets to be read outside their own country, and for overseas poets to become known (or better known) in New Zealand." **There is no payment to contributors and no complimentary copies. "The only 'reward' for contributing poets is the opportunity to be more widely read."** *Rhythm-and-Rhyme* publishes **"traditional rhyming poetry, blank verse, free verse, innovative (but not 'gimmickry') poetry on any subject; but no crude language."** As a sample I have selected the first stanza from "Sculpture (Henry Moore)" by the New Zealand poet William E. Morris:

> *It teases the mind with light and form*
> *an immovable object with unblinking face*
> *nestled in oblivion immune from time and place.*

The magazine is digest-sized, 48 pp. saddle-stapled, offset from typescript on white stock with colored paper cover, no graphics. It is published in April and October; subscription rate $5/year including surface mail postage to all countries outside New Zealand, or $7.60/year including airmail postage to North America. **Sample postpaid for half the above prices. They accept previously published poetry provided the post holds the copyright; simultaneous submissions OK, preferred length for poems is under 30 lines. They try to reply to all letters within 1 month.** The October 1985 issue included 48 New Zealand poets and 39 poets from 19 other countries. Mrs. Phillips says, "The Barhil Collective invites poets everywhere to participate in their venture of trying to establish global dialogue through poetry."

*RIDGE REVIEW MAGAZINE, RIDGE TIMES PRESS (IV, Regional/ Northern CA)**, Box 90, Mendocino, CA 95460, phone 707-937-1188, founded 1981, poetry editors Jim and Judy Tarbell and Lucie Marshall, is a "bio-regional quarterly looking at economic, political and social phenomena of the area" which uses **only poets from Northern California.** They have recently published poetry by Michael Sykes and Judith Tannenbaum. As a sample the editors chose these lines from "New Broom" by Kay Ryan:

> *New broom sweeps stiff,*
> *graceless thatch rakes,*
> *leaves tracks, but change*
> *comes unseen makes bristles*
> *sway that or this way*
> *turns tasks*
> *seque*

The 7x10" magazine, saddle-stapled, 50 + pp., matte card cover with art, photos and ads with text, circulation 3,500, 1,000 subscriptions, uses about 1 page of poetry per issue. Subscription: $7; per copy: $2. They use about 1 out of 20 poems submitted each year. Considers simultaneous submissions. **Sample: $2.85 postpaid. Photocopy, dot-matrix OK. Reports in about a week. Usually pays $10 per poem.**

‡*RIGHT HERE (THE HOMETOWN MAGAZINE) (I, IV, Regional, children)**, Box 1014, Huntington, IN 46750, phone 219-356-4223, founded 1984, editor Emily Jean Carroll, a general family magazine for northern Indiana that **accepts work from children as well as adults. "We use a variety of styles and lengths (up to 48 lines). Also story poems for children. Prefer easy to understand."** As a sample, I selected the first four lines from "Life's Growing Edge" by Carolyn A. Egolf:

> *Are you living out on life's growing edge?*
> *Does life hold excitement for you?*
> *Do you find new interest and challenge*
> *In the things you see and do?*

Right Here is a magazine-sized, 40 pp., offset in black and white with some drawings and photographs, two-color cover on same stock, saddle-stapled. It appears bi-monthly and has a circulation of 2,000, of which 200 are subscriptions. Price per issue is $1.25, subscription $6/year. **Sample available for $1.25 postpaid. Pay for poems is one copy or "$1-4 if featured separately," plus one copy. Poets should send a maximum of 6 poems with name and address on each page; reporting time is 1-2 months.**

RIVELIN GRAPHEME PRESS (II), 199 Greyhound Rd., London W14 9SD, England, founded 1984, poetry editors Snowdon Barnett and David Tipton, publishes **only poetry, hoping for 8 titles per**

year, approximately 68-120 pp. each (flat-spined, digest-sized quality paperbacks with glossy covers), illustrated. **One title each year will be of a Latin American poet translated into English, at least one by a woman, one anthology, one collected poems. Book-length poems considered**. I selected these lines as a sample from Philip Callow's "On the Raft" (in **New York Insomnia and Other Poems**):

> Lying on the hearthrug's raft of solitude
> she looked abandoned, but it was a safer thing
> to float on, wafted by heat and dreams,
> hair strewn on the thick river of sex . . .

These are obviously enthusiastic, ambitious publishers with an eye for quality. "We like to read poetry," they say, promising **immediate reports on submissions. Send book-length manuscript or about 10 poems for consideration for anthology, typed, double-spaced, photocopy OK. Payment: 20 copies of first printing of 600, then 5% royalties on subsequent printings. They prefer queries that contain biographical information, previous publications, and a photo, if possible**. Their advice: "Don't write about broken hearts, lost dogs or deceased grannies. Poetry is All!"

*RIVER CITY REVIEW, RIVER CITY REVIEW PRESS, INC. (II), Box 34275, Louisville, KY 40232, founded 1982, poetry editors Alan Naslund and Millard Dunn, appears twice yearly "published by a nonprofit corporation with a view to circulating and publishing fine contemporary poetry and fine fiction." They want "**free verse, any length, in the contemporary mode. We prefer poetry whose argument is carried by metaphor and image with little or no ancillary explanation or editorial voice**." They have recently published poetry by Richard Cecil and Lyn Lifshin. The editors selected these sample lines by Roger Mitchell:

> It was miles
> and the moonlight never stopped coming,
> and I never went back and I can't think, still,
> of her name, or why I never went back

RCR is magazine-sized with a two-column format, professionally typeset, using about 30 pp. of poetry per issue, circulation 500 + , 200 subscriptions of which 50 are libraries. Subscription: $10 per year; $3.50 per issue. **Sample: $3.50 postpaid. They receive about 200 submissions per year. "Prefer letter-quality print (but not crucial)." Photocopies and simultaneous submissions OK. Query in form of request for back issue. Rarely print only one poem, so make substantial submission. Usually reports within 6-8 weeks. Pays copies.**

*RIVER STYX MAGAZINE, BIG RIVER ASSOCIATION (II), 7420 Cornell, St. Louis, MO 63130, phone 725-0602, founded 1975, is "an international, multicultural journal publishing both award-winning and relatively undiscovered writers. We feature fine art, photography, poetry and short prose. **We publish original poetry of high quality and content**." They have recently published work by Adrienne Rich, Amy Clampitt, Toni Morrison, Amiri Baraka, Simon Ortiz and Margaret Atwood. As a sample the editors chose these lines by Derek Walcott:

> What's missing from the Charles is the smell of salt
> though the thawed river, muscling toward its estuary,
> swims seaward with the Spring, then with strong shoulders
> heaves up the ice. The floes crack like rifle fire.

River Styx is a digest-sized 112 + pp. biannual, circulation 1,500, 100 subscriptions of which 70 are libraries. Subscription $10; per copy: $5. They use about 100 of the 1,000 submissions each year. **Sample: $5 postpaid. Submit during September-October; notification in January. Send 4-6 poems. Prefers original typescript. Pays $7 per page plus 2 copies. Send SASE for guidelines. Editors sometimes comment on rejections.** They advise, "Be your own editor as much as possible! On a brighter note, we publish young writers."

*RIVERRUN (I, II), Glen Oaks Community College, Centreville, MI 49032, phone 616-467-9945, ext. 277, founded 1977, poetry editor Harvey Gordon, is a literary biannual, using **4-8 magazine-sized pp. of poetry in each issue—"no prejudices."** As a sample, I chose the complete poem, "Dissolve" by John Ditsky:

> The only poem finally's
> the face of a woman which, within
> the glare of this your gaze, seems
> melting, melting, down.

They have a printrun of 450-500. **Sample: $2 postpaid. They receive 60-80 poems per year, use "as much as possible," have a 6-12 month backlog, reports immediately. Pays 2 copies.**

*RIVERSIDE QUARTERLY (IV, Science fiction, fantasy), Box 833-044, Richardson, TX 75083, phone 231-9024, founded 1964, poetry editor Sheryl Smith (poetry submissions should be sent to her at

39090 Presidio Way, #132, Fremont, CA 94538), appears "irregularly, a critical magazine of **science fiction and fantasy.** Our relationship to these fields is the same as that of a journal like *Husdon Review* to literature in general." They **do not want to see "didactic or 'uplifting' verse; anything else permissible, 50 lines maximum length.**" They have recently published poetry by Neil Kvern, Edward Mycue, Peter Dillingham, Francis Blessington, John Ditsky and Doug Barbour. The editor selected these sample lines from "A Divine of the Black Hole Offers Mass" by Morgan Nyberg:

> May my prayer be drawn to the supersolid core
> Throne of transcending density
> Where light swallows itself
> And angels collapse inward

The 5x8" journal, photoreduced from typescript uses 10-12 pp. of poetry in each issue, circulation 1,100—800 subscriptions of which 200 are libraries. Subscription: $5. They receive 150-200 freelance submissions of poetry per year, use 10-15, have a 9-12 month backlog. **Sample: $1.25 postpaid. Contributors are advised to examine a sample copy before submitting. Reports in 10 days. Pays in copies. Editor comments on rejections.**

ROANOKE REVIEW (II), Roanoke College, Salem, VA 24153, phone 703-389-2351, ext. 367, founded 1968, poetry editor Robert R. Walter, is a semiannual literary review which uses **poetry that is "conventional; we have not used much experimental or highly abstract poetry."** They have recently published poetry by Peter Thomas, Norman Russell, Alan Seaburg, Mary Balazs and Irene Dayton. I selected as a sample the second of two stanzas of "Of Shoes and Ships" by Ernest Kroll:

> The shoes in snow divide a waveless sea
> Whose wake congeals as if it thought a trough
> Redress enough for snow's discourtesy,
> Redress enough—by fresh snow leveled off.

RR is 6x9", 52 pp., professionally printed with matte card cover with decorative typography, using 25-30 pp. of poetry in each issue, circulation 250-300, 150 subscriptions of which 50 are libraries. Subscription: $3; per copy: $2. They receive 200-250 freelance submissions of poetry per year, use 30-40, have a 6-12 month backlog. **Sample: $1 postpaid. Submit original typed MSS, no photocopies. Reports in 8-10 weeks. No pay.** The editor advises, "There is a lot of careless or sloppy writing going on. We suggest careful proofreading and study of punctuation rules."

‡*ROCKY MOUNTAIN REVIEW OF LANGUAGE AND LITERATURE (IV, Members)**, Boise State University English Dept., Boise, ID 83725, phone 208-385-1246, founded 1947, poetry editor, **Naomi Lindstrom, to whom poetry submissions should be sent directly, % Spanish-Portuguese Dept., University of Texas, Austin, TX 73712. Contributors to the literary quarterly must be members of Rocky Mountain Modern Language Association. Poetry should be "generally relatively short," but otherwise they will consider anything but "bad poetry."** The review has recently published Scott P. Sanders and translations of Antonio Cisneros and David Huerta. As a sample, the editor selected the following three lines (opening stanza) of "Autobiography, Chapter X: Circus in the Blood" by Jim Barnes:

> My father's blood is strong: my bones grow hard
> with stakes of things and my veins pulse with
> a lively red from his nomadic ways.

The 6x9", 276 pp. flat-spined quarterly publishes work of interest to college and university teachers of literature and language; **poetry may be in English or other modern languages. Contributors are not paid and do not receive extra copies; subscription is part of RMMLA membership. Poets should submit two copies,** *without author's name* **to Naomi Lindstrom at the address above. They report on submissions in 4-8 weeks and publish usually with 6 months but no more than 12 months after acceptance.** Circulation of the review is 1,100-1,200, all membership subscriptions. They accept a few ads from other journals and publishers.

‡*ROMANCE AND FICTION WORLD (I)**, Box 531, Station W, Toronto, ON M6M 5C3, Canada, founded 1984, editor Emanuela Palmacci, a "bimonthly magazine with 4 specials and an annual." The editors buy **3-6 poems per issue and want to see "romance, traditional, haiku, and free verse, length not more than 15 lines." They do not want "private poems, erotic."** They have recently published poems by C. Buckaway, Suzanne Summer, and Cassandra Lise Di Marco, from whose work the editors choose the following lines as a sample:

> she dances swiftly, then slowly, as if she was making love
> The ballerina shuddered, and all her emotions flowed to him

The first issue of *Romance and Fiction World* came out in February/March 1986; at this writing. Library subscriptions were expected to be 125 and newsstand sales 675. **Sample plus guidelines are available for $4.75 postpaid. Pay is $10/poem plus 4 copies. Submissions should be typed, double-**

spaced, with "your real name and address, area code and phone number." Reporting time is 3-12 weeks, backlog is 1-3 months. For publication in the annual volume, poets can enter a bimonthly contest. "We welcome new poets, but they must be a subscriber to the magazine or a member of the International Paperback Romance/Fiction/Poets Association."

*ROOM OF ONE'S OWN (IV, Feminist), Box 46160 Station G, Vancouver, B.C. V64 4G5, Canada, founded 1975, is a **feminist literary quarterly, pays $10-25**. They have a circulation of 1,200, 600 subscriptions of which 100 are libraries, use exchange ads with other periodicals, **sample: $3 postpaid**. They receive hundreds of submissions per year, use about 80, **report in three months**. I selected these lines as a sample, from "No Fear of Blood" by Kirsten Emmott:

> *I love the smell of labouring women, the amniotic fluid*
> *that soaks the bed, their earthy beauty.*

*THE ROUND TABLE: A JOURNAL OF POETRY AND FICTION (II), 206 Sherman St., Wayne, NE 68787, founded 1984, poetry editors Alan and Barbara Lupack. "We publish a journal of poetry and fiction. Currently, 2 issues a year—one devoted solely to poetry and one solely to fiction. We feature one poet (usually someone who has not published widely or who doesn't have a national reputation, but whose work is of very high quality). **Few restrictions on poetry—except high quality. We like forms if finely crafted. Very long poems could only be published in the featured poet section.**" They have recently published poetry by Kathleene West, John Tagliabue, James Humphrey and Paul Scott. As a sample I chose the opening lines of "Homestead in Union" by David Memmot:

> *We live in a house we did not build*
> *and cannot revise overnight*
> *generations of unfinished dreams.*
> *These walls recall many weavers . . .*

The Round Table is digest-sized, 40-44 pp., saddle-stapled, professionally printed (offset) with matte card cover. The new magazine had a circulation of 150 in its first year, 75 subscriptions of which 3 are libraries. Subscription: $6. **Sample: $3 postpaid. "We like to see about 5 poems (but we read whatever is submitted but only from Nov. 1-Feb. 28)—more for those wishing to be considered for featured writer section. Cover letter. Simultaneous submissions OK "But we expect to be notified if a poem submitted to us is accepted elsewhere." Quality of poetry, not format, is most important thing. We try to report in 1 month, but—especially for poems under serious consideration—it may take longer."** Pays copies.

‡*RUBICON (II), Box 835, Amherst, MA 01004, founded 1984, poetry editors Howard Dupuis, Laurie Hutchins, and Jeffrey Whitehead, a semi-annual magazine that publishes quailty contemporary poetry in English or translated into English. They have **"few restrictions; we tend to grimace when, upon opening an envelope, we find the poem flopping all over the page." They don't want to see** "poems which won't endure." Poets recently published include Michael Burnhard, Rolf Jacobsen, James Tate, Thomas Lux, Marilyn Hacher, and John Unterecter. The editors did not quote sample lines, and I have not seen the magazine. It has a circulation of 1,000, of which 600-700 are subscriptions and 100 are newsstand sales. Price per issue is $4, subscription $10 for 3 issues. **Sample available for $4 postpaid. Pay is 3 copies. Writers should send at least 5 poems, "crisp, readable." Reporting time is 1-8 weeks and time to publication 1-5 months.**

RUDDY DUCK PRESS, *ORO MADRE, SMALL PRESS TIMES, OXYURA JAMAICENSIS RUBIDA MONOGRAPHS IN POETRY(II), 4429 Gibraltar Dr., Fremont, CA 94536, phone 415-797-9096, founded 1980, poetry editors L. Glazier and J. L. Riley, publishes the quarterly *Oro Madre*, chapbooks and anthologies of poetry. It "is a small and fiercely independent press founded on the belief that literature is an alive, influential, and vital force historically, socially, and on a personal level. To this end, we operate as a source of *alternative* information, and are a key link internationally and nationally, between libraries, small presses, and writers. For this reason, we publish work that is multicultural in orientation, that shows a certain spirit of survival and triumph through literate, independent freethinking. We consider one of our strongest features to be our selection of materials that is regional in nature, and we select from a variety of regions. We hope to provide a rich, engaging alternative that might not otherwise be available to a culture that desperately needs it." They "**want: clean, evocative style; expert wordsmanship; poems that *evoke* feelings and images; do not want: over-personal, melodramatic or self-indulgent work, nor poems that 'recite' experiences. Form, length, style, subject matter not limited. Purpose: poems should exhibit a commitment to a philosophy or picture of the world in a larger sense.**" They have recently published poetry by Bukowski, Aguila, Glazier, Castano, Simon Hirschman and Arguelles. The editors selected these sample lines by Luke Breit:

> *. . . I wonder*
> *if the men with the bombs have ever spent a day*

> *looking at the world this slowly;*
> *how a girl walking by, or two children*
> *shrieking in the grass, or the good words*
> *of a friend, are the small flames*
> *that set the right kind of fire to the earth.*

Oro Madre is digest-sized, 50+ pp., professionally printed, card matte cover with art (uses b/w art throughout). There are about 44 pp. of poetry in each issue, circulation 500. Subscription: $12. They receive about 400 freelance submissions of poetry per year, use 100. **Sample: $3.50 postpaid. Prefer 3-4 poems per submission, no simultaneous submissions, legible photocopy or dot-matrix OK. "We pride ourselves on our commitment as editors and try to respond to each submission individually, therefore response times can sometimes be long, but poets can be sure that each submission is carefully read." Pays in copies. For book or chapbook consideration, query with 3-4 samples and cover letter giving publication credits, bio, personal or aesthetic philosophy, poetic goals and principles and whatever additional information seems relevant. Disc submission OK if compatible with Osborne 1 or IBM PC; hard copy preferred. 10% royalty contracts plus copies. Sample copy $3.50. Send SASE (2 oz.) for catalog to buy samples.**

‡**RUNA PRESS (V)**, Monkstow County Dublin, Dublin, Ireland, phone 801869, founded 1930, editor Tony Hughes, a small press that publishes hardbacks and paperbacks. **No unsolicited MSS are accepted.** The catalog I have lists books of poetry by Rupert Strong, Eithne Strong and Jonathan Hanaghan. Jonathan Hanaghan and Rupert Strong practiced as psychoanalysts and their poetry deals with the illumination that comes from lives lead at the core of the struggle for existence. Editors chose this sample:

> *The joy of the morning*
> *expires on the cross*
> *when monogamous lady*
> *makes of husband a daddy.*

S.O.S. (SULTAN OF SWAT) BOOKS (II), 1821 Kalorama Road NW, Washington, DC 20006, phone 202-638-1956, founded 1982, poetry editors Richard Flynn and Hugh Walthall, exists "to publish the best poetry we can find. **Poets without substantial publications in magazines are unlikely to be selected.** We believe our taste is excellent and the reviews of our first books seem to confirm our belief." **Query with 5-6 samples and cover letter with bio, publication record, personal or aesthetic philosophy, poetic goals and principles. Replies to query in 2-3 weeks. If invited to submit there is a $5 reading fee. Reports in 6 weeks or longer. MS should be neatly typed. Photocopy, simultaneous submissions OK. Pays at least 50 copies and "often" an honorarium. Send $6 for sample book.** The editors comment, "We are not impressed by what is currently fashionable, although our poets have been published in some of the better magazines. We depend on our own money to publish, and so far have neither applied for nor received grants. (One of our authors did, however, receive a state grant on the basis of the book we published.) We must reiterate that beginners and greeting card versifiers have no chance with us. We lose money on what we publish (though our first book sold well) and prefer to lose money on poets whose work we believe in. Also, though we feel somewhat reluctant to charge the reading fee, we feel that the careful reading we've given even mediocre MSS more than justifies the fee."

‡**SACHEM PRESS (II)**, Box 9, Old Chatham, NY 12136, phone 518-794-8327, founded 1980, editor Louis Hammer, a small-press publisher of poetry and fiction, both hardcover and flat-spined paperbacks. The editor wants to see "**strong compelling, even visionary work, English-language or translations**." He has recently published poetry by Cesar Vallejo, Yannis Ritsos, 24 leading poets of Spain, Peter Huchel, and himself. As a sample, he selected the following lines from a poem by Felix Grande in the anthology, *Recent Poets of Spain*, translated by Louis Hammer and Sara Schyfter:

> *I offend the way the cypresses offend. I'm*
> *the depressor. I'm the one who contaminates*
> *with his kisses a vomit of dark silences,*
> *a bleeding of shadows. I offend, love, I offend.*

I have 5 sample publications by Sachem Press, all handsome flat-spined paperbacks with glossy two- or four-color covers; all are translations (from Greek or Spanish) except one by Louis Hammer. The small paperbacks average 120 pp. and the anthology of Spanish poetry contains 340 pp. Each poem is printed in both Spanish and English, and there are biographical notes about the authors. The small books cost $6.95 and the anthology $11.95. **Writers wanting to be considered for book publication should submit 10-20 sample poems and bio. Mr. Hammer will consider simultaneous submissions, and photocopied, dot-matrix, or disc (IBM) MSS are acceptable. Royalties are 10% maximum, after expenses are recovered, plus 50 author's copies.** Book catlog is free "when available," and poets can purchase books from Sachem "by writing to us, 33⅓% discount."

SACKBUT PRESS, *SACKBUT REVIEW (II), 2513 E. Webster Pl., Milwaukee, WI 53211, founded 1978, poetry editor Angela Peckenpaugh. "I publish mainly **poem notecards. I take short, neatly-typed poems that lend themselves to illustration by line drawing or b/w photo.** I get the illustrations through *Artists Market.* These are not greeting cards! I publish occasional chapbooks but am not seeking MSS for chapbooks. **I like anything that leaves me with refreshment or delight.**" She has recently published poetry by Rachel Hadas, Cornelius Eady, Ron Ellis, Fae Korsmo, Ron Schreiber and Marcia Falk. She selected this sample by Kathleen Dale:

> Here is a coin newly struck
> ready to shine like sun
> polished by fog:
> a newborn tongued clean.

Submit no more than 3 poems for notecard series. Reports in 2 weeks. Payment is 25 cards.

*SAINT ANDREWS REVIEW, SAINT ANDREWS PRESS (II), St. Andrews College, Laurinburg, NC 28352, founded 1970. The *Review* is a literary biannual, 7x10", 120 pp., circulation 300-500, which **uses quality poetry. Sample: $2.50. Payment in copies; $100 prize to best poem printed in the year.** Saint Andrews Press does not consider unsolicited MSS but solicits often from those who have had work in the *Review*.

*ST. ANTHONY MESSENGER (IV, Religious), 1615 Republic St., Cincinnati, OH 45210, is a monthly magazine, circulation 417,000, 59 pp., for Catholic families, mostly with children in grade school, high school or college. In some issues, they have a **poetry page which uses poems appropriate for their readership.** In the issue I examined there were 2 poems of 11 and 30 lines each. As a sample I selected the first of six stanzas of "Iceflowers" by Ethel Marbach:

> Iceflowers bloom
> on midnight glass
> above the stove
> which sleeps now cold
> and white as death,

Pays $1 a line on acceptance. Send SASE for guidelines and free sample.

*ST. JOSEPH MESSENGER AND ADVOCATE OF THE BLIND (I), 541 Pavonia Ave., Box 288, Jersey City, NJ 07303, phone 201-798-4141, founded 1898, poetry editor Sister Ursula Maphet, C.S.-.J.P., is a 30 pp. regular-sized quarterly (16 pp., 8x11"), circulation 35,000, which wants **"brief but thought-filled poetry; do not want lengthy and issue-filled."** Most of the poets they have used are previously unpublished. The editor selected as a sample these lines by Charles Waugman:

> As sheer and improbable as a dream
> It looms far above my capability
> To stay sincere when honest looks wrong
> Is just the kind of strength for which I long

There are about 2 pp. of poetry in each issue. Subscription: $4. They receive 400-500 submissions per year, use 50. **Send SASE for guidelines and free sample. Reports within 2 weeks. Pays $5-20 per poem. Editor sometimes comments on rejections.**

*SALMAGUNDI (III), Skidmore College, Saratoga Springs, NY 12866, founded 1965, edited by Peggy and Robert Boyers, has long been **one of the most distinguished of the quarterlies** of the sciences and humanities, publishing poets such as Robert Penn Warren, Louise Gluck, John Peck, Howard Nemerov and W. D. Snodgrass. These lines, for instance, are by Robert Lowell:

> Pray for the grace of accuracy
> Vermeer gave to the sun's illumination
> stealing like the tide across a map
> to his girl solid with yearning.

Each issue is handsomely printed, a thick, flat-spined book, priced at $5-10 (**sample: $4 postpaid.**). Subscriptions are $15 a year, $18 for two years. The magazine has a paid circulation of 5,400, 3,800 subscriptions of which about 900 are libraries. **They use about 10-50 pages of poetry in each issue, receive 1,200 submissions per year and use about 20, have a year to 30 month backlog, and report in three months. Payment in copies only, no need to query, photocopies OK.**

*SALT LICK, SALT LICK PRESS, SALT LICK SAMPLERS, LUCKY HEART BOOKS (II), 1804 E. 38½ St., Austin, TX 78722, founded 1969, poetry editor James Haining, publishes "new literature and graphic arts in their various forms." They have published poetry by Michael Lally, Gerald Burns, Julie Siegel, Robert Trammell and Michaela Moore. As a sample I selected this poem, "Stride Time" by the editor, James Haining:

Close-up

Merritt Clifton
Samisdat

Artist: Lawrence Goodridge

Once a reader sent a complaint to the editor of *Writer's Digest* about my having described *Samisdat* in an article on small presses. She wrote, "I have never before discovered such an insolent publisher. In the least, Mr. Jerome should have warned his readers of the nature of this leftist/anarchist publisher."

Well, neither that label nor any other I know of quite describes Merritt Clifton, one of the most humane and gentlest violent men I have ever heard of, surely one of the most individualistic of publishers. In his early thirties, he is also one of the most thorough scholars (small press and other publishing, environmental issues, politics, baseball) outside the realms of academe.

As a ten-year-old, he witnessed the Free Speech Movement in Berkeley; as a young teenager, participated in the first Earth Day at a time when he was supporting himself by custodial work and rent collection in black slums. He founded *Samisdat* (Russian for self-publishing) at San Jose State University in 1973. There he met P. J. Kemp, a farm girl from Quebec and "a prolific writer." They married and went to help out on her family farm on the Quebec-Vermont border, where they still live, supporting themselves by writing and publishing.

Clifton writes news for papers in the region, articles on publishing history, baseball and other matters, fiction (much of it autobiographical) and, perhaps most centrally, poetry. "I was first attracted to writing for publication," he says, "by the discovery that words can have real power to change oppressive situations. Poetry, well-written, consists of concentrated word-power. A single poem rarely changes the whole world at once, but it can radically change individual perception, and that's where real change begins—in individual people's hearts and minds. For me, poems received at *Samisdat* tend to unlock areas of perception, which then color themselves in from news sources and result in changes in my own writing. Or, the poems I publish often become my direct inspiration for investigative journalism. If a poem is a mere distillation of journalism, on the other hand, it's dull as yesterday's news.

"Simultaneous submissions are automatically rejected, unread. Submissions without sufficient SASE are held for ransom. Poets who read a sample *Samisdat* stand a better chance of acceptance, simply because they have a much better idea of what I'm doing. *Samisdat* is, after all, a pretty unique rag. I don't really care about poetry for its own sake: I'm interested in what it can do. Merely 'publishing poems' seems a bit less meaningful to me than sorting out jars of nuts and bolts. Many poets claim in cover letters that they've read *Samisdat*, love what I'm doing, et cetera, when I know at a glance that they've never seen a copy. How do I know? When one prints only 300 of each issue, one knows exactly where each one's going, and if someone in Ketchum claims to have read an issue when one hasn't had a Ketchum subscriber since 1976, there's a 99.9% chance she's lying—even if her submissions are appropriate. In this case, one was, and I accepted it. But I let the young lady know she hadn't fooled me."

What makes you so feisty? I asked Merritt. "My brother Ted and sister Nicole are the same way. We just have a low tolerance for nonsense. We're also about 99% Irish, which might have something to do with it." Personally, I find it refreshing to have such a bull in the china-shop of literary publications.

—Judson Jerome

> *her walking into the*
> *room from the rain*
> *what you would*
> *in the length say*
> *I hear so time*
> *for time*

The magazine-sized journal, 48 pp., saddle-stapled, matte cover, experimental graphics throughout, appears irregularly, print run of 1,500. They receive 400-600 poems per year, use 1-2%. **Sample: $3 postpaid. Reports in 1-6 weeks. Pays copies. To submit for book publication under the Lucky Heart Books imprint, send 20 samples, cover letter "open." Simultaneous submissions, photocopies, dot-matrix OK. Pays copies.**

*SALTHOUSE (IV, Theme/style, historical, geographical, land-oriented), Box 11537, Milwaukee, WI 53211, founded 1975, is an irregularly published journal of "very tailored perspective," according to its editor, DeWitt Clinton. He calls it "A Journal of **Geopoetics—Where History and Imagination Meet**," and wants **free verse which is "historical, geographical, or land-oriented**." Poets he has published include Howard McCord, Robert Peters, Rochelle Ratner and Keith Wilson. He selected these lines as illustration:

> *Watching the Milky Way wheel*
> *across the sky*
> *the Hung River, the Chinese call it,*
> *we are a part of that.*

The magazine is thin, flat-spined, finely printed and bound, with a print run of about 500, circulation of 300, with 20 subscriptions of which 15 are libraries. **Sample: $6 postpaid**. He says that each issue uses 40-90 pages of material including poetry, but he has a two-year backlog, and that he gets about 30 submissions per year, of which he uses about three. **Reports in 3-5 months, no pay**. The editor's advice to contributors is **"Do not confuse us with a general-interest magazine**. Purchase latest issue."

*SAMISDAT (II), Box 129, Richford, VT 05476, founded 1973, is **one of the liveliest, least expensive publishing operations in the country**, edited by Merritt Clifton, author of the "Help!" column in *Small Press Review* and one of the most knowledgeable people I know about small presses and their history. He puts out a **quarterly magazine and monthly chapbook on an unusual subscription-payment arrangement**. You can get a **sample copy of the magazine for $2. For $2.50 you get the sample plus "our philosophy of writing," a sassy little chapbook** (*The Pillory Poetics*, by Robin Michelle Clifton) giving an irreverent but intelligent commentary on modern poetry. For $15 you get the next 500 pages of magazines and chapbooks, or $25 the next 1,000, and for $150 "all future items." If your poetry has been accepted for the magazine, you may be considered for one of the chapbooks, in which case **you pay for paper and printing supplies, Merritt Clifton does the printing, and you get half the press run**. The usual press run is 300 at a **cost to the poet of $35 for a 16-page book** ($42 for 20 pages, $7 for each additional 4 pages). Thus if you sell your 150 copies for a buck apiece, you've made a profit of $115 on a 16-page book. This plan was worked out for poets who want to have a modest sampling of their work to sell at readings. Merritt advises, "Ours is **not an appropriate system for authors who do not wish to get personally involved in distribution, nor for those hoping to distribute primarily to bookstores**." He says, "We want to see **direct, informed, memorable conscientious statement. We do not use patterned verse of any kind, shallow truisms, doggerel, or self-conscious artifice**," and he provides these lines as a sample of what he likes (by Haywood Jackson, writing of a Pittsburgh mill):

> *But for the faint thudding clang of heavy steel*
> *against steel, reverberating like a fading thunder,*
> *this is a tomb.*

Be sure to **study the guidelines (available for SASE) and a sample issue. They pay 2 complimentary copies; subscribers also receive a 1-issue subscription extension for each appearance**. Merritt adds, **"We actively seek reprints, reviews, (et cetera) for our contributors in other publications— most items first published here do eventually reach a wider audience." Don't be surprised by blunt or even indecent language on rejections**. Merritt Clifton speaks his mind plainly—**responds immediately, always with comments**. But, as he says, "We are not really eager to take on a whole lot of new people. We're always open to people of **compatible outlook and literary competence**, but they're a rare breed." As you might assume from the low production costs, the **printing is nothing fancy, stapled pamphlets**, with simple art, mostly composed on an IBM proportional typewriter. Merritt Clifton's advice for would-be contributors is, "Read poetry. Read good poetry. Remember that the object is to substantially **contribute to a better world by informing, inspiring, questioning; the object of great poets is not merely getting published or getting famous."**

SAN DIEGO POET'S PRESS (IV, watch *CODA* for submission requests), 7527 La Jolla Blvd., La Jolla, CA 92037, % D. G. Wills Books and Coffeehouse. Founded 1981 by poetry editors: Kathleen Iddings, Thomas L. Gayton, Ric Solano, Ron O. Salisbury, publishes poetry anthologies. The fifth, *Poets' Voices 1984*, subtitled: Social Issues by Contemporary Poets, included such poets as Galway Kinnell, Allen Ginsberg, Robert Pinsky, Carolyn Kiser, Carolyn Forché, Tess Gallagher, Charles Bukowski, Diane O'Hehir, and John Balaban. Poems from *Poets' Voices 1984* were nominated by Carolyn Kizer and Naomi Lazard for the 1985 Pushcart Award. As a sample of the type of poetry the editors wish to see, Kathleen Iddings selected these lines from the last stanza of John Balaban's "In Celebration of Spring":

> *Swear by the locust, by dragonflies on ferns,*
> *by the minnow's flash, the tremble of a breast,*
> *by the new earth spongy under our feet:*
> *that as we grow old, we will not grow evil,*

Editor Kathleen Iddings will critique manuscripts and individual poems for a fee. Query first with SASE. Simultaneous submissions OK.

*SAN FERNANDO POETRY JOURNAL, KENT PUBLICATIONS., INC., CERULEAN PRESS (MINI ANTHOLOGY SERIES), (I, IV, Social protest), 18301 Halsted St., Northridge, CA 91325, founded 1978, poetry editors Richard Cloke, Shirley Rodecker and Lori Smith (and, for the Mini Anthology Series, Blair H. Allen, 9651 Estacia Court, Cucamonga, CA 91730). The *San Fernando Poetry Journal* uses poetry **of social protest.** According to Richard Cloke, "Poetry, for us, should be *didactic* **in the Brectian sense. It must say something, must inform, in the spirit of Zeitgeist (the tenor of our time).** We follow Hart Crane's definition of poetry as architectural in essence, building upon the past but incorporating the newest of this age also, including science, machinery, sub-atomic and cosmic physical phenomena as well as the social convulsions wrenching the very roots of our present world." **Send SASE for guidelines which explain this more fully. Ask, also, for copies of their various rejection slips which elucidate their standards clearly. For example, I quote this passage from one of them for its general usefulness for poets: "In some, the end-line rhyming is too insistent, seeming** *forced;* in others the words are not vibrant enough to give the content an arresting framework. Others do not have any beat (cadence) at all and some are simply not well thought out—often like first drafts, or seem like prose statements. Please try reworking again to get some energy in your statement. If your poetry is to succeed in impelling the reader to act, it must electrify, or at least command interest and attention." **They welcome new and unpublished poets.** As a sample I chose these lines from "Poetry Reading '2075' " by Allen T. Billy:

> *on stage are antique toys*
> *speak 'n spell machines with memories and microchips*
> *reading poetry in electric fashion*

The flat-spined quarterly, photocopied from typescript, uses 100 pages of poetry in each issue, circulation 400, 350 subscriptions of which 15 are libraries. They use about 300 of the 1,000 submissions (the editor rightly prefers to call them "contributions") each year. **Sample: $2.50 postpaid. No specifications for MS form. Simultaneous submissions OK. Reports in 1 week, pays in copies.** The press, under its various imprints, also publishes a few collections by individuals. **Query with 5-6 pp. of samples. For the Mini Anthology Series, which will include poetry by Lyn Lifshin, Patti Renner Tana, Warren Woessner, Aaron Kramer, Bradley Strahan, Richard Weekley, Del Reitz, Richard Cloke, Blair H. Allen, John Brander, T. Kilgore Splake and Jennifer Welch, query Blair Allen at the address above.**

*SAN JOSE STUDIES (II), San Jose State University, San Jose, CA 95192, phone 408-277-2841, founded 1975, poetry editor O. C. Williams. This "journal of general and scholarly interest, featuring critical, creative and informative writing in the arts, business, humanities, science and social sciences" uses poetry of "**excellent quality—no kinds excluded. Tend to like poems with something to say, however indirectly it may be communicated. Usually publish 7-10 pp. of verse in each issue. We like to publish several poems by one poet—better exposure for the poet, more interest for the reader.**" They have recently published poetry by David Citino, Hank Lazer, Virginia de Araujo, Mordecai Marcus, Leonard Nathan and Adrienne Rich. As a sample the editor chose these lines from "Snake" by Virginia de Araujo:

> *Then there was a time he had four legs?*
> *Oh, primitive belief! If in the garden*
> *there was one perfect beast, he*
> *was it: he is oneness. Intact.*

SJS appears thrice yearly in a 6x9" flat-spined, 100 + pp. format, professionally printed, matte card cover, using b/w photos, circulation 350, 275 subscriptions of which 60-65 are libraries. Subscription: $12; per copy: $5. They receive about 120 submissions per year, use 6-8, have a 1 year backlog. **Sample: $4 postpaid. No simultaneous submissions. Reports in 4-6 weeks. Pays 2 copies. Annual award of a year's subscription for best poetry printed that year and a Casey Memorial Award of**

$100 for the best contribution in prose or poetry. O. C. Williams comments, "Poetry is both an art and a craft; we are not interested in submissions unless the writer has mastered the craft and is actually practicing the art."

*SANDS (II), Box 638, Addison, TX 75201, phone 214-931-1528, founded 1979, editor Susan Charles Baugh, translation editor Rainer Schulte "attempts to offer writers a forum for serious writing, for established writers and novices." They want poetry that is **"serious, some experimental, no contrived, sentimental or greeting card verse, no juvenile, erotic or commercial poetry; no length limit. Prefer to see 3-5 poems from poet."** They have recently published poems by Walter McDonald, Shane Dohey, Andree Chedid and Anthony Phelps. The editor selected these sample lines from "Primary Colors" by Mack Lewis:

> *Like falls by reds and springs by greens*
> *Our demarcations are not so keen*
> *As planet has them, as we would*
> *Draw them by reason, if reason's scape*
> *Could shape our tropics into seasons*

It is a digest-sized 90 pp. flat-spined format, professionally printed with matte card cover, using about 25 pp. of poetry in each issue, circulation 2,000, 500 subscriptions of which 30 are libraries. They receive about 400 freelance submissions of poetry per year, use about 35. **Sample: $3 postpaid to writers ($5.95 to others). No dot-matrix or handwritten MSS. Simultaneous submissions OK. Pays copies. Send SASE for guidelines. Editor comments on rejections "particularly for writers we think may be published in *Sands* or if requested by writer.** The editor advises: "target markets, send for copies, trade with fellow poets. We plan to do more poetry in future issues. We are concentrating on beginning poets, trying to develop talent that comes to us through the mails."

‡SANTA SUSANA PRESS (V), CSU Libraries, 18111 Nordhoff St., Northridge, CA 91330, phone 818-885-2271, founded 1974, editor Norman Tanis, a small-press publisher of limited edition fine print books, history, literature and art, some poetry, all hardcover editions. **They do not accept freelance submissions of poetry. Poets should query first, and queries will be answered in 2 weeks. Honorariums paid depend on grant money.** The press has recently published books by George Elliott, Ward Ritchie, and Ray Bradbury, from whose "The Last Good Kiss" the editor selected the following lines as a sample:

> *What's past is past*
> *And the memory of mouths*
> *In a dry season, soon or late,*
> *Makes salivate the mind*

Book catalog is free on request; prices are high. For instance, **Reaching: Poems by George P. Elliott**, illustrated, is published in an edition of 350 numbered copies at $35 and 26 lettered copies at $60.

*SAPIENS: A JOURNAL FOR HUMAN EVOLUTION (II, IV, Specialized), 3704 Hyde Park Ave., Cincinnati, OH 45209, phone 513-531-6378, founded 1983, poetry editor Edward Kaplan, is an irregularly appearing magazine (2nd issue 1985) of **"new writing which explores by example or subject, what we are becoming as a species.** *Sapiens* sees art as evolutionary. Unafraid. Our poets and writers are different, we're saying, in the structure of their consciousness, not just willful, but with brains exhibiting the next steps: the brain as a bag of knots they seek to untie with personal light. *Sapiens* seeks, then, to chart the impermanent. We want **anything original, transcending the word 'kinds,' incantory, non-linear, ESP. Poems should be 1-3 pp. average."** They have published poetry by Charles Bernstein, Norman Weinstein, Jayanta Mahapatra, Clayton Eshelman and Jed Rasula. As a sample the editor selected lines from his own "Joshua":

> *who assigns himself*
> *the flask of vision*
> *to drink from is*
> *a scout in front of*
> *us who only want*
> *ordinary things to*
> *mean*

The magazine-sized journal is flat-spined, 76 pp., offset from typescript, circulation 300, 100 subscriptions of which 10-20 are libraries, using 30-40 pp. of poetry in each issue. They receive 50-100 submissions per year, use 1-5. **Sample: $5. Photocopy OK. Reports "usually immediately." Pays copies.**

SATURDAY PRESS, INC., EILEEN W. BARNES AWARD SERIES, INVITED POETS SERIES (II, IV, Women's), Box 884, Upper Montclair, NJ 07043, phone 201-256-1731, founded 1975, poetry editor Charlotte Mandel with guest editors for contests which have included Maxine Kumin, Colette Inez, Maxine Silverman and Rachel Hadas. "Saturday Press, Inc., is a nonprofit literary organization. The Press has a **special—though not exclusive—commitment to women's poetry, and by sponsoring the Eileen W. Barnes Award Competition for first books by women over 40 seeks to offer opportunity for new poets who have delayed their writing careers.** Not an annual event, the contest is widely posted when announced. The Invited Poets Series offers publication to established or less-known poets. We want **authoritative craft, strong, fresh imagery, sense of imagination and a good ear for syntax, sounds and rhythms. Language should lead the reader to experience a sense of discovery. Any form, content or style, but do not want polemic, jingles or conventional inspiration**." They have recently published books of poetry by Colette Inez, Anneliese Wagner, Ghita Orth, Charlotte Mandel. Their **Saturday's Women** anthology includes work by Patricia Hooper, Lisa Ress, Janice Thaddeus, Geraldine C. Little and Jean Hollander. As a sample the editor chose these lines from Anne Carpenter's "Ma's Ram":

> *A scuffle in the multiflora. The shrieks stop all our blood.*
> *A rooster's crow is cut in two*
> *The shock waves gradually fade out.*
> *The air is loud with relief and night business winding up.*
> *The worst ,has happened, and it was none of us.*

Do not send book MS without query. Enclose 1-3 samples and minimum summary of publications. Replies to queries in 2 weeks. If invited, book MS may be photocopied; simultaneous submission OK. No dot-matrix. "Prefer no binder, simple folder or paper clip." Pays 25-50 copies and possible honorarium ("depends on grants"). Send SASE for catalog to buy samples.

SCARECROW PRESS (III), Box 4167, 52 Liberty St., Metuchen, NJ 08840, founded 1950, publisher William R. Eshelman, poetry editor Bob Peters. Scarecrow primarily publishes scholarly and critical works for libraries, but in 1981 they initiated a Poets Now Series, edited by Bob Peters, to provide libraries, especially, with 10 books a year of good, relatively inexpensive ($13.50) hardbound editions of poets at the height of their powers who have not recently been represented in anthologies and who have 5-6 books already published, striking a balance between the very well known and lesser known poets. In the first year of the series they published books by Jonathan Williams, Rochelle Ratner, Jerry Ratch, David Ray, Carolyn Stoloff and Edwin Honig. The next four volumes in the series are by Charles Plynell, Robin Magowan, Simon Perchik, and Kathleen Spivack. The well-known poet-editor, Bob Peters, is also the author of **The Great American Poetry Bake-Off** series of critical (and often satirical) discussions of American poets, also published by Scarecrow Press.

SCAVENGER'S NEWSLETTER (IV, Science fiction, fantasy, horror), 519 Ellinwood, Osage City, KS 66523 may seem an odd place to publish poems, but its editor, Janet Fox, uses 2-3 every month. The *Newsletter* is a **leaflet packed with news about science fiction and horror publications**, in tiny type, printed on a copier on both sides of a couple of sheets of legal sized paper. Janet prefers "poetry of the **mordant and macabre—not** poetry about writing, and the ones she has used so far are all very short—**under 10 lines**, like this complete poem "Terra Strains 26," by Wayne Allen Sallee:

> *bums rush mission full*
> *wind howls revenge*
> *what dead bag lady*
> *makes November headlines*

You can get a copy for 60¢ ($7 a year). She has 265 subscriptions, prints copies as needed, and at last report was **accepting about 1 out of 4 poems submitted. You can use photocopy, dot-matrix, multiple submissions, simultaneous submissions (if informed)—even reprints if credit is given. No need to query. Payment: $1 on acceptance plus one copy.**

SCIENCE FICTION POETRY ASSOCIATION, *STAR-LINE, THE RHYSLING ANTHOLOGY (IV, Science fiction), 8350 Poole Ave., Sun Valley, CA 91352 for membership information; **for submissions: Robert Frazier, Ed., Box 491, Nantucket, MA 02554**, founded 1979. The Association puts out two publications which use poetry: *Star*Line*, **a bimonthly magazine, and an annual, *The Rhysling Anthology*.** The magazine is the newsletter of the Association; the anthology is a yearly collection of final nominations from the membership "for the best SF/Fantasy long and short poetry of the preceding year." The Association also publishes a **postcard series and chapbooks**. The magazine has published poetry by Marge Piercy, Bruce Boston, Steve Rasnic Tem, Nancy Springer, Joe Haldeman, Jack Dann. Here are some sample lines from "The Last Planetarium Convention" by Elissa Malcohn:

> *We share our visions like reminiscent gods,*
> *teaching the art of ugly duckling tools*
> *that bedazzle the eyes in spite of themselves*
> *and put miracles in the palm of a hand.*

They have 200 subscribers (1 library) paying $6 for the 6 issues per year (**sample: $1 postpaid**). The editor says he gets two or three hundred submissions per year and uses about 80—**mostly short (under 50 lines). He reports in a month, likes 2-3 poems per submission, typed, single or double spaced, photocopy OK, dot-matrix "difficult but not refused," no simultaneous submissions, no queries, pays $1 for first 10 lines, 5¢/line thereafter**. The digest-sized magazines and anthologies are saddle-stapled, inexpensively printed, with numerous illustrations and decorations. (You can order the **anthology for $1.50**) Robert advises, "Know the language first. Communicate to others (not self). **We're really missing quality rhyme and meter. Light verse can be fun.**"

*SCOPE (IV, Christian women), 426 S. 5th St., Box 1209, Minneapolis, MN 55440, a monthly magazine of the American Lutheran Church women contains Bible study material and articles on women's concerns. They use **"very little" poetry and it must be appropriate to their function and readership. Pays $15-25/poem.**

*SCRIVENER (II), 853 Sherbrooke St. W., Montreal, Quebec, Canada H3A 2T6, founded 1980, produced by students at McGill University, is a literary semiannual, magazine-sized, 40 pp., glossy paper with b/w art and photography, circulation 1,000 (300 subscriptions of which 50 are libraries), which uses **"all types" of poetry**—about 7 pp. per issue. They have published poetry by Lyn Lifshin and Leonard Cohen. As a sample I selected the complete poem, "The Nude" by Antonia Cima:

> They say the artist
> exists in his canvases,
> and that is why
> I pose for you.

They use about 50 of 500 submissions received per year. **Sample: $2 postpaid. Submit 1 poem to a page. Photocopies, simultaneous submissions OK. Reports in 6 months. Pays $3-10 on publication. Editors sometimes comment on rejections.**

THE SEA HORSE PRESS LTD. (IV, Gay), 307 W. 11th St., New York, NY 10014, phone 212-691-9066, founded 1977, poetry editor Felice Picano, is dedicated "to publishing fine and accessible literature **by and for gays—also of interest to a wider literary audience. Gay poetry** *only*. **No erotica or porno. No 'coming out' poetry. Post-liberated** *only*." They have published poetry by Robert Peters, Gavin Dillard, Dennis Cooper, Rudy Kikel and Edward Field—and will be considering MSS again in 1987. **Query with 10-12 samples. No simultaneous submissions. No dot-matrix. Photocopies OK, discs compatible with Spellbinder SS/DS. Reports to queries in 1-3 weeks, submissions (if invited) in 1-3 months. Publishes on 6% royalty contract with $100-750 advance, 10 or more copies. Send SASE for catalog to buy samples.** "We suggest interested authors read at least two of our books before submission to see our tastes and interests."

SECOND COMING PRESS, INTEGRITY TIMES PRESS, *SECOND COMING (II, IV), Box 31249 (118 Laidley St.), San Francisco, CA 94131, founded 1972. A. D. Winans is poetry editor for **this distinguished publishing house and magazine, which has consistently brought out some of the best work from poets (primarily those who began to flourish in the '60s)** such as Charles Bukowski, Lawrence Ferlinghetti, Jack Micheline, Lynne Savitt, Terry Kennedy, Gene Fowler, and Winans himself. For a sample he selected these lines by Josephine Miles:

> The Day the winds went underground I gasped for breath
> Did not you? - oxygen gone from the chest wall,
> Nostrils pinched in the scant weather, strictest
> Sort of equilibrium at street corners.

The fat (96-112 pp.), flat-spined, quality-printed magazine comes out 1-2 times a year in print runs of a thousand or more (300 subscriptions, 100 libraries), and sells for $6 (but you can get a **sample for $3**). Winans says he gets over a thousand submissions a year, "uses 90% unsolicited work, 75% coming from writers who know of us and have read us over the years." He **reports in 1 day to 4 weeks. Any clear copy will do, but please let them know if it is submitted elsewhere. Sometimes accepts reprints (but query). Payment: 2 copies.** Second Coming Press publishes a chapbook (48 pp.)and a paperback (46-64 pp.) per year. **To submit for book consideration, send a sample of 6 poems and "brief background, including past credits and publications, including any awards."** If your book is published, you'll get **10% of the print run in copies—and "sometimes small honorarium if grant is involved**." In 1986 they started a poetry chapbook contest (48-pages maximum) with publication in 1987. They will repeat the procedure annually with publication in 1988, etc. Write for further information. The Second Coming Poetry and Fiction Book Contest has been discontinued. In 1984 Winans began Integrity Times Press "to publish occasional books, broadsides and postcards of 'political' importance to our times." The first book published by Integrity Times Press was Winans' own **The Regan Psalms** from which he selected these sample lines from "The Reagan Beatitudes":

> 1. blessed are the rich
> for they shall become richer

> 2. *blessed are the poor*
> *for they shall help the*
> *rich become richer*

Query with 6 samples and list of credits if you believe you have poetry relevent to their aims and goals. Sample of The Reagan Beatitudes (50% off): $3.50 plus $1.25 postage and handling. The editor advises, "There is a lot of political poetry being written today, but 99% of it isn't worth the paper it's written on. Will the poem endure and does it have something SIGNIFICANT to say is the question to ask yourself before submitting it to us, indeed before writing it. Study your market. We receive too many manuscripts from beginning writers who have no idea of what *Second Coming* is all about—such as religious and hardcore "porno" material, suggesting the poet is submitting to a NAME and not a publication."

*SEEMS (II), Box 359, Lakeland College, Sheboygan, WI 53081, founded 1971, published irregulary (18 issues in 13 years). This is a handsomely printed, nearly square (7x8¼") magazine, saddle-stapled, generous with white space on heavy paper. Two of the issues are considered chapbooks, and the editor, Karl Elder, suggests that a way **to get acquainted would be to order** *Seems #14, What Is The Future Of Poetry?* **for $3**, consisting of essays by 22 contemporary poets, and "If you don't like it, return it, and we'll return your $3." There are usually about 15 pages of poetry per issue. Karl Elder says, "**For a clear idea of what I'm after by way of submissions, see my essay 'The Possibilites of Poetry'** in #19-20, a special double issue of poetry." He has used poetry by Ed Engle, Jr., James Finnegan, J. B. Goodenough, Ernest Kroll and Walter MacDonald. He said it was "impossible" to select four illustrative lines, so I chose one of his own poems (in *Seems #16*):

> *"Crow's Feet (to Thomas James)"*
> *No sooner than vision*
> *began to ripen,*
> *the ravenous black dream*
> *straddled your eyes.*

The magazine has a print run of 350 for 150 subscriptions (40 libraries) and sells for $3 an issue (or $12 for a subscription—four issues). There is a **1-2 year backlog, reports in 1-8 weeks, pays copies.**

‡*SELF AND SOCIETY; EUROPEAN JOURNAL OF HUMANISTIC PSYCHOLOGY (IV, Humansitic psychology), 62 Southwark Bridge Road, London SE1 0A4, England, founded 1973, editor Vivian Milroy, a small-press publisher of "specialist material covering humansitic psychology and human potential; area includes human relationships, spiritual and esoteric experiences." The magazine is bi-monthly and prints **"occasional" poems relevant to these themes;** the issue I have contains two. As a sample, I selected these lines from "Myself I Sing" by Ann Castling:

> *I am a fernleaf, curled and uncurling,*
> *I am an embryo taking on form*
> *From the seed of my selfhood deeply embedded*
> *The sum of my being is born*

The digest-sized journal, about 56 pp., is offset with one b/w decoration, one-color matte card cover, saddle-stapled. Circulation is 2,500, of which 15 go to libraries and about 80 are newsstand sales. Subscription is $12/year. **Sample available for $3 postpaid. Pay is 5-10 offprints. Reporting time is 3 months and time to publication is 2-6 months after reporting. The editor wants "simplicity, honesty, relevance."**

SERPENT & EAGLE PRESS, SWAMP PRESS (II), 1 Dietz St., Oneonta, NY 13820, phone 607-432-5604, founded 1981, poetry editor Jo Mish. "Our aim is to print fine limited letterpress editions of titles worth printing in all subject areas." In poetry they like "Imagist—Ezra Pound's not Amy Lowell's type." They have published poetry by Jo Mish, Robert Bensen and Mike Newell. The chapbooks I have seen from this press are, indeed, elegantly designed and printed on handmade paper with hand-sewn wrappers. **For book consideration, query with 5 samples. No simultaneous submissions. Photocopy, dot-matrix OK. Pays 10 copies and $100 honorarium. Send SASE for catalog to buy samples.**

SEVEN, THE JESSE STUART CONTEST (II), 3630 NW 22, Oklahoma City, OK 73107-2893, founded 1930, poetry editor James Neill Northe. *Seven* is a 12 pp. digest-sized leaflet which appears irregularly, each issue with 7 poems. **Sample: $2. Pays $5/poem on acceptance. "*Please* no amateur verse. Study your market. Universal approach, no cataloging, but definite expression in finely written lines. Not impressed by the 'chopped prose' school or 'stream of consciousness' effusions."** As a sample, I chose the concluding lines of "Dream Doers" by Jesse Stuart:

> *Dream doers know the last is with them now*
> *When they must never let the dream escape;*

> *By watching those defeated youth learn how*
> *In their young years to forge good dreams in shape.*

The magazine conducts an annual, international Jesse Stuart Contest "for the best unpublished poems in the JESSE STUART tradition; any form or free verse; no restrictions as to length." Send SASE for contest rules and guidelines for *Seven*.

SEVEN BUFFALOES PRESS, HILL AND HOLLER ANTHOLOGY SERIES, BLACK JACK, VALLEY GRAPEVINE, *HARD ROW TO HOE (IV, Rural, regional/American West, Central California)**, Box 249, Big Timber, MT 59011, founded 1973. *Black Jack & Valley Grapevine* is an annual in 2 parts, circulation 750. *Black Jack* **uses rural material from anywhere, especially the American West;** *Valley Grapevine* **uses rural material from central California. They use poetry from these areas on rural themes. Sample: $4. Hill and Holler, Southern Appalachian Mountain series takes in rural mountain lifestyle and folkways. Sample copy: $4.** Seven Buffaloes Press does not accept unsolicited MSS but publishes books solicited from writers who have appeared in the magazines.

***SEVENTEEN (IV, Teen, teenage authors)**, 850 3rd Ave., New York, NY 10022, phone 212-759-8100, founded 1944, poetry editor Susan Butler Evans, is a slick monthly, circulation 1,750,000, for teenage girls which is open to "**all styles of poetry up to 40 lines by teenagers on subjects of interest to teens. We publish work by new young poets in every issue.**" Purchase sample ($1.50) at newsstands. **Reports in 4-6 weeks. Pays $10-25. Send SASE for guidelines.** They receive about 3,000 submissions per year, use 24-30, have a 12-18 month backlog.

***SEWANEE REVIEW (III), University of the South, Sewanee, TN 37375, founded 1892, thus being our nation's oldest continuously published literary quarterly, and one of the most awesome in reputation.** George Core is editor, Mary Lucia Cornelius, Managing Editor. Each of the four issues per year is a hefty paperback of nearly 200 pages, conservatively bound in matte paper, always of the same typography. Fiction, criticism and poetry are invariably of the **highest establishment standards. Poet Donald Hall once commented: "Writers tremble to submit to the *Sewanee Review*, for fear that the editor may discover them in a solecism**. For this reason, the bravest will send their work to *Sewanee*, finding editorial severity preferable to the embarrassment of perpetuated error. It is **the most *edited* of American quarterlies**." Most of our major poets appear here from time to time. Recent issues contain poetry by Howard Nemerov, John N. Morris and David Solway. In Paul Lindholdt's poem "Traveler to the Colonies" the sailor speaks to the 'flattering sea':

> *I will make me a cedar cabin*
> *At Hell's Gate, and there rest*
> *Cloistered from your strumpet ways.*
> *I will write the truth about this land*
> *And warn my countrymen to guard their eyes.*

In 1985 they had a total of 4,110 submissions and published 1.3% of the poems submitted. Circulation: 3,400. **Sample $4.75, pays 70¢/line, reports in 1-4 weeks.**

‡***SF SPECTRUM, *MACABRE (I, IV, Supernatural, science fiction, fantasy)**, 14 Sheerstock, Haddenham, Nr Aylesbury, Bucks HP 17 8EN, England, phone 01144 844 291996, founded in 1981, editor/publisher Wieslaw Tumulka, who says, "*SF Spectrum* publishes sci-fi, science fantasy, speculative fiction; *Macabre* publishes horror/fantasy/supernatural. **Length of poetry is up to the poet, subject matter must cover one of the areas listed above and style is also up to the poet. The purpose of the poetry should be to entertain and interest the reader.**" Poets he has published recently include Steve Sneyd, Christina Kiplinger, and Vonnie Crist. As a sample, I selected the beginning lines from "Lure of the Incubus" by t. Winter-Damon:

> *You who look on me—despair!*
> *Chaste temptress with your raven's hair*
> *That glistens with its blue-black sheen*
> *Behold the shimmering darkness of these gently beating*
> *wings*

SF Spectrum, which appears bi-monthly, is digest-sized offset from typed copy (very densely printed on the page), 22 pp., ordinary paper, folded and saddle-stapled, with one-color matte card cover decorated with a drawing in black. Circulation is 100-125, of which 85 are subscriptions. Price per issue is $1.25, subscription $7.50/year. **Sample available for $1.25 surface mail or $2.25 airmail. Pay is 1-3 copies.** *Macabre* appears quarterly. It is digest-sized, again very densely printed on thin paper, 15 pp. folded and saddle-stapled with one-color cover of the same paper, b/w illustration. **All submissions should include a brief note giving details about themselves (if they've had poetry published before, etc.)." No simultaneous submissions. Previously printed poetry will be considered if it was published at least 2 years prior to submission. "An airmail reply will be sent out within 48 hours."**

Time to publication is 1-2 issues. The editor says, *"SF Spectrum* (and *Macabre*) welcome any poets who wish to contribute . . . One of my aims is to print as many different poets of real worth that I genuinely believe could make it to the big time. [We] are ready and waiting for you to make that first important step on the way to success."

THE SHAKESPEARE NEWSLETTER (IV, Shakespeare), 1217 Ashland Ave., Chicago Circle, Evanston, IL 60202, founded 1951, editor Louis Marder, is a 12 pp. quarterly of short scholarly articles, abstracts of articles and lectures, notes and reviews which also uses some **poetry related to and inspired by Shakespeare and/ or Shakespeare studies. Poetry which is inspired by Shakespeare's plays, characters, critics which give new insights are welcome. No parodies of the sonnets or of "To be, or not to be," etc.** The editor chose as a sample the first five lines of "Ophelia" by Jean Cothary:

> *Love gone awry can wound the mind.*
> *A lover distracted.*
> *A brother gone,*
> *and all meaning shifts.*

"I am not an anthologist but I might print a short pithy poem in print if I thought it worthy to show to my 200 readers." Payment in 3 copies. Sample $1.50.

‡**SHAMAL BOOKS (IV, Ethnic)**, GPO Box 16, New York, NY 10116, phone 718-622-4426, founded 1976, editor Louis Reyes Rivera. Shamal Books is a small press whose purpose is **"to promote the literary efforts of African-American and Caribbean writers, particularly those who would not otherwise be able to establish their literary credentials as their concerns as artists are with the people."** The press publishes individual and "anthological" books and chapbooks, mostly flat-spined paper texts. Some poets recently published are SeKou Sundiata, Sandra Maria Esteves, Rashidah Ismaili, and the editor. As a sample, he selected the following lines by Zizwe Ngafua:

> *Tis the truth of cotton farms and*
> *muddied bloodied Mississippi rivers and tamborine blues*

The editor wants to see **"poetry that clearly demonstrates an understanding of craft, content, and intent as the scriptural source of the word guiding and encouraging the intellect of the people."** He does not consider freelance submissions of individual MSS, but will look at work only while anthologies are open. How many sample poems should you send? **"two is cool."** The cover letter should include a "leaning toward personal goals and poetic principles." The editor will reply to queries within 2 months; MSS of poetry should be **"neat and single-spaced." Royalties for book authors are 15%. The editor says that he will subsidy publish "delicately—depends on resources and interest in work."** His future projects include "an international anthology; drama; prison anthology; books on language as a weapon; a collectivized publisher's catalog of Third World presses working out of NYC." His advice to poets is, "Certainly to study the craft more and to research more into the historical role that has been the hallmark of poetry across class and caste conscious lines that limit younger perspectives. Not to be as quick to publish as to be in serious study, then while looking to publish, looking as well into collective ventures with other poets for publication and distribution. Above all, *READ!*"

SHAMELESS HUSSY PRESS (IV, Feminist), Box 3092, Berkeley, CA 94703, phone 415-547-1062, founded 1969, poetry editor Alta, is a **"feminist literary"** publisher. They want poetry which is *"feminist, yes. Sexist, racist, classist, ageist, etc., no. "* They have recently published books of poetry by Marilyn Krysl, Barbara Noda and John Oliver Simon. I selected these sample lines from **Neither of Us Can Break the Other's Hold: Poems For My Father** by John Oliver Simon:

> *I smoke*
> *in a sunny room*
> *wondering at my feelings*
> *& wait for a telephone to say*
> *you've gone back*
> *inside the darkness.*

For book publication, **query with about 5 samples. Reply to query in 6 months, to submission (if invited) in 6 months. Simultaneous submissions, photocopies OK. Pays 100 copies plus 10-12% net. Send SASE for catalog to buy samples.**

‡*SHARING THE VICTORY (IV, Christian athletes)**, 8701 Leeds Road, Kansas City, MO 64129, phone 816-921-0909, founded 1959, editor Skip Stogsdill. The bi-monthly magazine (circulation 47,000) is published by the Fellowship of Christian Athletes and uses only 2-3 poems/year. **They want free verse on themes of interest to Christian athletes. Pay is $15-30. Sample available for $1 with 8½x11" SASE (first class stamps for 3 oz.) Guidelines available free. Reporting time is 2 weeks and time to publication averages 3-4 months.**

‡HAROLD SHAW PUBLISHERS, WHEATON LITERARY SERIES (IV, Christian), Box 567, 388 Gundersen Dr., Wheaton, IL 60189, phone 312-665-6700, founded 1967, poetry editor Ramona C. Cramer, publishes anthologies and collections of poetry (1/year) which are "**fresh, innovative, 20th century, written from an evangelical perspective—poems that challenge living faith and meet the needs of Christians in today's world.**" **They do not want "trite 'my feelings' poems, hymns or devotional ramblings which some consider to be poetry.**" They have recently published poetry by Luci Shaw, Madelene L. Engle, John Leax, Sister Maura Eichner, Jean Janzen, Eugene H. Petersen, Chad Walsh and Eugene Warren. The editor selected these sample lines by Ruth El Saffar:

> *This body, servant*
> *to a begging bowl,*
> *battered in marketplace bustle,*
> *has toughened to the taunts,*
> *has turned to stone.*

That appears in a digest-sized, flat-spined, professionally printed anthology with glossy card cover, white with color type and painting: **A Widening Light: Poems of the Incarnation**, $6.95. They **accept freelance submissions for anthologies, but use mostly established poets. Send 2-3 sample poems with bio. "We will only seriously look at poets who have already published in many journals or magazines and have established a wide reading audience."** Simultaneous submissions, photocopy OK, no dot-matrix. Payment varies, depending on author, type of book or anthology. Editor sometimes comments on rejected MSS. Book catalog available. To order samples, call 1-800-SHAW-PUB. Ramona Cramer advises, "Be *concrete!* Too many 'poems' use abstract thoughts and feelings that may mean something to the author but convey nothing to the reader or his world."

‡*SHAWNEE SILHOUETTE (I), Shawnee State College, 940 Second St., Portsmouth, OH 45662, phone 614-354-3205, founded 1985, poetry editor Teresa Lodwick, a literary quarterly that publishes poetry, prose, art work, and photography and occasionally sponsors a poetry contest with an entry fee of $1/poem and a grand prize of $10. The editors want "**Any subject done in good taste; conventional, blank, and free verse forms; no restriction on length or subject matter, except no erotica.**" The issue I have contains work by sixteen different poets; as a sample the editors chose the following lines (poet unidentified):

> *I hear*
> *The voice of the river*
> *Calling me,*
> *Gentle waves whispering*
> *In soft tones . . .*

Shawnee Silhouette is digest-sized, offset from typed copy on fairly thin paper with b/w drawings and photographs, titles done in calligraphy, 40 pp. saddle-stapled, matte card cover with b/w decoration. It is published 3 times/year (fall, winter, and spring). Single copy price is $2, subscriptions $5/year. **Pay is 1 copy. Send 3 poems per mailing; typed double-spaced, no simultaneous submissions. Reporting time is normally 3 months and time to publication is 6 months.** The editors say, "We are interested only in quality material and try to provide a diversity of styles and topics in each issue."

*SHENANDOAH (II), Box 722, Lexington, VA 24450, founded 1950, fiction editor James Boatwright and editor Richard Howard, is one of the longest-standing literary quarterlies, one where some of my own early poems appeared in the '50s. They have recently published poetry by Richard Wilbur, Daniel Hoffman, Amy Clampitt, Joyce Carol Oates, Irving Feldman. The 100 pp. magazine is 6x9", circulation 1,000. **Sample: $3.50. Photocopy OK.**

‡*SHITEPOKE (II), Box 1086, Fairbanks AK 99707, founded 1983, editor Bob Ross, is "a very serious literary magazine," as it says on its cover. "**Very open as to form and content, looking for best contemporary work that doesn't take itself with life-and-death seriousness, do not want to see light verse, 'humor'.**" The editor selected these sample lines, poet unidentified:

> *That might have been the restoration of a potholder*
> *to its proper place on the kitchen pegboard*
> *as a favor to the Irish cook*
> *whose mother's name is Peg*

The digest-sized, flat-spined, 70 pp. review appears "sporadically." It is professionally printed (offset), with b/w glossy card cover, b/w photography and graphics. Circulation about 250. They have "five or six" subscriptions. **Sample: $4 postpaid. Pays 2 copies. "I do hate dot-matrix printing."** Bob Ross's advice to poets: "Stand up straight. Tuck in your shirttail. Eat your spinach. Get your teaching certificate first. Don't marry that dumb blonde. Start a savings account. Don't get your feet wet. Be sure your socks match."

THE SIGNPOST PRESS, *THE BELLINGHAM REVIEW (II), 412 N. State St., Bellingham, WA 98225, phone 206-734-9781, founded 1975, magazine editor Randy Jay Landon; book editor Knute Skinner. Publishes *The Bellingham Review* twice a year, runs an annual poetry chapbook competition, and publishes other books and chapbooks of poetry occasionally. "**We want well-crafted poetry but are open to all styles,**" **no specifications as to form.** Poets they have published recently include Paul Shuttleworth, Joseph Green, Sybil James, Phyllis Janik, Laurie Taylor, Stan Hodson and Marjorie Power. As a sample, Knute Skinner selected these lines by Richard Martin:

> Poets dwell too much
> on death.
> It's a sad occupation,
> with the obvious benefits.

Each issue of the *Review* has about 38 pp. of poetry. They have a circulation of 700, 500 subscriptions. It's a digest-sized, saddle-stapled, small-type, with art and glossy cover (**sample: $2 postpaid**). **Submit between September 1 and May 1 up to 10 pp. Photocopy, simultaneous submissions OK. Reports in 1-2 months, pays 1 copy plus a year's subscription**. Send SASE for rules for the chapbook competition and query regarding book publication.

*SILVER WINGS (I, IV, Christian), Box 5201, Mission Hills, CA 91345, phone 818-893-2889, founded 1983, poetry editor Jackson Wilcox. "As a committed Christian service we produce and publish a quarterly poetry magazine. We want **poems with a Christian perspective, reflecting a vital personal faith and a love for God and man. Will consider poems from 3-20 lines. Quite open in regard to meter and rhyme**." They have recently published poems by Michele J. Charvet, Ken Stone, Carmelita McKeever, Real Faucher. The editor chose these sample lines from "The Call," by Donna Miesbach:

> To know the truth
> When sense denies,
> To raise the thought
> And doubt defy,
> To see the Light
> Where all seems dark
> And, ever trusting,
> Love impart—

The 24 pp. magazine is digest-sized, offset from typescript with hand-lettered titles on tinted paper with cartoon-like art, circulation 350, 75 subscriptions. They receive 400 submissions per year, use 110. "Right now I have material enough for 2 issues, but will look at seasonal things right up to the last minute." Subscription: $5.10; per copy: $1.50. **Sample: $1 postpaid. Typed MSS, double-spaced. Reports in 3 weeks. Pays 5 copies. Occasionally comments on rejections**. The editor says, "If a poet has had a faith experience, share it freely from the heart, using whatever words are warm and expressive. Thus the shared message becomes a powerful communication to bless others."

*SILVERFISH REVIEW, SILVERFISH REVIEW PRESS (II), Box 3541, Eugene, OR 97403, phone 503-342-2344, founded 1979, poetry editor Rodger Moody, is an irregularly appearing digest-sized 48 pp. literary magazine, circulation 500. "The only criteria for selection is **quality. In future issues** *Silverfish Review* **wants to showcase translations of poetry from Europe and Latin America** as well as continue to print poetry and fiction of quality written in English." They have recently published poetry by John Woods, Dick Allen, Ivan Arguelles, D. M. Wallace, Debra Gregor, Melinda Kahn, Mary Tisera and Katharyn Machan Aal. As a sample the editor selected these lines by Edward Harkness:

> I think I understand how you
> all must have felt.
> I, too, have mixed feelings
> about mixed feelings.

There are 36-48 pp. of poetry in each issue. The magazine is professionally printed in dark type on quality, printed stock, matte card cover with art. Subscription: for institution $9; per issue: $3. They receive about 450 submissions of poetry per year, use 20, have a 6-12 month backlog. **Sample: $3 postpaid. Submit at least 5 poems to editor. Photocopies OK. No simultaneous submissions. Reports in 6 weeks. Pays 3 copies**. Silverfish Review Press will consider MSS for chapbook publication and conducts an annual chapbook competition with an award of $250 and 25 copies (with a press run of 250). Send SASE for rules.

*SING HEAVENLY MUSE! (IV, Feminist), Box 13299, Minneapolis, MN 55414, founded 1977, editor Sue Ann Martinson, fosters "the work of women poets, fiction writers, and artists. The magazine is feminist in an open, generous sense: we encourage women to range freely, honestly, and imaginatively over all subjects, philosophies, and styles. We do not wish to confine women to women's subjects, whether these are defined traditionally, in terms of femininity and domesticity, or modernly, from a sometimes narrow polemical perspective. We look for explorations, questions that do not come with ready-made answers, emotionally or intellectually. We seek out new writers, many before unpublished. The editors try to reduce to a minimum the common bureaucratic distance between a magazine and its readers and contributors. Although our staff is small, we encourage writers by discussing their work, and we solicit comments from our readers. This relationship makes *Sing Heavenly Muse!* a community where women with widely varying interests and ideas may meet and learn from one another.'' For poetry they have "**no limitations except women's writing.**" They have recently published poetry by Ellen Bass, Linda Hogan, Sharon Doubiago, Roberta Swarm and Patricia Hampl. The editor selected these sample lines by Linda Hogan:

> All bridges of flesh, all singing,
> all covering the wounded land,
> showing again, again
> that all boundaries are lies.

The magazine appears two or three times a year in a 6x9'' flat-spined, 125 pp. format, offset from type-script on heavy stock, b/w art, glossy card color cover, circulation 2,000, 275 subscriptions of which 40 are libraries. Subscription: $17 (3 issues); per copy: $6. They receive 1,500 + submissions per year, use 50-60, have a 5-6 month backlog. **Sample: $3.50 postpaid. Submit 3-10 pp., name and address on each page. Photocopy OK. No simultaneous submissions. Reports in 1-3 months, pays "usually $25 plus 2 copies." Generally accepts manuscripts for consideration in April and September. Inquire about special issues, contests. Send SASE for guidelines. Editors sometimes comment on rejections.**

SINGULAR SPEECH PRESS (II), 10 Hilltop Dr., Canton, CT 06019, phone 203-693-6059, founded 1976, editor Don D. Wilson. "This press began as a means of publishing the editor's verse translations, and it has continued, so far, along this line. It would be amenable to publishing other good poetry, however in stapled paperback chapbooks. I like **traditional and non-conventional verse, verse translations, any imaginative poetry—from haiku to sonnet and beyond, tightly written—anything good, but no self-indulgent stuff.**" As a sample he chose his translation from Omar Khayyam's Persian (with assistance):

> How sad youth's chapters have been riffled through;
> But yesterday the spring of life was new!
> That bird whose name was Youth, that joyous bird—
> I don't know when it came, alas, or flew!

For chapbook consideration, **query with a dozen or so samples, publication credits and bio. MS should be typed, double-spaced. Simultaneous submission, photocopies OK. Send for sample and list. Editor comments on rejections.**

‡*SINISTER WISDOM (IV, Lesbian, feminist), Box 1308, Monpelier, VT 05602, phone 802-229-9104, founded 1976, editor and publisher Melanie Kaye/Kantrowitz, a lesbian feminist journal. The editor says, "**We want poetry that reflects the diversity of women's experience—women of color, Third World, Jewish, old, young, working class, poor, disabled, fat, etc.—from a lesbian and/or feminist perspective. No heterosexual themes. We will not print anything that is oppressive or demeaning to women, or which perpetuates negative stereotypes.**" The journal has recently published work by Paula Gunn Allen, Cheryl Clarke, and Irena Klipfisz, from whose "I cannot swim" the editor chose the following lines as a sample:

> I cannot swim   but my parents
> say the land is less safe. And
> the first day the water was smooth
> like a slate I could walk on.

The quarterly magazine is digest-sized, 128 pp. flat-spined, with photos and b/w graphics; I have not seen it. Circulation is 3,500 of which 1,000 are subscriptions and 100 go to libraries; newsstand sales are 100. Price per issue is $4.75, subscription $15 US, $17 foreign. **Sample available for $5.75 postpaid. Pay is 2 copies. No simultaneous submissions. Reporting time is 6 months and time to publication 6 months-1 year.**

*SLIPSTREAM (II), Box 2071, New Market Station, Niagara Falls, NY 14301, phone 716-282-2616, founded 1980, poetry editors Dan Sicoli and Robert Borgatti, publishes "poetry and short fiction which reflects **contemporary urban lifestyles** although we hate to limit ourselves. Modern 'urban' poetry. No rhymes for sake of rhyming. No religious. We lean toward a contemporary feel rather than traditional. No line length restrictions. All styles but rarely use rhyming verse. No subject taboo except religious." They have recently published poetry by Arthur W. Knight, David Chorlton, Charles Bukowski, Todd Moore, Ron Androla, Belinda Subraman, Kurt Nimmo and Joe Semenovich. The editors

selected these sample lines by Emid Shomer:
> *where in shotgun houses*
> *tired men dream and wait*
> *for a woman*
> *whose car breaks down.*

Slipstream appears 1-2 times a year, 8½x7" format professionally printed, saddle-stapled, using b/w graphics, circulation 300, 200 subscriptions of which 10 are libraries. About 60 of the 80 + pp. are devoted to poetry. They receive about 700 freelance submissions of poetry per year, use 10%. **Sample: $3 postpaid. Reports in 2-8 weeks. Pays copies. Send SASE for guidelines. Some issues are on announced themes—e.g., for 1987, an "erotica/porn" issue is planned. Also producing an audio cassette series. Query for current needs. Query for current needs.**

‡**SLOUGH PRESS (II)**, Box 1385, Austin, TX 78767, editor Jim Cole, a small-press publisher of books of poetry, fiction, and non-fiction—chapbooks, flat-spined paperbacks, and hardcover books. **There are no limits on the type of poetry accepted; it must be "just good."** The editor says it is "too boring" to select a sample of the kind of poetry he publishes, and I have not seen any of his books, but he lists as some of the better-known poets published lately Cid Corman, Edward Field, Ricardo Sanchez, and Chuck Taylor. He publishes 3 books/year with an average page count of 60, digest-sized. **Freelance submissions are accepted. Writers should send 6 sample poems with credits and bio. Submissions will be reported on in 2 weeks. Simultaneous submissions and photocopied MSS are OK. Payment "varies with author."**

‡*SLOW DANCER, SLOW DANCER PRESS (II)**, Box 149A, RFD 1, Lubec, ME 04652, founded 1977, associate American editor Alan Brooks. *Slow Dancer* is an international magazine of English-language poetry published by John Harvey in Nottingham, England (address: 19 Devonshire Promenade, Lenton, Nottingham NG7); Slow Dancer Press publishes (very) occasional chapbooks of poetry and prose. The editor says, **"All types, lengths, subjects [of poetry] considered. We prefer to print multiple selections from contributors if the poems are sufficiently strong. We look for freshness of image and language, clarity and individuality, whatever the subject. We encourage submissions from previously unpublished poets and always judge the poem, not the 'name.' Prospective contributors should buy a sample copy if they want to learn our preferences. We will reject all poems which display knee-jerk alienation, cutesy formalism, or New Yorker-ese, as well as those which come with a cover letter explaining what they really mean."** He has recently published poems by Jack Anderson, David Kresh, Barry MacSweeney, Libby Houston, and Li Min Hua. As a sample, he selected the following lines from "Moonvines" by Nancy Nielseñ:
> *Under the moonvine shade, I sailed my summers.*
> *My grandfather walked west, toward the wheat;*
> *the freights slid through our small town*
> *and whistled my father away.*

Most issues of *Slow Dancer* "feature a mix of British and North American writers, with a smattering of writers (in English) from all over." The magazine is digest-sized, offset from typed copy, light peach-colored stock, some line drawings and photographs, 48 pp., saddle-stapled with two-color matte card cover. Circulation is about 500, of which approximately 300 are subscriptions. Price per copy is $2.50/ subscription $8/4 issues (2 years). **Sample available for $1 postpaid. Pay is 3 copies. Poems, previously unpublished, should be submitted one to a page, photocopy or dot-matrix OK if clear, simultaneous submissions OK. Reporting time is 2 months and accepted poems are published in the following issue.** Slow Dancer Press publishes 1 or 2 chapbooks of poetry per year, 12-48 pp., format like that of the magazine, but **freelance submissions for chapbooks are not accepted. "We publish manuscripts by poets who have regular appearances in the magazine." Pay is in author's copies.** The editor says, "Write what you like. Read the mag. If what you see connects with what you've got, send some poems. If not, try elsewhere. *Don't* send 3-page resumes of your life and works. *Do* check your spelling. And don't forget, you can always self-publish; Aunt Maud will love it."

*SMALL POND MAGAZINE OF LITERATURE, CIDER MILL PRESS (I, II)**, Box 664, Stratford, CT 06497, phone 203-378-4066, founded 1964, poetry editor Napoleon St. Cyr, a literary triquarterly that features poetry . . . "and anything else the editor feels is original, important." Poetry can be **"any style, form, topic, so long as it is deemed good, except haiku, but poems limit of about 100 lines."** Napoleon St. Cyr wants **"nothing about cats, pets, flowers, butterflies, etc. Generally nothing under 8 lines."** Although he calls it name-dropping, he "reluctantly" provided the names of Heather Tosteson, Deborah Boe, Richard Kostelanetz, Fritz Hamilton, and Emilie Glen as poets recently published. He preferred not to supply sample lines, but I have, from a recent issue, selected the opening stanza of "Corrida," by James Sallis:
> *The bull cannot find its wound.*

> *Again and again it lurches*
> *into the space where the wound*
> *should be, but the man's large feet*
> *bear it away each time.*

The magazine is digest-sized, offset from typescript on off-white paper, 40 pp. with matte card cover, saddle-stapled, art work both on cover and inside. Circulation is 300-325, of which about half go to libraries. Price per issue is $2.50; subscription $6.25 (for 3 issues). **Sample: $2 postpaid for a random selection. Guidelines are available in each issue. Pay is two copies. The editor says he doesn't want 60 pages of anything; dozen pages of poem max."** He reports on submissions in 3-15 days (longer in summer), and publication is within 3-18 months. Cider Mill Press publishes a poetry volume "once in a while—when money allows." No freelance submissions are accepted; poets must have a considerable number of magazine credits.

‡*THE SMALL TOWNER (II)**, Box 182, Glen Arbor, MI 49636, phone 616-334-4968, poetry editor William Shaw, contact editor Marianne Russell, is a quarterly magazine featuring articles on the environment, the arts, and interesting personalities, and includes fiction and poetry. **They will consider any kind of poetry that isn't sentimental.** The editor selected these sample lines from "The Running of the Mice" by Tom McKeown:

> *All night I hear small feet padding between walls.*
> *Sometimes there is a sudden stampede as if there has been*
> *an intrusion into their world. I think of mice walking*
> *all winter down lightless paths. shivering.*

The quarterly is magazine-sized, elegantly printed on heavy, glossy stock, using b/w and color graphics and photography and ads, 48-64 pp., saddle-stapled, circulation 3,000, 600 subscriptions of which 6 are libraries. $2.50 per issue, $10 subscription. **Sample: $3 postpaid. Pays $20/poem and up to 6 copies. Reports in 8-12 weeks. They have a 2 year backlog. Editor comments on rejections "if warranted."**

THE SMITH PUBLISHERS, *PULPSMITH MAGAZINE, THE GENERALIST ASSN. (II), 5 Beekman St., New York, NY 10038, founded 1964, Harry Smith publisher, Joe Lazarus poetry editor. "Especially dedicated to discovery of new talent and to humanistically-oriented subject matter. We publish the quarterly *Pulpsmith* (poetry, fiction, essays) plus a few books a year. As for poetry, **we like narrative, but not prosey, discursive poems. We like strong, original imagery in lyric poems. Our motto is, 'anything goes as long as it's good.' Please, no more than 5 pages at a time**." They have recently published poetry by Celia Watson Strome, Jared Smith and Menke Katz. *Pulpsmith* appears in a 5x7" 200 pp. format, pulp stock, flat-spined, circulation 6,000-7,000. **Pays $20-50 per poem plus 2 copies. Reports in 4-8 weeks.**

*SMOKE, WINDOWS PROJECT (II)**, 22 Roseheath Dr., Halewood, Liverpool, England L26 9UH, founded 1974, poetry editor Dave Ward, appears 2-3 times per year, digest-sized, 20 pp., b/w graphics, paper cover, circulation 1,500, 800 subscriptions of which 10 are libraries. They have recently published poetry by Douglas Dunn, Lorena Cassady, Matt Simpson and Frances Horovitz. Subscriptions: £1 for 4 issues (plus postage for foreign mailing); per issue 15p plus postage. They use about 50 of 1,000 submissions received annually. **Sample: 40p postpaid. Submit up to 6 poems. Simultaneous submissions, photocopy OK. Name and address on each poem. Reports "as soon as possible," pays £5 per contributor. Editor comments on rejections "only if asked to and if I've something helpful to say."**

*SNAPDRAGON (II, IV, Local material)**, English Dept., University of Idaho, Moscow, ID 83843, founded 1977, is a literary biannual, saddle-stapled, digest-sized, circulation 200, using at least **50% local material (college and community), but also open to contributions from outsiders. Simultaneous submissions OK. Sample: $2. Pays 1 copy.**

*SNOWY EGRET (IV, Nature)**, 205 S. 9th St., Williamsburg, KY 40769, phone 606-549-0850, founded 1922, poetry and fiction editor (to whom MSS should be addressed) Alan Seaburg, 67 Century St., W. Medford, MA 02155, is a semiannual mimeographed nature magazine which has persisted for over 60 years, regularly using poetry since 1952. **No restrictions on poetry "as long as it is about nature."** They have recently used poems by Dan Stryk, Richard Behm and Norma Farber. The editor selected these sample lines by Carole Glasser:

> *A beautiful bird*
> *flies through the garden. Its wings*
> *are the color of orange blossoms.*
> *You wake and the room is scented with orange.*

There are 3-10 pp. of poetry (of a total of 50 + magazine-sized pp.) in each issue, circulation 400. Subscription: $6. **Sample back copy: $2 postpaid. Photocopies, dot-matrix OK. Reports in 4-6 weeks. Pays $2/poem, $4 per magazine page on publication plus checking copy. Send SASE for guidelines.**

SOBRIETY HOUSE (II), Box 789, Station F, Toronto, Canada M4M 1H1, founded 1984, poetry editors j w curry, Mark Laba, Lillian Necakov and Stuart Ross, is a new endeavor which has so far published only one leaflet anthology of poetry by the editors, **Emo** (which you can order for a dollar, postpaid), but they are open to submissions of book MSS. **Send sample with covering letter. Replies "soonish." No simultaneous submissions. Dot-matrix OK. Terms negotiable.**

*SOCIAL ANARCHISM (IV, Political), 2743 Maryland Ave., Baltimore, MD 21218, founded (Vacant Lots Press) 1980, poetry editors Susan White and Howard J. Ehrlich, is a digest-sized 80 pp. biannual, printrun 1,000, using about 10 pp. of poetry in each issue which **"represents a political or social commentary that is congruent with a nonviolent anarchist and feminist perspective."** Issue #9 has poems by Paul Muolo, W.K. Buckley and Elsen Lubetsky. Sample is from "Greetings and/or Solicitations" by Elsen Lubetsky:

> *The world looks to you/me*
> *for a contribution to its/our*
> *existence. I look out*
> *see no golden daffodils but*
> *a host of misery: the*
> *daily mail is humanity's cry.*

Sample: $2.50 postpaid. Submit "not in crayon." Considers simultaneous submissions. Reports in 2-4 weeks. Pays in copies.

SOJOURNER (IV, Women), 143 Albany St., Cambridge, MA 02139, founded 1975, poetry editor Beverly J. Smith, is a 44 pp. national monthly tabloid providing an **open forum for writing by women of particular interest to women.** They have recently used poetry by Marge Piercy, Olga Broumas and Ruth Whitman. As a sample I chose these lines from "Still Unborn" by Kathi Gleason:

> *Each month, I let my blood go,*
> *casual as clockwork,*
> *the sudden stain, the ritual*
> *evidence, the child*
> *I keep choosing to not have.*

The newspaper has a printrun of 15,000, 3,000 subscriptions of which 10% are libraries. Subscription: $1.50 per copy. **Sample: $1.75 postpaid. Submit maximum of 4 pp. Photocopy, dot-matrix, simultaneous submissions OK. Reports in 1-2 months. Pays subscription plus 2 copies. Editors sometimes comment on rejections.**

SOMRIE PRESS (IV, Regional/Brooklyn), Ryder Street Station, Box 328, Brooklyn, NY 11234-0328, phone 718-763-0134, founded 1979, poetry editor Robert A. Frauenglas (publisher), is "a literary press, which is currently concentrating on publishing **works by and/or about Brooklyn and its people and places, urban gritiness and Jewish themes. Do NOT want classical poetry which I need a dictionary to understand. WANT poetry which hits at the emotions (any). No intellectual poetry! No epic poems."** They have recently published poetry by Lee Houston and Mel Waldbaum. The editors selected these sample lines from **A Park Slope Hipster Speaks Out, Again**, by Lee Houston (1985) poem: "Steamed Infancy":

> *you . . . bred a breed*
> *of creative verse makers*
> *free thinkers &*
> *freedom seekers*
> *color blinded by love*

The book is digest-sized, 56 pp., flat-spined, offset from typescript with b/w art, $4.95 **Query with cover letter. Replies to query in 2 weeks, to submission (if invited) in 4-6 weeks. Simultaneous submissions, photocopy, dot-matrix OK if readable. Payment depends on grant or award money.** "Writer shares my penury. Some copies left of Houston and Waldbaum books." Robert Frauenglas advises, "It's trite—but be true to yourself!" **Brooklyn Prospects: The First Annual Brooklyn Book Fair Anthology 1984** is in print, sells for $6 (80 pages); $3 for **PM** readers.

SONG, SONG PRESS (IV, Style), 1333 Illinois Ave., Stevens Point, WI 54481, phone 715-344-6836, founded 1976, poetry editors Richard Behm and Mary E. Norby, **"emphasizes traditional poetry, rhyme and meter.** Song Press publishes both the semiannual literary magazine, *Song,* and chapbooks.

Almost all of our chapbooks are solicited, often from contributors to *Song*. Therefore, your best bet is to submit to *Song* and mention that you have a chapbook. We look for a unified book with strong attention to the music of language, whether in free or traditional verse. Length is usually 16-24 pp. of poetry in a chapbook. They have recently published poetry by Hadrian Manske and Susan Katz. The editors selected these sample lines from "Open This Box" in **Leaving Dakota** by Lawrence Watson:

> *The goose feather, fox ruff, and snail shell,*
> *the oak leaf, thistle, and ash berries,*
> *the rattle of bean pod, the whip of willow,*
> *pine cone, snakeskin, and cough ball,*
> *all the world begging your forgiveness.*

Song is a digest-sized 40+ pp, professionally printed magazine, matte card cover with b/w art, circulation 150, 75 subscriptions of which 20 are libraries. Subscription: $5. They receive about 300 submissions per year, use less than 10%, have a 6 month or more backlog. **Sample: $2.50 postpaid. Submit 5-6 poems, no simultaneous submissions, no photocopies, dot-matrix OK. Name and address on each page. Reports in 6-8 weeks. Pays copies. "A cover letter including personal/ professional information is helpful sometimes but not required." For chapbooks payment is 25 copies and reduced price on additional copies. For sample, send $3. Editor tries to comment on all rejections.** Richard Behm comments, "Our emphasis on rhyme and meter means I inevitably get a lot of greeting card verse, but really the proportion of bad traditional poetry I receive is not higher than the bad free verse I used to get when a friend and I published a magazine of 'avant-garde' poetry."

‡*SONLIGHT CHRISTIAN NEWSPAPER, *SOLOING (I, IV, Christian), 4623 Forest Hill Blvd., West Palm Beach, FL 33415, phone 305-967-7739, founded 1980, editor and publisher Dennis Lombard. All Sonlight publications are "generally free tabloid newspaper circulated to singles, church members, and the general public." **All require inter-denominational, non-doctrinal viewpoint.** *Soloing* (first issue was October 1985) is "geared to Christian singles of all denominations." **Poetry should be 2-50 lines, inspirational/humorous, religious content generally. They do not want "flowery, amateurish. Poetry must have feeling, form 'begin in delight and end in wisdom' (Robert Frost), and dramatic conclusion."** The issue of *Soloing* I have contains one poem, "I Wish" by Rhode F. Ward. Its beginning lines are:

> *I wish I were a star to be closer to God*
> *I wish I were a cloud to be purer each day.*

The bi-monthly tabloid is 8 pp. offset on newsprint, folded, not stapled. Cover price is 50¢ subscription, $5 a year, but, as noted above, distribution is mostly free. Total circulation is 10,000. **Sample available for $1 postpaid, guidelines for SASE. Pay is $5-10, and contributors receive "as many copies as they want." Poems should be submitted 3 at a time, 2-50 lines, typed, no dot-matrix, simultaneous submissions and reprints accepted. Submissions are reported on "immediately" and time to publication averages 1-2 months.** The editor says, "It is simple for anyone with a flair for words to learn to write acceptable poems. All the theory one needs is contained in Robert Frost's 'The Figure a Poem Makes.' Poetry ceases to be poetry when it shuns form and discipline, begins in the mind instead of the heart, and leads nowhere."

SONO NIS PRESS, MORRISS PUBLISHING, DISCOVERY PRESS (II), 1745 Blanshard St., Victoria, BC, Canada V8W 2J8, phone 382-1024, founded 1968, poetry editors P.M. Sloan and outside board. They average 17 titles per year, 5 of which are poetry. "Other areas of interest: scholarship (2 titles yearly) and Canadian and Maritime History. **Rarely publish non-Canadian books."** Average 4 6x9" flat-spined paperbacks and 1 hardcover collected or selected poetry yearly. "We consider contemporary submissions. **Have yet to accept anything highly political. Have avoided concrete poetry. Emphasis on literary craftsmanship. Minimum MS length of 50 pp."** They have recently published poetry by Robin Skelton, Charles Lillard, Rona Murray and George Woodcock. The editors selected these sample lines (poet unidentified):

> *Who knows*
> *The hot stung days*
> *And brittle cold nights*
> *Of keeping a great poison pure*

Query with 6 samples, brief bio, publications credits. Replies to queries in 3 weeks, to submissions (if invited) in 3 months. "Reluctantly" considers simultaneous submissions. MS should be typed, double-spaced. Photocopy OK, no dot-matrix. Send 9x12" SASE for catalog to buy samples. The editor advises: "Beginners: gather a magazine publication/acknowledgments page before submitting to a book publisher. When submitting to a book publisher, study the work of that press before submitting. Don't submit if there is an obvious difference in your aims/their aims."

‡*SONORA REVIEW (II), Dept. English, ML445, University of Arizona, Tucson, AZ 85721, phone 602-621-1387, founded 1980, co-editors Scott Wigton and Julie Willson, a semi-annual literary journal

that publishes "non-genre" fiction and poetry. **The editors want "quality poetry, literary concerns."** They have recently published poems by Sharon Olds, William Matthews, Linda Pastan, Denis Johnson, and Marvin Bell. Some poems are published both in English and Spanish (with no indication as to which is the original). As a sample, the editors chose the following lines by John Anderson:

> At twilight you do what you can
> Which is almost nothing.
> For the coming night
> is childlike in its evocation

Sonora Review is a handsome magazine, 6x9", professionally printed on heavy off-white stock, 95 pp. flat-spined, with 2-color glossy card cover. Circulation is 1,000, of which 300 are subscriptions and 100 go to libraries. Price per copy is $3, subscription $5/year. **Sample available for $3 postpaid. Pay is 2 copies. Poets should submit typed copy, dot-matrix, simultaneous submissions OK. Reporting time is 6 weeks and time to publication 6 months.** The magazine sponsors annual poetry awards with prizes of $100 and $50. The editors' advice is "Send us your best work."

*SOUNDINGS EAST (II), Salem State College, Salem, MA 01970, phone 745-0556, founded 1973, advisory editor Claire Keyes. "*SE* is published by Salem State College and is staffed totally by students. We accept short fiction (15 pp. max) and **(primarily free verse) poetry (5 pp. max).** Purpose is to promote poetry and fiction in the college and beyond its environs. We **do not want graphic profanity. We do not restrict poems if profanity is appropriate and not just for 'shock value.'** " They have recently published poetry by Seamus Heaney, Terry Cader, Nancy Lagomarsino and Michael Madonick. The editor selected these sample lines from "Winterset" by Mary Driscoll:

> Laundered January afternoon.
> Towels on your clothesline lick at the north wind
> like iceboat sails

SE appears twice a year, 64-68 pp. digest-sized, flat-spined, b/w drawings and photos, glossy card cover with b/w photo, circulation 2,000, 120 subscriptions of which 35 are libraries. They receive about 500 submissions per year, use 40-60. **Sample: $2 postpaid. Fall deadline November 15; Spring March 15. Submit maximum of 6 poems. Photocopies, dot-matrix, simultaneous submissions OK. Reports within 4 months. Pays 2 copies. "When writer shows merit, a critique is enclosed."** The editor advises, "Beginning poets should write about things they *know and feel strongly about*. Poetry with interesting and varied vocabulary captures our attention. Forced rhyme detracts from a poem."

THE SOUNDS OF POETRY, THE LATINO POETS ASSOCIATION (I, IV, Ethnic), 2076 Vinewood, Detroit, MI 48216, phone 313-841-9742, founded 1983, poetry editor Jacqueline Sanchez. *The Sounds of Poetry* is a photocopied newsletter, stapled at the corner, which **"is mainly to publish lesser known poets/writers."** They publish **"whatever poet wishes to express as long as it does not have explicit sexual overtones. Nothing political."** They have recently published Jacqueline Sanchez, Trinidad Sanchez, Jose Garza, Sanchez Sisters and Myron W. McCurtis. The editor selected the second stanza of this sample poem by Jose Garza, "To the Maker":

> make of this life a conscious life
> dwelling in purpose and peace
> faithfully cleansed by the pure rains
> that all worldly temptations might cease . . .

Some of the poems are in Spanish. There are 5 issues a year ranging from 4-10 pp. each. They have 50 subscribers of which 2 are libraries. Subscription: $2 per year; 50¢ per issue. They publish "most of whatever material comes in." **Sample: 25¢ plus SASE. Submit up to 5 pp., 1 poem per page. Reports in 2-8 weeks. Pays 1 copy to non-subscribers, 2 copies to subscribers.** Jacqueline Sanchez explains, "We, as a family, work together to put together *The Sounds of Poetry*, an outlet for poets, writers who are looking for approval. Sometimes a writer cannot be objective about his/her work unless seen in print. Only then can the writer go on to improve his/her work. All readings are done by myself and 5 high school students and 1 graduate. There are no profits here, just sincere dedication to what we do. We are not perfect and to 'err is human.' Advice for new poets: Keep writing. Never give up and never accept a no. There are other editors, other minds willing to accept your material. Just keep on submitting. Rewrite only when necessary." (This is not advice many editors would agree with!)

*SOUTH CAROLINA REVIEW (II), English Dept., Clemson, U., Clemson, SC 29631, phone 803-656-3151, founded 1973, is a biannual literary magazine "recognized by the *New York Times Books Review* as one of the top 20 of this type." They will consider **"any kind of poetry as long as it's good. Format should be according to MLA Stylesheet."** They have recently published poems by F. C. Rosenburg, J. W. Rivers and Angela Walton. The editor selected these sample lines by John Lane:

> Who is to say if bodies wraped in a slow roll
> are mounted rock in a spreading floor,

> *or if he did see a child grind off a bench*
> *like a loose glacier? I loved him with all his faults.*

It is a 6x9", 130 + pp., flat-spined, professionally printed magazine which uses about 10 pp. of poetry in each issue, has a circulation of 600, 400 subscriptions of which 200 are libraries. Subscription: $5. They receive about 1,000 freelance submissions of poetry per year of which they use 10, have a 1-6 month backlog. **Sample: $1 postpaid. Reports in 1-6 months, pays in copies.**

‡*SOUTH COAST POETRY JOURNAL (II), English Dept., CSUF, Fullerton, CA 92634, phone 714-773-2651, editor John J. Brugaletta. At present time the twice-yearly (fall and spring) magazine publishes poetry only. **"We'd like to see poems with strong imagery and a sense that the poem has found its best form, whether that form is traditional or innovative. We prefer poems under 40 lines, but we'll look at others. Any subject-matter or style. We are not impressed by poetry that intends to shock or confuse the reader for no artistic purpose."** As a sample, the editor selected four lines by an unidentified poet:

> *I buried her in the filthy smock*
> *she wore. As she went into the grave,*
> *her hand in rigor mortis sent a rigid wave,*
> *white and fluid as a masterpiece in stone.*

The journal is digest-sized, 40 pp., saddle-stitched. Circulation is 500. **Sample: $2 postpaid. Guidelines are available for SASE. Pay is one copy. No simultaneous submissions, no dot-matrix. Submissions will be reported on in 4-6 weeks. They conduct a poetry contest for which the entry fee is $2/poem.**

*SOUTH DAKOTA REVIEW (II), Box 111, University Exchange, Vermillion, SD 57069, phone 605-677-5229, founded 1963, editor John R. Milton, is an academic quarterly, 6x9", 100 + pp., flat-spined, professionally printed, glossy card cover with b/w art, circulation 600, 450 subscriptions. The editor prefers **"formal free verse. We do not want merely descriptive or self-therapy poems."** They have recently published poetry by Lloyd Van Brunt, Imogene Bolls, Joseph Hansen, Thom Tammaro, and Simon Perchik. The editor selected these sample lines by David Citino:

> *Swear no oath to mean forever,*
> *No one's made to stay so long,*
> *and promise unfulfilled can leave*
> *your children full of scorn*
> *or bloated and pale in the dust,*
> *wounds blooming red as poppies.*

Subscription: $10; per copy: $3. **Sample: $3 postpaid. No simultaneous submissions. Reports in a few weeks for rejections, longer for poems being considered for publication. Pays copies. There is a $100 award for the best poem each year.**

SOUTH END PRESS (V), 302 Columbus Ave., Boston, MA 02116, founded 1977, is "a **political press publishing books on various aspects of the movements for social change.**" They have published 2 books of poetry, but are **not currently reading poetry MSS**.

*THE SOUTH FLORIDA POETRY REVIEW, SOUTH FLORIDA POETRY INSTITUTE (I, IV, Regional), Box 7072, Hollywood, FL 33081, *Review* founded 1983, poetry editors Michael Cleary, Ligia Saricyan-Jamieson and Magi Schwartz, S.A. Stirnemann, is a magazine-sized triquarterly, 52 pp. (including tinted paper cover), offset from typescript, circulation 300, 180 subscriptions of which 8 are libraries. "We try to attract a variety of poetic styles with a common denominator of quality. We admit to encouraging 'new' writers from anywhere; we also admit to delight in publishing Florida poets who deserve the recognition. **Any type. Not crazy about religious or inspirational. We seem to be publishing a number of humorous and tropical poems, but this is not by design.**" They have recently published poetry by Hans Juergensen, William White, Marcia Kester, Malcolm Glass, Joan Colby, Eileen Eliot and Larry Rubin. The editors selected these sample lines from "Christmas Scene," by Malcolm Glass:

> *This was the landscape I was taught*
> *to dream, through Florida winter*
> *rains, though I knew the sun*
> *would never be cold enough,*
> *nor my bones so small.*

They receive about 1,200 submissions per year, use 130. **Sample: $2 postpaid. "We read in September, January and April. Submit 4-6 poems, unpublished. Simultaneous submissions OK if noted. Brief bio sketch usually containing previous publications, awards, anything else." Reports within 3 months. Pays 2 copies. "If we are attracted to a good MS we sometimes reject with suggestions."**

SOUTH HEAD PRESS, *POETRY AUSTRALIA (II), Berrima NSW 2577, Australia, founded 1964, poetry editors Grace Perry and John Millett. "We have published 102 issues of *Poetry Australia* (5-6 per year), minimum of 80 pp. per issue, and many books of poetry." 30-50 poets appear in each issue of *PA*. As a sample I selected the first two (of 8) stanzas of "Right Winger" by David Ray:

> 1
> *On planes*
> *he always sat*
> *over the right wing.*
> 2
> *When he went hunting*
> *he always shot*
> *the duck in the left wing.*

PA is professionally printed, 6x9¾" flat-spined, glossy card cover, $7.50 per copy. They invite "**unpublished verse in English from writers in Australia and abroad. MSS should be typed double-spaced on one side of paper with name and address on reverse side. Overseas contributors are advised that sufficient money for return postage should accompany poems. Stamps of one country are not legal tender in another. Rates for poems: $10 or 1 year's subscription. Overseas poets are paid in copies. South Head Press will consider submissions for book publication. Query with 3 samples. They pay advance and copies. Editor sometimes comments on rejections.** There is a list of books of poetry they have published in *Poetry Australia*, which serves as their catalog. The editor advises, "Read all you can of the best that has been published in the last 20 years. Include *PA*, *Hudson Review*, etc."

‡SOUTH WESTERN ONTARIO POETRY (II), 764 Dalkeith Ave., London, Ontario, Canada N5X 1R8, founded 1978, editor/publisher Sheila Martindale, a small press publisher of chapbooks. The editor wants "**poems which are intelligent and intelligible; prefer poems which will fit on a 5x7 page when typewritten; 20-30 poems on one theme preferred.**" She has recently published chapbooks by George Swede, Robert Sward, and LeRoy Gorman. As a sample she selected (although she protested that a 4-line sample out of context could not be representative) the following lines from "Heavy Seasoning & Heavenly Bodies" by Jan Figurski:

> *the son is not born to his father*
> *he is grafted onto thigh*
> *a quiver at his side*
> *where he grows his own branches*

Sheila Martindale publishes 3-4 chapbooks per year, digest-sized, offset from typed copy, 24 pp., matte card covers with b/w illustrations, saddle-stapled, priced at $2/each. She says that she **accepts freelance submissions "in theory, but I am so overstocked that I send most of it back." Writers should query first; she will answer queries in 2 weeks and report on MSS in 4 weeks. Royalties are 10%. "Our books are often first books by emerging authors, who have already established a list of magazine credits.**" Ms. Martindale advises beginning poets, "Before you write anything else READ as much contemporary poetry as you can find. Subscribe to litmags, buy chapbooks, study current styles. Go to readings, and discuss poetry with established poets there. Support poetry in your area."

*SOUTHERN HUMANITIES REVIEW (II), 9088 Haley Center, Auburn University, AL 36849, founded 1967, is a 100 + pp. 6x9" literary quarterly, circulation 800, using **quality poetry. Sample copy, $4, subscription $12, 1 year. Pays $50 for best poem published during the year.**

*SOUTHERN POETRY REVIEW (II), English Dept., University of North Carolina, Charlotte, NC 28223, phone 704-597-4225, editor Robert Gray, founded 1958, a semi-annual literary magazine "with emphasis on effective poetry. **Not a regional magazine, but a natural outlet for new Southern talent.**" There are no restrictions on form, style, or content of poetry; length subject to limitations of space. They do not want to see anything "**cute, sweet, sentimental, arrogant or preachy.**" They have recently published work by Linda Pastan, Karen Swenson, Peter Wild, Peter Cooley, Betty Adcock, and Fred Chappell. As a sample, I chose the first stanza from "Museum Piece" by Barbara Fritchie:

> *Past survival, he killed for*
> *trophies. His wife said dead things*
> *have no decorative value.*
> *She never understood*
> *the importance of a good mount.*

Southern Poetry Review is 6x9", handsomely printed on buff stock, 78 pp. flat-spined with textured, one-color matte card cover. Circulation is 1,000 +, price per copy $2.50, subscription $5/year. **Sample available for $2 postpaid; no guidelines, but will answer queries with SASE. Pay is $5/poem** "when funds are available" plus 1 copy. Writers should submit no more than 3-5 poems. Reporting time is 4-6 weeks, and poems should be printed within a year of acceptance. There is a yearly contest, the Guy Owen Poetry Prize of $500, to which the entry fee is a subscription; deadline is normally about May 1.

*THE SOUTHERN REVIEW (II)**, 43 Allen Hall, Louisiana State University, Baton Rouge, LA 70803, phone 504-388-5108, founded 1935 (original series); 1965 (new series), poetry editors James Olney and Lewis Simpson, "is a literary quarterly which publishes fiction, poetry, critical essays, book reviews, with emphasis on contemporary literature in the US and abroad, and with special interest in southern culture and history. Selections are made with careful attention to craftsmanship and technique and to the seriousness of the subject matter." By general agreement this is one of the most distinguished of literary journals. Joyce Carol Oates, for instance, says, "Over the years I have continued to be impressed with the consistent high quality of *SR's publications and its general 'aura,' which bespeaks careful editing, adventuresome tastes, and a sense of thematic unity. SR* is characterized by a refreshing openness to new work, placed side by side with that of older, more established, and in many cases highly distinguished writers." The editors say they want "**No particular kinds of poetry. We are interested in any formal varieties, traditional or modern, that are well crafted, though we cannot normally accommodate excessively long poems (say 10 pp. and over).**" They have recently published poetry by Joyce Carol Oates, Daniel Haberman, Michael Van Walleghen, Robert Duncan, James Merrill and Monroe Spears. The editors selected these sample lines by Robert Penn Warren:

> Another land, another age, another self
> Before all had happened that has happened since
> And is now arranged on the shelf
> Of memory in a sequence that I call Myself.

The beautifully printed quarterly is massive: 6¾x10", 240+ pp, flat-spined, matte card cover, print-run 3,600, 2,300 subscriptions of which 70% are libraries. Subscription: $12. They receive about 2,000 freelance submissions of poetry, use 20%. **Sample: $5 postpaid. Prefer 1-4 pp. submissions. Reports in 2 months. Pays $20/printed page plus 2 copies. Send SASE for guidelines.**

SOUTHPORT PRESS (IV, Theme, style, historical)**, English Dept., Carthage College, Kenosha, WI 53141, founded 1977, poetry editors Travis DuPriest, is a "hand press which prints limited runs on quality paper. We print broadsides and small books, all hand work and binding. We publish poetry, historical reprints and theology. **We do not read unsolicited MSS.**" They have published poetry by Wilma Tague and Lilie Chaffin and prose by Krister Stendahl; and will publish short collections of thematic verse by individuals and historical —chapbooks of 10-15 pp. **Query. Replies in 1 month. To submission, if invited, reports in 1 month. Pays copies.** "Inactive at present, will resume operation in near future."

*SOU'WESTER (II)**, English Dept., Southern Illinois University, Edwardsville, IL 62026-1438, phone 618-692-2289, founded 1960, poetry editor Dickie Spurgeon, appears 3 times a year. "**No preferences" regarding kinds of poems. "We don't publish many that are shorter than 10 lines or so.**" They have recently published poetry by Ronald Wallace, X. J. Kennedy, R. T. Smith, Victoria McCabe, J. B. Goodenough, Robert Lietz, Shelley Ehrlich, Major Ragain, Fleda Brown Jackson, Howard Winn and E. Kroll. I selected the first stanza of "Muskellunge" by Robert Gibb as a sample:

> God, I had forgotten
> How much they heave forward
> Into their jaws, everything
> From the gills on back.

There are 25-30 pp. in each 6x9" 80 pp. issue. The magazine is professionally printed, flat-spined, with textured matte card cover, circulation 300, 110 subscriptions of which 50 are libraries. Subscription: $4 (3 issues). They receive some 2,000 poems (from 600 poets) each year, use 36-40, have a 4 month backlog. **Sample: $1.50 postpaid. Simultaneous submission, photocopy, dot-matrix submissions OK. Rejections usually within a week. Pays 2 copies.** Editor comments on rejections "usually, in the case of those that we almost accept."

*SOVEREIGN GOLD LITERARY MAGAZINE, SOVEREIGN GOLD AWARD PROGRAM, GALLANT KNIGHT PRINTING PRESS (I)**, Box 1631, Iowa City, IA 52244, phone 319-354-1191, founded 1975, poetry editor Gary J. King. "Goals are to provide an outlet for writers and poets and to help them market their work and to publish their books where otherwise they could not afford it." Gary King says he wants to see "**all forms in good taste—no off-beat or sex. I would like to see some sonnets, haiku—all forms." He publishes 99% of what he receives. As a sample he offers these lines by himself:**

> If I were a lemon

> *And you a peach*
> *what do you suppose*
> *our minds would compose?*

Sovereign Gold Literary Magazine comes out 3 times a year, 40 pp., digest-sized, offset from typescript on gold-colored paper with line-drawings. (He says he is switching to letterpress in 1985). **Sample: $3.50 plus postage. Submit 2 pp. maximum, 1 poem to page, double-spaced. No simultaneous submissions. Note with submission preferred. Reports in 2-3 weeks.** No pay, but "copy given in most cases. Since *Sovereign Gold* provides as many free copies to the elderly as it can, those submitting are asked to subscribe but it is not mandatory." Some issues are devoted to writing by school children. For chapbook consideration, query with 5 sample poems and cover letter "to include poetic goals, desire or diligence of poets and their outlook on life and POETRY. Good poets and those with good ideals may be invited to become a Staff Member! Sovereign Gold Award Program—World-wide = $10\frac{1}{2}$x13" plaques (gold, silver and bronze awards), highly sought after and very stiff competition. Information available for SASE." Gary King **always provides criticism and "never a charge. Will recommend another publication if not suited for mine. Suggest poets who have not been published try** *SGLM*. **99% chance of being published.** Publication is distributed to over 40 states in US and Canada and 8 foreign countries. Will also help them and make comments."

*SPACE AND TIME (IV, Science fiction, fantasy), #4B, 138 W. 70th St., New York, NY 10023-4432, founded 1966, poetry editor Gordon Linzner, is a biannual "publishing **science fiction & fantasy material—particularly hard-to-market mixed genres and work by new writers. Will look at all kinds of poetry but would like to see narrative poems. Should be SF-fantasy and not just using SF-fantasy imagery as metaphor**." They have published poetry by Steve Eng, Denise Dumars and Neal F. Wilgus. The editor selected these sample lines from "At the Bus Stop" by Ralph E. Vaughan:

> *They sit on bus benches in every step*
> *and their eyes glow in the night;*
> *their gaze is steady and without pity*
> *and they inspire emotions greater than fright.*

The 118 pp. digest-sized journal, saddle-stapled, photo reduced from typescript with b/w drawings, has a circulation of 400-500, 150 subscriptions of which 5 are libraries. They receive about 250 submissions of poetry per year, use 15-20. **Sample: $4 postpaid. No simultaneous submissions. Reports in 2 months maximum, usually sooner. Pays 2 copies. "Overstocked through 1987 except for narrative poems."**

SPARROW PRESS, SPARROW POVERTY PAMPHLETS, VAGROM CHAPBOOKS (II), 103 Waldron St., West Lafayette, IN 47906, phone 317-743-1991, founded 1954, poetry editors Felix and Selma Stefanile. This is one of the oldest and most highly respected small press publishers of poetry in the country. "We publish the best unsolicited poetry we can find. We are **unabashedly in favor of poetry that uses melody and rhetoric: language that pushes 'language' around in lively, sensitive and seriously artistic ways. Not interested in feelings but spirit's attempt to control or register feelings; mind over gut. We deliberately try to be eclectic in our choices of technique or theme or authorial attitude, but we demand skill, as well as sentiment.** We publish only poetry, translations of poetry and occasionally deeply concerned literary criticism that itself becomes a creative response to poetry. No hardbacks. We sometimes publish special books that become experiments in fine printing. (We've been favorably reviewed in *Fine Print* magazine). Our poets sometimes win distinguished awards: The Mills book won the Carl Sandburg Memorial Award in 1984, in open competition. Suffice it to say we usually publish in clean, neat, pretty durable offset, both perfect-bound for our larger books, the Vagroms, and side-stitched with decent cover for the Poverty pamphlets. We publish only *one* poet an issue. Our pamphlets run 24-26 pp. of poetry, our chapbooks 48-72. These formats accommodate standard lyrics and longer poems. We won't consider picture or 'concrete' poems, or prose poetry." They have recently published poetry by Roger Finch, Ralph J. Mills Jr., Sister Maura, Christopher Bursk, Geraldine C. Little, Gail White and Norbert Krapf. Felix Stefanile selected these sample lines from "The Sun Inflates the Sky" by Gael Turnbull:

> *An envelope pops through the letterbox and I hear*
> *it shouting my name from the floor, Destiny!*
> *but my wife picks it up and tears out its tongue and hands me, A Circular!*

"We don't want 'samples'; we're busy enough. Send us 20-24 pages of your work, and let the MS stand or fall on its own. Please note: we have a specific reading period, April and May. Only one condition, and it's more a desperate hope. I wish most people who submit knew what kind of press Sparrow is. Too many submissions quite simply should not be sent to us." **Send at least $2 for sample publication or SASE for catalog. Submit complete MS. Reports in 6 weeks. No simultaneous submissions. We are adamant about accepting only clearly typed copy, one poem per page. No photocopy or dot-matrix. Pays $25 advance, 20% royalties after costs recovered, 5 copies.** Felix Stefanile comments,

"Every successful writer I know, and I know quite a few, is a voracious reader, even a bookworm. Young poets should read, the way beginning athletes study the films of the pros. That's my veteran advice. They should also buy books, and I know most poets don't!"

*SPECTACULAR DISEASES, *LOOT (II), 83B London Rd., Peterborough, Cambridgeshire, UK, founded 1974, Paul Green editor (various invited poetry editors). "The press presents **experimental writing with bias to the current French scene and to current, and past scenes, in the US, and Britain. Most poetry is solicited by the editors.** Long poems will be clearly accepted, if falling in the special categories." They have recently published poetry by Saúl Yurkievich Jackson MacLow, Armand Schewner, Bernard Noël. *Spectacular Diseases* is an annual digest-sized 40-60 pp. *Loot* is a supplement to *SD*, free to subscribers, 4 issues per year, each issue limited to 1 author, "long poems preferred but not a requisite of acceptance." **Sample of** *SD* **£1.75 postpaid. Query before submitting as most material is invited. Pays in copies.** Under the Spectacular Diseases imprint a number of books and anthologies are printed. For book consideration, **query with about 16 samples; letter helpful but not essential. Pays 10% of run. Send postage for catalog to buy samples. Editor comments "if desired."**

‡*SPHINX—WOMEN'S INTERNATIONAL LITERARY/ART REVIEW (IV, Women), 175 Avenue Ledru-Rollin, Paris, France 75011, phone 43.67.31.92, editor/publisher Carol A. Pratl, who says "*Sphinx* is an innovative women's review [in English and some French] designed for everyone with fiction, poetry, art and photography **by women and by men about women.**" The editor wants **"poetry previously unpublished in English from around the world. We print the original version plus English translation (which should be provided). We seek poetry preferably of an experimental nature which avoids typical feminine themes (love, marriage, separation, family, etc.)—work should be thought-provoking with a consistent and developed form."** She does not want to see **"love poetry, overly autobiographical work, family portraits, work that reflects little or no research in content and style; no classical metric forms."** She has recently published poems by Michele LaForest, Grace Paley, Kathy Acker, and Luisa Futoransky. As a sample, she selected the following lines from "White Beauty Drinks Water," by the French poet Rosita:

> *Marrakeshramadan*
> *th' desert*
> *'s onli me onli me jes' me*
> *out strollin, I se so adorab'*
> *hey, gal, like steppin' out*

Sphinx is handsomely printed, 8¼" square, 78 pp. flat-spined, with glossy card cover and b/w art work. Illustrations within the magazine include b/w photographs and reproductions of paintings; the last four pages carry ads. One-third of each issue features work from a particular country. Circulation is 1,500, of which 200 are subscriptions and 900 are newsstand sales in 7 countries. Price per issue is $5, subscription (3 issues) $15. **Sample: $5. Guidelines available for SASE—or IRC if the inquirer is not in France. Contributors receive 2 copies. They are not expected to subscribe, but 'it is preferable that they've seen a copy and read it thoroughly before they submit any work." Writers should send no more than 3 poems (any length), typed, preferably photocopies, previously unpublished only. Submissions are reported on within 4-5 months, and the publication backlog is 3-4 months. "Each MS is commented on individually and personally."** Carol Pratl says "I believe it's essential for today's poets to read continually on diverse topics and by all means numerous poetry reviews and anthologies. They should research the themes of their poems, work and re-work them. Too many people today consider themselves poets without qualifications, they think it's simply a matter of sitting down at the desk for a half hour and writing (in poetic form) what they did the day before. They should also have read the reviews they're submitting work to."

SPIDER PLOTS IN RAT-HOLES (I, II), 729A Queen St. East, Toronto, Ontario, Canada M4M 1H1, founded 1982, phone 416-463-5867, poetry editors j w curry, Mark Laba and Steve Venright. This group of friends publish themselves and others in "fringe activity" publications—anthologies, postcards, books, leaflets, pamphlets and "facsimile bookworks." Send for list of publications to buy samples. Query if interested. SASE always. Pays in copies. "Personal contact is desired."

‡SPINSTERS INK (IV, Women), Box 410687, San Francisco, CA 94141, phone 415-558-9655, founded 1978, publisher Sherry Thomas, a small-press publisher of paperback books of fiction, nonfiction, some poetry—**by and for women.** "Publishes 8-10 books a year." As a sample, the publisher selected the following lines by Minnie Bruce Pratt:

> *getting to be a grown girl, I iron the cotton sheets*
> *into perfect blankness. No thump shakes Laura, dreaming in the straight-backed chair, up-*
> *right, eyes closed, dark brown*
> *face crumpled in an hour's rest from generations of children*

That is from **We Say We Love Each Other** a handsomely printed and designed flat-spined 6x9" paperback, glossy card cover with two-tone photograph, 100 pp. with b/w photo of author on last page. The publisher accepts freelance submissions but writers should query first. She reports on queries in 2 weeks, MS in 2 months. Photocopied MSS are OK, dot-matrix OK if double-strike. The cover letter should include credits and bio. Royalties are 8-12%. The press publishes only one poetry title every two years.

*SPIRIT: THE CHRISTIAN MAGAZINE ABOUT CAREER LIFESTYLE AND RELATION-SHIPS, Box 1231, Sisters, OR 97759, phone 503-549-0443, executive editor Jerry Jones, art director Denis Moretenson, is "to help guide today's new generation of adults toward a more Biblical life-style and philosophical perspective; to provide a framework for making decisions and wise choices in an increasingly complicated and challenging world; to explore these exciting, unique opportunities God has provided for this generation. **We prefer free verse, poetry that's feeling-oriented and relational. We don't want greeting card-type verse. Don't use much rhyming poetry. Poems should be 20 lines or less, should deal with life from a Christian world view.**" They have recently published poetry by Mari Hanes, Calvin Miller and Barbara Penwarden. The magazine-sized quarterly, 56 pp., glossy paper, circulation 40,000, uses less than 1 page of poetry per issue. (The issue I examined had none.) They receive 150 + submissions of freelance poetry per year, use 3-4. **Sample: $2 plus 9x12" SASE. Submissions should be double-spaced, no more than 2 at a time. "Query preferred but not required." Dot-matrix OK. Reports in 60-90 days. Pays $15-75 per poem. Send SASE for general writers' guidelines.** The editor comments, "I see a lot of poetry, but very little that is creative in ideas or artfully crafted."

*THE SPIRIT THAT MOVES US, THE SPIRIT THAT MOVES US PRESS (II), Box 1585, Iowa City, IA 52244, phone 319-338-7502, founded 1974, poetry editor Morty Sklar. *The Spirit That Moves Us* is a biannual literary magazine often on announced themes. "Poets should **query first with SASE to see what our theme/needs are**." They have recently published poetry by Margaret Randall, Jimmy Santiago Baca, Marge Piercy and William Stafford and Jaroslav Seifert (*The Casting of Bells*, winner of 1984 Nobel Prize). Morty Sklar selected these likes from "Strategic Air Command" by Gary Snyder as a sample:

> These cliffs and the stars
> Belong to the same universe.
> This little air between
> Belongs to the twentieth century and its wars.

Issues vary in size and price, and all issues are simultaneously released and marketed as books. **Sample:** *The Spirit That Moves Us Reader*, **an anthology of reprints from the magazine, is offered as a sample for $4.50 postpaid. Submit 3-5 poems at a time on current theme (except for long poems). Single-spaced (unless the poem's format is not). Simultaneous submissions OK if author notifies us. Photocopies OK. Reports within a month. Pays 1 paper, 1 cloth copy plus 40% discount on extra copies. Editor comments on rejections "when I really like something but not enough to accept, or when someone asks for criticism—if I have time."** Morty Sklar also publishes a few collections by individuals. **Query with 5 samples and cover letter containing "whatever the poet would like to communicate, but I hate long lists of credits without other info or personal expression."** The editor's advice: "Write what you would like to write, in a style (or styles) which is/are best for your own expression. Don't worry about acceptance, though you may be concerned about it. Don't just send work which you think editors would like to see, though take that into consideration. Think of the relationship between poem, poet and editor as personal. You may send good poems to editors who simply do not like them, whereas other editors might."

*SPITBALL (IV, Baseball), 1721 Scott Blvd., Covington, KY 41011, phone 606-261-3024, founded 1981, poetry editor Mike Shannon, is "a unique literary magazine devoted to poetry, fiction and book reviews *exclusively* about baseball. We enjoy publishing poetry the most. But sometimes do not receive as many submissions of good baseball poetry as we'd like to. Newcomers are very welcome, but remember that you have to know the subject. We do & our readers do. Perhaps a good place to start for beginners is one's personal reactions to the game, *a* game, a player, etc. & take it from there." As a sample I selected the opening lines of "From Fields Where Glory Does Not Stay" by David Craig:

> He was just an ol Okie,
> Country-shy with a cow-lick
> and a crooked smile.
> He hit homers left and right,
> Ran a hole in the wind.

The digest-sized 40 pp. quarterly, saddle-stapled, matte card cover, offset from typescript, has a circulation of 500, 250 + subscriptions of which 25 are libraries. Subscription: $8. They receive about 1,000 submissions per year, use 40—very small backlog. "Many times we are able to publish accepted work almost immediately." **Sample: $2.50 postpaid. "We are not very concerned with the technical details of submitting, but we do prefer a cover letter with some bio info. We also like batches of poems and prefer to use several of same poet in an issue rather than a single poem." Reports "immediately if we don't like the poetry. If we hold it more than a week, we usually publish it." Pays 2 copies. Send SASE for guidelines. "We annually sponsor a poetry contest. No entry fees. Baseball merchandise prizes as awards. Winner published in October-World Series Issue, deadline October 15 each year.** "We encourage anyone interested to submit to *Spitball*. We are always looking for fresh talent. Those who have never written 'baseball poetry' before should read some first probably before submitting. Not necessarily ours. Kerrane & Grossinger's **Baseball Diamonds** will demonstrate to anyone what wonderful things can be done with the subject from a poetic standpoint. We sponsor the Spitball Baseball Book of the Year Award and banquet every January. Any chapbook of baseball poetry should be sent to us for consideration for the 'Casey' statue that we award to the winner each year. New contest: Imitation 'Casey at the Bat' Contest, until Feb. 1, 1988. Details for SASE."

‡*SPOKES (I), #15, The Ridgway, Flitwick, Bedfordshire MK45 1DH, England, phone Flitwick (0525) 713699, founded 1985, joint editors Julius Smit and Colin Blundell, a quarterly journal of new poetry, information and articles on poetry, and art. The editors want **"all types of poetry, form and style. No limit on length. All kinds of subjects!"** As a sample, I chose the beginning lines from Colin Blundell's "Apologia," which is printed in a brochure for the magazine:

> So what counts, then, as a decent poem?
> What gets printed, for what reasons?
> Well, doesn't a decent poem choose itself?
> Doesn't it leap off the page
> with a sprightly   Voila!   Here I am! Print me!
> even if it's the saddest thing on earth?

Spokes is digest-sized, "offset litho printed," 48 pp., with picutres, stiff colored cover. Its circulation is in the UK, Europe, North America, and Australia. Price per issue is £2, subscription £6.50/year. **Sample available for £2.50; "if cheques are sent, we must ask for an additional £3 to cover UK bank exchange charge." There are no particular specifications for submissions. Reporting time is 6-8 weeks and time to publication approximately 2 months.**

‡*STAND MAGAZINE (I, II), 179 Wingrove Rd., Newcastle on Tyne, England NE4 9DA, phone 091-273-3280, founded by Jon Silkin in 1952, is a highly esteemed literary quarterly. They want **" verse that tries to explore forms. No formulaic verse."** The issue of *Stand* I have (Autumn 1984) contains poems by Rolf Jacobsen, Ken Smith, Robert Dana, Alison Brackenbury, Barry Spacks, and Richard Eberhart, from whose "Throwing Yourself Away" I selected the beginning lines as a sample:

> To throw yourself away
> Is to throw yourself into everybody
>
> A part of embracing the world,
> Not self-embrace, close embrace, wide embrace
>
> As if everyone in the world were open to love,
> Your love was unasked for, a gratuity, essential

Stand is 8x6", 80 pp., flat-spined, professionally printed, with ads, two-color matte card cover with photo of a writer. Circulation 4,500; 2,600 subscriptions of which 600 are libraries. Subscription $12.50 (£5.80). **Sample: $3 postpaid. Pays £30/poem (unless under 6 lines) and one copy (⅓ off additional copies).**

‡STAR BOOKS, INC. (IV, Religious), 408 Pearson St., Wilson, NC 27893, phone 919-237-1591, founded 1982, president Irene Burk Harrell, a small-press publisher of Christian books, including poetry. They are planning to start a magazine, perhaps in 1986, which will include poetry. **"We want to see poems that are specifically Christian in content. Form and style may vary, length as appropriate. Particularly interested in 'God-given' poetry. If poet has to ask what we mean by that, his stuff is probably not for us."** The press's first two books of poetry were by Dorothy Clements and Maureen Arthur-Lynch (both previously unpublished). As a sample, the editor chose the following lines from Ms.

ALWAYS submit MSS or queries with a stamped, self-addressed envelope (SASE) within your country or International Reply Coupons (IRCs) purchased from the post office for other countries.

Arthur-Lynch's **To Lift Your Heart**.
> *I walked today through fields of green*
> *That God had made for me,*
> *And wondered at the miracle*
> *Of all that I could see.*

Freelance submissions are accepted for book publication and, of course, will be accepted for the magazine when it appears. Writers should send 5 sample poems and bio, 1 poem/page, "no bad dot-matrix." Royalties are paid on books (amount varies), plus "a certain number of free copies." Queries will be answered in 1-4 weeks and MSS reported on in 1-2 months. The editors say, "Sometimes author helps with costs of first printing, sometimes not. Neither of our about-to-be published books of poetry had any author financing. Next one might or might not, 'as the Lord leads'."

*START: MAGAZINE OF LITERATURE AND THE ARTS (I), Queen's Chambers, King St., Nottingham, England, founded 1978, editor Carole Baker, is a digest-sized 48 pp. magazine appearing 4 times a year, circulation 500, uses **British and international material.** It is "first of all a place where writers, poets, critics, essayists and artists can **start** writing or drawing. You can try out your creative ideas on *Start's* pages." They are very open to beginners and want feedback from readers on material which has appeared in the magazine. "In 1985 START published poetry by Glyn Jones, Susan Bassnett, Jennifer Brice; short stories by Mansfield, Fay Prendergast; translations from German and Italian writers and articles on poetry composition and criticism. We also profiled famous authors: Fay Weldon by Carole Baker, Hermann Hesse, Coleridge and would like to see more." I chose three sample lines from "He's Gone Out" by Jaynie Mansfield:
> *In these aching heavy evenings*
> *hearts contract and sigh,*
> *some drown in moods of ashen lace*
> *in pale and holy vacuum space . . .*

Associate editor Charles Mansfield says, "We're looking for **modern writing that's not choked with sentimentality or old-fashioned chauvinism. We're trying to break down the established order of sexism and militarism in English literature." Submit, if possible, neatly-typed work which can be reproduced as is on digest-sized paper. Considers simultaneous submissions. Illustrate with b&w line drawings if you want to. They do *not* return work or send letters of acceptance or rejection. "Just watch out in the next issue of the magazine for your work. New writers: study back copies of** *Start* **for inspiration." Sample: $3 plus postage or order through your city library ISSN 0267-2502. New York Public Library have back issues, too.**

STATE STREET PRESS (II), 67 State St., Pittsford, NY 14534, phone 716-244-4850, founded 1981, poetry editor Judith Kitchen, "publishes **chapbooks of poetry (20-24 pp.) usually chosen in an anonymous competition**. State Street Press hopes to publish emerging writers with solid first collections and to offer a format for established writers who have a collection of poems that work together as a chapbook. We have also established a full-length publication—for those of our authors who are beginning to have a national reputation. We want **serious traditional and free verse. We are not usually interested in the language school of poets or what would be termed 'beat.' We are quite frankly middle-of-the-road. We ask only that the poems work as a collection, that the chapbook be more than an aggregate of poems—that they work together.**" They have recently published poetry by Christopher Bursk, Liz Rosenberg, Keith Ratzlaff, Kevin Clark, Stephen Corey and Nancy Simpson. Lines from "Forgetting" by Stan Sanuel Rubin:
> *It isn't as hard as you think, it's easy*
> *as spilling milk on a white cloth,*
> *as memory, the same dull breath repeated*
> *over and over. The pain that won't go away*

The sample chapbook I have seen is beautifully designed and printed, 6x9", 30 pp., with textured matte wrapper with art. **Send SASE for guidelines and contest rules. There is a $5 entry fee, for which you receive one of the chapbooks already published. Simultaneous submissions encouraged. Photocopies OK. Dot-matrix OK "but we don't like it." Pays 15 copies, and authors buy additional ones at cost, sell at readings and keep the profits.** Judith Kitchen comments, "State Street Press believes that the magazines are doing a good job of publishing beginning poets and we hope to present published and unpublished work in a more permanent format, so we do reflect the current market and tastes. We expect our writers to have published individual poems and to be considering a larger body of work that in some way forms a 'book.' We have been cited as a press that prints poetry that is accessible to the general reader."

‡STEP LIFE (IV, Step-parenting), 901 Ivy Court, Eaton, OH 45320, phone 513-456-6611, founded 1983, editor Carla Wall. The newsletter takes **"short poems dealing with step-parenting or remar-**

riage theme *only.*" Pay is 1 copy. Submissions are reported on within 1 month, and time to publication is no longer than 6 months. The magazine-sized, folded newsletter is offset from typed copy, with b/w illustrations. Subscriptions are $15. There was no poetry in the sample copy I saw.

‡THE STEVAN COMPANY (I), The Westwoods Center, 3253 Bee Cave Road, Austin, TX 78746, editor Kathryn S. McDonald. The company publishes an annual anthology of poetry built around a theme; 1987 will be Oriental influences. A reading fee of $2 per submission of 5 poems is charged. "We frown on profanity, look for forms of thoughtful open verse. No poetry with racist, religious bigotry or sexist overtones will be accepted." The last 1985 anthology, called Neutron, contains work by 18 poets, including David Wevell ("muse in residence" at the University of Texas), Ken Fontenot, and Bob Wolfkill. As a sample, the editor chose the opening lines from "Landscape" by Bob Wolfkill:

> The circumstance of winter
> is emotion. To feel
>
> that certain element curling
> around your limbs,

The next anthology will be 8x10¼", offset on ordinary white paper, cover printed on card stock with b/w photograph, 55 pp., perfect spine. The Steven Company sponsors various poetry readings in the Austin area and does videotapes of readings for Community Television. Stevan titles are distributed locally; "poets from other areas whose work is accepted will be asked to accept 10 free copies to distribute in their area. Back issues are available for $2 as the supply lasts. Poets are paid in contributor's copies." The editor says, "We continue to promote poetry as a labor of commitment to the ideals of literature as it represents free speech in the ultimate sense of the word, but do not wish to serve as a political mouthpiece for any particular special interest. If the poem has a political message avoid rhetoric."

*STONE COUNTRY, STONE COUNTRY PRESS, THE PHILLIPS POETRY AWARD (II), Box 132, Menemsha, MA 02552, phone 617-693-5832 or 645-2829, founded 1974, poetry editor Judith Neeld. "*Stone Country* magazine and Stone Country Press have consistently aspired to the publication of poetry (and related reviews, essays, special features) reflecting the craft and vision of its time. Our purpose in publishing poetry is to be an outlet for achieving poets whose work deserves serious and growing attention. Concomitant with this purpose is that of offering perspectives in contemporary poetry for poets at every degree of development. To this end, we publish special features in the magazine such as the series 'Currents in Poetry of the 80's,' forums on writers workshops, poetry of 'Wars & Rumors,' regional poets, etc. Whatever the feature section may be, *SC* always carries a general poetry selection and The Phillips Poetry Award. This latter is given to one or two poems, nominated by an independent panel, as best in the previous issue ($25 each). No restrictions on poetry used, but we must be made to see the common experience from a new perspective. We want unpredictable yet immediate images, mystery, the immersive strategies. We are open to all subjects and styles, usually not more than 40 lines in length, though we have published longer poems of irresistible qualities." They have recently published poetry by Linda Pastan, Jane Somerville, Robert Pinsky, David Hopes and Elizabeth Bartlett. The editors selected these sample lines from "Menses" by Robert Gibb:

> This dark which keeps
> On bleeding, these petals
> Which are always healing
> Within themselves.

Stone Country appears twice annually, digest-sized, 80-88 pp., glossy card cover with colored ink, printrun per issue 500, annual circulation 800, 250 subscriptions of which 50 are libraries. Majority of sales is single copy. Subscription $8.50; per copy $4.75. They receive 5,000-6,000 submissions per year, use 100-150, have a 5-10 month backlog. Sample: $3.50 postpaid. "We prefer 5 poems per submission; we read continuously throughout the year; if poems are more than one page each, then a total of 5 pp. is preferred. Simultaneous submissions considered provided we are advised. However, we will not publish work accepted by another journal unless we specifically request it." Reports in 2 months. Pays 1 copy (but note Phillips Award described above). Send SASE for guidelines. Editors "always comment briefly on submissions. Criticism is intended to encourage and/or instruct, never defeat. Criticism fee occasionally arranged, as time permits, to provide intensive help requested by a poet. Fee depends upon number of poems to be critiqued. The Press, a cooperative, publishes chapbooks and flat-spined paperback collections. Not presently considering submissions for book publication. When they do publish books they are on a "variable cooperative cost-sharing arrangement in which arrangements are made to keep an agreed-upon percentage of pressrun for the fulfillment of mail orders and issuance of review copies. The author then receives the balance of the books for local sales. The author receives 100% of all sales, including mail order, in this way." In 1982 *Stone Country* became a "self-supporting entity of The Nathan Mayhew Seminars, a non-profit educational group on the island of Martha's Vineyard." The editors comment, "As is true of every art, poetry requires commitment. The poem itself should be the principal goal, but publication is important as well. Though art—at its best—does not preach and pontificate but, rather, surprises and mystifies, it needs an audience in order to develop. The poet must, from beginning to end, be a serious student of all ages, stages, practices and practitioners of poetry. And at all times must be read as committedly into current poetry publications as the editors and publishers give of their own commitment."

‡*STONE SOUP, THE MAGAZINE BY CHILDREN (IV, Children), Box 83, Santa Cruz, CA 95063, founded 1973, editor Ms. Gerry Mandel. *Stone Soup* publishes **writing and art by children to age 13; they want to see free verse poetry but no rhyming poetry, haiku, or cinquain.** The editor chose as a sample these four lines from "Cancun, a Paradise" by 9-year-old Lisa Osornio:

> Dangling of the blue
> Drops of water splashed from the cool pool,
> orange ice drinks cool, going down into the water
> and swimming eight different ways.

Stone Soup, published 5 times a year, is a handsome 6x8¾" magazine, professionally printed on heavy stock with b/w drawings and a full-color illustration on the matte card cover, saddle-stapled. A membership in the Children's Art Foundation at $18.00/year includes a subscription to the magazine, each issue of which contains an Activity Guide. There are 2 pp. of poetry in each issue. Circulation is 8,000, all by subscription; 1,000 go to libraries. **Sample: $3.75 postpaid. Submissions can be any number of pages, any format, but no multiple submissions. The editor receives 2,000 submissions/year and uses only 10; she reports in 6-8 weeks. Guidelines are available for SASE. Pay is 2 copies plus discounts. Criticism will be given when requested.**

STONY HILLS, SMALL PRESS NEWS (II), Weeks Mills, New Sharon, ME 04955, phone 207-778-3436, founded 1981, poetry editor Diane Kruchkow. Both of these publications are primarily concerned with small press news and reviews and thus are more important as resources than markets for poets, but both use some short poems, **"less than 32 lines. More OK, if poem is superb." As a sample I chose the opening of "whine" by Steve Richmond:**

> it's all he does
> in his writings
> on the streets
> to his friends

Stony Hills is a tabloid, 16 pp. "full of energetic and often unconventional reviews and commentary, with photos, poems, listings, interviews, etc." It has a circulation of 2,500, appears irregularly. **Sample: $1.50 postpaid. Send no more than 5 poems. "Sometimes I pay $5-10/article or poem; if not at least 5 copies."** *Small Press News* is a mimeographed newsletter, 8 pp. on colored mimeo paper, stapled at the corner, appearing 10 times a year, circulation 290. **Sample: $1.25 postpaid. Submit no more than 5 poems. Reports within 2 months. Pays copies.** Diane Kruchkow advises, "Try not to associate with too many other poets, and keep your ego in check (seriously)."

‡STORMLINE PRESS, INC. (V, IV, Rural), Box 593, Urbana, IL 61801, phone 217-328-2665, founded 1985, publisher Ray Bial, an independent press publishing fiction, poetry, and photography, **ordinarily only by invitation. Mr. Bial prefers poetry on rural and small town themes; he does not want anything experimental. Writers interested in publishing with him should consider simultaneous submissions. Hard copy MSS are preferred, but photocopied or dot-matrix MSS are OK, as are discs if they are compatible with Kaypro 16. Royalties will be 15% after production costs are covered, plus 20 author's copies.** The press publishes 2-4 books of poetry each year with an average page count of 72. They are 6x9", some flat-spined paperbacks and some hardcover.

‡*STRAIGHT, STANDARD PUBLISHING CO. (IV, Christian, teens), 8121 Hamilton Ave., Cincinnati, OH 45231, editor Dawn B. Korth. Standard is a large, religious publishing company. *Straight* is a weekly take-home publication (digest-sized, 12 pp., color newsprint) for teens. Poetry is *by* teenagers, any style, **religious or inspirational in nature. No adult-written poetry.** As a sample I selected the complete poem, "Love is . . . by Laura L. Nelson (15):

> puppies to cuddle
> friends to enjoy
> memories to cherish
> nature to explore
> a beautiful rainbow
> a Man on a cross

Guidelines available for SASE. **Pays $5/poem plus 5 copies, reports in 4-6 weeks, publishes acceptances in 9-12 months. Teen author must include birthdate. Photocopy, dot matrix, simultaneous submissions OK.**

STREET PRESS, *STREET MAGAZINE, (II, IV Regional/eastern Long Island), Box 555, Port Jefferson, NY 11777, founded 1973, poetry editors Graham Everett, Leonard Greco and Marge Miller. The press publishes anthologies, postcard series, posters, chapbooks, pamphlets and flat-spined paperbacks. They want poetry which is **"clear and authentic, as short as necessary."** They have published poetry by Bud Navero, Fred Byrnes and William Brown. Their magazine, *Street*, "a voice for and to the people of eastern Long Island and the rest of the world," appears irregularly, digest-sized, 48-120 pp. of which 85-90% are poetry, circulation 500-750, 75 subscriptions of which 25 are libraries. Subscription: $10 for 4 issues. They use about 25 of 250 submissions per year, have a year's backlog. **Sample: $3 postpaid. Submit 3-6 pp. "Issues have been thematic—query first." Reports in 2 months. No pay. For book publication, query with 6 samples, $10 reading fee. Payment for books: 10% of run. Send for catalog to buy samples.**

‡*STRIDE MAGAZINE, STRIDE PUBLICATIONS, STRIDE CASSETTES (II), 80 Lord St., Crewe, Cheshire CW2 7DL, England, phone Crewe 216-710, founded 1981, editor R.M. Loydell. *Stride* magazine publishes art, prose, poetry, reviews, interviews, music, and features. Stride Publications publishes translations, poetry, and poetry sequences. **The editor wants to see any poetry that is "well written, interesting, experimental."** He has recently published work by R.S. Thomas, Brian Louis Pearce, Matt Simpson, and John Gimlett. I have not seen a copy of the magazine; it is digest-sized, offset, 100 pp. with b/w artwork—drawings, photos, cartoons, etc.—matte card cover. *Stride* appears quarterly and has a circulation of 500, of which 250 are subscriptions, 11 go to libraries, and 150 are newsstand sales. Price per issue is £1.50, subscription £5 (£6.50 Europe, £7.50 USA). **Sample available for £1.25 England or £1.50 rest of world. Pay is currently 1 copy. MSS should be typed with name and address on every sheet. Reporting time is 6 weeks maximum and accepted poems appear in the next issue.** Stride Publications publishes 10-20 poetry chapbooks/year with an average page count of 40, digest-sized, paperback, saddle-stapled. **Freelance submissions for book publication are accepted.** Authors should query first, sending sample poems. The editors **"usually publish authors known to us from magazine submissions but open to anyone (we have to have a market)." Queries will be answered in 1 week and MSS reported on in 3 months or more. Photocopied MSS are OK. Pay is in author's copies, 10% of the press run.** Book catalog is available for large SASE. The editor says, "Check basics—much spelling and grammar wrong in received MSS. Say something *new* in a *new* way. Read magazine first before submitting. Support the smaller presses—we support you."

STRONGHOLD PRESS, *PLAINS POETRY JOURNAL (II), Box 2337, Bismarck, ND 58502, founded 1982, editor Jane Greer, publishes "meticulously crafted, language-rich poetry which is demanding but not inaccessible. **We love rhyme and meter and poetic conventions if they are used in vigorous and interesting ways.** I strive to publish unpublished poets as well as old pros. **I do NOT want broken-prose 'free verse' or greeting card-type traditional verse. I want finely-crafted poetry which uses the best poetic conventions from the past in a way that doesn't sound as if it were *written* in the past. No specifications except that very few villanelles are interesting to me. Our credo is, 'no subject matter is taboo; treatment is everything.' "** They have recently published poetry by Robert N. Feinstein, Thomas Fleming, John Moffitt, Richard Moore, Margherita Faulkner, Nancy G. Westerfield and R. L. Barth. As a sample Greer chose the opening quatrain of "Last Minute" by Gary Selden:

> He walks, each step a stumbling.
> The warped oak boards go soft as air.
> Eight steps, nine, ten, and the warden fumbling
> Behind the chair.

Plains Poetry Journal is a quarterly, digest-sized, 44 pp. (of which about 40 are poetry), saddle-stapled, professionally printed on tinted paper with matte card cover, graphics, circulation 300, 250 subscriptions of which 25 are libraries. Subscription: $14. They receive 1,500-2,000 submissions per year, use about 200, seldom have more than 3 month backlog. **Sample: $3.50 postpaid. Submit "not less than 3 poems, not more than 10 at a time. Photocopy, hand-written, dot-matrix, simultaneous submissions, all OK." Reports usually same day, never more than a week on borderline poems "unless I'm out of town, which is seldom." Pays copies. Send SASE for guidelines. "Although I am still marketing books I have already published, I have had to make the hard decision to publish no more books for some time. It costs me too much. Considering the rude and totally unnecessary slowness of most publishers, an author is *crazy* not to submit simultaneously."** Jane Greer says she comments on rejections "often, especially if the MS is especially promising or if I think the poet is a child or teen (it happens)." She will criticize for a fee "only if I've said that I'm not able to publish the work and the poet wants me to criticize it anyway; the fee depends on the length of the MS and the amount of work to be done." She comments, "There is no excuse for not sending a SASE with submissions, and I'm getting to the point where I regretfully file such submissions in the trash. Don't bother with cover letters explaining what you're 'trying' to do in your poetry; if it's there, an editor with brains will see it, and if it isn't, no amount of explaining will help you."

STUDIA HISPANICA EDITORS, PRICKLY PEAR PRESS (IV, Ethnic), 502 Irma Dr., Austin, TX 78752, founded 1978, poetry editors Luis A. Ramos-Garcia and Dave Oliphant, is "a non-profit international cultural exchange organization interested in **regional literature (Texas) and in translations into English, Spanish and Portuguese** from the USA and Latin American writers. It works closely with Prickly Pear Press (Austin-Ft. Worth), producing anthologies and flat-spined paperbacks of **Texas and Latin American poetry.**" They have recently published poetry by William Barney, Naomi Shihab Nye, David Yates, James Hoggard, Edgard O'Hara, Antonio Cisneros, Javier Heraud, Silva-Santisteban, Dave Oliphant and R. G. Vliet. The editors selected these sample lines by Vassar Miller from "Reconciled":

> *Now I lay claim to this my native land*
> *planting my flag in the province of my dying,*
> *where I grow by diminution, am enriched*
> *by my renunciations, name myself . . .*

Query with 5 samples, bio, publication credits. "Writers should have grants/fellowships/personal money, etc. to pay for printing expenses. Editing and designing are free." Replies to queries in 4 weeks. Simultaneous submissions, photocopies OK. Send for booklist to buy samples.

*STUDIA MYSTICA (IV, Mystical experience), California State University, Sacramento, CA 95819, phone 916-278-6444, founded 1978, poetry editor Kathryn Hohlwein, is "a quarterly journal whose purpose is to **express mystical experience** through creative art, essay and scholarly articles. **We accept poetry that expresses the subtlety of mystical (not occult) experience, that in the tradition of the Sufi mystic poets, John of the Cross, the Biblical 'Song of Songs.' We do not want to see poetry that is obviously devotional or religious.**" They have recently published poetry by Raymond Roseliep, Dennis Schmitz, Ralph Slotten, Elizabeth Searle Lamb, Jeremy Ingalls and Jessica Powers. The editors selected these sample lines by Ted Lovington Jr.:

> *Once, as a dolphin of the Lord*
> *I moved in seas of light,*
> *Savoring lucid dawn and render day,*
> *Splendors of star-luminous night.*

The 80 pp. flat-spined, digest-sized journal has a circulation of 400, 300 subscriptions of which 150 are libraries. Subscription $14; per copy: $4. They use about a fifth of the 150-200 submissions received annually. **Sample: free for SASE. Submit no more than 10 poems. Simultaneous submissions OK. Reports in 3 weeks. No pay.**

SUBURBAN WILDERNESS PRESS, SUBURBAN WILDERNESS BROADSIDE OF A BARN SERIES, *POETRY MOTEL, OUTPOSTS, POETRY MOTEL CHAPS (II), 430 S. 21st Ave. E., Duluth, MN 55812, 218-724-6153, founded 1984, poetry editors Andrea and Patrick McKinnon, graphic editor Steven Grandell, associate editor Buddy Backen, aims "to publish contemporary literature, especially work that large houses won't consider. We are not in this for profit. We are in it because we have to be. **Don't want to see anything safe. We want poetry that takes risks. No specifications except that prose poems should not exceed 2 pages double-spaced.**" They have recently published poetry by James, Androla, Peters, Moffeit, Moore, Glass, Fox, Equi and "many new voices." The editors selected these sample lines by Tony Moffeit:

> *in this dance hall*
> *of time it's enough*
> *to race the trains*
> *to all-night cafes*

Poetry Motel appears 3 times a year, digest-sized , saddle-stapled, matte card cover, offset from typescript, includes 1-3 mini-chaps with each issue (to subscribers only), circulation 350 (to 350 subscriptions), 40-60 pp. of poetry, prose, essays and reviews in each issue. Subscription: $5 for 3 issues. They receive about 1,250 submissions per year, take 150, have no more than 2-3 month backlog. **Sample: $2 postpaid. Submit 6-10 pp., informal cover letter, name and address on each page. Photocopy OK. Simultaneous submissions OK. Reports in 1-3 weeks. Pays 1 copy. Editors are "always glad to comment, on request."** They advise, "Poets should read as much poetry as they can lay their hands on. And not just stuff that was written 50-150 years ago. If you want to write contemporary poetry, it only stands to reason that you need to read contemporary poetry."

*SUCCESS MAGAZINE, SUCCESS POETRY PUBLICATIONS (II), 17 Andrews Crescent, Peterborough, England PE4 6XL, founded 1968, poetry editor Michaela Edridge, is "a general writers' magazine with a large section devoted to poetry," appearing quarterly. "**Any kind of poetry is consid-**

ered, but for space reasons shorter work has a greater chance of acceptance." They have recently published poetry by Malc Payne, Margaret Munro Gibson, Cy Patterson, Irene Twite, Peggy George, Paul Renshaw and Ian Gordon. Michaela Edridge selected these sample lines from "The Night You Slept" by Edmund Henderson:

> The night too recalls you to me
> it is remote and its cries echo
> as though from far away
> as though from deep within a heart's cold tomb

There are 10-12 pp. of poetry in each issue, circulation 600, 520 subscriptions of which 6 are libraries. Subscription: $17. They receive 50-100 submissions per year, use 10-20, have a 3-6 month backlog. **Sample: $5 postpaid. Submit no more than 6 poems at a time, 1 per page. Reports within 2 weeks. Pays 1 copy.** Success Poetry Publications are anthologies and chapbooks for members only. They conduct an annual Open Poetry competition plus quarterly competitions for members. "We publish in the magazine articles about presentation, modern and traditional poetry, Form, Imagery etc. Also a regular 'Poetry Markets' column."

SUMMER STREAM PRESS (II), Box 6056, Santa Barbara, CA 93160-6056, phone 805-682-4626, founded 1978, poetry editor David Duane Frost, publishes a series of books in hardcover and softcover, each presenting 6 poets, averaging 70 text pp. for each poet. "The mix of poets represents many parts of the country and many approaches to poetry. The poets in the initial two volumes have been published, but that is no requirement. We present 1-2 traditional poets in the mix and thus offer them a chance for publication in this world of free-versers. The **6 poets share a 15% royalty. We require rights for our editions worldwide, and share 50-50 with authors for translation rights and for republication of our editions by another publisher. Otherwise all rights remain with the authors.** The first book features Martha Ellis Bosworth and poetry by Ruthann Robson, Clarke Dewey Wells, Robert K. Johnson, David Duane Frost and Ed Engle, Jr., from whose "Baking Catholic (Infallibility)" I selected these lines as a sample:

> The nun says the Catechism's true
> because the Pope's infallible.
> Gaylon passes me a note:
> God made his father that way, too.

To be considered for future volumes in this series, **query with about 12 samples, no covering letter. Replies to query in 30 days, to submission (if invited) in 6 months. Published poetry, simultaneous submissions, photocopy OK. Editor sometimes comments on rejections.**

*THE SUN (II), 412 W. Rosemary St., Chapel Hill, NC 27514, phone 919-942-5282, founded 1974, editor Sy Safransky, is "a monthly magazine of ideas" which uses "**all kinds of poetry.**" They have recently published poems by David Citino, Hal. J. Daniels III, Cedar Koons, Robert Bly, Michael Shorb, Roger Sauls, Alan Brilliant and Christopher Bursk. The editor selected these sample lines from "Two People At Dawn" by Robert Bly:

> His hand remains firm.
> Her courage shines
> the whole length of her body.

The Sun is magazine-sized, 40 pp., printed on 50 lb. offset, saddle-stapled, with b/w photos, graphics and ads, circulation 2,500, 1,500 subscriptions of which 25 are libraries. Subscription: $28. They receive 500 submissions of freelance poetry per year, use 25, have a 1-3 month backlog. **Sample: $3 postpaid. Submit no more than 6 poems. Reports within 1 month. Pays $5 on publication and in copies and subscription. Send SASE for guidelines.**

*SUNRUST MAGAZINE, DAWN VALLEY PRESS (II, IV, Rural), Box 58, New Wilmington, PA 16142, press founded in 1976, magazine in 1983, editors Nancy E. James and James A. Perkins. *Sunrust Magazine* is "a collection of poetry, prose, art and photography emphasizing the **moods, people and places of rural America.** The words and images in *Sunrust* express a uique identity and provide an adventure to capture impressions that are rich in life and spirit." Dawn Valley Press publishes chapbooks of poetry, usually 2/year, by individual arrangements. The type of poetry wanted for the magazine is **"in keeping with the theme, in good taste, preferably in free verse form (no greeting card verse), and no longer than 75 lines."** Poets recently published include Ed Ochester and James Deahl. As a sample the editor chose these lines from "View from a Red Chair" by Walt Phillips:

> The lake was as clear
> as the snow of a Christmas memory
> and the trees were the kind
> that bathe a fever away

The magazine is digest-sized, 72 pp. saddle-stapled, offset from typed copy on heavy stock with b/w drawings and photographs, two-color matte card cover. It appears twice a year and has a circulation of 400, of which 90 are subscriptions and 220 are mail order sales. Price per issue is $4.50, subscription $8/ year. **Sample $3 postpaid. Guidelines are available for SASE. Contributors receive 1 copy and may purchase additional copies at half price. Poets should submit no more than 10 poems, typed or photocopied; they prefer not to have simultaneous submissions. Reports are in 2-3 months, and accepted poems are published in the next issue. Dawn Valley Press usually does not accept freelance submissions of MSS for chapbooks; writers should query first.** The chapbooks are also digest-sized, 64 pp., flat-spined paperbacks.

*SUNSHINE MAGAZINE, *GOOD READING MAGAZINE, THE SUNSHINE PRESS, HENRICHS PUBLICATIONS, INC. (I), Box 40, Litchfield, IL 62056, phone 217-324-3425, founded 1924, poetry editor Peggy Kuethe. *Sunshine Magazine* "is almost entirely a fiction magazine; *Good Reading* is made up of short, current interest factual articles." Both magazines **use some poetry. "We do** *not* **publish free verse or abstract poetry, no haiku, no negative subjects, no violence, sex, alcohol. We use only uplifting, inspirational poetry that is of regular meter and that rhymes. Inspirational, seasonal, or humorous poetry preferred. Easy to read, pleasantly rhythmic. Maximum 16 lines—no exceptions."** They have recently published poems by Angie Monnens, Alice Mackenzie Swaim, Ruth M. Walsh and E. Cole Ingle. The editor selected these sample lines by Starrlette L. Howard:

> We cannot all own a garden
> or pantry behind a cellar door.
> We can't all see the harvest
> from seed to field to store.
> Yet the golden days of harvest
> and the goodness that you measure
> Can be stored within your hearts
> as your own supply of treasure

Both magazines are monthlies. *Sunshine* is 5¼x7¼, saddle-stapled, 36 pp., of which 5 are poetry, circulation to 75,000 subscribers. Subscription: $9. They use about 7% of 2,500 submissions of poetry each year. **Sample: 50¢. Send SASE for guidelines. Absolutely no queries. Submit typewritten MS, 1 poem per page. Reports in 6-8 weeks. Pays 1 copy.** *Good Reading* uses about 4 poems per issue, circulation to 7,200 subscribers. Subscription: $8. **Sample: 50¢. Submission specifications like those for *Sunshine*. Pays 1 copy.** The editors comment, "We strongly suggest authors read our guidelines and obtain a sample copy of our magazines. Our format and policies are quite rigid and we make absolutely no exceptions. Many authors submit something entirely different from our format or from anything we've published before—that is an instant guarantee of rejection."

SUNSTONE PRESS (IV, Regional/southwest), Box 2321, Santa Fe, NM 87504-2321, founded 1971, poetry editor Marcia Muth. "Since its beginning Sunstone Press has felt an obligation and commitment to poetry. Of their 96 published titles, 23 are poetry. Poets represent Anglo, Spanish and Indian cultures. Unfortunately inflation and rising costs have meant that fewer books of poetry are published by the Press since poetry is less of a commercial success than other books. To alleviate to some extent this financial burden, **we now also offer a form of cooperative publishing for some titles. Part of the expense is furnished by a grant or a sponsor (individual or corporate). In some cases the sponsor's money is returned as the books are sold. The author, of course, receives a regular royalty contract with the usual royalty agreement. We are interested in good literary quality and have, in general, tended to publish poetry with a Southwestern emphasis."** They have recently published poetry by Gerald Hausman, Phillips Kloss and Linda Monacelli Johnson. I selected as a sample the opening lines of "The Shining Mountains" by Cynthia Grenfell:

> The mountain peaks gleam and sparkle
> Gifts to the eyes and heart
> The big dog of heaven licks them clean
> Wagging his feathered tail.

That's from a collection, **Stone Run: Tidings**, a 76 pp. flat-spined paperback, printed mostly in a 2 column format on yellow-tinted paper in italic type with some ink drawing illustrations, matte card cover, $11.95. **Query with 3 samples, bio. Replies to queries "at once," to submissions, if invited, in 6 weeks. Photocopies, dot-matrix OK. Contracts are on 10% of wholesale price.**

SUPERINTENDENT'S PROFILE & POCKET EQUIPMENT DIRECTORY (IV, Specialized), 220 Central Ave., Box 43, Dunkirk, NY 14048, phone 716-366-4774, founded 1978, poetry editor Robert Dyment, is a "monthly magazine, circulation 2,500, for town, village, city, and county highway superintendents and DPW directors throughout New York State," and uses "**only poetry that pertains to highway superintendents and DPW directors and their activities."** Submit no more than one

page double-spaced. Subscription: $10. They receive about 15 freelance submissions of poetry per year, use 10, have a 2 month backlog. **Sample: 80¢ postage. Reports within a month. Pays $5/poem.**

‡**SWAMP PRESS (II)**, 323 Pelham Rd., Amherst Rd., Amherst, MA 01002, founded 1977, editor-in-chief Ed Rayher, a small-press publisher of poetry, fiction, and illustration. The press publishes 1-5 poetry chapbooks per year, with an average page count of 24, paperbacks and hardcovers. **Freelance submissions are accepted; the author should send chapbook MSS. Queries will be answered in 10 weeks and MSS reported on in the same amount of time. Photocopied or dot-matrix MSS are OK, as are discs if compatible with Wordstar, but hard copy is preferred. Pay will be in author's copies, 10% of press run.**

‡*****SYNTHESIS—A NEWSLETTER AND JOURNAL FOR SOCIAL ECOLOGY, DEEP ECOL-OGY, AND BIOREGINALISM (IV, Ecology)**, Box 1858, San Pedro, CA 90733, phone 213-833-2633, founded 1975, edited by an editorial committee, "**only occasional publication of a poem relat-ed to our interests—ecological, nature, non-violence, freedom, self-initiative, goodwill towards all species, uniqueness of our planet, physical and mental emancipation.**" They do not want "**vio-lence, mysticism.**" They have recently published poetry by Walt Franklin. As a sample, the editors chose the following lines by an unidentified poet:

> *I shall not believe*
> *In the law of the jungle*
> *In the language of weapons*
> *In the power of the mighty.*

Synthesis, which appears quarterly, is 22 pp., mimeographed, with art, no ads. Its circulation is 800, of which about 15 are library subscription. Price per copy is 75¢, subscription $3/year in the US and $4/year elsewhere. **Sample available for 75¢ US or $1 foreign. Pay is as many copies as wanted. Their backlog is small, and submissions are reported on at publication.**

*****TANDAVA (II)**, 25521 Hoffmeyer, Roseville, MI 48066, founded 1982, poetry editors Tom and Leona Blessing, is "primarily a poetry magazine, although we will print fiction dealing with India or the Great Lakes region. Poets should avoid the trite and outworn. We are looking for fresh images." They have recently published poetry by Arthur Winfield Knight, Ligi, todd moore, John Ditsky, Harry Calhoun and D.E. Steward. The editors selected these sample lines by Tim Peeler:

> *I thought I saw fire once.*
> *trees split with sparks*
> *glaring convulsively,*
> *maybe coon eyes*
> *hiding from Winchester's echo*
> *and the hunt*

The magazine appears in various inexpensive formats, devoting 28-50 pp. per issue to poetry, circula-tion 100, 35 subscriptions of which 2 are libraries. They receive about 100 submissions of freelance poetry per year, use 40, have a 6-12 month backlog. **Sample: $2 postpaid. Reports in 1-6 weeks. Pays 2 copies. Editors sometimes comment on rejections.**

*****TAR RIVER POETRY (II)**, English Dept., East Carolina University, Greenville, NC 27834, phone 757-6041, founded 1960, editor Peter Makuck, associate editor Phyllis Zerella. "**We are not interested in sentimental, flat-statement poetry. What we would like to see is skillful use of figurative lan-guage.**" They have recently published poetry by William Matthews, Richard Jackson, Leslie Norris, Carolyn Kizer, Michael Waters, Paula Rankin, Fred Chappell, Brendan Galvin, A. Poulin, Jr., and Pa-tricia Goedicke. The editors selected these sample lines from "Wrinkles" by Judith Sornberger:

> *. . . even for the cruel things—*
> *the network of lines crossing my face,*
> *birds gathering there for a song*
> *that, at twenty, I never could have heard*

Tar River appears twice yearly, digest-sized 52 pp., professionally printed on salmon stock, some deco-rative line drawings, matte card cover with photo, circulation 900 +, 500 subscriptions of which 125 are libraries. Subscription: $5. They receive 6,000-8,000 submissions per year, use 150-200. **Sample: $2.50. "We do not consider simultaneous submissions. Double or single-spaced OK. We prefer not more than 6 pp. at one time. We do not consider MSS during summer months." Reports in 3-6 weeks. Pays copies. Send SASE for guidelines. Editors will comment "if slight revision will do the trick."** They advise, "Read, read, read. Saul Bellow says the writer is primarily a reader moved to emu-lation. Read the poetry column in *Writer's Digest*. Read the books recommended therein. Do your homework."

‡**TAXVS PRESS, APRIL BOOKS (II)**, 30 Logan St., Langley Park, Durham, England DH7 9YN, phone 0385-732296, poetry editor Michael Farley, is a small press publisher of book-length collections of poetry and short-stories, publishing paperback, hardcover and some chapbooks. "Taxus Press is named after the yew-tree, *taxus* in Latin (hence the 'V' when the word is set in upper case—classical Rome had no 'U' in the alphabet. We have a very Catholic editorial policy: **open to all manner of serious, intelligently written work—slight, far from exclusive, bias in favour of work reflecting Christian faith, but not 'greeting-card' verse! We do not want to see light verse, doggerel, extreme beginners' first attempts, obscene (as opposed to erotic!) work, overtly anti-Christian work, or anything reflecting any real bigotry.**" They have recently published poetry by Anne Stevenson, Peter Redgrove, Jon Silkin, Norman Nicholson and Richard Caddel. The editor selected these sample lines from "Aditum per me," in the collection **Lake & Labyrinth** (1985) by Sally Purcell:

> *The Janus Joseph rules every entrance,*
> *and the hinges of death's door,*
> *borrows a cradle, lends a tomb, preparing*
> *thresholds for God.*

They publish 2 chapbooks, 10 64-pp. flat-spined, 2 hardcover books per year. **Query with 10 sample poems, bio and credits, including "details of previous (including magazine) publications, readings, broadcasts, etc." Reports to queries in 2 weeks, to MSS in 2 months. Simultaneous submissions acceptable if arrangements are explicitly made for simultaneous publication in another country. Photocopy, dot-matrix OK, also discs compatible with Acorn/BBC (hard copy preferred). Pays 5-10% royalties, 10 copies (or "up to full value of royalty on first edition")** Book catalog available; books distributed in US by SPD INC., 1784 Shattuck Ave., Berkeley, CA 94709. **"If criticism seems likely to benefit a 'near miss' author, or if a beginner shows real promise, advice may be offered** *gratis*." Michael Farley offers this general advice, which applies to many publishers: "*Submissions*: The most important thing about manuscripts submitted to any publisher is that they should be legible. In my opinion it is a matter of indifference whether they are printed by typewriter, daisy-wheel, or dot-matrix, original or photocopied—the sole criterion is legibility. A photocopy of good crisp NLQ dot-matrix print is far more legible than an original from a 1940 portable typewriter with clogged type-bars and a ten-month-old ribbon; but work from an old single-strike dot-matrix with a tired ribbon isn't easy to read either, and those grey, slippery electrostatic photocopies aren't any better. Don't forget binding on long MSS—something that holds together, but is removable if need be (e.g., for editing, or for fitting into a copyholder when typesetting) is best—plastic strip or spring binders are therefore better than (admittedly elegant) comb binders. *The work:* An editor is about all a reader—in many ways he or she could be said to be a reader for readers. Remember that it is highly unlikely (Emily Dickinson notwithstanding) that a poet will suddenly emerge in total darkness, ready to spring a big fat book on the world out of nowhere. Being part of a literary community is vital to the development of most writers, and to their subsequent growth and progress. Take every opportunity to learn—attend workshops, creative writing courses, anything available, and to publish with magazine and chapbook publishers; and don't forget that you can learn as much from people with whom you disagree as with ones with whom never a cross word is exchanged—often more, because healthy controversy stimulates the mind when a mutual admiration society may send it to sleep! And do read the work of potential publishers wherever possible—the local public or university library can often help here—get to know a possible editor through the work he/she publishes. That's why this book you're reading was published in the first place!"

‡***TEARS IN THE FENCE (II)**, 38 Hodview, Stourpaine, Nr. Blandford Forum, Dorset DT11 8TN, England, phone 0258-56803, founded 1984, poetry editor Sarah Hopkins, a "small press magazine of poetry, fiction, interviews, articles, reviews, and graphics. **We are open to a wide variety of poetic styles. Work of a social, political, ecological and feminist awareness will be close to our purpose. However, we like to publish a balanced variety of work.**" The editors do not want to see "didactic rhyming poems." They have recently published Jack Clemo, Gerald Locklin, Tina Morris, and Shiela E. Murphy. As a sample, they selected the following lines from "The Nature of Wood" by John Walsh:

> *Nature is like a giant wooden*
> *statue that walks blindly on*
> *while man chips away at its legs.*

Tears in the Fence appears two times a year. It is magazine-sized, offset from typed copy on lightweight paper with b/w cover art and graphics, 60 pp., one-color matte card cover with black spiral binding. It has a print run of 525 copies, of which 86 go to subscribers and 146 are sold on newsstands. Price per issue is $2, **sample available for same price. Pay is 1 copy.** Writers should submit 5 typed poems with IRC's to Sara Hopkins, 29 Chapel St., Buckfastleigh, **South Devon TQ11 0AB, England. Reporting time is 2 months and time to publication 6-8 months "but can be much less."** The editor says, "I think it helps to subscribe to several magazines in order to study the market and develop an understanding of what type of poetry is published. Use the review sections and send off to magazines that are new to you."

TELS, TOKYO ENGLISH LITERATURE SOCIETY, TELS POETRY CONTEST, *PRINTED MATTER (IV, Specialized), TELS "Tomeoki," Koishikawa Post Office, Bunkyo-Ku, Tokyo, Japan 112, phone 03-380-1831, founded 1977, poetry editor Steven Forth. **"Our main purpose is to give people writing in English in Japan a place to present their work** and to provide information on literary events in the Tokyo area." *Printed Matter* is a bimonthly newsletter, 16 pp., 7x10", circulation 200 subscriptions of which 2 are libraries, uses 4-6 pp. of poetry in each issue. "**There are no limitations as to subject matter or style, but we receive a fair amount of high quality work, and are unlikely to publish pieces just because they are in a Japanese form, or deal with Japan. 'Haiku' would have to be exceptionally good to be published. Poems over 150 lines are unlikely to be accepted.**" They have recently published poetry by Henry Braun and Joseph Simas. The editors selected these sample lines by Eric Selland:

> *Nothing matters in an earthquake*
> *the planets collect like*
> *magnetic clusters,*
> *sand perhaps*
> *or bundles of wire.*

They receive 100-200 submissions of freelance poetry per year, use 25%. **Sample: $2 (or 3 IRCs).** "**Poets may submit as many poems, preferably typed, as they wish. People in Japan should enclose a SASE, those abroad should send 3 IRCs. Reports in about 1 month. Payment: two copies.** They also publish collections by individuals and anthologies. **Query with 10-15 samples for a book, cover letter with publication credits, bio and other information. Membership in TELS preferred, as is residence in Japan at time of publication of book. Response to query in 6 weeks, to submission (if invited) in 3 months. Simultaneous submission, photocopies, dot matrix OK. Pays 10-15% royalties plus a maximum of 50 copies (10% of printing).** They occasionally are open to subsidy arrangements on negotiable terms. They hold an annual poetry contest in March, 20 line maximum, sometimes with theme. Send SASE/IRC for entry form. The editor's advice: "Network—it's a big world."

*TERRITORY OF OKLAHOMA: LITERATURE & THE ARTS (IV, Regional), Box 60824, Oklahoma City, OK 73146, is an occasional (4-8 times a year) publication, 28 pp., circulation 500-1,200, using **poetry by present or former residents of Oklahoma.** "Most issues are single page, 11x17" folded, newsletter format with 1-2 chapbooks per year: 8½x5½", 20-32 pp. Recently published Mary McAnally, Rochelle Owens, Larry D. Griffin and Norman Russel. Considers simultaneous submissions. Sample: $10.**

*THE TEXAS REVIEW, THE TEXAS REVIEW CHAPBOOK AWARD (II), English Dept., Sam Houston State University, Huntsville, TX 77341, Paul Ruffin, Editor, founded 1976, is a biannual, 6x9", 140+ pp., circulation 750-1,000, has recently published poetry by Ernest Kroll, Tom Sexton, William Stafford and Philip St. Clair. I selected these sample lines from "When Insanity Comes a Knocking Throw Away the Door, The Log of the *Pequod 2*" by D. C. Berry:

> *The Japanese Magnolia is sheathed in amethyst.*
> *It's tighter than Dixie's hands at Vicksburg.*
> *It unknobs its bulge. It's a pure kamikaze fist*
> *socked into obtuse Mississippi.*

Sample: $2 postpaid. Submit 3-4 poems. No simultaneous or photocopied submissions. Reports in 4 weeks, pays 2 copies, one-year subscription. Send SASE for chapbook competition rules.

TEXTILE BRIDGE PRESS, *MOODY STREET IRREGULARS: A JACK KEROUAC NEWSLETTER (II, IV, Working class), Box 157, Clarence Center, NY 14032, founded 1978, poetry editor Joy Walsh. "**We publish material by and on the work of Jack Kerouac, American author prominent in the fifties. Our chapbooks reflect the spirit of Jack Kerouac. We use poetry in the spirit of Jack Kerouac, poetry of the working class, poetry about the everyday workaday life. Notice how often the work people spend so much of their life doing is never mentioned in poetry or fiction. Why? Poetry in any form.**" They have recently published poetry by Joseph Semenovich, Marion Perry, Bonnie Johnson, Boria Sax, Michael Basinski, Emanuel Fried, Mildred Crombie, Ted Joans, Michael Hopkins, Tom Clark, Jack Micheline, Carl Solomon and ryki zuckerman. Joy Walsh selected these sample lines from "Indefinite Layoff" by Delores Rossi Script:

> *How desperately man*
> *needs to work.*
> *Society has shaped it so.*
> *Without it, it diminishes*
> *his existence.*

Moody Street Irregulars is a 28 pp. magazine-sized newsletter, biannual, circulation 700-1,000 (700 subscriptions of which 30 are libraries), using 3-4 pp. of poetry in each issue. Subscription: $7. They receive about 50 freelance submissions of poetry per year, use half of them. **Sample: $3.50 postpaid. Reports in 1 month. Pays copies.** Textile Bridge Press also publishes collections by individuals. For book publication, **query with 5 samples. "The work speaks to me better than a letter." Replies to query in 1 week, to submission (if invited) in 1 month. Simultaneous submission OK for "some things yes, others no." Photocopy, dot-matrix OK. Pays copies. Send SASE for catalog to buy samples. Editor comments on rejections "if they ask for it."**

THIRD WOMAN PRESS, *THIRD WOMAN (IV, Minority women), % Chicano-Riqueno Studies, BH 849, Indiana University, Bloomington, IN 47405, phone 812-335-5257, founded 1981, poetry editors Norma Alarcon and Luz Maria Umpierre. **"Presently we are primarily interested in publishing the literary and artistic work of U.S. Latinas, Hispanic, Native American, and other US minority women in general. The journal as well as our publications are in Spanish or English. We prefer poetry that employs well-crafted images and metaphors and pays attention to musical rhythms."** They have recently published poetry by Pat Mora, Margarita Lopez Flores, Achy Obejas, Margie Agosin, Luz Ma. Umpierre and Sandra Esteves. The editors selected these sample lines by Sandra Cisneros:

> *Pink like a Starfish's belly*
> *or a newborn rat,*
> *she hid the infected hand*
> *for some time*
> *before they noticed.*

Third Woman appears twice a year, digest-sized, flat-spined, 130 pp., professionally printed, glossy card cover with b/w art, circulation 750, 250 subscriptions of which 75 are libraries, 20-25 pp. of poetry per issue. Subscription: $7. They receive about 100 freelance submissions of poetry per year, use 10-15. **Sample: $5 postpaid. Submit at least 5 poems with short bio and past publications. Acknowledgment immediately, acceptance in about 6 weeks. No pay. Editors sometimes comment on rejections. For chapbook publication, query with 5-10 samples. "Poets may have to invest in publication or participate in fundraising events." Simultaneous submissions "not preferred." MS should be "error free, clean type." Send SASE for catalog to buy samples.**

*13TH MOON (IV, Feminist), Box 309, Cathedral Station, New York, NY 10025, editor-in-chief Marilyn Hacker, is a **feminist literary semiannual using writing by women for a well-read audience. 50% of material used is poetry. Open to all styles. Prefers poetry written by women who** *read* **contemporary poetry. Poetry submissions should be double-spaced with extra space between stanzas. "We would like more submissions from women of color,"** the editors comment. "Independent literary magazines cannot continue to exist unless those people so eager to send their MSS and be read and criticized, if not published, by editors, are equally eager to purchase, subscribe to and read such periodicals." **Sample: $6.50 plus 75¢ postage.**

THIS IS IMPORTANT, IMPORTANT POETRY PRESS (II), % Illumanti, Box 67e07, Los Angeles, CA 90067, founded 1980, poetry editor F. A. Nettlebeck. *This Is Important* is "patterned after a religious tract and features one poem from 6 different poets in each issue. The pamphlets are distributed free on buses, subways, toilet floors, in bars, laundramats, etc. **Mostly want to see experimental poetry,** *no* **religious. Poems should be short and to the point."** F. A. Nettlebeck has recently published in this fashion poetry by Kostelanetz, Giorno, Lifshin, Micheline, Burroughs, Clark, Androla and Blazek. These sample lines were taken from "Father's Tooth" by Todd Moore:

> *he'd been working*
> *it w/a pliers*
> *all afternoon*
> *sd when it finally*
> *gave he could*
> *almost hear those*
> *roots pop loose*

Each leaflet is printed offset from typescript on a 4¼x11" piece of paper folded twice to make 8 panels. The black title-panel says "This Is Important" in white type. There are concrete poems (experimental typography) and other varieties, with the note that "Publishable poems are *always* welcome" on the back. F. A. Nettlebeck puts out 4 of these per year, printrun 5,000. As the *Los Angeles Times Book Review* noted, "A gift of $25 will support his costs for a run of 5,000 pamphlets, while $10 will assure you a year's subscription. If you can't afford that, a pamphlet is free for the asking." **Send $1 for samples. Reports in 1 month. Pays 200 copies. Editor sometimes comments on rejections.** His advice: "Don't give up, follow your heart and stick with it."

THISTLEDOWN PRESS LTD. (IV, Canadian authors), 668 East Place, Saskatoon, Saskatchewan, Canada S7J 2Z5, phone 306-477-0556, founded 1975, Patrick O'Rourke, Editor-in-Chief, is "a literary press that specializes in **quality books of contemporary poetry by Canadian authors. Only the best of contemporary poetry that amply demonstrates an understanding of craft with a distinctive use of voice and language. Only interested in full-length poetry MSS with a 60-80 pp. minimum.**" Each title is published in both hardback and paperback editions. They have recently published books of poetry by John V. Hicks, Patrick Lane, Andrew Wreggitt, Gerald Hill and Doris Hall. Canadian poets may **query with 6-10 pp. of sample poems, bio and publication credits. Replies to queries in 2-3 days, to submissions (if invited) in 2-3 months. No simultaneous submissions, photocopies or dot-matrix. Contract is for 10% royalty plus 10 copies. Editors sometimes comment on rejections.** They comment, "Poets submitting MSS to Thistledown Press for possible publication should think in 'book' terms in every facet of the organization and presentation of the MSS: poets presenting MSS that *read* like good books of poetry will have greatly enhanced their possibilities of being published."

THE THOMAS HARDY YEARBOOK (IV, Theme/Thomas Hardy), The Toucan Press, St. Peter Port, Guernsey, C.I. via Britain, founded 1970, editors J. Stevens Cox, F.S.A. and G. Stevens Cox M.A., "is devoted to publishing essays and articles about the life, times and works of Thomas Hardy; about the writer's environment, both physical and cultural; and about Dorset writers, especially those of the 19th century." **They use some poetry about or related to Thomas Hardy.** I selected as a sample the opening lines on "December 31st, 1974" by John Doheny:

Thomas Hardy leaned on a gate
Seventy-four years ago today
Viewing bleak and desolate life
Through the veil of Dorset winter,

The yearbook is 6x9", saddle-stapled, 116 glossy pp., mostly offset from typescript, double-spaced, the text appearing to be a camera-ready research paper. It is "virtually a nonprofit making enterprise. We solicit no subsidies from any quarter but rely entirely on subscriptions and advertisements." **Sample:** £3 plus postage. Payment by arrangement.

THREE CONTINENTS PRESS INC. (IV, Non-western), 5th Floor, 1646 Connecticut Ave., NW, Washington, DC 20009, phone 202-332-3886, founded 1973, poetry editors Donald Herdeck and Norman Ware: "**We publish literature by creative writers from the non-western world (Africa, the Middle East, the Caribbean, and Asia/Pacific)—poetry** *only* **by non-western writers, or good translations of such poetry if original language is Arabic, French, African vernacular, etc.**" They have recently published poetry by Derek Walcott, Khalil Hawi, Mahmud Dawish and Julia Fields. As a sample "The Wind" from **Burden of Waves and Fruit** by the Indian poet Jayanta Mahapatra:

My eyes are getting used to the dark.
From time to time
My old father comes at me
with outstretched arms of judgement
and I answer from no clear place I am in.

This collection is a digest-sized 98 pp. flat-spined book professionally printed, glossy card cover with art. They also publish anthologies focused on relevant themes. **Query with 4-5 samples, bio, publication credits. Replies to queries in 5-10 weeks, to submissions (if invited) in 4-5 weeks. 10% royalty contract (5% for translator) with $100-200 advance plus 10 copies.** Send SASE for catalog to buy samples.

‡*3 SCORE & 10 (IV, Elderly)**, Box 103, RD #2, Boswell, PA 15531, phone 814-629-9815, founded 1984, editor Joseph Kaufman, a monthly aimed at readers over 70 years of age—"general interest/inspirational/ informative/educational/helpful/humorous/seek wisdom." Poems wanted are **"short, any style"** but nothing **"depressing/distasteful/negative."** *3 Score & 10* is saddle-stapled, offset from typed copy, matte card cover. The issue I saw has a picture on the cover of an Elder Hostel group looking very happy. It contains no poetry. Subscription rate is $7/year. **Sample $1 postpaid, guidelines available for SASE. Simultaneous submissions OK. Pay is $3/poem plus 1 copy. Submissions are reported on in 2-3 weeks and publication takes 3-6 months, possibly longer.**

***THE THREEPENNY REVIEW (II)**, Box 9131, Berkeley, CA 94709, phone 415-849-4545, founded 1980, poetry editor Wendy Lesser, "is a quarterly review of literature, performing and visual arts, and social articles aimed at the intelligent, well-read, but not necessarily academic reader. Nationwide circulation. **Want: formal, narrative, short poems (and others); not want: confessional, no punctuation, no capital letters. Prefer under 50 lines but not necessary. No bias** *against* **formal poetry, in fact a slight bias in favor of it.**" They have recently published poetry by Thom Gunn, Frank Bidart, Robert Haas, Czeslaw Milosz, Brenda Hillman and Louise Gluck. and Charles Wright. There are about 7-8 poems in each 28 pp. tabloid issue, circulation 7,500, 6,000 subscriptions of which 300 are libraries. Subscription: $8. They receive about 4,500 submissions of freelance poetry per year, use 12. **Sample:**

$3 postpaid. **Send 5 poems or fewer per submission. Reports 2-8 weeks. Pays $30/poem. Send SASE for guidelines.**

THRESHOLD BOOKS (IV, Spiritual, translations), Box 1350, RD #3, Dusty Ridge Rd., Putney, VT 05346, phone 802-387-4586 or 254-8300, founded 1981, poetry editor Edmund Helminski, is "a small press dedicated to the publication of quality works in metaphysics, poetry in translation, and literature with some spiritual impact. **We would like to see poetry in translation of high literary merit with spiritual qualities, or original work by established authors.**" They have recently published poetry by Rainer Maria Rilke. The editor selected these sample lines by Jelaluddin Rumi, translated by John Moyne and Coleman Barks:

> *We have this way of talking, and we have another.*
> *Apart from what we wish and what we fear may happen,*
> *We are alive with other life, as clear stones*
> *take form in the mountain.*

That comes from a collection **Open Secret, Versions of Rumi**, published in a beautifully printed flat-spined, digest-sized paperback, glossy color card cover, 96 pp., $7. **Query with 10 samples, bio, publication credits. Replies to queries in 1-2 months, to submissions (if invited) in 1-2 months. Simultaneous submissions, photocopies OK, or discs compatible with CPM (Morrow Decision), hard copy preferred. Publishes on 15% contract plus 10 copies (and 40% discount on additional copies). Send SASE for catalog to buy samples.**

THUNDER CITY PRESS, FORD-BROWN & CO., AMERICAN POETS PROFILE SERIES, (II), Box 600574, Houston, TX 77260, founded 1975 (in Birmingham, AL), poetry editor Steven Ford Brown, is dedicated "to publish innovative fiction and poetry in finely published books; also to publish profiles of contemporary poets in the American Poets Profile Series. We want contemporary, experimental, surrealism, dada, prose poetry and innovative fiction." They have recently published poetry by Dave Smith, Peter Cooley, Georg Trakl, Thomas Transtromer and Andrew Glaze. The editor selected these sample lines by Michael Waters:

> *When this slow heart was raging*
> *and I could tell no one, especially you,*
> *I would abandon the exhaustion of sheets,*
> *this woman tossing like damp leaves,*
> *and storm a few miles into the country.*

The sample book I examined is **The Empire of Summer** by M. R. Doty, a 56 pp., flat-spined digest-sized format, professional printing (small type), glossy card cover with color and b/w photo—$4.50. **Query with 5 sample poems, bio, publication credits. Replies to query in 1 month, to submission (if invited) in 2 month. No simultaneous submissions. "There will be no replies or returns without SASE." Photocopy OK. No dot-matrix. Pays 10% of press run. Editor "sometimes" comments on rejections. Send SASE for catalog to buy samples.** The editor advises, "seek out other writers for feedback. Purchase, borrow or steal books of contemporary poetry to read and be influenced by. Don't isolate yourself against the other poets of the world."

‡*THURSDAYS POETRY MAGAZINE (I), 70 Poplar Road, Bearwood, Warley, West Mids. B66 4AN, England, phone 021-429-9806 or 021-622-3462, founded 1985, current editors John Denny and Kath West. Thursdays Poetry Group was formed to encourage beginners to discuss and develop their work, to promote poetry events locally, and to establish contact with poets from different areas or countries. The magazine "began to encourage 'unknowns' to submit for publication and simply to show it could be done without grant aid, sponsorship, etc." They take "**all types of poetry as long as it is written in the language of today, except long poems (prefer maximum length one page), any poetry written deliberately to shock or indoctrinate others politically or emotionally. Prefer social comment to be offered in a manner which encourages readers to form their own views on any subject.**" They have recently published work by Michael Henry, Geoff Stevens, Tom Bingham, Leslie A. Richardson, John Daunt, and Denise Bennett. As a sample, they chose the following lines from "Through the eyes of the Bull" by John Gross Birmingham:

> *Hot sand blots up the dregs*
> *Of blood clotting in the sun*
> *That tans your oily skins*
> *Your sins are watching you . . .*

Thursdays is magazine-sized, photocopied on colored and white ordinary paper with some b/w graphics, about 20 pages, colored cover (same paper), side-stapled. It appears quarterly and has a circulation of approximately 200. Price per issue is 60p in the UK, subscription £1.50/3 issues. **Pay is 1 copy. A maximum of 4 poems should be submitted. Reporting time is 2-3 weeks and time to publication is a maximum of 3 months. "All poems returned if they are not to be published in next issue."** The editors say, "For beginners would recommend discussion of their work with other poets either in a formal established group, or informally, before attempting to get published; see a copy of the magazine before submitting to get a general idea of content; do not send more poems than requested; don't see rejections as personal insults; don't assume that editors are experts to anything and everything; don't be in too much of a rush to publish yourself—if you have a selection of poems you want to inflict on the world, put them away for a year to see if they can stand the test of time. Suprising how your work can develop in that period!"

THE TIDAL PRESS (II), Box 150, Portsmouth, NH 03801, founded 1977, poetry editors Jean and Charles Wadsworth and Leslie Norris, wants **"poetry which makes one sit up and take notice, not by lamenting or shocking but by its superb use of words. The shock should be in the poetic perfection of choice—and one should not forget the music. The poetry itself is more important than form, length, style, subject-matter or purpose."** They have recently published books of poetry by Charles Wadsworth, William H. Matchett, Paul Petrie and Charles Pratt. The editors selected these sample lines from "Islands off Maine" by Leslie Norris:

> Dawn moves briskly
> Among the rugosas.
> The harbour lights take back
> Their shaken images.

Query with 4 samples, bio, publication credits, statement of your poetic goals and principles. Replies to queries in 1-2 months, to submissions (if invited) in 1-2 months. No simultaneous submissions. No dot-matrix. Photocopies OK. Pays 10 copies and share of profits when and if the book makes any (seldom does). Send SASE for catalog to buy samples. The editors comment, "We will not follow trends."

TILTED PLANET PRESS (II), Box 8646, Austin, TX 78712, phone 447-7619, founded 1983, poetry editor Robin Cravey, wants to see **"clear, vigorous poems on social and cultural comment, nature observation, personal growth. Rhyme, meter and other devices welcome. So is free verse. Poems should be accessible to the average reader."** So far the press has published work by local writers Isabella Russell-Ides, Chuck Taylor, Robert Ayres and Heronius Gotha. The editor, Robin Cravey, selected these lines by Chuck Taylor as a sample:

> i see poor men's flesh
> up against all this grey and steel;
> i imagine one, just one man,
> when the sub lies under water,
> turning in the dark of his narrow bunk
> high there by the ceiling
> so his face almost bumps pipes
> and tubes and wires

Query with 3-5 samples. Reply in 3 weeks, report on submission (if invited) in 2 months. Photocopies OK. No simultaneous submissions or dot-matrix. Pays 1-5% royalties, 2-5 copies. Sample book for $6. Editor comments on rejection. He advises, "Western Culture cries out for a literature that will show the way out of our dead end materialism."

TIMBERLINE PRESS (II), Box 327, Fulton, MO 65251, phone 314-642-5035, founded 1975, poetry editor Clarence Wolfshohl. "We do limited letterpress editions with the goal of blending strong poetry with well-crafted and designed printing. We lean toward **natural history or strongly imagistic nature poetry, but will look at any good work. Also, good humorous poetry. MSS of less than 50 (preferably 25-30) pp. No other preconceived notions."** They have recently published poetry by Virginia Brady Young, Michael Burns, Gary Metras, Rochelle Lynn Holt and Conger Beasley Jr. The editor selected these sample lines from "Center of the Spiral" by Gary Metras:

> The hawk is full of spirals
> The eye is the center
>
> Trees hardly flutter
> as they fatten with sparrows
> who've renounced air.

The sample publication I have seen is **Timber: 1st Addition** by Robert A. Davies. It is about 20 unnumbered pp., handset and printed by letterpress on quality buff stock, flat-spined, matte wrapper with art, no price indicated. **Query with 5 samples, bio, publication credits. Replies to query in 1 week, to submission (if invited) in 1 month. Simultaneous submissions, photocopies OK. No dot-matrix. Splits profits 50-50 with poet. Send SASE for catalog to buy samples—or $3 (average price) for sample.**

*TIME OF SINGING, A MAGAZINE OF CHRISTIAN POETRY (I, IV, Religious), Box 211, Cambridge Springs, PA 16403, founded 1958-1965, revived 1980, poetry editor Charles A. Waugaman. "The viewpoint is **unblushingly Christian—but in its widest and most inclusive meaning**. Moreover, it is believed that the vital message of Christian poems, as well as inspiring the general reader, will give pastors, teachers, and devotional leaders rich current sources of inspiring material to aid them in their ministries. We tend to have a Fall-Christmas issue, a Lent-Easter one, and a Summer one. But **we do have themes quite often. We tend to value content, rather than form. I hope we have variety.**" They have recently published poetry by Tony Cosier, Benedict Auer, Luci Shaw and Nancy Ester James. The editor selected these sample lines by Alice Mackenzie Swain:

> The traffic pours, a steady waterfall,
> past corpses where Confederate soldiers lay.
> The lily pond is gone; the roses all
> unkempt reminders of a gentler day.

The triquarterly is digest-sized 32 pp., offset from typescript with decorative line-drawings of flowers scattered throughout, circulation 200 + , 138 subscriptions. Subscription: $7; per copy: $3. They receive over 500 submissions per year, use about 140, have a 6-8 month backlog. **Sample: $1. Prefer about 5 poems, double-spaced, no simultaneous submissions. Reports in 1-2 months. Pays 1 copy. Send SASE for guidelines. Editor frequently comments with suggestions for improvement for publication. "We tend to be traditional. We like poems that are aware of grammar. Collections of uneven lines, series of phrases, preachy statements, unstructured 'prayers,' and trite sing-song rhymes usually get returned. We look for poems that 'show' rather than 'tell.'** " They also publish chapbooks of poets of the editor's selection.

*TIME WARP, *DARK VISIONS, VISIONS PUBLICATIONS (I, IV, Science fiction), Box 1291, Ottawa, Ontario, Canada K1P 5R3, founded 1984, poetry editor Bruce Brown. *Time Warp* is a science fiction quarterly which wants "**speculative fiction poetry. Good poetry with viewpoint of future/ space/time. 40 line maximum; prefer short poems. I like poetry that leaves you thinking about it.**" As a sample I chose these lines from "The Moon" by Pramil:

> The Moon let loose and shook her locks
> full of night and perfumed stars
> untied her velvet bodice tight
> shyly but wantonly exposing
> small white breasts
> tipped with fire-enamelled roses.

The digest-sized 48 pp. quarterly, offset from typescript, matte card cover, uses 4-6 pp. of poetry in each issue, printrun 500. Subscription: $6.95. They recieve about 150 submissions of freelance poetry per year, use 20%. **Sample: $1.95. Reports in 2 weeks. Pays 2 copies. Send SASE for guidelines. Editor comments on rejections.** He advises, "Poetry ought to be stimulating to a reader and leave an impression. Experimental poetry is OK, but it is a sin to leave a reader wondering what you're talking about. Write with consideration for your reader, not for other writers. Don't stuff poetry with 5 syllable words."

‡*TIN WREATH (I), Box 13401, Albany, NY 12212, founded 1985, "editor/janitor" David Gonsalves. "*Tin Wreath* appears quarterly with selected late 20th century American visions of the actual and the possible." **The editor wants to see poetry that is "both representational and non-representational; tend to favor short over long pieces; appreciate the imaginary and visionary challenge to the public consensus." He does not want "greeting card, narrative, rhymed, formal."** He has recently published work by Lyn Lifshin, B. Z Niditch, Alan Catlin, and Sheila E. Murphy. As a sample, he chose the following lines by Walt Franklin:

> Thinking about James Wright
> Then returning to this place
> where nothing will appear except
> the moon above the evergreens

Tin Wreath is digest-sized, photocopied from handsome, large type on ordinary paper, about 20 pp., folded and saddle-stapled; it has no frills. Circulation is 250. **"*Tin Wreath* is available free upon request and is sent to everyone who submits. There are no subscriptions per se or sales." Contributors receive 3 copies. Writers should send 5 or fewer poems; photocopy, dot-matrix, and simultaneous submissions are all OK. Reporting time is "13 days to 13 months" and time to publication is 3-6 months. All MSS receive some form of handwritten reply/criticism.** The editor comments, "Believe we are in the midst of a transitory phase in American and world poetics (and politics). The movement seems now to be away from the absolute master and masterpiece and toward visionary landscapes both personal and inclusive."

*TOUCH (IV, Christian girls, themes), Box 7244, Grand Rapids, MI 49510, phone 616-241-5616, founded 1970, poetry editor Carol Smith: "Our magazine is a 24 pp. edition written **for girls 7-14 to show them how God is at work in their lives and in the world around them.** *Touch* **is theme-orientated. We like our poetry to fit the theme of each. We send out a theme update biannually to all our listed freelancers. We prefer short poems with a Christian emphasis that can show girls how God works in their lives.**" They have recently published poetry by Lois Walfrid Johnson, Mercedes Johnston and Trudy Vander Veen. The editor selected these sample lines by Clare Miseles:

> God help me know
> And understand
> When a friend needs
> A helping hand.

Touch is published 10 times a year, magazine-sized, circulation 13,850, 13,000 subscriptions. Subscription: $7 US, $8 Canada, $9 foreign. They receive 150-200 freelance submissions of poetry per year, use 2 poems in each issue, have a 6 month backlog. **Sample and guidelines free with 8x10 SASE. Poems must not be longer than 20 lines—prefer much shorter. Simultaneous submissions OK. Query with SASE for theme update. Reports in 6 weeks. Pays $5-10 and copies. "We have a rejection sheet that states the reason we have done so."**

TOUCHSTONE PRESS, *TOUCHSTONE (II), Box 42331, Houston, TX 77042, founded 1975, poetry editor William Laufer, "is committed to publishing poetry which most commercial magazines no longer publish. We are non-commercial, sponsored by the Houston Writers Guild, and we are in our 10th year of publication. We publish nascent poets as well as established authors. While we accept **poetry that is mainstream, we enjoy the experimental and that which ventures into risk. We do not wish to see the sentimental, the saccharine nor that which is 'inspirational.' Looking for translations. Our average length is 20 lines; however we will accept work up to 50 lines if the artist has presented us with a work of literary merit.**" They have recently published poetry by Lyn Lifshin, Ramona Weeks, Sandra Scofield, Karla Hammond, Walter McDonald, Gary Fincke and Chris Woods. The editor selected these sample lines from "Los Pobres" by Milt McLeod:

> . . . tired doors
> stand open to those whose clothing,
> whose flesh,
> have been eaten by the years

Touchstone appears quarterly, digest-sized, 40 pp., printed on heavy, textured buff stock, perfect bound, matte card cover with art, circulation to 975 subscriptions of which 5 are libraries. Subscription: $10. They receive about 2,000 freelance poetry submissions per year, use 115, have a 6-8 month backlog. **Sample: $3 postpaid. Submit clean copy, single-spaced. "We copyright to protect our authors, but return copyright upon publication; hence, we cannot accept simultaneous submissions." Reports in 6-8 weeks. Pays 1 copy. Send SASE for guidelines.** "*We encourage contributors to subscribe*, but this is not a prerequisite for acceptance." Touchstone Press publishes chapbooks. For consideration, query with 5 samples. "We are interested in original artwork as illustration for the poetry." Photocopies, dot-matrix OK. "We provide a free market newsletter and free critique to subscribers requesting these services. We do not reject MSS, but rather return them with personal, hand-written comments." The editor comments, "We enjoy helping the unpublished poet in breaking into print. We enjoy minority viewpoints, and we would like to see more of them. We ask that contributors do not take advantage of our good nature, yet attempt to understand the hard realities of publishing—finance. Also, all of us at *Touchstone* are working writers—established authors and artists."

TOWER POETRY SOCIETY, PINE TREE SERIES, *TOWER (II), Dundas Public Library, 18 Ogilvie St., Dundas, Ontario, Canada L9H 2S2, founded 1951, editor-in-chief Vincent Francis. "the press is an outgrowth of Tower Poetry Society, started by a few members of McMaster University faculty to promote interest in poetry. We publish *Tower* twice a year and a few chapbooks. We want **rhymed or free verse, traditional or modern, but not prose chopped into short lines, maximum 35 lines in length, any subject, any comprehensible style.**" They have recently published poetry by Sparling Mills, John Ferns, Kenneth Samberg, Tony Cosier and Catherine Bankier. The editor selected these sample lines by Tony Cosier:

> From forging brass he took to forging soul,
> gave up plowing soil to plow his skull,
> ripped open the eye that never closed again
> and took for tongue the howl of the beast in pain.

Tower is digest-sized, 40 pp., circulation 150, 60 subscriptions of which 8 are libraries. Subscription: $5.50 including postage. They receive about 400 freelance submissions of poetry per year, use 30, no backlog. **Sample: $1.50 postpaid. Limit submissions to 4 poems. Submit during April or September. Reports in 2 months. Pays 1 copy. "Comment if requested—no charge."** The editor advises, "Read a lot of poetry before you try to write it."

*TRADESWOMEN (IV, Women), Box 40664, San Francisco, CA 94140, phone 415-989-1566, founded 1981, poetry editors Sandra Marilyn and Joss Eldredge: "We are an advocacy magazine for **women who do skilled trades jobs (carpentry, electricians, mechanics, etc).** We publish fiction and nonfiction dealing with the problems and pleasures of these types of specific non-traditional jobs. We have **1-3 poems each issue dealing with women in non-traditional jobs.**" They have recently published poetry by Donna Langston. The editors selected these sample lines (poet unidentified):

> Risks. I'm ready for a job that
> Walks a tall plank. Rickety ladders—
> All week—40 hours—suspension . . .
> "Cool" art poses

The magazine appears quarterly, circulation to 600 subscriptions of which 10% are libraries. Subscription: $10. They receive about 20 freelance submissions of poetry per year, take 8-10. **Sample: $1 postpaid. Simultaneous submissions OK. Reports in 1-2 months. Pays copies. Send SASE for guidelines. The editors make personal comments concerning most rejected material.** They comment, "By using poetry about women who pioneer in extremely difficult non-traditional jobs we hope to show the importance of their roles in our society. We also hope to show that the emotions of our work lives are as important to write about as the other emotions which dominate our lives."

*TRADITION (IV, Music), 106 Navajo, Council Bluffs, IA 51501, phone 712-366-1136, founded 1976, editor Robert Everhart, a quarterly magazine that publishes **short poetry about traditional things—mostly music. The magazine covers "old-time music, folk-bluegrass-country, and lifestyles."** It is digest-sized, offset (I have not seen a sample copy.) Circulation is 1,000-1,500, price per issue $1. **Sample: $1 postpaid, guidelines available for SASE, pays 10 copies. The editor reports on submissions in 6 months.** He says, "We have a poetry reading championship every Labor Day weekend in conjunction with our annual old-time country music festival. Poets are encouraged to participate for judging, publication, and prizes."

TRANSITION PUBLICATIONS, *NEW OREGON REVIEW (II), 537 NE Lincoln St., Hillsboro, OR 97124, phone 503-640-1375, founded 1977, editor-in-chief Dr. Steven Dimeo, currently publishing just *New Oregon Review* semiannually. **"We prefer only poetry of exceptional merit, usually by well-established writers who demonstrate careful attention to rhyme, rhythm, internal tonal integrity and progressive development. We automatically reject poems imitating e. e. cummings and seldom consider poems over 40 lines and none that are either trite or moralistic."** They have recently published poetry by John Ditsky, J. B. Goodenough, Elizabeth Bartlett and Marianne Andrea. The editor selected this example of *slant* rhyme from the opening passage of Stuart Silverman's "The Making":

> I was cauterized by a fatherly knife when I was seven.
> Dad's iron jaws clamped me down, and his hand moved in
> Steady as a spider riding its silk life-line in the wind.

New Oregon Review is digest-sized, 28 pp., saddle-stapled, professionally printed on good stock, paper cover with b/w photography and graphics, circulation 150, 100 subscriptions of which 5% are libraries, using 3-4 pp. of poetry in each issue. Subscription: $4.50. They receive 500 + freelance submissions of poetry per year, use 6-8, have a 6-12 month backlog. **Sample: $3 postpaid. Poems should not be longer than one page. Photocopies OK, no dot-matrix, no simultaneous submissions. "It's always best for poets to query whenever possible since we're always overstocked in this category."** Reports within 2 weeks if rejected; 2-3 months if poetry is being seriously considered. **Pays $10/poem. Send SASE for guidelines. Magazine now requires a reading fee of $3 per submission (3 poems maximum) for which the prospective contributor receives 1 back issue of his/her choice. Fee is waived for subscribers and those purchasing 2 or more back issues.** Such supporters also are eligible for the annual $50 best poem award beginning in 1986. They also will consider unsolicited MSS between Sept. 1 and Nov. 30 each year. "We admire poetry written in the tradition of classical poets like Emily Dickinson, W. B. Yeats, Robert Frost, T. S. Eliot, E. A. Robinson, W. H. Auden and Theodore Roethke. Those not familiar with these names shouldn't bother submitting."

TRANSLATION CENTER, *TRANSLATION (IV, Translations), 307A Mathematics Bldg., Columbia University, New York, NY 10027, phone 212-280-2305, founded 1972, managing editor Diane G. H. Cook. "Translation Center publishes only excerpted foreign contemporary literature in English language translations and also gives annual awards and grants to translators. *Translation* magazine uses **contemporary foreign poetry/literature in English language translations.** (Note: we do not review and do not accept translated plays.)." They have recently published translations of poetry by Yannis Ritsos, Badawi al-Jabal, Christoph Meckel, Osip Mandelstam, Nikos Kavadias and Gunars Salins. *Translation* is a biannual, circulation 1,500. Subscription: $15. **Sample: $8-9 postpaid. Translators should query. Up to 6 poems may be submitted at a time, letter-quality MS. Translators must include**

with MS: (a) copy of original text (in the foreign language); (b)5 line bio of translator; (c) 5 line bio of author/ poet; (d) statement of copyright clearance. Payment is 2 copies of the magazine to translators. Send SASE for guidelines and descriptions of the various award programs they administer.

TRANS-SPECIES UNLIMITED, ONE WORLD (IV, Ecology), Box 1351, State College, PA 16804, phone 814-238-0793, founded 1981, poetry editor Dana Marie Stuchell. *One World* is a periodic news journal which uses **only poetry of high quality having a direct relevance to the concerns of animal rights, environmental protection and ecology.** They have recently published poetry by Rainer Marie Rilke, Robinson Jeffers and the editor, Dana Marie Stuchell, who selected these sample lines:

> *His sight from ever gazing through the bars*
> *has grown so blunt that it sees nothing more.*
> *It seems to him that thousands of bars are*
> *before him, and behind them nothing merely.*

The newsletter has a circulation of 5,000, uses 1-2 poems per issue. Membership in Trans-Species Unlimited: $10 per year. **Sample: $1 postpaid. Reports in 2 weeks. No pay. Editor comments on rejections.**

‡*TREETOP PANORAMA (I), Box 160, RR 1, Payson, IL 62360, founded 1983, editor Jared Scarborough, an "aesthetic/political/cultural magazine carrying some poetry in each issue. **Poetry accepted is usually rural, international, or/and environmental." The editor wants "subtle, concise, well-proportioned and rhythmically pleasing" poetry. Avoids verse that is self-conscious, sad with no relief, stumbling, awkward, indulgent."** He has recently published work by Walt Franklin and Ruth Wildes Schular. As a sample, he selected the following lines by an unidentified poet:

> *Come, sit by quiet, country lane*
> *Read these pages, and sip again*
> *A cup full blessed with risen grain.*

The sample of *Treetop Panorama* that I have is magazine-sized, offset in brown on white ordinary paper ("brown ink in fall, green in spring"), folded and not stapled. It is only 4 pp., although the editor says the magazine contains 36 pp. Circulation is "500-1,000," introductory subscription $2.85/year (2 issues). **Current issue available in lieu of guidelines for $1. Pay is a minimum of $1/poem plus 2 copies. "Reasonable, legible submissions appreciated." Reporting time is 1-2 weeks and accepted poems are published as soon as possible. "Careful, considerate comments offered on all poetry submitted. A thorough critique may be had for $5/poem (less than 2 dozen lines)."** The editor says, "Tip: include personal letter that is open and honest, expect same. Comment: female voices encouraged (50% minimum female poets published). Advice: Get to know good music (aboriginal as well as classical). Attempt to forge the elemental with the reasoned, creating balance."

*TRESTLE CREEK REVIEW (II), 1000 West Garden, Coeur d'Alene, ID 83814, phone 769-3300, ext. 384, founded 1982-3, poetry editor M. Fay Wright et al, is a "2 year college creative writing program production. Purposes: (1) expand the range of publishing/ editing experience for our small band of writers; (2) expose them to editing experience; (3) create another outlet for serious, beginning writers. **We favor poetry strong on image and sound, the West and country vs. city; spare us the romantic, rhymed cliches (in other words, send quality). We can't publish much if it's long (more than 2 pp.)"** They have recently published poetry by Louis Phillips, Jim Bertolino, Donnell Hunter, Elsie Pankowski, Greg Keeler, Wilham Studebaker and Tim Ranick. M. Fay Wright selected these lines by Louis Phillips:

> *It is summer and*
> *The pines hold a murder of crows*
> *Better than the sky holds silence.*

TCR is a digest-sized 57 pp. annual, professionally printed on heavy buff stock, saddle-stapled, matte cover with art, circulation 400, 6 subscriptions of which 4 are libraries. They receive freelance poetry submissions from about 100 persons per year, use 30. **Sample: $3.50. Submit before March 1 (for May publication) no more than 5 pp., no simultaneous submissions. Reports by March 30. Pays 2 copies.** The editor advises, "Be neat, be precise, don't romanticize or cry in your beer, strike the surprising, universal note. Know the names of things."

*TRIQUARTERLY MAGAZINE (II), 1735 Benson Ave., Evanston, IL 60201, phone 312-492-3490, founded 1964, editor Reginald Gibbons, is one of the most distinguished journals of contemporary literature, now publishing poetry again (after excluding it for a 10 year period). Some issues are published as books on specific themes. They have recently published poetry by C. K. Williams, Alane Rollings, Lisel Mueller, George Starbuck, William Heyen, Bruce Weigl, Maxine Kumin and Marvin Bell. I selected this sample stanza of "Moon" by Josephine Jacobsen:

> *It has a hundred ways: to pull water*

and women; to shatter in wells; to glare on fugitives,
stain clouds, trouble the mad. It can call
cats and coyotes, touch insomniacs, light
a hyena's eyeball. Be men's trampoline.

Triquarterly's three issues per year are 6x9", 200 + pp., flat-spined, professionally printed with b/w photography, graphics, glossy card cover with b/w photo, circulation 3,500 + , 2,000 subscriptions of which 35% are libraries, using about 24 pp. of poetry in each issue. Subscription: $16; per copy: $6.95. They receive about 3,000 freelance submissions of poetry per year, use 20, have about a 6 month backlog. **Sample: $3 postpaid. No photocopy, dot-matrix or simultaneous submissions. Reports in 8-10 weeks. Payment varies. "We** *suggest* **prospective contributors examine sample copy before submitting."**

TROUT CREEK PRESS, *DOG RIVER REVIEW, DOG RIVER REVIEW POETRY SERIES (II), Box 125, Parkdale, OR 97041-0125, founded 1981, poetry editor Laurence F. Hawkins, Jr., prefers **"shorter poems (to 30 lines) but will consider longer. No restrictions on form or content but look for emotional honesty. Would like to see more lyric poetry and traditional forms. No pornography or religious verse."** They have recently published poetry by Lyn Lifshin, Roger Weaver, Gerald Locklin, Louis McKee, Connie Fox, David Chorlton and Joseph Semenovich. Laurence Hawkins selected these sample lines by Roger Weaver:

A man opens his throat to sing,
he takes you in. The instant
you stand inside his song you travel
his country, learn it like second skin,

Dog River Review is a semiannual, digest-sized, 60 pp., saddle-stapled, offset from typescript with b/w graphics, circulation 200, 40 subscriptions of which 5 are libraries. Subscription: $6. They receive 2,000-2,500 freelance submissions of poetry per year, use 80-90. **Sample: $2 postpaid. "Prefer to see no more than 5 poems at a time. Will consider anything we can read—prefer typewritten copy." Reports in 1 week-3 months. Payment in copies. Send SASE for guidelines. For book publication by Trout Creek Press, query with 4-6 samples. Replies to queries immediately, to submission (if invited) in 1-2 months. No simultaneous submissions. Photocopy, dot-matrix OK. No payment until "material costs recovered."** The sample chapbook I examined, **the peter poems and other disgraces** by Joseph Semenovich, is digest-sized, 40 pp., high-quality stock, decorated with b/w graphics, matte card cover with line-drawing, $4 postpaid, "Dog River Review Poetry Series #1." Send SASE for catalog to buy samples. Editor sometimes comments on rejections.

TROUVERE COMPANY, *TROUVERE'S LAUREATE, *WRITERS GAZETTE, JUST A LITTLE POEM (I), Box 290, Rt. 2, Eclectic, AL 36024, founded 1981, poetry editor Brenda Williamson. "Trouvere Company works mainly with new writers and offers different publications to help promote their work. All of the publications listed above use poetry and most poetry used has never been published before, by inexperienced and experienced poets. *Writer's Gazette* is an incentive, encouraging format, used to display work by new writers as well as experienced and is open to criticism by fellow writers. Hopefully this will act as a continuing learning newsletter. **I want to see meaningful poetry that has dimension shown in its words. And what I don't like to see is abstract poetry, with words jumbled around a page that has no meaning, format, style, or concrete reason for being, nothing but some words randomly written down. No specifications as to form, length, style, subject-matter or purpose except in the case of contests which usually have a length of no more than 24 lines. Topics pertain to outlined guidelines for different ones."** They have recently published poetry by Denver Stull, Illeana Fitzpatrick, Merle Beckwith, Gene Boone, Flora Kosoff, Amelia Ferencz, Aggie McKeever, Jay Giammarino and Mildred Fisher. The editor selected these sample lines by Gary W. Fort:

Poetry is the motivating force
the flaming spear
that strikes deep into the heart
and stirs the creative juices

Writer's Gazette is a magazine-sized quarterly newsletter, 16 pp. center-stapled, which uses 5-15 poems throughout, 700 subscriptions of which 5 are libraries. **Sample: $1.50 postpaid. Submit any number of pp, photocopies OK, simultaneous and previously published submissions OK. Reports in 4-8 weeks, pays 10¢-$1 per line. Send SASE for guidelines.** *Trouvere's Laureate* is a digest-sized 16 pp. tri-annual, saddle-stapled, offset from typescript, 400 subscribers. **Sample: $2.50 postpaid. Pays $1-3/poem on acceptance or publication.** *Just a Little Poem* is a quarterly contest newsletter for **poems 2-12 lines. Subscribers may enter without fee; for all others the entry fee is 75¢ per poem. Subscription: $7.50. Pays copies and 1 prize of $20 for the best poem of the month.** *Short Story Review*, is a triannual, first issue March 1985, centering on short stories, including the poetic story, with articles about writing short stories and reviews of each story constructed from comments and criticism of fellow writers. **Story length: 500-3,000 words. Submissions are accepted only from subscribers. Subscription: $12 per year; sample copy: $2.50. No payment-prize awarded. Send SASE for guidelines.** For all other publications and contests, send SASE. "Most individual book MS contracts are worked on subsidy publishing—anthologies, chapbooks, etc. There are no conditions or requirements to purchase copy or copies." Brenda Williamson comments, "Everyone wants to be a poet. And in most cases that is possible if they take time to read poetry and study what poetry is. It isn't simply a means of getting published by throwing together a few paragraphs quickly. It is more an expression of yourself in a short non-direct way, because there is no really financial support for most poets. This only comes to very few, and most of them are dead. Poetry is expression and self reward."

TURKEY PRESS (V), 6746 Sueno Rd., Isla Vista, CA 93117, founded 1974, poetry editor Harry Reese, "is involved with publishing contemporary literature, producing traditional and experimental book art, one-of-a-kind commissioned projects and collaborations with various artists and writers. **We do not encourage solicitations of any kind to the press. We seek out and develop projects on our own.**" They have published poetry by James Laughlin, Sam Hamill, Edwin Honig, Glenna Luschei, Tom Clark, Michael Hannon, Keith Waldrop, David Ossman, Peter Whigham, Jack Curtis, Kirk Robertson and Anne E. Edge. Harry Reese says, "I've been making my own paper since 1979, and use it frequently in the books. My books have been exhibited widely throughout the country, usually as book art or as traditional fine printing. I try to make the book come out of the text, though it is often elaborate or at least much more elaborate than the author would have imagined. . . . We 'privish,' a term I've heard David Godine use disparagingly, rather than 'publish'; but our intentions are with making a quality book, and we start out by trying not to compromise. We don't put out collections of poems; we put out *books*. They have texture, feel, visual meanings. And they have words, most of the time. I salute the work of other presses who do work differently from ours, while doing it well. If everyone in the book business set about to do an honest day's work with their books, we'd all be better off." He advises poets to "study a publication (magazine/anthology) or press before submitting anything to it. Encourage your library to order books you want to see. Use the library and it will expand its collection. Poets need to read more and look at more books. Of course, they can't afford to buy them all, but that shouldn't stop a poet from looking."

‡**22 PRESS (II)**, Box 6236, Wilmington, DE 19804, phone 215-891-9046, founded 1978, publisher-editor Terry Persun, is a small press publisher of poetry and fiction asking a **reading fee of $3 for chapbook consideration**. "We consider collections of approximately 40 pp. at present and hope to publish flat-spined paperbacks at a later date. **Type is open, but I like well-crafted material bordering on academic, nothing flighty. No short love poems, pornographic scenes or weak images.** We have recently published poetry by Harold Witt, Gerald Locklin and Rafael Zapeda." Terry Persun selected these sample lines by Ken Poyner:

> I cannot think that after all of it
> The river will run any other way.
> The bones of Jane McClellan will still
> In the bottom mud be odd mineral.

22 Press publishes 3-5 chapbooks per year, saddle-stapled, with matte card cover with line-drawings, heavy stock. **Send SASE for catalog to buy samples ($3-6.95). Submit 40 pp. of poetry with bio, statement of philosophy, $3 reading fee. Simultaneous submissions, photocopies, dot-matrix OK. Reports in 3 months. Pays 25 copies plus 10% royalties for those which sell over 1,000 copies. Poet should send mailing list to publisher. Terry Persun "often" comments on rejected MSS.** He advises, "Read everything you can."

‡*****TYRO MAGAZINE (I)**, 194 Carlbert St., Sault Ste. Marie, Ontario P6A 5E1, Canada, phone 705-253-6402, founded 1984, editor Stan Gordon, who says, "This bimonthly is a practice, learning and discussion medium for developing writers, publishing poetry, fiction and nonfiction submitted by members of Tyro Writers' Group. Widely published professionals provide advice, feedback on mail, and market opportunities." **Lifetime membership in the group costs $4, and you must be a member to submit. The magazine publishes "all types" of poetry, but does not want "anything that is morally offensive, legally dangerous, or wildly experimental."** As a sample I selected the first lines of "Dream #12" by Denis Robillard:

> Girl, do you see me floating out of my house,
> my warm bed, and into my car travelling
> the dark funnel of nightness
> to reach your little life,

The magazine is digest-sized, offset from typed copy with some b/w graphics, 80-120 pp. flat-spined, one-color matte card cover. Circulation is "about 500 and growing." Price per issue is $4, subscription $21/year. **Sample available for $4, guidelines for SASE. Contributors receive no pay or free copies.**

Submissions are reported on in 1 month. Time to publication is 6 weeks. Criticism is "always" provided on rejected MSS. The editor says, "Writers develop skill through imitation, practice, exposure, and feedback. They learn to write by writing, become more published by getting published. We try to provide these experiences to writers with a wide range of skills, from frequently-published to never-been-published."

‡ULTRAMARINE PUBLISHING CO., INC. (II), Box 303, Hastings-on-Hudson, NY 10706, founded 1974, editor C. P. Stephens, who says "We mostly distribute books for authors who had a title dropped by a major publisher—the author is usually able to purchase copies very cheaply. We use existing copies purchased by the author from the publisher when the title is being dropped." Ultramarine's recent list includes 250 titles, 90% of them cloth bound, one-third of them science fiction and 10% poetry. The press pays 10% royalties. "Distributor terms are on a book by book basis, but is a rough split." Authors should query before making submissions; queries will be answered in 1 week. Simultaneous submissions are OK, as are photocopied or dot-matrix MSS, but no discs.

‡*UNCLE, HEART'S DESIRE PRESS (I, IV, Humor), RR #4, Box 798, Springfield, MO 65802, founded 1981, poetry editor Mr. Lynn Cline. *Uncle* is "humor magazine open to any sort of submission. A typical issue is about ½ fiction, ¼ poetry, and the rest might be anthing at all." The editors say, "**Free verse or rhymed poetry is acceptable, though what we see of the latter is usually doggerel. Light or satirical poetry is what we want. We don't want religious verse, poems brimming over with allusions, or doggerel. We like 'language' poems if they absolutely** *sing*. Wry prose poems are read with favor." Poets recently published include Elisavietta Ritchie, Karl Elder, Paul Hoover, and Hal Daniel. As a sample, the editors selected the following lines by an unidentified poet:

> *May the plane of the other woman explode*
> *with just one fatality*
> *but, if not, may she spew*
> *dysentry from*

The digest-sized magazine has 60-90 pp. saddle-stapled, offset (rather faintly) from typed copy, with b/w or sometimes blue illustrations, one-color matte card cover. Frequency is twice yearly, circulation is 250, of which 50+ are subscriptions, 30 are newsstand sales, and 50-60 are distributed to editors, friends, and at writer's conferences. Price is $2.50, subscription $5/year. **Sample: $2.50 postpaid. Guidelines are available for SASE, but the editors say "we're so loose that guidelines are meaningless. We just want it to be funny, and we don't care who you are or aren't. Pay is 2 copies. Submissions are reported on in 1 week to 2 months, and time to publication is never more than 5 months.** The editors' advice is: "Be elegant, but not 'literary'."

‡UNDERWHICH EDITIONS, PHENOMENON PRESS, GRONK, ANONBEYOND PRESS, TEKSTEDITIONS (II), Box 262, Adelaide St. Station, Toronto, Ontario, Canada M5C 2J4, phone 416-536-9316, founded 1978, poetry editors Richard Truhlar, Michael Dean, bp Nichol, Brian Dedora, Steven Smith, Paul Dutton, John Riddell and Steve McCaffery, is "dedicated to presenting in diverse and appealing physical formats, new works by contemporary creators, focusing on formal invention and encompassing the expanded frontiers of literary endeavor" in chapbooks, pamphlets, flat-spined paperbacks, posters, cassettes, records and anthologies. They have recently published poetry by Victor Coleman, John Riddell, bp Nichol and Karen MacCormack. The editors selected these sample lines from "From the Dark Wood" by Victor Coleman:

> *My losses are all artifice*
> *I shaped my life to fit the square,*
> *the spare tire, the fire, the ire*
> *of mothers' despair at the violent*
> *death of their sons, the volunteer Army.*

Query with 5-10 sample poems, cover letter and curriculum vitae. Reports in 6 months. Photocopy, dot-matrix, discs compatible with Apple OK. No simultaneous submissions. Pays percent of run. Catalog available to buy samples.

THE UNITED METHODIST REPORTER, THE NATIONAL CHRISTIAN REPORTER (IV, Religious), Box 660275, Dallas, TX 75266-0275, phone 214-630-6495, founded 1847, editor/ general manager Spurgeon M. Dunnam III, managing editor John A. Lovelace, is "a non-profit company which exists for the purpose of publishing weekly and biweekly newspapers for a number of the United Methodist Churches throughout the US via the *United Methodist Reporter, the UM Review* and for congregations of other denominations via the *National Christian Reporter.* There is a weekly broad sheet newspaper and a biweekly tabloid newspaper. **At most we use one poem per week as filler. Poetry using concrete, fresh imagery. Prefer single effect rather than general; specific rather than vague. 4-12 lines, free verse or rhymed but no contrived, rhyme, or archaic language. Must have explicit**

Christian theme/ message. Most poems we reject are too long, too general, too trite, or substitute sound for meaning."

UNITY SCHOOL OF CHRISTIANITY, *UNITY, *DAILY WORD, *WEE WISDOM (II, IV, Religious), Unity Village, MO 64065, founded 1893. "Unity periodicals are devoted to spreading the truth of practical Christianity, the everyday use of Christ principles. The material used in them is constructive, friendly, and unbiased as regards creed or sect, and positive and inspirational in tone. We suggest that prospective contributors study carefully the various publications before submitting material. **Sample copies are sent on request. Complimentary copies are sent to writers on publication. MSS should be typewritten in double space. We accept MSS only with the understanding that they are original and previously unpublished. Unity School pays on acceptance $1 a line for verse."** *Unity Magazine* is a monthly journal which publishes "poems that give a clear message of Truth and provide practical, positive help in meeting human needs for healing, supply, and harmony." *Daily Word* is a "monthly manual of daily studies" which "buys a limited number of short devotional articles and poems." *Wee Wisdom* is a monthly magazine for boys and girls. **"Its purpose is character-building. Its goal is to help children develop their full potential. Short, lively poems, readable by a third-grader. Character-building ideals should be emphasized without preaching. Language should be universal, avoiding the Sunday-school image."** As a sample I selected the last of three stanzas of "The Prayer of Faith" by Hannah More Kohaus:

> God is my health, I can't be sick;
> God is my strength, unfailing, quick; God is my all, I know no fear,
> Since God and love and Truth are here

Many of the poems in the magazine are by children, submitted to the section called "Writers' Guild," edited by Verle Bell. There is no payment for poems in this section except for complimentary copies and an award word certificate and letter. Here is a sample, "I Love," by Wendy Strickland (Grade 4):

> I love the sand,
> I love the sea,
> I love the waves so high;
> But then I saw an airplane
> And wished that I could fly.

Wee Wisdom is 48 pp. saddle-stapled, digest-sized, with colorful art and graphics. **They also buy "rhymed prose for 'read alouds' " for which they pay $15 minimum.**

‡**UNIVERSITY EDITIONS (I)**, 4937 Humphrey Road, Huntington, WV 25704, phone 304-429-7204, publisher Ira Herman. **"University Editions will be primarily doing subsidized books of poetry [by the author], with a payback plan."** The press is "committed to assisting and establishing new and published poets. **No firm prejudices as to style or kind of poetry—we'll consider everything that comes in."** The press's current catalog lists two books of poetry, **Weights and Measures** by Paul Christensen and **Hearing the Light** by Robert Bowie. From the latter, Mr. Herman selected the following lines as a sample:

> Among fields of grasses so tall
> the elk seem only a herd of barren
> branches in a kind of migration . . .

The slim books are digest-sized, nicely printed, 60 pp., flat-spined with one-color glossy card covers, priced at $5/each. **Sample available for $5 plus $1 postage. The payback plan works like this: "author receives all sales proceeds until his subsidy has been repaid; remaining unsold copies belong to him. Marketing program includes submission to distributors, other publishers, agents, bookstores, and libraries."** Simultaneous and photocopied submissions are acceptable.

***THE UNKNOWNS, ABRI PUBLICATIONS, AN ATLANTA CREATIVE ALLIANCE PUBLICATION (I)**, Suite #1, 1900 Century Blvd NE, Atlanta, GA 30345, phone 404-636-3145, founded 1973, is a magazine-sized 64 pp. quarterly, circulation 500, "to encourage writers who must be fed recognition." I selected these sample lines, the conclusion of "Towel Me Dry, Lord" by Lenore Turkeltaub:

> Lord, stay awhile with me
> and listen to my outpourings
> You'll understand. Listen, please.
> Then towel me dry.

Subscription: $15. **Sample: $1 postpaid. Reports within a month. Payment: contributor's copy. Send SASE for guidelines. Editors comment on rejections.** They advise, "Do not hide your message—point—in vagueness not even understood by the individual."

***UNMUZZLED OX (II)**, #311, 105 Hudson St., New York, NY 10013, founded 1971, poetry editor, Michael Andre is a digest-sized 100 + pp. literary biannual. **Sample: $7. SASE must be 9x12" with at**

least 69¢ postage. They have also published **The Poets' Encyclopedia,** 310 pp., "World's basic knowledge transformed by 225 poets, artists, musicians and novelists."

THE UNSPEAKABLE VISIONS OF THE INDIVIDUAL (IV, Beat), Box 439, California, PA 15419, phone 412-938-8956, founded 1971, poetry editors Arthur & Kit Knight, is an "ongoing compendium of writings on, about and for the Beat Generation" publishing anthologies, postcards, posters and annually, the unspeakable visions of the individual. **Poetry must be Beat-oriented, generally free verse, confessional.** They have published poetry recently by Allen Ginsberg, Diane di Prima, Gregory Corso and Michael McClure. Each issue of *TUVOTI* uses 60-176 pp. of poetry, circulation 2,000, 150 subscriptions of which half are libraries. Subscription: $10. **Sample: $3.50 postpaid. Submit maximum of 10 pp. Photocopy OK; no dot-matrix. Pays 2 copies and occasionally small cash payment, i.e. $10.** The editors advise, "Write honestly out of your own experience."

*THE UPPER ROOM, *ALIVE NOW!, *POCKETS (IV, Religious, theme, style), 1908 Grand Box 189, Nashville, TN 37212, phone 615-327-2700. This publishing company brings out about 20 books a year and three magazines: *The Upper Room, Alive Now!,* and *Pockets.* Of these, two use freelance poetry. *Pockets, Devotional Magazine for Children,* which comes out 11 times a year, circulation 78,000-80,000, is for children 6-12, "offers stories, activities, prayers, poems—all geared to giving children a better understanding of themselves as children of God. Some of the material is not overtly religious but deals with situations, special seasons and holidays, ecological concerns from a Christian perspective." It uses 3-4 pp. of poetry per issue. **Sample: $1.50 plus 73¢ postage. Ordinarily 24 line limit on poetry. Pays $25-50. Send SASE for themes and guidelines.** The other magazine which uses poetry is *Alive Now!*, a bimonthly, circulation 75,000, for a general Christian audience interested in reflection and meditation. **Sample and guidelines free. They buy 30 poems a year, avantgarde and free verse. Submit 5 poems, 10-45 lines. Pays $10-25.**

SHERRY URIE (V), Box 63, RFD 3, Barton, VT 05822, phone 802-525-4482, founded 1974, poetry editor Sherry Urie, publishes mostly **Vermont and New England work. Poetry not likely to be considered at present.**

UNIVERSITY OF UTAH PRESS (II), 101 University Service Bldg., Salt Lake City, UT 84112, phone 801-581-6771, publishes a poetry series under the editorship of the poet and critic Dave Smith. Each year a volume of original poetry is chosen from submitted MSS. **MSS are invited** *during the month of March only;* the volume selected for publication is announced the following September with other MSS returned during the summer. **Poetry collections should be at least 60 pp. in length and should be sent to Acquisitions Editor—Poetry, University of Utah Press, USB 101, University of Utah, Salt Lake City, Utah 84112. "We are not reading any MSS for the spring of 1986, but will accept them in 1987." They will accept MSS which are simultaneous submissions "provided we are notified that this is the case."**

UTAH STATE UNIVERSITY PRESS (II, IV, Regional/Western Americana), UMC 95, Logan, UT 84322, phone 801-750-1362, founded 1972, is a "scholarly press producing 6-10 titles a year. Emphasis on regional and Western Americana." They publish poetry in hardbacks and paperbacks—**"no restrictions at this time."** They have recently published books of poetry by Kenneth Brewer and Keith Wilson, from whose **Stone Roses: Poems From Transylvania** I selected these sample lines (opening of "The Casino at Constanta"):

> Here is where that I stood,
> its hand upon this railing,
> cigarette in hand thinking
> of a woman, fingers, candlelight.

That volume is hardback, flat-spined, in an unusual format—9" wide x 6" high, with b/w surreal photos—$12.95. Wilson is a New Mexican poet. **Query with cover letter discussing scope and focus of the MS and attached vita listing other publications and biographical background. The only condition for acceptance is that the MS successfully pass through the three-tiered review process used by the USU Press. Reply to queries in 2-3 weeks, to submission (if invited) in 2-4 months. Prefer not to review simultaneous submissions. Photocopy, dot-matrix OK, or discs compatible with Televideo 803 (hard copy preferred). Contract is for 10% after 500 copies are sold plus 10 author's copies. Send SASE for catalog to buy samples. Editors comment on rejections of MSS accepted for the three-tiered review process.** The editor advises, "Learn how to write GREAT letters of inquiry! Send complete, clean MSS."

*VALLEY SPIRIT (II), Box 1145, Corrales, NM 87048-1145, founded 1981, poetry editor Sabra Basler, is an "irregular quarterly of poetry and essays on the role of art in our lives to let each other see where we are coming from . . . as human beings first. **Want hard & clear poetry that has to do with either the noumenal or phenomenal worlds that believes in love over evil . . . but that accepts truth—truthful representations of the human condition in any form and on any topic . . . NO SENTIMENTAL.**" They have recently published poetry by Sheila Clark, Ed Mycue, Jack Hirschman and Jim Normington. The editor selected these sample lines by Julia Connor:

> *or,*
> *think of the poet's lament*
> *I cannot name it*
> *there is no name*
> *to which the wise physician counseled*
> *you must invent it.*

Valley Spirit is magazine-sized, side-stapled ("not fancy, but it gets the work out to the public"), using about 40 pp. of poetry in each issue, circulation 99, 25 subscriptions of which 1 is a library. Subscription: $16; per copy: $4 They use about 3-5% of the hundreds of poems submitted each year, have a 3-6 month backlog. **Sample: $2 postpaid. Submit typed or photocopied MS—no dot-matrix. Reports in 1-3 months. Pays "rarely." Editor "frequently" comments on rejections.** Sabra Basler advises, "Do not be afraid to live in the unknown. Form and content are born from Chaos. Write from your heart and not for any magazine . . . you know the old addage . . . the truth will set you free . . .truth and social justice and working for both in writing."

VEGETARIAN JOURNAL, JEWISH VEGETARIANS (I, IV, Specialized), Box 1463, Baltimore, MD 21203, founded 1982, poetry editor Debra Wasserman. These are newsletters (*Journal* monthly, *Jewish* quarterly) serving as "an educational resource for vegetarianism, involved in issues of health, nutrition, ecology, world hunger and animal rights." They also publish occasional pamphlets and paperback books. They use poetry on these subjects, such as these sample lines selected by the editor:

> *Place two of us in a small tank*
> *More money to put in a bank*
>
> *People come to stare*
> *You'd think they really care*
> *They say it's to promote respect*
> *Instead we survive, but feel neglect*

Jewish Vegetarians is a newsletter, 16 pp., with a circulation of 500. *Vegetarian Journal* is a magazine-sized 16 pp. newsletter (folded, stapled) with a circulation of 600. **Poetry for** *Jewish Vegetarians* **should have a Jewish slant. Sample: free for SASE. For either, simply submit appropriate poems. Considers simultaneous submissions; photocopy, dot-matrix OK. Reports in 2-3 weeks. No pay. They sponsor a yearly essay contest for students 19 and under, and entries may be poems; $50 savings bond price.**

VEHICLE PRESS, SIGNAL EDITIONS (II), Box 125 Station Place du Parc, Montreal, Quebec, Canada H2W 2M9, poetry editor Michael Harris, editorial contact: editor Margaret Christatos; publisher Simon Dardick, is a "literary press with poetry series." They publish flat-spined paperbacks and hardbacks. Among the poets published recently are Michael Harris, Anne McLean, David Solway and Susan Glickman. They want poetry which is **"first-rate, original, content-conscious." Query with 20 poems ("a good proportion of which should already have been published in recognized literary periodicals")as sample, bio, statement of aesthetic or poetic aims. Reports in 6 weeks. Photocopy, dot-matrix OK. "***Signal Editions'*** emphasis is on Canadian-authored manuscript. Poets appearing in** *Signal Editions* **usually have wide magazine publication."**

‡*VER POETS, *POETRY POST (I, IV, Members),, Haycroft, 61/63 Chiswell Grn. Lane, St. Albans, County Herts. AL2 3AG, England, founded 1965, editor/organizer May Badman, a poetry group **"publishing members' work if it has reached a good standard.** We publish *Ver Poets Voices, Poetry Post*, and *Poetry World*, the last being an information sheet. **"We aim at bringing members' work up to professional literary standards if it is not already there. All members receive our publications free and can buy further copies." Membership costs £4.** They have recently published work by Meg Seaton, John Cotton, John Mole, and Howard Sergeant. As a sample, they selected the following lines from "Genesis" by Richard Ball:

> *The black book hangs open,*
> *weighted by a stone. a black line*
> *splits the chapters, that split the*
> *globe clenched by creation.*

Ver Poets Voices, which appears about twice a year, is digest-sized with a stapled card cover. It goes to the 250 members plus about 50 copies to shops, etc. *Poetry Post*, also a semi-annual, is magazine-sized with a card front cover. It reports on Ver Poets competitions and other matters concerning poetry. *Poetry World*, which appears 4 times/year, is a series of information sheets on national competitions and poetry events. The group sponsors the Ver Poets Open Competition (an annual event), which has prizes of £100, £50, and £25. They also organize six competitions per year for members only; winners are published in *Poetry Post*. **"All members are encouraged to send work for comment." Not more than 6 clearly typed or reproduced poems should be submitted at once. Reporting time is "by return of post" and time to publication is 6 months or less.** The editors say, "A lot of work is being done in England by small presses such as ourselves, and we provide continually the first few rungs of the ladder to success as poets. Members are offered free advice on their work and how to present it to editors. Also information on publishing opportunities."

*VERSE & UNIVERSE (I), #3, 1780 McKinley, Wyandotte, MI 48192, founded 1985, poetry editors Tammy Anderson at that address or Blaine Francis at 18340 Alvaro, phone 313-285-9384, is a literary quarterly looking for **strong, intense poetry of any length.** They use poetry in each issue, printrun 200-300. **"We answer all letters within a week or two, will comment on all poetry submitted if requested. Submit as many poems as one wishes. All we ask is that the poet's name appear on each sheet, typed neatly." Pays in copies.**

‡*VIAZTLAN: AN INTERNATIONAL JOURNAL OF THE ARTS AND LETTERS (II), 122 N. Cherry St., San Antonio, TX 78202, phone 512-227-2751, founded 1981, editor-in-chief Rafael C. Castillo, poetry editor Jesus Cardona, a bi-monthly journal which publishes serious fiction and poetry. **"We try to look for a particular slant toward issues affecting American society. We do not publish inspirational poems, pornography, etc. The audience is college [students].** *"ViAztlan* is mailed to our correspondents in France, Italy, Germany and England." We publish free verse, rhyme and concrete poetry . . . we look for individuality, character and imagery. 'A poem should be palpable and mute/As a globed fruit (Archibald MacLeish)'." *ViAztlan* has recently published Debra Meadows, Ricardo Sanchez, Yolanda Porros Lopez, Jose Montalvo, Rudolfo Anaya, and Edward Meeks. As a sample, the editors selected the following lines by Gary Soto:

> In this moment when the light starts up
> In the east and rubs
> The horizon until it catches fire,
> We enter the fields to hoe,
> Row after row, among the small flags of onion.

ViAztlan (I have not seen it) is magazine-sized, 40 pp. with b/w graphics. Circulation is 5,000, including 1,500 subscriptions ("and growing"); 20% of the subscriptions go to university libraries. Single copy price is $1. **At present contributors receive 10 copies, but "pending CCLM, NEH [grants] will allow payment." Writers should "send neat typewritten poems only, original material only." Reporting time is 3-5 weeks, and "backlog is not big yet."** Mr. Castillo says, "Preparations are under way for publication of a chapbook series in 1986." **For chapbook publication, writers should query, sending credits, 4 sample poems, bio, and poetic aims. "We do not publish previously published poetry." Queries will be answered in 4-5 weeks and MSS reported on in 1 month.** As of 1986, they offer poetry and fiction prizes. The editor comments, "Poets have probably heard much of 'finding your own voice' and 'focusing in on an image. We, at ViAztlan, feel that American poets should be less metaphysical, philosophical; more lucid in their quest for bridging common everyday experiences with the common man. We particularly recommend a thorough reading of Kenneth Rexroth's 'Why is American poetry culturally deprived?' (TriQuarterly, Winter 1967). If all else fails, follow your path."

*THE VILLAGER (II), 135 Midland Ave., Bronxville, NY 10707, phone 914-337-3252, founded 1928, editor Amy Murphy, poetry editor Josephine Colville, a publication of the Bronxville Women's Club for club members and families, professional people and advertisers, circulation 750, appears in 9 monthly issues, October-June. **Sample: $1.25 postpaid. They use 1 page or more of poetry per issue, prefer short poems "in good taste only," seasonal (Thanksgiving, Christmas, Easter) 3 months in advance. They copyright material but will release it to author on request. Pays 2 copies.**

*VINTAGE '45, A UNIQUELY SUPPORTIVE QUARTERLY FOR WOMEN (IV, Midlife women), Box 266, Orinda, CA 94563, phone 415-254-7266, founded 1983, editor Susan L. Aglietti, is for "active, introspective women who have outgrown traditional publications. From time to time I will publish a literary anthology on a topic relevant to my readership." A recent example is *Maternal Legacy*, a 104 pp. mother-daughter anthology (primarily composed of poetry), which includes 24 essays, poems and short stories, none of which had previously appeared in print. Susan L. Aglietti was herself born in 1945, which explains the title of the quarterly. She says, **"I seek well-reasoned, understandable poems directly relevant to mid-life women. No jingles, erotica or abstruse messages. My format is**

small so poems need to be relatively short (no longer than 2 typed pages) Anthologies allow for greater length." As a sample is the first stanza of "Target Practice" by Mindy Kronenberg:

> *It is visiting time again*
> *I sit across from my sister*
> *and we warm up*
> *by loosely discussing our lives*

Vintage '45 is digest-sized, 28 pp., offset from typescript, matte card cover, saddle-stapled, using an average of 2 pp. of poetry per issue. They receive 40-50 freelance submissions of poetry per year, use 5-8 **by women writers only. Sample: $2.50 postpaid. Submit up to 5 poems, typed or computer-printed. No simultaneous submissions. Preference for unpublished work. Pre-published MSS must be labeled as such. Reports in 1-2 months (shorter if totally unsuitable). Pays 1 year's subscription. Send SASE for guidelines. "I like to know what motivated the writer to compose her work, something about her life which would be relevant to me and to my readers. I always try to comment on rejections; I have no form rejection letter. But I am not a poetry critic by training."** Susan L. Aglietti advises, "When an editor offers to read other material you have written, take him/ her up on it! There are so many reasons work is not accepted apart from its intrinsic qualities."

*THE VIRGINIA QUARTERLY REVIEW (III), 1 West Range, Charlottesville, VA 22903, founded 1925, is one of the oldest and most distinguished literary journals in the country. It is digest-sized, 220 + pp., flat-spined, circulation 4,000. **They use about 15 pp. of poetry in each issue, pay $1/line, no length or subject restrictions.**

*VOICES INTERNATIONAL (II), 1115 Gillette Dr., Little Rock, AR 72207, editor Clovita Rice, is a quarterly poetry journal, 32-40 pp., 6x9" saddle-stapled, professionally printed with b/w matte card cover. **Subscription: $10 per year. Sample: $2 postpaid (always a back issue). Prefers free verse but accepts high quality traditional, 200-300 unsolicited poems per year. Limit submissions to batches of 5, double-spaced, 3-40 lines (will consider longer if good). Publishes an average of 18 months after acceptance. Pays copies.** "We accept poetry with a new approach, haunting word pictures and significant ideas. Language should be used like watercolors to achieve depth, to highlight one focal point, to be pleasing to the viewer, and to be transparent, leaving space for the reader to project his own view. Our own trend is toward shorter poems—30 lines or less. Space is vital to us, and it's harder to sustain interest and impact in a longer poem." I selected the first stanza of "Unity" by James A. Bateman as a sample:

> *The pleasure, first, is in the writing:*
> *making things—words into phrases,*
> *phrases into lines; also giving*
> *feelings and thoughts a shapeliness.*

*VOICES ISRAEL (I), 38 Nehemia St., Nave Sha'anan, Haifa, 32 295 Israel, phone 04/223332, founded 1972, editor Reuben Rose, with an editorial board of 7, is an annual anthology of poetry in English coming from all over the world. **You have to pay $2/poem (up to 4) to submit and buy a copy to see your work in print. Price for 1987: $20 airmail, $10 surface mail. Submit all kinds of poetry no longer than a sheet of typing paper. The editor does not want "smut, perversity, obscenity, or fanatical religiosity."** He has recently published poetry by Ada Aharoni, Ruth Finer Mimtz, Roger White and Elias Pater. As a sample he selected these lines by Eva Avi-Yonah:

> *Crushed by the force of events*
> *I shall rise again,*
> *Shake the shards and the dust off my garment*
> *And, not heeding my wounds, go on.*

The annual *Voices Israel* is 6¼x8", offset from typed copy on ordinary paper, 81 pp. flat-spined with glossy white card cover printed in blue. The magazine is "16x20 cm., saddle-stapled, offset from photographic plates." Circulation 350-500, subscription $20. **Sample: $10 postpaid. Back copies $4 airmail, $2 surface mail. Evaluation $3 per poem. Reports in 6 months, has at least 6 month backlog.** The editor advises, "Try all magazines all over the world; in short, collect magazines."

VOL. NO. MAGAZINE (II), 24721 Newhall Ave., Newhall, CA 91321, phone 805-254-0851, founded 1983, poetry editors Richard Weekley, Jerry Danielsen, Tina Megali and Bob Brown. "*Vol. No.* publishes lively and concise works. Zippery connections to the unsung world. **Each issue has a theme, such as 'Intuition' and 'Under Observation' and 'Water, Wind, and Stone' scheduled for 1986-87. Send SASE for descriptions of these. No trivial, unthoughtout work. Work that penetrates the feelings-mind. 1 page poems have the best chance.**" They have recently published poetry by John Brander, Jennifer Grace Welch and Robin B. Martinez. The editors selected these sample lines by Marcia Van Wyak:

Close-up

John Stone M.D.
Poet

William Carlos Williams was a doctor. So were Chekhov, Keats and Maugham. Surprisingly, the medical-literary combination is not such an unusual one. Nor is the writing incidental, for as Poet Williams said, "When they ask me . . . how I have for so many years continued an equal interest in medicine and the poem, I reply that they amount to nearly the same thing."

"It's a natural marriage," says Dr. John Stone, author of the 1985 Mississippi Institute of Arts and Letters award-winning *Renaming the Streets*, his third book of poems. "There are interesting commonalities between academics and poetry; they both come out of the human experience. Each patient, each medical problem is a short story or a poem—small remarkable unwritten novels."

Poet John Stone, a cardiologist, writes straight from the heart—as an affirmation of life, a way to find order and meaning in the world. His poetry also helps him come to terms with mortality and his limitations as a physician. Today more medical schools, including the one at Emory University where Stone is Director of Admissions, are acknowledging the importance of art in medicine as a way of seeing, observing. Literature courses are more frequently a part of the medical curriculum to help bridge the widening gap, which sophisticated technology is creating, between doctor and patient.

For Stone poetry preceded medicine—since high school at the encouragement of an English teacher. During his decade-plus of medical training, poetry took a necessary hiatus. Today, along with his administrative duties, Dr. Stone sees patients and teaches classes. After work, on weekends or alone on trips for readings, speaking engagements, medical or writing seminars, his "peripheral brain" goes to work.

Moving, accessible, entertaining, Stone's poetry is diverse in form as are his subjects—from life's familiar circumstances to troubling medical cases. Inspiration—a special expression, line or a germ of a poem—usually begins on 3x5 cards which he always carries in his shirt pocket, because, as he says, "When the Muse whispers in your ear, you'd better have something to write on."

Sometimes, says Stone, a poem begins with a *donnée*, an unexplainable "gift" to which other lines naturally stick and decide they want to be a poem—"and you know it's just right." Poems are also the work of serendipity, the result of an auspicious incident which triggers verse, such as Stone's highly metaphorical pigeon sonnets, written in Oxford where he taught one summer. Poems also evolve out of sheer musicality, he says, when meter and sound join in song. On occasion complete poems simply "arrive" and must be written that moment.

After med school Stone immersed himself in contemporary poetry—his prescription to understanding and defining a poet's interest in writing. Read literary magazines and know what's being done today; continue to send out poems and get published in little magazines, the doctor orders. Editors seldom agree on what makes a good poem, but "when they see your poems have been published, that is, tested by other editors, they take notice." Don't be discouraged by rejection slips. Everyone gets them. "Publication will come," maintains Atlanta's Dr. Zhivago. Patience is the best medicine.

—Jean M. Fredette

No heart will catch fire in the bedroom haze.
In the vacuum left by a smile there is no sound.
Nothing can burn like silence.
This is what it sounds like.

Vol.No. is a digest-sized, saddle-stapled, 32 pp. semiannual, circulation 300. Subscription: $5. They receive about 200 freelance submissions of poetry per year, use 40, have a 6 month backlog. **Sample: $3 postpaid. Submit limit of 6 poems. Photocopy and simultaneous submissions OK. Reports in 3-5 months. Pays 2 copies.**

WAMPETER PRESS, *TENDRIL MAGAZINE (II), Box 512, Green Harbor, MA 02041, phone 617-834-4137, founded 1978, poetry editor George E. Murphy Jr. *Tendril* "publishes 3 issues per year of poetry and fiction. Each issue contains a chapbook-length collection of poems from a 'Feature Poet.' Recent Featured Poets have included Denis Johnson, Jorie Graham, Susan Wood, Raymond Carver and Robert Long. We also publish special anthology issues, e.g. 'The Poet's Choice,' in which 100 major poets chose their favorite of their own poems. We are **open to poetry of any style or length. Though we are not interested in light verse, experimental work, etc., our tastes are eclectic.**" In addition to those listed above, they have recently published poetry by Linda Gregg, William Matthews, Maxine Kumin, Linda Pastan and James Tate. George Murphy selected these sample lines by Denis Johnson:

I will always love you and think of you with bitterness
and when someone offers a remark in a voice
that brings back your loosened voice and your inebriated
fear,
I'll be wounded along scars.

Tendril is a 6x9" flat spined, 200+ pp. triquarterly with color matte cover, circulation 1,800, 1,300 subscriptions of which 520 are libraries. Subscription: $12; per copy: $5.95. They receive some 12,000+ freelance submissions of poetry per year, use 350. **Sample: $3 postpaid. Submit 3-5 pp. Photocopy, dot-matrix OK. Reports in 1-8 weeks. Pays copies. For book publication by Wampeter Press, query with 10 samples. Replies to queries in 3 weeks, to submissions (if invited) in 2 months. Simultaneous submissions OK if so designated. Photocopy, dot-matrix, discs compatible with Macintosh OK (hard copy preferred). Publishes on 7% contract plus 10% of the run in copies.** They are open to subsidy arrangements with author helping with the production expenses. George Murphy advises: "Don't worry about publishing. Instead, work on improving your craft. Publication will take care of itself in time."

WARTHOG PRESS (II), 29 South Valley Rd., West Orange, NJ 07052, phone 201-731-9269, founded 1979, poetry editor Patricia Fillingham, publishes books of poetry "**that is understandable, poetic.**" She has published poetry by Barbara A. Holland, Penny Harter and Marta Fengues. **Query with 5 samples, cover letter "saying what the author is looking for." Simultaneous submissions OK. MS should be "readable." Pays copies, but "I would like to get my costs back." Comments on rejections, "if asked for. People really don't want criticism." Send SASE for catalog to buy samples.** Patricia Fillingham advises, "The best way to sell poetry still seems to be from poet to listener. I wish more people would buy poetry."

*WASCANA REVIEW (II), University of Regina, Saskatchewan, Canada, editor-in-chief Joan Givner, emphasizes literature and the arts for readers interested in serious poetry, fiction and scholarship. Semiannual, circulation 300. **Photocopies OK. Buys 10-15 poems per issue, any form, 2-100 lines, pays $10/page.**

*WASHINGTON REVIEW (II, IV, Regional), Box 50132, Washington, DC 20004, phone 202-638-0515, founded 1974, poetry editor Beth Joselow, is a bimonthly journal of arts and literature published by the Friends of the Washington Review of the Arts, Inc., a non-profit, tax-exempt educational organization, tabloid-sized, saddle-stapled on high-quality newsprint, circulation 2,000, 700 subscriptions of which 10 are libraries, using 2 of the large pp. per issue for poetry. **They publish primarily local Washington metropolitan area poets.** Payment in copies. They have recently published poems by Paul Genega and Jerry Ratch. The editor selected these sample lines by Robert McDowell:

Someone else can claim his lean-to
And lie awake reading the news he used for warmth.
Walking north against the suction-slap of semis,
He imagines a pal released from jail,

Sample: $2.50 postpaid. Pays 5 copies.

WASHINGTON WRITERS' PUBLISHING HOUSE (IV, Regional), Box 50068, Washington, DC 20004, founded 1975. An editorial board is elected annually from the collective. "We are a poetry publishing collective who publishes outstanding poetry collections in flat-spined paperbacks by **individual authors from the greater Washington DC area (60 mile radius, excluding Baltimore) on the basis of competitions held once a year.**" They have recently published poetry by Ann Darr, Barbara X. Lefcowitz, David McAleavy, Elaine Magarrell, Eric Nelson, Catherine Harnett and Paul Estaver. The editors chose this sample from "Do You Take This Woman":

> *Eat your muse*
> *and your mouth is melted shut.*
> *All you can do, ever again, is beckon.*

Submit 50-60 pp. MS with SASE only between July 1 and September 1. $5 reading fee. A poet contributes $300 toward cost of publication and is then reimbursed in copies which sell for $5.

*WATERWAYS: POETRY IN THE MAINSTREAM, TEN PENNY PLAYERS (I), 799 Greenwich St., New York, NY 10014, phone 212-929-3169, founded 1977, poetry editors Barbara Fisher and Richard Spiegel, "publishes poetry by adult and child poets in a magazine that is published 11 times a year. We do theme issues and are trying to increase an audience for poetry and the printed and performed word. The project produces performance readings in public spaces and is in residence year round at our local library with workshops and readings. We publish the magazine, *Waterways*, **anthologies of child poets; child poetry postcard series; chapbooks (adults & child poets). We are not fond of haiku or rhyming poetry; never use material of an explicit sexual nature.** We are open to reading material from people we have never published writing in traditional and experimental poetry forms. While we do 'themes' sometimes an idea for a future magazine is inspired by a submission so we try to remain open to poets' inspiration. Poets should be guided however by the fact that we are children's and animal rights advocates & are a NYC press." They have recently published poetry by Albert Huffstickler, Joanne Seltzer, Robert Lime, Lillian Morrison, Sarah Brown Weitzman, Arthur Knight and Kit Knight. As a sample, the editors chose the opening lines of "Sojourner" by Albert Huffstickler:

> *The lady who went to Hell came back*
> *with scars on her eyes*
> *soul limp as a ragdoll, gums bleeding.*

Waterways is published in a 40 pp. 4¼x 7" wide format, saddle-stapled, offset from various type styles, using b/w drawings, matte card cover, circulation 150, 30 subscriptions of which 4 are libraries. Subscription: $20. **Sample: $2.54 postpaid. They use 60% of freelance poems submitted. Submit less than 10 poems for first submission. No dot-matrix. Simultaneous submissions OK. Send SASE for guidelines for approaching themes. Reports in less than a month. Pays 1 copy. Editors sometimes comment on rejections.** They hold contests for children only. Chapbooks published by Ten Penny Players are "by children only—and not by submission; they come through our workshops in the library and schools." The editors advise, "We suggest that poets attend book fairs, particularly the major ones such as the New York Book Fair and the other larger regional events. It's a fast way to find out what we are all publishing."

WAV PUBLICATIONS, *WORDS AND VISIONS (WAV) MAGAZINE, WAV POETRY SERIES (IV, Regional), Box 545 Norwood, Adelaide, South Australia 5067, phone 08-3329529, founded 1983, poetry editors Martin Brakmanis and Span. "Publishing art and literature for the Australian market (predominantly—at this stage). Books include fiction, poetry and children's titles. The magazine has suspended publication, perhaps permanently." They want to see "**anything stimulating, interesting and fresh. No pornography. We do publish conceptual series. Prefer individual poems to have less than 70 lines.**" They have recently published poetry by Jenny Boult, Pauline Wardenworth, Rob Knottenbelt, Mick Bocchino, Jeff Nuttal, Josef Raffa, Jeff Guess, John Griffin, Rory Harris, Jeri Kroll and Bruce Holling Rooers. The editors selected hese sample lines from "The Heat" by Mike Ladd:

> *between the galvanised iron fence and the street*
> *the heat comes down like a punch from behind,*
> *rolling the eyes back to the whites of the sky . . .*
> *the sea on the western horizon*
> *is a samurai sword*
> *and the hills are screaming at the plains . . .*

Query with sample poems. They publish books of poetry by Australians only. Editor comments on rejections "always for individual pocms but not for entire MSS." The editors advise, "Accessibility for the layman is important—without divorcing the content or style from its literary or artistic traditions. Experimentation does not mean incomprehensibility. Ideas and images and lucidity are vital. Humour often helps."

THE WAVE PRESS, *THE WAVE (II), 95 Tussel Lane, Scotch Plains, NJ 07076, phone 201-382-8450, founded 1982, poetry editor Michael E. Napoliello Jr. "By printing the finest poetry available to us from in and out of state, we help NJ understand the Nation, and the Nation understand NJ." The Wave Press publishes posters and anthologies in addition to *The Wave,* a tabloid weekly, distributed free, circulation 50,000 (750 subscriptions of which 12 are libraries), "a popular lifestyle paper that also reports on and influences culture through the presentation of fine arts and folk literature. **We accept all types of poetry in light of the fact that what's experiment becomes tradition; tradition, experiment."** No specifications as to form, length, style, subject-matter or purpose: "We, of course, leave that up to the poet." They have recently published poems by Mark Stuart, Gregory Waryas and Lynn Becker. The editor, Michael Napoliello Jr., selected these sample lines from his own "The Newark Refinery Fires":

> *Huddled about the blaze, I saw old Anscilla,*
> *Forty years on the assembly line, her Newark factory was now burning—*
> *In her eyes I could see the flames tear the constellations from the sky;*
> *And I knew the poets would have to start again . . .*

Sample: $1 postpaid plus a large envelope with 3 first class stamps. They use half of the 150 submissions of freelance poetry submitted yearly. Reports in 2 months. Pays 25-75¢ per line. Editor comments on rejections if requested. He says, "We look for and love the poetry that bridges the inner world of self to the outer world of reality. This is what is starting to happen today in poetry and what needs to happen if tomorrow is to be more than just a promise."

*WAVES (II), 79 Denham Dr., Richmond Hill, Ontario, Canada L4C 6H9, phone 416-889-6703, founded 1972, poetry editor Gay Allison, is a triannual literary journal "publishing the best of emerging and established writers. We want poetry with **an exciting use of language and technique, as well as insights into the 'human condition.'** 4-100 lines. Avoid: clichés, literal, cut-up prose.** Many writers do not know what literary means! Many cannot 'sense' the difference between literary sonnets & *Reader's Digest* humorous jingles!." They have recently published such Canadian poets as Al Purdy, Margaret Atwood, Dorothy Livesay, Irving Layton as well as many other nationalities. The editor selected the concluding lines of "We Are Those" by Fred Cogswell:

> *We are those whose lives are restless ever,*
> *The hero-gods in us are ever killed*
> *In the space between our space and that space*
> *Whose face we close when we deny our dreams*

Waves is digest-sized 115 pp. average, flat-spined, professionally printed on heavy stock, glossy card cover, circulation 1,000 + , 700 subscriptions of which 300 are libraries. They receive "nearly 1,000" freelance submissions of poetry per year, use "less than 100." **Sample: $2 postpaid. Submit 4-8 poems, tyed, name and address on each poem, single-spaced (double between stanzas). Photocopy, dot-matrix OK. Reports in 2-6 weeks. Pays $10/page plus 1 copy. Send SASE for guidelines. Editor comments on rejections "if asked/ pushed. Helpful comments often make enemies."** Editor Bernice Lever advises, "READ contemporary books and magazines and go to readings—even if only 1 book, 1 magazine and 1 reading a month by established poets. You can hate their style and content, but do learn what is published today. Visit your library. They have some literary magazines. We were listed in the top 50 markets and get dozens more US poetry submissions per week with US return stamps (which are useless to us). Basic return cost is 39¢ Canadian if a few poems—or 53¢ if more—a financial drain, as most are not 'literary' writers. Send IRC's."

*WEBSTER REVIEW (II), Webster University, 470 E. Lockwood, Webster Groves, MO 63119, founded 1974, poetry editors Pamela Hadas and Jerred Metz, is a literary semiannual. They want **"no beginners. We are especially interested in translations of foreign contemporary poetry."** They have recently published poetry by Bertolt Brecht, Therese Plantier, Robert Rack, A.F. Moritz and George Bilgere. I selected as a sample the first stanza of "Six Sense" by Devon Jersild:

> *I seem to love you, love, with a sixth sense*
> *beyond my ken, beyond my power to see.*
> *It's soft and brutal, it teases a keen smell,*
> *it cloys and sours on the tongue—a taste*
> *like light to carry home, like air to touch,*
> *It's higher, lower than the ear can hear.*

Webster Review is 112 pp. digest-sized, flat-spined, professionally printed with glossy card cover, circulation 1,000, 500 subscriptions of which 200 are libraries. Subscription: $5; per copy: $2.50. They receive about 1,500 submissions of freelance poetry per year, use 120. **Sample free for SASE. Reports "within a month, usually." Pays $25-50, if funds permit. Contributors receive 2 copies. Editors comment on rejections "if time permits."**

*THE WEIRDBOOK SAMPLER (IV, Fantasy), Box 149, Amherst Branch, Buffalo, NY 14226, is a "modern pulp magazine" emphasizing **weird fantasy (swords and sorcery, supernatural horror, pure fantasy) for educated, mature readers of all ages, and uses some poetry, 20 lines maximum,** similar in nature. **Sample: $2.75 postpaid. No pay for poetry. Send SASE for guidelines.** It is "published randomly," circulation 200, has a 3 year backlog.

*WELLSPRING (IV, Religious), 321 O'Connor St., Menlo Park, CA 94025, phone 415-326-7310, founded 1978, poetry editor Tim Chown, "is a forum for **Christian poets** and their work. We strive to publish poetry that transcends the 'religious' cliché; poetry that touches the spirit of the reader with its artistic beauty as well as its content. We want **poems in any form or length with strong imagery and fresh use of language. No 'jokes' or 'play on words'.**" They have recently published poetry by Paul Weinman, John Leax, Grace Cash, Fred Zydek and Viola Jacobson Berg. The editor selected these sample lines by Luci Shaw:

> *I am listening, still,*
> *for the edges of*
> *colored*
> *wing feathers.*

Wellspring is a quarterly, 32 pp., digest-sized, professionally printed with b/w drawings, colored mat card cover, circulation 250, 200 subscriptions of which 10-15 are libraries. Subscription: $9. They receive about 4,000 poems submitted freelance each year, use 120-150. **Sample: $2.50 postpaid. Send SASE for guidelines. Name and address on upper left corner of each poem, each poem on a separate sheet. Previously published and simultaneous submissions OK. Reports in 6-8 weeks. Pays 1 copy. Editor sometimes comments on rejections.**

‡*WELLSPRING MAGAZINE, GREAT AUK PUBLISHING (II, IV, Regional/Texas), U.T. Texas Union #282, Box 7338, Austin, TX 78713, phone 512-467-1321, founded 1983, editors John Stearle and Edward Pittman, a literary magazine that appears Fall and Spring each year and publishes poetry, fiction, art, and photography, both mainstream and experimental. The editor says, **"We prefer 40% Texas writing per issue. No length restrictions [on poetry]. Any subject or style. Highest quality only. Very open to freelancers. Prose-poetry also. Send only best work because we've seen some great things."** *Wellspring* has recently published poetry by Albert Huffstickler, Fred Asnes, and Thomas Whitbread. As a sample, I've selected the following excerpt from "Somewhere" by Kenneth Fontenot:

> *But now a song ends somewhere, somewhere*
> *a pillow is being fluffed for the night.*
> *Somewhere a young girl is beginning to know*
> *her own blood.*

Wellspring is digest-sized, 100 + pp. per issue including 10 or more pages of art, four-color cover. The print run is 850-1,000, of which 300 are subscriptions, 300 newsstand sales, 10 library subscriptions, and the remainder direct sales to friends, relative, co-workers and students. Price per issue is $5. **Sample available for $5 postpaid, guidelines for $1 to cover copying costs. Pay is 2 copies. "Writers should submit a maximum of 6 poems, letter-quality preferred to dot-matrix, no simultaneous submissions. MSS should be typed single-spaced, double-spaced between stanzas, no length restrictions. Reporting time is 2 months and time to publication 6-12 months. Freelance submissions for poetry books are accepted; writers should query first, sending credits. Queries will be answered in 1 month and MSS reported on in 2 months. Pay for books is 5 author's copies plus 10% of the profits."** The press publishes one poetry collection about every 2 years. The books are digest-sized, average page count 50, flat-spined paperbacks. The editor says, "Would like them [poets] in the magazine first. Books are not our primary concern, so we will select only the finest writing available and forego a book rather than print something that doesn't meet our standards." Book catalog is available for an 8½x11" SASE and 50¢. The editor advises, "Be persistent, and never stop trying to improve. You must never be satisfied with what you're doing. If you get lazy, you won't write anything good again. We like poetry that is precise, with limited philosophizing and sharp inspiring images. I want the poetry we print to be so good that it's scary."

WESLEYAN UNIVERSITY PRESS, WESLEYAN NEW POETS (III), 110 Mt. Vernon, Middletown, CT 06457, director Jeannette Hopkins, is one of the major publishers of poetry in the nation. **Query or send complete MS.** I selected as a sample from the Wesleyan New Poets Series ($15 submission fee), **Green Dragons**, by Richard Katrovas, the opening lines of "Father, I Know":

> *that I have changed,*
> *you have changed,*
> *and the spoiled meat*
> *that is my love for you*
> *sways on hooks in a chilled room*
> *of a woman's life*

Like other books in that series, this is a 6x8" flat-spined paperback, 62 pp., professionally printed with glossy card cover. "We discourage multiple submissions. No fee for the Established Poets Series, for poets who have already published one or more books." Poetry publications from Wesleyan tend to get widely (and respectfully) reviewed.

WEST ANGLIA PUBLICATIONS, BEN-SEN PRESS (II), Box 2683, La Jolla, CA 92038, phone 619-453-0706, Ben-Sen founded 1978, West Anglia founded 1982, poetry editor Helynn Hoffa. "Ben-Sen is a working print shop and does books for a fee. West Anglia is a publishing company and assumes the cost of putting out the book and pays the author royalties or in books. In most cases publicity and distribution rests with the author." They publish anthologies, chapbooks, flat-spined paperbacks and pamphlets. "**We look for authors who know the English language and how to use it correctly. Form, length, style is for the poet to decide. We do not want pornography, Marxist revolutionary, or how America oppresses the world.**" They have recently published Gary Morgan, Wilma Lusk, Kathleen Iddings, John Theobald and Kenneth Morris. "Poets we wish we had printed: Sappho, Homer, John Keats, Marianne Moore, Alexander Pope, Elizabeth Barrett Browning and Philip Larkin." And that takes JJ's prize for the most original and effective way of indicating the range of editorial taste that I have encountered. The editor chose these sample Haiku by Wilma Lusk, from her collection **Cat's Paws and Morning Glories**:

> *cats scratching at the door*
> *after a night out*
> *fog seeps through the window*
>
> *cat in the cupboard*
> *hunting breakfast*
> *among the cans*
> *birds flying by*

The book is a 5½x8" flat-spined format, 61 pp., professionally printed, black ink on quality white stock, matte card cover: $4.95. **Query with 5 sample poems. Cover letter "should include previous publication credits, awards." $10 reading fee with submissions. Simultaneous submissions, photocopies OK. No dot-matrix. Discs compatible with Apple IIE OK. Send SASE for catalog to buy samples. Editor supplies criticism at author's request for $15 per poem.** She advises, "Keep writing. Learn the language. English is our most important tool: hone it, study it, use it properly."

*WEST BRANCH (II), English Dept., Bucknell University, Lewisburg, PA 17837, founded 1977, is a literary biannual. Recently published poems by Martha Collins, Brigit Pegeen Kelly, Timothy Russell, David Citino, Hayden Carruth, Len Roberts, Betsy Sholl, Jill Stein, and Howard Nelson. 90+ pp., digest-sized, circulation 500, using **quality poetry. "In special circumstances we will consider simultaneous submissions; however, we prefer not to receive them."** Reports in 4-6 weeks. Payment in contributors' copies and a subscription to the magazine. One-year's subscription: $5. Two year (4 issues): $8. Sample: $2.

*WEST COAST REVIEW (IV, Canadian poets), English Dept., Simon Fraser University, Burnaby, British Columbia, Canada V5A 1S6, poetry editor Tom Martin, is a "quarterly magazine of the arts which favors work by *new* **Canadian artists, especially of the West Coast**, but it observes no borders in encouraging *original* creativity. Our focus is on *contemporary* poetry, short fiction, drama, music, graphics, photography, criticism, and reviews of books on *modern* art. The *Review* is *unique* in its continuing programme of publishing West Coast Review Books as part of the regular offering to subscribers." The magazine is 8x8", flat-spined, 64 pp., elegantly printed in 2 columns, b/w photography and graphics, glossy card cover with b/w photo. As a sample I selected the first of 3 stanzas of "Poem For Sylvia" by Pat Lane:

> *I loved the spite of your secret celibacy,*
> *the thick meat-soup of your self-pity.*
> *How you wanted to eat men. How you cried out*
> *the word, sorry, sorry, sorry,*
> *loving your revenge.*

‡WEST END PRESS (IV, Social), Box 291477, Los Angeles, CA 90029, founded 1976, editor and publisher John Crawford, a small-press publisher of socially conscious poetry and prose. They publish flat-spined paperbacks with an average print run of 1,200 to 2,000. They want "**politically or socially active poetry, preference given to working class, women, people of color, midwest or southwest or Pacific coast. No limitation on form, but we have not stressed post-modernist experimentation.**" They do not want "**Elitist, trivial, self-indulgent, 'cute,' amateur, racist, sexist, or very prolix.**" Recently they have published work by Nellie Wong, Cherrie Moraga, and Wendy Rose, from whose "Yurike" they chose the following lines as a sample:

> *I am the sound of crackling flesh,*
> *I was born of her drizzle,*
> > *your fire.*

The press publishes 3-4 books or poetry each year with an average page count of 48 to 96, usually digest-sized. **Freelance submissions are accepted. Writers should query, sending 6 sample poems, bio, philosophy, and poetic aims. Queries will be answered in 3 weeks and MSS reported on in 3 months. Simultaneous submissions will be accepted "only if you explain this." Photocopied MSS are OK but dot-matrix MSS are "Yuk!" Royalties are 6-10% or, in author's copies, 10% of print run. "We expect reprint rights to the book and will negotiate translations, anthology rights, etc. for you on a 50/50 basis. You retain copyright to the poems."** I have not seen samples of the books, just their catalog, which indicates that the books are priced from $3.25 to $9.95. The logo on the catalog is a cartoon of Karl Marx with a guitar.

‡*WEST HILLS REVIEW (II)**, 246 Walt Whitman Rd., Huntington Station, NY 11746, phone 516-299-2391, editor William A. Fahey, founded 1979, is a literary annual featuring poetry on any theme and essays on Walt Whitman. The editor wants **"lyric poetry primarily; not over 1-2 pp. in length. No restrictions as to style or subject matter. Looking for imagination, intelligence, vigor, emotional range or depth, music. I want a line that sings. Poetry should be *presentational*, not talky. If there must be talk, let it be witty or wise, gnomic, pithy, mysterious."** The magazine has recently published poetry by David Ignatow, William Stafford, James Schevill, John Ciardi, X. J. Kennedy, Edward Field, Richard Eberhart and Louis Simpson. The editor selected these sample lines (poet unidentified):

> More than a throat-saver, it muffles
> The face against enemies and fog.
> Drapes the chest, warms the head,
> Guards ears from frost and castigation.

The review (which I have not seen) is digest-sized, flat-spined, with a "Whitman print on cover." It uses art. "photographs, reproductions of paintings, sculpture, prints." Circulation 1,000, $4 copy. **Sample: $3 postpaid. Pays 1 copy. Reports in 2 weeks; no longer than 1 year before publication. "Prefer to receive 4-5 poems. No simultaneous submissions."** Editor sometimes comments on rejections.

WEST OF BOSTON (II), Box 2, Cochituate Station, Wayland, MA 01778, phone 617-653-7241, founded 1983, poetry editor Norman Andrew Kirk, "is re-evaluating its activities and purposes. Thus far has published paperback and hardcover books." As a sample of poetry he likes the editor selected these lines (poet unidentified):

> Come to my museum of poetry.
> The masterpieces of my mind
> are cast about like the misplaced
> children of a mad whore.

Query with 3-5 samples, bio, publication credits, and statement of poetic goals. Replies to queries in 1 month, to submissions, if invited, in 2 months. Query regarding simultaneous submissions. Photocopies, dot-matrix OK. Pays copies. Editor sometimes comments on rejections.

WESTBURG ASSOCIATES PUBLISHERS, *NORTH AMERICAN MENTOR MAGAZINE (I, II), 1745 Madison St., Fennimore, WI 53809, phone 608-822-6237, founded 1964, poetry editors John Edward and Mildred W. Westburg. "Despite its ambitious name, Westburg Associates Publishers is a small, family, cottage-type 'industry,' an amateurish kind of firm. Our 'products,' (booklets and a magazine) are of the hand-and-home-made kind and very serious so far as concerns the literary works that we strive to publish. Our purpose has always been to seek, encourage, and to publish 'the best' kind of literary and humanities works that we could obtain. We **prefer poetry in the traditional poetic forms that deal with the human condition and that are rich in metaphors.** The readers should not be made to decipher a poem like they would a crossword puzzle nor feel the slightest bit of debasement after reading the poem but rather should feel delighted, amused, good, and hopeful. The work should be literate, artful if not artistic, and in general clean and decent. We might respond with criticism sometimes, but only if the author specifically requests it. Some poets we have published include Merrill G. Christophersen, Branley Allan Branson, Pearl Newton Rook, William Laufer, Virginia E. Smith, Mary Jane Barnes, Edna Jones, Jean Bouhier, Tony Kellman and Wilma H. Clements." These sample lines are from "Orpheus and Constanza" by Arthur Avergun:

> . . . and suddenly,
> Out of the ground, Orpheus, laughing and free,
> Astounding our Milton, shows us how to be,
> Twines time with eternity. . . .

North American Mentor is published quarterly by seasons, a magazine-sized side-stapled format, typeset with b/w graphics, average 32 pp. of which 7-15 pp. are poetry, circulation 450-475, 300 subscriptions including 6 libraries. Subscription: $11 per year: $4 per issue. "Approximately 200 poets submit a total of about 2,000 poems each calendar year. Our backlog is 'seasonal,' for most of the poems are chosen from poetry contest entries in our annual contest, the deadline being September 1, which means that we hold those entries for possible publication in the next year." **Sample: $2.75. Photocopy submissions OK. Prefer under 50 lines. Pays in copies. "We return freelance submissions that we cannot publish within a few days. Contest entries we hold until after the contest deadline." Subscribers pay no contest fees. Non-subscribers pay $1 for each poem submitted (up to 50 poems), minimum fee $5.** Westburg Associates publishes collections of poetry by individuals. **Submit whole MS with bio background, publications. "Obviously, if a poet can assure us that he can provide us a reasonably good market for his books, he stands the best chance of being published. For example, does he hold a lot of public poetry readings with a good turnout at each one? We reply to queries almost immediately. Works that are under active consideration may be studied for several weeks before a decision is made about them."** Poets and writers may examine copies of our publications by obtaining them via interlibrary loan from the University of Wisconsin-Madison library. In New York some copies may be examined in the library of the Coordinating Council of Literary Magazines; in California from the University library of the University of California at Santa Barbara or from Len Fulton, Dustbooks, Paradise, CA." John Westburg comments, "I have examined hundreds of small press poetry books and anthologies. Many are well-manufactured, handsome, artistic, and expensive. Yet many are lacking in literacy, good taste, art, skill, or even humanity. I advise a poet to write in his own mood and spirit and not try to emulate the passing trends of the moment. For example, poems that are obscene or scatological which some believe mistakenly makes them in vogue. I have rejected MSS that had redundant obscenities which but for the obscenities might have been seriously considered, and some fiction writers have responded that they used foul language because they thought that it would help modernize their work and make it more suitable for the trends of the times whereas they would be more successful by omitting the obscenities and scatology!"

‡*WESTERLY (II),** Dept. of English, University of Western Australia, Nedlands 6009, Australia, phone (09) 380-2101, founded 1956, editors Dennis Haskell, Peter Cowan, and Bruce Bennet. *Westerly* is a literary quarterly publishing quality short fiction, poetry, literary critical and socio-historical articles, and book reviews on subjects of interest to people in Western Australia. **"No restrictions on creative material. Our only criterion [for poetry] is literary quality. We don't dictate to writers on rhyme, style, experimentation or anything else. We are willing to publish short or long poems. We do assume a reasonably well read, intelligent audience.** Past issues of *Westerly* provide the best guides. No consciously an academic magazine." They have recently published work by Bruce Dawe, Diane Fahey, Dimitris Tsaloumas, Nicholas Hasluck, and Chris Wallace-Crabbe. As a sample, they chose the following lines by an unidentified poet:

> Under WA's blitz of blue skies,
> skies like an endless promise,
> skies of a perpetual
> shrugging of the shoulders . . .

The quarterly magazine (which I have not seen) is 7x10", "electronically printed," 96 pp. with some photos and graphics. circulation is 1,000. Price per copy is $5 (Aus.) plus overseas postage of approximately $1/issue, subscription $16 (Aus.)/year. **Sample available for $6 (Aus.) surface mail, $7 (Aus.) airmail. Pay for poetry is $40 plus 1 copy. "Please do not send simultaneous submissions." Reporting time is 1-2 months and time to publication approximately 6 weeks.** The advice of the editors is: "Be sensible. Write what matters for you but think about the reader. Don't be swayed by literary fashion. Read magazines if possible before sending submissions. Read. Read. Read poetry of all kinds and periods."

*WESTERN HUMANITIES REVIEW (II),** University of Utah, Salt Lake City, UT 84112, phone 801-581-7438, founded 1947, poetry editor Larry Levis, is a quarterly "printing articles on the humanities, short stories, poetry, book- and film-reviews." In poetry they want **"nothing sentimental or boringly and didactically moral."** They have recently published poems by Mary Oliver, Hayden Carruth, T. R. Hummer and Ed Ochester. The magazine is 96 pp., flat-spined, 6³/₄x10", circulation to about 1,000 subscribers of which 90% are libraries, using 3-6 submissions of poetry per year, use 12-20. **Sample: Inquire for copy. Pays $50/poem.**

WESTERN PRODUCER PUBLICATIONS, WESTERN PEOPLE (IV, Regional/Western Canada), Box 2500, Saskatoon, Saskatchewan, Canada S7K 2C4, phone 306-665-3500, founded 1923, managing editor Mary L. Gilchrist. *Western People* is a magazine supplement to *The Western Producer*, a weekly newspaper, circulation 144,000, which uses **"poetry about the people, interests and environment of rural Western Canada."** I selected the first of 9 stanzas of "The Tribute" by Byron Anderson as a sample:

> "Those years were hard," the farmer said to me,
> And hardened lines then deepened round his eyes,

> *Which narrowed like he read each memory*
> *From chalky scrawls that streaked the prairie skies.*

The magazine-sized supplement is 16 pp., newsprint, saddle-stapled, with color and b/w photography and graphics. They receive about 800 submissions of freelance poetry per year, use 40-50. **Sample free for postage (2 oz.)—and ask for guidelines. One poem per page, maximum of 3 poems per submission. No dot-matrix. Name, address, telephone number upper left corner of each page. Reports within 4 weeks. Pays $10-35 per poem.** The editor comments, "It is difficult for someone from outside Western Canada to catch the flavor of this region; almost all the poems we purchase are written by Western Canadians." They also publish books—but not of poetry.

‡**WESTGATE PRESS (IV, Fantasy, supernatural)**, 8 Bernstein Blvd., Center Moriches, NY 11934, associate editor Eldine Crowley, a small-press publisher **"in the field of dark fantasy and supernatural poetry."** The chapbook I have seen is **Amethyst & Lampblack** by Leilah Wendell. As a sample I selected the following lines from "Yesterday's Ghost":

> *Vampire's blood & Alchemic wine!*
> *Drink, my children, for Auld Lang Syne!*
> *Another year leaving youth behind,*
> *a worn cloak we sadly unwind.*

The book is digest-sized, offset from typed copy on fairly thin paper with b/w illustrations, 80 pp. flat-spined, with black matte card cover printed in gold; price is $5. **"Authors can query us regarding their own project along the lines of *Amethyst & Lampblack* type material, we would be happy to respond. A query is a must!"**

***WEYFARERS, GUILDFORD POETS PRESS (II)**, 9, White Rose Lane, Woking, Surrey, U.K. GU22 7JA, founded 1972, poetry editors John Emuss, Susan James, Margaret Pain. They say, "Our main activity is publication of *Weyfarers* magazine (its name a pun on the river Wey) three times a year. We occasionally publish booklets for contributors. All our editors are themselves poets and give their spare time free to help other poets." They describe their needs as **"probably be considered 'mainstream' but should be modern and have lift-off. Excellence main consideration. Traditional if top-class. NO hard porn, graphics, way-out experimental. Any subject publishable, from religious (in the widest sense) to humour and satire. Not more than 40 lines including spaces preferred, though longer poems considered if excellent."** They have recently published poetry by David Radavich, Dale Loucareas, John Drexel, Douglas Owen Pitches, Brian Mitchell and S. L. Henderson-Smith. As an example the editors chose the last two stanzas of David R. Morgan's "A 30th Birthday":

> *Salt light rubs its hide against the bedroom wall,*
> *Exhales rough sweetness on a morning mirror.*
> *Nearer the sea sleeps another me, all mist*
> *Locked fast inside a dream with stone gates.*

The inexpensively produced digest-sized saddle-stapled format contains about 29 pp. of poetry (of a total of 32 pp.) The magazine has a circulation of "about 225," including about 140 subscriptions of which 4 are libraries. They use about 125 of 1,200-1,500 submissions received each year. Sample: $1 in cash (or 50 UK); current issue $2 in cash (or 90 UK) postpaid. Submit no more than 6 poems, one poem per sheet. No previously published or simultaneous submissions. Payment 1 copy. "We are associated with Surrey Poetry Center, who have an annual Open Poetry Competition. The prize-winners are published in *Weyfarers*." They sometimes **comment briefly, if requested** on rejections. And their advice to poets is, "Always read magazine before submitting. And read plenty of published modern poetry. Remember there are thousands of other people writing poetry, though beginners seem to find this hard to believe!"

WHEAT FORDER'S PRESS, PRIMERS FOR THE AGE OF INNER SPACE (IV, Modern thought), Box 6317, Washington, DC 20015-0317, founded 1974, poetry editor Renée K. Boyle. This is a 100% subsidy press, asking for camera-ready copy. "We publish for embassies on topics of interest to 3rd world countries. We have a series called Frontiers for the Age of Inner Space. **We seek poetry and book-length essays for this which reflects ideas in sciences, psychology, metahistory reflecting modern thought *at its leading edges*.**" As a sample the editor selected these lines from "Graffiti on the Wall of Time":

> *That man himself is dead, who being yet in life*
> *reports that God no longer lives, because in him*
> *the image of that God*
> *no longer rises.*

Query with 5-10 samples and cover letter giving "publication record, precise aim in writing poetry (as fanciful as you wish), express modern thought. Skip modern vulgarities, sex, pot and all that jazz—it's going nowhere." Terms for cooperative publishing, author paying all costs, worked out individually.

‡**WHETSONE (I, II)**, Department of English, University of Lethbridge, 4401 University Drive, Lethbridge, Alberta, Canada T1K 3M4, editor Marlene Graveland, appears twice a year with writing by beginners and published authors. **"Open to any kind of poetry, as long as it's of good quality."** They have recently published poems by Robert Kroetsch, bp Nichol and Kim Maltman. As a sample the editor selected lines from "The Technology of Arrogance Which Enters the Mind Unasked and Poisons it with Visions of Paradise" by Kim Maltman:

> . . . *the use of wood becomes like*
> *faith, or love, or sorrows,*
> *that once-removed shadow world in which objects*
> *are inseparable from our desires* . . .

The review is digest-sized, 80 + pp. saddle-stapled, professionally printed in bold face type with 2-color matte card cover, circulation 150, 50 subscriptions of which 2 are libraries, $3/copy, subscription $5. **Sample: $2.50 postpaid. Guidelines available for SASE. Pays 1 copy. Any length of poetry. Photocopy, dot-matrix OK. Editor sometimes comments on rejections.** They have competitions with $100 for best poem, $10 entry fee (which includes subscription) for up to 4 poems. Marlene Graveland advises, "Poetry is meant to be read by others. Don't write something so obscure and esoteric that it has *no* meaning for anyone else."

WHIMSY, WORLD HUMOR AND IRONY MEMBERSHIP (WHIM) (IV, Humor), English Dept., Arizona State University, Tempe, AZ 85287, phone 602-965-7592, founded 1981, poetry editor Don L. F. Nilsen. "Every year we have a humor conference with about 1,000 participants, over the April 1st weekend. A year following each conference we publish the proceedings. The conference is called WHIM; the proceedings are called *Whimsy.*" They are looking for **humorous poetry, no restrictions on form, length, style, subject-matter or purpose.** They have recently published poetry by Eve Merriam, Lee Bennett Hopkins, Mike Thaler, Clinton Larson and Ric Masten. I selected these sample lines from "Past & Repast" by Guy Bensusan:

> *So, imagine Cortez, Bernal Diaz and flock,*
> *after Cholula, and in culture shock,*
> *each wanting his woman, to let his wounds heal,*
> *rest, relaxation, and a good home-cooked meal.*

The annual publication is 320 pp. magazine-sized flat, taped spine, neatly offset from justified typescript, using about 10 pp. of poetry in each issue, circulation 1,000, 200 subscriptions of which 50 are libraries. **Sample: $10 postpaid. Submit by January 1 each year, any format. Simultaneous submissions OK, but we must know in order to get permission. Reports immediately. Pays 1 copy.** Contributors are expected to attend the conference. **"We read only material sent with registration fee of $35."** Don Nilsen adds, "On my car we have a personalized license plate: WHIM. It's called our 'Poetic License.' "

***WHISKEY ISLAND MAGAZINE (I, II)**, Cleveland State University, UC 7, Cleveland, OH 44115, phone 687-2056, founded 1978, poetry editor Leah Borovich, appears 2-3 times per year, "**using any type of poetry excluding those that use too much profane language and are disgusting in their theme.**" The editor selected these sample lines from "Witchdoctor," by Andrew Oerke:

> *I crawl on my knee-caps into the hut's*
> *Hot, breathless yet breathing darkness. She breathes*
> *A denser darkness round her: Wrists of smoke,*
> *Charcoal eyes, winds of moonless midnight, smock*
> *Of terror as my bird mask cheeps the birth of all birds.*

The journal is digest-sized, 84 pp., flat-spined, elegantly printed on heavy glossy stock with glossy card cover, b/w photos and graphics, circulation 1,500, using 70-84 pp. of poetry in each issue. **Sample: free. They accept more than half the 300 freelance poetry submissions they receive each year. Multiple and simultaneous submissions OK. Reports in 2-3 months. Pays 2 contributor's copies. Send SASE for guidelines.**

***THE WHITE LIGHT (IV, Occult)**, Box 93124, Pasadena, CA 99109, founded 1973, poetry editor N. White: "**Our principal interests are Ceremonial Magick & Occultism; and Survival.** *The White Light*, **a quarterly magazine of Ceremonial Magick, occasionally prints poetry.**" I selected these sample lines from "The Obscurati" by H. R. Felgenhauer:

> *Illuminatti takes the heat.*
> *Illuminatti's really neat.*
> *Illuminatti rise so high.*
> *Illuminatti fry your eyes.*

The White Light is a digest-sized 12 pp. publication, offset from typescript, circulation 200, 100 subscriptions of which 2 are libraries. Subscription: $5. They receive 1-2 freelance submissions of poetry and use some. Simultaneous submissions OK. **Pays 5 copies. Sample: $1.25.**

WHITE PINE PRESS (V, IV, Translations), 76 Center St., Fredonia, NY 14063, phone 716-672-5743, founded 1973, poetry editors Dennis Maloney, Steve Lewandowski and Elaine La Mattina. White Pine Press publishes poetry, fiction, literature in translation, essays, Eastern philosophy and photography—mainly chapbooks and flat-spined paperbacks. "At present we are **not accepting unsolicited MSS. Inquire first. We are looking for translations of contemporary writers from other languages and translations of historical writers of Japan and China.**" They have recently published poetry by Basho, Antonio Machado, Pablo Neruda, Yosano Akiko, Francis Ponge, Maurice Kenny and James Wright. As a sample I chose this stanza of "Poems at the Edge of Day" by John Brandi:

> Poems are acts of death
> burning clean
> at the edge of day
> to renew life.

The book is 44 pp., flat-spined, digest-sized, professionally printed with b/w drawings, colored matte card cover with photo, $4.50. **Query with 4-5 samples, brief cover letter with bio and publication credits. Reply to queries in 2-4 weeks, to submissions (if invited) in 4 weeks. Simultaneous submissions, photocopy, dot-matrix OK. Pays 5-10% of run. Send SASE for catalog to buy samples.**

*JAMES WHITE REVIEW, A GAY MEN'S LITERARY QUARTERLY (IV, Gay), Box 3356 Traffic Station, Minneapolis, MN 55403, phone 612-291-2913, founded 1983, poetry editor Greg Baysans **uses all kinds of poetry for gay men.** They have published poetry by Ian Young, Antler Steve Abbott and Jim Holmes. The magazine has a circulation of 2,000, 400 subscriptions of which 15 are libraries. They receive about 1,000 submissions per year, use 100, have a 6 week backlog. **Sample: $2 postpaid. Submit a limit of 10 poems or 250 lines. A poem can exceed 250 lines, but it "better be very good."** They report in 4 months. Not paying currently but "hope to in the near future." Send SASE for guidelines. Subscriptions $6/year (US).

‡*THE WHITE ROSE LITERARY MAGAZINE (I), 14 Browning Rd., Temple Hill, Dartford DA1 5ET, Kent, England, editor Mrs. Nancy Whybrow. The magazine, planned as an annual, was first published in January, 1986; I have not seen a copy. The editor asked for **contributions of poems, short stories, anecdotes relating to local history; she planned to include a section of entries by disabled people. Poems could be of any length, form, or subject. She was sponsoring a contest in memory of her son, Kim, killed in an automobile accident; entry fee was £1/poem.** Price of the magazine is £1.50.

*WHITE WALLS: A MAGAZINE OF WRITINGS BY ARTISTS (IV, Visual artists), Box 8204, Chicago, IL 60680, founded 1978, publishes "essays, journals, fiction, and other prose works by visual artists (i.e., painters, sculptors, graphic artists, photographers, conceptual, performance and other experimental artists). **We will occasionally publish concrete or other visually-oriented experimental poetry if it is by visual artists.**" They have published poems by these artists: Dick Higgins, Scott Helmes, Davi Det Hompson and Ellen Lanyon. As a sample I selected these lines from "Phrases and Revisions for Progress Backstroke," a long poem accompanying a set of instructional photos for the backstroke by Robert C. Morgan:

> The stroke looks effortless . . .
> arms overhead . . . four or five
> inches from the ears . . . the head
> is inclined . . . a double chin

White Walls is digest-sized, 80+ pp., flat-spined, elegantly printed with high-quality b/w photos and graphics, circulation 650, 250 subscriptions of which 45 are libraries. Subscription: $10 for 3 issues. They receive about 50 freelance poetry submissions per year, use 1-2. **Sample: $4 postpaid. Photocopies OK. Reports in 1 month. Pays $2.50 per page plus 5 contributor's copies.**

‡*WHOLE EARTH REVIEW (V), 27 Gate Five Road, Sausalito, CA 94965, is a merger of the previous titles *Whole Earth Software Review* and *Coevolution Quarterly*, published by Stewart Brand, editor Kevin Kelly. **"We do *not* accept unsolicitied MSS."** It is a quarterly which the editor describes as "a refresing juxtaposition of the practical and the unpredicatable. It challenges familiar assumptions, explores unorthodox topics, and offers cutting-edge ideas. It also continues the *Whole Earth Catalog* practice of reviewing books, tools, computer software and accessories, magazines and mail-order suppliers." It is flat-spined, 144 pp., 7¾x10½", circulation of 25,000 to newsstands and 25,000 to subscribers. Subscription: $18; single issues: $4.50. They have recently published poetry by Gary Snyder and Ursula Le Guin. **Sample: $4.50 postpaid.**

*WIDE OPEN MAGAZINE (I), 326 I St., Eureka, CA 95501, phone 707-445-3847, founded 1984, poetry editors Clif and Lynn L. Simms. "**We want to publish as many poets as possible with a mini-**

mum of 100 each issue. We want to give exposure to as many poets as we can. We want poetry in all forms, styles and contents, maximum of 16 lines per poem. We like concrete images, wit, irony, humor, paradox and satire." They have recently published poetry by Patricia Lawrence, Helen Bradford, Robert Randloph and Ted Yund. The editors selected these sample lines from "Night of the Locust" by Robert Begley:

> Great friends as we are
> we pass the static in the dark
> our words hard as fleas
> jump cracking back and forth

Wide Open is a quarterly, magazine-sized, 48 pp. saddle-stapled, offset from photo reduced typescript, many poems to a page, card cover with graphics, circulation 500, subscriptions including 5 libraries. Subscription: $20; per issue: $7.50. They use 90% of the 800 submissions received per year, have a 3 month maximum backlog. **Sample: $5 postpaid. Submit 5 poems at a time, one per page, name and address on each page. Simultaneous submissions, photocopy, dot-matrix, neat handwriting all OK. Reports usually within 1 week. No pay. Contributors may buy copy at one-third discount (i.e., $5 instead of $7.50). There is a quarterly poetry contest, $150 prize, $2 per poem entered. But contributors *do not* have to enter contest to be considered for the magazine.** This magazine obviously offers beginners an easy way to get into print, though $5 seems an excessive charge for a 20 pp. inexpensively produced magazine. The editors advise, "Submit, submit, submit. Use concrete images. Avoid Latinate diction."

*WIDENER REVIEW (II), Humanities Division, Widener University, Chester, PA 19013, phone 215-499-4266, founded 1984, poetry editor Michael Clark, a literary annual, wants poetry with "**hard imagery, intellectual clarity.**" They have recently published poetry by Lyn Lifshin, Gary Fincke, Ann Michael and Patricia Farewell. *Widener Review* is digest-sized, 100 pp., flat-spined, offset from typescript, white glossy card cover, printrun 250. They used 25-30 of 300 freelance poetry submissions their first year. **Sample: $3.50 postpaid. Reports in 2-3 months. Pays 2 copies. Send SASE for guidelines. Editor sometimes comments on rejections.**

‡THE WILLOW BEE PUBLISHING HOUSE, *WYOMING, THE HUB OF THE WHEEL . . . A JOURNEY FOR UNIVERSAL SPOKESMEN (I, II), Box 9, Saratoga, WY 82331, phone 307-326-5214, founded 1985, managing editor Lenore A. Senior, who says "We publish a semi-annual literary-art magazine devoted to themes of Peace, The Human Race, Positive Relationships & The Human Spirt and all its Possibilities. We have a general audience interested in peace, humanism, the environment, society, and universal messages." The editor's instructions are: **"Poetry should be real. We look for a haunting quality in the work which makes the reader want to read each piece again, and again. Usually accept work which is personal & creates emotion in the reader (yet *says* something rather than works which are purely intellectual, factual. We're especially open to high quality work from minority writers from the U.S. or anywhere in the world." Her negatives are: "Don't list emotions. Don't sum up' what it is you are saying. Leave some mystery. Strong images, natural rhythms, use of metaphor are necessary; without them, it's merely verse or an editorial."** She has recently published poetry by Ann Fletcher, Richard Shaw, Rochelle Lynn Holt, Joanne Seltzer, and B. J. Buckley. As a sample, she chose the following lines by Gabriel Okara:

> And I lost in the morning mist
> Of an age at a riverside keep
> Wandering in the mystic rhythm
> Of jungle drums and the concerto

Wyoming, The Hub of the Wheel is a 6x9" paperback, flat-spined, 64 pp., offset with b/w artwork, glossy card cover with b/w illustration. It appears semi-annually (the premier issue was winter/spring 85/86), and the editor expects a circulation of about 500, of which 40% will be subscriptions. Price per issue is $5, subscription $9. **Sample $5 postpaid, guidelines available for SASE. Pay is 2 copies. Writers should submit up to 5 poems, maximum of 80 lines. Photocopies, dot-matrix, and simultaneous submissions are OK. "Prefer unpublished poems, but will accept previously published works acknowledged as such." Submissions will be reported on in 4 weeks or sooner, and time to publication is 6-12 months.** The editor says, "About 50% of our publication is open to new and/or previously unpublished writers. Our editorial biases preclude our accepting material which lauds alcohol or drugs, or which contains sexually explicit passages of a coarse nature. We would reject outright any material which in subject, thought, or language is contrary to our themes. No religious material. Humor is welcome if it is poetry and not verse. If you like our approach, send us something and see what happens. We also offer an annual award of $50, plus publication. No reading fee. SASE for guidelines."

*WILLOW SPRINGS, (I) Box 1063, Eastern Washington University, Cheney, WA 99004, phone 509-458-6429, founded 1977, poetry editor Edward Hausken, editor Bill O'Daly, who is "the only paid member of the staff as well as the only 'permanent' staff member. The remainder of the staff consists primarily of students in EWU's MFA Program in Creative Writing. We also sponsor public readings. **We prefer to publish poetry which speaks for something essential in the human experience, and which is well-crafted, no matter the form, content, etc.**" They have recently published poetry by Denise Levertov, Carolyn Kizer, Sam Hamill, Hayden Carruth, Al Young, Emily Warn, David Citino, Odysseas Elytis, and Thomas McGrath. The editors selected these sample lines by James J. McAuley:

> Yet, repeating these signs so often, you know
> Better than kelp-gatherer or beachcomber, sand
> Is matter, process, and the word for these.
> Sand is history: it has none of its own.

Willow Springs is a semiannual, 6x9", 90 pp., flat-spined, professionally printed, with glossy 2-color card cover with art, circulation 800, 230 subscriptions of which 30% are libraries. Subscription: $8. They use 1-2% of some 4,000 freelance poems received each year. **Sample: $4 postpaid. Submit any time, name on every page, address on first page of each poem. No simultaneous submissions. Brief cover letter saying how many poems on how many pages. Reports in 1-3 months. Pays 2 copies, others at half price, and pays cash when funds available. Send SASE for guidelines. Editor comments on rejections "if requested."** Bill O'Daly comments, "We believe poetry is a *vocation* and not a career. It is especially important for young poets to read the classics, poetry in translation, the Modernists, the academics, feminists, naturalists, the Beats and the Buddhists, as well as their peers, and to examine inherited attitudes and habits. As Czeslaw Milosz says, 'Poetry is the passionate pursuit of the real.'"

*WIND MAGAZINE (I, II), Box 809K, RFD #1, Pikeville, KY 41501, phone 606-631-1129, founded 1971, poetry editor Quentin R. Howard. "*Wind* since 1971 has published hundreds of poets for the first time and today there are at least 125 who are publishing widely in many magazines & have books to their credit. I have also published about 15 people who had stopped writing and submitting to 'little' magazines because many young editors were not acquainted with much of their work. There's nothing unique about *Wind*; like all 'little' magazines it is **friendly (too friendly at times) toward beginning writers who have something to say and do so effectively and interestingly. I have no taboos. I invent my own taboos on reading each MS. But plain old raw vulgarity for shock effect is out. Save your postage!** Those who are acquainted with *Wind* know it has no Victorian characteristics; here I remember 3 people who cancelled their subscriptions because they thought *Wind* was too vulgar. One lady recently said: 'Cancel. I'd simply fall dead if my dear grandchildren found *Wind* on the coffee table.' *Wind* has subscribers in Australia, Germany, France, Kuwait, and several Central American countries, plus Japan and Hong Kong. **I don't want simple broken prose, neither greeting card-type verse; nor please no love verse & soothing graveyard poetry; none please enamoured of death; believe me it's still being written. I'm not picky about form, style, subject matter nor purpose; but length (pages and pages) makes me frown no matter how much I love it. 'Little' magazines are a squeamish group when it comes to space.**" They have recently published poetry by J. B. Goodenough, H.L. Van Brunt, Hans Ostrom, Peter Brett, Rennie McQuilkin, John O'Brien, Simon Perchik, Larry Rubin. The editor selected these sample lines by Charles Semones:

> Summer is the bad word in our yearly grammar.
> It fits no sensible sentence. No one can write the syntax
> of summer right. Our shared radio clears its throat nightly:
> static the thickness of phlegm drowns out Beethoven and conmen peddling Jesus.

Wind appears 3 times a year, digest-sized, averaging 86 pp. per issue of which 60 are poetry, saddle-stapled, professionally printed with matte card cover, circulation 575, subscriptions 412 of which 29 are libraries. Subscription: $6. They use about 200 of 3,600 freelance submissions of poetry per year, sometimes have as much as a year backlog. **Sample: $2 postpaid. Submit at least 3-6 poems. "Photocopies and simultaneous submissions scare me." Shorter poems of 1½ pp. or under have a better chance here. Reports in 2-4 weeks. Pays contributors copies. Editor comments on rejections "Now & then when time permits. There's many pitfalls about this."** Quentin Howard advises, "Presentation is all-important in deciding on poems."

*WINDFALL, WINDFALL PROPHETS CHAPBOOK SERIES (II), English Dept. University of Wisconsin at Whitewater, Whitewater, WI 53190, phone 472-1036, founded 1979, poetry editor Ron Ellis. **Windfall** is a "semi-annual magazine of intense, highly crafted lyrics with occasional longer poems. Both mag and chapbook series sponsored by non-profit Friends of Poetry and UW-Whitewater English Department. **We want a fusion of craft and imagination, controlled daring. Don't want generalized 'wisdom,' workshop poetry, contrived excitement. 1-100 lines. Dislike imitative but enjoy snycretic styles. Any subject or purpose: the inevitable and inimitable expression of the subject.**" They have recently published poetry by ivan arguelles, Margot Treitel, Martha Mihalyi, Jack Barrack, Will Inman and Arthur Madson. The editor selected these sample lines from "Words for the Pine Barrens" by Thomas Reiter:

> *What can be said of us*
> *when the roots of conifers go down*
> *a tandem-wheeled incinerator's*
> *auger throat?*

Windfall is 40-50 pp., digest-sized, circulation 200, 50 subscriptions, using 40-45 pp. of poetry in each issue. Subscription: $5. They receive about 700 submissions of freelance poetry per year, use 70, have a 4-6 month backlog. **Sample: $1 postpaid. Submit 4-6 poems before March for mid-year issue, before October for year-end issue. Pays 2 copies.** Windfall Prophets Press publishes chapbooks for which **poet must pay $200 toward production costs ("more or less, subject to negotiation"). Query with 2-3 samples. $10 reading fee for submission (if invited). Simultaneous submissions, crisp, clear photocopy or dot-matrix OK, or discs compatible with Applewriter II. Poet receives all copies except 20, is responsible for promotion and distribution of the chapbook under Windfall Prophets logo. Editor comments on rejections "when MS shows sufficient excellence."**

‡*THE WINDHAM PHOENIX (I, II)**, Box 752, Willimantic, CT 06226, founded 1985, poetry editor Michael J. Westerfield, a monthly news/feature magazine (local news) about one-quarter of which is devoted to poetry and fiction; the poetry section usually has 4-8 poems. **Poetry can be of any kind but not "overly lengthy—i.e. exceeding 3 typed pages."** The magazine has recently published poems by Leo Connellan and Noel Manning, whose lines from "Little Christmas" the editor chose as a sample:

> *So cold*
> *Even smoke moves slow*
> *Up one side of the roof*
> *Down the other*

The monthly periodical is 6x9", offset, flat-spined, with line drawings and illustrations on the cover and throughout. Circulation is 950, of which about 650 are subscriptions and 200 are newsstand sales. Price per issue is $1.25, subscription $12/year. **Sample $1.50 postpaid. Contributors receive 5 copies and "we hope to begin payment shortly." They report on submissions in 6 weeks and time to publication is 2 months. The editors comment on rejected MSS "whenever we feel the author shows promise."** They say, "**The Phoenix** is unique in that it presents the ordinary citizens of the community with an exposure to literature. The magazine is always read from cover to cover and local writers who have never before received feedback on their published works have been immensely pleased by the 'man in the street' response to publication in **The Phoenix**."

*THE WINDLESS ORCHARD, THE WINDLESS ORCHARD CHAPBOOKS (II)**, English Dept., Indiana University, Fort Wayne, IN 46805, phone 219-481-6100, founded 1970, poetry editor Robert Novak, a "shoestring labor of love—chapbooks only from frequent contributors to magazine. Sometimes publish calendars." They say they want "**heuristic, excited, valid non-xian religious exercises. Our muse is interested only in the beautiful, the erotic, and the sacred,"** but I could find **nothing erotic or sacred in the sample issue sent me, and the kinds of beauty seemed about like those in most literary journals,** as these lines by Wayne Kvam, selected by the editors as a sample, indicate:

> *Wolfgang, the waiter comes over*
> *red shirt bulging*
> *like an apple*
> *says "crisp oak, birch, and lime"*
> *into this thin air.*

The Windless Orchard appears 3-4 times a year, 50+ pp., digest-sized, offset from typescript, saddle-stapled, with matte card cover with b/w photos. The editors say they have 100 subscriptions of which 25 are libraries, a printrun of 300, total circulation: 280. There are about 35 pp. of poetry in each issue. Subscription: $7. They receive about 3,000 freelance submissions of poetry per year, use 200, have a 6 month backlog. **Sample: $2 postpaid. Submit 3-7 pp. Reports in 1 day-4 months. Pays 2 copies. Chapbook submissions by invitation only to contributors to the magazine. Poets pay costs for 300 copies, of which The Windless Orchard Chapbook Series receives 100 for its expenses. Sample: $3. Editors sometimes comment on rejections.** They advise, "Memorize a poem a day, do translations for the education."

WINSTON-DEREK PUBLISHERS, INC., SCYTHE BOOKS, MAGGPIE PUBLICATIONS, HOMESPUN ANTHOLOGY SERIES, (IV, Religious), Box 90883, Nashville, TN 37209, phone 615-321-0535, founded 1977, "is a religious and traditional trade publishing house. Our publications are for a general, intellectual, and church audience. Even our mystery series is slanted for a Christian. We accept no MSS that are vulgar (in the common sense of the term), use cheap language or are derogative of other cultures, races and/ or ethnic origins. We have accounts with more than 5,000 Christian Books stores in America and abroad. We want to see **poetry that's inspirational, religious, family life,**

academic and/ or scholarly. **We do not accept poetry of the avant-garde type, sensuous or erotic.**"
They have recently published poetry by Rose Marie Walch, Michele Joubert, Alyce C. Lunsford, Helen
Pendergraft, Sharon Boswell, and Dorothea McHugh. The editors selected these sample lines from
"Sonnets from the Studio" by Rose Marie Walch:

> My spirit kneels within. Awareness shrinks
> To pinpoint center. Mind no longer thinks,
> Engulfed by You. A vortex dark and deep,
> Pathway to life while all the senses sleep.
> Black Hole of Faith. The stars do but rehearse
> The riddle-solving of the universe.

**Submit complete book MS. "A good cover letter is always in order. Although we sponsor a liter-
ary guild, The Poets Herald, this is not a requirement." Reply to query in 4 weeks, to submission
in 4-6 weeks. MS should be "preferably typed, single-spaced. No simultaneous submissions. Photocopy, dot-matrix OK. Pays 10-25% royalties plus 20 copies. To "established poets with track records" an average advance of $1,500. Send 9x12" SASE and $1 for catalog to order samples. You
may request a 50% discount.** They offer a "best poetry MS of the year award—a poetry workshop
scholarship. Judges: Robert Earl and Marjorie Staton. The editors advise, "Write poetry that is literate.
Stay with a definite style. Poetry is more than prose writing, one either has to be gifted or well trained or
both. Our poetry is distributed by the publisher, The Baker & Taylor Company, and The Poet's Herald.

‡***THE WIRE, PROGRESSIVE PRESS (I)**, 7320 Colonial, Dearborn Heights, MI 48127, phone
517-394-3736, founded 1981, editor Sharon Wysocki. *The Wire* is an "alternative arts" publication that
appears 2-3 times a year. **It publishes "language and experimental poetry" but no sonnets.** Poets recently published include Lyn Lifshin, Ivan Arguelles, Doug Draime, and Joseph Raffa. As a sample, the
editor selected the following lines by an unidentified poet:

> The empty hum
> of a numbered mind
> The unsure fairies
> remembering a place.

The Wire is photocopied on 8½x11" offset paper, 9 pp., with graphics, stapled at the top left corner.
Price per issue is 80¢ and a subscription is $3.75 (checks should be made out to Progressive Press.
**Guidelines are available for SASE. Contributors receive 1 copy. Photocopied and simultaneous
submissions are OK, but print must be dark enough for photocopying.** Submissions are reported in
6 months and time to publication is the same. Criticism of rejected MSS is provided. "*The Wire* attempts to print a sample of all submissions in order to coincide with its non-censorship in art philosophy.

***WISCONSIN ACADEMY REVIEW (IV, Regional)**, 1922 University Ave., Madison, WI 53705,
phone 608-263-1692, founded 1954, poetry editor Patricia Powell, "distributes information on scientif-
ic and cultural life of Wisconsin & provides a forum for **Wisconsin (or Wisconsin background) artists
and authors. They want good lyric poetry; traditional meters acceptable if content is fresh. No
poem over 65 lines.**" They have recently published poetry by Bink Noll, Felix Pollak, Ron Wallace and
John Bennett. I selected these sample lines from "Indian Summer" by Ingrid Swanberg:

> The oaks are alive in the half dark,
> the wind shakes out their gold
> & roils it with indigo & rust

Wisconsin Academy Review is a magazine-sized 64 pp. quarterly, professionally printed on glossy
stock, glossy card cover with b/w photo, circulation 1,800, 1,500 subscriptions of which 109 are libraries. They use 4-12 pp. of poetry per issue. Of over 100 freelance submissions of poetry per year they use
about 15, have a 6-12 month backlog. **Sample: $2 postpaid. Submit 5 pp. maximum, double-spaced.
Photocopy, dot-matrix OK. Must contain Wisconsin connection if not Wisconsin return address.
Reports in 4-6 weeks. Pays 5 copies. Editor sometimes comments on rejections.**

***THE WISCONSIN RESTAURATEUR (IV, Food service)**, 122 W. Washington, Madison, WI
53703, phone 608-251, 3663, founded 1933, poetry editor Jan LaRue is a "trade association monthly
(except November-December combined), circulation 3,400-3,500, for the promotion, protection and
improvement of the WI foodservice industry." They use "**all types of poetry, but must have food
service as subject. Nothing lengthy or off-color (length 10-50 lines)." Reports in 1-2 months. They
buy 6-12 per year, pay $2.50-7.50/poem. Sample: $1.75 plus postage. Send SASE for guidelines.
Editor sometimes comments on rejections.** She advises, "Study many copies of the mag."

‡***WISCONSIN REVIEW, WISCONSIN REVIEW PRESS (II)**, Box 158, Radford Hall, University
of Wisconsin-Oshkosh, Oshkosh, WI 54901, 414-424-2267, founded 1966, poetry editor Patricia
Haebig. The elegantly printed *WR* is published 3 times a year, 32-48 pp. **"In poetry we publish mostly**

free verse with strong images and fresh approaches. We want new turns of phrase." Some poets recently published are Dan Gerber, Diana Chang, Jim Heynen, Laurel Mills, Walter Griffin, William Silver. As a sample the editors selected these lines from "Early Morning of Another World" by Tom McKeown:

> After squid and cool white wine there is
> no sleep. The long tentacles uncurl
> out of the dark with all that was left behind.
> Promises expand promises. A frayed mouth
> loses its color in the dawn.

They use 18-30 pp. of poetry in each issue; total circulation is 2,000, with 50 subscriptions, 30 of which go to libraries. Price per issue is $2, subscription $6. **Sample copy: $2 postpaid. The *Review* receives 700-1,500 poetry submissions per year, of which it publishes about 75. Editor requests no more than 4 poems per submission, one poem per page, single spaced with name and address of writer on each page, simultaneous submissions OK; reports to writer within 1-6 months. Pays 2 contributor's copies; guidelines available for SASE.** Magazine-sized, quality buff stock, glossy card cover with colored art.

*THE WISHING WELL (IV, Lesbian), Box G, Santee, CA 92071-0167, founded 1974, is a quarterly directory of gay women, self-described, listed by code number, 38 pp., 7x8½", subscriptions 4,000. They use **some poetry by gay women who are current members. Sample: $5.**

‡*WITHOUT HALOS (II), Box 1342, Point Pleasant Beach, NJ 08742, founded 1983, editor-in-chief Frank Finale, an annual publication of the Ocean County Poets Collective; it prints "good contemporary poetry and short fiction." The magazine **"accepts all genres, though no obscenity. Prefers poetry no longer than 2 pages. Wants to see strong, lucid images ground in experience."** They do not want "badly rhymed, cliched poetry, concrete poetry, religious verse, or greeting card lyrics." Some Poets published recently are Lora Dunetz, Lyn Lifshin, Bradley Strahan, and Arthur Winfield Knight. As sample, the editor selected the following lines by Barbara A. Holland:

> I was lace last evening
> a collection of some thousand holes
> through which the North wind
> poked the energy of chilly fingers.

Without Halos is digest-sized, handsomely printed with b/w artwork inside and on the cover, 48 pp. saddle-stapled with matte card cover. Circulation is 1,000, of which 50 are subscriptions and 100 are sold on newsstands; other distribution is at cultural events, readings, workshops, etc. Price per issue is $2.75. **Sample available for $2.75 postpaid, guidelines for SASE. Pay is 1 copy. The editors "prefer letter-quality printing, double-spaced, no more than 3-5 pages per poem. Name and address should appear in top left-hand corner. Sloppiness tossed back." Reporting time is 1-3 months and all acceptances are printed in the next annual issue, which appears in the fall. Deadline for submissions is June 30.**

WOLFSONG (II), 3123 S. Kennedy, Sturtevant, WI 53177, founded 1978, poetry editor Gary Busha, primarily publishes chapbooks of poetry—irregularly. They have recently published **Root River**, a Racine-area poetry anthology. As a sample I selected the first of two stanzas of "Old Lady at a Concert" by Travis Du Priest:

> As if to music by Schumann
> the black sequined crab
> nestles deep into her sleepy
> head with its claws of pearl.

That poem appears in the chapbook, **Soapstone Wall**, 20 pp., digest-sized, offset from typescript with blue matte card cover, $2.50, press run 300. The Wolfsong Series includes 11 others, including chapbooks by Peter Wild, Dave Etter and Arthur Winfield Knight. **Query with 20-30 samples. Cover letter not necessary. Simultaneous submissions, photocopy, dot-matrix OK. Reports in 2-3 weeks. Pays 20-30 copies. Send $2.50 for sample.**

*WOMAN OF POWER, A MAGAZINE OF FEMINISM, SPIRITUALITY AND POLITICS (IV, Feminist), Box 827, Cambridge, MA 02238-0827, founded 1983, poetry editor Linda Roach. "The purpose of *Woman of Power* is to give women a voice. We do not accept submissions from men at this time. We honor the collective and individual, and **encourage women from all backgrounds, classes, religions, races, and spiritual paths to submit work.** We read everything that is submitted and try to respond personally to each submission. We answer all queries with specifics. We are a quarterly publication and each issue has a theme. Interested poets are encouraged to write (with SASE) for the upcoming themes, for our selection of works greatly depends on how well the poem fits the theme of each issue. We do not want to see poetry which serves to further separate us from each other, work that could be seen as racist, classist, homophobic or part of any other 'ism.' We encourage work that is sensitive, imaginative, sensual, erotic, clear and that speaks of a woman's experience in the world. It can be all or any one of these, and can be of any length, except MS length. We ask that each poet only submit 5 poems per issue. We have no style specifications. Subject matter should relate to the theme, but it is in each woman's interpretation that we build the diversity of work. The purpose should be to entertain, enlighten, make the reader laugh or cry, transform or point out something she has discovered that she wishes to share. We are not interested in work that is anti-male or angry." They have recently published poetry by Marge Piercy, Barbara Deming, Mary Moran and Ellen Bass. As a sample the editors selected these lines by Nicole d'Entremont:

> The mapmaker knows it's easier
> to understand the immensity of sky
> if you look at it through a crack
> in the barnboards.

The quarterly is magazine-sized, 96 pp., saddle-stapled, professionally printed in 2 columns, b/w graphics, photos and ads, matte card cover with photos, circulation 15,000, 3,000 subscriptions of which 100-200 are libraries. Subscriptions: $18 regular (4 issues). They use 10-20 of 200 submissions of free lance poetry per year. **Sample: $6 US, $7.50 Canada. "Send for deadlines and themes. Thematic quality very important. Photocopy OK. Send only 5 poems, any length. Simultaneous submissions OK, but we must know in the cover letter. Reports within 1 month of deadline. Pays 2 copies. Send SASE for guidelines. Editor comments on rejections.**

WOMEN WRITERS ALLIANCE (IV, Members), Box 2014, Setauket, NY 11733, is a national nonprofit support group for all ("we have male membership") writers which occasionally publishes collections of poetry by members. **Membership: $10/year, which includes quarterly newsletter, ivitations to meetings and events and discounts on Alliance publications.** For a sample, order the anthology, **Island Women, Poems and Stories**, $4.95 postpaid, $3.50 for members, a 7x8½" flat-spined, 140 pp. book, offset from typescript, from which I selected this sample poem, "Eros and Civilization," by Renner-Tana:

> There he sat: Eros.
> There I sat: Civilization.
> He wanted to seed;
> I wanted to read.
> After dialectical struggle
> I decided to yield
> my field to his plow.
> When I satisfied
> his need to breed;
> I bred; he read

WOMEN-IN-LITERATURE, INC., WOMAN POET (IV, Women), Box 60550, Reno, NV 89506, phone 702-972-1671, founded 1978, editor-in-chief Elaine Dallman. Women-in-Literature is "a literary service organization established as a non-profit educational organization. Its sole purpose is to encourage, develop and promote public interest in women in all fields of literature. All money earned over and above the cost of manufacturing and marketing a new book is designated for the production of subsequent books. On the national level, poetry and drama comprise a tiny fraction of the 40,000 new books published each year in the United States. Yet much of our culture at its best is preserved and passed on to following generations in our poetry. Because poetry in the USA at present has a limited audience, however, commercial publishers are seldom interested in handling works of poets, which do not return large profits to their corporations. So it is up to the small, often non-profit, publishers to present these works. Women-in-Literature has begun its publishing program by presenting its first series of four regional anthologies: **Woman Poet—The West, Woman Poet—The East, Woman Poet—The Midwest** and **Woman Poet—The South.** The regional focus of these anthologies is a useful one: studying women writers by their regions, and providing information about their lives, as well as their written work, enables both writer and reader to be drawn out of their isolation. Not only readers, but poets' peers learn of each other and make contact; the resultant meetings and exchanges are productive. The ongoing relationship between poets and poetry discussed in **Woman Poet** provides important information for those, both young and old, just beginning to write. The biographical material throws light not only onto individual poems, but on the entire field of poetry. Each book in the current series comprises the previously unpublished poetry of approximately 30 women, of whom 2-3 are featured. . . ." For more information about the work of Women-in-Literature, send SASE. **"Unpublished fine poetry of any length by women will be considered. No particular political leanings or thematic bent.**" They have recently published poetry by Ann Stanford, Madeline De Frees, Josephine Miles, June Jordan, Audre Lorde, Li-

328 *Poet's Market '87*

sel Mueller, Judith Minty and Marie Ponsot. The editor selected these sample lines from "The Gorge" by Mary Barnard:

> Light has the dull luster of pewter
> and the clouds move sidewise clawing
> the tops of the crags,
> resting their soft gray bellies
> briefly in high valleys.

The anthologies are published in both hardback and paper editions, 100 pp., 8x9½", flat-spined, professionally printed in 1 and 2 columns, with b/w photos of poets. **Sample: $8.50 plus $1.50 handling for paperback; complete set: $30; $27 for students.**

*WOMEN'S QUARTERLY REVIEW (IV, Feminist), Box 708, New York, NY 10150, phone 212-675-7794, founded 1984, poetry editor Michelle Tokarczyk, "publishes both articles and literature relating to women's changing roles in politics, society and the arts. **We would like to see poetry that is feminist but are open to very good poetry by women. We are open to various styles. Shorter pieces preferred. Absolutely no sexist material. We publish mainly new poets and writers.**" The magazine is a quarterly tabloid using 1-2 pp. of poetry per issue, circulation 1,000, 200 subscriptions. They use about 25 of some 300-400 submissions of freelance poetry received per year. **Sample: $2.75 plus SASE. Photocopy OK. Submit no more than 5 poems at a time. Reports in 6-8 weeks. Pays in contributor's copies. Send SASE for guidelines.**

‡*WOMENWISE (IV, Women), 38 South Main St., Concord, NH 03301, phone 603-225-2739, founded 1980, editor Susan A. Janicki, "a quarterly newspaper that deals specifically with issues relating to women's health—research, education, and politics." They want "**poetry reflecting status of women in society, relating specifically to women's health issues.**" They do not want "**poetry that doesn't include women or is written by men; poetry that degrades women or is anti-choice.**" They have recently published poems by Marge Piercy. *WomenWise* (which I have not seen) is a tabloid newspaper, 12 pp. with b/w art and graphics. Its circulation is 3,000 +. Price per copy is $2, subscription $7/year. **Sample available for $2 postpaid. Pay is a 1-year subscription. Submissions should be typed double-spaced. Reporting time is 1-2 months and time to publication "depends."**

WONDER TIME (IV, Religious), 6401 The Paseo, Kansas City, MO 64131, phone 816-333-7000, founded 1969, poetry editors Evelyn Beals and Patty L. Hall, a publication of the Children's Ministries Department, Church of the Nazarene, "**is committed to reinforcement of the Biblical concepts taught in the Sunday School curriculum, using poems 4-8 lines, simple, with a message, easy to read, for 1st and 2nd graders. It should not deal with much symbolism.**" They have recently published poems by Helen Kitchell Evans, Sandra Liatsos and Minni Wells. The editors selected this sample poem by Helen Kitchell Evans:

> Thank you for helping me make new friends,
> And learn new things to do.
> Thank You, God, for help at school
> With all of my lessons, too.

Wonder Time is a weekly 4 pp. leaflet, magazine-sized, newsprint, circulation 37,000. **Sample free for SASE. Reports in 6-8 weeks. Pays minimum of $2.50, 25¢/line, and 4 contributor's copies. Send SASE for guidelines.**

*THE WOOSTER REVIEW (I, II), The College of Wooster, Wooster, OH 44691, founded 1983, poetry editor Michael Allen (faculty; student editorship changes), "publishes poetry and fiction accessible to a wide audience, including work by students at college and graduate school level, and runs an annual high school contest for Ohio students. Poetry should be **not too literary, sexy or overly posed; no John Ashbery, please. But competent, contemporary poetry. Free verse, closed forms, blank verse. Is it interesting? Is there some emotional response elicited with some artfulness?**" They have recently published poetry by William Stafford, Cary Waterman, Jack Myers, Ron Wallace, Deb Burnham, Christopher Bursk, Mary Crow, Reg Saner and Ron Koertge. As a sample the editor selected these lines by Cary Waterman:

> It is always and only this:
> rowers on a pond at dawn,
> their darkness muffled by mist.
> What approaches them is the promise
> of light, a slender bridge
> under which the morning comes.

The Wooster Review appears twice a year, 6x9", 120 pp., flat-spined, professionally printed, matte card cover, about 30 pp. of poetry per issue, printrun 400, paid circulation 50-100 (many used in classes and as college copies), 50 subscriptions of which 5 are libraries. They use about 60 of 500 freelance submissions of poetry per year. **Sample: $2 postpaid. Simultaneous submissions. Double-spaced, 3-6 poems, photocopies, dot-matrix OK. Payment 3 copies.** The Ohio High School Creative Writing Contest offers prizes of $100, $65 and $35 and publication in *The Wooster Review*. **The editor advises, "Forget New York; forget 'the Big Time.' Read to develop an ear for sound, then write to find out what you know; the real poem is usually not the one you think you want to write."**

‡**WORD EXCHANGE (I)**, Furbringerstrasse 17, 1000 Berlin 61, West Germany, editor Suzan Letham. **"Word Exchange is a service for poets who wish to exchange copies of their work for those of other poets.** Communication is the main principle; to bring new poets into contact with each other, help them to overcome shyness about showing their work to others. Reciprocal criticism is encouraged and wished-for." **There is no charge for using the services of Word Exchange; contributors should enclose two IRC's. No limit to number of poems submitted; whenever possible the exchange is on a 1 to 1 basis.** Twice a year selected poems are collected in a folder, which is available to contributors at $3 or £3, or locally in Berlin at $4, £4, or DM12.

THE WORD SHOP, SINS OF THE MORNING ANTHOLOGIES, SENIOR CITIZEN MONTHLY (IV, Senior Citizens), 11 Ridge Rd., 2 Q South, Ridgewood, NJ 07450, founded 1980, poetry editors Juanita Tobin, Fran Portley and Virginia Gaechter. *Senior Citizen Monthly* is an 8 pp. photocopied newsletter of activities of the Senior Citizen Center, 46-50 Center St., Midland Park, NJ 07432. Each issue has 2 pp. of poems by members of the center. They publish anthologies of their work, **Sins of the Morning**, financed by craft sales and flea markets, **Anthology 3** and **JOY (Joining Old & Young)**, the latter published May 1985 made possible by a Local Arts Development Grant awarded by Bergen County Office of Cultural & Historic Affairs through the New Jersey State Council on the Arts Block Grant Funding. **JOY** contains poems by students of the 6th and 7th grades and members of The Word Shop. "We want the writer to attend The Word Shop and workshop the poem to be considered for our next anthology, which we plan for June 1986." Simultaneous submissions OK. **Length of poetry used restricted to 35 lines, which includes the title and any spaces between lines or stanzas as required.** They have used poetry by Van Dee Sickler, Eugenie Porter Cowell, Dorothy Starzyk, Marueen Cannon and 50 others in the last Anthology. The editor selected as a sample these lines by Eberhard Gormanns:

> One Sunday afternoon on the side
> of the road in the grass
> I looked into her eyes
> and saw my image.

The Word Shop poets are mostly older Americans living close enough to the Senior Citizen Center to attend weekly poetry workshops and learn the craft often from scratch. Attendance at the workshops is the only requirement. No money is involved unless they want to buy a copy or copies of Anthologies which contain their work. The anthologies are professionally printed, flat-spined, 58 pp. volumes, glossy card cover: $5.

THE WORD WORKS (II), Box 42164, Washington, DC 20015, founded 1974, poetry editors Karren Alenier, Deirdra Baldwin, J. H. Beall and Robert Sargent, "is a nonprofit literary organization publishing contemporary poetry in single author editions usually in collaboration with a visual artist. We sponsor ongoing poetry reading and performance programs as well as archival projects and the Washington Prizes—an award of $1,000 for a single poem by a living American poet." They publish flat-spined paperbacks and occasional anthologies and want **"well-crafted poetry, open to most forms and styles (though not political themes particularly). Experimentation welcomed."** The editors chose these passages as examples:

> Details are important
> . . . the little things, like having an extra
> child.—Grace Cavalieri
> I want to see the world through your eyes,
> . . . How the Fly was chatting to the Other Bug
> How I resemble you by virtue of loving you—John (Mack) Wellman

Query with 5 sample poems, publication credits, brief bio, brief philosophic outlook/ principles, statement of how poet will help in distributing the book (readings, etc.) "We recommend purchase of Word Works publications so author understands what we do. (Not a prerequisite.)" Replies to queries, submissions in 3 months. Simultaneous submissions OK if so stated. Photocopy OK, no dot-matrix. Discs compatible with 8" CP/M format TRS80 or MSDOS 5¼ (hard copy preferred). Payment is 15% of run (usually of 500). Send SASE for catalog to buy samples. Occasionally comment on rejections. The editors advise, "don't work in a void, gather community support for your work. See if your poetry stands up in time, read voraciously, support contemporary literature by buying and reading small press."

‡*WORD-FIRES (II)**, 695 Charlotte St., Sudbury, Ontario, Canada P3E 4C1, is a **literary journal on television** begun in 1985 by Robert L. J. Zenik, its executive producer, director and editor. **He selects poems from those submitted and reads them on the air.** He hopes to reach a national (Canadian) and eventually international audience of millions with this alternative to the printed journal. **No pay, and obviously no free copies—but with 2 months notice and $30 you can purchase a VHS tape of the show on which your poem(s) are read.**

‡* **WORDS: THE NEW LITERARY FORUM (III)**, 7 Palehouse Common, Framfield, Uckfield, East Sussex, UK TN22 5QY, phone 082-582-490, editor Philip Vine, is a literary monthly publishing criticism, poetry, fiction and drama with lavish use of illustrations—and plans to begin publishing books in 1986. They welcome **all types of poetry** and have recently published poems by Jon Silkin, John Mole, D. J. Enright, Lawrence Sail, Peter Redgrove, David Holbrook and Spike Milligan. The editor selected these sample lines by Norman MacCraig:
> The way of going
> wanders in my mind.
> It writhes slowly.
> It won't lie still in the grasses.

The magazine-sized publication is 64 pp., glossy, with color and b/w illustrations and cover, circulation 10,000, 1,500 subscriptions of which 350 are libraries, subscriptions $26 (£15). **Sample: $3.50 postpaid. Pays "by negotiation" and one contributor's copy. Reports in 1 month maximum. Comments on MSS as a free service to those who subscribe for 2 years.** They offer competitions to those in the U.K. with entry fees of £1.25 and prizes of £15-500, 50 lines maximum. Philip Vine advises, "study your magazines and study other poets, and then follow your dream!"

‡**WORDWRIGHTS CANADA (IV, Theme)**, Box 456, Station O, Toronto, Ontario, Canada M4A 2P1, director Susan Ioannou, is a "small press with an interest in **poetry on a single theme** and books on poetics in layman's not academic, terms. Susan Ioannou selected these sample lines from Joseph Maviglia's "Mother Sits" in **The Crafted Poem: A Step by Step Guide to Writing And Appreciation**.
> Mother sits. The time knits on her hands
> Hands that fed and warmed.
> Around the moon with patience
> she navigates unchartered regions for her children.

The book is a large digest-sized, photocopied from typescript, 74 pp., saddle-stapled with blue matte card cover with line drawing. She wants to see **book-length manuscripts on a single theme to be published as 64 pp. paperback, saddle-stapled chapbooks. Send complete MS and cover letter giving credits, philosophy, aesthetic or poetic aims. Responds in 6 weeks. Photocopy, dot-matrix OK. Pays $50 advance, 10% royalties, and 5% of press run in copies. Editor rarely comments on rejections, but Wordwrights offers a separate "Manuscript Reading Service." Request order form to buy samples.** The editor comments, **"We have no interest in narcissistic poetry of despair. Instead of mirrors of the brooding self, we seek windows on the wider world of shared human experience. We want poetry founded in courage and insight. Also, small books on the aesthetics of writing poetry—both craft and reflection."**

WORLD POETRY SOCIETY, *POET, INTERNATIONAL (I), 208 W. Latimer Ave., Campbell, CA 95008, phone 408-379-8555, founded 1960, managing editor Edwin A. Falkowski. *Poet, International* is funded by the World Poetry Society, Intercontinental, to promote the translation and interchange of verse between diverse peoples of the world. Send SASE for brochures indicating special issues, anthologies and activities. **They accept for publication "all but .1%" of poetry submitted. Guidelines indicate exact format for submission. Sample: 75¢ for 1, $1 for 2. Pays 1 copy.** Editor Edwin Falkowski says he wants poetry with **"clarity of hot ice, not dissertations on sewer outfalls of futilities in free (?) verse. Partial to forms, free form, within length of 3 sonnets or 42 lines. We do not edit for style, subject or any purpose other than inherent zen."** As a sample he selected these lines from "The Challengers" by Ruth Newton Mattos:
> The world is after all a testing place
> a dot among Utopias of space.
> When by design Earth's transients must depart
> new runners grasp the torch and run the race.

Poet, International is a monthly, printed in India on newsprint, average of 90 pp. digest-sized saddle-sewn, matte paper cover, circulation 750, 550 subscriptions of which 10% are libraries. Subscription: $18. The editor advises, they plan to graft in Thai and Korean prosody through an English competition for promotion and publication in *Poet* as done with contest results in a special issue of March 1982 on the *Lachian* language nations of East Europe, the *Poet Laureate* status of all 50 states in March 1981 copy, or the Trans-World Poetry Exposition results of 8 categories of entries published in the March 1987 issue.

WORMWOOD REVIEW PRESS, *THE WORMWOOD REVIEW (II), Box 8840, Stockton, CA 95208-0840, phone 209-466-8231, founded 1959, poetry editor Marvin Malone. This is one of the oldest and most distinguished literary journals in the country. "The philosophy behind *Wormwood:* (i) avoid publishing oneself and personal friends, (ii) avoid being a 'local' magazine and strive for a national and international audience, (iii) seek unknown talents rather than establishment or fashionable authors, (iv) encourage originality by working with and promoting authors capable of extending the existing patterns of Amerenglish literature, (v) avoid all cults and allegiances and the you-scratch-my-back-and-I-will-scratch-yours approach to publishing, (vi) accept the fact that magazine content is more important than format in the long run, (vii) presume a literate audience and try to make the mag readable from the first page to the last, (viii) restrict the number of pages to no more than 40 per issue since only the insensitive and the masochistic can handle more pages at one sitting, (ix) pay bills on time and don't expect special favors in honor of the muse, and lastly and most importantly (x) don't become too serious and righteous." Marvin Malone (who happens to be a professor of pharmacology) wants "**poetry and prose poetry that communicate the temper and range of human experience in contemporary society; don't want religious poetry and work that descends into bathos; don't want imitative sweet verse. Must be original; any style or school from traditional to ultra experimental, but *must* communicate; 3-600 lines.**" He has recently published poetry by Ron Koertge, Charles Bukowski, Edward Field, Lyn Lifshin and Gerald Locklin. As a sample he offers these lines of haiku by William Marsh:

> A snake in one stroke
> wiggles off the old man's brush
> on sale at the shrine

The digest-sized quarterly, offset from photo reduced typescript, saddle-stapled, has a usual printrun of 700—400 subscriptions of which about 175 are libraries. Subscription: $6. Yellow pages in the center of each issue feature "one poet or one idea"—in the issue I examined, 8 pp. devoted to Jennifer Stone's "Notes From the Back of Beyond" passages from her diary. **Sample: $3 postpaid. Submit 2-10 poems on as many pages. No dot-matrix. Reports in 2-8 weeks, pays 2-10 copies of the magazine or cash equivalent ($5-25). Send SASE for guidelines. For chapbook publication, no query; send 40-60 poems. "Covering letter not necessary—decisions are made solely on merit of submitted work." Reports in 4-8 weeks. Pays 25-30 copies or cash equivalent ($62.50-75).** Send $3 for samples or check libraries. They offer the Wormwood Award to the Most Overlooked Book of Worth (poetry or prose) for a calendar year, judged by Marvin Malone. He comments on rejections if the work has merit. He advises, "Have something to say. Read the past and modern 'master' poets. Absorb what they've done, but then write as effectively as you can in your own style. If you can say it in 40 words, do *not* use 400 or 4,000 words."

‡**WPBS POETRY (I)**, Suite 1091, 377B Somerset St. W, Ottawa, Ontario K2P 0K1 Canada, phone 613-521-0713, founded 1974 (publishing poetry since 1982), editor Hubert Dewey Joy. This press publishes poetry books only and holds poetry contests. They will publish "**any good quality poetry. Prefer traditional rhyming work, which is not excessively long. Some longer poems are published but they are the exception. Prefer poetry from 4-40 lines." They won't publish "anything that is racist or vested interest slanted.**" As a sample, the editor chose these lines by an unidentified poet:

> They looked into
> The darkened sky
> To ask questions
> and wonder why

The press plans to publish 4 chapbooks each year with a page count of 800-500. The format is either digest- or magazine-sized paperbacks or hard covers, flat-spined. **Writers should query first, sending 4 or 5 poems at a time if unsolicited. Reading fees are charged "by arrangement—generally $2 per volume considered. Format is not important, but typed copy 8½x11" paper is best for our needs. We are interested in good poetry and new poets from whatever source, without obligation." Queries will be answered in 1-2 weeks and MSS reported on in 1 month. Simultaneous submissions, photocopied MSS, or dot-matrix are OK but discs are not. No pay. There are monthly and annual poetry contests with cas and book awards.** The editor observes, "We believe poetry is entering a 20th Century renaissance. Free verse, and other artifical forms of poetry are giving way to the living forms of skillfully constructed rhymed and well metered poetry. Tense forms of poetry are presently popular. Publishers like them because of today's space limitations and printing formats. Concentrate on good rhyme, poetic license and having something to say beyond and above the truth or history and nature. Be original, but not totally descriptive of the physical. Express the 'heart of the poet.' "

‡***WRIT (II)**, 2 Sussex Ave., Toronto, Ontario, Canada M5S 1T5, phone 416-978-4871, founded 1970, editor Roger Greenwald, associate editor Richard Lush, is a "literary annual publishing new fiction, poetry and translation of high quality; has room for unestablished writers." **No limitations on kind of poetry sought; new forms welcome. "Must show conscious and disciplined use of language."**

They do not want to see "haiku, purely formal exercises, and poetry by people who don't bother reading." They have recently published poems by Rolf Jacobsen, Harry Martinson, Werner Asperstrom, Hebrik Nordbrandt, Reiner Kunze, Nichita Stanescu, Yannis Kondos, Richard Lush and Sharon Dunn. As a sample I selected the first stanza of "Body of Water" by Elaine Schwager:

Children's laughter leaves the beach at seven p.m.
The sand is silent. Bulging with blood, eyes
popping, dragonflies riding in tandem
nip at the water. A million bubbles appear.

The magazine is 6x9", 96 pp. flat-spined, professionally printed on heavy stock, matte card cover with color art, circulation 500-600, 125 subscriptions of which 75 are libraries, about 50 newsstand sales, $6/copy. **Sample: $6 postpaid. Pays 2 copies and discount on bulk purchases. Reports in 6-8 weeks** (longer in summer). Acceptances appear in the next issue published. **Poems must be typed and easily legible, close to letter quality as possible with new ribbon. Photocopies OK. Editor "sometimes" comments on rejections."** The editor advises, "Read a copy of the magazine you're submitting to. Let this give you an idea of the quality we're looking for. But in the case of *WRIT*, don't assume we favor only the styles of the pieces we've already published (we can only print what we get and are open to all styles). We will probably do more translation issues in the future. Read."

WRITE NOW BOOKS, ASTRA PUBLICATIONS, *REBIRTH OF ARTEMIS, *NEW VOICES (I, IV, Women), 24 Englewood Ter. Methuen, MA 01844, phone 617-685-3087, founded 1979, poetry editors Lorraine Laverriere and Terry Kelley. Their purpose is "to encourage new poets to 'break in,' as well as publish established poets." *New Voices*, an annual, is all poetry. Lorraine Laverriere says, **"I prefer contemporary poetry or free verse. I don't usually publish rhymed poetry because it is usually written so badly. I accept lengths from 3 lines to 2 pp., free style. Any subject matter if original and well-written and expressed..**" The editors selected these sample lines by John Kristofco:

Caught in the net of years,
she stares out to the street
where children and their mothers
stir with wandering men
in the concrete hand of time.

New Voices is a digest-sized with about 48 pp. of poetry in each issue, circulation 375, 140 subscriptions of which 3 are libraries. They use about 40 of 500 freelance submissions of poetry per year. **Sample: $2 postpaid. Poems can be in "any form so long as they're legible. I prefer batches of 6—strongly dislike only 1 poem in a submission. I try to at least send a card informing the poet that the submission was received within a month." Pays 1 copy. Send SASE for guidelines.** Astra Publications is an all-women press. The poetry published in *Rebirth of Artemis*, also an annual, "is devoted to **poetry written by women about women.** The purpose is for women to identify with each other and to share this identification with each other in an art form such as poetry. **I don't want to see poetry that puts down the male gender or 'I'm-just-a-housewife-martyr type theme. I like well-written work that addresses women in today's world in pride as well as stress. All relationships imaginable are acceptable. No long epics. Contemporary or free verse is preferred."** *Rebirth of Artemis* has published poetry by Judith Arcana, Arlyn, Lyn Lifshin, Janine Canan and Elaine Dollman. It is similar in size and format to *New Voices*, **has a circulation of 200, 60 subscriptions of which 3 are libraries, uses about 40 of 600 freelance submissions of poetry per year. Sample: $2.50 postpaid. See instructions above for *New Voices*, which apply also to *Rebirth of Artemis*, which also pays 1 copy and offers guidelines.** Lorraine Laverriere advises, "Don't get discouraged by rejections; be encouraged by acceptances, regardless of how few. Stay away from vanity presses and consider a copy of the magazine you're published in as reasonable payment since editors/publishers in the small presses are barely staying alive but *do not* charge poets to be published." Write Now Books has published a directory of autobiographies of poets, writers, editors and publishers.

‡*WRITE ON (I)**, Box 344A, Route 6, Carthage MO 64836, phone 417-358-3621, founded 1985, editor Judy St. John. *Write On* is a mimeographed "newsletter" that "provides the opportunity for the beginner and the contest winner to become published, as long as it is in 'good taste'." **Poems are "usually 24 lines or less, any style, but nothing vulgar."** As a sample, the editor selected the following lines by L. Lane:

Christmas bulbs hung up high.
Little fingers stretch and try.
Momma know; and that is why—
Christmas bulbs are hung up high.

The monthly newsletter consists of 10 pp. of colored 8½x11 paper, side-stapled. Circulation is "growing!" Price per issue is $1, subscription $10/year. **Sample available for $1 postpaid, guidelines for SASE. Pay is 1 copy. Poems should be submitted up to 6 per envelope; photocopies, print-outs, si-**

multaneous submissions are OK. Reporting time is within a month and time to publication is 6-8 weeks. Contests are listed in each *Write On*. The editor says, "You'll never get published unless you submit or enter a contest. Subscribe to *Write On*—get the 'feel'—then send in some of your work. You might well be in the next issue.

‡*THE WRITER (I)**, 120 Boylston St., Boston MA 02116, phone 617-423-3157, founded 1887, "The Poet's Workshop" author Florence Trefethen. This monthly magazine for literary workers and freelance writers publishes a bi-monthly column called **"The Poet's Workshop" that makes a "selection of the month"** from submissions and analyzes selected poems in the column. **Poems must be original, submitted by the author, unpublished and not under consideration by another publisher. They must be typewritten, 1 poem to a page, poet's name and address on each sheet, no longer than 20 lines, no more than 10 poems in one submission.** *Do not send SASE*; no poems will be acknowledged or returned. Guidelines are available for SASE, but you must buy a copy of the magazine to see your work in print; poems are discarded after each bimonthly selection. There is no payment for selected poems." Circulation of *The Writer* is 56,000.

‡*THE WRITERS' BLOC (I)**, Box 212, Marysville, OH 43040, phone 513-642-8019, founded 1985, poetry editors Jennifer Comer and Sharon Lawson, a literary quarterly **catering to the beginning writer. The editors say, "Anything more than 30 lines will have a tough time getting into print in our publication; any subject matter as long as in good taste. Shaped poetry not accepted. We like poetry that conveys a feeling—even if it is humor. Although the meaning of a lot of poetry is hidden, we would prefer not to see something that is completely over everyone's head, although we like something that is thought-provoking. Nothing that makes a political statement."** They have recently published work by Joyce Chandler, Ellen Sandry, and Kenneth Geisert. As a sample, the editors selected the following lines by an unidentified poet:

> *Our words connect on white paper,*
> *In voices inky black and ballpoint blue.*
> *My heart is opened once again*
> *As we read each others soul,*

The Writers' Bloc is digest-sized, offset in different sizes of type on ordinary paper with b/w decorations throughout, 40 pp. saddle-stapled, one-color matte card cover. Circulation is 200, of which 100 are subscriptions; 10 go to libraries and 30 are sold on newsstands. Price per issue is $3, subscription $10/year. **Sample available for $3 postpaid, guidelines for SASE. Pay is 1 copy. Submit "letter quality printing, 1 poem per page, no more than 5 per envelope. Reporting time is 3-6 weeks and time to publication 3-6 months.** The magazine sponsors an annual contest; one must be a subscriber to enter. The editors say, "Don't give up if we reject you the first time. We want to see your work. For most of our beginning contributors, the shorter the poem the better. Send us more than one so we have something by which to gauge your talent."

*WRITER'S DIGEST, WRITER'S DIGEST WRITING COMPETITION, *WRITER'S YEAR-BOOK (IV, Writing, publishing)**, 9933 Alliance Rd., Cincinnati, Ohio 45242, phone 513-984-0717, founded 1921. *Writer's Digest,* editor William Brohaugh, is a monthly magazine for freelance writers— fiction, nonfiction, poetry and drama. "All editorial copy is aimed at helping writers to write better and become more successful. **Poetry is part of 'The Writing Life' section only. These poems should be "generally light verse concerning 'the writing life'—the foibles, frenzies, delights and distractions inherent in being a writer. Don't want poetry unrelated to writing. Some 'literary' work is used, but must be related to writing. Preferred length: 4-20 lines."** They have recently published poems by Charles Ghigna, Willard R. Espy and Marcia Kruchten. As a sample, William Brohaugh chose this poem, "For Love Alone" by John D. Engle Jr.:

> *"I write for love alone,"*
> *he said.*
> *Then with a smile*
> *both fake and funny,*
> *he said again,*
> *"I write for love—*
> *the love of fame,*
> *the love of money."*

 The double dagger before a listing indicates that the listing is new in this edition. New markets are often the most receptive to freelance contributions.

They use 2 short poems per issue, about 25 per year of the 1,000 submitted. *Writer's Digest* has a circulation of 200,000. Subscription: $17. **Sample: $2.50 postpaid. Submit to Sharon Rudd, Submissions Editor, each poem on a separate page, no more than 4 per submission. Dot-matrix is discouraged, photocopy OK. Previously published, simultaneous submissions OK if acknowledged in covering letter. Reports in 3 months. Pays $20-50 per poem. Send SASE for guidelines. Editor comments on rejections "when we want to encourage or explain decision."** Poetry is also eligible for the annual Writer's Digest Writing Competition—poetry judge for 1985, John D. Engle. Watch magazine for rules and deadlines.

WRITERS FORUM (II, IV. Theme/contemporary Western living), University of Colorado, Colorado Springs, CO 80933-7150, phone 303-599-4023, founded 1974, poetry editor Victoria McCabe. This distinguished literary annual publishes both beginning and well-known writers, giving "**some emphasis to contemporary Western literature**, that is, to representation of living experience west of the 100th meridian in relation to place and culture. We collaborate with authors in the process of revision, reconsider and frequently publish revised work. We are open to **experimental work, to long poems— solidly crafted imaginative work that is verbally interesting and reveals authentic voice. We do not seek MSS slanted for popular appeal, the sentimental, or gentle, pornographic or polemical, and work primarily intended for special audiences such as children, joggers, gays and so on is not for us. Send 3-5 poems.**" They have recently published poems by William Stafford, David Ray, Yusef Komunyakaa, Bill Tremblay and Carolyne Wright. As a sample I chose the opening lines from 'Oblomor" by David Ray:

> *Sometimes I turn to stone, cannot unfreeze*
> *the fear, unlock what it would take*
> *to lift a teabag, walk the block. The status*
> *quo alone seems the great goal to move*

The annual is digest-sized, 225w pp., flat-spined, professionally printed with matte card cover, using 40-50 pp. of poetry in each issue, circulation 800, 100 subscriptions of which 25 are libraries. **The list price is $8.95 but they offer it at $5.95 to readers of *Writer's Digest*.** They use about 25 of 500 freelance submissions of poetry per year. **Pays 1 copy. For chapbook or book submission, query with 5 samples, bio, publication credits. Response to queries in 3-6 weeks. Simultaneous submissions OK if acknowledged. Photocopy, dot-matrix OK. No payment.**

WRITERS HOUSE PRESS, COMMUNITY WRITERS ASSOCIATION, *BEGINNING MAGAZINE (I), Box 3071, Iowa City, IA 52244, phone 319-337-6430, founded 1982, poetry editor John Wilder. "Community Writers Association and its parent organization, The Institute for Human Potential and Social Development does not solicit funds so much as people, young and old, new and established, who wish to contribute their efforts in the arts to *Beginning*, the periodic magazine of the organization. For those who are beginning, CWA provides criticism of works for members of the association who require it and publishes the results in *Beginning*. We solicit all forms of artistic endeavor which can fit in to the two-dimensional space of a quarterly: poetry, fiction, essays, criticism, commentaries, review, photos, prints and poetry and prose by children. Membership dues for the Community Writers Association, which include a subscription to *Beginning* and many other benefits, are $25 a year, $15 a year for students and fixed income. "One does not need to be a member or subscriber to submit manuscripts." Children may participate through a program and magazine entitled *The Very Beginning*. Send SASE for details. **Unsolicited MSS are welcomed and must include SASE, a one paragraph biography of the author, and a telephone number. Name and address of author must be on each page of the MS. Submit no more than 4 poems. Dot-matrix, photocopy, simultaneous submissions OK. Reports in 3 minutes-3 months. Pays 2 contributor's copies and money when grants make that possible. All MSS must be double-spaced. Prefer contemporary free verse to traditional rhyme and meter. No haiku, but will consider most other styles.**" They have recently published poetry by Morty Sklar and Jim Mulac. As a sample the editors selected the opening lines of "Elegy (for Helen)" by Phoebus Delphis, translated by George Gott and Fotioula Letsos:

> *Your shadow appears to me*
> *at nightfall;*
> *alive and eloquent*
> *she fills me*
> *with the fear of loneliness.*

Beginning is a digest-sized periodical, 56 pp., professionally printed, saddle-stapled, with matte card cover with photo, circulation 150, 100 subscriptions of which 5 are libraries. Subscription: $10. They receive about 100 freelance submissions of poetry per year, use 20-40. **Sample: $3 postpaid. They also publish collections by individuals. Query with 10 samples, cover letter giving bio, publication credits, personal or aesthetic philosophy, poetic goals and principles. Replies to queries in 1 month, to submission (if invited) in 3-4 months. Terms of publication depend upon grants or** award money. "Non-members receive moderate feedback on their MSS. Members receive detailed workshop-style feedback and criticism, as explained in our brochure. We do not believe in the form rejection letter." Writers House Press occasionally publishes quality book-length manuscripts written by CWA members and *Beginning* readers and others. Some of these books will be included in the subscription to *Beginning*. Send SASE for guidelines and brochure.

*WRITERS WEST(II), Box 16097, San Diego, CA 92116, phone 619-278-6108, founded 1982, poetry editor E.I.V. von Heitlinger. *Writers West* is a bimonthly which "publishes articles of interest to professional, working writers and the informed literate public. "Poetry may be on any subject in any style, 50 lines maximum. No hard-core pornography, but tasteful erotica will be considered. Looking for well-crafted, tight, polished poems of clarity and force of visions." No epics, or poems about 'the writing life'." They have recently published poetry by Robert D. Hoeft, Jonathan Lowe, Heidi Hart and Albert Pertha. von Heitlinger chose these lines by Albert Pertha as a sample:

> Close the doors and play fugues
> On the strings of madness
> Smash the cracked podium
> and compose toccatas
> On deadly violins

Writers West is 16-20 pp. magazine-sized, professionally printed in 2 columns on matte paper, glossy paper cover with b/w photos, graphics, ads, circulation 2,500, using half a page or less of poetry in each issue. Subscription: $10. **Sample: $2 postpaid. Submit no more than 6 poems, any format. Simultaneous submissions, photocopy, dot-matrix OK. Reports in 2 weeks. Pays 3 copies and possible token payment.**

*XANADU, A LITERARY JOURNAL, LONG ISLAND POETRY COLLECTIVE INC., PLEASURE DOME PRESS, *PROCESS, POEMCARD SERIES, LIPC NEWSLETTER (II), Box 773, Huntington, NY 11743, phone 516-746-4203, founded 1975, poetry editors Anne-Ruth Baehr, Mildred M. Jeffrey, Barbara Lucas, and Pat Fisher. "The LIPC is essentially a not-for-profit organization which publishes an informational newsletter (which sometimes uses a poem or two), *Xanadu*, an annual with worldwide submissions, *Process* (peer workshop magazine), *Poemcard* series (membership contest or reading fee), and Pleasure Dome Press, which publishes books of poetry but is not currently active. We promote readings, sponsor open readings and art festivals. **We want quality work that shows real sensitivity to language as well as the human condition. A well-focused poem will get a good reading. We are open to formal poetry with fresh language and insights, as well as open forms. We consider visual-shaped poems from time to time. Any length, but successful long submission are rare.**" They have recently published poetry by Chris Bursk, Hillel Schwarz, Margot Treitel, Brown Miller, R.T. Smith, Jimmy Aubert, Michael Blumenthal and Virginia Terris. The editors selected these sample lines by Lois V. Walker:

> Time and each I rise up out of
> shallow graves to break the heavy waves
> of dust, whispering a wasted liturgy—
> names, places, dates—a verbal collage
> with instant paper replay for a shroud.

Xanadu is a digest-sized, 72 pp., flat-spined, professionally printed on good stock with glossy card cover with b/w art, circulation 500, 250 subscriptions of which 20 are libraries. "We make a real effort to give poets a good showcase with careful production work. Good art work is always included." There are about 60 pp. of poetry in each issue. They receive over a thousand submissions of freelance poetry per year, use 50-55. **Sample: $3.50 postpaid. "Send a batch of 3-5 poems neatly typed on 8½x11" paper. Type your name and address in the upper left corner of each sheet. Fold the sheets together (not separately) in thirds. Do not mail poems flat. Use only #10 business envelopes, not large manila envelopes. No letter is necessary. We are not interested in simultaneous submissions or work that has been published elsewhere." Reports in 3 months. Pays 3 copies—and, when funded, $5 per poem and 2 copies. Editors sometimes comment on rejections. Send SASE for guidelines.** Pleasure Dome Press is not presently considering unsolicited MS. The editors advise, "Poets just starting out should certainly read a great deal of poetry, should listen to a wide range of established poets. This not to control their work, but rather to be aware of what has been and is in order to create for the future of their actual context."

*X-IT MAGAZINE (II), Box 102, St. John's, New Foundland, Canada A1C 5H5, phone 709-753-8802, founded 1984, poetry editor Ken J. Harvey, is a magazine-sized, 40 pp. arts and entertainment journal for the average person appearing 3 times a year. "**We accept all lengths and types of poetry although our minds move toward a contemporary mode.**" They have recently published poetry by

John Ditsky, Lesley Choyce and Helen Porter. The editors selected these sample lines from "Fireman" by Ken J. Harvey:

> *I put out a fire last night*
> *The smoke is still in my breath*
> *I can taste it when I eat*
> *I can hear screams when*
> *I spark a match*

There are approximately 5 pp. of poetry in each issue, circulation 3,000, "hundreds" of subscriptions of which one third are libraries. Subscription: $10 for two years. They receive "hundreds" of freelance submissions of poetry, use about 15 per year, have a 2-3 month backlog. **Sample: $3 postpaid. Photocopy, simultaneous submissions OK. Include covering letter. Reports in 3-4 weeks. Pays $10-50 depending on success of particular issue. Editors "most always" comment on rejections.** They advise, "Keep at it. Don't get discouraged. Do not follow other styles. Write exactly how you feel, then craft it. Forget standards and guidelines—just do as it feels. Always send covering letter; no covering letter projects an uncaring sentiment." Submissions without proper return envelope and postage will not be returned.

YALE UNIVERSITY PRESS, THE YALE SERIES OF YOUNGER POETS, *THE YALE RE-VIEW (III), 92A Yale Station, New Haven CT 06520, phone 203-436-7881, founded 1908, poetry editor (Yale University Press) Charles Grench. First I would like to report on *The Yale Review*, one of our most important intellectual quarterlies. Penelope Laurans, Associate Editor, responds in a way that will help many readers understand why so many of our major markets are "drying up" because of inappropriate submissions by too many poets. She writes, "Our experience with listings in books like **Poet's Market** is so unhappy—literally hundreds of submissions which we do not have the staff to handle—that I feel at the moment we should decline your offer. I am sorry about this because it certainly seems that you are making an admirable effort to publish a responsible, accurate book—but our recent experiences with floods of mail have frightened us." Good poets will continue to place some of their best work with *YR*, and they will continue to publish some of the most outstanding poetry in the country. But I join Penelope Laurans in begging most of you to stop pestering these high-prestige publications until you have good, objective reason to believe that your work measures up to the quality of the poetry published there. Otherwise you make it difficult for yourself and all of us. Similar warnings should probably apply to the Yale Series of Younger Poets, which is one of the most prestigious means available to launch a book publishing career. It is **open to poets under 40 who have not had a book previously published— a book MS of 48-64 pp. Entry fee: $5. Submit February 1-28 each year. Send SASE for rules and guidelines.** Recent winners have been Richard Kenney, Kathy Song, Pamela Alexander and George Bradley. Publication of the winning volume each year is on a standard royalty contract plus 10 authors' copies, and the reputation of the contest guarantees more than the usual number of reviews. The editor advises, "Work hard. Have faith. Rewrite often."

YE OLDE NEWS, SHELF IMAGE, *PRINTER'S NEWS (IV, Renaissance), 1002 South, Lufkin, TX 75901, phone 409-637-7468, founded 1969. *Printer's News* is a trade journal for the printing industry. *Ye Olde News*, a "historical/hysterical annual about the Renaissance, circulation 60,000, uses very little poetry, and that which is used is used as filler and deals with the period 1300-1650 AD. Of several hundred freelance submissions of poetry each year they use a dozen or so. "Don't send originals, not in the position to assure the return of material." Sample: $3 postpaid. Submit short fillers. Dot-matrix, photocopy, simultaneous submissions OK. Reports in 30 days. No pay. Send SASE for guidelines. Editor sometimes comments on rejections.**

‡YELLOW PRESS (V), 2394 Blue Island, Chicago, IL 60608, founded 1972, editor Peter Kostakis, a small-press publisher of flat-spined paperbacks and occasionally hardcovers. **Freelance submissions are not accepted.** They have published poetry books by Tod Borrican, Paul Carroll, Alice Notley, Paul Hoover, and Maxine Chernoff. The book they sent me is **Evidence**, by Art Lange. As a sample I chose the beginning lines from his "Sonnet After Rilke":

> *Black bushes as a signal floating*
> *suddenly in the ephemeral air like fame*
> *and in the anxiety of the long year*
> *our playing of pure*
> *song is existence.*

The book is digest-sized, nicely printed on buff stock, 58 pp., flat-spined with two-color glossy card cover, illustration on front, picture of author on back. The press publishes 1-2 books per year, paperbacks priced from $2.50-3.50, clothbound editions priced at $6.95-7.95, and signed editions at $12-15. Their catalog, which is very handsomely printed on glossy stock, is free on request.

*YELLOW SILK: JOURNAL OF EROTIC ARTS (IV, Erotic), Box 6374, Albany CA 94706, phone 415-841-6500, founded 1981, poetry editor Lily Pond, publishes the quarterly *Yellow Silk* and a possible future anthology. They want **"no porn; all forms of erotic poetry (traditional, experimental) from the exquisitely subtle to the graphically explicit; literary excellence always the first consideration. Any form, length, style or subject matter so long as it is erotic."** They have recently published poetry by Ntozake Shange, Ivan Argüelles, W.S. Merwin, Mary Mackey, Arlene Stone, Jane Hirshfield and James Broughton. The editor selected these sample lines from "Seedbed" by Noelle Caskey:

> On my belly as you enter me,
> I think in flowers,
> taste names of roses:
> Glorie de Dijon, Crimson. Starburst.

"Editorial policy: all persuasions, no brutality." *Yellow Silk* is magazine-sized, about 52 pp. of which 20 are poetry, circulation 9,000, professionally printed mostly in 2-3 columns with much b/w art, a few ads, 4-color gloss cover with art. Subscription: $12-40 (pay what you can). Lily Pond says she receives 10,000 submissions of freelance poetry per year, uses 100, a 1-month-3 year backlog. **Sample: $3.50 postpaid. Submit any time, "eightish pages, one poem per page, name and address and phone on each page, photocopy fine, hate dot-matrix." Reports in 6-8 weeks. Pays 3 copies (additional copies for half-price) plus $5/poem. She occasionally comments on rejections.** Lily Pond's advice: "Most of the writers I publish regularly write several hours every day for years. I don't. I guess that's what makes them so good. Don't expect a payoff on any less an investment." Cody's Books of Berkeley sponsors annual *YS* poetry contest.

YES PRESS, CAMBRIDGE COLLECTION (I), Box 91 for Yes Press, Box 866 for Cambridge Collection, Waynesboro, TN 38485, founded 1983, editor Glenn Gallahcr, is a **subsidy publisher which publishes virtually all poetry submitted. They want to see "traditional and free verse, haiku, light verse, all themes except porno. Length is limited to 18 lines. We like to see a variety of styles in our general anthologies.** They have recently published poetry by Gayle Elen Harney, Diana Kwiatkowski, B. Z. Niditch and Paula Christian. The editor selected these sample lines (poet unidentified):

> Maw,
> I never know
> running the blood
> in her strange canoe

I will quote Gleen Gallaher at length because he addresses a common problem many beginning poets encounter with various publishing arrangements. "My wife and I are printers here in the small town of Waynesboro. We make a living by job printing. As English majors and published poets ourselves in many of the better poetry journals during past years, we decided we'd like to help beginning poets 'get started'. We both started out that way years ago and truly believe it's a worthwhile thing to do—publishing new poets in paperback anthologies. **The majority of books we print are simply anthologies of new and beginning poets who submit as a result of our advertising in *Writer's Digest*, our direct mail notifying past contributores of new books, and those who have been published by us before. We *do not* require poets to buy copies.** On the other hand, we just cannot afford to send 500 poets contributors' copies every 4 months (that's our schedule for each new book). In short runs like these books, the initial set-up costs us more than anything else. I suppose poets let us publish their work because they need their first publication credits, want to see their work in print, want an audience for their work, etc. And many of these writers turn out to be really good ones who need the experience of publication to learn from their own strengths and/or mistakes. The "subsidy books" we publish contain mini-books of 4 poets' work. Each poet in these has his own title page, list of credits, and about 22-23 poems in his own book selection. It's the same thing as selfpublishing, really, except they share the total book with two or three others. Each poet only pays for the typesetting, layout, printing, and shipping of his 75 copies of the book with his 25 pages contained. This is a new project we just started because so many new poets write us, asking our help in publishing "their own" book of poetry. The Cambridge Collection is a response to poet's requesting more substantial and permanent books. The series includes general poetry from the same sources as the rest of our antholgies; only the very best of submissions will be taken for these books. No purchase of a book is required for this series either. The sample anthology I have seen is professionally printed in small type, several poems to the page, in a flat-spined format, 130 + pp., decorated with b/w drawings. In the back a number of poets (who probably paid extra) are featured with bios and some with photos.

‡*YESTERDAY'S MAGAZETTE (I), Independent Publishing Co., Box 15126, Sarasota, FL 34277, editor and publisher Ned Burke, founded 1973. This bi-monthly tabloid says that it is aimed at "plain folks" but it seems to be mainly for the elderly; there is a large "Memories" section. The issue I have contains poems on its "Quills, Quips, & Quotes" page as well as a 28-page insert section which is a complete rendering of the Bible in verse by George E. Cook. As a sample of the "Quills, Quips, & Quotes," I chose the following lines from "The Backyard Pump" by J.E. Coulbourn:

> *With two small hands you'd*
> *grasp the monster's tail*
> *And try to pump the water in the pail,*
> *But if his darned esophagus got dry*
> *No water came no matter how you'd try.*

Without the insert, the tabloid is 10-12 pp., printed on newsprint, folded, not stapled. A year's subscripton is $6. **Submissions for "Quills, Quips, & Quotes" should be "thoughtful, amusing, or just plain interesting for our 'plain folks' readers. No SASE is required as short items are generally not returned nor acknowledged, unless requested by the contributor. SASE for longer articles. $2 for sample copy and details.**

YOUNG AMERICAN PUBLISHING CO., INC., *YOUNG AMERICAN: AMERICA'S NEWS-MAGAZINE FOR KIDS (IV, Children), Box 12409, Portland OR 97212, phone 503-230-1895, founded 1983, managing editor Kristina T. Linden, is a 16 pp. tabloid monthly of "information/news/entertainment/fiction/games for youth, **looking for light and humorous poetry that kids from 7-16 might enjoy reading. Because of our format, we generally opt for short poems. Exception for something really teriffic. In addition to above, we would like to see seasonal and holiday related poetry.**" They use about a fourth of a page of poetry in each issue, circulation, 100,000. Subscription: $9. **Sample: 50¢ with 10x12" SASE. Reports in 4 months. Pays 7¢ per word.**

THE YOUNG CRUSADER (IV, Youth, religious), National Woman's Christian Temperance Union, 1730 Chicago Ave., Evanston, IL 602011, is a monthly publication for members of the Loyal Temperance Legion and young friends of their age—about 6-12 years. The digest-sized leaflet, 12 pp., uses short poems appropriate for the temperance and high moral value and nature themes and their young audience. I selected as a sample the first of 5 stanzas of "Leprechaun's Gold" by Dianne W. Shauer:

> *On the 17th day of March, two*
> *days past the ides, look for wee,*
> *little old men, who, when they see*
> *you, will hide.*

They pay 10¢/line for poetry.

ZEPHYR PRESS (II), 13 Robinson St., Somerville, MA 02144, founded 1981, poetry editor Miriam Sagan, publishes chapbooks and books, including poetry. The sample I have examined is by the editor, Miriam Sagan, **Aegean Doorway,** 6x9" flat-spined, 44 pp., professionally printed on acid-free matte stock, 1,000 copies, with glossy 3 color card cover: $3.95. I selected these sample lines, the second of 5 stanzas, from "South Ridge Zendo":

> *Tears begin when I sit with incense*
> *Like the smell of you late last night*
> *Hair full of smoke and earth*

Query. Charges $12 reading fee for book MS. Query regarding simultaneous submissions. Photocopy, dot-matrix OK. Pays 20% royalties and 100 copies (10% of run). Editor supplies full critique for the $12 reading fee.

*ZEST (II), Box 339, Station P, Toronto, Ontario, Canada M5S 2S8, founded 1981, poetry editor Jim Roberts, is a quarterly of poetry, stories and visual art. They want to see "**highly crafted poems with impact. No specifications as to form, length, style, subject-matter or purpose.**" They have recently published poems by Fred Wah, Tom Wayman, David McFadden and George Bowering. The editor selected these sample lines by Erin Mouré:

> *The encroachment of particulars, your hand*
> *lifting the beer in the room's light*
> *afraid at last of anger, your one small skin ·*
> *stretched to its limit*

Zest is magazine-sized 34 pp., using 15-20 pp. of poetry in each issue, circulation 150, 80 subscriptions of which 5 are libraries. Subscription: $10. They use about 5 of 50 freelance poetry submissions per year, have a 1 issue backlog. **Sample: $3 postpaid. Submit any time, no page limit, photocopy fine. Reports in 3 months. Pays 3 copies. Editor sometimes comments on rejections.**

‡*ZINDY (I), 15, Mersey Rd., Liverpool £17 6A9, England, phone 051-427-1625, founded 1985, editor Mark Roberts a semi-annual magazine that publishes "very short fiction, poetry, cartoons, satire, English soccer, pop music reviews/interviews, jokes, ranting verse." The editor says, "**Funny poetry stands a great chance. Political/socially biting—but not whining poetry; short pieces; style—any-**

thing. *Immediate* impact is appreciated, be it a love poem or doggerel." He does not want "arty-farty nonsense; long streams of windy words that mean nothing." He has recently published poems by Attila the Stockbroker, Swift Nick, Belinda Subraman, and Brendan Behan. As a sample, he quoted the following lines from "Industrial Estates" by David R. Hannah:

> I can see there's money in Exploitation—especially the young
> when Ambitions are high—they're easily strung,
> bought and then sold with low interest rates
> And the Dole ques grow longer on the   Industrial Estates

Zindy (which I have not seen) is digest-sized, 24 pp., b/w or color, with photo or art on cover. Its circulation is 200-300 and there are no subscriptions; single copy price is 35p. **Guidelines available for SASE. Pay is "nothing but glory" and 1 or 2 copies. Reporting time is 1 day-1week and time to publication is 6 months.** The editor says, "A light-hearted covering letter makes a welcome change from curt invitations to publish 'me'!

Additional Poetry Publishers

In preparing **Poet's Market: 1987** we contacted all major and minor book and magazine publishers in the United States, Canada, the United Kingdom, Australia, New Zealand, and numerous other countries at least once—and in most cases two or three times. Most responded and their listings appear in the preceding Publishers of Poetry section. However, others, including some major publishers of poetry, did not fill out a questionnaire, return an updated verification, could not be reached by phone or specifically asked not to be included for one or more of the following reasons:

- They are not actively seeking submissions of poetry. They publish poetry but are not planning to add any new poets to their list in the near future.
- They will consider submissions of poetry but believe that they receive sufficient material without listing in this directory.
- They solicit al the material they publish.
- They consider submissions only from agents or established poets whose names they recognize.
- They don't have a staff large enough to handle the increased number of submissions a listing would create.
- They publish only the work of the editor(s) and friends.
- Their experience with listings in other directories has been a deluge of inappropriate submissions.
- They choose not to make public information about their publishing policies.

The following names and addresses of the *most commonly known* poetry publishers are included for the sake of completeness, as you may well encounter books or magazines they publish which include poetry and wonder why you cannot find them in **Poet's Market**. Also, in some cases, the reasons some of these publishers are not included in the directory are temporary (e.g., overstocked, temporarily suspending publication, etc.). Before submitting to any of the following, I suggest you write a brief query letter (enclosing SASE) to determine whether they are now interested in receiving submissions.

Abatis
UT Review Press
University of Tampa
Tampa, FL 33600

Andrew Mountain Press
Yet Another Small Magazine
Lamont Hall Chapbook Series
Box 14353
Hartford, CT 06114

Artful Dodge
Box 1473
Bloomington, IN 47402

The Atavist
Box 5643
Berkeley, CA 94705

August House Publishers
Box 3223
Little Rock, AR 72203-3223

Black Willow
401 Independence Dr.
"Sunrise"
Harleysville, PA 19438

George Braziller
1 Park Ave.
New York, NY 10016

Burning Deck Books
71 Elmgrove Ave.
Providence, RI 02906

Camus Editions
Box 687
Tiburon, CA 94920.

Canadian Literary Review
Box 278
Scarborough, Ont., Canada M1N 1S6

Chelsea
Box 5880
Grand Central Station, New York, NY 10163

Chicago Review
Faculty Exchange Box C
University of Chicago
Chicago, IL 60637

Chicago Review Press
213 West Institute Pl.
Chicago, IL 60610

Cider Mill Press
Box 664
Stratford, CT 06497

Cincinnati Poetry Review
Dept. of English (069)
University of Cincinnati
Cincinnati, OH 45221

Coydog Review
203 Halton Ln.
Watsonville, CA 95076

The Dalhousie Review
Killam Library
Dalhousie University Press
4413 Halifax, NS, Canada B3H 4H8

Dolphin-Moon Press
Signatures
Box 22262
Baltimore, MD 21203

Elizabeth Street Press
Unpublished Poets Series
Contemporary Writers Series
240 Elizabeth St.
New York, NY 10012

Equivalencias
%Fernando Rielo Foundation
380 Burns St.
Forest Hills, NY 11375

Faber & Faber, Inc.
39 Thompson St.
Winchester, MA 01890

Farrar, Straus and Giroux
19 Union St.
New York, NY 10003

University of Central Florida
Contemporary Poetry Series
%Dept. of English
University of Central Florida
Orlando, FL 32816

The Hampden-Sydney Poetry Review
Box 126
Hampden-Sydney, VA 23943

Harper's
2 Park Ave.
New York, NY 10016

Hermes House Press
Kairos, *Apt. 3F*
127 W. 15th
New York, NY 10011

Holt, Rinehart & Winston
521 5th Ave.
New York, NY 10175

The Hudson River
684 Park Ave.
New York, NY 10021

The Johns Hopkins University Press
Baltimore, MD 21218

The Kenyon Review
Gambier, OH 43022

Alfred A. Knopf, Inc.
201 E. 50th St.
New York, NY 10022

Lieb-Schott Publications
Pteranodon
Box 229
Bourbonnais, IL 60914

Macmillan Publishing Co.
866 3rd Ave.
New York, NY 10022

The Manhattan Review
304 3rd Ave.
New York, NY 10010

MSS
SUNY
Binghampton, NY 13901

Nantucket Review
Box 1234
Nantucket, MA 02554

New Directions Publishing Co.
80 8th Ave.
New York, NY 10011

North American Review
University of Northern Iowa
Cedar Falls, IA 50614

Ohio State University Press
1050 Carmack Rd.
Columbus, OH 43210

Orion Press
Eureka Review
16 Samuelson Rd.
Weston, CT 06883

Owl Creek Press
The Montana Review
Box 2248
Missoula, MT 59806

Pacific Quarterly
626 Coate Rd.
Orange, CA 92669

Persea Books, Sheep Meadow Press, Flying Point Books
225 Lafayette St.
New York, NY 10012

The Poetry Miscellany
English Dept.
University of Tennessee at Chattanooga
Chattanooga, TN 37403

Poetry Now
3118 K St.
Eureka, CA 95501

Riverstone Press
809 15th St.
Golden, CO 80401
Rowan Tree Press
124 Chestnut St.
Boston, MA 02108.
Rutledge and Kegan Paul
9 Park St.
Boston, MA 02108
St. Martin's Press
175 5th Ave.
New York, NY 10010
Separate Doors: A Journal of Contemporary Poetry
911 WT
Canyon, TX 79106
Southwest Review
Box 4374
Southern Methodist University
Dallas, TX 75275
The Stone
Stone Press
J. Postcard Series
Full Circle Press
1112-B Ocean St.
Santa Cruz, CA 95060

Stone Press
Happiness Holding Tank
1790 Grand River
Okemos, MI 48864
Sulphur Magazine
852 S. Bedford St.
Los Angeles, CA 90035
Taurus
Box 28
Gladstone, OR 97027-0028
Vanity Fair
350 Madison Ave.
New York, NY 10017
White Rock Review
16W481 Second Ave.
Bensenville, IL 60106
Woodrose Editions
Woodbooks
Woodcards
Box 2537
Martison, WI 53701
Yellow Moon Press
1725 Commonwealth Ave.
Brighton, MA 02135

66 *The trend to traditional poetry is due to return. Very little of the poetry written today would lend itself to memorization or recital. We think of the many students who are being deprived of learning the beauty of poetry. Many of the poems we receive are nothing more than prose broken down into lines. Surely poetry should be more than that.*

Ruth Lamb, Alura **99**

Contests
and Awards

Contests ranked (III) are reputable, offer substantial prizes or awards, and are respected in the literary community. Those marked (V) are also prestigious, though they cannot be entered by individuals; you have to be selected by a panel of judges, or your work must be submitted by your publisher. For example, The Academy of American Poets offers a variety of prizes to individuals selected by panels of judges, but for only two of these, the Lamont Poetry Selection and Walt Whitman Award, may individuals submit manuscripts. Most of our best known poets have been granted such awards or entered such contests as those in categories (III) and (V) at one time or another in their careers. Note, also, the separate list of state and provincial awards (following this section), all of which are prestigious.

Category (II) contests are quite reputable, though the prizes are generally smaller than those in (III), and they are not as widely known. Often such contests are conducted by good literary journals as a means of raising money through entry fees to keep the magazine afloat. For example, the editor of *Blue Unicorn*, one of our better journals, tells me they would have folded long ago if it were not for their annual contest. No great literary reputation is to be gained by winning them, and the awards are not great, but even a small prize is better than no payment other than copies. But most important, it always feels good to have the quality of one's work acknowledged by a judge's choice.

Contests marked (I) or (IV) should be approached with more caution. They are as various in quality as they are numerous. I am especially amused by the Chaucer Award, in which the winning poem is chosen by a blindfolded student, and the winner gets half the entry fees; the rest goes to support the Poetry Festival offered annually by St. Mary's College of Maryland. At least it is honest—and there is no pretense that the judge has selected the best. Like most of the contests ranked (I), it is frankly a fundraiser. And the cause is one with which poets can identify.

The same is true of many contests sponsored by state poetry societies, writers' groups, magazines and publishers of poetry. Some have prizes as high as a hundred or more dollars and offer publication in respected magazines. The entry fees are not excessive, and they raise money for a good cause. Some, though, are run by individuals (sometimes calling themselves "publishers," though they publish nothing but advertisements for their contests), presumably for financial gain.

One explanation I offer for these contests flourishing, as many apparently do (dozens more emerge each year), is that many poetry hobbyists enjoy the game. Tens of thousands of poets enter such contests annually. Some devote more time and attention to these contests than to seeking publication in magazines. Obviously the contests fulfill a need. Most welcome beginners (category I). Some are specialized (category IV) by theme, form, or other considerations. Send SASE for the rules and judge each individually.

That applies to all the contests listed here. I have not tried to summarize the rules for each because they are often complex, and they change from year to year, as do the deadlines. I have given only names, addresses and very general summaries. **In each case, do not enter until you have found out the current rules and deadlines.**

‡**AAA ANNUAL NATIONAL LITERARY CONTEST (I)**, Box 10492, Phoenix AZ 85064, sponsoring organization Arizona Authors' Association, award director Boye Lafayette De Mente. 42 lines maximum, $3 entry fee, submit between Jan. 1 and July 29. Prizes are $100, $50, $25, 3 honorable mentions $10 each. Include SASE with entry for contest results; no material will be returned. Winners are announced and prizes awarded in October at an awards banquet in Phoenix; winning entries are published in a special edition of *Arizona Literary Magazine*. Entries must be typed, double-spaced on 8½x11" paper.

THE ACADEMY OF AMERICAN POETS (III), 177 E. 87 St., New York, NY 10128, award director Nancy Schoenberger. The Academy gives 4 annual awards, the most prestigious of which is the Academy of American Poets Fellowship of $10,000, given to an American citizen "in recognition of distinguished poetic achievement" by nomination of the Academy's Chancellors. The Walt Whitman award pays $1,000 plus publication of a poet's first book by a major publisher (Viking Penguin in 1986). MSS of 50-100 pp. must be submitted between September 15 and November 15 with a $5 entry fee. Request entry form in August or September. The Lamont Poetry Selection, for a poet's second book under contract and scheduled for publication, is again a prize of $1,000. Peter I.B. Lavan Younger Poets Awards: three younger poets selected annually by Academy Chancellors (no applications taken); prize $1,000 each. The academy supports publication by purchasing 1,500 copies of the book for distribution to its members. Submissions must be made by a publisher, in MSS form, prior to publication. Poets entering either contest must be American citizens. The Academy also sponsors the Harold Morton Landon Translation Award ($1,000) for a published book-length translation of poetry from any language into English. Entry forms for the Whitman and Lamont awards are available at the Academy.

ALL SEASONS POETRY CONTESTS (I), Box 9314, Jacksonville, FL 32208, offers 2 prizes of $25, $10, and one subscription to the *All Seasons Poetry Promoter* Newsletter at least 2 honorable mentions, and a $5 prize for poems in tune to the times. Send SASE to All Seasons Poetry for details, and a free copy of the newsletter.

‡**ETHAN B. ALLEN (IV, "Dutiful is Beautiful")**, "author's interpretation, any form, 32 line limit. Prizes $25, $15. $10. See National Federation of State Poetry Societies.

THE AMERICAN ACADEMY & INSTITUTE OF ARTS & LETTERS (III), 633 W. 155th St., New York, NY 10032, offers annual awards in the arts, several of which are given to poets—by nomination only. These are: The Arts & Letters Awards of $5,000 each, given to 10 writers annually, some poets; The Gold Medal of the American Academy and Institute of Arts and Letters, given to a poet every 6 years; Award of Merit of $2,500 for an outstanding artist in one field of the arts, given to a poet once every 6 years; the Witter Bynner Foundation Poetry Prize of $1,500; a fellowship to the American Academy in Rome, including lodging and a stipend to a poet or fiction writer; the Jean Stein Award of $5,000 given every 3rd year to a poet whose work takes risks in expressing its commitment to the author's values and vision; the Morton Dauwen Zabel Prize of $2,500 given every 3rd year to a poet of "progressive, original and experimental tendencies rather than of academic and conservative tendencies." The 7 members of the jury are all Academy-Institute members appointed for a 3-year term. **No applications for these awards are accepted. Candidates (only published writers are considered) must be nominated by a member of the academy-institute.**

‡**AMERICAN POETRY ASSOCIATION POETRY CONTESTS (I)**, Dept. PM-87, Box 2279, Santa Cruz, CA 95063. Though the primary business of the American Poetry Association is publishing anthologies which poets have to buy to be included—at the cost of $35—their biannual contests are a genuine opportunity for poets to win substantial cash awards. I will go into the matter at length, because these contests resemble a number of similar plans offered by other companies, not listed in this book, operating for profit, though their names sound like those of nonprofit organizations. The APA's biannual contests (deadlines June 30 and December 31) have no entry fees, and most of their invitational contests (held 2-3 times per year, all entrants of the biannual contest are invited to enter) require no entry fee. The APA says that winners need not purchase books to win and "the considerable majority of winners have

ALWAYS submit MSS or queries with a stamped, self-addressed envelope (SASE) within your country or International Reply Coupons (IRCs) purchased from the post office for other countries.

not bought anything at all. All winners, in both the biannual and invitational contests are published without any need to buy a book." However, a poet reports in the poetry society newsletter that she edits: "I enter my 20 line poem with $3 entry fee in a contest proposed by The American Poetry Association. The poem is returned with congratulations on its acceptance in their current anthology. I may make my last minute corrections and return it *with* my order for a copy of the anthology. I write politely stating that I can't afford their $40 book, but here's the poem. The editor John Frost [a fictitious name, by the way] sends a second letter—with the poem attached—suggesting that I save and return the poem with *my* order. The grand prize, he reminds me, is $1,000. Since I still don't want to buy a $40 book, I return the poem, saying I don't need to be published, thanks. I was merely entering their contest. The poem returns with a note saying that it is indeed being considered for the contest, but can't be published unless I order a book. Presto: the entry fee for the contest has jumped from $3 to $43, since the poem is back on *my* desk." In fact the poem was entered and considered in the contest. The judges make photocopies of promising poems; the originals are returned for proofreading by those who want to pay to be published. Contest entry is simple and automatic. Every submission follows the APA guidelines of 1 poem only, no more than 20 lines, is entered when it first arrives. What poets need to know is that they will be tempted to buy to get published, and many poets find the temptation irrestible. The stakes are high. According to the APA, "950 poets have received over $25,000 from the APA's contests over the past 3 years." Winners are published in the *American Poetry Anthology* and most receive a copy free. Each entrant to the biannual contest is sent a copy of *The Poet's Guide to Getting Published*, a four-page flyer with some practical tips about such things as public readings and other ways of becoming published and known.

ANHINGA PRIZE FOR POETRY (II), The Anhinga Press, Box 10423, Tallahassee, FL 32302, is awarded annually—$500 and publication by Anhinga Press of a book (48-64 pp.) of poetry. Deadline January 31. $10 entry fee. Send SASE for submission guidelines and entry form.

‡**ANNUAL INTERNATIONAL NARRATIVE CONTEST (IV, Story poem)**, sponsored by Poets and Patrons, Inc., 13942 Keeler Ave., Crestwood, IL 60445, Mary Mathison, chairman. A yearly contest for previously unpublished narrative (story) poems of 40 lines or less; prizes of $75, $25, and honorable mentions without cash. Submit two copies: one an original with no identification; one carbon with name, address, contest name and title. There are no entry forms or fees. Only one poem may be entered in each annual contest, postmarked no later than September 1. The poem must not have won a cash award in any previous Poets and Patrons contests.

‡**APPRECIATION AWARD (I)**, any subject, any form, 40 line limit. Prizes of $100, $35, $15. See National Federation of State Poetry Societies.

ARTEMIS POETRY CONTEST (I), Box 945, Roanoke, VA 24005, offers an annual poetry contest with 1st prize, $100; 2nd, $50; 3rd, $25; fee $2 per poem or 3 poems/$5, deadline January 15. "Poems not previously published, two copies of each poem with name and address appearing on one copy. No poems will be returned. Winning poems published in *Artemis IX*. SASE for list of winning poems."

ATLANTA WRITING RESOURCE CENTER (I), Room 206, The Arts Exchange, 750 Kalb St., Atlanta, GA 30312. Sponsors annual contest for previously unpublished original poems of any style, 8-40 lines, fee $2 for first poem, $1 each additional. Small cash prizes and honorable mentions. Winners published in *The Chattahoochee Review* and in *Thunder & Honey*. Send 2 copies of each entry with 1 copy unidentified. No returns.

THE AWP AWARD SERIES, THE EDITH SCHIFFERT PRIZE IN POETRY (II), Old Dominion University, Norfolk, VA 23508-8510, selects a volume of poetry each year to be published by University Press of Virginia ($10 entry fee).

‡**GORDON BARBER AWARD (III)**, $200, see Poetry Society of America.

EMILY CLARK BALCH AWARDS, VIRGINIA QUARTERLY REVIEW (III), 1 West Range, Charlottesville, VA 22903, $500 given for the best poem and $500 for the best short story published in *VQR* during the year, as judged by the editors.

 The double dagger before a listing indicates that the listing is new in this edition. New markets are often the most receptive to freelance contributions.

EILEEN W. BARNES AWARD, SATURDAY PRESS, INC. (IV, Women/Feminist), Box 884, Upper Montclair, NJ 07043, editor Charlotte Mandel, annually publishes a first book of poetry by a woman over 40. The MS is selected by means of open competition or, in alternate years, by editorial board decision. The contest is widely posted when announced. Query for current information.

GEORGE BENNETT FELLOWSHIP (II), Phillips Exeter Academy, Exeter, NH 03833 provides a $5,000 fellowship plus room and board to a writer with a MS in progress. The Fellow's only official duties are to be in residence while the Academy is in session and to be available to students interested in writing. The committee favors writers who have not yet published a book-length work with a major publisher. Send SASE after September 1 for application materials. Deadline early December.

‡**BENSALEM ASSOCIATION OF WOMEN WRITERS ANNUAL COMPETITIONS (I)**, Box 236, Croydon, PA 19020-0940. Each year on a different theme (1986: Scintillations), $2/poem entry fee, 16 line limit, any form, may be previously published, cash prizes "based on total entry fees—plus" and publication.

‡**BEYMORLIN SONNET AWARD (IV, Sonnet)**, Shakespearean or other sonnet. Prizes $50, $30, $20. See National Federation of State Poetry Societies.

BLUE UNICORN POETRY CONTEST (II), 22 Avon Rd., Kensington, CA 94707, holds an annual contest with prizes of $100, $75 and $50 (and publication in *Blue Unicorn*), deadline February 1. Entry fee: $3 for first poem, $2 for others to a maximum of 5. Write for current guidelines.

BOLLINGEN PRIZE (V), Yale University Library, New Haven, CT 06520, $5,000 to an American poet for the best poetry collection published during the previous two years, or for a body of poetry written over several years. By nomination only. Judges change biennially. Announcements in January of odd-numbered years.

‡**BRITTINGHAM PRIZE IN POETRY (III)**, University of Wisconsin Press, 114 N. Murray St., Madison, WI 53706, award director Ronald Wallace. An annual award of $500 is given to a book-length poetry MS (50-80 pp.), which will be subsequently published by the press. MSS are considered from Sept. 1-30 each year; there is a $10 reading fee. Entries should be typed (MS-size SASE included) and previously unpublished, though they can be entered in other contests.

‡**JOSEPH E. BRODINE MEMORIAL AWARDS (I)**, See Connecticut Poetry Society Awards.

‡**BUCKNELL SEMINAR FOR YOUNGER POETS (IV, College students)**, Bucknell University, Lewisburg, PA 17837, director John Wheatcroft. This is not a contest for poems but for fellowships to the Bucknell Seminar, held four weeks in January every year. Seniors and second-semester juniors from American colleges are eligible to compete for the ten fellowships, which consist of tuition, room, board, and spaces for writing. The staff, which includes Professor Wheatcroft plus Bucknell's Poet-in-Residence and visiting seminar poets, conduct workshops, offer readings, and available for tutorials. Application deadline for each year's seminar is November 1 of the previous year. Students chosen for fellowships will be notified on November 20.

BUSH FOUNDATION FELLOWSHIPS FOR ARTISTS (IV, Regional), E-900 First National Bank Bldg., St. Paul, MN 55101, are for Minnesota residents over 25 years of age to help writers, (poetry, fiction, literary nonfiction and playwriting), visual artists, choreographers and composers set aside time for work-in-progress or exploration of new directions. Maximum of 15 awards of a maximum of $20,000 (and up to $5,000 additional for production and traveling expenses) are awarded each year for 6-18 month fellowships. Deadline November 15.

BYLINERS OF CORPUS CHRISTI (IV, Regional), Box 6015, Corpus Christi, TX 78411, a 45-year-old writer's group, sponsors an annual "Texas-wide" writer's competition for state residents, winter Texans or out-of-state members. Awards in rhymed, unrhymed and short poetry (and fiction and non-fiction). Deadline is March 31. For rules send SASE.

‡**CALIFORNIA FEDERATION OF CHAPARRAL POETS, ROBERT FROST CHAPTER, ANNUAL POETRY CONTEST (I)**, c/o Katharine Wilson, 1652 Bel Air Ave., San Jose, CA 95126. This annual contest has 6 categories; a part of California; triolet; free verse; haiku/senryu; sonnet; and humorous. Prizes are $25, $15, and $10 in each category. Entry limit 2 poems in each category, entry fee $1/poem for nonmembers. Submissions may be previously published or unpublished, "in good taste," and

original. Students, 9-12 grades, may enter. Deadline mid-August. The Federation also sponsors monthly contests.

‡**CALIFORNIA WRITERS' ROUNDTABLE POETRY CONTEST (I)**, sponsored by the California Writers' Roundtable, Lou Carter Keay, chairman, Suite 807, 11684 Ventura Blvd., Studio City, CA 91604-2652. An annual contest with $10-20 cash prizes for unpublished poems on any subject, in various forms, no length limit. Members may submit free; nonmembers pay an entry fee, usually $4. Deadline is April 30. Send SASE for guidelines.

‡**MELVILLE CANE AWARD (III)**, $500 for a book, see Poetry Society of America.

‡**CANTERBURY PRESS LIMERICK CONTEST (IV, Limericks)**, 5540 Vista Del Amigo, Anaheim, CA 92807, phone 714-637-1266, editor Jay Cotter. Annual contest for limerick form only; not previously published; any subject, style, or treatment; fees $2/limerick or $5 for three on one page by same author. Prizes: $500, $400, $300, $250, $150, 6th-10th places, $25/each. No limit on submissions. Deadline July 15.

CINCINNATI POETRY REVIEW (II), English Dept. 069, University of Cincinnati, Cincinnati OH 45221, offers in each issue a poetry contest for poems of all types, prizes of $150 and $50 and publication in the magazine. Continual deadline.

CINTAS FELLOWSHIP PROGRAM (IV, Regional), Institute of International Education, 809 United Nations Plaza, New York, NY 10017, makes awards of $7,500 to young professional Cuban writers and artists living outside of Cuba. Deadline for applications March 1.

‡**GERTRUDE B. CLAYTON AWARD (III)**, $250, see Poetry Society of America.

COLUMBIA UNIVERSITY TRANSLATION CENTER (IV, Translations), 307A Mathematics, Columbia University, New York, NY 10027, send SASE for guidelines and descriptions of various award programs.

CONNECTICUT POETRY SOCIETY (I), % Pat McDonald, Box 93, Poquanock, CT 06064, annually offers The Joseph E. Brodine Memorial Award of $50-150, entry $2/poem, July deadline.

‡**BERNARD F. CONNERS PRIZE (III)**, c/o The Paris Review, 541 East 72nd St., New York, NY 10021. This is an annual award that offers a prize of $1,000 and publication in *The Paris Review*. Submissions must be 200 + lines and previously unpublished; no entry forms are necessary, and there are no entry fees. Deadline is May 1 each year.

‡**INA COOLBRITH CIRCLE ANNUAL POETRY CONTEST (IV, Regional)**, c/o Tom Berry, 761 Sequoia Woods Place, Concord, California, annual for California residents only, Prizes $10-50, for poems up to 42 lines in several categories, August deadline. Entry fee $2/poem except for members of the Ina Coolbrith Circle.

‡**CRITERION WRITING CONTEST (I)**, Box 16315, Greenville, SC 29606, award director Terri McCord. An annual contest for poems of any length and form; awards certificates and prizes of $50, $25, and $10, plus certificates for 5 honorable mentions. Entry fee $1/poem, deadline Dec. 31.

‡**GUSTAV DAVIDSON AWARD (III)**, $500, see Poetry Society of America.

‡**MARY CAROLYN DAVIES AWARD (III)**, $250, see Poetry Society of America.

‡**BILLIE MURRAY DENNY POETRY AWARD (I, III)**, c/o Janet Overton, Lincoln College, Lincoln, IL 62656, prizes of $1,000, $450 and $200. Open to poets who have not previously published a book of poetry with a commercial or university press (except for chapbooks with a circulation of less than 250). Enter up to 3 poems, 100 lines or less at $2/poem. Poems may be on any subject, using any style, but may not contain "any vulgar, obscene, suggestive or offensive word or phrase. Entry form and fees, payable to Poetry Contest, Lincoln College, must be postmarked no later than May 30. Winning poems are published in *The Denny Poems*, an annual anthology available for $3 from Lincoln College. Write for entry form.

DEVIS AWARD (II), University of Missouri Press, Breakthrough Editor, 200 Lewis, Columbia, MO 65211. Judging in odd-numbered years; one award chosen for each year; $500 advance on book publication by the University of Missouri Press, for a poet who has not previously published in book form or for an established writer who is using a form for the first time. For rules and entry fee send SASE in fall.

‡**ALICE FAY DI CASTAGNOLA AWARD (III)**, $200, see Poetry Society of America.

‡**DIAL-A-POEM CONTEST (I)**, 475 Chestnut Ave., Bakersfield, CA 93305, award directors Helen Shanley and Mary Laird. An annual contest wanting poems suitable for telephone listening; prizes are $150, $100, and $50. Poems may be published or unpublished. Entry fee $2/poem; checks or money orders made out to Mary Laird; deadlines March 15 and September 15.

‡**EMILY DICKINSON AWARD (III)**, $100, see Poetry Society of America.

THE DISCOVERY/*THE NATION (III), The Poetry Center of 92nd St. YM-YWHA, 1395 Lexington Ave., New York, NY 10128, offers a contest for poets whose work has not yet been published in book form. Submit 4 complete sets of 10 poems, no more than 500 lines total. Previously published poems are acceptable. Put name, address and phone numbers (day and evening) on cover sheet, not on poems. Entries will not be returned. Prizes: $200 and invitation to read at Poetry Center. Deadline February. Write for complete information.

‡**DOUBLE-EDGE POETRY CONTEST (I)**, 3210 W. Antoinette St., Peoria, IL 61605, sponsored by Peoria Poetry Club, an irregularly held contest ("when club elects to have a contest") offering prizes of $50, $30, and $20 in each of two categories: short verse (not more than 12 lines, humor preferred), and open (not more than 44 lines, any form). Entry fees: $1 for each of first and second entries, 50¢ for each additional, up to six. Send entries to Ctlenna Lamb at address above.

ELECTRUM MAGAZINE, ALICE JACKSON POETRY PRIZE (II), 2222 Silk Tree Dr., Tustin, CA 92680-7129. Maximum 10 poems, fee is $2 per poem. Entries must not have been previously published. Annual contest. Prizes: $200, $100, $50 plus publication in *Electrum*. Deadline is August 30. SASE for return of manuscript.

‡**EVE'S LEGACY . . . ADAM'S APPLE (I)**, c/o Midwood Post Office, Box 366, Brooklyn, NY 11230, is an annual contest, April 15 deadline, $25 prize, 32 line limit, unpublished, in English, any style or subject. Entry fee $2 for first poem, $1 for others up to a total of 5.

‡**NORMA FARBER AWARD (III)**, $1,000 for a first book, see Poetry Society of America.

FLORIDA STATE POETS ASSOCIATION (I), Box 387, Beverly Hill, FL 32665, an annual contest with awards of from $5 to $100 in each of 22 different categories. Entry fee, categories 1 and 2, $2/poem; 3 through 17, $1/poem; 18 through 22 (student categories, including grade school students), no entry fee. Send entries to: Agnes Homan, FSPA Poetry Contest Chairman, 99 Spring Garden Road, Sebring, FL 33870.

‡**FOR POETS ONLY (I)**, Box 1382, Jackson Heights, NY 11372, director Lillian Walsh. A quarterly contest with $2/poem entry fee and prizes of $50, $25, and $10; poems are published in *For Poets Only*, a photocopied, digest-sized collection; deadline for the January 1 issue, December 1.

‡**CONSUELO FORD AWARD (III)**, $250, see Poetry Society of America.

GALAXY OF VERSE (I, IV, Black American). Prizes $30-10. See National Society of State Poetry Societies.

GEORGIA STATE POETRY SOCIETY, INC., DANIEL WHITEHEAD HICKY NATIONAL AWARDS (I), % Edwin Davin Vickers, Suite 111, 1421 Peachtree St. NE, Atlanta, GA 30309, offers an annual poetry competition, $500 in prizes, August 20 deadline.

‡**GREAT LAKES COLLEGES ASSOCIATION NEW WRITERS' AWARDS (IV, First Books)**, %English Dept., Albion College, Albion, MI 49224. Publisher of first collections of poetry may submit proofs or published books by February 28 each year. The poet selected will tour the 12 GLCA colleges, receive an honorarium of at least $150 from each. Travel and entertainment expenses will be paid by GLCA.

GUGGENHEIM FELLOWSHIPS (III), John Simon Guggenheim Foundation, 90 Park Ave., New York, NY 10016. Approximately 280 Guggenheims are awarded each year generally to persons between the ages of 30-45 who have already demonstrated unusual capacity for productive scholarship or unusual creative ability in the arts. The amounts of the grants vary. The average grant is about $20,000. Application deadline October 1.

‡HACKNEY LITERARY AWARDS (II), Birmingham-Southern College, Box A-3, Birmingham, AL 35254. This competition, sponsored by the Cecil Hackney family since 1969, offers $2,000 in prizes for poetry and short stories as part of the annual Birmingham-Southern Writer's Conference. Poems with a maximum of 50 lines must be postmarked by December 31; only original, unpublished manuscripts may be entered. Winners are announced at the conference, which is held in March.

‡RALPH HAMMOND POETRY CONTEST (II), Alabama State Poetry Society, Box 486, Arab, AL 35016, award director R.C. Hammond. The contest is open to members and nonmembers; prizes $75, $50, $25, $15, $10, and 5 honorable mentions at $5 each. Entry fee $1/poem, payable to Alabama State Poetry Society, deadline February 15, no limit on number of entries, line limit 42. Any form, style, or theme. Top 5 winners will be published in *The Sampler*, anthology of the Society, unless publication is declined by the author.

‡ETHEL EIKEL HARVEY MEMORIAL AWARD (IV), lyric form, 24 lines maximum. Prizes $75, $50, $25. See National Federation of State Poetry Societies.

‡CECIL HEMLEY AWARD (III), $300, see Poetry Society of America.

‡DANIEL WHITEHEAD HICKY NATIONAL AWARDS (I), Georgia State Poetry Society, Inc., Box 120, Epworth, GA 30541, award director Ethelene Dyer Jones. An annual contest with prizes of $250, $100, $50, and for best sonnet $50; 5 special recognitions of $10 each. "Beginners may enter; experienced have better chance for prizes." Poems must be unpublished, no more than 50 lines, in any form. Entry fee $5 for first poem, $1 for each additional. Deadline August 19. Each entrant will receive a hardback copy of *Poems of Daniel Whitehead Hicky*.

‡INDIANA FALL POET'S RENDEZVOUS CONTEST (I), 808 East 32nd St., Anderson, IN 46014, contest director Glenna Glee Jenkins, an annual award that offers approximately $350 or more in 10 or more categories. Entry fee is "usually $2-3 for entire contest," deadline September 1. Poems can be up to 40 lines in any one of 10 specified forms. Send SASE for brochure.

INTERNATIONAL SHAKESPEAREAN SONNET CONTEST (IV, Form), 2546 Atlantic, Franklin Park, IL 60131, an annual contest sponsored by Poets Club of Chicago. Prizes: $50, $35, $15, no entry fee, deadline Sept. 1. For details and rules, send SASE to contest chairman, Agnes Wathall Tatera, at the address above.

‡IOWA ARTS COUNCIL LITERARY AWARDS (IV, Iowa), Iowa Arts Council, State Capitol Complex, Des Moines, IA 50319, award director Marilyn Parks. Annual awards in two categories, poetry and fiction, with prizes of $1,000 and $500. Contestants must be legal residents of Iowa. Poems may be 50-150 lines and must be previously unpublished. No entry fee, deadline July 31.

THE CHESTER H. JONES FOUNDATION NATIONAL POETRY COMPETITION (III), Box 43033, Cleveland, OH 44143, an annual competition for persons in the USA or American citizens living abroad; lower age limit 16. Prizes: $1,000, $500, $250, and $50 honorable mentions. Winning poems plus others called "commendations" are published in a chapbook available for $2 from the foundation. Entry fee $1/poem, no more than 10 entries, deadline March 15. Distinguished poets serve as judges.

JUNIPER PRIZE (II), University of Massachusetts Press, % Mail Room, Amherst, MA 01003, is an annual award of $1,000 and book publication in cloth and paperback editions of a book of poetry (need not be a first book). Entry fee $7 and for return of manuscript a SASE. Deadline October 1.

KENTUCKY STATE POETRY SOCIETY (I), % James W. Proctor, 505 Southland Blvd., Louisville, KY 40214, offers an annual contest with 31 categories and over $1,000 in prizes. Any subject, traditional rhymed form, 28-line limit. Prizes $25, $15, $10.

‡JOHN KERR MEMORIAL AWARD (I), any subject, any form. 40 line limit. Prizes of $150, $100, $50. See National Federation of State Poetry Societies.

‡RUTH LAKE AWARD (III), $100, see Poetry Society of America.

‡**THE LAMONT POETRY SELECTION (III)**, for a second book, $1,000 plus publication, see The Academy of American Poets.

‡**HAROLD MORTON LANDON TRANSLATION AWARD (IV, Translation)**, $1,000 for a book-length translation of poetry from any language into English, see The Academy of American Poets.

‡**PETER I.B. LAVAN, YOUNGER POETS AWARDS (V)**, three younger poets selected annually for $1,000 prize to each, see The Academy of American Poets.

‡**ELIAS LIEBERMAN AWARD (III)**, $100, see Poetry Society of America.

‡**LEONA LLOYD MEMORIAL AWARD (I)**, any subject, any form, 30 lines or less contestants must not have won a previous award of $25 or less. Prizes $25, $15, $10. See National Federation of State Poetry Societies.

THE LOFT-MCKNIGHT WRITERS AWARDS (IV, Minnesota), 2301 E. Franklin Ave., Minneapolis, MN 55406 are 8 grants of $6,000 each to Minnesota poets and creative writers. Applicants must be state residents for at least 1 year prior to applying. Writers who have received grants in literature totaling $12,000 or more over the 2 years prior to applying are not eligible. Writers should write or call for guidelines.

LOUISIANA STATE SOCIETY POETRY DAY CONTEST (I), c/o Glen Swetman, President, Box 1162, Thibodaux, LA 70302, award director Jessica Gonsoulin, #L-201, 2300 Severn Ave., Metairie, LA 70001, to whom contest entries should be sent. The annual "Poetry Day Contest" offers awards in ten categories; entry fee, category 1, $3/poem, $5/2 poems; all other categories, $1/poem. Deadline Aug. 19. Prizes range from $5 to $30.

‡**JOHN A. LUBBE MEMORIAL AWARD (I)**, any subject, any form, prizes $20-50, see National Federation of State Societies.

LYRIC ANNUAL COLLEGIATE POETRY CONTEST, THE LYRIC (IV, Traditional), 307 Dunton Dr. SW, Blacksburg, VA 24060, deadline postmark June 1, offers a poetry contest in traditional forms for fulltime undergraduate students enrolled in any 4-year American or Canadian college or university, prizes totaling $500. Send SASE for rules.

MACOMB FANTASY FACTORY, EGO FLIGHTS (I), 13532 Terry Dr., Utica, MI 48087, award director Del Corey, offers two annual poetry contests, one for adults with prizes of $50, $25 and $10, and youth division (18 and under) with prizes of $30, $20 and $10. 10 honorable mentions in each category. All winners and honorable mentions are published in the club's annual book, **Ego Flights**. 30-line limit. Entry fee is $1 for each poem by an adult, 50¢ for each poem by a youth. Deadline April 1. Associate memberships and critiquing services available.

‡**MAPLECON SF, FANTASY, AND SCIENCE POETRY COMPETITION (IV, Science fiction, fantasy)**, 2105 Thistle Cr., Ottawa, ON Canada K1H 5P4, no entry fee. Send SASE for rules.

LENORE MARSHALL/NATION PRIZE FOR POETRY (III), c/o Emily Sack and *The Nation*, 72 Fifth Ave., New York, NY 10011, phone 212-242-8400. Co-sponsored by the New Hope Foundation and The Nation magazine, the Lenore Marshall/*Nation*, prize is $7,500 award for the outstanding book of poems published in the United States during the previous year. Books of poetry must be submitted by the publisher to each of the judges at addresses listed in an April press release; deadline early June.

‡**JOHN MASEFIELD AWARD (III)**, $500, see Poetry Society Award.

‡**MASSACHUSETTS STATE POETRY SOCIETY AWARD (I)**, any form, any subject, 40 line limit. Prizes $25, $15, $10. See National Federation of State Poetry Societies.

‡**LUCILLE MEDWICK AWARD (III)**, $500, see Poetry Society of America.

‡**MID-SOUTH POETRY FESTIVAL (I, IV)**, The Poetry Society of Tennessee, 811 Pope, Memphis, TN 38112, is an annual event sponsoring a wide range of contests with small prizes (up to $50, including jewels and other items). Some are open to all poets, some only to those attending the festival, some to mid-south poets, some to students (grades 1-12). Most are for poems on specific themes or in specific forms, but some are for any subject in any form, 50 line limit. Prizes total more than $1,200.

‡**THE MYSTICAL UNICORN (I)**, Box 1580, New Albany, IN 47150, holds two contests per year, deadlines at the end of March and October, any style, subject, no line limit, unpublished, entry fee $3/poem, prizes: $200, $50, $25 plus 5 Awards of Merit at $5 each.

NASHVILLE NEWSLETTER POETRY CONTEST (I, II), Box 60535, Nashville, TN 37206, Robert Dale Miller, Editor/Publisher. Any style or subject up to 40 lines. One unpublished poem to a page with name, address in upper left corner. Entry fee of $5 for up to 3 poems. Must be sent all at once. Prizes of $50, $25, and $10 with at least 50 Certificates of Merit.

NATIONAL ENDOWMENT FOR THE ARTS (III), Literature Program, 1100 Pennsylvania Ave. NW, Washington, DC 20506. The Fellowships for Creative Artists comprise the largest program for individual grants available for poets (and other writers and artists). Dozens of awards of $20,000 are made each year to poets who have published a book or at least 20 poems in magazines in the last 10 years. Decisions are made solely on the quality of the submitted material. Deadline March 3. They also offer grants of up to $10,000 to nonprofit organizations to support residencies for published writers of poetry, Fellowships for Translators ($10,000 or $20,000), and other programs to assist publishers and promoters of poetry. Write for complete guidelines.

NATIONAL FEDERATION OF STATE POETRY SOCIETIES PAST PRESIDENT'S AWARD (I), any subject, any form, 40 line limit. Prizes $50, $30, $20. See Federation Listing in Organizations.

‡**NATIONAL FEDERATION OF STATE POETRY SOCIETIES PRIZE (III)**, $1,000, any subject to 100 line, $5 entry fee, See Federation listing in Organizations.

NATIONAL POETRY SERIES ANNUAL OPEN COMPETITION (II, III), 18 W. 30th St., New York, NY 10001, between January 1 and February 15 considers book-length (approximately 48-64 pp.) MSS, entry fee $10. Must send SASE for return of manuscript. The five winners are published by participating small press, university press and trade publishers.

‡**NATIONAL WRITERS CLUB ANNUAL POETRY CONTEST (I)**, Suite 620, 1450 S. Havana, Aurora, CO 80012, award director Donald E. Bower, an annual contest with prizes of $100, $50, $25, $10, and $5 plus honorable mentions. Entry fee $5/poems; additional fee charged if poem is longer than 40 lines. Deadline August 3, 1987. All subjects and forms are acceptable.

‡**NEVADA POETRY SOCIETY ANNUAL CONTEST (I)**, 1470 Kirkham Way, Reno, NV 89503, award director Ida E. Sprague. This contest offers cash awards of $50, $25, and $10 in each of three categories: sonnet; free verse (40-line limit); and any other form. Entry fee is $2 for each of the first 3 poems, $1 for each additional. Entries must be received by August 1. Winning poems are read at the September meeting of the Nevada Poetry Society.

NEW ENGLAND SAMPLER CREATIVE WRITING CONTEST (I), Box 306, RFD # 1, Belfast, ME 04915, deadline June 15, poems up to 30 lines relating to New England. Entry fee $3/3 poems. Prizes $100, $50 and $25.

‡**NEW MADROS WRITERS AWARD (IV)**, any form, 40 line limit. Prizes $25, $15, $10. See National Federaton of State Poetry Societies.

‡**NEW YORK POETRY FORUM ANNUAL AWARDS CONTEST (1)**, Box 855, Madison Square Station, 149 E. 23rd St., New York, NY 10159. First-place awards from $10 to $35 are offered in 34 categories; apply to Dr. Dorothea Neale, 3064 Albany Crescent, Bronx, NY 10463. Deadline for nonmembers, March 20, for members, April 5. Winning poems are read at various awards programs. No entry fee.

‡**NEW ZEALAND LITERARY FUND**,   The Secretary, New Zealand Literary Fund Advisory Committee, Department of Internal Affairs, Private Bag, Wellington, New Zealand. A brochure entitled "Sources of Support for New Zealand Writing" is available from the Literary Fund at the address above.

NORTHEASTERN STATES POETRY CONTEST (IV, Regional), % Charles M. Henry Printing Co., Box 68, Greensburg PA 15601. To be eligible to enter you must live or attend school in the Middle Atlantic States, including MD, District of Columbia or New England. You can enter if you can list an address in the Northeast. Limit: 25 lines, any style or subject. Entries not returned. Entry fee $6 per 3 poems. Prizes: $500, $250 and $100. Deadline November 1. Winners' collection published and distributed free to all entrants.

OBSERVER & RONALD DUNCAN FOUNDATION INTERNATIONAL POETRY COMPETI-TION (III), % Faber and Faber, Inc., 39 Thompson St., Winchester, MA 01890. It is intended that this competition, which is one the largest in the world in terms of money awarded and number of entries, will be held every two years; the first was in 1985. The competition is open to the world but poems must be in English. First prize is £5,000, and there are five prizes of £200 and 10 prizes of £100. Distinguished poets serve as judges. "Competitors may submit as many entries as they wish, provided that each poem is accompanied by an entry fee of $5 (U.S. dollars)."

‡**OHIO POETRY DAY ASSOCIATION (I)**, 3520 St. Rt. 56, Mechanicsburg, OH 43044, contest chairman Amy Jo Zook. 30-35 contests/year with prizes ranging from "$75 down." Requirements vary with contest, $5 fee covers all contests, no fee for students, deadline July 10. Contest information available after April 16. Money-winning poems are printed in a copyrighted "Best of 19—" chapbook (85 pp., one-color matte card cover, saddle-stapled), $5 postpaid.

‡**OPEN MIND, INTERNATIONAL LITERARY COMPETITION (I)**, Box 1557, Pascagoula, MS 39567, award director Nina T. Bratt. There are competitions in 5 categories: limerick, dirty limerick, January haiku, July haiku, and "open mind—anything goes." Prizes in first 4 categories are $10 and $5, $20 and $10 in the open mind category. Entry fee $1/poem, or one entry in each category for $3. Deadline for all categories is March 13.

OWL CREEK PRESS POETRY BOOK COMPETITON (II), Box 2248, Missoula, MT 59806, is an annual competion in which 1-3 books are chosen for publication.Unpublished poems in submitted MSS are considered for publication for *The Montana Review*. MSS should be a minimum of 50 typed pages and should include an acknowledgments page for previous publications. Deadline December 31; entry fee $8, for which winners receive a copy of the winning book. Winners receive 100 copies of published book. Write for information on Owl Creek Poetry Book Contest.

‡**PENNSYLVANIA POETRY SOCIETY ANNUAL CONTEST, WINE AND ROSES POETRY CONTEST, PEGASUS CONTEST FOR STUDENTS, FULL MOON POETRY CONTEST (I, IV, Members)**, 623 N. 4th St., Reading, PA 19601, award director Leonard Paul Harris. The deadline for the society's annual contest, which has 12 categories open to nonmembers and 4 to members only, is January 15. Grand prize in category 1 (open) will be $100 in 1987; prizes in other categories range from $10-25. Entry fees are $1/poem for nonmembers except for the grand prize, which requires an entry fee of $2/poem for everybody. The Wine and Roses poetry contest, sponsored by the Wallace Stevens Chapter, has prizes of $50, $25, and $15 plus newspaper publication and telecast; entry fee $1/poem; deadline June 1; address same as above. For information about the Pegasus Contest for Students, write to Toni-Francoise Lyons at the same address. For information about the Full Moon Poetry Contest (deadline April 1), send SASE to Ken Mullen, Delco Dept. of Parks and Recreation, 1671 N. Providence Rd., Media, PA 19603.

‡**PERRYMAN-VISSER NATIONAL POETRY AWARD (IV, Visser Sonnet)**, Italian-like sonnets but most of the rhymes are not at the end of lines but scattered internally, Prizes $25, $15, $10. See National Federation of State Poetry Societies.

PITT POETRY SERIES (II, III), University of Pittsburgh Press, 127 N. Bellefield Ave., Pittsburgh, PA 15260, editor Ed Ochester. Poets **who have not previously published a book of poetry may submit to the Agnes Lynch Starrett Poetry Prize, 48-120 typed pages, $7.50 handling fee, postmark during March or April, $1,000 + publication. Do not submit MS before requesting and reading rules.** They also publish 4-5 books a year of at least 48 pp. by **poets who have previously published one book or more. Submit during September and October only. Before sending MS, send SASE for complete information.**

‡**PLAINS POETS AWARD (IV, Change)**, any form. Prizes $25, $15, $10. See National Federation of State Poetry societies.

‡**PLUMA DE ORO WRITING COMPETITION (IV, Spanish)**, c/o Amber H. Moss, Dean of Graduate School of International Studies, University of Miami, Miami, FL 33168, offers annual awards of $2,000 first place and a $500 student prize to anyone living in the United States or Puerto Rico, writing in Spanish. Deadline October 12. Co-sponsored by the American Express Co. and University of Miami.

THE POETRY CENTER BOOK AWARD (III), 1600 Holloway Ave., San Francisco, CA 94132, director Frances Phillips. Method for entering contest is to submit a published book and a $4 entry fee; book must be published and copyrighted during the year of the contest and submitted by Dec. 31. "Beginners may enter but in the past winners have published several previous books." Deadline Dec. 31. Translations are acceptable but "we cannot judge works that are not in English." Books should be by an individual living writer, and must be entirely poetry. Prize (only one) is $500 and an invitation to read for the Poetry Center. No entry form is required.

POETRY SOCIETY OF MICHIGAN (I), 825 Cherry Ave., Big Rapids, MI 49307, The Open Contest has a January 15 deadline—no restrictions, $2/poem for all entries, prizes of $100, $30, $20. The Annual Contest, November 15 deadline, has a fee of $1/poem except for members of PSM. Poems for the Annual must be unpublished and may be entered in any of 9 categories, prizes of $25, $15, $5 and lesser prizes. PSM also publishes a quarterly, *Peninsula Poets*, for members' poems.

‡POETRY SOCIETY OF TENNESSEE AWARD (I), any subject, any form, 40 line limit. Prizes $25, $15, $10. See National Federation of State Poetry Societies.

POETRY SOCIETY OF TEXAS (I), any subject, any form, 40 line limit. Prizes of $100, $35, and $15. See National Federation of State Poetry Societies.

‡POETRY SOCIETY OF VIRGINIA CONTEST (I), Box 55, Llanarth Rt. 1, Esmont, VA 22937, contest chairman Elizabeth D. Solomon, offering awards for unpublished poems in English. Prizes range from $10 to $100; most contests are open to anyone, but some are open only to members of The Poetry Society of Virginia, and one is for students in a public or private secondary school. Entry fee $1/ poem; poems may not be submitted elsewhere until contest results are announced. Deadline Jan. 31. Send SASE for rules.

‡POETS' DINNER CONTEST (IV), 2214 Derby St., Berkeley, CA 94705. Since 1926 there has been an annual awards banquet sponsored by the ad hoc Poets' Dinner Group, usually at Spenger's Fish Grotto (a Berkeley Landmark). Three typed copies of poems in any form or length on any subject are submitted anonymously (January 15 deadline), and the winning poems (grand prize), 1st, 2nd, 3rd, and honorable mentions in 8 categories) are read at the banquet; contestant must be present to win.

‡POETS OF THE VINEYARD CONTEST (I), %Winnie E. Fitzpatrick, Box 77, Kenwood, CA 95452, an annual contest sponsored by the Sonoma County Chapter of the California Federation of Chaparral Poets with entries in 7 categories: traditional forms; free verse, 16 lines or less; free verse, 17-32 lines; light or humorous; short verse (maximum of 12 lines); haiku/senryu and tanka; theme poem (grapes, vineyards, wine, viticulture). Prizes in each category are $20, $15, and $10, with a grand prize chosen from category winners ($50.) Deadline March 1, entry fee $2/poem. Prize winning poems will be published in the annual **Winners Anthology**.

‡PRO DOGS NATIONAL CHARITY OPEN POETRY COMPETITION (I, IV, Dogs), New Road, Ditton, nr Maidstone, Kent, England. The Pro Dogs National Charity is an organization that promotes taking pet dogs to visit elderly and disabled people. The contest, deadline July 31, is open to anyone, poems on any subject, in any style, up to a maximum of 32 lines. There is a special category of poems dedicated to or about a dog. Fee £1 for first poem, 25p for any others (or, for those under 16, 40p for the first, 10p for others). Prizes: 100£ for overall winner, 25£ and trophy for best poem about a dog, 5£ for runner up poems selected for publication, 10£, 5l and 3£ prizes in "Under 16-year-old" category.

‡PRUNE POETRY CONTEST (I, IV, "Prunes and others"), sponsored by the Robert Frost chapter of the California Federation of Chaparral Poets and the Campbell Historical Museum Association, % Eulah H. Blaine, 91 S. 4th St., Campbell, CA 95008. A contest (1986 was the third annual) held in collaboration with the Campbell, California Wine, Art and Prune Festival. Prizes are $15, $10, and $5; winning poems will be read during the festival and later bound into an anthology for the Historical Museum. Deadline is April 7. Specified form for poems varies from year to year; line limit is 32. (See other contests listed under California Federation of Chaparral Poets.)

‡PSYCH IT (I, IV, Psychology), %Charlotte L. Babicky, 6507 Bimini Court, Apollo Beach, FL 33570, who says "I am considering holding contests twice a year; depends on poet response." Entry fee, $1/poem, prizes $10, $7, and $5. Any form, 25 lines maximum, on themes of indulgence and/or overindulgence, deadline Jan. 15. Make checks or money orders payable to Charlotte L. Babicky.

PTERANODON AWARD (II), Lieb-Schott Publications any subject free style, 40 line limit. Prizes $25, $15, $10. See National Federation of State Poetry Societies.

PULITZER PRIZE IN ARTS AND LETTERS (III), % Secretary of the Pulitzer Prize Board, 702 Journalism, Columbia University, New York, NY 10027 offers 5 $1,000 prizes each year, including one in poetry, for books published in the calendar year preceding the award. Submit 4 copies of published books (or galley proofs if book is being published after November) before December 31. Deadline November 1.

‡**RHODE ISLAND STATE POETRY SOCIETY AWARD (I)**, any form, any subject 40 line limit. Prizes $25, $15, $10. See National Federation of State Poetry Societies.

‡**FERNANDO RIELO PRIZE FOR MYSTICAL POETRY (IV, Mystical))**, Fernando Rielo Foundation, Jorge Juan, 102-2—B, 28009 Madrid, Spain. The sixth annual competition, for which the prize is 600,000 Spanish pesetas, is for "Any unpublished poem or group of poems with a total length of 600 to 1,300 lines, written in or translated into Spanish." The winning entry will be published by the Fernando Rielo Foundation one year after the awarding of the prize. Fernando Rielo, who selects and presides over the jury, says of the prize: ". . . an effort will be made to award it to true poets who, though not regarded as mystics in terms of a typical definition, nevertheless harbor intimate dreams reflecting an essential datum of art: the mystery of suffering is the poet's companion."

MARY ROBERTS RINEHART FOUNDATION AWARD (III), % Richard Bausch, Mary Roberts Rinehart Fund, English Dept., George Mason University, 4400 University Dr., Fairfax, VA 22030. Two $2,500 grants are made annually to writers who need financial assistance "to complete work definitely projected." Grants in fiction and poetry will be given in even-numbered years, those in drama and nonfiction will be made in odd numbered years. A writer's work must be nominated by an established author or editor; no written recommendations are necessary. Nominations must be accompanied by a sample of the nominee's work, up to 25 pp. of poetry and 30 pp. of fiction. Deadline November 1.

CARL SANDBURG AWARDS (III), sponsored by Friends of the Chicago Public Library, 78 E. Washington St., Chicago, IL 60602, are given annually to Chicago-area writers for new books in 4 categories including poetry. Each author receives $500. Publisher or authors should submit two copies of books published between June 1 of one year and June 30 of the next. Deadline October 1.

SECOND COMING (II), Box 31249, San Francisco CA 94131. "Poetry chapbook" (maximum 48 pp.) contest with winner published in 87, 87 poetry winners published in 88, etc." Send SASE for details.

‡**SHELLEY MEMORIAL AWARD (III)**, $2,000, see Poetry Society of America.

THE SIGNPOST PRESS POETRY CHAPBOOK COMPETITION (II), 412 N. State St., Bellingham, WA 98225, is an annual contest for 20 pp. MS of poetry. Winner receives $100 and 50 copies of a 500 print run. No fee if you subscribe to *The Bellingham Review* ($8 for 4 issues); fee for nonsubscribers $5. Submission period is from October 1 to December 31 (postmark).

‡**BESSIE ARCHER SMITH MEMORIAL AWARD (IV, Narrative, Women/Feminist)**, 40 line limit. Prizes $25, $15, $10. See National Federation of State Poetry Societies.

‡**SOUTHERN CALIFORNIA CHAPTER, ANNUAL NATIONAL CONTEST (I)**, 2266 6th St., La Verne, CA 91750, award director Ernestine Hoff Emrick. An annual contest for previously unpublished poems of any form, on any theme (40-line limit) with prizes of $100, $50, $25, and five at $5. No limit on number of entries, entry fee $1/poem, deadline August 15. Poems must not have been awarded a previous money prize. (Also see Dial-A-Poem).

SOUTHERN CALIFORNIA POET'S PEN (I), Box 85152-187, San Diego, CA 92138, award director Jerine P. Watson-Miner. A semi-annual contest (deadlines May 31 and Dec. 31) with prizes of $100, $75, $50, and 10 honorable mentions of $10 each. Submissions must be previously unpublished, of any length or style (but "prefer no haiku, no epics"). Entry fee $5/poem. Name and address on back of sheet only.

SOUTHWEST REVIEW, ELIZABETH MATCHETT STOVER MEMORIAL AWARD (II), Box 4374, Southern Methodist University, Dallas, TX 75275. This $100 award is given annually for the best poem published in the quarterly during the year as judged by the editors.

‡**THE STAR FOUNDATION POETRY AWARDS (I)**, Box 111627, Nashville, TN 37222, award director Melissa A. Cannon, sponsors cash awards for poetry in twelve categories (deadlines 15th of various months) as well as in monthly (deadline 1st of month) unrestricted contests. Prizes: $70, $40, $20, and citations for honorable mentions. Entry fee is $5 for each three poems. Submissions may be previ-

ously published and can be entered in other contests. Winning poems are not published. Send for complete guidelines and contest categories.

‡**JESS STRADER POETRY CONTEST (I)**, Aberdeen Fireside Group, 418 9th Ave. SE, Aberdeen, SD 57401, award director Kent Hyde, 321 Citizens Bldg., Aberdeen, SD 57401. An annual contest with a specific theme each year offering prizes of $50, $25, and $15. No entry fees. Deadline Feb. 1, submit up to 3 unpublished poems, length and form are open.

‡**STUDENT AWARD (IV, Student)**, for students in grades 6-12, no entry fee, any theme or form, 32 lines or less. Prizes $25, $15, $10. See National Federation of State Poetry Societies.

‡**SWALLOW'S TALE POETRY CONTEST (III)**, Swallow's Tale Press, Box 930040, Norcross, GA 30093, offers a prize of $500 plus paper and hardback book publication under royalty contract: 48 + pp., deadline May 29, $6 entry fee—no entry form necessary. The final judge in 1986 was poet David Bottoms.

TEXAS INSTITUTE OF LETTERS POETRY AWARD (IV, Regional), c/o J.E. Weems, Box 8594, Waco, TX 76714. The Institute gives annual awards for books by Texas authors in 8 categories, including a $200 award for best volume of poetry. Books must have been first published in the year in question, and entries may be made by authors or by their publishers; deadline Jan. 15 of the following year. One copy of each entry must be mailed to each of three judges, with "information showing an author's Texas association . . . if [it] is not otherwise obvious." Poets must have been in Texas, have spent formative years there, or currently reside in the state. Write for complete instructions.

‡**TRI-CITY POETRY SOCIETY AWARD (IV, Haiku)**, Prizes $25, $15, $10. See National Federation of State Poetry Societies.

*****VIRGINIA PRIZE (IV, Regional)**, sponsor Virginia Commission for the Arts, administered by Virginia Center for the Creative Arts, Mt. San Angelo, Sweet Briar, VA 24595, award administrator Cary Kimble. A bi-annual (even-numbered years) award of $8,000 for a previously unpublished collection of poems, no more than 40 pages, open to Virginia residents only. No special format for entry, no entry fees; write for rules.

‡**CELIA B. WAGNER AWARD (III)**, $250, see Poetry Society of America.

‡**WASHINGTON POETS ASSOCIATION ANNUAL POETRY CONTESTS: WILLIAM STAFFORD AWARD (I, IV, Members), JUNIOR HIGH AND HIGH SCHOOL STUDENT CONTESTS (IV, Students, members), TRADITIONAL VERSE FORMS (I, IV Traditional, members)**, 2540 122nd Ave., SE, Bellevue, WA 98005. For the William Stafford contest, entry fee is $1/poem plus membership of $10 ($5 for seniors); students pay adult fees. Deadline April 1. Cash prizes for 1st, 2nd, and 3rd places plus honorable mentions. The junior high and high school divisions sponsor 2 free verse and 2 traditonal verse contests; deadline April 1; first poem entered free, then membership of $5 plus $1/poem plus $10 membership ($5/seniors); deadline 1 April. As before, 3 cash prizes plus honorable mentions.

WASHINGTON PRIZE (I), Word Works, Box 42164, Washington, DC 20015, $1,000 for an unpublished poem (12-24 lines). Submission open to any American writer except those connected with Word Works. Entries must be submitted in duplicate. The original typed MS must be signed by the poet with name, address, and telephone printed on the back of the page. The other copy should contain the poem and title only with no identification. All entries *must* be accompanied by SASE for entry acknowledgement. Maximum entry is 3 poems. Entry free is $2/poem. Entries accepted between September 1 and November 1 of each year. Deadline is November 1 postmark.

‡**WEST VIRGINIA POETRY SOCIETY AWARD (IV, Regional)**, Mountain folk, their homelife, customs, history. Any form, 40 line limit. Prizes $25, $15, $10. See National Federation of State Poetry Societies.

WESTERN STATES ARTS FOUNDATION (IV, Regional), #200, 207 Shelby St., Santa Fe, NM 87501, gives book awards to outstanding authors (including poets) and publishers from the west. Authors receive $2,500; publishers get $5,000. MSS must be written by an author living in Arkansas, Arizona, Colorado, Hawaii, Idaho, Montana, Nevada, New Mexico, Oregon, Utah, Washington, or Wyoming. Publishers must have published at least 3 books in the last 2 years and be able to print a first edition of 2,500 to 5,000 copies. Publishers submit MS. Write for guidelines.

‡**MRS. GILES WHITING FOUNDATION (V)**, Room 3500, 30 Rockefeller Plaza, New York NY 10112, Gerald Freund, Director of the Writers' Program, beginning in 1984-5, made awards of $25,000 to 10 candidates chosen by a Selection Committee of recognized writers, literary scholars, and editors, serving anonymously. The program places special emphasis on exceptionally promising emerging talent (which may not mean "young"), though "proven authors" are also eligible. Direct applications and informal nominations are not accepted by the Foundation.

‡**WALT WHITMAN AWARD (III)**, $1,000 plus book publication, see The Academy of American Poets.

‡**WILLIAM CARLOS WILLIAMS AWARD (III)**, book royalties, see Poetry Society of America.

WORLD ORDER OF NARRATIVE POETS (II), Box 174, Station A, Flushing, NY 11358, contest chairman Dr. Alfred Dorn. This nonprofit organization sponsors contests in 14 categories of traditional poetic forms (rhyme royal, Petrarchan or Shakespearean sonnet, sestina, villanelle, etc.). Prizes total $1,300 and range from $20 to $200. "We look for originality of thought, phrase and image, combined with masterful construction. Trite, trivial or technically inept work stands no chance." Deadline April 30.

YALE SERIES OF YOUNGER POETS (II), Yale University Press, 92A Yale Station, New Haven CT 06520, selects annually a first book (48-64 pp.) of poetry by an applicant under 40, U. S. citizen or resident. (Poets are not disqualified by previous publication of limited editions of more than 300 copies or previously published poems in newspapers and periodicals, which may be used in the book MS if so identified.) Submissions February 1-28. $5 entry fee must accompany MS. For rules and guidelines send SASE to above address.

Additional Contests and Awards

The following publishers and organizations also offer contests. Read their listings for contest information.

Ahnene
Alice James
Amelia
American Scholar
Arthur Press
Arts Insight
Atlanta Writing Resource Center
Aztec
Bay Area Poets Coalition
Beach & Co.
Bitterroot
Black Warrior
Blue Unicorn
Breakthrough
Bumpershoot
Caesara
Calliope
Candle
The Cape Rock
Ceilidh
Chattahooche
Chimera Connections
Christians Writing
Co-Laborer
Colonnades
Columbia
Connecticut River
Connecticut Writer
Cotton Boll
Creative Urge

Creative with Words Publications
Criterion Review
Cross-Canada Writer's Quarterly
Croton
Cutbank
DeLong & Associates
Dream
Earthwise
Embers
Explorer
Federation for the Advancement of Independent
  Magazines
Fine Madness
Fireweed
First Time
Flume
Folio
Forum
A Galaxy of Verse
University of Georgia
Gila
Golden Isis
The Green Book
Greensboro
Haiku Society of America
Hat
The Haven
University of Hawaii Press
Horizons SF
Inkling Publications

Inky Trails
The Inside from the Outside
International Poetry Review
INT
IWI Review
Jewish Currents
Kaleidoscope Press
Kansas
Lake Shore
The Literary Review
The Lyric
M.O.P.
Maat
The MacGuffin
Manna
The University of Massachusetts Press
Matrix
Memphis State Review
Midwest Poetry Review
Milkweed
University of Missouri Press
Mr. Cognito Press
Mythopoeic Society
The Nation
National Federation of State Poetry Societies
Negative Capability
New Departures
New Worlds Unlimited
Nimrod
Nit & Wit
Northeastern
Odessa
Ohio Journal
Ommation Press
Orbis
Outposts
Ozark Creative Writers
Paris Review
Paris/Atlantic
Parnassus
Passages North
Pegasus
Piedmont
Pitt Poetry Series
Poet Lore
Poetry Nippon
Poetry Northwest
Poetry Nottingham
Poetry Press
Poetry Review
Poetry: San Francisco Publications
Poets at Work
Prairie Schooner
Princeton University Press
Purple Heather

Quarry
Quarterly Review
R.S.V.P.
Rainbow
Rambunctious Press
Red Candle
Red Key
Reiman
Rhiannon
Rhino
Rhyme Time
Romance and Fiction World
San Jose
Saturday Press
Second Comind
Seven
Shawnee
Signpost
Silverfish
Sing Heavenly Muse
Sonora
South Coast
South Dakota
Southern Humanities
Southern Poetry Review
Spitball
State Street
Stone Country
Success
Tels
Texas Review
Transition
Translation
Trouvere
University of Utah
Vegetarian Journal
Ver
Washington Writers
Westburg
Weyfarers
Wide Open
Willow Bee
Winston-Derek
Wooster
Word works
Words
World Poetry Society
Wormwood Review
WPBS Poetry
Write On
Writer's Bloc
Writer's Digest
Yale Unversity Press
Yellow Silk
Xanadu

State and Provincial Grants

Most states in the United States and provinces in Canada have arts councils which provide assistance to artists (including poets), usually in the form of fellowships or grants. Only residents of the state or province are eligible.

These grants are often substantial and confer some prestige upon recipients, and should be considered as comparable to category (III) contests. Because deadlines for applications and the amount and nature of available support vary annually, I provide here only the addresses to which you should send queries in your own state or province:

United States Art Agencies

Alabama State Council on the Arts and Humanities
114 N. Hull St.
Montgomery, AL 36130

Alaska State Council on the Arts
Suite 220, 619 Warehouse Ave.
Anchorage, AK 99501

Arizona Commission on the Arts
Suite 201, 2024 N. Seventh St.
Phoenix, AZ 85006

Arkansas Arts Council
Suite 500, Continental Bldg.
Little Rock, AR 72201

California Arts Council
Suite A, 1901 Broadway
Sacramento, CA 95818

Colorado Council on the Arts and Humanities
770 Pennsylvania St.
Denver, CO 80203

Connecticut Commission on the Arts
340 Capitol Ave.
Hartford, CT 06106

Delaware State Arts Council
State Office Bldg.
Wilmington, DE 19801

DC Commission on the Arts And Humanities
2nd Floor, 420 7th St., NW
Washington, DC 20004

Arts Council of Florida
Dept. of State, The Capitol
Tallahassee, FL 32304

Georgia Council for the Arts and Humanities
Suite 100, 2082 E. Exchange Pl.
Tucker, GA 30084

Hawaii State Foundation on Culture and the Arts
Suite 202, 355 Merchant St.
Honolulu, HI 96813

Idaho Commission on the Arts
304 W. State St.
Boise, ID 83720

Illinois Arts Council
Suite 700, 111 N. Wabash Ave.
Chicago, IL 60602

Indiana Arts Commission
155 E. Market St.
Indianapolis, IN 46204

Iowa Arts Council
State Capitol Bldg.
Des Moines, IA 50319

Kansas Arts Commission
112 W. Sixth St.
Topeka, KS 66603

Kentucky Arts Council
Berry Hill
Frankfort, KY 40601

Louisiana State Arts Council
Box 44247
Baton Rouge, LA 70804

Maine State Commission on the Arts and Humanities
55 Capital St.
State House Station 25,
Augusta, ME 04333

Maryland State Arts Council
15 W. Mulberry
Baltimore, MD 21201

Massachusetts Council on the Arts and Humanities
One Ashburton Pl.
Boston, MA 02108

Michigan Council for the Arts
1200 Sixth Ave.
Executive Plaza
Detroit, MI 48226

Minnesota State Arts Board
432 Summit Ave.
Saint Paul, MN 55102

Mississippi Arts Commission
301 N. Lamar St.
Box 1341
Jackson, MS 39205

Missouri Arts Council
Suite 105, 111 N. Seventh St.
St. Louis, MO 63101

Montana Arts Council
1280 S. Third St. W.
Missoula, MT 59801

Nebraska Arts Council
1313 Farnam-on-the-Mall
Omaha, NE 68102

Nevada State Council on the Arts
329 Flint St.
Reno, NV 89502

New Hampshire Commission on the Arts
Phenix Hall
40 N. Main St.
Concord, NH 03301

New Jersey State Council on the Arts
109 W. State St.
Trenton, NJ 08608

New Mexico Arts Division
113 Lincoln
Santa Fe, NM 87503

New York State Council on the Arts
80 Centre St.
New York, NY 10013

North Carolina Arts Council
Dept. of Cultural Resources
Raleigh, NC 27611

North Dakota Council on the Arts
Suite 811, Black Bldg.
Fargo, ND 58105

Ohio Arts Council
727 E. Main St.
Columbus, OH 43205

Oklahoma State Arts Council
Room 640, Jim Thorpe Bldg.
Oklahoma City, OK 73105

Oregon Arts Commission
835 Summer St. NE
Salem, OR 97301

Pennsylvania Council on the Arts
Room 216, Finance Bldg.
Harrisburg, PA 17120

Rhode Island State Council on the Arts
312 Wickenden St.
Providence, RI 02903

South Carolina Arts Commission
1800 Gervais St.
Columbia, SC 29201

South Dakota Arts Council
108 W. 11th St.
Sioux Falls, SD 57102

Tennessee Arts Commission
Suite 1700, 505 Deaderick St.
Nashville, TN 37219

Texas Commission on the Arts
Box 13406 Capitol Station
Austin, TX 78711

Utah Arts Council
617 East South Temple St.
Salt Lake City, UT 84102

Vermont Council on the Arts
136 State St.
Montpelier, VT 05602

Virginia Commission for the Arts
1st Floor, 400 E. Grace St.
Richmond, VA 23219

Washington State Arts Commission
Mail Stop GH-11
Olympia, WA 98504

West Virginia Arts and Humanities Division
Dept. of Culture & History
Capitol Complex
Charleston, WV 25305

Wisconsin Arts Board
123 W. Washington Ave.
Madison, WI 53702

Wyoming Council on the Arts
2nd Floor, Equality State Bank Bldg.
Cheyenne, WY 82002

Canadian Provinces Art Agencies

Alberta Arts Council
12th Floor, 20004 204th Ave., CN Tower
Edmonton, AB, Canada T5J 0K5

British Columbia Arts Council
3rd Floor, 820 Pandora Ave.
Victoria, BC Canada V8W 1P3

Canada Council, Writing and Publications Section
Box 1047
Ottawa, ON Canada K1P 5J3

Canadian Ministry of Citizenship and Culture, Arts Service Branch
7th Floor, 777 Bloor St., W.
Toronto, ON Canada M7A 2K9

Manitoba Arts Council
123-555 Main St.
Winnipeg, MB Canada $3B 1C3

New Brunswick Culture Development, Youth, Recreation and Culture
Centennial Bldg.
Fredericton, NB Canada E3A 4G7

Newfoundland-Labrador Arts Council
Box 4750, Confederation Bldg.
St. John's, NF Canada A1C 5T7

Nova Scotia Arts Council
Box 864
Halifax, NS Canada B3J 2V2

Ontario Arts Council
Suite 500, 151 Bloor St. W.
Toronto, ON Canada M5S 1T6

Prince Edward Island Council of the Arts
Box 2234
Charlottestown, PIE Canada C1A 8B9

Quebec aide a la creation
255 Grande Allee, est
Quebec, PQ Canada G1R 5G5

Saskatchewan Arts Board
2550 Broad St.
Regina, SK Canada S4P 3V7

Alternative Writing Opportunities

Making a Living

I have often said there is no such thing as a fulltime poet. You simply cannot think of poetry as a way to make a living. Even the greatest of our poets figure out first how to support themselves and, in doing so, support their poetic habit. Poets may be engineers or doctors or computer programmers or receptionists or school bus drivers or teachers—or be supported by their mates or inheritances. But poetry is not a profession in itself.

But a poet is a writer, and you might want to know how you can support yourself that way. It took me some forty years of professional writing to learn that, short of writing a bestseller, it is actually possible to earn a living by writing. To do that, though, you have to take a step which seems not to come naturally to many poets: *Subdue thy vanity*. The writing which really pays—steadily and dependably—requires supression of your ego. The bread-and-butter work I presently do as a writer is mostly as one of a stable of writers working on a freelance basis for a foundation. If you have the skills, you might find similar opportunities in your own area.

Freelance Writing

First of all for work such as I am doing—as much editing as writing—you need precise editorial skills. Not only must you be expert in the fundamentals of grammar, punctuation and usage, but you know the **Chicago Manual of Style** or similar editorial guides inside out. Freelance writers must understand better than corporate or institutional executives, administrators, scientists and technicians the mysteries of getting ideas into language and then into print. You have to know how to grasp and convey the spirit and values of an organization with which you may not personally identify. Sometimes you must capture the personality and style of an individual—someone you may not like, or even know. You must be able to write rapidly, briefly, clearly, effectively—and, above all, accurately.

To build up a portfolio of such writing, start with the hundreds of listings of trade publications in **Writer's Market**. There you will find magazines that pay better and reach a larger audience than the mostly literary magazines listed in **Poet's Market** (though some of those magazines use poetry and are listed here). I open **Writer's Market** literally at random, and my eye falls on *Heating, Plumbing, Air Conditioning*, a magazine with a circulation of 14,500 that pays 10-20¢ a word and sometimes pays expenses of writers on assignment. Our little village has a plumbing supply house. In an hour I could make an appointment with the manager, interview him—for example on the uses of infrared heating in our area. I might take a few pictures of the installation process. In another hour I could write up a 1,500 story that might sell for $150 or more—especially with photos—to that magazine. If it is rejected, there are other publications in the same section of **Writer's Market** which might take it; and if I were to plumb the field of plumbing I know I would discover hundreds of additional potential markets.

Competent writers should be able to sell an article a day of that sort—building up their skills and credits in the process. You don't need a lot of technical knowledge to do such writing: The whole point is that if the people in the field can explain their business so that *you* can understand the technical elements, you can write about them clearly enough that you can help others understand.

Once you have developed a portfolio illustrating what you can do, move on to the more profitable work available around you. For example, many hospitals these days publish magazines with feature articles about individual doctors or other medical personnel, equipment, procedures, and other such topics. They usually contract for these articles through advertising agencies, which, in turn, contract for freelancers, paying $1,000 per article or more. Ad agencies also place articles for corporations or industries in the trade magazines. The money comes from the client, who also supplies all the research material, so the writer needn't leave the study. Or perhaps the company will pay the expenses of a writer to visit the plant and interview key personnel.

I learned such things by getting together with writers in my area. One woman has been making over $30,000 a year for many years as a freelance writer for such organizations; yet she has only occasionally seen her own name in print. Like most of us, however, she steadily submits poetry and fiction to the literary magazines, considering her "real" writing that which she does on weekends—with little expectation of pay.

At my suggestion some of us in our area have formed an informal group, Wordsmiths, to meet regularly as a support system, to exchange tips and experiences, socialize, and pass around work that we individually can't take or don't want. You could do the same—if you live in or near a metropolitan area. If you have a rural or small-town home, you might organize by mail. But first of all, get out and find out where writing is being done in our society and find how to tap into it.

Greeting Cards

Some call this hack writing. I prefer the term *transparent writing*. On a recent visit to the corporate headquarters of Hallmark Cards in Kansas City, Missouri, where dozens of writers work in little cubicles, practicing their highly specialized, demanding trade, I thought of an analogy between writing and carpentering. Carpenters may love and respect wood and the ancient and honored techniques for working it, putting it together, and finishing it. They feel about wood just as writers feel about language, yet they rarely sign their names to their products. When they make, say, chairs, they are not thinking of self-expression. The chairs may not even be of a style or design they would select for their own homes. The products may have style, character, taste, distinction, but the individual personalities of the carpenters who make them have been deliberately suppressed. They think of utility, of the taste and needs of those who will ultimately use the chairs. They think of their customers. They carry their love for wood, their knowledge and skill, into serving the needs of others.

And though many creative people pretend to scorn commercial or market values, most of them, I notice, have to eat. There need be no compromise of values in making a living, even as a writer. And there can be no shoddiness in such work—if you are going to succeed at it. Transparent writing requires talent—specifically the same talents required for good poetry— even if the copy produced is mostly prose.

Greeting cards these days have, for the most part, moved far beyond the hearts and flowers of yesteryear (though some are still in the old-fashioned style, which best serves the needs of many customers). Most are not in verse. To write them requires wit, compassion, a genuine identification with the communication needs of customers, precision, craft, and sometimes bizarre imagination. As I mentioned, most greeting card manufacturers use primarily inhouse material because there must be very close coordination between art, design and text. But some also accept freelance work. Many provide potential contributors with "tipsheets" highlighting their current needs.

For a good overview of the field and instruction about how to break into it, see **A Guide to Greeting Card Writing**, published by Writer's Digest Books. Here are names and addresses of some greeting card companies (and their editors) that are interested in freelance submissions. Study their products in a greeting card store, write for their tipsheets, and try your hand:

AMBERLEY GREETING CARD CO., Box 36159, Cincinnati, OH 45236. Editor: Ned Stern.

AMERICAN GREETINGS, 10500 American Rd., Cleveland, OH. Contact: Director, Creative Recruitment. (Does not accept unsolicited material; wants only resumes initially.)

ARGUS COMMUNICATIONS, 1 DLM Park, Allen, TX 75002. Editor: Martee Phillips.

CAROLYN BEAN PUBLISHING, LTD., 120 2nd St., San Francisco, CA 94105. Chief Executive Officer: Lawrence Barnett.

BLUE MOUNTAIN ARTS, INC., Box 1007, Boulder, CO 80306. Contact: Editorial Staff.

BRILLIANT ENTERPRISES, 117 W. Valerio St., Santa Barbara, CA 93101. Contact: Editorial Dept.

CONTENOVA GIFTS, 1239 Adanac St., Vancouver, British Columbia V6A 2C8 Canada. Editor: Jeff Sinclair.

CURRENT, INC., Box 2559, Colorado Springs, CO 80901. Editor: Nancy McConnell.

DRAWING BOARD GREETING CARDS, INC., 8200 Carpenter Freeway, Dallas, TX 75247. Editorial Director: Jimmie Fitzgerald.

D. FORER & CO., INC., 105 E. 73rd St., New York, NY 10021. Editor: Barbara Schaffer.

FREEDOM GREETING CARD CO., Box 715, Bristol, PA 19007. Editor: J. Levitt.

LEANIN' TREE PUBLISHING CO., Box 9500, Boulder, CO 80301. Contact: Editor.

MAINE LINE CO., Box 418, Rockport, ME 04856. Editor: Marjorie MacClennen.

ALFRED MAINZER, INC., 27-08 40th Ave., Long Island City, NY 11101. Art Director: Arwed Baenisch.

OATMEAL STUDIOS, Box 138, Rochester, VT 05767. Editor: Helene Lehrer.

PARAMOUNT CARDS, INC., Box 1225, Pawtucket, RI 02862. Editorial Director: Dolores Riccio.

PAWPRINTS, Box 446, Jaffrey, NH 03452. Editor: Mary Tripp.

RED FARM STUDIO, Box 347, 334 Pleasant St., Pawtucket, RI 02862. Editor: Mary M. Hood.

RED/ETER KARDZ, Box 231015, Pleasant Hill, CA 94523. Editor: Ed Kennedy.

REED STARLINE CARDS CO., Box 26247, Los Angeles, CA 90026. Editor: Barbara Stevens.

RENAISSANCE GREETING CARDS, Box 126, Springvale, ME 04083. Editor: Ronnie Sellars.

ROUSANA CARDS, 28 Sager Place, Hillside, NJ 07205. Editor: Janice E. Thurmond.

SUNRISE PUBLICATIONS, INC., Box 2699, Bloomington, IN 47402. Product Manager: Ken Illingworth.

VAGABOND CREATIONS, INC., 2560 Lance Dr., Dayton, OH 45409. Editor: George F. Stanley, Jr.

WARNER PRESS, INC., Box 2499, Anderson, IN 46018. Editor: Jane H. Wendt.

CAROL WILSON FINE ARTS, INC., Box 17394, Portland, OR 97217. Editor: Gary Spector.

And here is a final—and most unusual—market for greeting card verse:

THE COMPUTER POET CORPORATION has thousands of MacIntosh computers in greeting card stores and other retail outlets around the country. The customer keys in individual names to whom the card is addressed, traits, and the occasion for the card, then gets an individualized card printed out. The verses used are all limericks, many written by freelancers. For guidelines, send SASE to The Magical Poet, 4339 N. 39th St., Phoenix, AZ 85018.

Resources

Conferences and Workshops

I don't know whether writers' workshops and conferences are an American invention, but they are certainly a characteristically American phenomenon. The most important opportunity such workshops offer is not the instruction, nor the readings, nor the public performances, nor the criticism of manuscripts. It is the chance to rub elbows with other writers, to create a temporary literary community in which unknowns can meet the better known, in which associations and friendships may form to generate the literature of the future.

Some of this association may occur when writers visit campuses or make local appearances. Some of it occurs through the mail. But writers' conferences and workshops are the primary way in which unknown writers can associate, however briefly, with those who have achieved some reputation. Even if nothing much comes of the association, we learn a great deal about the way the literary world works by being around such writers—hearing how they field questions, what their casual conversation is like, seeing how they behave at parties, how they view their fellow-writers—including conference participants.

The pattern of these workshops varies widely. Some are one-day affairs in which participants simply listen to presentations by knowledgeable speakers who give their insights into the writing business. Longer ones typically have separate meetings for those interested in poetry, fiction, nonfiction, screenwriting, children's literature and other genres. The workshop may offer you the opportunity to submit a manuscript for criticism by a staff member, usually in a private session. And the workshop may be enhanced by public readings, performances, panel discussions, or other features. Usually there are representatives of magazine and book publishers present, literary agents and others associated with publication.

Above all, these workshops enable one to escape, at least for a while, the pervasive loneliness of the writer's life. There you find a lot of other people like yourself, people struggling daily with submissions and rejections, with fitting writing into busy schedules, people searching for the right books to read, magazines to subscribe to, experiences to pursue. Often participants organize readings among themselves—chances to perform before a sympathetic and interested audience.

You may find many participants who actually do very little writing. These are often the most interesting of all. They are people for whom literature is an important element in their lives, though their participation in writing is largely vicarious. They've read a lot. (And what poet doesn't favor the proliferation of readers?) They *know* writing. They like to talk about it and bask a while in the dubious aura of glamour they find in published writers. You may not meet many people like that in your home setting. Get acquainted. Keep your ears open.

The information given here is approximate. Dates, fees, and other details change from year to year, but the dates and fees given are those of a recent year—enabling you to guess at least the approximate timing and cost of the conference. In each case, send a SASE for information about the current year.

Arizona

Arizona Christian Writers Seminar
Donna Goodrich
648 S. Pima St.
Mesa, AZ 85202
Nov. 7-8

Tucson Writers' Conference
Rolly Kent, Tucson Public Library
Box 27470
Tucson, AZ 85726
Dec. 27-31, $195
Held at Sheraton

Arkansas

Ozark Creative Writers, Inc.
Box 391
Eurekea Springs, AR 72632
Oct. 10-12, $15

California

Annual Christian Writers Conference
Mt. Hermon Christian Conference Center
Box 413
Mt. Hermon, CA 95041
March 24-29, $100-250
MS eval for 15 participants

California Writers Club Conference at Asilomar, Pacific Grove
2214 Derby St.
Berkeley, CA 94705
July 12-14, $190-210 includes room/board

Forest Home's Christian Writers' Conference
Forest Home Christian Conference Center
Forest Falls, CA 92339
Oct. 13-16, $250 includes room/board

International Women's Writing Guild Early Spring California Conference
Westerbeke Ranch, 2300 Grove
Sonoma, CA 95476
Feb. 28-March 2, $35-170
Write IWWG, Box 810
Gracie Station, NYC 10028

Napa Valley Poetry Conferences
Conference Director, Napa Valley College
Napa, CA 94558
Aug., $95-410. Series of 2-week workshops featuring major poets

Pasadena Annual Writers Forum
Nino Valmasoi
Pasadena City College
1570 E. Colorado Blvd.
Pasadena, CA 91106

UCLA Extension
Poets-in-Residence
10995 Le Conte Ave.
Los Angeles, CA 90024
Oct.-June, $4-40 for readings
Poets give readings, hold classes

Colorado

National Writers Club
James Lee Young
Suite #620,1450 S. Havana
Aurora, CO 80012
April 4-5, July 18-20

Summer Festival of Arts Writers Conference
Steamboat Arts Council
Box 771913
Steamboat Springs, CO 80477
Aug. 1-2, $40-50

Connecticut

Connecticut Writers Conference
George W. Earley
Box 10536
West Hartford, CT 06110
May 2, Nov. 17, Spring: $25, Fall: free

Wesleyan Writers Conference
Wesleyan University
Middletown, CT 06457
July 7-12, $250
5-6 poems evaluated

Florida

Florida Freelance Writers Conference
Box 9844
Ft. Lauderdale, FL 33310
May 16-18, $65-160
Includes banquets
MS critique $10/15 minutes

Florida Suncoast Writers' Conference
University of South Florida
830 First St. S.
St. Petersburg, FL 33701
Jan. 23-25, $50-100
MS evaluated $35 up to 5 pp.

Illinois

Christian Writers Institute
June Eaton, Director
396 E. Charles Rd.
Wheaton, IL 60188
June 3-6, $12-120

International Black Writers Conference
Mable Terrell
Box 1030
Chicago, IL 60690
February 15, $15, $6 to attend plays

McKendree Writers' Association Writers' Conference
M. Bracken, Director
McKendree College, E 30, Lot 32
Glen Carbon, IL 62034
June 8-9, $5-30

Mississippi Valley Writer's Conference
College Center
Augustana College
Rock Island, IL 61201
June 9-14, $45-85

Indiana

Indiana University Writers Conference
Sharon Shaloo, Ballantine Hall
Indiana University
Bloomington, IN 47405
June 22-27, $100-275
MS evaluation

Ohio River Writers' Conference
Evansville Arts and Education Council
16 ¹/₃ SE 2nd St.
Evansville, IN 47708
Aug. 2-4, $50-75 with MS

Kansas

Butler County Creative Writing Workshop
Lois Friesen, Coordinator
901 S. Haverhill Rd.
El Dorado, KS 67042-9989
Nov. 7-8, $5-10
1-3 poems (up to 20 lines) evaluated

Kentucky

Carter Caves Writer's Workshop
Lee Pennington
Carter Caves State Resort Park
Olive Hill, KY 41164
June 2-8, $60
Tours and workshops with Lee Pennington

Eastern Kentucky University
William Sutton, Creative Writing
Eastern Kentucky University
Richmond, KY 40475
June 17-23, $38-156
Submit MSS for critique

Massachusetts

Cape Cod Writers' Conference
at Olde Colonial Courthouse
Box 111
W. Hyannisport, MA 02672
July 27-31, Aug. 17-21
Planning 1987 mid-Jan. cruise on Cunard Countess from San Juan PR, 7 days, about $1,000

Maryland

St. Mary's College of Maryland
Intensive Poetry Writing Workshop and Festival of Poets and Poetry
St. Mary's City, MD 20686
May 23-June 4, $225 + $30 books

Maine

State of Maine Writers Conference
Richard F. Burns
Box 296
Ocean Park, ME 04063
Holds contests in conjunction with annual conference, 46th year

Michigan

Bay de Noc Writers' Conference
Bay de Noc Community College
Escanaba, MI 49829
June 14-15, $50-65

Michigan Northwoods Writers Conference
Leelanau Center for Education
Glenn Arbor, MI 49636
July 13-18, $333-495 includes room/board
Send sample

Midland Writers Conference
Matrix-Midland Festival
Grace A. Dow Memorial Library
Midland, MI 48640
June 8, $32-40

Minnesota

Minnesota Writers Conference
Judy Mans, Box 109
Mankato State University
Mankato, MN 56001
April 26, $35

Minnesota Writers' Conference
College of St. Teresa, Winona
Rochester Center, U. of MN
Rochester, MN 55904
June 21-26, $260 includes room/
board
MS critique
Registrar in Rochester, conference
held at St. Teresa in Winona

Split Rock Arts Program
Duluth Campus, U. of MN
320 Westbrook Hall, 77 Pleasant St.
SE
Minneapolis, MN 55455
June-August, series of workshops

Upper Midwest Writers' Conference
Bill Elliott, Box 48, Hag Sauer
Bemidji State University
Bemidji, MN 56601
July 14-25, 3 2-credit courses

Missouri

Avila College Writers Conference
Marcy Caldwell
11901 Wornall Rd.
Kansas City, MO 64145-9990
Aug. 14-15, $150 or $55 day
MS evaluated free, poetry 3rd day

Mark Twain Writers Conference
Jim Hefly
Hanibal-LaGrange College
Hanibal, MO 63401
June 23-27, $275 includes dorm/
meals
Daily workshops in fiction, nonfic-
tion, poetry

New Jersey

New Jersey Writers Conference
Alumni Association
New Jersey Inst. of Technology
Newark, NJ 07102
Mar. 8, $20

Trenton State College Annual Writ-
ers' Conference
Jean Hollander, English Dept.
Trenton State College, Hillwood
Lakes CN550
Trenton, NJ 08625
April 14-15, $3-30
May submit 1-2 poems for evaluation

New Mexico

Santa Fe Writers Conference
Recursos de Santa Fe
Dept. T
Santa Fe, NM 87501
Aug. 4-8, $325
At St. John's College
Submit 5 pp. poetry

New York

Chautauqua Writers' Workshops
Box 1095
Chautauqua, NY 14722
July 22-Aug. 9, $80-190

Cornell University Writers Program
Dean Charles W. Jermy, Jr.
B12P Ives Hall, Cornell University
Ithaca, NY 14853
June and Aug., 3 and 6 week ses-
sions

Feminist Women's Writing Work-
shops
held at Wells College, Aurora
Box 456
Ithaca, NY 14851
July 13-23, $325-575
MS critique

Generoso Pope Foundation
Writing Workshops
Manhattanville College
Purchase, NY 10577
June 22-24, 24-28, $100-275

Hofstra University Summer Writers
Conference
Dr. James J. Kolb
017 Weller
Hofstra University
Hempstead, NY 11550
July 7-18, $405
May submit 5 pp. poetry for critique

International Women's Writing
Guild
Conf/Retreat, Skidmore College
Box 810, Gracie Station
New York, NY 10028
July 25- Aug. 3, $206-470 includes
room/board

Long Island University/Southhamp-
ton Campus
Writers' Conference & Workshops
Southhampton Campus LIU
Southhampton, NY 11968
July 8-19, credit or noncredit
Must submit 5-8 pp. poetry

New York University Summer Writ-
er's Conference
School of Continuing Education
Susan Edelmann, Director
331-2 Shimkin Hall, Washington
Square
New York, NY 10003
July 7-18, $650
Sample required (20-40 pp.)

Write Associates Writers' Work-
shops
Buffalo Convention Center
Box 132
Grand Island, NY 14072
April 12, $50-55

Ohio

Antioch Writers Workshop
Bill Baker, Chairman
Antioch University
Yellow Springs, OH 45387
July 20-26, $200-400
Scholarships for area residents
DAWN-Dayton Area Writer's Nexus
Ruth Innis Quast
2086 Settlers Trail
Vandalia, OH 45377
Jan. 19, $12.50

Oregon

The Flight of the Mind
Summer Writing Workshop for Women
622 SE 28th
Portland, OR 97214
July 21-28, $350-375
Scholarships, college credit

Pennsylvania

Madwomen in the Attic
Jane Coleman, Dept. of English
Carlow College, 3333 Fifth Ave.
Pittsburgh, PA 15213
Jan. 21-April 8, $60
12 sessions taught by Jane Coleman

South Carolina

Francis Marion Writers' Retreat
Bob Parham
Francis Marion College
Florence, SC 29501
May 23-25, $60 (+ $10 for critique)

Virginia

Christopher Newport College
Writers' Conference
50 Shoe Lane
Newport News, VA 23606
April 12, $65

Washington

Port Townsend Writers' Conference
Centrum
Box 1158
Port Townsend, WA 98368
July 11-12, $55-200
Financial aid available
Spectrum Summer Writers Conference
Carol Orlock, Arts & Humanities
U. Ext GH-21, U. of Washington
Seattle, WA 98195
July 18-20, $95-110
May submit up to 5 poems

Wisconsin

The Clearing
Writing Workshops
Box 65
Ellison Bay, WI 54210
June 15-21, $303-325 includes room/board
Classes with Norbert Blei
Green Lake Christian Writers Conference
Arlo R. Reichter
Green Lake Conference Center,
American Baptist Association
Green Lake, WI 54941
Aug. 9-16, $70
Rhinelander School of Arts
UW Extension
726 Lowell Hall, 610 Langdon St.
Madison, WI 53703
July 28-Aug. 1, $100
Responsible for own MS evaluation

Canada

Cross-Canada Writer's Workshop
Box 277, Station F
Toronto, Ont., Canada M4Y 2L7, is a continual workshop-by-mail. For $75/year you can submit up to 5 copies every 3 weeks for evaluation by other workshop members.

Writing Colonies

‡**ATLANTIC CENTER FOR THE ARTS**, 1414 Art Center Ave., New Smyrna Beach, FL 32069, phone 904-427-6975. The Center was founded in 1979 by a sculptor and painter, Doris Leeper, who secured a seed grant from The Rockefeller Foundation. That same year the Center was chartered by the state of Florida and building began on a 10-acre site. The Center was officially opened in 1982. Beginning in 1986, 5 Master Artists-in-Residence sessions were held. At each of the 3-week sessions internationally known artists from different disciplines conduct interdisciplinary workshops, lectures, critiques of work in progress. They also give readings and recitals, exhibit their work, and develop projects with their "fellows"—artists who come from all over the US to work with the Masters. The Center is run by an advisory council which chooses Masters for residencies, helps set policies, and guides the Center in its growth. The brochure I have gives no information on the process of becoming a fellow—whether one has to apply, or whether anyone can attend by paying a fee. In 1985 one session included a Master in poetry—William Stafford. No poets were listed in 1986.

DORLAND MOUNTAIN COLONY, Box 6, Temecula, CA 92390, established 1979, is a 300 acre Nature Conservancy which offers 1-2 month residences for writers, visual artists and composers in a rustic environment with oil lamps and wood stoves. Residents provide their own meals. No fee, but established writers are encouraged to make tax-deductible contributions. The facilities encourage collaborative applications. Write for application form. Deadlines the first of September and March.

FINE ARTS WORK CENTER IN PROVINCETOWN, Box 565, 24 Pearle St., Provincetown, MA 02657, provides monthly stipends of $375 and studio/living quarters for 7 uninterrupted months for 20 young artists and writers (10 of each) who have completed their formal training and are capable of working independently. The Center has a staff of writers and artists who offer manuscript consultations, arrange readings and slide presentations and visits from other distinguished writers and artists. Several established writers are invited each year for extended residencies. Each year they publish *Shankpainter*, a magazine of prose and poetry by the writing fellows. Sessions run from October 1-May 1. Applications, accompanied by a $15 processing fee, must be received by February 1.

‡**HAWK, I'M YOUR SISTER, WOMEN'S WILDERNESS CANOE TRIPS**, %Beverly Antaeus, Box 9109, Santa Fe, NM 87504. Most of the trips led by Beverly Antaeus have special themes in addition to the conventional (if there is such a thing) wilderness adventure—one of them is a "vision quest," one is a photography workshop, one shares personal experiences and writings of women who traveled through the wilderness, and one is called "Writing Retreat: The River as Metaphor." The 1986 writing retreat took place on the Green River in Utah in June (6 days, 65 miles, cost $500); an earlier writing retreat was on the Penobscot River in Maine. Co-guide for these trips is Alice Swinger, a professor of literature and writing at Wright State University in Ohio. College credit (3 hours) is available through Wright State; tuition fees are in addition to the fee for the trip.

THE MACDOWELL COLONY, 100 High St., Peterborough, NH 03458, founded 1907, offers residencies to established writers and artists. Over 2,000 of our major poets, authors and artists have stayed there, many of them producing major works. Apply 8 months before desired residency. No residence fee. Meals provided.

THE MILLAY COLONY FOR THE ARTS, INC., Steepletop, Austerlitz, NY 12017, founded 1973 at the 600-acre estate which is the former home of Edna St. Vincent Millay. Provides 1 month residencies for writers, composers and visual artists. No residence fee. Meals provided.

MONTALVO CENTER FOR THE ARTS, Box 158, Saratoga, CA 95071, presents theatre, musical events and other artistic activities. (I once was on the panel of a poetry workshop there.) They have an Artist-in-Residence program which has 6 apartments available for artists (including poets) for 3-6 month periods ($100 single, $115 for a couple. No children or pets). Limited financial assistance available.

NETHERS, Box 41, Woodville, VA 22749, director Carla Eugster, is a farm retreat for poets and classical musicians offering 1-4 week residencies to fellows on the basis of merit and promise. Carla Eugster (herself a poet) tries to maintain a balance of known and unknowns, males and females, poets, musicians and other artists, and "exceptional people." Minorities are welcome. Instead of applying for a residency, guests may choose to come by self-selection (as paying or working guests). One week is the minimum stay for working guests. No one is denied a residency because of inability to pay "but contributions keep Nethers going, and fellows are expected to contribute what they can either at the time of their residency or after they get back home."

‡**NIANGUA COLONY**, %Wilhelmine Bennett, Route 1, Stoutland, MO 65567, "a place of quiet and beauty where artists may spend time concentrating on their work;" the Colony is located on 15 acres of forest and meadow. Each resident has a private room and studio space; kitchen and common room are shared, and residents cooperate on food preparation. They are expected to donate 8 hours/week to Colony work: building, maintenance, gardening, etc. At present the Colony can accomodate 3 residents; two additional studios are being constructed. Residents pay $65/month; any additional amount paid is tax-deductible as a contribution to the Colony. The regular season is from April 15 to November 1; residents may stay for 2 weeks to 2 months, or longer by special arrangement. Admission is by application; a record of past achievement is helpful, and recommendations must be included. Application forms are available from the address above. Acceptance is based upon whether the proposed project is feasible in that setting and whether the directors feel that residence at Niangua would contribute to the project.

THE NORTHWOOD INSTITUTE ALDEN B. DOW CREATIVITY CENTER, Midland, MI 48640, founded 1979, director Judith O'Dell, offers fellowships for 3-month residencies at the Northwood Institute Campus. Travel and all expenses are paid. Applicants can be undergraduates, graduates, or those without any academic or institutional affiliation, including citizens of other countries (if they can communicate in English). Projects may be in any field.

RAGDALE FOUNDATION, 1260 N. Green Bay Rd., Lake Forest, IL 60045, founded 1976, President Alice Ryerson, provides through the year a peaceful place and uninterrupted time for 12 writers, scholars, composers and artists. Meals, linen and laundry facilities are provided. Each resident is assigned private work space and sleeping accommodations. Couples are accepted if each qualifies independently. Residents may come for 1 week to 2 months. The fee is $70 per week. The Foundation also sponsors poetry readings, concerts, workshops and seminars in writing.

MILDRED I. REID WRITERS COLONY IN NEW HAMPSHIRE, Penacook Rd., Contoocook, NH 03229, phone 603-746-3625. winter address Apt. 5, 917 Bucida Rd., Delray Beach, FL 33444, phone 305-278-3607. The Mildred Reid Writers Colony is run as a private enterprise; there are weekly sessions from July 7 to August 8. The sessions are held at a chalet in the country, 10 miles west of Concord, NH. Cost of a week at the Colony ranges from $120 for a single room and shared bath in the chalet to $210 double rate for a log cabin in the pines. Fees include room, breakfast, two private conferences and two class sessions weekly. Kitchen facilities are available, and a village with restaurants within walking distance. Ms. Reid gives private consultations at $5/half hour.

YADDO, Box 395, Saratoga Springs, NY 12866-0395, founded 1926, executive director Curtis Harnack, offers residencies to writers and artists who have already achieved some recognition in their field and have new work under way. During the summer 19 writers can be accommodated, during the winter 4-8. Guests live in rooms in the mansion or, during the summer, in cottages around the estate; in the winter the mansion is closed, but some guests live and work in West House, Pine Garde, and adjoining studios. The hours 9-4 are a quiet period reserved for work. There is no fixed charge for a guest stay, but voluntary contributions to help defray costs of the program are expected—either at the time of the visit or later in the year.

Organizations Useful to Poets

The road to poetry seems such a lonely one it is sometimes surprising to look up and discover that we are, in fact, surrounded by a vast support system of groups which have been formed to share, encourage and foster our work. There is probably a writers' group or club in your area. If not, it is easy to form one. Just put up notices on public bulletin boards, or take out an ad in your local paper, suggesting that interested writers get together at some specific time and place. (Often public libraries have rooms available for such purposes if you don't want to use your home.) There are many more closet poets (and other writers) around the country than you might believe.

I have listed here some of the major organizations which offer support of various kinds to poets, and some representative samples of smaller groups. Most states have state poetry societies (see National Federation of State Poetry Societies), and these have local chapters in many towns and cities. New ones can always be formed. Special interest groups such as those for women, for blacks and other minorities, for romance writers, for haikuists, are proliferating daily. Some such groups sponsor local festivals of the arts and garner support from local businesses or other organizations.

One early step I recommend toward sensing your position as a professional in the field is to subscribe to *Coda: Poets and Writers Newsletter* (see in Publications Useful to Poets). In *Coda* you will find ads and announcements from a wide range of organizations which may be helpful to you. There, too, appear announcements of the many grants and awards offered by state arts councils (see in State and Provincial Grants) and some of the organizations listed here.

ACADEMY OF AMERICAN POETS, 177 E. 87th St., New York, NY 10128, founded 1910. I quote Robert Penn Warren, from the *Introduction to Fifty Years of American Poetry*, an anthology published in 1984 containing one poem from each of the 126 Chancellors, Fellows and Award Winners of the Academy: "What does the Academy do? According to its certificate of incorporation, its purpose is 'To encourage, stimulate, and foster the production of American poetry. . . . The responsibility for its activities lies with the Board of Directors (with Mrs. Hugh Bullock as president and many board members of distinguished reputation) and the Board of 12 Chancellors, which has included, over the years, such figures as Louise Bogan, W. H. Auden, Witter Bynner, Randall Jarrell, Robert Lowell, Robinson Jeffers, Marianne Moore, James Merrill, Robert Fitzgerald, F. O. Matthiessen, and Archibald MacLeish—certainly not members of the same poetic church." They award fellowships, currently of $10,000 each, to distinguished American poets—48 to date—and other annual awards. The Walt Whitman Award pays $1,000 plus publication of a poet's first book by a major publisher (Viking-Penguin in 1986). MSS of 50-200 pp. must be submitted between September 15 and November 15 with a $5 entry fee. The Lamont Poetry Selection, for a poet's second book, is again a prize of $1,000 and publication. The Academy supports distribution to its members. Submissions must be made by a publisher, in MSS form, prior to publication. Poets entering either contest must be American citizens. The Peter I.B. Lavan Younger Poets Awards of $1,000 each are given annually to three younger poets selected by Academy Chancellors (no applications taken). *Envoi* and *Poetry Pilot* are informative periodicals sent to those who contribute $10 or more per year or who are members.

ALWAYS submit MSS or queries with a stamped, self-addressed envelope (SASE) within your country or International Reply Coupons (IRCs) purchased from the post office for other countries.

APPALACHIAN POETRY ASSOCIATION, Box 1358, Middlesboro, KY 40965, conducts activities to promote literary talent in the Appalachian region.

ASSOCIATED WRITING PROGRAMS, AWP NEWSLETTER, INTRO, WORD BEAT, THE AWP AWARD SERIES, Old Dominion University, Norfolk, VA 23508-8510, founded 1967, offers a variety of services to the writing community, including information, job placement assistance, publishing opportunities, literary arts advocacy and forums, and publishes frequent samples of student work. Annual membership is $40. For $12 you can subscribe to the *AWP Newsletter* (quarterly), containing information about grants and awards, publishing opportunities, fellowships, and writing programs. They have a catalog of over 250 college and university writing programs. *Intro* is an annual of student writing, accepting submissions in poetry and other creative writing each March for fall publication. The AWP Award Series selects a volume of poetry each year to be published by University Press of Virginia ($10 entry fee). Their placement service helps writers find jobs in teaching, editing and other related fields. *Word Beat* is a quarterly magazine mailed to over 250 US colleges that offer courses and degrees in creative writing. It is a general writers' service magazine, circulation 1,000, containing news and information about awards, publications, markets, deadlines and reviews of small and university press publications.

‡**ATLANTA WRITING RESOURCE CENTER, INC.**, Room 206, The Arts Exchange, 750 Kalb St., Atlanta, GA 30312, "is for everyone with an interest in writing, whether for print or electronic media or simply for personal satisfaction. The Center will provide reference materials, guidelines information, samples, standard writing formats, and other resources for effective writing and marketing." They hold meetings on the second Thursday of each month, a biweekly critique group for poets and short story writers, and a monthly open house called "Writers' Brawl" on the fourth Wednesday of each month. The Center has regular open hours (staffed by volunteer hosts) with personal work space including typewriters, reference books, and other resources. They publish a bimonthly newsletter highlighting Center activities and Atlanta's literary events, and they provide news of contests, writers' conferences, etc. They also sponsor contests (see entry in Contests section). Literary magazines and journals as well as their writers' guidelines are available at the Center. They also hold workshops aimed at improving literary and marketing skills.

‡**THE BASEMENT WORKSHOP**, 3rd Floor, 22 Catherine St., New York, NY 10039, phone 212-732-0770, writers' center.

‡**BEYOND BAROQUE LITERARY/ARTS CENTER**, 681 Venice Blvd., Box 806, Venice, CA 90291, phone 213-822-3006, director Dennis Phillips, a foundation established in 1968 that has been funded by the NEA, state and city arts councils, and corporate donations. Foundation members get a calendar of events, discounts on regularly scheduled programs, and borrowing privileges in the small-press library of 23,000 volumes of poetry, fiction, and reference materials, including audio tapes of Beyond Baroque readings. The library contains a bookstore open 4 days a week, including Friday evenings to coincide with regular readings and performances. About 130 writers are invited to read each year; there are also open readings. Beyond Baroque, according to its director, is "the only literary focal point in all of Los Angeles."

‡**BURNABY WRITERS' SOCIETY**, 6450 Gilpin St., Burnaby, BC, V5G 2J3, Canada, contact person Eileen Kernaghan. Corresponding membership in the society, including a newsletter subscription, is open to anyone, anywhere. Yearly dues are $15. The Society holds monthly meetings at The Burnaby Arts Centre (address above), with a business meeting at 7:30 followed by a writer-speaker. Occasionally members of the society gather to read their own work.

‡**THE WHITTER BYNNER FOUNDATION FOR POETRY, INC.**, Box 2188, Santa Fe, NM 87504, phone 505-988-3251, president Douglas W. Schwartz. The Foundation awards grants exclusively to nonprofit organizations for the support of poetry-related projects in the area of: 1) support of individual poets through existing nonprofit institutions; 2) developing the poetry audience; 3) poetry translation and the process of poetry translation; and 4) uses of poetry. The Foundation "may consider the support of other creative and innovative projects in poetry." Grant applications must be received by February 1 each year; requests for application forms should be submitted to Steven Schwartz, Administrator, at the address above.

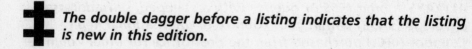

The double dagger before a listing indicates that the listing is new in this edition.

THE CATHEDRAL CHURCH OF ST. JOHN THE DIVINE AMERICAN POETS' CORNER, Cathedral Heights, 1047 Amsterdam Ave. at 112 St., New York, NY 10025, initiated in 1984 with memorials for Emily Dickinson, Walt Whitman and Washington Irving. It is similar in concept to the English Poets' Corner in Westminster Abbey, and was established and dedicated to memorialize this country's greatest writers.

THE CENTER FOR CREATIVE WRITING, Hope Center, Box 586, Houghton Lake Heights, MI 48630, offers workshops, information and occasional contests for writers in its area.

COMMITTEE OF SMALL MAGAZINE EDITORS AND PUBLISHERS, COSMEP NEWSLETTER, Box 703, San Francisco, CA 94101. If you are starting a small press or magazine or are embarking on self-publication, you should know about the advantages of membership in COSMEP. Send SASE for brochure. They publish a number of chapbooks on various aspects of small-press publishing which are distributed free to members and a monthly *COSMEP Newsletter*, mailed to members, with current publishing needs of small presses and other news and commentary.

COORDINATING COUNCIL OF LITERARY MAGAZINES, THE 1987 DIRECTORY OF LITERARY MAGAZINES, CCLM NEWS, CCLM CATALOG OF COLLEGE LITERARY MAGAZINES, 666 Broadway, New York, NY 10012 provides annual grants to various literary magazines and publishes two directories useful to writers: *The 1986 Directory of Literary Magazines*, which has detailed descriptions of 350 fiction and/or poetry magazines which are supported by CCLM and *CCLM Catalog of College Literary Magazines*, which covers the 250 undergraduate literary magazines which participate in CCLM's literary award contest as well as the quarterly CCLM News, listing manuscript requests, and grants and award deadlines. They also administer the General Electric Foundation Awards for Younger Writers, designed to recognize excellence in younger and less established creative writers and to support the literary magazines that publish their work. Nominations are accepted before April 30 from editors of noncommercial literary magazines published in the US and its territories. Up to 6 prizes of $5,000 each are given to the writers and $1,000 is given to the literary magazine in which the writer's work appeared.

ELLISTON POETRY COLLECTION, 646 Central Library, University of Cincinnati, Cincinnati, OH 45221, has one of the most comprehensive collections of current poetry.

‡F.A.I.M. (FEDERATION FOR THE ADVANCEMENT OF INDEPENDENT MAGAZINES), Geoff Stevens, 8 Beaconview House, Charlemont Farm, West Bromwich, West Midlands, England, is "an attempt to help member magazines to help themselves and each other at a time when production costs, postal rates and threats of V.A.T. are against them." It is a loose organization of small magazines, each retaining its own editorial policy, helping one another by trading advertising, sharing information, and general mutual support. They hold an annual poetry contest conducted by *Hat* magazine.

‡THE H.E.L.P. CENTER (HELPING THROUGH EDUCATING, LINKING AND PREVENTING), 598 Sixth St., Brooklyn, NY 11214, Joe Molnar, M.S.W., Director, provides "personal counseling by mail, for a fee, and all our psychotherapists are also experienced writers who are sensitive to the special needs and concerns of poets and creative writers."

‡INTERNATIONAL WOMEN'S WRITING GUILD, Box 810, Gracie Station, New York, NY 10028, phone 212-737-7536, founded 1976, "an alliance of women who value creativity and mutual support"; the women can write either for publication or for personal growth. The Guild publishes a bimonthly 16-20 page newsletter which includes member's needs, achievements, contests, and publishing information. A manuscript referral service introduces members to New York City literary agents. Other activities are writing conferences and retreats (they give $2,000 in scholarships to these conferences each year); "regional clusters" (independent regional groups); a talent bank for job referrals and a volunteer bank; a special member emergency fund for members who find themselves in crisis situations; group health and life insurance and a dental benefit plan. Membership in the nonprofit Guild costs $25/year in the US and $31/year foreign.

‡INTERSECTION FOR THE ARTS, 13 Columbus Ave., San Francisco, CA 94111, phone 415-397-6061, a writers' center.

‡ITHACA COMMUNITY POETS, Box 456, Ithaca, NY 14851, founded in 1974 by a number of local writers (most of them poets) who began meeting for discussion and support of their efforts and soon sponsored a series of readings that present Ithaca's own writers as well as others. Selection of writers for these readings (which are paid) is competitive. Ithaca Community Poets is supported by the NY State

Council on the Arts, the Tompkins Country Arts Council, Tompkins County Friends of the Library, and local merchants. Members of the group periodically offer workshops in areas of their own expertise, such as "Writing and Publishing Your Poems." They also sponsor the Ithaca Poetry Theatre, and they publish a poetry postcard series and a collection of poem-posters. At social gatherings, members read their poetry, short fiction, or other form of literature to the group.

‡**JUST BUFFALO**, 111 Elmwood Ave., Buffalo, NY 14201, phone 716-885-6400, founded in 1975 by Debora Ott, is now a permanent part of Buffalo's Allentown Community Center. Just Buffalo, with Ott as a full-time employee and one part-time assistant, offers a variety of programs including numerous readings, a monthly calendar of events, an annual writing competition, a weekly half-hour public radio show, and a program of writers in the public schools. Every program features a book sale, with a local bookstore handling the sale and splitting profits with Just Buffalo.

‡**THE LEAGUE OF CANADIAN POETS**, 24 Ryerson Ave., Toronto, Ontario M5T 2P3, Canada, phone 416-363-5047, founded 1966, executive director Angela Rebeiro. The League's aims are the advancement of poetry in Canada and promotion of the interests of serious, committed Canadian poets. Information on full and associate membership can be obtained by writing for the brochure, League of Canadian Poets: Services and Membership. The League publishes a quarterly newsletter (magazine-sized, 30 pp.); the *New Poet's Handbook*, which concerns itself with the personal, technical, and business aspects of a poetry career and is available for $5 from the Society; *When is a Poem*, on teaching poetry to children; a directory volume called *The League of Canadian Poets* that contains one page of information, including a picture, bio, publications, and "what critics say" about each of the members, plus information about educational services, workshops, seminars, etc.; and *Here is a Poem*, a companion anthology of League members and poets who contributed their techniques to the first publication. The League's members go on reading tours, and the League encourages them to speak on any facet of Canadian literature at schools and universities, libraries, or organizations. The League has arranged "thousands of readings in every part of Canada"; they are now arranging exchange visits featuring the leading poets of such countries as Great Britain, Germany, and the U.S. The League co-sponsors a World Poetry Festival with Harbourfront Corporation. Write for information. *Canadian Author and Bookman* is published at this address. It is also the address of Writers Union of Canada.

‡**THE LOFT**, 2301 E. Franklin Ave., Minneapolis, MN 55406, phone 612-341-0431, founded 1974, executive director Susan Broadhead. The Loft began as a group of poets looking for a place to give readings and conduct workshops and evolved into a sophisticated hub of activity managed by an 18-member board of directors. A staff of 5 persons is assisted by more than 200 volunteers who contribute more than 4,000 hours annually. One thousand members contribute $25/year to The Loft; it is further supported by $7,000 from donor funds. The Loft features regular readings, some of them open to all who wish to participate and others, such as the Mentor series, that feature nationally known writers. The Center publishes a monthly newsletter called *A View from the Loft*. The Loft's present quarters are in an old church, which has offices and classrooms in the basement and performance areas on the main floor. See also The Loft-McKnight Writers Awards under Contests and Grants.

‡**NATIONAL ASSOCIATION FOR POETRY THERAPY**, 1029 Henhawk Rd., Baldwin, NY 11510. In many mental and other hospitals, schools, clinics, prisons, nursing homes, half-way houses, recreation and community centers, drug and alcohol addiction centers, hospice programs and other settings professional poetry therapists engage in "the intentional use of poetry and the interactive process to achieve therapeutic goals and personal growth." If you are such a professional you are probably aware of the national organization. If you are not, you may wish to find out about it for many reasons, including the possibility of training and employment. You can become an Associate Member for $20 and receive their *NAPT Newsletter* and other publications and attend their meetings.

‡**NATIONAL FEDERATION OF STATE POETRY SOCIETIES, INC.**, 1121 Major Ave. NW, Albuquerque, NM 87107, phone 505-344-5615. Most reputable state poetry societies are members of the National Federation and advertise their various poetry contests through their quarterly bulletin, *Strophes*, available without cost to members of the societies, 10¢ per copy to others. Beware of organizations calling themselves state poetry societies (however named) that are not members of NFSPS, as such labels are sometimes used by vanity schemes trying to sound respectable. Others, such as the Oregon State Poetry association, are quite reputable, but they don't belong to NFSPS because the don't want to pay their dues. NFSPS holds an annual meeting in a different city each year with a large awards banquet, addressed by an honorary chairman. There are 50 different contests with entry fees ($3 for nonmembers, except $5/each for NFSPS Award entries; $1/poem for members except $5/poem for NFSPS award). Rules for all contests are given in a brochure available from *Strophes* at the address above.

THE NORTH SHORE WOMEN WRITERS ALLIANCE, Box 2014, Setauket, NY 11733, is a support group for writers and artists of all callings, male or female. Membership is $8 yearly ($20 for 3 years) and entitles members to a quarterly newsletter with marketing information; news about small and large presses and other writers, artists, magazines, and newspapers. They provide feedback on the work of members, writer-referral services, instruction in research techniques, and low-cost critique/editing services. They publish work by their members, sometimes in the newsletter and sometimes in anthologies.

‡**THE OREGON STATE POETRY ASSOCIATION**, 10058 SE 100th Dr., Portland, OR 97266, phone 503-775-2232, founded 1956 for "the promotion and creation of poetry," has over 300 members, $10 dues, publishes a quarterly *OSPA Newsletter*, and sponsors contests twice yearly with total cash prizes of $300 (no entry fee to members). Guidelines available in February and August for SASE. The association coordinates opportunities for its member poets and teachers of poets who are available on request for readings and seminars throughout the state and provides occasions for members to showcase and sell their books.

PASSAIC COUNTY COMMUNITY COLLEGE POETRY CENTER LIBRARY, College Blvd., Paterson, NJ 07509, has an extensive collection of contemporary poetry and seeks small press contributions to help keep it abreast.

‡**PENINSULA WRITERS**, Box 88012, Kentwood, MI 49508, founded 1984. Many of the teacher-members meet regularly in small groups to write and to share their writing. Peninsula Writers' activities include membership workshops, small-group writing, publication of anthologies of member and student works, recognition programs for student and teacher writers, and a Peninsula Writers Conference. Inquiries about memberships, programs, and their summer writing retreat are invited.

PERSONAL POETS UNITED, 860 Armand Ct. NE, Atlanta, GA 30324, c/o Jean Hesse. Ms. Hesse started a business in 1980 writing poems for individuals for a fee (for greetings, special occasions, etc.). Others started similar businesses, after she began instructing them in the process, especially through a Cassette Tape Training Program and other training materials. She then organized a support group of poets around the country writing poetry-to-order, Personal Poets United, hoping to have local chapters in key areas and a national conference. Send SASE for free brochure.

‡**THE POETRY CENTER OF THE 92ND STREET Y**, 1395 Lexington Ave., New York, NY 10128, phone 212-427-6000, was founded in 1939 by William Kolodney and for 47 years has presented a model repertoire of programs and services to writers. The Y's ongoing series of poetry readings is today the leading platform for international literary figures. The series of readings is frequently sold out, and the Center sells some 2,000 books by the visiting writers each season. Kolodney also established a wide range of workshops and seminars that often incorporate poetry with dance, music, film, and theater. The Poetry Center's programs are advertised in the New York newspapers, or you can join the Center to participate in and be informed about their activities.

‡**THE POETRY PROJECT AT ST. MARK'S CHURCH IN THE BOWERY**, 10th St. and 2nd Ave., New York, NY 10003, phone 212-674-0910, was established in 1966 by the US Dept. of H.E.W. in an effort to help wayward youths in the East Village. It is now funded by a variety of government and private sources. Eileen Myles is the artistic director. From October through May the project offers workshops, talks, staged readings, performance poetry, and a series of featured writers who bring their books to sell at the readings. If the reading is a publication party, the publisher handles the sales.

POETRY RESOURCE CENTER OF MICHIGAN, 621 S. Washington, Royal Oak, MI 48067, phone 313-399-6163, "is a nonprofit organization which exists through the generosity of poets, writers, teachers publishers, printers, librarians, and others dedicated to the reading and enjoyment of poetry in Michigan. The PRC Newsletter and Calendar, published with the cooperation of the Detroit Public Library, is available by mail [monthly] for an annual membership donation of $15 or more, and is distributed free of charge at locations throughout the state. To obtain copies for distribution at poetry functions, contact the editor or any member of the PRC Board of Trustees.

‡**POETRY SOCIETY OF AMERICA**, 15 Gramercy Park, New York, NY 10003, phone 212-254-9628, is a membership organization of professional poets sponsoring readings, lectures and workshops both in New York City and around the country. Their Van Voorhis Library of 7,000 volumes of poetry is open for research and scholarly works. They publish the quarterly *Poetry Review* (see under publishers), and a newsletter of their activities. And they sponsor a wide range of contests, most of them open only to

members, but four of them are (in 1987) open to nonmembers as well, as are three awards for books. Contests deadlines are December 31 each year, and the awards are made at a banquet in the spring. For rules and guidelines for submission to their various contests, send SASE after September 1.

POETS & WRITERS, INC., 201 W. 54 St., New York, NY 10019, is the major support organization for writers of poetry and fiction in the US. Phone 212-757-1766 between 11 and 3 EST for addresses, facts or referrals from their nationwide Information Center. They also conduct a Readings/Workshop Program in New York State. Their primary function is publication of aids for writers.

POETS FOR PEACE, 508 Lincoln St., Port Townsend, WA 98368, an organization of poets protesting nuclear armaments and war, publishes *Give Peace a Chance* quarterly, newspaper ads of protest, and conducts readings.

THE SEGUE FOUNDATION, 300 Bowery, New York, NY 10012, distributes books and magazines from the small presses that are rarely available in commercial bookstores, with the aid of the National Endowment for the Arts and the New York State Council on the Arts. Send SASE for catalog.

‡**THE THURBER HOUSE**, 77 Jefferson Ave., Columbus, OH 43215, phone 614-464-1082, officially opened in 1985, executive director Donn Vickers, who says that it is "one of the most diversely active of all restored writer's homes." The Thurber Center has a staff of 2 people plus 17 volunteers and a 9-person regional advisory board. Half of its budget comes from state, local, and national arts councils; 35 percent from foundations; and the rest from sales. The house includes a bookstore which distributes the best small press books the Midwest has to offer. They sponsor a writer-in-residence program which provides 3-month retreats. The house also includes performance spaces and offices. Local writers are invited to use the house as a place to "come together with others who care."

‡**UNITED AMATEUR PRESS**, c/o Velma Lamoreaux, 8 South 5th St., Marshalltown, IA 50158, a group requiring a membership fee of $7 plus a "credential," which can be a poem, essay, or story written by the applicant, or any item edited, published, or printed by the applicant. The press accepts "bundles"—"an envelope of papers with writings authored by members," and then circulates these bundles to other members. There is a publication called *The United Amateur*, which appears quarterly and publishes winners of "Laureate Awards" in 8 categories including both serious and humorous poetry.

‡**THE WRITER'S CENTER**, 7815 Old Georgetown Road, Bethesda, MD 20814, phone 301-654-8664, founder and chairman of the board Allan Lefcowitz, director Jane Fox. This is an outstanding resource for writers not only in Washington DC but in the wider area ranging from southern Pennsylvania to North Carolina and West Virginia. The Center offers 150 multi-meeting workshops each year in writing, typesetting, word processing, and graphic arts, and provides a research library and printing equipment. It is open 7 days a week, 10 hours a day. Some 2,200 members support the Center with $15 annual donations, which allows for 4 paid staff members. There is a book gallery at which publications of small presses are displayed and sold. The Center's publication, *The Carousel*, is an 8-page tabloid that comes out 8 times a year. They also sponsor 40 annual performance events, which include presentations in poetry, fiction, and theater.

‡**WRITERS UNION OF CANADA**, 24 Ryerson Ave. Toronto, Ontario M5T 2P3 Canada, provides services and information to members, including a writer's guide to Canadian publishers ($3) and a variety of other publications to assist writers.

Additional Organizations Useful to Poets

Also read the following listings for other information on organizations for poets:

Calliope
Channels
Haiku Society of America
IWI Review
Konglomerati
Legerete
Maine Writers Workshop
Matilda

Midwest Arts & Literature
Piedmont
Poetry Nippon
Science Fiction Poetry Association
Women-in-Literature
Women Writer's Alliance
Writers House Press

Publications Useful to Poets

R. R. BOWKER CO., LITERARY MARKET PLACE, MAGAZINE INDUSTRY MARKET PLACE, MAGAZINES FOR LIBRARIES, 205 E. 42 St., New York, NY 10017. **LMP** is an annual, $45 in paperback, covering all aspects of trade book and university press publishing in the US, listing about 1,700 book publishers, 350 of which publish fiction and/or poetry. Only the 300 commercial and better known literary magazines are listed in **LMP** because Bowker covers the others in **Magazine Industry Market Place. LMP** "yellow pages" give the addresses and telephone numbers of most publishers, editors and agents; many services offered by typesetters, printers and binders; and miscellaneous information such as TV and film outlets, literary organizations, writing conferences, award and book clubs. **MIMP** is an annual, $45 in paperback, which is to US magazines what **LMP** is to books. About 2,500 magazines are listed alphabetically, a quarter of which publish fiction and/or poetry. **MFL** is designed primarily to help librarians decide which magazines to purchase, but writers should know about it because of the vast number of magazines—6,500 in 117 subject areas, about 1,000 using poetry and/or fiction—which are listed. These are standard reference works which can be consulted in the library.

THE BUCKLEY-LITTLE BOOK CATALOGUE, Box 512, Canal St. Station, New York, NY 10013, is an annual publication listing remaindered and out-of-print books available from their authors. Bookdealers use this resource to find out-of-print books for specific customers and it is a means by which authors, for an annual fee, may maintain listings of their books and make them available by mail-order.

CANADIAN POETRY, English Dept., University of Western Ontario, London, Ontario, Canada N6A 3K7, phone 519-679-3403, founded 1977, editor Prof. D.M.R. Bentley, is a biannual journal of critical articles, reviews, historical documents (such as lettter), and an annual bibliography of the year's work in Canadian poetry studies. It is a professionally printed, scholarly edited, flat-spined 100 + pp. journal which pays contributors in copies. Subscription: $10. Sample: $5. Note that they publish no poetry except in quotations in articles.

THE CHRISTIAN WRITER, THE PROFESSIONAL WRITING MAGAZINE FOR CHRISTIANS, Box 5650, Lakeland, FL 33807, circulation 15,000, is a monthly how-to magazine for Christian writers. Free sample and writer's guidelines.

CODA: POETS AND WRITERS NEWSLETTER, see Poets & Writers, Inc. in this section.

DUSTBOOKS, INTERNATIONAL DIRECTORY OF LITTLE MAGAZINES AND SMALL PRESSES, SMALL PRESS REVIEW, Box 100, Paradise, CA 95960. Dustbooks publishes a number of books useful to writers. Send SASE for catalog. Among their regular publications, **International Directory** is an annual directory of all small presses and literary magazines, about 3,000 entries (many of them repetitive), about half being magazines, a fourth being book publishers, and the other fourth being both. There is very detailed information about what these presses and magazines report to be their policies in regard to payment, copyright, format and publishing schedules. *Small Press Review* is a monthly magazine, newsprint, carrying current updating of listings in **ID**, small press needs, news, announcements and reviews—a valuable way to stay abreast of the literary marketplace. I have a regular column in this magazine carrying information on poetry markets.

‡GEM'S NEWSLETTER FOR AUTHORS, Box 1417, Marietta, GA 30061, a 4-page newsletter "published irregularly but about 2-3 times each calendar year." Subscription (5 guaranteed issues) costs $6. The newsletter publishes short paragagraphs about current markets for writers, contests, directories, etc.

GOLDEN EAGLE NEWSLETTER, 50 Canterbury Rd., New Milford, CT 06776, editor Tom Morris, 6 issues for $7.50, 12 issues for $13.50, lists a wide range of contests: rules, deadlines and prizes. Sample book issue free for SASE. Subscription: $7.50 for 6 issues, $13.50 for 12.

GRANTS AND AWARDS AVAILABLE TO AMERICAN WRITERS, PEN, 47 5th Ave., New York, NY 10003, $6 postpaid, is an annual directory with up-to-date listings on award programs, key information on deadlines, guidelines, and a complete list of state and provincial arts councils in the US and Canada.

‡**THE INSIDE FROM THE OUTSIDE: AN INTERNATIONAL NEWSLETTER FOR WRITERS**, Box 3186, Bloomington, IN 47402, editor Normajean MacLeod, is a 6 pp. magazine-sized newsletter of columns and reviews of interest to writers, subscription: $3/1 year, $5/2 years. It is photocopied from typescript on heavy grey stock. The publication conducts an annual writing competition a $50 Grand Prize (plus publication), entry fee of $1/poem for non-subscribers, reduced rates for subscribers.

‡**THE LETTER EXCHANGE**, published by The Readers' League, c/o Stephen Sikora, Box 6218, Albany, CA 94706. Published 3 times each year, *The Letter Exchange* is a digest-sized magazine, 30 pp., that publishes four types of listings: regular (which are rather like personal classifieds); ghost letters, which contain lines like "Send news of the Entwives!"; amateur magazines, which publicizes readers' own publishing ventures; and sketch ads, in which readers who would rather draw than write can communicate in their chosen mode. All ads are coded, and readers respond through the code numbers. Subscription to *The Letter Exchange* is $9/year, and sample copies are $3.50 postpaid. Poets who are so inclined often exchange poems and criticism with each other through this medium.

‡**LITERARY MAGAZINE REVIEW**, %The English Dept., Denison Hall, Kansas State University, Manhattan, KS 66506, founded 1981, editor G.W. Clift, a quarterly magazine (digest-sized, 76 pp.) that publishes critiques, 2-5 pp. long, of various literary magazines, plus shorter "reviews" (about ½ page), directories of literary magazines (such as British publications), and listings of new journals during a particular year. Single copies are available for $3 or subscriptions for $10 year.

LITERARY MARKETS, Suite 105, 725 South Beach Rd., Point Roberts, WA 98281 or 4340 Coldfall Rd., Richmond, British Columbia, Canada V7C 1P8, is a bimonthly newsletter, usually about 6 pp., stapled at the corner, which is packed with information about new publications, changes and current needs. I was guided to many of the listings in this directory by this newsletter. They also have market lists available and carry information about literary activities and resources other than markets.

‡**UNIVERSITY OF MICHIGAN PRESS, POETS ON POETRY, UNDER DISCUSSION**, 839 Greene St., Ann Arbor, MI 48106, phone 313-764-4388, founded 1930, managing editor LeAnn Fields. The press publishes scholarly work including the Poets on Poetry series and the Under Discussion series, which are books of poetry criticism.

‡**ORYX PRESS, STYLE MANUALS OF THE ENGLISH-SPEAKING WORLD: A GUIDE, WOMEN'S POETRY INDEX**, 2214 North Central at Encanto, Phoenix, AZ 85004-1483, toll-free order number 800-457-ORYX. *Style Manuals of the English-Speaking World* ($32.50) describes nontechnical, nonliterary style manuals and author's guides from English-speaking communities, including government, commercial, and university press style manuals and a second section on manuals for individual disciplines. *Women's Poetry Index* ($65) is "the first and only index devoted exclusively to anthologies of women's poetry." It covers collections published between 1945 and 1982. The scope is international and poetry in translation is included.

POESIS, English Dept., Bryn Mawr College, Bryn Mawr, PA 19066, founded 1973, is a quarterly of contemporary poetry criticism.

‡**POETRY BOOK SOCIETY**, 21 Earls Court Square, London SW5 9DE, England, a book club with an annual subscription rate of £15.50, which covers 4 books of new British poetry at discount prices, the *PBS Bulletin*, the annual *Poetry Supplement*, a £2.50 book voucher or a free copy of *The Rattle Bag* (for new members or those enrolling new members), and free surface postage and packing to anywhere in the world. A quarterly choice of a new book of poetry is made, and all members receive it. The selectors also recommend other books of special merit, which are obtainable at discount prices. The Poetry Book Society is subsidized by the Arts Council of Great Britain.

‡**POETRY EXCHANGE**, c/o Horizon Books, 425 15th Ave. E., Seattle, WA 98112, a 4-page monthly newsletter that includes a calendar of happenings in the Seattle area as well as listings of manuscripts wanted, workshops, announcements, and "views and reviews." The newsletter is supported by donations and published by volunteers. It is distributed at various locations in Seattle, including bookstores, coffeehouses, libraries, etc.

Use an up-to-date Market Directory!

Don't let your Poet's Market turn old on you.

You may be reluctant to give up this copy of Poet's Market. After all, you would never discard an old friend.

But resist the urge to hold onto an old Poet's Market! Like your first typewriter or your favorite pair of jeans, the time will come when this copy of Poet's Market will have to be replaced.

In fact, if you're still using this 1987 Poet's Market when the calendar reads 1988, your old friend isn't your best friend anymore. Many of the publishers listed here have moved. Many of the contact names are now incorrect, and even the publisher's needs have changed since last year.

You can't afford to use an out-of-date book to plan your publishing efforts. But there's an easy way for you to stay current—order the 1988 Poet's Market. All you have to do is complete the attached postcard and return it with your payment or charge card information. Best of all, we'll send you the 1988 edition at the 1987 price—just $16.95. The 1988 Poet's Market will be published and ready for shipment in October 1987.

Make sure you have the most current marketing information—order the new edition of Poet's Market now.

To order simply drop this postpaid card in the mail.

☐ YES! I want the most current edition of Poet's Market. Please send me the 1988 Poet's Market at the 1987 price—$16.95. I have included $2.00 for postage and handling. (Ohio residents add 5½% sales tax.) NOTE: 1988 Poet's Market will be ready for shipment in October 1987.

☐ Payment enclosed (Slip this card and your payment into an envelope.)

☐ Please charge my: ☐ Visa   ☐ MasterCard

Account #_____ Exp. Date_____

Signature_____

Name_____

Address_____

City_____ State_____ Zip_____

(This offer expires August 1, 1988. Please allow 30 days for delivery.)

2158

9933 Alliance Road
Cincinnati, Ohio 45242

Make sure you have a current edition of Poet's Market

Each edition of Poet's Market contains hundreds of changes to give you the most current information to work with. Make sure your copy is the latest edition.

This card will get you the 1988 edition... at 1987 prices!

POETS & WRITERS, INCL., 201 W. 54th St., New York, NY 10019, is our major support organization (see listing in Organizations Useful to Poets section). Their many helpful publications include *Coda: Poets & Writers Newsletter*, which appears 5 times a year ($12.50, or $2.50 for a single copy), magazine-sized, 32 pp., newsprint, has been called *The Wall Street Journal* of our profession, and it is there that one most readily finds out about resources such as I am listing here, current needs of magazines and presses, contests, awards, jobs and retreats for writers, and discussions of business, legal and other issues affecting writers. Subscription $12 a year. P&W also publishes a number of valuable directories such as **A Directory of American Poets and Fiction Writers ($8 paperback),** which editors, publishers, agents and sponsors of readings and workshops use to locate over 8,000 active writers in the country. (You may qualify for a listing if you have a number of publications.) They also publish **A Writer's Guide to Copyright; Sponsors List** (of over 600 organizations which sponsor readings and workshops involving poets and fiction writers); **Literary Agents: A Complete Guide; Literary Bookstores: A List in Progress**; and many reprints of articles from *Coda* which are useful to writers, such as "Jobs for Writers"; "How to Give an Unsolicited Manuscript the Best Chance"; "Fifteen Heavens"; information on writers' colonies; "On Giving Readings"; "The Quest for a Publisher": etc.

‡**POETS' AUDIO CENTER, THE WATERSHED FOUNDATION**, Box 50145, Washington, DC 20004, toll-free number for charge orders 800-824-7888; minimum phone order $15. This is an international clearinghouse for ordering any poetry recording available, from both commercial and noncommercial producers. Catalog available free ("an introduction to our collection"); they stock over 700 titles. Complete listing available for $3, or free to acquisitions librarians. Members of Watershed Associates get a 10 percent discount on everything; you are invited to join.

STRUGGLING WRITER, Box 16315, Greenville, SC 29606, is a bimonthly publication carrying articles (and poems up to 16 lines) about writing, presses, publications, reviews, and other information especially of value to beginning writers.

‡**THE UPPER LEFT-HAND CORNER**, published by International Self-Counsel Press, Ltd., 306 W. 25th St., North Vancouver, BC, V7N 2G1, Canada, edited by E. Kernaghan, E. Surridge, P. Kernaghan, and R. Westergaard, a book designed for writers "looking to the growing markets in the upper left-hand corner of North America." It includes a comprehensive list of regional publishers and contains basic information useful to both the beginning and professional writer. Price is $10.95 plus $1 postage. A 1986 edition was to be published soon after **Poet's Market** press time.

‡**WORDS IN OUR POCKETS: THE FEMINIST WRITERS GUILD HANDBOOK ON HOW TO GAIN POWER, GET PUBLISHED AND GET PAID**, edited by Celeste West and available from Dustbooks, Box 100, Paradise, CA 95969, phone 916-877-6110 or 415-641-5816, price $9.95 paper, or $15.95 cloth. This is a 368-page guide book "for the woman who hopes to make the world more whole through her writing." The first section is "Finding your way around establishment publishing" and the second is on "Women's publishing." In section three, a dozen writers discuss their own genres, and section four is a discussion of "The community of the book and our support systems." See also The Feminist Writers Guild under Organizations Useful to Poets.

THE WRITER, 8 Arlington St., Boston, MA 02116, is a monthly magazine about writing techniques and experience with a regular poetry column in which poems from readers are analyzed, evaluated and discussed.

WRITER'S DIGEST, WRITER'S YEARBOOK, WRITER'S DIGEST BOOKS, 9933 Alliance Rd., Cincinnati, OH 45242, phone 800-543-4644 outside Ohio, or 513-984-0717. *Writer's Digest* is a monthly magazine about writing with frequent articles and much market news about poetry in addition to my monthly column and Poetry Notes. See entry in Publishers of Poetry section. *Writer's Yearbook* is a newsstand annual for freelance writers, journalists and teachers of creative writing, with articles and market information regarding poetry. Writer's Digest Books publishes and distributes a remarkable array of books useful to writers, such as *Writer's Market*, a general guide to about 750 book publishers, of which about 450 publish fiction and/or poetry. They publish my books about writing poetry: *The Poet and the Poem, On Being a Poet* and *The Poet's Handbook* and distribute Robert Wallace's *Writing Poems*, a book I recommend, and *Wood's Unabridged Rhyming Dictionary*, as well as a number of other books about writing poetry.

WRITER'S JOURNAL, Lynnmark, Box 2922T, Livonia, MI 48150 is a newsletter with articles, essays and fillers to help inform, direct, encourage and inspire aspiring writers. They use some poetry on their Poets Page.

WRITER'S LIFELINE, Box 1641, Cornwall, Ontario, Canada K6H 5V6, Canada, is a monthly magazine aimed at freelance writers of all ages and interests.

WRITERS WEST, FOR WORKING WRITERS, see entry in Publishers of Poetry section.

WRITEWAY, POETRY CONTEST CALENDAR, Box 199, 3421 N. 1st Ave., Tucson, AZ 85705, publishes an annual calendar ($6.95) giving the dates and rules for over 70 annual contests.

WRITING!, Curriculum Innovations, Inc., 3500 Western Ave., Highland Park, IL 60035, is a monthly magazine (September through May) covering writing skills for junior and senior high school students.

Additional Publications Useful to Poets

Also read the following listings for other publications of interest to poets:

Academy of American Poets
Ahnene
American Poetry Review
Associated Writing Programs
Bay Area Poets Coalition
Bloomsburg Review
Byline
Committee of Small Magazine Editors and Publishers
Coordinating Council of Literary Magazines
Creative Urge
Cross-Canada Writer's Quarterly
Dear Contributor
Inkling
Konocti Books
Neophytes
Pacific Arts & Letters
Philadelphia Poets
Piedmont
Poet & Critic
Poet Tree
Poetry Canada
Poetry Flash
Poetry Nippon
Princeton University Press

Printers Pie
Published!
Rainbow
Rhyme Time
Scarecrow
Seems
Spokes
Stone Country
Stony Hills
Success
Trouvere Company
Tyro
Unmuzzled Ox
Word Exchange
Wordwrights Canada
Write Now Books
Write On
The Writer
Writer's Bloc
Writers House Press
Writers West
Ye Olde News
Xanadu

Close-up

Noel Peattie
Sipapu

Artist: Lawrence Goodridge

Noel Peattie, of Konocti Books also writes and publishes (a one-man operation) *Sipapu*, a journal of small press reviews which appears twice a year. I was so fascinated by the first issue I saw, I sat and read it cover-to-cover, then subscribed. Though it is aimed primarily at librarians, my guess is that many poets will be as fascinated by it as I was. There they will find an insider's look at many of the presses and publications listed in **Poet's Market**—and sensitive reviews of what they publish.

Although Noel's parents were both well-known writers, he became a librarian. In 1969, at a meeting of the California Library Association, the members were concerned about how they could monitor and collect the vast amount of underground and anti-Establishment literature that had been pouring out of the small presses during the late 60s. Noel volunteered to do a newsletter and though the organization dissolved, *Sipapu* continues. He explains, "In Hopi and Apache lore *sipapu* is the place of emergence of the tribes from underground.

"I hadn't written poetry," he says, "since my teens, but the assignment of selecting poetry for U.C. Davis revived my interest. Now it was possible for anyone to write poetry—Blacks, prisoners, housewives, even librarians. I sent my own out to magazines—mostly local, but I have also appeared in *Pulpsmith*, *Second Coming*, and *Greenfield Review*."

Sipapu is distinguished by its candid, scholarly and critical tone. In each issue he interviews at length an unusual publisher, librarian, or similar small press figure. The other publications in the field (primarily *Small Press Review* and *Small Press*) are aimed at the small press world itself. Noel's aim is in helping librarians make choices in the bewildering profusion in the field.

I asked him what he thought was happening in the small presses today. He said, "My own sense of the poetry and small press scene is that poet, editor, publisher, distributor, librarian/bookseller, and reader are all on an endless merry-go-round in which no one is actually winning." (My own opinion is that it can be explained by the atmosphere of "anything goes" which Ginsberg and others of the 60s introduced—the very atmosphere which encouraged Noel to take up poetry again.)

Noel continued, "Even the few well-known poets spend a lot of time giving readings around the country. Poets have manuscripts they can't get published; publishers have manuscripts they can't afford to publish; editors get manuscripts they absolutely refuse to publish; librarians are asked to subscribe to periodicals that come from clear across the country and that they can't understand (or don't want to try); and the reader—ah, where is he? In the wilderness, I fear."

But Noel does what he can to make sense of all this publishing hurly-burly, and he brings it to you in the pages of *Sipapu*.

—Judson Jerome

Glossary

Digest-size. 5½ x 8½", the size of a folded sheet of conventional typing paper.

Flat-spine. What many publishers call "perfect-bound," glued with a flat edge (usually permitting readable type) on the spine.

IRC. International Reply Coupon, postage for return of submissions from another country. One IRC is sufficient for one ounce *by surface mail.* If you want an air mail return, you need one IRC for each half-ounce. An English editor comments, "We get only 22p for an IRC you paid 65¢ for—a big rip-off by the PO." Do not send checks or cash for postage to foreign countries: the exchange rates are so high it is not worthwhile for editors to bother with. (Exception: many Canadian editors do not object to US dollars; use IRCs the first time and inquire.) When I am submitting to foreign countries—or submitting heavy manuscripts within the US—I am likely to instruct the editor to throw the manuscript away if it is rejected, and to notify me by air mail, for which I provide postage. It is cheaper to make another print-out or photocopy than to pay postage for such manuscripts.

Magazine-size. 8½ x 11", the size of conventional typing paper unfolded.

MS, MSS. Manuscript, manuscripts.

Multiple submission. Submission of more than one poem at a time; most publishers of poetry *prefer* multiple submissions and many specify how many poems should be in a packet.

Saddle-stapled. What many publishers call "saddle-stitched," folded and stapled along the fold.

SAE. Self-addressed envelope.

SASE. Self-addressed, stamped envelope. *Every* publisher requires, with any submission, query, request for catalog, or sample, a self-addressed, stamped envelope. This information is so basic I exclude it from the individual listings but repeat it in bold type at the bottom of many pages throughout this book. The return-envelope (usually folded for inclusion) should be large enough to hold the material submitted or requested, and the postage provided—stamps if the submission is within your own country, IRCs if it is to another country—should be sufficient for its return..

Simultaneous submission. Submission of the same manuscript to more than one publisher at a time. Most magazine editors *refuse to accept* simultaneous submissions. Some book and chapbook publishers do not object to simultaneous submissions. In all cases, notify them that the manuscript is being simultaneously submitted elsewhere if that is what you are doing.

Tabloid-size. 11x15" or larger, the usual size of tabloid newspapers.

US State Codes

AL	Alabama	AK	Alaska	ME	Maine
AZ	Arizona	AR	Arkansas	MA	Massachusetts
CA	California	CO	Colorado	MN	Minnesota
CT	Connecticut	DE	Delaware	MS	Mississippi
FL	Florida	GA	Georgia	NE	Nebraska
GU	Guam	HI	Hawaii	NH	New Hampshire
ID	Idaho	IL	Illinois	NM	New Mexico
IN	Indiana	IA	Iowa	NC	North Carolina
KS	Kansas	KY	Kentucky	OH	Ohio
LA	Louisiana	OK	Oklahoma	OR	Oregon
MD	Maryland	PA	Pennsylvania	PR	Puerto Rico
MI	Michigan	RI	Rhode Island	SC	South Carolina
MO	Missouri	SD	South Dakota	TN	Tennessee
MT	Montana	TX	Texas	UT	Utah
NV	Nevada	VT	Vermont	VI	Virgin Islands
NJ	New Jersey	VA	Virginia	WA	Washington
NY	New York	DC	Washington DC	WV	West Virginia
ND	North Dakota	WI	Wisconsin	WY	Wyoming

Canadian Provinces

AB	Alberta	PQ	Quebec	NS	Nova Scotia
LB	Labrador	YT	Yukon	PEI	Prince Edward
NB	New Brunswick	BC	British Columbia		Island
NT	North West Territories	MB	Manitoba	SK	Saskatchewan
ON	Ontario	NF	Newfoundland		

Indexes

Subject Index

The following index is a general guide to help save you time in your search for the proper market for your poem(s).

The categories are listed alphabetically and contain the magazines, publishers and contests and awards that buy or accept special categories of poetry, most of which are coded IV in their listing. The presses and magazines for a particular subject are listed together; the contests and awards follow separately, marked (C&A).

Check through the index first to see what subjects are represented. Then, if you are seeking a magazine for your poem on fantasy, for example, look at the section under Science Fiction/Fantasy/Horror. After you have selected a possible market, refer to the General Index for the correct page number. Then find the listing and read the requirements *carefully*.

In the section *Specialized*, there are publishers and magazines which publish a particular theme or subject or publications directed to a special audience. The poetry these markets accept would therefore be subject-related. The *Regional* section lists those outlets which publish poetry about a special geographic area or poetry by poets from that region; and the category *Form/Style* contains those magazines and presses that prefer a specific poetic style or form; haiku, sonnets, epic, narrative, etc. The last two sections are of magazines and publishers located in Canada and in other English-speaking countries, and they all demand a SAE with IRC's for return of your poetry.

We do not recommend that you use this index exclusively in your search for a market. Most of the magazines and publishers are very general in their specifications, and they don't choose to be listed by category. Also, many publishers specialize in one subject area but are open to other subjects as well. Reading *all* the listings is still your best marketing tool.

ANTHOLOGY
International Publishers Co., Inc.

CHILDREN/TEEN
Alive! For Young Teens
Brilliant Star
Children's Better Health Institute
Cobblestone Publishing Co.
District Lines
Green Tiger Press
Harcourt Brace Jovanovich
Insight
Just About Me
Pennywhistle Press
Reflections
Seventeen
Stone Soup
Straight
Young American
The Young Crusader

CHILDREN/TEEN (C&A)
Student Award

ETHNIC
Adrift (Irish)
Akwekon Literary Journal (Native American)
Ashod Press (Armenian)
Black American Literature Forum
Blackberry Books
Blind Beggar Press
Blue Cloud Quarterly Press (Native American)
Caribbean Review (Caribbean, Latin American)

The Celtic League (Ireland)
Cencrastus (Scottish)
Chandrabhaga (Third World)
Chapman (Scottish)
The Clyde Press (folklore)
Confluence Press (Native American, Western)
Cordillera Press (Spanish)
The Italian Times of Maryland
Japanophile (Japan)
Kitchen Table: Women of Color Press (Third World)
Miorita (Romanian)
NBJ (French)
New Yarn (Asian, Japanese women)
Notebook: A Little Magazine (Chicano)
Ore (American Folklore)
Outrigger Publishers Ltd. (Third World and Pacific cultures)

Path Press, Inc. (Black American, Third World)
Pella Publishing Company (Greek)
Poetry Ireland Review (Irish)
Poetry Wale Press (Welsh, Anglo-Welsh)
Shamal Books (Afro-American, Caribbean)
The Sounds of Poetry (Latino)
Studia Hispanica Editors (Texas Hispanics)
Third Woman Press (minority women)

ETHNIC (C&A)
Cintas Fellowship Program (Cuban)
Galaxy of Verse (Black American)
Pluma De Oro Writing Competition (Spanish)

FORM/STYLE
All in Wall Stickers
The Arthur Press
Assembling Press
Burnt Lake Press
Colorado-North Review
The F. Marion Crawford Memorial Society
Dragonfly: A Quarterly of Haiku
The Gamut (experimental)
Gandhabba (post-beat)
Haiku Society of America
Haiku Zasshi Zo
High/Coo Press
Inkblot Publications (avant-garde)
Inkstone (haiku)
James Joyce Broadsheet
Kaldron (visual)
Luna Bisonte Prods
M.A.F. Press
Me Magazine (visual art)
Modern Haiku
Mosaic Press
The Mountain Laurel (traditional, nostalgic)
New Cicada (haiku)
The North Carolina Society Press
Northern Light (Neo-Surrealistic)
Oink! Magazine (New York school, post-moderism)
Ouroboros (visual, experimental)
Phoebus (illustrated poetry)
Phoenix Broadsheets (descriptive)
Place Stamp Here (visual)
The Red Candle Press (traditional)

The Red Pagoda, A Journal of Haiku
The Shakespeare Newsletter (Shakespeare)
Song (traditional)
The Unspeakable Visions of the Individual (beat oriented)

FORM/STYLE (C&A)
Annual International Narrative Contest
Beymorlin Sonnet Award
Canterbury Press Limerick Contest (limericks)
Ethel Eikel Harvey Memorial Award (lyric)
International Shakespearean Sonnet Contest
The Lyric Annual Collegiate Poetry Contest (traditional)
Perryman-Visser National Poetry Award (Visser, sonnet)
Bessie Archer Smith Memorial Award (narrative)
Tri-City Poetry Society Award (haiku)

GAY/LESBIAN
Bay Windows
The Body Politic
Common Lives/Lesbian Lives
First Hand
GMP Publishers
Pacific Bridge
RFD: A Country Journal for Gay Men Everywhere
The Sea Horse Press Ltd.
Sinister Wisdom
James White Review
The Wishing Well

HUMOR
Barrington Press
Bits Press
Candle: An International Ragazine
Ladies' Home Journal
Lonestar Publications of Humor
M.O.P. Press
Raw Dog Press
Rhyme Time Poetry Newsletter
Uncle
Whimsy

LOVE/ROMANCE/EROTICA
Apaeros: Reader-Written Forum About Sex and Erotica
Bride's
Brush Hill Press, Inc.
Modern Bride
Red Alder Books
Yellow Silk

MEMBERSHIP
Folio: An International Literary Magazine
IWI Review
Red Herring Press
Rocky Mountain Review of Language and Literature
Ver Poets
Women Writers Alliance

MEMBERSHIP (C&A)
Pennsylvania Poetry Society Annual Contest
Washington Poets Association Annual Poetry Contests

NATURE/RURAL/ECOLOGY
Action
Allegheny Press
The Amicus Journal
Arachne
Bear Tribe
Bird Watcher's Digest
Calli's Tales
The Countryman
Fruition
Great Elm Press
Hot Springs Gazette
Snowy Egret
Sunrust Magazine
Synthesis
Trans-Species Unlimited

PSYCHIC/OCCULT
Studia Mystica (mystical experience)
The White Light (occult)

PSYCHIC/OCCULT (C&A)
Fernando Rielo Prize for Mystical Poetry (mystical)

POLITICAL
Broadside Magazine
Central Park: A Journal of the Arts and Social Theory
Kropotkin's Lighthouse Publications
North American Political Spectrum
Quixote Press
Red Bass
Second Coming Press
Social Anarchism

REGIONAL
Ahsahta Press (Western American)
Alice James Books (New England)
Appalachian Heritage (Southern Appalachian)

Artemis (Virginia)
Arts Insight (Indiana)
The Augusta Spectator (southeastern US)
Bamboo Ridge (Hawaii)
Big Two-Hearted (Michigan)
Blueline (Adirondacks)
Bottom Dog Press (Ohio)
Callaloo Poetry Series
Cape Cod Life
Carolina Wren Press (North Carolina)
City Miner Books (northern California)
Cold-Drill Books (Idaho)
Cotton Boll/The Atlanta Review (Georgia)
Cottonwood Press (Midwest)
Delta Scene (Mississippi)
Dickenson Press (Appalachian)
The Dragonsbreath Press
Duende Press (New Mexico)
Expressions (Delaware)
Farmer's Market (Midwest)
Fireweed Press (Alaska)
Gambit (Kentucky, Ohio, Pennsylvania, Virginia, W. Virginia)
Georgia Journal (the South)
Great River Review (Midwest)
Journal of New Jersey Poets
Katuah (southern Appalachians)
Kennebec (Maine)
The Laurel Review (Appalachia)
Little Balkans Press (Kansas)
Midwest Arts & Literature (Midwest)
Mother Duck Press (Southwest)
New Mexico Humanities Review (Southwest)
New Southern Literary Messenger
Northwest Magazine (Pacific Northwest)
Now and Then (Appalachian)
Petronium Press (Hawaii)
The Poet Tree, Inc. (Sacramento)
Poetry/LA (Los Angeles)
Point Riders Press (Midwest)
Prescott Street Press (Northwest)
The Puckerbrush Press (Maine)
The Redneck Review of Literature (West)
Rhiannon Press (Midwest)
Ridge Review Magazine (northern California)
Right Here (northern Indiana)
Seven Buffaloes Press (rural American West and central California)
Snapdragon (Idaho)
Somrie Press (Brooklyn)
The South Florida Poetry Review
Southern Review, The (Louisiana)

Street Press (eastern Long Island)
Sunstone Press (Southwest)
Territory of Oklahoma: Literature & The Arts
Utah State University Press (western Americana)
Washington Review (Washington DC area)
Washington Writers' Publishing House (Washington DC area)
Wellspring Magazine (Texas)
Wisconsin Academy Review

REGIONAL (C&A)
Bush Foundation Fellowships for Artists (Minnesota)
Byliners of Corpus Christi (Texas)
INA Coolbrith Circle Annual Poetry Contest (California)
Iowa Arts Council Literary Awards
The Loft-McKnight Writers Award (Minnesota)
Mid-South Poetry Festival
Northeastern State Poetry Contest (Middle Atlantic States)
Texas Institute of Letters Poetry Award
Virginia Prize
West Virginia Poetry Society Award
Western States Arts Foundation

RELIGIOUS
Agada
The Awakener Magazine
Baptist Sunday School Board
Broken Streets
Channels
Choice Magazine
Christian Educators Journal
Christians Writing
Co-Laborer
Cornerstone: The Voice of this Generation
Dialogue: A Journal of Mormon Thought (Latter-Day Saints)
European Judaism
Evangel
The Evangelical Beacon
The Friend
Gesar: Buddhism in the West
Harold Shaw Publishers
The Inquirer
Issues (Judaism)
Jewish Currents
The Lutheran Journal
Lutheran Women
Marriage and Family Living
Mennonite Publishing House
Midstream: A Monthly Jewish Review
On Being

The Other Side Magazine
Our Family
Pentecostal Evangel
Queen of All Hearts
Reconstructionist (Judaism)
Reform Judaism
St. Anthony Messenger
Sharing The Victory
Silver Wings
Sonlight Christian Newspapers
Star Books, Inc.
Time of Singing
Touch
The United Methodist Reporter
Unity School of Christianity
The Upper Room
Wellspring
Wonder Time

SCIENCE FICTION/FANTASY/HORROR
Amazing Stories
Beyond
Bifrost
Bill Munster's Footsteps
The Creative Urge
Empire
Fantasy and Terror
Fantasy Book
Fantasy Review
Grue Magazine
Horizons S F
Infinitum
The Mage
The Mythopoeic Society
Night Cry
Pandora
Riverside Quarterly
Scavenger's Newsletter
Science Fiction Poetry Association
SF Spectrum
Space and Time
Time Warp
The Weirdbook Sampler
Westgate Press

SCIENCE FICTION/FANTASY/HORROR (C&A)
Maplecon SF, Fantasy, and Science Poetry Competition

SENIOR CITIZEN
Artful Codger and Codgerette
Heartland Journal
Modern Maturity
Muscadine
Prime Times
3 Score & 10
The Word Shop

SOCIAL ISSUES
Aim Magazine
Alcoholism & Addiction Magazine. Recovery!

Anti-Apartheid News
Before the Rapture Press
Cathedral Voice
Five Fingers Review
Laughing Waters Press
Pudding Publications
San Fernando Poetry Journal
West End Press
Wheat Forder's Press

SPECIALIZED

AG-Pilot International Magazine
The Allegheny Review
Alta Napa Press
American Atheist Press
American Land Forum (landscape)
American Rowing
American Studies Press, Inc. (Americana)
& (Ampersand) Press
Arete: The Journal of Sport Literature
Arjuna Library Press (critical surrealism, social topology, fine arts)
As Is/So & So Press (idiosyncratic)
Balance Beam Press, Inc. (children, feminism, peace)
Baseball: Our Way (baseball, football)
Black Bear Publications
Bowbender (archery)
Byline Magazine (writer's, writing)
Cabaret 246 (friends)
Colonnades (college students)
Creative with Words Publications
Crown Creations Associates (mytho-poeic)
Dear Contributor (publishing)
Dialogue (visually impaired)
Dickinson Studies (Emily Dickinson)
Dream International Quarterly
Ear Magazine (music)
Handicap News
Heresies
His Magazine (college life)
Hoofstrikes Newsletter (equine)
Ideals (nostalgia)
Iron Mountain: A Journal of Magical Religion
Joyful Noise (handicapped writers)
Kaleidoscope Press (disability)
La Jolla Poets' Press (established poets)
Latin American Literary Review Press (romance language)
The Lockhart Press (dreams)
The Lookout (merchant marine)
Ludd's Mill (music)
Minas Tirith Evening-Star: The Journal of the

American Tolkien Society (J.R.R. Tolkien)
Miriam Press (Viet Nam, women)
Music Works
New Methods (animals)
Nightsun
Ommation Press (dance)
One Shot (rock and roll)
The Pet Gazette
Philosophy and the Arts (philosophy, Bertrand Russell)
The Pipe Smoker's Ephemeris
The Poetry Connexion (radio)
Poetry Flash
Prime Time Sports & Fitness (humor, sports)
Processed World (work, information handling)
Reflect (Spiral Movement literature)
Religious Humanism
Salthouse (theme)
San Diego Poet's Press
Sapiens: A Journal for Human Evolution
Self and Society: European Journal of Humanistic Psychology
Southport Press (theme, historical)
Spitball (baseball)
Step Life (step-parenting)
Superintendent's Profile & Pocket Equipment Directory (highway superintendents, DPW directors)
Tels
Textile Bridge Press (working class)
Thomas Hardy Yearbook
Three Continents Press Inc. (non-Western)
Tradition (music)
Vegetarian Journal
White Walls: A Magazine of Writings by Artists
The Wisconsin Restaurateur
Writer's Digest (writing/publishing)
Ye Olde News (Renaissance)

SPECIALIZED (C&A)

Allen, Ethan B. (theme)
Bucknell Seminar for Younger Poets (college students)
Plains Poets Award (change)
Poet's Dinner Contest
Pro Dogs National Charity Open Poetry Competition
Prune Poetry Contest (prunes & others)
Psych It (psychology)

SPIRITUALITY/INSPIRATIONAL

Aries Productions
Decision
Lapis
One Earth
The Presbyterian Record
Regression Therapy (spirituality)

TRANSLATIONS

Chinese Literature
The Classical Outlook
International Poetry Review
Mundus Artium Press
New Rivers Press, Inc.
Northeastern University Press
Osiris, An International Journal/ Revue Internationale
Poetry World
Pressed Curtains
Threshold Books
Translation Center
White Plain Press

Translations (C&A)

Columbia University Translation Center
Harold Morton Landon Translation Award

WOMEN/FEMINIST

Anima: An Experiential Journal
Atlantis, A Women's Studies Journal
Bloodroot, Inc.
Calyx, A Journal of Art & Literature by Women
The Celibate Woman
Changing Men: Issues in Gender, Sex and Politics
Crone's Own Press
Daughters of Sarah
Deviance
Expecting
Feminist Studies
Fighting Woman News
Frontiers
Helicon Nine
Hurricane Alice
Hysteria
Kalliope
Ms. Magazine
Primavera
Reiman Publications
Room of One's Own
Saturday Press, Inc.
Scope
Shameless Hussy Press
Sing Heavenly Muse!
Sojourner
Sphinx-Women's International Literary/Art Review
Spinsters Ink
13th Moon
Tradeswomen

Vintage '45
Woman of Power
Women-in-Literature Inc.
Women's Quarterly Review
Womenwise

WOMEN/FEMINIST (C&A)
Eileen W. Barnes Award

CANADA
Ahnene Publications
The Alchemist
The Antigonish Review
Atlantis, A Women's Studies
    Journal
Aya Press Poetry Series
The Body Politic
Borealis Press
Bowbender
Breakthrough
Burnt Lake Press
Canadian Literature
Cannon Press
Coach House Press
Cobblestone Publishing Co.
Coteau Books
Cross-Canada Writers' Quarterly
Curvd H & Z
CV2
Daybreak
Descant
Dinosaur Review
Event
Fiddlehead Poetry Books
The Fiddlehead
Four by Four
Gamut
Grain
Green's Magazine
Guernica Editions
Horizons S F
Hysteria
Impulse
Inkstone
Just About Me
Koyo
Lucky Jim's Journal of Strange-
    ly Neglected Topics
The Malahat Review
Matrix
McClelland and Stewart Limited
Mosaic Press
Music Works
NBJ
Next Exit
Northern Light
Our Family
Ouroboros
Poetry Canada Review
Poetry Toronto
Porcupine's Quill, Inc.
Prairie Fire
The Prairie Journal
The Presbyterian Record
Press Porcepic Ltd.

Prism International
Proper Tales Press
Public Works
Quadrant Editions
Quarry Magazine
Queens Quarterly
The Raddle Moon
Romance and Fiction World
Room of One's Own
Scrivener
Sobriety House
Sono Ris Press
South Western Ontario Poetry
Spider Plots in Rat-Holes
Thistledown Press Ltd.
Time Warp
Tower Poetry Society
Tyro Magazine
Underwhich Editions
Vehicule Press
Wascana Review
Waves
West Coast Review
Western Producer Publications
Whetstone
Word-Fires
Wordwrights Canada
WPBS Poetry
Writ
X-It Magazine
Zest

FOREIGN
Agenda Editions (England)
All in Wall Stickers (England)
Allardyce (England)
& (Ampersand) Press (England)
Anti-Apartheid News (England)
Aquarius (England)
Aquila Publishing Co.
    (Scotland)
Argo, Incorporating Delta (En-
    gland)
Barenibs (England)
BB Bks (England)
Blind Serpent (Scotland)
Cabaret 246 (United Kingdom)
The Celtic League (Ireland)
Cencrastus (Scotland)
Chandrabhaga (India)
Chapman (Scotland)
Chinese Literature (China)
Christians Writing (Australia)
Compass: Poetry & Prose (Aus-
    tralia)
Coop. Antigruppo Siciliano (Ita-
    ly)
The Countryman (England)
Curlew Press (United Kingdom)
Dream International Quarterly
    (Japan)
Editions Nepe (France)
Ember Press (England)
Encounter (England)
Envoi (Wales)
Euroeditor (Germany)

European Judaism (England)
First Time (England)
Flame Poetry Magazine (En-
    gland)
The Folio (England)
Frank (France)
Galaxy Books (Australia)
Geneva Review (Switzerland)
Giant Steps (England)
GMP Publishers (England)
Gold Athena Press (Australia)
The Green Book (England)
Handshake Editions (France)
Hat (England)
Hippopotamus Press (United
    Kingdom)
The Inquirer (England)
Iron Press (England)
Islands (New Zealand)
Issue One (England)
Jackson's Arm (England)
James Joyce Broadsheet (En-
    gland)
Johnston/The Moorlands Re-
    view, Anne (England)
The Keepsake Press (England)
Krax (England)
Kropotkins' Lighthouse Publica-
    tions (England)
Label Magazine (England)
London Review of Books (En-
    gland)
Ludd's Mill (England)
The Mandeville Press (England)
Maroverlag (West Germany)
Matilda Publications (Australia)
Mensuel 25 (Belgium)
New Cicada (Japan)
New Departures (England)
New Hope International (United
    Kingdom)
New Yarn (Japan)
Ninth Decade (England)
Oasis Books (England)
On Being (Australia)
The Oleander Press (England)
One Earth (Scotland)
Orbis (England)
Ore (England)
Other Poetry (England)
Outpost Publications
Outrigger Publishers Ltd. (New
    Zealand)
Panorama of Czech Literature
    (Czechoslovakia)
Parallel Projects (Belgium)
Paris/Atlantic International Mag-
    azine of Poetry (France)
Pennine Platform (England)
Permanent Press (England)
Phoenix Broadsheets (England)
Plantagenet Publications (En-
    gland)
Poetry Durham (England)
Poetry Ireland Review (Ireland)
Poetry Kanto (Japan)
Poetry Nippon Press (Japan)

Poetry Nottingham (England)
Poetry Now (England)
Poetry Review (England)
Poetry Wales Press (Wales)
Pressed Curtains (England)
Proof (England)
Purple Heather Publications (England)
Purple Patch (England)
The Red Candle Press (England)
Rhythm-and-Rhyme (New Zealand)
Rivelin Grapheme Press (England)
Runa Press (Ireland)
Self and Society; European Journal of Humanistic Psychology (England)
SF Spectrum (England)

Smoke (England)
South Head Press (Australia)
Spectacular Diseases (United Kingdom)
Sphinx-Women's International Literary/Art Review (France)
Spokes (England)
Stand Magazine (England)
Start: Magazine of Literature and the Arts (England)
Stride Magazine (England)
Success Magazine (England)
Taxvs Press (England)
Tears in the Fence (England)
Tels (Japan)
The Thomas Hardy Yearbook (England)
Thursdays Poetry Magazine (England)

University of Queensland Press (Australia)
Ver Poets (England)
Voices Israel (Israel)
Wav Publications (Australia)
Westerly (Australia)
Weyfarers (England)
The White Rose Literary Magazine (England)
Word Exchange (West Germany)
Words: The New Literary Forum (England)
Zindy (England)

Contests (C&A)
New Zealand Fund (New Zealand)

State Index

Use this State Index to locate small presses and magazines in your region. Much of the poetry being published today reflects regional interests; also publishers often favor poets (and their work) from their own regions.

The publications in this index are arranged alphabetically; refer to the General Index for specific page numbers. Also check your neighboring states for other regional opportunities and the Subject Index for Canadian and foreign listings.

Alabama
Aura Literary/Arts Magazine
The Black Warrior Review
Caesura
College English
Epos
Explorations 87
Legerete
Negative Capability
Poem
Southern Humanities Review
Trouvere Company
University of Alabama Press

Alaska
Fireweed Press
Intertext
Permafrost
Shitepoke

Arizona
Arizona Quarterly
Aztec Peak

Bisbee Press Collective
Cache Review
Chimera
Gila Review
Ironwood
Keith Publications
Mother Duck Press
Nebo
Sonora Review
Whimsy

Arkansas
Literaria
The University of Arkansas Press
Voices International

California
Acts
Agada
Alchemy Books
Alta Napa Press
The Altadena Review

Am Here Books
Amelia
Androgyne Books
Applezaba Press
Arete: The Journal of Sport Literature
As Is/So & So Press
Athena Incognito Magazine
The Awakener Magazine
Axios
Barque
Barrington Press
Bay Area Poets Coalition
Berkeley Poets Cooperative (Workshop & Press)
Bizarre Press
Black Sparrow Press
Blue Unicorn, A Triquarterly of Poetry
Blue Wind Press
Bottomfish
Caravan Press
Ceilidh: An Informal Gathering for Story & Song

Christian Educators Journal
City Light Books
City Miner Books
Comet Halley Press
Conditioned Response Press
Crazy Quilt Quarterly
The Creative Urge
Creative With Words Publica-
tions
Crosscurrents
Crowdancing
Dragon's Teeth Press
Electrum
Embers Press
Empire
Fantasy Book
Fat Tuesday
Five Fingers Review
Flume Press Annual Poetry
Chapbook Contest
Fruition
The Galley Sail Review
Gaz Press
Gesar: Buddhism in the West
Green Tiger Press
The Grendhal Poetry Review
Harcourt Brace Jovanovich
Hartmus Press
The Heyeck Press
Hibiscus Press
Aaron W. Hillman, Ph.D., Pub-
lisher
Holmgangers Press
Hot Springs Gazette
Illuminati
Illuminations Press
Inkblot Publications
Insight Press
Issue Magazine
Issues
Kaldron
Konocti Books
La Jolla Poets' Press
Libra Publishers, Inc.
Magical Blend
Manic D Press
Mendocino Graphics
Mina Press
Minotaur Press
Modern Maturity
Monitor Book Company, Inc.
The Mythopoeic Society
Nancy's Magazine
New Methods
Notebook: A Little Magazine
Pacific Arts & Letters
Pacific Bridge
Pancake Press
Pangloss Papers
Panjandrum Books
Perivale Press
Players Press
The Poet Tree, Inc.
Poetic Justice
The Poetry Connexion
Poetry Flash
The Poetry Letter

Poetry: San Francisco Publica-
tions
Poetry/LA
The Press of MacDonald &
Reinecke
Processed World
Prophetic Voices
Published!
Quintessence Publications
Realities Library
Red Alder Books
Ridge Review Magazine
Ruddy Duck Press
San Diego Poet's Press
San Fernando Poetry Journal
San Jose Studies
Santa Susana Press
Science Fiction Poetry Associa-
tion
Second Coming Press
Shameless Hussy Press
Silver Wings
South Coast Poetry Journal
Spinsters Ink
Stone Soup, The Magazine by
Children
Studia Mystica
Summer Stream Press
Synthesis
This is Important
The Threepenny Review
Tradeswomen
Turkey Press
Vintage '45
Vol. No. Magazine
Wellspring
West Anglia Publications
West End Press
The White Light
Whole Earth Review
Wide Open Magazine
The Wishing Well
World Poetry Society
Wormwood Review Press
Writers West
Yellow Silk

Colorado
Arjuna Library Press
The Bloomsbury Review
Blue Light Books
Blue Mountain Arts, Inc.
Cloud Ridge Press
Colorado Review
Colorado-North Review
Denver Quarterly
Frontiers
Handicap News
High Country News
High/Coo Press
Iron Mountain
Laughing Waters Press
Maize Press
Metrosphere Literary Magazine
Mountain Cat Review
Muscadine

Writers Forum

Connecticut
A Letter Among Friends
Broken Streets
Chicory Blue Press
Clock Radio
The Connecticut Poetry Review
Connecticut River Review
The Connecticut Writer
Connections Magazine
Embers
Muse's Brew Poetry Review
Poets ON:
Potes & Poets Press, Inc.
Singular Speech Press
Small Pond Magazine of Litera-
ture
Wesleyan University Press
The Windham Phoenix
Yale University Press

Delaware
Expressions
22 Press

District of Columbia
The American Scholar
The Celibate Woman
The City Paper
District Lines
Folio
The New Republic
Paycock Press
Pennywhistle Press
Poet Lore
S.O.S. (Sultan of Swat) Books
Three Continents Press Inc.
Washington Review
Washington Writers' Publishing
House
Wheat Forder's Press
The Word Works

Florida
American Studies Press, Inc.
Anhinga Press
Audio/Visual Poetry Foundation
Calli's Tales
Caribbean Review
The Cathartic
Chimera Connections
Earthwise Publications/Produc-
tions
Fantasy Review
Gryphon
Kalliope
Konglomerati Press
M.O.P. Press
Moonsquilt Press
New Collage Magazine
North American Political Spec-
trum
The Pet Gazette

Rainbow Books
Red Bass
Red Key Press
Sonlight Christian Newspapers
The South Florida Poetry Review
Yesterday's Magazette

Georgia
The Augusta Spectator
Changing Men: Issues in Gender, Sex and Politics
The Chattahoochee Review
The Classical Outlook
Cotton Boll/The Atlanta Review
Creative Loafing
The Dekalb Literary Arts Journal
Georgia Journal Agee Publishers, Inc.
Ishtar Press
James Dickey Newsletter
The Old Red Kimono
Parnassus Literary Journal
University of Georgia Press
The Unknowns

Hawaii
Bamboo Ridge
Hawaii Review
Petronium Press
University of Hawaii Press

Idaho
Ahsahta Press
Cold-Drill Books
Confluence Press
Inky Trails Publications
Limberlost Press
Mother of Ashes Press
The Redneck Review of Literature
Rhyme Time Poetry Newsletter
Rocky Mountain Review of Language and Literature
Snapdragon
Trestle Creek Review

Illinois
Aim Magazine
Angeltread
Another Chicago Press
Before The Rapture Press
Broken Whisker Studio
Chicago Sheet
Cornerstone: The Voice of this Generation
Crawlspace
Daughters of Sarah
Dialogue, The Magazine for the Visually Impaired
Erie Street Press
Farmer's Market
Golden Isis

His Magazine
IWI Review
Karamu
Lake Shore Publishing
Lapis
Magic Changes
Midwest Poetry Review
Mississippi Valley Review
Nit&Wit
No Magazine
Oink! Magazine
Ommation Press
Oyez Review
Path Press, Inc.
Phoenix Poets
The Pikestaff Forum
Poetry
Primavera
Prime Time Sports & Fitness
Rambunctious Press
Red Herring Press
Rhino
The Shakespeare Newsletter
Harold Shaw Publishers
Sou'wester
Stormline Press, Inc.
Sunshine Magazine
Treetop Panorama
Triquarterly Magazine
University of Illinois Press
White Walls: A Magazine of Writings by Artists
Yellow Press
The Young Crusader

Indiana
Action
American Rowing
Arts Insight
Barnwood Press Cooperative
Black American Literature Forum
Channels
Chariot
Children's Better Health Institute
Evangel
Explorer Magazine
Forum (Ball State University)
Indiana Review
Joyful Noise
Marriage
Marriage and Family Living
Meridian
Neophytes
Oppossum Holler Tarot
The Poet
Right Here
Sparrow Press
Third Woman Press
The Windless Orchard

Iowa
Ansuda Publications
Blue Buildings
Common Lives/Lesbian Lives

Iowa Review
Luna Tack
Poet and Critic
Poetry World
Sovereign Gold Literary Magazine
The Spirit That Moves Us
Tradition
Writers House Press

Kansas
Capper's Weekly
Cottonwood Press
Kansas Quarterly
The Kindred Spirit
Little Balkans Press
The Midwest Quarterly
Naked Man
Scavenger's Newsletter

Kentucky
Apalachee Quarterly
Appalachian Heritage
Artful Codger and Codgerette
Callaloo Poetry Series
Kentucky Poetry Review
Pandora
Plainsong
River City Review
Snowy Egret
Spitball
Wind Magazine

Louisiana
Exquisite Corpse
Louisiana State University Press
The New Laurel Review
New Orleans Poetry Journal Press
The Southern Review

Maine
The Beloit Poetry Journal
Blackberry Books
Dan River Press
Kennebec
Maine Writers' Workshop
Northwoods Press
The Puckerbrush Press
Slow Dancer
Stony Hills

Maryland
Abbey
Acheron Press
American Land Forum
Antietam Review
Aqua/Art Node
Celebration
Delong & Associates
Dickinson Studies
Feminist Studies
The Galileo Press

The Italian Times of Maryland
Kavitha
Linden Press
The New Poets Series, Inc.
Nightsun
Quixsilver Press
Social Anarchism
Vegetarian Journal

Massachusetts
Adastra Press
The Agni Review
Alice James Books
The Ark
Arts End Books
The Atlantic
Bay Windows
Boston Review
Branden Publishing Co., Inc.
Brush Hill Press, Inc.
Cape Cod Life
The Christian Science Monitor
Cordillera Press
Day Tonight/Night Today
The Harbor Review
Houghton Mifflin Co.
Loom Press
The Massachusetts Review
Moment Magazine
New Age Journal
the new renaissance
New Traditions Press
Northeastern University Press
O.Ars
On the Edge
Osiris, An International Journal/
    Une Revue Internationale
Partisan Review
Ploughshares
Rubicon
Sojourner
Soundings East
Stone Country
Swamp Press
The University of Massachusetts
    Press
Wampeter Press
West of Boston
Woman of Power
Write Now Books
The Writer
Zephyr Press

Michigan
Alura
Beatniks From Space
Big Two-Hearted
The Centennial Review
Clubhouse
Expedition Press
Heirloom Books
Hoofstrikes Newsletter
Howling Dog
Insight
Japanophile

Katydid Books
Lotus Press
The MacGuffin
Michigan Quarterly Review
Minas Tirith Evening-Star: The
    Journal of the American
    Tolkien Society
Nada Press
Passages North
Rackham Journal of the Arts
    and Humanities (RAJAH)
Riverrun
The Small Towner
The Sounds of Poetry
Tandava
Touch
Verse & Universe
The Wire

Minnesota
Ally Press Center
Balance Beam Press, Inc.
Coffee House Press
Crown Creations Associates
Decision
The Evangelical Beacon
Graywolf Press
Great River Review
Hurricane Alice
Inkling Publications
James White Review
Lake Street Press
The Lutheran Journal
Mankato Poetry Review
Milkweed Chronicle
New Rivers Press
Northern Lit Quarterly
Rag Mag
Scope
Sing Heavenly Muse!
Suburban Wilderness Press

Mississippi
Delta Scene
Mississippi Review

Missouri
Alive! For Young Teens
Aries Productions
The Cape Rock
Cathedral Voice
The Chariton Review Press
Cornerstone Press
Helicon Nine
International University Press
Midwest Arts & Literature
Missouri Review
New Letters
Odessa Poetry Review
Open Places
Pentecostal Evangel
Regression Therapy
River Styx Magazine
Sharing the Victory

Timberline Press
Uncle
Unity School of Christianity
University of Missouri Press
Webster Review
Wonder Time
Write On

Montana
Corona
Cutbank
Multiples Press
Seven Buffaloes Press

Nebraska
Abattoir Editions
Best Cellar Press
The Nebraska Review
The Penumbra Press
Plainsongs
Prairie Schooner
The Round Table

Nevada
Duck Down Press
Interim
Women-in-Literature

New Hampshire
Golden Quill Press
Kenyon Hills Publications
The Tidal Press
Womenwise

New Jersey
Chantry Press
First Hand
From Here Press
Hoboken Terminal
Journal of New Jersey Poets
King and Cowen Press
Lips
The Literary Review
Merging Media
New Worlds Unlimited
The Ontario Review
Passaic Review
Pegasus Review
Pella Publishing Company
Place Stamp Here
Princeton University Press
Ptolemy/The Browns Mill Re-
    view
Quarterly Review of Literature
St. Joseph Messenger and Ad-
    vocate of the Blind
Saturday Press, Inc.
Scarecrow Press
Warthog Press
The Wave Press
Without Halos
The Word Shop

New Mexico

Duende Press
The Haven; New Poetry
The Lightning Tree
New Mexico Humanities Review
Orphic Lute
Sunstone Press
Valley Spirit

New York

Adrift
Akwekon Literary Journal
America
The Amicus Journal
Arachne
Art Times
Ashley Books, Inc.
Ashod Press
Assembling Press
Atheneum Publishers
The Basilisk Press
Beach & Co., Publishers
Bellevue Press, The
Beyond
Bill Munster's Footsteps
Bitterroot
Blind Beggar Press
Blueline
Boa Editions
Box Turtle Press
Breathless Magazine
Bride's
Broadside Magazine
Brooklyn Review
Buffalo Spree Magazine
Central Park: A Journal of the Arts and Social Theory
The Clyde Press
Columbia: A Magazine of Poetry & Prose
Confrontation Magazine
Cosmopolitan Magazine
Credences: A Journal of 20th Century Poetry & Poetics
Croton Review
Dear Contributor
Ear Magazine
Ecco Press
Epoch
Exit
Expecting
Fighting Woman News
The First East Coast Theater and Publishing Co.
Folder Editions
Full Court Press
Gandhabba
Good Housekeeping
Graham House Review
Great Elm Press
The Greenfield Review Press
Grinning Idiot
Grove Press
Grue Magazine

Gull Books
Haiku Society of America
Hard Press
Harper and Row
Helikon Press
Heresies
Hermes House Press
Home Planet News
Indra's Net
International Publishers Co., Inc.
Ithaca House
Jewish Currents
Kitchen Table: Women of Color Press
Ladies' Home Journal
Lionsong Magazine
The Loft
The Lookout
M.A.F. Press
MacFadden Women's Group
The Mage
Manhattan Poetry Review
McCall's
Me Magazine
Midstream: A Monthly Jewish Review
Miorita
Modern Bride
Ms. Magazine
The Nation
The New York Quarterly
The New Yorker
Night Cry
W.W. Norton & Company, Inc.
Oovrah
Out There
Outerbridge
The Overlook Press
Oxford University Press
Parabola
The Paris Review
Parnassus: Poetry in Review
Philosophy and the Arts
The Pipe Smoker's Ephemeris
The Poetry Review
Printable Arts Society, Inc.
Queen of all Hearts
Random House
Reconstructionist
Reform Judaism
Sachem Press
Salmagundi
The Sea Horse Press Ltd.
Serpent & Eagle Press
Seventeen
Shamal Books
Slipstream
The Smith Publishers
Somrie Press
Space and Time
State Street Press
Street Press
Superintendent's Profile & Pocket Equipment Directory
Textile Bridge Press
13th Moon

Tin Wreath
Translation Center
Ultramarine Publishing Co., Inc.
Unmuzzled Ox
The Villager
Waterways: Poetry in the Mainstream
The Weirdbook Sampler
Westgate Press
Westhills Review
White Pine Press
Women Writers Alliance
Women's Quarterly Review
Xanadu; A Literary Journal

North Carolina

The Black Mountain Review
Carolina Quarterly
Carolina Wren Press
Colonnades
Crone's Own Press
The Greensboro Review
Gypsy
Hieroglyphics Press
International Poetry Review
Katuah
Manna
The North Carolina Haiku Society Press
Nycticorax
Pembroke Magazine
RFD: A Country Journal for Gay Men Everywhere
Saint Andrews Review
Southern Poetry Review
Star Books, Inc.
The Sun
Tar River Poetry

North Dakota

Bloodroot, Inc.
North Dakota Quarterly
Stronghold Press

Ohio

The Antioch Review
Bird Watcher's Digest
Bits Press
Black River Review
Bottom Dog Press
Gambit
The Gamut
Green Feather Magazine
Hiram Poetry Review
Images
Implosion Press
Kaleidoscope Press
Luna Bisonte Prods
Mid-American Review
Mosaic Press
Nexus
The Ohio Journal
Ohio Renaissance Review

The Ohio Review
One Shot
Passion for Industry
Pudding Publications
Reflections
Religious Humanism
St. Anthony Messenger
Sapiens: A Journal for Human
    Evolution
Shawnee Silhouette
Step Life
Straight
Whiskey Island Magazine
The Wooster Review
The Writer's Bloc
Writer's Digest

Oklahoma

The Arthur Press
Byline Magazine
Cardinal Press
Cimmaron Review
Midland Review
Nimrod Magazine Pablo Neruda
    Prize for Poetry
Point Riders Press
Seven
Territory of Oklahoma: Litera-
    ture & The Arts

Oregon

Apaeros: Reader-Written Forum
    About Sex and Erotica
Calyx, A Journal of Art and
    Literature by Women
Camus Press
Choice Magazine
Grey Whale Press
Mr. Cogito Press
Northwest Magazine
Northwest Review
Prescott Street Press
Silverfish Review
Spirit: The Christian Magazine
    About Career Lifestyle and
    Relationships
Transition Publications
Trout Creek Press
University of Portland Review
Young American Publishing
    Co., Inc.

Pennsylvania

Allegheny Press
The Allegheny Review
American Poetry Review
Anima; An Experiential Journal
Axe Factory Review
Bifrost
Black Bear Publications
Calliope, Bensalem Association
    of Women Writers
Carnegie-Mellon Magazine
Carnegie-Mellon University
    Press

Creeping Bent
Grit
Hob-Nob
The Lancaster Independent Press
Latin American Literary Review
    Press
Lutheran Women
Mennonite Publishing House
Northern Pleasure
Painted Bride Quarterly
Paper Air Magazine
The Pennsylvania Review
Philadelphia Poets
Pitt Poetry Series
Poetry Newsletter
Poets at Work
Potpourri International
Raw Dog Press
Sunrust Magazine
3 Score & 10
Time of Singing, A Magazine
    of Christian Poetry
Trans-Species Unlimited
The Unspeakable Visions of the
    Individual
West Branch
Widener Review

Rhode Island

Aldebaran
Copper Beech Press
Deviance
Frugal Chariot
Rhode Island Review

South Carolina

Criterion Review
Linwood Publishers
R.S.V.P. Press
South Carolina Review

South Dakota

Blue Cloud Quarterly Press
South Dakota Review

Tennessee

Baptist Sunday School Board
Co-Laborer
The F. Marion Crawford Memo-
    rial Society
Cumberland Poetry Review
Ideals
Memphis State Review
Now and Then
Raccoon Books
The Red Pagoda, A Journal of
    Haiku
Sewanee Review
The Upper Room
Winston-Derek Publishers, Inc.
Yes Press

Texas

A Galaxy of Verse
Aileron Press
American Atheist Press
The Body Eclectic, Newsletter
    of the Gimlet Press
Brilliant Star
Chawed Rawzin Press
Cross Timbers Review
Descant
Infinitum
Interstate
Inverted-A, Inc.
Jean's Journal
Lonestar Publications of Humor
Maat
Mundus Artium Press
Piddiddle
Poetry Press
Quixote Press
RE:AL (Re: Artes Liberales)
Riverside Quarterly
Salt Lick
Sands
Slough Press
The Stevan Company
Studia Hispanica Editors
The Texas Review
Thunder City Press
Tilted Planet Press
Touchstone Press
The United Methodist Reporter
Viaztlan: A Journal of the Arts
    and Letters
Wellspring Magazine
Ye Olde News

Utah

Dialogue: A Journal of Mormon
    Thought
Dragonfly: A Quarterly of Hai-
    ku
The Friend
Quarterly West
University of Utah Press
Utah State University Press
Western Humanities Review

Vermont

Anemone Press
Awede Press
Jam To-Day
Samisdat
Sherry Urie
Sinister Wisdom
Threshold Books

Virginia

Aerial
Artemis
Black Buzzard Press
Bogg Publications
Brunswick Publishing Company
The Hague Review
The Hollins Critic

Inlet
Lintel
The Lyric
Miriam Press
Mockersatz Zrox
The Mountain Laurel
New Southern Literary Messen-
   ger
The Other Side Magazine
Phoebe
Phoebus
Piedmont Literary Review
Poetry East
Proof Rock Press
Reflect
Roanoke Review
Shenandoah
The Virginia Quarterly Review

Washington
AG-Pilot International Magazine
Alcoholism & Addiction Maga-
   zine, Recovery!
Bear Tribe
Bellowing Ark
Bumbershoot
Candle: An International Raga-
   zine
Crab Creek Review
Dragon Gate, Inc.

Fantasy and Terror
Fine Madness
Globe Publishing
Haiku Zasshi Zo
Home Edition Magazine
Home Education Magazine
L'Epervier Press
The Lockhart Press
Poetry Northwest
Poets. Painters. Composers.
The Signpost Press
Willow Springs

West Virginia
Aegina Press
Dickenson Press
The Laurel Review
University Editions

Wisconsin
Abraxas Press, Inc.
Amazing Stories
Aurora: Speculative Feminism
Baseball: Our Way
Clockwatch Review
Cream City Review
The Dragonsbreath Press
Ghost Pony Press
Heartland Journal

Juniper Press
Lionhead Publishing
The Madison Review
The Magazine of Speculative
   Poetry
Modern Haiku
Pentagram
Prime Times
Reiman Publications
Rhiannon Press
Sackbut Press
Salthouse
Seems
Song
Southport Press
Westburg Associates Publishers
Windfall
Wisconsin Academy Review
The Wisconsin Restaurateur
Wisconsin Review
Wolfsong

Wyoming
The Willow Bee Publishing
   House

General Index

A

AAA Annual National Literary
   Contest 343
Abacus (see Potes & Poets
   Press, Inc. 235)
Abatis 339
Abattoir Editions 14
Abbey 14
Abraxas Press, Inc. 14
Abri Publications (see The Un-
   knowns 306)
Academy of American Poets,
   The 343, 369

Acheron Press 15
ACM (Another Chicago Maga-
   zine), (see Another Chicago
   Press 28)
Action 15
Acumen (see Ember Press 102)
Adastra Press 15
Adrift 16
Aegina Press 16
Aerial 16
AG-Pilot International Magazine
   17
Agada 16
Agee Publishers (see Georgia
   Journal 117)

Agenda (see Agenda Editions
   17)
Agenda Editions 17
Agni Review, The 17
Ahnene Publications 17
Ahsahta Press 18
Aileron: A Literary Journal (see
   Aileron Press 18)
Aileron Press 18
Aim Magazine 18
Airplane Press, The (see New
   Southern Literary Messenger
   194)
Akwekon Literary Journal 19
Akwesasne Notes (see Akwekon

Literary Journal 19)
Alabama State Council on the Arts and Humanities 357
Alaska State Council on the Arts 357
Alberta Arts Council 358
Alchemist, The 19
Alchemy Books 20
Alcoholism & Addiction Magazine, Recovery! 20
Aldebaran 20
Alice James Books 20
Alive! For Young Teens 20
Alive Now! (see The Upper Room 307)
All in Wall Stickers 21
All Seasons Poetry Contests 343
Allardyce 21
Allegheny Press 21
Allegheny Review, The 21
Allen, Ethan B. 343
Ally Press Center 22
Alps Monthly (see Pacific Arts & Letters 211)
Alta Napa Press 22
Altadena Review, The 22
Alura 22
Am Here Books 23
Amazing Stories 23
Amberley Greeting Card Co. 361
Amelia 23
America 24
American Academy & Institute of Arts & Letters, The 343
American Atheist (see American Atheist Press 24)
American Atheist Press 24
American Greetings 361
American Land Forum 25
American Poetry Association Poetry Contests 343
American Poetry Review 25
American Poets Profiles Series (see Thunder City Press 297)
American Rowing 25
American Scholar, The 25
American Studies Press, Inc. 26
Amicus Journal, The 26
& (Ampersand) Press 26
And Still It Moves (see As Is/So & So Press 35)
Andrew Mountain Press 339
Androgyne Books 26
Anemone (see Anemone Press 26)
Anemone Press 26
Angeltread 27
Anhinga Press 27
Anhinga Prize for Poetry 344
Anima; An Experiential Journal 27
Annual Christian Writers Conference 363
Annual International Narrative Contest 344
Anonbeyond Press (see Underwhich Editions 305)

rwhich Editions 305)
Another Chicago Press 28
Ansuda Publications 28
Antaeus (see Ecco Press 102)
Anthology of Magazine Verse (see Monitor Book Company 184)
Anti-Apartheid News 28
Antietam Review 29
Antigonish Review, The 29
Antioch Review, The 29
Antioch Writers Workshop 366
Apaeros: Reader-Written Forum About Sex and Erotica 29
Apalachee Quarterly 29
Appalachian Heritage 29
Appalachian Poetry Association 370
Applezaba Press 30
Appreciation Award 344
Aqua/Art Node 30
Aquarius 30
Aquarius Anthology (see Golden Isis 120)
Aquila Publishing Co. 30
Arachne 31
Archer, The (see Camas Press 66)
Arete: The Journal of Sport Literature 31
Argo (Incorporating Delta) 32
Argus Communications 361
Aries Productions 32
Aril Books (see Taxvs Press 293)
Arizona Christian writers Seminar 363
Arizona Commission on the Arts 357
Arizona Quarterly 32
Arjuna Library Press 33
Ark, The 33
Arkansas Arts Council 357
Art Times 34
Artemis 34
Artemis Poetry Contest 344
Artful Codger and Codgerette 34
Artful Dodge 339
Arthur Press, The 34
Arts Council of Florida 357
Arts End Books 35
Arts Insight 35
As Is/So & So Press 35
Ashley Books, Inc. 36
Ashod Press 36
Assembling Annual (see Assembling Press 36)
Assembling Press 36
Associated Writing Programs 370
Astra Publications (see Write Now Books 332)
Atavist, The 339
Atelier De L'Agneau (see Mensuel 25, 176)
Athena Incognito Magazine 37

Atheneum Publishers 37
Atlanta Creative Alliance Publications, An (see The Unknowns 306)
Atlanta Writing Resource Center 344
Atlanta Writing Resource Center, Inc. 370
Atlantic Center for the Arts 367
Atlantic, The 37
Atlantis, A Women's Studies Journal 37
Audio/Visual Poetry Foundation 39
August House Publishers 339
Augusta Spectator, The 39
Aura Literary/Arts Magazine 39
Aurora: Speculative Feminism 40
Australasian Writing (see Compass: Poetry & Prose 83)
Avila College Writers Conference 365
Awakener Magazine, The 40
Awede Press 40
AWP Award Series, The 344
AWP Award Series, The (see Associated Writing Programs 370)
AWP Newsletter (see Associated Writing Programs 370)
Axe Factory Review 40
Axios 40
Aya Press Poetry Series 41
Aztek Peak 41

B

Bad Breath Magazine (see As Is/So & So Press 35)
Balance Beam Press, Inc. 41
Balch Awards, Emily Clark 344
Bamboo Ridge 42
Baptist Sunday School Board 42
Barber Award, Gordon 344
Barenibs 42
Barnes Award, Eileen W. 345
Barnes Award Series, Eileen W. (see Saturday Press Inc. 264)
Barnett Publishers (see Allardyce 21)
Barnwood (see Barnwood Press Cooperative 42)
Barnwood Press Cooperative 42
Barque 43
Barrington Press 43
Baseball: Our Way 43
Basement Workshop, The 370
Basilisk Press, The 44
Bay Area Poets Coalition 44
Bay Area's Poetry Calendar & Review, The (see Poetry Flash 228)

Bay de Noc Writers' Conference 364
Bay Windows 44
BB Bks 45
Beach & Co., Publishers 45
Bean Publishing, Ltd., Carolyn 361
Bear Tribe 45
Beatniks From Space 46
Before the Rapture Press 46
Beginning Magazine (see Writers House Press 334)
Bellevue Press, The 46
Bellingham Review, The (see The Signpost Press 271)
Bellowing Ark 46
Beloit Poetry Journal, The 47
Ben-Sen Press (see West Anglia Publications 316)
Bennett Fellowship, George 345
Bensalem Assocation of Women Writers Annual Competitions 345
Berkeley Poets Cooperative (Workshop & Press) 47
Best Cellar Press 47
Beymorlin Sonnet Award 345
Beyond 48
Beyond Baroque Literary/Arts Center 370
Bibliotherapy (see Aaron W. Hillinon Ph.D 133)
Bifrost 48
Big River Association (see River Styx Magazine 256)
Big Scream (see Nada Press 188)
Big Two-Hearted 48
Bird Watcher's Digest 50
Birth of America (see Inky Trails Publications 142)
Bisbee Press Collective (see Mother Duck Press 185)
Bits Press 50
Bitterroot 51
Bizarre Press 51
Black American Literature Forum 51
Black Bear Publications 51
Black Bear Review (see Black Bear Publications 51)
Black Buzzard Illustrated Poetry Chapbook Series, The (see Black Buzzard Press 52)
Black Buzzard Press 52
Black Mountain Review, The 53
Black River Review 53
Black Sparrow Press 53
Black Warrior Review, The 54
Black Willow 340
Blackberry Books 54
Blind Beggar Press 54
Blind Serpent 54
Bloodroot (see Bloodroot, Inc. 54)
Bloodroot, Inc. 54
Bloomsbury Review, The 55

Blow (see Grey Whale Press 123)
Blue Buildings 55
Blue Cloud Quarterly (see Blue Cloud Quarterly Press 55)
Blue Cloud Quarterly Press 55
Blue Glow/Egad!, The (see Bizarre Press 51)
Blue Light Books 56
Blue Light Review (see Blue Light books 56)
Blue Moon Press, Inc. (see Confluence Press 83)
Blue Mountain Arts, Inc. 56, 361
Blue Unicorn 56
Blue Unicorn Poetry Contest 345
Blue Wind Press 56
Blueline 57
Boa Editions 57
Body Eclectic 57
Body Politic, The 58
Bogg (see Bogg Publications 58)
Bogg Publications 58
Bollingen Prize 345
Bonus Books (see Minotaur Press 180)
Borealis Press 58
Boston Review 59
Bottom Dog Press 59
Bottomfish 59
Bowbender 60
Bowker Co., R.R. 375
Box 749 (see Printable Arts Society, Inc. 240)
Box Turtle Press 60
Branden Publishing Co., Inc. 60
Bravo (see King and Cowen Press 156)
Braziller, George 340
Bread Loaf Quarterly (see Kenyon Hills Publications 155)
Breakthrough 60
Breathless Magazine 60
Bride's 61
Brilliant Enterprises 361
Brilliant Star 61
British Columbia Arts Council 358
Brittingham Prize in Poetry 345
Broadman Press (see Baptist Sunday School Board 42)
Broadside Magazine 61
Brodine Memorial Awards, Joseph E. 345
Broken Images Editions (see Guernica Editions 125)
Broken Streets 61
Broken Whisker Studio 62
Brooklyn Review 62
Broukal Press, Gustav (see American Atheist Press 24)
Brunswick Poetry Workshop (see Matilda Publications 174)

Brunswick Publishing Company 62
Brush Hill Press, Inc. 62
Buckley-Little Book Catalogue, The 375
Bucknell Seminar for Younger Poets 345
Buffalo Spree Magazine 62
Bumbershoot 63
Burnaby Writers' Society 370
Burning Deck Books 340
Burnt Lake Press 63
Bush Foundation Fellowships for Artists 345
Butler County Creative Writing Workshop 364
Byline Magazine 63
Byliners of Corpus Christi 345
Bynner Foundation for Poetry, Inc., The Whitter 370

C

Cabaret-246 64
Cache Review 64
Caesura 64
California Arts Council 357
California Federation of Chaparral Poets, Robert Frost Chapter, Annual Poetry Contest 345
California Writers Club Conference 363
California Writer's Roundtable Poetry Contest 346
Callaloo (see Callaloo Poetry Series 64)
Callaloo Poetry Series 64
Calliope, Bensalem Association of Women Writers 65
Calli's Tales 65
Calyx, A Journal of Art & Literature by Women 65
Camas Press 66
Cambridge Collection (see Yes Press 337)
Camus Editions 340
Canada Council, Writing and Publications Section 358
Canadian Literary Review 340
Canadian Literature 66
Canadian Ministry of Citizenship and Culture, Arts Service Branch 358
Canadian Poetry 375
Candelabrum (see The Red Candle Press 250)
Candle: An International Ragazine 66
Cane Award, Melville 346
Cannon Press 67
Cannonade Press (see Konocti Books 157)
Canterbury Press Limerick Contest 346

Cape Cod Life 67
Cape Cod Writers' Conference 364
Cape Rock, The 67
Capper's Weekly 67
Caravan Press 68
Cardinal Press 68
Caribbean Review 68
Carn (see The Celtic League 70)
Carnegie-Mellon Magazine 68
Carnegie-Mellon University Press 68
Carolina Quarterly 69
Carolina Wren Press 69
Carter Caves Writer's Workshop 364
Cassette Gazette (see Handshake Editions 127)
Cathartic, The 69
Cathedral Church of St. John the Divine American Poets' Corner, The 371
Cathedral Voice 70
CCLM Catalog of College Literary Magazines (see Coordinating Council of Literary Magazines 371)
CCLM News (see Coordinating Council of Literary Magazines 371)
Ceilidh: An Informal Gathering for Story & Song 70
Celebration 70
Celibate Woman; A Journal for Women who are Celibate or Considering this Liberating Way of Relating to Others, The 70
Celtic League, The 70
Cencrastus 71
Centennial Review, The 71
Center for Creative Writing, The 371
Central Park: A Journal of the Arts and Social Theory 71
Cerulean Press (Mini Anthology Series) (see San Fernando Poetry Journal 263)
Chandrabhaga 71
Changing Men: Issues in Gender, Sex and Politics 71
Channels 72
Chantry Press 72
Chapman 72
Chariot 72
Charioteer, The (see Pella Publishing Company 216)
Chariton Review, The (see The Chariton Review Press 73)
Chattahoochee Review, The 73
Chattahoochee Review Press, The 73
Chautauqua Writers' Workshops 365
Chawed Rawzin Press 73
Chelsea 340
Cherry Valley Editions (see

Beach & Co., Publishers 45)
Chestnut Hills Press (see The New Poets Series, Inc. 193)
Chiaroscuro (see Ithaca House 147)
Chicago Review 340
Chicago Review Press 340
Chicago Sheet 74
Chicago Tower Press (see Prime Time Sports & Fitness 239)
Chicory Blue Press 74
Child Life (see Children's Better Health Institute 74)
Children's Better Health Institute 74
Children's Digest (see Children's Better Health Institute 74)
Children's Playmate (see Children's Better Health Institute 74)
Chimera 74
Chimera Connections 74
Chinese Literature 76
Choice Magazine 76
Christian Educators Journal 76
Christian Living (see Mennonite Publishing House 175)
Christian Science Monitor, The 77
Christian Writer, The 375
Christian Writers Institute 363
Christians Writing 77
Christmas in Watertown (see Clockwatch Review 78)
Christopher Newport College 366
Cider Mills Press 340
Cimmaron Review 77
Cincinnati Poetry Review 340, 346
Cintas Fellowship Program 346
City Light Books 77
City Miner Books 77
City Paper, The 78
Classical Outlook, The 78
Clayton Award, Gertrude B. 346
Clearing, The 366
Clock Radio 78
Clockwatch Review 78
Cloud Ridge Press 79
Clover Press (see Green's Magazine 122)
Club Leabhar (see Aquila Publishing Co. 30)
Clubhouse 80
Clyde Press, The 80
Coach House Press 80
Cobblestone (see Cobblestone Publishing Co. 80)
Cobblestone Publishing Co. 80
CODA: Poets and Writers Newsletter 375
Coffee House Press 80
Co-Laborer 81
Cold-Drill (see Cold-Drill Books 81)

Cold-Drill Books 81
College English 81
Colonnades 81
Colophon Books (see Harper and Row 128)
Colorado Council on the Arts and Humanities 357
Colorado Review 81
Colorado State Review (see Colorado Review 81)
Colorado-North Review 82
Columbia: A Magazine of Poetry & Prose 82
Columbia University Translation Center 346
Comet Companion (see Comet Halley Press 82)
Comet Halley Magazine (see Comet Halley Press 82)
Comet Halley Press 82
Comet With No Name (see Comet Halley Press 82)
Committee of Small Magazine Editors and Publishers 371
Common Lives/Lesbian Lives 82
Community Writers Association (see Writers House Press 334)
Compass: Poetry & Prose 83
Computer Disc Series (see Guernica Editions 125)
Computer Poet Corporation, The 361
Conditioned Response (see Conditioned Response Press 83)
Conditioned Response Press 83
Confluence Press 83
Confluent Education Journal (see Aaron W. Hillman Ph.D., Publisher 133)
Confrontation Magazine 83
Connecticut Commission on the Arts 357
Connecticut Poetry Review, The 84
Connecticut Poetry Society 346
Connecticut River Review 84
Connecticut Writer, The 84
Connecticut Writers Conference 363
Connections Magazine 84
Conners Prize, Bernard F. 346
Conservatory of American Letters (see Northwoods Press 200)
Contemporary Writers Series 340
Contenova Gifts 361
Contests & Contacts (see Keith Publications 154)
Coop. Antigruppo Siciliano 85
Coordinating Council of Literary Magazines 371
Copper Beech Press 85
Cops Going For Doughnuts Editions (see Proper Tales Press 241)

Cordillera Press 85
Cornell University Writers Program 365
Cornerstone Press 86
Cornerstone: The Voice of this Generation 86
Corona 86
COSMEP Newsletter (see Committee of Small Magazine Editors and Publishers 371)
Cosmopolitan 86
Cosmos Prime (see Crown Creations Associates 92)
Coteau Books 86
Cotton Boll/The Atlanta Review 87
Cottonwood (see Cottonwood Press 87)
Cottonwood Arts Foundation, The (see Point Riders Press 234)
Cottonwood Press 87
Countryman, The 87
Coydog Review 340
Crab Creek Review 87
Crawford Memorial Society, The F. Marion 88
Crawlspace 88
Crazy Quilt Quarterly 88
Cream City Review 89
Creative Loafing 89
Creative Urge, The 89
Creative with Words Publications 89
Credences: A Journal of 20th Century Poetry & Poetics 90
Creeping Bent 90
Criterion Review 90
Criterion Writing Competition (see Criterion Review 90)
Criterion Writing Contest 346
Crone's Own Press 90
Cross Timbers Review 91
Cross-Canada Writers' Quarterly 91
Cross-Canada Writer's Workshop 366
Cross-Cultural Communications (see Coop. Antigruppo Siciliano 85)
Crosscurrents 91
Croton Review 91
Crowdancing 92
Crown Creations Associates 92
Cumberland Poetry Review 92
Curlew Press 92
Current, Inc. 361
Curtains (see Pressed Curtains 238)
Curvd H & Z 93
Cutbank 93
CV2 93

D

D.D.B. Press (see Apalachee Quarterly 29)

Daily Word (see Unity School of Christianity 306)
Dalhousie Review, The 340
Dalhousie University Press 340
Dan River Press 93
Dante University of America Press (see Banden Publishing Co., Inc. 60)
Dark Star (see The Creative Urge 89)
Dark Visions (se Time Warp 299)
Daughters of Sarah 94
Davidson Award, Gustav 346
Davies Award, Mary Carolyn 346
Dawn Valley Press (see Sunrust Magazine 290)
DAWN-Dayton Area Writer's Nexus 366
Day Tonight/Night Today 94
Daybreak 94
DC Commission on the Arts and Humanities 357
Dear Contributor 94
Decision 94
DeKalb Literary Arts Journal, The 95
Delaware State Arts Council 357
Delong & Associates 95
Delta Scene 95
Dennis A. Dorner Communications (see Prime Time Sports & Fitness 239)
Denny Poetry Award, Billie Murray 346
Denver Quarterly 95
Deros; Up Against the Wall (see Miriam Press 180)
Descant 96
Deviance 96
Devis Award 346
Dharma Publishing (see Gesar: Buddhism in the West 118)
Di Castagnola Award, Alice Fay 347
Dial-A-Poem Contest 347
Dialogue: A Journal of Mormon Thought 96
Dialogue, The Magazine for the Visually Impaired 96
Dickenson Press 97
Dickinson Award, Emily 347
Dickinson Studies 97
Dickinson-Higginson Society Press (see Dickinson Studies 97)
Dinosaur Review 97
Discovery Press (see Sono Nis Press 276)
Discovery, The 347
District Lines 98
Dog River Review (see Trout Creek Press 303)
Dog River Review Poetry Series (see Trout Creek Press 303)
Dolphin-Moon Press 340

Door County Almanak (see The Dragonsbreath Press 99)
Doorways to the Mind: Journey into Psychic Awareness (see Aries Productions 32)
Dorland Mountain Colony 367
Double-Edge Poetry Contest 347
Dragon Gate, Inc. 98
Dragonfly: A Quarterly of Haiku 98
Dragon's Teeth Press 99
Dragonsbreath Press, The 99
Drawing Board Greeting Cards, Inc. 361
Dream International Quarterly 99
Drift Shop, The (see Hot Springs Gazette 136)
Duck Down Press 99
Duende Press 100
Dustbooks 375

E

Ear Magazine 100
Earthwise Publications/Productions 100
Eastern Kentucky University 364
Ecco Press 102
ECW Press (see Poetry Canada Review 227)
Ego Flights (see Macomb Fantasy Factory 349)
Eidos Magazine; Erotic Entertainment for Women (see Brush Hill Press, Inc. 62)
Eight Miles High Home Entertainment (see Ludd's Mill 167)
Electrum 102
Electrum Magazine 347
Elizabeth Street Press 340
Elliston Poetry Collection 371
Ember Press 102
Embers 103
Embers Press 103
Empire Books (see Pandora 212)
Empire for the Science Fiction Writer 103
Encounter 103
Envelope Book Library (see Green Tiger Press 122)
Envoi 103
Envoi Poets Publications (see Envoi 103)
Eon Publications (see Issue One 147)
Epoch 104
Epos 104
Equivalencias 340
Erie Street Press 104
Esoterica Press (see Notebook: A Little Magazine 201)

Essential Poet Series (see
  Guernica Editions 125)
Eureka Review 340
Euroeditor 105
European Judaism 105
Evangel 105
Evangelical Beacon, The 105
Eve's Legacy . . . Adam's Apple 347
Event 105
Exit 106
Expecting 106
Expedition Press 106
Explorations 87 106
Explorer Magazine 106
Explorer Publishing Co. (see
  Explorer Magazine 106)
Expressions 107
Exquisite Corpse 107

F

F.A.I.M. (Federation for the
  Advancement of Independent
  Magazines 371)
Faber & Faber 340
Faces (see Cobblestone Publishing Co. 80)
Fallot Poetry Competition,
  Edward A (see Rainbow
  Books 248)
Fantasy and Terror 107
Fantasy Book 108
Fantasy Review 108
Farber Award, Norma 347
Farm Woman (see Reiman Publications 252)
Farmer's Market 108
Farrar, Straus and Giroux 340
Fat Tuesday 108
Feminist Studies 108
Feminist Women's Writing
  Workshop 365
Fiddlehead Poetry Books 109
Fiddlehead, The 109
Fighting Woman News 110
Findhorn Press, The (see One
  Earth 205)
Fine Arts Society (see The Poet
  226)
Fine Arts Work Center In Provincetown 367
Fine Madness 110
Fireweed Press 110
First East Coast Theater and
  Publishing Co., The 111
First Hand 111
First Time 111
Five Fingers Poetry (see Five
  Fingers Review 111)
Five Fingers Review 111
Five Leaves Left (see Purple
  Heather Publications 242)
Flame Poetry Magazine 112
Fleur De Leaf Worldwide Inc.

(see North American Political Spectrum 198)
Flight of the Mind, The 366
Florida Freelance Writers Conference 363
Florida State Poetry Assoc. (see
  Earthwise Publications/Productions 100)
Florida State Poets Association
  347
Florida Suncoast Writers' Conference 363
Flume Press Annual Poetry
  Chapbook Contest 112
Flying Point Books 340
Folder Editions 112
Folio: A Literary Journal 113
Folio: An International Literary
  Magazine 113
Football: Our Way (see Baseball: Our Way 43)
Footsteps (see Bill Munster's
  Footsteps 50)
For Poets Only 347
Ford Award, Consuelo 347
Ford Brown & Co. (see Thunder City Press 297)
Forer & Co., Inc., D. 361
Forest Home's Christian Writers' Conference 363
Forum (Ball State University)
  113
Four By Four 113
Francis Marion Writers' Retreat
  366
Frank 114
Franklin Literary and Medical
  Society, Benjamin (see Children's Better Health Institute
  74)
Freedom Greeting Card Co. 361
Freelance Writer (see Inkling
  Publications, Inc. 141
Friend, The 114
Frogpond (see Haiku Society of
  America 126)
From Here Press 114
Frontiers 114
Frugal Chariot 114
Fruition 115
Full Circle Press 341
Full Court Press, Inc. 115
Full Moon Poetry Contest (see
  Pennsylvania Poetry Society
  Annual Contest 351)

G

Galaxy Books 115
Galaxy of Verse 347
Galaxy of Verse, A 115
Galileo Book Series (see The
  Galileo Press 116)
Galileo Press, The 116
Gallant Knight Printing Press

(see Sovereign Gold Literary
  Magazine 280)
Galley Sail Review, The 116
Gambit 116
Gamut 116
Gamut, A Journal of Ideas and
  Information 117
Gandhabba 117
Gargoyle Magazine (see Paycock Press 215)
Gaz Press 117
Gemini Press (see Lake Shore
  Publishing 159
Gem's Newsletter for Authors
  375
Generalist Ass'n., The (see The
  Smith Publishers 274)
Generoso Pope Foundation 365
Geneva Review, The 117
Georgia Council for the Arts
  and Humanities 357
Georgia Journal 117
Georgia State Poetry Society,
  Inc. 347
Gesar: Buddhism in the West
  118
Ghost Pony Press 118
Giant Steps 118
Gifts of the Press (see Juniper
  Press 151)
Gila Review 119
Gimlet Press/Gimlet Publishing
  (see The Body Eclectic 57)
Glens Falls Review (see The
  Loft Press 165)
Global Tapestry Journal (see BB
  Bks 45)
Globe Publishing 119
GMP Publishers 119
Gold Athena Press 120
Golden Eagle Newsletter 375
Golden Isis 120
Golden Quill Press 120
Good Housekeeping 120
Good Reading Magazine (see
  Sunshine Magazine 291)
Goose Lane Editions (see
  Fiddlehead Poetry Books
  109)
Gospel Herald (see Mennonite
  Publishing House 175)
Graham House Review 120
Grain 121
Grants and Awards Available to
  American Writers 375
Graywolf Press 121
Great Auk/Guana Publishing
  (see Wellspring Magazine
  315)
Great Elm Press 121
Great Lakes Colleges Association New Writers' Awards
  347
Great River Review 121
Green Book, The 122
Green Feather Magazine 122
Green Lake Christian Writers

Conference 366
Green Tiger Press 122
Greenfield Review Press, The 122
Green's Magazine 122
Greensboro Review, The 123
Greenwood St. Press (see Prime Time Sports & Fitness 239)
Grendhal Poetry Review, The 123
Grey Whale Press 123
Grinning Idiot 123
Grit 124
Gronk (see Underwhich Editions 305)
Groovy Gray Cat Publications (see The Kindred Spirit 155)
Grove Press 124
Grue Magazine 124
Gryphon 125
Guernica Editions 125
Guggenheim Fellowships 347
Guildford Poets Press (see Wey-farers 319)
Gull Books 125
Gypsy 125

H

H.E.L.P. Center (Helping Through Education, Linking and Preventing), The 371
Hackney Literary Awards 348
Had We But, Inc. (see Fine Madness 110)
Hague Review, The 126
Haiku Review (see High/Coo Press 132)
Haiku Society of America 126
Haiku Zasshi Zo 127
Haiku-Short Poem Series (see Juniper Press 151)
Hammond Poetry Contest, Ralph 348
Hampden-Sydney Poetry Review, The 340
Handicap News 127
Handshake Editions 127
Happiness Holding Tank 341
Harbor Review, The 127
Harcourt Brace Jovanovich 128
Hard Press 128
Hard Row to Hoe (see Seven Buffaloes Press 268)
Harper and Row 128
Harper's 340
Hartmus Press 128
Harvey Memorial Award, Ethel Eikel 348
Hat 129
Haven: New Poetry, The 129
Hawaii Review 129
Hawaii State Foundation on Culture and the Arts 357
Hawk, I'm Your Sister 367

Heartland Journal 130
Heart's Desire Press (see Uncle 305)
Heirloom Books 130
Heldref Publications (see Poet Lore 226)
Helicon Nine 130
Helikon Press 131
Hemley Award, Cecil 348
Henderson Award, Harold G. (see Haiku Society of America 126
Henrichs Publications, Inc. (see Sunshine Magazine 291)
Heresies 131
Heritage Trails Press (see Prophetic Voices 242)
Hermes House Press 131, 340
Heyeck Press, The 131
Hibiscus Magazine (see Hibiscus Press 131)
Hibiscus Press 131
Hieroglyphics Press 132
Higginson Journal (see Dickinson Studies 97)
High Country News 132
High/Coo Press 132
Hill and Holler Anthology Series (see Seven Buffaloes Press 268)
Hillman, Ph.D., Publisher, Aaron W. 133
Hippopotamus Press 133
Hiram Poetry Review 133
His Magazine 133
Hob-Nob 133
Hoboken Terminal, The 134
Hofstra University Summer Writers Conference 365
Hollins Critic, The 134
Holmgangers Press 134
Holt, Rinehart & Winston 340
Home Life (see Baptist Sunday School Board 42)
Home Planet News 135
Homespun Anthology Series (see Winston-Derek Publishers, Inc. 324)
Hoofstrikes Newsletter 135
Horizons S F 135
Hot Springs Gazette 136
Houghton Mifflin Co. 136
Howling Dog 136
Hudson River, The 340
Humpty Dumpty's Magazine (see Children's Better Health Institute 74)
Huntsville Literary Associates (see Poem 225)
Hurricane Alice 136
Hydraulics Poetry Publishing Co. (see Northern Pleasure 199)
Hysteria 136

I

Idad Press (see Hat 129)
Idaho Commission on the Arts 357
Ideals 138
Illinois Arts Council 357
Illinois Writers, Inc. (see IWI Review 148)
Illuminati 138
Illuminations Press 139
Image Magazine (see Cornerstone Press 86)
Images 139
Impetus (see Implosion Press 140)
Implosion Press 140
Important Poetry Press (see This is Important 295)
Impulse Magazine 140
INA Coolbrith Circle Annual Poetry Contest 346
Indiana Arts Commission 357
Indiana Fall Poet's Rendezvous Contest 348
Indiana Review 140
Indiana University Writers Conference 364
Indra's Net 140
Industrial Sabotage (see Curvd H & Z 93)
Infinitum 141
Infinity Publications (see Ohio Renaissance Review 202)
Inkblot Publications 141
Inkling Literary Journal (see Inkling Publications, Inc. 141)
Inkling Publications, Inc. 141
Inkstone 141
Inky Trails Publications 142
Inland Series (see Juniper Press 151)
Inlet 142
Inquirer, The 142
Inside from the Outside, The 376
Insight 142
Insight Press 142
Integrity Times Press (see Second Coming Press 266)
Interim 144
International Black Writers Conference 364
International Creative Yearbook (see Parallel Projects 213)
International Directory of Little Magazines and Small Presses (see Dustbooks 375)
International Pocket Library (see Branden Publishing Co., Inc. 60)
International Poetry Review 144
International Publishers Co., Inc. 144
International Shakespearean Sonnet Contest 348

International University Poetry Quarterly (see International University Press 144)

International University Press 144

International Women's Writing Guild 363, 365, 371

International Young Writers Award for Poetry (see Paris/Atlantic International Magazine of Poetry 213)

Intersection for the Arts 371

Interstate 144

Intertext 145

Intro (see Associated Writing Programs 370)

Inverted-A Horn (see Inverted-A 145)

Inverted-A, Inc. 145

Invited Poets Series (see Saturday Press 264)

Iolaire Arts Foundation (see Aquila Publishing Co. 30)

Iowa Arts Council 357

Iowa Arts Council Literary Awards 348

Iowa Review 145

Iron (see Iron Press 145)

Iron Mountain 145

Iron Press 145

Ironwood 146

Ironwood Press (see Ironwood 146)

Ishtar Press 146

Islands 146

Issue Magazine 146

Issue One 147

Issues 147

Italian Times of Maryland, The 147

Ithaca Community Poets 371

Ithaca House 147

IWI Poetry Contest (see IWI Review 148)

IWI Review 148

J

J Postcard Series 341

Jack and Jill (see Children's Better Health Institute 74)

Jack Kerouac Awards (see Beach & Co., Publishers 45)

Jackson Poetry Prize, Alice (see Electrum Magazine 347)

Jackson's Arm 148

Jam To-Day 148

James Dickey Newsletter 149

James Joyce Broadsheet 149

Japanophile 149

Jean's Journal 149

Jewish Currents 150

Jewish Educational Ventures, Inc. (see Moment Magazine 184)

Jewish Vegetarians (see Vegetarian Journal 308)

Johns Hopkins University Press, The 340

Johnston/The Moorlands Review, Anne 150

Jones Foundation National Poetry Competition, The Chester H. 348

Journal of Canadian Poetry (see Borealis Press 58)

Journal of New Jersey Poets 150

Journal of Regional Criticism (see Arjuna Library Press 33)

Joyful Noise 150

Judson Series of Contemporary American Poetry, The William N. (see Juniper Press 151)

Junior High and High School Student Contests (see Washington Poets Association Annual Poetry Contest 354)

Juniper Books (see Juniper Press 151)

Juniper Press 151

Juniper Prize 348

Juniper Prize, The (see The University of Massachusetts Press 173)

Just A Little Poem (see Trouvere Company 303)

Just About Me 151

Just Buffalo 372

K

Kairos 340

Kairos (see Hermes House Press 131)

Kaldron 151

Kaleidoscope (see Kaleidoscope Press 151)

Kaleidoscope Press 151

Kalliope 152

Kansas Arts Commission 357

Kansas Quarterly 152

Karamu 153

Katuah 153

Katydid Books 154

Kavitha 154

Keepsake Press, The 154

Keith Publications 154

Kennebec 155

Kent Publications, Inc. (see San Fernando Poetry Journal 263)

Kentucky Arts Council 357

Kentucky Poetry Review 155

Kentucky State Poetry Society 348

Kenyon Hills Publications 155

Kenyon Review, The 340

Kerr Memorial Award, John 348

Kestrel Chapbook Series (see Holmgangers Press 134)

Killam Library 340

Kindred Spirit, The 155

King and Cowen Press 156

Kitchen Table: Women of Color Press 156

Knopf, Inc., Alfred A. 340

Konglomerati (see Konglomerati Press 156)

Konglomerati Press 156

Konocti Books 157

Koyo 157

Krax 157

Kropotkin's Lighthouse Publications 158

L

La Jolla Poets' Press 158

La Nouvelle Barre Du Jour (see NBJ 188)

Label Magazine 158

Ladies' Home Journal 158

Lake Aske Memorial Open Poetry Competition (see Poetry Nottingham 230)

Lake Award, Ruth 348

Lake Country Christmas, A (see Clockwatch Review 78)

Lake Shore Publishing 159

Lake Street Press 159

Lake Street Review (see Lake Street Press 159)

Lakes and Prairies Series (see Milkweed Chronicle 179)

Lamont Hall Chapbook Series 339

Lamont Poetry Selection, The 349

Lamplight Editions (see Blind Beggar Press 54)

Lancaster Independent Press, The 159

Landon Translation Award, Harold Morton 349

Lapis 160

Lapis Educational Association, Inc. (see Lapis 160)

Latin American Literary Press 160

Latin American Literary Review (see Latin American Literary Review Press 160)

Latino Poets Association, The (see The Sounds of Poetry 277)

Laughing Waters Press 160

Laurel Review, The 160

Lavan, Younger Poets Awards, Peter I. B. 349

League of Canadian Poets, The 372

Leanin' Tree Publishing Co. 361

Legerete 161

L'Epervier Press 161
Letter Among Friends, A 161
Letter Exchange, The 376
Letters Magazine (see Maine Writers' Workshop 172)
Libra Publishers, Inc. 161
Lieberman Award, Elias 349
Lieb-Schott Publications 340
Light and Life Press (see Action 15)
Light Year (see Bits Press 50)
Lightning Tree, The 162
Limberlost Press 162
Limberlost Review, The (see Limberlost Press 162)
Linden Press 162
Lintel 162
Linwood Publishers 163
Lionhead Publishing 163
Lionsong Magazine 163
Lionsong Press (see Lionsong Magazine 163)
LIPC Newsletter (see Xanadu 335)
Lips 163
Literaria 164
Literary Magazine Review 376
Literary Market Place (see R.R. Bowker Co. 375)
Literary Markets 376
Literary Review, The 164
Little Balkans Press 164
Little Balkans Review (see Little Balkans Press 164)
Little Father Time Society (see The Hoboken Terminal 134)
Living Poets Series (see Dragon's Teeth Press 99)
Living with Children (see Baptist Sunday School Board 42)
Living with Preschoolers (see Baptist Sunday School Board 42)
Living with Teenagers (see Baptist Sunday School Board 42)
Lloyd Memorial Award, Leona 349
Lockert Library of Poetry in Poetry in Translation (see Princeton University Press 239)
Lockhart Press, The 164
Loft Press, The 165
Loft, The 372
Loft-McKnight Writers Awards, The 349
London Review of Books 165
Lone Star Comedy Monthly, The (see Lonestar Publications of Humor 165)
Lonestar: A Comedy Service and Newsletter (see Lonestar Publications of Humor 165)
Lonestar: Humor Digest (see Lonestar Publications of Humor 165)

Lonestar Publications of Humor 165
Long Island Poetry Collective Inc. (see Xandu 335)
Long Island University/Southampton College 365
Lookout, The 166
Loom (see Loom Press 166)
Loom Press 166
Loot (see Spectacular Diseases 282)
Lorien House (see The Black Mountain Press 53)
Lost and Found Times (see Luna Bisonte Prods 167)
Lothlorien (see Chapman 72)
Lotus Press 166
Louisiana State Arts Council 357
Louisiana State Society Poetry Day Contest 349
Louisiana State University Press 167
Lubbe Memorial Award, John A. 349
Lucky Heart Books (see Salt Lick 260)
Lucky Jim's Journal of Strangely Neglected Topics 167
Lucky Star (see Erie Street Press 104)
Ludd's Mill 167
Luna Bisonte Prods 167
Luna Tack 167
Lutheran Journal, The 168
Lutheran Women 168
Lyrian Ruse, The (see Angeltread 27)
Lyric Annual Collegiate Poetry Contest 349
Lyric, The 168
Lyric, The (see Lyric Annual Collegiate Poetry Contest 349)

M

M.A.F. Press 168
M.O.P. Press 169
Maat 169
Macabre (see SF Spectrum 268)
MacDowell Colony, The 367
MacFadden Women's Group 169
MacGuffin, The 170
MacMillan Publishing 340
Macomb Fantasy Factory 349
Madison Review, The 170
Madwomen in the Attic 366
Magazine Industry Market Place (see R.R. Bowker Co. 375)
Magazine of Speculative Poetry, The 171
Magazines for Libraries (see R.R. Bowker Co. 375)
Mage, The 171

Magic Changes 171
Magical Blend 172
Magpie Publications (see Winston-Derek Publishers, Inc. 324)
Maine Line Co. 361
Maine State Commission on the Arts and Humanities 357
Maine Writers' Workshop 172
Mainespring Press (see Maine Writers' Workshop 172)
Mainzer, Inc., Alfred 361
Maize Press 172
Malahat Review, The 172
Mandeville Press, The 172
Manhattan Poetry Review 172
Manhattan Review 340
Manic D Press 172
Manila Series, The (see The Penumbra Press 218)
Manitoba Arts Council 358
Mankato Poetry Review 173
Manna 173
Maplecon SF, Fantasy, and Science Poetry Competition 349
Marijuana Moments (see Northern Pleasure 199)
Marilu Books (see American Studies Press, Inc. 26)
Mark Twain Writers Conference 365
Maroverlag 173
Marriage and Family Living 173
Marshall/Nation Prize for Poetry, Lenore 349
Maryland State Arts Council 357
Masefield Award, John 349
Mason Review, The George (see Phoebe 219)
Massachusetts Council on the Arts and Humanities 357
Massachusetts Review, The 173
Massachusetts State Poetry Society Award 349
Mati Magazine (see Ommation Press 204)
Matilda Literary & Arts Magazine (see Matilda Publications 174)
Matilda Publications 174
Matrix 174
Matrix Anthology (see Red Herring Press 251)
Mayfly (see High/Coo Press 132)
McCall's 174
McClelland and Stewart Limited 175
McKendree Writers' Association Writers' Conference 364
Me Magazine 175
Medina Press (see Electrum 102)
Medwick Award, Lucille 349
Memphis State Review 175
Mendocino Graphics 175
Mendocino Review, The (see

Mendocino Graphics 175)
Mennonite Publishing House 175
Mensuel-25 176
Merging Media 176
Meridian 176
Metrosphere Literary Magazine 176
Miami-Earth Chapter (see Earthwise Publications/Productions 100)
Michigan Council for the Arts 357
Michigan Northwoods Writers Conference 364
Michigan Quarterly Review 177
Microcosm (see Quixsilver Press 246)
Mid-American Review 177
Midland Review 177
Midland Writers Conference 364
Mid-South Poetry Festival 349
Midstream: A Monthly Jewish Review 177
Midwest Arts & Literature 178
Midwest Farmer's Market, Inc. (see Farmer's Market 108)
Midwest Poetry Review 178
Midwest Quarterly, The 178
Milkweed Chronicle 179
Milkweed Editions (see Milkweed Chronicle 179)
Millay Colony for the Arts, Inc., The 367
Mina Press 179
Minas Tirith Evening-Star: The Journal of the American Tolkien Society 180
Minnesota State Arts Board 357
Minnesota Writers Conference 364
Minnesota Writers' Conference 365
Minotaur (see Minotaur Press 180)
Minotaur Press 180
Miorita 180
Miriam Press 180
Mississippi Arts Commission 358
Mississippi Review 182
Mississippi Valley Review 182
Mississippi Valley Writer's Conference 364
Missouri Arts Council 358
Missouri Review 182
Mockersatz Zrox 183
Modern Bride 183
Modern Haiku 183
Modern Maturity 183
Modern Poetry Association, The (see Poetry 227)
Modern Poetry in Translation (see Poetry World 233)
Modern Romances (see MacFadden Women's Group 169)

Moment Magazine 184
Mondo Hunkamooga (see Proper Tales Press 241)
Monitor Book Company, Inc. 184
Montalvo Center for the Arts 367
Montana Arts Council 358
Montana Review, The 340
Moody Street Irregulars: A Jack Kerouac Newsletter (see Textile Bridge Press 294)
Moonjuice Collective (see Embers Press 103)
Moonsquilt Press 184
Moorlands Press, The (see Aquila Publishing Co. 30)
Morning Coffee Chapbooks (see Coffee House Press 80)
Morriss Publisher (see Sono Nis Press 276)
Mosaic Press (Canada) 185
Mosaic Press (Ohio) 184
Mother (see Miriam Press 180)
Mother Duck Press 185
Mother of Ashes Press 185
Mountain Cat Press (see Mountain Cat Review 185)
Mountain Cat Review 185
Mountain in Minnesota Series (see Milkweed Chronicle 179)
Mountain Laurel, The 186
Mr. Cogito (see Mr. Cogito Press 182)
Mr. Cogito Press 182
Ms. Magazine 186
MSS 340
Mudfish (see Box Turtle Press 60)
Multiples (see Multiples Press 186)
Multiples Press 186
Mundus Artium Press 187
Munster's Footsteps, Bill 50
Muscadine 187
Muse's Brew Poetry Review 187
Music Works 187
Mystery Time (see Rhyme Time Poetry 254)
Mystical Unicorn, The 350
Mythellany (See The Mythopoeic Society 187)
Mythlore (see The Mythopoeic Society 187)
Mythopoeic Fantasy Award (see The Mythopoeic Society 187)
Mythopoeic Scholarship Award (see The Mythopoeic Society 187)
Mythopoeic Society, The 187
Mythos (see Crown Creations Associates 92)
Mythprint (see THe Mythopoeic Society 187)

N

Nada Press 188
Naked Man 188
Nalanda University Press (see Gandhabba 117)
Nancy's Magazine 188
Nantucket Review 340
Napa Valley Poetry Conference 363
Nashville Newsletter Poetry Contest 350
Nation Christian Reporter, The (see The United Methodist Reporter 305)
Nation, The 189
Nation, The (see The Discovery 347)
National Association for Poetry Therapy 372
National Association of Retired Credit Union People (see Prime Times 239)
National Endowment for the Arts 350
National Federation of State Poetry Societies, Inc. 372
National Federation of State Poetry Societies Past President's Award 350
National Federation of State Poetry Societies Prize 350
National Poetry Series Annual Open Competition 350
National Writers Club 363
National Writers Club Annual Poetry Contest 350
NBJ 188
Nebo 189
Nebraska Arts Council 358
Nebraska Review, The 189
Negative Capability 189
Negative Capability Press (see Negative Capability 189)
Neither/Nor Press (see Beatniks from Space 46)
Neophytes 190
Nethers 367
Nevada Poetry Society 350
Nevada State Council on the Arts 358
New Age Journal 190
New Broom Private Press (see Phoenix Broadsheets 220)
New Brunswick Culture Development, Youth, Recreation and Culture 358
New Cicada 190
New Collage Magazine 190
New Departures 191
New Directions Publishing 340
New England Review (see Kenyon Hills Publications 155)
New England Sampler Creative Writing Contest 350
New Europa (see Euroeditor 105)

New Hampshire Commission on the Arts 358
New Hope International 191
New Jersey State Council on the Arts 358
New Jersey Writers Conference 365
New Laurel Review, The 191
New Letters 192
New Madros Writers Award 350
New Methods 192
New Mexico Arts Division 358
New Mexico Humanities Review 192
New Oregon Review (see Transition Publications 301)
New Orleans Poetry Journal Press 192
New Poetic Drama (see Dragon's Teeth Press 99)
New Poets Series (see Paris/Atlantic International Magazine of Poetry 213)
New Poets Series, Inc., The 193
New Rain (see Blind Beggar Press 54)
new renaissance, the 193
New Republic, The 194
New Rivers Press, Inc. 194
New Southern Literary Messenger 194
New Traditions Press 194
New Voices (see Write Now Books 332)
New Worlds Unlimited 194
New Yarn 195
New York Poetry Forum 350
New York Quarterly, The 195
New York State Council on the Arts 358
New York University Summer Writer's Conference 365
New Yorker, The 195
New Zealand Literary Fund 350
Newfoundland-Labrador Arts Council 358
Next Exit 196
Nexus 196
Niangua Colony 368
Night Cry 196
Nightsun 196
Nimrod Magazine Pablo Neruda Prize for Poetry 196
1987 Directory of Literary Magazines, The (see Coordinating Council of Literary Magazines 371)
Ninth Decade 197
Nit&Wit 197
No Magazine 197
North American Mentor Magazine (see Westburg Associates Publishers 317)
North American Political Spectrum 198
North American Review 340
North Carolina Arts Council 358

North Carolina Haiku Society Press, The 198
North Dakota Council on the Arts 358
North Dakota Quarterly 198
North Shore Women Writers Alliance, The 373
Northeast (see Juniper Press 151)
Northeastern States Poetry Contest 350
Northeastern University Press 199
Northern Light 199
Northern Lit Quarterly 199
Northern Panic Mail (see Northern Pleasure 199)
Northern Pleasure 199
Northern Pressure Press (see Northern Pleasure 199)
Northwest Magazine 200
Northwest Review 200
Northwood Institute Alden B. Dow Creativity Center, The 368
Northwoods Press 200
Norton & Company, Inc. W.W. 200
Nostoc Magazine (see Arts End Books 35)
Notebook: A Little Magazine 201
Nottingham Poetry Society (see Poetry Nottingham 230)
Nova Scotia Arts Council 358
Now and Then 201
Nycticorax 201

O

O Books Series (see Oasis Books 202)
O.Ars 201
Oasis (see Oasis Books 202)
Oasis Books 202
Oatmeal Studios 361
Observer & Ronald Duncan Foundation International Poetry Competition 351
Ocean Monographis (see Outrigger Publishers Ltd. 210)
Odessa Poetry Review 202
Offset Offshoots (see Ommation Press 204)
Ohio Arts Council 358
Ohio Journal, The 202
Ohio Poetry Day Association 351
Ohio Renaissance Review 202
Ohio Review Books (see The Ohio Review 203)
Ohio Review, The 203
Ohio River Writers' Conference 364
Ohio State University Press 340
Oink! Magazine 203

Oklahoma State Arts Council 358
Old Plate Press (see From Here Press 114)
Old Red Kimono, The 203
Oleander Modern Poets (see The Oleander Press 204)
Oleander Press, The 204
Ommation Press 204
On Being 204
On the Edge 204
One Earth 205
One Shot 205
One World (see Trans-Species Unlimited 302)
Ontario Arts Council 358
Ontario Review, The 205
Oovrah 205
Open Mind, International Literary Competition 351
Open Places 206
Open Windows (see Guernica Editions 125)
Oppossum Holler Tarot 206
Orbis 206
Ore 206
Oregon Arts Commission 358
Oregon State Poetry Association, The 373
Orion Press 340
Oro Madre (see Ruddy Duck Press 258)
Orpheus (see Illuminati 138)
Orphic Lute 207
Oryx Press 376
Osiris, An International Journal/ Une Revue Internationale 207
Other Poetry 207
Other Side Magazine, The 208
Our Family 208
Our Way Publications (see Baseball: Our Way 43)
Ouroboros 208
Out There 209
Out There Productions, Inc. (see Out There 209)
Outerbridge 209
Outposts (see Suburban Wilderness Press 289)
Outposts Poetry Quarterly (see Outpost Publications 209)
Outposts Publications 209
Outrigger (see Outrigger Publishers Ltd. 210)
Outrigger Publishers Ltd. 210
Overlook Press, The 210
Owl Creek Press 340
Owl Creek Press Poetry Book Competition 351
Owlflight (see Empire for the Science Fiction Writer 103)
Oxford University Press 210
Oxyura Jamaicensis Rubida Monographs in Poetry (see Ruddy Duck Press 258)
Oyez Review 210
Ozark Creative Writers, Inc. 363

P

Pacific Arts & Letters 211
Pacific Bridge 211
Pacific Poetry Series (see University of Hawaii Press 129)
Pacific Quarterly 340
Pacific Quarterly Moano (see Outrigger Publishers Ltd. 210)
Paintbrush (see Ishtar Press 146)
Painted Bride Quarterly 211
Pan-Erotic Review (see Red Adler Books 249)
Pancake Press 212
Pandora 212
Pandrama of Czech Literature 212
Pangloss Papers 212
Panjandrum Books 212
Paper Air Magazine 213
Parabola 213
Parabola Books (see Parabola 213)
Parallel (see Parallel Projects 213)
Parallel Projects 213
Paramount Cards, Inc. 361
Paris Exiles (see Handshake Editions 127)
Paris Review, The 213
Paris/Atlantic International Magazine of Poetry 213
Parnassus Literary Journal 214
Parnassus: Poetry in Review 214
Partisan Review 214
Pasadena Annual Writers Forum 363
Passages North 215
Passaic County Community College Poetry Center Library 373
Passaic Review 215
Passion for Industry 215
Path Press, Inc. 215
Pathways (see Inky Trails Publications 142)
Pawprints 361
Paycock Press 215
Peace & Pieces Books (see Pacific Arts & Letters 211)
Pebble (see Best Cellar Press 47)
Pegasus Contest for Students (see Pennsylvania Poetry Social Annual Contest 351)
Pegasus Review, The 216
Pella Publishing Company 216
Pembroke Magazine 216
Peninsula Writers 373
Pennine Platform 217
Pennsylvania Council on the Arts 358
Pennsylvania Poetry Society Annual Contest 351

Pennsylvania Review, The 217
Pennywhistle Press 217
Pentagram 217
Pentecostal Evangel 217
Penumbra Press, The 218
Penway Books (see Lotus Press 166)
Perivale Press 218
Permafrost 218
Permanent Press 218
Perryman-Visser National Poetry Award 351
Persea Books 340
Personal Poets United 373
Pet Gazette, The 219
Petronium Press 219
Phaeton Press (see Aquila Publishing Co. 30)
Phenomenon Press (see Underwhich Editions 305)
Philadelphia Poets 219
Phillips Poetry Award, The (see Stone Country 286)
Philosophy and the Arts 219
Phoebe 219
Phocbus 220
Phoenix Broadsheets 220
Phoenix Poets 220
Pictograms (see Illuminati 138)
Piddiddle 220
Piedmont Literary Review 220
Piedmont Literary Society (see Piedmont Literary Review 220)
Pikestaff Forum, The 222
Pikestaff Poetry Chapbooks (see The Pikestaff Forum 222)
Pikestaff Press, The (see The Pikestaff Forum 222)
Pikestaff Publications, Inc. (see The Pikestaff Forum 222)
Pine Tree Series (see Tower Poetry Society 300)
Pipe Smoker's Ephemeris, The 222
Pitt Poetry Series 224, 351
Place Stamp Here 224
Plains Poetry Journal (see Stronghold Press 288)
Plains Poets Award 351
Plainsong 224
Plainsongs 224
Plantagenet Productions 224
Platen Publishing Company (see Published! 248)
Players Press 225
Pleasure Dome Press (Xanadu 335)
Ploughshares 225
Pluma De Oro Writing Competition 351
Pockets (see The Upper Room 307)
Poem 225
Poemcard Series (see Xanadu 335)
Poesis 376

Poet and Critic 225
Poet International (see World Poetry Society 330)
Poet Lore 226
Poet Lore Narrative Poetry Prize (see Poet Lore 226)
Poet News (see The Poet Tree, Inc. 226)
Poet, The 226
Poet Tree, Inc., The 226
Poetalk (see Bay Area Poets Coalition 44)
Poetic Justice 226
Poetry 227
Poetry Australia (see South Head Press 279)
Poetry Book Society 376
Poetry Canada Review 227
Poetry Center Book Award, The 351
Poetry Center of the 92nd Street Y, The 373
Poetry Connexion, The 227
Poetry Durham 228
Poetry East 228
Poetry Exchange 376
Poetry Flash 228
Poetry in Review Foundation (see Parnassus: Poetry in Review 214)
Poetry Ireland Review 228
Poetry Kanto 228
Poetry Letter, The 229
Poetry Miscellany 340
Poetry Motel (see Suburban Wilderness Press 289)
Poetry Motel Chaps (see Suburban Wilderness Press 289)
Poetry 'N Prose (see Ahnene Publications 17)
Poetry Newsletter 229
Poetry Nippon (see Poetry Nippon Press 230)
Poetry Nippon Newsletter (see Poetry Nippon Press 230)
Poetry Nippon Press 230
Poetry Northwest 230
Poetry Nottingham 230
Poetry Now (CA) 340
Poetry Now (UK) 231
Poetry Post (see Ver Poets 308)
Poetry Press 231
Poetry Project at St. Mark's Church in the Bowery, The 373
Poetry Quarterly (see Curlew Press 92)
Poetry Resource Center of Michigan 373
Poetry Review 231
Poetry Review, The 231
Poetry: San Francisco Publications 232
Poetry: San Francisco Quarterly (see Poetry: San Francisco Publications 232)
Poetry Society of America 373

Poetry Society of America (see The Poetry Review 231)
Poetry Society of Japan, The (see Poetry Nippon Press 230)
Poetry Society of Michigan 352
Poetry Society of Tennessee Award 352
Poetry Society of Texas 352
Poetry Society of Virginia Contest 352
Poetry Toronto 232
Poetry Wales (see Poetry Wales Press 233)
Poetry Wales Press 233
Poetry World 233
Poetry/LA 229
Poets & Writers, Inc. 374
Poets & Writers, Incl. 377
Poets at Work 233
Poets' Audio Center 377
Poets' Dinner Contest 352
Poets Eleven . . . Audible (see Black Bear Publications 51)
Poets for Peace 374
Poets for Peace (see Poetry: San Francisco Publications 232)
Poet's Magazine, The (see King and Cowen Press 156)
Poets of the Vineyard Contest 352
Poets On 233
Poets on Poetry (see University of Michigan Press 376)
Poets. Painters. Composers 234
Poet's Showcase (see Quixsilver Press 246)
Point Riders Press 234
Porcupine's Quill, Inc. 234
Port Townsend Writers' Conference 366
Post Me Stamp Series (see Me Magazine 175)
Post Poems (see Raw Dog Press 248)
Potes & Poets Press, Inc. 235
Potpourri International 235
Prairie Fire 235
Prairie Journal Press (see The Prairie Journal 236)
Prairie Journal, The 236
Prairie Schooner 236
Presbyterian Record, The 236
Prescott Street Press 238
Press Me Close (see Place Stamp Here 224)
Press of MacDonald & Reinecke 238
Press Porcepic Ltd. 238
Pressed Curtains 238
Press-Press Press (see Northern Pleasure 199)
Prickly Pear Press (see Studia Hispanica Editors 289)
Primavera 239
Prime Time Publications (see Prime Time Sports & Fitness 239)

Prime Time Sports & Fitness 239
Prime Times 239
Primers for the Age of Inner Space (see Wheat Forder's Press 319)
Prince Edward Island Council of the Arts 358
Princeton Series of Contemporary Poets (see Princeton University Press 239)
Princeton University Press 239
Printable Arts Society, Inc. 240
Printed Matter (see Tels 294)
Printer's News (see Ye Olde News 336)
Printers Pie (see Aquila Publishing Co. 30)
Prism International 240
Pro Dogs National Charity Open Poetry Competition 352
Process (see Xanadu 335)
Processed World 240
Professional Writing Magazine for Christians, The (see The Christian Writer 375)
Progressive Press (see The Wire 325)
Proof 240
Proof Rock (see Proof Rock Press 241)
Proof Rock Press 241
Proper Tales Postcards (see Proper Tales Press 241)
Proper Tales Press 241
Prophetic Voices 242
Prospice (see Aquila Publishing Co. 30)
Prune Poetry Contest 352
Psassaic Review 215
Psych It 352
Pteranodon 340
Pteranodon Award 352
Ptolemy/The Browns Mill Review 242
Pub (see Ansuda Publications 28)
Public Works 243
Published! 234
Puckerbrush Press, The 243
Puckerbrush Review, The (see The Puckerbrush Press 243)
Pudding Magazine (see Pudding Publications 243)
Pudding Publications 243
Pulpsmith Magazine (see The Smith Publishers 274)
Pulitzer Prize in Arts and Letters 352
Punclips (see M.O.P. Press 169)
Purple Heather Publications 242
Purple Patch 242
Purpose (see Mennonite Publishing House 175)

Q

Quadrant Editions 244
Quality Publications (see Green Feather Magazine 122)
Quarry Magazine 244
QuarryPress (see Quarry Magazine 244)
Quarterly Review of Literature 245
Quarterly West 245
Quebec aide a la creation 358
Queen of All Hearts 245
Queenie Lee Competition (see Poetry Nottingham 230)
Queens Quarterly 245
Quercus (see The Poet Tree, Inc. 226)
Quintessence Publications 245
Quixote (see Quixote Press 246)
Quixote Press 246
Quixotl (see Quixote Press 246)
Quixsilver Press 246

R

R.S.V.P. Press 246
Raccoon (see Raccoon Books 247)
Raccoon Books 247
Rackham Journal of the Arts and Humanities (RAJAH) 247
Raddle Moon, The 247
Rag Mag 247
Ragdale Foundation 368
Rainbow Books 248
Rambunctious Press 248
Rambunctious Review (see Rambunctious Press 248)
Random House 248
Raw Dog Press 248
RE: AL (Re: Artes Liberales) 249
Realities Library 249
Rebirth of Artemis (see Write Now Books 332)
Reconstructionist 249
Red Alder Books 249
Red Bass 250
Red Candle Press, The 250
Red Farm Studio 361
Red Herring Chapbook Series (see Red Herring Press 251)
Red Herring Press 251
Red Key Press 251
Red Pagoda, A Journal of Haiku, The 251
Red Sharks Press (see Cabaret 246, 64)
Red/Eter Kardz 361
Redneck Review of Literature, The 251
Reed Starline Cards Co. 361

Reflect 251
Reflections 252
Reform Judaism 252
Regression Therapy 252
Reid Writers' Colony in New Hampshire, Mildred I. 368
Reiman Publications 252
Religious Humanism 253
Renaissance Greeting Cards 361
Renegade (see Point Riders Press 234)
Re:Print (see Printable Arts Society, Inc. 240)
Revue D'Etudes Sur LA Femme (see Atlantic, A Women's Studies Journal 38)
RFD: A Country Journal for Gay Men Everywhere 253
Rhiannon Press 253
Rhinelander School of Arts 366
Rhino 254
Rhode Island Review 254
Rhode Island State Council on the Arts 358
Rhode Island State Poetry Society Award 353
Rhyme Time Poetry Newsletter 254
Rhysling Anthology, The (see Science Fiction Poetry Association 265)
Rhythm-and-Rhyme 255
Ridge Review Magazine 255
Ridge Times Press (see Ridge Review Magazine 255)
Rielo Prize for Mystical Poetry, Fernando 353
Right Here 255
Rimu (see Outrigger Publishers Ltd. 210)
Rimu Publishing Co. Ltd. (see Outrigger Publishers Ltd. 210)
Rinehart Foundation Award, Mary Roberts 353
Rivelin Graphene Press 255
River City Publications (see Midwest Poetry Review 178)
River City Review 256
River City Review Press, Inc. (see River City Review 256)
River Styx Magazine 256
Riverrun 256
Riverside Quarterly 256
Riverstone Press 341
Road Runner (see Insight Press 142)
Roanoke Review 257
Roar Recording (see Lionhead Publishing 163)
Rochester Routes/Creative Arts Projects (see Exit 106)
Rocky Mountain Review of Language and Literature 257
Romance and Fiction World 257
Romantist, The (see The F. Marion Crawford Memorial Society 88)
Room of One's Own 258
Round Table, The 258
Rousana Cards 361
Rowan Tree Press 341
Rowing USA (see American Rowing 25)
Rubicon 258
Ruddy Duck Press 258
Rump Booklets (see Krax 157)

S

S.O.S. (Sultan of Swat) Books 259
Sachem Press 259
Sackbut Press 260
Sackbut Review (see Sackbut Press 260)
Sacramento Poetry Center, The (see The Poet Tree, Inc. 226)
Saint Andrews Press (see Saint Andrews Review 260)
Saint Andrews Review 260
Saint Anthony Messenger 260
Saint Joseph Messenger and Advocate of the Blind 260
Saint Martin's Press 341
Saint Mary's College of Maryland 364
Saint Willibrod Press (see Cathedral Voice 70)
Salmagundi 260
Salome: A Literary Dance Magazine (see Ommation Press 209)
Salt Lick 260
Salt Lick Press (see Salt Lick 260)
Salt Lick Samplers (see Salt Lick 260)
Salthouse 262
Samisdat 262
San Diego Poet's Press 262
San Fernando Poetry Journal 263
San Jose Studies 263
Sandburg Awards, Carl 353
Sanctuary (see Gypsy 125)
Sands 264
Santa Fe Writers Conference 365
Santa Susana Press 264
Sapiens: A Journal for Human Evolution 264
Saskatchewan Arts Board 358
Saturday Press, Inc. 264 (also see Eileen W. Barnes Award 345)
Scarecrow Press 265
Scavenger's Newsletter 265
Schiffert Prize in Poetry, The Edith (see The AWP Award Series 344)
Science Fiction Poetry Association 265
Scope 266
Scrivener 266
Scythe Books (see Winston-Derek Publishers, Inc. 324)
Sea Horse Press Ltd., The 266
Seattle Pulp (see Globe Publishing 119)
Second Coming 353 (also see Second Coming Press 266)
Second Coming Press 266
Seems 267
Segue Foundation, The 374
Self and Society: European Journal of Humanistic Psychology 267
Senior Citizen Monthly (see The Word Shop 329)
Separate Doors 341
Serpent & Eagle Press 267
Seven 267
Seven Buffaloes Press 268
Seventeen 268
Sewanee Review 268
SF Spectrum 268
Shakespeare Newsletter, The 269
Shamal Books 269
Shameless Hussy Press 269
Sharing The Victory 269
Shaw Publishers, Harold 270
Shawnee Silhouette 270
Sheba Review, Inc. (see Midwest Arts & Literature 178)
Sheep Meadow Press 340
Shelley Memorial Award 353
Shenandoah 270
Shitepoke 270
Shorelines (see Delong & Associates 95)
Shotgun Poetry Series (see Cannon Press 67)
Signal Editions (see Vehicule Press 308)
Signpost Press Poetry Chapbook Competition, The 353
Signpost Press, The 271
Silver Wings 271
Silverfish Review 271
Silverfish Review Press 271)
Sing Heavenly Muse! 271
Singing Horse Press (see Paper Air Magazine 213)
Singular Speech Press 272
Sinister Wisdom 272
Sins of the Morning Anthologies, The (see The Word Shop 329)
Sipapu (see Konocti Books 157)
Slippery People Press (see Aerial 16)
Slipstream 272
Slough Press 273

Slow Dancer 273
Slow Dancer Press (see Slow Dancer 273)
Small Pond Magazine of Literature 273
Small Press, A (see Heirloom Books 130) .
Small Press News (see Stony Hills 287)
Small Press Review (see Dustbooks 375)
Small Press Times (see Ruddy Duck Press 258)
Small Towner, The 274
Smith Memorial Award, Bessie Archer 353
Smith Publishers, The 274
Smoke 274
Snapdragon 274
Snowy Egret 274 (also see Artful Codger and Codgerette 34)
Sobriety House 275
Social Anarchism 275
Society for the Furtherance & Study of Science Fiction (see Aurora: Speculative Feminism 40)
Sojourner 275
Soloing (see Sonlight Christian Newspapers 276)
Somrie Press 275
Song 275
Song Press (see Song 275)
Sonlight Christian Newspapers 276
Sono Nis Press 276
Sonora Review 276
Soundings (see Lake Shore Publishing 159)
Soundings East 277
Sounds of Poetry, The 277
South Carolina Arts Commission 358
South Carolina Review 277
South Coast Poetry Journal 278
South Dakota Arts Council 358
South Dakota Review 278
South End Press 278
South Florida Poetry Institute (see The South Florida Poetry Review 278)
South Florida Poetry Review, The 278
South Head Press 279
South Western Ontario Poetry 279
Southern California Chapter, Annual National Contest 353
Southern California Poets' Pen 353
Southern Humanities Review 279
Southern Poetry Review 279
Southern Review, The 280
Southport Press 280
Southwest Review 341

Southwest Review, Elizabeth Matchett Stover Memorial Award 353
Sou'wester 280
Sovereign Gold Award Program (see Sovereign Gold Literary Magazine 280)
Sovereign Gold Literary Magazine 280
Space and Time 281
Sparrow Poverty Pamphlets (see Sparrow Press 281)
Sparrow Press 281
Spectacular Diseases 282
Spectrum Summer Writers Conference 366
Sphinx-Women's International Literary/Art Review 282
Spider Plots in Rat-Holes 282
Spinsters Ink 282
Spirit That Moves Us Press (see The Spirit That Moves Us 283)
Spirit That Moves Us, The 283
Spirit: The Christian Magazine About Career Lifestyle and Relationships 283
Spitball 283
Split Rock Arts Program 365
Spokes 284
Spoofing (see Creative with Words Publications 89)
Stafford Award, William (see Washington Poets Association Annual Poetry Contests 354)
Stand Magazine 284
Standard Publishing Co. (see Straight 287)
Star & Elephant Books (see Green Tiger Press 122)
Star Books, Inc. 284
Star Foundation Poetry Awards, The 353
Star-Line (see Science Fiction Poetry Association 265)
Starrett Poetry Prize, Agnes Lynch (see Pitt Poetry Series 224)
Start: Magazine of Literature and the Arts 285
State of Maine Writers Conference 364
State Street Press 285
Step Life 285
Stevan Company, The 286
Stone Country 286
Stone Country Press (see Stone Country 286)
Stone Press 341
Stone Roller Press (see Black River Review 53)
Stone Soup, The Magazine by Children 287
Stone, The 341
Stony Hills 287
Stormline Press, Inc. 287

Story Friends (see Mennonite Publishing House 175)
Strader Poetry Contest, Jess 354
Straight 287
Street Magazine (see Street Press 288)
Street Press 288
Stride Cassettes (see Stride Magazine 288)
Stride Magazine288
Stride Publications (see Stride Magazine 288)
Stronghold Press 288
Struggling Writer 377
Stuart Contest, The Jesse (see Seven 267)
Student Award 354
Studia Hispanica Editors 289
Studia Mystica 289
Style Manuals of the English-Speaking World (see Oryx Press 376)
Suburban Wilderness Broadside of a Barn Series (see Suburban Wilderness Press 289)
Suburban Wilderness Press 289
Success Magazine 289
Success Poetry Publications (see Success Magazine 289)
Sulphur 341
Summer Festival of Arts Writers Conference 363
Summer Stream Press 290
Sun, The 290
Sunrise Publications, Inc. 361
Sunrust Magazine 290
Sunshine Magazine 291
Sunshine Press, The (see Sunshine Magazine 291)
Sunstone Press 291
Superintendent's Profile & Pocket Equipment Directory 291
S-W Enterprises (see Green Feather Magazine 122)
Swallow's Tale Poetry Contest 354
Swamp Press, NY 292 (see Serpent & Eagle Press 267)
Swamp Press, MA 292
Sylvia Beach (see Beach & Co., Publishers 45)
Synthesis 292

T

T.S. Eliot Chapbook Contest (see Earthwise Publications/Productions 100)
Tadbooks (see Illuminati 138)
Talltales (see Illluminati 138)
Tandava 292
Tar River Poetry 292
Taurus 341
Taxvs Press 293

Tears in the Fence 293
Tecumseh Press Ltd. (see Borealis Press 58)
Teksteditions (see Underwhich Editions 305)
Tels 294
Tels Poetry Contest (see Tels 294)
Tempest Review (see Earthwise Publications/Productions 100)
Ten Million Flies Can't Be Wrong (see Clock Radio 78)
Ten Penny Players (see Waterways: Poetry in the Mainstream 313)
Tendril Magazine (see Wampeter Press 312)
Tennessee Arts Commission 358
Territory of Oklahoma: Literature & The Arts 294
Texas Commission on the Arts 358
Texas Institute of Letters Poetry Award 354
Texas Review Chapbook Award, The (see The Texas Review 294)
Texas Review, The 294
Textile Bridge Press 294
Third Woman (see Third Woman Press 295)
Third Woman Press 295
Thirteen Poetry Magazine (see M.A.F. Press 168)
13th Moon 295
This Is Important 295
Thistledown Press Ltd. 295
Thomas Hardy Yearbook, The 296
Three Continents Press Inc. 296
Three Rivers Poetry Journal (See Carnegie-Mellon University Press 68)
3 Score & 10 296
Threepenny Review, The 296
Threshold Books 297
Thunder City Press 297
Thunder Creek Publishing Co-op (see Coteau Books 86)
Thurber House, The 374
Thursdays Poetry Magazine 297
Tidal Press, The 297
Tilted Planet Press 297
Timberline Press 297
Time of Singing, A Magazine of Christian Poetry 299
Time to Pause (see Inky Trails Publications 142)
Time Warp 299
Tin Wreath 299
Tiptoe Publishing (see Candle: An International Ragazine 66)
Tokyo English Literature Society (see Tels 294)
Tokyo Women's Arts Festival (see New Yarn 195)

Toll Gate Journal, The (see Purple Heather Publications 242)
Touch 300
Touchstone (see Touchstone Press 300)
Touchstone Press 300
Tower (see Tower Poetry Society 300)
Tower Poetry Society 300
Tradeswomen 301
Tradition 301
Traditional Verse Forms (see Washington Poets Association Annual Poetry Contests 354)
Trans-Species Unlimited 302
Transition Publications 301
Translation (see Translation Center 301)
Translation Center 301
Treetop Panorama 302
Trenton State College Annual Writers' Conference 365
Trestle Creek Review 302
Tri-City Poetry Society Award 354
Triquarterly Magazine 302
Trout Creek Press 303
Trouvere Company 303
Trouvere's Laureate (see Trouvere Company 303)
True Experience (See MacFadden Women's Group 169)
True Love (see MacFadden Women's Group 169)
True Story (see MacFadden Women's Group 169)
Tryo Magazine 304
Tucson Writers Conference 363
Turkey Press 304
Turtle Magazine for Preschool Kids (see Children's Better Health Institute 74)
Tusk Books (see The Overlook Press 210)
22 Press 304

U

UCLA Extension 363
Ultramarine Publishing Co., The 305
Uncle 305
Under Discussion (see University of Michigan Press 376)
Underwhich Editions 305
Unique Graphics (see Empire for the Science Fiction Writer 103)
United Amateur Press 374
United Methodist Reporter, The 305
Unity (see Unity School of Christianity 306)
Unity School of Christianity 306

University Editions 306
University of Alabama Press 19
University of Arkansas Press, The 33
University of Central Florida 340
University of Chicago Press, The (see Phoenix Poets 220)
University of Georgia Press 105
University of Illinois Press 138
University of Massachusetts Press, The 173
University of Michigan Press 376
University of Missouri Press 182
University of Pittsburgh Press (see Pitt Poetry Series 224)
University of Portland Review 235
University of Queensland Press 245
University of Utah Press 307
Unknowns, The 306
Unmuzzled Ox 306
Unpublished Poets Series 340
Unspeakable Visions of the Individual, The 307
Upper Left-Hand Corner, The 377
Upper Midwest Writers' Conference 365
Upper Room, The 307
Urie, Sherry 307
Utah Arts Council 358
Utah State University Press 307

V

Vagabond Creations, Inc. 361
Vagrom Chap Books (see Sparrow Press 281)
Valley Editions (see Mosaic Press 185)
Valley Spirit 308
Vanessapress (see Fireweed Press 110)
Vanity Fair 341
Vegetarian Journal 308
Vehicule Press 308
Ver Poets 308
Vergin' Press see Gypsy 125)
Vermont Council on the Arts 358
Verse & Universe 309
Viaztlan: A Journal of the Arts and Letters 309
Village Idiot, The (see Mother of Ashes Press 185)
Villager, The 309
Villeneuve Publications (see Four By Four 113)
Vintage Books (see Random House 248)
Vintage '45 309
Virginia Commission for the Arts 358

Virginia Prize 354
Virginia Quarterly Review, The 310 (also see Emily Clark Balch Awards 344)
Visions (see Black Buzzard Press 52)
Visions Publications (see Time Warp 299)
Voices International 310
Voices Israel 310
Vol. No. Magazine 310

W

Wagner Award, Celia B. 354
Wampeter Press 312
Warner Press, Inc. 361
Warthog Press 312
Wascana Review 312
Washington Poets Association Annual Poetry Contest 354
Washington Prize 354
Washington Review 312
Washington State Arts Commission 358
Washington Writers' Publishing House 312
Watershed Foundation, The (see Poets Audio Center 377)
Waterways: Poetry in the Mainstream 313
Wav Poetry Series (see Wav Publications 313)
Wav Publications 313
Wave Press, The 313
Wave, The (see The Wave Press 313)
Waves 314
Webster Review 314
Wee Wisdom (see Unity School of Christianity 306)
Weeping Monk Editions (see Proper Tales Press 241)
Weirdbook Sampler, The 314
Wellspring 315
Wellspring Magazine 315
Wesleyan New Poets (see Wesleyan University Press 315)
Wesleyan University Press 315
Wesleyan Writers Conference 363
West Anglia Publications 316
West Branch 316
West Coast Review 316
West End Press 316
West Hills Review 317
West of Boston 317
West Virginia Arts and Humanities Division 358
West Virginia Poetry Society Award 354
Westburg Associates Publishers 317
Westerly 318
Western Humanities Review 318

Western People (see Western Producer Publications 318)
Western Producer Publications 318
Western States Arts Foundation 354
Western World Haiku Society (see Dragonfly: A Quarterly of Haiku 98)
Westgate Press 319
Weyfarers 319
Wheat Forder's Press 319
Wheaton Literary Series (see Harold Shaw Publishers 270)
Whetstone 320
Whimsy 320
Whiskey Island Magazine 320
White Light, The 320
White Pine Press 321
White Review, James 321
White Rock Review 341
White Rose Literary Magazine, The 321
White Walls: A Magazine of Writings by Artists 321
Whitehead Hicky National Awards, Daniel 348
Whiting Foundation, Mrs. Giles 355
Whitman Award, Walt 355
Whole Earth Review 321
Wide Open Magazine 321
Widener Review 322
Wildfire Networking Magazine (see Bear Tribe 45)
Williams Award, William Carlos 355
Willow Bee Publishing House, The 322
Willow Springs 322
Wilson Fine Arts, Inc., Carol 361
Wind Magazine 323
Windfall 323
Windfall Prophets Chapbook Series (see Windfall 323)
Windham Phoenix, The 324
Windless Orchard Chapbooks, The (see The Windless Orchard 324)
Windless Orchard, The 324
Windows Project (see Smoke 274)
Windriver Series (see Duck Down Press 99)
Wine & Roses Poetry Contest (see Pennsylvania Poetry Society Annual Contests 351)
Winston-Derek Publishers, Inc. 324
Wire, The 325
Wisconsin Academy Review 325
Wisconsin Arts Board 358
Wisconsin Restaurateur, The 325
Wisconsin Review 325

Wisconsin Review Press (see Wisconsin Review 325)
Wishing Well, The 326
With (see Mennonite Publishing House 175)
Without Halos 326
Wolfsong 326
Woman of Power 326
Woman's National Auxilary Convention (see Co-Laborer 81)
Women Poet (see Women-in-Literature, Inc. 327)
Women Writers Alliance 327
Women-in-Literature, Inc. 327
Women's Quarterly Review 328
Women's Wilderness Canoe Trip (see Hawk, I'm Your Sister 367)
Womenwise 328
Wonder Time 328
Woodbooks 341
Woodcards 341
Woodrose Editions 341
Wooster Review, The 328
Word Beat (see Associated Writing Programs 370)
Word Exchange 329
Word Shop, The 329
Word Works, The 329
Word-Fires 330
Words and Visions (WAV) Magazine (see Wav Publications 313)
Words in our Pockets: The Feminist Writers Guild Handbook on How to Gain Power, Get Published and Get Paid 377
Words: The New Literary Forum 330
Wordwrights Canada 330
World Humor and Irony Membership (see Whimsy 320)
World Order of Narrative Poets 355
World Poetry (see American Poetry Review 25)
World Poetry Society 330
Wormwood Review Press 331
Wormwood Review, The (See Wormwood Review Press 331)
Worthies Library, The (see The F. Marion Crawford Memorial Society 88)
WPBS Poetry 331
Writ 331
Write Associates Writers' Workshops 365
Write Now Books 332
Write On 332
Write to Fame (see Keith Publications 154)
The Writer 333, 377
Writer's Block, The 333
Writer's Center, The 374

Writer's Digest 333, 377
Writer's Digest Books (see Writer's Digest 377)
Writer's Digest Writing Competition (see Writer's Digest 333)
Writers Forum 334
Writers Gazette (see Trouvere Company 303)
Writers House Press 334
Writer's Journal 377
Writer's Lifeline 378
Writer's Rescue (see Keith Publications 154)
Writers Union of Canada 374
Writers West 335
Writer's West, For Working Writers 378
Writer's Yearbook (see Writer's Digest 333, 377)
Writeway, Poetry Contest Calendar 378
Writing! 378

Writing Update (see Inkling Publications, Inc. 141)
Wyoming (see The Willow Bee Publishing House 322)
Wyoming Council on the Arts 358

X

Xanadu 335
X-it Magazine 335
Xtras (see From Here Press 114)

Y

Yaddo 368
Yale Review, The (see Yale University Press 336)
Yale Series of Younger Poets, The 355 (also see Yale University Press 336)

Yale University Press 336
Ye Olde News 336
Yearbook of American Poetry (see Monitor Book Company Inc. 184)
Yellow Moon Press 341
Yellow Press 336
Yellow Silk 337
Yes Press 337
Yesterday's Magazette 337
Yet Another Magazine 339
Young American Publishing Co., Inc. 338
Young Crusader, The 338
Your Story Hour (see Clubhouse 80)

Z

Zephyr Press 338
Zindy 338

Judson Jerome has been writing poetry for fifty-one years and seeing it in print for over forty in dozens of popular and literary magazines. His monthly column in Writer's Digest, *which he has written for twenty-five years, is widely read and respected for its insight and its relevance to working poets. His writing on poetry is dedicated to encouraging other poets and promoting the qualities he sees missing in much of today's poetry—meter, beauty of language, and honest communication.*

Jerome was Professor of Literature at Antioch College for twenty years until he left for life on a communal farm in the Alleghenies. His books include a study of communes, a novel, and collections of his poetry and verse plays, as well as three books on the technical aspects of poetry, The Poet and the Poem, The Poet's Handbook, *and* On Being a Poet. *He now lives with his family—he's been married to Marty since 1948—in Ohio.*

Notes

_____ **Notes**

Other Books of Interest

Computer Books
  The Complete Guide to Writing Software User Manuals, by Brad M. McGehee (paper) $14.95
  The Photographer's Computer Handbook, by B. Nadine Orabona (paper) $14.95
General Writing Books
  Beginning Writer's Answer Book, edited by Polking and Bloss $14.95
  Getting the Words Right: How to Revise, Edit and Rewrite, by Theodore A. Rees Cheney $13.95
  How to Become a Bestselling Author, by Stan Corwin $14.95
  How to Get Started in Writing, by Peggy Teeters (paper) $8.95
  How to Write a Book Proposal, by Michael Larsen $9.95
  How to Write While You Sleep, by Elizabeth Ross $12.95
  If I Can Write, You Can Write, by Charlie Shedd $12.95
  International Writers' & Artists' Yearbook (paper) $12.95
  Law & the Writer, edited by Polking & Meranus (paper) $10.95
  Knowing Where to Look: The Ultimate Guide to Research, by Lois Horowitz $16.95
  Make Every Word Count, by Gary Provost (paper) $7.95
  Pinckert's Practical Grammar, by Robert C. Pinckert $12.95
  Teach Yourself to Write, by Evelyn Stenbock (paper) $9.95
  The 29 Most Common Writing Mistakes & How to Avoid Them, by Judy Delton $9.95
  Writer's Block & How to Use It, by Victoria Nelson $12.95
  Writer's Guide to Research, by Lois Horowitz $9.95
  Writer's Market, edited by Becky Williams $21.95
  Writer's Resource Guide, edited by Bernadine Clark $16.95
  Writing for the Joy of It, by Leonard Knott $11.95
  Writing From the Inside Out, by Charlotte Edwards (paper) $9.95
Magazine/News Writing
  Basic Magazine Writing, by Barbara Kevles $16.95
  How to Sell Every Magazine Article You Write, by Lisa Collier Cool $14.95
  How to Write & Sell the 8 Easiest Article Types, by Helene Schellenberg Barnhart $14.95
  Writing Nonfiction that Sells, by Samm Sinclair Baker $14.95
Fiction Writing
  Creating Short Fiction, by Damon Knight (paper) $8.95
  Fiction Writer's Help Book, by Maxine Rock $12.95
  Fiction Writer's Market, edited by Jean Fredette $18.95
  Handbook of Short Story Writing, by Dickson and Smythe (paper) $8.95
  How to Write & Sell Your First Novel, by Oscar Collier with Frances Spatz Leighton $14.95
  How to Write Short Stories that Sell, by Louise Boggess (paper) $7.95
  One Way to Write Your Novel, by Dick Perry (paper) $6.95
  Storycrafting, by Paul Darcy Boles $14.95
  Writing Romance Fiction—For Love And Money, by Helene Schellenberg Barnhart $14.95
  Writing the Novel: From Plot to Print, by Lawrence Block (paper) $8.95
Special Interest Writing Books
  Complete Book of Scriptwriting, by J. Michael Straczynski $14.95
  The Craft of Comedy Writing, by Sol Saks $14.95
  The Craft of Lyric Writing, by Sheila Davis $18.95
  Guide to Greeting Card Writing, edited by Larry Sandman (paper) $8.95
  How to Make Money Writing About Fitness & Health, by Celia & Thomas Scully $16.95
  How to Make Money Writing Fillers, by Connie Emerson (paper) $8.95
  How to Write a Cookbook and Get It Published, by Sara Pitzer $15.95
  How to Write a Play, by Raymond Hull $13.95
  How to Write and Sell Your Personal Experiences, by Lois Duncan (paper) $9.95
  How to Write and Sell (Your Sense of) Humor, by Gene Perret (paper) $9.95

How to Write "How-To" Books and Articles, by Raymond Hull (paper) $8.95
How to Write the Story of Your Life, by Frank P. Thomas $12.95
How You Can Make $50,000 a Year as a Nature Photojournalist, by Bill Thomas (paper) $17.95
Mystery Writer's Handbook, by The Mystery Writers of America (paper) $8.95
Nonfiction for Children: How to Write It, How to Sell It, by Ellen E.M. Roberts $16.95
On Being a Poet, by Judson Jerome $14.95
The Poet's Handbook, by Judson Jerome (paper) $8.95
Poet's Market, by Judson Jerome $16.95
Sell Copy, by Webster Kuswa $11.95
Successful Outdoor Writing, by Jack Samson $11.95
Travel Writer's Handbook, by Louise Zobel (paper) $9.95
TV Scriptwriter's Handbook, by Alfred Brenner (paper) $9.95
Writing After 50, by Leonard L. Knott $12.95
Writing and Selling Science Fiction, by Science Fiction Writers of America (paper) $7.95
Writing for Children & Teenagers, by Lee Wyndham (paper) $9.95
Writing for the Soaps, by Jean Rouverol $14.95
Writing the Modern Mystery, by Barbara Norville $15.95
Writing to Inspire, by Gentz, Roddy, et al $14.95

The Writing Business

Complete Guide to Self-Publishing, by Tom & Marilyn Ross $19.95
Complete Handbook for Freelance Writers, by Kay Cassill $14.95
Editing for Print, by Geoffrey Rogers $14.95
Freelance Jobs for Writers, edited by Kirk Polking (paper) $8.95
How to Bulletproof Your Manuscript, by Bruce Henderson $9.95
How to Get Your Book Published, by Herbert W. Bell $15.95
How to Understand and Negotiate a Book Contract or Magazine Agreement, by Richard Balkin $11.95
How You Can Make $20,000 a Year Writing, by Nancy Hanson (paper) $6.95
Literary Agents: How to Get & Work with the Right One for You, by Michael Larsen $9.95
Professional Etiquette for Writers, by William Brohaugh $9.95

To order directly from the publisher, include $2.00 postage and handling for 1 book and 50¢ for each additional book. Allow 30 days for delivery.

Writer's Digest Books, Department B
9933 Alliance Road, Cincinnati OH 45242

Prices subject to change without notice.